COMPLETE
COLLECTED
STORIES

By the same author

SHORT STORIES
The Spanish Virgin
You Make Your Own Life
It May Never Happen
Collected Stories (1956)
Sailor, Sense of Humour and Other Stories
When My Girl Comes Home
The Key to My Heart
Blind Love and Other Stories
The Camberwell Beauty and Other Stories
Selected Stories
On the Edge of the Cliff
Collected Stories (1982)
More Collected Stories
A Careless Widow and Other Stories

NOVELS
Clare Drummer
Shirley Sanz
Nothing Like Leather
Dead Man Leading
Mr Beluncle

BIOGRAPHY
Balzac
The Gentle Barbarian: The Life and Work of Turgenev
Chekhov: A Spirit Set Free

MEMOIRS
A Cab at the Door
Midnight Oil

LITERARY CRITICISM
In My Good Books
The Living Novel and Later Appreciations
Books in General
The Working Novelist
George Meredith and English Comedy
The Myth Makers
The Tale Bearers
A Man of Letters
Lasting Impressions

TRAVEL
Marching Spain
The Spanish Temper
London Perceived (with photographs by Evelyn Hofer)
Foreign Faces
New York Proclaimed (with photographs by Evelyn Hofer)
Dublin: A Portrait (with photographs by Evelyn Hofer)
At Home and Abroad

COMPLETE COLLECTED STORIES

V. S. PRITCHETT

Random House
NEW YORK

All rights reserved under International and Pan-American Copyright Conventions.
Published in the United States by Random House, Inc., New York.
Originally published in Great Britain by Chatto and Windus Ltd., London, in 1990.

Library of Congress Cataloging-in-Publication Data

Pritchett, V. S. (Victor Sawdon), 1900–
[Short stories]
Complete collected stories / by V. S. Pritchett.
p.   cm.
ISBN 0-679-40215-2
I. Title
PR6031.R7A15   1991   90-47478
823'.912—dc20

Manufactured in the United States of America
24689753
First U.S. Edition

For Dorothy as always

Contents

Contents

Sense of Humour

―――――

It started one Saturday. I was working new ground and I decided I'd stay at the hotel the weekend and put in an appearance at church.

'All alone?' asked the girl in the cash desk.

It had been raining since ten o'clock.

'Mr Good has gone,' she said. 'And Mr Straker. He usually stays with us. But he's gone.'

'That's where they make their mistake,' I said. 'They think they know everything because they've been on the road all their lives.'

'You're a stranger here, aren't you?' she said.

'I am,' I said. 'And so are you.'

'How do you know that?'

'Obvious,' I said. 'Way you speak.'

'Let's have a light,' she said.

'So's I can see you,' I said.

That was how it started. The rain was pouring down on to the glass roof of the office.

She'd a cup of tea steaming on the register. I said I'd have one, too. What's it going to be and I'll tell them, she said, but I said just a cup of tea.

'I'm TT,' I said. 'Too many soakers on the road as it is.'

I was staying there the weekend so as to be sharp on the job on Monday morning. What's more it pays in these small towns to turn up at church on Sundays, Presbyterians in the morning, Methodists in the evening. Say 'Good morning' and 'Good evening' to them. 'Ah!' they say. 'Church-goer! Pleased to see that! TT, too.' Makes them have a second look at your lines in the morning. 'Did you like our service, Mister – er – er?' 'Humphrey's my name.' 'Mr Humphrey.' See? It pays.

'Come into the office, Mr Humphrey,' she said, bringing me a cup. 'Listen to that rain.'

I went inside.

'Sugar?' she said.

'Three,' I said. We settled to a very pleasant chat. She told me all about herself, and we got on next to families.

'My father was on the railway,' she said.

'"The engine gave a squeal," I said. '"The driver took out his pocket-knife and scraped him off the wheel".'

'That's it,' she said. 'And what is your father's business? You said he had a business.'

'Undertaker,' I said.

'Undertaker?' she said.

'Why not?' I said. 'Good business. Seasonable like everything else. High class undertaker,' I said.

She was looking at me all the time wondering what to say and suddenly she went into fits of laughter.

'Undertaker,' she said, covering her face with her hands and went on laughing.

'Here,' I said. 'What's up?'

'Undertaker!' she laughed and laughed. Struck me as being a pretty thin joke.

'Don't mind me,' she said. 'I'm Irish.'

'Oh, I see,' I said. 'That's it, is it? Got a sense of humour.'

Then the bell rang and a woman called out 'Muriel! Muriel!' and there was a motor bike making a row at the front door.

'All right,' the girl called out. 'Excuse me a moment, Mr Humphrey,' she said. 'Don't think me rude. That's my boy friend. He wants the bird turning up like this.'

She went out but there was her boy friend looking over the window ledge into the office. He had come in. He had a cape on, soaked with rain and the rain was in beads in his hair. It was fair hair. It stood up on end. He'd been economising on the brilliantine. He didn't wear a hat. He gave me a look and I gave him a look. I didn't like the look of him. And he didn't like the look of me. A smell of oil and petrol and rain and mackintosh came off him. He had a big mouth with thick lips. They were very red. I recognised him at once as the son of the man who ran the Kounty Garage. I saw this chap when I put my car away. The firm's car. A lock-up, because of the samples. Took me ten minutes to ram the idea into his head. He looked as though he'd never heard of samples. Slow, – you know the way they are in the provinces. Slow on the job.

'Oh Colin,' says she. 'What do you want?'

'Nothing,' the chap said. 'I came in to see you.'

'To see me?'

'Just to see you.'

'You came in this morning.'

'That's right,' he said. He went red. 'You was busy,' he said.

'Well, I'm busy now,' she said.

He bit his tongue, and licked his big lips over and took a look at me. Then he started grinning.

'I got the new bike, Muriel,' he said. 'I've got it outside.'

'It's just come down from the works,' he said.

'The laddie wants you to look at his bike,' I said. So she went out and had a look at it.

When she came back she had got rid of him.

'Listen to that rain,' she said.

'Lord, I'm fed up with this line,' she said.

'What line?' I said. 'The hotel line?'

'Yes,' she said. 'I'm fed right up to the back teeth with it.'

'And you've got good teeth,' I said.

'There's not the class of person there used to be in it,' she said. 'All our family have got good teeth.'

'Not the class?'

'I've been in it five years and there's not the same class at all. You never meet any fellows.'

'Well,' said I. 'If they're like that half-wit at the garage, they're nothing to be stuck on. And you've met me.'

I said it to her like that.

'Oh,' says she. 'It isn't as bad as that yet.'

It was cold in the office. She used to sit all day in her overcoat. She was a smart girl with a big friendly chin and a second one coming and her forehead and nose were covered with freckles. She had copper-coloured hair too. She got her shoes through the trade from Duke's traveller and her clothes, too, off the Hollenborough mantle man. I told her I could do her better stockings than the ones she'd got on. She got a good reduction on everything. Twenty-five or thirty-three and a third. She had her expenses cut right back. I took her to the pictures that night in the car. I made Colin get the car out for me.

'That boy wanted me to go on the back of his bike. On a night like this,' she said.

'Oh,' she said, when we got to the pictures. 'Two shillings's too much. Let's go into the one-and-sixes at the side and we can nip across into the two-shillings when the lights go down.'

'Fancy your father being an undertaker,' she said in the middle of the show. And she started laughing as she had laughed before.

She had her head screwed on all right. She said:

'Some girls have no pride once the lights go down.'

Every time I went to that town I took a box of something. Samples, mostly, they didn't cost me anything.

'Don't thank me,' I said. 'Thank the firm.'

Every time I took her out I pulled the blinds in the back seat of the car to hide the samples. That chap Colin used to give us oil and petrol. He used to give me a funny look. Fishy sort of small eyes he'd got. Always looking miserable. Then we would go off. Sunday was her free day. Not that driving's any holiday for me. And, of course, the firm paid. She used to take me down to see her family for the day. Start in the morning, and taking it you had dinner and tea there, a day's outing cost us nothing. Her father was something on the railway, retired. He had a long stocking, somewhere, but her sister, the one that was married, had had her share already.

He had a tumour after his wife died and they just played upon the old man's feelings. It wasn't right. She wouldn't go near her sister and I don't blame her, taking the money like that. Just played upon the old man's feelings.

Every time I was up there Colin used to come in looking for her.

'Oh Colin,' I used to say. 'Done my car yet?' He knew where he got off with me.

'No, now, I can't Colin. I tell you I'm going out with Mr Humphrey,' she used to say to him. I heard her.

'He keeps on badgering me,' she said to me.

'You leave him to me,' I said.

'No, he's all right,' she said.

'You let me know if there's any trouble with Colin,' I said. 'Seems to be a harum-scarum sort of half-wit to me,' I said.

'And he spends every penny he makes,' she said.

Well, we know that sort of thing is all right while it lasts, I told her, but the trouble is that it doesn't last.

We were always meeting Colin on the road. I took no notice of it first of all and then I grew suspicious and awkward at always meeting him. He had a new motor bicycle. It was an Indian, a scarlet thing that he used to fly over the moor with, flat out. Muriel and I used to go out over the moor to Ingley Wood in the firm's Morris – I had a customer out that way.

'May as well do a bit of business while you're about it,' I said.

'About what?' she said.

'Ah ha!' I said.

'That's what Colin wants to know,' I said.

Sure enough, coming back we'd hear him popping and backfiring close behind us, and I put out my hand to stop him and keep him following us, biting our dirt.

'I see his little game,' I said. 'Following us.'

So I saw to it that he did follow. We could hear him banging away behind us and the traffic is thick on the Ingley road in the afternoon.

'Oh let him pass,' Muriel said. 'I can't stand those dirty things banging in my ears.'

I waved him on and past he flew with his scarf flying out, blazing red into the traffic. 'We're doing 58 ourselves,' she said, leaning across to look.

'Powerful buses those,' I said. 'Any fool can do it if he's got the power. Watch me step on it.'

But we did not catch Colin. Half an hour later he passed us coming back. Cut right in between us and a lorry – I had to brake hard. I damn nearly killed him. His ears were red with the wind. He didn't wear a hat. I got after him as soon as I could but I couldn't touch him.

Nearly every weekend I was in that town seeing my girl, that fellow was hanging around. He came into the bar on Saturday nights, he poked his head into the office on Sunday mornings. It was a sure bet that if we went out in the car he would pass us on the road. Every time we would hear that scarlet thing roar by like a horse-stinger. It didn't matter where we were. He passed us on the main road, he met us down the side roads. There was a little cliff under oak trees at May Ponds, she said, where the view was pretty. And there, soon after we got there, was Colin on the other side of the water, watching us. Once we found him sitting on his bike, just as though he were waiting for us.

'You been here in a car?' I said.

'No, motor bike,' she said and blushed. 'Cars can't follow in these tracks.'

She knew a lot of places in that country. Some of the roads weren't roads at all and were bad for tyres and I didn't want the firm's car scratched by bushes, but you would have thought Colin could read what was in her mind. For nine times out of ten he was there. It got on my nerves. It was a red, roaring, powerful thing and he opened it full out.

'I'm going to speak to Colin,' I said. 'I won't have him annoying you.'

'He's not annoying me,' she said. 'I've got a sense of humour.'

'Here Colin,' I said one evening when I put the car away. 'What's the idea?'

He was taking off his overalls. He pretended he did not know what I was talking about. He had a way of rolling his eyeballs, as if they had got wet and loose in his head, while he was speaking to me and you never knew if it was sweat or oil on his face. It was always pale with high colour on his cheeks and very red lips.

'Miss MacFarlane doesn't like being followed,' I said.

He dropped his jaw and gaped at me. I could not tell whether he was being very surprised or very sly. I used to call him 'Marbles' because when he spoke he seemed to have a lot of marbles in his mouth.

Then he said he never went to the places we went to, except by accident. He wasn't following us, he said, but we were following him. We never let him alone, he said. Everywhere he went, he said, we were there. Take last Saturday, he said, we were following him for miles down the by-pass, he said. But you passed us first and then sat down in front, I said. I went to Ingley Wood, he said. And you followed me there. No, we didn't, I said, Miss MacFarlane decided to go there.

He said he did not want to complain but fair was fair. I suppose you know, he said, that you have taken my girl off me. Well, you can leave *me* alone, can't you?

'Here,' I said. 'One minute! Not so fast! You said I've taken Miss MacFarlane from you. Well, she was never your girl. She only knew you in a friendly way.'

'She was my girl,' was all he said.

He was pouring oil into my engine. He had some cotton wool in one hand and the can in the other. He wiped up the green oil that had overflowed, screwed on the cap, pulled down the bonnet and whistled to himself.

I went back to Muriel and told her what Colin had said.

'I don't like trouble,' I said.

'Don't you worry,' she said. 'I had to have someone to go to all these places with before you came. Couldn't stick in here all day Sunday.'

'Ah,' I said. 'That's it, is it? You've been to all these places with him?'

'Yes,' she said. 'And he keeps on going to them. He's sloppy about me.'

'Good God,' I said. 'Sentimental memories.'

I felt sorry for that fellow. He knew it was hopeless, but he loved her. I suppose he couldn't help himself. Well, it takes all sorts to make a world, as my old mother used to say. If we were all alike it wouldn't do. Some men can't save money. It just runs through their fingers. He couldn't save money so he lost her. I suppose all he thought of was love.

I could have been friends with that fellow. As it was I put a lot of business his way. I didn't want him to get the wrong idea about me. We're all human after all.

We didn't have any more trouble with Colin after this until Bank Holiday. I was going to take her down to see my family. The old man's getting a bit past it now and has given up living over the shop. He's living out on the Barnum Road, beyond the tram stop. We were going down in the firm's car, as per usual, but something went wrong with the mag. and Colin had not got it right for the holiday. I was wild about this.

[7]

What's the use of a garage who can't do a rush job for the holidays! What's the use of being an old customer if they're going to let you down! I went for Colin bald-headed.

'You knew I wanted it,' I said. 'It's no use trying to put me off with a tale about the stuff not coming down from the works. I've heard that one before.'

I told him he'd got to let me have another car, because he'd let me down. I told him I wouldn't pay his account. I said I'd take my business away from him. But there wasn't a car to be had in the town because of the holiday. I could have knocked the fellow down. After the way I'd sent business to him.

Then I saw through his little game. He knew Muriel and I were going to my people and he had done this to stop it. The moment I saw this I let him know that it would take more than him to stop me doing what I wanted.

I said:
'Right. I shall take the amount of Miss MacFarlane's train fare and my own from the account at the end of the month.'

I said:
'You may run a garage, but you don't run the railway service.'

I was damned angry going by train. I felt quite lost on the railway after having a car. It was crowded with trippers too. It was slow – stopping at all the stations. The people come in, they tread all over your feet, they make you squeeze up till you're crammed against the window, and the women stick out their elbows and fidget. And then the expense! A return for two runs you into just over a couple of quid. I could have murdered Colin.

We got there at last. We walked up from the tram stop. Mother was at the window and let us in.

'This is Miss MacFarlane,' I said.

And mother said:

'Oh, pleased to meet you. We've heard a lot about you.'

'Oh,' mother said to me, giving me a kiss, 'Are you tired? You haven't had your tea, have you? Sit down. Have this chair, dear. It's more comfortable.'

'Well, my boy,' my father said.

[8]

'Want a wash?' my father said. 'We've got a wash basin downstairs,' he said. 'I used not to mind about washing upstairs before. Now I couldn't do without it. Funny how your ideas change as you get older.'

'How's business?' he said.

'Mustn't grumble,' I said. 'How's yours?'

'You knew,' he said, 'we took off the horses: except for one or two of the older families we have got motors now.'

But he'd told me that the last time I was there. I'd been at him for years about motor hearses.

'You've forgotten I used to drive them,' I said.

'Bless me, so you did,' he said.

He took me up to my room. He showed me everything he had done to the house. 'Your mother likes it,' he said. 'The traffic's company for her. You know what your mother is for company.'

Then he gives me a funny look.

'Who's the girl?' he says.

My mother came in then and said:

'She's pretty, Arthur.'

'Of course she's pretty,' I said. 'She's Irish.'

'Oh,' said the old man. 'Irish! Got a sense of humour, eh?'

'She wouldn't be marrying me if she hadn't,' I said. And then I gave *them* a look.

'Marrying her, did you say?' exclaimed my father.

'Any objection?' I said.

'Now Ernest dear,' said my mother. 'Leave the boy alone. Come down while I pop the kettle on.'

She was terribly excited.

'Miss MacFarlane,' the old man said.

'No sugar, thank you, Mrs Humphrey. I beg your pardon, Mr Humphrey?'

'The Glen Hotel at Swansea, I don't suppose you know that?' my father said.

'I wondered if you did being in the catering line,' he said.

'It doesn't follow she knows every hotel,' my mother said.

'Forty years ago,' the old man said. 'I was staying at the Glen in Swansea and the head waiter . . .'

'Oh no, not that one. I'm sure Miss MacFarlane doesn't want to hear that one,' my mother said.

'How's business with you, Mr Humphrey?' said Muriel. 'We passed a large cemetery near the station.'

'Dad's Ledger,' I said.

'The whole business has changed so that you wouldn't know it, in my lifetime,' said my father. 'Silver fittings have gone clean out. Everyone wants simplicity nowadays. Restraint. Dignity,' my father said.

'Prices did it,' my father said.

'The war,' he said.

'You couldn't get the wood,' he said.

'Take ordinary mahogany, just an ordinary piece of mahogany. Or teak,' he said. 'Take teak. Or walnut.'

'You can certainly see the world go by in this room,' I said to my mother.

'It never stops,' she said.

Now it was all bicycles over the new concrete road from the gun factory. Then traction engines and cars. They came up over the hill where the AA man stands and choked up round the tram stop. It was mostly holiday traffic. Everything with a wheel on it was out.

'On this stretch,' my father told me, 'they get three accidents a week.' There was an ambulance station at the crossroads.

We had hardly finished talking about this, in fact the old man was still saying that something ought to be done when the telephone rang.

'Name of MacFarlane?' the voice said on the wire.

'No. Humphrey,' my father said. 'There is a Miss MacFarlane here.'

'There's a man named Colin Mitchell lying seriously injured in an accident at the Cottage Hospital, gave me the name of MacFarlane as his nearest relative.'

That was the Police. On to it at once. That fellow Colin had followed us down by road.

Cry, I never heard a girl cry, as Muriel cried, when we came back from the hospital. He had died in the ambulance. Cutting in, the old game he used to play on me. Clean off the saddle and under the Birmingham bus. The blood was everywhere, they said. People were still looking at it when we went by. Head on. What a mess! Don't let's talk about it.

[10]

She wanted to see him but they said 'No.' There wasn't anything recognisable to see. She put her arms round my neck and cried, 'Colin. Colin,' as if I were Colin and clung to me. I was feeling sick myself. I held her tight and I kissed her and I thought 'Holiday ruined.'

'Damn fool man,' I thought. 'Poor devil,' I thought.

'I knew he'd do something like this.'

'There, there,' I said to her. 'Don't think about Colin.'

Didn't she love me, I said, and not Colin. Hadn't she got me? She said, yes, she had. And she loved me. But, 'Oh Colin! Oh Colin!' she cried. 'And Colin's mother,' she cried. 'Oh it's terrible.' She cried and cried.

We put her to bed and I sat with her and my mother kept coming in.

'Leave her to me,' I said. 'I understand her.' Before they went to bed they both came in and looked at her. She lay sobbing with her head in the pillow.

I could quite understand her being upset. Colin was a decent fellow. He was always doing things for her. He mended her electric lamp and he riveted the stem of a wine glass so that you couldn't see the break. He used to make things for her. He was very good with his hands.

She lay on her side with her face burning and feverish with misery and crying, scalded by the salt, and her lips shrivelled up. I put my arm under her neck and I stroked her forehead. She groaned. Sometimes she shivered and sometimes she clung to me, crying, 'Oh Colin! Colin!'

My arm ached with the cramp and I had a crick in my back, sitting in the awkward way I was on the bed. It was late. There was nothing to do but to ache and sit watching her and thinking. It is funny the way your mind drifts. When I was kissing her and watching her I was thinking out who I'd show our new Autumn range to first. Her hand held my wrist tight and when I kissed her I got her tears on my lips. They burned and stung. Her neck and shoulders were soft and I could feel her breath hot out of her nostrils on the back of my hand. Ever noticed how hot a woman's breath gets when she's crying? I drew out my hand and lay down beside her and 'Oh, Colin, Colin,' she sobbed, turning over and clinging to me. And so I lay there, listening to the traffic, staring at the ceiling and shivering whenever the picture of Colin shooting right off that damned red thing into the bus came into my mind – until I did not hear the traffic any more, or see the ceiling any more, or think any more,

[11]

but a change happened – I don't know when. This Colin thing seemed to have knocked the bottom out of everything and I had a funny feeling we were going down and down and down in a lift. And the further we went the hotter and softer she got. Perhaps it was when I found with my hands that she had very big breasts. But it was like being on the mail steamer and feeling engines start under your feet, thumping louder and louder. You can feel it in every vein of your body. Her mouth opened and her tears dried. Her breath came through her open mouth and her voice was blind and husky. Colin, Colin, Colin, she said, and her fingers were hooked into me. I got out and turned the key in the door.

In the morning I left her sleeping. It did not matter to me what my father might have heard in the night, but still I wondered. She would hardly let me touch her before that. I told her I was sorry but she shut me up. I was afraid of her. I was afraid of mentioning Colin. I wanted to go out of the house there and then and tell someone everything. Did she love Colin all the time? Did she think I was Colin? And every time I thought of that poor devil covered over with a white sheet in the hospital mortuary, a kind of picture of her and me under the sheets with love came into my mind. I couldn't separate the two things. Just as though it had all come from Colin.

I'd rather not talk any more about that. I never talked to Muriel about it. I waited for her to say something but she didn't. She didn't say a word.

The next day was a bad day. It was grey and hot and the air smelled of oil fumes from the road. There's always a mess to clear up when things like this happen. I had to see to it. I had the job of ringing up the boy's mother. But I got round that, thank God, by ringing up the garage and getting them to go round and see the old lady. My father is useless when things are like this. I was the whole morning on the phone: to the hospital, the police, the coroner – and he stood fussing beside me, jerking up and down like a fat india-rubber ball. I found my mother washing up at the sink and she said:

'That poor boy's mother! I can't stop thinking of her.' Then my father comes in and says, – just as though I was a customer –

'Of course if Mrs Mitchell desires it we can have the remains of the deceased conveyed to his house by one of our new specially sprung motor hearses and can, if necessary, make all the funeral arrangements.'

[12]

I could have hit him because Muriel came into the room when he was saying this. But she stood there as if nothing had happened.

'It's the least we can do for poor Mrs Mitchell,' she said. There were small creases of shadow under her eyes which shone with a soft strong light I had never seen before. She walked as if she were really still in that room with me, asleep. God, I loved that girl! God, I wanted to get all this over, this damned Colin business that had come right into the middle of everything like this, and I wanted to get married right away. I wanted to be alone with her. That's what Colin did for me.

'Yes,' I said. 'We must do the right thing by Colin.'

'We are sometimes asked for long-distance estimates,' my father said.

'It will be a little something,' my mother said.

'Dad and I will talk it over,' I said.

'Come into the office,' my father said. 'It occurred to me that it would be nice to do the right thing by this friend of yours.'

We talked it over. We went into the cost of it. There was the return journey to reckon. We worked it out that it would come no dearer to old Mrs Mitchell than if she took the train and buried the boy here. That is to say, my father said, if I drove it.

'It would look nice,' my father said.

'Saves money and it would look a bit friendly,' my father said. 'You've done it before.'

'Well,' I said. 'I suppose I can get a refund on my return ticket from the railway.'

But it was not as simple as it looked, because Muriel wanted to come. She wanted to drive back with me and the hearse. My mother was very worried about this. It might upset Muriel, she thought. Father thought it might not look nice to see a young girl sitting by the coffin of a grown man.

'It must be dignified,' my father said. 'You see if she was there it might look as though she were just doing it for the ride – like these young women on bakers' vans.'

My father took me out into the hall to tell me this because he did not want her to hear. But she would not have it. She wanted to come back with Colin.

'Colin loved me. It is my duty to him,' she said. 'Besides,' she said, suddenly, in her full open voice – it had seemed to be closed and carved and broken and small – 'I've never been in a hearse before.'

'And it will save her fare too,' I said to my father.

That night I went again to her room. She was awake. I said I was sorry to disturb her but I would go at once only I wanted to see if she was all right. She said, in the closed voice again, that she was all right.

'Are you sure?' I said.

She did not answer. I was worried. I went over to the bed.

'What is the matter? Tell me what is the matter,' I said.

For a long time she was silent. I held her hand, I stroked her head. She was lying stiff in the bed. She would not answer. I dropped my hand to her small white shoulder. She stirred and drew up her legs and half turned and said, 'I was thinking of Colin.'

'Where is he?' she asked.

'They've brought him round. He's lying downstairs.'

'In the front room?'

'Yes, ready for the morning. Now be a sensible girl and go back by train.'

'No, no,' she said. 'I want to go with Colin. Poor Colin. He loved me and I didn't love him.' And she drew my hands down to her breasts.

'Colin loved me,' she whispered.

'Not like this,' I whispered.

It was a warm grey morning like all the others when we took Colin back. They had fixed the coffin in before Muriel came out. She came down wearing the bright blue hat she had got off Dormer's millinery man and she kissed my mother and father good-bye. They were very sorry for her. 'Look after her, Arthur,' my mother said. Muriel got in beside me without a glance behind her at the coffin. I started the engine. They smiled at us. My father raised his hat, but whether it was to Muriel and me or to Colin, or to the three of us, I do not know. He was not, you see, wearing his top hat. I'll say this for the old boy, thirty years in the trade have taught him tact.

After leaving my father's house you have to go down to the tram terminus before you get on to the by-pass. There was always one or two drivers, conductors or inspectors there, doing up their tickets, or changing over the trolley arms. When we passed I saw two of them drop their jaws, stick their pencils in their ears and raise their hats. I was so surprised by this that I nearly raised mine in acknowledgment, forgetting that we had the coffin behind. I had not driven one of my father's hearses for years.

Hearses are funny things to drive. They are well-sprung, smooth-running cars, with quiet engines and, if you are used to driving a smaller car, before you know where you are, you are speeding. You know you ought to go slow, say 25 to 30 maximum and it's hard to keep it down. You can return empty at 70 if you like. It's like driving a fire engine. Go fast out and come back slow – only the other way round. Open out in the country but slow down past houses. That's what it means. My father was very particular about this.

Muriel and I didn't speak very much at first. We sat listening to the engine and the occasional jerk of the coffin behind when we went over a pot hole. We passed the place where poor Colin – but I didn't say anything to Muriel, and she, if she noticed – which I doubt – did not say anything to me. We went through Cox Hill, Wammering and Yodley Mount, flat country, don't care for it myself. 'There's a wonderful lot of building going on,' Muriel said at last.

'You won't know these places in five years,' I said.

But my mind kept drifting away from the road and the green fields and the dullness, and back to Colin, – five days before he had come down this way. I expected to see that Indian coming flying straight out of every corner. But it was all bent and bust up properly now. I saw the damned thing.

He had been up to his old game, following us, and that had put the end to following. But not quite; he was following us now, behind us in the coffin. Then my mind drifted off that and I thought of those nights at my parents' house, and Muriel. You never know what a woman is going to be like. I thought, too, that it had put my calculations out. I mean, supposing she had a baby. You see I had reckoned on waiting eighteen months or so. I would have eight hundred then. But if we had to get married at once, we should have to cut right down. Then I kept thinking it was funny her saying 'Colin!' like that in the night; it was funny it made her feel that way with me, and how it made me feel when she called me Colin. I'd never thought of her in that way, in what you might call the 'Colin' way.

I looked at her and she looked at me and she smiled but still we did not say very much, but the smiles kept coming to both of us. The light-railway bridge at Dootheby took me by surprise and I thought the coffin gave a jump as we took it.

'Colin's still watching us,' I nearly said.

There were tears in her eyes.

'What was the matter with Colin?' I said. 'Nice chap, I thought. Why didn't you marry him?'

'Yes,' she said. 'He was a nice boy. But he'd no sense of humour.'

'And I wanted to get out of that town,' she said.

'I'm not going to stay there, at that hotel,' she said.

'I want to get away,' she said. 'I've had enough.'

She had a way of getting angry with the air, like that. 'You've got to take me away,' she said. We were passing slowly into Muster, there was a tram ahead and people thick on the narrow pavements, dodging out into the road. But when we got into the Market Square where they were standing around, they saw the coffin. They began to raise their hats. Suddenly she laughed. 'It's like being the King and Queen,' she said.

'They're raising their hats,' she said.

'Not all of them,' I said.

She squeezed my hand and I had to keep her from jumping about like a child on the seat as we went through.

'There they go.'

'Boys always do,' I said.

'And another.'

'Let's see what the policeman does.'

She started to laugh but I shut her up. 'Keep your sense of humour to yourself,' I said.

Through all those towns that run into one another as you might say, we caught it. We went through, as she said, like royalty. So many years since I drove a hearse, I'd forgotten what it was like.

I was proud of her, I was proud of Colin and I was proud of myself. And, after what had happened, I mean on the last two nights, it was like a wedding. And although we knew it was for Colin, it was for us too, because Colin was with both of us. It was like this all the way.

'Look at that man there. Why doesn't he raise his hat? People ought to show respect for the dead,' she said.

A Spring Morning

After many days of rain came a cleansed and miraculous morning when the larks went up straight from the dykes, lifting the sky higher with every leap. They stayed there singing; while above them the planes of the aviators droned like metallic bees and the air thrilled in a fine breeze from the sea. People walking in the village dipped their bodies in the sunlight and raised their faces to the perfectly blue sky with pleasure for the first spring sun was shining.

A girl was whistling loudly at the door of a shop. She whistled through a gap between two prominent front teeth. She was a thin girl, ill-nourished, with blue eyes too close together and fair hair chopped short and brushed off her bony face. Over her body was a long pink evening dress and on her feet was a frayed pair of evening shoes which slopped about as she pretended to waltz to her whistles.

One side of the village street was in the sun and the other in shadow. It was a quiet place, yet sounds came from it, sounds by which were measured its great quietness. Here a window squealed open, here a carpet was beaten, here the double tap of a boatman's hammer, the step of a man in the street, the sudden rattle of a car, the throb of the hourly bus, or even the sound of the girl whistling – all these sounds came singly, exceptionally, measuring off the silence of the village and the people possessed by the first sun of the year.

Soon a youth wearing a dirty pair of canvas shoes came shuffling up the street with a puppy tearing at his shoe laces. The girl, who was alone in the shop, stopped whistling when she saw this fat, pale youth with his thick unbrushed hair and his pimpled skin. He was wearing oil-stained trousers and jersey and he slouched along with his hands in his pockets. His eyes were so pale that they scarcely showed in his freckled unshaven face.

'Minding the shop?' he called.

He grinned as he nodded to the door, showing his very yellow teeth.

'Take care that don't run away,' he said. He gave her a look up and down from the points of her half-formed breasts to her feet, and then with a spit, moved on, ignoring her, but when he had got ten yards away he stopped dead to stare at an aeroplane in the sky.

The girl recovered and stiffened.

'Eh!' she screeched. '*You* take care or you might get a job of work.'

'Nothing doing,' he said, speaking up at the aeroplane. When he turned he caught the scornfulness in her look and slowly, smiling, threatening, he came back towards her. He came nearer and nearer and when he was so close that she could smell the breakfast tea in his warm breath on her cheeks, he took one hot fat freckled hand out of his pocket, and leaned it on the doorpost above her head. Then he looked over her shoulder impertinently into the shop. She was alarmed because he was nearly touching her.

'You can't come in,' she said.

'Who said so?'

'You can't come in.'

She barred the way but he was smiling and not even looking at her.

'How much is that bit of firewood?' he asked, pointing to a chair in the shop.

'I shan't tell you.'

He took no notice, with his shadow on her, staring over her shoulder into the shop and giving a nod to each thing there, the china, the glass, the mirrors, the desks, mockingly.

'Don't want nothing,' he said at last.

His face was nearly touching hers; slowly he took down his arm from the doorpost and, for a moment, his hand hovered as if to touch her. Then it dropped and he whistled up his dog, and without moving a step away from the girl, he bent down with his back to her. The dog was a small, black and grey spaniel and he rolled the creature over and over, tickling its mottled belly, running his fingers into its mouth and making it snap and slobber and bark.

'Here,' she said. 'Get out of the light.'

[19]

He went on rolling the puppy over and over and took no notice of her. At last he yawned and got up, still with his back to her.

'Coming out?' he said without interest.

'No,' she said at once with satisfaction.

It was a slow morning, slow with the sun, slow the tide opening its fan of water in the creek, slow the hours and slow the breeze. When the church clock struck, the green bus came down and was backed round at the bottom of the road by the sea. The driver got off and walked round to the sunny side of the bus in pursuit of the conductor. They followed each other round like two dogs.

The girl gazed at them. They were men in uniform, working to time. The driver, who was always looking at his watch, said the word and the conductor gave the engine a turn, the bell struck and off they went, sticking up their thumbs as they passed their friends. 'Thumbs up,' they called to the postman, the policeman, the passing bus drivers on their route, and the sunlight sizzled on the radiator caps. 'Thumbs up,' they repeated.

The girl gazed where the men had been and where they had been the youth was standing. His dusty shoulders were in a lump and, although she tried, she could not stop looking at him. She looked at the way he planted his legs, at the set of his buttocks, at his neck, the bow of his calves, at the back, broad, dusty, indolent, and the hang of his heavy arms.

'Afraid to come in?' she taunted.

He looked round at once but she was not there because she dodged back quietly to hide in the shop. He kicked the dog away from him and went to the door.

'Gerout!' he said to the dog.

The moment he went in he hesitated because he was awed by the valuable things in the shop and because he did not know who might come out of the inner door, but in the half darkness, her pink dress was brilliant and he could not resist her stiff, glittering cunning. All he could do was to laugh and take her wrist. She tried to pull herself away.

'Leave me be.'

'Leave you be!'

'There's someone coming.'

'No there ain't.'

'You're not to. I shall call out . . .'

Now he got hold of both wrists. His mouth was open. She was angry and helpless, her fingers crooked, trying to scratch at his face. He laughed at her with what breath he had.

'Huh! Huh! Skinny,' he laughed.

He did not know what he wanted to do and she did not know what she did not want him to do. They just stood fighting.

At last, with a push, he sat her into a chair and dropped her wrists. The moment he did so she flew at him like a cat and smacked him on the face.

'Here, hold on!' he said. And after a pause: 'What's the big idea?'

'You dirty beast,' she said.

'I never touched you,' he said.

'Chance is a fine thing, isn't it?' she taunted.

Her lips quivered until she grinned as he stared back at her staring, narrow, combative, hungry face. Then he made a leap at her. He had his arm round her waist and his fingers on the hollow of her spine at once. She was dragged and rubbed in confusion against him. He kissed her roughly on the lips and would not release her, though she pushed with her knees and her hands against him. There was the smell of tobacco from his mouth and the smell of oil on his clothes. Then suddenly he released her and stood without anything to say. He laughed. His eyes were sparkling. Her lips were wet; her face was marked red and startled; and her child's eyes, which had the cunning-old-woman-look of a child, were now the melting blue, hazy eyes of a young woman. She propped her heels on the step and made herself tall so that she could look at him proudly. But her heart was striking against her chest, and her aching lips were bruised with kissing.

When he had gone away up the street to sit on the kerb with his puppy once more, she could still feel the fading mark of his lips. She crinkled her eyes in the sunlight, swaying and dipping her arms in the white warmth. In the sky droned the men from the aerodrome. Their planes slid down the face of the sky, making scars of pale exhaust. They roared up again, twirled slowly over and whined down in

[21]

long dives which scribbled their flight over the sky, until they set off once more in their formations and their roar rained down upon other country.

She was driven straight out of the shop towards him and he stood up waiting for her to come and be near to him. But a gate clicked and another girl, a dark and placid one, came out of a garden, and the two girls ran to each other with shouts. They put their hands on each other's shoulders and whispered bending together and laughing over their shoulders at him. He stepped across to them. They gave screams and ran for the shop. There in the doorway they laughed and then disappeared laughing into the shop, laughing and laughing. Twice they came to the door and laughed and then screaming ran to laugh inside. She stood and laughed in the face of the dark girl and the dark girl laughed in her face too.

'Whoop,' shrieked the girl, driving the dark one before her and bringing a pail of water out of the shop. A chair was brought out too and she climbed on to it to clean the window, watching her reflection dance from one small pane to the next as she worked. When she reached for the higher panes she hoped her dress was not caught up because she could see him in the glass still lounging there.

'You do hang around,' she bawled at his reflection. He let all that die away.

'Why don't you go for a soldier!' she yelled. Dragging his feet he came slouching across to her, grinning, kicking the puppy, spitting.

'Eh?' she screamed. She picked up the pail and lugged it to the gutter. Then she lifted it. 'Wake up,' she cried suddenly and emptied the whole pailful over him.

A white flash of water, a shout, a flop as the water fell, the roar from him and the yelp of the puppy scampering out of the mess. She stared. She dropped the pail. She went white. She gave a choking laugh and then she bolted. Into the shop she rushed, slamming and locking the door. The soaked youth rushed after her, but she was safe, white, startled, putting her tongue out at him. He flew at the door and rattled its handle. Water was running off his face, dripping from his nose.

'You wait,' he shouted. 'You wait.'

Then the green bus came down and the twelve o'clock whistle blew. She saw him go off. Very hot, her heart beating loudly, she waltzed in the room with stupefied gaiety and whistled through her big teeth.

Main Road

At the close of a December evening when the roads are like slugs, oozy and gleaming in the cold, two workless and sodden men were shambling along, lost in the side lanes of silent country. The darkness had come down to the roots of the trees and the fields. The houses with their yellow dabs of oil light had scattered and thinned away. Blistered and squelching and gone past the cravings of hunger into a hunched, mechanical misery, the two men went on. It was their third day on the road, and, no longer exchanging any words, cursing the lanes which had snared them into homeless, foodless darkness, they seemed to be groping round and round in a pit. Now, they would almost sooner have found a main road than a plate of beef.

Suddenly the old one who was ahead stopped dead and then broke into a weak, gasping hobble.

' 'Ere y'are,' he called.

Without warning, after a sudden rise, the lane had finished. They were out of it. They stood – oh miracle of miracles! – upon a main road. They gazed upon it with awe. Straight as a dull sword it carved the country in two, lightless, soundless, without signposts; and with it the double rows of telegraph poles and the low chopped hedges went. And now the two men were appalled. Which way? After the winding roads this great one seemed to strike them like a plank flat in the face. It jerked the knees in their sockets. It was as hard as iron to the weak bones.

On this third day the object of their journey had been driven from their minds altogether. They did not care if they never got to the town where the factory and the jobs were said to be, nor where they slept. They had eaten poorly on the first two days when the adventure was young, but on this day the singing had stopped and the whistling. The only sounds all day had been the dazed singing in their heads, the gritting of their teeth.

During the daytime, not work nor towns, but food had been their only thought. They ached and craved for it. Every step was for food, every glance sharpened the search for it, every sound was passed in judgement, every sight was questioned. The anarchy of hunger was in their bubbling bellies which blew weakly out or cavernously sank.

Most of the time the younger one walked behind. Sometimes he had been only a few yards behind, sometimes the distance was twenty or thirty yards, once or twice it had been a quarter of a mile. He walked with belt tight and his hands in the sodden pockets of his overcoat, his straight shoulders rounded over his chest. He was a man of thirty with spikes of grey about the ears, his eyes were steely, the skin of his face stretched over the set bones. In his hunger he had begun to hate the man who was always in front.

He was a man near fifty, the older one, a man whose one-time florid corpulence had declined, like a leaking balloon, in two years of famine, to a bluish wobbling windiness. Dazed, vague, dreamy, his big arms, lolling about loose and with a lost look in his eyes, he stumbled ahead. Even when their hunger had started to put out claws he had continued to make jokes. They were always the same kind of joke.

'Cows doin' nicely,' was one of them.

'Show me a stew now an' I'd throw it back at you,' was another.

First of all the younger man had begun hating him because he always got ahead. Then he hated his back and his figure and his ridiculous top-heavy way of walking on his toes. He hated him because, in the intolerable space and emptiness of the country and of the sky, it was necessary to hate someone. He hated him for being so bloody cocksure and humorous. He hated him for hearing of the job, thinking of the journey, for drinking their money on the second day, for leading this dance over the lanes when hunger had made them wander off the main road, so they were going round in circles, no doubt, like men lost in a forest – the forest of the cravings of hunger where everything reminds you of only one thing – looking for houses where there was food. But most of all he grew to hate the older man for begging. The young one had never begged, refused to beg, hung back if begging was on the cards. 'The bloody old tramp!' he chewed away. 'I'd sooner sock a man in the jaw than beg.'

'And,' he would add when the old man came away from a back door, where he had been refused, 'he doesn't get anything when he does beg.' Throughout the day the young one had looked at the baldish head of the older one as he bared it with an absurd touch of ceremony at kitchen doors, with intensified disgust. He hated him when he tried, he hated him when he failed, and, finally, even more he got to hate him when, discouraged and dazed, he passed houses without begging at all.

The older man was innocently unaware of all this. In the afternoon they had come among people who lived in scattered shacks and bungalows. There were small holdings and gardens of vegetables, with patches of glass frame, and everyone had a few chickens. They were small careful people, with a little nervous independence – small builders, small shopkeepers, small coal merchants, small pensioners. They bent digging in their holdings and spoke arrogantly with fright when the big fellow went to a back door and asked for food. They had small, raging dogs. The two men walked closer together in these places. Lights were now lit, the yellow country lights, dabbed among the smeared blackness of the trees. The older man set the course. Instinctively he walked from light to light, stopping when he got to a lamp, wonderstruck because there was no food under it. Then on he went, lifting his feet high because of his blisters, the damp under his arms propping up his shoulders with spears of cold. Loosely his top teeth slid about on the lower ones; dazed and dreamy he walked. Tinned salmon, cabbage, suet pudding and cheese, he dreamed. Fish and chips, ham and eggs, spaghetti. Grass and rubbish heaps, dogs and cats. Thrushes, sparrows, chickens and canaries. In imagination he was grazing off everything he saw.

'We had a goat when I was a boy,' he said. 'And when it got a bit past it my ol' dad killed and skinned it.' He jogged on ruminating. 'Show me a bit of goat and I'd throw it back in your face.'

The other one didn't answer. Their breath was short. In a weak voice the big one continued:

'Seagull. I knew a man who ate a seagull. The French eat horse.'

'Goose is another tough thing. Wild goose. When we was boys . . .'

'It's a bleedin' pity you're not a boy now,' called the younger man.

'What?' called back the old one over his shoulder, still walking.

And now the old fool was deaf. The young one strained himself to catch up. He gasped along with his mouth open. At last he got within a couple of yards of the old man.

'A bleedin' pity you're not a boy now,' the young one shouted out in a rage. Having got it home, he dropped back yard by yard.

After this they had been silent. The old one wobbled along, deeply injured by the reproach; no more he laughed, no more he begged.

Then, suddenly they had come upon the main road. It was empty now. But when life came to this road it was not mean and made of little sounds, spade strokes and footsteps as it had been in the lanes.

Here, when life came, it was brilliant and roaring. Every few minutes fans of light would open slowly in the elms a mile ahead and then abruptly narrow and close; a few seconds would pass and then the long beams of a car's head-lights would leap out and paint the poles and hedges gaudily with light. Long shadows rushed back from the two men, and then new shorter shadows jumped out of them, until in a cascade of rushing brilliance, the car roared by and they were left like men slapped in the face, awakened. Gliding more slowly towards them and sloping to the camber of the road came soft two-decker buses. Like meat in a shop window the passengers seemed, women with full baskets, men with food inside them and pipes in their mouths. The two men stood upon the grass verge exalted by the light.

Now they were on the main road, the younger one took the lead. He lifted his head and stepped out. This was what he wanted. After the rasp of the wheels on this road its silences were icy and momentous. The cars whined and expired like shells across an empty planet wilderness. There was no sound of people. There were no animals moving in the fields. An appalling inhuman vacancy opened in the road. The younger one understood this. But before they had gone a mile the old man was craving for the sight of a lane in which, broken at last but sheltered, he could crawl and hide from these blinding lights that seemed to go clean through his mind, from these silences of iron. He was paralysed. At the sight of the first signpost he hurried after his companion and got there with him.

'Lane,' he said breathlessly, lifting an arm. The hedges were high, a friendly warmth seemed to come from them. The young one was startled into stopping. The last mile had been vehement. Lane must lead some-where. House? Light?

The old one's eyes swung about helplessly, pleading. 'Bloke,' he said. He hadn't strength to say more.

The young one was compelled to listen. The sound of footsteps was distinctly heard. He, too, heard the footsteps distantly in the lane coming nearer. The two men listened, the only sounds were from their breathing and the steps. Suddenly, the old man stumbled off down the lane towards the steps. The young one gaped but did not move. A figure dimly appeared in the darkness. It was a man. It was a youth. It was a youth with a small playful ball of light from a torch dancing round his feet.

'God!' exclaimed the young man, all the hatred of the day returning to his body, so that he clenched his fists. 'The old fool's going to beg! God, I'll . . .' He raised his fists.

But in spite of this he found himself making a few steps after the old man. He saw the youth coming out of the black silence with a small raffia bag in his hand. He saw the old man move nearer the youth. He saw the youth stop. The younger one sidled up slowly, but, still hanging aloof, as he always did when the old one begged. He stood scowling, with tears of craving in his eyes, and a cold shiver of rage and shame sprang through him when he heard the old man's voice.

'No. I haven't.' Distinctly he heard the youth's answer. The young man's held breath went out and he unclenched his fists at the reply. He was beaten. He could have broken into tears; but when he saw the youth step aside making a half circle round the big fellow, afraid to lift the torch to his face, but half raising it instead to shine on his stomach and neck, a wild contempt, a rage before prey flung itself into his blood. Impelled by his day-long hatred of the old man he stepped forward, taking a cold breath. 'I'll show you,' he muttered. There was the smell of cows, the smell of chickens, the smell of a farm, where animals and birds had been feeding all day. 'Leave the bastard alone,' he rapped out loudly to the old man. He strode forward into the circle of light and stopped the youth.

'What's that?' he said sharply, knocking the bag.

'Hyur' . . . blustered the young man, but his opened mouth would not make any more words. He flashed the light helplessly about him.

'Been pinching?' said the younger man.

The older man gaped but said nothing.

'Chicken,' stammered the youth. 'Mrs Ross gave me a chicken.'

'That's not a chicken,' said the younger man.

The youth looked helplessly up and down the lane. He tried to skip away, but the older one woke up and stopped him.

'That's not a chicken.' A sudden change had come over the older man. He copied the younger man's words. A feeling of intense new wakefulness was in both of them.

'Ah . . .' The youth tried to shout.

'Bleedin' thief,' shouted the younger man. He trembled for a second and then suddenly let out a hard punch to the youth's wind and tripped him up. He went down flat in the mud.

Now there was no doubt about it. It was as if silently under all their talk and in all their silence they had been rehearsing this all day, working out every detail to perfection. They said nothing but sprang to it. The big fellow went down gay and hard on the gasping youth and sat on him. The younger one snatched up the bag and rummaged in the youth's coat pocket for a handkerchief. Money chinked. The youth feebly kicked. Without a word, the older man stuffed a bit of the handkerchief between the youth's teeth and tied it round his neck. A look of extraordinary pale, breathless gaiety rose in the older man's exhausted face; a look of keenness and shrewd skill sprang up in the eyes of the other. Their breath came in helpless gasps.

' 'Ere y'are,' they gasped together.

They lifted the youth up, giving a glance apiece up the lane.

'There's a bus coming,' said the older one. They pitched the youth at the top of their strength through the hedge and into the ditch and ran for the bus.

Out of the lane and across the road they went. They were babbling, choking, half laughing. They waved their arms to signal to the large green bus softly swerving towards them.

They grabbed frantically at the rail.

'Just in time,' grinned the older man to the conductor.

The conductor, noting the numbers of tickets, hardly smiled.

The big one flopped into a seat on one side of the gangway. He had the bag on his knee. The younger one sat on the opposite side. They sat panting quietly. The passengers stared at them stupidly. The dry warmth of the bus entered into the bodies of the two men and the pounding of their hearts slackened. Their heads lolled weakly, luxuriously on their necks.

'Two to the finish,' said the older man in a hoarse voice.

The younger one paid up. What was more, there was a shilling change. The older man glanced at the empty road behind and then settled comfortably down. With its warm soft roar the bus broke the dull air of the open country. What a change! He winked at the younger one.

'Got a fag?' he teased.

The shadow of the grin he had had when he was a much fatter and less crafty man came on his face. It made the passengers smile. Reassured, the older man felt the bag with his fingers. Cautiously he drew out the skewer and looked down. He signalled across the gangway like a schoolboy.

'Nt. Chkn. Fsnt,' he was signalling with his lips. Not chicken, pheasant.

This made the passengers laugh. The grin on the older man's face became broader and deeper, feeding on his face. He loved the world. The light vans of tradesmen began to spin by, passing the speeding bus. There was light, speed, hilarity everywhere. A feeling of wild irresponsibility overcame the older man. Amid the laughter of the passengers, he pulled the pheasant's tail out of the bag.

But the younger one ignored all this. Crouching in his seat, he sat alert in the bitter vividness of his vengeance and his pride. There goes the bloody butcher, the bloody baker, money streaming down the world in petrol. Food! He looked at the old man with contempt. What he wanted, his tortured hating soul cried out within him, was not food.

The Evils of Spain

We took our seats at the table. There were seven of us.

It was at one of those taverns in Madrid. The moment we sat down Juliano, the little, hen-headed, red-lipped consumptive who was paying for the dinner and who laughed not with his mouth but by crinkling the skin round his eyes into scores of scratchy lines and showing his bony teeth – Juliano got up and said, 'We are all badly placed.' Fernando and Felix said, 'No, we are not badly placed.' And this started another argument shouting between the lot of us. We had been arguing all the way to the restaurant. The proprietor then offered a new table in a different way. Unanimously we said, 'No,' to settle the row; and when he brought the table and put it into place and laid a red and white check tablecloth on it, we sat down, stretched our legs and said, 'Yes. This table is much better.'

Before this we had called for Angel at his hotel. We shook his hand or slapped him on the back or embraced him and two hung on his arm as we walked down the street. 'Ah, Angel, the rogue!' we said, giving him a squeeze. Our smooth Mediterranean Angel! 'The uncle!' we said. 'The old scoundrel.' Angel smiled, lowering his black lashes in appreciation. Juliano gave him a prod in the ribs and asked him if he remembered, after all these years, that summer at Biarritz? When we had all been together? The only time we had all been together before? Juliano laughed by making his eyes wicked and expectant, like one Andalusian reminding another of the great joke they had had the day poor So-and-So fell down the stairs and broke his neck.

'The day you were nearly drowned,' Juliano said.

Angel's complexion was the colour of white coffee; his hair, crinkled like a black fern, was parted in the middle, he was rich, soft-palmed and patient. He was the only well-dressed man among us, the suavest shouter. Now he sat next door but one to Juliano. Fernando was between them, Juan next to me and, at the end, Felix. They had put Caesar at the head of the table, because he was the oldest and the largest. Indeed at his age he found his weight tiring to the feet.

Caesar did not speak much. He gave his silent weight to the dinner, letting his head drop like someone falling asleep, and listening. To the noise we made his silence was a balance and he nodded all the time slowly, making everything true. Sometimes someone told some story about him and he listened to that, nodding and not disputing it.

But we were talking chiefly of that summer, the one when Angel (the old uncle!) had nearly been drowned. Then Juan, the stout, swarthy one, banged the table with his hairy hands and put on his horn-rimmed glasses. He was the smallest and most vehement of us, the one with the thickest neck and the deepest voice, his words like barrels rumbling in a cellar.

'Come on! Come on! Let's make up our minds! What are we going to eat? Eat! Eat!' he roared.

'Yes,' we cried. 'Drink! What are we going to drink?'

The proprietor, who was in his shirt sleeves and braces, said it was for us to decide. We could have anything we wanted. This started another argument. He stepped back a pace and put himself in an attitude of self-defence.

'Soup! Soup? Make up your minds about soup! Who wants soup?' bawled Juan.

'Red wine,' some of us answered. And others, 'Not red, white.'

'Soup I said,' shouted Juan. 'Yes,' we all shouted. 'Soup.'

'Ah,' said Juan, shaking his head, in his slow miserable disappointed voice. 'Nobody have any soup. I want some soup. Nobody soup,' he said sadly to the proprietor.

Juliano was bouncing in his chair and saying, God he would never forget that summer when Angel was nearly drowned! When we had all been together. But Juan said Felix had not been there and we had to straighten that matter out. Juliano said:

'They carried him on to the beach, our little Angel on to the beach. And the beach superintendent came through the crowd and said, "What's happening?" "Nothing," we said. "A man knocked out." "Knocked out?" said the beach superintendent. "Nothing," we said. "Drowned!" A lot of people left the crowd and ran about over the beach saying, "A man has been drowned." "Drowned," said the beach superintendent. Angel was lying in the middle of them all, unconscious, with water pouring out of his mouth.'

'No! No!' shouted Fernando. 'No. It wasn't like that.'

'How do you mean, it wasn't like that?' cried Juliano. 'I was there.' He appealed to us, 'I was there.'

'Yes, you were there,' we said.

'I *was* there. I was there bringing him in. You say it wasn't like that, but it was like that. We were all there.' Juliano jumped protesting to his feet, flung back his coat from his defying chest. His waistcoat was very loose over his stomach, draughty.

'What happened was better than that,' Fernando said.

'Ah,' said Juliano, suddenly sitting down and grinning with his eyes at everyone, very pleased at his show.

'It was better,' he said. 'How better?'

Fernando was a man who waited for silence and his hour. Once getting possession of the conversation he never let it go, but held it in the long, soothing ecstasy of a pliable embrace. All day long he lay in bed in his room in Fuencarral with the shutters closed, recovering from the bout of the day before. He was preparing himself to appear in the evening, spruce, grey-haired and meaty under the deep black crescents of his eyebrows, his cheeks ripening like plums as the evening advanced, his blue eyes, which got bloodshot early, becoming mistier. He was a man who ripened and moistened. He talked his way through dinner into the night, his voice loosening, his eyes misting, his walk becoming slower and stealthier, acting every sentence, as if he were swaying through the exalted phase of inebriation. But it was an inebriation purely verbal; an exaltation of dramatic moments, refinements upon situations; and hour after hour passed until the dawn found him sodden in his own anecdotes, like a fruit in rum.

'What happened was,' Fernando said, 'that I was in the sea. And after a while I discovered Angel was in the sea. As you know there is nothing more perilous than the sea, but with Angel in it the peril is tripled; and when I saw him I was preparing to get as far away as possible. But he was making faces in the water and soon he made such a face, so inhuman, so unnatural, I saw he was drowning. This did not surprise me for Angel is one of those men who, when he is in the sea, he drowns. There is some psychological antipathy. Now when I see a man drowning my instinct is to get away quickly. A man drowning is not a man. He is a lunatic. But a lunatic like Angel! But unfortunately he got me before I could get away. There he was,' Fernando stood up and raised his arm, confronting the proprietor of the restaurant, but staring right through that defensive man, 'beating the water, diving, spluttering, choking, spitting, and, seeing he was drowning, for the man *was* drowning, caught hold of me, and we both went under. Angel was like a beast. He clung to me like seaweed. I, seeing this, awarded him a knock-out – zum – but as the tenacity of man increases with unconsciousness, Angel stuck to me like a limpet, and in saving myself there was no escape from saving him.'

'That's true,' said Angel, admiring his finger nails. And Caesar nodded his head up and down twice, which made it true.

Juan then swung round and called out, 'Eat! Food! Let us order. Let us eat. We haven't ordered. We do nothing but talk, not eat. I want to eat.'

'Yes, come on,' said Felix. 'Eat. What's the fish?'

'The fish,' said the proprietor, 'is bacalao.'

'Yes,' everyone cried. 'Bacalao, a good bacalao, a very good one. No, it must be good. No. I can't eat it unless it's good, very good *and* very good.'

'No,' we said. 'Not fish. We don't want it.'

'Seven bacalaos then?' said the proprietor.

But Fernando was still on his feet.

'And the beach inspector said, "What's his name and address and has he any identity papers?" "Man," I said, "he's in his bathing dress. Where could he keep his papers?" And Juan said, "Get a doctor. Don't stand there asking questions. Get a doctor."'

'That's true,' said Juan gloomily. 'He wasn't dead.'

'Get a doctor, that was it,' Angel said.

'And they got a doctor and brought him round and got half the Bay of Biscay out of him, gallons of it. It astonished me that so much water could come out of a man.'

'And then in the evening,' Juliano leaped up and clipped the story out of Fernando's mouth, 'Angel says to the proprietor of the hotel . . .'

Juan's head had sunk to his chest. His hands were over his ears.

'Eat,' he bawled in a voice of despair so final that we all stopped talking and gazed at him with astonishment for a few moments. Then in sadness he turned to me appealing. 'Can't we eat? I am empty.'

'. . . said to the proprietor of the hotel,' Fernando grabbed the tale back from Juliano, 'who was rushing down the corridor with a face like a fish, "I am the man who was drowned this morning." And the proprietor who looked at Angel like a prawn, the proprietor said, "M'sieu, whether you were drowned or not drowned this morning you are about to be roast. The hotel is on fire."'

'That's right,' we said. 'The hotel was on fire.'

'I remember,' said Felix. 'It began in the kitchen.'

'How in the kitchen?'

This then became the argument.

'The first time ever I heard it was in the kitchen.'

'But no,' said Angel, softly rising to claim his life story for himself. Juliano clapped his hands and bounced with joy. 'It was not like that.'

'But we were all there, Angel,' Fernando said, but Angel who spoke very rapidly said:

'No and no! And the proof of it is. What was I wearing?' He challenged all of us. We paused.

'Tripe,' said Juan to me hopelessly wagging his head. 'You like tripe? They do it well. Here! Phist!' he called the proprietor through the din. 'Have you tripe, a good Basque tripe? No? What a pity! Can you get me some? Here! Listen,' he shouted to the rest of the table. 'Tripe,' he shouted, but they were engrossed in Angel.

'Pyjamas,' Fernando said. 'When you are in bed you wear your pyjamas.'

'Exactly, and they were not my pyjamas.'

'You say the fire was not in the kitchen,' shouted Fernando, 'because the pyjamas you were wearing were not yours!' And we shouted back at Angel.

'They belonged to the Italian ambassador,' said Angel, 'the one who was with that beautiful Mexican girl.'

Then Caesar, who, as I have said, was the oldest of us and sat at the head of the table, Caesar leaned his old big pale face forward and said in a hushed voice, putting out his hands like a blind man remembering:

'My God – but what a very beautiful woman she was,' he said. 'I remember her. I have never in my life,' he said speaking all his words slowly and with grave concern, 'seen such a beautiful woman.'

Fernando and Angel, who had been standing, sat down. We all looked in awe at the huge, old-shouldered Caesar with his big pale face and the pockets under his little grey eyes, who was speaking of the most beautiful woman he had ever seen.

'She was there all that summer,' Caesar said. 'She was no longer young.' He leaned forward with his hands on the table. 'What must she have been when she was young?'

A beach, the green sea dancing down white upon it, that Mexican woman walking over the floor of a restaurant, the warm white houses, the night glossy black like the toe of a patent shoe, her hair black. We tried to think how many years ago this was. Brought by his voice to silence us, she was already fading.

The proprietor took his opportunity in our silence. 'The bacalao is done in the Basque fashion with peppers and potatoes. Bring a bacalao,' he snapped to a youth in the kitchen.

Suddenly Juan brought his fists on the table, pushed back his chair and beat his chest with one fist and then the other. He swore in his enormous voice by his private parts.

'It's eleven o'clock. Eat! For God's sake. Fernando stands there talking and talking and no one listens to anybody. It is one of the evils of Spain. Someone stop him. Eat.'

We all woke up and glared with the defiance of the bewildered, rejecting everything he said. Then what he said to us penetrated. A wave roared over us and we were with him. We agreed with what he said. We all stood up and, by our private parts, swore that he was right. It was one of the evils of Spain.

The soup arrived. White wine arrived.

'I didn't order soup,' some shouted.

'I said "Red wine",' others said.

'It is a mistake,' the proprietor said. 'I'll take it away.' An argument started about this.

'No,' we said. 'Leave it. We want it.' And then we said the soup was bad, and the wine was bad and everything he brought was bad, but the proprietor said the soup was good and the wine was good and we said in the end it was good. We told the proprietor the restaurant was good, but he said not very good, indeed bad. And then we asked Angel to explain about the pyjamas.

Handsome Is As Handsome Does

In the morning the Corams used to leave the Pension which was like a white box with a terra-cotta lid among its vines on the hill above the town, and walk through the dust and lavish shade to the beach. They were a couple in their forties.

He had never been out of England before but she had spent half her youth in foreign countries. She used to wear shabby saffron beach pyjamas with a navy blue top which the sun had faded. She was a short, thin woman, ugly yet attractive. Her hair was going grey, her face was clay-coloured, her nose was big and long and she had long yellowish eyes. In this beach suit she looked rat-like, with that peculiar busyness, inquisitiveness, intelligence and even charm of rats. People always came and spoke to her and were amused by her conversation. They were startled by her ugly face and her shabbiness but they liked her lazy voice, her quick mind, her graceful good manners, the look of experience and good sense in her eyes.

He was a year older. On the hottest days, when she lay bare-backed and drunk with sunlight, dozing or reading a book, he sat awkwardly beside her in a thick tweed jacket and a white hat pulled down over his eyes. He was a thickset, ugly man; they were an ugly pair. Surly, blunt speaking, big boned, with stiff short fair hair that seemed to be struggling and alight in the sun, he sat frowning and glaring almost wistfully and tediously from his round blue eyes. He had big hands like a labourer's. When people came to speak to her, he first of all edged away. His instinct was to avoid all people. He wanted to sit there silently with her, alone. But if the people persisted then he was rude to them, rude, uncouth and quarrelsome. Then she had to smooth away his rudeness and distract attention from it. But he would ignore the person to whom she was talking and looking down at her would say, 'What are you getting at me for, Julia?' There was a note of angry self-pity in his voice. She liked a man of spirit.

This started quarrels. They were always quarrelling. They quarrelled about their car, their food, where they would sit, whether on the beach or at cafés, whether they would read upstairs or downstairs. He did not really know he was quarrelling. The trouble was that everything seemed difficult to him.

He had thoughts but he could not get them out. They were tied up in knots like snakes, squeezing and suffocating him. Whenever he made a suggestion or offered an opinion, his short brow became contorted with thick frowns, like a bull's forehead, and he coloured. He lowered his forehead, not as if he were going to charge with fury, but as if he were faced with the job of pushing some impossible rock uphill. He was helpless.

She would see this and, cunningly, tactfully, she would make things easy for him. They had no children and, because of the guilt she felt about this and because of the difficulties he saw everywhere, they had become completely dependent on each other.

First of all they were alone at the Pension. There were themselves and M. Pierre. He was the proprietor. At meal times they all sat together. M. Pierre was a plump grey man of sixty, with a pathetic, mean little mouth, a monocle in his eye. He was a short and vain little dandy and was given to boastfulness. The town was a gay place in the summer like a pink flower opening by the peacock sea and M. Pierre was the butterfly that flutters about it. He had the hips of a woman. He was full of learned little proverbs, and precise little habits. Certain hours he would devote to lying on a couch and reading detective stories in a darkened room. At another time he would sit in his dining room with a patent cigarette-making machine, winding the handle, meddling with the mechanism, turning out the cigarettes. He gave a lick to each one as it came out. 'So he won't have to offer you one,' Coram said.

In the afternoon M. Pierre made a great fuss. Appearing in yellow vest and red trousers he took out a new bicycle done in grey enamel and glittering with plated bars, gears, brakes, acetylene lamps and elaborate looped wires. He mounted by a tree and, talking excitedly as if he were about to depart on some dangerous journey to the Alps or the Himalaya, he would whizz giddily down to the beach with his towel and striped gown on the carrier.

'You are going to bathe this afternoon?' M. Pierre asked. 'I am going.' It was a question he put to the Englishman regularly at lunch time. M. Pierre would boast of his love of the sea.

Coram frowned and coloured and a veil of wetness, as if tears were being generated by the struggle within, came to his eyes.

'What's he say?' he asked his wife at last, for he understood French poorly.

'He wants to know whether we are going to bathe with him.'

'Him!' said Coram in a surly voice. 'Him bathe! He can't swim. He can't swim a yard. He just goes down to look at the women.'

'Please Tom!' she said in a sharp lowered voice. 'You mustn't say that in front of him. He understands more than you think.'

M. Pierre sat at the head of the table, grey hair parted in the middle, monocle on expressionless face.

'He's a fraud,' Coram said in his blunt grumbling voice. 'If he understands English why does he pretend he don't?'

'Parlez français, Monsieur Coram,' came the neat, spinsterly correcting voice of the Frenchman.

'Oui,' said the wife very quickly, smiling the long enchanting smile which transformed her ugly face. 'Il *faut*.'

M. Pierre smiled at her and she smiled at him. He liked her bad accent. And she liked him very much but for her husband's sake she had to pretend to dislike him. Her life was full of pretences, small lies and exaggerations which she contrived for her husband's sake.

But Coram disliked the Frenchman from the beginning. When M. Pierre saw the Corams had a car he persuaded them to take him about the country; he would show them its beauties. Sitting like a little duke in the car he pointed out the torrid towns raked together like heaps of earthenware in the mountain valleys, the pale stairways of olives going up hills where no grass grew and the valleys filled with vines. Driving in the fixed, unchanging sunlight, M. Pierre directed them to sudden sights of the sea in new bays more extravagant in colour. Coram frowned. It was all right for his wife. She had been to such places before. Her family had always been to such places. This was the thing which always awed him when he thought about her; pleasure had been natural to her family for generations. But for him it was unnatural. All this was too beautiful. He had never seen anything like it. He could not speak. At noon when the mountains of the coast seemed to lie head down to the sea like savage, panting and silver animals, or in the evening when the flanks and summits were cut by sharp purple shadows and the sea became like some murmuring lake of milky opal, he felt the place had made a wound in him. He felt in his heart the suspended anger of a man torn between happiness and pain. After his life in the villas and chemical factories of the Midlands, where the air was like an escape of gas and the country brick-bruised and infected, he could not believe in this beautiful country. Incredulous, he mistrusted.

'Garsong!' (There was a café near the harbour where the Corams used to sit for an hour before dinner.) 'Garsong – Encore – drinks!' That was the only way he could melt his mistrust.

Coram could not explain why. He was thwarted like his country. All he could do was frown and take it out on M. Pierre.

'He's a mean squirt,' Coram said.

'He's a liar,' he said.

'Look at him making those cigarettes.'

'We've known him a week and what's he do but cadge drinks and rides in the car. He's a fraud.'

His wife listened. Her husband was a man without subtlety or wit, quite defenceless before unusual experience. He was a child. Every day she was soothing this smouldering aching struggle that was going on inside him.

After they had been there a week a newcomer arrived at the Pension. He arrived one morning by the early train walking down from the station with his new light suitcase. He was a young man in his twenties, tall, dark, aquiline, a Jew.

'We will call you Monsieur Alex,' said M. Pierre with his French love of arranging things.

'That is charming,' said the Jew.

He spoke excellent English, a little too perfect, a little too round in the vowels, and excellent French, almost too pure. He talked easily. He had heard, he said, that there were some excellent pictures in the churches of the mountain towns.

'Rather sweet isn't he?' said Mrs Coram. The Jew was grave and handsome. Coram was admiring too, but he was more cautious.

'Yeah. He looks all right,' he said.

His mother was French, the young Jew told them on the first evening, his father German. But they had both come from Austria originally. He had cousins in every country in Europe. He had been educated in England. Slender, with long hands, a little coarse in complexion in the Jewish way, he had grey and acute sepia eyes. He was so boyish, so free in his talk about himself, so shy and eager in his laugh – and yet – how could Mrs Coram describe it? – he seemed ancient, like some fine statue centuries old that has worn and ripened in the sun. He was thick-lipped and had a slight lisping hesitance of speech and this sense of the ancient and profound came perhaps from his habit of pausing before he spoke as if judiciously cogitating. Mrs Coram would sit there expectant and curious. She was used to the hesitations, the struggles with thought of her husband; but there was this difference: when the Jew spoke at last, what he said was serious, considered, a charming decoration of commentary upon their discussions.

M. Pierre always longed for fresh worlds to patronise; he was delighted with Alex. Too delighted for Coram and even for his wife. She could not help being on the point of jealousy when Alex sat and talked to the Frenchman. Coram bluntly wanted to rescue the young man from 'the fraud'.

'You know what's wrong ... with this place,' Coram said to Alex. 'There's no industry.'

'Oh, but surely agriculture, the wine,' said Alex.

'Yeah, I know,' said Coram. 'I mean real industry ...'

'My husband's a chemist, industrial chemist,' she explained.

'I mean,' said Coram grinding on and frowning quizzically, 'they just sit around and grow wine and batten on the visitors, like this feller. What a town like this wants is a couple of good whore shops and a factory ...'

'Tom!' said Mrs Coram. 'How exotic you've become.'

'I expect ample provision has been made,' said the Jew.

'No,' said Coram, in his halting, muddling, bullying tone, 'but you see what I mean.'

He screwed up his eyes. He wished to convey that he had not quite found the words for what he had meant really to say.

The odd thing about the young Jew was that although he seemed to be rich and was cultivated, he had no friends in the town. The young always arrived in troops and car loads at this place. The elderly were often in ones and twos but the young – never. Mrs Coram detected a curious loneliness in him. Polite and formal, he sometimes seemed not to be there. Why had he come? Why to this Pension? It was a cheap place and he obviously had money. Why alone? There were no relations, no women. When he went out he saw no one, spoke to no one. Why not? Alone he visited the mountain churches. He was equable, smiling, interested, happy – yet alone. He liked to be alone, it seemed, and yet when they spoke to him, when Coram – urged by her – asked him to come down to the beach or drive in the car, he came without hesitation, with the continuous effortless good manners and curious lack of intimacy that he always had. It baffled her. She wanted to protect and mother him.

'The Jewboy,' Coram called him. His wife hated this. They quarrelled.

'Stop using that stupid expression,' she said.

'He is,' said her husband. 'I've nothing against him. He's clever. But he's a Jewboy. That's all.' He was not against the Jewboy. He even liked him. They talked together. Coram almost felt protective to him too.

'Aren't you being rather vulgar?' she said to her husband.

One effect the Jew had on them was to make them stop having this kind of quarrel in public. Coram did not change. He was as uncouth as ever. But his wife restrained herself. In mortification she heard his crude stumbling words and quickly interrupted them, smoothed them away hastily so that Alex should not notice them. Either she was brushing her husband away out of hearing, first of all, or she was working with every nerve to transform her husband in the young man's eyes. At the end of the day she was exhausted.

One evening when they went up to bed in the hot room at the top of the house, she said to her husband:

'How old is he, Tom? Twenty-two?'

Coram stared at her. He did not know.

'Do you realise,' she said, 'we're nearly old enough to be his parents.' She had no children. She thought about him as her son.

She took off her clothes. The room was hot. She lay on the bed. Coram, slow and methodical, was taking off his shoes. He went to the window and emptied out the sand. He did not answer. He was working out how old he would have been if the young man had been his son. Before he found an answer, she spoke again.

'One forgets he must think we're old,' she said. 'Do you think he does? Do you think he realises how much older we are? When I look at him it seems a century and then other times we might all be the same age . . .'

'Jews look older than they are,' said Coram.

Her questioning voice stopped. Tom was hanging up his jacket. Every time he took off a garment he walked heavily across the room. Her questions went on silently in her mind. Twenty-two? And she was forty. What did he think of her? What did he think of her husband? Did her husband seem crude and vulgar? Did he seem slow-minded? What did the young man think of both of them? Did he notice things? Did he notice their quarrels? And why did he like to spend time with them, talk to them, go about with them? What was he thinking, what was he feeling? Why was he so friendly and yet ultimately, so unapproachable?

She lay on her side with her slight knees bent. Out of her shabby clothes her body was thin but graceful. Her shoulders were slender, but there were lines on her neck, a reddish stain spreading over her breastbone, a stain hard with exposure to years. Her small breasts were loose and slack over the ribs. The skin creasing under them was sallow. She ran her hands over her hips. She moved her hands round and round on her small flat belly caressing herself where she knew her body was beautiful. It seemed only a few days ago that this had been the body of a young girl. She was filled with sadness for her husband and herself. She could hear the beating of her heart. She found herself listening for the steps of the young man on the stairs. Her heart beat louder. To silence it she said in an anxious voice to her husband, lowering her knees:

'Tom – you haven't stopped wanting me.' She knew her voice was false.

He was taking off his shirt.

'What do you want?' he said.

His face looked grotesque as it looked out of the shirt top.

'Nothing,' she said.

Tom took off his shirt and looked out of the window. You could see the white farms of the valley with their heavy walls from the window. The peasants kept their dogs chained and when there was a moon they barked, a dozen or more of them, one after the other, all down the valley.

'If those dogs – start tonight – we won't sleep,' he said. He came to the bed and waited for her to get under the sheet. She felt his big-boned body beside her and smelled his sharp, curious smell.

'God,' he said. He felt stupefied in this place. In five minutes he was asleep. But she lay awake. Forty she was thinking. A woman of forty with a son. No son. She heard, as she lay awake, the deep breathing of her husband, the curious whistlings of his breath. She lay thinking about her life, puzzling, wondering. Why had she no son? She dozed. She awakened. She threw back the sheet and sleeplessly sighed. If she slept it was only in snatches and she woke up with her heart beating violently and to find herself listening for the sound of a step on the stairs. There was a sensation of inordinate hunger and breathlessness in her body.

Sometimes the young Jew waited for them in the morning and went down with them to the beach. He carried her basket for her or her book. He went back for things.

'Tom,' she said in front of her husband, 'has no manners.'

She walked between them and talked excitedly to the young man about characters in books, or foreign towns, or pictures. She laughed and Coram smiled. He listened with wonder to them.

They sat on the beach. Under his clothes the Jew wore a black bathing suit. He undressed at once and went into the water. His body was alien and slender, the skin burned to the colour of dark corn. He dived in and swam far out into the blue water, beyond the other bathers. He did not laugh or wave or call back, but in his distant, impersonal way he swam far out with long easy strokes. After a mile he lay floating in the sun. He seemed to pass the whole morning out there. She could see his black head. To be young like that and lie in the sea in the sun! And yet how boring to lie there for so long. She would have sudden pangs of anxiety. She would talk of the cold current that came out in the deeper water, from the harbour. She was always glad and relieved when she saw his head moving towards the shore. When he came out of the water he seemed to be dry at once, as if some oil were in his skin. She would see only beads of water at the back of his neck on the short black hair.

'You can swim!' she said.

He smiled.

'Not much,' he said. 'Why don't you?'

The question pleased her. She was astonished by the pleasure it gave her.

'I'm not allowed,' she said with animation. 'Tell me what were you doing out there? You were such a long time.'

His dark eyes were large and candid as he turned to her and she caught her breath. There were three or four black freckles on his skin. Her older yellow eyes returned his innocent gaze. 'Good heavens,' she thought. 'With eyes like that he ought to be a girl.' But she did not know and did not feel that her eyes were older than his.

'I was nearly asleep,' he said. 'The sea is like a mattress.'

He and Coram had a scientific discussion about the possibility of sleeping on the sea.

It was absurd of her, she knew, but she was disappointed. Had he not thought of them, of her? She had been thinking of him all the time.

Coram sat beside them. He talked about the business scandals and frauds in the chemical trade. The quick-minded Jew understood all these stories long before Coram got to their elaborate end. Coram had an obsession with fraud. His slow mind was angry about that kind of quickness of mind which made fraud possible. Coram sat inert, uncomprehending, quite outside the gaiety on the beach. He was not gloomy or morose. He was not sulking. His blue eyes glistened and he had the wistful face of a dog trying to understand. He sat struggling to find words which would convey all that he had felt in this fortnight. He considered the sea and the young man for a long time. Then he undressed. Out of his dark red bathing dress his legs were white and were covered with thick golden hairs. His neck was pink where the sun had caught it. He walked down awkwardly over the pebbles, scowling because of the force of the sun, and straddled knee deep into the water. Then he flung himself on it helplessly, almost angrily and began clawing at it. He seemed to swim with clenched fists. They could see him clawing and crawling as the slow blue swell lifted him up. For a hundred yards he would swim not in a straight line but making a half circle from the beach, as if he were incapable of swimming straight or of knowing where he was going. When he waded out with the water drenching from him there was a look of grievance on his face.

'That water's dirty,' he said when he got back. The Mediterranean was a fraud: it was too warm, thick as syrup. He sat dripping on his wife's books.

One morning when he came back and was drying himself, rubbing his head with the towel, he caught sight of M. Pierre. The Frenchman was sitting not many yards away. Short-sighted, no doubt M. Pierre had not seen them. Beside him were his towels, his red slippers, his red swimming helmet, his cigarette case, his striped bathing gown and his jar of coconut oil. He was in his bathing dress. More than ever, but for his short grey hair, he looked like a pot-bellied middle-aged woman as he rubbed coconut oil on his short brown arms. His monocle was in his eye. He looked like a Lesbian in his monocle.

Coram scowled.

'You see,' he blurted in a loud voice. 'He hasn't been in. He won't go in either. He just comes – down here – all dolled up – to look at the women.'

'Not so loud,' his wife said. 'Please.' She looked with anxiety at the Jew. 'Poor Monsieur Pierre,' said Mrs Coram. 'Remember his age. He's sixty. Perhaps he doesn't want to go in. I bet you won't be swimming when you're sixty.'

'He can swim very well,' said the young Jew politely. 'I went out with him a couple of days ago from the other beach.' He pointed over the small headland. 'He swam out to the ship in the bay. That is three miles.'

'There Tom!' cried his wife.

She was getting bored with these attacks on M. Pierre.

'He's a fraud, a rotten fraud,' said Tom in his smouldering, struggling voice.

'But Alex was with him!' she said.

'I don't care who was with him,' said Tom. 'He's a fraud. You wait till you know him better,' said Tom bluntly to the Jew. 'Believe me he's a rotten little blackmailer.'

'Ssh. You don't know that. You mustn't repeat things,' she said.

'Well, you know it as well as I do,' Tom said.

'Quiet Tom, please,' his wife said. 'He's sitting there.'

'He blackmails his brother-in-law,' Tom persisted. He was addressing himself to the Jew.

'Well, what of it?'

She was angry. M. Pierre could easily hear. And she was angry, trembling with anger, because she did not want the young man to see the uncouthness of her husband and her mortification at it.

'Pierre's sister married a motor millionaire. That's where Pierre gets his money. He waits till his brother-in-law has a new woman and then goes to his sister and pitches the tale to her. She goes to her husband, makes a jealous scene and, to keep her quiet, he gives her what she wants for Pierre.'

'You don't know that,' she said.

'I know it as well as you do,' he said. 'Everyone in the town knows it. He's a fraud.'

'Well don't *shout*. And use some other word. It's a bore,' she said.

'I've no respect for a man who doesn't earn his living,' Coram said. Oh God, she thought, now he's going to quarrel with this boy.

The Jew raised an eyebrow.

'Doesn't he keep the Pension?' the Jew enquired calmly.

'You mean his servants keep it,' blustered Coram. 'Have you ever seen him do a stroke?'

'Well,' his wife said, 'we can't all be like you, Tom. My family never earned a penny in their lives. They would have been horrified at the idea.'

She was speaking not with irony but with indignation. At once she knew she had gone too far. She had failed for once to soothe, to smooth away.

'Ay! Didn't want the dirty work,' Coram said, dropping into his Midland accent. He was not angry. He was, from his own stolid point of view, reasonable and even genial. He wondered why she was 'getting at' him.

'Why dearest,' she said, knowing how irony hurt his vanity. 'You've hit it. You've hit it in one. Bravo. They had no illusions about the nobility of work.' She was ridiculing him.

[48]

'You don't believe in the nobility of work, do you?' she said to the Jew. 'My husband's got a slave's mind,' she said.

'Working is a habit, like sleeping and eating,' said the Jew seriously in his lazy and too perfect enunciation. It had the well-oiled precision of a complexity of small pistons in an impersonal machine. She had heard him speak French and German with an equal excellence. It was predestined.

Living with her husband, always dealing with the inarticulate, she had injured her own full capacity to speak. The Jew stirred her tongue and her lips. She felt an impulse to put her lips to his, not in love, but to draw some of the magic of exposition from him. She wanted her head to be joined to his head in a kiss, her brow to be against his. And then his young face and his dark hair would take the lines from her face and would darken her greyness with the dark, fresh, gleaming stain of youth. She could never really believe that her hair was grey. Her lips were tingling and parted, as lost in this imagination, she gazed at him; innocent and cool-eyed he returned her look. She did not lower her eyes. How young she had been! A shudder of weakness took her shoulders and pain spread like a burn from her throat and over her breasts into the pit of her stomach. She moistened her lips. She saw herself driving in the August sun on an English road twenty years ago, a blue tarred road that ran dazzling like steel into dense trees and then turned and vanished. That day with its climate and the resinous smells of the country always came back when she thought of being young. She was overwhelmed.

The sun had gone in and the sea was grey and sultry and, in this light, the water looked heavier and momentous, higher and deeper at the shore, like a swollen wall. The sight of the small lips of foam was like the sight of thirst, like the sudden inexplicable thirst she had for his lips.

Then she heard Tom's voice. It was explanatory. Sitting with people who were talking he would sometimes slowly come to conclusions about a remark which had struck him earlier in the conversation. He would cling to this, work upon it, struggle with it. She often laughed affectionately at this lagging of his tortoise mind.

The frowns were deep in the thick pink skin of his forehead, the almost tearful glare was in his eyes:

'They didn't want the dirty work,' he said. He was addressing the young man. 'They have butlers. They have a grown man to answer door bells and bring letters. Her family had. They corrupt people by making them slaves . . .'

The Jew listened politely. Coram felt he hadn't said what he meant. The frown deepened as the clear eyes of the Jew looked at his troubled face.

'I was on a jury,' Coram said. 'We had to try a man . . .'

'Oh Tom, not that story about the butler who stole elevenpence. Yes, Tom was on a jury and a man got six months for obtaining a meal value elevenpence from an ABC or a Lyons or some place . . .'

'Yes,' said Coram eagerly, his glaring eyes begging the Jew to see his point.

He wanted to explain that a man corrupts by employing servants. No, not that. What Coram really meant in his heart was that he would not forgive his wife for coming from a rich family. And yet something more than that too, something not so ridiculous, but more painful. He was thinking of some fatal difference between his wife and himself and their fatal difference from society. He was thinking of the wound which this place by the beautiful sea had made in him. He struggled, gave it up.

But she looked scornfully at him. She wiped him out of her sight. She was angry with him for exposing his stupidity before the young Jew. She had fought against it in the last few days; she had been most clever in concealing it. But now she had failed. The thing was public.

She got up angrily from the beach.

'Pick up my book,' she said to her husband. The Jew did not quite hide his astonishment. She saw him gaze and was angrier still with herself. Tactfully he let her husband pick up the book.

They walked back to the Pension. All the way along the road she scarcely spoke to her husband. Once in their room she pulled off her hat and went to the mirror. She saw him reflected in the glass, standing with a look of heavy resentment on his face, bewildered by her.

She saw her own face. The skin was swollen with anger and lined too. Her grey hair was untidy. She was shocked by her physical deterioration. She was ugly. When she heard the young man's step on the stairs she could have wept. She waited: he did not close his door. This was more than she could bear. She turned upon her husband. She raised her voice. She wanted the young man to hear her rage.

Why had she married such an oaf, such a boor!

Her family had begged her not to marry him. She mocked him. He failed at everything. There he was stuck at forty, stuck in his career, stuck for life.

Sometimes he blurted out things in the quarrel but most of the time he was speechless. He stood at the foot of the bed with his tweed coat in his hand, looking at her with heavy blue eyes, his face reddening under the insults, his tongue struggling to answer, his throat moving. He was not cold, but hot with goading. Yet he did nothing. The forces inside him were locked like wrestlers at each other's throats, muddled, powerless. As the quarrel exhausted itself she sank on to the bed. She was fascinated by his hulking incapacity. She had always been fascinated. From the very beginning.

He had not moved during all this but when she lay down on the bed with her head in the pillow he went quietly to the clothes peg and hung up his coat. He stood there rolling up his sleeves. He was going to wash. But she heard him move. She suddenly could not bear that he moved away, even those two steps, from her. She could not bear that he should say to himself, 'One of Julia's scenes. Leave her alone. She'll get over it,' and, taking his opportunity, slip away and go on as if nothing had happened.

She sat up on the edge of the bed. Tears were stinging her cheeks.

'Tom!' she called out. 'What are we going to do? What are we going to do?'

He turned guiltily. She had made him turn.

'I want a child, Tom. What are we going to do? I must have a child.'

Her tone made his blood run cold. There was something wild and horror-struck in her voice. It sounded like a piercing voice crying out in a cavern far away from any other living creature, outraged, animal and incomprehensible.

'God,' he thought. 'Are we going over all that again. I thought we'd resigned ourselves to that.'

He wanted to say, 'You're forty. You can't have a child.' But he could not say that to her. He suspected that she was acting. He said instead what she so often said to him; it seemed to be the burden of their isolated lives.

'Quiet,' he said. 'People will hear.'

'All you ever think of!' she cried out. 'People. Drift. Do nothing.'

They went down the tiled stairs to the dining-room. The sun had come out again but it was weak. A thin film of cloud was rising in the east. The shutters of the dining-room were always closed early in the morning and by noon the house was cool and dark. Before his guests came down, M. Pierre used to go round the room with a fly swatter. Then the wine was brought in a bucket of water and he put it down beside his chair and waited. A clock clucked like some drowsy hen on the wall and the coloured plates, like crude carnival wheels, glowed in the darkened room on the black carved shelves of the cupboard. Mrs Coram came into the room and she heard the dust blowing outside in the breeze and the leaves moving in the vines. A bolt tapped on the shutters.

Their faces were dark in the room, all the faces except Mrs Coram's. Her face was white and heavily powdered. She had been afraid that when she saw Alex she would be unable to speak, but would choke and have to run from the table. To her surprise when she saw him standing by his chair in the room, with his brown bare arm on the chair top, she was able to speak. So easily that she talked a great deal.

'Red wine or white? The wishes of women are the wishes of God,' said M. Pierre to her, paying himself a compliment at the same time.

She began to mock the young man. He laughed. He enjoyed the mockery. 'The wishes of women are the sorrows of Satan,' he said satanically. She went on to mockery of M. Pierre. He was delighted. She repeated in her own way the things which her husband said about him.

'Monsieur Pierre is a fraud,' she said. 'He goes to the beach. He pretends he goes there to swim. Don't you believe it! He goes there to look at the girls. And Alex – he has got a motor inside him. He goes straight out and anchors. You think he's swimming. But he's only floating.'

'I can swim ten miles,' said M. Pierre. He took a small mouthful of wine and boasted in a neat, deprecating way. 'I once swam half across the Channel.'

'Did you?' said the young man with genuine interest.

And once M. Pierre had started to boast he could not be stopped. She egged him on.

'Challenge him,' said Coram morosely to the young man, chewing a piece of meat.

'I challenge him,' said M. Pierre.

But not at the town beach, he said, at the one beyond. It was true he rarely swam at the town beach. He liked to be alone when he swam . . . solitude . . . freedom . . .

'You bet he does,' grunted Coram.

'And Monsieur Coram too,' said M. Pierre.

'I have been in once,' Coram said.

'So have they!' she exclaimed.

When they got up from the table, Coram took his wife aside. He saw through it all, he said to her; it was a device of M. Pierre's to get a drive in his car. She was astonished at this remark. Before today she would not have been astonished, she would have tried to smooth away the difficulties he saw and the suspicions. But now everything was changed. He was like a stranger to her. She saw it clearly; he was mean. Men of his class who had worked their way up from nothing were often mean. Such a rise in the world was admired. She had once admired it. Now it amused her and made her contemptuous. Mean! Why had she never thought of that before? She had been blind.

When lunch was over it was their habit in the house to go to their rooms and sleep. She waited. First M. Pierre went into his room, with his yellow novel. The Jew and her husband lingered. 'The best thing about this place is the drinks,' he was saying. 'They're cheap. You can have as much as you like. Down at those hotels in the town they don't leave the bottle on the table.' He was flushed and torpid. After a while he said:

'I'm going up.'

'I'm staying here. I shall take a deck chair outside. That room's too hot,' she said.

He hesitated. 'Go, go,' she almost cried. She looked at the black shining hair of the young man, his full lips, the brown bare arms that came out of the blue vest, the large darker hands, redder with the flush of blood. They were spread on the table, stroking the cloth. She could feel, in imagination, those palms on her body. Her heart raced and shook her. She and he would be alone. She would talk to him, she would not listen to him, he should not have his own words, perfect, predestined and impersonal. It was she who would talk. She would make him halt and stammer. She would break through this perfection of impersonal speech. She would talk and make him know her. She would bring herself close to him with words, and then with touch. She would touch him. He was young, he was without will: he would touch her. She saw in her mind the open door of his room. She thought all this as her husband hesitated, stupefied, by the table.

But when he went and she was alone with Alex her heart stopped and there were no words in her throat. Her whole body was trembling, the bones of her knees were hard to her hands.

'I think,' Alex suddenly said as he had often said before. 'I think I shall go for a walk. I'll be back for the swim,' he said.

She gasped. She looked with intent irony at him. She saw him get up from the table and, in his oddly studied way, as if there were meat in his solitude no one else could know, he went.

'You fool,' she said to herself. But as she stared out of the open door and heard his cool footsteps on the gravel outside until the sound of the breeze in the vines licked them away, she felt lost with relief.

In a deck chair under the mulberry tree she thought about herself and her husband. It was the time of year when the fruit of the mulberry falls. The berries dropped on to the gravel, into the tank where the frogs croaked at night and on to the table. They broke there. Sometimes they dropped like small hard hearts into her lap and when she picked them off they crushed in her fingers and the red juice ran out. She breathed deeply, almost panting in her chair.

She had married an outcast. Her relations had said that and they had been right. Some of those who had been right – her mother and father, for example, – were dead. Tom's father had had a small boot-repairing business in Leicester. He worked in the front room of their house, with its bay window. Coram. Repairs While You Wait. That man and his wife had had seven children. Imagine such a life! Tom had studied, won scholarships, passed examinations. All his life he had been different from his brothers and sisters. Now his job was chemistry. Once he was going to be a famous chemist. Instead he got commercial jobs in the laboratories of big firms. He did not belong to the working class any more. He did not belong to her class. He did not belong to the class of the comfortable professional people he now met. He did not belong anywhere. He was lost, rough, unfinished, ugly, unshaped by the wise and harmonious hand of a good environment.

And she had really been the same. That was what had brought them together. He was ugly in life, she was ugly in body; two ugly people cut off from all others, living in their desert island.

Her family were country gentry, not very rich, with small private incomes and testy, tiresome genteel habits. The males went into the army. The females married into the army. You saw one and you had seen them all. She had always been small and thin; her long nose, her long mouth, her almost yellowish eyes and dead clay skin made her ugly. She had to be clever and lively, had to have a will or no one would have noticed her. At one time she supposed she would marry one of those tedious young men with dead eyes and little fair moustaches who were 'keen' on gunnery and motor cars. She had thrown herself at them – thrown herself at them, indeed, like a bomb. That didn't suit the modern militarists. They had the tastes of clerks. They fingered their moustaches, looked dead and embarrassed at her, said they couldn't bear 'highbrow' girls and got away as quickly as they could. They were shocked because she didn't wear gloves. The naked finger seemed an indecency to them. 'I could be a General's wife by now if I'd worn gloves,' she used to say. Before they could throw her out and treat her as the bright, noisy impossible woman who appears in every family, she threw them out.

So she married Tom. She got away from her home, went to live with a friend, met Tom and married him. There was a row. 'The toothpaste man,' her relations called him. Thought she was going to live in a chemist's shop. He became a stick to beat her family with; he was going to be a great man, a great scientist – she flogged them. He was going to be a much greater man than those 'keen' subalterns with their flannel bags, dance records and little moustaches or those furtive majors, guilty with self-love.

She looked back on these days. She had always expected something dramatic and sudden to happen. But – what was it? – Tom had not become a great man. The emergence from his class had become really an obsession, and a habit. He was struggling to emerge long after he had emerged. He was always spending his energy on reacting from something which no longer existed. He lived – she could never quite understand it – in the grip of some thwarting inward conflict, his energy went into this invisible struggle. The veins and the muscles swelled as if they would burst. Torn between dealing with her, that is with the simple business of giving her simple natural happiness, and himself, he was paralysed. And they had had no children. Whose fault was that? At first it was a mercy because they were poor, but later? She slept with him. Her body had grown old trying to tear a child from him. Afterwards she attacked him. He listened stupefied.

Why had this happened to her? And why had she this guilt towards him so that now she pitied him and spent all her day coming between him and difficulty? She had sown her disappointment in him, he had sown his frustration in her. Why? And why did they live in a circle they could not break? Why did they live so long in it until suddenly she was forty, a grey-haired woman?

She went over these things but she was not thinking and feeling them only. There was the soft stroke of a pulse between her breasts, making her breathless with every throb. Movement came to her blood from the sight of the blowing vines and the red soil of the olive fields and out of the wind-whitened sky. Her lips parted in thirst for the articulate lips of the young Jew. She could not sleep or read.

At last she went into the cool house. The flies, driven indoors by the wind, were swimming in the darkness. She went up the stairs to her room.

'Get up,' she said to her husband. 'We must go.'

He couldn't go in these clothes, she said. He must get the car. She bullied him. She changed into a green dress. Grumbling, he changed.

She looked out of the window. Alex was not coming. She could see the valley and the trees flowing and silvered by the wind. Dust was blowing along the roads between the earth and sun giving it a weird and brilliant light like the glitter of silica in granite.

Tom went downstairs. His clothes were thrown all over the room.

'We're waiting,' he said when she came down. The black car was there and M. Pierre. He stood by it as if he owned it.

'Women,' said M. Pierre, 'are like the bon Dieu. They live not in time but in eternity.'

Coram glared at him. Alex was there, tall and impersonal. He had come back, he said, some other way. He gravely considered M. Pierre's remark. He made a quotation from a poet. This was obscure to her and everyone.

'Where the hell's this picnic going to be,' said Coram.

They disputed about where they should sit. That is, she said one thing and her husband another. At last M. Pierre was in front and she and the young man were at the back. Coram got in and sulked. No one had answered his question. 'If anyone knows where they're going they'd better drive,' he said. 'The far beach,' she called out. 'Well, in God's name!' he muttered. Still he drove off.

'Are you crowded at the back?' he said later in a worried voice. A sudden schoolgirl hilarity took her.

'We like it,' she cried loudly, giggling. And pressed her legs against Alex.

She was immediately ashamed of her voice. Before she could stop herself she cried out: 'I've got my young man.'

She swaggered her arm through his and laughed loudly close to his face. She was horrified at herself. He laughed discreetly, in a tolerant elderly way at her. So they bumped and brushed over the bad roads to the beach. Coram swore it would break the springs of his car, this damfool idea. She could see the sweat on her husband's thick pink neck. She goaded him. She called to him not to crawl, not to bump them about, not to take the town road but the other. Coram turned angrily to her.

She wanted to show the young man: 'You see, I don't care. I don't care how revolting I am. I don't care for anything, I hate everything except a desire that is in me. There is nothing but that.'

[57]

The car topped the hill and she turned her head to look back upon the town. She was surprised. Two belfries stood above the roofs. She had never seen them before. The clay-coloured houses were closely packed together by the hills and those that were in the sun stood out white and tall. The roofs went up in tiers and over each roof a pair of windows stared like foreign eyes. The houses were a phalanx of white and alien witnesses. She was startled to think that she had brought her life to a place so strange to her. She and her husband had lived in the deeply worn groove of their lives even in this holiday, and had not noticed the place. Her mood quietened.

The outlying villas of this side of the town were newer and the air burned with the new resinous odour of the pines and the two flames of sea and sky.

'I often come this way,' said the Jew, 'because there is more air. Do you know the waiter in the café by the harbour? On one hot day last year he chased his wife's lover down the street, loosing off a revolver. He breaks out once a year. The rest of the time he is the perfectly contented complaisant husband. If the café were up here, it would not happen. Or perhaps he might only be complaisant once a year. Probably our whole emotional life is ruled by temperature and air currents.'

She looked at him. 'You have read your Huxley,' she said dryly, 'haven't you?' But afterwards she felt repentant because she thought if he was showing off, it was because he was young. '*I* could cure him of that.'

Presently the car stopped. They had got to the beach. They sat for a minute in the car studying it. It was a long beach of clean sand, looped between two promontories of rock, a wilder beach than the one by the town where people came to picnic. Now there was no one on it. And here the sea was not the pan of enamelled water they had known but was open and stood up high from the beach like a loose tottering wall, green, wind-torn, sun-shot and riotous. The sky was whitened on the horizon. The lighthouse on the red spit eight miles across the bay seemed to be racing through the water like a periscope. The whole coast was like groups of reddened riders driving the waves into a corral.

'The east wind,' said M. Pierre, from his window, considering it.

They got out of the car. They walked on the sand and the waves unrolled in timed relay along the shore. The three men and Mrs Coram stood singly, separated by the wind, gazing at the tumult. They spoke and then turned to see where their words had gone. The wind had swept them from their lips and no one could hear.

Alex stayed behind but soon he ran forward in his bathing dress.

'You're not going!' Tom said. The sea was too wild. The Jew did not hear him and ran down to the shore.

'Oh!' Mrs Coram said anxiously and moved to Pierre.

Without a word the Jew had dived in. Now he was swimming out. She held Pierre's arm tightly and then slowly the grip of her fingers relaxed. She smiled and then she laughed. It was like watching a miracle to see Alex rise and sink with those tall waves, strike farther out and play like some remote god with their dazzling falls. Sometimes he seemed to drop like a stone to the sea's floor and then up he shot again as if he had danced to the surface. She watched him, entranced.

'He's fine,' she called. She looked for Tom. He was standing back from them, looking resentfully, confusedly, at the sea. Suddenly all her heart was with the swimmer and her mind felt clean by the cleansing sea. Her fear for him went. She adored his danger in the water and the way he sought it, the way he paused and went for the greatest waves and sailed through.

'Tom!' she called.

Before he knew what she wanted Coram said:

'I'm not going out in that.'

'Pierre is,' she called. 'Aren't you?'

The old man sat down on the shingle. Yes, he was going in, he said.

Alex came back. He came out and stood by the water, unable to leave it. He was fifty yards from them. Suddenly he had dived in again. Then he came out once more and stood throwing stones into the sea. She saw him crouch and his long arm fling out as he threw the stone. He was smiling when he came back to them.

They sat down and talked about the rough water. They were waiting for Pierre to go. He did nothing. He sat down there and talked. The Jew eyed him. Eagerly he wanted Pierre to come. The time passed and Pierre said this sea was nothing. He began to boast of a time when he had been in a yacht which had been dismasted in a gale. 'I looked death in the face,' he said. Coram glowered, and winked at the Jew.

The Jew grew tired of waiting and said he was going to try the other end of the beach. She watched him walk away over the sand. Like a boy he picked up stones to throw as he went. She was hurt that he went away from her and yet she admired him more for this. She leaned back on her elbow; the soft stroke of pleasure and pain was beating between her breasts, a stroke for every step of his brown legs across the sand, a stroke for every fall of the sea on the shore. She saw him at last run down to the water and go in. He went far out of sight until there was a crest of fear to every breath of longing in her. He has gone far enough, she thought, far enough away from me.

She stood up. If she could fly in this wind over the sea and, like a gull, call to him from overhead and, pretending to be pursued, make him follow her to the shore! Then, to her surprise, he was suddenly on the shore again, standing as he had done before, studying the waves he had just been through. He stood there a long time and afterwards sat down and watched them. She called to him. It was too far. Timelessly he lived in his far away youth. What was he doing, what was he thinking as he sat there remote in the other world of his youth?

Now M. Pierre had the beach to himself and there were no near competitors, he walked away and undressed. Presently he came back, short and corpulent in his bathing dress and his red slippers. He asked particularly that Mrs Coram should be careful with his eyeglass. He fastened his helmet. Dandified, deprecating, like the leading dancer in a beauty chorus he stood before them.

'I float naturally in the sea,' he observed as if he were a scientific exhibit, 'because the balance of displacement in my case is exact.'

He went to the sea's edge like royalty pausing every few yards to nod.

'Look,' she said.

It was odd, for the moment, to be alone with her husband, to feel that just he and she saw this as they alone had seen many other things in the world.

'He won't go in,' said Coram.

M. Pierre had reached the sea's edge. Impertinently a large wave broke and he stood, surprised, like an ornament in a spread lace doily of surf.

It swilled his ankles. He waited for it to seethe back a little and then he bent and wetted his forehead. He paused again. A green wave stood up on end, eight feet high, arched and luminous like a carved window in a cathedral. It hung waiting to crash. But before it crashed an astonishing thing happened. The fat little man had kicked up his heels and dived clean through it. They saw the soles of his red rubber shoes as he went through and disappeared. There he was on the other side of the wave in the trough and then, once again, he dived through the next wave and the next, clambering over the surf-torn ridges like a little beetle. The foam spat round him, suds of it dabbed his face. Now his head in its blue bathing helmet bobbed up in dignified surprise at the top of a wave, now he was trudging out further and further into the riotous water.

'He's floating,' said Tom.

'He's swimming,' she said.

They talked and watched. She looked down the beach for Alex. He was lying full length in the sun.

Pierre was far out. How far they could not tell. Sometimes they saw the head bobbing in the water, sometimes they could not see him. They lost him. It was difficult to see against the flash of the sun. Nearer to them the emerald water fell in its many concussions on the shore and the shingle sang as the undertow drew back. She saw with surprise the lighthouse still racing, periscope-like, through the waves, dashing through the water and yet going nowhere. Why does he stay there, why doesn't he come back? She looked avidly to the young man stretched on the shore.

'Let's go up to the car and have a drink,' said Tom.

'No,' she said. 'Wait.'

She looked up for Pierre. He was not straight ahead of them.

'Where is Pierre?'

Ah, there he was; he was far out, swimming as far as they could see parallel to the beach.

She got up and walked along the beach. The mounting chaos of the sea was like the confusion of her heart. The sea had broken loose from the still sky and the stable earth; her life was breaking loose too from everything she had known. Her life was becoming free and alarmed. The prostration of each wave upon the sand mocked her with the imagination of desire for ever fulfilling and satiate; satiate and fulfilling. She walked dazed and giddily towards Alex as if she were being blown towards him. Her dress blew and the wind wetted her eyes. She lifted her arms above her head and the wind blew into her legs, drove back her skirts. She paused. Did he see her? Did he see her miming her passion, with the wind?

She marched back to her husband. The wind caught and blew her almost unwillingly fast towards him.

'Tom!' she said. 'I shall have a child by someone else.'

He looked at her, in his habitual startled stupor. He hated this sea, this beach, this extraordinary country. He simply did not believe in it. Those words seemed like the country, wild and incredible. He just did not believe them, any more than he believed that the wind could speak. God, he thought she'd had her scene for the day and had got over it.

He was struggling.

'I have decided,' she said. It was an ultimatum.

He smiled because he could not speak.

'You don't believe me.'

'If you say so, I believe you.'

She had terrified him. He was like a man blundering about a darkened room. Say? What could he say? She'd be crying before the night was out that she could never leave him. Or would she? He was relieved to see her walk away and to sink back into his habitual stupor. When she had gone he wanted to seize her and shake her. He saw another man lying naked on her; the picture enraged him and yet it gave him the happiness of an inexpressible jealousy. Then tears came to his eyes and he felt like a child.

She was walking away looking for Pierre and thinking, 'He doesn't believe me. He's a lout.'

She watched Pierre as she walked. An old man, a nice old man, a funny old man. And very brave. Two unconcerned men, making no fuss, one old and one young: Pierre and the Jew.

The grace of the Jew, the comic strength of Pierre – they belonged to a free, articulate world. She was opposite to Pierre now. The sea was heavy in his course, the waves weightier there and once or twice a roller cracked at the crest as he was swimming up it. But he was coming in, she saw, very slowly coming in. He was coming in much farther down. She came back to Tom.

'Look,' she jeered. She seemed to have forgotten her earlier words. 'You said he couldn't swim!' Coram screwed up his eyes. She walked down once more to the place where Pierre would land. The roar of the waves was denser and more chaotic. Tom followed her down. Pierre hardly seemed nearer. It was long waiting for him to come in.

At this end of the beach there was rock. It ran out from the promontory into the water. She climbed up to get a better view. Suddenly she called out in a controlled voice:

'Tom. Come here. Look.'

He climbed up and followed her. She was looking down. When he got there he looked down too. 'Hell,' he said.

Below them was a wide cavern worn by the sea with two spurs of rock running out into the water from either side of it. The enormous waves broke on the outer spurs and then came colliding with each other and breaking against the tables of rock submerged in the water, jostled, punched and scattered in green lumps into the cave. With a hollow boom they struck and then swept back on the green tongue of the undertow. The place was like a wide gulping mouth with jagged teeth. Mr and Mrs Coram could not hear themselves speak, though they stood near together looking down at the hole with wonder and fear.

'Tom,' she said, clutching his arm. He pulled his arm away. He was frightened too.

'Tom!' she said. 'Is he all right?'

'What?'

'Pierre – he's not coming in here?' she said.

He looked at the hole and drew back.

'Tom, he is. He is!' she cried out suddenly in a voice that stopped his heart. 'He's drifting. He's drifting in here. These rocks will kill him.'

Tom glared at the sea. He could see it as plainly as she. He backed away.

'The damn fool,' Tom said. 'He's all right.'

'He's not. Look.'

He was drifting. He had been drifting all the time they had talked. They had thought he was swimming parallel to the beach but all the time he had been drifting.

They could see M. Pierre plainly. In five minutes he would be borne beyond the first spur and would be carried into the hole.

As he came nearer they saw him at battle. They saw him fighting and striking out with his arms and legs. His cap had come loose and his grey hair was plastered over his head. His face had its little air of deprecation, but he was gasping and spitting water, his eyes were stern and bewildered as if he had not time to decide which of the waves that slapped him on the face was his opponent. He was like a man with dogs jumping up at his waving arms. The Corams were above him on the rock and she called out and signalled to him but he did not look up.

'Are you all right?' she called.

'Course he's all right,' said Coram.

It seemed to her that Pierre refused to look up but kept his eyes lowered. Increasingly, as he got into the outer breakers he had the careless, dead look of a body that cannot struggle any more and helplessly allows itself to be thrown to its pursuers. The two watchers stood hypnotised on the rock. Then Mrs Coram screamed. A wave, larger than the rest, seemed to dive under Pierre and throw him half out of the water. His arms absurdly declaimed in space and a look of dazed consternation was on his face as he dropped into the trough. The sun in the sky flashed like his own monocle upon him and the rich foam.

'Quick. He is going,' she cried to her husband, clambering down the rock to the beach.

'Come on,' she said. He followed her down. She ran towards the surf. 'We'll make a chain. Quick. Take my hand. He's finished. We'll get him before he goes.'

She stretched out her hand.

'Get Alex,' she said. 'Run and get him. We'll make a chain. Quickly run and get him.'

But Tom drew back. He drew back a yard, two yards, he retreated up the beach backing away.

'No,' he said angrily waving his arm as though thrusting her away. Yet she was not near him or touching him.

'Tom!' she called. 'Quick. You can swim. I'll come.'

'No,' he said.

She did not see for a moment that the look of angry stupor on his face was fear, that he was prepared to let Pierre drown; and then, as he half ran up the beach she saw it. He would not go in himself. He would not fetch Alex. He was going to stand there and let Pierre drown. 'Tom,' she called. She saw his thick red glistening face, his immovable glowering struggling stare. He stood like a chained man. He would stand there like that doing nothing and let Pierre drown. She was appalled.

So she ran. She ran down the beach, calling, waving to the Jew.

It happened that he had got up and was wandering idly along the surf towards them. He heard her cry and thought she was calling out with the excitement of the wind. Then he saw.

'Quick,' she called. 'Pierre is drowning.'

She clutched his arm as the Jew came up to her. He gave a glance, jerked away her arm, and ran swiftly along the beach. She followed him. She saw him smile as he ran, the slight gleam of his teeth. When he got near the rock he broke into a short laugh of joy and rushed into the water. In two strokes he was there.

She feared for both of them. She saw a wave rise slowly like an animal just behind Pierre and a second greater one, green as ice and snowy with fluttering spume, following it closely. The two swimmers stared with brief, almost polite surprise at each other. Then the Jew flung himself bodily upon Pierre. An arm shot up. Their legs were in the air. They were thrown like two wrestlers in the water. There was a shout. The Jew came up, his arm went out and his hand – the big hand she had seen upon the table that morning in the Pension – caught the old man under the armpit. They were clear of the rock. They swayed like waltzing partners and then the enormous wave picked them both up, tossed them to its crest and threw them headlong over and over on the shore. The falling wave soaked Mrs Coram as they fell.

M. Pierre crawled dripping up the shingle and sank down panting. His face was greenish in colour, his skin purple with cold. He looked astonished to be out of the sea. The Jew had a lump the size of an egg on his shin.

[65]

'I thought I was finished,' Pierre said.

'I'll get some brandy,' Mrs Coram said.

'No,' he said. 'It is not necessary.'

'You saved his life,' she said excitedly to the Jew.

'It was nothing,' he said. 'I found myself the current out there is strong.'

'I could do nothing against the current,' Pierre said. 'I was finished. That,' he said in his absurd negligent way, 'is the second time I have looked death in the face.'

'Rub yourself with the towel,' she said.

He did not like being treated as an old man.

'I'm all right,' he said. After all, once he had attempted to swim the Channel. Perhaps they would believe now he was a swimmer.

'It is always you good swimmers who nearly drown,' she said tactfully.

'Yes,' Pierre boasted, becoming proud as he warmed up. 'I nearly drowned! I nearly drowned! Ah yes, I nearly drowned.'

The emotion of the rescue had driven everything else from her mind. The scene was still in front of her. She looked with fear still at the careless water by the rock where only a few minutes ago she had seen him nearly go. Never would she forget his expressionless head in the water. With the eyelids lowered it had looked grave, detached, like a guillotined head. She was shivering: her fingers were still tightly clenched. Supposing now they had M. Pierre dead beside them. How near they had been to death! She shuddered. The sea, green and dark as a blown shrub, with its slop of foam, sickened her.

'He is not very grateful,' she thought. And she said aloud:

'Monsieur Pierre, but for Alex you would be dead.'

'Ah yes,' said M. Pierre turning to the Jew not very warmly. 'I must express my warmest thanks to you. That is the second time I have looked . . .'

'You get no credit,' she said to Alex in English just in her husband's way. It was odd how she had his habit in a time of stress. 'He thinks he's immortal.'

'Parlez français,' said M. Pierre.

'She says,' said Alex quickly, 'that you are immortal.'

All this time she was standing up. One side of her dress had been soaked by the wave which had borne them in. As she talked she could see Tom standing forty yards off. He was standing by the car as if for protection and half turned from the sight of the sea. She was still too much in the excitement of the rescue, going over it again and again, to realise that she was looking at him or to know what she thought of him.

'We must get you home,' she said to M. Pierre, 'quickly.'

'There is no hurry,' he said with dignity. 'Sit down, Madame. Calm yourself. When one has looked death in the face . . .'

She obeyed. She was surprised they thought her not calm. She sat next to Alex as all the afternoon, when he had gone off, she had wished to do. She looked at his arms, his chest and his legs as if to find the courage shining on his body.

'It was nothing.' She could see that this was true. It had been nothing to him. One must not exaggerate. He was young. His black hair was thick and shining and young. His eyes were young too. He had, as she had always thought, that peculiarly ancient and everlasting youth of the Greek statues that are sometimes unearthed in this Mediterranean soil. He was equable and in command of himself, he was at the beginning of everything, at the beginning of the mind and the body. There was no difficulty anywhere, it was all as easy as that smile of his when he ran into the water. Had she been like that when she was young? How had she been? Had everything been easy? No, it had been difficult. She could not remember truly, but she could not believe she had ever been as young as he was young. Without knowing it she touched his bare leg with two of her fingers and ran them down to his knee. The skin was firm.

'You're cold,' she said. The coldness startled her. He had probably never slept with a woman. She found herself, as she touched that hard body which did not move under her touch, pitying the woman who might have slept with this perfect, impersonal, impenetrable man.

There was resentment against his perfection, his laugh in the water, his effortless achievement. He showed no weakness. There was no confusion in him. There was no discernible vice. She could not speak.

And now, as she calmed down and saw Tom, her heart started. She saw, really saw him for the first time since the rescue and went up the tiring shingle to him. He was still standing against the car.

[67]

'The damn fool,' Coram said before his wife could speak. 'Trying to drown others beside himself. They're all alike.'

'It is no thanks to you that we saved him,' she said. 'Leave it to me! You ran away!' she said angrily.

'I didn't,' he said. 'Drown myself for a fool like that. What do you take me for? He wasn't drowning anyway.'

'He was,' she said. 'And you ran away. You wouldn't even go for Alex. I had to go.'

'No need to shout,' he said. She stood below him on the shingle and he winced as if she were throwing stones at him. 'These people get me down in this place,' he said, 'going into a sea like that.'

'You ran away when I called,' she insisted.

'Are you saying I'm a coward?' he said.

He looked at her small, shrilling figure. She was ugly when she was in a temper, like a youth, gawky, bony, unsensual. Now she had joined all the things that were against him. The beauty of this country was a fraud, a treachery against the things he had known. He saw the red street of his childhood, heard the tap of his father's hammer, the workers getting off the trams with their packages and little bags in their hands, the oil on their dungarees. He heard the swing door of his laboratory, the drum of machines and smoke drooping like wool through the Midland rain, saw the cold morning placards. That was his life. The emeralds and ultramarine of this sea and the reddened, pine-plumed coast made him think of those gaudy *cocottes* he had seen in Paris. The beauty was corruption and betrayal.

He did not know how to say this. It was confused in his mind. He blustered. He glared. She saw through the glowering eyes the piteous struggle, the helpless fear. He was ugly. He stood there blustering and alone with his dust-covered car, an outcast.

'I'm saying you could have helped,' she said.

She looked in anger at him. Her heart was beating loudly, her blood was up. It was not the rescue – she half realised now – which had stirred her – but the failure to rescue. From the very moment when he had run away, something in her had run after him, clamouring for him, trying to drag him back. Now, his muddle seemed to drag her in too.

'Help that swine!' he said.

M. Pierre and Alex came to the car carrying their towels.

'You think of no one but yourself,' she said to her husband in front of them. 'For God's sake let's get home.'

Everyone looked at her apprehensively. Coram got into the car and she, determined not to let him escape one moment of her contempt, sat beside him. Pierre and Alex were at the back. In silence they drove from the beach and over the hill from which the white town could be seen stacked closely in the sun, like a pack of tall cards. As the car crawled through the narrow streets which were crowded in the evenings with holiday makers and workers who came up from the harbour or down from the fields, Pierre put his head out of the window. He waved to friends sitting in cafés.

'I nearly drowned!' he called out. 'I nearly drowned.'

'Drowned?' people laughed, getting up from their tables.

'For the second time in my life,' he called, 'I have looked death in the face.'

'Tiens!'

'Yes, I nearly . . .'

Coram trod on the accelerator. M. Pierre fell back into his seat, his little scene cut short, as they swerved up the dusty road to the Pension.

Coram was silent. They got out and he went to put the car away. Pierre went to his room and she and Alex went up the stairs of the shuttered house to their rooms. She was ahead of him. When she got to his landing she saw his door was open. She turned and said:

'May I see what you are like?'

'Of course,' he said.

She went into his room and he followed her. The shutters were closed and the room was dark and cool. There was the white shape of the bed, the pile of books by its side, the white enamel basin on its iron stand and his suitcase on a chair. He went to push open the shutters.

'Oh don't do that,' she said. But one shutter slipped open. Her face was white and hard, tragically emptied of all expression as she looked at his polite face.

There was nothing.

She went over and lay on the bed. He raised his eyebrows slightly. She saw him raise them.

'They are hard in this house,' she said. 'The beds.'

'A bit,' he said.

She leant up on one elbow.

'You were plucky,' she said, 'this afternoon. But my husband ran away.'

'Oh no,' he said. 'He had not changed. He had not been in.'

'He ran away,' she said. 'He wouldn't even go and fetch you.'

'One could not expect . . .' Alex began.

'You mean you are young?' she said.

'Yes,' said Alex.

'My husband is my age,' she said in a hard voice. 'Turned forty.'

'I admired what you did,' she said.

He murmured something politely. She got up and sat on the edge of the bed.

'My skirt,' she said, 'was soaked. Look.'

She pulled it above her knees. 'Feel it,' she said.

He came close to her and felt the frock. She stared into his eyes as he touched the cloth. She was shivering.

'Close the door,' she said suddenly. 'I must take it off. I don't want Monsieur Pierre to see me.' He closed the door. While his back was turned she picked up the hem of her frock and pulled it over her head. She stood bare-legged in her white underclothes. The shoulder strap slipped over her arm. She knew that he saw her white breast.

'In England this might be misunderstood,' she said, with a loud nervous laugh. 'But not in France.' She laughed and stared, frightened, at him.

'I'm old enough to be your mother, aren't I?'

'Well, not quite,' he said.

She was nearly choking. She could nearly scream. She was ugly and hideous. She had wanted to show him what she was. 'Feel how cold I am,' she said putting out her leg. He put his hand on her white thigh. It was soft and warm. He was puzzled.

'Do you mind?' she said. She lay back on the bed. Tears came into her eyes when she spoke.

'You are young,' she said. 'Come and sit here.'

He came and sat on the edge of the bed beside her. He was very puzzled. She took his hand. But there was no desire in her. It had gone. Where had it gone? She dropped his hand and stared helplessly at him. She saw that he did not want her and that it had not occurred to him to want her. If she had drawn his head down to her breast she would have been cold to his touch. There was no desire, but only shame and anger in her heart.

'I suppose,' she said suddenly, with a false yawn, 'that this is a little unconventional.'

To her astonishment he got up.

'Have you ever been in love?' she asked in a mocking voice to call him back. 'Hardly, I expect, not yet. You are only a child.'

Before he could answer she said:

'Too young to sleep with a woman.'

Now he looked embarrassed and angry. She laughed. She got up. She was delighted she had made him angry.

She took her frock and waited. Perhaps he would attempt to kiss her. She stood waiting for him. But he did not move. Slowly a horror of what she was doing came over her. There was no desire. She saw too a remote fear of her in his brown eyes.

'Thank you,' she said. She put the frock against her breast and went to the door. She hoped for one more humiliation when she opened it: that she should be seen, half naked, leaving his room. But there was no one on the stairs.

From the landing window as she went up she saw the familiar picture. The military rows of the vines in the red soil. The shadow-pocked mountains, the pines. It was like a postcard view taken in the sun, the sun not of today but of other days, a sun which was not warm but the indifferent, hard, dead brilliance of the past itself, surrounding her life.

She lay down on her bed and sobbed with misery and shame as a broken creature will abase itself before a bloodless, unapproachable idol. She sobbed because of her ugliness and of the ugliness of having no desire. She had abased and humiliated herself. When had the desire gone? Before Alex had rushed to the rescue into the sea it had been there. When?

[71]

It had gone when she had heard her husband's refusal and had seen the fear and helplessness in his eyes, the muddle in his heart. Her desire had not gone winged after the rescuer, but angry, hurt, astounded and shocked towards her husband. She knew this.

She stopped weeping and listened for him. And in this clarity of the listening mind she knew she had not gone to Alex's room to will her desire to life or even to will it out of him, but to abase herself to the depths of her husband's abasement. He dominated her entirely, all her life; she wished to be no better than he. They were both of them like that; helpless, halted, tangled people, outcasts in everything they did.

She heard him coming up the stairs.

'Tom,' she called. 'Tom.'

She went avidly to the door.

That evening in the quietness after dinner some friends of M. Pierre's came in to hear about his escape. He wore his yachting cap that night. Death, he said, had no terrors for him, nor had the sea. In his case the balance of displacement was exact; once already he had looked death in the face . . . He was the hero. He did not once refer to his rescuer. Two of the guests were English, a Colonel and his wife, and to them Coram, also, told the story. He stumbled over his words. He lumbered on. They sat under the massed black leaves of the mulberry tree.

Mrs Coram sat there calm, clever and experienced, as she always was. Here and there, as she always did, she helped her husband over the story. 'Let me tell you what happened,' she said smiling. They turned to her with relief and Coram himself was grateful.

Wonderful story she always tells, they said. Ought to write. Why didn't she take it up? 'Go on, Mrs Coram, give us the lowdown.'

They all laughed, except Pierre, under the trees. He was out of his depth in so much quick English.

It was ridiculous, she said, in her quickest voice, glancing at Alex, to go out in a sea like that. She described the scene.

'Tom tried to persuade him not to go, but he would. You know how vain they are,' she said. 'And then,' she said as they laughed with approval and caught the excitement of her story. 'Poor Tom had to go in and rescue him.'

She looked at them. Her eyes were brilliant, her whole body alive with challenge as she glanced from her visitors to Alex and Tom.

'B ...' Tom began.

'Alex was at the other end of the beach and Tom had to go in and rescue him,' she repeated.

She looked at all of them with defiance and a pause of pity for Alex; at Tom, like a cracking whip before a too docile lion. The Corams against the world.

The Aristocrat

It was at two o'clock and after a good lunch that Mr Murgatroyd went into The Prince of Denmark and took his stand four-square and defensive against the bar. The time was seven minutes past two by the clock above the bottles, but by his gold watch, which he slipped out of its chamois case, it was two. He remarked upon this to Mrs Pierce, the publican, who was leaning with her fat forearms on the bar, musing like a cat; and she croaked out a long story about her husband winding up the clock on Saturday nights. The usual people were on the bench in the small bar, crowded, cheerful and comfortable. Mr Sanders with a red carnation in his buttonhole, squeezing his little legs together with glee, like a house fly in the sun, in the midst of three women and not sitting next to his wife. They all heard the conversation with Mrs Pierce and they heard her say:

'Bit of an 'eat wave isn't it, Mr Murgatroyd?' nodding to the first flakes of March snow in the street.

To this Mr Sanders added his news:

'Couple of cases of sunstroke in the Theobald's Road they tell me.'

The presence of Mr Murgatroyd brought out Mr Sanders's wit. He was a dogged little man with a waxed moustache and tobacco-stained fingers, one to nudge the ladies in the ribs with his sharp elbows, a jumping cracker at three-ten a week in the provision trade. And bald.

Mr Murgatroyd was wearing a smart, new grey flannel suit. A pair of yellow gloves drooped in one hand like the most elegant banana skins. He was a shy and important man. His eloquence was in the breadth of his shoulders, in the thick pink of his face after the first drink, in the full-moon expansion of his stomach under the smooth waistcoat and in the polish of his shoes. Mrs Sanders, a woman pushed to the outskirts of everything and sitting on the extreme edge of the bench, was ashamed

[74]

of her wriggling husband when Mr Murgatroyd, blue-eyed, shy and impressive, stood with his lids lowered, gazing at the floor, secure and silent in his substance. The young Jewess who was always there on Saturday afternoon got up and opened her fur coat when Mr Murgatroyd came in. She rested one hand on her hip, gave a long look into the mirror and began walking up and down, almost touching Mr Murgatroyd when she turned. Mr Murgatroyd lowered his eyes when she came, rolling her lips, humming and laughing towards him.

It was Mr Sanders's round. Mr Murgatroyd took a deep drink, faced the eyes of the dancing Jewess for a second, and then, as the beer sank down in him, grew heavy in the head, solid in his silence and vague in his vision.

It was at this moment when they were busy with their glasses, all talking at once, when Mr Murgatroyd unbuttoned his new coat and was easing out his disclaiming stomach and when the Jewess gave it a tap on the fourth button, with the words:

'What you got in there Mr Murgatroyd?' – it was at this moment that a stranger came into the bar. He was a tall, white-haired man and was among them just as Mr Sanders was pulling the money out of his pocket. Mr Sanders was bobbing about, standing in his way.

'Jim,' whispered Mrs Sanders, anxiously leaning across to pull her husband's coat tails. 'There's a gentleman wants to get past.'

'Excuse me, mister,' said Mr Sanders, holding a full glass in each hand and abashed by the height of the stranger. A quiet, slightly wavering voice replied and the stranger walked past them to the bar.

'A beer if you please,' he said. He turned round and all talk stopped. They saw the old man looking at them, counting them, giving each one of them a fine, quick calculating stab of his eyes. There were wet points of thawed snow on his long shabby green overcoat. Without a word he took his glass and walked slowly over to the mirror and put his glass down on the shelf. They watched him. His clothes were worn but they were carefully kept.

One hand was fidgeting in his overcoat pocket as he stood. He was an old man; he might have been seventy, even seventy-five. He was thin, rigid and austere, a soldierly old man with quick crafty eyes. His lips were pared away to two thin, stiff lines, he carried his chin high like a sentry. His nose was lean and aquiline and he wore a long, carefully clipped moustache which curled with a military flourish. It was the alertness of the grey threadbare eyes of the old man and something supple and gentle in him that silenced everyone.

Mr Murgatroyd lowered his eyes and studied the old man's clothes. They were old and respectable. Mr Sanders was silenced by the aristocratic curve, the disciplined richness of that white moustache. Mrs Tagg jostled her various selves together within her corsets and stared. Mrs Sanders timidly admired. The Jewess stood yielding, softening her gaiety before his white age.

'Cold day,' said the old man to them all. They were all surprised. Only the Jewess and Mrs Tagg murmured a reply.

Although he stood still he was a restless old man. He moved his feet a little as he stood and one of his hands was continually fingering something hidden in his pocket. Everybody noted this. Then his eyes moved in soft, darting glances at them all, so that they shifted their eyes. By those razor-cut glances he seemed to observe not their faces but things on their persons. Mr Sanders straightened his carnation after one of these looks and Mrs Tagg felt for her black beads. When he turned to Mr Murgatroyd he looked straight into the middle of Mr Murgatroyd's fine grey flannel stomach. Mr Murgatroyd leaned back rather more defensively against the bar; then he relented; being a very shy man he could not resist the chance of a conversation when someone had got over the first difficulties.

'Was it snowing still?' Mr Murgatroyd asked.

'It was,' said the old man.

Mr Murgatroyd wagged his head impressively.

'This wind finds out all your weak spots,' said the old man. There was a movement of sympathy; he drew himself up with dignity to repel it.

Then the old man, with some deliberation, opened his overcoat and he was seen to be even thinner than he had at first appeared. His long hand went into the pocket of his carefully darned jacket and he drew out something which amazed them all.

It was a very large green silk handkerchief with a brilliant pattern of red and yellow suns on it, rich, exotic and expensive. Mrs Tagg reckoned out the price at once. He let the handkerchief fall to its full length and caught it with his other hand. He gave it a small shake and gathered it up, clutching it tightly and watching it spring out and open like a gorgeous flower. Mr Sanders had expected to see it lifted straight to the beads of foam on the old man's fine moustache; but now he was playing with it, showing it off, conjuring with its brilliant lightness in the snowy darkness of the bar. Would it fall to the dirty floor?

But the old man did not let it fall. He lightly touched his moustache with it and put it not into the inner pocket, but into the outside pocket of his overcoat. It hung out and Mr Murgatroyd looked down his own chest and gave a touch to his own handkerchief in his breast pocket. The old man took one of his economical drinks and then smiled a friendly, faintly triumphant smile.

Mrs Tagg smiled back at him. She was gazing at the handkerchief hanging far out of the pocket.

'Mind you don't drop that handkerchief of yours,' said Mr Murgatroyd with great difficulty.

The old man, still smiling, drew back before this friendliness and straightened himself.

'You don't want to lose a nice one like that,' said Mrs Tagg.

The old man surveyed them all and murmured something impatiently as if resenting interference. Rebuked, they watched. Presently, eyeing them all, he drew out of his other pocket the thing he had been fingering for so long. It was a short smooth stick about a foot long, like a wooden whistle.

It was not a whistle, but merely a stick. He took it out and ran it through his hands, smoothing it and stroking it, and with every touch his thin, stiff hands seemed to become lighter and softer and more pliable. He passed the stick from one hand to the other, sometimes holding it only between the tips of his two forefingers. The Jewess came forward to watch this.

'Nice bit of wood,' said Mr Murgatroyd enquiringly.

'Uh,' grinned the old man and then with a severe look put the stick back in his pocket. There was disappointment in the wondering eyes of Mrs Sanders. But the old man was fumbling and muttering:

[77]

'Yes, yes,' and went on fumbling.

'Your handkerchief is in the other pocket,' said Mr Sanders eagerly. The Jewess looked admiringly at Mr Sanders for being so quick to read her thoughts.

'I know,' said the old man, giving him a severe glance, and still fumbling and frowning now with irritation.

Mr Murgatroyd expanded and said with amusement:

'Lost something?'

The old man looked round sharply.

'Have you got a sixpence?' he jerked.

Mr Murgatroyd's smile died in his soul but remained fixed on his face. He coloured. He moved his lips. He concealed a swallow. He leaned further back against the counter. Everyone was watching the crisis in Mr Murgatroyd.

'I want a sixpence,' said the old man and appealed to the others. 'A sixpence,' he said quickly. And at the same time he drew out the brilliant handkerchief and caught it with the other hand.

'I'll show you something. I'll show you what I can do with this handkerchief.'

His whole manner had changed. He had become sharp and assertive.

The Jewess saw it at once. Her eyes woke up.

'You are going to do a trick,' she said.

He looked at her with contempt and a smile on the tail of it.

'A conjuring trick?' asked Mr Murgatroyd widening his eyes. 'What are you going to do? Sixpence and a handkerchief?' he said deprecatingly.

'You know it?' said the old man.

'Everyone knows it. Everyone sees it. The vanishing sixpence.'

'There's nothing new in that,' laughed Mr Sanders. 'Eh, ma?' he said.

They all laughed. God, the old man was a conjurer. Mrs Pierce, without unfolding her arms, slid them further down the bar. The old man's eyes glittered.

'I'll bet you a tanner,' said the old man, 'you don't see it.' And he stared full and unanswerably at Mr Murgatroyd. Mr Murgatroyd stared back with all his might. He entrenched himself against the counter. Mrs Pierce stepped nearer on her side and he entrenched himself against the support of Mrs Pierce and the bar. He went very red and a mist came into his eyes.

'You want my sixpence,' he said in a stupor, strenuously defending himself.

'No, I'll make a bet,' the old man said, 'with anyone.' He snapped his fingers at them all. 'You'll get it back,' he said softly, smiling. They were ashamed of their suspicions. They gazed with command at Mr Murgatroyd hemmed in against the bar. He was obliged to hand the old man a sixpence.

The old man looked at the sixpence on the pink palm of Mr Murgatroyd's hand. Very reluctantly he took it and held it in his fingers.

'It's a funny thing,' he said, 'but you see all kinds of handkerchief tricks, but no one sees this.'

'Let's see it,' interrupted Mr Murgatroyd and was frowned on for interrupting.

'Some of these men you see on the halls are quick.' He chattered away and he told them of ways of doing the trick, ways of folding the handkerchief and of concealing the coin.

'There, hold it a minute,' he said, giving the sixpence back to Mr Murgatroyd to the astonishment of all. And his fingers captivated them with the play of his handkerchief as he illustrated his points.

They all leaned forward.

'Well, let's see it,' said Mr Murgatroyd from his defence. But the old man went on talking. And then he insisted on Mr Murgatroyd holding the handkerchief. The Jewess came forward and wanted to hold it too.

'Now watch,' said the old man. And he took back the sixpence and placed it in the handkerchief and began to knot it in. Mr Murgatroyd held one end of the handkerchief while the old man got to work with both his nimble hands. He folded and knotted. He stopped to explain.

'Get on with it,' said Mr Sanders.

'Shut up. You watch,' said Mrs Tagg, sitting vast in nervous judgment.

'Well, there you are,' said the old man. 'The sixpence is in there, isn't it? You saw me put it in.'

'I saw it,' said Mr Murgatroyd very hot.

'It was his sixpence, he ought to know,' said Mr Sanders.

The old man smiled along his lips. Mrs Sanders gazed sadly at her husband. The Jewess watched like a jackdaw for brightness.

'Feel it,' said the old man.

Reluctantly, ashamed of suspicion, Mr Murgatroyd put out his hand. He could feel the hard round coin.

'It's there,' he said to the others.

'Oh!' said the old man coldly, whipping the handkerchief open.

It was empty. There was no sixpence. The beautiful rich, green handkerchief with the yellow suns on it waved. Mrs Sanders was glad the poor old gentleman had a beautiful silk handkerchief.

'There!' said Mrs Pierce gloomily from the bar.

'That's done it,' said Mr Sanders, screwing up his legs.

Mrs Tagg made more room for herself on the bench and then breathed deeply.

'A man who can do that,' she frowned, 'is a clever man.'

'He had it in his hand all the time,' said the Jewess.

The old man showed her his empty hands.

'Eh?' said the old man, faintly smiling. He began absently to fold up the handkerchief with his rippling hands which never ceased in their movements.

'Yes,' said Mr Murgatroyd, rather proud of himself. 'Yes,' he said, shaking his head.

The handkerchief was whipped open again and there was the sixpence in it.

'You see!' Mrs Pierce murmured miserably.

They all began to talk at once.

The old man put his handkerchief back into his pocket and reached for his drink. He listened to the arguments and explanations.

'Oh, I must give you your sixpence,' he said to Mr Murgatroyd. But Mr Murgatroyd recoiled. He was shamed by the sight of his coin. He thickened with generosity, his skin gleamed with admiration and the flush of his second pint. He felt he was the leader of a delegation, the master of ceremonies, the mayor of a town; but too much of a man of the world to show it crudely. He condescended in a knowing, intimate, chatty way with the sparse of speech old man.

'No, that's your sixpence,' said Mr Murgatroyd casually. 'You won it.'

'Oh . . .', the old man hesitated.

'Yes go on. You take it. Go on,' said Mrs Tagg firmly, shaking her head. Mrs Tagg was proud of being out for justice.

The old man drew the stick from his pocket and began sliding it to and fro and shyly pocketed the sixpence. Mrs Sanders smiled wistfully and gladly at him when he did this.

'There's nothing in it,' said the old man. 'It's all a swindle. The quickness of the hand deceiving the eye. And human nature,' he said. 'Take the stick and tumbler trick.' He picked up an empty glass and rammed the stick several times at the bottom of it. The third or fourth time it appeared to go through.

'Gawd,' said Mr Sanders with admiration.

'That's clever. See how he done that? Do it again! There now.'

'Dear me. Look at that,' said Mrs Tagg.

They all saw it. They all felt warm and intimate.

'There's a trick in everything,' said the old man.

'A man with a brain can diddle anyone,' said Mr Sanders nodding intimately to the old man, whose eye faintly fluttered and then ignored him.

Somehow a ring had come into the old man's hand. The Jewess was the first to notice it.

'A ring and a stick,' said the old man. 'Get it off without moving your hands.' He slid the ring up and down the stick and then slipped it off.

It was the maddening way of this old man to start a trick and then stop and talk and begin all over again.

Now he was off again and he got Mr Murgatroyd to hold one end of the stick, while he took out this handkerchief again. He covered the stick up. The ring was on it. The handkerchief in all its colours covered the stick and Mr Murgatroyd's hand was resting pressed against his waistcoat. The old man kept altering the position of Mr Murgatroyd's hand, pulling the stick away to show the ring was still on it, and then giving it back again.

'The chair trick now,' he was saying. 'They tie a man up to a chair with his arms behind his back. You can go up and see he's properly knotted, and yet he just steps out of it. What's the explanation? Trick knots.'

'They're not real knots, then?' accused Mr Sanders.

'He's knotted up,' said the old man.

"But not with real knots,' said the Jewess.

"They're knots all right,' said the old man. 'He's got a couple of tapes up his sleeve coming out in slits in his coat.'

They exclaimed. He was fidgeting all the time, straightening out his handkerchief. He even gave Mr Murgatroyd a tap in the ribs and said he was sorry. Mr Murgatroyd smiled pityingly at the poor fussy old conjurer with all his tricks. Suddenly the old man said 'Look!' and whipped off the handkerchief. There was no ring on the stick.

'What are you drinking?' said Mr Murgatroyd with embarrassment.

The old man hesitated. 'No, thank you,' he said. 'Not before my dinner. I haven't had my dinner yet.'

'Oh I see,' murmured Mr Murgatroyd with embarrassment.

No dinner! What did he mean, no dinner? Did he mean he was earning his dinner? They were all very comfortable people with full stomachs. It was embarrassing to sit there full of food while an old man going on for seventy-five stood there empty, a fine old man like that. An aristocratic old man and nothing inside him. Mr and Mrs Sanders, they had had a stew. Mrs Tagg had had a nice bit of crab and a Guinness. Crab didn't agree with the Jewess. 'It isn't that it repeats, but, you know, I know I've had it.' So she had had spaghetti. As for Mr Murgatroyd, he had been built up on steak and two vegetables and raisin roll. They were diffusing their goodness in him.

All were touched when the old man gave a short bow and murmured in his quavering dignified voice that an old soldier would be grateful for a copper or two. His quick eyes watched their hands.

A handsome old man like that doing this for a living! Mrs Sanders signalled to her husband. The Jewess opened her handbag.

'An old soldier did you say?' asked Mrs Tagg on behalf of everyone.

'The East Kents,' said the old man, straightening.

'The Buffs!' she smiled with sudden reminiscent warmth, imperiousness vanishing in a glitter of long-forgotten gaiety.

'Yes, that's it. The Buffs,' the old man repeated mechanically. His thin, long, clever, hungry hands!

'Steady, the Buffs!' exclaimed Mrs Tagg, with a shake of her head and tears of pleasure in her eyes.

'Oh, ah . . .' murmured the old man.

'Chatham?' said Mr Sanders. 'Nice place. The Bells, Chatham. Know that?'

'Twenty-five years' service,' said the old man. 'Not so young now.'

'I could tell you was an old soldier,' said Mrs Tagg with pride.

He stood there talking to them as he put the few coppers in his pocket. Mr Sanders began to remember the good old days at Chatham during the War.

'I was talking about the Boer War,' said the old man.

Mrs Sanders raised her head high in shame for her husband. She was proud of the heroic old man.

'Well,' he said, after a while. 'I suppose I'd better be moving along to my dinner.'

They were sad. But they understood. They realised he was a hungry old man.

'Good day, and I thank you,' he said.

Mr Murgatroyd put out his hand. The old man was surprised by this handshake. It was the only time he had been taken aback. Raising his hat he went slowly out of the bar. The swing door bumped after him and Mrs Pierce raised herself from the counter and went to the window to see the tall, upright figure walk away. When she came back she said: 'It's snowing hard now.'

They all sat in silence staring into the tops of their glasses. Except the Jewess, who took off her hat and combed her hair by the mirror. There on the mantelpiece was the froth-laced glass the old man had used.

'Well, well,' said Mr Murgatroyd uncomfortably. He relaxed from the slanting position into which he had recoiled before the old man. 'He gets a living,' said Mr Murgatroyd.

There was a long silence. The bar seemed to be much darker now that the old man had gone. They were thinking about Mr Murgatroyd's words. Mr Murgatroyd was all right, he had a new suit of clothes, gloves in his hand, a fountain pen in his pocket, a car outside and a new Trilby hat. But everyone had to get a living. Mrs Sanders moved at the end of the bench and pulled up the collar of her coat with a shiver.

'Hunger,' said Mrs Sanders in her timid voice. 'That's the worst thing.'

They all looked at her with curiosity and reproof for speaking that word.

And that uncomfortable word reminded Mr Murgatroyd of something. His shyness and importance were moving inside him. It was his round.

'What's everyone having?' he said at last, looking away up at the clock among the bottles. Mrs Pierce looked up, too.

'Guinness, ma'am. Time for another, I think. Your clock's fast, Mrs Pierce . . .'

And his hand went down his waistcoat for his watch. Down and down it went. And as it went down he seemed to feel a nudge in his stomach and a look of consternation came on his face. The watch was not there. His hand dug in his other pocket.

'Well I'm . . .' he said aloud. The watch had gone. His eyes popped wide and hard, his jaw dropped. He went very pale and then flushed to the colour of a beetroot.

'Here,' he blurted out, starting from the counter. 'My watch. It was here. I know it was. It's gone. You saw it, Mrs Pierce. You saw me take it out. It's gone. That artful old swine has pinched my watch!'

He glared at them all.

'Where is he?' he shouted. 'Which way did he go? Look for him! Of all the thieves . . .'

Unable to do more because of the vast heaving and of his rage, Mr Murgatroyd looked as though he would burst.

The Two Brothers

The two brothers went to Ballady to look at the house. It was ruinous but cheap, there were miles of bog and mountain alive with birds, there was the sea and not a soul living within two miles of it. As had always happened in their childhood and as had repeatedly happened since the war when 'the Yank' had returned to the Old Country to look after his sick brother, 'the Yank,' with his voracious health, had his way.

'Sure it's ideal,' yelled the Yank.

The time was the Spring.

'We'll take it for six months,' he exclaimed.

'And after that?' asked Charlie, watching him like a woman for plans and motives he had not got.

'Och, we'll see. We'll see. Sure what's the use of worrying about the future?' said the Yank.

He knew and Charlie knew the question hung over them; the future watching them like an eagle on a rock, waiting to shadow them with its wing. In six months he would be left alone. He knew how the Yank, his brother, dealt with time. Out came his gun and he took a pot shot at it, went after it, destroyed it and then laughed at his own skill and forgot.

In the sky and land at Ballady there was the rugged wildness of farewell. This was the end of the land, prostrating itself in rags before the Atlantic. The wind stripped the soil so that there was no full-grown tree upon it, and rocks stood out like gravestones in the bigoted little fields. A few black cattle grazed, a few fields of oats were grown, the rest was mountain and the wide empty pans of bog broken into eyes of water. The house lay in a hollow out of sight of the sea, which was only half a mile away. It was a grey, rambling place of two storeys with outhouses and stables all going to pieces. It was damp, leaky and neglected and barely furnished. There were fuchsia bushes growing right up to the windows, beating against them and blinding them in the gales, pressed close as people in the night. The garden was feet deep in grasses, the gravel drive had become two grass ruts, and for a gate there was an iron hurdle propped against a gap in the stone wall. From the hill above Ballady Charlie and Micky had made out its slate roof silvery in the light, the ribs of the roofless stable, like a shining skeleton.

'The way it is,' the Yank explained when he went in to Ballady alone for a drink now and then. 'The poor bloody brother he's after having a breakdown.' The Yank was a wild, tall, lean, muscular fellow, straight and springy as a whip, with eyes like dark pools, with bald brows, lips loose and thin, and large ears protruding from his bony skull. His black hair stood up straight and was cropped close like a convict's, so that the skin could be seen through it; his nose was straight and his face was reddened by the wind. He went about with a cigarette in the corner of lips askew in a conquering grin, and carried a gun all day. A breezy, sporting chap. He wandered up and down the bog and the fields or lay in the dunes waiting; then, bang went his gun, the sea-birds screamed over the sand and up he got from his knees to pick up a rabbit or a bird. The sun burned him, the wind cut him, the squalls pitted him like shot. He had no secrets from anyone. Fifteen years of Canada, he told them, four years of war and now for a good time while his money lasted. Then, he said publicly to all, he would go back. All he wanted now was a bit of rough country, a couple of drinks, and a gun; and he had got them. It was what he had always wanted. He was out for the time of his life.

How different Charlie was, slight and wiry, nervous and private as a silvery fish. His hair was fair, almost white, and his eyes were a keen dark blue in the pupils and a fairer blue was ringed round them. His features were sharp and he kept his lips together and his head down as he walked, glancing nervously about him. He looked like a man walking in his thoughts. If, when he returned from the sea, he saw someone in his path, he dodged away and made a long detour back to the house. If taken by surprise and obliged to talk to a stranger, he edged away murmuring something. His voice was quiet, his look shrill, pleading and shy. He was absorbed in the most private of all pieties, the piety of fear to which his imagination devoted a rich and vivid ritual.

He did not badger his brother with speech. He followed him about the house, standing near him, asking with his eyes for the virtue of his

[86]

brother's strength, courage, company and protection. He asked no more than his physical presence and to watch. In the mornings at first, after they had established themselves in the house, there was always this situation: Micky restless, burning to be out with his gun and Charlie's eyes silently asking him not to go. Micky bursting to be free, Charlie worrying to hold him. Sometimes Micky would be melted by an unguarded glance at his brother. For a moment he would forget his own strength and find himself moved by an awed tenderness for this clever man who had passed examinations, stayed in the Old Country, worked his way up in a bank and then, when the guns had started to popple, and 'the troubles' began, had collapsed.

Micky was kind and humoured him. They would sit for hours together in the house, with the Spring growing in the world outside, while Charlie cajoled him with memories of their boyhood together, or listened to Micky's naive and boasting tales of travel. In those hours Charlie forgot the awful years, or he would have the illusion of forgetting. For the two surrounded themselves with walls of talk, and Charlie, crouching round the little camp fire of his heart, used every means to keep the talk going, to preserve this picture of life standing as still as a dreamy ship in haven and himself again a child.

But soon the sun would strike through the window and the fairness of the sky would make Micky restless. He would lead his brother, by a pretext, into the garden and slyly get him to work there, planting lettuces or digging, and when he had got him to work he would slip away, pick up his gun and be off to the dunes.

Shortly after moving into the house Micky went into Dill, got drunk as was his habit, and returned with a dog, a young black retriever very strong, affectionate and lively. He did not know why he had bought it and could hardly remember what he had paid for it. But when he got home he said on the impulse to Charlie:

'Here, Charlie boy. I've bought you a dog. One of the priest's pups.'

Charlie smiled slightly and looked in wonder.

'There y'are, man,' Micky cried. 'Your dog.

'Hup! Go to your master,' said Micky, giving the dog a push and sent it over to Charlie, who still incredulously gazed.

'Now that's kind of you,' he murmured, flushing slightly. He was

[87]

speechless with pleasure. Micky, who had given the animal to his brother on the spur of the moment, was now delighted with himself, sunned in his generosity.

'Sure now ye've got yer dog,' Micky kept saying, 'ye'll be all right. Ye'll be all right now ye've got the dog.'

Charlie gazed at Micky and the animal, and slyly he smiled to himself; Micky had done this because he had a bad conscience. But Charlie put these thoughts aside.

Both brothers devoted themselves to the retriever, Micky going out and shooting rabbits for it, and Charlie cooking them and taking out the bones. But when Micky got up and took his gun and the retriever jumped up to go out with him, Charlie would whistle the dog back and say:

'Here! Stay here. Lie down. Ye're going out with me in a minute.'

It was his dog.

At last Charlie went out and the watchful creature leaped out with him. Charlie drew courage from it as it loped along before him, sniffing at walls and standing stiff with ears cocked to see the sudden rise of a bird. Charlie talked to it in a low running murmur hardly made of words but easing to the mind. When it stopped he would pass his clever hands over its velvety nose and glossy head, feeling the strange life ripple under the hair and obtaining a curious strength from the tumult. Then he would press on and whistle the creature after him and make across the fields to the long finger bone of rock that ran down to the sea; but as the retriever ran it paused often, as Charlie began to note with bewilderment and then with dread, to listen for Micky's voice or the sound of his gun.

When he saw this Charlie redoubled his efforts to win the whole allegiance of the dog. Power was renewing itself in him. And so he taught the dog a trick. He called it over the rocks, slipping and yelping to the sea's edge. Here the sand was white, and as the worlds of clouds bowled over the sky to the mountains where the light brimmed like golden bees, the sea would change into deep jade halls, purple where the weeds lay and royal blue under the sparkling sun, and the air was sinewy and strong. Charlie took off his clothes and, shivering at the sight of his own thin pale body, his loose queasy stomach and the fair sickly hairs now picking up gold from the light, and with a desire to cleanse himself of sickness and fear, lowered himself cautiously into the green water, and wading out with beating heart called to the dog. It stood up whining and barking for a while, running up and down the rock, and at last plunged in pursuit. Then the man caught hold of its tail and let himself be towed out to sea, and for minutes they would travel out and out until, at a word, the dog returned, snorting, heart pumping, shoulders working and eyes gazing upwards and the green water swilling off its back until it had pulled Charlie back into his depth.

Then Charlie would sit drying himself and listening to the scream of the birds while the black retriever yelped and shivered at his side. And if Micky were late for his meal when he returned, through drinking with the schoolmaster or going away for a day to the races, Charlie would say nothing. He would build up a big turf fire in the empty room and wait with the dog at his side, murmuring to it.

But it took Charlie hours to make up his mind to these expeditions, and as time went on they became irregular. There were days when the absences of his brother left him alone with his fears, and on these days he would helplessly see the dog run after Micky and go off with him. Soon it would hardly obey Charlie's call.

'You're taking the dog from me,' Charlie complained.

'Sure if ye'd go out the dog'd follow you,' said Micky. 'Dammit, what's the use of staying inside? I don't want the dog, but the poor bloody creature needs a run an't follows me. It's only natural.'

'Natural. That's it,' Charlie reflected. From him that hath not shall be taken even that which he hath. But he cried out sharply:

'Sure you have it trained away from me.'

Then they quarrelled, and Micky, thinking his head was getting too hot for his tongue, went out to the dunes and stood in the wind staring at the sea. Why was he tied to this weak and fretful man? For three years since the end of the war he had looked after Charlie, getting him out of hospital and into a nursing home, then to houses in the country, sacrificing a lot of his own desire to have a good time before he returned to Canada, in order to get his brother back to health. Micky's money would not last for ever; soon he would have to go, and then what would happen?

But when he returned with cooler head, the problem carelessly thrown off, he was kind to his brother. They sat in eased silence before the fire, the dog dreaming at their feet, and to Charlie there returned the calm of the world. His jealousies, his suspicions, his reproaches, all the spies sent out by his reconnoitring fears, were called in and with Micky he was at peace and no shadow of the future was on him.

Yet as the months climbed higher out of July into August and swung there awhile, enchanted by their own halcyon weather, before declining into the cooler days, the question had to be faced. Micky knew and Charlie knew, but each wished the other to speak.

It was Micky who, without warning, became impatient and spoke out.

'Lookut here, Charlie,' he said one evening as he washed blood off his hands in the kitchen – he had been skinning and cleaning a couple of rabbits – 'are you coming back to Canada with me in September?'

'To Canada is it?' said the brother putting his thin fingers on the table and speaking in a gasping whisper. He stood incredulous. Yet he had expected this.

'And leave me here alone!'

'Not at all,' said Micky. 'I said "You're coming with me." You heard me. Will ye come with me to Canada?'

Charlie drew in his lips and his eyes were restless with agony.

'Sure, Micky, ye know I can't do that,' he said.

'But what's to stop ye? Ye're all right. Ye're well. Ye've got your bit of pension and ye'll be as comfortable as in your own home. Get out of this damn country, that's what ye want. Sure 'tis no good at all except for old people and children,' cried Micky.

But Charlie was looking out of the window towards the mountains. To go out into the world, to sit in trains with men, to sleep in houses with them, to stand bewildered, elbowed and shouldered by men in a new country! Or, as the alternative, to stay alone without Micky, left to his memories.

'You'll not leave me, Micky boy?' he stammered in panic.

Micky was bewildered by the high febrile voice, the thin body shivering like a featherless bird. Then Charlie changed. He hunched his shoulders, narrowing himself and cowering round his heart, hardening himself against the world, and his eyes shot out suspicions, jealousies, reproaches, the weapons of a sharp mind.

' 'Tis the schoolmaster has been putting you against me,' he said.

Micky ridiculed the idea.

'Ye knew as well as I did, dammit, when we took the place, that I'd be going now,' he said. Yes, this was true, Charlie had known it.

Micky took the matter to his friend the schoolmaster. He was a stout, hard-drinking old man with a shock of curly grey hair. His manner was theatrical and abrupt.

' 'Tis the poor bloody brother,' Micky said. 'What am I to do with him at all?'

'Ye've no more money,' said the schoolmaster.

'Ye've been with him for years,' he went on. He paused again.

'Ye can't live on him.'

'And he must live with you.'

He glowered at Micky and then his fierce look died away.

'Sure there's nothing you can do. Nothing at all,' said the school-master.

Micky filled their glasses again.

He continued his life. The Summer glided down like a beautiful bird scooping the light. The peasants stood in their long shadows in the fields and fishermen left their boats for the harvest. Micky was sad to be leaving this beautiful isolation.

But he had to return to the question. He and Charlie began to argue it continually day and night. Sometimes Charlie was almost acquiescent, but at last always retired within himself. Since he could not sit in the safety of the old talk, his cleverness found what comfort it could for him in the new. Soon it was clear to Micky that Charlie encouraged the discussion, cunningly played with it, tortured him with vacillations, cunningly played on his conscience. But to Charlie it seemed that he was struggling to make his brother aware of him fully; deep in the piety of his fear he saw in Micky a man who had never worshipped at its icy altars. He must be made to know. So the struggle wavered until one night it came out loudly into the open.

'God Almighty,' cried out Micky as they sat in the lamplight. 'If you'd been in France you'd have had something to cry about. That's what's wrong with this bloody country. All a pack of damn cowards, and ye can see it in their faces when they stare at you like a lot of bleating sheep.'

'Oh, is that it?' said Charlie gripping the arms of his chair. 'Is that what you're thinking all these years? Ye're saying I'm afraid, is it? You're saying I'm a coward. Is that what you were thinking when you came home like a red lord out of hell in your uniform, pretending to be glad to see me and the home? But thinking in your own heart I'm a coward not to be in the British army. Oh, is that it?'

His voice was quiet, high and monotonous in calculated contrast to Micky's shouting anger. But his body shook. A wound had been opened. He *was* a coward. He *was* afraid. He was terrified. But his clever mind quickly closed the wound. He was a man of peace. He desired to kill no one. He worshipped the great peace of God. This was why he had avoided factions, agreed with all sides, kept out of politics and withdrawn closer and closer into himself. At times it had seemed to him that the only place left in the world for the peace of God was in his own small heart.

And what had Micky done? In the middle of the war he had come home, the Destroyer. In five minutes by a few reckless words in the drink shop and streets of the town he had ruined the equilibrium Charlie had tended for years and had at last attained. In five minutes Charlie had become committed. He was no longer 'Mr Lough the manager', a man of peace. No, he was the brother of 'that bloody pro-British Yank'. Men were boycotted for having brothers in the British army, they were threatened, they were even shot. In an hour a village as innocent-looking as a green and white place in a postcard had become a place of windows hollow-eyed with evil vigils. Within a month he had received the first note threatening his life.

' 'Twas yourself,' said Charlie – discovering at last his enemy. ' 'Twas yourself, Micky, that brought all this upon me. Would I be sick and destroyed if you hadn't come back?'

'Cripes,' said Micky, hearing the argument for the first time and pained by this madness in his brother. 'Cripes, man, an' what was the rest of ye up to? Serving God Almighty like a lot of choir boys, shooting up some poor lonely policeman from a hedge and driving old women out of their homes.'

'Stop it,' shouted Charlie, as the memories broke upon him and he put his fingers to his ears.

Micky threw his cigarette into the fire and took his brother by the shoulder in compassion. He was sorry for having spoken so; but Charlie ignored him. He spoke, armouring himself.

'So it's a coward I am, is it!' he said. 'Well, I stayed when they threatened me and I'll stay again. You're thinking I'm a coward.' He was resolute. But behind the shrubs brushing against the window, in the spaces between the cool September stars, were the fears.

There was nothing else for it. Charlie watched Micky preparing to go, indifferent and resigned, feeding his courage on this new picture of his brother. He turned to it as to a secret revelation. Micky was no longer his brother. He was the Destroyer, the Prince of this World, the man of darkness. Micky, surprised that his good intentions were foiled, gave notice to the landlord, to force Charlie. Charlie renewed the agreement. He spoke little; he took no notice of the dog, which had now completely deserted him. When Micky had gone it would be his. Charlie kicked it once or twice as if to remind it. He gave up swimming in the sea. He was staying here. He had all the years of his life to swim in the sea.

Micky countered this by open neglect of his brother. He entered upon a life of wilder enjoyment. He gave every act the quality of a reckless farewell. He was out all day and half the night. In Ballady he drank the schoolmaster weeping under the table and came staggering home, roaring like an opera, and was up at dawn, no worse for it, after the duck.

'This is a rotten old wall,' Micky said in the garden one day, and started pushing the stones off the top of it. A sign it was his wall no longer. He chopped a chair up for firewood. He ceased to make his bed. He took a dozen empty whisky bottles and, standing them at the end of the kitchen garden, used them as shooting targets. He shot three rabbits and threw two of them into the sea. He burned some old clothes, tore up his letters and gave away a haversack to the fisherman and a second gun to the schoolmaster. A careless enjoyment of destruction seized him. Charlie watched it, saying nothing. The Destroyer.

One evening as the yellow sun flared in the pools left by the tide on the sand, Micky came upon Charlie.

'Not a damn thing,' Micky said, tapping his gun.

But as they stood there, some gulls which had been flying over the rocks came inland and one fine fellow flew out and circled over their heads, its taut wings deep blue in the shadow as it swung round. Micky suddenly raised his gun and fired and, before the echoes had broken in the rocks, the wings collapsed and the bird dropped warm and dead.

'God Almighty, man,' cried Charlie, turning away with nausea, 'is nothing sacred to ye?'

'It's no damned good,' grinned Micky, picking up the bird by the wing, which squeaked open like a fan. 'Let the fish have it.' And he flung it into the sea. This was what he thought of wings.

Then with a week to go, without thinking he struck a bad blow. He went off to Dill to say good-bye to the boys, and the retriever followed him although Charlie called it back. The races were on at Dill, but Micky spent most of the time in the pubs telling everyone he was going back to Canada. A man hearing this said he'd change dogs with him. His dog, he said, was a spaniel. He hadn't it with him but he'd bring it down next fair. Micky was enthusiastic.

'I know ye will,' said Micky. 'Sure ye'll bring it.'

'Ah, well now,' said the man. 'I will bring it.'

''Tis a great country the west,' said Micky. 'Will ye have another?'

'I will,' said the man, and as he drank: 'In the three countries there is not a place like this.'

Micky returned the next day without the dog.

'Where's the dog?' said Charlie suspiciously.

'Och sure,' began Micky evasively, realising for the first time what he had done. 'D'you see the way it is, there is a man in Dill –'

'Ye've sold it. Ye've sold my dog,' Charlie shouted out, rushing at his brother. His shout was the more unnerving because he had spoken so little for days. Micky drew back.

'Ah now, Charlie, be reasonable now. Sure you never did anything for the dog. You never took it out. You didn't care for it . . .'

Charlie gripped a chair and painfully sat down, laying his head in his hands on the table.

'You brought the war on me, you smash me up, you take the only things I have and leave me stripped and alone,' he moaned. 'Oh, God in heaven,' he half sobbed in pleading voice, 'will ye give me gentleness and peace!'

Now the dog was gone Charlie sat still. He would not move from the house, nor even from the sitting-room except to go to bed. He would scarcely speak. Sulking, Micky repeated to his uneasy conscience, sulking, sulking. He's either mad or he's sulking. What could he do? They sat estranged, already far apart, impatient for the act of departure.

When the eve of his departure came Micky was relieved to see that Charlie accepted it, and was even making it easy: and so touched was Micky by this that he found no difficulty in promising to spend that last night with Charlie alone. He remained in the house all day, and when the night came a misted moonlight gleamed on the cold roof and the sea was as quiet as the licking of a cat's tongue. Charlie drew the curtains, made up the fire and there they sat silently listening to the clock. They were almost happy: Charlie pleased to have this final brief authority over Micky; Micky relieved by the calm, both disinterested. Charlie spoke of his plans, the work he would do in the garden, the furniture he would buy, the girl he would get in to cook and clean.

' 'Twould be a fine place to bring a bride to,' said Micky, giving Charlie a wink, and Charlie smiled.

But presently they heard footsteps on the drive.

'What's that?' exclaimed Charlie sharply, sitting up. The mild mask of peace left his face like a light, and his face set hard.

Without knocking at the door, in walked the schoolmaster. He was in the room before Charlie could get out. He stood up and retreated to the corner.

'Good evening to ye,' said the schoolmaster, pulling a bottle out of his pocket, and spreading himself on to a seat. 'I came to see your brother on his last night.'

Charlie drew in his lips and gazed at the schoolmaster.

'Will ye have a drink?' said Micky nervously.

That began it. Gradually Micky forgot his promise. He paid no attention to Charlie's signs. They sat drinking and telling stories. The world span round. The alarm clock on the little bamboo table, the only table in the bare room, ticked on. Charlie waited in misery, his eyes craving his brother's, whose bloodshot eyes were merry with drinking and laughter at the schoolmaster's tales. The man's vehement voice shook the house. He told of the priest at Dill who squared the jockeys and long thick stories about some Archbishop and his so-called niece. The air to Charlie became profane.

'Isn't your wife afraid to be up and alone this time of night?' Charlie ventured once.

'Och, man, she's in bed long ago,' shouted the schoolmaster. 'She is that.'

And Micky roared with laughter.

At two o'clock Charlie went to bed and left him to it. But he was awake at five when Micky stumbled into his room.

'Before God, man,' Micky said. 'I'm bloody sorry, Charlie man. Couldn't turn out a friend.'

'It's too late now,' said Charlie.

Micky left at seven to catch a man who would give him a lift to the eight-o'clock train.

The Autumn gales broke loose upon the land a month after Micky's departure and the nights streamed black and loud. The days were cold and fog came over the sea. The fuchsias were blown back and the under leaves blew up like silver hands. The rain lashed on the windows like gravel. There were days of calm and then the low week-long mist covered the earth, obliterating the mountains, melting all shapes. All day long the moisture dripped from the sheds and windows and glistened on the stone walls.

At first Charlie did not change. Forced to go to the village for groceries he would appear there two or three times a week, saying little and walking away quickly. A fisherman would call and the post-boy lingered. Letters came from Micky. Charlie took little heed of all this. But as the weather became wilder he hung curtains over the windows day and night and brought his bed down to the sitting-room. He locked the doors upstairs, those that had still keys to them. He cooked on the sitting-room fire. He was narrowing his world, making a smaller and closer circle to live in. And as it grew smaller, the stranger the places beyond its boundaries seemed. He was startled to go into the empty kitchen, and looked with apprehension up the carpetless stairs to the empty landing where water dripped through the fanlight and was already staining the ceiling below. He lay awake in the night as the fire glowed in the room.

One morning when he found the noises of his isolation supportable no more, he put on his hat and coat and packed his things and walked out of the house. He would stay no longer. But with his fear his brain had, as always, developed a covering cunning. He went up the lane to see if anyone was coming first. He wanted to be away from people, yet among them; with them, yet alone. And on this morning the Ballady sailor was reloading a load of turf that had fallen off his cart. Charlie returned into the house. He took off his hat and coat. He had not been out for a week because of this dread.

There was still food in tins for a few days. It was the thought that he could last if he liked, that he could keep the world off, that made him satisfied. No letters came now. Micky no longer wrote; effusive in the first weeks, his letters had become rare. Now there had been no news for a month. Charlie scarcely thought of him.

But when late in December the mists held the country finally, the twigs creaked on the drive like footsteps and the dark bushes divided in the wind as if they had been parted by hidden hands, he cowered into his beating heart, eating little, and the memories began to move and creep in his head. A letter threatened him with death. He drove alone with the bank's money. At Carragh-cross road the signpost stood emptily gesticulating like some frightened speaker with the wind driving back the words into his mouth, and the two roads dangling from its foot. He knew what had happened at Carragh-cross road. He knew what had been found there lying with one leg out of the ditch. He saw it. And Micky, the Destroyer, with his convict's head and his big red ears, shooting down the Holy Ghost like a beautiful bird, grinned there blowing smoke down his nose.

These memories came and went. When they came they beat into his head like wings, and though he fought them off with prayers, they beat down and down on him and he cried out fast to the unanswering house:

'God give me peace,' he prayed. 'Holy Mother of God, give me peace for the sake of thy sweet Son . . .'

When the beating wings went his cleverness took possession of him again. He prepared a little food, and once or twice walked around the garden within the shelter of the walls. The ground was frozen, the air still and a lace of snow was on the paths. But if the days passed in peace, his heart quickened at the early darkness, and when the turf smoke blew back down the chimney it was as if someone had blown down a signal.

One night he had a terrible dream. He was dead, he had been caught at last on the road at Carragh-cross. 'Here's the man with the pro-British brother,' they cried and threw him into a bog pool, sinking deeper and deeper into soft and sucking fires that drew him down and down. He was in hell. And there in the flames calling to him was a woman with dark hair and with pale insects walking over her skin. It was the schoolmaster's wife. 'And he thinking you were in bed,' said Charlie, amazed by the justice of revenge. He woke up gasping in the glow of the sitting-room fire, and feeling that a load was still pressing down on his chest.

In the morning the dream was still in his mind; mingling with some obscure sense of triumph it ceased to be a dream and became reality. It became like a new landscape imposed upon the world. The voice of the woman was more real to his ear than his own breathing.

He felt free, was protected and cleansed, and his dream seemed to him like an impervious world within a world, a mirage in which he musically walked. In the afternoon he was exalted. He walked out of the house and taking the long way round by the lanes went to the schoolmaster's. The frost still held and the air was windless, the land fixed and without colour. As it happened the schoolmaster had taken it into his head to go as far as his gate.

'Man, I'm glad to see ye about,' cried the schoolmaster at the sight of Charlie. 'I meant to see ye. Come in now. Come in. 'Tis terrible lonely for you in that place.'

Charlie stood still and looked icily through him.

'Ye thought she was in bed,' he said. 'But I'm after seeing her in the flames of hell fire.'

Without another word he walked away. The schoolmaster made a rush for him. But Charlie had climbed the stone wall and had dropped into the field opposite.

'Come here. Come back. What's that you say?' called the schoolmaster. But Charlie walked on, gathering speed as he dropped behind the hill out of sight going to his house. Then he ran for his life.

The schoolmaster did not wait. He went in for his coat, bicycled into Ballady Post Office and rang up the Guards at Dill.

'There's a poor feller here might do harm to himself,' he said. 'Will you send someone down?'

But on the way back to the house Charlie's accompanying dream and its dazed exaltation left him. Speaking had dissolved it. It lifted like a haze and suddenly he was left alone, exposed, vulnerable in the middle of the fields. He began to run, shying at every corner, and when he got to the house he clawed at the door and ran in gasping to throw himself on the bed. He lay there on his face, his eyes closed. There had been brief excitement in the run, but as he recovered his breath the place resumed its normal aspect and its horror became real as slowly he turned over and opened his eyes to it. And now they were open he could not close them again. They stared and stared. Slowly it came to him there was nothing in life left for him but emptiness. Career gone, peace gone, God gone, Micky gone, dog – all he had ever had trooped with bleak salute of valediction through his mind. He was left standing in the emptiness of himself. And then a shadow was cast upon the emptiness; looking up he saw the cold wing of a great and hovering bird. So well he knew it that in this last moment his mind cleared and he had no fear. ' 'Tis yourself, Micky, has me destroyed,' he said. He took out a razor and became absorbed in the difficulty of cutting his throat. He was not quite dead when the Guards broke in and found him.

X-ray

The X-ray department in the hospital is reached by tepid corridors. A swing door admits the noises of the street and with a gulp swallows you and rejects them. You are cut off from the world. Stairways lead upwards to the regions of pain, six floors carefully labelled and distributed; yet, passing the open doors of laboratories, seeing instruments and retorts, smelling ether which excites the nostrils, the body begins to feel important. It is bringing its talent of pain to the total.

The waiting-room stands between two doors; one swings and gulps like the street door, the other is fixed open and leads into a long room which is unnaturally light. The X-ray machine is screened by long brown curtains. There are four benches in the waiting-room and a high window, and none of the waiting people are speaking though the air is nervous with their wanting to speak. They look at one another and down at the light reflected in diagram on the polished floor. But it is not sun that lies there in a pool, you feel, but mere evidence of the existence of light. If to escape you look outside it is to see on one of the higher floors in another wing a man in a white coat holding up a test tube – a god, and the nurses who come and go up the iron fire escapes outside are angels on Jacob's Ladder.

The immediate noises are particular and lively; the high heels of the starched nurses on the floor, the suction of the swing door when a patient is wheeled in on a stretcher or in a bath chair, the fizzling, electric frying noise of the X-ray machine behind the curtain. It might be a steam press in a cleaner's shop and you expect to see a cloud of steam blow up over the top of the curtain. The disembodied voice of a nurse says, 'Lie down. Pull down the trousers to the knees. When I say, "Breathe gently," hold the breath and do not breathe till I tell you. Put the arms above the head (this patient knows). Now breathe . . .'

The frying begins.

'Breathe out. Pull up the trousers. Get down. Dress. Go outside and wait. You may put your coat on.' Each sentence is exact and part of a formula.

A nurse comes out and goes to the telephone. 'X-ray department speaking. Is Sister there? Oh, Sister, you know that little boy Reeves? Well, we'll have to have him down again. The films haven't come out. His stomach's all full of gas.'

A human expression of guilt comes over the waiting people. Are they, too, grossly and unscientifically full of gas? This starts conversation. The women are sitting opposite the men on different benches, in voluntary segregation. Among the women by mistake sits one chicken-breasted, trembling little man, stringy of skin, red-nosed and wearing a white choker. His knees are drawn up and are tight together. When the nurse comes in and says without interest, 'Beale? Patient called Beale?' and there is no answer, a dozen heads naturally turn upon him. He must be Beale. And he is squeezing himself into his corner. 'Beale?' The nurse steps forward to accuse him. He makes a noise that is Beale. She bends over him like a large white intoxicating flower. 'Are you Beale?' He squeezes himself and makes another noise. 'Beale,' she says sternly, 'you have come on the wrong day.' He cowers. 'You ought to have come last Thursday, not this.' He stares at her and murmurs. 'Why didn't you?' she says.

There is a movement of delight and pity. All gaze at Beale the hero, the idiot, the man who HAS COME ON THE WRONG DAY. The hospital goes on humming. The sunlight is still being generated. 'I don't know what we shall do about you, Beale.' And outside: 'What's to be done about this man Beale, Sister?' His lot is beyond desolation. Other nurses come in and gaze at him. When *she* comes in again Beale grips his cap and thinks he ought to stand up when a lady is talking to him. 'Sit down,' says the nurse. 'Don't stand, Beale. Sit down.' It is terrifying for him to sit down. Then she says in a deep enticing voice, 'Go into that room.' He stares. 'Get up and go into that room.'

He gets up and hesitates in a muddle, trembling and looking at the doors and window.

'Over here, Beale,' she says. 'Into that dressing-room.'

He is shuffling about the room quite lost, glancing at her like a dog.

Now his lips are tight, now they are loose. She leads him by the elbow as he stutters something. 'Beale, take off your coat and waistcoat, loosen your trousers, put on a dressing-gown. When you have done that come out and wait.'

The door closes on Beale. Everyone waits and waits for him to come out. But he does not come out. People begin to smile and nod significantly at the door. 'Coo,' says a girl, who is very pale and has large round dark eyes like a surprised half-caste doll. She has her hand over her lips. 'Oh, dear,' she says. She cannot stop giggling with awe. 'I'm that hungry,' she says. 'They do play you up. No breakfast. Did they make you take some stuff?'

This, of course, to the strong man of the room. He sits like a cowed boxer gone to fat, a massive mottled man with a broken nose, rather scared and absurdly friendly. He is always jumping up to open doors for nurses and wants to talk to everyone. 'You have to take it,' he says with authority. 'Yes,' says the girl, shocked at herself. 'I'm going to have something quick when I get out of this.'

'They're not open yet,' says the bruiser. People sigh and smile. Their eyes shine for a moment and go dead again. 'Oh, dear,' says the girl, rolling her eyes and holding her empty stomach. 'Yus,' says the bruiser, shaking his head.

The door opens and in comes a woman who knows what she is doing, walks straight to the bench, gives it a whisk with a newspaper, sits down and puts her bright pop eyes into the *Daily Mirror*, and hums. In a moment she might twitter like a canary. She wears a bright blue dressing-gown and nods to all the nurses. She is the efficient spinster settling with the glee of a bird. She has come to stay. But she is only the harbinger of a richer disturbance. Far doors are heard swinging. The curtains suck in and belly out wide, a warm cyclone is coming. Nurses scatter to the walls, and suddenly there appears with great strides a tall red-haired doctor, fat, whiskered and gleaming, cannibal, with his white coat flying behind him and out of it great legs leaping with the gusto of striped tigers. He dashes through the sun, a hand covered with golden hairs shoots out of his sleeve, back flies the swing door and he is gone, the spices of the Indies with him. Thermometers have risen. But when the air has settled again the nurse comes and intones, 'Beale,' looking at the empty corner. Where is Beale? What is he doing in that room? Is he praying or weeping or has he hanged himself? With what awful garments is he struggling? Will he be found crushed on the heel of the doctor's shoe?

'He hasn't come out, miss,' says the bruiser, the reformed boy of the class. Everyone is smiling with expectation except the spinster, wetting their lips for the entrance of Beale. A lanky man with a lot of hair who wriggles, smells of tobacco, bites his nails and looks like a barber, slaps his knee with a long hand and says, 'Oh, flick!'

'Ssh,' says the bruiser. The nurse opens the dressing-room door and although it is a room no bigger than a bathing box her voice sounds as if she were bending down and talking to something under the seat. 'Come on, Beale,' she says. 'Come with me.' And out comes Beale with his trousers collapsing and his braces on the floor, lost in the huge dressing-gown except for a head that is like that of an unfledged bird. He opens his mouth several times, but no words come, only noise. The women are now very pitiful as he is led into the next room behind the curtain. The bruiser spreads his legs and puts his hands on his knees. The barber doubles himself up with expectancy. An old man who has been wheeled in a bath chair snuffles. The spinster goes on reading. From behind the curtain come the familiar voices, the familiar hum of the hospital. Up the iron staircase outside a nurse rises with a tray, an offering to the god.

Suddenly there is a loud humming sound, a cool voice, 'When I say "Breathe gently," breathe gently and hold it till I tell you to breathe out. The arms at the sides. Now "Breathe gently." Hold it . . .'

'Whoops! Off we go,' exclaims the bruiser in a loud voice, as the electricity crackles. 'He's copped it.'

'Oooh dear,' says the girl, showing large foolish teeth. Perhaps Beale has been sawn in two. But Beale returns whole, looking behind him suspiciously and takes his seat among the women at the back, sitting in the sunlight at the window like a fly. The spinster goes. 'Me?' she says, brightly. She takes her *Daily Mirror* with her. It is she who never returns. They have probably put her to sing in a golden cage. The bruiser is called. He swallows and grimaces at the girl who watches him go from the room. In a few minutes he returns, smiling sheepishly. 'It don't hurt,' he boasts to her. 'They put something on top of you. Pouf, it's heavy, but that's all.'

[103]

But he is surprised he is still alive and so is everyone else. Beale was half dead already – but this man: it had sounded as if he were being ironed out flat and here he is in three dimensions the whole seventeen stone of him. When he sits down he looks back to the curtain rather pleased with himself, nodding his head with approval of the process as it is repeated, rather like someone who has been called on to the stage by a conjurer. What happens next? Can he help again?

'Do they let you see yourself?' asks the barber.

'Nao,' says the bruiser. 'What you think you are inside? A family group?'

The bruiser and the barber go, the women go, only Beale is left. After a long while the nurse says, 'Oh, Beale, we shall want you on Saturday at nine. Will you remember Saturday at nine? This Saturday. Take no aperient.' Beale looks up through his long eyelashes with eyes so tightly crinkled that they are no bigger than a pair of fleas. Very slowly his lips draw back and show six strong yellow teeth. He makes a noise. He is called back from three wrong doors. 'This way, Beale,' says the nurse.

The Scapegoat

There were long times when we were at peace and when the world left us alone. We could go down Earl Street and, although we did not like the place and it felt strange to us and the women stared down from the windows and a child here and there might call out a name after us, we just walked on thinking of something else. But we were always more at ease and more ourselves, even in the quietest times of truce, when we had turned the corner by the hop warehouse and had got back into Terence Street which was our own. The truth is that you can't live without enemies and the best enemies are the ones nearest home; and though we sometimes went out to the Green to boo the speakers and some of our lads went after the Yids or joined a procession up West, that was idleness and distraction. The people we hated were not a mile away on the main road where the trams and the buses are and you don't know one man from the next; no, the people we hated were round the corner, next door, in Earl Street. They were, we used to say, a different class of people from ourselves altogether.

I don't know why but if there was any trouble in the world, we turned out and attacked them. I don't know either how these things began. You would know there was trouble coming when you heard the voices of the children getting shriller and more excited, until their cries became rhythmic like the pulse of native war cries in the forest. We were, indeed, lost in a *jungle* of streets. Somehow the children would have sticks, old pieces of board and stones in their hands and they would be rushing in groups to the hop warehouse and jeering and then scattering back. A similar thing would be happening in Earl Street. Usually this happened in the warm long evenings of the summer. Then, after the children, the thing got hold of the women and they came down from their windows where they had been watching and scratching their arms, very hot and restless, and would stand at their doorsteps and start shouting at their children. A stone would fly up and then the women would be down in the middle of the street.

It might take a day to work up or it might take longer. You would get the Earl Street girls going down our street talking in loud voices daring us, and our young lads would stand by saying nothing until the girls got to the corner. And then those girls would have to bolt. Towards closing time the Gurneys, the fighting family in Earl Street, would be out and we had our Blackers and then it was a question of who came out of the Freemasons and how he came out. But perhaps nothing would happen and we would just go down Earl Street after dark and merely kick their milk bottles down the basements.

This has been going on ever since the old people can remember. When the war came we knew everyone in Earl Street was a spy or a Hun or a Conchie. The Great War, for us, was between Earl Street and Terence Street. They had a VC and we hadn't, though we had a bunch of other stuff and one man who escaped from the Turks and was in the papers; and, though we did our best, the tea we gave was nothing to the tea they did in Earl Street for their VC. Where they got the money from was the puzzle. Thirty-two pounds. Some of our women said the Earl Street girls must have been on the streets; and at the Freemasons, the men said half of Earl Street were nothing but bloody pensioners. The police came in before we had the question settled. But when the war ended things changed. Half of our lot was out of work and when we went down Earl Street we would see half of their lot out of work too, and Earl Street did not seem quite so strange to us. One street seemed to blend into the other. This made some of our lot think and they gave their steps an extra clean to show there was a difference between Earl Street and Terence Street after all.

In the years that followed sometimes we were up on Earl Street, sometimes we were down. We were waiting for some big event. It did not come for a long time and a stranger might have thought that the old frontiers had gone and the reign of universal peace was upon us. It was not. The Jubilee came and we saw our chance. Earl Street had collected thirty-two pounds for its VC's tea party. We reckoned we would top that for the Jubilee. We would collect forty.

There was a red-haired Jew in our street called Lupinsky. He was a tailor. He was round-shouldered from bending over the table and his eyes were weak from working by gas at night. In the rush season he and his family would be up past midnight working. He was a keen man. He came out in pimples – he was so keen. Lupinsky saw everything before any of us. He saw the Jubilee before the King himself. He had got his house full of bunting and streamers and Union Jacks. 'Get in at the early doors,' he said. 'What'll you have,' he used to say to us when we went to his shop. 'Rule Britannia or God Save the King.' 'Who's that?' we said. 'The King of the Jews?' 'Getcha,' said Lupinsky. 'He's dead. Didn't you hear?' He raked in the money. They had another Jew in Earl Street doing the same. 'I say!' called Lupinsky. 'I say!' – we used to call him 'I-say-what'll-you-have' – 'Cohen's sold 120 yards to Terence Street and you've only done 70.' So we doubled. 'I say,' says Lupinsky. 'I say. When you going to start collecting? They got ten quid in Earl Street and you haven't started.'

And this was true. The trouble was we couldn't agree upon who should collect. We had had a nasty experience with the Club a few years back. And then Lupinsky was hot for doing it himself. He'd got the bunting. He'd seen it coming. He'd even got boxes. He'd thought of everything. We had nothing against Lupinsky but when we saw him raking in the money on his God Saves and Kiss-me-quicks and his flags of all the nations, we thought he was collecting enough as it was. He might mix up the two collections. 'No,' we said to Lupinsky. 'You're doing your bit, we'll do the rest.' 'That's OK,' Lupinsky said. He never bore resentment, he was too keen. 'But I hear Earl Street's up to twelve ten.' He wasn't upset with us but he couldn't bear to see us shilly-shallying around, while Earl Street walked away with it. 'If you don't trust me,' he said, 'can't you trust yourselves? I don't know what's happened to this street.' And he spat from the top of his doorstep into the gutter.

Lupinsky was wrong about us. We trust each other. There is not a man in Terence Street you cannot trust. In that nasty business we had with the Club, the man was not a Terence Street man. We could trust one another. But we were frightened. Forty pounds! We thought. That's a big sum. We didn't like the handling of it. There wasn't one of us who had seen forty pounds in his life. The Blackers, a good fighting lot, were terrified. Albert Smith and his uncle were the most likely but they said they were single and didn't like the idea. And we, for some reason, thought a single man wasn't right for the job. And the wives, the married ones, though eagerly wanting their husbands to do it, were so afraid the honour would go to someone else that they said to give it to a married man was tempting Providence. Lupinsky went down the street almost in tears saying Earl Street had touched seventeen ten.

Then suddenly we saw the right man had been staring us in the face all the time. He was not single and he was not married. He was a widower, made serious by death: Art Edwards. We chose Art Edwards and he agreed.

Art Edwards was a man of forty-seven and the moment he agreed we were proud of him. He was a grey-haired man, not very talkative and of middle height, very patient and looked you straight in the face. He lived with his sister who looked after his two children, he had a fruit stall in the main road – he had been there for twenty years – and every Sunday he used to go alone with a bunch of flowers for his wife's grave at the cemetery. The women admired him very much for doing this. He never changed. His house was the neatest house in our street and he never seemed to get richer or poorer. He just went on the same.

He had been a widower a good long time, too, and some thought he ought to marry again. The women were curious about him and said you couldn't but respect a man who didn't take a second and Art was held up as a model. This didn't prevent many of them running after him and spreading the rumour afterwards that his sister was a woman who wouldn't let a man call his soul his own. But the way Art mourned for the dead and kept faithful to The First, the ONE AND ONLY, as the women said, was striking. Some of the men said that being a model wasn't healthy and that if they had been in Art's shoes they would muck around on the quiet. They wondered why the hell he didn't, yet admired him for his restraint. Some of us couldn't have lived with temptation all those years without slipping up.

Art had put a black band on his sleeve when his wife died and had worn it ever since. But when he started collecting for the tea we had the feeling he had put off his mourning and had come alive again. We were pleased about this because, with his modest, retiring ways we hardly knew him. 'It will bring him out,' we said. He came round with his little red book and his tin and we said, 'What's it now, Art? How we doin'?'

Art was slow at adding up but accurate. He told us. We made a big effort and we touched the ten-pound mark pretty soon.

This woke us up and made us feel good, but Lupinsky came round and said it wasn't any bloody good at all. They'd touched nineteen pounds in Earl Street. So one of the women said they'd help Art. He didn't want this, or his sister didn't. So she joined in, too, to keep the other women off him. They knocked at his door at all hours and stopped him in the street. And when she saw this his sister put on her best hat and coat and went round and stopped their men. The result was everyone was collecting and came round to Art and said:

'Here y'are, Art. One and eight,' or

'Here y'are, Art, eight and six.'

And two of the Blacker girls had a fight because one said the other wasn't collecting fair but was cheapening herself to get the money. For we touched seventeen and went on to twenty-one.

The night we passed Earl Street some of our girls went out and just walked down Earl Street telling them. They didn't like it. A crowd from Earl Street came round and called 'Down with the Yids,' outside Lupinsky's. Then Earl Street picked up and passed us again. We went round to Art and planked down more money. Art got out his book and he couldn't write it down fast enough.

'Where do you keep it, Art?' we said.

He showed us a box in the cupboard. It was a fine sight all that money. His sister said:

'Art's picked up a bit in the High Street.' We looked at him as if he were a hero. ''Slike business,' he said. 'You've got to go out for it.'

We looked with wonder at him. We had chosen the right man. It was bringing him out. And he had ideas too. He got some of the kids to go out at night with tins.

We passed Earl Street and they passed us. Then we passed them again. It was ding-dong all the time. Lupinsky flew in and out with the latest like a wasp and stung us to more. Art Edwards, he said, had no life in him. After this, it became madness. People got out their savings.

There was a funny case at Harry Law's. He was a boozer, a big, heavy man, very particular in the house and very religious. Some nights when he was bad he used to beat his wife and we used to look down into their basement window wondering what would be happening inside, for something usually was happening. There were often shouts and curses and screams coming from that room and then times, which made you uncomfortable, when everything was quiet. Harry Law was often out of a job. Mrs Law was a timid woman and everyone was sorry for her. She used to go up to the Freemasons and look through the door at him. She was a thin, round-shouldered woman, always anxious about her husband and sorry that he made a fool of himself, for he got pompous when he was drunk and she hated the way people laughed at him. He used to say she had no ambition and he had dragged her out of the gutter. She said, '*Down* into the gutter, you mean.' They used to have guilty arguments like this for hours, each boasting they were better than the other and wondering all the time why they had got into their present situation. Then Harry Law would go to church so as to feel good and find out why and his wife used to stop at home and think about it, too. She would put her arms round him and love him when he came back. And he would be all right for a few days until he got some scheme into his head for making money. When he had the scheme he would go out and get drunk again.

Harry Law wanted to show everyone that he was a man of ideas and ambitions, and better than the rest of us in Terence Street. He used to dress up on Sundays. He used to say he had been better off once and had had a shop. The truth was, as his wife bitterly told everyone, he'd always been the same; up and down all his life. She couldn't bear other people laughing at him but she used to tear his reputation to bits herself and get great pleasure out of doing it.

It was just at the height of our madness that he came into the Freemasons and instead of cadging for drinks, he began to order freely. A funny thing had happened, he said. And he said, in his lordly voice, 'I want Art Edwards.' It turned out that he had been going across the room while his wife was out and had tripped up on something on the floor. There was a bump in the lino. Being a very inquisitive man who never had anything to do, he knelt down and felt the lump. 'I thought it was dirt,' he said. One of the things he always said about his wife was that she was dirty. He was a very clean man himself. He decided to take up the lino and underneath he found a lump of money wrapped up in notes. It was his wife's savings.

That was why Harry Law was lording it at the Freemasons. He had hardly given a penny to the Collection, but now, when everyone was present, he was going to make a great gesture and show his greatness. When Art came in, he said, 'Here, Art. Have a fiver.'

We all stared. Harry Law was leaning against the bar with the notes in the tips of his fingers as if they were dirt, like a duke giving a tip.

At that moment his wife came in.

'That's mine,' she screamed. 'It's mine.'

There was a row and Art wouldn't take the money. Everyone said that a man hadn't the right to take his wife's money. But Harry said, 'What!' Wasn't his money as good as anybody's and we said, 'Yes, Harry, but that belongs to your missus.' She was crying and he kept saying, 'Go home. I'll teach you to come round here. It is my money. I earned it.'

This was awkward. Between her tears, with her hands covering her face, Mrs Law was saying she had saved it. He was always ruining them, so she had to save. Still, if he'd earned it, it was his.

'Take that money,' says Harry, dropping it like a lord on the floor. The notes fell down, we all looked at them and no one moved. Mr Bell of the Freemasons got a laugh by saying we were littering up his bar with paper. Then Harry turned his back and we picked it up and were going to give it to Mrs Law, but Harry says in a threatening voice, 'That's Art's. For the Collection. I reckon I got Earl Street knocked silly.'

That part of the statement was irresistible. While we hesitated, Art said:

'Give it here then. I'll look after it.' Lupinsky, who had been sitting there all the time clutching his hands and his eyes starting out of his head with misery at the sight of money lying in the sand, gave a shout.

'That's the boy,' he said. 'We've got 'em.'

We all felt uncomfortable with Harry and we went away in ones and twos and Mrs Law went out still crying. After she went out, Art went too and when we got down the street Art stopped and told Mrs Law he wasn't going to take the money and he made her take it back. She clutched it with both hands and looked at him like a dog with gratitude.

That night half the men in Terence Street wanted to take up their lino and sat up late arguing with their wives: but the madness was still in the air, especially when Earl Street, hearing our news, sent all their kids up

West and passed us. There was a fight in the High Street between our kids and the Earl Street kids and one of ours lost her box. But there was nothing in it except stones. They put stones in to make a rattle so that people would think they were doing well. If there had been any money in that box there wouldn't have been a pane of glass in Earl Street left.

'They've passed us,' the cry went down our street. In the middle of this Mrs Law came over to Art and gave him back the money. She made him take it.

'Your husband made you,' says Art.

'Him,' she said scornfully. 'He don't know anything about it. I told him you gave it me back and he said, "A good thing too," he's feeling sorry for himself. I'll teach him to touch my money, I said. If there's going to be any giving in this house, it's me that's got the money. I'm going to teach my husband a lesson', she said.

This surprised Art for he had been very sorry for poor Mrs Law and had shown it. But I've no doubt she was tired of being pitied. That money was all she had. She was going to show us that the Laws had their pride and she wasn't going to let them down. Only *she* was going to give it.

Her eyes shone and were sharp. They were greenish miserly grey eyes yet she was not miserly. Now she was proud and not bedraggled with tears and misery, she looked jubilant and cunning. She had been a gay, quick-tongued woman in her time.

'I kept it under the floor. That was wrong of me,' she said. 'I oughter have put it in the Post Office.'

She said she knew her husband was right. It was not right to hide money.

Everyone in Terence Street had supposed Mrs Law to be a poor, timid, beaten soul and Art had always thought the same, he said; but now he said that she had some spirit. She had opened her heart to him because he had been kind to her and now she said, very proudly, that he should come and have a chat with her husband. She took Art triumphantly to her basement just to show her husband there were other men in the world. Old Harry Law saw this at once – he was always on his dignity – so he just talked largely to Art about the shops he had had, the ups and downs, his financial adventures. Investments, he called them. We had all heard of investments but none of us had ever had any. If he had his life over again, Harry Law said, he'd invest every penny.

'There's a man,' Art said when he went, 'who doesn't practise what he preaches.' But he respected Harry's preaching though he despised him a bit. And Harry said, 'There's a man who stays the same all his life. Never made a penny, never lost a penny. The only money he's got,' said Harry, 'isn't his – this collection.'

And Harry asked him how much it was. There were some thirty-odd pounds, Art said.

Harry respected him when he heard that and said with a sigh, 'Money makes money.'

When Art got back his sister was short with him. 'Going after other men's wives,' she said. And she lectured him about Mrs Law. It had been such a warm, pleasant, friendly evening over at Harry Law's that Art was hurt about this.

'Him and her,' he said, 'has got more brains than you think. They've lived, all right. They've had their ups and downs.'

'He's a boozer.'

'We've all got our faults. He's had his ups and downs.'

And that was the phrase that he kept repeating. It fascinated him. He felt generous. It came to him that he had never felt anything for years. He had just gone on standing in the High Street by the stall. He had never taken a holiday. He had never bought himself anything he wanted. He had never done anything. It startled him – but he suddenly did not want his wife who was in the grave. The street had chosen him, singled him out above all others, and there he stood naked, nothing. He was shy about his nonentity. He felt a curious longing for ups and downs.

You will say, 'How did we know what Art Edwards thought?' That was the strange thing: we did know. We knew as if he had told us, as if we were inside him. You see, because we had singled him out he was, in a sense, ourselves. We could see him thinking and feeling and doing what we would. He had taken the burden off us. By doing that he had become nearer and more precious to us than any other person.

And there was Terence Street two pounds ahead of Earl Street, drunk with the excitement of it. Art used to get out the money and count it – it was the biggest sum of money he had ever seen – and a sober pride filled him. He had done this. People like Mrs Law had just thrown in all they had. He had put in his bit cautiously, but everyone had scraped and strained and just wildly thrown in the cash. It made him marvel. He marvelled at us, he marvelled – as his hands trembled over the money – that he had been picked out by us to hold it.

We went round once or twice to look at the money too. What a nest egg, what an investment! Over thirty pounds! We said we wished it was ours. We said we wished we could give more, or double it. We all wanted to double it. We looked at it sadly. 'If that thirty pounds had been on the winner today,' someone said. 'Or on the dogs.'

We laughed uneasily. And we dreamed. The more we looked at that money the more we thought of things you could do with it – mad things like backing a horse or sensible things like starting a business or having a holiday.

When we got up in Art's kitchen and saw him put the money in the cupboard and lock the door, we nodded our heads sadly. It was like burying the dead.

'It's sad it's got to go,' we thought.

And it seemed to us fitting that Art, who had buried the dead and who was a dour man with iron-grey hair and level-looking eyes, should have the grim task of keeping that money, like some sexton. And we were glad to have him doing it, to have him be responsible instead of us. For some of us had to admit we'd go mad at times with temptation tingling in our fingers and hissing like gas in coal in our hearts.

When we left him we felt a kind of sorrow for Art for bearing our burden, for being the custodian of our victory over Earl Street.

It made us all very friendly to Art. The time went by. We used to stop and have a word with him in the street. And Art became friendly too. But he wasn't at the Freemasons much. He went over to Mrs Law's. And Harry Law didn't go on the booze. He stayed at home talking largely to Art. Once or twice Art went out in the evenings with Mr and Mrs Law. Lupinsky used to see them up at the Pictures.

Lupinsky was our reporter of everything and gradually, expressing no doubt the instinct of the street, he had become our reporter on Art Edwards. We wanted a friendly eye kept on him not because he was valuable but because he was – well, as you would keep an eye on a sick man, say, a man who might have a heart attack or go dizzy in the street. When Lupinsky came back and said: 'I see Art Edwards getting on a tram,' we used to look up sharply and then, annoyed with ourselves, say, 'What of it? What was he doing, having a ride?'

That Jew used to make us tired. And he'd started worrying already about the catering. They'd started arranging about the catering already in Earl Street. 'It's a funny thing,' we said, 'about the Yids. He's only been here fifteen years and you'd think he'd been here for ever. Anyone'd think he'd been born in the street. You'd bloody well think it was Jerusalem.'

We had been born there, most of us, and we said:

'It *will* be Jerusalem soon.'

But we would have been nowhere without Lupinsky.

And then one morning he came along and said:

'Seen Art?'

'No,' we said.

'He's not up in the High Street,' said Lupinsky. 'And he's not at his house.'

'What of it?' we said.

Lupinsky was breathless. All the pimples on his face seemed about to burst. He had the kind of red hair that is coarse and stands up on end and thick arched eyebrows which were raised very high but were now higher for his eyes were starting out of his head. There were always bits of cotton from tailoring on his clothes and he was as I have said rather hump-backed from leaning all day over his machine.

'I saw him last night at the station. Nine o'clock. He took a ticket on the North London and hasn't been back.'

'Smart baby,' we said. But we were thinking of Lupinsky. We didn't believe him and yet we did believe him. 'What were you doing up at the station – brother had another fire?' we said. Lupinsky's brother was always having fires.

But it was true. Art hadn't been home that night and his sister was very shifty when we went to see her. We never liked Art's sister and we grinned to think he'd got away from her for a night.

'Art had to go away on business,' she said.

Theirs was a tidy house and Art's sister worked hard in it. The window sills were hearth-stoned. That woman never stopped. She always came to the door with an iron in her hand or a scrubbing-brush or with something she was cleaning or cooking. She was a tall, straight-nosed woman and she had the best teeth I've ever seen, but there was no thickness in her, no give.

She used to say, 'I've never had justice done me.'

And Art used to sigh and say, 'I can never do justice to her.'

'What about it now?' said Lupinsky, who was waiting for us.

'Art can go away if he likes,' we said. 'Why not?'

'Sure, yes, why not?' said Lupinsky. 'What you worrying about?'

Later on Lupinsky came and told us Art was still away. His stall was still in the lock-up and he hadn't been down to the market. Lupinsky had a friend who had told him. Then Lupinsky had another friend who said he'd seen Art at Wembley.

'Too many Yids here,' said Albert Blacker. 'You can't move but you catch one in your clothes. What's up with Wembley?'

We went over to Mrs Law's and called down to her. She was ironing in the light of the window.

'Seen Art Edwards?' we said.

'No,' she said. 'He hasn't been here for two or three days.'

'Oh,' we said.

Then Harry Law got up from his chair by the stove and said:

'Art gone?'

'We're just looking for him. Thought he might be with you?'

Mrs Law gazed at us and then she looked at her husband. She was one of those women who when anything serious or unexpected happens, when they don't know what to think, when they are bewildered, always turn to their husbands; as if by studying him she would always know the worst about any event in the world and would be prepared. It was like looking up something in a book or gazing into a crystal. And when she had gazed at her husband and thought about him, she said:

'Oh dear.' And she put down her iron and her shoulders hunched up. She looked accusingly at her husband and he lowered his eyes. He knew she could read him like that.

We did not think so at the time but afterwards we said we had the feeling that when Mrs Law looked at her husband in that accusing way, she knew something about Art Edwards that we did not know. It turned out that she did not know. I looked out of the window that night when I went to bed. It was a warm night. I work in a fur-warehouse and the air had the close, dead, laid-out smell of ladies' furs. There was a cold hollow lilac light over the roofs from the arc lamps in the High Street. At night our street is quiet and often you can hear the moan of a ship's siren from the river like the hoarse voice of someone going away. But the commonest sound is the clinking of shunting trucks on the railway – a sound that is meaningless as if someone who couldn't play the piano had struck the keys anyhow, trying to make a tune. It is a sound which makes you think the city has had an attack of nerves. As I stood there on one leg, undoing my boots, I heard quick footsteps coming along. They were Lupinsky's. Lupinsky was always up late.

'I say. I say,' he called up to me. 'Art's come back. I just seen him. He came back and let himself in.'

That night Art Edwards went into the lock-up in his yard and, attaching his braces to a hook in the roof, he hanged himself. The box in the cupboard was empty. He had gone off to Wembley and lost all the money on the dogs.

We went out into the street in the morning and stood outside the house and stared at the windows. The people from Earl Street came too. All the children came and stared and no one said anything in the street. Albert Blacker went into the yard at the back and Lupinsky was there with the police. Mrs Law would not leave her house but stood on her doorstep holding the railing tightly, watching from a distance. Harry Law would not come out. He walked up and down the room and called up to his wife to come down. He could not bear being left alone. She was afraid to leave her house and yet, I thought, wanted to be with Art.

'The bloody twister,' we said between our teeth.

'That bloody widower,' we said.

'Takes our money and has a night out. Our savings! Our money!'

'The rotten thief.'

We muttered like this standing in front of the house. We were sorry for the police who had to touch the body of a man like that.

'You wouldn't trust me,' Lupinsky said.

We looked at him. We turned away. We couldn't bear the sight of that man's pimples.

'I'm used to money,' Lupinsky said.

I could not repeat all the things we said. I remember clearly the red, white and blue streamers drooping over the street and looking dirty, with 'God Save the King' on them. 'God Save Art Edwards,' said Harry Law coming up. He was tight.

We thought of the spirit of Art Edwards's sister being humbled. All down the street, at all the windows, the women leaned on their bare arms thinking about this. They cuffed their children and the children cried. There was the low murmur of our voices in the street and then the whining voices of children. Presently a couple of women came down, pushed their way through the crowd and went in to help Art's sister. We gaped at them.

And then Lupinsky, who gave the lead to everything and always knew what we were thinking underneath, said:

'They're jeering at us in Earl Street.'

They were. We set our teeth. Kids came round shouting, 'Who swiped the money box! Who swiped the money box!' Our kids did nothing for a long time. Then they couldn't stand it. Our kids went for the Earl Street kids. Some of our women came down to pull their kids off and this drew out the Earl Street women. In half an hour Albert Blacker came out of the Freemasons with his sleeves rolled up, just when the Earl Street men were getting together and then Harry Law came out roaring. Mrs Law ran towards him. But it was too late. A stone went and a window crashed and that brought out the rest of the Blacker family. We got it off our chests that night and we crowded into Earl Street. Half their milk bottles had gone before the police whistles went.

And then it was clear to us. We knew what to do. Lupinsky headed it. Art Edwards was suddenly our hero. We'd kill the man who said anything against Art Edwards. In our hearts, we said, it might have been ourselves. Thirty pounds, we remembered the sight of it! We even listened to Harry Law.

'He was trying to double it at the dogs,' he said. 'Investing it. Every man has . . .'

His wife pulled his coat and tried to stop him.

'Every man,' continued Harry Law, 'has his ups and downs.'

And to show Earl Street what we were and to show the world what we thought of Art Edwards we got up the biggest funeral that has ever been seen in our street. He was ourselves, our hero, our god. He had borne our sins. You couldn't see the hearse for flowers. The street was black with people. The sun shone. We'd been round and got every stall holder, every barrow man in the neighbourhood. That procession was a mile long when it got going. There was a Jubilee for you, covered in red, white and blue wreaths. Art Edwards our king. It looked like a wedding. The great white trumpets of the lilies rocked thick on the coffin. Earl Street couldn't touch that. And Lupinsky collected the money.

Eleven o'Clock

From years of habit the mare stopped a minute or two at the right houses in all the streets waiting for the milkman's voice to call: 'Good day, ma'am, thank you, ma'am,' in the alleys. Then she gave a slouching heave, the cans and bottles would start jingling, and, with the man following, she was off to the next stop. But when eleven o'clock came she stopped dead. She knew the house they were at now. She knew it well. An ungainly, warty and piebald creature, she loosened her shoulders, her head and neck hung to the ground, her forelegs splayed out, and she looked old, rakish and cynical.

For here was no stop of a minute or two. Down the passage strode the milkman, his lips whistling. Five minutes passed into ten, ten into twenty. Some mornings it was half an hour, three-quarters or the full hour. And when the milkman came back he was not whistling.

He was a short, ruddy man in a brown dustcoat with the firm's name on it and a hat like a police inspector's. But there is nothing like a uniform for concealing the soul. He was bald and battered under his hat and his eyebrows were thick and inky. If he took his hat off in the middle of a sentence, that sentence would become suddenly very easy and rather free: if he wiped his bald head with his handkerchief, *that* was a sign he might get freer.

The first time the milkman went to the house a woman came across the kitchen towards him. The fire was murmuring in the range and a pot of coffee was standing on it. A tray of cakes had just been taken out of the oven and was standing on the table. The milkman's nostrils had small sensitive black hairs in them, and they quivered.

'Oh, I do like a nice mince-pie,' said the milkman.

She was a kind woman. 'The early bird catches the worm,' she said. 'Have one.'

She was a big creature, lazy and soft in the arms and shoulders. She had several chins. The small chin shook like a cup in its saucer on the second chin that was under it, and she had freckles on her neck. She was warm and untidy with cooking, and her yellow hair was coming undone at the back. Her mouth was short and surly, but now it softened in harmony with the rest of her into an easy placid smile; the rest of her body seemed to be laughing at her fatness, and the smile broadened from her lips to her neck and so on downwards, until the milkman put his foot on the doorstep, took off his hat and wiped his bald head with pleasure.

'I'm a rollin' stone, ma'am,' said the milkman. 'I don't mind if I do.'

She turned round and walked slowly to the table and the cakes. They were small cherry cakes. When she turned, the crease in the back of her neck seemed to be a smile and even her shoes seemed to be making smiles of pleasure on the floor.

'Come in,' she said. 'I'm Yorkshire. I'm not like the people round here. I'm neighbourly.'

'I'm Yorkshire. I'm neighbourly too,' said the milkman, rubbing his hands, and he stepped in. It was warm and cosy in the kitchen, warm with the smell of the cakes and the coffee, and warm with the good-natured woman.

'Take a seat,' said the woman. 'I'm sitting down myself. I've been on my feet all morning. I come from Leeds and this is my bake.'

'I come from Hull,' said the milkman. 'We never say "no" and we never say die. I've been on my feet too. What I mean to say – in my job, you can't ride because you're always stopping and you can't stop because you've got to keep moving, if you get me.' The milkman sat down opposite to her.

'I could tell you were from the north,' said the hospitable woman. She pushed the cakes towards him. 'Go on,' she said. 'Take one. Take two. They're a mean lot of people down here. There's nothing mean about me.'

'After you, ma'am,' he said.

'No,' she said. 'I dassn't.'

She laughed.

'Slimming?' said the milkman.

'Oh, ha ha,' laughed the woman. 'That's a good one. Look at me. I've got the spread. I don't get any exercise.' She went into a new peal of laughter. 'And I don't want it.'

'We're as God made us,' said the milkman. 'All sizes.'

'And all shapes,' said the woman, recovering. 'It wouldn't do for all of us to be thin.'

'You want some heavyweights,' said the man.

'They're all thin round here, and mean,' said the woman.

The woman laughed until tears came into the small grey eyes which were sunk like oyster pearls between her plump fire-reddened cheeks and her almost hairless brows. She laughed and laughed, and her laughter was like her smile. She laughed not only with her mouth, but her cheeks gave a jump and her chins jumped together and her big breasts shook, and she spread her legs with laughter, too, under the table.

'Oh dear! Oh dear!' she said. 'When I was a girl I was in the catering business and they starved me. One house I was in the boss used to follow me into the kitchen when I was putting away the snacks to see I didn't pinch anything. And I can tell you it was a work of art slipping a bit of cheese down the neck of me blouse to eat when I got up to bed, it was.'

The milkman looked at her blouse.

The milkman widened one eye and winked with the other.

'Oh, don't!' cried the woman, going off again. 'Don't! Stop it! Don't start me off.'

'Don't mind me,' said the woman wiping her eyes. 'I've been here seven weeks and this is the first laugh I've had. My husband's a cripple. He's a watchmaker. Tick-tock, tick-tock, tick-tock, all day long. He hangs up the watches on the wall and that's all I've heard for seven weeks! Tick-tock, tick-tock, tick-tock.'

She wiped the tears from her eyes with her apron and waved an arm to the wall.

There were four clocks on the kitchen wall and three on the mantelpiece, and there were watches hanging on nails. The tall brown clock with the pendulum gave a slow grating 'Tock'; the blue alarm on the mantelpiece went at a run; the big wooden clock next to it made a sweet sound like a man sucking a pipe, and the rest croaked, scratched, ticked and chattered. Carved in fretwork was a small cuckoo clock beside the door.

'Who winds them?' asked the milkman with his mouth full of cake.

'Who winds them?' said the woman. 'He winds them. He comes home and spends all night winding them. Have some coffee. You ought to see what I've got inside and upstairs.'

'I bet,' said the milkman, gazing at her from his still wide eyes. 'If there's a drop of coffee I'll have it.'

'Laugh,' said the woman. 'You can't tell night from day in this house. They all say something different. I've been seven weeks here, but it might be seven years. It's a good thing I can laugh.'

'It's slimming,' he said.

'It's spreading,' she said.

'Well, I like a bit of spread myself,' said the milkman.

The milkman watched her go to the range. He watched her bring the coffee-pot over and bring a couple of white cups from the dresser. He got up and went to the door.

'My Jenny,' he said. 'My mare. Whoa! Listen to her. She's kicking up the pavement.'

The mare was kicking the kerb. She was standing with her forelegs on it, gazing down the alley and striking a hoof on the pavement.

'She knows I'm in here,' he said, coming back. 'I bet she knows I'm having a cup of coffee. I bet she's wondering what's happening. I bet she's thinking it out. Wonderful things horses are. Jealous, you know, too,' he said. 'If she knew you was in here, I'd never hear the last of it.

'Eating's her trouble. She's old,' said the milkman. 'She's terrible. I've never seen an animal eat what she does. I bet she knows there's something going on.'

The milkman sipped his coffee. His lips made bubbling sounds as he drank. Soon there were no sounds in the room but the ticking of the clocks and the bubbling noise of the woman's lips and the man's lips at their cups, and a click of the cups and a murmur of laughter from the woman.

Then the little fretwork clock which hung by the door gave a small sneezing buzz, a door clipped open, a tiny hammer rang and out bobbed the bird. 'Cuckoo! Cuckoo!' it called, and 'Clap' went the door. The milkman put down his cup with a start and gaped.

'They're all wrong,' said the woman. 'Sit down. Have another cake, just a little one. Have a tart? That cuckoo's never right. "Oh, shut up," I tell it. "Keep quiet."'

'I used to do fretwork myself,' said the milkman. 'Sit down,' she pressed him. 'Another cup will warm you up.'

'You're warm in here,' said the milkman.

'I'm warm anywhere,' the woman said.

'Don't want winding up, I bet,' said the milkman with a wink. He was short beside her and he took a long easy look at her. He wiped his bald head and put on his hat.

'Well,' he said. 'Talking of time, one thing leads to another.'

She looked at him sadly, and with a lazy yawn raised her big arms above her head.

'Come and see those clocks.'

The milkman had his pencil in his ear, a small red stump of pencil. He took it out and, quickly, he gave her a soft poke in the waist with it and went off.

'Good day, ma'am, thank you, ma'am,' he called, and went off whistling.

The next day the milk-cart stopped again at the house. Behind the cart the milkman walked, humming to himself. He looked up at the house. There was the short brick wall and the iron rail on top of it. There was the green hedge coming into leaf. He took his basket, he swung open the gate and he went down the alley. There was a smell of pastry just out of the oven. For a long time while he was gone the mare stood, then she stepped on to the kerb and began knocking her hoof upon it. The sound could be heard down the deserted road. 'Whoa!' shouted the milkman down the alley. The mare stretched her neck and sniffed the ground and then began pawing again. She got both forefeet on the pavement and kept stretching and shaking her smooth white neck. 'Whoa!' shouted the milkman's voice. She pricked her ears. He was shouting from the front room window.

Half an hour passed. The mare had now stepped farther on to the pavement. Her neck was stretched out to its full length. She was sniffing the wall, the iron rail, and behind it the juicy green shoots of the hedge. She strained, her nostrils trembling, her soft mouth opening to seize a shoot in her old yellow teeth. She paused and made a greater effort, pulling the cart, and now her nose was over the top of the railing.

Grunting, chewing, slopping, crunching sounds came from her mouth. She had bitten off her first piece. And, once on it, appetite leapt. She gave a wilder tug and now she could get at the hedge. Her teeth dragged at the hedge and crunched. She raised her neck, looked with discrimination at the shoots, then went on quietly browsing.

No sounds came from the house, no sound from the road but the chewing of the horse, the bit chinking like marbles in her slobber. Hearing him come at last, she backed on to the road. He came out very thoughtful and not whistling.

And some mornings there was the smell of cake in the alley, sometimes it was pie and sometimes it was coffee. Again a quarter of an hour passed, or maybe twenty minutes or half an hour, and often enough a full hour, and a shout of 'Whoa!' came from an upstairs window. He had his coat off. 'That clock's wrong,' said the woman. 'They're all wrong.' The mare's neck was right over the railings and this was necessary because, as she chewed, the hedge got lower and lower.

'Eh, whoa there!' the milkman shouted down from the top floor of the house one morning and, looking in amazement at the torn and bitten green hedge and the mare still tearing it, he came down to the street.

'What's the idea? Come off it,' he said, taking the mare by the bridle and jerking her head off the hedge.

He drew her off the pavement and went back and looked over the railings at the hedge, ruined by weeks of eating.

'Been getting your greens, haven't you?' he said. He stared at the mare and, bright under their blinkers, he saw the eyes of that cynical animal, secretive and glistening, gazing back at him.

The Upright Man

Calvert was an upright man, tall, shy, short-stepping. His eyes were lowered and his narrow shoulders square. Proud in his poverty he kept to himself, he feared to know himself to be known. He came to the office punctually, he hung up his raincoat and hat in the cloakroom reserved for the male staff, he changed into a grey jacket in order to save his better one, he used his own towel when he washed his thin hands. He did not stand as the other clerks did, with dejected buttocks to the cashier's fire, defying him in his absence and scattering to their stools when the blowing of a nose announced that he had arrived. Calvert did not spend himself in gestures or extravagances. He kept himself apart. He went straight to his desk, took out his blotting paper, cleaned his pens, took down his books and, before all others, bent his body and bowed his head. The clerks smiled at him. He was fair.

The carpenter bends over his bench, the cobbler over his shoe, the mechanic over his machine, the priest over his altar, the clerk over his desk. By day, the heads of all men are bowed and their bodies bent. Not one of them is upright. Yet Calvert, the first to bow, was an upright man. Soldierly in duty, remembering his mother, scrupulous in poverty, when others laughed only smiling, saying two words while others spoke ten, eating sparingly alone, secret in life and parsimonious of himself. He trod the path of a single preoccupation, an instinctive loneliness. He conserved himself, every sinew was restraining. There were iron bars to the windows of his office. Through them if a bowed man looked up, he saw not the sky but across the street the flat walls of windows where other bowed men worked.

At first he had been restless, his mouth had the desire to speak, his legs fidgeted on the stool – the chains unfamiliar – his hands reckoning his money, his grey eyes looking at the window-bars for a space to squeeze through and escape. 'Calvert,' the cashier warned him. And the chant of the office went on. He bowed his head and ducked with the rest repentant. Then cautiously at twenty-two he let a little of himself go. He lit his eyes, guiltily conscient of his mother and their poverty, permitted himself a little of the great secrecy of love. He cautiously looked up at the bars expecting to see a miracle, a vision, the appearance of an angel. For months he continued this deep espionage. No vision came. He bowed his head at last. He was an upright man.

Now there were two women, his mother and this other. It was his duty not to look up. She and he must save themselves. They must not speak too much, nor smile too much, nor touch too much each other's skin, in case they should love too much and exclaim out of their hearts. How long the old live! They sat in the evenings with his mother and with hers, looking through the fine lace curtains to the sky, waiting for the miracle. But there was no sky. There were the walls of lace curtains in the houses opposite and behind them invisible presences looking up. For ten years looking through lace curtains for a miracle they brought laughter to others.

Clerks flung their lives about and committed follies. One married to a voracious wife drank on Thursdays a glass of stout. One who copied weighing slips gave imitations of the voice of the cashier. One who was bald put his hand down the blouse of his secretary and was slapped in the face. One would absent himself for twenty minutes in the morning to read the newspaper in the lavatory. One going deaf turned to an Oriental religion. One made use of the office telephone to communicate with a bookmaker. One told the Port of London Authority of an error in demurrage; it was his own. One staying after six lit his pipe. The oldest, in charge of stamps, went up in an aeroplane for a few minutes at a resort; he had married a widow. But Calvert did not so defy the gods, his gaolers.

So the gods, his gaolers, got drunk and went mad. They opened the doors of the cell, they flung in the keys. 'You are not a slave. You are not a tame man,' they whispered in his ears. 'You are a beast and brute fighting for survival. You have saved yourself too long. Go outside,' they said to him, patting him on the back. 'Stand out in the air, draw yourself up to your full height, take a deep breath. Do you see? You are a man already. Your pale face is tanned by the sun, your neck is golden. Your hair which had gone dead and greasy is alive again like corn. Your shoulders are like walls, your muscles are hard. Do not lower your eyes! Do not bow your head any more! That day has passed and gone. My dear fellow, those red spots in front of your eyes have nothing to do with your liver, they are made of blood.'

'Blood?' murmured Calvert incredulously.

'Yes, yes,' they said. 'Blood. Life. You're a hero. Go and kill.'

Women, above all, they said, expected this of him. Now was the time to save nothing but to spend all.

He mistrusted them until they said, remembering his tradition, that it was his duty. He had bowed but now at last had come the time of freedom and uprightness.

And indeed the whole world of men was changed. The carpenter no longer bent over his bench, nor the mechanic over his screw, nor the cobbler at his last, nor the clerk at his desk. They were not many bowed men. They were all upright, bolt upright, chins up, shoulders back, forefinger on the seam of trousers, and they marched on grass under the sky. Like upright gods they marched, strong, healthy and beautiful. Women watched them. They would never go back they said. Many indeed did not.

For it appeared that this was a trick. They were made to stand in rows in trenches as they had sat in rows at desks, but the pens they now used required two arms to lift. The cashiers had three stripes on their arms, the partners red bands to their hats. The bars of the office windows had become bars of wire. Accounts were opened and kept, but not of bales. It soon became the habit not to be an upright man, but to duck the head once more. Looking at the sky, they saw miracles but they were sulphurous, and there was a tone of hoarse, consumptive wailing in the voices of the angels as they passed over to be entertained unawares.

But Calvert was an upright man. He had waited long with great passion. He had waited to make a life for himself. He had come to the end of his loneliness. Recklessly he talked, loudly he laughed. He entered into fellowship. He had to spend himself and all his life, to laugh with his whole body, to love and die and live again with his whole nature. This was a supreme duty. All his life he had waited, to stand in all his stature and fullness, attending the Passion. And after sundown between the lights of day and night when the bowed men stand up, he looked up through the wire bars at the sky, and the miracle occurred. He was shot by a sniper in the head.

First of all it was as if, angered with his standing, the earth had swung up with all its metals like a pick and hit with full might upon the head, that his life leapt from his feet and all parts of his body to that place. He fell. It seemed he was whipped off his feet while his head pealed like a helpless belfry. Now there was nothing left of him, he was scattered into fragments and flung together in an iron ball of pain, to be struck and struck until he broke into nothing but clangorous and bloody echoes; and then great toothed pliers picked him up by the skull and flung him away down into a black pit that had no end to it and measured only by the wail of his pain as he dropped down. He had not imagined a death so extravagant.

They carried Calvert away on a stretcher. He was written off the books. His name appeared in many entries. By goods, cash. His account closed, he entered into heaven where all men were lying down full length and only the angels bowed their heads over them. For a long time the hammer-on-anvil clangour of the earth was there, but slowly as he sank into heaven there was the tolerable melody of bells and endurable singing. God came in white coat and held his head together by the pressure of his hands so that these sounds died and after God had held his head it was rigid. Calvert slept, and in his sleep lived many lives and enacted dreams. After many months his eyes, which had long been open, saw a white ceiling and a human face looking down at him. He closed his eyes, unwilling to return from the fevers of heaven from which he was drifting on the sweet stream of sleep. He could have wept that he was not dead. When again he opened his eyes two women were looking at him. One of them was old and one desired. 'Save yourself,' their eyes pleaded. He had nothing now to save. He had spent. 'Do not let him bend his head,' they said in one voice. 'HE CANNOT MOVE HIS HEAD,' said the doctor. 'The bullet is still in it.'

At this the gods sobered and grabbed back the keys. 'All men to the cells,' they said. 'All men back to the bars. No more holidays – work!' The clerks in this new freedom were gay. One who had come to suspect Divine Justice took to games of chance. One who was bald consummated love with a telephone operator and was presented with a clock on his marriage; one saddened by an adding machine took drugs which gave him visions; one moved into a town whose train service had been electrified; one who could imitate the voice of the cashier played in an orchestra; one sold his house at a profit; a typist given to the circulation of religious pamphlets had a week's leave to serve on a jury; many grew flowers and had newborn children.

But what can a man do in the world who cannot bend his head? Even the inspired blind are led erect, tapping, can bend their heads and work. They can lean down to kiss, they can grope into the convulsions of love. But a man screwed upright by a bullet in his neck, a bullet like the clot of a spirit level to be steadily carried, cannot bend over tools or ledger, nor grovel with fingers.

In this new world returning to life Calvert walked now rigid as the memory of the fear of death. Eyes now wide open, face narrow, shoulders fixed, body bleak, he was fixed in uprightness for ever. Many pitied him. But life requires pliable men. Regimentation of the pliable, they said; it was the lesson of the war. All must bend to the wheel together. No head out of alignment.

What could he do, fixed now in the discipline of uprightness for ever, not of men, lately of heaven, but not of the angels, needing to eat? He sank from plane to plane. There were two women. He had been, he said, staring, a clerk. He went from place to place asking. 'There,' they said, 'that is what you can do.' He could go from place to place, he could be a pair of hands, impersonal. Take this. Bring that. Fetch me ... Give him ... A messenger, walking from room to room, standing in lifts, waiting at desks, an intermediary, lifeless. Not a live man, not a dead man, a man now without all means of desiring anything, a man indelibly alone not looking up nor down. An upright man.

Page and Monarch

Ten days before Christmas, Schneider went. His departures like his arrivals were orgiastic, and between them was a three-months orgy of work. All day between Schneider House and his suite at the hotel, the messengers, the secretaries, the managers, the legal and advertising men, went. Jewellers, picture dealers, stockbrokers, women, sailed up to his suite in the hushed warm lifts. There were nights in restaurants, theatres and night clubs. Telephone bells rang in Manchester, Paris, Rome and New York calling people to the eager guttural splutter of Schneider's voice. Up to the last moment he was working and playing at once, flopping like a sea-lion in his chair. A cigar was in his mouth, a bottle of champagne was on his desk, a pen was in his hand signing letters and contracts, while he talked to Lippott who was behind him, his three secretaries, to people more remote in the blue haze of cigar smoke: and all the time into another telephone he was gurgling thick, sentimental nonsense to Lola in the bedroom next door who was sitting like a cross bird of paradise at her dressing-table. He had been up till four the night before, dancing. And now, while the cars waited below and the heavy luggage was being loaded, he was rolling in his chair. His black hair curled over the astrakhan collar of his overcoat. The smiles that sent ripples into the bay of sallow baldness in the head seemed to flow from his voracious lips all over his body. His very arms smiled when he smiled, his whole body grunted when he grunted.

Then when all was done he and his court sailed down in the lifts and he walked out of the hotel to his car like a squat prince in horn-rimmed spectacles, still giving orders, shaking hands, bowed to by the manager and the staff; and two cars followed the Rolls with the luggage. Lippott, as was fitting in the man who was closer to Schneider than any man, knowing more than his mistresses, more than his directors, knowing more about his money, his clothes, his very underclothes, more about his

tempers, his tricks, his swindles, his schemes – Lippott, who was as vital
to him as the braces which held up his trousers – was the last to speak
to him through the car window.

'And a merry Christmas!' Lippott said in a voice which was like the
icing on a small cake.

'Vot's that, Lippott?'

'A merry Christmas. Compliments of the season.' Lippott, though he
was stiff and clever with other people, wriggled like a confused girl when
he spoke to Schneider.

'Oh ha ha,' came the roar of Schneider's laugh from the car. 'Merry
compliments. No?'

Schneider had a lifelong difficulty with English greetings. And so, like
a cat, the car went off, taking Schneider to Italy. Schneider House would
not be disturbed for another two or three months.

After the departure of Schneider came the departure of Lippott: a liner
is launched and after it comes an outboard, methodically chugging
and drawn out with deceptive speed into the immense swell. Lippott
went back with the manager into the hotel. The servants, who were left,
bowed. In a more practical way there was a similar if smaller deference
to Lippott. Lippott arranged about bills and tips. Lippott scrutinised,
organised and paid. Lippott was Schneider's shadow. Schneider was a
dream, a fantasy like an enormous electric sign on the front of a building;
but Lippott, the exact man in the bowler hat, the restrained expensive
clothes, and the small culture-pearl laugh, was the reality. He was the
Code Book. There was a deference to the man who paid in hundreds or
in thousands on behalf of Schneider and after he had received his deference
he left. No car waited for him.

'Good day Mr Lippott,' from three, not ten servants, and a look from
bowler brim to rubber-tipped heels after he passed.

Lippott walked. He walked because he was a frugal man and because
he was a free man now Schneider had gone, and also because it took
hours, after these launchings, for the swell of departure to die down. One
was borne along and out with Schneider on a wave that rose and dived
like a dolphin. Then at last the wave weakened and the pace lagged;
gradually Schneider got away and Lippott was left bumping about in the
wake of Schneider, to the long musing row back to familiar waters.

But the wave was not weakening yet and Schneider was, so to speak, in sight. Continually, as Lippott walked back to the office, as he sat drinking coffee and eating a sandwich there, as lunch time passed and the afternoon began, Lippott was seeing Schneider on the boat, the Schneider cabins, the Schneider lunch at Calais, the Schneider nights in Paris, the Schneider villas. (Lippott had done it all more than once with Schneider.) He was filled with Schneider. This was like being filled with Schneider's champagne. In this state of intoxication, Lippott could not settle to his work. He had never been able to work on the days when Schneider left.

'Oh, Miss Anderson' (Lippott was speaking into an instrument on his desk. His 'Oh, Miss Anderson' always sounded like the restive appeal of a man being tickled), 'I am going out,' he said.

He put on his hat and coat and left the office.

'I am sorry there is no reply from the secretary's room,' the operators said. 'Schneiders. Schneiders,' the voices chimed in the telephone exchange. 'The secretary is out.'

Lippott went down by the stairs. Now Schneider must be racing down the long march of poplars to Abbeville. The chalk dust would be fainter in the winter. If it were raining the cars would arrive white with mud in Paris. Lippott preferred the stairs to the lift because he liked no one to see what he was doing. Schneider was the voluptuary of lifts; on the stairs, the ascetic Lippott. He was the private, confidential man, the secretary of the company – the one who came round corners surprising people, noting who they are, pleased that they stop talking. They were afraid, in spite of their large Public School voices, of the busy Board School Lippott. Even the directors were cautious with the unobtrusive, omnipresent secretary with the shaky accent.

He went through the swing doors that seemed to flash messages of the wealth and cleverness of Schneider into the city. He went into the street. In the approaching dusk he was a short man who might have been mistaken for Schneider; but Lippott was lean, and, for the rest, no more than a sedate dark coat, smart dark trousers, a bowler hat, a collar and a tie and pair of boots, with a face put in precisely the right place among them. He had tired, well-fed creases in the skin of his face, the London pallor.

[133]

If Lippott looked pleased as he walked past the shops it was from no personal vanity. He had leisure because trade was slack and it was slack at Christmas because the shops had filled up with Schneider materials in the late autumn. Now the crowds in the streets were looking at them in the shop windows. Whenever he saw lights of shop windows he partook of the pleasure of being attached to the brilliance of Schneider.

The afternoon was closing. After the morning fog there had been a few hours of grey daylight over the roofs and then at three the street lamps were lit and the lamps of cars and buses. The shops threw out weak fans of light from their windows. There was a hoarse evanescent tenderness in the air which makes many people think of the winters of their childhood, and they look into the shop windows as they used in those days to look into the fire. There was the sound of thousands of footsteps, the sea-roar of engines. Many people were going home. The lights of the cars moved smoothly like pairs of cat's eyes out of the slowly sinking fog. As he crossed the side streets, Lippott would see the moist horn-coloured vapour, with its core of weak pink or lilac light where the arc lamps hung. The corners of buildings were smudged and broken off in the upper air and, in the lower, the fog was like a damp sand, the vapour of a million individual breaths. Gaiety was about, as if this too were the orgiastic wake of Schneider and the traffic were his music. Lippott stepped out. There was the restaurant where Schneider dined. There was the shop where Schneider had bought Lippott his Daimler. There Schneider bought his orchids, his wine, his cigars, his perfumes – the smell of the Schneider women – the street was rich and dazzling with the folly of Schneider.

Lippott had three thousand a year now, and his shares, and there were all those private speculations where, if Schneider had put down ten thousand, a hundred thousand or half a million, Lippott had followed with his occasional hundreds, a mouse nibbling where a rat had gnawed. He belonged to two clubs now, he had his clothes made at the tailors which Schneider had found too cheap ten years before. His signet ring was from Schneider and so was his cigarette case. Schneider had bought him his house and given him his Daimler. Once – this was one of the earliest presents and Lippott had refused it because he had seen at once it might put sand into the oil of their intimacy – Schneider had offered him a mistress he was tired of. Women for Lippott were items of Schneider's accountancy; a new pair of eyes, a new account.

Lippott stopped beside the window of a piano shop. He had not been thinking of Schneider at all. He had been thinking of Lola, sitting beside him racing through the chalk dust of the road to Abbeville, the value of whose shoes he knew, the price of whose fur coat and diamonds he knew, the rent of whose villa he paid; and of her voice which was like the tinkling of wine glasses. He had stopped.

The piano shop was graver than the other shops in the street and its lights were dimmer. In dull pools they were reflected on the level tops of the instruments. The shop was as solemn as an undertaker's and had the dreary luxury of a mausoleum. Chinese urns had indeed been placed in the windows and the ivory keyboards were like the long teeth of the dead. Lippott looked through the window and under the strong low light of an inner room he could see the grey, waved hair of a woman. Younger women stood idle at the counters. Lippott stood in the shadow watching her, and as he watched her he felt himself deeper in voice and growing in height and stoutness. He felt his hair curl at the back and his small hands grow thicker. The sensation grew as he approached the door. It was opened by a man with a chest of medals. Lippott, on the impulse, was Schneider. This was the woman Schneider had offered him. Schneider gone, he had come out to look at her.

'I want to speak to Mrs Cambery,' he said. He lowered his dark eyelids as he said the name and then looked up and began whistling softly. Still he was Schneider. He saw her rise from her desk and come out to him, a tall woman taking small steps toward him, like a smile on stilts.

'It's a long time since you've been in here, Mr Lippott,' she said in a high voice like the voice of Schneider's Lola, but an older and harder voice. 'Have you come to wish me a happy Christmas? How nice of you.' She looked down upon him trying to guess his errand.

And he was Schneider no more. Of course he had not come to wish her a happy Christmas. He had taken off his hat and he could see his short straight black hair shining in the dreary gilded mirror which accentuated his leanness. His voice was the voice of the secretary of the company, being charming to a one-time client.

'I came in,' he said, 'to buy a gramophone.'

He looked at her. She was taller than he. Like all the women in the shops in this part of London she was expensively dressed. She was a woman in her late forties and her grace had stiffened and quickened with an exaggerated animation, her beauty remaining in her long cold eyes.

'Little Lippott,' she thought. 'Money. Still with Schneider. Out-lasted me with Schneider. What's he after?'

'They are making some lovely things nowadays,' she said, glancing at him, to read what he wanted. He saw this. Lippott never missed a look of this kind. She, like the rest, had to be careful of Lippott. But her talk seemed to him like the crisp, clean-petalled forced flowers in the florists where Schneider bought his roses, his bouquets, his orchids. She was the woman Schneider had offered him, one of the earliest women of the days when Schneider was emerging from the period of East End fires and dubious liquidations. Lippott watched her as she walked to a gramophone. He smiled to think she did not know that Schneider had offered her to him.

'It is in walnut,' she said. 'The grain is like smoke.'

'Holy smoke,' he had his little joke, 'if I know anything about the price.'

'It gives a richness to the tone which I don't think any other wood gives.' The voice went on skilfully arranging its words like flowers about every object.

He listened to her heels on the polished floor. He noted her sharp orders to the assistants, the swing of her ear-rings.

'She's a good saleswoman,' Lippott thought. 'And she's done well for herself. He put her in this shop; and she has her money, her flat. An ordinary girl from Kentish Town who sold programmes in the theatre. She has got on. Schneider's doing, but even Schneider could not have given her her chance if she hadn't had talent. It was the same with me. She had brains and Schneider spotted them.'

He knew all about her. She was not Mrs Cambery, of course. Edwards was her real name. Like him she had risen from nothing, absolutely nothing. They had worked their way up. They had travelled far, so far that no one would have known that she was a Board school girl and he was a Board school boy, both of them from a slum. There was the bond of Schneider between them. Lippot warmed.

This was in his mind all the time she was showing him the gramophones, pretending she did not know the prices and asking her assistants in a drawling voice. That pleased him. And yet there was one difference between them. Schneider had offered her to him and she did not know it. She did not know he was thinking, 'I could have had this woman.'

Could he have had her? Of course. Schneider had said so. Everything belonged to Schneider, that was the wonderful thing about him. Yet one had to *be* Schneider to have everything Schneider offered. And Lippott knew as he saw her long, slender back arch over the instruments, and the ear-rings swing, that he could not be Schneider. She did not move to him as she would have moved instinctively had Schneider come into the shop, but she had stepped back, she had stopped, she had exclaimed and he had seen in her eyes the look he was used to seeing in the eyes of everyone, 'What's he up to? What is Schneider doing?'

Music was playing. She went to the instruments, raising the lids, putting on records, making music.

'Listen to this,' she said.

'What is it?'

'A carol.'

A lid was closed, there was the faint hiss of a record. Lippott sat down. He was already thinking he must get back. He placed his umbrella between his knees and stared at the carpet. For many years he had seen carpets and heard music together. Music meant hotels and restaurants, business lunches, evenings with Schneider's parties when he looked through the glass door after his own meal alone to see Schneider with his guests. The sound of music meant to him the spending of money. One could reckon up the price per bar, bill totals by the top notes. There was an instant association of a five-pound bill with the figure of the orchestra leader moving forward to the tables. The music waiter. There were orchestras whose music brought to the mind the price of champagne; there were Italian operas like the increment on private investments, with that sparkling beauty.

But the music which came from this gramophone had no financial context. Without warning men stood up. Their voices were loud, sudden and deep. They seemed to leap upon his breast and tear his shirt front open, going straight for his heart.

'Good King Wenceslas looked out
On the feast of Stephen,
When the snow lay round about
Deep and crisp and even.'

He saw the snow.
'They're good,' said Mrs Cambery. 'Don't you think?'
He nodded.

'Brightly shone the moon that night
Though the frost was cruel,
When a poor man came in sight,
Gathering winter fuel.'

He was at the Abbey Road school. The class was singing. He was working for his scholarship. The poor man gathering the fuel was Chas. Lippott. He was sorry for him. He was stirred by the memory of his miserable origins. In his childhood most of the days had been dark, he thought. There used to be continual fog. Then suddenly Schneider appeared.

'Bring me flesh and bring me wine,'

and,

'Thou and I shall see him dine.'

And dine they had. He would never forget the first time he had been taken to dine by Schneider. He knew he was going up in the world then. He knew it had paid him to obliterate everything for Schneider. He had saved money on his own dinner that night and had drunk wine for the first time. Tears of pride were concealed in Lippott's eyes. He was an errand boy in a shop. He had worked at evening classes and he had become a clerk. He went earlier to the office than everyone and he left latest. He worked till his eyes ached. At night he studied for his account-ancy examinations. Slowly he advanced, eating no more than a bar of chocolate every day, never smoking, never drinking, never going to football matches or cinemas, never seeing girls. He worked. He saved. His mother was left £50 and he re-invested it for her; he saw to it that money was put by for the funerals of his parents. He thought of everything. There were steps: from 27s. 6d. a week to 30s. a week, from 30s. a week to 35s., a sudden spring to £2: 5s., a leap to £4. Then Schneider had appeared and there was a jump to £300 a year. That was the real beginning. For ten years he had had no holiday and had worked three Sundays out of four. And now he knew the truth of the last verse, Schneider triumphant, Lippott as close as the glove of his right hand.

'Page and Monarch forth they went
Forth they went together.'

It took a full male choir to sound like the reverberant voice of Schneider, hoarse and loud, a choir not a man.

Lippott said, 'I'll buy it. What do I get – three months? Any discount for thirty days?' he said to Mrs Cambery.

'Makes one think of old times,' she said, 'doesn't it? Do you think we'll have snow?'

'No,' he laughed mildly. 'There is never any snow. We only get slush.'

He left the shop. The roar of the street was sudden like the voices of the singers. He felt tired and irritable. In an obscure way he knew what was happening because he had known it before. It had gone four o'clock. The Schneider wave had passed. He had been borne out and now he floundered. Schneider must be near Paris now, but Lippott could not even imagine him there. The air was cold and rough to the throat, the pavements were chilled. Schneider had gone and there was the long row back. Lippott did not mind that he had paid 120 guineas for a gramophone, indeed he was proud of that. He knew, after a few yards, that Schneider working through the art of Mrs Cambery had seduced him into spending this money and he liked that. There was the pleasure of being secretly seduced by Mrs Cambery, of sharing her in this way with Schneider. Where Schneider went, where Schneider had paid his thousands, Lippott had pushed his little one hundred and twenty less discount. He was satisfied as he walked. But there was the Schneider who lived and the Schneider who had to be paid for. As he walked back to his office, through the caves of shop light that had become more dazzling with the closing of the darkness, he felt himself the private custodian, the accountant of life and folly. His department went beyond Schneider into the world at large.

It was the end of the year and the accounts were being made. It was the time of the year when, at last, Lippott used to think, 'we get down to bedrock, to the real thing.' He was happiest at this time. Everyone who came to his office brought him long sheets of foolscap covered with figures. He turned the corner and came down into the square where the Schneider House stood. The bare trees hung a net of branches against the dark lilac night and dripped on to the cab rank. Through the branches, like lanterns hanging among them, were the windows of the offices opposite. There was a building there like a cage of light floating over the earth. All the electricity, all the Schneider in the world had to be paid for.

He passed the Trade Entrance. The loading bay was empty. There were cones of dim light over the empty loading platform. The goods lifts were stationary and in the hollow of the fog were the figures of men in brown overalls. There were five of them, young men with cigarettes in their ears, and they were talking, doing nothing. By the entrance was the machine which punched their time-tickets and in the wall was a small office where the yard foreman sat. It was like a signal box and a green shaded lamp was shining on the man's bald head bent over his book. (Mrs Cambery under another light did not know that Schneider had offered her to him.) No one knew what Schneider offered him. The workmen looked as they saw Lippott pass. He glanced at them and then went by towards the swing doors of the main entrance. They did not know who he was. It was ten days before Christmas, the slack time. One hundred and twenty pounds. Schneider must be paid for.

He nodded to the commissionaire and went up the stairs. Typists were laughing on the first landing. Quickly they ran away when they saw him. He went through glass doors and passed the frosted windows of corridors. An office door was open and he saw a pipe on a desk but no one there. Schneider must be paid for. He went along to his own office. On his desk were the foolscap sheets. He drew in his lips as if he were sipping tea, pleased by the sight of these papers. He knew the cost of everything, everything in the world.

In half an hour the building knew that he was the man who knew the cost of everything.

'Some people,' he was saying in his office to one of the younger managers, 'have got the wrong idea about this firm. They think it's just a milch cow. I don't care if it is a week before Christmas.'

The bell rang in the time-keeper's office. He was a heavy man who wrote with difficulty in a small round hand.

'Yeah,' he said. Then he was sitting bolt upright in his chair. 'Yes, sir. Yes, sir,' he said. A voice made neat by the telephone said:

'How many men have you got on the lifts?'

'Five, sir.'

'Sack three,' the voice said.

'Now, sir? This week, sir? Right, sir. I'll bring the names.'

He put down the receiver and stared at the telephone. He closed up his delivery book, got down from his stool and went out, first of all, to have a look at the fog. Lippott, up above, was humming a tune he could not get out of his head.

Miss Baker

When Easter came she knew that her time of fasting was drawing to a close; for three weeks she had not spoken. God had given her nothing to say to the world. She had prayed – for prayer always transposed her great sorrow – but He had become very small and far away like a very high and soundless bird. Yet in these days of the triumph of Spring and of His Son she had heard Him moving. On Easter Monday she got up from her chair and looked into the mirror and spoke for the first time.

'There you are, Miss Baker!' she said to her image. 'Your hair is beautiful and yellow.'

She watched the image, expectantly crinkling her pale eyes – there might be a miracle – but her lips in the mirror did not move.

'Poor darling,' said Miss Baker to the image at last. 'You are caught.' And she smiled sadly though there was a fine curl of slyness at the corner of her lips. It was at this point when she might have broken down in a passion of sadness, when she had already the silver hairbrush in her hand raised to smash the mirror into a great gasping star that the Voice of God stopped her with a whisper. So quietly the Voice spoke that for the moment she might have been deceived. It said, 'Go ye into all the world.' That was all. She wanted to hear more but when nothing came she understood.

She washed her face and brushed back her yellow hair over her ears to hear and understand the Voice again. She put on her white dress for her purity. 'You are good to me, too good to me, Miss Baker,' she said to the image in the mirror, thanking it with her repentance.

Then with a devout languor, very slowly before the glass she raised her arms in their long white sleeves, leaned back and closed her eyes; she was crucified upon herself.

When she came down from the cross the devils had gone. She put on a white straw hat with a broad brim and daisies round the crown. She took her umbrella, saw that the gas was turned off and that her key was in her bag and every window closed, and went out. To her surprise night had already fallen and the stairs were dark. Down six flights of stairs she went lower and lower into all the world. Sounds of traffic and of people walking came nearer and nearer from the street, starting like birds from her descending feet and rising in flocks until as she stepped down on to the pavement she was surrounded by them.

But like a ghost in her white dress she moved untouched by the things and creatures she touched. It was a cold night and people were wearing coats and hurrying. Their breath puffed out in clouds. The world smelled. It smelled of beer and frying meat, of vegetables in the market, of motor cars and oil, and the steam of a laundry. The world made noises. The scrawling noise of boots on the pavement, the sizzle of motor-car wheels, the deep mayoral bark of horns, the vicissitudes of voices. She walked through the music of a barrel organ, through halls and fountains of music, but her mind listened to none of the sounds that her ears heard. When she stopped dead still and listened, it was to hear again the guiding Voice.

She prayed in these moments humbly, not with the arrogance of expecting to be heard, though when she opened her eyes again it seemed the world was more contented and long and happily married. The eyes of the houses were alight and in the early darkness, she thought, they looked so nice and comfortable like old gentlemen with spectacles on, smoking their pipes. She walked on and on, from street to street, going into as many streets as she could and saying nothing, her lips very full and still and slightly smiling and the colour of her eyes fading as the inner light shone brighter. Wherever she took her whiteness she could feel the pain of the world going away.

Yet she was not white and pure enough for the Voice did not come again though she listened for it. Why did the Voice not speak again? Perhaps an hour had passed or two or three hours. People looked at her. Then when she opened her eyes from prayer she saw on the opposite side of the street a shining pool. I do not hear His Voice, she said, but He leadeth me beside still waters, even though it is only a puddle. And she had a very clever pouting and joking look on her face as she waited for the traffic to pass and crossed the street. On the pavement she found a dry, clean spot, dusted it with her handkerchief and sat down. 'It is not very comfortable,' she said aloud in case people should think her foolish, 'but it will do.' Very decently she pulled her dress down to her ankles and sighed, closing her eyes but too tired for prayer, and in those unguarded minutes an errand boy went by and staggered into a long, walking-backwards stare. An old woman passed with a chain of three children walking backwards, too. A young man in a mackintosh took his pipe out of his mouth, swivelled round and then turned back to her:

'Excuse me – er – miss,' he said. 'Allow me,' he said touching her shoulder. 'Are you ill?'

She was charming and frigid to him. His face was stupid with health.

'No, I am merely resting, thank you,' she said.

A fat carpenter with a sandy moustache and a bag of tools in his hand came up and nudged the young man.

'What's up?' he asked. 'Bin knocked down?'

'Dunno,' said the young man. 'Says she's resting.'

The carpenter stared and then bent down himself.

'Anything the matter, miss?' he said.

'Nothing, thank you. It's not very comfortable but I am resting,' she said.

Oh, for five minutes' rest! Would God not give her just five minutes? Great weariness was streaming up out of the pavement into her and the street was heaving as if in it some tide had turned. Three young girls from a factory stopped chattering to look at her. Two of them giggled with embarrassment, but the third who was dark and compassionate knelt at Miss Baker's feet and looked clearly into her eyes.

'There is nothing the matter,' said Miss Baker before the girl could speak. 'I am only waiting for Someone. Please go!' she said, turning to the small crowd. They were very startled because she had a ladylike voice. They shifted their feet, glanced up and down the empty street looking out for danger, saw people in the distance and re-encouraged by the sight closed round her again.

'Where do you live?' asked the kneeling girl. 'Let me take you home.'

'Where do she live?' asked the carpenter.

'She says she's waiting for someone,' said the girl.

'For Someone,' Miss Baker subtly corrected. They were puzzled and abashed. Malign, she studied their feet to embarrass the people and when she put on the look of adding up their faces they turned away. But they did not go. The crowd had greatly increased. There was the inner ring composed of the young man, the carpenter, the kneeling girl and two or three others at the heart of the mystery. There was the second ring. There was a third ring which, between trying to reply to the outer ring and ask the second ring for information at the same time, got no satisfaction and could not get away either. The crowd stood there like oxen with all their weight. Their pipes smoked. Their breath steamed. Their eyes, like bright creeping things, she felt, wandered over her. 'It's a girl,' said the carpenter, swelling out in the chest. At last the outer ring forced a victory. 'Here's a copper,' cried a boy at the back and the circles opened to admit the weight of the policeman. They made way for him and closed in after him. He was a young policeman with very clean cheeks and all his weight went from one foot to the other. He was very heavy and calm, but he was blushing.

'Stand back,' he said raising his voice, to give himself more space to be calm in. He put his hands on his knees and bent down to Miss Baker.

'Please, officer,' she said. 'Tell all these people to go away.'

'Stand back,' said the policeman again to cover his bewilderment.

'If you are all right you must move on, ma'am,' he said uncertainly. 'You are obstructing, miss.'

'I am not obstructing,' said Miss Baker very sharply and tightening her long white gloves on her fingers.

'Causing a crowd to collect . . .' said the policeman in his quoting voice. 'Causing an obstruction . . .'

'I am not obstructing. It is all these people who are obstructing. Please, officer,' said Miss Baker with imperious lucidity, 'please tell them to go away.'

The policeman swallowed and stood up because his back was uncomfortable and so was his reason. He advanced upon the crowd waving his arms. 'Move along there,' he said. 'Move along now. Hear what I say?'

[145]

The ranks thinned out before him and as they did so Miss Baker very quickly, quietly and cleverly got up and walked away in the opposite direction, at first lightly shaking the looks of the gaping crowd off her back. She walked on twenty or thirty yards and one or two ran on to get ahead of her and some nervously followed to be within reach but without responsibility if something happened again. The rest had wavered backwards and forwards and the policeman stood in the middle of the pavement, his head held together by his helmet strap. She walked on blindly straight. The heads of the crowd still seemed to her to be stretching after her like the shooting heads of serpents. She waved her umbrella to beat them off, but the miserable heads came on. She hurried to get out of reach. If she could only get a few yards ahead of them into solitude and into the charmed circle of prayer. If she could stop and hear the Voice. If only she could hear the Voice!

But now the invisible serpents had caught her and were in her head, filling it with their thoughts. She struggled bravely against them. And it was this struggle which filled her with towering rage. They were slaves. She was free. What right had the slaves of the serpent over the free? She trembled with rage. Defiantly sure of her right, she sat down on the pavement again.

She sat down and her spirit darkened with passionate affirmations of her freedom. It was her pavement as much as anyone else's. She had a right in law. Her cheeks flushed and she felt giddiness and darkness of blood in her head and the answering heat of defiance in her hands, her bosom and throat. She gathered all her forces into this narrow compass of personal assertion and defiance and magnified herself until there was no room for the Voice of God; and only the roar of the world was in her ears. She pushed back her white hat and her yellow hair began to fall over her face. She dug her nails into her umbrella. She was weeping passionately, and with shudders of hatred, abandoning herself to sin; beside her now was no healing pool. In the bars of the drain of the gutter beside her was the entrance into hell and the fingers of Anti-Christ were clawing at the bars. Down and down she was being dragged. It was with unspeakable gratitude she rose to go away with the policeman when he came again.

The following crowd stared at the empty door of the police station long after she had gone in. Generations of minutes bred and passed like ants. She seemed to be sitting on a bench in the police station and sometimes she was interested when a face with moving lips came nearer to her, but she could not think about the questions the lips asked her. She saw a man with a number on his collar, scratching his head, staring at his writing and two or three times he spoke into the telephone. It did seem that they wanted something that she could give, but when she gave them her handbag they returned it to her. The policeman with the clean face who had brought her took her umbrella. When she got her handbag back she opened it and looked into the mirror.

'Oh, Miss Baker, you are a dear to come with me,' she murmured, glancing slyly to see if anyone was watching her. 'Where would I be without you! You and I in a police station, Miss Baker!'

She tidied her hair and before she had done this – which was very embarrassing – the man with the number on his collar put down his glasses and got down from his high desk. He walked across to her quietly and again began to ask her things. And at last it came to her very clearly that he wanted to know her name. Clearly as she heard the Voice speaking she heard another voice speak distinctly in her throat: 'Legion,' it answered. 'L-E-G-I-O-N?' spelled the surprised officer. 'And what address?'

But the other voice saw the trap and would not answer. Inside her it laughed like a flame.

They led her into an inner room and gave her some tea. She heard them telephoning again, far away the voices alighting in the places where the bells had rung, clapping down upon them quickly. Her mind drifted through parks and gardens and fountains which slowly quenched her inward flame. The room was peaceful and she could feel peace returning. And then, far away among the telephoning voices she heard a stirring in the air like the movement that came when the Voice was going to speak. She looked up quickly in this direction. And she saw a man in the room. There was peace in him she saw at once. He was huddled on a bench near her, his legs sprawling wide. His body lay in big, smiling curves of fatness. His sandy hair was sprinkled neatly and thinly over his head and in the gaslight gleamed like a halo. But his features were ugly, brutal and sodden, his thick mouth had dropped open, many of his front teeth were chipped and he grunted half-asleep with the snort of a pig. His little blue eyes were half-blindly peeping. Once or twice he muttered and wagged his head and the policeman who was at the door of the room grinned.

She smiled and gazed at the man, not pushing herself out to him, but casting aside all aggression of the bodily will so that it was Sight that saw him and not herself. There poured out love and compassion for the man who was drowned in sleep. Out of him the Voice could speak. And in this knowledge she forgot about herself and her right, about drunkenness; and where the drunk man was, was a shape that would become the figure of God. The Voice was coming. Distantly like a high bird descending she could see the Voice; nearer and near it circled down, till as pure as a far away bugle the sound came into her, saying to all her blood:

'Speak to me.'

Speak to Him. She who had always listened *for* Him, now to speak *to* Him! She rose up with no hesitation and touched the drunk man on the shoulder and shook him. His eyes opened and quivered and closed again. She took him by his hand and his eyes opened very wide and stared. Then slowly he gave a long, creeping, dirty grin.

'This is Peniel,' she said, 'the place of names. What is your name?' she asked him earnestly.

He stared and his face sank deeper and deeper, more satiate into his folds of smile, and a sparkle of wetness came on the corner of his lower lip.

'Tell me your name,' she begged.

He looked at her doubtfully and at last muttered thickly: 'Shepherd.'

Her face became radiant. Her neck was pale and her throat beseeching as she took his hand in both of hers and said rapturously:

'Then I am one of Your Sheep!'

'Here,' muttered the drunk man, pulling his hand away and recoiling at the meaning in her eyes and lips. 'You know shlot 'bout this shex stuff, donchyer.'

And pushed her violently away. But she stood up and said aloud, laughing mildly in the duplicity of the revelation her great sorrow had given her and holding out her arms in trembling white sleeves and raising her head:

'I have found my Lord! Miss Baker, darling, we have found our Lord.'

You Make Your Own Life

Upstairs from the street a sign in electric light said 'Gent's Saloon'. I went up. There was a small hot back room full of sunlight, with hair clippings on the floor, towels hanging from a peg and newspapers on the chairs. 'Take a seat. Just finishing,' said the barber. It was a lie. He wasn't anywhere near finishing. He had in fact just begun a shave. The customer was having everything.

In a dead place like this town you always had to wait. I was waiting for a train, now I had to wait for a haircut. It was a small town in a valley with one long street, and a slow mud-coloured river moving between willows and the backs of houses.

I picked up a newspaper. A man had murdered an old woman, a clergyman's sister was caught stealing gloves in a shop, a man who had identified the body of his wife at an inquest on a drowning fatality met her three days later on a pier. Ten miles from this town the skeletons of men killed in a battle eight centuries ago had been dug up on the Downs. That was nearer. Still, I put the paper down. I looked at the two men in the room.

The shave had finished now, the barber was cutting the man's hair. It was glossy black hair and small curls of it fell on the floor. I could see the man in the mirror. He was in his thirties. He had a swarthy skin and brilliant long black eyes. The lashes were long too and the lids when he blinked were pale. There was just that suggestion of weakness. Now he was shaved there was a sallow glister to his skin like a Hindu's and as the barber clipped away and grunted his breaths, the dark man sat engrossed in his reflection, half smiling at himself and very deeply pleased.

The barber was careful and responsible in his movements but nonchalant and detached. He was in his thirties too, a young man with fair receding hair, brushed back from his forehead. He did not speak to his customer. His customer did not speak to him. He went on from one job to the next silently. Now he was rattling his brush in the jar, wiping the razor, pushing the chair forward to the basin. Now he gently pushed the man's head down, now he ran the taps and was soaping the head and rubbing it. A peculiar look of amused affection was on his face as he looked down at the soaped head.

'How long are you going to be?' I said. 'I've got a train.'

He looked at the clock. He knew the trains.

'Couple of minutes,' he said.

He wheeled a machine on a tripod to the back of the man. A curved black thing like a helmet enclosed the head. The machine was plugged to the wall. There were phials with coloured liquids in them and soon steam was rushing out under the helmet. It looked like a machine you see in a Fun Fair. I don't know what happened to the man or what the barber did. Shave, hot towels, haircut, shampoo, this machine and then yellow liquid like treacle out of a bottle – that customer had everything.

I wondered how much he would have to pay.

Then the job was over. The dark man got up. The clippers had been over the back of his neck and he looked like a guardsman. He was dressed in a square-shouldered grey suit, very dandyish for this town, and he had a silk handkerchief sticking out of his breast pocket. He wore a violet and silver tie. He patted it as the barber brushed his coat. He was delighted with himself.

'So long, Fred,' he smiled faintly.

'Cheero, Albert,' said the upright barber and his lips closed to a small, hardly perceptible smile too. Thoughtfully, ironically, the barber watched his handiwork go. The man hadn't paid.

I sat in the chair. It was warm, too warm, where the man had sat. The barber put the sheet round me. The barber was smiling to himself like a man remembering a tune. He was not thinking about me.

The barber said that machine made steam open the pores. He glanced at the door where the man had gone. 'Some people want everything,' he said, 'some want nothing.' You had to have a machine like that.

He tucked in the cotton wool. He got out the comb and scissors. His fingers gently depressed my head. I could see him in the mirror bending to the back of my head. He was clipping away. He was a dull young man with pale blue eyes and a look of ironical stubbornness in him. The small dry smile was still like claw marks at the corners of his lips.

'Three bob a time,' he said. He spoke into the back of my neck, and nodded to the door. 'He has it every week.'

He clipped away.

'His hair's coming out. That's why he has it. Going bald. You can't stop that. You can delay it but you can't stop it. Can't always be young. He thinks you can.' He smiled drily but with affection.

'But he wasn't so old.'

The barber stood up.

'That man!' he said. He mused to himself with growing satisfaction. He worked away in long silence as if to savour every possible flavour of my remark. The result of his meditation was to make him change his scissors for a finer pair.

'He ought to be dead,' he said.

'TB,' he said with quiet scorn.

He looked at me in the mirror.

'It's wonderful,' he said, as if to say it was nothing of the sort.

'It's wonderful what the doctors can do,' I said.

'I don't mean doctors,' he said. 'Consumptives! Tuh! They're wonderful.' As much as to say a sick man can get away with anything – but you try if you're healthy and see what happens!

He went on cutting. There was a glint in his pale-blue eyes. He snipped away amusedly as if he were attending to every individual hair at the back of my head.

'You see his throat?' he said suddenly.

'What about his throat?' I asked.

'Didn't you notice anything? Didn't you see a mark a bit at the side?' He stood up and looked at me in the mirror.

'No,' I said.

He bent down to the back of my neck again. 'He cut his throat once,' he said quietly. 'Not satisfied with TB,' he said with a grin. It was a small firm, friendly grin. So long, Fred. Cheero, Albert. 'Tried to commit suicide.'

'Wanted everything,' I said.

'That's it,' he said.

'A girl,' the barber said. 'He fell in love with a girl.'

He clipped away.

'That's an item,' said the barber absently.

He fell in love with a local girl who took pity on him when he was in bed, ill. Nursed him. Usual story. Took pity on him but wasn't interested in him in that way.

'A very attractive girl,' said the barber.

'And he got it badly?'

'They get it badly, consumptives.'

'Matter of fact,' said the barber, stepping over for the clippers and shooting a hard sideways stare at me. 'It was my wife.'

'Before she was my wife,' he said. There was a touch of quiet, amused resolution in him.

He'd known that chap since he was a kid. Went to school with him. Used to be his best friend. Still was. Always a lad. Regular nut. Had a milk business, was his own guv'nor till he got ill. Doing well.

'He knew I was courting her,' he smiled. 'That didn't stop him.' There was a glint in his eye.

'What did you do?' I asked.

'I lay low,' he said.

She had a job in the shop opposite. If you passed that shop you couldn't help noticing her in the cash desk near the door. 'It's not for me to say – but she was the prettiest girl in this town,' he said. 'Still is,' he mused.

'You've seen the river? You came over it by the station,' he said. 'Well he used to take her on the river when I was busy. I didn't mind. I knew my mind. She knew hers. I knew it was all right.'

'I knew him,' he grinned. 'But I knew her. "Let him take you on the river," I said.'

I saw the barber's forehead and his dull blue eyes looking up for a moment over my head in the mirror.

'Damp river,' he said reflectively. 'Damp mists, I mean, on the river. Very flat, low lying, unhealthy,' he said. 'That's where he made his mistake. It started with him taking her on the river.'

'Double pneumonia once,' he said. 'Sixty cigarettes a day, burning the candle at both ends.'

He grunted.

[153]

'He couldn't get away with it,' he said.

When he got ill, the girl used to go and look after him. She used to go and read to him in the afternoons. 'I used to turn up in the evenings too when we'd closed.'

The barber came round to the front and took the brushes lazily. He glanced sardonically at the door as if expecting to see the man standing there. That cocksure irony in the barber seemed to warm up.

'Know what he used to say to her?' he said sharply and smiled when I was startled. '"Here, Jenny," he used to say. "Tell Fred to go home and you pop into bed with me. I'm lonely."' The young barber gave a short laugh.

'In front of me,' he said.

'What did you say?'

'I told him to keep quiet or there'd be a funeral. Consumptives want it, they want it worse than others, but it kills them,' he said.

'I thought you meant *you'd* kill him,' I said.

'Kill him?' he said. 'Me kill him?' He smiled scornfully at me: I was an outsider in this. 'He tried to kill *me*,' he said.

'Yeah,' he said, wiping his hands on a towel. 'Tried to poison me. Whisky. It didn't work. Back OK?' he said, holding up a mirror. 'I don't drink.'

'I went to his room,' he said. 'I was his best friend. He was lying on the bed. Thin! All bones and blue veins and red patches as if he'd been scalded and eyes as bright as that bottle of bath salts. Not like he is now. There was a bottle of whisky and a glass by the side of the bed. He wanted me to have a drop. He knew I didn't drink.

'"I don't want one," I said. "Yes, you do," he said. "You know I never touch it," I said. "Well, touch it now," he said. "I tell you what," he said; "you're afraid." "Afraid of what?" I said. "Afraid of catching what I've got." "Touch your lips to it if you're not afraid. Just have a sip to show."

'I told him not to be a fool. I took the bottle from him. He had no right to have whisky in his state. He was wild when I took it. "It'll do some people a bit of good," I said, "but it's poison to you."

'"It *is* poison," he said.

'I took the bottle away. I gave it to a chap in the town. It nearly finished him. We found out it *was* poison. He'd put something in it.'

I said I'd have a singe. The barber lit the taper. I felt the flame warm against my head. 'Seals up the ends,' the barber said. He lifted up the hair with the comb and ran the flame along. 'See the idea?' he said.

'What did you do?'

'Nothing,' he said. 'Just married my girl that week,' the barber said. 'When she told him we were going to get married he said, "I'll give you something Fred won't give you." We wondered what it would be. "Something big," he said. "Best man's present," he said. He winked at her. "All I've got. I'm the best man." That night he cut his throat.' The barber made a grimace in the mirror, passed the scissors over his throat and gave a grin.

'Then he opened the window and called out to a kid in the street to fetch *her*. The kid came to me instead. Funny present,' he said. He combed, he patted, he brushed. He pulled the wool out of the back of my neck. He went round it with the soft brush. Coming round to the front he adroitly drew off the sheet. I stood up.

'He got over it,' he said. 'Comes round and plays with my kids on Sundays. Comes in every Friday, gets himself up. See him with a different one every week at the Pictures. It's a dead place this, all right in the summer on the river. You make your own life. The only thing is he don't like shaving himself now, I have to go over every morning and do it for him.'

He stood with his small grin, his steady eyes amused and resolute. 'I never charge him,' he said. He brushed my coat, he brought my hat.

The Sailor

He was lifting his knees high and putting his hand up, when I first saw him, as if, crossing the road through that stinging rain, he were breaking through the bead curtain of a Pernambuco bar. I knew he was going to stop me. This part of the Euston Road is a beat of the men who want a cup of tea or their fare to a job in Luton or some outlying town.

'Beg pardon, chum,' he said in an anxious hot-potato voice. 'Is that Whitechapel?'

He pointed to the traffic clogged in the rain farther down where the electric signs were printing off the advertisements and daubing them on the wet road. Coatless, with a smudged trilby hat on the back of his head so that a curl of boot polish black hair glistered with raindrops over his forehead, he stood there squeezing the water in his boots and looking at me, from his bilious eyes, like a man drowning and screaming for help in two feet of water and wondering why the crowd is laughing.

'That's St Pancras,' I said.

'Oh, Gawd,' he said, putting his hand to his jaw like a man with toothache. 'I'm all messed up.' And he moved on at once, gaping at the lights ahead.

'Here, wait,' I said. 'Which part of Whitechapel do you want? Where have you come from?'

'Surrey Docks,' he said. 'They said it was near Surrey Docks, see, but they put me wrong. I bin on the road since ten this morning.'

'Acton,' he read a bus sign aloud, recalling the bottom of the day's misery. 'I bin there,' and fascinated, watched the bus out of sight.

The man's worried mouth dropped open. He was sodden. His clothes were black with damp. The smell of it came off him. The rain stained from the shoulders of his suit past the armpits over the ribs to the waist. It spread from dark blobs over his knees to his thighs. He was a greasy-looking man, once fat and the fat had gone down unevenly like a deflating bladder. He was calming as I spoke to him.

A sailor, of course, and lost. Hopelessly, blindly lost. I calculated that he must have wandered twenty miles that day exhausting a genius for misdirection.

'Here,' I said. 'You're soaked. Come and have a drink.'

There was a public-house nearby. He looked away at once.

'I never touch it,' he said. 'It's temptation.'

I think it was that word which convinced me the sailor was my kind of man. I am, on the whole, glad to say that I am a puritan and the word temptation went home, painfully, pleasurably, excitingly and intimately familiar. A most stimulating and austerely gregarious word, it indicates either the irresistible hypocrite or the fellow-struggler with sin. I couldn't let him go after that.

Presently we were in a café drinking acrid Indian tea.

'Off a ship?' I said.

He looked at me as if I were a magician who could read his soul.

'Thank Gawd I stopped you,' he said. 'I kep' stopping people all day and they messed me up, but you been straight.'

He gave me his papers, his discharge paper, his pension form, official letters, as he said this, like a child handing himself over. Albert Edward Thompson, they said, cook, born '96, invalided out of the service two years before. So he was not just off a ship.

'They're clean,' he said suspiciously when I asked him about this. 'I got ulcers, riddled with ulcers for fourteen years.'

He had no job and that worried him, because it was the winter. He had ganged on the road, worked in a circus, had been a waiter in an Italian restaurant. But what worried him much more was getting to Whitechapel. He made it sound to me as though for two years he had been threshing about the country, dished by one job and another, in a less and less successful attempt to get there.

'What job are you going to do?' I said.

'I don't know,' he said.

'It's a bad time,' I said.

'I fall on my feet,' he said, 'like I done with you.'

We sat opposite to each other at the table. He stared at the people in the café with his appalled eyeballs. He was scared of them and they looked scared too. He looked as though he was going to give a yell and spring at them; in fact, he was likelier to have gone down on his knees to them and to have started sobbing. They couldn't know this. And then he and I looked at each other and the look discovered that we were the only two decent, trustworthy men in a seedy and grabbing world. Within the next two hours I had given him a job. I was chum no longer, but 'Sir'. 'Chum' was anarchy and the name of any twisty bleeder you knocked up against, but 'sir' (for Thompson, out of the naval nursery) was hierarchy, order, pay-day and peace.

I was living alone in the country in those days. I had no one to look after me. I gave Albert Thompson some money, I took him to Whitechapel and wrote down the directions for his journey to my house.

The bungalow where I lived was small and stood just under the brow of a hill. The country was high and stony there. The roads broke up into lanes, the lanes sank into woods and cottages were few. The oak woods were naked and as green as canker. They stood like old men, and below them were sweet plantations of larch where the clockwork pheasants went off like toys in the rainy afternoons. At night you heard a farm dog bark like a pistol and the oceanic sound of the trees and sometimes, over an hour and half's walk away, the whistle of a train. But that was all. The few people looked as though they had grown out of the land, sticks and stones in cloth; they were old people chiefly. In the one or two bigger houses they were childless. It was derelict country; frost with its teeth fast in the ground, the wind running finer than sand through a changeless sky or the solitary dribble of water in the butts and the rain legging it over the grass – that was all one heard or saw there.

'Gawd!' said Thompson when he got there. 'I thought I'd never strike the place.' Pale, coatless again in the wet, his hat tipped back from a face puddingy and martyred, he came up the hill with the dancing step of a man treading on nails. He had been lost again. He had travelled by the wrong train, even by the wrong line, he had assumed that, as in towns, it was safest to follow the crowd. But country crowds soon scatter. He had been following people – it sounded to me – to half the cottages for miles around.

'Then I come to the common,' he said. 'I didn't like the look of that. I kept round it.'

At last some girl had shown him the way.

I calmed him down. We got to my house and I took him to his room. He sat down on the bed and told me the story again. He took off his boots and socks and looked at his blistered feet, murmuring to them as if they were a pair of orphans. There was a woman in the train with a kid, he said, and to amuse the kid he had taken out his jack-knife. The woman called the Guard.

After we had eaten and I had settled in, I went for a walk that afternoon. The pleasure of life in the country for me is in its monotony. One understands how much of living is habit, a long war to which people, plants and animals have settled down. In the country one expects nothing of people; they are themselves, not bringers of gifts. In towns one asks too little or too much of them.

The drizzle had stopped when I went out, the afternoon was warmer and inert and the dull stench of cattle hung over the grass. On my way down the hill I passed the bungalow which was my nearest neighbour. I could see the roof as pink as a slice of salt ham, from the top of my garden. The bungalow was ten years old. A chicken man had built it. Now the woodwork was splitting and shrinking, the garden was rank, two or three larches, which the rabbits had been at, showed above the dead grass and there was a rose-bush. The bush had one frozen and worm-eaten flower which would stick there half the winter. The history of the bungalow was written in the tin bath by the side door. The bath was full of gin, beer and whisky bottles, discarded after the week-end parties of many tenants. People took the place for ever and then, after a month or two, it changed hands. A business man, sentimental about the country, an invalid social worker, a couple with a motor bicycle, an inseparable pair of school-teachers with big legs and jumping jumpers; and now there was a woman I hardly saw, a Colonel's daughter, but the place was said to belong to a man in the Northampton boot trade.

A gramophone was playing when I walked by. Whenever I passed, the Colonel's daughter was either playing the gramophone or digging in the garden. She was a small girl in her late twenties, with a big knowledgeable-looking head under tobacco-brown curls, and the garden fork was nearly as big as herself. Her gardening never lasted long. It consisted usually of digging up a piece of the matted lawn in order to bury tins; but she went at it intensely, drawing back the fork until her hair fell over her face and the sweat stood on her brow. She always had a cigarette in her mouth, and every now and then the carnation skin of her face, with its warm, dark blue eyes, would be distorted and turned crimson by violent bronchial coughing. When this stopped she would straighten up, the delicacy came back to her skin and she would say, 'Oh, Christ. Oh, bloody hell' and you noticed at the end of every speech the fine right eyebrow would rise a little and the lid of the eye below it would quiver. This wink, the limpid wink of the Colonel's daughter, you noticed at once. You wondered what it meant and planned to find out. It was as startling and enticing as a fish rising, and you discovered when you went after it that the Colonel's daughter was the hardest drinking and most blasphemous piece of apparent childish innocence you had ever seen. Old men in pubs gripped their sticks, went scarlet and said someone ought to take her drawers down and give her a tanning. I got a sort of fame from being a neighbour of the Colonel's daughter. 'Who's that piece we saw down the road?' people asked.

'Her father's in the Army.'

'Not,' two or three of them said, for this kind of wit spreads like measles, 'the Salvation Army.' They said I was a dirty dog. But I hardly knew the Colonel's daughter. Across a field she would wave, utter her obscenity, perform her wink and edge off on her slight legs. Her legs were not very good. But if we met face to face on the road she became embarrassed and nervous; this was one of her dodges. 'Still alone?' she said.

'Yes. And you?'

'Yes. What do you do about sex?'

'I haven't got any.'

'Oh, God, I wish I'd met you before.'

When I had friends she would come to the house. She daren't come there when I was alone, she said. Every night, she said, she locked and bolted up at six. Then the wink – if it was a wink. The men laughed. She did not want to be raped, she said. Their wives froze and some curled up as if they had got the blight and put their hands hard on their husbands' arms. But the few times she came to the house when I was alone, the Colonel's daughter stood by the door, the full length of the room away, with a guilty look on her face.

When I came back from my walk the gramophone had stopped. The Colonel's daughter was standing at the door of her bungalow with her sleeves rolled up, a pail of water beside her and a scrubbing brush in her hand.

'Hullo,' she said awkwardly.

'Hullo,' I said.

'I see you've got the Navy down here. I didn't know you were that way.'

'I thought you would have guessed that straight away,' I said.

'I found him on the common crying this morning. You've broken his heart.' Suddenly she was taken by a fit of coughing.

'Well,' she said. 'Every day brings forth something.'

When I got to the gate of my bungalow I saw that at any rate if Thompson could do nothing else he could bring forth smoke. It was travelling in thick brown funnel puffs from the short chimney of the kitchen. The smoke came out with such dense streaming energy that the house looked like a destroyer racing full steam ahead into the wave of hills. I went down the path to the kitchen and looked inside. There was Thompson, not only with his sleeves rolled up but his trousers also, and he was shovelling coal into the kitchener with the garden spade, the face of the fire was roaring yellow, the water was throbbing and sighing in the boiler, the pipes were singing through the house.

'Bunkering,' Thompson said.

I went into the sitting-room. I thought I had come into the wrong house. The paint had been scrubbed, the floors polished like decks, the reflections of the firelight danced in them, the windows gleamed and the room was glittering with polished metal. Door-knobs, keyholes, fire-irons, window-catches, were polished; metal which I had no idea existed flashed with life.

'What time is supper piped – er ordered,' said Thompson, appearing in his stockinged feet. His big round eyes started out of their dyspeptic shadows and became enthusiastic when I told him the hour.

A change came over my life after this. Before Thompson everything had been disorganised and wearying. He drove my papers and clothes back to their proper places. He brought the zest and routine of the Royal Navy into my life. He kept to his stockinged feet out of tenderness for those orphans, a kind of repentance for what he had done to them; he was collarless and he served food with a splash as if he allowed for the house to give a pitch or a roll which didn't come off. His thumbs left their marks on the plates. But he was punctual. He lived for 'Orders'. 'All ready, sir,' he said, planking down the dish and looking up at the clock at the same moment. Burned, perhaps, spilling over the side, invisible beneath Bisto – but on time!

The secret of happiness is to find a congenial monotony. My own housekeeping had suffered from the imagination. Thompson put an end to this tiring chase of the ideal. 'What's orders for lunch, sir?'

'Do you a nice fried chop and chips?' he said. That was settled. He went away but soon he came back.

'What pudding's ordered, sir?' That stumped both of us, or it stumped me. Thompson watched me to time his own suggestion.

'Do you a nice spotted dick?' So it was. We had this on the second day and the third, we changed on the fourth, but on the fifth we came back to it. Then Thompson's mind gave a leap.

'Do you grilled chop, chips, spotted dick *and custard?*' he said. That became almost our fixed menu. There were bouts of blancmange, but spotted dick came back.

Thompson had been sinking towards semi-starvation, I to the insidious Oblomovism of the country. Now we were reformed and happy.

'I always fall on my feet,' he said, 'like I done with you.' It was his refrain.

The winter dripped like a tap, the fog hardly left our hill. Winter in England has the colourless, steaming look of a fried-fish shop-window. But we were stoking huge fires, we bunkered, the garden spade went through coal by the hundredweight. We began to talk a more tangy dialect. Things were not put away; they were 'stowed'. String appeared in strange knots to make things 'fast', plants were 'lashed' in the dying garden, washing was 'hoist' on the lines, floors were 'swabbed'. The kitchen became the 'galley'. The postman came 'alongside', all meals were 'piped' and at bedtime we 'piped down'. At night, hearing the wind bump in the chimneys and slop like ocean surf in the woods, looking out at the leather darkness, I had the sensation that we were creeping down the Mersey in a fog or lumping about in the Atlantic swell off Ushant.

I was happy. But was Thompson happy? He seemed to be. In the mornings we were both working, but in the afternoons there was little more to do. He sat on a low chair with his knees close to the bars of the range or on the edge of his bed, darning his clothes. (He lived in a peculiar muddle of his own and he was dirty in his own quarters.) In the evenings he did the same and sometimes we talked. He told me about his life. There was nothing in it at all. It was buried under a mumble of obscurity. His memories were mainly of people who hadn't 'behaved right', a dejecting moral wilderness with Thompson mooching about in it, disappointed with human nature. He didn't stay to talk with me much. He preferred the kitchen where, the oil-lamp smoking, the range smoking and himself smoking, he sat chewing it all over, gazing into the fire.

'You can go out, you know,' I said, 'whenever you want. Do what you like.'

'I'm OK,' he said.

'See some of the people,' I said. Thompson said he'd just as lief stand by.

Everyone knows his own business best. But I was interested one night when I heard the sound of voices in the kitchen. Someone had come in. The voices went on on other nights. Who was it? The milker from the farm probably or the cowman who cleaned out cess pits by lantern light at night and talked with nostalgia about burying bodies during the war. 'If there hadn't been a war,' this man used to say, 'I wouldn't have seen nothing. It was an education.'

I listened. Slow in question, slow in answer, the monotonous voices came. The woodcutter, the postman? I went into the kitchen to see who the profound and interminable crony was.

There was no one. There was only Thompson in the kitchen. Sitting close to the fire with all windows closed, a sallow, stupefied, oil-haired head in his own fug, Thompson was spelling out a story from a *Wild West Magazine*. It was old and dirty and his coal-blackened finger was moving from word to word.

So far Thompson had refused to go out of the house except as far as the coal-shed, but I was determined after this discovery that he should go out. I waited until pay-day.

'Here's your money,' I said. 'Take the afternoon off.'

Thompson stepped back from the money.

'You keep it,' he said, in a panic. 'You keep it for me.'

'You may need it,' I said. 'For a glass of beer or cigarettes or something.'

'If I have it I'll lose it,' he said. 'They'll pinch it.'

'Who?' I said.

'People,' Thompson said. I could not persuade him.

'All right, I'll keep it for you,' I said.

'Yes,' he said eagerly. 'If I want a bob I'll ask you. Money's temptation,' he said.

'Well, anyway,' I said, 'take the afternoon off. It's the first sunny afternoon we've had. I'll tell you where to go. Turn to the right in the lane . . .'

'I don't like them lanes,' said Thompson, looking suspiciously out of the window. 'I'll stay by you.'

'Well, take a couple of hours,' I said. 'We all need fresh air.'

He looked at me as if I had suggested he should poison himself; indeed as if I were going to do the poisoning.

'What if I do an hour?' he began to bargain.

'No, the afternoon,' I said.

'Do you half an hour?' he pleaded.

'All right, I don't want to force you,' I said. 'This is a free country. Go for an hour.'

It was like an auction.

'Tell you what,' he said, looking shifty. 'I'll do you twenty minutes.' He thought he had tricked me, but I went back into the kitchen and drove him to it. I had given him an overcoat and shoes, and it was this appeal to his vanity which got him. Out he went for his twenty minutes. He was going straight down the lane to where it met the main road and then straight back; it would take a smart walker about twelve minutes on a winter's day.

When an hour passed I was pleased with myself. But when four hours had gone by and darkness came I began to wonder. I went out to the gate. The land and the night had become one thing. I had just gone in again when I heard loud voices and saw the swing of a lamp. There came Thompson with a labourer. The labourer, a little bandy man known as Fleas, stood like a bent bush with a sodden sack on his shoulders, snuffling in the darkness, and he grinned at me with the malevolence of the land.

'He got astray,' he said, handing Thompson over.

'Gawd,' exclaimed Thompson, exhausted. His face was the familiar pale suety agony. He was full of explanations. He was sweating like a scared horse and nearly hysterical. He'd been on the wrong course. He didn't know where to steer. One thing looked like another. Roads and lanes, woods and fields, mixed themselves together.

'Woods I seen,' he said in horror. 'And that common! It played me up proper.'

'But you weren't anywhere near the common,' I said.

'Then what was it?' he said.

That night he sat by the fire with his head in his hands.

'I got a mood,' he said.

The next morning cigarette smoke blew past my window and I heard coughing. The Colonel's daughter was at the kitchen door talking to Thompson. 'Cheero,' I heard her say and then she came to my door and pushed it open. She stood there gravely and her eye winked. She was wearing a yellow jersey and looked as neat as a bird.

'You're a swine,' she said.

'What have I done?'

'Raping women on the commons,' she said. 'Deserting your old friends, aren't you?'

'It's been too wet on the common,' I said.

'Not for me,' she said. 'I'm always hopeful. I came across last night. There was the Minister's wife screaming in the middle of it. I sat on her head and calmed her down and she said a man had been chasing her. "Stop screaming," I said. "You flatter yourself, dear." It was getting dark and I carried her shopping-bag and umbrella for her and took her to her house. I often go and see her in the evenings. I've got to do something, haven't I? I can't stick alone in that bungalow all day and all night. We sit and talk about her son in China. When you're old you'll be lonely too.'

'What happened on the common?'

'I think I'm drunk,' said the Colonel's daughter, 'but I believe I've been drunk since breakfast. Well, where was I? I'm losing my memory too. Well, we hadn't gone five minutes before I heard someone panting like a dog behind us and jumping over bushes. Old Mrs Stour started screaming again. "Stand still," I said, and I looked and then a man came out of a tree about ten yards away. "What the hell do you want?" I said. A noise came back like a sheep. "Ma'am, ma'am, ma'am, ma'am," it said.'

'So that's where Thompson was,' I said.

'I thought it was you,' the Colonel's daughter said. '"There's a woman set about me with a stick on the common," he said. "I didn't touch her, I was only following her," he said. "I reckoned if I followed her I'd get home."

'When they got to the wood Thompson wouldn't go into it and she had to take his hand; that was a mistake. He took his hand away and moved off. So she grabbed his coat. He struggled after this, she chased him into the thicket and told him not to be a fool, but he got away and disappeared, running on to the common.

'You're a damn swine,' the Colonel's daughter said to me. 'How would you like to be put down in the middle of the sea?'

She walked away. I watched her go up the path and lean on the gate opposite to stroke the nose of a horse. She climbed into the field and the horses, like hairy yokels, went off. I heard her calling them but they did not come.

When she was out of sight, the door opened behind me and Thompson came in.

'Beg pardon, sir,' he said. 'That young lady, sir. She's been round my kitchen door.'

'Yes,' I said.

He gaped at me and then burst out:

'I didn't touch her, straight I didn't. I didn't lay a finger on her.'

'She didn't say you did. She was trying to help you.'

He calmed down. 'Yes, sir,' he said.

When he came back into the room to lay the table I could see he was trying to catch my eye.

'Sir,' he said at last, standing at attention. 'Beg pardon, sir, the young lady . . .'

His mouth was opening and shutting, trying to shape a sentence.

'The young lady – she'd had a couple, sir,' he said in a rush.

'Oh,' I said, 'don't worry about that. She often has.'

'It's ruination, sir,' said Thompson evangelically.

She did not come to the house again for many days, but when she came I heard him lock both kitchen doors.

Orders at the one extreme, temptation at the other, were the good and evil of Thompson's life. I no longer suggested that he went out. I invented errands and ordered him to go. I wanted, in that unfortunate way one has, to do good to Thompson. I wanted him to be free and happy. At first he saw that I was not used to giving orders and he tried to dodge. His ulcers were bad, he said. Once or twice he went about barefoot, saying the sole was off one of his boots. But when he saw I meant what I said, he went. I used to watch him go, tilted forward on his toes in his half-running walk, like someone throwing himself blindly upon the mercy of the world. When he came back he was excited. He had the look of someone stupefied by incomprehensible success. It is the feeling a landsman has when he steps off a boat after a voyage. You feel giddy, canny, surprised at your survival after crossing that bridge of deep, loose water. You boast. So did Thompson – morally.

'There was a couple of tramps on the road,' Thompson said. 'I steered clear. I never talked to them,' he said.

'Someone asked me who I was working for.' He described the man. 'I never told him,' he said shrewdly. 'I just said "A gentleman". Meaning you,' he said.

There was a man in an allotment who had asked him for a light and wanted to know his business.

'I told him I didn't smoke,' said Thompson. 'You see my meaning – you don't know what it's leading up to. There warn't no harm, but that's how temptation starts.'

What was temptation? Almost everything was temptation to Thompson. Pubs, cinemas, allotments, chicken-runs, tobacconists – in these, everywhere, the tempter might be. Temptation, like Othello's jealousy, was the air itself.

'I expect you'd like to go to church,' I said. He seemed that kind.

'I got nothing *against* religion,' Thompson said. 'But best keep clear. They see you in church and the next thing they're after you.'

'Who?' I asked.

'People,' he said. 'It's not like a ship.'

I was like him, he said, I kept myself to myself. I kept out of temptation's way. He was glad I was like that, he said.

It was a shock to me that while I observed Thompson, Thompson observed me. At the same time one prides oneself, the moment one's character is defined by someone else, on defeating the definition. I kept myself to myself? I avoided temptation? That was all Thompson knew! There was the Colonel's daughter. I might not see her very often; she might be loud, likeable, dreary or alarming by turns, but she was Temptation itself. How did he know I wasn't tempted? Thompson's remark made me thrill. I began to see rather more of the Colonel's daughter.

And so I discovered how misleading he had been about his habits and how, where temptation was concerned, he made a difference between profession and practice. So strong was Thompson's feeling about temptation that he was drawn at once to every tempter he saw. He stopped them on the road and was soon talking about it. The postman was told. The shopkeepers heard all his business and mine. He hurried after tramps, he detained cyclists, he sat down on the banks with roadmakers and ditchers, telling them the dangers of drink, the caution to be kept before strangers. And after he had done this he always ended by telling them he kept himself to himself, avoided drink, ignored women and, patting his breast pocket, said that was where he kept his money and his papers. He behaved to them exactly as he had behaved with me two months before in the Euston Road. The Colonel's daughter told me. She picked up all the news in that district.

'He's a decent, friendly soul,' muttered the Colonel's daughter thickly. 'You're a prig. Keep your hair on. You can't help it. I expect you're decent, too, but you're like all my bloody so-called friends.'

'Oh,' I said hopefully, 'are prigs your special line?'

I found out, too, why Thompson was always late when he came home from his errands. I had always accepted that he was lost. And so he was in a way, but he was lost through wandering about with people, following them to their doorsteps, drifting to their allotments, backyards and, all the time, telling them, as he clung to their company, about the dangers of human intercourse. 'I never speak to nobody' – it was untrue, but it was not a lie. It was simply a delusion.

'He lives in two worlds at once,' I said to the Colonel's daughter one

[168]

morning. I had sent Thompson to the town to buy the usual chops, and I was sitting in her bungalow. This was the first time I had ever been in it. The walls were of varnished match-boarding like the inside of a gospel hall and the room was heated by a paraffin stove which smelled like armpits. There were two rexine covered chairs, a rug and a table in the room. She was sorting out gramophone records as I talked and the records she did not like she dropped to the floor and broke. She was listening very little to what I said but walked to the gramophone, put on a record, stopped it after a few turns and then, switching it off, threw the record away.

'Oh, you know a hell of a lot, don't you?' she said. 'I don't say you're not an interesting man, but you don't get on with it, do you?'

'How old are you? Twenty-five?' I said.

Her sulking, ironical expression went. She was astonished.

'Good God!' she exclaimed with a smile of sincerity. 'Don't be a damn fool.' Then she frowned. 'Or are you being professionally clever?'

'Here,' she said. 'I was damn pretty when I was twenty-five. I'm thirty-nine. I've still got a good figure.'

'I would have put you at twenty-seven at the most,' I said truthfully.

She walked towards me. I was sitting on the arm-chair and she stood very close. She had never been as close to me before. I had thought her eyes were dark blue but now I saw they were green and grey, with a moist lascivious haze in them and yet dead and clock-like, like a cat's on a sunless day. And the skin, which had seemed fresh to me, I saw in its truth for the first time. It was clouded and flushed, clouded with that thickened pimpled ruddiness which the skin of heavy drinkers has and which in middle-age becomes bloated and mottled. I felt: this is why she has always stood the length of the room away before.

She saw what was in my mind and she sat down on the chair opposite to me. The eye winked.

'Keep control of yourself,' she said. 'I came down here for a rest and now you've started coming round.'

'Only in the mornings,' I said.

She laughed. She went to a bookshelf and took down a bottle of whisky and poured out half a tumblerful.

'This is what you've done coming in here, early bird,' she said. 'Exciting me on an empty stomach. I haven't touched it for ten days. I had a letter this morning. From my old man.'

'Your father?'

I had always tried to imagine the Colonel. She gave a shout of cheerful laughter and it ended in coughing till tears came to her eyes.

'That's rich. God, that's rich. Keen observer of women! No, from my husband, darling. He's not my husband, damn him, of course, but when you've lived with someone for ten years and he pays the rent and keeps you, he is your husband, isn't he? Or ought to be. Ten years is a long time and his family thought he ought to be married. He thought so too. So he picked up a rich American girl and pushed me down here to take it easy in the country. I'm on the dole like your sailor boy. Well, I said, if he felt that way, he'd better have his head. In six months he'll tire of the new bitch. So I left him alone. I didn't want to spoil his fun. Well, now, he writes me, he wants to bring his *fiancée* down because she's heard so much about me and adores the country . . .'

I was going to say something indignant.

'He's nice too,' she said casually. 'He sells gas-heaters. You'd like him all the same. But blast that bloody woman,' she said raising her cool voice. 'She's turned him into a snob. I'm just his whore now.

'Don't look so embarrassed,' she said. 'I'm not going to cry.'

'For ten years,' she said, 'I read books, I learned French, educated myself, learned to say "How d'you do", instead of "Pleased to meet you", and look down my nose at everything in his sort of way. And I let him go about saying my father was in the Army too, but they were such bloody fools they thought he must be a Colonel. They'd never heard of sergeant-majors having children. Even my old man, bless his heart,' she smiled affectionately, 'thought or let himself think they did. I was a damn silly little snob.'

'I don't know him,' I said. 'But he doesn't sound much good to me.'

'That's where you're wrong,' she said sharply. 'Just weak, poor kid, that's all. You don't know what it is to be ashamed your mother's a housemaid. I got over it – but he didn't, that's all.'

She paused and the wink gave its signal.

[170]

'This is more embarrassing than I thought,' she said.

'I am very sorry,' I said. 'Actually I am in favour of snobbery, it is a sign of character. It's a bad thing to have, but it's a bad thing not to have had. You can't help having the diseases of your time.'

'There you go,' she said.

The suffering of others is incredible. When it is obscure it seems like a lie; when it is garish and raw, it is like boasting. It is a challenge to oneself. I got up from my chair and went towards her. I was going to kiss her.

'You are the sentimental type,' she said.

So I didn't kiss her.

Then we heard someone passing the bungalow and she went to the window. Thompson was going by. The lock of black hair was curling over his sweating forehead and he gave a hesitant staggering look at the bungalow. There was a lump of fear on his face.

'He'd better not know where you've been,' she said. She moved her lips to be kissed, but I walked out.

I was glad of the steady sense of the fresh grey air when I got outside. I was angry and depressed. I stood at the window of my house. Thompson came in and was very talkative. He'd been lost, of course. He'd seen people. He'd seen fields. He'd heard trees. He'd seen roads. I hardly listened. I was used to the jerky wobbling voice. I caught the words 'legion' and 'temptation', and thought he was quoting from the Bible. Presently I realised he was talking about the British Legion. The postman had asked him to go to a meeting of the British Legion that night. How simple other people's problems are! Yet 'No' Thompson was saying. He was not going to the British Legion. It was temptation.

I ought to have made love to her and kissed her, I was thinking. She was right, I was a prig.

'You go,' I said to Thompson, 'if you want to. You'd enjoy it.'

But how disgusting, obvious, stupid, to have made love to her then, I thought.

'Do as you like,' I said.

'I'm best alongside you,' said Thompson.

'You can't always be by me,' I said. 'In a month, perhaps less, as you know, I'll be leaving here and you'll have to go.'

'Yes,' he said. 'You tol' me. You been straight. I'll be straight with you. I won't go to the Legion.'

We ate our meal and I read.

'In every branch of our spiritual and material civilisation we seem to have reached a turning point,' I read. 'This spirit shows itself not only in the actual state of public affairs . . .'

Well, I thought, I can ask her over tonight. I needn't be a fool twice. I went out for an hour. When I returned Thompson was fighting Temptation hard. If he went to the Legion how would he get back? No, best not. He took the Legion on in its strength. (She is a type, I thought.) At four he was still at it. At five he asked me for his money. (Well, we are all types, I was thinking.) Very shortly he brought the money back and asked me to keep his pension papers. At half-past six I realised this meant that Thompson was losing and the Legion and all its devils winning. (What is a prig, anyway?) He was looking out at the night. Yet, just when I thought he had lost, he had won. There was the familiar sound of the Wild West monologue in the kitchen. It was half-past eight. The Legion was defeated.

I was disappointed in Thompson. Really, not to have had more guts than that! Restlessly I looked out of the window. There was a full moon spinning on the tail of a dying wind. Under the moonlight the fields were like wide-awake faces, the woods like womanish heads of hair upon them. I put on my hat and coat and went out. I was astonished by the circle of stars. They were as distinct as figures on a clock. I took out my watch and compared the small time in my hand with the wide time above. Then I walked on. There was a sour smell at the end of the wood, where, no doubt, a dead rabbit or pigeon was rotting.

I came out of the wood on to the metalled road. Suddenly my heart began to beat quickly as I hurried down the road, but it was a long way round now. I cut across fields. There was a cottage and a family were listening to a dance-band on the wireless. A man was going the rounds of his chickens. There was a wheelbarrow and there were spades and steel bars where a water mill was being built.

Then I crossed the last fields and saw the bungalow. My heart throbbed heavily and I felt all my blood slow down and my limbs grow heavy. It was only when I got to the road that I saw there were no lights in the bungalow. The Colonel's daughter, the Sergeant's daughter, had gone to bed early like a child. While I stood I heard men's voices singing across the fields. It must have gone ten o'clock and people were coming out of the public-house. In all the villages of England, at this hour, loud-voiced groups were breaking up and dispersing into the lanes.

I got to my house and lit a candle. The fire was low. I was exhausted and happy to be in my house among my own things, as if I had got into my own skin again. There was no light in the kitchen. Thompson had gone to bed. I grinned at the thought of the struggles of poor Thompson. I picked up a book and read. I could hear still the sound of that shouting and singing. The beer was sour and flat in this part of the country but it made people sing.

The singing voices came nearer. I put down the book. An argument was going on in the lane. I listened. The argument was nearing the cottage. The words got louder. They were going on at my gate. I heard the gate go and the argument was on my path. Suddenly – there could be no doubt – people were coming to the door. I stood up, I could recognise no voice. Loud singing, stumbling feet, then bang! The door broke open and crashed against the wall. Tottering, drunk, with their arms round each other, Thompson and the Colonel's daughter nearly fell into the room.

Thompson stared at me with terror.

'Stand up, sailor,' said the Colonel's daughter, clinging to him.

'He was lonely,' she said unsteadily to me. 'We've been playing gramophone records. Sing,' she said.

Thompson was still staring.

'Don't look at him. Sing,' she said. Then she gave a low laugh and they fell, bolt upright on the sofa like prim, dishevelled dolls.

A look of wild love of all the world came into Thompson's eyes and he smiled as I had never seen him smile before. He suddenly opened his twitching mouth and bawled:

'You've robbed every tailor,
And you've skinned every sailor,
But you won't go walking Paradise Street no more.'

'Go on. That's not all,' the Colonel's daughter cried and sang, 'Go on – something – something, deep and rugged shore.'

She put her arms round his neck and kissed him. He gaped at her with panic and looked at her skirt. It was undone.

He pointed at her leg in consternation. The sight sobered him. He pulled away his arms and rushed out of the room. He did not come back. She looked at me and giggled. Her eyes were warm and shining. She picked leaves off her skirt.

'Where's he gone? Where's he gone?' she kept asking.

'He's gone to bed,' I said.

She started a fit of coughing. It strained her throat. Her eyes were dilated like an animal's caught in a trap, and she held her hand to her chest.

'I wish,' she cried hysterically, pointing at me in the middle of her coughing, 'I wish you could see your bloody face.'

She got up and called out.

'Thompson! Thompson!' And when he did not answer she sang out, 'Down by the deep and rugged shore – ore-ore-ore.'

'What's the idea?' I said.

'I want Thompson,' she said. 'He's the only man up here.'

Then she began to cry. She marched out to his room, but it was locked. She was wandering through the other rooms calling him and then she went out, away up the path. She went calling him all the way down to her bungalow.

In the morning Thompson appeared as usual. He brought the breakfast. He came in for 'orders'. Grilled chop, did I think? And what about spotted dick? He seemed no worse. He behaved as though nothing had happened. There was no guilty look in his eyes and no apprehension. He made no apology. Lunch passed, tea-time and the day. I finished my work and went into the kitchen.

'Tell me,' I said, 'about last night.'

Thompson was peeling potatoes. He used to do this into a bucket on the floor, as if he were peeling for a whole crew. He put down the clasp-knife and stood up. He looked worried.

'That was a terrible thing,' Thompson said, as if it was something he had read about in the papers.

'Terrible, sir. A young lady like that, sir. To come over here for me, an educated lady like that. Someone oughter teach her a lesson. Coming over and saying she wanted to play some music. I was took clean off my guard.

'It wasn't right,' said Thompson. 'Whichever way you look at it, it wasn't right. I told her she'd messed me up.'

'I'm not blaming you. I want to know.'

'And she waited till you was out,' Thompson said. 'That's not straight. She may class herself as an educated young lady, but do you know what I reckon she is? I reckon she's a jane.'

I went down to the bungalow. I was beginning to laugh now. She was in the garden digging. Her sleeves were rolled up and she was sweating over the fork. The beds were thick with leaves and dead plants. I stood there watching her. She looked at me nervously for a moment. 'I'm making the garden tidy,' she said. 'For Monday. When the bitch comes down.'

She was shy and awkward. I walked on and, looking back, saw her go into the house. It was the last I ever saw of her. When I came back the fork she had been using was stuck in the flower bed where she had left it. She went to London that night and did not return.

'Thank Gawd,' Thompson said.

There was a change in Thompson after this and there was a change in me. Perhaps the change came because the dirty February days were going, the air softer and the year moving. I was leaving soon. Thompson mentioned temptation no more. Now he went out every day. The postman was his friend. They used to go to the pub. He asked for his money. In the public-house the labourers sat around muttering in a language Thompson didn't understand. He stood them drinks. At his first pint he would start singing. They encouraged him. He stood them more drinks. The postman ordered them for him and then tapped him on the pocket book. They emptied his pockets every night. They despised him and even brought complaints to me about him after they had emptied his pockets.

Thompson came back across the common alone, wild, enthusiastic and moaning with suspicion by turns. The next day he would have a mood. All the countryside for ten miles around knew the sailor. He became famous.

Our last week came. He quietened down.

'What are you going to do?' I asked.

'I'll stay by you.'

'You can't,' I said. 'I'll be going abroad.'

'You needn't pay me,' he said. 'I'll stay by you.' It was hard to make him understand he could not stay with me. He was depressed.

'Get me out of here safe,' he pleaded at last. 'Come with me to the station.' He could not go on his own because all the people he knew would be after him. He had told them he was going. He had told them I was saving his pension and his last fortnight's pay. They would come creeping out of cottage doors and ditches for him. So I packed his things and got a taxi to call for us. How slowly we had lived and moved in these fields and lanes. Now we broke through it all with a rush as the car dropped down the hill and the air blew in at the window. As we passed the bungalow with the sun on its empty windows I saw the fork standing in the neglected bed. Then we swept on. Thompson sat back in the car so that no one should see him, but I leaned forward to see everything for the last time and forget it.

We got to the town. As the taxi slowed down in the streets people looked out of shops, doors, a potman nodded from the pub.

'Whatcha, Jack,' the voices called.

The police, the fishmonger, boys going to school, dozens of people waved to him. I might have been riding with royalty. At the station a large woman sweeping down the steps of the bank straightened up and gave a shout.

'Hi, Jacko!' she called, bending double, went into shrieks of laughter and called across to a friend at a first-floor window. It was a triumph. But Thompson ignored them all. He sat back out of sight.

'Thank Gawd I've got you,' he said. 'They skin you of everything.'

We sat in the train. It was a two-hour journey.

'Once I strike Whitechapel,' he said in the voice of one naming Singapore, 'I'll be OK.' He said this several times, averting his face from the passing horror of the green fields.

'Don't you worry,' he said. 'Don't fret yourself for me. Don't you worry.' His optimism increased as mine dwindled as we got nearer London. By the time we reached London he was almost shouting. 'I'll fall on my feet, don't you worry. I'll send you my address.'

We stood on the kerb and I watched him walk off into the yellow rain and the clogged, grunting and mewing traffic. He stepped right into it without looking. Taxis braked to avoid him. He was going to walk to Whitechapel. He reckoned it was safer.

The Lion's Den

'Oh, there you are, that's it, dear,' said the mother, timidly clawing her son out of the darkness of the doorway and kissing him. 'You got here all right. I couldn't look out for you; they've boarded up the window. We've had a land-mine. All the glass went last week. Have you had your tea? Have a cup of tea?'

'Well, let's see the boy,' said the father. 'Come in here to the light.'

'I've had tea, thanks,' Teddy said.

'Have another cup. It won't take a tick. I'll pop the kettle on . . .'

'Leave the boy alone, old dear,' the father said. 'He's had his tea. Your mother's just the same, Teddy.'

'I only thought he'd like a cup of tea. He must be tired,' said the mother.

'Sit down, do, there's a good girl,' said the father.

'Now – can Father speak? Thank you. Would you like to wash your hands, old chap?' the father said. 'We've got the hot water back, you know.'

'Yes, go on,' said the mother, 'wash your hands. They did the water yesterday.'

'There she goes again,' the father said. 'Wonderful, isn't it?'

'No, I don't want to wash,' said Teddy.

'He doesn't want to wash his hands,' said the father, 'so leave him alone.'

'It's hot if he wants to.'

'We know it's hot,' said the father. 'Well, my boy, sit down and make yourself comfortable.'

'Take this chair. Don't have that one. It's a horrible old thing. Here, take this one,' the mother said.

'He's all right. He's got a chair,' the father said.

'Let him sit where he likes,' the mother said. 'You do like that chair, Teddy, don't you?'

'Well,' said Teddy, 'you're looking well, Mother.' This was not true; the mother looked ill. Her shoulders were hunched, her knees were bent and her legs bowed stiffly as she walked. When she smiled, tears ran to the corners of her eyes as if age were splitting them; and dirty shadows like fingermarks gave them the misplaced stare of anxiety. Her fingers, too, were twisting and untwisting the corners of her cardigan.

'Of course she's looking well. Nothing wrong with her, is there? What I keep saying,' the father said.

He was a bit of a joker. He resembled a doll-like colonel from a magazine cover, but too easy in manner for that.

'I'm well now,' said the mother. 'It's just these old raids. They upset me, but I get over it.'

'We worry about you,' Teddy said.

'You shouldn't worry,' said the father. 'There's nothing to worry about, really. We're here, that's the chief point. We just don't worry at all.'

'It doesn't do any good, Teddy dear,' said the mother. She was sitting by the fire and she leaned over to him and gripped his knee hard. 'We've had our life. I'm seventy, don't forget.'

'Seventy,' laughed his father. 'She can't forget she's seventy. She doesn't look it.'

'But I am,' said his mother fiercely.

'Age is what you make it,' the father said. 'That's how I feel.'

'There's a lot in that,' said the son.

'I go to bed . . . and I lie there listening,' the mother said. 'I just wait for it to go. Your father, of course, he goes to sleep at once. He's tired. He has a heavy day. But I listen and listen,' the mother said, 'and when it goes I give him a shake and say "It's gone."'

'I don't want to sound immodest,' the father laughed, 'but she nearly has my – my confounded pyjamas off me sometimes.'

'He just lies there. He'd sleep through it, guns and all,' the mother went on. 'But I couldn't do that. I sit on the edge of the bed. If it's bad I sit on the top of the stairs.'

'We both do if it's bad,' the father said. 'I get up if it's bad.'

'You ought to sit under the staircase, not on top,' said Teddy.

'Just in case,' said the mother. 'I like to feel I can get out.'

'You see, you want to get out,' the father said. 'It isn't that one's afraid, but – well – you feel more comfortable.'

'I sit there and I know it's wrong of me, I think of you all, if I'll ever see any of you again. I wish you were with me. I never see you all, not together like we used to be ...'

'It is natural for a mother to feel like that,' said the father.

'I mean if we could be not so far apart.'

'We wish you'd come down to us,' Teddy said.

'I wish I could, dear,' said the mother.

'Why don't you? You could, easily.'

'I'd like to, but I can't.'

'I don't see why not. Why don't you send her, Dad? Just for the rest.'

'I've got to stay with Dad,' she said.

'Your mother feels she's got to stay with me.'

'But,' Teddy said, 'you could look after yourself for a while.'

'I could look after myself all right,' said the father. 'Don't you worry about that.'

'Well,' said Teddy, 'what's against it?'

'Nothing's against it,' said his father. 'Just herself. She feels her place is here. She just feels this is her place.'

His father raised his chin and lowered his eyes bashfully. He had a small white moustache as slight as a monkey's, and it seemed to give a twist to the meaning of his words, putting them between sets of inverted commas.

The mother read his eyes slowly and fidgeted on her stool by the fire. She nodded from habit when she had got through her husband's words, but she glanced furtively at her son. She put on an air of light-heartedness, to close the subject.

'Some day I'll come,' she said. 'The Miss Andersons are very kind. They had us down last Sunday when the windows went ... It's safer downstairs.'

'You know what I feel?' said his father, in a sprightly way. 'I feel it's safe everywhere.'

The son and the mother both looked at the father with very startled concern and sympathy, recognising that in danger everyone lives by his own foible. Then guiltily they glanced at each other.

'I feel it,' said the father apologetically, when he saw their expression.

'I know it,' he asserted, feebly scowling. Seeing he had embarrassed them, he escaped into a business-like mood. 'Now I'm going down to see about the coal for the morning. I always do it at this time.'

'He's wonderful,' said the mother. 'He always does the coal.'

When the father left the room a great change came over the mother and son.

'Come nearer the fire, dear,' said the mother. They were together. They came closer together like lovers.

'Just a minute, dear,' she said. And she went to the curtains and peeped into the night. Then she came back to the stool.

'You see how it is, dear,' she said. 'He has faith.' The son scowled.

'It's wonderful, his faith,' she said. 'He trusts in God.'

A look of anger set on the son's jaw for a moment, then he wagged his head resignedly.

'He always did. You remember, when you were a boy?' said the mother, humouring her son. 'I never could. He did from the beginning when I met him. Mind you, Teddy, I don't say it's a bad thing. It's got him on. When one of those old things starts he goes to his room and he prays. I know he's praying. Really he's praying all the time, for me, for you children . . .'

'For us!' exclaimed the son.

'Yes, for everyone,' said the mother. 'The world – oh, I don't understand. If there's a God why did He let it happen in the first place? – but your father, he always did do things on a big scale.'

She was speaking in a whisper and glancing now and then at the door.

'Too big,' she murmured.

'If there is a God,' said the son. 'He is pitiable, weak, small. Hardly born . . .'

He checked himself when he saw that his mother looked at him without comprehension. 'I am old,' she shivered and he saw the tears cracking in her eyes. 'I used to live in hope – you know for the future. You know, hope things would go right, hoping things for you children, but now I haven't even got hope.' She looked wildly. 'It's gone.'

She stared over his shoulder to the walls of the room and the heavy curtains.

'It isn't this old war and these old raids,' she said. 'Life's gone, it's gone

[181]

too quickly. There's nothing, Ted, that's how it seems to me, except if we could just be together as we were.'

'Don't cry, Mother.'

'No, mustn't cry, mustn't let him see I cried. Women do cry. It's silly. What shall we talk about? Let's think of something else.'

She became sly and detached like a young girl running away, daring him to catch her. He knew these changes of mood in his mother very well. She began to talk in a bold taunting way.

'It's the house,' she said scornfully. 'He doesn't like the house to be left. Someone must be in the house. It won't run away I tell him. Good thing if it was bombed. But his mother was just the same, cling on, cling on, scrubbing, polishing. "You can't take it with you," I used to say to her. She used to give me a look. "Eh," she said, "you want me to die." I can see her now. "You wicked woman," I said. And when they carried her out, the men bumped the coffin, dear, on the chest of drawers and I thought: "If you could see that scratch!" Some call it faith. I call it property. Property.'

His mother's eyes became sly and malicious. She laughed.

'Oh, there are things I could tell you,' she cried recklessly, looking at the door. 'When it starts and I hear the guns, I think of you. Things you don't know about, you were just a baby at the time. No one knows them. It's my life. All those years. Can you hear him? Is he coming upstairs?'

'No, I don't hear him.'

'No, he'll be another minute or two. Quick, I'll show you something. Come along.'

She got up and seizing her son's sleeve she nearly ran with him from the room.

'You're not to say anything,' she said.

'His bedroom,' she said. 'Look at it.'

It was simply a bedroom with too much furniture in it.

'Three chests of drawers,' the son said. 'What does he want with three?'

A look of wicked delight came into his mother's face, a look so merry that he knew he was saying what she wanted him to say.

'Two wardrobes,' he exclaimed.

'Three with this!' exclaimed his mother, touching a cupboard in the corner, as if she were selling it.

'And then – just in case you want to read,' his mother said satirically. She pointed one by one to several reading lamps by the bed, on the chests, on the dressing-table.

'What's he want five for?' said the son.

'Shave?' said his mother excitedly, opening a heavy drawer. Inside was a number of razors and shaving things of all kinds. She bent to the drawer below.

'Locked,' she said. Undismayed, she led him to the far wall. 'Count,' she said. The son began to count. At seventeen he stopped. There were many more than seventeen pairs of boots lined up, and at the end the son stopped with astonishment.

'Riding-boots. When does he ride?'

'He's never ridden in his life, my dear.'

'Waders, climbing boots . . .' the son began to laugh. 'He never fished, did he? – '

'When did he buy all this gear?'

'Oh, we haven't begun, dear. Look at this.'

One by one she opened the wardrobes swiftly, allowed her son to glance, even to touch for a moment, and then swiftly closed the door. She showed him some thirty suits of clothes and more hats than he could count.

'I'll try one on,' said the son laughing.

'No,' said the mother, 'he'd know you'd touched them.'

'What's the idea of this hoard? It's madness,' he said.

The word madness came to his head because, at this triumph of her secret-telling, she looked mad herself. Her eyes stared with all the malice of the mad, intent on their message. Then quickly as a mouse she scurried to the door and listened.

The son stood by the fireplace when she went to the door and looked at a picture over the mantelpiece. It was the only picture in the room. It was a picture of a tall, bareheaded, austere man in ancient robes, standing in the shadows of a crowded place, alone. And in those shadows crouched a prowling group of lions, their surly faces barred with scowls of anger and fear.

'Daniel in the Lion's Den. He loves old Daniel,' said his mother, coming up behind him. 'He's always talking of Daniel.'

The son gaped at the picture. The room was filled with his father's life, but this picture seemed to be more profoundly his father's life than anything in the room. He suddenly felt ashamed of being in his father's room.

'Let's go back to the fire,' the son said.

'Look, dear,' the mother was pulling at his sleeve. 'Something else, quick.'

She took him to a chest of drawers and opened the drawers one by one.

'Pants,' she said in her deceptive voice, and as she spoke she carefully lifted one or two of the garments. Underneath them was a silver cruet.

'Solid silver,' she said. 'Wait. Two dozen teaspoons. A set of fish-knives. All silver.'

'Come along, Mother. I know, I know.'

'Silver tea-tray. Kettle,' she was at another drawer, ignoring him.

'Fish-knives, spoons, ink-stands . . .'

'Mother, stop . . .'

'You move this. It's heavy. Look at this one. Shirts.' She was lifting the shirts and revealing under them a cache of silver cream-jugs, hot-water jugs . . .

'Oh dear,' said his mother. 'We never use them. We never see them. He thinks I don't know. He just comes home and goes straight to his bedroom and slips them in.'

'Where does he pick up all this?' said the son.

'Ask no questions, hear no lies,' said his mother.

'No, seriously, what's the idea?'

The old lady's face was marked suddenly by all the bewilderment of a lifetime. She was helpless.

'Don't ask me, dear,' she said. 'It's him. It's how he's always been.'

She looked at her son, exhausted and enquiring. She had suddenly lost interest. She was also frightened.

'Come out, in case he comes. You see, dear, how it is. We couldn't leave all that.'

She turned out the lights and they walked back into the sitting-room.

'You're looking tired, dear,' she said, in an unnatural voice, making conversation. 'Do you sleep well?'

She went over to the curtain again and peeped out as she said this.
'Pretty well.'
She came back to the fire.
'I know. You dream. Do you dream? I dream something chronic. Every night. Your father doesn't dream, of course. He just sleeps. He's always been like that. Sometimes I have a terrible dream. I dream, dear, that I'm in a palace, a king's palace, something like Windsor Castle, and I go into a great hall and it's filled with – treasure: well, things, beautiful – you know, armour, pictures, china, and I stand there and I can't get my breath and I say "Oh. I must get out." And I go out of a door just to get air to breathe . . .'
'Indigestion,' said her son.
'Is it? Well, through this door there's another room, just the same, but it's filled with commoner things – crockery, ironmongery, furniture – just like a second-hand shop, but thousands, dear, and I think, "Oh, let me breathe," and I hurry out of it by the door, and beyond that door,' said the mother, holding his hand, 'is another room. Ted, it's full of everything decaying, filthy. Oh, it's horrible, dear. I wake up feeling sick.'
'What is that?' asked the son, nodding to the ceiling. 'Up there.'
'On the ceiling?' she said. 'Oh, that's our crack. It's getting bigger,' she said. 'It's a bad one.'
'That was the land-mine, dear, the one that broke the windows. The one that killed old Mrs Croft . . .'
'I know, Mother, don't . . .'
'I thought we had gone and I said, "Oh Dad. We've gone." Ted, dear, the dust!'
They looked at the ceiling. Beginning at the wall by the window, the crack was like a cut that has not closed.
'And perhaps it would have been a good thing if we had gone,' she said, narrowing her eyes and searching her son's face with a look that terrified him. 'We've had our life. What is your life? I watch that old crack and I say, "Let's see. Are you getting larger?" But he sits there, quiet at his table, and says "Remember Daniel. There's nothing to be afraid of." It's wonderful, really. He believes it. It does him good. There's just ourselves, dear, you see. You've all grown up, you've gone your own ways, you can't be here with me and it wouldn't be right if you could be.

I always feel I've got you. I think to myself, I've got something, I've got you children. But he's got nothing. You mustn't take any notice of the things I say. I expect you know women just say things and don't know why they say them ... When I see him sitting there under the lamp, praying for me and you and all of us, I think, "Poor old Daddy, that's all he's got – his faith. But I've got him."'

'Ssh, Mother, don't cry. He's coming now,' the son said. Quickly she sat on the stool by the fire and put her head forward so that the disorder of her face should be hidden in the glow of the flame.

The father tapped his fingers comically on the panel of the door.

'May I come in? Sure I'm not interrupting? Thank you. Mother and son,' he smiled, nodding his head. 'The old, old story, mother and son.'

A flush of annoyance and guilt passed over the son's body and came to his lips in a jaunty, uneasy laugh.

The father frowned.

'I say, old girl,' he said. 'I've just been outside. There was a chink of light showing in my room. We must be careful . . .'

'I was just showing Ted round,' said the mother.

'Showing me round the estate,' Ted said.

'I've switched it off,' the mother said.

'Switch it on, old girl. Let's have that tea.' He settled himself innocently on the edge of his chair with his legs tucked under it, and his pleased fingers joined over his waistcoat.

'It's a good thing I know your mother. How old are you, my boy – forty? In forty-five years I've got to know her,' the father smiled.

The old lady nodded her head as she went over his words, and then she got up from her stool to make the tea.

'I don't think they'll come tonight, dear,' she said with spirit.

'I'm here,' the son laughed.

'Run along, old girl. Of course they won't,' the father said, ordering and defending his own. 'I just *know* they won't.'

The Saint

When I was seventeen years old I lost my religious faith. It had been unsteady for some time and then, very suddenly, it went as the result of an incident in a punt on the river outside the town where we lived. My uncle, with whom I was obliged to stay for long periods of my life, had started a small furniture-making business in the town. He was always in difficulties about money, but he was convinced that in some way God would help him. And this happened. An investor arrived who belonged to a sect called the Church of the Last Purification, of Toronto, Canada. Could we imagine, this man asked, a good and omnipotent God allowing his children to be short of money? We had to admit we could not imagine this. The man paid some capital into my uncle's business and we were converted. Our family were the first Purifiers – as they were called – in the town. Soon a congregation of fifty or more were meeting every Sunday in a room at the Corn Exchange.

At once we found ourselves isolated and hated people. Everyone made jokes about us. We had to stand together because we were sometimes dragged into the courts. What the unconverted could not forgive in us was first that we believed in successful prayer and, secondly, that our revelation came from Toronto. The success of our prayers had a simple foundation. We regarded it as 'Error' – our name for Evil – to believe the evidence of our senses and if we had influenza or consumption, or had lost our money or were unemployed, we denied the reality of these things, saying that since God could not have made them they therefore did not exist. It was exhilarating to look at our congregation and to know that what the vulgar would call miracles were performed among us, almost as a matter of routine, every day. Not very big miracles, perhaps; but up in London and out in Toronto, we knew that deafness and blindness, cancer and insanity, the great scourges, were constantly vanishing before the prayers of the more advanced Purifiers.

'What!' said my schoolmaster, an Irishman with eyes like broken glass and a sniff of irritability in the bristles of his nose. 'What! Do you have the impudence to tell me that if you fell off the top floor of this building and smashed your head in, you would say you hadn't fallen and were not injured?'

I was a small boy and very afraid of everybody, but not when it was a question of my religion. I was used to the kind of conundrum the Irishman had set. It was useless to argue, though our religion had already developed an interesting casuistry.

'I *would* say so,' I replied with coldness and some vanity. 'And my head would not be smashed.'

'You would not say so,' answered the Irishman. 'You would not say so.' His eyes sparkled with pure pleasure. 'You'd be dead.'

The boys laughed, but they looked at me with admiration.

Then, I do not know how or why, I began to see a difficulty. Without warning and as if I had gone into my bedroom at night and had found a gross ape seated in my bed and thereafter following me about with his grunts and his fleas and a look, relentless and ancient, scored on his brown face, I was faced with the problem which prowls at the centre of all religious faith. I was faced by the difficulty of the origin of evil. Evil was an illusion, we were taught. But even illusions have an origin. The Purifiers denied this.

I consulted my uncle. Trade was bad at the time and this made his faith abrupt. He frowned as I spoke.

'When did you brush your coat last?' he said. 'You're getting slovenly about your appearance. If you spent more time studying books' – that is to say, the Purification literature – 'and less with your hands in your pockets and playing about with boats on the river, you wouldn't be letting Error in.'

All dogmas have their jargon; my uncle as a business man loved the trade terms of the Purification. 'Don't let Error in,' was a favourite one. The whole point about the Purification, he said, was that it was scientific and therefore exact; in consequence it was sheer weakness to admit discussion. Indeed, betrayal. He unpinched his pince-nez, stirred his tea and indicated I must submit or change the subject. Preferably the latter. I saw, to my alarm, that my arguments had defeated my uncle. Faith and doubt pulled like strings round my throat.

'You don't mean to say you don't believe that what our Lord said was true?' my aunt asked nervously, following me out of the room. 'Your uncle does, dear.'

I could not answer. I went out of the house and down the main street to the river where the punts were stuck like insects in the summery flash of the reach. Life was a dream, I thought; no, a nightmare, for the ape was beside me.

I was still in this state, half sulking and half exalted, when Mr Hubert Timberlake came to the town. He was one of the important people from the headquarters of our Church and he had come to give an address on the Purification at the Corn Exchange. Posters announcing this were everywhere. Mr Timberlake was to spend Sunday afternoon with us. It was unbelievable that a man so eminent would actually sit in our dining-room, use our knives and forks, and eat our food. Every imperfection in our home and our characters would jump out at him. The Truth had been revealed to man with scientific accuracy – an accuracy we could all test by experiment – and the future course of human development on earth was laid down, finally. And here in Mr Timberlake was a man who had not merely performed many miracles – even, it was said with proper reserve, having twice raised the dead – but who had actually been to Toronto, our headquarters, where this great and revolutionary revelation had first been given.

'This is my nephew,' my uncle said, introducing me. 'He lives with us. He thinks he thinks, Mr Timberlake, but I tell him he only thinks he does. Ha, ha.' My uncle was a humorous man when he was with the great. 'He's always on the river,' my uncle continued. 'I tell him he's got water on the brain. I've been telling Mr Timberlake about you, my boy.'

A hand as soft as the best quality chamois leather took mine. I saw a wide upright man in a double-breasted navy blue suit. He had a pink square head with very small ears and one of those torpid, enamelled smiles which were said by our enemies to be too common in our sect.

'Why, isn't that just fine?' said Mr Timberlake who, owing to his contacts with Toronto, spoke with an American accent. 'What say we tell your uncle it's funny he think's he's funny.'

The eyes of Mr Timberlake were direct and colourless. He had the look of a retired merchant captain who had become decontaminated from the sea and had reformed and made money. His defence of me had made me his at once. My doubts vanished. Whatever Mr Timberlake believed must be true and as I listened to him at lunch, I thought there could be no finer life than his.

'I expect Mr Timberlake's tired after his address,' said my aunt.

'Tired?' exclaimed my uncle, brilliant with indignation. 'How can Mr Timberlake be tired? Don't let Error in!'

For in our faith the merely inconvenient was just as illusory as a great catastrophe would have been, if you wished to be strict, and Mr Timberlake's presence made us very strict.

I noticed then that, after their broad smiles, Mr Timberlake's lips had the habit of setting into a long depressed sarcastic curve.

'I guess,' he drawled, 'I guess the Al-mighty must have been tired sometimes, for it says He re-laxed on the seventh day. Say, do you know what I'd like to do this afternoon,' he said turning to me. 'While your uncle and aunt are sleeping off this meal let's you and me go on the river and get water on the brain. I'll show you how to punt.'

Mr Timberlake, I saw to my disappointment, was out to show he understood the young. I saw he was planning a 'quiet talk' with me about my problems.

'There are too many people on the river on Sundays,' said my uncle uneasily.

'Oh, I like a crowd,' said Mr Timberlake, giving my uncle a tough look. 'This is the day of rest, you know.' He had had my uncle gobbling up every bit of gossip from the sacred city of Toronto all the morning.

My uncle and aunt were incredulous that a man like Mr Timberlake should go out among the blazers and gramophones of the river on a Sunday afternoon. In any other member of our Church they would have thought this sinful.

'Waal, what say?' said Mr Timberlake. I could only murmur.

'That's fixed,' said Mr Timberlake. And on came the smile as simple, vivid and unanswerable as the smile on an advertisement. 'Isn't that just fine!'

Mr Timberlake went upstairs to wash his hands. My uncle was deeply offended and shocked, but he could say nothing. He unpinched his glasses.

'A very wonderful man,' he said. 'So human,' he apologised.

'My boy,' my uncle said. 'This is going to be an experience for you. Hubert Timberlake was making a thousand a year in the insurance business ten years ago. Then he heard of the Purification. He threw everything up, just like that. He gave up his job and took up the work. It was a struggle, he told me so himself this morning. "Many's the time," he said to me this morning, "when I wondered where my next meal was coming from." But the way was shown. He came down from Worcester to London and in two years he was making fifteen hundred a year out of his practice.'

To heal the sick by prayer according to the tenets of the Church of the Last Purification was Mr Timberlake's profession.

My uncle lowered his eyes. With his glasses off the lids were small and uneasy. He lowered his voice too.

'I have told him about your little trouble,' my uncle said quietly with emotion. I was burned with shame. My uncle looked up and stuck out his chin confidently.

'He just smiled,' my uncle said. 'That's all.'

Then we waited for Mr Timberlake to come down.

I put on white flannels and soon I was walking down to the river with Mr Timberlake. I felt that I was going with him under false pretences; for he would begin explaining to me the origin of evil and I would have to pretend politely that he was converting me when, already, at the first sight of him, I had believed. A stone bridge, whose two arches were like an owlish pair of eyes gazing up the reach, was close to the landing-stage. I thought what a pity it was the flannelled men and the sunburned girls there did not know I was getting a ticket for *the* Mr Timberlake who had been speaking in the town that very morning. I looked round for him and when I saw him I was a little startled. He was standing at the edge of the water looking at it with an expression of empty incomprehension. Among the white crowds his air of brisk efficiency had dulled. He looked middle-aged, out of place and insignificant. But the smile switched on when he saw me.

'Ready?' he called. 'Fine!'

I had the feeling that inside him there must be a gramophone record going round and round, stopping at that word.

He stepped into the punt and took charge.

'Now I just want you to paddle us over to the far bank,' he said, 'and then I'll show you how to punt.'

Everything Mr Timberlake said still seemed unreal to me. The fact that he was sitting in a punt, of all commonplace material things, was incredible. That he should propose to pole us up the river was terrifying. Suppose he fell into the river? At once I checked the thought. A leader of our Church under the direct guidance of God could not possibly fall into a river.

The stream is wide and deep in this reach, but on the southern bank there is a manageable depth and a hard bottom. Over the clay banks the willows hang, making their basket-work print of sun and shadow on the water, while under the gliding boats lie cloudy, chloride caverns. The hoop-like branches of the trees bend down until their tips touch the water like fingers making musical sounds. Ahead in midstream, on a day sunny as this one was, there is a path of strong light which is hard to look at unless you half close your eyes and down this path on the crowded Sundays, go the launches with their parasols and their pennants; and also the rowing boats with their beetle-leg oars, which seem to dig the sunlight out of the water as they rise. Upstream one goes, on and on between the gardens and then between fields kept for grazing. On the afternoon when Mr Timberlake and I went out to settle the question of the origin of evil, the meadows were packed densely with buttercups.

'Now,' said Mr Timberlake decisively when I had paddled to the other side. 'Now I'll take her.'

He got over the seat into the well at the stern.

'I'll just get you clear of the trees,' I said.

'Give me the pole,' said Mr Timberlake standing up on the little platform and making a squeak with his boots as he did so. 'Thank you, sir. I haven't done this for eighteen years but I can tell you, brother, in those days I was considered some poler.'

He looked around and let the pole slide down through his hands. Then he gave the first difficult push. The punt rocked pleasantly and we moved forward. I sat facing him, paddle in hand, to check any inward drift of the punt.

'How's that, you guys?' said Mr Timberlake looking round at our eddies and drawing in the pole. The delightful water sished down it.

'Fine,' I said. Deferentially I had caught the word.

He went on to his second and his third strokes, taking too much water on his sleeve, perhaps, and uncertain in his steering, which I corrected, but he was doing well.

'It comes back to me,' he said. 'How am I doing?'

'Just keep her out from the trees,' I said.

'The trees?' he said.

'The willows,' I said.

'I'll do it now,' he said. 'How's that? Not quite enough? Well, how's this?'

'Another one,' I said. 'The current runs strong this side.'

'What? More trees?' he said. He was getting hot.

'We can shoot out past them,' I said. 'I'll ease us over with the paddle.'

Mr Timberlake did not like this suggestion.

'No, don't do that. I can manage it,' he said. I did not want to offend one of the leaders of our Church, so I put the paddle down; but I felt I ought to have taken him farther along away from the irritation of the trees.

'Of course,' I said. 'We could go under them. It might be nice.'

'I think,' said Mr Timberlake, 'that would be a very good idea.'

He lunged hard on the pole and took us towards the next archway of willow branches.

'We may have to duck a bit, that's all,' I said.

'Oh, I can push the branches up,' said Mr Timberlake.

'It is better to duck,' I said.

We were gliding now quickly towards the arch, in fact I was already under it.

'I think I should duck,' I said. 'Just bend down for this one.'

'What makes the trees lean over the water like this?' asked Mr Timberlake. 'Weeping willows – I'll give you a thought there. How Error likes to make us dwell on sorrow. Why not call them *laughing* willows?' discoursed Mr Timberlake as the branch passed over my head.

'Duck,' I said.

'Where? I don't see them,' said Mr Timberlake turning round.

'No, your head,' I said. 'The branch,' I called.

'Oh, the branch. This one?' said Mr Timberlake finding a branch just against his chest and he put out a hand to lift it. It is not easy to lift a willow branch and Mr Timberlake was surprised. He stepped back as it gently and firmly leaned against him. He leaned back and pushed from his feet. And he pushed too far. The boat went on, I saw Mr Timberlake's boots leave the stern as he took an unthoughtful step backwards. He made a last minute grasp at a stronger and higher branch, and then, there he hung a yard above the water, round as a blue damson that is ripe and ready, waiting only for a touch to make it fall. Too late with the paddle and shot ahead by the force of his thrust, I could not save him.

For a full minute I did not believe what I saw; indeed our religion taught us never to believe what we saw. Unbelieving I could not move. I gaped. The impossible had happened. Only a miracle, I found myself saying, could save him.

What was most striking was the silence of Mr Timberlake as he hung from the tree. I was lost between gazing at him and trying to get the punt out of the small branches of the tree. By the time I had got the punt out there were several yards of water between us and the soles of his boots were very near the water as the branch bent under his weight. Boats were passing at the time but no one seemed to notice us. I was glad about this. This was a private agony. A double chin had appeared on the face of Mr Timberlake and his head was squeezed between his shoulders and his hanging arms. I saw him blink and look up at the sky. His eyelids were pale like a chicken's. He was tidy and dignified as he hung there, the hat was not displaced and the top button of his coat was done up. He had a blue silk handkerchief in his breast pocket. So unperturbed and genteel he seemed that as the tips of his shoes came nearer and nearer to the water, I became alarmed. He could perform what are called miracles. He would be thinking at this moment that only in an erroneous and illusory sense was he hanging from the branch of the tree over six feet of water. He was probably praying one of the closely reasoned prayers of our faith which were more like conversations with Euclid than appeals to God. The calm of his face suggested this. Was he, I asked myself, within sight of the main road, the town Recreation Ground and the landing-stage crowded with people, was he about to re-enact a well-known miracle? I hoped that he was not. I prayed that he was not. I prayed with all my will that Mr Timberlake would not walk upon the water. It was my prayer and not his that was answered.

I saw the shoes dip, the water rise above his ankles and up his socks. He tried to move his grip now to a yet higher branch – he did not succeed – and in making this effort his coat and waistcoat rose and parted from his trousers. One seam of shirt with its pant-loops and brace-tabs broke like a crack across the middle of Mr Timberlake. It was like a fatal flaw in a statue, an earthquake crack which made the monumental mortal. The last Greeks must have felt as I felt then, when they saw a crack across the middle of some statue of Apollo. It was at this moment I realised that the final revelation about man and society on earth had come to nobody and that Mr Timberlake knew nothing at all about the origin of evil.

All this takes long to describe, but it happened in a few seconds as I paddled towards him. I was too late to get his feet on the boat and the only thing to do was to let him sink until his hands were nearer the level of the punt and then to get him to change hand-holds. Then I would paddle him ashore. I did this. Amputated by the water, first a torso, then a bust, then a mere head and shoulders, Mr Timberlake, I noticed, looked sad and lonely as he sank. He was a declining dogma. As the water lapped his collar – for he hesitated to let go of the branch to hold the punt – I saw a small triangle of deprecation and pathos between his nose and the corners of his mouth. The head resting on the platter of water had the sneer of calamity on it, such as one sees in the pictures of a beheaded saint.

'Hold on to the punt, Mr Timberlake,' I said urgently. 'Hold on to the punt.'

He did so.

'Push from behind,' he directed in a dry businesslike voice. They were his first words. I obeyed him. Carefully I paddled him towards the bank. He turned and, with a splash, climbed ashore. There he stood, raising his arms and looking at the water running down his swollen suit and making a puddle at his feet.

'Say,' said Mr Timberlake coldly, 'we let some Error in that time.'

How much he must have hated our family.

'I am sorry, Mr Timberlake,' I said. 'I am most awfully sorry. I should have paddled. It was my fault. I'll get you home at once. Let me wring out your coat and waistcoat. You'll catch your death . . .'

I stopped. I had nearly blasphemed. I had nearly suggested that Mr Timberlake had fallen into the water and that to a man of his age this might be dangerous.

Mr Timberlake corrected me. His voice was impersonal, addressing the laws of human existence, rather than myself.

'If God made water it would be ridiculous to suggest He made it capable of harming his creatures. Wouldn't it?'

'Yes,' I murmured hypocritically.

'OK,' said Mr Timberlake. 'Let's go.'

'I'll soon get you across,' I said.

'No,' he said. 'I mean let's go on. We're not going to let a little thing like this spoil a beautiful afternoon. Where were we going? You spoke of a pretty landing-place farther on. Let's go there.'

'But I must take you home. You can't sit there soaked to the skin. It will spoil your clothes.'

'Now, now,' said Mr Timberlake. 'Do as I say. Go on.'

There was nothing to be done with him. I held the punt into the bank and he stepped in. He sat like a bursting and sodden bolster in front of me while I paddled. We had lost the pole of course.

For a long time I could hardly look at Mr Timberlake. He was taking the line that nothing had happened and this put me at a disadvantage. I knew something considerable had happened. That glaze, which so many of the members of our sect had on their faces and persons, their minds and manners, had been washed off. There was no gleam for me from Mr Timberlake.

'What's the house over there?' he asked. He was making conversation. I had steered into the middle of the river to get him into the strong sun. I saw steam rise from him.

I took courage and studied him. He was a man, I realised, in poor physical condition, unexercised and sedentary. Now the gleam had left him one saw the veined empurpled skin of the stoutish man with a poor heart. I remembered he had said at lunch:

'A young woman I know said, "Isn't it wonderful. I can walk thirty miles in a day without being in the least tired." I said, "I don't see that bodily indulgence is anything a member of the Church of the Last Purification should boast about."'

Yes, there was something flaccid, passive and slack about Mr Timberlake. Bunched in swollen clothes, he refused to take them off. It occurred to me, as he looked with boredom at the water, the passing boats and the country, that he had not been in the country before. That it was something he had agreed to do but wanted to get over quickly. He was totally uninterested. By his questions – what is that church? Are there any fish in this river? Is that a wireless or a gramophone? – I understood that Mr Timberlake was formally acknowledging a world he did not live in. It was too interesting, too eventful a world. His spirit, inert and preoccupied, was elsewhere in an eventless and immaterial habitation. He was a dull man, duller than any man I have ever known; but his dullness was a sort of earthly deposit left by a being whose diluted mind was far away in the effervescence of metaphysical matters. There was a slightly pettish look on his face as (to himself, of course) he declared he was not wet and that he would not have a heart attack or catch pneumonia.

Mr Timberlake spoke little. Sometimes he squeezed water out of his sleeve. He shivered a little. He watched his steam. I had planned when we set out to go up as far as the lock but now the thought of another two miles of this responsibility was too much. I pretended I wanted to go only as far as the bend which we were approaching, where one of the richest buttercup meadows was. I mentioned this to him. He turned and looked with boredom at the field. Slowly we came to the bank.

We tied up the punt and we landed.

'Fine,' said Mr Timberlake. He stood at the edge of the meadow just as he had stood at the landing-stage – lost, stupefied, uncomprehending.

'Nice to stretch our legs,' I said. I led the way into the deep flowers. So dense were the buttercups there was hardly any green. Presently I sat down. Mr Timberlake looked at me and sat down also. Then I turned to him with a last try at persuasion. Respectability, I was sure, was his trouble.

'No one will see us,' I said. 'This is out of sight of the river. Take off your coat and trousers and wring them out.'

Mr Timberlake replied firmly:

'I am satisfied to remain as I am.'

'What is this flower?' he asked to change the subject.

'Buttercup,' I said.

'Of course,' he replied.

I could do nothing with him. I lay down full length in the sun; and, observing this and thinking to please me, Mr Timberlake did the same. He must have supposed that this was what I had come out in the boat to do. It was only human. He had come out with me, I saw, to show me that he was only human.

But as we lay there I saw the steam still rising. I had had enough.

'A bit hot,' I said getting up.

He got up at once.

'Do you want to sit in the shade,' he asked politely.

'No,' I said. 'Would you like to?'

'No,' he said. 'I was thinking of you.'

'Let's go back,' I said. We both stood up and I let him pass in front of me. When I looked at him again I stopped dead. Mr Timberlake was no longer a man in a navy blue suit. He was blue no longer. He was transfigured. He was yellow. He was covered with buttercup pollen, a fine yellow paste of it made by the damp, from head to foot.

'Your suit,' I said.

He looked at it. He raised his thin eyebrows a little, but he did not smile or make any comment.

The man is a saint, I thought. As saintly as any of those gold-leaf figures in the churches of Sicily. Golden he sat in the punt; golden he sat for the next hour as I paddled him down the river. Golden and bored. Golden as we landed at the town and as we walked up the street back to my uncle's house. There he refused to change his clothes or to sit by a fire. He kept an eye on the time for his train back to London. By no word did he acknowledge the disasters or the beauties of the world. If they were printed upon him, they were printed upon a husk.

[198]

Sixteen years have passed since I dropped Mr Timberlake in the river and since the sight of his pant loops destroyed my faith. I have not seen him since, and today I heard that he was dead. He was fifty-seven. His mother, a very old lady with whom he had lived all his life, went into his bedroom when he was getting ready for church and found him lying on the floor in his shirt-sleeves. A stiff collar with the tie half inserted was in one hand. Five minutes before, she told the doctor, she had been speaking to him.

The doctor who looked at the heavy body lying on the single bed saw a middle-aged man, wide rather than stout and with an extraordinarily box-like thick-jawed face. He had got fat, my uncle told me, in later years. The heavy liver-coloured cheeks were like the chaps of a hound. Heart disease, it was plain, was the cause of the death of Mr Timberlake. In death the face was lax, even coarse and degenerate. It was a miracle, the doctor said, that he had lived as long. Any time during the last twenty years the smallest shock might have killed him.

I thought of our afternoon on the river. I thought of him hanging from the tree. I thought of him, indifferent and golden in the meadow. I understood why he had made for himself a protective, sedentary bland-ness, an automatic smile, a collection of phrases. He kept them on like the coat after his ducking. And I understood why – though I had feared it all the time we were on the river – I understood why he did not talk to me about the origin of evil. He was honest. The ape was with us. The ape that merely followed me was already inside Mr Timberlake eating out his heart.

It May Never Happen

I shall not forget the fingers that fastened me into the stiff collar. Or how I was clamped down under the bowler-hat which spread my rather large ears outwards and how, my nose full of the shop smell of new suit, I went off for the first time to earn my living.

'You are beginning life,' they said.

'You have your foot on the first rung of the ladder,' they said.

'Excelsior,' my new Uncle Belton said.

I was going to work in the office of one of my uncles, a new uncle, the second husband of my mother's sister, who had just married into the family. His name was Belton, a man of forty-four with a tight, bumptious little business in the upholstery trade, a business that sounded so full of possibilities that it would blow up and burst, out of sheer merit. The push of Mr Belton, the designing of Mr Phillimore, his partner, made it irresistible. The name of the firm was Belton and Phillimore.

On my first day I met Mr Belton outside our railway station. I watched a horse eating and I read all the hoardings while I waited. Mr Belton was half an hour late. He was one of those cheerful, self-centred men whose tempers shorten when they are in the wrong. They put themselves right by sailing out into general reflections.

'Punctuality, Vincent, is everything,' said Mr Belton, bitterly. 'How long have you been here?'

'Half an hour.'

'*Why* have you been here half an hour?'

Mr Belton was looked upon as a sharp-shooter, a raider in our family. He had been around his new relations trying to raise capital for his business, he had carried off my mother's sister, in marriage, he was carrying me off to his office. He was a small, round, dominant and smartly dressed man, who usually wore brown. His black hair was parted in the middle and when he arrived anywhere he arrived with aplomb, bouncing down as hard as a new football on asphalt and very nearly on one's toes.

A new business, a new marriage, a new outlook on life – my brand new uncle looked as though he had come straight out of a shop-window. He had been hardly more than a quarter of an hour in our house before we thought our paint looked shabby and the rooms small. The very curtains seemed to shrink like the poor as he talked largely of exports, imports, agencies, overheads, discounts, rebates, cut prices and debentures. And when he had done with these he was getting at what we paid for meat, where we got our coal and how much at a time, telling us, too, where to buy carpets and clothes, gas-fires, art pottery and electric irons. He even gave us the name of a new furniture polish. It sounded like one of the books of the Old Testament. He walked about the house touching things, fingering picture-frames, turning chairs round, looking under tables, tapping his toes thoughtfully on the linoleum. Then he sat down and lifting his foot restfully to his knee and exposing the striking pattern of his socks, he seemed to be working out how much we would get if we sold up house and home. The message 'Sell up and begin again' flashed on and off in the smiles of his shining new face like Morse.

'I can get all these things,' he said, 'in the trade.'

When he and I sat in the train that morning I thought Mr Belton looked larger.

'I don't want you to think I'm lecturing you, boy,' he said, 'but there are many boys who would give their right hand to walk straight into this business as you are doing.'

'Yes, Uncle,' I said.

'A little thing – you must call me "sir".'

'Yes, Uncle,' I said, 'sir.'

'And you must call Mr Phillimore "sir".'

I had forgotten all about Mr Belton's partner.

'But for Mr Phillimore you would not have this chance,' Mr Belton said, detecting at once that I had forgotten. 'It's a very remarkable thing, it's really wonderful, some people would think more than wonderful, that Mr Phillimore agreed to it. He's a very busy man. A man with a great deal on his mind. There are people in the trade who would be glad to pay for the privilege of consulting Mr Phillimore. His word is law in the firm and I want you to be most respectful to him. Don't forget to say

[201]

"Good morning, sir" to him when you see him, and if he should offer to shake hands you must, of course, shake hands with him. I think he may offer to shake hands, but he may not. If he rings his bell or asks you to do anything you must do it at once. Be quick and mind your manners. If he is going out of the room, open the door for him. Mr Phillimore notices everything.'

Naturally, Mr Belton had seemed all-powerful to me, and it awed me to hear that behind this god was yet another god to whom even he deferred.

It distressed me that there were other people in the compartment who might hear this conversation. The day was damp and a low smoke from the train blew along the window as though we were travelling through cloud into another universe.

My face must have looked strained and pale. I had eaten very little for breakfast and my head ached where the bowler-hat pressed a red mark on my forehead. My uncle relaxed a little. At the next station two girls got out and we were alone in the compartment.

'I shall always remember the first time I stayed with Mr Phillimore and his mother.' So far my uncle had been hectoring and glum; but now a luminous gravity of expression came on his big experienced face and covered it like the skin on a balloon. He looked curiously light, as if he had been inflated with hydrogen and would rise from the seat of the empty railway carriage and blow away out of the window. He had what is called a common accent, none too certain about aitches and double negatives, but his voice was musical and now became rarefied when he spoke of his partner.

'In Mr Phillimore's 'ouse – ahem, house, the gentlemen give up their chairs to the ladies when they come into the room. And when the ladies leave the room you have to let them walk in front of you,' my uncle said. He stared at this picture in his memory with wonder. He seemed to hang in the higher air and then gradually he subsided and became himself again, a shade coarser than he had been before. His brown eyes looked unsteadily, a thick smile began nervously by his nose and slowly spread over his face, and a twist of deprecation came to the corners of his lips.

'You see, Mr Phillimore is a gentleman. It may seem peculiar to you and me,' he said.

'But people are peculiar,' he said. And the smile slowly deepened as it will on the face of a baby until he began to look fondly and sentimentally at me.

'I'll give you a little tip, boy,' he said, putting his hand on my knee, a touch that sent an uncomfortable thrill through my body and flushed me with all the shyness of my age. 'Do you mind if I give you a little piece of advice, something helpful?'

'No, Uncle,' I murmured. 'Sir.'

'You needn't call me sir, now,' he said kindly. 'If Mr Phillimore should ring for you,' he said, 'just remember the infant Samuel. You remember how when our Lord called Samuel the boy said, "Speak Lord, Thy Servant heareth." Well, just pause and say that, just quietly to yourself, before you go and see what Mr Phillimore wants. Don't hang around, of course. Sharp's the word. But say it.'

My throat pinched, my tongue went dry. I should have said that Mr Belton was a religious man. His expression became dreamy.

'I think there'd be no harm in your saying it if I ring, too,' he said. Even he looked surprised after making this suggestion.

The office and workshops of Belton and Phillimore, makers of Butifix furniture and especially of the Butifix armchair and sofa, were at No. 7, in a row of old stained houses standing behind railings. The street was flogged by trams and drayhorses. Dust flew into one's eyes from the vans. The doorstep of No. 7 was the only whitened one in the street.

'Step over it,' Mr Belton said. I nearly fell over it. From Mr Belton's manner, from his militant walk, I had imagined I was going to work in a large factory, where hundreds of workers were frizzling under acres of glass roof. But Belton and Phillimore occupied only the ground floor of this old house whose window-sills slanted and gave a leer of depression to its aspect. A number of small businesses – a tailor or two, a lamp-shade manufacturer, and agents for pulleys, gloves and shop-fittings worked in single rooms above. A smell of glue hung like a dead animal about the doorway and there were packing-cases stored in the hall. A notice which was never taken down all the time I was there said, 'Young Improvers Wanted. Apply Schenk.' Someone had written 'April 26 Holborn Baths' in pencil underneath. On my uncle's floor there was first a small room, made by new glass partitions, where a typist sat. She was a large-boned, round-shouldered girl of seventeen with fine yellow hair, who worked in a green overcoat. Her office smelled of gas, paint and tea. Next door was the room occupied by Mr Belton and Mr Phillimore and beyond, down the passage, was the large workroom under a top light where one could hear the sound of a turning machine, the swish of a plane and the noise of hammering. Patterns of cloth, samples of hair, kapok and down were on the large desk where the two partners sat in their office, and there I waited alone listening to the typewriter – an old-fashioned one – clumping up and down like the police. My uncle had changed into a white dust-coat and marched out to find Mr Phillimore. Before he went he leant down and smelled a bowl of flowers on the table. 'Colour,' he smiled patrioti-cally, 'we're colourful people.'

'Speak Lord . . .' I gabbled, but I was too afraid to get to the end of the sentence. I had had many daydreams about Mr Phillimore. He was a myth in our family. No one had ever seen him; but it was agreed that he had been the making of my uncle. Indeed, people said, he had been my uncle's salvation. I foresaw a tall, clean, sarcastic man with a deep stiff collar, as clean as a doctor. Or perhaps one of those bullying, morally overweighted figures from the north of England whose minds pass like soft steam-rollers over you, suffocating rather than flattening you with the eiderdown gospel of work and righteousness. The door opened. I was startled by a high-pitched, eager feminine giggle; a small man stumbled towards me.

'Er – er – hullo, 'llo, my dear,' the voice said. I saw a white dust-coat. I saw a pair of agonised yellow-blue eyes popping with an expression of helplessness out of a badly pimpled face. Really, Mr Phillimore looked raw and bleeding. Then I saw his untidy wheat-coloured hair, with a pink scalp showing through it; and after that, loose lips drawn back, rabbit fashion, from a set of protruding teeth, each tooth shooting out in a different direction. It was a mouth which looked ravenous and could not close; and saliva, therefore, fizzed out of it, when he was excited. He was young, no more than thirty-five, and my first sight of Mr Phillimore suggested the frantic, yelping disorganised expression of a copulating dog.

Before he got to me Mr Phillimore caught the pocket of his white dust-coat on the door-handle, dropped a ruler from his pocket and trod on a pencil.

'Oh dear, oh dear!' cried Mr Phillimore, going down on his knees with a sigh of inexpressible fatigue.

'Pick it up,' said my uncle to me bitterly, giving me a push.

'Oh no, *no*, my dear!' said Mr Phillimore from the floor. 'My fault, Mr B. I'm most frightfully sorry. How are you? At last, after all these months! Are you quite recovered from your illness?' He was on his feet now, a weak damp hand clung will-lessly to mine and he gazed eagerly into my eyes.

'I haven't been ill, sir,' I said.

'You don't look well,' he said doubtfully. Then his spirit rose again: 'The moment I heard of you I *longed* for you to come. We've been waiting for you for months. We're simply *killed* with work, my dear, you've no idea.'

Mr Phillimore sat down at the partner's desk and looked at me reproachfully. He looked congenitally exhausted.

'Ah Vernon,' he said.

'Vincent, sir,' I murmured.

'Vincent,' he said. 'You and I have not the energy, the decision of the remarkable Mr B. He is a remarkable man, Vernon, he has been my salvation. Vincent, I mean, I'm *so* sorry.'

My uncle, who had sat down at his desk and was tapping a sheet of figures with a pencil, glanced up at this remark and smiled mechanically. My confusion was natural. I had always gathered Mr Phillimore was the saviour; now I heard the rôles reversed. I blinked. The two men were saving each other.

'With two more machines, Phillimore,' my uncle said, ignoring the worship of his partner and acting a part, 'we could treble these figures.' And he brought his soft fist down like a sponge on the desk, not heavily, but strongly enough to make Phillimore strain to attention.

Though I had been only a few minutes in the office I felt already (when I heard those words) the swirl of urgency and importance in the affairs of Belton and Phillimore. I stared at Mr Phillimore until he must have thought I was trying to get instructions from him by hypnosis. To my disappointment a look of despair and appeal came into Mr Phillimore's

[205]

face. The telephone bell rang and, with a shudder, Mr Phillimore took up the telephone, saying before he answered it:

'P'please, Mr B, don't expand the business any more for a moment.' Then, mastering his stammer, dropping his voice into his throat, Mr Phillimore concentrated on answering the telephone efficiently. Copying and practising Uncle Belton's gesture, Phillimore weakly hammered the air with *his* fists as he talked, glancing at my uncle nervously as he did so. When he had finished his telephone conversation and had told my uncle about it, Mr Phillimore looked at me and said:

'It is true. I'm not exaggerating.' He nodded towards my uncle, who was still tapping his pencil on the figures. 'He saved my life.' Then he smiled and said to my uncle: 'Do you like the flowers I brought for us?'

'I'd sooner you brought me an order, Phillimore,' said my uncle.

Nothing happens in an office. One day is like another. When I look back upon that year the only thing I see is a love-affair – the love-affair of Mr Belton and Mr Phillimore. They sat in their office like husband and wife in a sitting-room. It was not really a love-affair, but a salvation affair. Mr Belton had the rippling mind of the natural salesman and, strengthening it, was a powerful evangelical notion that he must save people from their own undoing. He did not sell: he saved. He saved people, when he was travelling in towels or electric irons or cretonne for example, from the sadness of not having these things. When he was in the stocking business, he rescued people from the misery of not having so many hundreds of dozens of stockings. The world needed to be saved from its parsimony, its uncreative caution. Mr Belton pumped salvation into the world, rescued men from the Slough of Despond. Giant Despair – I have heard him say to customers – is man's greatest enemy. And when he came to have businesses or agencies of his own after he had married my mother's sister, and his relations put money into these enterprises, he was rescuing *them*. He was rescuing their savings from the ignominy of 2½ per cent or whatever it was, in some prim nibbling bank.

'Oh, ye of little faith,' he said, cocking his dark eyebrow. And if things went wrong the eyebrow would straighten.

'It was an experience,' he would rebuke his critics. 'I had to buy *mine*.'

It was my new Uncle Belton's gift of salvation which had captured Mr Phillimore.

Now that I had seen Mr Phillimore, Uncle Belton modified the Philli-more myth and said to me when I went home with him in the tobacco smoke of the train:

'Mr Phillimore is peculiar. We all have our peculiarities. He is really an artist. He does our designs. When I met Mr Phillimore three years ago he had a tiny chair-making, arts and craft shop in Somerset. He was living under his mother's thumb. Imagine a man of thirty-five who can't go out in the evening without his mother's permission. Terrible.'

Uncle Belton scowled.

'The poor devil was drinking himself to death,' he said. 'He shut himself in his room and drank whisky out of a hot-water bottle.'

Uncle Belton's face went pale as lichen.

'It might have led to women – anything,' he said. Then he blinked. He had evidently been struck by the thought that he ought not to have said this to me about his partner. His voice became bland and expansive.

'There he was – and independent, mind you, he had money – going downhill as fast as I have ever seen a man go – a gentleman, paralysed, hypnotised, you might call it. I told him straight what was the matter with him. I saw it at once – he had to get away from that mother. I told her, "You're a mother. You don't know nothing about your son."'

His voice now became merry. 'It's marvellous, reely,' he said. 'Marvel-lous the way things work out. I just went down there to look around.'

Uncle Belton saw those two provincial people with their neat lifeless little business. He saw in them a temporary gold-mine. But there was more in my uncle's passion than acquisitiveness. He had a horror of drink; he had a greater horror of spiritual disasters. He stepped back from the catastrophic crashes of the inner life. His remedy lay in that part of the Protestant tradition which deals with the conflicts of the inner life by annihilating the inner life altogether. When Uncle Belton and Mr Philli-more left Somerset to start the firm of Belton & Phillimore their departure was like an elopement.

'It has been an experience for me, knowing your uncle,' said Mr Phillimore to me again and again. He had borrowed the word 'experience' from Mr Belton. His voice rose into the treble. 'What drive, Vernon, Vincent – which is it? Vincent! What drive!'

My day's work at the office was monotonous, like family life. For if my new Uncle Belton and Mr Phillimore were husband and wife, I was the only child who strays listlessly from room to room trying to find something to do. I stuck on stamps, I copied letters. I put clean water in the flower-bowl which Mr Phillimore kept filled. They were a love-offering. I took messages. I went across the road to buy buns for the typist, or my uncle would send me out to collect a shirt from a shop or to buy a bottle of hair-cream at his barbers. My uncle had thick glossy hair as still as glass on his head. We lived in all the intensity of domestic life. Uncle was always willing to stop his work and address a manly mid-week sermon to Mr Phillimore. Mr Phillimore was always willing to stop what he was doing and talk to me. He would follow me ravenously about open-mouthed as if he would graze on my hair. We had been brought up on the myth of the unapproachability of Mr Phillimore: the myth had a germ of truth: it was he, who, continuously, made the approaches.

'Ah youth, youth, golden-headed youth,' he would say as he passed me in the workshop. I had thick black hair not unlike my uncle's and I was trying to make it look glossy. Through the window in the partition Miss Croft, the typist, kept her little eyes on all of us. One of my anxieties was to make Miss Croft smile, but she was in her wooden teens, and her lips set firmly when I stood in the room with her. She looked at me with the swollen face of an elder sister. It was a long time before I saw that she was piqued because once *she* had been the only child in this family and that I had supplanted her. A woman's life is swayed by her feelings, but Miss Croft was not yet a woman: she was learning about her feelings, how to use them, like a young girl who is learning to play scales on the piano, and she was still awkward with them.

Mr Phillimore would often stand at the door of her room talking to me and as he did so, his look would pop anxiously, intimately, apologetically in Miss Croft's direction. Mr Phillimore's eyes seemed to say, 'In my life I need all the help I can get from *everyone*. Don't be jealous and hurt!' One could see what had happened. Miss Croft silently reproached him.

'You are wasting Mr Phillimore's time. That poor man is run off his feet,' she said abruptly to me.

'*He* started talking to *me*,' I said.

Miss Croft sat back from her typewriter.

'He is the brains of this firm,' Miss Croft said. 'I have been here from the beginning. I've seen it all. That man,' she was developing her simple possessive instinct as if she were doing arm exercises, 'tells me everything.' She always called him 'that man'.

Yes, and now Mr Phillimore had started telling me everything.

Miss Croft gave her head a short upward jerk. She put a lump in her chin by running her tongue round her lower gum, and began typing again with her big red fingers. I loved watching the quickness of her fingers. There were two or three other things about her that were pretty; her little starry violet eyes and her small waist; the curve of her legs was becoming lovely. And she had a lisping childlike voice. But she was changing; what was pretty one week became plain the next. She was like a creature in a chrysalis.

'One thing,' she said complacently, 'that man won't be here long. I can see things.'

When she saw how astonished and impressed I was by this remark, Miss Croft was very satisfied.

'Why do you say that?' I asked.

There were things, she said primly to me, that were confidential.

My Uncle Belton was a man who was unaware of the little situations that were simmering all day long around him. He lived juicily, like an orange, within the containing rind of his objects in life. He was out two or three times a week seeing customers and walking in his dream of making the business larger and getting larger premises. When he wasn't tapping his pencil on columns of figures or abusing someone on the telephone, he was gazing vehemently at the plans of new premises he had seen. One afternoon he came back in a hearty mood and sent me to tell Mr Phillimore he had brought him a present.

'A present,' cried Mr Phillimore, who was working on the frame of a sofa. Up he jumped. 'How exciting,' he said.

We had a foreman with bloodshot eyes, who always winked at me when I came with a message for Mr Phillimore. He winked now.

'You've got a present for me!' cried Mr Phillimore, almost running to Uncle Belton's office. 'What a thrill.'

My uncle did not give Mr Phillimore the parcel. He wanted some of the surprise for himself. He wanted a part of everything for himself; it was not greed but part of his gregarious generosity. He would have eaten your lunch for you so that you and he could feel more genially at one. We watched Uncle undo the parcel. It contained a small framed picture. He stood it on the desk and turned it to face Mr Phillimore.

'Just made for you, Phillimore,' he said. The picture was simply a text done in poker work. The words were: 'Don't Worry – It May Never Happen.'

'Don't worry – it may never happen,' Phillimore read with delight and he rubbed his hands together.

'Don't Worry – it may never happen,' ruminated my uncle in his deep, golden, optimistic voice.

'Wonderful,' cried Phillimore. 'Oh, good.' Like a boy clapping a catch at cricket. Then he looked serious. He shook his head. 'Very true. Very true,' he said thoughtfully.

'I'll tell you what – we'll hang it on the wall.'

'That's an idea,' said Uncle.

'Over the mantelpiece? Or over the desk, do you think?' said Mr Phillimore.

He danced about holding the picture now in this place and now in the other. Uncle helped him. They were like a newly married couple hanging up a picture.

'Over the mantelpiece, where you can see it,' said Mr Belton.

'Here, do you think?'

'No – a little higher. There! No, a bit to the left.' Yes, it was a marriage. Mr Phillimore and Mr Belton sat down exhausted gazing at the picture now hanging on the wall. Phillimore read it aloud again.

'True,' he said. 'Very true.'

'Yes,' he sighed, shaking his head. 'It's just made for me. Why worry? There's no need to. One's desires, one's wishes, one's hopes – they won't come off. Nothing changes.'

'Here,' cried my uncle. 'It doesn't say that. It says don't be held back by your fears, the thing you're afraid of just won't occur. You're not afraid of what you want coming true, are you? That would be ridiculous.'

'My dear Vincent,' said Mr Phillimore, getting my name right for once, 'that only shows how different Mr B. is from the rest of us.'

'Good godfathers,' cried my uncle. 'Phillimore, you're morbid.'

[210]

'Yes, yes, I know,' said Mr Phillimore with a primness and secretiveness I had never noticed before. 'But one preserves one's integrity.'

And Phillimore lifted his nose and one could hear a hissing intake of air like a gas escape. It was a little terrifying. Uncle scowled playfully but he was put out. For a few seconds the two men considered each other and my uncle, being by far the shorter and stouter, had the advantage of weight. Many men who were taller than my new Uncle Belton were intimidated by his vehement shortness. He seemed to be shooting upwards at one like a howitzer.

After his expeditions to the warm and buzzing platters of the world, Belton was often irritable; when he came back, he was obliged to return to earth where he found an order had been delayed, or some timber had a flaw in it, or they were short of cloth because Phillimore had advised Belton to go easy on the buying. And now after the difference over the meaning of the picture, Belton went irritably off to the workroom.

'I hope,' said Mr Phillimore, 'dear Mr B. won't upset the hands. I shall feel it is my fault.' And then turning to me, begging for support, he said, 'Yet how frightful, how terrifying it would be, Vincent, if what one wished came true. How futile life would be if one's fears were not realised. Don't you think?' He watched me.

'I should die!' he cried and his hands hung limply from the wrist like wet leaves.

This kind of conversation was beyond me. And he often spoke like this in front of the workers who winked at me all the time. On the other hand, I could not be sure that Mr Phillimore wasn't mocking me. And then I suppose in our family – my own and my uncle's – we were stamped with a reserve about our personal lives. We had no private lives. We simply had secret lives, like secret drinkers. We were the natural opponents of private life. We regarded ourselves as units of will or energy directed upon our various purposes. Mr Belton saw himself (for he was religious) as a new kind of fusion of science and religion, a successful sperm, fertilising the Christian endeavour. Contact with a man like Phillimore, who appeared to put feebleness, illness, fright, incapacity and failure in life first, was bewildering. Phillimore's eagerness to cut a bad figure was like an indecent physical exposure. He was the sperm which fails.

So when Mr Phillimore cried out, 'I should die,' I saw something new

[211]

in his expression, something watchful, crystalline, and with the madman's order, in his eye. For a second or two I had the impression that Mr Phillimore was *not* a fool; that he was cunning and obstinate, and longsighted. The impression dissolved and indeed I forgot about it or he made me forget it by a sudden change of his mood. He was as limp as a willow. What I would call his good-bye air appeared. I mean that after some gust of confidence, some anxious tail-wagging spaniel-like prance of intimacy, Mr Phillimore would draw back and fade. He would gradually back to the door and stand there getting dimmer. It was like being in a train which is moving out and Mr Phillimore stood on the platform stammering about how lucky you were to be going away, while he was left behind. The weak hands seemed to wave. It was his vanity to be left behind.

'Ah well, Vernon,' he said (I was beginning to think he got my name wrong out of malice), 'where shall we all be in ten years' time? You – I see you – rich, successful, in the arms of some superb mistress – Miss Croft, shall we say, but in a tiger skin. And I . . . alas, in my solitary room . . .'

He had gone.

Every firm has its Devil, that is to say, its chief competitor. And this Devil is always a firm of the same size or perhaps a little more important. Belton and Phillimore were not afraid of their big competitors: the huge furniture manufacturers and upholsterers who devoured the trade like ranging wolves. Belton and Phillimore admired these great firms. They were afraid of the little ones and especially of one little one.

If my uncle wanted to give Mr Phillimore a fright he would say:

'Salter's on the move again. He's cut his prices.' Or, holding up a letter: 'Look at this. Salter's giving six months' credit.'

My uncle would look bitter and belligerent. One was warring against Sin. Salter, my uncle conveyed, was a cheat, a fraud, a sinister figure who was plotting against their lives. Salter copied our designs and cheapened them. He stole our customers. He would try and get hold of our workers. Like a highwayman, he preyed on our labour. He wanted to strangle us. My uncle was not eloquent about this; he was as curt, as stubborn as a soldier. Salter might have been outside on the street sniping at him.

'We can't fight *that*,' my uncle would say, meaning, of course, the opposite.

'That defeats us,' Phillimore eagerly agreed. He put down his ruler and his pencil, leaned back in his chair and made a noise in his throat like the death-rattle – a noise natural to him. He also had an irritating habit of whistling through the gap in his front teeth, a whistle of surrender. It was he, at these times, who appeared to be 'saving' my uncle; one saw the emergence of Phillimore's hatred of success, the trembling of compassion in his nature. An expression of one lying blissfully in hospital came on Phillimore's face. He would have done anything for Belton at that moment, and if Belton had observed the character of his partner – which, of course, he had not; he did not believe in any one's character but his own – he would have chosen this moment to say to Mr Phillimore:

'Go down to your mother, tell her we are on the edge of bankruptcy, get her to give us this extra capital we need. Tell her it is a terrible risk, that we may very likely lose it. Tell her it's desperate. Tell her we may not last another month. Go out and get drunk, it's the only thing to do.'

The prospect of ruin would have been irresistible to Mr Phillimore. He would have done in this mood what in a more confident one he would have resisted. Alas, Belton was no reader of the heart. He turned and attacked Phillimore.

'Defeat us,' he said, setting his chin. 'I don't understand the meaning of the word, Phillimore. There is no defeat. What's Salter? A draper' – Uncle's lowest word of contempt – 'a draper, Phillimore. Give me the price list. Get me Dobson's on the 'phone. Miss Croft, come and take these letters. Boy, take this note up to the bank . . .'

The crisis of sacrifice, loss, abandonment was passed. Like a wife who sees her husband recover and so free himself from helpless reliance on her, Phillimore saw his compassion scattered. Phillimore would have liked to rock my uncle like a baby – and indeed Belton often looked like one. But optimism had won. And when my uncle did raise the question of getting more capital, Mr Phillimore became evasive. The 'good-bye' look came back. He admired my uncle's resilience, but the admiration itself exhausted him and left him – how shall I say it? I can remember only his appearance, the open mouth, the choking open mouth under the dropping teeth – it left him in a condition of – nausea. And one heard the sound, the sinister air rushing up his nostrils, like a preparation for suicide.

About this time I used to go out to lunch with Mr Phillimore and one day I saw this Devil who haunted our firm and planned our destruction. Phillimore and I were in a teashop.

'Oh dear,' said Phillimore, 'there's that poor wretch, Salter.' My heart jumped. The devilries of Salter had so impressed me that I was ready to run out of the place.

'Has he seen us?' I said, trying to look undisturbed. I ought not to have been surprised by the self-possession of Phillimore: Salter meant disaster.

'That man might have ruined us,' said Phillimore sadly. 'But for your wonderful uncle, Vernon, we should be in Queer Street, up the spout, right in the middle of the purée.'

Phillimore sighed and shook his head. He gazed in Salter's direction with affection. He gazed, I now suspect, with nostalgia. And I, gazing there too, saw a stringy and dejected man, bald but not sufficiently so, with pince-nez like a dismal pair of birds on either side of his nose, and a grey moustache, damp with tea. The teashop was under a railway arch and we could hear the trains rumbling over our heads like rollers. They seemed to flatten and crush the figure of Mr Salter in his old raincoat. I suppose he knew us, for he looked at us miserably and I have never seen a figure which conveyed more resignation to injustice, more passive disquiet. To judge by the look he gave us, this hypocrite Salter was muttering aloud that we were cheating and ruining him. We were copying *his* designs, undercutting *his* prices, stealing *his* customers. He got up and went to pay his bill listlessly just as I was putting a spoonful of Queen's pudding into my mouth. I was relieved when he gave an accusing nod to Phillimore as he passed our table. He did not speak. We saw him stand on the step of the restaurant for a moment, looking at the traffic; and when he at last chose to cross the road and walked northward, I tried to work out which of our customers he was going to steal. But Phillimore said:

'Salter has an ulcerated stomach through living on tinned food on a hospital ship in the war. He was in the Middle East.'

Phillimore said this in a subdued enthusiastic voice. The illness, the cheatings, the plots of Salter excited Phillimore's imagination. To my uncle he talked about nothing else for days.

The year passed and another year began. I found myself growing. I spent more time in the workroom now working with my hands. I would check the timber or the cloth or help with the packing or sort certain kinds of hair and down. I was not penned in the little glass room with Miss Croft. I was free to walk about. I liked the workroom because it had a glass roof and through that one sometimes saw the white clouds smoking in the sky and I would think of the country you would be able to see if you could lie on top of one of those clouds. I liked to think that fields and woods existed, but that I too existed and was working. I wished I was in love and the wish itself was delightful, for there was no pain nor melancholy in it, no emptiness and defeat. I was in love already. I had fallen in love with myself, a lover as close as my own skin.

One morning in May the firm was delivering some chairs in the West End, and I was sent in a hired van with them, riding high up with the driver, to see that the chairs were delivered without damage to an important special customer. I did not go straight back to the office. I left the van. Up till then I had never been in a restaurant north of the Thames, but now I decided to try a place in some narrow alley of the city. One after the other I rejected. The thoughtless traveller wanders in circles. I was delighted to wander and, in fact, wandered so long that I found myself near the office and in the teashop under the arches. There I saw a most remarkable person. No, not Salter. I saw Miss Croft.

A Miss Croft I had never seen in my life before because I had never seen her outside the office. As surprised as I was, she blushed like a country rose, she smiled, she beckoned to me. Her awkwardness had gone, mine went too. Our eyes, our tongues were excited. I sat down at her table.

'Don't have the fish. It's awful,' she said. 'Dry.'

'I won't have the poached egg, either,' I said.

These two sentences seemed brilliant to us. A beautiful waitress, much more beautiful than Miss Croft, came up and looked at us sulkily. And the sneer on the waitress's face made us feel we were even more brilliant. We were escaped prisoners.

The new thing about Miss Croft was that she had put her hair up. Before it had hung, tied in a schoolgirlish black bow, on her shoulders. Now her head was lighter, like a flower which had long been sheathed

by its leaves; and her body was lighter too. She parted her lips when she
spoke instead of mumbling; the sisterly, sermonising line had gone from
her brows and she looked arch when she caught me looking at the two
small hills in her white blouse and even leaned forward to tempt and
confuse me more. For my part, I made one or two brilliant remarks about
the people in the restaurant, remarks which made her say, 'Oh, you are!'

'I'm coming to sit on your side of the table,' I said, very encouraged,
for I had the insane idea of putting my arm round her waist; but a waitress
dropped a tray and I think Miss Croft did not hear me, for she began to
talk very quickly about the only subject that really interested us: our daily
bread, the air we breathed, the latest instalment of the inner story of
Belton and Phillimore.

'Where did you take those chairs this morning?' she asked me. I parried
this. I was not sure whether I was supposed to say.

'To Naseley, wasn't it?' she said.

'Yes.'

'Mr Phillimore has gone to Somerset,' she said, 'to get money. Dadda
says there's something going on.' I ought to have said that when she
wanted to give authority to anything she said she always quoted her
father. She called him Dadda.

'Dadda says "You wait – there's another man."' She said this in the
voice a woman uses when she says 'There is another woman.'

'I don't believe it,' I said, not because I did not believe it, but because
I did not like the idea of Miss Croft having a father.

'Mr Belton and Mr Naseley are on the 'phone to each other every day.
When he says he's going out to a customer, he's going to see this Naseley.
He knows I know. I can read faces.'

She said this not in the moralising, maternal way she had had a year
before, but with a new feminine recklessness. She was tasting the new
feminine delight in saying anything that came into her head; and as she
said this she leaned forward, touching the back of her hair and looking
over the faces of the people in the restaurant, so that she could give me
another chance of looking at her throat and her neck and have the pleasure
of catching me do so.

'I can,' she said, catching me. I coloured. And then she went on to
soothe the wound:

'Why are you so vain?' she said. Then quickly changed to: 'I said to Mr Phillimore, when he left to catch the train, "I can read faces, Mr Phillimore." He looked at me. You should have seen the look he gave. Really I'm sorry for that man. He said to me, "Can you?" Just that, nothing more,' she said, her small eyes brightening. She closed her handbag and said firmly:

'Dadda says Naseley and Belton will buy him out if he doesn't get that money from his mother.' And she got up to go.

Two days later Phillimore returned from Somerset. It was clear, after he came out of my uncle's office, that there was a change in him. He had always been anxious to chatter with me, but for a while he said nothing to me. He nodded, stared, paused: there was that hissing intake of breath and then he said nothing. I became familiar.

'Coming out to lunch?' I called to him, forgetting to call him 'sir'. He looked at me coldly.

'No, Vincent,' he said, 'go to your beautiful waitress alone.'

And the next day.

'Not today, Vernon,' he said, 'but beware of the auburn glory at the Dyers and Cleaners.'

And his Adam's apple came up offensively over the top of his collar.

He said these things before Miss Croft, who laughed at me. 'Vincent is so susceptible,' she said. She looked with yearning at Mr Phillimore. Always Mr Phillimore had made the advances to everyone; now when Miss Croft seemed to be lifting herself on a dish towards him, he was taken aback. He hesitated, open-mouthed. He looked around him, like a man surrounded by plots and enemies and worked his way back to the door.

And now Miss Croft talked of nothing but Mr Phillimore. She would not leave till he left in the evening. She followed him to the end of the street. She watched his moods. She set her own by them. If he came into the room and went out without speaking – she refused to speak to me or to answer my uncle. If he spoke she would flirt with me, saying:

'He's so *serious*, Mr Phillimore. What shall we do with him?'

'Ah, youth!' began Mr Phillimore. Then he changed his mind and said in a savage way, 'I'd know what I'd do with him if I were you, Miss Croft. Look into his eyes.'

'Oh, don't, you'll make him shy.'

'Innocent!' said Mr Phillimore. 'Innocent eyes! How can you allow him to be innocent?'

Miss Croft blushed and turned indignantly away; but the indignation was for me. Both Phillimore and I gazed at her waist as she turned her back to us.

'Go away both of you,' said Miss Croft, stamping her foot. We both, to her annoyance, looked with astonishment at her foot and went away.

'The Croft,' said Phillimore, bitterly to me. 'Do you fancy the embraces of the Croft?' In his most withering way, 'All the indiscriminate vitality of a girl's secondary school going to waste,' he said. 'One almost has a duty ... No, Vernon ... With your energy, Vernon ...'

It struck me that Mr Phillimore was a man to avoid. He felt himself betrayed and looked as though, now, blindly, he would betray us all. One morning he arrived at the office a little late. His hat was on the back of his head and he had a spectacle-case in his hand. It had a spring in the lid which made it go 'Pop' when he closed it.

'Pop,' said Mr Phillimore, snapping the spectacle-case at me.

'Pop,' he said again, pointing it at Miss Croft. And then he put it to his forehead and said, 'Pop. Brains everywhere. "The balance of his mind was disturbed."'

He smelled of peppermint. I followed him out of the room. He had an attaché case in his hand. He half opened it; it was full of papers.

'Shall I just empty the lot on the top of the head of the chaste Miss Croft? Wager me I won't. Go on – wager me.'

I was alarmed, but luckily Uncle was not there. We could hear his voice in the workshop. It really was remarkable that my Uncle Belton had no idea of what was going on.

'All right,' I said.

Gloomily Phillimore picked up the attaché case, held it upside down with a finger on the lid and went back into Miss Croft's room.

'Good-bye, Mother' were the strange words which Mr Phillimore was muttering as he went in. Then he came out with the case still in his hands. 'Vernon, the bird – if that is the word – has flown.'

Poor Miss Croft had gone to cry in the lavatory.

Phillimore sat down for a little while nodding his head, and slowly his vacant face settled into a terrifying scowl. He went out to the workroom and at last Miss Croft came out. Her little eyes seemed to be full of pins and were pink-lidded with crying.

'He's drinking. Mr Belton knew he would start drinking if he went down to see his mother. He knew it. Where is he? Oh, I'm frightened. Don't let him come near me.'

I left her biting her lips. I put my arm round her, but she pushed me away.

'Dadda will make me give my notice when I tell him,' she was sobbing. 'He won't have me insulted.'

'I didn't insult you,' I said.

'Don't be a fool,' said Miss Croft.

In the workshop when I went there I heard the sound of snoring. The packer was nailing up a case, hitting the nails as loudly as he could and giving a huge wink and a nod to the other men. They were nodding at Mr Phillimore fast asleep on the heap of kapok. It was clinging to his trousers like burrs.

'He's been boozed up since four o'clock yes'day,' said the foreman. He winked. 'He's a case.'

Mr Phillimore left the office when he woke up and went away with the foreman who beckoned to two of his mates to come with them. Miss Croft and I stood on the step watching Mr Phillimore's hat, tipped back, wagging in a slowly advancing group of caps. Sometimes he stopped to put a hand on the foreman's shoulder and make a speech to him. A roar of laughter ended the speech and a man on the outside of the group swivelled round with his hands in his pockets and made a flying kick at a stone. We saw no more of Mr Phillimore for a week. The people at the boarding-house where he lived telephoned to say he had influenza.

In the early days of their marriage my Uncle Belton would have called a taxi and raced to Mr Phillimore's bedside; but now, bemused by the advance of his infidelities with Mr Naseley, he did nothing. But he did make a speech to me in the train, for the motion of a train and its isolation from the world encouraged moral reflection in my uncle.

'The important thing in life,' Uncle Belton said to me, getting out a toothpick, 'is to do the right thing. The Devil is always on the look out for our weaknesses. Two and two make four, you can't argue with the law of progress. Phillimore can't argue with it any more than I can or you can, Vincent. I am disappointed in Mr Phillimore. I said to him, multitudes, multitudes in the valley of decision, the servant who buried his talents was made to give to the others. Thou base and foolish servant. I don't want to influence nobody. I'm just putting the case as God sees it; and when Mr Naseley said something the other day about the partners in his firm, two brothers who don't get on – pretty dreadful that, isn't it, two brothers – I said, "God is my partner." Naseley said to me, "By God, Belton, you're right." I said, "*I'm* not right. God is right. He will guide us." By the way I shouldn't mention Mr Naseley's name at the office . . .'

After a week Mr Phillimore came back. He was wearing a new suit. He had a flower in his button-hole. He whistled quietly to himself. Phillimore had improved his appearance by clipping his moustache. I do not know what passed between himself and my uncle except that I heard my uncle say, 'Pull yourself together, Phillimore.'

Phillimore's manner to me was an indication: 'How's the Queen of Clapham, Vernon?' he said. 'Dusting and tidying the eternal mantelpiece of her virginity?' Then he put his fingers under my chin and tipped it up. 'What a bitch she must be, my poor boy,' he said and walked away.

Miss Croft kept the door of her room open, hoping to catch sight of him. He came in at last. She was wearing a new, pale blue frock and when she walked she made sudden half turns so that we saw the silk swimming over the full line of her leg, and she frowned when she looked back. Phillimore stopped in the doorway and clicked his tongue loudly.

'Woman,' he said, giving me a nudge. He looked very vulgar. She put on a puzzled expression which asked Mr Phillimore to explain. He just rolled his eyes. It was more than vulgar. She sat down quickly and began to type.

'I'm busy,' she said. 'Haven't you anything better to look at?'

'N'no. N'no,' said Phillimore, advancing a step and leering.

'You are being rude, Mr Phillimore,' she said. He was punctured. His boldness went. He tried to explain. She became angrier. He went.

'Sometimes,' sighed Miss Croft, 'I'm frightened of what that man will do.' And added: 'It's a new dress. Dadda says blue is my colour.'

Phillimore said to me: 'What have I done? What have you done, Vernon? Why is it that you and I are unspeakable in the eyes of that virgin? Because we must, a little while longer, presume she is one. We are innocent. We are children, Vernon. She plays with us. I beg of you, Vernon,' he said, seizing me by the shoulders and looking into my eyes: his own eyes were wild as though a pack of wolves were racing out of them towards me. 'I beg of you for the sake of the peace of this office, save us from that torture.'

I laughed. I laughed and stepped away because I thought he was going to cry and to kiss me: no, chiefly because I thought by all this acting he was laughing at me.

The hours went slowly. I did the stock books, the invoice books; then in the late afternoon I had to go and help Uncle and Phillimore in the workroom. Phillimore left us. Uncle had taken it into his head to investigate a collection of chairsprings. He hated being helped, but if you were there he obliged you to stand there and watch. I had to wait a long time before I could get step by step away from him, but at last I managed it and got back to his office. The workmen had gone and I sat reading a trade paper. Phillimore was in Miss Croft's office, sitting in his hat and coat. He too was waiting for my uncle. Miss Croft was not there. She was washing her hands and I saw her, through the open door, pass across the room and go to get her hat and coat. It was very quiet now the lathes had stopped and the evening cries of children in the street could be heard now the traffic had gone.

Suddenly I heard Mr Phillimore's voice. It was bold and decisive, the voice he had been training for use on our telephone.

'Duckie,' I heard him say. 'Don't be cross.' No answer.

'I say don't be cross.'

'I'm not cross.'

'You look it.'

Miss Croft was picking up her things.

'I must fly,' she said.

'Fly, fly,' he said. 'My wings are broken. The wings of youth are strong.'

'Don't,' said Miss Croft.

'Take me in your strong wings,' said Mr Phillimore.

'Oh, don't,' said Miss Croft.

Phillimore had got up and they were now both out of my sight.

'On your strong wings . . .' he was saying.

'I must catch my train,' she said.

'I am wrecked. My life is ruined . . .'

'I'll miss it if I don't dash,' she said.

'Dash,' he muttered very loudly. 'Yes, dash. Don't you understand, I love you!' The sounds suggested that Mr Phillimore had jumped across the room, or was about to do so. A chair fell over. 'You say, dash,' I heard him say.

And then a screech came from Miss Croft. I ran into the room. There was Mr Phillimore with one foot standing on his hat, holding Miss Croft in his arms and trying to kiss her, and she was pushing away from him not with anger, but with an unnecessarily helpless, sulky expression.

'I'll miss my train,' she was saying breathlessly. And then her face settled, she looked him in the eyes, stiffened, opened her mouth in a manner that I thought was inviting, but instead of a kiss, a high, pure, perfectly calculated and piercing scream came out of her. It was a marvel. By the fight in her little eyes I would have said it was a challenge. She waited to see what Mr Phillimore would do. My uncle came running up the passage and arrived with a plonk like a bouncing ball in the room.

Phillimore loosened his grip and the girl wriggled away. At the sight of my uncle she broke into tears.

'I . . .' gasped Phillimore. 'I – I – was – saying – good-bye – to Miss Croft.'

'Phillimore,' said my uncle.

'Good-bye,' said Phillimore to me. He did not look at my uncle. 'Dash,' he said.

And before we knew more about it, he *had* dashed. He dashed from the room and Uncle's new horn-rimmed glasses fell off.

'Oh – he's gone,' said Miss Croft, looking at the empty doorway. We all looked at it. But in a second he was back, a scornful face printed with derision which did not look at Miss Croft or myself but stared at Uncle Belton.

'I forgot to tell you I'm joining Salter's,' he said ironically. And then his self-control went: 'That's what you've all done to me.' This time he went for good. Uncle Belton and Miss Croft stepped towards each other instinctively.

'Oh, Mr Belton, did you hear?' she said. 'How awful.

'Mr Belton,' she said, 'the deceit.' She put her hand on my uncle's coat-sleeve; but he was simply staring. He always stood square-shouldered and now his shoulders seemed to spread wider. He was very pale, as pale as a loaf of bread. He still did not speak, but slowly sat down in a chair.

'The double-crossing swine,' he said.

It was quite simple, my Uncle Belton explained to me. When he had seen that Mr Phillimore was not going to keep his promise and bring in more capital, he had had to look elsewhere. It was hard to credit, but Mr Phillimore thought he had been badly treated – said 'I wasn't open with him' – and all the time he was seeing Salter! 'But there is a law of justice in the world,' Uncle said with a smile. 'Salter is on the point of bankruptcy.'

There were no more flowers on the desk now until Miss Croft started bringing them. She devoted herself to my uncle and every day came out with little pieces of news about the wickedness of Mr Phillimore. I saw him once, it must have been eighteen months later. He was standing on London Bridge looking up at a high building where a man was cleaning windows.

'I should die,' I heard him say to someone in the crowd. Then he saw me. He bared his teeth as if he were going to spit, but changed his mind. His look suggested that I was the most ridiculous thing on earth, as he turned away.

Pocock Passes

—

The cities fall, but what survives? It is the common, patient, indigenous grass. After Mr Pocock's death this thought lay in a muddle in Rogers's mind; if Rogers had a mind. He was enormously fat; a jellyfish which is washed and rocked by sensations and not by thought. The Wilcoxes, the Stockses and Rogerses, the three ordinary, far-back tribes who made the village, alone had history; and this plain corporate history, like the eternal grass, choked out the singular blooms. The death of a Rogers is something. A card is shuffled into another pack and he joins the great phalanx of village Rogerses beyond the grave, formidable in their anonymity. But the death of a stranger like Pocock, who had been in the place only a few months, was like a motor smash. Vivid but trivial, it sank out of village memory to the bottom of time.

Rogers admitted to himself that he had had a fright. Mr Pocock had been a man of fifty like himself, as fat as Rogers was, too – they had compared waist measurements once – and he drank heavily: that came home rather close. So close that although Rogers was Mr Pocock's only friend in the last months of his life, Rogers could not bring himself to go to the funeral. He put on his black to show willingness, but at the hour of the funeral slipped on the doorstep and twisted his knee and had to be kept in his house. With a sort of penitence or hoping for a last order, Askew, the village publican, went – he followed all his customers to the end – and came back saying:

'Mr Pocock, he drank too much. I often tried to stop him.'

Then it was that Rogers, who had gone down to the pub once the funeral was over and Pocock was set in his grave – then it was that Rogers saw a profound truth:

'You're wrong there,' he said.

'He didn't drink too much,' he said. 'The trouble with Mr Pocock was that he didn't drink enough.'

One thing the death of Mr Pocock did for Rogers was to make him stay at home. There was nothing to go out for. Outside was the road, the village, the four-eyed faces of the villas called Heart's Desire Estate which Rogers had built on the flat fields and had sold before anyone had discovered that the site was a water meadow. There was his wooden hut too, where he slept over the typewriter sometimes, and with its Estate Agent's plate on the door. His wife ran his business now – such as it was. Above all this was the sky. He was inclined to see a hole in things like the street or sky after Pocock's death, a hole with simply nothing beyond it. Staying at home with his family kept Rogers from seeing the hole. Hearing his wife use the typewriter or telephone in the office, drinking a cup of tea, listening to his two girls, torpidly watching them, his slow mind lay down like a dog in the domestic basket. 'Wife and family – you're lucky, ol' boy,' Mr Pocock had said many times in his husky, half-rapacious voice. Rogers brooded. Perhaps he, surviving, was the better man.

Yet with all his heart and with some plain builder's shrewdness and village vanity, Rogers had wanted to believe in the singularity of Mr Pocock. People came down from London and took a house in old age, and when they died, these strangers always turned out to be less than they had at first seemed to be. He was used to that. A handful of dust – often scandalous dust – was all they were against the great tribal burial mound of the village Wilcoxes, Stockses and Rogerses. Pocock had not only looked different but had sounded different and behaved accordingly. Yet the death of Pocock had left in Rogers's mind some suspicion of fraud – indeterminate yet disturbing, like waking in the night and thinking you smell a carpet smouldering, and yet no coal on it when you get out to look.

Pocock was a painter. Not only that, he was a well-known painter from London; he knew other painters. Not only other painters, but studios and actresses. He knew the stage. Yet after the ambulance went like a soft clap of low white wings between the hedges of the main road, taking Pocock to the hospital and his end, Rogers said to people who had come to look at property: 'We had Pocock here.' They merely said blankly, 'What's that? Never heard of him.' No one at all had heard of Mr Pocock, the famous painter.

Rogers and Mr Pocock had come together not because of their minds or tastes, but because of their bodies. They were drawn will-lessly together by the magnetic force of their phenomenal obesities. There is a loneliness in fat. Atlas met Atlas, astonished to find each saddened by the burden of a world. Rogers was short and had that douce, pleading melancholy of the enormous. His little blue eyes, above the bumps of fat on his cheek-bones, looked like sinking lights at sea; and he had the gentle and bewildered air of a man who watches himself daily getting uncontrollably and hopelessly fatter. His outsize navy blue jacket hung on him like another man's overcoat. The coarseness and grossness of his appearance, the spread of his nostrils, the crease of his neck, gave him a pathos: there is an inherent delicacy, a dignity and spirituality in pork. He lived in a quiet sedentary fever in which, as his own bounds daily grew, the world seemed farther away to him. His gentleness was like that of the blind, indicating how far he was from other people. There was no one like him in the village. Rogers was a show-piece. His visits to the public-house were a hopeless try for gregariousness, but there were no seats broad enough in the tap, it didn't 'do' for him to go to the bar where his workmen were and, anyway, there were no seats in it. He went instead to the small parlour and was usually there alone, like a human exhibit, with an aspidistra and a picture of Edward VII.

Rogers's first impression, as he came into the parlour one night, was that an enormous bull terrier in a black-and-white chessboard jacket had got up on to a chair in the darker corner.

Rogers's perceptions were slow; but at last he saw the figure was a man and not a dog. Between the check suit and check cloth-hat was a face, a raw-meat face which had grown a grey moustache, and under that was a small, furiously proud and querulous mouth. An old dog who would fly out at you if spoken to. The check coat went on to check knickerbockers. There was a rose in Pocock's buttonhole – the smell of the rose and of Turkish cigarettes in the room – and he had a spotted bow to his collar. But what surprised Rogers, after he had said 'good evening' and was leaning forward with the usual difficulty to tap the bell on the table, was the stranger's voice. Husky, swaggering, full-tempered, it said, daring you to contradict and yet somehow weary: 'What are you having, old boy?'

Deep called unto deep: Rogers saw to his astonishment, not a stranger, but a brother. Not his blood brother, of course, but something closer – a brother in obesity.

Mr Pocock's was a different kind of fatness, tight where Rogers's was loose, dynamic where Rogers's was passive and poetic, aggressive where Rogers's was silkily receptive. Mr Pocock's pathos was fiery and bitter. A pair of stiffly inflated balloons seemed to have been placed, one under and one above Mr Pocock's waist-line, and the load forced his short legs apart on either side of the chair, like the splayed speckled legs of a frog. And there was another bond. Mr Pocock, it was evident, was a drinker. A gentleman, too (Rogers observed), as the evening went on, arrogantly free with money. A sportsman also. There were a couple of illustrated papers on the table and one had a photograph of tropical game. A peeress had taken these photographs. One showed a hippopotamus rising like a sofa out of a lake.

'Damn' cruel, old boy,' said Mr Pocock in a grating gasp, having an imaginary row with the aristocracy and Rogers about it. 'All these bloody white women following poor defenceless animals around with cameras, old boy. Bloody hippopotamus can't even drink in peace. Animals much sooner be shot, old boy – what?'

Yes, Mr Pocock was a sportsman, a blaspheming sportsman of some elegance, for now Rogers noticed a couple of rings on one hand.

Yet not a sportsman, after all, for he looked bored when Rogers spoke of the duck and snipe and the teal which float like commas on the meres at the back of the village.

'Can't eat it, old boy,' replied Pocock. 'Game's poison to me. Bloody waste of time following birds, if you ask me. Need every ounce of daylight for my work.'

The bell on the table was tapped again and again. In and out went Askew, the publican. Even he straightened up under the snapping orders of Mr Pocock.

And there was no reserve in Mr Pocock. His talk was free and self-explanatory. 'I've come down here to see if there is anything,' said Pocock. 'If there is, well and good. If not, all right. There may be something.'

('What?' wondered Rogers.)

'I've got to, old boy,' said Mr Pocock. 'I've got to cut down the overheads. Have another, old boy? With this bloody crisis,' he said with an angry and frightened look in his eyes. 'I had my own studio in London and a housekeeper, but with this crisis, and the critics in league against you, the bottom's gone out of things. There may be something here – I don't know – two rooms, a bed, a table, do my own cleaning up and cooking – that's all I want and no women about. No,' said Mr Pocock, 'no more women.'

'You married, old boy?' asked Mr Pocock.

'Yes,' said Rogers.

'You're lucky, old boy,' said Mr Pocock. 'Bloody lucky. Excuse my language, old boy, but woman's a b . . .'

'Oh, fifty-fifty,' said Rogers, not clear whether he meant only half lucky or wholly lucky to have a wife he could share everything with, she doing the office work and looking after his house while he built up his figure and did the drinking. For Rogers had reached the point of saturation in his own life when drinking was work. It never stopped.

Rogers's slow mind wanted to explain, but Pocock interrupted.

'I know, old boy. You can't tell me anything about women. They're a bloody question-mark, old boy. There's two answers to it, one's right and one's wrong. When I want what I want, I don't ask anyone's opinion, I go and get it.'

'What?' added Mr Pocock.

'You're right,' said Rogers in his slow, groping voice. 'You know the story of the couple who . . .'

They didn't laugh out loud at the story. Rogers shook and shook and his eyes sank out of sight. Mr Pocock strained in his chair and seemed to fizz with austere pleasure like a bottle of soda-water.

'It's nature,' said Mr Pocock when his head stopped fizzing.

Rogers was out of his depth here. His head was lolling forward. He had reached the stage when Mr Pocock had a tendency to rise to the ceiling and then to drift away sideways towards the door in great numbers.

'Take salmon,' said Rogers heavily, this coming into his mind at the moment.

'Salmon, old boy? Why bloody salmon?' said Mr Pocock.

'They go . . .' said Rogers. 'They go – up fresh water.'

'Salmon?' said Mr Pocock. 'Salmon? They come from the sea.'

'They don't breed in it,' said Rogers uncertainly. He was beginning to forget why he had mentioned them.

'I know,' said Mr Pocock peremptorily. 'They live in the sea and go up the river when they feel like it.'

'Feel like it,' repeated Rogers. Somewhere near here was the reason for raising the matter.

'. . . I've seen 'em, old boy,' continued Mr Pocock, putting down his glass with a bang.

'Out of the sea,' insisted Rogers.

'Don't be bloody funny, old boy,' said Mr Pocock, banging his glass again. 'We know they do.'

The landlord called 'Time'.

Rogers and Mr Pocock got up with common difficulty, exchanging a look of sympathy. Foot by foot, after they had unbent, stopping between paragraphs, they talked and stopped their way out of the public-house and outside its door. Facing the night, surprised by it, they halted again. The moon arrested them. It was a white full moon, the most obese of planets, with its little mouth open in the sad face.

'Just made for an artist, I should say,' said Rogers, slapped across the face by the cold wind, but warm within in his linings. Yet as a villager he had an obscure feeling that for a London stranger to paint the place insulted it. His feeling was primitive; he did not want the magic of an alien eye upon his home.

'It *used* to be pretty, old boy,' said Mr Pocock. 'Till some bastard ran up those bloody villas.'

'I put them up ten years ago', said Rogers dispassionately; and he meant that time justified and forgave all things.

'Good God, old boy. Bloody ugly,' fizzed Mr Pocock.

They stared at the villas and grinned, almost sniggered, like boys peeping through a fence at something shocking. It gave Rogers and Mr Pocock pleasure, they being human, to know the worst about each other. And as they gazed with tenderness upon the raped virgin, the sight started Pocock's mind on his own affairs and prompted him to the words which were the final thing to bind Rogers to him.

'I don't mind telling you, old boy, I've been hurt,' Mr Pocock said. 'I've had a jerk. I haven't told a bloody soul so far, but I'll tell you. *Last year I started living on my capital.*'

Rogers turned his back on Mr Pocock and affected to look up the road for traffic. It was empty. All lights in the village houses were out. He felt a stirring of the bowels. His wife did not know, he hardly let himself know – but he, too, had passed the crest of his life, he, too, was beginning the first harassed footsteps downhill, crumbling away to pieces like a town in a fog, and no one, hitherto, to watch or share the process. Rogers also had started living on his capital.

After this, day by day, they sought each other out like two dogs. First of all they were halting and suspicious. Rogers said: 'Have you been painting, Mr Pocock?' but this was not, he discovered, a welcome question. Mr Pocock replied that he was sizing up the situation. Midday, Mr Pocock could always be found sizing things up at The Grapes or The Waggoner. He was sizing up and settling in. And, anyway, he hadn't been feeling too well lately.

'Been having trouble with my foot,' said Mr Pocock defiantly at Rogers.

'It's the weight you carry,' said Rogers. 'I get it myself.'

Mr Pocock, as one heavy drinker to another, appreciated the tact of that lie.

'I keep clear of doctors, old boy,' said Mr Pocock. 'Always have.'

'They cut you down,' said Rogers, emptying his glass.

'All wrong, old boy,' said Mr Pocock. 'Want to kill you.'

At night they met like lovers. They were religious drinkers. Whisky was Mr Pocock's religion, beer was the faith of Rogers. An active faith ranges widely. After the public-houses of the village there were two or three on the main road. The headlights of cars howling through the dark to the coast picked out two balloons in coats and trousers, bouncing and blowing down the road. Dramas halted them.

'What's that, old boy?'

'Rabbit.'

'No, old boy, not a rabbit. It was a fox. I know a fox.'

'I reckon it was a stoat.'

The point became intricate under the stars.

'Bring Mr Pocock in to supper one evening,' Mrs Rogers said. She was a plump, practical woman, with hair set like a teacake. She was a one-time nurse, abnormally good-tempered, pleasantly unimaginative. She ate well and enjoyed the anxiety of being the business management of an exhibit-like her husband. Incapable herself of his deterioration, hers was the craving, so strong in the orderly and new, for its opposite, the romantic ruin. Rogers, like many men, and especially drinking men, who neglect their wives and are slowly ruining their families, had an ideal picture of his family in his mind, a picture to which his fancy was always putting more delicate touches of reminiscence. For, like all the world beyond his hazy corpulence, his family became remote, a little farther away each day, like a memory or an old master.

'Bloody funny thing, old boy,' Mr Pocock said. 'When I paint a picture, I get the feeling I have for a woman.'

It was Rogers's feeling about his own picture, of his family, that private masterpiece of his. Rogers wasn't interested in any other pictures; Mr Pocock wasn't interested in domestic life. And The Crown was placed strategically between their homes.

About once every couple of months, Mr Pocock hinted, he 'broke out'. He always had. He always would. There was a large manufacturing town with a river, pleasure-boats and a Hippodrome twenty miles away, where life, said Rogers, abounded. He and Mr Pocock put roses in their buttonholes, cigars in their mouths and went. Rogers explained that he hadn't seen quite so much life since he was married, but when he was a youngster ... Oh, dear. This stirred up memories in Mr Pocock. They arrived and, to make a start, went to the station buffet. After this the past was vivid. They went to the Hippodrome for the second act of a play about divorce. The seats were narrow and Mr Pocock said he couldn't breathe. They left. Mr Pocock said all this modern stuff was dirty. Nothing but sex. (What's yours, old boy?) Dirt, like Epstein and Cézanne.

The last train back was the 12.17. It brought the Hippodrome people. For a long time the station with its hoardings and iron and glass façade seemed unattainable, but at last, after a long time on the kerb opposite, they rushed it. The train was crowded. Rogers had been sorry to leave the Hippodrome. He smiled, wagging his head, thinking about it, then he began to laugh and nudge his neighbours. They were soon entertained by Rogers. It was like the old days.

[231]

'I've been divorced today,' Rogers suddenly said; 'and he's my co-respondent.' Mr Pocock at once offered him a cigarette. Rogers refused.

'Why do you refuse my cigarettes, old boy?' Mr Pocock asked abruptly. He was out for a quarrel.

'Do you think I want your wife?' exclaimed Mr Pocock angrily. Rogers laughed idiotically.

'Because you're a swine if you do,' said Mr Pocock.

But they didn't fight. They got out at their station, helped out by the passengers, and the guard, while the engine-driver watched from the cab. They passed Rogers's villas.

'Damned awful, old boy,' said Mr Pocock.

'Come in,' said Rogers when they got to his house.

A look of sobered terror came into Mr Pocock's face.

'Your wife in?' he said.

'She's in bed,' Rogers said.

'Thank God,' said Mr Pocock. 'I'm drunk.'

'Come in,' said Rogers.

'She'd hear my language,' said Mr Pocock. Rogers opened the door and led the way into the sitting-room.

Mr Pocock sat down while Rogers went to the whisky-bottle.

'It's empty, old man,' Rogers said, looking blankly at Mr Pocock.

'Thank God, old boy.' Mr Pocock stood appalled, like a man who had never been in an inhabited house before. He looked shocked. He saw with horror the cretonne-covered sofa, the photographs, the slim silver vases with maidenhair fern in them.

'She's taken the other one away and put this one here.'

'Women,' said Mr Pocock.

They stared at each other.

'Come round to my place,' said Mr Pocock.

Still talking, they went out, leaving the door open. A woman's head appeared at the window.

'Alfred!' the voice called.

Rogers stopped and stared at Mr Pocock. Mr Pocock stared back like a fierce dog at Rogers.

'Better answer, old boy,' said Mr Pocock, banging his stick on the ground.

'Yes,' called Rogers.

'Had a good time?' said the woman's voice. They could not see her in the darkness, but Mr Pocock raised his hat.

'Better go,' he whispered.

He went off alone. Rogers followed him at last. Mr Pocock's house was the last of a row of labourers' cottages, one room and the scullery downstairs and two little rooms up. Now Rogers was shocked by what he saw. In the downstairs room was an old bit of carpet laid to the edge of a cooking range, and the carpet was stained with grease. Tins and the remains of a meal were on the table. Mr Pocock used only one of the rooms upstairs. They went up. Its boards were bare. There was a suitcase on the floor and there was an iron bed and a chair. The place smelled of mice and also of the smoking candle stuck on the mantelpiece. They sat down.

'That's what I ought to have done – got married,' said Mr Pocock. His face looked greenish in the candlelight. 'Bloody lonely without a woman, old boy.'

'There's a woman,' Mr Pocock exclaimed violently. There were canvases stacked against the dirty wall. He turned one round. He filled his glass. What Rogers saw shocked him. It was the picture of a thin, dark-haired woman sitting on a bed, naked. Not lascivious, not beautiful, not enticing, just naked and seeming to say, 'It don't feel natural, I mean having nothing on.'

'Oh dear, oh dear,' was all Rogers could say. He went hot. It was the painting of the bed that shocked him. Mr Pocock seemed to him a monster.

Mr Pocock began to boast and Rogers hardly listened. There was a bottle of whisky. Rogers's eye kept going with astonishment to the picture. A dancer, Mr Pocock said. He knew all the stage crowd, he said. Could have had her, he said. Words and words came out of Mr Pocock, gobbling and strutting like a blown-out turkey in the room, words making an ever-softening roar in the set, cold silence of the cottage where no clock ticked.

Suddenly Rogers had a shock. It was daylight. He had been asleep on the floor and the sun was shining on him. He gaped. There was Mr Pocock on the bed. Still holding his cane, the rings shining on his podgy fingers which had grey hair at the knuckles, Mr Pocock lay. He was

[233]

snoring. His body heaved up and down in the loud suit, like a marquee with the wind loose in it. Remote in sleep with his picture above him, Mr Pocock looked sacred and innocent, in the bare room.

The spring came with its glassy winds, its air going warm and cold and the lengthening light becoming frail in the evenings. Rogers and Mr Pocock were both ill. Rogers received illness as part of his burden; he was more aware of his wife and of his children when he was ill. But Mr Pocock was an aggressive invalid. He saw conspiracy. He was terrified and he blustered to conceal this and made war on the doctor. He would not stay in bed.

'Kimble thinks he's got me, old boy. Knocked off my beer and cut me down to two whiskies a day. It isn't right! It isn't human! He's got to be fair.'

When Rogers got up they met in the pub.

'I've had seven, old boy,' Mr Pocock said. 'But if Kimble says anything to you about what I drink – it's two. I've treated him fairly. I've been reasonable. That man wants to kill me. But not a word to him! You've got to deal with these doctors.'

First of all when he had come to the village Mr Pocock had a charwoman to clean and wash up for him, but he was hardly ever in his cottage and he ate at any time. He had got rid of the charwoman and looked after himself. He had brought his bed downstairs when he was first ill because he had been frightened in the upstairs room. One night he felt tired and low. A bus-ride had upset him. He went to bed early. In the middle of the night he woke up in black terror. He felt sick and he was fainting, and he was sure he was in London. He reached for his stick and knocked on the floor to make the woman come up to him, the woman whose portrait Rogers had seen and who lived downstairs. All the night sleeping and waking he dreamed he was knocking to make himself heard on the floor. For the model, then for Mrs Rogers, then for his mother.

In the morning he could hardly move. Then he remembered he was on the ground floor and had been knocking on the carpet which covered the flags, which covered the earth. He had been knocking on the hard crust of the earth. All he could do was to crawl from his bed to the cupboard where the whisky-bottle was and then crawl back. But he called no one; he stiffened with anger if there were any signs of anyone coming to the door. He was not going to be caught like this. He was not going to admit anything. He cursed the doctor.

It was two days before Mr Pocock's illness was discovered.

'Mr Pocock's ill,' Rogers's wife brought the news. She knew all the illnesses of the village.

Rogers sat up, alert. He was at once frightened for himself. He did not want to see Mr Pocock before the doctor had been. Rogers sat in his chair, unable to move. He wanted to do something for Mr Pocock, but he was paralysed. He sat in a stupor of inertia and incompetence. He looked appealingly at his wife. She got a car and had Mr Pocock brought to the house.

'It's the bloody sugar, old boy,' murmured Mr Pocock with a regal weariness as three men carried him upstairs.

Mrs Rogers was glad when the ambulance came that, for once in his life, Mr Pocock had had a real home with a woman to look after him.

That was the last of him.

A dealer came down to look at the pictures after the funeral, but he would not take them. One or two others came hoping for frames. But the twenty-odd canvases there had no frames on them. A brother came down to clear up Mr Pocock's affairs.

'We never corresponded,' said the brother. Of all things he was a clergyman.

Two fair and tall young men in suede shoes and pullovers, so alike they looked like a pair of tap dancers, turned up at the same time. They *were* tap-dancers.

'Terrible,' they said. They were looking at the pictures; but Rogers supposed they referred to the death, the poverty of the house – or perhaps the clergyman. Rogers had been told by Mr Pocock that in reward for his kindness he might have one of the pictures, but he did not know which to choose. The only picture he felt anything about was the picture on the bedroom wall, the nude. He detested it.

'Women,' he thought, 'that must have been Mr Pocock's trouble. Not drink. Oh dear, not drink, women.' So when everyone had gone, he took the small picture, wrapped it in newspaper and put it in a shed in his garden. That picture, and a corkscrew which he stuffed in his pocket, because a corkscrew was useful. He took the picture because, without knowing it, he felt it symbolised the incomprehensibility of the existence of other people. The corkscrew was the man he knew, the picture the man he did not know at all. He thought that one day he had better destroy the picture – in case a bad impression of his friend was formed.

And so, slipping out of the funeral, keeping in the background afterwards, staying in his own house, Rogers eluded the memory of Mr Pocock. Rogers was forgetting everything as he grew larger. He forgot yesterday, last week, last year – he dreamed through time like an idle whale, with its mouth open, letting what would come into it. He contemplated through a haze his own work of art – his family. He watched his wife's second chin when she gave her practical laugh. His two girls swam up to him like fish. They were an extra pair of eyes and ears for him. They saw things quickly. They laughed at things long before he heard them. On Saturdays he took them to the cinema. Every Saturday. A year passed, and then two years. He never said now: 'We had Mr Pocock, the painter, here.' He had learned his lesson.

And then came the most extraordinary fortnight of Rogers's life. He was with his daughters in the cinema. They were watching a gangster film. A film four years old: they only got the old films in these country towns. Two men were going quietly up the stairs of an hotel and then along a corridor. It was at night. They were making for the room where a Mexican, behind closed doors, was covering a girl with a gun. But they were not sure of the room. They hesitated at doors. It was trying for Rogers, because his mind was still in the pillared lounge below, reminded by it that he was living on his capital. How had the Mexican got the girl in the room? Then the two men stopped. One said 'OK,' and they pushed open a door marked 13 and switched on the light. Rogers's daughters jumped in their seats and a shout of laughter came from the audience. A large, round-faced man with a huge stomach was lying on a bed in check suit and knickerbockers, asleep and snoring, with a bottle, rolled on its side, near by.

'Mr Pocock!' the girls shouted.

It was. Rogers's heart went small in his chest and seemed to shoot like a stone in his throat. The gangsters rolled their eyes ironically. The audience laughed. One of the gangsters picked up the bottle and made to prod Mr Pocock with it. The audience sent up blast after blast of laughter;

especially shrill laughter went up first from the children in front. The other gangster touched his friend's arm, raised his eyes to the ceiling and said: 'RIP.' Wave after wave of laughter passed by as the snores stopped and then began again like a car toiling and missing up hill.

'It's Mr Pocock, Mr Pocock, Dad,' Rogers's daughters cried, jumping on their seats. And the laughter went on. For the achievement of Mr Pocock was that he did nothing, nothing at all. He just lay and snored, the human balloon.

Rogers couldn't believe it.

It became urgent for him after this to decide the matter. Films in the town moved down the road, ten or twenty miles to the next place in the week. Four times he followed that film in a fortnight. Four times he saw that scene. It was unmistakably Pocock. And each place the audience roared until one night at the Hippodrome where it was the big picture, he heard a packed house shout out with enthusiasm at Pocock's sublime unconsciousness. He had three minutes of the film, but those three minutes brought the house down.

It terrified Rogers. Pocock was lying exactly as Rogers had seen him that morning after the binge when he had woken up in Pocock's cottage. He dreaded that the eyes would open, the voice speak. And then, after the sixth time of seeing the film, as he walked home down the village street he longed to meet that preposterous figure, to slap him on the back and tell him. He longed for him to wake up on the screen and hear that helpless applause, to see those wide open laughing mouths. 'He kept it quiet,' thought Rogers. And the drowning soul saw no irony in it all; but rather felt that life was incomprehensible no more. Something had been settled.

When he took the picture from his garden shed and burned it on the rubbish heap soon after, Rogers heard in the husky roar of the flame the sound of a soul set free, all stain removed.

The Oedipus Complex

─────

'Good morning, Mr P.,' said Mr Pollfax, rinsing and drying his hands after the last patient. 'How's Mr P.?' I was always Mr P. until I sat in the chair and he switched the lamp on and had my mouth open. Then I got a peerage.

'That's fine, my lord,' said Mr Pollfax, having a look inside.

Dogged, with its slight suggestion of doggish, was the word for Mr Pollfax. He was a short man, jaunty, hair going thin with jaunty buttocks and a sway to his walk. He had two lines, from habitual grinning, cut deep from the nostrils, and scores of lesser lines like the fine hair of a bird's nest round his egg-blue eyes. There was something innocent, heroic and determined about Mr Pollfax, something of the English Tommy in tin hat and full pack going up the line. He suggested in a quiet way – war.

He was the best dentist I ever had. He got you into the chair, turned on the light, tapped around a bit with a thing like a spoon and then, dropping his white-coated arm to his side, told you a story. Several more stories followed in his flat Somerset voice, when he had your mouth jacked up. And then removing the towel and with a final 'Rinse that lot out', he finished with the strangest story of all and let you go. A month or so later the bill came in. Mr Pollfax presents his compliments and across the bottom of it, in his hand, 'Be good.' I have never known a dentist like Mr Pollfax.

'Open, my lord,' said Mr Pollfax. 'Let's see what sort of life his lordship has been leading. Still smoking that filthy pipe, I see. I shall have to do some cleaning up.'

He tapped around and then dropped his arm. A look of anxiety came on his face. 'Did I tell you that one about the girl who went to the Punch and Judy show? No? Nor the one about the engine-driver who was put on sentry duty in Syria? You're sure? When did I see you last? What was the last one I told you? That sounds like last April? Lord, you *have* been letting things go. Well,' said Mr Pollfax, tipping back my head and squirting something on to a tooth, 'we'll have a go at that root at the back. It's not doing you any good. It was like this. There was a girl sitting on the beach at Barmouth with her young man watching a Punch and Judy show . . .' (Closer and closer came Mr Pollfax's head, lower and lower went his voice.)

He took an instrument and began chipping his way through the tooth and the tale.

'Not bad, eh?' he said, stepping back with a sudden shout of laughter.

'Ah,' I mouthed.

'All right, my lord,' said Mr Pollfax, withdrawing the instrument and relapsing into his dead professional manner. 'Spit that lot out.'

He began again.

There was just that root, Mr Pollfax was saying. It was no good there. There was nothing else wrong; he'd have it out in a couple of shakes.

'Though, my lord,' he said, 'you did grow it about as far back in your throat as you could, didn't you, trying to make it as difficult as you could for Mr Pollfax? What we'll do first of all is to give it a dose of something.'

He swivelled the dish of instruments towards me and gave a tilt to the lamp. I remembered that lamp because once the bulb had exploded, sending glass all over the room. It was fortunate, Mr Pollfax said at the time, that it had blown the other way and none of it had hit me, for someone might have brought a case for damages against someone – which reminded him of the story of the honeymoon couple who went to a small hotel in Aberdeen . . .

'Now,' said Mr Pollfax, dipping things in little pots and coming to me with an injection needle; 'open wide, keep dead still. I was reading Freud the other day. There's a man. Oedipus complex? Ever read about that? Don't move, don't breathe, you'll feel a prick, but for God's sake don't jump. I don't want it to break in your gum. I've never had one break yet, touch wood, but they're thin, and if it broke off you'd be in a nursing home three weeks and Mr Pollfax would be down your throat looking for it. The trouble about these little bits of wire is they move a bit farther into the system every time you swallow.

'There now,' said Mr Pollfax.

'Feel anything? Feel it prick?' he said. 'Fine.'

He went to a cupboard and picked out the instrument of extraction and then stood, working it up and down like a gardener's secateurs in his hand. He studied my face. He was a clean-shaven man and looked like a priest in his white coat.

'Some of the stories you hear!' exclaimed Mr Pollfax. 'And some of the songs. I mean where I come from. "The Lot that Lily Lost in the Lottery" – know that one? Is your skin beginning to tingle, do you feel it on the tip of your tongue yet? That's fine, my lord. I'll sing it to you.'

Mr Pollfax began to sing. He'd give it another minute, he said, when he'd done with Lily; he'd just give me the chorus of 'The Night Uncle's Waistcoat Caught Fire'.

'Tra la la,' sang Mr Pollfax.

'I bet,' said Mr Pollfax sadistically, 'one side of his lordship's face has gone dead and his tongue feels like a pin cushion.'

'Blah,' I said.

'I think,' he said, 'we'll begin.'

So Mr Pollfax moved round to the side of me, got a grip on my shoulders and began to press on the instrument in my mouth. Pressing and drawing firmly he worked upon the root. Then he paused and increased the pressure. He seemed to be hanging from a crowbar fixed to my jaw. Nothing happened. He withdrew.

'The Great Flood begins,' said Mr Pollfax putting a tube in my mouth and taking another weapon from the tray.

The operation began again. Mr Pollfax now seemed to hang and swing on the crowbar. It was not successful.

'Dug himself in, has he?' muttered Mr Pollfax. He had a look at his instruments. 'You can spit, my lord,' he said.

Mr Pollfax now seized me with great determination, hung, swung, pressed and tugged with increased energy.

'It's no good you thinking you're going to stay in,' said Mr Pollfax in mid-air, muttering to the root. But the instrument slipped and a piece of tooth broke off as he spoke.

'So that's the game is it?' said Mr Pollfax withdrawing. 'Good rinse, my lord, while Mr Pollfax considers the position.'

He was breathing hard.

Oh well, he said, there were more ways than one of killing a cat. He'd get the drill on it. There were two Jews standing outside Buckingham Palace when a policeman came by, he said, coming at me with the drill which made a whistling noise like a fishing line as he drew it through. The tube gurgled in my mouth. I was looking, as I always did at Mr Pollfax's, at the cowls busily twirling on the chimneys opposite. Wind or no wind these cowls always seemed to be twirling round. Two metal cowls on two yellow chimneys. I always remember them.

'Spit, my lord,' said Mr Pollfax, changing to a coarser drill. 'Sorry old man, if it slipped, but Mr Pollfax is not to be beaten.'

The drill whirred again, skidding and whining; the cowls twirled on the chimneys, Mr Pollfax's knuckles were on my nose. What he was trying to do, he said, was to get a purchase.

Mr Pollfax's movements got quicker. He hung up the drill, he tapped impatiently on the tray, looking for something. He came at me with something like a button-hook. He got it in. He levered like a signal man changing points.

'I'm just digging,' he said. Another piece of tooth broke off.

Mr Pollfax started when he heard it go and drew back.

'Mr Pollfax in a dilemma,' he said.

Well, he'd try the other side. Down came the drill again. There were beads of sweat on his brow. His breath was shorter.

'You see,' exclaimed Mr Pollfax suddenly and loudly, looking angrily up at his clock. 'I'm fighting against time. Keep that head this way, hold the mouth. That's right. Sorry, my lord, I've got to bash you about, but time's against me.'

'Why, damn this root,' said Mr Pollfax, hanging up again. 'It's wearing out my drill. We'll have to saw. Mr Pollfax *is* up against it.'

His face was red now, he was gasping and his eyes were glittering. A troubled and emotional look came over Mr Pollfax's face.

'I've been up against it in my time,' exclaimed Mr Pollfax forcefully between his teeth. 'You heard me mention the Oedipus complex to you?'

'Blah,' I managed.

'I started well by ruining my father. I took every penny he had. That's a good start, isn't it?' he said, speaking very rapidly. 'Then I got married. Perfectly happy marriage, but I went and bust it up. I went off with a French girl and her husband shot at us out in the car one day. I was with that girl eighteen months and she broke her back in a railway accident and I sat with her six months watching her die. Six ruddy months. I've been through it. Then my mother died and my father was going to marry again, a girl young enough to be his daughter. I went up and took that girl off him, ran off to Hungary with her, married her and we've got seven children. Perfect happiness at last. I've been through the mill,' said Mr Pollfax, relaxing his chin and shining a torch down my mouth, 'but I've come out in the end.

'A good rinse, my noble lord,' said Mr Pollfax.

'The oldest's fourteen,' he said, getting the saw. 'Clever girl. Very clever with her hands.'

He seized me again. Did I feel anything? Well, thank God for that, said Mr Pollfax. Here we'd been forty minutes with this damned root.

'And I bet you're thinking why didn't Lord Pollfax let sleeping dogs lie, like the telephone operator said. Did I tell you that one about the telephone operator? That gum of yours is going to be sore.'

He was standing legs apart, chin trembling, eyes blinking, hacking with the button-hook, like a wrestler putting on a headlock.

'Mr Pollfax with his back against the wall,' he said, between his teeth.

'Mr Pollfax making a last-minute stand,' he hissed.

'On the burning deck!' he gasped.

'Whence,' he added, 'all but he had fled.

'Spit,' he said. 'And now let's have another look.' He wiped his brow. 'Don't say anything. Keep dead still. For God's sake don't let it hear you. My lords, ladies and gentlemen, pray silence for Mr Pollfax. It's coming, it isn't. No, it isn't. It is. It is. There,' he cried, holding a fragment in his fingers.

He stood gravely to attention.

'And his chief beside,
Smiling the boy fell dead,'

said Mr Pollfax. 'A good and final spit, my lord and prince.'

The Voice

A message came from the rescue party who straightened up and leaned on their spades in the rubble. The policeman said to the crowd: 'Everyone keep quiet for five minutes. No talking, please. They're trying to hear where he is.'

The silent crowd raised their faces and looked across the ropes to the church which, now it was destroyed, broke the line of the street like a decayed tooth. The bomb had brought down the front wall and the roof, the balcony had capsized. Freakishly untouched, the hymnboard still announced the previous Sunday's hymns.

A small wind blew a smell of smouldering cloth across people's noses from another street where there was another scene like this. A bus roared by and heads turned in passive anger until the sound of the engine had gone. People blinked as a pigeon flew from a roof and crossed the building like an omen of release. There was dead quietness again. Presently a murmuring sound was heard by the rescue party. The man buried under the debris was singing again.

At first difficult to hear, soon a tune became definite. Two of the rescuers took up their shovels and shouted down to encourage the buried man, and the voice became stronger and louder. Words became clear. The leader of the rescue party held back the others and those who were near strained to hear. Then the words were unmistakable:

'Oh Thou whose Voice the waters heard,
And hushed their raging at Thy Word.'

The buried man was singing a hymn.

A clergyman was standing with the warden in the middle of the ruined church.

'That's Mr Morgan all right,' the warden said. 'He could sing. He got silver medals for it.'

The Rev Frank Lewis frowned.

'Gold, I shouldn't wonder,' said Mr Lewis, dryly. Now he knew Morgan was alive he said: 'What the devil's he doing in there? How did he get in? I locked up at eight o'clock last night myself.'

Lewis was a wiry, middle-aged man, but the white dust on his hair and his eye-lashes, and the way he kept licking the dust off his dry lips, moving his jaws all the time, gave him the monkeyish, testy and suspicious air of an old man. He had been up all night on rescue work in the raid and he was tired out. The last straw was to find the church had gone and that Morgan, the so-called Rev Morgan, was buried under it.

The rescue workers were digging again. There was a wide hole now and a man was down in it filling a basket with his hands. The dust rose like smoke from the hole as he worked.

The voice had not stopped singing. It went on, rich, virile, masculine, from verse to verse of the hymn. Shooting up like a stem through the rubbish the voice seemed to rise and branch out powerfully, luxuriantly and even theatrically, like a tree, until everything was in its shade. It was a shade that came towards one like dark arms.

'All the Welsh can sing,' the warden said. Then he remembered that Lewis was Welsh also. 'Not that I've got anything against the Welsh,' the warden said.

'The scandal of it,' Lewis was thinking. 'Must he sing so loud, must he advertise himself? I locked up myself last night. How the devil did he get in?' And he really meant: How did the devil get in?

To Lewis, Morgan was the nearest human thing to the devil. He could never pass that purple-gowned figure, sauntering like a cardinal in his skull cap on the sunny side of the street, without a shudder of distaste and derision. An unfrocked priest, his predecessor in the church, Morgan ought in strict justice to have been in prison, and would have been but for the indulgence of the bishop. But this did not prevent the old man with the saintly white head and the eyes half-closed by the worldly juices of food and wine from walking about dressed in his vestments, like an actor walking in the sun of his own vanity, a hook-nosed satyr, a he-goat significant to servant girls, the crony of the public-house, the chaser of bookmakers, the smoker of cigars. It was terrible, but it was just that the bomb had buried him; only the malice of the Evil One would have thought of bringing the punishment of the sinner upon the church as well. And now, from the ruins, the voice of the wicked man rose up in all the elaborate pride of art and evil.

Suddenly there was a moan from the sloping timber, slates began to skate down.

'Get out. It's going,' shouted the warden.

The man who was digging struggled out of the hole as it bulged under the landslide. There was a dull crumble, the crashing and splitting of wood and then the sound of brick and dust tearing down below the water. Thick dust clouded over and choked them all. The rubble rocked like a cake-walk. Everyone rushed back and looked behind at the wreckage as if it were still alive. It remained still. They all stood there, frightened and suspicious. Presently one of the men with the shovel said: 'The bloke's shut up.'

Everyone stared stupidly. It was true. The man had stopped singing. The clergyman was the first to move. Gingerly he went to what was left of the hole and got down on his knees.

'Morgan!' he said, in a low voice.

Then he called out more loudly:

'Morgan!'

Getting no reply, Lewis began to scramble the rubble away with his hands.

'Morgan!' he shouted. 'Can you hear?' He snatched a shovel from one of the men and began digging and shovelling the stuff away. He had stopped chewing and muttering. His expression had entirely changed. 'Morgan!' he called. He dug for two feet and no one stopped him. They looked with bewilderment at the sudden frenzy of the small man grubbing like a monkey, spitting out the dust, filing down his nails. They saw the spade at last shoot through the old hole. He was down the hole widening it at once, letting himself down as he worked. He disappeared under a ledge made by the fallen timber.

The party above could do nothing. 'Morgan,' they heard him call. 'It's Lewis. We're coming. Can you hear?' He shouted for an axe and presently they heard him smashing with it. He was scratching like a dog or a rabbit.

A voice like that to have stopped, to have gone! Lewis was thinking. How unbearable this silence was. A beautiful proud voice, the voice of a man, a voice like a tree, the soul of a man spreading in the air like the cedars of Lebanon. 'Only one man I have heard with a bass like that. Owen the Bank, at Newtown before the war. Morgan!' he shouted. 'Sing! God will forgive you everything, only sing!'

One of the rescue party following behind the clergyman in the tunnel shouted back to his mates.

'I can't do nothing. This bleeder's blocking the gangway.'

Half an hour Lewis worked in the tunnel. Then an extraordinary thing happened to him. The tunnel grew damp and its floor went as soft as clay to the touch. Suddenly his knees went through. There was a gap with a yard of cloth, the vestry curtain or the carpet at the communion rail was unwound and hanging through it. Lewis found himself looking down into the blackness of the crypt. He lay down and put his head and shoulders through the hole and felt about him until he found something solid again. The beams of the floor were tilted down into the crypt.

'Morgan. Are you there, man?' he called.

He listened to the echo of his voice. He was reminded of the time he had talked into a cistern when he was a boy. Then his heart jumped. A voice answered him out of the darkness from under the fallen floor. It was like the voice of a man lying comfortably and waking up from a snooze, a voice thick and sleepy.

'Who's that?' asked the voice.

'Morgan, man. It's Lewis. Are you hurt?' Tears pricked the dust in Lewis's eyes and his throat ached with anxiety as he spoke. Forgiveness and love were flowing out of him. From below the deep thick voice of Morgan came back.

'You've been a hell of a long time,' it said. 'I've damn near finished my whisky.'

'Hell' was the word which changed Mr Lewis's mind. Hell was a real thing, a real place for him. He believed in it. When he read out the word 'Hell' in the Scriptures he could see the flames rising as they rise out of the furnaces at Swansea. 'Hell' was a professional and poetic word for Mr Lewis. A man who had been turned out of the church had no right to use it. Strong language and strong drink, Mr Lewis hated both of them. The idea of whisky being in his church made his soul rise like an angered stomach. There was Morgan, insolent and comfortable, lying (so he said) under the old altar-table, which was propping up the fallen floor, drinking a bottle of whisky.

'How did you get in?' Lewis said, sharply, from the hole. 'Were you in the church last night when I locked up?'

The old man sounded not as bold as he had been. He even sounded shifty when he replied, 'I've got my key.'

'*Your* key. I have the only key of the church. Where did you get a key?'

'My old key. I always had a key.'

The man in the tunnel behind the clergyman crawled back up the tunnel to the daylight.

'OK,' the man said. 'He's got him. They're having a ruddy row.'

'Reminds me of ferreting. I used to go ferreting with my old dad,' said the policeman.

'You should have given that key up,' said Mr Lewis. 'Have you been in here before?'

'Yes, but I shan't come here again,' said the old man.

There was the dribble of powdered rubble, pouring down like sand in an hour-glass, the ticking of the strained timber like the loud ticking of a clock.

Mr Lewis felt that at last after years he was face to face with the devil and the devil was trapped and caught. The tick-tock of the wood went on.

'Men have been risking their lives, working and digging for hours because of this,' said Lewis. 'I've ruined a suit of . . .'

The tick-tock had grown louder in the middle of the words. There was a sudden lurching and groaning of the floor, followed by a big heaving and splitting sound.

'It's going,' said Morgan with detachment from below. 'The table leg.' The floor crashed down. The hole in the tunnel was torn wide and Lewis grabbed at the darkness until he caught a board. It swung him out and in a second he found himself hanging by both hands over the pit.

'I'm falling. Help me,' shouted Lewis in terror. 'Help me.' There was no answer.

'Oh, God,' shouted Lewis, kicking for a foothold. 'Morgan, are you there? Catch me. I'm going.'

Then a groan like a snore came out of Lewis. He could hold no longer. He fell. He fell exactly two feet.

The sweat ran down his legs and caked on his face. He was as wet as a rat. He was on his hands and knees gasping. When he got his breath again he was afraid to raise his voice.

'Morgan,' he said quietly, panting.

'Only one leg went,' the old man said in a quiet grating voice. 'The other three are all right.'

Lewis lay panting on the floor. There was a long silence. 'Haven't you ever been afraid before, Lewis?' Morgan said. Lewis had no breath to reply. 'Haven't you ever felt rotten with fear,' said the old man, calmly, 'like an old tree, infested and worm-eaten with it, soft as a rotten orange?'

'You were a fool to come down here after me. I wouldn't have done the same for you,' Morgan said.

'You would,' Lewis managed to say.

'I wouldn't,' said the old man. 'I'm afraid. I'm an old man, Lewis, and I can't stand it. I've been down here every night since the raids got bad.'

Lewis listened to the voice. It was low with shame, it had the roughness of the earth, the kicked and trodden choking dust of Adam. The earth of Mr Lewis listened for the first time to the earth of Morgan. Coarsened and sordid and unlike the singing voice, the voice of Morgan was also gentle and fragmentary.

'When you stop feeling shaky,' Morgan said, 'you'd better sing. I'll do a bar, but I can't do much. The whisky's gone. Sing, Lewis. Even if they don't hear, it does you good. Take the tenor, Lewis.'

Above in the daylight the look of pain went from the mouths of the rescue party, a grin came on the dusty lips of the warden.

'Hear it?' he said. 'A ruddy Welsh choir!'

Aunt Gertrude

The name of the street where my Aunt Gertrude lived was Dorinda Gardens. The house was a new one with builders' putty, a tin of undercoating and a roll of wallpaper in the attic. A smell of paint and size was on the stairs, and a shop smell still in the carpets, the upholstery and the new furniture. Uncle owned the house, too, as a mortgagee, and that, Aunt said, was a new thing for him. There was the pride of being one of a regiment in this house, for it was one of several hundred, each with a small white balcony over the front door. The balcony had seduced Uncle. He said one could have breakfast on it 'like they did on the Riveera', and in his imagination I am sure he did so, though there was room for only one person to stand on it and certain there was no room for a table. A railway lay in a shallow green cutting at the end of the back garden and in front were two plots of waste land which had not yet been sold. From the bedroom, where I sometimes went in the afternoon when Aunt Gertrude was lying down, one could see a hoarding standing in the field, with the words Easipay Estates Ltd. Ideal Sites for Ideal Houses. The waste grass was spiked with thistles, lumpy with old horse manure, where yellow flies congregated. From Uncle we understood we were in Ideal Surroundings, but to us three boys the paddock was the snag of evil. Its wildness fascinated us and we loosened a paling in order to creep in and smoke our first cigarettes among its dungy stench, feeling that here was the native place of sin. Rusted kettles, a sour heap of old rags and the sight of a prowling dog which looked savage, as it ran sniffing in the hot climate of this enclosure, gave us the fright we longed for. One day as we looked through, Harold said, 'There's a man.' The man was making water in a corner. We moved off. The man had confirmed our belief in the horror of the place.

There was a small passe-partout picture in the hall of my aunt's house which defined our lives. It was a picture of a letter-box with a letter sticking out of it and on the letter in good writing was the address:

Messrs Sell and Repent,
Prosperous Place,
The Earth.

'Some sell and wish they hadn't,' said Uncle Smith, cocking a shrewd, pleased eyebrow at the picture.

'Buy and repent you mean,' said Aunt Gertrude, whose face used to puff into small lumps when she was contradicting. If Uncle Smith was the sun of the house, Aunt Gertrude was the critical and watery moon, ringed with omens of bad weather.

There was a canal at the end of Dorinda Gardens, the road went over it by a bridge, and from the bridge one saw the slow worm of water pass under the girders of the railway. The days were warming and summer was blistering the new paint of the doors. One Sunday Aunt Gertrude said to Harold, her eldest son:

'Where's your dad? What's he doing?'

'S'upstairs, mum.'

'He's a long time,' said Aunt Gertrude.

She was tied to her husband by fear. He was out all day and sometimes he would be away for two or three nights, and in these absences she sank back into an undercurrent of uneasiness. His absences, even in another room, had the same effect on her as the silences of a child. What calamity had occurred? She was far from being one of those women who have the pose of treating their husbands as children. She was afraid of him and she knew it.

'Pop up and see,' said Aunt to Harold, but he did not want to go.

A time passed and then Uncle came downstairs. He was a quiet and secretive walker. He opened the kitchen door.

'Gert,' he said.

We gaped at him. He had dressed himself in a dark blue blazer with the initials H.B.S. worked on the pocket, white flannel trousers, white boots and on his head was a yachting cap. He kept his right hand in his blazer pocket.

He smiled shyly and modestly.

[250]

'I thought I'd take you for a row on the canal.'

We all laughed until he blushed like a boy. He had to laugh too.

'What's the joke? I see no joke,' he said grinning.

'Where did you get that hat?' called Harold.

'No need to be vulgar,' Uncle said, with a smirk. 'We may not have a yacht, but we're close to the water.'

Aunt stopped laughing and into her face came a glint of fear such as she always had whenever he did a new thing.

'Look at your mother,' said Uncle to Leslie. 'Pretending she's never been in a boat. We used to go out every Sunday when we were courting.'

'I was a young limb,' said Aunt Gertrude tenderly and dreamily; but while there was a glow in Uncle's dreams, Aunt Gertrude's had an edge to them and suggested that if anyone went back with her into her memories, they would get their hands scratched or their clothes torn.

We did not go rowing on the canal. There were no boats. But we walked down to the bridge, Uncle still in his regalia. We saw men fishing in the oil-green water and the thundery marble of summer clouds crested as white as cherry blossom and very still over our heads, as if the London sky were in a glass case. The men sat in the stillness smoking their pipes and watching their floats. Or, leaving their rods, they went for short circular walks and grunted to one another. While we watched from the bridge one of the men whipped up his line. There was the squeal of rapid winding and at the end of the line was a fish like a slip of dancing tin. Uncle took us down to the towpath and the man showed us the fish.

'That's what we ought to do,' said Uncle. 'We're on the water. We ought to catch our own fish. Imagine herrings straight out of the river.'

He said this to Aunt Gertrude when we got back. 'You don't get herrings in rivers,' she said tartly.

This genuinely astonished Uncle, but he recovered.

'Imagine it!' he cried, giving her a smack on the bottom.

'Ah, come on, old girl,' he bullied. 'Cheer up. Imagine it!'

Our only visitor at Dorinda Gardens was my Grandma Carter. She came in her black bead bonnet, her red nose and the red-rimmed eyes showing like knife-cuts through her black veil, and wearing a black cape of some shiny material, the deathwatch beetle of grief. She carried a string bag with her, for wherever she went she seemed always to travel with a few groceries, some sewing and a bottle of stout. There was the smell of the sharp grocer's about her, something compounded of tea, biscuits, bacon and pickles, and her tongue was the vinegar. Grief, one thinks, should purge and exalt the soul, but it had made her ugly, bad-tempered and given her also a morbid shuffling humility, a look of guilt and shame. She came every Wednesday to see us and she would suddenly appear, letting herself in by the back door and saying every time apologetically:

'I came round the back, Gert dear, because I see you done your front.' Then she pushed back her veil to the bridge of her nose, and turning slowly in a circle as a dog does before it lies down to sleep, she would give a sniff and put her string bag down on a chair. Her loneliness, her unhappiness and her snuffling made us afraid.

Aunt Gertrude was very guarded with her mother, for Gran had a tongue.

'Where d'you get that from?' Grandma Carter would exclaim at once, pointing perhaps at the coat and umbrella stand in the hall. She was very jealous of her daughter's new furniture.

'Horace bought it at Freebody's.'

'What's wrong with a hook and two nails?' Gran sniffed. 'Now I've come round to see what's happening to my boy's money.' I, of course, was her boy; but so many she had loved had repaid her treacherously by dying that she was distant and suspicious and erratic in the show of affection to me. She had had a scare when she thought she might be landed with me when my mother died. Gran gave me a whiskered kiss which smelled of sugar-bags, and tears came off her face on to mine. She was small but there was something muscular in her grip when she hugged me and she would tell Aunt of the dozens of times when 'the poor lamb' (myself) had shown that I regarded her as a second mother – a delusion, for Gran terrified me. Gran's life was filled with guilt towards the living, whom she looked at slyly, and her tears were not tears of sorrow, but issued to conceal this guilt. She was guilty because she forgot the living and neglected them in her absorption with the dead.

When they had settled down and Grandma Carter had asked perfunctorily after her son-in-law with a 'How's Smith?' Aunt Gertrude asked after Gran's lodgers. They were never called lodgers.

'How is . . . er . . .' Aunt said, not finishing the sentence and looking up at the silk shade over the gas-bracket in the middle of the room.

'Studying for his . . .' Gran replied, nodding with a genteel expression. The word 'examination' suggested a rare, upper atmosphere which it did not become her to investigate or even mention.

After this Aunt and Gran got down to the dead. The two women raised them and wept. Poor Flo, how she had suffered; my father's cough, that horse which had kicked my grandfather – the horse had died too, for they had had it shot – then Harry being taken and the brightness of my mother, her last words – some dispute about them – and then poor Great Aunt Emily, her last years darkened, and her brother Wilf, the deaf fishmonger. Having exhausted the human dead, unwrapping the cerements of memory and gazing at the closed faces, Aunt and Gran would feel hungry, as if death had been their appetiser, and would get out the beetroot, the vinegar and the mutton bone. Aunt called from the kitchen in a high giggling voice.

'Gran! Gran!'

'Yes, dear?'

'I was thinking of Aunt Emily's dog Rover.' And Aunt went off into a shriek of laughter. 'How it went away that night, do you remember? And they found it two days later drowned in the canal!'

Aunt came in holding the mutton bone in her hand, waving it as she laughed, and they both laughed and laughed till they had to sit down.

'Don't be so reel, Ma,' said Aunt Gertrude. 'It's wicked to laugh. She loved that dog. Oh, don't, I'll die . . .'

'Emily was a fool about that dog,' said Gran Carter to steady their laughter.

But Aunt was 'off' now, 'off' being Gran's word for it. She remembered other dogs, then Wilf's jackdaw, Flo's goldfish, my mother's canary, which Aunt Gertrude's cat had got when they were young – for there was a jealousy between the sisters and Aunt was always guilty about having left the cage door open – human beings had given place to the animals and birds. And then Aunt's face and Gran's straightened and the two women ended with the horse which had given Gran's husband the fatal kick.

[253]

'I'll never forget the day poor Jessie was shot.' The purgation was complete, Gran started to admire all the new furniture now and said, 'Smith's paid for it, I hope,' and a defiance came into Aunt Gertrude's salty green eyes and she said, 'Yes, he has.' And then Gran went. She took a roll of wallpaper that day to paper her closet. She was an active woman and a natural picker up of trifles by the way.

Women are the terrors, the sergeant majors of childhood. Their hard quick fingers pull at the neck, get at your ears, strain at buttons, one moment they are cuffing, the next they are hugging. Their moods last about a quarter of an hour. It's easy to scare them, simple to delude them . . . Not all women. My mother was not like this. Our shop must have put some order into her femininity. But Aunt Gertrude had the disorder of a story. When she wasn't weeping, she was laughing, swaying up and down and covering her face with her hands, or she was in a temper, or she was sulking. She sulked when she was tired of us, especially when Uncle was away for a day or two, waiting for him to come home. She was not a beautiful woman, but the nearer the time of his return came, her restless face calmed in a sulk which was a kind of beauty. She set her yellow hair under a net until it was as firm as a scone, her underlip drooped and the pupils of her grey eyes turned darker, almost blue. She put on her best dress and watered a small fern in the middle of the table and sat in the front room without moving. It made her rather impressive that in the middle of the afternoon she had had a bath and we had to keep away from her so as not to spoil her clothes. She was one of those fair, freckled women who sweat easily and after a bath the smell, half of soap, and half hay-like, of her skin put an excitement into the air, as if we were walking in a summer field. Harold, her son, was in love with her at these times, and spoke very piously and devotedly and kept us away from her. He wanted her to stay like this and did not want his father to return. But she was not in love with her son.

'Why don't you behave yourself like this all the time?' she said sarcastically to him. Harold had the sanctimoniousness of a once-spoiled and now easily envious eldest child. She preferred Leslie, the younger boy, at this moment because he too was longing for Uncle to come back and stood for hours at the window. The time when she was in love with

Harold was just after Uncle had gone away; but Harold was excited by freedom then and did not want her.

Aunt Gertrude was like a book of stories to me. When there were holidays I would leave the boys who were playing in the garden or the kitchen, pretending to them I was going to the lavatory. I would go upstairs and try to get into Aunt Gertrude's bedroom where she used to lie down in the afternoon.

'Who's that? Stop fiddling at the door. What do you want?'

I got into the habit of going there and standing at the window, watching the road and telling her what was happening. A wide road, sandy; the hoarding opposite; a dog in the paddock; a pile of new bricks in the lot which had been sold.

'There goes the lady with the dog.'

Once or twice Aunt got off the bed when I said this. She lay on the bed in a pair of grey bloomers and a loose vest with her thick hair down over her shoulders so that her face seemed to be looking out of the flap of a hairy tent, like a savage's. She got off the bed and kicked the chamber pot and peeped through the curtains. The tall grey-haired woman with the dog fascinated my aunt.

'There she goes,' she repeated to herself. 'Look at her. And the dog.' It was a fox terrier.

'She's a lady,' Aunt Gertrude said in a dreamy voice, coming away and pushing the chamber pot under the bed in a refined way. 'She spoke to me in the grocer's. Her little dog got its lead all twisted up round me and she said' – here Aunt imitated the woman's accent – '"Oooh, Ai'm soo sorr'eh." "Oh noo reely, it's quite all right," I said. I could see she was a lady. "Ooh, but mai leetle dawg is being ai nuis-ance. Come heah, Tiny." And she smiled. "Ooh, don't mention it," I said.'

Now she was out of bed, Aunt sat at her dressing table. Like all the other furniture it was new; the price of the dressing table was marked in blue chalk on the back of the mirror. I looked at her. She had slim arms and small shoulders and the skin, except at the armpits where it was the colour of dry yellow grass, was very white. She told me to have another look at the window, and, when I obeyed, with a furtive blush, she took her clothes off and put on the new ones in a hurry in case I should see. I turned to watch her brush her straight thick hair.

One afternoon she was doing her hair like this when an accident happened, something which dominated her thoughts for months afterwards. She was holding her hand-mirror in one hand and talking to herself in it while she did her hair at the back.

'Is it right at the back? There's another bit. Let's put a pin in it. Here,' she said, handing me a hairpin over her shoulder, 'put it in, do you see? No, not there. That bit. Oh come on, give it to me.'

She had quick nervy hands, and she put out her hand for the pin and placed the mirror on the table.

'Here it is,' I said. She was trying to get the pin from me without looking round and then she turned round with one of her sudden movements. Her elbow caught the mirror and it fell to the floor.

Aunt Gertrude's face changed.

'Don't touch it,' she said.

I stood back, startled by the crash. She stared down at the mirror which was lying on its face. Her manner frightened me.

'It's gone,' she exclaimed. 'I heard it go.' Her face went very red and her cheeks became lumpy as she bent down and picked up the mirror. The glass had cracked across the face.

'Oh, I wish I hadn't done that,' she said, gazing at the crack.

It was nothing for Aunt to smash things, tear things, drop things. She was a careless woman. And she did not mind except to say to the boys: 'Don't tell your father.' But as she held the mirror, she looked with helpless appeal at it, blown out with unbelief.

'That's seven years' bad luck to me,' she said.

'Don't be silly,' I said.

'You see. I know it,' she said. 'I broke one before my wedding-day. And for seven years your uncle had nothing but trouble.'

Then she stood up and got in a temper with me and everything, telling me to pick up her clothes and fold them straight and muttering such things as: 'Where's your uncle? Brush your hair before he comes. Three late nights this week! Look at my hair – it's coming down again.'

And suddenly she pulled half her hair down, picked up the cracked mirror and started again angrily. Half her face was swollen and the other half looked fierce, distraught and mad, as she picked up lengths of hair and pulled them into place on top.

'Trouble the whole time. Never in the same job five minutes,' she spat at the mirror. 'That's your uncle. What's he doing now?'

She had hairpins in her teeth and pulled one out after every sentence.

'Pay as you go,' she said. And out came a hairpin.

'That's how us girls were brought up. If you haven't got it, don't spend it.' Another pin.

'It's robbery. They say I don't understand these things, but right's right.' Another pin.

Aunt began to talk to invisible presences in the room.

'If your precious son's so perfect why did I have to come up here with a babe in arms begging for bread and say "Thank you" for every mouthful? "Eh," *she* says. "There's some have no business to get married and may be some *has* to get married." Vernon,' she swung round to me, taking out the remaining pins and holding them wildly. 'I could have skinned the old bitch. "You mind what you're saying," I said. "A better-living lot of girls you won't find. Gran had her troubles as we all know, but us girls were straight."'

The temper went and she sulked dreamily into the mirror. 'It's a good thing he met a straight girl like me,' she said quietly. 'A young country boy like that, he might have had someone who would have got hold of him. There was one or two in the shop. But I could stick up for myself. It was my hair,' she said, lifting up the final strand and curling it round her finger, 'he fell in love with, your poor mother could sit on hers.

'Vernon,' she said, turning round again. 'He had the cleanest hands I've ever seen on a man. I'll never forget in all my natural how clean his hands were. That was the first thing I noticed. Your dead dad used to say Horace Smith's the only man in this shop that washes.

'He got that from old Mrs Smith, of course. She scrubbed Horace and Mildred when they were kids till they were as clean as her kitchen. Too clean, if you ask me. But, of course, I didn't go out with him for the asking. I led him on. I didn't half make him jealous. There he was in his spats – a regular k-nut, shop-walker, see – of course, he would have everything just so, your uncle! – and he says, "Buttons forward, Miss Carter," I can see him now. "Gloves here, not buttons, caught you bending," I said. The cheek of me when you come to think of it. I was terrible.' Aunt's eyes flashed green as the sea.

[257]

'Girl-like,' she said dreamily. And then she saw the crack in the mirror and tears came into her eyes, large tears like the pearl buttons in her blouse. To me they were not like the tears I had seen before, for her common tears were hardly personal, but a general oblation to the unexplainable coming and going of woe in the world.

Many Are Disappointed

Heads down to the wind from the hidden sea, the four men were cycling up a deserted road in the country. Bert, who was the youngest, dreamed:

'You get to the pub, and there's a girl at the pub, a dark girl with bare arms and bare legs in a white frock, the daughter of the house, or an orphan – may be it's better she should be an orphan – and you say something to her, or better still, you don't say anything to her – she just comes and puts her arms round you, and you can feel her skin through her frock and she brings you some beer and the other chaps aren't there and the people don't say anything except laugh and go away, because it's all natural and she doesn't have a baby. Same at the next place, same anywhere, different place, different girl, or same girl – same girl always turning up, always waiting. Dunno how she got there. Just slips along without you knowing it and waiting like all those songs . . .'

And there the pub was. It stood on the crown of the long hill, straight ahead of them, a small red brick house with outbuildings and a single chimney trailing out smoke against the strong white light which seemed to be thrown up by great reflectors from the hidden sea.

'There's our beer, Mr Blake,' shouted Sid on his pink racing tyres, who was the first to see it, the first to see everything. The four men glanced up.

Yes, there's our beer, they said. Our ruddy beer. They had been thinking about it for miles. A pub at the cross-roads, a pub where the old Roman road crossed this road that went on to the land's end, a funny place for a pub but a pub all right, the only pub for ten miles at Harry's ruddy Roman road, marked on the map which stuck out of the backside pocket of Harry's breeches. Yes, that was the pub, and Ted, the oldest and the married one, slacked on the long hill and said all he hoped was that the Romans had left a drop in the bottom of the barrel for posterity.

When they had left in the morning there had been little wind. The skylarks were over the fields and the sun itself was like one of their steel wheels flashing in the sky. Sid was the first, but Harry with the stubborn red neck and the close dull fair curls was the leader. In the week he sat in the office making the plan. He had this mania for Roman roads. 'Ask our Mr Newton,' they said, 'the man with the big head and the brain.' They had passed through the cream-walled villages and out again to pick up once more the singing of the larks; and then cloud had covered the sun like a grey hand, west of Handleyford the country had emptied and it was astonishing to hear a bird. Reeds were in the small meadows. Hedges crawled uncut and there had been no villages, only long tablelands of common and bald wiry grass for sheep and the isolated farm with no ivy on the brick.

Well, they were there at last. They piled their bicycles against the wall of the house. They were shy before these country places. They waited for Ted. He was walking the last thirty yards. They looked at the four windows with their lace curtains and the varnished door. There was a chicken in the road and no sound but the whimper of the telegraph wire on the hill. In an open barn was a cart tipped down, its shaft white with the winter's mud, and last year's swallow nests, now empty, were under the eaves. Then Ted came and when he had piled his bicycle, they read the black sign over the door. 'Tavern,' it said. A funny old-fashioned word, Ted said, that you didn't often see.

'Well,' Sid said, 'a couple of pints all round?'

They looked to Harry. He always opened doors, but this door was so emphatically closed that he took off his fur gauntlet first and knocked before he opened it. The four men were surprised to see a woman standing behind the door, waiting there as if she had been listening to them. She was a frail, drab woman, not much past thirty, in a white blouse that drooped low over her chest.

'Good morning,' said Sid. 'This the bar?'

'The bar?' said the woman timidly. She spoke in a flat wondering voice and not in the sing song of this part of the country.

'Yes, the bar,' Ted said. 'It says "Tavern,"' he said, nodding up at the notice.

'Oh, yes,' she said, hesitating. 'Come in. Come in here.'

She showed them not into the bar but into a sitting-room. There was a bowl of tomatoes in the window and a notice said 'Teas'.

The four men were tall and large beside her in the little room and she gazed up at them as if she feared they would burst its walls. And yet she was pleased. She was trying to smile.

'This is on me,' Sid said. 'Mild and bitter four times.'

'OK, Mr Blake,' Ted said. 'Bring me my beer.'

'But let's get into the bar,' said Bert.

Seeing an armchair, Ted sank into it and now the woman was reassured. She succeeded in smiling but she did not go out of the room. Sid looked at her and her smile was vacant and faint like the smile fading on an old photograph. Her hair was short, an impure yellow, and the pale skin of her face and her neck and her breast seemed to be moist as if she had just got out of bed. The high strong light of this place drank all colour from her.

'There isn't a bar,' she said. 'This isn't a public-house. They call it the Tavern, but it isn't a tavern by rights.'

Very anxiously she raised her hands to her blouse.

'What!' they exclaimed. 'Not a pub! Here, Harry, it's marked on your map.' They were dumbfounded and angry.

'What you mean, don't sell beer?' they said.

Their voices were very loud.

'Yes,' said Harry. 'Here it is. See? Inn.'

He put the map before her face accusingly.

'You don't sell beer?' said Bert. He looked at the pale-blue-veined chest of the woman.

'No,' she said. She hesitated. 'Many are disappointed,' she said, and she spoke like a child reciting a piece without knowing its meaning. He lowered his eyes.

'You bet they ruddy well are,' said Ted from the chair.

'Where is the pub?' said Sid.

She put out her hand and a little girl came into the room and clung close to her mother. Now she felt happier.

'My little girl,' she said.

She was a tiny, frail child with yellow hair and pale blue eyes like her mother's. The four men smiled and spoke more quietly because of the resemblance between the woman and her child.

'Which way did you come?' she asked, and her hand moving over the child's hair got courage from the child. 'Handleyford?' she said. 'That's it. It's ten miles. The Queen's Arms, Handleyford, the way you came. That's the nearest pub.'

'My God!' said Bert. 'What a country!'

'The Queen's Arms,' said Ted stupefied.

He remembered it. They were passing through Handleyford. He was the oldest, a flat wide man in loose clothes, loose in the chin too, with watery rings under his eyes and a small golden sun of baldness at the back of his head. 'Queen's Arms' he had called. 'Here, what's the ruddy game?' But the others had grinned back at him. When you drop back to number four on the hills it comes back to you: they're single, nothing to worry about, you're married and you're forty. What's the hurry? Ease up, take what you can get. 'Queen's Arms' – he remembered looking back. The best things are in the past.

'Well, that's that!' said Sid.

'Queen's Arms, Harry,' Ted said.

And Bert looked at the woman. 'Let's go on,' he said fiercely. She was not the woman he had expected. Then he blushed and turned away from the woman.

She was afraid they were going and in a placating voice she said, 'I do teas.'

Sid was sitting on the arm of a chair and the child was gazing at a gold ring he wore on his little finger. He saw the child was gazing and he smiled.

'What's wrong with tea?' Sid said.

'Ask the man with the brain,' said Ted. 'Ask the man with the map.'

Harry said, 'If you can't have beer, you'd better take what you can get, Mr Richards.'

'Tea,' nodded Sid to the woman. 'Make it strong.'

The woman looked at Sid as if he had performed a miracle.

'I'll get you tea,' she said eagerly. 'I always do teas for people.' She spoke with delight as if a bell had suddenly tinkled inside her. Her eyes shone. She would get them tea, she said, and bread and butter, but no eggs, because the man had not been that morning, and no ham. It was too early, she said, for ham. 'But there are tomatoes,' she said. And then, like a child, 'I put them in the window so as people can see.'

'OK,' Sid said. 'Four teas.'

She did not move at once but still, like a shy child, stood watching them, waiting for them to be settled and fearful that they would not stay. But at last she put out her hand to the child and hurried out to the kitchen.

'Well, Mr Blake,' said Ted, 'there's a ruddy sell.'

'Have a gasper, Mr Richards,' said Sid.

'Try my lighter,' said Ted.

He clicked the lighter but no flame came.

'Wrong number,' said Ted. 'Dial O and try again.' A steak, said Sid, had been his idea. A couple of pints just to ease the passage and then some real drinking, Ted said. But Bert was drumming on a biscuit tin and was looking inside. There was nothing in it. 'Many,' said Bert, 'are disappointed.'

They looked at the room. There were two new treacle-coloured armchairs. There was a sofa with a pattern of black ferns on it. The new plush was damp and sticky to the hands from the air of the hidden sea. There was a gun-metal fender and there was crinkled, green paper in the fireplace. A cupboard with a glass door was empty except for the lowest shelf. On that was a thick book called *The Marvels of Science*.

The room was cold. They thought in the winter it must be damn' cold. They thought of the ten drizzling miles to Handleyford.

They listened to the cold clatter of the plates in the kitchen and the sound of the woman's excited voice and the child's. There was the bare linoleum on the floor and the chill glass of the window. Outside was the road with blown sand at the edges and, beyond a wall, there were rows of cabbages, then a bit of field and the expressionless sky. There was no sound on the road. They – it occurred to them – had been the only sound on that road for hours.

The woman came in with a cup and then with a plate. The child brought a plate and the woman came in with another cup. She looked in a dazed way at the men, amazed that they were still there. It seemed to Ted, who was married, that she didn't know how to lay a table. 'And now I've forgotten the sugar,' she laughed. Every time she came into the room she glanced at Bert timidly and yet pityingly, because he was the youngest and had been the most angry. He lowered his eyes and avoided her look. But to Ted she said, 'That's right, you make yourselves comfortable,' and at Sid she smiled because he had been the kindest. At Harry she did not look at all.

She was very startled then when he stood at the door and said, 'Where's this Roman road?'

She was in the kitchen. She told him the road by the white gate and showed him from the doorway of the house.

'There he goes,' said Sid at the window. 'He's looking over the gate.'

They waited. The milk was put on the table. The woman came in at last with the bread and butter and the tea.

'He'll miss his tea next,' Ted said.

'Well,' Ted said, when Harry came back. 'See any Romans?'

'It's just grass,' Harry said. 'Nothing on it.' He stared in his baffled, bull-necked way.

'No beer and no Romans,' Ted said.

The woman, who was standing there, smiled. In a faltering voice, wishing to make them happy, she said:

'We don't often get no Romans here.'

'Oh God!' Bert laughed very loudly and Ted shook with laughter too. Harry stared.

'Don't take any notice of them, missus,' Sid said. And then to them: 'She means gypsies.'

'That come with brooms,' she said, bewildered by their laughter, wondering what she had done.

When she had gone and had closed the door, Bert and Ted touched their heads with their fingers and said she was dippy, but Sid told them to speak quietly.

Noisily they had drawn up their chairs and were eating and drinking. Ted cut up tomatoes, salted them, and put them on his bread. They were good for the blood, he told them, and Harry said they reckoned at home his grandad got the cancer he died of from eating tomatoes day after day. Bert, with his mouth full, said he'd read somewhere that tea was the most dangerous drink on earth. Then the child came in with a paper and said her mother had sent it. Sid looked at the door when it closed again.

'Funny thing,' he said. 'I think I've seen that woman before.'

That, they said, was Sid's trouble. He'd seen too many girls before.

He was a lanky man with a high forehead and a Hitler moustache and his lips lay over his mouth as if they were kissing the air or whispering to it. He was a dark, harsh-looking, cocksure man, but with a gentle voice and it was hard to see his eyes under his strong glasses. His lashes were long and his lids often half lowered which gave him an air of seriousness and shyness. But he stuck his thumbs in his waistcoat and stuck out his legs to show his loud check stockings and he had that ring on his finger. 'Move that up a couple and he'd be spliced,' they said. 'Not me,' he said. 'Look at Ted.' A man with no ideals, Bert thought, a man whose life was hidden behind the syrup-thick lens of his glasses. Flash Sid. See the typists draw themselves up, tilt back their heads and get their hands ready to keep him off. Not a man with ideals. See them watch his arms and his hands, see them start tapping hard on the typewriter keys and pretending to be busy when he leant over to tell them a story. And then, when he was gone, see them peep through the Enquiry window to watch where he went, quarrel about him and dawdle in the street when the office closed, hoping to see him.

'Well,' said Harry when they had cleared the table and got out the map. Sid said:

'You gen'lemen settle it. I'll go and fix her up.'

Sid's off, they said. First on the road, always leading, getting the first of the air, licking the cream off everything.

He found her in the kitchen and he had to lower his head because of the ceiling. She was sitting drably at the table which was covered with unwashed plates and the remains of a meal. There were unwashed clothes on the backs of the chairs and there was a man's waistcoat. The child was reading a comic paper at the table and singing in a high small voice.

A delicate stalk of neck, he thought, and eyes like the pale wild scabious you see in the ditches.

Four shillings, she said, would that be too much?

She put her hand nervously to her breast.

'That's all right,' Sid said and put the money in her hand. It was coarsened by work. 'We cleared up everything,' he said.

[265]

'Don't get many people, I expect,' he said.

'Not this time of year.'

'A bit lonely,' he said.

'Some think it is,' she said.

'How long have you been here?' he said.

'Only three years. It seems,' she said with her continual wonder, 'longer.'

'I thought it wasn't long,' Sid said. 'I thought I seen you somewhere. You weren't in . . . in Horsham, were you?'

'I come from Ashford,' she said.

'Ashford,' he said. 'I knew you weren't from these parts.'

She brightened and she was fascinated because he took off his glasses and she saw the deep serious shadows of his eyes and the pale drooping of the naked lids. The eyes looked tired and as if they had seen many things and she was tired too.

'I bin ill,' she said. Her story came irresistibly to her lips. 'The doctor told us to come here. My husband gave up his job and everything. Things are different here. The money's not so good . . .' Her voice quickened, 'But I try to make it up with the teas.'

She paused, trying to read from his face if she should say any more. She seemed to be standing on the edge of another country. The pale blue eyes seemed to be the pale sky of a faraway place where she had been living.

'I nearly died,' she said. She was a little amazed by this fact.

'You're OK now,' Sid said.

'I'm better,' she said. 'But it seems I get lonely now I'm better.'

'You want your health but you want a bit of company,' Sid said.

'My husband says, "You got your health, what you want company for?"'

She put this to Sid in case her husband was not right, but she picked up her husband's waistcoat from the chair and looked over its buttons because she felt, timorously, she had been disloyal to her husband.

'A woman wants company,' said Sid.

He looked shy now to her, like Bert, the young one; but she was most astonished that someone should agree with her and not her husband.

Then she flushed and put out her hand to the little girl who came to her mother's side, pressing against her. The woman felt safer and raised her eyes and looked more boldly at him.

'You and your friends going far?'

He told her. She nodded, counting the miles as if she were coming along with them. And then Sid felt a hand touch his.

It was the child's hand touching the ring on his finger.

'Ha!' laughed Sid. 'You saw that before.' He was quick. The child was delighted with his quickness. The woman put the waistcoat down at once. He took off the ring and put it in the palm of his hand and bent down so that his head nearly brushed the woman's arm. 'That's lucky,' he said. 'Here,' he said. He slipped the ring on the child's little finger. 'See,' he said. 'Keeps me out of mischief. Keep a ring on your little finger and you'll be lucky.'

The child looked at him without belief.

'Here y'are,' he said, taking back the ring. 'Your mother wants it,' he said, winking at the woman. 'She's got hers on the wrong finger. Little one luck, big one trouble.'

She laughed and she blushed and her eyes shone. He moved to the door and her pale lips pouted a little. Then, taking the child by the hand, she hurried over to him as if both of them would cling to him. Excitedly, avidly, they followed him to the other room.

'Come on, Mr Blake,' said Ted. The three others rose to their feet.

The child clung to her mother's hand and danced up and down. She was in the midst of them. They zipped up their jackets, stubbed their cigarettes, folded up the map. Harry put on his gauntlets. He stared at the child and then slowly took off his glove and pulled out a sixpence. 'No,' murmured Ted, the married man, but the child was too quick.

They went out of the room and stood in the road. They stretched themselves in the open air. The sun was shining now on the fields. The woman came to the door to see them. They took their bicycles from the wall, looked up and down the road and then swung on. To the sea, the coast road and then perhaps a girl, some girl. But the others were shouting.

'Good-bye,' they called. 'Good-bye.'

And Bert, the last, remembered then to wave good-bye too, and glanced up at the misleading notice. When they were all together, heads down to the wind, they turned again. 'Good God,' they said. The woman and the child had come out into the middle of the road hand in hand and their arms were still raised and their hands were fluttering under the strong light of that high place. It was a long time before they went back into the house.

And now for a pub, a real pub, the three men called to Harry. Sid was ahead on his slim pink tyres getting the first of the new wind, with the ring shining on his finger.

The Chestnut Tree

━━━━━

The first firm I worked for was a leather merchants' in the south of London. To look at, their place was like a pair of muddy Methodist chapels with a jail attached; there were bars to the windows and, inside, the office smelled of feet, ink and boots. The name of the firm was Greenhythe & Co. They had been established for 150 years.

I was fifteen when my father took me there. I had never been to London before and, in the train, after the ticket collector had passed, we walked down the corridor to an empty first-class carriage, pulled down the blinds and then knelt in prayer. Afterwards we read the 91st Psalm. I had diarrhœa that morning because I was afraid.

When we came to the office we were shown at once to Mr Greenhythe's room.

'I want this boy to begin at the bottom of the ladder,' my father said, speaking as a self-made man.

'Do you speak French, boy? *Parlez-vous français?*' said Mr Greenhythe. I could not answer. He was a very old man with long white hair which was the colour of Vaseline at the roots. He had a hump on one shoulder and the head of a lion.

He then said there was a French proverb which went: '*C'est le premier pas qui coûte.*'

After that my father and Mr Greenhythe exchanged memories about the Wesleyan movement and the two men walked to the door. There was something noble, savage and prophet-like about Mr Greenhythe. But as he walked nimbly and cautiously to the door, with his bearded head sunk forward, his long arms hanging loosely, his old, cracked blue eyes raised and his boots hissing on the ground like a boxer's in the sawdust, I noticed he had the punched-in face of a fighter and wicked little teeth. Only people, he said, who had been recommended by the chapel and were known for their seriousness ever worked for the firm of Greenhythe &

Co. And so it seemed. Ten clerks were bending over their ledgers as if over the Scriptures when I was led to the cashier's desk.

My work began at eight in the morning. First of all I went down into the basement where the lavatory was to collect the pads used for copying the letters. The pads had been soaking all night. A smell of cigar smoke and scent came from the water-closet and the sound of a newspaper being unfolded. Then of singing. Out came Mr Cook, a fat bald man of sixty with a pair of nostrils like pink bubbles, and as fresh and perfumed as a flower; he had indeed a carnation in his buttonhole for he grew these plants in his garden. 'La da, di da, hijorico,' he sang and stood biting his finger-nails sulkily and scratching his womanish backside. Mr Cook opened the office every morning at half-past seven. Later, when we went upstairs and while I was filling the ink wells, this old man would lift up his desk lid, peep over the top and shout 'Ya! Ya! Ya!' and duck again. Then, once more, he sat biting the nails of his short dirty fingers.

At ten to nine the clerks began to arrive. When they had hung up their coats and hats they came to the fireplace and stood warming themselves. If there was no fire, they stood there all the same. Williams, the sandy, flat-footed one, with a sneering voice and misery in his skinny legs; Hodgkin, like a young actor, raising dark eyebrows as if he were looking at himself sideways in a mirror, and very stage-struck; Porter, the shipping clerk, with food stains on his waistcoat, the puffing father of a large family who was often making mistakes in an authoritative way, sending bills of lading to the wrong ports, delivery orders to the wrong wharves and who sat among the muddle of his papers like a hen having a dust bath; Turpin, the limp dandy in patent shoes, lined and sick-looking, always with a smile stamped dead on his face, and smelling of cachous; then Sawston. Cook did not join them. Popping his head above his desk lid he shouted out: 'Ha ya! Ha ya!' And when they turned in condescension, some word like 'Flambustigation'. Sawston used to turn to him and tell him, in a dry, morose voice, to shut up. Cook put down his lid and laughed till the tears ran down his face.

Then the outer door swung and in came Drake, the cashier and head of the office. All the clerks moved guiltily to their desks. Except Sawston. He glanced up at the clock. If it wanted two minutes or one minute of nine, he stayed where he was and watched Drake, a tall man with a gloomy voice like a chapel organ and grizzled hair and gold-rimmed glasses, come glowering towards him, clearing his throat.

'Good morning, Mr Drake,' said Mr Sawston with loud effrontery. Drake looked at the clock; Sawston's small black eyes in his baldish bullet head dared Mr Drake to have the courage to tell him to go to his desk. Mr Drake blew his nose and did not dare. 'Um. Um. Umph.' Mr Drake made a characteristic sigh on three notes, a noise famous in the office, and at once perfectly imitated by Mr Cook, who again lifted his desk lid, ducked his head and spluttered with laughter. Nine o'clock struck and slowly Mr Sawston walked to his desk, carefully cleaned his pens, wiped his ruler, sharpened his pencils, put a pile of invoices tidily on his blotter and began writing in his small girlish hand. Moodily Mr Drake gazed at the back of Mr Sawston's cheap grey suit and shook his head.

In Greenhythe's office the hours were long. At seven in the evening when I left, Williams and Sawston were still at their books under the green shades of the lights, Porter the shipping clerk was sunk in his muddle; the partners, Mr Greenhythe's sons, had gone, but a bell which snapped outside his office and a weak bad light shining through the glass door showed that Mr Greenhythe was still working. On Saturdays we left early – four o'clock. Only Mr Cook enjoyed this régime. Leaving the office at eleven o'clock in the morning to take documents or large cheques to the City, he would waggle his rump as he went out, saying 'Ya! Ya! dears!' and would spend the next few hours in the West End, sometimes at theatres for an act or two, somtimes in pubs and occasionally with girls. He came back, short-tempered, rosy and smelling of cigars.

One Monday when I had been four or five months in the firm, a woman came to the office counter. She was a tall, soft woman who wore a big floating hat with flowers on it and a blue serge coat and skirt. She had the bust of a draper's model. 'I have an appointment with Mr Greenhythe,' she said in a delicate, aloof and dreamy voice, looking down at me as if I were a fly on the counter. She was touching her nose affectedly with a handkerchief and I thought she was a royalty with a cold.

'What name, please?'

'Miss Browne,' she said. 'Browne with an "e".'

After an hour she came out of Mr Greenhythe's room with Mr Drake as well and they led her to the street door. They were talking about Mr

Greenhythe's Bible class. A week later she came again and then two days running. In his harmonium voice, Mr Drake murmured to Mr Porter that the firm were thinking of employing 'a lady book-keeper'.

The word 'lady' fell like a boulder upon us. There were typists upstairs who arrived late and who never spoke to us; in the General Office there were no women at all.

'A leedy book-keepah!' called Mr Cook from his desk. 'Ya ha!'

'Who's getting the sack?' said Williams.

'Who's getting the bird?' said Hodgkin and hummed an air from *La Bohème*.

'There are two,' said Turpin, the tired sick young man who always knew everything. 'She said she could not work in an office unless she were chaperoned by her sister.'

'One for you, one for Mr Turpin,' sneered Williams.

'Let us pray,' called Mr Cook, hiding behind his desk lid.

Mr Drake was coming in. The clerks moved to their desks. The lines on Mr Turpin's face became deep seams. He was a martyr to the seduction of women. Women set him off, like a machine, against his will. They confided in him at once; just as Mr Drake confided to him the worries of a cashier, Mr Porter the muddles of his shipping, Mr Williams his troubles with his stomach, Mr Greenhythe the number of well-known preachers he had heard. The bold sick eyes of Mr Turpin, the sympathy of his manners, even his large ears which stuck out like comical microphones from his long head, the smile which was the tired smile of a man with a headache, brought men and women to him helplessly. He was a clever man from the flat, sing-song Midlands, but he had the long stupid face of an animal that is mindless and sad.

The two lady book-keepers arrived. Miss Browne the elder, whom we had seen, was like a swan and thought so herself. Her fair hair, she conveyed to you, was her glory. She was curving and sedate. With the sleepy smile of one lying on a feather bed in Paradise, with tiny grey eyes behind the pince-nez which sat on her nose, with the swell of long low breasts balanced by the swell of her dawdling rump, she moved swan-like to her desk. But not like a swan in the water; like a swan on land. She waddled. Her feet were planted obliquely. One would have said that they were webbed.

Behind her came the cygnet and chaperone, her sister and protector. When I saw her I felt I had been struck in the heart by a stone. Mr Drake frowned and drummed his fingers, Mr Cook began biting his thumb-nail and leered in fury, Mr Porter became homely and paternal, Williams gave a scheming look at her legs, the stage-struck Hodgkin took a comb out of his pocket and ran it through his waved hair. Turpin and Sawston, who were on opposite sides of the same high, tilted desk, looked at each other fixedly. They looked as though they were trying to hypnotise each other. Taking small hard steps, her red lips pettishly drooping, her head in a cap of short black curls, her small breasts, her hips, her waist, set off by her silk dress, the sister of Miss Browne walked as if at any moment, if she shrugged her shoulders again, she could make her clothes fall off her. Her dress had some small design of red and white daisies. She looked at us tenderly and without innocence. She was as hard as a bird. When she spoke her voice was like a high cross voice in a garden.

Turpin put one leg down from his stool at once. He was about to introduce himself to the women; to walk between them with his hand just touching their waists. In such times his limpness went; he was decided. The dull buzz of his voice was the sound of the machine which had started inside him. But this time he sat back on his stool. Sawston was looking at him. Sawston's face was bloodless, as set and chalky as a clown's. The thick black brows were rigid and seemed to have been painted on, his eyes had a light so peremptory in them that one might have been looking into a pair of pistol barrels. Turpin was arrested by Sawston's eyes.

'OK, laddie,' Turpin said. A slight smile came to Sawston's face and he went on staring with indulgence at Turpin whom he had silently conquered. Sawston's eyes appeared to be printing off thousands of words which Turpin read as rapidly as they were printed. Sawston folded his arms and his fists were clenched. His coat sleeves were short and his wrists were spidery with black hair. The smile became fainter, more ironically acid and delighted.

At the end of the morning Sawston, who had worked very little – and ordinarily he worked hard – but had sat staring defiantly at his own life, got down from his stool and walked back to the desk by the fireplace where Mr Drake ruled. Drake was tall. Sawston was a short man, wide for his size, and he wore collars so low that they did not show above his jacket. This gave the impression that he was a collarless workman or was perhaps wearing a boxer's sweater. He was one of those men who have to shave twice a day and whose beard leaves a dark indigo stain like ink on a blotter. He was a curt man, blunt and independent.

'I think, Mr Drake,' he said, 'I think the younger Miss Browne had better work with me.'

It was a demand, an order. Drake's jaws chewed, he blew into his moustache and was flustered. He tried to glower. He looked sideways up at the bars of the window, he made his harmonium noises. In the office he had the kind of authority which is despised but obeyed. But with Sawston Mr Drake could do nothing. He looked down resentfully at Sawston as if Sawston were a bear who had put him up a tree.

'Obviously,' continued Sawston, 'the girl hasn't got a brain in her head. I'll teach her.'

Sawston had a cocky habit of clicking his tongue in his mouth when he was amused by his own self-possession. Having said this he walked back to his desk.

After lunch Sawston called across two rows of desks in a clear voice which was much louder than the tone which was thought suitable in this office:

'Miss Browne. Will you come over here, please.'

She pouted and, affecting lack of interest, walked over to him. The black curls shook on her head, the small breasts pushed like nuts against her blouse. Her eyes were hot-blue with freckles on the pale skin under them and her clockwork voice said, 'Yes, what do you want?'

'Call over these invoices,' he said. She shrugged her rounded shoulders and held a pencil in her teeth. Sawston put his hand out and took the pencil out of her mouth. She was astonished. Sitting behind them the elder Miss Browne saw this incident and awoke from her dream. She gazed at Sawston's shiny back with dislike.

We were afraid of Sawston, all of us. Without authority he suggested independent power. He was small, but our fear was physical. His walk, for example – he walked, not as some swaggerers did, who thought the place belonged to them, but as if he owned the precise yard of floor he happened to stand on. That was a vaster claim. His desk was his, not the firm's. His pens were his. He sharpened *his* pencils. He made no mistakes in his books – well, once a year he might make a mistake and no one cared to mention it to him. He would admit it. This was inhuman and alarming; there was no one else in the building who did not make a scene about their mistakes and try to argue them on to someone else. A peculiar physical thing about him was the smallness of his wrists and his hands. Then of what were we afraid? His indifference. He was a man, Mr Turpin said admiringly, who would ruin himself. And Mr Turpin understood ruin.

Sometimes the two sisters sat together, sometimes the elder Miss Browne sat beside Mr Drake, calling over the big ledgers. High on their stools these two looked like a King and Queen. Mr Drake was respectful to her. She had a romantic queenly air, sighed majestically or made little regal yawns behind her hands, sometimes stretching her arms to the back of her head and looking at us from a great, pale pillow of voluptuousness through her rimless glasses. No one, not even Mr Turpin, responded to the voluptuousness of the elder Miss Browne. She dropped her pens, but only Mr Drake grovelled on the floor for them. She watched him grovelling, thanked him with languor, spoke in the exhausted voice of a great hostess. Her favourite subject was Woman.

When the sisters sat together was the time to attempt a flirtation with the younger one. The swan prevented it. She had a weary musical sarcasm:

'Have you nothing else to occupy yourself with, Mr Williams?'

One day she said:

'Heestings is a beautiful spot. One can have any kind of holiday there – quiet, noisy or musical.'

'Quiet with her about,' said Williams, digging his pen in the younger one's ribs. The younger one astonished us, as pretty women do, by making a horrible face, squaring her mouth as if she were going to be sick and nodding at her sister. Delight! The two sisters detested each other. The great actress was jealous; the chaperone was venomous. Left alone together they bickered in refined voices.

'But you did, Hester, you said so yourself.'

'I didn't.'

'You did. You said he said . . .'

'I said nothing of the sort.'

We rolled our eyes. Lovely! Lady book-keepers! The young one saw

[275]

me listening and turned and smiled intimately at me. I went scarlet and when she spoke to me I could not answer. The elder sister looked over the young one's black curls at me and said remotely: 'He's only a child.' She pronounced it 'charld'.

Turpin and I sat opposite Sawston and when the young one was with him we heard him reading the invoices and she copying or checking; but between the dates and the figures, a low conversation was interpolated. Sitting side by side they did not look at each other but looked across at Turpin and me, or at their books. But all the time, like the dry mutter of a telegraph, their talk went on.

Lady book-keepers! What happiness it was to see them arrive in the morning. The elder one, holding her hair at the back and tilting her flowery hat forward, came in with her coat flying and swayed as if drunk to the cloakroom, murmuring loudly to the young one who came pattering trimly, crossly, shrugging her shoulders and snapping out words, behind.

'Ha ya,' called Mr Cook. 'Late again.'

'And hot,' said Mr Williams. Covering his mouth with his hand he added to the remark.

'Sisters, sisters,' called Mr Cook when they came to their desk. 'Do not quarrel.' The young one ignored him and went to Sawston and started intense whispering.

'The big cow,' said Sawston aloud one morning.

'What do you want?' he snapped at me seeing I was listening. She smiled at me. She reached across to the library book I had on the desk and said:

'What are you reading?'

It was poetry, the poetical works of Sir Walter Scott. I was reading *The Lay of the Last Minstrel*.

'Pooh,' she said. 'Dry.'

Sawston looked quizzically at me.

'The boy's brain will bust,' he said.

They both smiled, united by the same irony. I felt sad; I might have been their son.

But the cashier was watching our little group. 'Press on, Mr Sawston,' he moaned. 'Press on! Boy. Come here.' Colouring I went to the side of his desk. He had his pen longways in his teeth and he went on turning the pages of his ledger.

'I do not want you to waste Miss Hester's time,' he said. 'We are very busy. How old are you?'

'Sixteen,' I lied. I was fifteen years and two months old. I stood there waiting for his next remark. He went on turning the pages of his ledger. 'Um. Um. Um,' he sighed on his three notes. I had never been so near to this legendary noise before. It was like the rumination of humanity. A cage had been opened and out had come the humdrum rumour of the human race, the neutral, aimless, mindless rumble of the ape, digesting its inexplicable years on earth.

'Yes?' said Mr Drake, observing me again, surprised to see me still there. Then: 'That's all.' I went back in a sulk. My cheeks were hot. I scowled at Miss Hester Browne. She had been my undoing.

In the garden of the house where I lodged was a chestnut tree. In the morning when I left to catch my train the sky was clear and blue and against it the leaves of the tree hung down like the tongues of dark green dogs and the pink candles of blossom stood up from among them. I listened to the sound of my feet on the pavement. It was without will of mine that they touched the ground. There was a throbbing in my ears, so that I could hear only my own body, the clapping of my heart. I seemed to be flying, not walking. Would people in the train be uneasy because I was mad? The spirit and the flesh – two animals that were always in my head – were pulling me apart. The spirit was desire, the spirit was Hester Browne; the flesh had no desire, it clothed the torpor and the innumerable dreads of the mind and body.

My train went on to London, past the factories. Why were there no lakes, no mountains? For: 'He, neglected and oppressed, wished to be with them and at rest.' And why was great literature so boring? Into the pages of *The Lay of the Last Minstrel* I had put a folded sheet of the *Windsor Magazine* with a poem printed on it.

Stars of the heavens I love her
Spread the glad news afar,

it began. I was ashamed to think that terrible poem described my feelings better than anything in Scott.

'I should say you were an idealist,' Mr Turpin said gravely to me while he opened the firm's letters. In the morning, when he was tired, he used to talk about life.

But now, Mr Drake had broken me. I was watched. Shame, vanity, spite thickened my head and bit my throat. The spirit and the flesh turned a somersault inside me, I tore up my cutting from the magazine; the flesh triumphed. I hated Hester Browne. My desire had become a poison. I saw the deadly nightshade shadows under her eyes and I was pleased by what Mr Turpin had said.

Turpin wore a small, mauve silk handkerchief in his breast pocket, and it was very long. An idealist! I bought myself a handkerchief and wore it like his. Williams shuffled over to me and, putting his hand over his mouth in his secretive way, bent towards me slyly so that I could smell the tobacco on his breath.

'Imitation,' he sneered, 'is the sincerest form of flattery.'

Giving a sharp look back at me, he went off.

Now I hated Hester Browne I had the courage to observe her. She began to arrive after her sister and went breathless and damp-skinned to her desk. The pretty eyes were sticky with sleep as if she hadn't washed. To a connoisseur like Turpin this was very attractive. Her dress, the one with the small daisies, had scores of small creases in it. There was a week like this, her lips sulked and an exciting hay-like smell followed her in a warm current as she walked.

'Do you notice, Mr Turpin, anything about the atmosphere?' said Williams.

'Yes, I do,' said Mr Turpin shortly. 'Pleasanter than leather, isn't it?'

'A matter of opinion,' leered Mr Williams. Up went the inevitable hand to his lips. 'Perhaps a matter of experience.'

There was a lift up to the top floor of the warehouse and sometimes I had to take messages there. I was waiting on the third floor when the lift went groaning past me. Inside were two people, a man and a woman. The man was limp and tall and his head was close to her looking down at her neck. She was the elder Miss Browne. She was talking violently and the man was Mr Turpin who paid no attention to what she said but kept murmuring:

'You great big doll.'

'He's a married man,' she was saying. 'Look at his face. It's a cruel face. The way he speaks to her even.'

Two coats, a skirt, and a pair of trousers were carried upstairs out of my sight.

'I can be cruel too, duckie,' Mr Turpin was saying as his patent shoes went up beyond me.

It was August. Mr Cook put his carnation in a glass of water and smelled it from time to time. He was 62 on the Bank Holiday and went up in an aeroplane. Mr Greenhythe's secretary, an elderly woman who looked like Queen Victoria, put a pamphlet with the heading *Repent Ye* on our desks. Turpin read it through carefully. Then he lit his cigarette with it and said respectfully:

'I must go upstairs and thank her.' Hodgkin took a clean sheet of paper and wrote with flourishes the words *The Marriage of Figaro*. Underneath he wrote in smaller letters: The Count: Rupert Hodgkin. He looked in a pocket mirror and watched the movements of his mouth. 'Press on, Mr Hodgkin,' said Mr Drake. Mr Sawston and Hester Browne went out to lunch together, waiting for Mr Drake to go first.

On an afternoon in the middle of that week children in the street began shouting at a balloon in the sky. 'Listen to those children,' said Mr Porter tenderly, making a mistake in a weighing slip as he spoke. Between two and three was a slow hour; we all went to look at the balloon.

'Before the war,' said Mr Drake, unbending, 'there used to be a number of balloons.' We did not notice the elder Miss Browne get down from her desk and go into Mr Greenhythe's room and so we were astonished to see her coming out of it. The top part of her was gliding in a drowsy and smiling dream. She had the smile of one who has opened a bazaar, of a boa-constrictor that has fed.

Mr Drake pulled himself together.

'March 1,' came Mr Drake's voice. 'By goods, cash. £26 17s. 1d.' And her voice repeated, '£26 17s. 1d.'

'March 3,' Mr Drake went on. 'By goods, cash. £462 16s. 3d. March 14,' the voice was chanting the office litany. 'Have you got March 14, Miss Browne? Goods, thirteen and a penny? Put a query against that.'

He peered over Miss Browne to the page to see she had done this. As she wrote in the great ledger she was looking at the childish pink and white frock of her sister like a woman who is thinking of lengthening the sleeves. She also looked ironically at the slack, shiny coat of Mr Sawston.

There was a bell over Mr Greenhythe's door and it snapped two or three times. It was my business to answer the bell and sometimes the old man used to ring it by mistake or forget what he wanted. I went into his office which had a green light, for the sun-blind was down. His elderly secretary was just leaving the room. The old lion put down the telephone.

'Boy,' he said breathlessly, 'the *Alexandra Castle* has docked.'

I stared at him. He looked at me suspiciously.

'Is your father well?' he asked.

I said he was.

He looked absently at his secretary.

'What was I thinking about?' he asked pathetically.

'Mr Sawston,' she said.

'Ah, boy!' he barked at me, showing his little teeth. 'Send Mr Sawston to me.'

Mr Sawston went into Mr Greenhythe's room.

'Sawston's on the carpet,' Williams said.

'Hi yi,' said Cook, smelling his carnation. 'What do I ca-ah? What do I ca-ah? I've got tickets for the Palladium.'

Turpin leaned across to Hester Browne, who was looking resentfully towards Mr Greenhythe's door and straightening her shoulder straps.

'Keep on doing that,' said Mr Turpin in a dead voice. 'And I will bite your shoulders.'

'I was thinking, Mr Drake,' said the elder Miss Browne with a yawn, 'what thousands of people there must be at the sea.'

A pencil rolled down the desk and dropped on to the floor. 'Boy,' called a curt voice. 'Pick up my pencil.' It was Sawston. He was back again. Suddenly sitting at the desk. His eyebrows appeared to be stamped an inch higher on his forehead. His eyes seemed to be filled with points of flint. I picked up the pencil.

'The damned, impudent old man,' he said so loudly that everyone looked up. He did not look at Hester Browne. She spoke to him.

'Shut up,' he said very loudly.

[280]

He collected his invoice forms together, folded his blotter and put those into his desk. Then he put away his pens and his round ruler.

The girl put her hand on his sleeve, but he lifted it off. Then he got down, looked round the office, taking in every detail of it, and after that walked to the cloakroom. He came out in his bowler-hat with his mackintosh over his shoulder. He stopped, lit a cigarette and threw the match-stick over the counter. We all stared. At three o'clock in the afternoon, smoking without permission, Mr Sawston walked out of the office.

A moan, indignant, and forlorn, like the sound of a ship's siren as it goes out with foreboding into the ruin of the sea, went up from Mr Drake.

'Mr Sawston!' called the appalled voice. Mr Sawston glanced back, showed the whites of his eyes and raised his bowler-hat. He was gone. Hester Browne jumped down, knocked her stool over and ran to the counter.

'Hetty,' shouted her sister and came heavily after her. 'Leave that man alone!'

She was in time to catch Hester by the sleeve.

'Stop it,' shouted Hester and, turning like a rat, struck at the elder one's face.

'Ooh you, you . . . you,' cried Miss Browne and hit out. The young one's sleeve tore, down went the elder's glasses.

'Just look at that,' said Williams.

They were at each other's hair, screeching and shouting.

'You little tart! You little tart! You – you – you – little tart!' screamed Miss Browne.

The swing door on the counter flew open and Miss Browne fell through on to the floor.

We rushed to them. Their blouses were ripped, their hair was down, their faces were bleeding. The little one underneath was biting her sister's wrist, the big one was striking out and hitting the counter. They rolled.

'Miss Browne. Miss Hester,' sobbed Mr Drake shaking his pen at them and spattering them with ink. He bent to pull down Miss Browne's skirt which was round her waist and exposing thighs whose might astonished us.

At once the pair of them got free and flew at Mr Drake. This was

[281]

beyond us. Mr Hodgkin stepped back, Mr Cook lowered his head and blushed, Mr Williams cried out.

'Remove them, remove them,' pleaded Mr Drake. Mr Porter, eternally wrong, began to pull at Mr Drake. A loud slap startled us. Miss Hester had caught Mr Drake on the cheek. There was silence. And then we saw Mr Turpin. Sitting sideways on his stool, detached, interested and thoughtful, he was watching us.

'Mr Turpin!' Drake and Porter called out together. It was a cry to the expert. Sadly he got down from his stool and came to the two panting girls.

'Darlings . . .' he began and put his arms round their waists, but at this word the big one swooned and hung on him so that he was hardly able to support her. 'I told Mr Greenhythe,' she was gasping quietly. 'Save her, save her. He's a married man.'

But the little one had jumped away. Screeching, she escaped us and ran into the street to follow Mr Sawston. And that was the last we saw of either of them. The thing that struck us all dumb was that Mr Sawston had not fallen to the fear that hung over all of us: he had not been sacked. He had sacked himself.

The Ape

The fruit robbery was over. It was the greatest fruit robbery, and from our point of view, the most successful ever known in our part of the jungle. Not that we can take all the credit for that, for it was not ourselves who started the fight, but our enemies, a colony of apes who live in another tree. They were the first to attack and by the time the great slaughter was over hundreds of their dead, of both sexes, lay on the ground, and we had taken all their fruit. It was a fortunate triumph for us.

But apes are not a complacent or ungrateful race. Once we were back in our tree binding up our wounds, we thought at once of commemorating our victory and thanking our god for it. For we are aware that if we do not thank our god for his benefactions he might well think twice before he sent us another fruit robbery of this triumphant kind. We thought therefore of how we might best please him. We tried to put ourselves in his place. What would most impress him? There were many discussions about this: we screamed and screeched in passionate argument and the din grew so loud – far louder than the noise we make in the ordinary business of eating or defending our places in the tree or making love and dying – that at last our oldest and wisest ape, who lived at the very top, slyly observed: 'If I were god and had been looking down at this tree of screeching monkeys for thousands of years, the thing that would really impress me would be silence.' We were dumbfounded. Then one or two of us shouted: 'That's got it. Let silence be the commemoration of our victory.'

So at last it was arranged. On the anniversary of the day when the great fruit robbery began, we arranged that all of us would stop whatever we were doing and would be silent.

But nothing is perfect in the jungle. You would think that all apes would be proud to be alike, and would have the wisdom to abide by the traditions of their race and the edicts of their leader. You would think all would destroy the individual doubt with the reflection that however different an ape may fancy he is, the glory of the ape is that as he is now so he always has been, unchangeable and unchanged. There were, however, some and one in particular as you will see, who did not think so.

We heard of them from a pterodactyl, a rather ridiculous neighbour of ours.

The pterodactyl lived on a cliff just above our tree and often, scaly and long-necked, he would flop clumsily down to talk to us. He was a sensationalist and newsmonger, a creature with more curiosity than brains. He was always worried. What (he would ask us) is the meaning of life? We scratched our heads. Where was it all leading? We spat out fruit pips. Did we apes think that we would always go on as we were? That question was easy. Of course, we said. How fortunate we were, he said, for he had doubts about himself. 'It seems to me that I am becoming – extinct,' he said.

It was all very well of us to make light of it, he said, but 'if I had not lived near you such an idea would never have entered my head.' We replied that we did not see what we had done to upset him. 'Oh, not you in particular,' he said. 'It is your young apes that are worrying me. They keep talking about their tails.' – 'No livelier or more flourishing subject,' we said. 'We apes delight in our tails.' – 'As far as I can see,' the pterodactyl said, 'among your younger apes, they are being worn shorter and will soon be discarded altogether.' – 'What!' we exclaimed – he could have touched us on no more sensitive spot – 'How dare you make such a suggestion!' – 'The suggestion,' the pterodactyl said, 'does not come from me but from your young apes. There's a group of them. They caught me by the neck the other day – I am very vulnerable in the neck – and ridiculed me publicly before a large audience. "A flying reptile," they said. "Study him while you can for the species won't exist much longer – any more than *we apes shall go about on four legs and have tails*. We shall, at some unknown time in the future, but a time that comes rapidly nearer, cease to be apes. We shall become man. The pterodactyl, poor creature, came to the end of his evolutionary possibilities long ago."'

'Man!' we exclaimed. 'Man! What is that?' And what on earth, we asked the pterodactyl, did he mean by 'evolution'? We had never heard of it. We pressed the pterodactyl to tell us more, but he would only repeat what he had already said. When he had flopped back to his cliff again we sat scratching ourselves, deep in thought. Presently our old and wisest ape, a horny and scarred old warrior who sits dribbling away quietly to himself all day and rubbing his scars on the highest branch of all, gave a snigger and said, 'Cutting off their tails to spite the ape.' We did not laugh. We couldn't take the matter as lightly as he took it. We, on the contrary, raged. It was blasphemy. The joy, the pride, the whole apehood of us apes is in our tails. They are the flag under which we fight, the sheet-anchor of our patriotism, the vital insignia of our race. This young, decadent post-fruit-robbery generation was proposing to mutilate the symbol which is at the base of all our being. We did not hesitate. Spies were at once sent down to the lower branches to see if what the pterodactyl had told us was true and to bring the leader into our presence.

But before I tell what happened I must describe what life in our tree is like. The tree is a vast and leafy one, dense in the ramification of its twigs and branches. In the upper branches, where the air is freer and purer and the sunlight is plentiful, live those of us who are called the higher apes; in the branches below, and even to the bottom of the trunk, swarm the thousands of lower apes, clawing and scrambling over one another's backs, massing on the boughs until they nearly break, clutching at twigs and leaves, hanging on to one another's legs and tails and all bellowing and screeching in the struggle to get up a little higher and to find a place to sit, so that when we say, as we do, that the nature of life is struggle and war we are giving a faithful report from what is going on below us.

We in the upper branches eat our fruit in peace and spit out the pips and drop the rind upon the crowd below. It is they who, without of course intending to do so, bring us our food. Each of them carries fruit for himself, but the struggle is so violent that it is hard for them to hold the fruit or to find a quiet place where they can eat it. Accordingly we send down some of our cleverer apes – those who are not quite at the top of the tree yet and perhaps will never get there because they have more brain than claw – and these hang down by their tails and adroitly flick the fruit out of the hands of the climbers. Very amusing it is to watch the astonishment of the climbers when they see their fruit go, because a minute before, they were full of confidence; then astonishment changes to anger and you see them grab the fruit from their nearest neighbours who in turn grab from the next. Failing in this, they have to go down once more to the bottom to get more fruit and begin again; and as no part of the struggle is more difficult than the one which takes place at the bottom, an ape will go to any lengths, even to the risk of his life, to avoid that catastrophe. So for thousands of years have we lived and only when fruit on our own tree is short or when we can bear no longer the sight of an abundance of fruit on another tree, occupied by just such a tribe of apes as ourselves, do our masses cease their engaging civil struggle and, at an order from us higher apes above, go forth upon our great fruit robberies. It is plain that if in any respect an ape ceased to be an ape, our greatness would decline, and anarchy would follow, i.e. how would we at the top get our food? – and we should lose our tree and be destroyed by some stronger tribe. Our thoughts can therefore be imagined when the spies brought before us the leader of that group of apes who were preparing to monkey with our dearest emblem. He stood before us – and that is astonishing, for we apes do not habitually stand for long. Then he was paler than our race usually is, less hairy, fearless – very un-ape like that – and upright on his hind legs, not seeking support for his forelegs on some branch. These hung at his side or fidgeted with an aimless embarrassment behind his back. We growled at him and averted our eyes from his stupidly steadfast stare – for as a fighting race we are made subtle by fear and look restlessly, suspiciously around us, continually preparing for the sudden feint, the secret calculation, the necessary retreat, the unexpected attack. Nothing delivers an ape more readily to his enemy than a transparently straightforward look; but this upright ape had already lost so much of his apehood that he had forgotten the evasions of a warrior race. He was not even furtive. And in another way, too, he had lost our tradition. He spoke what was in his mind. This, I need hardly say, is ridiculous in a warrior whose business is to conceal his real purpose from his enemy. I note these facts merely as a matter of curiosity and to show how this new ape, from the very beginning, gave himself helplessly into our hands. We had supposed him to be guilty of race-treachery only, a bodily perversion which is, perhaps, a sin and not a crime – but the moment he spoke he went much further. He accused himself of sedition from his own mouth. He spoke as follows:

'Since my arrest has given me an opportunity of speaking to higher apes for the first time in my life, I will speak what (perhaps unknown to you) has been in the minds of us who are lower in the tree for hundreds of years. We think that there is no greater evil than the vast fruit slaughters. Now there could be no slaughter if our teeth and claws were not sharp, and they would not be sharp if we were not perpetually engaged in struggle. We believe that a crucial time has arrived in the evolution' (we pricked up our ears at that word) 'of the ape. Our tails, that used to swirl us (as they waved above our heads) into blood-thirsty states of mind, are shortening; we have not shortened them ourselves by any act of will. If we apes will work to order our lives in a new way, the struggle will cease, no more great fruit slaughters will be necessary and everyone will have all the fruit he needs and can eat in peace in his appropriate place in the tree. For we do not think that even you in the higher branches for whom unconsciously we labour, really benefit by the great slaughters. Some of you are killed as thousands of us are, many of you are maimed and carry unbeautiful scars. From what we below hear of your private lives and talk in the upper branches, your privileges do not make you either sensible or happy.'

We were ready to fall upon him after this blasphemous speech, but our oldest ape, steeped in the wisdom and slyness of his great age, silenced us. 'And when there is a shortage of fruit for everyone in the tree, high and low alike?' he asked. 'If our teeth and claws are not sharpened,' replied the new ape, 'we shall not want to attack other trees but, when we need fruit, we shall go to the others and instead of tearing them apart we shall talk to them, stroke them and persuade them. They, seeing how gentle our hands are, will like being stroked and will smile and coo in their pleasure; for, as all of us apes know from intimate experience, there is nothing more delightful than a gentle tickling and scratching – and then they will share their fruit with us.' – 'What a hope!' we laughed. And some cried with disgust, 'That ape's a pansy!' But a shout went up from the lower branches where a mass of his supporters were gathered. 'You'd better do as he says,' the cry came, 'or soon there will be none of

[287]

us left to bring you your fruit.' 'Yes,' said the leader, 'another fruit robbery and there will be no more workers for you to steal from.'

'Now,' we whispered to our oldest ape on the highest branch, 'now let us kill him.'

'Remember,' said the old one, 'that he has followers. They are too many for us and we are unprepared.'

This was true, so, reluctantly, we let the leader go and swing back down the branches to his own people.

After he had gone we gathered in conference in the upper branches. When we were seated our oldest ape said, 'No doubt to you there seems to be something new, startling and dangerous in the speech you have just heard. I expect you think it the speech of a revolutionary. So it is – but there's nothing new in that. From the beginning of time there have been revolutions and what difference do they make? None whatever. Everything goes on afterwards exactly as it went on before. Do not worry therefore about revolutionaries. I have seen dozens of such people and with a little art they can be made to die very comfortably of their own enthusiasm. And, in one way, I agree with what that strange ape said. He said that violence is wasteful. It is – for to exterminate our own workers would mean that we would be without food or would have to go down out of our comfortable places in the tree and get it for ourselves. That would indeed be a calamity. No, I think if we wish to remove the danger from this particular movement we should support it.'

'Support blasphemy and treachery!' we cried with indignation.

'Ah!' exclaimed the old ape wistfully. 'There speaks the honest warrior. But I am old and political and it would seem to me a mistake to let all that enthusiasm get out of our hands. After our last great fruit robbery we are rather tired, you know, and enthusiasm is not easily come by again.'

'But our tails!' we shouted.

'Your honour and your tails!' said our weary and ancient one. 'I guarantee to show you such a display of tails wagging, curling, prehensile and triumphant as you have never seen before.'

'Well, if your plan will safeguard our sacred tails and preserve us from evolution,' we said, 'there may be something in it. Tell us what it is.'

'It is very simple,' he said. 'First of all we shall announce the end of all fruit robbery . . .'

'Impossible,' we interrupted.

'It is never impossible to *announce* anything,' he said. 'I repeat we shall announce the end of all fruit robbery. But the lower ape is an emotional creature. It is useless to argue with him – indeed we know that the free interchange of ideas in open argument is extremely dangerous, for the lower apes are hungry and hunger sharpens the mind, just as it sharpens the claws. No, we must appeal to his emotions, for it is here that he is untrained and inexperienced. So when we announce the end of all fruit robbery we must perform an act which shall symbolise our intention. That is easy. Almost anything would do. The best, I think, would be merely to alter the date of the commemoration of our last robbery from the anniversary of its call to battle to the day on which it ended and when peace was declared. I'll lay you a hundred to one in pomegranates that you will see the tails wag on that day.'

We who listened were doubtful of the success of a trick so simple and, moreover, we were disappointed not to have the opportunity of killing the rebel ape. But when we heard the enthusiasm in the lower branches, we realised that our oldest ape had judged rightly. Those short-tailed evolutionists were so diddled that they shouted for joy. 'Peace!' 'The end of all fruit robberies,' 'To each according to his needs' – we above heard their delirious cries and winked. And when the inquisitive pterodactyl came down to see what it was all about, we slapped him on the back and pulled his wings about merrily and nearly choked him with pomegranate seeds which do not agree with him. 'Cheer up, you're not extinct yet,' we said. And even that cheerless reptile, though he said his nerves couldn't stand monkey tricks any more, had to smile.

And the ceremony took place. We appointed the day, and just before noon the yelling ceased and all the struggling and climbing. Just where they were, on whatever twig or branch, our apes coiled their tails and squatted in silence. The only movement was the blinking of our eyes, thousands of eyes in the hot rays of the sun. I do not know if you have ever seen a tree full of apes squatting in silence on their haunches. It is an impressive sight. There was our oldest ape on the topmost branch; a little beneath him was our circle of privileged ones, and below, thick in the descending hierarchy, were the others.

And then, before a minute had gone by, an event occurred which filled us with horror. The lengths to which blasphemy will go were revealed to us. Taking advantage of the stillness of the multitude, an ape leapt up the tree, from back to back, from branch to branch, and burst through our unprepared ranks at the top. It was the leader to whom we had spoken.

'This is a fraud,' he shouted. 'You are pretending to commemorate peace when all the time you are planning greater robberies. You are not even silent. Listen to the grinding and sharpening of your claws and teeth.'

It was, of course, our habit. We do it unconsciously.

Too startled for a moment to act, we hesitated. Then: 'Lynch him. Kill him,' cried the crowd with a sudden roar. We hesitated no more and at least a score of us leapt upon him. You would think we had an easy task. But there was extraordinary strength in that creature. He fought like a god, skilfully, and he had laid out half of our number with a science and ferocity such as we had never seen before our numbers overwhelmed him. Some spirit must have been in him and we still wonder, not without apprehension, if that spirit is lying asleep in his followers. However that may be, we threw him down at last upon the branch. Our oldest ape came down to look upon the panting creature and then what we saw made us gasp. He was lying on his face. There was a backside bare and hairless – he had no tail. No tail at all.

'It is man!' we cried. And our stomachs turned.

The Clerk's Tale

There were two railway stations in the town where I lived when I was a boy, the Junction and the East station, and from both of them the surburban trains went up to London. It was during the war, when I was sixteen, that I last used that line. I used to go from the East station and the trains were very crowded. We all sat or stood, jammed against each other, and people rarely talked.

There was, nevertheless, one talker, if what he said can be called talk. He started with us at the East station. The moment he got into the compartment he would begin. 'Must we have that window open?' he would say. Or, 'Will you kindly move up and give me more room. Five passengers are allowed each side.' Or, 'Kindly sit on the opposite side, your smoke is annoying me.' Or, if a woman opened the door, he would say, 'This is a smoking compartment. Can't you go to the special compartment for ladies?' He hated women. All these things he planked down like a man throwing aside a spade in a temper. And after he said them he took off his glasses, showed his large, cold, snail-grey naked eyes, jerked back his shoulders and spread his fingers as if preparing to slap someone hard on the face. He was a hard-chinned, greyhaired man of fifty. People turned away to the window, raised their papers, looked more closely at their books and said nothing.

One day somebody said to me, 'You should be sorry for that man. You should not mock him. One of his sons has been killed in the war. And the other has been wounded.' I was silent. This conveyed little to me. I was sixteen. The world, the war – I hardly saw or heard of them. The mark of the war on that train meant nothing. I lived in a different world. I lived in a dream. Looking out of the carriage window, sunk in some book, watching the slow clock in the warehouse where I worked, I lived only for one thing in those days: that time should be urged on and the week pass.

So that it would be Sunday once more. For on Sunday, during one hour on Sunday morning, I saw Isabel Hertz. She was in my class at Sunday School, a girl who was half-Swedish, with hair as yellow as thick sunflowers and candid eyes like blue pebbles of ice. Her throat, her lips which broke apart in piety when she sang the hymns, and her silk legs, intoxicated me. Once I fell down the Sunday School stairs when I heard her voice in the doorway below. When she spoke I thought of a crystal of snow falling on a warm hand and instantly melting; a particle of herself melted away with every word and passed with a sigh to Heaven. There, ardent but purified by her purity, I joined her in melodious, fleshless and speechless union. In one of those northern landscapes of snow, perhaps, where time is frozen in the sky, where sleigh-bells ring and there is the dry mutter of skates saying, 'Inevitable, for ever. Inevitable, for ever,' like our love, over iron lakes of ice.

It was a very small incident which had started my love for Isabel Hertz. It occurred one Sunday at the school. With her Bible on her lap she was sitting opposite to me, for I was afraid to sit next to her.

'Isabel, dear,' the teacher said, 'what is God?' Isabel, who always held her head a little to one side as if her small ears were listening to the spring sky, turned her head. She hesitated, as if waiting for the voice of Heaven; then she replied, 'God is love.'

I was looking at her, waiting for her to speak, and she caught my eye and smiled. A pain like hunger pinched my throat.

All that day, I could eat nothing, but my mouth seemed to drink and eat the air because she, miles away, was breathing it. There was a laburnum tree in our garden, and I cut her initials, I.H., on the trunk and went to have a look at them every hour. I even went out after dark before I went to bed and struck a match to see them. I told my parents I had dropped a pencil there and was looking for it. I was awake all night and horses seemed to be galloping over my heart.

I longed to dream at night about Isabel Hertz, but this never happened. I was dreaming about her all day; but when the next Sunday and the next came I felt my body was covered with the garish tattoo of guilt and I could not speak. I never spoke to her. Once when she spoke to me, I choked.

Man cannot live by the spirit alone. It was about this time that, thinking always of the face and walk of Isabel Hertz, I started imagining things I could do with girls with round shoulders and protruding upper teeth. The uglier the better. I used to follow them. There was a girl who got into the train at the next station one morning. She carried a small cardboard attaché case which had the initials D.O.M. on it. At the London station, some nights after, I saw her again. The fact that I had now seen her twice, by accident, overruled everything. I dropped all other girls with protruding teeth and followed D.O.M. *Her* teeth stuck out like tusks.

D.O.M. was a dark, shabby, stumpy girl with thin legs and high scared shoulders. Her hollow, sparrow-brown eyes and those teeth, which spread her lips and left her mouth open, gave her an expression of craving and hunger. The thing about her that moved me was the sad wideness of her white forehead. She was always with a tall friend and as they walked up the platform they bumped their hips against each other or pushed and pinched. They were always laughing and made people stare.

I used to follow in the evenings. My technique was like this. I got out at her station and gave her about fifty yards start and then I went after her. She and her friend went first down the station road; then they turned to the left and went up a long street of small villas. At the two corners I used to put on speed when she and her friend were out of sight; but when, racing round the corner, I found I was only ten yards behind them, I eased off and let them go ahead. At last they would turn inside a side street where, I supposed, she lived. There I left her and went on home. The idea of knowing exactly where D.O.M. lived was repugnant.

At first there was excitement in this pursuit; then dead but obliged boredom and finally the humiliation of secrecy. For the more I saw of D.O.M. the more I disliked her. I shuddered at the worn fur collar of her coat, her bad complexion, her giggle, the silly way in which she was always bumping into her friend, her bad, scraping walk which turned over the heel of her left shoe. All these things gave me a horror which I could not resist for I felt in my own mouth the hunger which I saw in hers. But once she had gone, there were freedom, weariness and relief. I went home exhausted. Once more I could dream freely about Isabel Hertz.

This went on into the summer. It was a bondage. I believed that D.O.M. did not know I followed her. But one evening towards the end of September something did happen which changed the situation and altered my life. Just as we were all at the end of the long straight road of villas and D.O.M. was about to turn into her street and set me free, she gave a sudden twist to her shoulders, as a pomeranian does when it starts prancing and yapping, opened her mouth wide and put her tongue out at me three or four times. After this she put her hand to her throat and pretended to be sick. She knew. She had known all the time. I felt deep shame and anger. But this soon gave place to a decisive bombast and brutality. The next time I saw her I was determined to speak.

The following evening I walked past the barrier on to the platform of the London station and searched for D.O.M. She was at her usual place near the indicator. I was late in getting there and I had not reached it when the train came in. I saw her get into a compartment and I was going to join her but, at the last moment, I was afraid. I pretended to myself I would be more subtle. I would get into the next compartment. I opened the door and got in and, as I did so, I heard a voice shout: 'Full up here.' I saw the violent man. He was wearing a light grey pistol-coloured suit.

But the train moved. There was nothing to be done. He couldn't turn me out. I stayed at the window. The draught of the rushing train was blowing in my face. One of those yellow sunsets of the autumn, with cloud like the brown smoke that runs off paraffin flares in the street markets, was painted over the manure-coloured brick of London and the approaching pink brick of the suburbs. The train snuffled on. I looked out of the window and then I saw D.O.M. at the next one, not her face but the elbow of her green coat and the fur of her collar. She was standing too. I stared until the wind made my eyes sting. Presently her head showed. But she did not turn, the metals crossed like scissors under the train at the points outside the coming station. Someone got out of our compartment at this station and I went to take his place. In doing so I kicked the violent man's toe. He dropped his paper, stiffened his chin and muttered. I apologised and sat down.

At the next station another person got out and left the door open. 'Close the door!' shouted the man. I was glad to curry favour. I stood up, closed the door and looked out. I saw her head again. I stared and stared and waited. She did not look my way. I went back to my place. But I couldn't stay there. I had to get up again. She was there. She saw me. She affected not to see me. I was excited. I had entirely lost all sense of the people in the compartment. They were nothing but wagging and shaking sacks. I went back, got up again, a half-dozen times. I opened and closed the window, stepped across people's legs, gazed out, sometimes rewarded and sometimes disappointed. As I went to my seat once more I hardly heard the man opposite to me say:

'What the devil do you think you're doing, you young fool. Can't you sit still?'

'This is not your compartment,' I said.

The wind in my eyes and the sight of D.O.M. at the window had given me defiance. All the brutality that lies under humiliation was ready.

'Perpetually getting up and treading on my feet,' said the man.

'There is no need to lose your temper,' I said. I was swept into another world, away from everything I had known. I felt the recklessness of a blasphemer in defying a man thirty years older than myself, a man with grey hair. I felt I had grown up ten years with a word.

'You dare talk to me like that,' said the man, removing his pince-nez and showing me his naked grey eyes.

The other passengers looked at us in a stupor of displeasure.

'If you were my son,' he said, 'I'd thrash you within an inch of your life.'

'Try,' I said. 'Go on.' I felt about thirty. I suddenly felt I had fought in the war. 'Why aren't you in the army, anyway?' I said. It was a phrase I had often heard.

The man threw down his paper, jumped up and was about to strike me when a passenger touched his arm.

'I shall call an inspector,' he said.

An expression of bliss came over the faces of the others in the compartment. There was a worship of inspectors on our line.

'Call a dozen inspectors,' shouted the man, still standing and threatening me. Before I knew what I was doing I gave him a push in the waistcoat, the train suddenly stopped with a jerk and he fell back into his seat. In our quarrel we had passed D.O.M.'s station where I always got out. We had arrived at the East station, the terminus.

This put me in a panic because I did not want to be seen quarrelling in the town where my home was. The passengers had risen and one, a woman, was between me and the man. He was trying to get at me. I pushed and got out on to the platform first, but my enemy was on me. He tumbled out and hit hard. The blow hit my shoulder. And he grabbed my arm, too. He was savage and unguarded. I saw his mouth like a flattened rose and landed my knuckles on it. This knocked him into the crowd and his spit was on my hand.

I knew I was for it now and had not a chance against this man and I was scared by what I had done. I got a burning blow on the ear that nearly knocked me senseless. I swung back at him and perhaps I hit him or one of the people who were trying to get between us and the barrier. It wasn't a fight.

'You young swine. You young hound.' I heard his shouts. A passenger muddled the next swing of his arm and I caught him on the collar. The blow was not as wonderful to me as the first one; it made me feel dizzy. His spit on my hand had gone cold. I dodged away quickly, jumped on to a truck, climbed over the low fence and got down into the coal yard. A number of people were arguing with the man. His hat had fallen off and had been kicked and he was holding it crumpled in his hand and shouting at the person who had trodden on it. Someone said, 'Striking a boy like that!' and this made me feel heroic now I was safe. I walked away with the feeling that I was treading through flames and one side of my face seemed to be like a football. Then I felt horror at myself; and at the whole human race. I had struck a man whose son had been killed. I suddenly knew what the war was. I went home and was sick.

After this, I did not use the East station any more. I got up earlier and used the Junction. For two years I dared not go near the East station and I did not see D.O.M. again. I found a new girl on the new line and went out arm-in-arm with her. That had an unhappy ending, too – unhappy for the girl. None of this would have happened if Isabel Hertz had not known what God is.

The Fly in the Ointment

It was the dead hour of a November afternoon. Under the ceiling of level mud-coloured cloud, the latest office buildings of the city stood out alarmingly like new tombstones, among the mass of older buildings. And along the streets, the few cars and the few people appeared and disappeared slowly as if they were not following the roadway or the pavement, but some inner, personal route. Along the road to the main station, at intervals of two hundred yards or so, unemployed men and one or two beggars were dribbling slowly past the desert of public buildings to the next patch of shop fronts.

Presently a taxi stopped outside one of the underground stations and a man of thirty-five paid his fare and made off down one of the small streets.

'Better not arrive in a taxi,' he was thinking. 'The old man will wonder where I got the money.'

He was going to see his father. It was his father's last day at his factory, the last day of thirty years' work and life among these streets, building a business out of nothing, and then, after a few years of prosperity, letting it go to pieces in a chafer of rumour, idleness, quarrels, accusations and, at last, bankruptcy.

Suddenly all the money quarrels of the family, which nagged in the young man's mind, had been dissolved. His dread of being involved in them vanished. He was overcome by the sadness of his father's situation. 'Thirty years of your life come to an end. I must see him. I must help him.' All the same, knowing his father, he had paid off the taxi and walked the last quarter of a mile.

It was a shock to see the name of the firm, newly painted too, on the sign outside the factory and on the brass of the office entrance, newly polished. He pressed the bell at the office window inside and it was a long time before he heard footsteps cross the empty room and saw a shadow cloud the frosted glass of the window.

'It's Harold, father,' the young man said. The door was opened.

'Hullo, old chap. This is very nice of you, Harold,' said the old man shyly, stepping back from the door to let his son in, and lowering his pleased, blue eyes for a second's modesty.

'Naturally I had to come,' said the son, shyly also. And then the father, filled out with assurance again and taking his son's arm, walked him across the floor of the empty workroom.

'Hardly recognise it, do you? When were you here last?' said the father.

This had been the machine-room, before the machines had gone. Through another door was what had been the showroom where the son remembered seeing his father, then a dark-haired man, talking in a voice he had never heard before, a quick, bland voice, to his customers. Now there were only dust-lines left by the shelves on the white brick walls, and the marks of the showroom cupboards on the floor. The place looked large and light. There was no throb of machines, no hum of voices, no sound at all, now, but the echo of their steps on the empty floors. Already, though only a month bankrupt, the firm was becoming a ghost.

The two men walked towards the glass door of the office. They were both short. The father was well-dressed in an excellent navy blue suit. He was a vigorous, broad man with a pleased impish smile. The sun-burn shone through the clipped white hair of his head and he had the simple, trim, open-air look of a snow man. The son beside him was round-shouldered and shabby, a keen but anxious fellow in need of a hair cut and going bald.

'Come in, Professor,' said the father. This was an old family joke. He despised his son, who was, in fact, not a professor but a poorly paid lecturer at a provincial university.

'Come in,' said the father, repeating himself, not with the impatience he used to have, but with the habit of age. 'Come inside, into my office. If you can call it an office now,' he apologised. 'This used to be my room, do you remember, it used to be my office? Take a chair. We've still got a chair. The desk's gone, yes that's gone, it was sold, fetched a good price – what was I saying?' he turned a bewildered look to his son. 'The chair. I was saying they have to leave you a table and a chair. I was just going to have a cup of tea, old boy, but – pardon me,' he apologised again, 'I've only one cup. Things have been sold for the liquidators and they've cleaned out nearly everything. I found this cup and teapot upstairs in the foreman's room. Of course he's gone, all the hands have gone, and when I looked around just now to lock up before taking the keys to the agent when I hand over today, I saw this cup. Well, there it is. I've made it. Have a cup?'

'No, thanks,' said the son, listening patiently to his father. 'I have had my tea.'

'You've had your tea? Go on. Why not have another?'

'No really, thanks,' said the son. 'You drink it.'

'Well,' said the father, pouring out the tea and lifting the cup to his soft rosy face and blinking his eyes as he drank, 'I feel badly about this. This is terrible. I feel really awful drinking this tea and you standing there watching me, but you say you've had yours – well, how are things with you? How are you? And how is Alice? Is she better? And the children? You know I've been thinking about you – you look worried. Haven't lost sixpence and found a shilling have you, because I wouldn't mind doing that?'

'I'm all right,' the son said, smiling to hide his irritation. 'I'm not worried about anything, I'm just worried about you. This –' he nodded with embarrassment to the dismantled showroom, the office from which even the calendars and wastepaper basket had gone – 'this –' what was the most tactful and sympathetic word to use? – 'this is bad luck,' he said.

'Bad luck?' said the old man sternly.

'I mean,' stammered his son, 'I heard about the creditors' meeting. I knew it was your last day – I thought I'd come along, I . . . to see how you were.'

'Very sweet of you, old boy,' said the old man with zest. 'Very sweet. We've cleared everything up. They got most of the machines out today. I'm just locking up and handing over. Locking up is quite a business. There are so many keys. It's tiring, really. How many keys do you think there are to a place like this? You wouldn't believe it, if I told you.'

'It must have been worrying,' the son said.

'Worrying? You keep on using that word. I'm not worrying. Things are fine,' said the old man smiling aggressively. 'I feel they're fine. I *know* they're fine.'

'Well, you always were an optimist,' smiled his son.

[299]

'Listen to me a moment. I want you to get this idea,' said his father, his warm voice going dead and rancorous and his nostrils fidgeting. His eyes went hard, too. A different man was speaking, and even a different face; the son noticed for the first time that like all big-faced men his father had two faces. There was the outer face like a soft warm and careless daub of innocent sealing wax and inside it, as if thumbed there by a seal, was a much smaller one, babyish, shrewd, scared and hard. Now this little inner face had gone greenish and pale and dozens of little veins were broken on the nose and cheeks. The small, drained, purplish lips of this little face were speaking. The son leaned back instinctively to get just another inch away from this little face.

'Listen to this,' the father said and leaned forward on the table as his son leaned back, holding his right fist up as if he had a hammer in his hand and was auctioning his life. 'I am 65. I don't know how long I shall live, but let me make this clear: if I were not an optimist I wouldn't be here. I wouldn't stay another minute.' He paused, fixing his son's half averted eyes to let the full meaning of his words bite home. 'I've worked hard,' the father went on. 'For thirty years I built up this business from nothing. You wouldn't know it, you were a child, but many's the time coming down from the North, I've slept in this office to be on the job early the next morning.' He looked decided and experienced like a man of forty, but now he softened to sixty again. The ring in the hard voice began to soften into a faint whine and his thick nose sniffed. 'I don't say I've always done right,' he said. 'You can't live your life from A to Z like that. And now I haven't a penny in the world. Not a cent. It's not easy at my time of life to begin again. What do you think I've got to live for? There's nothing holding me back. My boy, if I wasn't an optimist I'd go right out. I'd finish it.' Suddenly the father smiled and the little face was drowned in a warm flood of triumphant smiles from the bigger face. He rested his hands on his waistcoat and that seemed to be smiling too, his easy coat smiling, his legs smiling and even winks of light on his shining shoes. Then he frowned.

'Your hair's going thin,' he said. 'You oughtn't to be losing your hair at your age. I don't want you to think I'm criticising you, you're old enough to live your own life, but your hair you know – you ought to do something about it. If you used oil every day and rubbed it in with both hands, the thumbs and forefingers is what you want to use, it would be better. I'm often thinking about you and I don't want you to think I'm lecturing you because I'm not, so don't get the idea this is a lecture, but I was thinking, what you want, what we all want, I say this for myself as well as you, what we all want is ideas – big ideas. We go worrying along but you just want bigger and better ideas. You ought to think big. Take your case. You're a lecturer. I wouldn't be satisfied with lecturing to a small batch of people in a university town. I'd lecture the world. You know, you're always doing yourself injustice. We all do. Think big.'

'Well,' said his son, still smiling, but sharply. He was very angry. 'One's enough in the family. You've thought big till you bust.'

He didn't mean to say this because he hadn't really the courage, but his pride was touched.

'I mean,' said the son, hurriedly covering it up in a panic, 'I'm not like you ... I ...'

'What did you say?' said the old man. 'Don't say that.' It was the smaller of the two faces speaking in a panic. 'Don't say that. Don't use that expression. That's not a right idea. Don't you get a wrong idea about me. We paid sixpence in the pound,' said the old man proudly.

The son began again, but his father stopped him.

'Do you know,' said the bigger of his two faces, getting bigger as it spoke, 'some of the oldest houses in the city are in Queer Street, some of the biggest firms in the country? I came up this morning with Mr Higgins, you remember Higgins? They're in liquidation. They are. Oh yes. And Moore, he's lost everything. He's got his chauffeur but it's his wife's money. Did you see Beltman in the trade papers? Quarter of a million deficit. And how long are Prestons going to last?'

The big face smiled and overflowed on the smaller one. The whole train, the old man said, was practically packed with bankrupts every morning. Thousands had gone. Thousands? Tens of thousands. Some of the biggest men in the City were broke.

A small man himself, he was proud to be bankrupt with the big ones; it made him feel rich.

'You've got to realise, old boy,' he said gravely, 'the world's changing. You've got to move with the times.'

The son was silent. The November sun put a few strains of light through the frosted window and the shadow of its bars and panes was weakly placed on the wall behind his father's head. Some of the light caught the tanned scalp that showed between the white hair. So short the hair was that his father's ears protruded and, framed against that reflection of the window bars, the father suddenly took (to his son's fancy) the likeness of a convict in his cell and the son, startled, found himself asking: Were they telling the truth when they said the old man was a crook and that his balance sheets were cooked? What about that man they had to shut up at the meeting, the little man from Birmingham, in a mackintosh . . .?

'There's a fly in this room,' said the old man suddenly, looking up in the air and getting to his feet. 'I'm sorry to interrupt what you were saying, but I can hear a fly. I must get it out.'

'A fly?' said his son listening.

'Yes, can't you hear it? It's peculiar how you can hear everything now the machines have stopped. It took me quite a time to get used to the silence. Can you see it, old chap? I can't stand flies, you never know where they've been. Excuse me one moment.'

The old man pulled a duster out of a drawer.

'Forgive this interruption. I can't sit in a room with a fly in it,' he said apologetically. They both stood up and listened. Certainly in the office was the small dying fizz of a fly, deceived beyond its strength by the autumn sun.

'Open the door, will you, old boy,' said the old man with embarrassment. 'I hate them.'

The son opened the door and the fly flew into the light. The old man struck at it but it sailed away higher.

'There it is,' he said, getting up on the chair. He struck again and the son struck too as the fly came down. The old man got on top of his table. An expression of disgust and fear was curled on his smaller face; and an expression of apology and weakness.

'Excuse me,' he said again, looking up at the ceiling.

'If we leave the door open or open the window it will go,' said the son.

'It may seem a fad to you,' said the old man shyly. 'I don't like flies. Ah, here it comes.'

They missed it. They stood helplessly gaping up at the ceiling where the fly was buzzing in small circles round the cord of the electric light.

'I don't like them,' the old man said.

The table creaked under his weight. The fly went on to the ceiling and stayed there. Unavailingly the old man snapped the duster at it.

'Be careful,' said the son. 'Don't lose your balance.'

The old man looked down. Suddenly he looked tired and old, his body began to sag and a look of weakness came on to his face.

'Give me a hand, old boy,' the old man said in a shaky voice. He put a heavy hand on his son's shoulder and the son felt the great helpless weight of his father's body.

'Lean on me.'

Very heavily and slowly the old man got cautiously down from the table to the chair. 'Just a moment, old boy,' said the old man. Then, after getting his breath, he got down from the chair to the floor.

'You all right?' his son asked.

'Yes, yes,' said the old man out of breath. 'It was only that fly. Do you know, you're actually more bald at the back than I thought. There's a patch there as big as my hand. I saw it just then. It gave me quite a shock. You really must do something about it. How are your teeth? Do you have any trouble with your teeth? That may have something to do with it. Hasn't Alice told you how bald you are?'

'You've been doing too much. You're worried,' said the son, soft with repentance and sympathy. 'Sit down. You've had a bad time.'

'No, nothing,' said the old man shyly, breathing rather hard. 'A bit. Everyone's been very nice. They came in and shook hands. The staff came in. They all came in just to shake hands. They said, "We wish you good luck"'.

The old man turned his head away. He actually wiped a tear from his eye. A glow of sympathy transported the younger man. He felt as though a sun had risen.

'You know –' the father said uneasily, flitting a glance at the fly on the ceiling as if he wanted the fly as well as his son to listen to what he was going to say – 'you know,' he said. 'The world's all wrong. I've made my mistakes. I was thinking about it before you came. You know where I went wrong? You know where I made my mistake?'

The son's heart started to a panic of embarrassment. 'For heaven's sake,' he wanted to shout, 'don't! Don't stir up the whole business. Don't humiliate yourself before me. Don't start telling the truth. Don't oblige me to say we know all about it, that we have known for years the mess you've been in, that we've seen through the plausible stories you've spread, that we've known the people you've swindled.'

'Money's been my trouble,' said the old man. 'I thought I needed money. That's one thing it's taught me. I've done with money. Absolutely done and finished with it. I never want to see another penny as long as I live. I don't want to see or hear of it. If you came in now and offered me a thousand pounds I should laugh at you. We deceive ourselves. We don't want the stuff. All I want now is just to go to a nice little cottage by the sea,' the old man said. 'I feel I need air, sun, life.'

The son was appalled.

'You want money even for that,' the son said irritably. 'You want quite a lot of money to do that.'

'Don't say I want money,' the old man said vehemently. 'Don't say it. When I walk out of this place tonight I'm going to walk into freedom. I am not going to think of money. You never know where it will come from. You may see something. You may meet a man. You never know. Did the children of Israel worry about money? No, they just went out and collected the manna. That's what I want to do.'

The son was about to speak. The father stopped him.

'Money,' the father said, 'isn't necessary at all.'

Now like the harvest moon on full glow the father's face shone up at his son.

'What I came round about was this,' said the son awkwardly and drily. 'I'm not rich. None of us is. In fact, with things as they are we're all pretty shaky and we can't do anything. I wish I could but I can't. But' – after the assured beginning he began to stammer and to crinkle his eyes timidly – 'but the idea of your being – you know, well short of some immediate necessity, I mean – well, if it is ever a question of – well to be frank, *cash*, I'd raise it somehow.'

He coloured. He hated to admit his own poverty, he hated to offer charity to his father. He hated to sit there knowing the things he knew about him. He was ashamed to think how he, how they all dreaded having the gregarious, optimistic, extravagant, uncontrollable disingenuous old man on their hands. The son hated to feel he was being in some peculiar way which he could not understand mean, cowardly and dishonest.

The father's sailing eyes came down and looked at his son's nervous, frowning face and slowly the dreaming look went from the father's face. Slowly the harvest moon came down from its rosy voyage. The little face suddenly became dominant within the outer folds of skin like a fox looking out of a hole of clay. He leaned forward brusquely on the table and somehow a silver-topped pencil was in his hand preparing to note something briskly on a writing pad.

'Raise it?' said the old man sharply. 'Why didn't you tell me before you could raise money? How can you raise it? Where? By when?'

The Night Worker

A marriage was in the air. In a week the boy's Cousin Gladys was going to be married. The boy sat in a corner of the room out of the way. Uncle Tom and Aunt Annie danced round the girl all day, pushing her this way, pulling her that; only a week to go and now – as the boy watched them in the little dark kitchen, out of the way of people's feet – the dance got fiercer, gayer, rougher. 'Do what you like, you're free already,' they seemed to say to her. And then: 'You dare! You wait! You're still our daughter. Do as you're told.' The boy watched them. He was seven. He did not know what a marriage was, and he gazed at them, expecting it to come into the room like a bird, or to be put on the table like a cake.

Aunt Annie stood at one end of the table with her back to the window, making a pie. He watched the mole move on her bony arm as she rolled the pastry.

'Hurry up with that sleeve, my girl. Haven't you taken out the tacking?'

'It's a fiddling job,' said Gladys, holding up her needle.

'Here, give it us,' said Aunt Annie, wiping the pastry off her fingers and snatching the needle. 'Who's taking the Bible class on Sunday, then?'

'Not me,' said Gladys.

Aunt Annie flopped the pastry over the pie-dish and the boy saw it hang in curtains over the edge, while his Aunt stood straight looking down at the parting in Gladys's thick hair. Aunt Annie's grey hair was screwed back and in her bony face she had bold false teeth, so that she clucked when she talked and had the up and down smile of a skull. She had the good nature of a skeleton.

The boy was waiting for her to trim the pastry on the pie-dish. When she had done this she opened the oven door and a smell of hot cake came across the room. In came the boy's Uncle Tom, a sad, cake-eating man. How did a man so short come to marry a woman so tall? It must have been because Uncle Tom looked like a crouching animal who lived by making great jumps. He was a carpenter, whose skin was the colour of chapel harmonium keys; a yellow, Chinese-looking man with split thumb nails and a crinkled black beard and he frightened because he never quite came into the room, but stood in the doorway, neither in nor out, with a hammer or a chisel in his hand.

'I done them stair-rods, my girl,' he said. It was like a threat.

'I'll take them round,' Gladys said.

'She's going at twelve,' said Aunt Annie.

'Jim be there?' asked her father.

'Yes,' said Aunt Annie. She seemed to the boy to have the power to make her tall teeth shine on the scowl of Uncle Tom, and to put the idea of springing on us all out of his head. 'Jim'll be there. She's taking the boy.'

Then Gladys laughed and, leaning down the table, put her soft arm round the boy's waist and rubbed her cheek in his hair.

'I'm taking my young man round. You'll look after me, won't you?' she said. One of their inexplicable fits of laughter started. Aunt Annie's teeth clucked and clicked. Uncle Tom went, 'Ha, Ha, Ha,' like a saw and lit a pipe.

'Only another week, Glad. It's just because of the neighbours,' said Aunt Annie.

'Ay, my girl, neighbours talk,' said Uncle Tom, and blew out violet smoke as if he were smoking the neighbours out.

The girl put on a prim, concealing expression. One minute she was a girl and the next a woman, then a girl again.

'Stars above, look at the time. Quick,' she cried to the boy, getting up from the table.

They ran upstairs to her room at the back where he slept too, a room which did not smell of camphor like his Aunt's room. He did not like to see Gladys take off her kitchen dress and stand, with bare shoulders and bare arms, in her petticoat, and bare-legged too, because then she became a person he did not know. She was shorter and more powerful. But when her Sunday blue dress was over her head and after she had said, 'Oh these blooming things,' when the hooks caught in her hair, he liked her again.

'How do I look?' she said, when she had her straw hat on, and, not waiting for an answer, she said, 'Now, there's you! Brush your jersey! Quick.'

Jim was waiting, she said. They went out of the room like the wind and the text 'Honour Thy Father' swung sideways on the wall. Down those dark stairs, they went, two at a time, and were half out of the door, when Uncle Tom made his great jump after them.

'Don't forget them stair-rods.'

'Goodness,' she said, grabbing them, 'I'm going dippy.'

And then she was going down the street so fast that the boy had to trot.

'Oh!' She breathed more easily when they had got out of her street. 'That's better. You ain't seen my new house.' But she was talking to the street, not to him, smiling at it. She went along, smiling at the sky and the children playing hopscotch on the pavement, and the greengrocer's cart, as though she were eating the world like an orange and throwing away the skin as she went along. And her breasts and her plump chin jumped in time with her step.

'Which house is it?' the boy said.

'Not yet. Round the corner.'

They turned the corner and there was another long street. 'In this street?' he said.

'No. Round another corner.'

He took her hand. She was walking so fast he was afraid of being lost. And then, down the next street, she calmed down.

Her face became stern. 'Look at him, standing like a dummy! He hasn't seen us.'

A man in a grey cap and a blue serge suit was standing on the pavement.

'Smoking,' she said. 'Bold as brass. There's men for you. He promised he'd give it up. Standing there daft and idle.'

They were all workers in this family. Everything was work to them. Uncle Tom was always sawing and hammering. He had made the chests of drawers and the tables in his house. Aunt Annie scrubbed and cooked. Cousin Gladys was always sewing and even when she came in from her factory, she had, as they said, 'something in her hands' – a brush, a broom, a cleaning cloth or scissors. Jim was a worker, too. He worked at the post office in the middle of the town. One day Uncle Tom took the boy on top of a tram and when they came near the post office, he said: 'Eh, look out this side and you'll see Gladys's Jim working. He's got a good job. Sometimes he's on nights. He's a night worker. Now, look out for him when the tram slows down.' The boy looked into the grey window of the post office as the tram passed by. Inside were dim rows of desks and people and presently he saw Jim in his shirt sleeves. He was carrying a large wastepaper basket.

'What's he doing?' said the boy.

'Sorting,' said Uncle Tom. 'Sorting the mail. His father put him into that job when he was fourteen.'

The boy saw Jim lift the wastepaper basket and then suddenly empty it over the head of another man who was sitting at a desk. He saw Jim laughing. He saw the man jump down and chase Jim across the office, laughing too.

'Larking about,' said Uncle Tom indignantly. 'That's government work.'

The boy stopped laughing. He was scared of Jim after this. Jim was a tall man with a hungry face, but there was a small grin on his lips and after seeing him empty the wastepaper basket the boy did not know what to make of him. It made him feel there was something reckless and secretive in the lives of Cousin Gladys and Jim.

Jim stood outside the gate of the house.

'You come to see the house?' he said to the boy. The boy murmured.

'Lost his tongue,' said Jim.

'I've been in,' he said to Gladys.

Gladys took his arm.

'Have you brought the things? I've got the stair-rods.'

'I put them inside,' he said.

'Oh, let me see,' she said eagerly. The three went to the green front door of the house and Jim let them in. It was a small house of grey brick with a bay window.

'There,' Jim said, pointing to the things. 'I didn't take them upstairs. I waited for you.'

On the floor was a wash-basin and a jug.

'I must wash them before we go,' she said. 'Take them to the kitchen.'

Jim stood and winked at the boy.

'Orders,' said Jim.

'I can't stand dirt,' she said, getting up.

'Well,' said Jim, 'I'm waiting, aren't I?' He put this question to the boy and winked again.

'Oh,' Gladys said, 'don't be soft.'

'Don't look,' said Jim to the boy.

And then Gladys and Jim put their arms round each other and kissed. He saw her heels come off the ground and her knees bend. Gladys blushed and stepped back.

'Oh no, you don't, does she?' Jim said to the boy. And he pulled Gladys and gave her another kiss.

'Jim!' she cried. 'You'll have me over.'

The boy laughed and pulled at her waist from behind and they were all laughing until her shoe kicked the china basin on the floor. That stopped them.

'What'll Ma say when she sees my dress?' Gladys said.

'Oh,' said Jim. '*He* won't tell.' Winking again at the boy. 'Here's a penny. Go into the garden and see if you can find some chocolate.'

'No,' said Gladys, kissing the boy and holding his hand. 'He's my young man. He's looking after me.'

They walked from room to room in the house. After Uncle Tom's house it was bare and smelled of size and new paint. The curtains were up but there was very little furniture. In the sitting-room there was only a blue carpet and a small settee. Jim and Gladys stood at the door and took deep breaths when they looked at this room. There was a vase on the mantelpiece and Gladys moved the vase from the middle to the end.

'Now I've made it lopsided,' she said. 'It wants two.'

'It wants a picture,' said Jim, looking at the bare, lilac-coloured walls. 'It looks bare.'

'Don't complain,' said Gladys pouting.

'I'm not. I was only thinking,' he said, putting his arm round her waist, but she stepped away. Jim gave her a look. The boy had seen her sulk before. He loved her and when she sulked he was frightened.

Jim went out into the hall and while he was out she stroked the boy's head and pressed him against her leg.

'You like it, don't you?' she said. 'You don't think it's bare?'

'No,' he said.

'I'll marry you. You don't grouse.'

'Here – Glad – what's this here?' called Jim sharply from the hall. 'When you've done spooning . . .'

Her sulk went at once. She went out. Jim and she were looking at a small dark spot on the ceiling.

'A leak!' she cried.

'From the bathroom,' he said.

'Who left the water on last time?' she said.

'Your mother – washing things,' Jim said.

'She never,' Gladys said.

They both rushed upstairs. The carpet was not yet down on the stairs and their steps and voices echoed. It was a house of echoes. The boy did not follow. He went to see the painters' pails in the kitchen and to stir the oily remains of paint in them with a stick. He looked into the clean sink. He could not understand why Gladys and Jim were going to live in this house. He wanted to live there with them. He could not understand the laugh of his Aunt and Uncle, that peculiar laughter, so pleased and yet jealous, so free and yet so uneasy, when they talked about Gladys living in this house. It was a laughter marked by side glances. The boy couldn't understand why it was important for him to be there, and he felt lost. He went at last upstairs and on the landing he heard them in the bathroom. They were talking. They had forgotten him. In the evasive way of grown-up people they had gone upstairs to look at the cause of the water coming through the ceiling and, now they were there, they were not talking about that at all. They were talking about people, about some person. The boy stood still and listened.

'They don't want him. *He's* away all the time travelling and she's having another, that'll be the fifth. Terrible, isn't it? Five, imagine it,' Gladys was saying.

'Can't someone put her wise,' Jim said.

'I'd throw myself in the river.'

The boy saw Gladys falling into the river. He thought, I wonder why Gladys wants to get her clothes wet and what will Aunt Annie say.

'I dunno. Kids are nice. I'd like one like that,' Jim said.

'Nobody's kid. That's what he is,' Gladys said. When he heard the word kid, the boy seemed to himself to swell and to lean and to topple with importance towards the bathroom door, but some fear of a woman's hand catching him by the leg or the arm made him seem to go thin again and lean away, till he crept quickly to the landing. There were two doors. Quietly he opened one door and went into a small room. There was nothing in it at all, no curtains to the windows, no linoleum on the floor, no firegrate either, but only a mousehole. He looked down the mousehole and watched it for a long time but nothing came out of it. There was a smell of mouse which reminded him of his home and he looked out of the window down into three back gardens but no child was there. He wondered where nobody's kid was, but no child came. So he went to another room, for this was the house he wanted to live in with one room after another, if people would come and live in it and silence the echoes. Quietly he edged out of the room and guiltily looked into the next one. It was in the front of the house and looked on to the street. Each thing in the room seemed to look at him. There was a small carpet on the floor. There was a wardrobe, a dressing table and a large bedstead with a mattress on it, but no sheets or blankets. It was like his mother's and father's room, but this one was cold and smelled of the furniture shop. It had the mystery and watchful quietness of an empty bedroom.

'Where are you?' called Gladys. 'Where's the boy gone?'

'He's round about,' said Jim easily. They were walking towards the room. The boy could not escape. He stood still.

'Ah, there he is,' Gladys cried. And they were both in the room with him.

'Who sleeps in this bed?' said the boy. Gladys went red. Jim winked.

'Gladys, who sleeps here?' Jim said.

'I don't know,' said Gladys.

'Getcha, she does. She knows,' Jim said. 'Ask her.'

'You do,' the boy said, pointing at Gladys. 'She does.'

'I don't,' said Gladys sternly.

'Jim does,' she said sharply.

'He doesn't,' the boy said. He had seen the lies rolling in their glances at each other.

'I do,' said Jim.

'You don't,' said the boy. 'You're a night worker.'

'That's a good one,' said Jim, who never laughed but only smiled at the corner of his lips, and now suddenly shouted with laughter. 'That's it. That's where I do my work. A night worker, that's where I do my work. Eh, Glad?'

'Jim, shut up,' said Gladys primly. 'Don't tease.'

'I'm not teasing,' laughed Jim. 'I'm a hell of a night worker.' And he made a grab at Gladys who moved away.

'Jim,' she said, 'the neighbours. They can hear everything. These walls are like paper.'

'You and the neighbours,' laughed Jim and he caught up the boy high in the air and sat on the side of the bed. 'One, two, three,' he said, and at three he brought the boy down on the bed.

'Come here, Glad,' he said, 'you have a go. He's ticklish.'

The boy called out and kicked.

'Don't,' said Gladys, coming to rescue him.

'Ticklish yourself,' said Jim, catching her arm and pulling her on the bed. The boy was free.

'Kiss her. Kiss her,' cried the excited boy.

'Don't,' said Gladys.

'I'll neighbour you,' said Jim.

The boy watched them struggling and then he saw Jim was not kissing her but whispering in her ear.

'You are too real, Jim,' she said tenderly. And then they were all lying quiet, Jim in the middle of them, with one arm round Gladys's neck and one arm round the boy and the boy wishing he could get away.

'Family already,' Jim said. 'You must have been on night work, Glad.'

'Oh, give it a rest,' said Glad. 'Remember everything is taken back home. Little pigs have big ears.'

'Very nice work too,' said Jim.

'Don't be so awful,' she pleaded.

'What's awful about it?'

A sigh came from Gladys.

'Very nice, I was saying,' said Jim. 'Sunday morning. Who's getting up to light the fire?'

'You.'

'Me? – No you.'

'Married life,' said Jim. 'Hear that?'

'Who does sleep here truthfully?' said the boy.

'Nobody does,' said Gladys. 'But Jim and me are going to when we are married. That satisfy you?'

The boy knew it was true. It was true because it was far beyond his understanding. Jim and Gladys watched him silently, but Jim's arm tightened on her. They nodded to each other watching the boy.

'And we'll have you for our little boy,' said Gladys.

He knew this was not true. He did not want to be their little boy. They cuddled and kissed and danced about too much; and then people smiled and laughed at them.

'Leave him alone,' said Jim. And they all lay there silently, but he was aching to move from Jim's arm and to go. He was thinking of nobody's child and wishing he could find him, see him, watch him, talk to him.

'First question when I get back,' Gladys said. '"Did you put the stair-rods down?" They think it's *their* house.'

Yes, the boy wanted to get away from this house that wasn't a house yet, from this bed that was not a bed, and to see Aunt Annie and Uncle Tom who sat still for hours after they had worked. He was going to ask her who nobody's child was and how big he was, where he lived, to see him, to watch for a long time what he did, to throw something to him to see if he moved, to see if he talked and how his mouth looked when he talked.

'When are we going home?' he said.

Double Divan

——

Two workmen were carrying a double divan bed, slung on ropes from their shoulders, down the busy streets in the warm fume of a London dusk. The man behind was ginger-haired. He had a moustache of sweat, a hard, factory mouth, and blue, unwilling eyes. The weight of the bed kept his head down, and the pace of the big-potato-bummed man in front was dragging him along on the tips of his toes almost at a trot. They were travelling fast.

Presently the traffic lights were against them and they stood still.

'How much farther?' said the man in front. He could not turn his head.

'You're bloody right,' said the man behind.

The lights changed, the traffic gave a loud swallow and moved forward, and the two men were driven over the crossing. On they raced, not daring to stop. They came to a wide road-junction and then the lights went red again. The man behind felt the warm radiator of a lorry toasting his backside.

'Gone deaf or something; how much farther?' called back the man in front.

'What d'you mean, how much farther? You got the paper,' said the man behind.

'What bleeding paper?' said the man in front.

'The address she give you,' said the man behind.

'Who?' said the man in front.

'The paper she give you,' said the man behind.

'I haven't got no bleeding paper,' said the man in front.

The man behind rolled his eyes and wagged his knees about. The bed swayed with him and the man in front went as pink as a sausage in the neck as he steadied it.

'Call the keeper, lock me up, I'm barmy,' said the man behind.

Motor horns started blowing, the lorry radiator pressed closely on the trousers of the man behind. A bus driver put his head out and shouted: the lights had changed. The two heaved at the bed and rushed over the crossing. They advanced to the next side-turning and the leader swung round there, put his end of the bed down and they faced each other.

'She spoke to you. You was the last to see her,' said the leader. 'She didn't give me no address.'

'You fixed the job. All she said to me was, "Be careful. Be careful," she said, "and mind the casters,"' said the man behind.

The man in front was large and dazed. He wiped his forehead and felt in his jacket pockets. A pigeon came down in the dusk and he looked at the bird enquiringly. He felt in his waistcoat pocket and looked up to the rows of windows for help. All knowledge of where he had been told to take the bed had gone. The man behind took the rope off his aching shoulders and threw it on the bed.

'What name was it?' said the man behind.

'Ida or Mary or like that,' said the man in front.

'Ida or Mary, very tasty, very sweet,' jeered the man behind. 'Ida what?'

'I'm trying to think,' said the man in front.

'You'd better stop thinking and go back and find her,' said the man behind.

'She's left. Moved out,' said the man in front.

The man behind sat down on the bed and took his cap off. 'Is she waiting there – where we're going, this woman, this Ida, this party?'

'I got it!' exclaimed the man in front. 'Robinson – that's the name. Mrs Robinson. There was two of them.'

The man behind got up and rolled his eyes and put his tongue out. 'Open the door,' he cried. 'Open the door and let me out.'

The large man stood searching his mind.

'She came over to the yard in the morning,' the man in front said. '"The name is Robinson, Mrs Robinson," she says. "My sister is moving her flat and I want you to get a bed out for her, a big one." Married woman, see, giving orders, doesn't tell you anything and expects you to know the lot. "I can't do that," I says, "I work all day." "I don't want it moved in the daylight," she says. "It's not my bed, it's my sister's." "I don't want to know your business," I says. "I'll move what you like, but

I can't do it till the evening." "What are we arguing about?" she says. "That's what I want you to do."'

'Get on,' said the man. 'I don't half sweat.'

'She give me the address. Next thing, after work, I go up to the flat. Number twenty-six. Top floor. She comes out with glasses on. The carpets are gone, all the furniture, just the bed in the back room. "I'll tell my sister," she says. "Ida," she calls out. "Here's the man." Ida – that's the sister, see – comes out of the kitchen. "What man, Mary?" says the sister. "The man about the bed," says this Mrs Robinson.'

'Step on it,' said the man behind.

'I can't,' said the man in front, 'or you won't follow. This Ida wasn't like the other. She had a fur coat on and first of all I thought she was sweating, her face was red and steamy, only a girl. She had a handkerchief in her hand and she dropped it. "Excuse me," I said, and picked it up. It was wet. She was crying. She gives one look at me and then the waterworks start up again and she goes off to the kitchen, leaving me, see, with the other one. "Wait here," Mrs Robinson says. "I must go to my sister. She's not very well. She's upset." "Oh," I says, "having trouble . . . ?"'

'Here,' said the man behind. 'Pack it in. Here's a van coming. We got trouble here.'

The two men put the ropes round their necks and moved on to the entrance to a public-house yard. The dray horses struck with bearded hoofs at the cobbles as they strained past.

'Put her here,' said the man behind, lowering his end. 'I'm going to have a beer.'

The two men stood the striped bed on end against the side wall of the public-house. They looked at the bed, silently telling it not to move while they were gone, and they went into the public-house. The shadow of the bed could be seen against the frosted glass of the bar window.

'Know anyone of the name of Robinson round here?' said the man behind. 'Number twenty-six, The Terrace?'

'You see hundreds of faces, you never know the names,' the barman said, picking up his cigarette from the bar.

'We're moving a bed,' said the man behind, 'for a Mrs Ida something.'

'Miss, not Mrs,' said the man in front. 'She wasn't married.'

'Mrs, must be,' said the man behind. 'Double bed.'

'That don't follow,' said the barman, winking at the customers.

'It'd be a funny thing for a single woman to have a double bed,' a man said.

'What's funny in that?' the barman said.

'When his old woman rolls on him,' the customer said. 'I sleep with myself.'

'I lay you do, Jim,' said the barman.

Two squeaks of laughter went up from two old women sitting on a bench.

'She is a young woman and she isn't married,' said the man in front.

'It must be,' said the man behind, 'some tart.'

'Oh dear,' said one of the women on the bench, hiding her face in the top of her glass. 'Language, now we hear it.'

'Ginger,' said the leader, taking his beer to a table, 'you're right. That Mrs Robinson must have given me the paper and it has dropped out. She wrote it down on the mantelpiece, and while she was writing her sister called out from the kitchen and Mrs Robinson put the pencil down and says, "I'll be back. My sister wants to talk to me."'

He sat down, the man in front said, and he waited in the flat. He sat on the bed; it was the only thing in the room to sit on. 'The only furniture they hadn't moved,' he said, 'was a brass coal-scuttle with some fire-irons and an electric kettle in it.' He knew about that because he had had an eye on the electric kettle, and Mrs Robinson knew he had because she said to him, 'Don't you touch those. They are mine.' The flat was a pretty place; to give an example, the paint was green, but not the common green, and the walls were pink, but not what you would call right out pink: a lady's place. You could tell that by Ida's voice.

'Perhaps,' said the man behind, going up to the bar for two more pints and speaking over his shoulder as though he were spitting, 'she couldn't pay the rent. Was it a shop? Did she give you the address of a shop?'

'No,' said the man in front, 'it wasn't a shop. I had a look out of the window. You could see the canal through the tops of the trees. And that's what messed me up. They were having an argument next door. I could hear them carrying on. The next thing the door bangs. Mrs Robinson shouts out in a temper, "I'll tell him to go." There's a sort of free-for-all in the door and in comes the sister, Ida, still crying. She marches up to me and she says, very sharp, "Give me a pencil. I want you to take this bed to Mrs Robinson's house." Of course, I hadn't got a pencil. But before I could tell her this, Mrs Robinson comes in. She was shouting. "No, Ida," she says, "I won't have it. Not after what you said. You're a pig. Keep your beastly bed." Your beastly bed, oh dear, that's what she said. She says, "I am only trying to help you. If you haven't got any reputation to think of," she says, "the rest of the family have. What would the neighbours say if they saw a double bed go out of a single girl's flat into the van with the rest in broad daylight? There," she says, "Ida, I've told you the plain truth. Someone's got to tell you."'

'Oh dear, oh dear, oh dear,' said the man behind. 'Sisters, you say.'

'Taking no notice of me,' said the man in front. 'I'm the wall. "Now which of you ladies is having it?" I says. "I'm having these," says Mrs Robinson, picking up the scuttle and things in both arms like someone was robbing her. "My sister's having it," says Ida, opening her bag and looking for a pen. "No," says Mrs Robinson, putting down the scuttle and snatching her pen from her. "Not after what you said. We've slept in a single bed all the time we've been married and we can carry on." A regular ding-dong. And then Mrs Robinson says, "What are you going to sleep on tonight, Ida?"'

'Ah!' said the man behind.

'Oh dear,' said the man in front. 'You ought to have seen Ida's face. She stops talking, her mouth stays open. She gives a hoot as if she had struck a mine. "Ooh! Oooh!" she goes. There's a flood again. "Oooh," she hoots, "what shall I do, what shall I do? I don't care where I sleep. I don't care what happens to me." And then she goes over to the window and cries out, "I shall throw myself in the canal. I shall kill myself. I don't want to live. I told him I would, he's broken my heart."

'Mrs Robinson says, "The number of times you've hanged yourself, drowned yourself, and put your head in the gas oven, Ida, you'd fill a cemetery. He was a married man and you knew it. You said the same after Arthur and after Len. Please excuse me," she says to me.

'And, Ida answers back: "You're married, Mary. You've got a husband and children. Won't anyone marry me? I came home from the office and I cooked him a meal every night."

'"That was Philip, not this one," Mrs Robinson calls out. "Because of his stomach."

'Ida looks at her sister and stops crying at this. Annoyed. "There were two with bad stomachs," Ida says sharp. "You're always unfair to me. They said it was because of their wives."

'That's what she said,' said the man in front, looking at his untouched beer with indignation, indignant with himself. He took a long swallow of it.

'Straight,' he said, watching the beads of froth float on the dark current towards his lips. He put the glass down; he had finished it. 'Two married men with bad stomachs.

'And then,' he said, 'Ida, the single girl, began to laugh, not a laugh in the ordinary way . . .'

'Hysterics,' said the man behind. 'My wife's sister does it.'

'No,' said the man in front. 'Too dry. More like a bark than a laugh. She laughed at Mrs Robinson, she laughed at me. "Oh dear," she laughed. She couldn't stop. "It's all because I had a double bed," she says, "I ought to have kept to singles."

'You ought to have seen the married one's face when she said this. Didn't like it. In front of me, see. I couldn't help it, could I? "Oooh, Ida," she says, "how can you?" Very classy. "Don't mind me," I says. Ida gives me a wink. "Oh yes it is," Ida says. "Ask this gentleman. I'll never get married till I get a single, will I?" she says. "Ida, shut up!" says Mrs Robinson. "It's no good rushing things, miss," I says. "There you are!" says Ida.

'She comes up to me,' said the man in front, 'this Ida, and she says, "Take this bed and the coal-scuttle and things to my sister's address. She's a respectable married woman." And then she turns on her sister and says, "You had the fender when Arthur left me and the armchair, Mary. I'm keeping the rest till next time. You've furnished your flat bit by bit out of my broken heart." You ought to have seen the look she gave her sister; sarcastic, it wiped the floor up with a wet rag all round her. If looks could kill.'

'I know what I'd do,' said the man behind, 'with a girl like that Ida if she was my daughter. I'd take her knickers down and I'd paste her. What's class? A tart's a tart anywhere. My wife's sister is one – talk of love, it's turned on like a tap.'

'There was the best electric kettle in that scuttle that I ever see,' said the man in front.

The two men studied the shadow of the bed on the window. It did not seem to them like the bed they had been talking about and they bought two more drinks in order to be able to look it in the face. They went outside and they were astonished to find the dusk had gone – the London night was in full bud and blossom. They swayed down the yard entrance and considered the bed with many renewed attempts at impartiality. With its very wide stripes it was an object now hard to focus.

'Better lift it into the yard,' said the man in front, 'so's no one will touch it while we go back to the house.'

They lifted the bed and lowered it again in the yard at the back of the public-house.

'A bed like that's worth a bit of money,' said the man behind. 'It's worth fifteen quid.'

'Twenty,' from the man in front.

'Seven years ago, before the war, you'd have given ten pounds for it,' said the man behind.

'Talk sense,' said the man in front, suddenly lighting with rage. 'The war didn't last seven years.'

A quarrel broke out between the two men. Their shouts banged about up and down the yard until the dogs barked at them.

'Where's the money for this job?' shouted the man behind. 'I don't let go of this bed till I get my money.'

The man in front suddenly sat down.

'You'll get your money,' he said.

'Too true I will,' said the man behind. 'I'm going back to the house to see if they're there.'

And he went. The man in front watched him go without surprise. When he was out of sight the man in front began to feel the springs, and then gently to bounce up and down. He smiled as he bounced and then the smile grew to a laugh. 'Oh dear, what a disappointment for Mrs Robinson,' he said. And to spite her he put his feet up on the bed and lay down. 'I wonder,' he said, 'what that other poor girl is doing now?'

He was asleep when Mrs Robinson, Ida, and the man behind returned. They found the bed in the darkness by his snores.

'Mary,' cried out Ida, clapping her hands, 'there's a man in it.'

The Landlord

It was due to the boldness of Mrs Seugar, who always got what she wanted, that they came to live in the semi-detached house called East Wind. They were driving through that part of the town one Sunday. Mrs Seugar was bouncing on the seat and sighing: 'Snobby district. I like it snobby, refined, a bit of class.' And her little eyes, like caterpillars' heads, began eating up everything they passed until she saw East Wind. The adjoining house was called West Wind. 'Oh stop!' she called out. 'Look – posh! That's the house I want. You could live in a house like that. I mean, be one of the toffs and look down your nose at everyone. I don't mean anything nasty. Get out and see if they'll sell it.'

Wherever Mrs Seugar moved, a spotlight played on her; but Mr Seugar lived in a deep, damp-eyed shade of shame, the shame of always obliging someone. Unable to step out of it, he had shuffled a lot of money out of his shop into his pocket and piled it on to Mrs Seugar, who stood out in the spotlight seeing that she was taken notice of. Mr and Mrs Seugar left the car, went to the house, and were asked in by the man who was to be their landlord. He was having tea in a shabby room, with pictures and books, a very tall man with nothing to remark about him except that as the Seugars advanced he retreated, slipped back like a fish with eyes like lamps and with a coarse little open mouth. Mrs Seugar sat herself down and let her legs fall open like a pair of doors.

'I have set my heart on your house. Oh, it's posh, cute,' she said. 'Isn't it? Haven't I?' Mr Seugar with his knees together confirmed it.

'Would you sell it to us?' Mrs Seugar said.

The landlord poured them out two cups of tea and slipped back into the corner watching them as if he were having a dream of being robbed. (In the end, it was he who robbed them. A scholar and gentleman, he asked a tremendous price: Mrs Seugar was knobbed with jewellery.) But first of all he put them off. They could have, not this house, but the one next door, he said.

'I own both.'

'Who lives next door?' said Mrs Seugar. 'Ask him who lives next door. Why should *I* talk – oh, it's so posh,' she said, elbowing her husband. 'You make me wear out my voice.'

'Who . . .' began Mr Seugar.

'No one,' said the landlord.

'Then you can move in next door and we can move in here,' cried Mrs Seugar. 'What did I say? Would you believe it – I said to my husband, "That's the house I want, go and ask," but he wouldn't. He makes objections to everything – well, I call it daft to make objections all the time. It makes people look down on me for marrying him. I don't mean anything nasty.'

The shadow of shame came down like a dark shop blind over Mr Seugar, and indeed that is where his mind was – in his shop. In half an hour the landlord was showing them round the house, Mr Seugar following them like a sin, giving a glance into every room after the other two had gone on, being called forward for lagging behind. When the visit was done, Mr Seugar bought the house, wiping his feet up and down on the carpet as he did so, crying inside himself at the tremendous price, and bewildered because, in buying something that could not be wrapped up in paper and slipped into his overcoat pocket, he felt exposed.

When they got home and shut their door, Mrs Seugar began to shout everything she said. He was snobby (the landlord); it was a pleasure to hear him talk the way the snobs talk, la-di-da. It was lovely; but if you haven't the cash it doesn't help you being a snob. She felt at ease having someone to look down on straight away.

'He's a recluse,' said Mr Seugar.

'He isn't,' shouted Mrs Seugar, grabbing him back from her husband. 'He never stopped staring at me. I could have died,' shouted Mrs Seugar. 'Fancy him letting us have the house like that, no questions. It's barmy. Funny thing him living in that house all his life – he must have got pig-sick of it – and me killing myself to have it, it shows what I say, you never know. You say I'm mad.'

At the end of the month Mrs Seugar led her furniture into East Wind, and when it was all in, Mr Seugar followed it like a mourner. They settled in and Mrs Seugar sat there with her legs wide open and her shoes kicked off, going through the names of all the people she was going to look down her nose at. 'Listen,' said Mr Seugar from the shade. No shop bell to call them, no one popping in from down the street; they were hearing the only sound in their lives: the landlord poking his fire in the house next door.

'Talk!' said his wife to him. 'But for me you wouldn't be here, say something. Not business. Talk. Talk snobby. Oh,' sighed Mrs Seugar, 'I bet you talk in the shop. I've got everything on,' she said, having a look at her gold watch, her diamond brooch, and so on, 'and I feel a fool, you sitting with your trap closed. A snob would talk.'

At that moment they both started. The front door was being opened, shoes were being wiped on the mat, there were steps in the hall.

'What's that?' said Mr Seugar.

'Burglars, I'd welcome it,' said Mrs Seugar.

Mr Seugar went out and met their landlord walking down the hall. He was just putting a key into his pocket. He was surprised by Mr Seugar, murmured something, walked on, and then was stopped by the sight of their stair carpet. Murmuring again, he flicked like a fish sideways into the sitting-room, looked at Mrs Seugar in a lost way, and then sat down.

'I've been for a walk,' he said.

'A constitootional,' said Mr Seugar.

'Shut up, Henry,' said Mrs Seugar, 'until remarks are addressed to you.'

The landlord looked round the room where his pictures and his books had been and then glanced at the Seugars.

'Dreadfully late,' he said suddenly, went to the window, which was a low one, opened it, and stepped over the sill. Once over, he walked down the garden into his own garden next door.

'Dreadfully, awfully, frightfully – late,' Mrs Seugar was repeating in ecstasy.

Mr Seugar came out of his shame. 'Blimey. See that? Forgot he's moved! He's still got the key.'

A terrible quarrel broke out between the Seugars. That was a call, Mrs Seugar said. No, it wasn't, said Mr Seugar, it was a mistake. Mr Seugar was so ill-bred he hadn't realised it was a call, but must pass remarks. If a visitor says 'walk' you don't say 'constitootional' afterwards, correcting him. Why repeat? It's daft. Not only that, he came to see her, not Mr Seugar. A man, Mrs Seugar said, was what she wanted, her ideal, who talked soft and gave you a good time, a lovely man, not the fairy prince and all that twaddle, but a recluse who could fascinate you and give you things.

'Out of mean spite you gave him the bird,' she said to Mr Seugar. Mr Seugar did not know what to do. At last he got a spade and went out to the garden to dig.

The next day just as lunch was put on the table, in came the landlord, walked straight into the dining-room, ahead of Mr Seugar, sat down in Mr Seugar's place before the joint, and started to carve.

'Henry!' Mrs Seugar warned her husband.

Mr Seugar said nothing. Their landlord handed them their plates and then rang the bell for an extra one. Mrs Seugar talked about her summer holiday. People were stand-offish there, she said, and she couldn't get a corset.

'I apologise for the beef,' said the landlord.

Mrs Seugar kicked Mr Seugar under the table.

'D'you believe millions now living will never die?' asked Mrs Seugar to keep conversation going. 'I mean they'll live, not pass out. It sounds daft. We had a circular. We put up a notice saying: No Hawkers. No Circulars; but that doesn't stop some people. Not never die, they must be fools to think that, what some people's minds get on, they must be empty. I want a bit of life. I'm not morbid.'

'Millions now living?' said the landlord. 'Will never die?'

'I'm surprised,' said Mrs Seugar, 'they are allowed to give out circulars like that in a neighbourhood like this.'

'I am sorry, I do apologise for the sweet,' said the landlord. 'It is my fault. I am awfully thoughtless. I will make a confession.'

'A confession. Oh!' cried Mrs Seugar, clapping her hands.

'It is terrible,' said the landlord. It was one of his longest speeches. 'I forgot I asked you to lunch.'

'Henry,' said Mrs Seugar. 'Close your mouth, we don't want to see what you've eaten.'

Presently the landlord looked at the pattern on the plates, then at the table, then at the walls. He got up and, murmuring, went suddenly out.

'You can see what has happened,' said Mrs Seugar.

'What I said yes'day, day before,' said Mr Seugar.

They sat there dwindling at the table, terrified.

'He's barmy,' said Mr Seugar humbly – the customer is always right. 'He's forgot he's moved. Like people who order the same groceries twice.'

'Father,' said Mrs Seugar – she always called him Father when she was accusing him: he had failed in this respect. 'Ever since we've been up here you've shown you're not used to it. Why didn't you tell me you asked him in for a bite?'

'Who carved the joint? Am I barmy or is he?' said Mr Seugar.

'I was glad for him to carve. It used to be his house. I have manners if some people haven't,' said Mrs Seugar.

Mr Seugar began one of his long, low, ashamed laughs, a laugh so common that Mrs Seugar said he could keep that for the next time. Mr Seugar stopped suddenly and kept it for that. He had kept so many things for the next time in his life that they got stale.

'If any person calls to be laughed at, it's you, Father,' said Mrs Seugar. Mr Seugar waited till she went out of the room and then did a small dance, which he stopped in alarm when he caught sight of himself in the mirror. A blush darkened his face and he went out to dig in the garden. Later his wife brought out a cap for him to wear; she didn't, she said, like to see a man digging without his cap.

If they had had a cat or a dog, Mrs Seugar said, it would have been just the same; why make a difference when it was a human being who came in at the front door, said a word or two in the sitting-room, and went out by the window? For all the time she was left alone, Mrs Seugar said, it was company.

'It's a man,' said Mrs Seugar.

'What's he say?' said Mr Seugar.

'It isn't what he says,' Mrs Seugar said. 'With those snobby ones it is the way they say it, it's what d'you call it, that pansy drawl. I love it. He likes to hear me talk.'

'Oh,' said Mr Seugar.

'Yes,' said Mrs Seugar. 'Why?'

'I just said "Oh,"' said Mr Seugar. 'I'll try the window myself.' And copying the landlord, Mr Seugar himself stepped over the sill into the garden to his digging.

'That isn't funny, it's vulgar,' called Mrs Seugar after him.

Mr Seugar said: 'Oh, sorry. No harm,' and came back over the sill into the room and went out the proper way to put things right.

One evening the following week he met their landlord coming down-stairs fast in his slippers.

Mr Seugar went into his store-room at the shop on early closing day and sat on a sack of lentils. He was trying to get a few things clear in his mind. 'He sold me the house. I bought it. But I hadn't the right to buy it, there was no notice up.' Suddenly the truth was clear to him. 'I bought *him* as well. He was thrown in. It's like sand in the sugar.'

And then the cure occurred to him. Mr Seugar went home to his wife and said:

'We must arst him in. We've never arst him in. If we arst him he'd see his mistake.'

'He never wanted us to have this house,' said Mrs Seugar. Once a month she suffered from remorse. 'We oughtn't to have done it. It's a judgment.'

'Arst him.'

They laid out a table of ham and cake and tea and put a bottle of port wine on the sideboard. Mr Seugar lit a whiff to make the hall smell and went all over the house to be sure the landlord wasn't there already and then walked up and down there until he arrived. He came at last and gave a long hand to Mr Seugar.

'I hope you are comfortably settled. I ought to have come before but I have been very busy. I must go and present my apologies to Mrs S . . .' said the landlord.

'We have been meaning to ask you a long time,' said Mrs Seugar.

'I go away so often,' said the landlord.

'You live next door to people all your life and never see them,' said Mrs Seugar, 'yet someone from the other end of the earth you keep running into. How long is it since you've spoken a word to the people in the fish shop next door, Henry?'

'This morning,' said Mr Seugar.

'Don't tell lies,' Mrs Seugar said. 'Ten years more like it.'

The Landlord

Mrs Seugar drank a glass of port and went red. An evening of pleasure succeeded. They were celebrating the normality of their landlord.

'Is a woman's life what you call over at forty-five?' asked Mrs Seugar. 'You work and what is there? You can't settle, you wish you could, but no, you must be up looking out of the window. *You* have settled. You've got your books, you can read. I can't, it's daft, I can't lose myself in something. If I could *lose* myself!'

Their landlord looked at Mr and Mrs Seugar and they could see he was appreciating them. Mrs Seugar's voice went like a lawn-mower running over the same strip of grass, up and down, up and down, catching Mr Seugar like a stone in the cutters every now and then, and then running on again. They had a long conversation about boiler coke. It turned out that their landlord used anthracite, which did not affect the lungs, and Mr Seugar said they had paraffin at the shop in his father's time.

There was a pause in the conversation. The landlord looked at the clock and yawned. Presently he knelt down and they thought he was tying his bootlaces; he was untying them. He took his shoes off, then his collar and tie, unbuttoned his waistcoat.

'If you will forgive me,' he said, 'I'll go to bed now. Don't let me break up the party. I'll just slip off. You know your rooms.'

'Sssh,' said Mrs Seugar when he had gone. 'Say nothing. Listen.'

Mr and Mrs Seugar sat like the condemned in their chairs. They heard their landlord go upstairs. They heard him walking in their rooms above. Then evidently he discovered his mistake, for they heard him rush downstairs and out of the house, banging the door after him. The following night Mr Seugar went up to their bedroom at nine o'clock to get some matches and found their landlord fast asleep, in their bed.

Service was always Mr Seugar's motto. He bent slightly over the bed, rubbing his hands. 'And the next pleasure?' he appeared to say.

Mrs Seugar came in. When she saw their landlord lying in his shirt, half out of the bedclothes, she made one of her sudden strides forward, squared her chins and her cheeks, and made a grab at her husband's pyjamas, which had been thrown on the bed. At the same time she gave him a punch that sent him through the doorway and threw the pyjamas after him. 'Take those things away,' she said.

Mr Seugar was an inhuman man; he was not sorry for himself, but he

[329]

was sorry for his pyjamas. He picked them up. As he did this, he saw Mrs Seugar settling into an attitude of repose and heaving her breath into position. From Mr Seugar's point of view, on the fourth stair outside and on an eye level with his wife's ankles, never had Mrs Seugar seemed more beautiful; it was as if she were eating something that agreed with her and that other people could not get.

'Where are yours?' whispered Mr Seugar emotionally.

Mrs Seugar never answered questions. Now she came out of the room and quietly closed the door. 'So refined!' she said. 'His mouth was shut.'

Mr Seugar opened his mouth at once. He and Mrs Seugar had not slept apart for twenty-eight years and, in a voice irrigated by what with him passed for feeling, Mr Seugar mentioned this fact.

A new contralto voice came from Mrs Seugar's bosom. 'There are times,' she said, 'when a woman wants to be alone. I'll take the spare room.'

And what Mrs Seugar said she would take, she always took. In the spare room she lay awake half the night going over the past twenty-eight years of her life with a tooth comb. You make your circumstances or they make you, she thought. Which is it?

By 'circumstances', she meant, of course, Mr Seugar, who lay on the living-room sofa frivolously listening to the varying notes of the springs. An extraordinary dream came to him that night. He dreamed that thieves had removed the ham-and-bacon counter from his shop. At six o'clock he woke up, put on an overcoat, and went up to what was, after all, his bedroom. The landlord had gone. Mr Seugar put his hand under one of the pillows and pulled out his wife's nightdress and threw it into the corner with his pyjamas when he had taken them off. Unfairness was what he hated.

'If I had had a different life,' said Mrs Seugar to her friends, 'things would have been different for me. I sacrificed myself, but when you're young you don't know what you're doing. I don't mean anything nasty against Father, he's done what he could, it's wonderful, considering ...'

Mr Seugar went out and played bowls when the shop was closed. He pitched the ball down the green, watching it as it rolled, and when it stopped he called out: 'How does that smell?'

The fishmonger at the other end called back: 'Strong.'

But what Mr Seugar was really thinking as he pitched the ball was: 'I lay he's in the kitchen making tea.' Or 'I lay a pound he's having a bath.' Or 'What you bet he's gone to bed?' Mr Seugar was a betting man by nature. He would bet anyone anything, only they did not know he was doing so. 'It's a mug's game,' Mr Seugar said, knowing that he was a mug. He did not bet only on the bowling green; he betted while he was digging in the garden, turning round suddenly and looking at the windows of both houses to see if anything had happened while his back was turned. A starling on the chimney would give him a start and he would stick the spade in the ground and go inside to see what had happened. One day when he thought he had betted on everything his landlord could possibly do, he met him upstairs on the landing of the house.

'Are you looking for someone?' said Mr Seugar, leaning forward over an imaginary counter as he spoke.

'Yes,' said the landlord and walked on, disregarding Mr Seugar as he always did, like a customer moving on to the next counter.

'My wife,' said Mr Seugar, always one to oblige, 'is in the sitting-room.'

The landlord stopped and considered Mr Seugar with astonishment.

'*Your* wife!' he said.

'Oh,' screamed Mr Seugar – the scream was inside him, in his soul, and was not audible. 'Oh,' he screamed. 'The deception. I never thought of that.'

He saw how he had been diddled. He went out into the garden and dug, dug, dug. Worm after worm turned in the damp soil. 'I am mad,' said Mr Seugar. Mr Seugar dropped his spade and, pulling out his key, he opened his mouth, put on a fish-like expression, and went round to his landlord's house. He let himself in. Out of the study came the landlord.

'Good morning,' said the landlord.

Mr Seugar did not answer, but marched up the stairs and had a bath. After that he came down to the study. His landlord had gone, but Mr Seugar sat there in front of the fire. Then, in order to annoy them next door, poked the fire.

Passing the Ball

—

Two years ago, when I had finished at the hospital and was waiting for a grant to come through, I put in a month as a locum for a country doctor.

When I first went to see him the doctor switched on his desk lamp, turned it to shine full in my face, and said in a rough voice, as if he were finishing a mouthful of hay:

'How old are you?' he said. 'If I may ask? Married? Do you hunt? I mean where were you at school?'

He began pulling out the drawers of his desk one by one and, shutting them recklessly with a number of bangs, rang for his dispenser and said something to her about a horse. After this he leaned forward and fell to tapping the side of his tin wastepaper basket with a riding-crop in slow, trotting time. His look was uninterested.

'Yes, yes, yes,' he said lazily from the saddle. 'We don't want a lot of your new-fangled ideas here. This isn't the usual kind of practice. The man I have here has got to be a gentleman. You can hand out your penicillin and your M & B. You can put the whole parish in an iron lung, fill them with American drugs – I know that's the modern idea – but it's my experience of forty years of doctoring that a gentleman's worth the lot. Have a drink? Do you know the Fobhams?'

I could see up the doctor's meaty nose and underneath his chin when he raised it to utter this name in the voice of one who had suddenly put on court dress. By nature Dr Ray was a man of disguises, and a new one with every sentence. Two whiskies stabilised him. A heavy, guilty blush came down from the middle of his head, enlarged his ears, and went below his collar. His hands became confidential; one of them was put on my shoulder; his voice lowered and, if shrewdness was in one blue eye as sharp as a pellet, the other became watery with anxiety.

'What it boils down to, old man, is this,' he said, sneering at himself. 'Half the village at the surgery door thinking they're going to die because they've cut their fingers, and threatening to write to the Ministry of Health because you won't issue free crutches and corsets. The usual thing. The day's work, eh? All in it. Forget it. The important thing is this.'

'Yes?' I said.

'I'm telling you.' He sharpened. 'The only people who count here are fifteen families: the private patients. That's where the living is. I've been here most of my life and I've made quite a nice thing out of it. I don't want it spoiled. They're the people to watch. I get a call from them – I go at once. I don't want anyone coming in here and ruining it with a lot of new-fangled stuff.

'Frankly,' he added, 'I can't afford it.'

The doctor stepped back, opened his mouth wide and felt his face in several places.

'I think you're the right sort of chap,' he said. 'Have another drink? There are only three illnesses in this place – bridge, horses, and marriage – you're not married? Glad to hear it. And there's only one medicine: tact. In any case,' he said, 'it's August. Everyone's away.'

In that month the woods in the small estates seemed to lie under glass. The cottages fluffed like hens in the sun; the large houses had a sedate and waxen gleam. The air seemed to hang, brocaded, from the enormous trees. I drove on my rounds from one tropical garden to the next. Men like cock pheasants drove out of Georgian houses in their shooting brakes; their women's voices went off like the alarm call of game. In the rivers, large, clever trout, living like *rentiers* on their capital, put themselves at the disposal of the highly taxed fishermen on the banks of the beautiful river. There was the warm bread smell of the harvest in the fields and of tweed, roses, and tobacco in the bars. In their houses, most of them built in the eighteenth century, the fifteen families were hidden. There Mrs Gluck ordered more honeysuckle so that next year it would climb into *every* bedroom; there the Admiral did his jigsaw puzzle and the young Hookhams came down from the week's climb towards the Cabinet in London; two miles off, Lord Fobham, wearing plimsolls, let off a wing of his house at a tremendous rent and spent his evenings stiffening himself with gin in the company of Mr Calverley, a cultivated alcoholic who often – I was to discover – lost his clothes and had slept, against the will of their owners, in most of the houses round about. Mrs Luke sat moustached and quietly chewing on her fortune in a house famous for its monkey puzzles. At Upley was the financier Hicks, who had shot the head off the stone pelican on the gate of his drive; in the mill house near the water meadows was Mrs Scarborough ('Pansy') Flynn, three times divorced, nesting like a moorhen and listening for the voices of men. And then there were the Bassilleros, who brought into the country an odour of Claridges; indeed, his violet complexion gave 'Jock' Bassillero's face the surprised appearance of one cut out of a hotel carpet and seen in fluorescent light.

I have conveyed an impression of tropical luxury in my account of this August, but in fact it was the coldest August for many years. We had influenza in the village. The tropical quality came from the fifteen families; at a certain stage, portions of civilisation reach a Tahitian condition and are hot enough to be moved to a climate less mild than the English one; indeed, there was a good deal of talk among the fifteen families of emigrating to Jamaica. I found this tropical tendency almost at once. A few days after I had taken over from the doctor, there was a party at the Hickses'.

I heard there had been a party when Mr Calverley was brought into the surgery. He had a cut on top of his head and was supported by a few friends. Mrs Bassillero was among them.

'What have you been up to?' I said as I dressed the wound.

Mr Calverley was wearing no collar and no jacket and smelled strongly of ivy. He had curling black hair and looked gentle, savage, and appealing.

'The gutter fell on him,' said one of the women. 'Is it deep? Is it all right? Poor Tommy. He was climbing after Pansy Flynn.'

The sympathy annoyed Calverley. He knocked the dressing out of my hand, jumped up, and drove his friends back to the door.

'I'll kill you all,' he said.

Hicks, the financier, a man who illustrated the Theory of Conspicuous Waste, by the habit of dropping the first letter of many of his words, said: ''hut up, Tommy. 'it down. 'ook at Ray, he's making 'ight of it.'

'That's not Ray,' someone said. 'Ray's on holiday.'

''ood 'od,' said Hicks. ' ''an't have quacks here.'

I had got Calverley back in the chair.

' ''ight poison us. State 'octor? No?'

[334]

Calverley looked up at me with a quiet, intimate, head-hunting smile.

'I'll kill you,' he said to me in a soft and cultivated voice.

Mrs Bassillero started talking loudly to someone on the other side of the surgery about the sexual life of a couple called Pip and Dottie.

I found Calverley's tie on my carpet the next morning.

In the next two or three days I heard odds and ends about the Hickses' party. Calverley had got half-way up the ivy at the side of the house. Hicks had put his foot through his drawing-room window. One or two cars were having their wings straightened at the garage and Lady Fobham, to whom I was called, had been in the lily pond.

And then there was a telephone call from the Bassilleros. I was out on my rounds and the message followed me from house to house. It was half past twelve before I got to the Bassilleros'. Mr Bassillero (the message said) had had 'one of his attacks'.

The Bassilleros lived in a house built in 1740. I noticed, as I went in, paintings of several famous dead horses, a great many medals. With its white and its gold, the house was a pretty example of the architecture of the period. A Spanish servant let me into a wide hall where a large naval battle was going on in a gilt frame on the wall opposite the door. It was a picture filled with impudent little waves, clouds, and sails, like Mrs Bassillero's blue-grey curls. She came to me wearing a smart, sand-coloured version of the county's tweed uniform. She walked with the artificial jerk of the hips taught to débutantes in her time. One eyelid was lowered in a little, trained, quarter-wink. She was five feet high, broad-chinned, thin-limbed, and narrow like a boy.

'I had a message at the surgery . . .' I began. Mrs Bassillero had a pretty voice and the seductive, abrupt, bad manners of her generation which set it off.

'I rang for Ray.'

'He's on holiday,' I said.

'That's a body blow,' she said. 'We always have Ray.' She stood there, her violet eyes picking me over, preparing to haggle with me, do a deal, or ask me what I bet her that she could not get Ray back at once from the other end of the earth if she wished to.

'You're using Ray's car,' she accused me. 'He said he'd lend it to me.'

Mrs Bassillero put her head on one side to see if this 'try on' would succeed.

'It belongs to the practice,' I said.

Mrs Bassillero gave the faintest jerk to her head and one eyebrow moved, as if she were shaking off a very close bullet.

'Hard luck on me,' she said.

'I am sorry about Mr Bassillero,' I said. 'May I see him? What is the trouble?'

Mrs Bassillero considered me and hummed. Then again came that jerk of the head, shaking off the bad news: the bad news was myself.

'I rang up to ask Ray to luncheon,' she said. 'I forgot he's away.' And then, doing a deal again: 'Will you stay?'

'I was told Mr Bassillero had had an attack,' I said.

'He has,' she said. 'He's lost his voice again.'

'He can't speak,' she said. Her direct eyes now were made to mist with skilful appeal.

'I had better look at his throat,' I said.

Mrs Bassillero suddenly laughed like a man.

'If you really want to,' she said. 'You don't understand. What a bore Ray isn't here! When I say he can't speak, I mean he *won't* speak. We're not on speaking terms. We had a row after the party at the Hickses'. You must stay to luncheon. There's no one to pass the ball. Everyone's away. We always get Ray when my husband's voice goes. You'll stay? Now I will take you to my husband.'

She trod out of the room slowly like a cat and I followed her to the door of her husband's study.

'Look at his throat, Doctor,' she said loudly as she opened the door.

Mr Bassillero was a short person, too. He was considering his fishing rods and did not look up at once when I came into the room.

'Damn glad you're here, Doctor,' he said. 'Trouble.'

'I'm sorry to hear that,' I said.

Then Mr Bassillero looked up and said: 'Who are you?'

Tact, I remembered, was the thing. I did not say Mrs Bassillero had sent for me. Mr Bassillero had that kind of dark handsomeness which is fixed like a pain to one aspect of a luxurious head. He was only about forty-five, but he seemed to have receded into the loud pattern of his clothes. He was wearing a plum-coloured tweed suit with green lines squared on it, a design that made him nearly invisible in any well-furnished room. His violet cheeks had been embossed on him twenty-five years ago. Mr Bassillero, I was to find out, had undergone a severe cure for drinking. His cure had left him stupefied. His main occupation during the day, I soon gathered, was to consider whether he would change his clothes. He was a man who knew he was dressed for something – but for what escaped his mind.

'I think I shall go in and change,' was one of his frequent sentences. Or 'I shall put on my other boots and go down to the village.'

Mr Bassillero was looking at my worn grey suit.

'Mrs Bassillero has very kindly asked me to luncheon,' I said.

'We usually have Ray,' said Bassillero. 'Always passes the ball. Understands women. Can cap anything. She,' Mr Bassillero pointed a neutral finger at the door, 'better warn you – has lost her voice. Can't speak.'

'It is damp weather for August,' I said.

'Yes, put on a Burberry this morning,' Mr Bassillero agreed. 'Cold enough for a coat. Difficult speaking to someone who doesn't answer, difficult to keep it up. We've got Spanish servants – never stop.'

Mr Bassillero had talked a lot, but now his supply of words went. We stared at a silver dog on his desk. We were saved by one of the Spaniards calling us to luncheon.

We went into a room so high and large that the Bassilleros were like a pair of mere anemones at the bottom of a tank. I, on the contrary, had the sensation of growing uncomfortably tall; one of my difficulties during the meal was a dread that I would shoot up and hit the ceiling.

'If you will ask my husband he will, I am sure, give you something to drink,' Mrs Bassillero said as we sat down.

'I wonder if I could get you to trouble *her* to pass us down the bread. Spanish servants always forget something,' said Mr Bassillero.

I had become wired in as a telephone for Mr and Mrs Bassillero. I found myself bobbing in my chair from right to left, collecting one set of remarks, passing them on, and then collecting and disposing again. I found myself very soon telling Mr Bassillero that his wife was going to London on the evening train, I found myself telling her that Mr Bassillero was going to Scotland. Mr Bassillero told me he had found 'some damn

Spanish thing' in his cutlets; Mrs Bassillero asked *if* I had just bought a new motor mower, *would* I allow it to be left out in the rain, considering the price of things now. I sat trying to make myself shorter. We had arrived, I thought, at last at a safe topic: the weather. As I have said, it was a cold August. The Bassilleros had put on their heating. Mr Bassillero eased now that we had returned to his favourite, indeed his only, subject.

'Thought of changing my shirt this morning,' he said. 'Putting on a warmer one. Not a single warm shirt in my drawer.'

If the Bassilleros could not speak they could, of course, hear.

'I imagine, Doctor, when you can't find a shirt where you are lodging, you go to the linen room or you go to Mrs Thing?' said Mrs Bassillero.

Mr Bassillero asked me if I did not agree that in a properly run house, as my lodgings probably were, there was a place for everything and you did not have to turn the house upside down to get it. Not only that, he said, my Mrs Thing probably spoke English.

Mr Bassillero spoke mainly to the salt at his end of the table; Mrs Bassillero looked at a large picture of a horse called Bendigo, which had won the Jubilee Stakes in the eighties.

Mrs Bassillero said: 'I'm sure you, Doctor, speak foreign languages well.'

A group of Cupids above my head seemed to be beckoning me up. I fought my way down to the subject of the weather.

'It is clouding over again,' I said.

The attempt did not help us.

'In any case,' said Mrs Bassillero, 'I'm sure you never change into warm shirts at this time of the year. You wear a light summer overcoat.'

'I haven't got one,' I said.

'What?' said Mr Bassillero.

I repeated the sentence to his end of the table.

'Good God,' he said.

'Did you lose it?' said Mrs Bassillero with sharp interest.

'Some fellow pinch it?' asked Mr Bassillero.

For a moment they were almost united. They even looked at each other for a second, then their glances skidded away.

'No, I just haven't got one,' I said.

Mr Bassillero sank back, like an invalid, into his handsomeness. He looked at me with total unbelief.

'I thought you were going to say,' he said bitterly, 'some fellow took it. Tom Calverley took mine at the Hickses' on Saturday. I took his. Only thing to do.'

'Men are too extraordinary, Doctor,' said Mrs Bassillero. 'You are no taller than my husband, but I'm sure you wouldn't be such a fool as to come home in Tommy Calverley's overcoat. He's six foot three. I mean right down to your boots. Polar. I mean, surely you'd pick one your own size. Even after a party.'

'Calverley took mine. I took his. Fair's fair,' said Bassillero, speaking to me.

'On a cold night,' I said.

'Two in the morning,' said Bassillero.

'I see you are not on my side, Doctor,' said Mrs Bassillero, giving the shake to her grey curls.

'After a party I might come away in mink,' I said. I risked a lie: 'I once did,' I said. I looked hopefully at both of them to see if we were happier now.

Mrs Bassillero had a gay but humourless manner; a joke about mink was unacceptable.

'What an *odd* thing to do,' she said coldly.

I had offended Mr Bassillero too; he looked at me with distaste. In mixing up men's and women's clothes, I had been sartorially disagreeable. He rang off, so to say, and spoke to himself. Mrs Bassillero said to me in her short, crushing style: 'I hope you returned the coat.'

'Of course,' I said.

'Because I do think if one wilfully takes someone else's coat one ought to return it, don't you? Or not? I don't know about men. I mean, there's Tommy Calverley's ridiculous coat hanging up in the cloakroom still. I expect you saw it?'

I don't like being snubbed. 'I thought of selling it,' I said.

Mr Bassillero looked up. His colour had become a darker violet.

'Sold it!' exclaimed Mr Bassillero.

'No,' I calmed him. 'I was speaking to Mrs Bassillero about a coat I took.'

'Oh,' said Mr Bassillero, 'if Tom Calverley's sold my coat . . .'

Mr Bassillero was unable to go on with this idea. He looked at me suspiciously: it appeared to him I was trying to get him away from the ground on which he was making his stand.

'Took my coat and hadn't the grace to bring it back,' he said to me.

Mr Bassillero became magnetic.

'Daren't,' he said. 'Daren't bring it back.'

There was a long silence at the table. At either end of it the Bassilleros had receded into the events of the Hickses' party. Mr Bassillero was the first to speak, and his voice seemed to come from three days away.

'Wouldn't pay him either,' he said.

He glanced at the window and the sky, looked at his jacket wondering if he would change again.

'Knows what he left in his pocket,' he said.

Mrs Bassillero's head made a small dodge. She got up.

'Shall we have coffee next door?' she said. She walked ahead and opened the door. Bassillero held me back.

'You a married man, Doctor?' he said.

'No,' I said.

'Neither is Ray,' he said.

Mr Bassillero looked lost, as if by some misfortune he was the only married man in the world.

'Are you coming?' called Mrs Bassillero.

'Engaged?' said Bassillero, recovering hope.

'No,' I said.

Mr Bassillero thought this over.

'It makes no odds,' said Mr Bassillero. 'A fellow takes your coat, eh? You take his? All right. You find your wife's gloves in his pocket. Now what do you do? Where are you, I mean to say – what? You've got a scientific brain – explain it. Eh? See what I mean?'

I passed into the drawing-room, where Mrs Bassillero's thin legs looked like scissors, and one cutting and racketing knee appeared from under her skirt as she sat pouring the coffee.

'Do sit down, you look so unsteady,' said Mrs Bassillero as I took my coffee. She poured out a cup for her husband and turned her back to him when he took it.

'I *do* think,' she said in a gush, turning to me. 'I *do* think it's too extraordinary about men. I mean the way they have become humble in the last two hundred years. I mean they used to dress up to please women and to be admired by them; hours doing their hair and their faces. Now it's the other way on. I do think it's sweet of you to give it all up. So self-effacing. I mean you all dress alike, and take each other's clothes.'

She paused. Not only her face, but the hard-headed knee seemed to be advancing at me. The dealer's voice in her suddenly came out.

'After a couple of martinis, when you've got one eye on the man who is making a pass at you and the other ripping around for somewhere to put your gloves, one has no idea which coat is which. You stick them anywhere. They all look alike. One might be married to anybody.'

When she said this, Mrs Bassillero's pleasant violet eye gave its trained quarter-wink.

'That, at any rate, is the story you've got to sell for me to Mr Bassillero,' she appeared to be signalling.

I saw that this was the crisis; this was where Ray, having 'passed the ball' for half an hour, would now rise to the occasion and administer his medicine. What would he do? Would he distract Mr Bassillero with some anecdote about a tailor, a horse, or a fish; or entangle Mrs Bassillero in some social crossword puzzle about the first Fobham marriage? To show how unsuited my mind was to the situation – I tried, as they say, to get at the facts and to reconstruct the incident. I got back to the scene in my surgery on the night of the Hickses' party. Who was there? What were they wearing? I went over the people one by one and then I saw Calverley sitting in my chair.

'Good heavens,' I said. 'I've just remembered something. You know when Calverley came to my surgery that night, he wasn't wearing an overcoat. Actually, he hadn't even got a jacket on.'

I didn't know what Mrs Bassillero's relations with Mr Calverley were; but Mrs Bassillero's startled eyes suddenly stared into a scene that neither Mr Bassillero nor I knew about; she was too taken aback to wink.

'I see,' she said. 'You mean he hadn't taken my husband's coat at all?'

'Or,' I said, making it worse, 'he'd probably left it somewhere.'

She looked at me scientifically in a way that suggested that I was the kind of man who couldn't keep his mouth shut even if it were stitched. Then she gave the small flick of her head and, turning to her husband, she spoke to him directly for the first time.

'That is why he hasn't brought it back,' she said. 'It's at Pansy Flynn's . . .'

Into that name Mrs Bassillero might have been pouring machine-gun fire.

'Not the first time your coat has been there, my dear,' she followed up. 'It probably walked there by itself, it knows the way.'

The astonishment in Mr Bassillero's face was chiefly that of a man who finds himself, through no fault of his own, suddenly on speaking terms with his wife again. He could not believe it. Then he slowly saw the innuendo. He appeared to be about to shoot back at his wife – indeed, his arms moved nervously; I suppose he felt he was not dressed in the right clothes for uttering a domestic sarcasm, for all he did was suddenly to pull down his two waistcoat ends with a force that made his collar stand out.

And then I had the only sensible idea that occurred to me during the luncheon party.

'I'm passing there' – I did not say where – 'on my way to the surgery. I will pick up your coat for you, Mr Bassillero. In fact, if you'd like to give me Mr Calverley's, I will make the exchange. I'll drop yours in for you this evening.'

I looked from one Bassillero to the other and I saw that, having done my worst, I was beginning to triumph. I saw the embarrassment of two people who are about to lose the object of a very satisfying quarrel. Reluctantly Mr Bassillero saw his grievance go; suspiciously Mrs Bassillero considered the peace. Presently they fell into an argument about who was going to London and who to Scotland and when. It ended where so many of the discussions of the Bassilleros must have done on the central situation of their marriage; that Mr Bassillero couldn't go to Scotland – indeed, anywhere else – until he could freely decide which coat to wear, and that Mrs Bassillero never made up her mind until she saw what he was doing first.

It is pleasant to do good to people. As I put Calverley's coat in the car and drove off from the Bassilleros', I felt that Dr Ray would congratulate me. I had been a telephone for the Bassilleros, I had been the catalyst, I had administered 'the only medicine'. Calverley's coat, like Calverley disembodied, sagged beside me on the seat. Long, a dim, grey herringbone cloth, it was not in fresh condition. The collar was greasy, there were the spots of Calverley's personal life on it; it was worn at the pockets and the second button hung loose. It had been left in so many places; it had been returned by so many hands; it had hung on so many alien hooks. It probably smelled of whisky. As it lounged there in its creases, I could imagine Calverley's head sticking out of the collar, the face with the gentle eyes, the violent mouth, and the head-hunting smile. An ordinary stretch of herringbone tweed, with its tradition of decorum, can never before have conveyed such sensations of rampage and free will, though now it lay sly, slothful – conceivably, I fancied, in remorse.

I drove for a couple of miles through the long settled greenery of this part of the country. It was the time of the year when the chestnut leaves are dark and drying. I had no intention of stirring up a mare's nest at Mrs Flynn's, but went to Calverley's house. He lived in a small white lodge, a pretty, even arty place with a peacock cut out of the yew hedge. I got out, picked up the coat, and knocked at the door and listened to the bees humming under the windows as I waited. A cottage woman who said she came in to clean and cook for Mr Calverley opened to me.

'I have brought back Mr Calverley's coat,' I said. 'I believe he and Mr Bassillero took the wrong ones the other day.'

The cottage woman took the coat in the guarded way of one who had been taking in the discarded clothes of Mr Calverley from all kinds of undesirable people for many years.

'Where is the jacket?' she said. 'He had a jacket.'

'I don't think they swapped jackets,' I said. 'Perhaps I could take Mr Bassillero's coat back, if you know where it is.'

The cottage woman became a defender of private property.

'Mr Calverley's gone to London,' she said.

She had stepped back to hang the coat up in the little hall of the house and I followed her in.

'He didn't say anything to me about a coat,' the woman said.

'Isn't it hanging up there?' I said.

'There's nothing there,' she said, pointing to the mackintoshes and jackets hanging on the pegs. There was, I saw at once, a short grey herringbone coat hanging among them.

'I think I *see* Mr Bassillero's coat behind the mackintosh,' I said, advancing eagerly.

The woman backed towards the peg, made herself swell, and barred the way.

'Oh no,' she said, 'that is Mr Calverley's coat.'

'Oh – I mean the one behind the mackintosh . . .'

The cottage woman folded her hands on her apron and stuck her elbows out.

'That's his best one,' she said. 'He only got it three days ago.'

'Three days – but that's extraordinary. Are you quite sure?'

'I look after all Mr Calverley's things. I'm mending it. It's the one,' she said, playing her trump card with dignity, 'that had the accident.'

The woman's cheeks puffed with offence.

'You can see for yourself,' she said, stepping scornfully out of the way.

I went to the peg and got the coat off the peg. As I did so, a peculiar thing happened. It divided into two pieces. It had been ripped almost in two from tail to collar. Half of one pocket was hanging off. The woman's face swelled with a purple blush.

'Mr Calverley had a few friends in and it got torn,' she said.

'No buttons either,' I said.

The woman did not like my grin.

'Mr Calverley,' she said, 'often buys new things and gets dissatisfied. He is very particular about his clothes. He said it was too short on him.'

Naturally, Bassillero was the name on the tape.

At the end of the month Dr Ray came back. My last interview was in some respects like the first. He had a new disguise; he was sunburned. He put his hands in the pockets of his navy-blue jacket, tightening it at the waist; on his head was an imaginary yachting cap; and he swung from side to side in his swivel chair. After hunting, he said, yachting was the finest training for any profession. It taught you not to cross the line before the gun goes off.

'Which is what you did,' he said; 'you weren't very bright when you let Calverley have his coat back before you got Bassillero's.'

'But how could I take that back?' I said. 'It was ripped to pieces.'

'Did you ever notice Calverley's hands?' said the doctor. 'Ever see him on a horse? Or pick up a head waiter by the collar?'

Dr Ray buzzed for his dispenser, and when the girl came in he asked her to find out whether Mr Bassillero was still in Scotland. Then, as it were, swinging the tiller over and coming round into the wind, Dr Ray looked me in the face.

'I think you've made the right decision. Keep out of general practice. Now did you have any other trouble? The Fobhams – all quiet there? No heavy weather? Very odd – perhaps they're away too.'

A Story of Don Juan

One night of his life Don Juan slept alone. Returning to Seville in the spring, he was held up, some hours' ride from the city, by the floods of the Quadalquivir, a river as dirty as an old lion after the rains, and was obliged to stay at the finca of the Quintero family. The doorway, the walls, the windows of the house were hung with the black and violet draperies of mourning when he arrived there. Quintero's wife was dead. She had been dead a year. The young Quintero took him in and even smiled to see Don Juan spattered and drooping in the rain like a sodden cockerel. There was malice in his smile: Quintero was mad with loneliness and grief. The man who had possessed and discarded all women was received by a man demented because he had lost only one.

'My house is yours,' said Quintero, speaking the formula. There was bewilderment in his eyes; those who grieve do not find the world and its people either real or believable. Irony inflects the voices of mourners, and there was malice, too, in Quintero's further greetings; he could receive Don Juan now without that fear, that terror which he brought to the husbands of Seville. It was perfect, Quintero thought, that for once in his life Don Juan should have arrived at an empty house.

There was not even (as Don Juan quickly found out) a maid, for Quintero was served only by a manservant, being unable any longer to bear the sight of women. This servant dried the guest's clothes and in an hour or two brought in a bad dinner, food which stamped up and down in the stomach, like people waiting for a coach in the cold. Quintero was torturing his body as well as his mind, and as the familiar pains arrived they agonised him and set him off about his wife. Grief had also made Quintero an actor. His eyes had the hollow, taper-haunted dusk of the theatre as he spoke of the beautiful girl. He dwelled upon their courtship, on details of her beauty and temperament, and how he had rushed her from the church to the marriage bed like a man racing a tray of diamonds through the streets into the safety of a bank vault. The presence of Don Juan turned every man into an artist when he was telling his own love-story – one had to tantalise and surpass the great seducer – and Quintero, rolling it all off in the grand manner, could not resist telling that his bride had died on her marriage night.

'Man!' cried Don Juan. He started straight off on stories of his own. But Quintero hardly listened; he had returned to the state of exhaustion and emptiness which is natural to grief. As Don Juan talked, the madman followed his own thoughts like an actor preparing and mumbling his next entrance; and the thought he had had, when Don Juan first appeared at the door, returned to him: a man must be a monster to make a man feel triumphant that his own wife was dead. Half-listening, and indigestion aiding, Quintero felt within himself the total hatred of all the husbands of Seville for this diabolical man. And as Quintero brooded upon this it occurred to him that it was probably not by chance that he had a vengeance in his power.

The decision was made. The wine being finished, Quintero called for his manservant and gave orders to change Don Juan's room.

'For,' said Quintero dryly, 'His Excellency's visit is an honour and I cannot allow one who has slept in the most delicately scented rooms in Spain to pass the night in a chamber which stinks to heaven of goat.'

'The closed room?' said the manservant, astonished that the room which still held the great dynastic marriage bed and which had not been used more than half a dozen times by his master since the lady's death was to be given to a stranger.

Yet to this room Quintero led his guest and there parted from him with eyes so sparking with ill-intention that Don Juan, who was sensitive to this kind of point, understood perfectly that the cat was being let into the cage only because the bird had long ago flown out. The humiliation was unpleasant. Don Juan saw the night stretching before him like a desert.

What a bed to lie in: so wide, so unutterably vacant, so malignantly inopportune! He took off his clothes, snuffed the lamp wick. He lay down knowing that on either side of him lay wastes of sheet, draughty and uninhabited except by bugs. A desert. To move an arm one inch to the side, to push out a leg, however cautiously, was to enter desolation. For miles and miles the foot might probe, the fingers or the knee explore a friendless Antarctica. Yet to lie rigid and still was to have a foretaste of the grave. And here, too, he was frustrated; for though the wine kept him yawning, that awful food romped in his stomach, jolting him back from the edge of sleep the moment he got there.

There is an art in sleeping alone in a double bed, but this art was unknown to Don Juan. The difficulty is easily solved. If one cannot sleep on one side of the bed, one moves over and tries the other. Two hours or more must have passed before this occurred to him. Sullen-headed, he advanced into the desert, and the night air lying chill between the sheets flapped and made him shiver. He stretched out his arm and crawled towards the opposite pillow. The coldness, the more than virgin frigidity of linen! He put down his head and, drawing up his knees, he shivered. Soon, he supposed, he would be warm again, but, in the meantime, ice could not have been colder. It was unbelievable.

Ice was the word for that pillow and those sheets. Ice. Was he ill? Had the rain chilled him that his teeth must chatter like this and his legs tremble? Far from getting warmer, he found the cold growing. Now it was on his forehead and his cheeks, like arms of ice on his body, like legs of ice upon his legs. Suddenly in superstition he got up on his hands and stared down at the pillow in the darkness, threw back the bedclothes and looked down upon the sheet; his breath was hot, yet blowing against his cheeks was a breath colder than the grave, his shoulders and body were hot, yet limbs of snow were drawing him down; and just as he would have shouted his appalled suspicion, lips like wet ice unfolded upon his own and he sank down to a kiss, unmistakably a kiss, which froze him like a winter.

In his own room Quintero lay listening. His mad eyes were exalted and his ears were waiting. He was waiting for the scream of horror. He knew the apparition. There would be a scream, a tumble, hands fighting for the light, fists knocking at the door. And Quintero had locked the door. But when no scream came, Quintero lay talking to himself, remembering the night the apparition had first come to him and had made him speechless and left him choked and stiff. It would be even better if there were no scream! Quintero lay awake through the night, building castle after castle of triumphant revenge and receiving, as he did so, the ovations of the husbands of Seville. 'The stallion is gelded!' At an early hour Quintero unlocked the door and waited downstairs impatiently. He was a wreck after a night like that.

Don Juan came down at last. He was (Quintero observed) pale. Or was he pale?

'Did you sleep well?' Quintero asked furtively.

'Very well,' Don Juan replied.

'I do not sleep well in strange beds myself,' Quintero insinuated. Don Juan smiled and replied that he was more used to strange beds than his own. Quintero scowled.

'I reproach myself; the bed was large,' he said.

But the large, Don Juan said, were necessarily as familiar to him as the strange. Quintero bit his nails. Some noise had been heard in the night – something like a scream, a disturbance. The manservant had noticed it also. Don Juan answered him that disturbances in the night had indeed bothered him at the beginning of his career, but now he took them in his stride. Quintero dug his nails into the palms of his hands. He brought out the trump.

'I am afraid,' Quintero said, 'it was a cold bed. You must have *frozen*.'

'I am never cold for long,' Don Juan said, and, unconsciously anticipating the manner of a poem that was to be written in his memory two centuries later, declaimed: 'The blood of Don Juan is hot, for the sun is the blood of Don Juan.'

Quintero watched. His eyes jumped like flies to every movement of his guest. He watched him drink his coffee. He watched him tighten the stirrups of his horse. He watched Don Juan vault into the saddle. Don Juan was humming, and when he went off was singing, was singing in that intolerable tenor of his which was like a cock-crow in the olive groves.

Quintero went into the house and rubbed his unshaven chin. Then he went out again to the road where the figure of Don Juan was now only a small smoke of dust between the eucalyptus trees. Quintero went up to the room where Don Juan had slept and stared at it with accusations and suspicions. He called the manservant.

'I shall sleep here tonight,' Quintero said.

The manservant answered carefully. Quintero was mad again and the moon was still only in its first quarter. The man watched his master during the day looking towards Seville. It was too warm after the rains, the country steamed like a laundry.

And then, when the night came, Quintero laughed at his doubts. He went up to the room and as he undressed he thought of the assurance of those ice-cold lips, those icicle fingers and those icy arms. She had not come last night; oh, what fidelity! To think, he would say in his remorse to the ghost, that malice had so disordered him that he had been base and credulous enough to use the dead for a trick.

Tears were in his eyes as he lay down and for some time he dared not turn on his side and stretch out his hand to touch what, in his disorder, he had been willing to betray. He loathed his heart. He craved – yet how could he hope for it now? – that miracle of recognition and forgiveness. It was this craving which moved him at last. His hands went out. And they were met.

The hands, the arms, the lips moved out of their invisibility and soundlessness towards him. They touched him, they clasped him, they drew him down, but – what was this? He gave a shout, he fought to get away, kicked out and swore; and so the manservant found him wrestling with the sheets, striking out with fists and knees, roaring that he was in hell. Those hands, those lips, those limbs, he screamed, were *burning* him. They were of ice no more. They were of fire.

The Ladder

'We had the builders in at the time,' my father says in his accurate way, if he ever mentions his second marriage, the one that so quickly went wrong. 'And,' he says, clearing a small apology from his throat as though preparing to say something immodest, 'we happened to be without stairs.'

It is true. I remember that summer. I was fifteen years old. I came home from school at the end of the term, and when I got to our place not only had my mother gone but the stairs had gone too. There was no staircase in the house.

We lived in an old crab-coloured cottage, with long windows under the eaves that looked like eyes half-closed against the sun. Now when I got out of the car I saw scaffolding over the front door and two heaps of sand and mortar on the crazy paving, which my father asked me not to tread in because it would 'make work for Janey'. (This was the name of his second wife.) I went inside. Imagine my astonishment. The little hall had vanished, the ceiling had gone; you could see up to the roof; the wall on one side had been stripped to the brick, and on the other hung a long curtain of builder's sheets. 'Where are the stairs?' I said. 'What have you done with the stairs?' I was at the laughing age.

A mild, trim voice spoke above our heads.

'Ah, I know that laugh,' the voice said sweetly and archly. There was Miss Richards, or I should say my father's second wife, standing behind a builder's rope on what used to be the landing, which now stuck out precariously without banisters, like the portion of a ship's deck. The floor appeared to have been sawn off. She used to be my father's secretary and I had often seen her in my father's office; but now she had changed. Her fair hair was fluffed out and she wore a fussed and shiny brown dress that was quite unsuitable for the country.

I remember how odd they both looked, she up above and my father down below, and both apologising to me. The builders had taken the old staircase out two days before, they said, and had promised to put the new one in against the far wall of the room behind the dust sheets before I got back from school. But they had not kept their promise.

'We go up,' said my father, cutting his wife short, for she was apologising too much, 'by the ladder.'

He pointed. At that moment his wife was stepping to the end of the landing where a short ladder, with a post to hold on to at the top as one stepped on the first rung, sloped eight or nine feet to the ground.

'It's horrible,' called my step-mother.

My father and I watched her come down. She came to the post and turned round, not sure whether she ought to come down the ladder frontwards or backwards.

'Back,' called my father.

'No, the other hand on the post,' he said.

My step-mother blushed fondly and gave him a look of fear. She put one foot on the step and then took her foot back and put the other one there and then pouted. It was only eight feet from the ground: at school we climbed half-way up the gym walls on the bars. I remembered her as a quick and practical woman at the office; she was now, I was sure, playing at being weak and dependent.

'My hands,' she said, looking at the dust on her fingers as she grasped the top step.

My father and I stopped where we were and watched her. She put one leg out too high, as if, artlessly, to show the leg first. She was a plain woman and her legs (she used to say) were her 'nicest thing'. This was the only coquetry she had. She looked like one of those insects that try the air around them with their feelers before they move. I was surprised that my father (who had always been so polite and grave-mannered to my mother, and had almost bowed to me when he had met me at the station and helped me in and out of the car) did not go to help her. I saw an expression of obstinacy on his face.

'You're at the bottom,' he said. 'Only two more steps.'

'Oh dear,' said my step-mother, at last getting off the last step on to the floor; and she turned with her small chin raised, offering us her helplessness for admiration. She came to me and kissed me and said:

'Doesn't she look lovely? You are growing into a woman.'

'Nonsense,' said my father. And, in fear of being a woman and yet pleased by what she said, I took my father's arm.

'Is that what we have to do? Is that how we get to bed?' I said.

'It's only until Monday,' my father said again.

They both of them looked ashamed, as though by having the stairs removed they had done something foolish. My father tried to conceal this by an air of modest importance. They seemed a very modest couple. Both of them looked shorter to me since their marriage: I was very shocked by this. *She* seemed to have made him shorter. I had always thought of my father as a dark, vain, terse man, very logical and never giving in to anyone. He seemed much less important now his secretary was in the house.

'It is easy,' I said, and I went to the ladder and was up it in a moment.

'Mind,' called my step-mother.

But in a moment I was down again, laughing. When I was coming down I heard my step-mother say quietly to my father, 'What legs! She is growing.'

My legs and my laugh: I did not think that my father's secretary had the right to say anything about me. She was not my mother.

After this my father took me round the house. I looked behind me once or twice as I walked. On one of my shoes was some of the sand he had warned me about. I don't know how it got on my shoes. It was funny seeing this one sandy footmark making work for Janey wherever I went.

My father took me through the dust curtains into the dining-room and then to the far wall where the staircase was going to be.

'Why have you done it?' I said.

He and I were alone.

'The house has wanted it for years,' he said. 'It ought to have been done years ago.'

I did not say anything. When my mother was here, she was always complaining about the house, saying it was poky, barbarous – I can hear her voice now saying 'barbarous' as if it were the name of some terrifying and savage Queen – and my father had always refused to alter anything. Barbarous: I used to think of that word as my mother's name.

'Does Janey like it?' I said.

My father hardened at this question. He seemed to be saying, 'What has it got to do with Janey?' But what he said was – and he spoke with amusement, with a look of quiet scorn:

'She liked it as it was.'

'I did too,' I said.

I then saw – but no, I did not really understand this at the time; it is something I understand now I am older – that my father was not altering the house for Janey's sake. She hated the whole place because my mother had been there, but was too tired by her earlier life in his office, fifteen years of it, too unsure of herself, to say anything. My father was making an act of amends to my mother. He was punishing Janey by 'getting in builders' and making everyone uncomfortable and miserable; he was making an emotional scene with himself. He was annoying Janey with what my mother had so maddeningly wanted and which he would not give her.

After he had shown me the house, I said I would go and see Janey getting lunch ready.

'I shouldn't do that,' said my father. 'It will delay her. Lunch is just ready.

'Or should be,' he said, looking at his watch.

We went to the sitting-room, and while we waited I sat in the green chair and he asked me questions about school and we went on to talk about the holidays. But when I answered I could see he was not listening to me but trying to catch sounds of Janey moving in the kitchen. Occasionally there were sounds: something gave an explosive fizz in a hot pan, and a saucepan lid fell. This made a loud noise and the lid spun a long time on the stone floor. The sound stopped our talk.

'Janey is not used to the kitchen,' said my father.

I smiled very close to my lips, I did not want my father to see it, but he looked at me and he smiled by accident too. There was understanding between us.

'I will go and see,' I said.

He raised his hand to stop me, but I went.

It was natural. For fifteen years Janey had been my father's secretary. She had worked in an office. I remember when I went there when I was young she used to come into the room with an earnest air, leaning her head a little sideways and turning three-quarter-face to my father at his desk, leaning forward to guess at what he wanted. I admired the great knowledge she had of his affairs, the way she carried letters, how quickly she picked up the telephone if it rang, the authority of her voice. Her strength was that she had been impersonal. She had lost that strength in her marriage. As his wife, she had no behaviour. When we were talking she raised her low bosom, which had become round and duck-like, with a sigh and smiled at my father with a tentative, expectant fondness. After fifteen years, a life had ended: she was resting.

But Janey had not lost her office behaviour: that she now kept for the kitchen. The moment I went to the kitchen, I saw her walking to the stove where the saucepans were throbbing too hard. She was walking exactly as she had walked towards my father at his desk. The stove had taken my father's place. She went up to it with impersonal enquiry, as if to anticipate what it wanted; she appeared to be offering a pile of plates to be warmed as if they were a pile of letters. She seemed baffled because the stove could not speak. When one of the saucepans boiled over she ran to it and lifted it off, suddenly and too high, with her telephone movement: the water spilled at once. On the table beside the stove were basins and pans she was using, and she had them all spread out in an orderly way like typing; she went from one to the other with the careful look of enquiry she used to give to the things she was filing. It was not a method suitable to work in a kitchen.

When I came in, she put down the pan she was holding and stopped everything – as she would have done in the office – to talk to me about what she was doing. She was very nice about my hair, which I had had cut last term; it made me look older and I liked it better. But blue smoke rose behind her as we talked. She did not notice it.

I went back to my father.

'I didn't want to be in the way,' I said.

'Extraordinary,' he said, looking at his watch. 'I must just go and hurry Janey up.'

He was astonished that a woman so brisk in an office should be languid and dependent in a house.

'She is just bringing it in,' I said. 'The potatoes are ready. They are on the table. I saw them.'

'On the table?' he said. 'Getting cold?'

'On the kitchen table,' I said.

'That doesn't prevent them being cold,' he said. My father was a sarcastic man.

I walked about the room humming. My father's exasperation did not last; it gave way to a new thing in his voice. Resignation.

'We will wait if you do not mind,' he said to me. 'Janey is slow. And by the way,' he said, lowering his voice a little, 'I shouldn't mention we passed the Leonards in the road when I brought you up from the station.'

I was surprised.

'Not the Leonards?' I said.

'They were friends of your mother's,' he said. 'You are old enough to understand. One has to be sometimes a little tactful. Janey sometimes feels . . .'

I looked at my father. He had altered in many ways. When he gave me this secret his small, brown eyes gave a brilliant flash and I opened my blue eyes very wide to receive it. He had changed. His rough black hair was clipped closer at the ears and he had that too young look which middle-aged men sometimes have, for by certain lines it can be seen that they are not as young as their faces. Marks like the minutes on the face of a clock showed at the corners of his eyes, his nose, his mouth; he was much thinner; his face had hardened. He had often been angry and sarcastic, sulking and abrupt, when my mother was with us; I had never seen him before, as he was now, blank-faced, ironical and set in impatient boredom. After he spoke, he had actually been hissing a tune privately through his teeth at the corner of his mouth. At this moment Janey came in with a smile but without dishes, and said lunch was ready.

'Oh,' I laughed when we got into the dining-room. 'It is like . . . it is like France.'

'France?' they both said together, smiling at me.

'Like when we all went to France before the war and you took the car,' I said. I had chosen France because that seemed as far as I could get from the Leonards.

'What on earth are you talking about?' said my father, looking embarrassed. 'You were only five before the war.'

'I remember every bit of it. You and Mummy on the boat.'

[356]

'Yes, yes,' said my step-mother with melancholy importance. 'I got the tickets for you all.'

My father looked as though he was going to hit me. Then he gave a tolerant laugh across the table to my step-mother.

'I remember perfectly well,' she said. 'I'm afraid I couldn't get the peas to boil. Oh, I've forgotten the potatoes.'

'Fetch them,' my father said to me.

I thought she was going to cry. When I came back, I could see she *had* been crying. She was one of those very fair women in whom even three or four tears bring pink to the nose. My father had said something sharply to her, for his face was shut and hard and she was leaning over the dishes, a spoon in her hand, to conceal a wound.

After lunch I took my case and went up the ladder. It was not easy to go up carrying a suitcase, but I enjoyed it. I wished we could always have a ladder in the house. It was like being on a ship. I stood at the top thinking of my mother leaning on the rail of the ship with her new husband, going to America. I was glad she had gone because, sometimes, she sent me lovely things.

Then I went to my room and I unpacked my case. At the bottom, when I took my pyjamas out – they were the last thing – there was the photograph of my mother face downwards where it had been lying all the term. I forgot to say that I had been in trouble the last week at school. I don't know why. I was longing to be home. I felt I had to *do* something. One afternoon I went into the rooms in our passage when no one was there, and I put the snap of Kitty's father into Mary's room – I took it out of the frame – and I put Mary's brother into Olga's, and I took Maeve's mother and put her into the silver frame where Jessie's mother was: that photograph was too big and I bent the mount all the way down to get it in. Maeve cried and reported me to Miss Compton. 'It was only a joke,' I said. 'A joke in very poor taste,' Miss Compton said to me in *her* voice. 'How would you like it if anyone took the photograph of your mother?' 'I haven't got one,' I said. Well, it was not a lie. Everyone wanted to know why I had an empty frame on my chest of drawers. I had punished my mother by leaving her photograph in my trunk.

But now the punishment was over. I took out her picture and put it in the frame on my chest, and every time I bent up from the drawers I looked at her, then at myself in the mirror. In the middle of this my step-mother came in to ask if she could help me.

'You are getting very pretty,' she said. I hated her for admiring me.

I do not deny it: I hated her. She was a foolish woman. She either behaved as if the house, my father and myself were too much hers, or as if she were an outsider. Most of the time she sat there like a visitor, waiting for attention.

I thought to myself: There is my mother, thousands of miles away, leaving us to this and treating us like dirt, and we are left with Miss Richards, of all people.

That night after I had gone to bed I heard my father and my step-mother having a quarrel. 'It is perfectly natural,' I heard my father say, 'for the child to have a photograph of her mother.'

A door closed. Someone was wandering about in the passage. When they had gone I opened my door and crept out barefoot to listen. Every step I made seemed to start a loud creak in the boards and I was so concerned with this that I did not notice I had walked to the edge of the landing. The rope was there, but in the dark I could not see it. I knew I was on the edge of the drop into the hall and that with one more step I would have gone through. I went back to my room, feeling sick. And then the thought struck me – and I could not get it out of my head all night; I dreamed it, I tried not to dream it, I turned on the light, but I dreamed it again – that Miss Richards fell over the edge of the landing. I was very glad when the morning came.

The moment I was downstairs I laughed at myself. The drop was only eight or nine feet. Anyone could jump it. I worked out how I would land on my feet if I were to jump there. I moved the ladder, it was not heavy to lift, to see what you would feel like if there were no ladder there and the house was on fire and you had to jump. To make amends for my wicked dreams in the night I saw myself rescuing Miss Richards (I should say my step-mother) as flames teased her to the edge.

My father came out of his room and saw me standing there.

'What are you pulling such faces for?' he said. And he imitated my expressions.

'I was thinking,' I said, 'of Miss Compton at our school.'

He had not foreseen the change in Miss Richards; how she would sit in the house in her best clothes, like a visitor, expectant, forgetful, stunned by leisure, watchful, wronged and jealous to the point of tears.

Perhaps if the builders had come, as they had promised, on the Monday, my step-mother's story would have been different.

'I am so sorry we are in such a mess,' she said to me many times, as if she thought I regarded the ladder as her failure.

'It's fun,' I said. 'It's like being on a ship.'

'You keep on saying that,' my step-mother said, looking at me in a very worried way, as if trying to work out the hidden meaning of my remark. 'You've never been on a ship.'

'To France,' I said. 'When I was a child.'

'Oh yes, you told me,' said my step-mother.

Life had become so dull for my father that he liked having the ladder in the house.

'I hate it,' said my step-mother to both of us, getting up. It is always surprising when a prosaic person becomes angry.

'Do leave us alone,' my father said.

There was a small scene after this. My father did not mean by 'us' himself and me, as she chose to think; he was simply speaking of himself, and he had spoken very mildly. My step-mother marched out of the room. Presently we heard her upstairs. She must have been very upset to have faced going up the ladder.

'Come on,' said my father. 'I suppose there's nothing for it. I'll get the car out. We will go to the builder's.'

He called up to her that we were going.

Oh, it was a terrible holiday. When I grew up and was myself married, my father said: 'It was a very difficult summer. You didn't realise. You were only a schoolgirl. It was a mistake.' And then he corrected himself. I mean that: my father was always making himself more correct: it was his chief vanity that he understood his own behaviour.

'I happened,' he said – this was the correction – 'to make a very foolish mistake.' Whenever he used the phrase 'I happened' my father's face seemed to dry up and become distant: he was congratulating himself. Not on the mistake, of course, but on being the first to put his finger on it. 'I happen to know ... I happen to have seen ...' – it was this incidental rightness, the footnote of inside knowledge on innumerable minor issues, and his fatal wrongness in a large, obstinate, principled way about anything important, which, I think, made my beautiful and dishonest mother leave him. She was a tall woman, taller than he, with the eyes of a cat, shrugging her shoulders, curving her long graceful back to be stroked and with a wide, champagne laugh. My father had a clipped-back monkeyish appearance and that faint grin of the bounder one sees in the harder-looking monkeys that are without melancholy or sensibility; this had attracted my mother, but very soon his youthful bounce gave place to a kind of meddling honesty, and she found him dull. And, of course, ruthless. The promptness of his second marriage, perhaps, was to teach her a lesson. I imagine him putting his divorce papers away one evening at his office and realising, when Miss Richards came in to ask if 'there is anything more tonight', that there was a woman who was reliable, trained and, like himself, 'happened' to have a lot of inside knowledge.

To get out of the house with my father, to be alone with him: my heart came alive. It seemed to me that this house was not my home any more. If only we could go away, he and I; the country outside seemed to me far more like home than this grotesque divorced house. I stood longing for my step-mother not to answer, dreading that she would come down.

My father was not a man to beg a woman to change her mind. He went out to the garage. My fear of her coming made me stay for a moment. And then (I do not know how the thought came into my head) I went to the ladder and I lifted it away. It was easy to move a short distance, but it began to swing when I tried to put it down. I was afraid it would crash, so I turned it over and over against the other wall, out of reach. Breathlessly, I left the house.

'You have got white on your tunic,' said my father as we drove off. 'What have you been doing?'

'I rubbed against something,' I said.

'Oh, how I love motoring,' I laughed beside my father.

'Oh, look at those lovely little rabbits,' I said.

'Their little white tails,' I laughed.

We passed some hurdles in a field.

'Jumps,' I laughed. 'I wish I had a pony.'

And then my terrible dreams came back to me. I was frightened. I tried to think of something else, but I could not. I could only see my step-mother on the edge of the landing. I could only hear her giving a scream and going over head first. We got into the town and I felt sick. We arrived at the builder's and my father stopped there. Only a girl was in the office, and I heard my father say in his coldest voice, 'I happen to have an appointment . . .'

My father came out, and we drove off. He was cross.

'Where are we going?' I said, when I saw we were not going home.

'To Longwood,' he said. 'They're working over there.' I thought I would faint.

'I – I . . .' I began.

'What?' my father said.

I could not speak. I began to get red and hot. And then I remembered. 'I can pray.'

It is seven miles to Longwood. My father was a man who enjoyed talking to builders; he planned and replanned with them, built imaginary houses, talked about people. Builders have a large acquaintance with the way people live; my father liked inside knowledge, as I have said. Well, I thought, she is over. She is dead by now. I saw visits to the hospital. I saw my trial.

'She is like you,' said the builder, nodding to me. All my life I shall remember his moustache.

'She is like my wife,' said my father. 'My first wife. I happen to have married again.'

(He liked puzzling and embarrassing people.)

'Do you happen to know a tea place near here?' he said.

'Oh no,' I said. 'I don't feel hungry.'

But we had tea at Gilling. The river is across the road from the tea-shop and we stood afterwards on the bridge. I surprised my father by climbing the parapet.

'If you jumped,' I said to my father, 'would you hurt?'

'You'd break your legs,' said my father.

Her 'nicest thing'!

I shall not describe our drive back to the house, but my father did say, 'Janey will be worried. We've been nearly three hours. I'll put the car in afterwards.'

When we got back, he got out quickly and went down the path. I got out slowly. It is a long path leading across a small lawn, then between two lime trees; there are a few steps down where the roses are, and across another piece of grass you are at the door. I stopped to listen to the bees in the limes, but I could not wait any longer. I went into the house.

There was my step-mother standing on the landing above the hall. Her face was dark red, her eyes were long and violent, her dress was dirty and her hands were black with dust. She had just finished screaming something at my father and her mouth had stayed open after her scream. I thought I could *smell* her anger and her fear the moment I came into the house, but it was really the smell of a burned-out saucepan coming from the kitchen.

'You moved the ladder! Six hours I've been up here. The telephone has been ringing, something has burned on the stove. I might have burned to death. Get me down, get me down. I might have killed myself. Get me down,' she cried, and she came to the gap where the ladder ought to have been.

'Don't be silly, Janey,' said my father. 'I didn't move the ladder. Don't be such a fool. You're still alive.'

'Get me down,' Janey cried out. 'You liar, you liar, you liar. You did move it.'

My father lifted the ladder, and as he did so he said:

'The builder must have been.'

'No one has been,' screamed my step-mother. 'I've been alone. Up here!'

'Daddy isn't a liar,' I said, taking my father's arm.

'Come down,' said my father when he had got the ladder in place. 'I'm holding it.'

And he went up a step or two towards her.

'No,' shrieked Janey, coming to the edge.

'Now, come on. Calm yourself,' said my father.

'No, no, I tell you,' said Janey.

'All right, you must stay,' said my father, and stepped down.

That brought her, of course.

'*I* moved the ladder,' I said when she came down.

'Oh,' said Janey, swinging her arm to hit me, but she fainted instead.

That night my father came to my room when I was in bed. I had moved

my mother's photograph to the bedside table. He was not angry. He was
tired out.

'Why did you do it?' he asked.

I did not answer.

'Did you know she was upstairs?' he said.

I did not reply.

'Stop playing with the sheet,' he said. 'Look at me. Did you know she
was upstairs?'

'Yes,' I said.

'You little cat,' he said.

I smiled.

'It was very wrong,' he said.

I smiled. Presently he smiled. I laughed.

'It is nothing to laugh at,' he said. And suddenly he could not stop
himself: he laughed. The door opened and my step-mother looked in
while we were both shaking with laughter. My father laughed as if he
were laughing for the first time for many years; his bounderish look, sly
and bumptious and so delicious, came back to him. The door closed.

He stopped laughing.

'She might have been killed,' he said, severely again.

'No, no, no,' I cried, and tears came to my eyes.

He put his arm round me.

My mother was a cat, they said, a wicked woman, leaving us like that.
I longed for my mother.

Three days later, I went camping. I apologised to my step-mother and
she forgave me. I never saw her again.

The Satisfactory

'When one says that what one is still inclined to call civilisation is passing through a crisis,' Mr Plymbell used to say during the last war and after it when food was hard to get, and standing in his very expensive antique shop, raising a white and more than Roman nose and watching the words go off one by one in the air and circle the foreign customer, 'one is tempted to ask oneself whether or not a few possibly idle phrases that one let fall to one's old friend Lady Hackthorpe at a moment of national distress in 1940 are not, in fact, still pertinent. One recalls observing, rightly or wrongly, at that time that one was probably witnessing not the surrender of an heroic ally but the defeat of sauces. Béarnaise, hollandaise, madère – one saw them overrun. One can conceive of the future historian's enquiring whether the wars of the last ten years, and indeed what one calls "the peace", have not been essentially an attack on gastronomy, on the stomach and palate of the human race. One could offer the modest example of one's daily luncheon . . .'

Mr Plymbell can talk like *The Times* forever. Not all the campaigns of our time have been fought on the battlefield. His lunch in those bad days was a study.

At two minutes before half past twelve every day, Plymbell was first in the queue in the foyer outside the locked glass doors of Polli's Restaurant, a few yards from his shop. On one side of the glass Plymbell floated – handsome, Roman, silver-haired, as white-skinned and consequent as a turbot of fifty; on the other side of the glass, in the next aquarium, stood Polli with the key in his hand waiting for the clock to strike the half hour – a man liverish and suspended in misanthropy like a tench in the weed of a canal. Plymbell stared clean through Polli to the sixty empty tables beyond; Polli stared clean through the middle of Plymbell into the miasma of the restaurant-keeper's life. Two fish gazed with the indifference of creatures who have accepted the fact that neither of them is edible. What they wanted, what the whole of England was crying for, was not fish but red meat, and to get meat at Polli's one had to be there at half past twelve, on the dot.

First customer in was Plymbell. He had his table, in the middle of this chipped Edwardian place, with his back to one of those white pillars that gave it the appearance of a shop-soiled wedding cake mounted on a red carpet, and he faced the serving hatch. Putting up a monocle to his more annoyed eye, he watched the chef standing over his pans, and while he watched he tapped the table with lightly frantic fingers. Polli's waiters were old men, and the one who served Plymbell had the dejected smirk of a convict.

Plymbell used hardly to glance at the farcical menu and never looked at the waiter when he coldly gave his order. 'Two soups,' said Plymbell. 'Two roast beefs ... Cheese and biscuits,' he added. 'Bring me mine now and you can bring the second order in a quarter of an hour, when my secretary arrives.'

It was a daily scene. Plymbell's waiter came forward with his dishes like one hurrying a funeral in a hot country, feebly averting his nose from the mess he was carrying on his dish. He scraped his serving spoons and, at the end, eyed his customer with criminal scorn. Plymbell's jaws moved over this stuff with a slow social agony. In fifteen minutes he had eaten his last biscuit and was wetting his finger to pick up the small heap of crumbs he had worked to one side of his plate. Plymbell looked at his watch.

Exactly at this moment Plymbell's assistant used to come in. Shabby, thin, with wrinkled cotton stockings and dressed in black, a woman of forty-five, Miss Tell scraped on poor shoes to the table. She carried newspapers in a bundle under an arm and a basket in her hand. He would look carefully away from her as she alighted like some dingy fly at the other side of the table. It was astonishing to see a man so well dressed lunching with a woman so bowed and faded. But presently she would do a conjuring trick. Opening her bundle, Miss Tell put a newspaper down on the roll of bread on her side plate and then she picked it up again. The roll of bread had gone. She had slipped it into her lap. A minute passed while she wriggled to and fro like a laying hen, and then she would drop the roll into the basket by the leg of her chair.

Plymbell would be looking away from her while she did this and, his lips hardly moving, he would speak one word.

'What?' was the word.

She replied also with one word – the word naturally varied – cringing toward him, looking with fear, trying to get him to look at her.

'Sausages,' she might whisper.

'How many?' Plymbell would ask. He still did not look at her.

'Half pound,' she said. On some fortunate days: 'A pound.'

Plymbell studied the domed skylight in the ceiling of the restaurant. The glass was still out in those days; the boards put there during the war when a bomb blew out the glass had not been replaced. Meanwhile the waiter brought a plate of soup to Miss Tell. She would stare at the soup without interest. When the waiter went, she lifted the plate across the table and put it in Plymbell's place and then lowered her head in case other customers had seen. Plymbell had not seen, because he had been gazing at the ceiling, but, as if absent-mindedly, he picked up a spoon and began to drink Miss Tell's soup, and when he had finished, put her plate back on her side of the table, and the waiter took it away.

Plymbell had been lunching at Polli's for years. He used to lunch there before the war with Lady Hackthorpe. She was a handsome woman – well-cut clothes, well-cut diamonds, brilliantly cut eyes, and sharply cut losses. Plymbell bought and sold for her, decorated her house.

Miss Tell used to go home to her parents in the evenings and say: 'I don't understand it. I make out her bill every month and he says: "Miss Tell, give me Lady Hackthorpe's bill," and tears it up.'

Miss Tell lived by what she did not understand. It was an appetite.

After 1940, no more Lady Hackthorpe. A bomb cut down half of her house and left a Hepplewhite bed full of broken glass and ceiling plaster on the first floor, and a servant's washstand on the floor above. Lady Hackthorpe went to Ireland.

Plymbell got the bed and a lot of other things out of the house into his shop. Here again there was something Miss Tell did not understand. She was supposed to 'keep the books straight'. Were Lady Hackthorpe's things being 'stored' or were they being 'returned to stock'?

'I mean,' Miss Tell said, 'if anyone was killed when a thing is left open it's unsatisfactory.'

Plymbell listened and did not answer. He was thinking of other things. The war on the stomach and the palate had begun. Not only had Lady Hackthorpe gone. Plymbell's business was a function of Lady Hackthorpe's luncheons and dinners, and other people's, too. He was left with his mouth open in astonishment and hunger.

'Trade has stopped now,' Miss Tell said one night when she ducked into the air-raid shelter with her parents. 'Poor Mr Plymbell never goes out.'

'Why doesn't he close the business, Kitty?' Miss Tell's mother said.

'And leave all that valuable stock?' said Mr Tell. 'Where's your brain?'

'I never could fathom business,' said Mrs Tell.

'It's the time to pick up things,' said Mr Tell.

'That's a way to talk when we may all be dead in a minute,' said Mrs Tell.

Mr Tell said something about prices being bound to go up, but a huge explosion occurred and he stopped.

'And this Lady Hackthorpe – is she *friendly* with this Plymbell?' said old Mrs Tell when the explosion settled in as part of the furniture of their lives.

'*Mr* Plymbell,' Miss Tell corrected her mother. Miss Tell had a poor, fog-coloured London skin and blushed in a patch across her forehead. 'I don't *query* his private life.'

'He's a man,' sighed Mrs Tell. 'To hear you talk he might be the Fairy Prince or Lord Muck himself. Listen to those guns. You've been there fifteen years.'

'It takes two to be friendly,' said Miss Tell, who sometimes spoke like a poem. 'When one goes away, it may be left open one way or another, I mean, and that –' Miss Tell searched for a new word but returned to the old one, the only one that ever, for her, met the human case. 'And that,' she said, 'is unsatisfactory.'

'You're neurotic,' her mother said. 'You never have any news.'

And then Miss Tell had a terrible thought. 'Mum!' she cried, dropping the poetic accent she brought back from the West End every night; 'where's Tiger? We've left him in the house.'

Her mother became swollen with shame.

'You left him,' accused Miss Tell. 'You left him in the kitchen.' She got up. 'No one's got any heart. I'm going to get him.'

'You stay here, my girl,' said Mr Tell.

'Come back, Kitty,' said Mrs Tell.

But Miss Tell (followed across the garden, as it seemed to her, by an aeroplane) went to the house. In her panic Mrs Tell had left not only the cat; she had left her handbag and her ration books on the kitchen table. Miss Tell picked up the bag and then kneeled under the table looking for Tiger. 'Tiger, dear! Tiger!' she called. He was not there. It was at this instant that the aeroplane outside seemed to have followed her into the house. When Miss Tell was dug out alive and unhurt, black with dust, six hours later, Mr and Mrs Tell were dead in the garden.

When Plymbell talks of that time now, he says there were moments when one was inclined to ask oneself whether the computed odds of something like eight hundred and ninety-seven thousand to one in favour of one's nightly survival were not, perhaps, an evasion of a private estimate one had arrived at without any special statistical apparatus – that it was fifty-fifty, and even providential. It was a point, he said, one recollected making to one's assistant at the time, when she came back.

Miss Tell came back to Plymbell's at lunch-time one day a fortnight after she had been dug out. She was singular: she had been saved by looking for her cat. Mr Plymbell was not at the shop or in his rooms above it. In the vainglory of her escape she went round to Polli's. Plymbell was more than half-way through his meal when he saw her come in. She was wearing no hat on her dusty black hair, and under her black coat, which so often had ends of cotton on it, she was wearing navy-blue trousers. Plymbell winced: it was the human aspect of war that was so lowering; he saw at once that Miss Tell had become a personality. Watching the wag of her narrow shoulders as she walked, he saw she had caught the general immodesty of the 'bombed out'.

Without being invited, she sat down at his table and put herself sideways, at her ease, crossing her legs to show her trousers. Her face had filled out into two little puffs of vanity on either side of her mouth, as if she were eating or were containing a yawn. The two rings of age on her neck looked like a cheap necklace. Lipstick was for the first time on her lips. It looked like blood.

[368]

'One enquired in vain,' said Plymbell with condescension. 'I am glad to see you back.'

'I thought I might as well pop round,' said Miss Tell.

Mr Plymbell was alarmed; her note was breezy. 'Aren't you coming back?'

'I haven't found Tiger,' said Miss Tell.

'Tiger?'

Miss Tell told him her story.

Plymbell saw that he must try to put himself for a moment in his employee's situation and think of her grief. 'One recalls the thought that passed through one's mind when one's own mother died,' he said.

'They had had their life,' said Miss Tell.

A connoisseur by trade, Plymbell was disappointed by the banality of Miss Tell's remark. What was grief? It was a hunger. Not merely personal, emotional, and spiritual; it was physical. Plymbell had been forty-two when his mother died, and he, her only child, had always lived with her. Her skill with money, her jackdaw eye had made the business. The morning she died in hospital he had felt that a cave had been opened inside his body under the ribs, a cave getting larger and colder and emptier. He went out and ate one of the largest meals of his life.

While Miss Tell, a little fleshed already in her tragedy, was still talking, the waiter came to the table with Plymbell's allowance of cheese and biscuits.

Plymbell remembered his grief. 'Bring me another portion for my secretary,' he said.

'Oh no, not for me,' said Miss Tell. She was too dazed by the importance of loss to eat. 'I couldn't.'

But Polli's waiter had a tired, deaf head. He came back with biscuits for Miss Tell.

Miss Tell looked about the restaurant until the waiter left and then coquettishly she passed her plate to Plymbell. 'For you,' she said. 'I couldn't.'

Plymbell thought Miss Tell ill-bred to suggest that he would eat what she did not want. He affected not to notice and gazed over her head, but his white hand had already taken the plate, and in a moment, still looking disparagingly beyond her, in order not to catch her eye, Mr Plymbell bit into one of Miss Tell's biscuits. Miss Tell was smiling slyly.

After he had eaten her food, Mr Plymbell looked at Miss Tell with a warmer interest. She had come to work for him in his mother's time, more than fifteen years before. Her hair was still black, her skin was now grey and yellow with a lilac streak on the jaw, there were sharp stains like poor coffee under her eyes. These were brown with a circle of gold in the pupils, and they seemed to burn as if there were a fever in their shadows. Her black coat, her trousers, her cotton blouse were cheap, and even her body seemed to be thin with cheapness. Her speech was awkward, for part of her throat was trying to speak in a refined accent and the effect was half arrogant, half disheartened. Now, as he swallowed the last piece of biscuit, she seemed to him to change. Her eyes were brilliant. She had become quietly a human being.

What is a human being? The chef, whom he could see through the hatch, was one; Polli, who was looking at the menu by the cash desk, was another; his mother, who had made remarkable ravioli; people like Lady Hackthorpe, who had given such wonderful dinner parties before the war – that circle which the war had scattered and where he had moved from one lunch to the next in a life that rippled to the sound of changing plates that tasted of sauces now never made. These people had been human beings. One knew a human being when the juices flowed over one's teeth. A human being was a creature who fed one. Plymbell moved his jaws. Miss Tell's sly smile went. He looked as though he was going to eat *her*.

'You had better take the top room at the shop,' he said. 'Take the top room if you have nowhere to live.'

'But I haven't found Tiger,' Miss Tell said. 'He must be starving.'

'You won't be alone,' said Plymbell. 'I sleep at the shop.'

Miss Tell considered him. Plymbell could see she was weighing him against Tiger in her mind. He had offered her the room because she had fed him.

'You have had your lunch, I presume,' said Plymbell as they walked back to the shop.

'No – I mean yes. Yes, no,' said Miss Tell secretively, and again there was the blush like a birthmark on her forehead.

[370]

'Where do you go?' said Plymbell, making a shameful enquiry.

'Oh,' said Miss Tell defensively, as if it were a question of chastity. 'Anywhere. I manage. I vary.' And when she said she varied, Miss Tell looked with a virginal importance first one way and then the other.

'That place starves one,' said Plymbell indignantly. 'One comes out of there some days and one is weak with hunger.'

Miss Tell's flush went. She was taken by one of those rages that shake the voices and the bones of unmarried women, as if they were going to shake the nation by the scruff of its neck. 'It's wrong, Mr Plymbell. The government ought to give men more rations. A man needs food. Myself, it never worries me. I never eat. Poor mother used to say: "Eat, girl eat." A tear came to Miss Tell's right eye, enlarged it, and made it liquid, burning, beautiful. 'It was funny, I didn't seem to fancy anything. I just picked things over and left them.'

'I never heard of anyone who found the rations too much,' said Mr Plymbell with horror.

'I hardly touch mine since I was bombed out,' said Miss Tell, and she straightened her thin, once humble body, raised her small bosom, which was ribbed like a wicker basket, gave her hair a touch or two, and looked with delicate resolution at Plymbell. 'I sometimes think of giving my ration books away,' she said in an offhand way.

Plymbell gaped at the human being in front of him. 'Give them away!' he exclaimed. '*Them*? Have you got more than one?'

'I've got Father's and Mother's, too.'

'But one had gathered that the law required one to surrender the official documents of the deceased,' said Plymbell, narrowing his eyes suggestively. His heart had livened, his mouth was watering.

Miss Tell moved her erring shoulders, her eyes became larger, her lips drooped. 'It's wicked of me,' she said.

Plymbell took her thin elbow in his hand and contained his anxiety. 'I should be very careful about those ration books. I shouldn't mention it. There was a case in the paper the other day.'

They had reached the door of the shop. 'How is Lady Hackthorpe?' Miss Tell asked. 'Is she still away?'

Miss Tell had gone too far; she was being familiar. Plymbell put up his monocle and did not reply.

[371]

A time of torture began for Plymbell when Miss Tell moved in. He invited her to the cellar on the bad nights, but Miss Tell had become light-headed with fatalism and would not move from her bed on the top floor. In decency Plymbell had to remain in his bed and take shelter no more. Above him slept the rarest of human beings, a creature who had three ration books, a woman who was technically three people. He feared for her at every explosion. His mouth watered when he saw her: the woman with three books who did not eat and who thought only of how hungry Tiger must be. If he could have turned himself into a cat!

At one point Plymbell decided that Miss Tell was like Lady Hackthorpe with her furniture; Miss Tell wanted money. He went to the dark corner behind a screen between his own office and the shop, where sometimes she sewed. When he stood by the screen he was nearly on top of her. 'If,' he said in a high, breaking voice that was strange even to himself, 'if you are ever thinking of *selling* your books . . .'

He had made a mistake. Miss Tell was mending and the needle was pointing at him as she stood up. 'I couldn't do that,' she said. 'It is forbidden by the law.' And she looked at him strictly.

Plymbell gaped before her hypocrisy. Miss Tell's eyes became larger, deeper, and liquid in the dusk of the corner where she worked. Her chin moved up in a number of amused, resentful movements; her lips moved. Good God, thought Plymbell, is she eating? Her thin arms were slack, her body was inert. She continued to move her dry lips. She leaned her head sideways and raised one eye. Plymbell could not believe what he saw. Miss Tell was plainly telling him: 'Yes, I *have* got something in my mouth. It is the desire to be kissed.'

Or was he wrong? Plymbell was not a kissing man. His white, demanding face was indeed white with passion, and his lips were shaped for sensuality, but the passion of the gourmet, the libidinousness of the palate, gave him his pallor. He had felt desire, in his way, for Lady Hackthorpe, but it had been consummated in *bisques*, in *crêpes*, in *flambées*, in *langouste* done in many manners, in *ailloli*, in *bouillabaisse* and vintage wines. That passion had been starved, and he was perturbed by Miss Tell's signal. One asks oneself (he reflected, going to his office and considering reproachfully his mother's photograph, which stood on his desk) – one asks oneself whether or not a familiar adage about Nature's abhorrence of a vacuum had not a certain relevance, and indeed whether one would not be justified in coining a vulgar phrase to the effect that when one shuts the front door on Nature, she comes in at the back. Miss Tell was certainly the back; one might call her the scullery of the emotions.

Plymbell lowered his pale eyelids in a flutter of infidelity, unable honestly to face his mother's stare. Her elderly aquiline nose, her close-curled silver hair tipped with a touch of fashionable idiocy off the forehead, her too-jewelled, hawking, grabbing, slapdash face derided him for the languor of the male symptom, and at the same time, with the ratty double-facedness of her sex, spoke sharply about flirtations with employees. Plymbell's eyes lied to her image. All the same, he tried to calm himself by taking a piece of violet notepaper and dashing off a letter to Lady Hackthorpe. Avocado pear, he wrote, whitebait (did she think?), *boeuf bourguignon*, or what about *dindonneau* in those Italian pastes? It was a letter of lust. He addressed the envelope, and, telling Miss Tell to post it, Plymbell pulled down the points of his slack waistcoat and felt saved.

So saved that when Miss Tell came back and stood close to his desk, narrow and flat in her horrible trousers, and with her head turned to the window, showing him her profile, Plymbell felt she was satirically flirting with his hunger. Indignantly he got up and, before he knew what he was doing, he put his hand under her shoulder blade and kissed her on the lips.

A small frown came between Miss Tell's eyebrows. Her lips were tight and set. She did not move. 'Was that a bill you sent to Lady Hackthorpe?' she asked.

'No,' said Plymbell. 'A personal letter.'

Miss Tell left his office.

Mr Plymbell wiped his mouth on his handkerchief. He was shocked by himself; even more by the set lips, the closed teeth, the hard chin of Miss Tell; most of all by her impertinence. He had committed a folly for nothing and he had been insulted.

The following morning Plymbell went out on his weekly search for food, but he was too presumptuous for the game. In the coarse world of provisions and the black market, the monocle was too fine. Plymbell lacked the touch; in a long day all he managed to get were four fancy cakes. Miss Tell came out of her dark corner and looked impersonally at him. He was worn out.

'No offal,' he said in an appalled, hoarse voice. 'No offal in the whole of London.'

'Ooh,' said Miss Tell, quick as a sparrow. 'I got some. Look.' And she showed him her disgusting, blood-stained triumph on its piece of newspaper.

Never had Miss Tell seemed so common, so flagrant, so lacking in sensibility, but also never had she seemed so desirable. And then, as before, she became limp and neutral and she raised her chin. There were the unmistakable crumb-licking movements of her lips. Plymbell saw her look sideways at him as she turned. Was she inviting him to wipe out the error of the previous day? With one eye on the meat, Plymbell made a step towards her, and in a moment Miss Tell was on him, kissing him, open-mouthed and with frenzy, her fingernails in his arms, and pressing herself to him to the bone.

'Sweetbreads,' she said. 'For you. I never eat them. Let me cook them for you.'

An hour later she was knocking at the door of his room, and carrying a loaded tray. It was laid, he was glad to notice, for one person only. Plymbell said: 'One had forgotten what sweetbreads were.'

'It was nothing. I have enjoyed your confidence for fifteen years,' said Miss Tell in her poetic style. And the enlarged eyes looked at him with an intimate hunger.

That night, as usual, Plymbell changed into a brilliant dressing gown, and, standing before the mirror, he did his hair, massaging with the fingers, brushing first with the hard ivory brush and then with the soft one. As he looked into the glass, Miss Tell's enquiring face kept floating into it, displacing his own.

'Enjoyed my confidence!' said Plymbell.

In her bedroom Miss Tell turned out the light, drew back the curtains, and looked into the London black and at the inane triangles of the searchlights. She stood there listening. 'Tiger, Tiger,' she murmured. 'Where are you? Why did you go away from me? I miss you in my bed.

Are you hungry? I had a lovely dinner ready for you – sweetbreads. I had to give it to him because you didn't come.'

In answer, the hungry siren went like the wail of some monstrous, disembodied Tiger, like all the dead cats of London restless beyond the grave.

Miss Tell drew the curtains and lay down on her bed. 'Tiger,' she said crossly, 'if you don't come tomorrow, I shall give everything to him. He needs it. Not that he deserves it. Filling up the shop with that woman's furniture, storing it free of charge, writing her letters, ruining himself for her. I hate her. I always have. I don't understand him and her, how she gets away with it, owing money all round. She's got a hold –'

The guns broke out. They were declaring war upon Lady Hackthorpe.

Tiger did not come back, and rabbit was dished up for Plymbell. He kissed Miss Tell a third time. It gave him the agreeable sensation that he was doing something for the war. After the fourth kiss Plymbell became worried. Miss Tell had mentioned stuffed veal. She had spoken of mushrooms. He had thoughtlessly exceeded in his embrace. He had felt for the first time in his life – voluptuousness; he had discovered how close to eating kissing is, and as he allowed his arm to rest on Miss Tell's lower-class waist, he had had the inadvertent impression of picking up a cutlet in his fingers. Plymbell felt he had done enough for the vanity of Miss Tell. He was in the middle of this alarmed condition when Miss Tell came into his office and turned his alarm to consternation.

'I've come to give my notice,' she said.

Plymbell was appalled. 'What is wrong Miss Tell?' he said.

'Nothing's wrong,' said Miss Tell. 'I feel I am not needed.'

'Have I offended you?' said Plymbell suspiciously. 'Is it money?'

Miss Tell looked sharply. She was insulted. 'No,' she said. 'Money is of no interest to me. I've got nothing to do. Trade's stopped.'

Plymbell made a speech about trade.

'I think I must have got –' Miss Tell searched for a word and lost her poetic touch – 'browned off,' she said, and blushed. 'I'll get a job in a canteen. I like cooking.'

Plymbell in a panic saw not one woman but three women leaving him. 'But you are cooking for me,' he said.

[375]

Miss Tell shrugged.

'Oh, yes, you are. Miss Tell – be my housekeeper.'

'Good God,' thought Plymbell afterwards, 'so that was all she wanted. I needn't have kissed her at all.'

How slowly one learns about human nature, he thought. Here was a woman with one simple desire: to serve him – to slave for him, to stand in queues, to cook, to run his business, do everything. And who did not eat.

'I shall certainly not kiss her again,' he said.

At this period of his life, with roofs leaving their buildings and servants leaving their places all round him, Plymbell often reflected guardedly upon his situation. There was, he had often hinted, an art in keeping servants. He appeared, he noted, to have this art. But would he keep it? What was it? Words of his mother's came back to him: 'Miss Tell left a better job and higher wages to come to me. This job is more flattering to her self-importance.' 'Never consider them, never promise; they will despise you. The only way to keep servants is to treat them like hell. Look at Lady Hackthorpe's couple. They'd die for her. They probably will.'

Two thousand years of civilisation lay in those remarks.

'And never be familiar.' Guiltily, he could imagine Lady Hackthorpe putting in her word. As the year passed, as his nourishment improved, the imaginary Lady Hackthorpe rather harped on the point.

There was no doubt about it, Plymbell admitted, he *had* been familiar. But only four times, he protested. And what is a kiss, in an office? At this he could almost hear Lady Hackthorpe laughing, in an insinuating way, that she hardly imagined there could be any question of his going any farther.

Plymbell, now full of food, blew up into a temper with the accusing voices. He pitched into Miss Tell. He worked out a plan of timely dissatisfaction. His first attack upon her was made in the shop in the presence of one of the rare customers of those days.

'Why no extra liver this week, Miss Tell? My friend here has got some,' he said.

Miss Tell started, then blushed on the forehead. It was, he saw, a blush of pleasure. Public humiliation seemed to delight Miss Tell. He made it harder. 'Why no eggs?' he shouted down the stairs, and on another day, as if he had a whip in his hand: 'Anyone can get olive oil.' Miss Tell smiled and looked a little sideways at him.

Seeing he had not hurt her in public, Plymbell then made a false move. He called her to his room above the shop and decided to 'blow her up' privately.

'I can't *live* on fish,' he began. But whereas, delighted to be noticed, she listened to his public complaints in the shop, she did not listen in his room. By his second sentence, she had turned her back and wandered to the sofa. From there she went to his writing-table, trailing a finger on it. She was certainly not listening. In the middle of his speech and as his astounded, colourless eyes followed her, she stopped and pointed through the double doors where his bedroom was and she pointed to the Hepplewhite bed.

'Is that Lady Hackthorpe's, too?' she said.

'Yes,' said Plymbell.

'Why do you have it up here?' she said rudely.

'Because I like it,' said Plymbell, snubbing her.

'I think four-posters are unhealthy,' said Miss Tell, and circled with meandering impertinence to the window and looked out on the street. 'That old man,' she said, admitting the vulgar world into the room, 'is always going by.'

Miss Tell shrugged at the window and considered the bed again across the space of two rooms. Then, impersonally, she made a speech. 'I never married,' she said. 'I have been friendly but not married. One great friend went away. There was no agreement, nothing said, he didn't write and I didn't write. In those cases I sympathise with the wife, but I wondered when he didn't communicate. I didn't know whether it was over or not over, and when you don't know, it isn't satisfactory. I don't say it was anything, but I would have liked to know whether it was or not. I never mention it to anyone.'

'Oh,' said Plymbell.

'It upset Dad,' said Miss Tell, and of that she was proud.

'I don't follow,' said Plymbell. He wanted to open the window and let Miss Tell's private life out.

'It's hard to describe something unsatisfactory,' said Miss Tell. And then: 'Dad was conventional.'

Mr Plymbell shuddered.

'Are you interested?' asked Miss Tell.

'Please, please go on,' said Plymbell.

'I have been "the other woman" three times,' said Miss Tell primly.

Plymbell put up his monocle, but as far as he could judge, all Miss Tell had done was make a public statement. He could think of no reply. His mind drifted. Suddenly he heard the voice of Miss Tell again, trembling, passionate, raging as it had been once before, at Polli's, attacking him.

'She uses you,' Miss Tell was saying. 'She puts all her rubbish into your shop, she fills up your flat. She won't let you sell it. She hasn't paid you. Storage is the dearest thing in London. You could make a profit, you could turn over your stock. Now is the time to buy, Dad said . . .'

Plymbell picked up his paper.

'Lady Hackthorpe,' explained Miss Tell, and he saw her face, small-mouthed and sick and shaking with jealousy.

'Lady Hackthorpe has gone to America,' Plymbell said, in his snubbing voice.

Miss Tell's rage had spent itself. 'If you were not so horrible to me, I would tell you an idea,' she said.

'Horrible? My dear Miss Tell,' said Mr Plymbell, leaning back as far as he could in his chair.

'It doesn't matter,' said Miss Tell, and she walked away. 'When is Lady Hackthorpe coming back?' she said.

'After the war, I suppose,' said Plymbell.

'Oh,' said Miss Tell, without belief.

'What is your idea?'

'Oh no. It was about lunch. At Polli's. It is nothing,' said Miss Tell.

'Lunch,' said Plymbell with a start, dropping his eyeglass. 'What about lunch?' And his mouth stayed open.

Miss Tell turned about and approached him. 'No, it's unsatisfactory,' said Miss Tell. She gave a small laugh and then made the crumb movements with her chin.

'Come here,' commanded Plymbell. 'What idea about lunch?'

Miss Tell did not move, and so he got up, in a panic now. A suspicion

[378]

came to him that Polli's had been bombed, that someone – perhaps Miss Tell herself – was going to take his lunch away from him. Miss Tell did not move. Mr Plymbell did not move. Feeling weak, Mr Plymbell decided to sit down again. Miss Tell came and sat on the arm of his chair.

'Nothing,' she said, looking into his eyes for a long time and then turning away. 'You have been horrid to me for ten months and thirteen days. You know you have.' Her back was to him.

Slices of pork, he saw, mutton, beef. He went through a nightmare that he arrived at Polli's late, all the customers were inside, and the glass doors were locked. The headwaiter was standing there refusing to open. Miss Tell's unnourished back made him think of this. He did no more than put his hand on her shoulder, as slight as a chicken bone, and as he did so, he seemed to hear a sharp warning snap from Lady Hackthorpe. 'Gus,' Lady Hackthorpe seemed to say, 'what are you doing? Are you mad? Don't you know why Miss Tell had to leave her last place?' But Lady Hackthorpe's words were smothered. A mere touch – without intention on Plymbell's part – had impelled Miss Tell to slide backward on to his lap.

'How have I been horrid to you?' said Plymbell, forgetting to put inverted commas round the word 'horrid'.

'You know,' said Miss Tell.

'What was this idea of yours,' he said quietly, and he kissed her neck. 'No, no,' she said, and moved her head to the other side of his neck. There was suddenly a sound that checked them both. Her shoe fell off. And then an extraordinary thing happened to Plymbell. The sight of Miss Tell's foot without its shoe did it. At fifty, he felt the first indubitable symptom. A scream went off inside his head – Lady Hackthorpe nagging him about some man she had known who had gone to bed with his housekeeper. 'Ruin,' Lady Hackthorpe was saying.

'About lunch – it was a good idea,' Miss Tell said tenderly into his collar.

But it was not until three in the morning that Miss Tell told Plymbell what the idea was.

And so, every weekday, there was the modest example of Mr Plymbell's daily luncheon. The waiter used to take the empty soup plate away from

Miss Tell and presently came forward with the meat and vegetables. He scraped them off his serving dish on to her plate. She would keep her head lowered for a while, and then, with a glance to see if other customers were looking, she would lift the plate over to Mr Plymbell's place. He, of course, did not notice. Then, absently, he settled down to eat her food. While he did this, he muttered, 'What did you get?' She nodded at her stuffed basket and answered. Mr Plymbell ate two lunches. While this went on, Miss Tell looked at him. She was in a strong position now. Hunger is the basis of life and, for her, a great change had taken place. The satisfactory had occurred.

But now, of course, French cookery has come back.

Things as They Are

Two middle-class women were talking at half past eleven in the morning in the empty bar of a suburban public house in a decaying district. It was a thundery and smoky morning in the summer and the traffic fumes did not rise from the street.

'Please, Frederick,' said Mrs Forster, a *rentier* who spoke in a small, scented Edwardian voice. 'Two more large gins. What were you saying, Margaret?'

'The heat last night, Jill. I tossed and I turned. I couldn't sleep – and when I can't sleep I scratch,' said Margaret in her wronged voice. She was a barmaid and this was her day off.

Mrs Forster drank and nodded.

'I think,' said Margaret, 'I mean I don't mean anything rude, but I had a flea.'

Mrs Forster put her grey head a little on one side and nodded again graciously under a flowered hat, like royalty.

'A flea, dear?' she said fondly.

Margaret's square mouth buckled after her next drink and her eyes seemed to be clambering frantically, like a pair of blatant prisoners behind her heavy glasses. Envy, wrong, accusation, were her life. Her black hair looked as though it had once belonged to an employer.

'I mean,' she began to shout against her will, and Frederick, the elderly barman, moved away from her. 'I mean I wouldn't have mentioned it if you hadn't mentioned it.'

Mrs Forster raised her beautiful arms doubtfully and touched her grey hair at the back and she smiled again.

'I mean when you mentioned that you had one yesterday you said,' said Margaret.

'Oh,' said Mrs Forster, too polite to differ.

'Yes, dear, don't you remember, we were in here – I mean, Frederick!

Were we in here yesterday morning, Frederick, Mrs Forster and me . . .'

Frederick stood upright, handsome, old, and stupid.

'He's deaf, the fool, that's why he left the stage,' Margaret said, glaring at him, knowing that he heard. 'Jill, yesterday? Try and remember. You came in for a Guinness. I was having a small port, I mean, or were you on gin?'

'Oh, gin,' said Mrs Forster in her shocked, soft, distinguished way, recognising a word.

'That was it, then,' said Margaret, shaking an iron chin up and down four times. 'It might have hopped.'

'Hopped,' nodded Mrs Forster pleasantly.

'I mean, fleas hop, I don't mean anything vulgar.' Margaret spread her hard, long bare arms and knocked her glass. 'Distances,' she said. 'From one place to another place. A flea travels. From here, at this end of the bar, I don't say to the end, but along or across, I mean it could.'

'Yes,' said Mrs Forster with agreeable interest.

'Or from a person. I mean, a flea might jump on you – or on me, it might jump from someone else, and then off that person, it depends if they are with someone. It might come off a bus or a tram.' Margaret's long arms described these movements and then she brought them back to her lap. 'It was a large one,' she said. 'A brute.'

'Oh, large?' said Mrs Forster sympathetically.

'Not large – I mean it must have been large, I could tell by the bites, I know a small flea, I mean we all do – don't mind my mentioning it – I had big bites all up my leg,' said Margaret, stretching out a long, strong leg. Seeing no bites there, she pulled her tight serge skirt up with annoyance over her knee and up her thigh until, halted by the sight of her suspender, she looked angrily at Frederick and furtively at Mrs Forster and pulled her skirt down and held it down.

'Big as pennies, horrible pink lumps, red, Jill,' argued Margaret. 'I couldn't sleep. Scratching doesn't make it any better. It wasn't a London flea, that I know, Jill. I know a London flea, I mean you know a London flea, an ordinary one, small beastly things, I hate them, but this must have been some great black foreign brute. Indian! Frederick! You've seen one of those things?'

Frederick went with a small business of finger-flicking to the curtains at the back of the bar, peeped through as if for his cue. All bars were empty.

'Never,' he said contemptuously when he came back, and turning his back on the ladies, hummed at the shelves of bottles.

'It's easy,' Margaret began to shout once more, swallowing her gin, shouting at her legs, which kept slipping off the rail of the stool and enraged her by jerking her body, 'I mean, for them to travel. They get on ships. I mean those ships have been in the tropics, I don't say India necessarily, it might be in Egypt or Jamaica, a flea could hop off a native onto some sailor in the docks.'

'You mean, dear, it came up from the docks by bus,' said Mrs Forster. 'You caught it on a bus?'

'No, Jill,' said Margaret. 'I mean some sailor brought it up.'

'Sailor,' murmured Mrs Forster, going pale.

'Ted,' said Margaret, accusing. 'From Calcutta. Ted could have brought it off his ship.'

Mrs Forster's head became fixed and still. She gazed mistily at Margaret and swayed. She finished her drink and steadied herself by looking into the bottom of the glass and waited for two more drops to come. Then she raised her small chin and trembled. She held a cigarette at the end of her thumb and her finger as if it were a stick of crayon and she were writing a message in blue smoke on the air. Her eyes closed sleepily, her lips sucked, pouted, and two tears rolled down her cheeks. She opened her large handbag and from the mess of letters, bills, money, keys, purses, and powder inside she took a small handkerchief and dabbed her eyes.

'Ah!' said Margaret, trying to get her arm to Mrs Forster, but failing to reach her because her foot slipped on the rail again, so that she kicked herself. 'Ah, Jill! I only mentioned it, I didn't mean anything, I mean when you said you had one, I said to myself: "That's it, it's an Indian. Ted's brought it out of the ship's hold." I didn't mean to bring up Ted, Jill. There's nothing funny about it, sailors do.'

Mrs Forster's cheeks and neck fattened amorously as she mewed and quietly cried and held her handkerchief tight.

'Here,' said Margaret, mastering her. 'Chin-chin, Jill, drink up, it will do you good. Don't cry. Here, you've finished it. Frederick, two more,' she said, sliding towards Mrs Forster and resting one breast on the bar.

[383]

Mrs Forster straightened herself with dignity and stopped crying.

'He broke my heart,' said Mrs Forster, panting. 'I always found one in the bed after his leave was over.'

'He couldn't help it,' said Margaret.

'Oh, no,' said Mrs Forster.

'It's the life sailors live,' said Margaret. 'And don't you forget, are you listening, Jill? Listen to me. Look at me and listen. You're among friends, Jill. He's gone, Jill, like you might say, out of your life.'

'Yes,' said Mrs Forster, nodding again, repeating a lesson. 'Out of my life.'

'And good riddance, too, Jill.'

'Riddance,' murmured Mrs Forster.

'Jill,' shouted Margaret. 'You've got a warm heart, that's what it is, as warm as Venus. I could never marry again after what I've been through, not whatever you paid me, not however much money it was you gave me, but you're not like me, your heart is too warm. You're too trusting.'

'Trusting,' Mrs Forster repeated softly, squeezing her eyelids.

'I tell you what it was,' Margaret said. 'You were in love, Jill,' said Margaret, greedy in the mouth. 'Can you hear me?'

'Yes, dear.'

'That's what I said. It was love. You loved him and you married him.'

Margaret pulled herself up the bar and sat upright, looking with surprise at the breast that had rested there. She looked at her glass, she looked at Mrs Forster's; she picked up the glass and put it down. 'It was a beautiful dream, Jill, you had your beautiful dream and I say this from the bottom of my heart, I hope you will have a beautiful memory.'

'Two months,' sighed Mrs Forster, and her eyes opened amorously in a grey glister and then sleepily half closed.

'But now, Jill, it's over. You've woke up, woken up. I mean, you're seeing things as they are.'

The silence seemed to the two ladies to stand in a lump between them. Margaret looked into her empty glass again. Frederick lit a cigarette he had made, and his powdered face split up into twitches as he took the first draw and then put the cigarette economically on the counter. He went through his repertory of small coughs and then, raising his statesman-like head, he listened to the traffic passing and hummed.

Mrs Forster let her expensive fur slip back from her fine shoulders and looked at the rings on her small hands.

'I loved him, Margaret,' she said. 'I really did love him.'

'We know you loved him. I mean, it was love,' said Margaret. 'It's nothing to do with the age you are. Life's never over. It was love. You're a terrible woman, Jill.'

'Oh, Margaret,' said Mrs Forster with a discreet glee, 'I know I am.'

'He was your fourth,' said Margaret.

'Don't, Margaret,' giggled Mrs Forster.

'No, no, I'm not criticising. I never criticise. Live and let live. It wasn't a fancy, Jill, you loved him with all your heart.'

Jill raised her chin in a lady-like way.

'But I won't be hit,' she whispered. 'At my age I allow no one to strike me. I am fifty-seven, Margaret, I'm not a girl.'

'That's what we all said,' said Margaret. 'You were headstrong.'

'Oh, Margaret!' said Mrs Forster, delighted.

'Oh, yes, yes, you wouldn't listen, not you. You wouldn't listen to me. I brought him up to the Chequers, or was it the Westmoreland? – no, it was the George – and I thought to myself, I know your type, young man – you see, Jill, I've had experience – out for what he could get – well, honest, didn't I tell you?'

'His face was very brown.'

'Brown! Would you believe me? No, you wouldn't. I can see him. He came up here the night of the dance. He took his coat off. Well, we all sweat.'

'But,' sighed Mrs Forster, 'he had white arms.'

'Couldn't keep his hands to himself. Put it away, pack it up, I said. He didn't care. He was after Mrs Klebs and she went potty on him till Mrs Sinclair came and then that Mr Baum interfered. That sort lives for trouble. All of them mad on him – I bet Frederick could tell a tale, but he won't. Trust Frederick,' she said with a look of hate at the barman, 'upstairs in the billiard room, I shan't forget it. Torpedoed twice, he said. I mean Ted said: he torpedoed one or two. What happened to him that night?'

'Someone made him comfortable, I am sure,' said Mrs Forster, always anxious about lonely strangers.

'And you were quite rude with me, Jill, I don't mean rude, you couldn't be rude, it isn't in you, but we almost came to words . . .'

'What did you say, Margaret?' said Mrs Forster from a dream.

'I said at your age, fifty-seven, I said you can't marry a boy of twenty-six.'

Mrs Forster sighed.

'Frederick. Freddy, dear. Two more,' said Mrs Forster.

Margaret took her glass, and while she was finishing it Frederick held his hand out for it, insultingly rubbing his fingers.

'Hah!' said Margaret, blowing out her breath as the gin burned her. 'You bowled over him, I mean you bowled him over, a boy of twenty-six. Sailors are scamps.'

'Not,' said Mrs Forster, reaching to trim the back of her hair again and tipping her flowered hat forward on her forehead and austerely letting it remain like that. 'Not,' she said, getting stuck at the word.

'Not what?' said Margaret. 'Not a scamp? I say he was. I said at the time, I still say it, a rotten little scamp.'

'Not,' said Mrs Forster.

'A scamp,' said Margaret.

'Not. Not with a belt,' said Mrs Forster. 'I will not be hit with a belt.'

'My husband,' began Margaret.

'I will not, Margaret,' said Mrs Forster. 'Never. Never. Never with a belt.

'Not hit, struck,' Mrs Forster said, defying Margaret.

'It was a plot, you could see it a mile off, it would make you laugh, a lousy, rotten plot,' Margaret let fly, swallowing her drink. 'He was after your house and your money. If he wasn't, what did he want to get his mother in for, a big three-storey house like yours, in a fine residential position? Just what he'd like, a little rat like that . . .'

Mrs Forster began a long laugh to herself.

'My grandfather,' she giggled.

'What?' said Margaret.

'Owns the house. Not owns. Owned, I say, the house,' said Mrs Forster, tapping the bar.

'Frederick,' said Mrs Forster. 'Did my grandfather own the house?'

'Uh?' said Frederick, giving his cuff links a shake. 'Which house?'

'My house over there,' said Mrs Forster, pointing to the door.

'I know he owned the house, dear,' Margaret said. 'Frederick knows.'

'Let me ask Frederick,' said Mrs Forster. 'Frederick, you knew my grandfather.'

'Uh?' said Frederick, leaning to listen.

'He's as deaf as a wall,' Margaret said.

Frederick walked away to the curtain at the back of the bar and peeped through it. Nervously he came back, glancing at his handsome face in the mirror; he chose an expression of stupidity and disdain, but he spoke with a quiet rage.

'I remember this street,' he raged, 'when you could hardly get across it for the carriages and the footmen and the maids in their lace caps and aprons. You never saw a lady in a place like this.'

He turned his back on them and walked again secretively to the curtain, peeped again, and came back stiffly on feet skewed sideways by the gravity of the gout and put the tips of his old, well-manicured fingers on the bar for them to admire.

'Now,' he said, giving a socially shocked glance over the windows that were still half boarded after the bombing, 'all tenements, flats, rooms, walls falling down, balconies dropping off, bombed out, and rotting,' he said. He sneered at Margaret. 'Not the same people. Slums. Riff-raff now. Mrs Forster's father was the last of the old school.'

'My grandfather,' said Mrs Forster.

'He was a gentleman,' said Frederick.

Frederick walked to the curtains.

'Horrible,' he muttered loudly, timing his exit.

There was a silence until he came back. The two women looked at the enormous empty public house, with its high cracked and dirty ceilings, its dusty walls unpainted for twenty years. Its top floor had been on fire. Its windows had gone, three or four times.

Frederick mopped up scornfully between the glasses of gin on the counter.

'That's what I mean,' said Margaret, her tongue swelling up, her mouth side-slipping. 'If you'd given the key to his mother, where would you have been? They'd have shut you out of your own house and what's the good of the police? All the scum have come to the top since the war. You were too innocent and we saved you. Jill, well, I mean if we hadn't all got together, the whole crowd, where were you? He was going to get into the house and then one night when you'd been over at the George or the Chequers or over here and you'd had one or two . . .'

Jill looked proudly and fondly at her glass, crinkled her childish eyes.

'Oh,' said Jill in a little naughty-faced protest.

'I mean, I don't mean plastered,' said Margaret, bewildered by the sound of her own voice and moving out her hand to bring it back.

'Not stinking, Jill, excuse me. I mean we sometimes have two or three. Don't we?' Margaret appealed to the barman.

'Uh?' said Frederick coldly. 'Where was this?'

'Oh, don't be stupid,' said Margaret, turning round suddenly and knocking her glass over, which Frederick picked up and took away. 'What was I saying, Jill?'

A beautiful still smile, like a butterfly opening on an old flower, came onto Mrs Forster's face.

'Margaret,' she confided, 'I don't know.'

'I know,' said Margaret, waving her heavy bare arm. 'You'd have been signing papers. He'd have stripped you. He might have murdered you like that case last Sunday in the papers. A well-to-do woman like you. The common little rat. Bringing his fleas.'

'He – was – not – common,' said Mrs Forster, sitting upright suddenly, and her hat fell over her nose, giving her an appearance of dashing distinction.

'He was off a ship,' said Margaret.

'He was an officer.'

'He said he was an officer,' said Margaret, struggling with her corsets.

Mrs Forster got down from her stool and held with one hand to the bar. She laughed quietly.

'He –' she began.

'What?' said Margaret.

'I shan't tell you,' said Mrs Forster. 'Come here.'

Margaret leaned towards her.

'No, come here, stand here,' said Mrs Forster.

Margaret stood up, also holding to the bar, and Mrs Forster put her hands to Margaret's neck and pulled her head down and began to laugh in Margaret's ear. She was whispering.

'What?' shouted Margaret. 'I can't hear. What is it?'

Mrs Forster laughed with a roar in Margaret's ear.

'He – he – was a man, Margaret,' she whispered. She pushed her away.

'You know what I mean, Margaret,' she said in a stern clear voice. 'You do, don't you? Come here again, I'll tell you.'

'I heard you.'

'No, come here again, closer. I'll tell you. Where are you?'

Mrs Forster whispered again and then drew back.

'A man,' she said boldly.

'And you're a woman, Jill.'

'A man!' said Mrs Forster. 'Everything, Margaret. You know – everything. But not with a belt. I won't be struck.' Mrs Forster reached for her glass.

'*Vive la France!*' she said, holding up her glass, drank, and banged it down. 'Well, I threw him out.'

A lament broke from Margaret. She had suddenly remembered one of *her* husbands. She had had two.

'He went off to his work and I was waiting for him at six. He didn't come back. I'd no money in the house, that was seventeen years ago, and Joyce was two, and he never even wrote. I went through his pockets and gave his coats a shake, wedding rings poured out of them. What do you get for it? Your own daughter won't speak to you, ashamed to bring her friends to the house. "You're always drunk," she says. To her own mother. Drunk!' said Margaret. 'I might have one or perhaps two. What does a girl like that know?'

With a soft, quick crumpling, a soft thump and a long sigh, Mrs Forster went to the floor and full-length lay there with a beautiful smile on her face, and a fierce noise of pleasure came from her white face. Her hat rolled off, her bag fell down, open, and spilling with a loud noise.

'Eh,' said Frederick, coming round from behind the counter.

'Passed out again. Get her up, get her up quick,' said Margaret. 'Her bag, her money.

'Lift her on the side,' she said. 'I will take her legs.'

They carried Mrs Forster to the broken leather settee and laid her down there. 'Here's her bag,' Margaret wrangled. 'It's all there.'

'And the one in your hand,' said Frederick, looking at the pound note in Margaret's hand.

And then the crowd came in: Mrs Klebs, Mrs Sinclair, Mr Baum, the one they called Pudding, who had fallen down the area at Christmas, and a lot more.

'What's this?' they said. 'Not again? Frederick, what's this?'

'They came in here,' Frederick said in a temper. 'Ladies, talking about love.'

The Sniff

—————

It is hard to say what the present situation is, whether it is improving or whether it is becoming one of those everlasting situations that mark the characters and memories of children. These have all noticed their mother's habit of looking up from her sewing, raising her straight nose and giving a sniff as if she were going to say 'Pop outside and see what's burning' – that sniff has become established since their father came back from the war. Her candid children glance at one another and then, without self-betrayal, they copy the sniff. The last one copies it loudly. It is not a snuffling nor a weeping sound; it is alert, questing and suspicious: 'I think I smell burning *again*.' After a few of these sniffs there is a look of wooden melancholy on her face and she sighs, she looks sullenly up at the window and the continuing daylight. She listens for foot-steps upstairs, and one would say that (for her) the ceiling is like dirty thawing snow, trodden all over by the hundreds of footmarks of some-one who will not come down. She is a woman of thirty-seven who has dull, fair hair, a long face, warm-tempered grey eyes, and her arms and elbows are going all day long. She has what she calls 'a woman's life'.

Mrs N.'s husband (who is the man upstairs) is her age and works in the boys' outfitting department of a big shop. He is one of those men who like to see other people promoted over their heads. The manager, Mr Frederick, for example, began in the shop, at the same counter with him. Between these two, Mr Frederick and her husband, Mrs N. feels – how can she put it? – she feels that her heart has become a cage and that she cannot get out of it. Perhaps 'cage' is the wrong word; for what she really feels is that she is enclosed not in bars but in a smell. She really means that: a literal smell. It is not a strong smell, for sometimes it is hardly noticeable; but it is always there, and on Saturdays and Sundays it is openly there, strong, animal and violent; so that she gets up restlessly and goes round the house unconsciously following it, searching for it, until at last she finds it. And when she finds it, she stands, as still as stone, unable to speak. Her husband looks up and tells her that what she needs is a holiday.

Mr N. is not as tall as she is; indeed, he is not as tall as most poeple. His large astounded dark blue eyes are raised under caterpillar eyebrows as if he were standing on tiptoe. He has a wide swarthy face – though he lost colour when he came back from the war – a low, monkeyish fore-head and a cap of black curls over his head. The widely opened eyes appear to be talking with astonishment, though in fact his lips hardly talk at all. He is astonished by the goods he sells, the customers he sees, by every woman he sees; by his wife, his children. Astonished at being married now fifteen years, astonished by what happened to him during the war. There is only one thing that does not astonish him.

When he came back from the war she saw with relief he had aged as much as she had. Those gazing doll's eyes of his, so childish and so surprised, were beginning to look out of the stupor of middle age. He looked like a man who is going to live on his kindness to himself. One good thing (she thought with pleasure, with pity and the spite that comes of dealing with children all day for years) – One good thing (she thought), the girls won't be after you. In the old days at the shop the girls were mad about him and he was mad about them. But only mad. Before she was married to him, she would have done any-thing to get him away from them; but once she was married she did not mind. That was the one certain control of him: the shop. The hate-ful thing about the war was that neither she nor the shop ruled him, and what he would be like then she could not imagine. What had happened to him during the war? He told her everything, but surely there was something else? He came back. She watched the crust of Italy and Africa pass from his skin and saw the paler man underneath appear.

'I used to think,' he would begin.

Think! Imagine it, he had time to think! For five years she had been trailing after children, cooking, cleaning, mending, queuing, and he came home and told her he used to 'think'. Well, what was the marvellous 'thought'? 'Five years out of our lives,' he said. Good heavens, do you call that a 'thought'? There was no time to waste, you must get what you can out of life, he said. The children might be calling and she would be glad to leave the room. No wonder he never got on at the shop, if that was what he called 'thinking'.

When she went out shopping, she listened to some of the other women. To the woman next door:

'They're lazy. The Army made them forget what life is like. They go round looking for one another like dogs. Don't worry. They'll settle down.'

What the other women were saying with their eyes and sometimes with their tongues was, 'I bet there's been another woman. They are doped with memory. Have *you* got a clear conscience?'

She almost wished there had been another woman, almost wished she had not got a clear conscience.

He was a good husband. On Saturday afternoons she went out and he stayed at home and looked after the children. She used to go out giving orders in all directions and came back to see which had been disobeyed. One of the satisfying things about him was that he was always reproachable. One Saturday when she came back from shopping and got to the gate of the house, she saw the lights were not lit. The curtains were not drawn.

In the hall no light, and in the house no sound. The air was still. The coats on their hooks, the closed doors of the rooms, the silence, indicated a place absorbed in itself. And then – her heart jumped. She was in the wrong house. This place did not *smell* like hers. She was treading on some other woman's floor-polish. She took a breath and the skin of her nostrils moved to the prick of some new smell that might have been the smell of an unsweet flower, like the garlic flower. She opened the sitting-room door and, for the first time, sniffed. The smell was not in the sitting-room. She went to the foot of the stairs and again she sniffed, but there too the scent weakened. For a moment she thought another woman was in the house and, trying the dining-room, she expected to find her sitting there, an odorous creature with bare, vaccinated arms and hot flowered lap, painting her nails, but the dining-room was empty. The scent strengthened as she approached the kitchen. Perhaps he had washed the dog, polished the brass. She opened the kitchen door and the wild smell raced to her.

'Where's the light?' she called out.

In the kitchen the daylight had decayed. He was sitting at the kitchen table with a box of oil-paints before him, his thumb in a gaudy palette. He was painting a small picture of the kitchen with its plate-rack and sink, and beside him the children stood watching silently. Even he did not look up, but went on painting.

'Ssh,' said the eldest girl, as her mother went to put her bag on the table. 'Don't jog him.'

The children moved nearer to protect the sacred figure of their father, who had suddenly, gloriously, without warning, taken up painting.

'Look,' the children said. They opened a roll of sketches he had done in the war: crayon drawings, water-colours of soldiers, the pyramids, sand dunes, Italian towns. She could not speak.

'You never told me,' she said.

She gazed at his secret life with consternation. The look of astonishment had gone from him. He looked determined, ashamed and unnaturally boastful.

'I thought I'd have a go at the old oils,' he said in a dishonest voice. She looked at the sink. The washing-up was done. The room was clean. Newspaper had been spread on the table. He was wearing an old jacket. Nothing (she had to agree) was 'wrong'.

She laughed.

'What a blessed kid you are,' she said. 'Where's these poor children's teas?'

'We don't want any tea,' the children said together.

'I bought myself some paints,' he said in an ashamed voice. 'Second-hand.'

He put his brushes down.

'No,' cried the children. 'You haven't finished.'

'The light's gone,' he said. And he spoke so sadly that the children turned indignantly towards the window at the fading sky. His wife switched on the light, and she could have died laughing when she saw his face change.

'It's wrong,' he said. 'It's the perspective. I'll have to start again.'

[394]

'Is this what they taught you in the Army?' she said.

'Yes,' he said. 'The only thing. Time drags, you've got to do something.'

Their neighbour was a dirty, gleeful woman bobbing up and down with curiosity about everything. She wore horn-rimmed spectacles and she used to stand on a box and look over the fence by the kitchen door. Her shoulders were out of sight and the head appeared to rest on top of the fence by itself, like a hairy bird's egg.

'We don't know what they've been through,' the neighbour said.

'A man wants a hobby,' his wife explained.

'Some men spend it on drink and some on women or the dogs,' said the neighbour.

'He' (his wife nodded to her husband, who was crouching over his oil-paints on a kitchen chair at the end of the garden) – 'He doesn't even smoke. Every night he comes home it's the same. I wish he'd paint the kitchen.'

'It keeps him in, mine's always out,' said the neighbour greedily. 'Has he done your picture?'

'Years ago,' said his wife, 'when I was in the shop, all the girls were after him, saying, "Draw me, draw me," posing for him, anyone would think they were – I don't know what they thought themselves.'

'Film stars,' said the neighbour, tidying her hair.

'Cheapening their faces I used to tell them,' his wife said, remembering.

'He asked me, but I wouldn't let him. It's funny how things begin. I said to him, "Can't you find something better to do? Or are you soft?"' She laughed.

'What did he say?' said the neighbour.

'That's how we got married. I made him stop it,' she said. He stopped drawing altogether when he was in love with her.

Now he came up from the bottom of the garden, astonished of course. Astonished by the sight of the neighbour's bodiless head balanced on the wooden fence; even more astonished when a hand came up from nowhere and removed the spectacles.

'When are you going to do my portrait?' said the neighbour, with a rich and sickly smile.

He had no sense. A few weeks passed and he showed his pictures to Mr Frederick, the manager.

'Mr Frederick says I have genius,' he said. That was the thing that did not astonish him.

'How that man's got on,' she said. 'Climbing on other people's shoulders,' she said.

'You're unfair to him,' he said.

'Only because he flatters you you like him,' she said.

The smell was the worst thing. Sometimes he painted flowers, sometimes a corner of the garden, sometimes he tried to turn his Italian sketches into a large oil-painting; and they all smelled. He took to standing his best ones on the mantelpiece, and she knew at once. They were awkward, living, chopped-off little pictures, unbearably new – not like pictures you see in a shop or a magazine – like small joints of meat. When she knew Mr Frederick had praised them, she saw that Mr Frederick had 'got on' by sheer unscrupulousness. Her husband came home, changed his jacket and went up to the box-room, and if she went there he was so absorbed he did not answer. The smell made her sniff, but he took no notice of that; he simply grunted. She sniffed. He grunted. He would sit there holding his breath for as much as a minute, and then puff it out with the labour of a man lifting a heavy piece of furniture upstairs. Sniff. Grunt. That animal grunt: that was their only conversation.

All these years trailing after children, all these years waiting for your husband to come home, all these years getting older – and then, when he did come, he didn't speak! Not much of a life for a woman.

'As long as it keeps him happy,' the neighbour said. 'I like a contented man.'

'By the pound, in a shop,' her husband said.

What began to alarm her was that this painting did not make him happy. Hear him! How he carried on, moaning and groaning! It was: 'I can't paint' or 'It's all wrong.' Or he got stuck and painted it all out (that was waste for you) and started again. 'Well,' she told him, 'if I couldn't do a thing, I'd give it up, not make myself miserable. I mean, what's the use of giving yourself the pip?'

He grunted.

'You say all your life you wanted to paint, if only you could paint

[396]

you'd be happy,' she said. 'You said I stopped you when we were married.'
She sniffed.

'I didn't say that,' he said with astonishment. She had got a reply from
him at last!

'It's what you meant,' she said.

He put his brush sideways in his mouth; the brush looked like a
moustache there; he gazed at her.

'Well, look at you,' she said. 'It makes you miserable and me miserable
and the children.' (That was untrue: the children loved him to paint. She
could not forgive them that.) 'You don't think of us. It's turned you
selfish. Always breathing that stuff into your system. It's poisoning
you.'

He put the brush down and started explaining to her about the picture.
She was not listening; she was riding her wrongs, galloping away on
them; but all the same, the words that caught her ear. Persp – what was
it? – Chiaro – how d'you do? His eyes got larger and larger, astonished
by the difficulty he had in trying to say what was in his mind.

'You're too trustful of people, showing that picture to Mr Frederick.
He'll genius you out of the shop,' she said.

'I'd be free then,' he said. 'An artist can't work without time and
freedom. I was sort of free in the Army,' he said.

'Free of me,' she said.

'No, free,' he said, 'for the first time in my life. That's what made me
start.'

'Give up the shop!' she cried out.

'That's what I want to do,' he said. 'I give up the shop or give up my
work.'

'Your work!' she said. 'Are you crazy or what? Here,' she said
in a panic. 'You're kidding yourself. You're not an artist. Not a real
artist.'

She waited for his answer, anxiously fixing her look upon him. He
waited a long time before answering. He seemed to be clambering over
obstacles, puffing and struggling to get to something that eluded him; he
failed. For he replied:

'No.'

'What?' she said to be sure of it.

'No,' he said. 'I'm not.'

'Oh!' she said. And then her argument died on her tongue. If he had said 'Yes,' she could have had it out with him then and there. He had always been a boaster – 'Look what I've done,' like a child. But his 'No' shocked her. It was spoken in such a cold voice out of a frozen, obdurate, empty desolation. He might have been a marooned man, someone who had been put off alone on an ugly island. She felt an emotion that was half pity and half rage at this denial of himself. It was frightening to her, now, that he should agree with her, and she said to soothe him after she had wounded him:

'Are you going to draw the woman next door? She asked you. You never offer to draw me.'

'That old owl,' he said. 'You said you hated being drawn.'

'You never asked me,' she said. 'Draw me – not my face.

'Like artists do,' she said. 'With nothing on.

'I'll let you,' she said eagerly.

'Now,' she said, when she had taken off her clothes and sat on a chair. 'This is not to be an excuse. The children will be back soon.'

He was shy and uncertain.

'A painter doesn't think like that,' he said. 'Move your arm back. He's thinking of the composition. He's thinking of beauty.'

'You don't love me,' she said. 'Not like you used, in the shop. You wanted to draw me then. Now any woman would do.

'I can't keep my arm like that all the time,' she said.

'Just a moment, only a moment,' he said.

It was terrible. The way his astonished eyes looked at her, how composed his astonishment was. The way he measured her, as though she was in some way wrong. Imagine what the neighbours would say. Suppose one of the children came in. He grunted as he drew.

'You have a hard life,' he said, suddenly talking, talking for the first time as he drew. 'Shut up with three children, always at the stove or at the sink. You don't have a chance. I often think,' he said, 'you never have a life, not to call it life.'

Her lips straightened.

'Go on telling me,' she said.

'You need a rest, a change,' he said, measuring her shoulders with the pencil.

'You don't say,' she said. 'And who's going to give it me?'

And then she slowly came to see what it was that she hated about this painting of his. *He* had a life, a life she couldn't share, a secret life she could not enter. Wonderfully kind he sounded – wonderfully kind, just like a man who is being unfaithful to you. Telling her. Telling her to go and have a life of her own. She sat there, naked, ironical, muttering her thoughts. You thank your stars, she said (but not to him), I don't go after a life of my own. A woman's life is a man, a child, another person. If I had had a life of my own it wouldn't be you.

'Oh, don't move,' he said.

If I had a life of my own, as you have, it would be a man. She saw now clearly how it was with him: this painting was an infidelity. It was like another woman. She took a long breath. She smelled the sharp smell of the paint and she remembered what she had thought at once when she smelled it in the house: another woman was there. He was unfaithful to her.

She got up without warning and covered herself with a vest. It humiliated her to sit before him.

That is still the situation. Mr Frederick, the manager, has been to the house. He is a shy, hard-mouthed man with a narrow face and grey hair. Unmarried. He is the kind of man who has to have some power, and usually you see his kind standing for hours outside chicken-runs at the end of a garden, fancying he is the cock. You can see he's gone farther with this husband of hers; leads him round like a tame bear. The fool! The enemy! 'Didn't I say he wished him no good?' He has bought one of her husband's pictures for £10.

'Your husband is a born artist,' he says to her. 'He needs time. He needs peace. He needs ... He needs...'

She can see he is dropping hints to her. What have they been saying about her? She says nothing. She just hates Mr Frederick. And yet – she can't understand why she does this, why she should enslave herself to this new mistress of his – she tiptoes to his room at dinner-time with a tray; if he is working, she puts the tray down without a word, so as not to disturb him, and goes out. She asks no questions. She makes no

[399]

difficulties. She keeps the children away. And then, one of the children begins to sniff, the next one sniffs, and the third one sniffs louder; she herself goes into the sitting-room and sniffs again, sniffing round the walls. Where is it? What has he done with it? Has he brought it down yet – the new picture?

The Collection

It happens (when it does happen) on Sunday mornings. On weekdays, when he has to go to his factory, he is the first up, but on Sunday mornings he lies in. He awakens and first of all he looks at his wife, who is curled up like a white grub, with her hair all over her eyes. Typical. What a muddle she makes of sleeping; not like other women he knows. Of course, he doesn't mean that he knows what other women are like in bed, never has; but that is one black mark against her: he has been faithful to her: she might at least keep her hair tidy. And then there was last night – surely at their age, forty-five or whatever it is, without being vulgar about it – well (he thinks), I married a woman who doesn't understand the word 'progress'. He turns his face away, looks at the starchy white ceiling and lies there disturbed by the strange silence of the house. That's it: just because it's Sunday and he's not getting up, *they* aren't getting up. Why shouldn't *they* get up for a change?

'Edward, Philip, Rose,' he shouts to the children. 'Get up.' And then to his wife, whose wakening eyes glitter like a pair of ants under her hair: 'Come on, girl.'

'Sunday,' he says poetically. 'Look at the sun. It is streaming in. Look at the sky. Listen to the birds. They're not wasting the day.'

But nobody moves.

After this the usual thing happens. It is surprising how no one understands him in the house; he has to lose his temper and start shouting at the lazy hounds, the curs, to get the family to their feet.

'Oh, you,' says his wife, to whom he has given a push. 'You never give anyone any peace.' And she gets out of bed stark naked. She is thin and round-shouldered and her neck is red.

'Here, here, I say,' he says jovially, but he hates that about her more than anything. He closes his eyes at the sight.

'Pah,' he says to himself. 'There's no getting away from it. I married beneath me.'

[401]

Downstairs in the kitchen the children are mooching, laying the table, kicking the furniture – he can hear that – cleaning his boots, scared that they are getting blacking on the laces or skimping the heels.

He is lying in bed, listening to them, when suddenly he remembers: 'Good God, this Sunday I'm taking the collection.'

He is out of bed at once, standing in his collapsing pyjamas. Why didn't someone remind him?

The children go to the bottom of the stairs and listen.

'He's in the bath,' they say.

Twenty minutes go by, half an hour, an hour. The mystery of his toilet reigns over it. One after another the children tiptoe and listen.

Enormous volumes of water, as if the Congo were pouring into the house, are heard in the bathroom, sounds like the breathing and thumping of boxers, silences so long that he may have drowned. Then, through the keyhole, they see him shave; the dark rhino cheek frilled by soap, straining, Christianwise, to turn from the mirror, while the sacrificial blade comes down. When he is back in his room, they see him put on his blue suit and blue shirt and then take them off again. A hot smell of scent fills his room as he rubs three different lotions into his black hair while he considers the problem. He is taking the collection. Would the brown or the grey be more suitable? Or would it not be best to wear his tail coat and his striped trousers? He puts on a wing collar which bites at his throat and slices into his jowl. He puts on a silvery tie. Then he goes and disdains himself in the mirror.

The spy creeps down and a stair-rod comes out on the last tread.

'Confound you, you clumsy hound, what are you doing?' he roars from the mirror.

'He's nearly ready, Mum,' the spy whispers.

Treading like a cat, floating silkily down, watching the amazing stripes of his trousers, with the gravity of a mourner, a little distracted, like a bridegroom by the flash of his spats which might make him misjudge the steps if he were not careful, he arrives downstairs and pauses in the doorway and puts on the impersonal yet benevolent scowl he intends to wear as he stands at the end of the pews waiting for the plate to come down the row. A plate in fact arrives; it is a plate of porridge rushed towards him by his wife.

'Oh,' she cries stopping dead, tipping the plate. 'You give me a fright.'

'Give!' he says. 'Gave. I'm taking the collection. Am I all right?'

Doesn't she know that it is an important thing to take the collection at the chapel, that people have their eye on you, that it has got to be done properly, and that people say, There's £20-a-week taking the collection? And in a sense, God is looking too. God is saying: That's it. Don't spare the expense. I want the best.

'Give me a brush,' he says. 'And the back. I look after *my* clothes. Where are those boys? Aren't they coming to church?'

'I don't know where they are,' she says.

'Give the brush to me,' he says.

'They were here,' she says. 'They're outside, I expect.'

'Outside!' he shouts, hitting himself with the brush, lashing himself up. 'I don't understand you, outside! The only day their father is home, they're outside . . .'

He bangs the brush down. He is beginning to sweat.

'You'll be late,' she says to him.

'Edward, Philip,' he roars at the door, wiping his hat. There is no answer. 'Come here when I call you.' He puts his hat on. No answer.

'Come and watch your father go. He's going. Come and watch.' She calls in her lighter voice. He stands there waiting, looking as though he will explode.

'If I had behaved like this to my father,' he raps out, 'I'd have been thrashed within an inch of my life.'

But he has marched off, slamming the gate, as they creep up from the back of the house.

The garrulous church bells are stirring up the morning heat. No obedience, he thinks (once he is out of the house), no discipline, no love. No religion. That's her doing. No God. No progress. You might as well cast your pearls before swine. Idle hounds lounging about in the shed. Slack, don't wash. I slave all the week for their education, and what do I get? They bleed you, that's what children do, bleed you white. The Government's the same, bleeds you with taxation. Who goes to church nowadays? No one. Who believes in God – look at the state of the world for the answer. Why did we have a war? Perhaps if it could be reckoned up, if you could get some really good accountant at it, it would turn out

that I am the only one who really believes in the Truth. Many think they
do; but do they?

Gradually, like the unfolding of a white rose in the sun, an intoxicating
sensation of conspicuousness opens in his mind. He feels that he is
flashing with sadness. And then as he gets near to the granite chapel he
is happy. He sees the shabby people go in. They turn to look at him and
whisper. Hard, severe, is he? Maybe.

He himself goes into the chapel and looks at the small congregation.
The believers are few. They are indeed the elect, but the elect look
dispirited. In the half-empty chapel he gazes at the red brick walls and he
is calmed. He rises to sing, he kneels to pray, he sits.

He is awakened by the organ. Before he is ready for it, the time to take
the collection has come. On the other side of the aisle he sees Mr
Doncaster – wearing an ordinary brown suit – begin his collection as the
organ mews and growls like an animal up in the loft. He stands up very
upright – unlike Mr Doncaster, who is round-shouldered; he puts on the
impersonal, official expression – not like Mr Doncaster's, who leans over
the congregation thanking them disgustingly like a grocer; he affects not
to hear the chink of coins in the plate and raises his eyes to the rafters if
there is the rustle of a note. He takes the plate and hands it to the next
row with a forbidding patience. He would like to take Mr Doncaster's
side as well, because the pleasure of being given money for nothing has
a touch of folly which only a man who has risen in the world can know.
And then, as the organ rolls, he and Mr Doncaster walk together, dead
level, slowly – he can feel the eyes of the congregation on him, almost
heavily on him, tipping the chapel down on his side like a scale pan –
he and Mr Doncaster, like bridegroom and bride, walk up the central
aisle; and, after placing their offerings, return with the same gravity.
And all the time he is thinking, Doncaster must feel a fool not being in
black.

A sensation of being swept upwards by his excellent shoes, upwards
toward some expensive radiance, cool, fleshless and flawless, overcomes
him as if he were drunk. His eyes shine and twinkle, his cheeks are pink
and happy. The sermon begins. The minister is barking away in the oak
pulpit. Soon he hears nothing, but he looks round the chapel. A house
with natural oak everywhere is what he would like, with tall, church-like

windows on the stairs, an organ in the wide entrance hall, an open fire as wide as the chapel at the communion rail; gradually the chapel turns into a feudal castle, armour everywhere, himself in a kilt. His wife and children drift about in it, delightful creatures. Yes, he thinks, they are the children of God, we have put off the old Adam. His dreamy eyes come down from the chapel walls and he sees the yellow bald head of old Doncaster. Yes, he says, poor old Doncaster who doesn't brush his coat – yes, God made him, too.

I'm hungry, he says. What an appetite! Going to chapel does you good, sets you up. I wonder what there is for lunch?

Reluctantly he leaves the chapel, the scene of his vision. He has been in heaven. He marvels at the contradictions of his nature, he walks back home. At first he notices how well all the houses are painted and then the pleasant accent of people. The neighbourhood is going up. Then, he notices, the property deteriorates. Fences are not so good, a gate-hinge has gone. It's the war. His temperature lowers a little. He arrives at his own house. It is at the corner of the street and he notices, for the first time, that a paling has gone. The hedge has not been cut. A bush at the corner rocks like a broom. The boys are trampling down the garden again. He goes to his high gate. It sticks. He has to shake and rattle and then call. 'Edward! Philip!' There is no answer. Yet distinctly he had heard them. He is obliged to dirty his gloves and his hands, forcing the confounded gate open. And what a sight: that paper left on the path.

'Edward,' he says. 'Come here. What's this?'

'Paper, Father.'

'What paper?'

'Just paper, Father.'

'Who put it there?'

'I don't know.'

Edward's alarmed eyes are fixed on his father's. He cannot take them away. In that coat, that collar, so naked at the neck, behind the bars of those striped trousers, he looks militant and tigerish.

'When did you clean your boots?' says the father, sudden in his attack.

The boy flinches.

'This morning.'

'Don't lie,' says the father. 'Why can't you tell the truth? A man who doesn't tell the truth, fearlessly, in all circumstances, come what may, forfeits my trust. If a man lies to me in my business I sack him – on the spot. Pick that paper up.'

He goes into the house.

'Philip,' he calls. 'Why isn't the table laid? Do you expect your father and mother to slave for you? Don't you know there are no servants? I suppose you think you are a lord or something. Let me tell you, in this world, we are all servants.'

He marches into the kitchen. As he advances, he notices a shadow goes with him. Smiles vanish; scowls, evasions, furtive, deceitful, lying looks pass over the faces of his family. It is all so unlike the communion of saints.

'Don't crash the forks on that table,' he calls back down the passage. 'You would have to pay £80 for it today.'

His wife is still in her old apron, the sweat from the heat of the fire is on her face as she kneels. He goes out of the kitchen as quickly as he can.

The family are sitting down to lunch.

'Stop kicking the table, Philip,' he says as he carves. He glares. They all lower their eyes.

'Take that plate, pass it down, it's not for yourself. Think of others,' he says. 'Others before self always, the golden rule.' And then he looks at Edward.

'Edward,' he says. 'What have you done to your hair?'

'Nothing.'

'I told you before about lying. Why have you got your best suit on, getting yourself up like that, what's the idea?'

'Edward wants to go out,' says Philip.

'What's that?' he says. 'What's that, Edward? Did I understand that you want to go out?

'On Sunday?' he says. 'Your father's only day at home, and you want to go out. I never heard of such a thing.'

The father goes pale as if he had cut himself with the carving knife.

'You stay in and shut up, Edward,' says his mother. 'You cause enough trouble as it is. Get on with your food.'

'Go out with who?' says the father. 'Who is it you value more than your father and mother? It's not some girl, is it? I won't have you go with girls. I don't want trouble with girls at your age. Oh, I'm glad to hear it. You're not telling me lies, are you? You tell lies. I know you deceive me, lie and deceive, but you can't deceive God. He sees, He knows when you're telling lies. I don't like people who tell lies. I don't like boys who aren't friends with their fathers. It's not some girl? Look me in the face.'

'No,' says Edward in a weak voice. Tears are very near his eyes. A light glints in the father's eyes. He has seen the son's weakness.

'N'no, n'no. I don't understand that language. Be straightforward. If you mean yes, say yes. If you mean no, say no. N'n'no. I never heard of it. Sit up straight and speak to your father. Go on now – what is it?'

Tears pour into Edward's eyes, tears of rage and shame, and rush down his cheeks.

'I just want to go out. I want to get away from this,' he shouts, but he is crying so hard that no one understands. He shouts and cries, starts up and goes out of the room, knocking his chair over.

'Look what you've done!' shouts the wife, banging down her knife and fork. 'I can't stand this. Every Sunday the same. I'm going too.'

And crying also, she leaves the table.

The father gapes at the astonishing scene. He looks down gently at the other children. What on earth have I done? he silently asks them. He suspects they are going to move too.

'Stop where you are,' he says.

He stands there. The food is going cold on his plate. It is all so stupefying, so sudden. He feels that lions are inside him rending him apart. He feels that he is like Samson, the hairy Samson of the Bible, who has pulled down the temple crashing on top of him. The day he has taken the collection, too.

Thank God, he thinks, I shall be at the office tomorrow. People understand me there.

Of course, he gets them back. It takes a bit of doing, the lunch is cold, but she heats it up again. Everyone has a good cry, and while they're at it, he goes up and changes into another suit. Everyone is shy and disappointed and sorry for him after that; and, not to annoy him, no one goes out. They stay in the room with him, all of them, and in their midst he falls asleep. He sleeps and sleeps and his snores rise and dive, cavort and turn over like fighters in the room. And waking at last at the end of the afternoon, he looks at them with surprise. It's all gone, he has forgiven them.

The Wheelbarrow

'Robert,' Miss Freshwater's niece called down from the window of the dismantled bedroom, 'when you have finished that, would you mind coming upstairs a minute? I want you to move a trunk.'

And when Evans waved back from the far side of the rumpled lawn where he was standing by the bonfire, she closed the window to keep out the smoke of slow-burning rubbish – old carpeting, clothes, magazines, papers, boxes – which hung about the waists of the fir trees and blew towards the house. For three days the fire had been burning and Evans, red-armed in his shirt sleeves and sweating along the seams of his brow, was prodding it with a garden fork. A sudden silly tongue of yellow flame wagged out: some inflammable piece of family history – who knew what? – perhaps one of her aunt's absurd summer hats or a shocking year of her father's day-dream accountancy was having its last fling. She saw Evans pick up a bit of paper from the outskirts of the fire and read it. What was it? Miss Freshwater's niece drew back her lips and opened her mouth expectantly. At this stage all family privacy had gone. Thirty, forty, fifty years of life were going up in smoke.

Evans took up the wheelbarrow and swaggered back with it across the lawn towards the house, sometimes tipping it a little to one side to see how the rubber-tyred wheel was running and to admire it. Miss Freshwater's niece smiled. With his curly black hair, his sun-reddened face and his vacant blue eyes, and the faint white scar or chip on the side of his nose, he looked like some hard-living, hard-bitten doll. 'Burn this? This lot to go?' was his cry. He was an impassioned and natural destroyer. She could not have found a better man. 'Without you, Robert,' she said on the first day and with real feeling, 'I could never have faced it.'

It was pure luck getting him but, lazy, smiling and drifting, she always fell on her feet. She had stepped off the morning train from London at the beginning of the week and had stood on the kerb in the station yard, waiting for one of the two or three taxi drivers who were talking there to take notice of her. Suddenly, Evans drove in fast from the street outside, pulled up beside her, pushed her in and drove off. It was like an abduction. The other taxi drivers shouted at him in the bad language of law-abiding men, but Evans slowly moved his hand up and down, palm downwards, silently and insultingly telling them to shut up and keep their hair on. He looked very pious as he did this. It made her laugh out loud.

'They are manner-less,' he said in a slow, rebuking voice, giving each syllable its clear value as if he were speaking the phrase of a poem. 'I am sorry I did not ask you where you want me to take you.'

They were going in the wrong direction and he had to swing round the street. She now saw him glance at her in the mirror and his doll's eyes quickly changed from shrewd pleasure to vacancy: she was a capture.

'This is not the first time you are here, I suppose?' he said.

'I was born here,' she said. 'I haven't been here for twenty-five years, well perhaps just for a day a few years ago. It has changed. All this building!'

She liked friendly conversations.

They were driving up the long hill out of the town towards her aunt's house. Once there had been woodland here but now, like a red hard sea flowing in to obliterate her memory, thousands of sharp villas replaced the trees in angular waves.

'Yes,' he said simply. 'There is money everywhere.'

The car hummed up the long, concrete hill. The villas gave way to ribbons of shacks and bungalows. The gardens were buzzing with June flowers. He pointed out a bungalow which had a small grocery shop in the lean-to at the side, a yard where a couple of old cars stood, and a petrol pump. That was his place, he said. And then, beyond that, were the latest municipal housing estates built close to the Green which was only half a mile from her aunt's house. As they passed, she saw a white marquee on the Green and a big, sagging white banner with the words Gospel Mission daubed on it.

'I see the Gospellers still keep it up,' she said. For it was all bad land outside the town, a place for squatters, poor craftsmen, smallholders, little men with little sheds, who in their flinty way had had for generations the habit of breaking out into little religious sects.

'Oh, yes,' said Evans in a soft voice, shocked that she could doubt it. 'There are great openings. There is a mighty coming to the Lord. I toil in the vineyard myself. You are Miss Freshwater's niece?' he said. 'She was a toiler too. She was a giantess for the Lord.'

She saw she had been reckless in laughing. She saw she was known. It was as if he had knowingly captured her.

'You don't come from these parts, do you?' she said.

'I am from Wales,' he said. 'I came here from the mines. I ob-ject-ed to the starvation.'

They arrived at the ugly yellow house. It could hardly be seen through the overgrown laurels and fir trees which in some places fingered the dirty windows. He steadied her as she got out for she had put on weight in the last year or so and while she opened her bag to find some money, he walked to the gate and looked in.

'It was left to you in the will, I suppose?' he said.

'Yes,' she said. She was a woman always glad to confide. 'I've come down to clear up the rubbish before the sale. Do you know anyone here who would give me a hand?'

'There are many,' he pronounced. 'They are too handy.' It was like a line from an anthem. He went ahead, opened the gate and led the way in and when she opened the front door, splitting it away from the cobwebs, he went in with her, walking into the stale, sun-yellowed rooms. He looked up the worn carpet of the stairs. He looked at the ceilings, measuring the size of everything.

'It will fetch a high price,' he said in a sorrowful voice and then, looking over her figure like a farmer at the market, in case she might go with the property, he added enthusiasm to his sorrow.

'The highest!' he said. 'Does this door go to the back?' She lost him for a while. When she found him he was outside, at the back of the house, looking into sheds. He had opened the door of one that contained gardening tools and there he was, gazing. He was looking at a new green metal wheelbarrow with a red wheel and a rubber tyre and he had even pulled it out. He pushed it back, and when he saw her he said accusingly:

'This door has no lock. I do not like to see a door without a lock. I will bring one this afternoon.'

It was how she knew he had appointed himself.

'But who will do your taxi work?'

'My son will do that,' he said.

From that moment he owned her and the house.

'There will be a lot of toil in this vineyard,' she said to him maliciously and wished she had not said it; but Evans's eyes lost their vacancy again and quickened and sparkled. He gave a shout of laughter.

'Oh boy, there will!' he said admiring her. And he went off. She walked from room to room, opening windows, and from an upper one she saw distantly the white sheet of the Gospel tent through the fir trees. She could settle to nothing.

It was an ugly house of large mean rooms, the landings dark, the stairs steep. The furniture might have come out of old-fashioned hotels and had the helpless look of objects too large, ill-met commercially and too gregarious. After her mother's death, her father had moved his things into his sister's house. Taste had not been a strong point in the family. The books, mainly sermons, were her grandfather's; his son had lived on a hoard of engineering textbooks and magazines. His sister read chiefly the Bible and the rest of her time changed her clothes, having the notion that she might be going out.

What paralysed Miss Freshwater's niece was the emptiness of the place. She had expected to disturb ghosts if she opened a drawer. She had expected to remember herself. Instead, as she waited for Evans to come on the first day she had the sensation of being ignored. Nothing watched in the shadows, nothing blinked in the beams of sunlight slanting across the room. The room she had slept in meant nothing. To fit memories into it was a task so awkward and artificial that she gave up trying. Several times she went to the window, waiting for Evans to walk in at the gate and for the destruction to begin.

When he did come he seized the idea at once. All files marked A.H.F. – that was her father – were 'rubbish'.

'Thorpe?' he said. 'A.H.F. more A.H.F.! Burn it?' He was off with his first load to lay the foundation to the fire.

'And get this carpet up. We shall trip on it, it is torn," she said. He ripped the carpet off the stairs. He tossed the door mats, which were worn into holes, outside. By the barrow load out went the magazines. Every now and then some object took his eye – a leather strap, a bowl, a pipe rack, which he put into a little heap of other perquisites at the back door.

But to burn was his passion, to push the wheelbarrow his joy. He swaggered with it. He unloaded it carefully at the fire, not putting it down too near or roughly tipping it. He often tried one or two different grips on the handles before he started off. Once, she saw him stop in the middle of the lawn and turn it upside down and look it over carefully and make the wheel spin. Something wrong? No, he lovingly wiped the wheel with a handful of grass, got an oilcan from his pocket, and gave the wheel a squirt. Then he righted the wheelbarrow and came on with it round the house, singing in a low and satisfied voice. A hymn, it sounded like. And at the end of the day, when she took him a cup of tea and they stood chatting, his passion satisfied for the time being, he had a good look at her. His eye was on the brooch she was carelessly wearing to fasten her green overall. He came closer and put his hand to the brooch and lifted it.

'Those are pearls, I shouldn't wonder?' he said.

'Yes,' she said. He stepped nimbly away, for he was as quick as a flea.

'It is beautiful,' he said, considering the brooch and herself together. 'You would not buy it for fifty pounds, nor even a hundred, I suppose. A present, I expect?' And before she could answer, he said gravely: 'Half past five! I will lock the sheds. Are you sleeping here? My wife would go off her head, alone in the house. When I'm at the Mission, she's insane!'

Evans stared at Miss Freshwater's niece, waiting for a response to his drama. She did not know what to do, so she laughed. Evans gave a shout of laughter too. It shook the close black curls of his hair and the scar on the side of his nose went white.

'I have the key,' he said seriously and went off.

'Robert,' Miss Freshwater's niece opened the window and called again. 'Can you come now? I can't get on.'

Evans was on his way back to the house. He stamped quickly up the bare stairs.

'I'm in here,' she called. 'If you can get in!'

There was a heap of old brown paper knee high at the door. Some of the drawers of a chest had been taken out, others were half open; a wardrobe's doors were open wide. There were shoes, boxes and clothes piled on the bed which was stripped. She had a green scarf in a turban round her head, and none of her fair hair could be seen. Her face, with its strong bones and pale skin marked by dirty fingers, looked hard, humorous and naked. Her strong lips were dry and pale with dust.

They understood each other. At first he had bossed her but she had fought back on the second day and they were equals now. She spoke to him as if they were in a conspiracy together, deciding what should be 'saved' and what should be 'cast into the flames'. She used those words purposely, as a dig of malice at him. She was taller than he. She couldn't get over the fact that he preached every night at the Mission and she had fallen into the habit of tempting him by some movement of arm or body, when she caught him looking at her. Her aunt had used the word 'inconvenient', when her niece was young, to describe the girl's weakness for dawdling about with gardeners, chauffeurs, errand boys. Miss Freshwater's niece had lost the sense of the 'convenient' very early in life.

'I've started upstairs now,' she said to Evans. 'It's worse than downstairs. Look at it.'

Evans came a step further into the room and slowly looked round, nodding his head.

She leaned a little forward, her hands together, eagerly awaiting for him to laugh so that they could laugh together.

'She never threw away a scrap of paper. Not even paper bags. Look at this,' she said.

He waded into the heap and peeped into a brown paper bag. It contained a bun, as hard as stone.

'Biscuits too,' she said. 'Wrapped up! Like a larder. They must have been here for years. In the top drawer.'

Evans did not laugh.

'She feared starvation,' he said, 'old people are hungry. They are greedy. My grandmother nibbled like a little rat, all day. And in the night too. They wake up in the night and they are afraid. They eat for comfort. The mice did not get in, I hope,' he said, going to look in the drawer.

'She was eighty-four,' she said.

'My grandmother was ninety,' he said. 'My father's mother. She liked to hear a mouse. It was company, she said.'

'I think my aunt must have been fond of moths,' she said. 'They came out in clouds from that wardrobe. Look at all those dresses. I can hardly bear to touch them.'

She shook a couple of dresses in the wardrobe and then took them out. 'There you are, did you see it? There goes one.'

She held up an old-fashioned silk dress.

'Not worn for twenty years, you can see by the fashion. There!' She gave the dress a pull. 'Did you hear? Perished. Rotten. They are all like that. You can't give them away. They'd fall off you.'

She threw the dresses on the floor and he picked up one and he saw where moths had eaten it.

'It is wicked,' he said. 'All that money has gone to waste.'

'Where moth and dust doth corrupt,' she mocked him, and took an armful of the clothes and threw them on the floor. 'Why did she buy them if she did not want them? And all those hats we had to burn? You haven't seen anything yet. Look at this.'

On the bed was lying a pile of enormous lace-up corsets. Evans considered them.

'The men had patience,' he said.

'Oh, she was not married,' she said.

He nodded.

'That is how all the property comes to you, I suppose,' he said. There was a shrewd flash in his blue eyes and she knew he had been gazing at her all this time and not at the clothes; but even as she caught his look the dissembling, still, vacant light slid back into it.

'Shoes!' she said, with excitement. 'Do you want any shoes?' A large number of shoes of all kinds, little worn or not worn at all, were rowed in pairs on the bed and some had been thrown into a box as well.

'Fifty-one pairs I counted,' she said. 'She never went out but she went on ordering them. There's a piece of paper in each pair. Have a look. Read it. What does it say?'

He took a piece of paper out of a shoe.

'"Comfortable for the evening",' he read out. He took another. '"For wet weather". Did it rain indoors?'

She took one and read out:

'"With my blue dress"! Can you imagine? "Sound walking pair",' she laughed but he interrupted her.

'In Wales they lacked them,' he said. 'In the bad times they were going barefoot. My sisters shared a pair for dances.'

'What shall I do with them?' she asked. 'Someone could wear them.'

'There are good times now. They have the money,' he said, snubbing her. 'They buy new.'

'I mean – anyone,' she said. 'They are too big for me. I'll show you.'

She sat down on a packing case and slipped her foot into a silver evening shoe.

'You can see, my feet are lost in them,' she said.

'You have small feet,' he said. 'In Wales the men would be chasing you.'

'After chapel, I've no doubt,' she said. 'Up the mountain – what was the name of it? You told me.'

'It has the best view in Wales. But those who go up it never see it,' he laughed. 'Try this pair,' he said, kneeling down and lifting her foot. 'Ah no, I see. But look at those legs, boy!'

Miss Freshwater's niece got up.

'What size does your wife take?' she asked.

'I don't know,' he said, very pleased with himself. 'Where is this trunk you said we had to move?'

'Out in the landing cupboard. I'll show you. I can't move it.'

She led the way to the landing and bent down to tug at it.

'You must not do that,' he said, putting his hands on her waist and moving her out of the way. He heaved at the trunk and tipped it on end. She wanted it, she said, in the light, where she could see.

'Here on the chest,' she said.

He lifted it up and planked it down on the chest.

'Phew!' he said. 'You have a small waist for a married woman. Soft. My wife is a giantess, she weighs thirteen stone. And yet, you're big, too, oh yes, you are. But you have light bones. With her, now, it is the bones that weigh. Shall we open it?'

She sat down on a chair and felt in her pocket for a mirror.

'Why didn't you tell me I looked such a sight?' she said, wiping her face. 'Yes, open it.'

The trunk was made of black leather: it was cracked, peeling, stained and squashed by use. Dimly printed on it was her father's fading name in white large letters. The trunk had been pitched and bumped and slithered out of ships' holds and trains, all over the world. Its lid, now out of the true, no longer met the lock and it was closed by a strap. It had lain ripening and decaying in attics and lofts for half a lifetime.

'What is in it?' she called, without looking from her mirror.

'Clothes,' he said. 'Books. A pair of skates. Did the old lady go skating?'

He pulled out a Chinese hat. There was a pigtail attached to it and he held it up.

'Ah,' he called. 'This is the job.' He put the hat on his head and pulled out a mandarin coat.

Miss Freshwater's niece stared and then she flushed.

'Where did you get that?' she cried jumping up, taking the hat from his head and snatching the coat. 'They're mine! Where were they?'

She pushed him aside and pulled one or two things from the trunk.

'They're mine!' she accused him. 'All mine.'

She aged as she looked at him. A photograph fell to the floor as she lifted up a book. 'To darling Laura,' she read out. 'Tennyson.'

'Who is this?' he said, picking up the photograph.

She did not hear. She was pulling out a cold, sequined evening dress that shrank almost to nothing as she picked it up.

'Good God,' she said and dropped it with horror. For under the dress was an album. 'Where,' she said, sharply possessive, 'did you put the skates?' She opened the album. She looked at a road deep in snow leading to an hotel with eaves a yard wide. She had spent her honeymoon there.

'Kitzbühel,' she said. 'Oh, no!'

She looked fiercely at him to drive him away. The house, so anonymous, so absurd, so meaningless and ghostless, had suddenly got her. There was a choke of cold wonder in her throat.

She turned on him: 'Can't you clear up all that paper in the room?' She did not want to be seen by him.

Evans went to the door of the bedroom and, after a glance inside, came back. He was not going to leave her. He picked up the book of poems, glanced at a page or two and then dropped it back in the trunk.

'Everyone knows,' he said scornfully, 'that the Welsh are the founders of all the poetry of Europe.'

She did not hear him. Her face had drained of waking light. She had entered blindly into a dream in which she could hardly drag herself along. She was looking painfully through the album, rocking her head slowly from side to side, her mouth opening a little and closing on the point of speech, a shoulder rising as if she had been hurt, and her back moving and swaying as she felt the clasp of the past like hands on her. She was looking at ten forgotten years of her life, her own life, not her family's, and she did not laugh when she saw the skirts too long, the top-heavy hats hiding the eyes, her face too full and fat, her plainness so sullen, her prettiness too open-mouthed and loud, her look too grossly sly. In this one, sitting at the café table by the lake when she was nineteen, she looked masterful and at least forty. In this garden picture she was theatrically fancying herself as an ancient Greek in what looked like a nightgown! One of her big toes, she noticed, turned up comically in the sandal she was wearing. Here on a rock by the sea, in a bathing dress, she had got thin again – that was her marriage – and look at her hair! This picture of the girl on skis, sharp-faced, the eyes narrowed – who was that? Herself – yet how could she have looked like that! But she smiled a little at last at the people she had forgotten. This man with the crinkled fair hair, a German – how mad she had been about him. But what pierced her was that in each picture of herself she was just out of reach, flashing and yet dead; and that really it was the things that burned in the light of permanence – the chairs, the tables, the trees, the car outside the café, the motor launch on the lake. These blinked and glittered. They had lasted and were ageless, untouched by time, and she was not. She put the album back into the trunk and pulled out an old tweed coat and skirt. Under it was an exercise book with the word 'Diary' written on it in a hand more weakly rounded than the hand she wrote today. Part of a letter fell out of the diary, the second page, it seemed, of a letter of her own. She read it.

'. . . the job at any rate,' she read. 'For a whole week he's forgotten his chest, his foot, his stomach. He's not dying any more!!! He conde (crossed out) congratulates himself and says it just shows how doctors are all fools. Inner self-confidence is what I need, he tells me!! It means giving up the flat and that's what I keep thinking – Oxford will be much more difficult for you and me. Women, he says, aren't happy unless they're sacrificing themselves. Darling, he doesn't know; it's the thought of You that keeps . . .'

She turned over the page. Nothing. She looked through the diary. Nothing. She felt sick and then saw Evans had not gone and was watching her. She quickly put the letter back into the diary.

'Ah,' she said nervously. 'I didn't know you were here. I'll show you something.' She laughed unnaturally and opened the album until she found the most ludicrous and abashing picture in the book, one that would humiliate her entirely. 'Here, look at this.'

There was a see-saw in the foreground surrounded by raucously laughing people wearing paper hats and looking as though they had been dipped in glycerine: she was astride at the higher end of the see-saw, kicking her legs, and on the lower end was a fat young man in a pierrot costume. On her short, fuzzy fair hair was a paper hat. She showed the picture to Evans and picked out the terrible sequin dress from the trunk.

'That's the dress!' she said, pointing to the picture. 'I was engaged to him. Isn't it terrible?' And she dropped the dress back again. It felt cold and slippery, almost wet. 'I didn't marry him.'

Evans scowled.

'You were naked,' he said with disgust.

'I remember now. I left it all here. I kept that dress for years. I'll have to go through it all.' And she pulled down the lid.

'This photograph fell out,' he said.

It was the picture of another young man.

'Is this your husband?' Evans asked, studying the man.

'My husband is dead,' she said sharply. 'That is a friend.' And she threw the picture back into the trunk. She realised now that Evans had been holding her arm a long time. She stepped away from him abruptly. The careless friendliness, the sense of conspiracy she had felt while they worked together, had all gone. She drew away and said, in the hostile voice of unnecessary explanation:

'I mean,' she said, 'my husband died a few years ago. We were divorced. I mustn't waste any more time.'

'My wife would not condescend to that,' he said.

'She has no reason, I am sure,' said Miss Freshwater's niece, severely, and returned to the bedroom.

'Now! We can't waste time like this. You'd better begin with what is on the bed. And when you've cleared it you can put the kettle on.'

When Evans had gone downstairs with his load, she went to the landing and glared at the trunk. Her fists were clenched; she wished it was alive and that she could hit it. Glancing over the banisters to be sure she was alone, she opened it again, took out the photograph and the letter from her diary and put them in her handbag. She thought she was going to be sick or faint for the past was drumming, like a train coming nearer and nearer, in her head.

'My God!' she said. And when she saw her head in its turban and her face hardened by shock and grief in her absurd aunt's dressing-table mirror, she exclaimed with real horror. She was crying. 'What a mess,' she said and pulled the scarf off her head. Her fair, thick hair hung round her face untidily. Not once, in all those photographs, had a face so wolfish with bitterness and without laughter looked back at her.

'I'm taking the tea out,' Evans called from below.

'I'm just coming,' she called back and hurriedly tried to arrange her hair and then, because she had cried a little, she put on her glasses. Evans gave a keen look at the change in her when she got downstairs and walked through the hall to the door.

He had put the tray on the grass near a yew hedge in the hot corner at the side of the house and was standing a few yards away drinking his tea. In the last two days he had never drunk his tea near her but had chatted from a distance.

In her glasses and with her hair girlishly brushed back, Miss Freshwater's niece looked cold, tall and grand, like a headmistress.

'I hope we shan't get any more smoke here,' she said. 'Sit down. You look too restless.'

She was very firm, nodding to the exact place on the lawn on which she required him to sit. Taken aback, Evans sat precisely in that place. She sat on the grass and poured herself a cup of tea.

'How many souls came to Jesus last night?' she asked in her ladylike voice. Evans got up and squatted cheerfully, but watchfully, on his heels.

[420]

'Seventeen,' he said.

'That's not very good,' she said. 'Do you think you could save mine?'

'Oh, yes,' he said keenly.

'You look like a frog,' she said mocking. He had told her miners always squat in this way after work. 'It's too late,' she went on. 'Twenty years too late. Have you always been with the Mission?'

'No,' he said.

'What was it? Were you converted, did you see the light?' she mocked, like a teacher.

'I had a vision,' he said seriously.

'A vision!' she laughed. She waved her hand. 'What do you mean – you mean, you – well, where? Up in the sky or something?'

'No,' he said. 'It was down the mine.'

'What happened?'

He put down his cup and he moved it away to give himself more room. He squatted there, she thought, not like a frog at all, but like an imp or a devil, very grave and carven-faced. She noticed now how wide his mouth was and how widely it opened and how far the lips drew back when he spoke in his declamatory voice. He stared a long time waiting for her to stop fidgeting. Then he began:

'I was a drunkard,' he declaimed, relishing each syllable separately. 'I was a liar. I was a hypocrite. I went with women. And married women too!' His voice rose. 'I was a fornicator. I was an adulterer. Always at the races, too, gambling, it was senseless. There was no sin the Devil did not lead me into, I was like a fool. I was the most noteworthy sinner in the valley, everyone spoke of it. But I did not know the Lord was lying in wait for me.'

'Yes, but what happened?' she said.

He got to his feet and gazed down at her and she was compelled to look up at him.

'I will tell you,' he said. 'It was a miracle.' He changed his manner and after looking round the garden, he said in a hushing and secretive voice:

'There was a disaster in the mine,' he said. 'It was in June. I was twenty-three and I was down working and I was thinking of the sunlight and the hills and the evening. There was a young girl called Alys Davies, you know, two or three had been after her and I was thinking I would take her up the rock, that is a quiet place, only an old mountain ram would see you . . .'

'You were in the mine,' she said. 'You are getting too excited about this Alys Jones . . .'

'Davies,' he said with a quick grin. 'Don't worry about her. She is married now.' He went back to his solemn voice.

'And suddenly,' he said, 'there was a fall, a terrible fall of rock like thunder and all the men shouting. It was at eleven in the morning when we stopped work for our tea. There were three men in the working with me and they had just gone off. I was trapped alone.'

'Were you hurt?' she said anxiously.

'It was a miracle, not a stone touched me. I was in a little black cave. It was like a tomb. I was in that place alone for twelve hours. I could hear them working to get at me but after the first fall there was a second and then I thought I was finished. I could hear nothing.'

'What did you do? I would have gone out of my mind,' she said. 'Is that how you got the scar on your nose?'

'That was in a fight,' he said, offhand. 'Madness is a terrible thing. I stared into the blackness and I tried to think of one thing to stop my mind wandering but I could not at first for the fear, it was chasing and jumping like a mad dog in my head. I prayed and the more I prayed the more it chased and jumped. And then, suddenly, it stopped. I saw in my mind a picture. I saw the mantelpiece at home and on it a photograph of our family – my father and mother, my four sisters and my brother. And we had an aunt and uncle just married, it was a wedding photograph. I could see it clearly as if I had been in my home. They were standing there looking at me and I kept looking at them and thinking about them. I held on to them. I kept everything else out of my mind; wherever I looked that picture was before my eyes. It was like a vision. It saved me.'

'I have heard people say they hear voices,' said Miss Freshwater's niece, kindly now.

'Oh, no! They were speechless,' said Evans. 'Not a word! I spoke to them,' he said. 'Out loud. I promised God in front of all my family that I would cleanse my soul when I got out.'

[422]

Evans stood blazing in his trance and then he picked up his cup from the grass and took it to her.

'May I please have some more tea?' he said.

'Of course,' she said. 'Sit down.'

He considered where he should sit and then put himself beside her.

'When I saw you looking at your photographs,' he said, 'I thought, "She is down the mine."'

'I have never been down a mine in my life. I don't know why. We lived near one once when I was in the north,' she evaded.

'The mine of the past,' he said. 'The dark mine of the past.'

'I can see why you are a preacher, Robert,' she smiled. 'It's funny how one cannot get one's family out of one's head. I could feel mine inside me for years – but not now.'

She had entirely stopped mocking him.

'I can't say they ever saved me,' she said. 'I think they nearly ruined me. Look at that ugly house and all that rubbish. Did you ever see anything like their furniture? When I was a girl I used to think, Suppose I got to look like that sideboard! And then money was all they ever talked about – and good and nice people, and nice people always had money. It was like that in those days, thank God that has gone. Perhaps it hasn't. I decided to get away from it and I got married. They ought to have stopped me – all I wanted was to get away – but they thought my husband had money, too. He just had debts and a bad stomach. When he had spent all my money, he just got ill to punish me . . . You don't know anything about life when you're young and when you are old it's too late . . .

'That's a commonplace remark,' she went on, putting her cup on the tray and reaching for his. 'My mother used to make it.' She picked up her scarf and began to tie it on her head, but as she was tying it Evans quickly reached for it and pulled it off. His hand held the nape of her neck gently.

'You are not old,' he shouted, laughing and sparkling. 'Your hair is golden, not a grey one in it, boy.'

'Robert, give me that scarf. It is to keep out the dust,' she said, blushing. She reached for the scarf and he caught her wrist.

'When I saw you standing at the station on Monday, I said, Now, there

is a woman! Look at the way she stands, a golden woman, that is the first
I have seen in this town, she must be a stranger,' he said.

'You know all the others, I expect,' she said with amusement.

'Oh, indeed, yes I do! All of them!' he said. 'I would not look at them
twice.'

His other hand slipped from her neck to her waist.

'I can trust myself with them, but not with you,' he said, lowering his
voice and speaking down to her neck. 'In an empty house,' he whispered,
nodding to the house, letting go of her hand and stroking her knee.

'I am far past that sort of thing,' said Miss Freshwater's niece, choosing
a lugubrious tone. She removed his arm from her waist. And she stood
up, adroitly picking up the tray, and from behind that defence, looked
round the garden. Evans sprang up but instead of coming near her, he
jumped a few yards away and squatted on his heels, grinning at her
confidently.

'You look like the devil,' she said.

He had placed himself between her and the way to the house.

'It is quiet in the garden, too,' he said with a wink. And then she saw
the wheelbarrow which he had left near the fire.

'That barrow ought to go well in the sale,' she said. 'It is almost new.
How much do you think it will fetch?'

Evans stood up at once and his grin went. An evasive light, almost the
light of tears, came into his hot blue eyes and he stared at her with an
alarm that drove everything else out of his head.

'They'll put it with the tools, you will not get much for it.'

'I think every man in the town will be after it,' she said, with malice.

'What price did you want for it?' he said, uncertain of her.

'I don't know what they cost,' she said carelessly and walked past him
very slowly back to the house, maddening him by her walk. He followed
her quickly and when she turned, still carrying the tray, to face him in
the doorway, she caught his agitation.

'I will take the tray to the kitchen,' he said politely.

'No,' she said, 'I will do that. I want you to go upstairs and fetch down
all those shoes. And the trunk. It can all go.'

And she turned and walked through the house to the kitchen. He
hesitated for a long time; at last she heard him go upstairs and she pottered

in the kitchen where the china and pans were stacked on the table, waiting for him to come down. He was a very long time. He came down with the empty trunk.

'It can all go. Burn it all. It's no good to anyone, damp and rotten. I've put aside what I want,' she said.

He looked at her sullenly. He was startled by her manner and by the vehemence of her face, for she had put on the scarf and her face looked strong-boned, naked and ruthless. She was startled herself.

His sullenness went; he returned to his old excitement and hurried the barrow to the fire and she stood at the door impatiently waiting for the blaze. When he saw her waiting he came back.

'There it goes,' he said with admiration.

The reflection of the flame danced in points of light in her eyes, her mouth was set, hard and bitter. Presently the flame dropped and greenish smoke came out thickly.

'Ah!' she gasped. Her body relaxed and she smiled at Evans, tempting him again.

'I've been thinking about the barrow,' she said. 'When we've finished up here, I'll make you a present of it. I would like to give it to you, if you have a use for it?'

She could see the struggle going on inside him as he boldly looked at her; and she saw his boldness pass into a small shrug of independent pride and the pride into pretence and dissembling.

'I don't know,' he said, 'that I have a use – well, I'll take it off you. I'll put the shoes in it, it will save bringing the car.' He could not repress his eagerness any longer. I'll put the shoes into it this evening. Thank you.' He paused. 'Thank you, ma'am,' he said.

It was the first time he had called her ma'am. The word was like a blow. The affair was over. It was, she realised, a dismissal.

An hour later she heard him rumbling the barrow down the path to the gate. The next day he did not come. He had finished with her. He sent his son up for his money.

It took Miss Freshwater's niece two more days to finish her work at the house. The heavy jobs had been done, except for putting the drawers back into the chests. She could have done with Evans's help there, and for the sweeping which made her hot but she was glad to be alone because she got on more quickly with the work. She hummed and even sang as she worked, feeling light and astonishingly happy. Once or twice, when she saw the white sheet of the Mission tent distantly through the trees, she laughed:

'He got what he wanted! And I'm evidently not as old as I look.'

The last hours buzzed by and she spun out the time, reluctant to go. She dawdled, locking the sheds, the windows and doors, until there was nothing more to keep her. She brought down a light suitcase in which she had put the few things she wanted to take away and she sat in the dining-room, now as bare as an office, to go through her money. After the destruction she was having a fit of economy and it had occurred to her that instead of taking a taxi to the station, she could walk down to the bus stop on the Green. She knew that the happiness she felt was not ebbing, but had changed to a feeling she had not had for many years: the feeling of expectancy, and as this settled in her she put her money and papers back into her bag. There was a last grain of rubbish here: with scarcely a glance at them, she tore up the photograph and the unfinished letter she had found in the trunk.

'I owe Evans a lot,' she thought.

Nothing retained her now.

She picked up her case. She left the house and walked down the road in the strong shade of the firs and the broad shade of the oak trees, whose leaves hardened with populous contentment in the long evening light. When she got to the open Green children were playing round the Gospel Tent and, in twos and threes, people were walking from the houses across the grass towards it. She had twenty minutes to wait until her bus arrived. She heard the sound of singing coming from the tent. She wondered if Evans would be there.

'I might give him the pleasure of seeing what he missed,' she thought.

She strolled across to the tent.

A youth who had watered his hair and given it a twirl with a comb was standing in his best clothes at the entrance to the tent.

'Come to Jesu! Come to Jesu!' he said to her as she peeped inside.

'I'm just looking for someone,' she said politely.

The singing had stopped when she looked in but the worshippers were still standing. They were packed in the white light of the tent and the hot smell of grass and somewhere at the far end, invisible, a man was shouting like a cheapjack selling something at an auction. He stopped suddenly and a high, powerful country voice whined out alone: 'Ow in the vale . . .' and the congregation joined in for another long verse.

'Is Mr Evans here tonight?' she asked the youth.

'Yes,' he said. 'He's witnessing every night.'

'Where is he? I don't see him.'

The verse came to an end and once more a voice began talking at the other end of the tent. It was a woman's voice, high and incomprehensible and sharp. The hymn began again and then spluttered into an explosive roar that swept across the Green.

'They've fixed it. The loudspeaker!' the youth exclaimed. Miss Freshwater's niece stepped back. The noises thumped. Sadly, she looked at her watch and began to walk back to the bus stop. When she was about ten yards from the tent, the loudspeaker gave a loud whistle and then, as if God had cleared his throat, spoke out with a gross and miraculous clearness.

'Friends,' it said, sweeping right across the Green until it struck the furthest houses and the trees. 'My friends . . .'

The word seemed to grind her and everyone else to nothing, to mill them all into the common dust.

'When I came to this place,' it bellowed, 'the serpent . . .' (An explosion of noise followed but the voice cleared again) '. . . heart. No bigger than a speck it was at first, as tiny as a speck of coal grit in your eye . . .'

Miss Freshwater's niece stopped. Was it Evans's voice? A motor coach went by on the road and drowned the next words, and then she heard, spreading into an absurd public roar:

'I was a liar. I was an adulterer. Oh my friends, I was a slave of the strange woman the Bible tells about, the whore of Babylon, in her palace where moth and dust . . .' Detonations again.

But it was Evans's voice. She waited and the enormously magnified voice burst through:

'And then by the great mercy of the Lord I heard a voice cry out, "Robert Evans, what are you doing, boy? Come out of it" . . .' But the voice exploded into meaningless concussions, suddenly resuming:

'. . . and burned the adulteress in the everlasting fire, my friends – and all her property.'

The hymn started up again.

'Well, not quite all, Robert,' said Miss Freshwater's niece pleasantly aloud, and a child eating an ice-cream near her watched her walk across the grass to the bus stop.

The Fall

It was the evening of the Annual Dinner. More than two hundred accountants were at that hour changing into evening clothes, in the flats, villas and hotel rooms of a large, wet, Midland city. At the Royal was Charles Peacock, slender in his shirt, balancing on one leg and gazing with frowns of affection in the wardrobe mirror at the other leg as he pulled his trousers on; and then with a smile of farewell as the second went in. Buttoned up, relieved of nakedness, he visited other mirrors – the one at the dressing table, the two in the bathroom, assembling the scattered aspects of the unsettled being called Peacock 'doing' – as he was apt to say – 'no so badly' in this city which smelled of coal and where thirty-eight years ago he had been born. When he left his room there were mirrors in the hotel lift and down below in the foyer and outside in the street. Certain shop windows were favourable and assuring. The love affair was taken up again at the Assembly Rooms by the mirrors in the tiled corridor leading towards the bullocky noise of two hundred-odd chartered accountants in black ties, taking their drinks under the chandeliers that seemed to weep above their heads.

Crowds or occasions frightened Peacock. They engaged him, at first sight, in the fundamental battle of his life: the struggle against nakedness, the panic of grabbing for clothes and becoming someone. An acquaintance in a Scottish firm was standing near the door of the packed room as Peacock went in.

'Hullo, laddie,' Peacock said, fitting himself out with a Scottish accent, as he went into the crowded, chocolate-coloured buffet.

'What's to do?' he said, passing on to a Yorkshireman.

'Are you well now?' he said, in his Irish voice. And, gaining confidence, 'Whatcha cock!' to a man up from London, until he was shaking hands in the crowd with the President himself, who was leaning on a stick and had his foot in plaster.

'I hope this is not serious, sir,' said Peacock in his best southern English, nodding at the foot.

'Bloody serious,' said the President sticking out his peppery beard. 'I caught my foot in a grating. Some damn fools here think I've got gout.'

No one who saw Peacock in his office, in Board Rooms, on committees, at meetings, knew the exhausting number of rough sketches that had to be made before the naked Peacock could become Peacock dressed for his part. Now, having spoken to several human beings, the fragments called Peacock closed up. And he had one more trick up his sleeve if he panicked again: he could drop into music hall Negro.

Peacock got a drink at the buffet table and pushed his way to a solitary island of carpet two feet square, in the guffawing corral. He was looking at the back of the President's neck. Almost at once the President, on the crest of a successful joke he had told, turned round with appetite.

'Hah!' he shouted. 'Hah! Here's friend Peacock again.'

Why "again"? thought Peacock.

The President looked Peacock over.

'I saw your brother this afternoon,' shouted the President. The President's injured foot could be said to have made his voice sound like a hilarious smash. Peacock's drink jumped and splashed his hand. The President winked at his friends.

'Hah!' said the President. 'That gave our friend Peacock a scare!'

'At the Odeon,' explained a kinder man.

'Is Shelmerdine Peacock your brother? The actor?' another said, astonished, looking at Peacock from head to foot.

'Shelmerdine Peacock was born and bred in this city,' said the President fervently.

'I saw him in *Waste*,' someone said. And others recalled him in *The Gun Runner* and *Doctor Zut*.

Four or five men stood gazing at Peacock with admiration, waiting for him to speak.

'Where is he now?' said the President, stepping forward, beard first. 'In Hollywood? Have you seen him lately?'

They all moved forward to hear about the famous man.

Peacock looked to the right – he wanted to do this properly – but there was no mirror in that direction; he looked to the left, but there was no mirror there. He lowered his head gravely and then looked up shaking his head sorrowfully. He brought out the old reliable Negro voice:

'The last time I saw l'il ole brudder Shel,' he said, 'he was being thrown out of the Orchid Room. He was calling the waiters goatherds.'

Peacock looked up at them all and stood, collected, assembled, whole at last, among their shouts of laughter. One man who did not laugh, and who asked what the Orchid Room was, was put in his place. And in a moment, a voice bawled from the door, 'Gentlemen. Dinner is served.' The crowd moved through two ante-rooms into the Great Hall where, from their portraits on the wall, Mayors, Presidents and Justices looked down with the complacent rosiness of those who have dined and died. It was gratifying to Peacock that the President rested his arm on his shoulder for a few steps as they went into the hall.

Shel often cropped up in Peacock's life, especially in clubs and at dinners. It was pleasing. There was always praise; there were always questions. He had seen the posters about Shel's film during the week on his way to his office. They pleased, but they also troubled. Peacock stood at his place at table in the Great Hall and paused to look around, in case there was one more glance of vicarious fame to be collected. He was enjoying one of those pauses of self-possession in which, for a few seconds, he could feel the sensations Shel must feel when he stepped before the curtain to receive the applause of some great audience in London or New York. Then Peacock sat down. More than two hundred soup spoons scraped.

'Sherry, sir?' said the waiter.

Peacock sipped.

He meant no harm to Shel, of course. But in a city like this, with Shel appearing in a big picture, with his name fifteen feet long on the hoardings, talked about by girls in offices, the universal instinct of family disparagement was naturally tickled into life. The President might laugh and the crowd admire, but it was not always agreeable for the family to have Shel roaming loose – and often very loose – in the world. One had to assert the modesty, the anonymity of the ordinary assiduous Peacocks. One way of doing this was to add a touch or two to famous scandals: to enlarge the drunken scrimmages and add to the divorces and the breaches of contract, increase the overdoses taken by flighty girls. One was entitled to a little rake off – an accountant's charges – from the fame that so often annoyed. One was entitled, above all, because one loved Shel.

'Hock, sir?' said the waiter.

Peacock drank. Yes, he loved Shel. Peacock put down his glass and the man opposite to him spoke across the table, a man with an amused mouth, who turned his sallow face sideways so that one had the impression of being inquired into under a loose lock of black hair by one sharp, serious eye only.

'An actor's life is a struggle,' the man said. Peacock recognised him: it was the man who had not laughed at his story and who had asked what the Orchid Room was, in a voice that had a sad and puncturing feeling for information sought for its own sake.

Peacock knew this kind of admirer of Shel's and feared him. They were not content to admire, they wanted to advance into intimacy, and collect facts on behalf of some general view of life's mysteriousness. As an accountant Peacock rejected mystery.

'I don't think l'il ole brudder Shel has struggled much,' said Peacock, wagging his head from side to side carelessly.

'I mean he has to dedicate himself,' said the man.

Peacock looked back mistrustfully.

'I remember some interview he gave about his schooldays – in this city,' said the man. 'It interested me. I do the books for the Hippo-drome.'

Peacock stopped wagging his head from side to side. He was alert. What Shel had said about his early life had been damned tactless.

'Shel had a good time,' said Peacock sharply. 'He always got his own way.'

Peacock put on his face of stone. He dared the man to say out loud, in that company, three simple English words. He dared him. The man smiled and did not say them.

'Volnay, sir?' said the waiter as the pheasant was brought. Peacock drank.

Fried Fish Shop, Peacock said to himself as he drank. Those were the words. Shel could have kept his mouth shut about that. I'm not a snob, but why mention it? Why, after they were all doing well, bring ridicule upon the family? Why not say, simply, 'Shop'. Why not say, if he had to, 'Fishmonger'? Why mention 'Frying'? Why add '*Bankrupt* Fried Fish Shop'?

It was swinish, disloyal, ungrateful. Bankrupt – all right; but some of that money (Peacock said, hectoring the pheasant on his plate) paid for Shel's years at the Dramatic School. It was unforgiveable.

Peacock looked across at the man opposite, but the man had turned to talk to a neighbour. Peacock finished his glass and chatted with the man sitting to his right, but he felt like telling the whole table a few facts about dedication.

Dedication – he would have said. Let us take a look at the figures. An example of Shel's dedication in those Fried Fish Shop days he is so fond of remembering to make fools of us. Saturday afternoon. Father asleep in the back room. Shel says, 'Come down the High Street with me, Tom. I want to get a record.' Classical, of course. Usual swindle. If we get into the shop he won't have the money and will try and borrow from me. 'No,' I say. 'I haven't got any money.' 'Well, let's get out of this stink of lard and fish.' He wears me down. He wore us all down, the whole family. He would be sixteen, two years older than me. And so we go out and at once I know there is going to be trouble. 'I saw the Devil in Cramers,' he says. We go down the High Street to Cramers, it's a music shop, and he goes up to the girl to ask if they sell bicycle pumps or rubber heels. When the girl says 'No', he makes a terrible face at her and shouts out 'Bah'. At Hooks, the stationers, he stands at the door, and calls to the girl at the cash desk: 'You've got the Devil in here. I've reported it,' and slams the door. We go on to Bonds, the grocers, and he pretends to be sick when he sees the bacon. Goes out. 'Rehearsing,' he says. The Bonds are friends of Father's. There is a row. Shel swears he was never anywhere near the place and goes back the following Saturday and falls flat on the floor in front of the Bond daughter groaning, 'I've been poisoned. I'm dying. Water! Water!' Falls flat on his back ...

'Caught his foot in a grating, he told me, and fell,' the man opposite was saying. 'Isn't that what he told you, Peacock?'

Peacock's imaginary speech came suddenly to an end. The man was smiling as if he had heard every word.

'Who?' said Peacock.

'The President,' said the man. 'My friend, Mr McAlister is asking me what happened to the President. Did he fall in the street?'

Peacock collected himself quickly and to hide his nakedness became Scottish.

'Ay, mon,' he nodded across the table. 'A wee bit of a tumble in the street.'

Peacock took up his glass and drank.

'He's a heavy man to fall,' said the man called McAlister.

'He carries a lot of weight,' said his neighbour. Peacock eyed him. The impression was growing that this man knew too much, too quietly. It struck him that the man was one of those who ask what they know already, a deeply unbelieving man. They have to be crushed.

'Weight makes no difference,' said Peacock firmly.

'It's weight and distance,' said the Scotsman. 'Look at children.'

Peacock felt a smile coming over his body from the feet upwards.

'Weight and distance make no difference,' Peacock repeated.

'How can you say that?'

An enormous voice, hanging brutally on the air like a sergeant's, suddenly shouted in the hall. It was odd to see the men in the portraits on the wall still sitting down after the voice sounded. It was the voice of the toastmaster.

'Gen – tle – men,' it shouted. 'I ask you. To rise to. The Toast of Her. Maj – es – ty. The Queen.'

Two hundred or more accountants pushed back their chairs and stood up.

'The Queen,' they growled. And one or two, Peacock among them, fervently added, 'God bless her,' and drained his glass.

Two hundred or more accountants sat down. It was the moment Peacock loved. And he loved the Queen.

'Port or brandy, sir?' the waiter asked.

'Brandy,' said Peacock.

'You were saying that weight and distance make no difference. How do you make that out?' the sidelong man opposite said in a sympathetic and curious voice that came softly and lazily out.

Peacock felt the brandy burn. The question floated by, answerable if seized as it went and yet, suddenly, unanswerable for the moment. Peacock stared at the question keenly as if it were a fly that he was waiting to swat when it came round again. Ah, there it came. Now! But no, it had gone by once more. It was answerable. He knew the answer. Peacock smiled loosely biding his time. He felt the flame of authority, of absolute knowledge burn in him.

There was a hammering at the President's table, there was hand-clapping. The President was on his feet and his beard had begun to move up and down.

'I'll tell you later,' said Peacock curtly across the table. The interest went out of the man's eye.

'Once more,' the President's beard was saying and it seemed sometimes that he had two beards. 'Honour,' said one beard. 'Privilege,' said the other. 'Old friends,' said both beards together. 'Speeches ... brief ... reminded of story ... shortest marriage service in the world ... Tennessee ...'

'Hah! Hah! Hah!' shouted a pack of wolves, hyenas, hounds in dinner jackets.

Peacock looked across at the unbeliever who sat opposite. The interest in weight and distance had died away in his face.

'Englishman ... Irishman ... Scotsman ... train ... Englishman said ... Scotsman said ... Och, says Paddy ...'

'Hah! Hah! Hah!' from the pack.

Over the carnations in the silver-plated vases on the table, over the heads of the diners, the cigar smoke was rising sweetly and the first level indigo shafts of it were tipping across the middle air and turning the portraits of the Past Masters into day dreams. Peacock gazed at it. Then a bell rang in his ear, so loudly that he looked shyly to see if anyone else had heard it. The voice of Shel was on some line of his memory, a voice richer, more insinuating than the toastmaster's or the President's, a voice utterly flooring.

'Abel?' Shel was saying. 'Is that you Abel? This is Cain speaking. How's the smoke? Is it still going up straight to heaven? Not blowing about all over the place ...'

The man opposite caught Peacock's eye for a second, as if he too had heard the voice and then turned his head away. And, just at the very moment, when once more Peacock could have answered that question about the effect of weight and distance, the man opposite stood up, all the accountants stood up. Peacock was the last. There was another toast to drink. And immediately there was more hammering and another speaker. Peacock's opportunity was lost. The man who sat opposite had moved his chair back from the table and was sitting sideways to the table, listening, his interest in Peacock gone for good.

Peacock became lonely. Sulkily he played with matchsticks and arranged them in patterns on the tablecloth. There was a point at Annual Dinners when he always did this. It was at that point when one saw the function had become fixed by a flash photograph in the gloss of celebration and when everyone looked sickly and old. Eyes became hollow, temples sank, teeth loosened. Shortly the diners would be carried out in coffins. One waited restlessly for the thing to be over. Ten years of life went by and then, it seemed, there were no more speeches. There was some business talk in groups; then twos and threes left the table. Others filed off into a large chamber next door. Peacock's neighbours got up. He, who feared occasions, feared even more their dissolution. It was like that frightening ten minutes in a theatre when the audience slowly moves out, leaving a hollow stage and row after row, always increasing, of empty seats behind them. In a panic Peacock got up. He was losing all acquaintance. He had even let the man opposite slip away, for that man was walking down the hall with some friends. Peacock hurried down his side of the long table to meet them at the bottom and when he got there he turned and barred their way.

'What we were talking about,' he said. 'It's an art. Simply a matter of letting the breath go, relaxing the muscles. Any actor can do it. It's the first thing they learn.'

'I'm out of my depth,' said the Scotsman.

'Falling,' said Peacock. 'The stage fall.' He looked at them with dignity, then he let the expression die on his face. He fell quietly full length to the floor. Before they could speak he was up on his feet.

'My brother weighs two hundred and twenty pounds,' he said with condescension to the man opposite. 'The ordinary person falls and breaks an arm or a foot, because he doesn't know. It's an art.'

His eyes conveyed that if the Peacocks had kept a fried fish shop years ago, they had an art.

'Simple,' said Peacock.

And down he went, thump, on the carpet again and lying at their feet he said:

'Painless. Nothing broken. Not a bruise. I said "an art". Really one might call it a science. Do you see how I'm lying?'

'What's happened to Peacock?' said two or three men joining the group.

'He's showing us the stage fall.'

'Nothing,' said Peacock, getting up and brushing his coat sleeve and smoothing back his hair. 'It is just a stage trick.'

'I wouldn't do it,' said a large man, patting his stomach.

'I've just been telling them – weight is nothing. Look.' Peacock fell down and got up at once.

'You turn. You crumple. You can go flat on your back. I mean, that is what it looks like,' he said.

And Peacock fell.

'Shel and I used to practise it in the bedroom. Father thought the ceiling was coming down,' he said.

'Good God, has Peacock passed out?' A group standing by the fireplace in the hall called across. Peacock got up and brushing his jacket again walked up to them. The group he had left watched him. There was a thump.

'He's done it again,' the man opposite said. 'Once more. There he goes. Look, he's going to show the President. He's going after him. No, he's missed him. The old boy has slipped out of the door.'

Peacock was staring with annoyance at the door. He looked at other groups of two and threes.

'Who was the casualty over there?' someone said to him as he walked past.

Peacock went over to them and explained.

'Like judo,' said a man.

'No!' said Peacock indignantly, even grandly. And in Shel's manner. Anyone who had seen Shelmerdine Peacock affronted knew what he looked like. That large white face trod on you. 'Nothing to do with judo. This is the theatre . . .'

'Shelmerdine Peacock's brother,' a man whispered to a friend.

'Is that so?'

'It's in the blood,' someone said.

To the man who had said 'judo', Peacock said, 'No throwing, no wrestling, no somersaulting or fancy tricks. That is not theatre. Just . . . simply . . .' said Peacock. And crumpling, as Shel might have done in *Macbeth* or *Hamlet*, or like some gangster shot in the stomach, Peacock once more let his body go down with the cynicism of the skilful corpse. This time he did not get up at once. He looked up at their knees, their waists, at their goggling faces, saw under their double chins and under their hairy eyebrows. He grinned at their absurdity. He saw that he held them. They were obliged to look at him. Shel must always have had this sensation of hundreds of astonished eyes watching him lie, waiting for him to move. Their gaze would never leave the body. He never felt less at a loss, never felt more completely himself. Even the air was better at carpet level; it was certainly cooler and he was glad of that. Then he saw two pairs of feet advancing from another group. He saw two faces peep over the shoulders of the others, and heard one of them say:

'It's Peacock – still at it.'

He saw the two pairs of boots and trousers go off. Peacock got to his feet at once and resentfully stared after them. He knew something, as they went, that Shel must have known: the desperation, the contempt for the audience that is thinning out. He was still brushing his sleeve and trouser legs when he saw everyone moving away out of the hall. Peacock moved after them into the chamber.

A voice spoke behind him. It was the quiet, intimate voice of the man with the loose lock of black hair who had sat opposite to him.

'You need a drink,' the man said.

They were standing in the chamber where the buffet table was. The man had gone into the chamber and, clearly, he had waited for Peacock. A question was going round as fast as a catherine wheel in Peacock's head and there was no need to ask it: it must be so blindingly obvious. He looked for someone to put it to, on the quiet, but there were only three men at the buffet table with their backs turned to him. Why (the question ran) at the end of a bloody good dinner is one always left with some awful drunk, a man you've never liked – an unbeliever?

Peacock mopped his face. The unbeliever was having a short disgusting laugh with the men at the bar and now was coming back with a glass of whisky.

'Sit down. You must be tired,' said the unbeliever.

They sat down. The man spoke of the dinner and the speeches. Peacock did not listen. He had just noticed a door leading into a small ante-room and he was wondering how he could get into it.

'There was one thing I don't quite get,' the man said. 'Perhaps it was the quickness of the hand deceiving the eye. I should say feet. What I mean is – do you first take a step, I mean like in dancing: I mean is the art of falling really a paradox – I mean the art of keeping your balance all the time?'

The word 'paradox' sounded offensive to Peacock.

The man looked too damn clever, in Peacock's opinion, and didn't sit still. Wearily Peacock got up.

'Hold my drink,' he said. 'You are standing like this, or facing sideways – on a level floor, of course. On a slope like this . . .'

The man nodded.

'I mean – well, now, watch carefully. Are you watching?'

'Yes,' said the man.

'Look at my feet,' said Peacock.

'No,' said the man, hastily, putting out a free hand and catching Peacock by the arm. 'I see what you mean. I was just interested in the theory.'

Peacock halted. He was offended. He shook the man's arm off.

'Nothing theoretical about it,' he said, and shaking his sleeves added: 'No paradox.'

'No,' said the man standing up and grabbing Peacock so that he could not fall. 'I've got the idea.' He looked at his watch. 'Which way are you going? Can I give you a lift?'

Peacock was greatly offended. To be turned down! He nodded to the door of the ante-room: 'Thanks,' he said. 'The President's waiting for me.'

'The President's gone,' said the man. 'Oh well, good night.' And he went away. Peacock watched him go. Even the men at the bar had gone. He was alone.

'But thanks,' he called after him. 'Thanks.'

Cautiously Peacock sketched a course into the ante-room. It was a

small, high room, quite empty and yet (one would have said), packed
with voices, chattering, laughing and mixed with music along the panelled
walls, but chiefly coming from behind the heavy green velvet curtains
that were drawn across the window at one end. There were no mirrors,
but Peacock had no need of them. The effect was ornate – gilded pillars
at the corners, a small chandelier rising and falling gracefully from a
carven ceiling. On the wall hung what, at first sight, seemed to be two
large oil paintings of Queens of England but, on going closer, Peacock
saw there was only one oil painting – of Queen Victoria. Peacock
considered it. The opportunity was enormous. Loyally, his face went
blank. He swayed, loyally fell, and loyally got to his feet. The Queen
might or might not have clapped her little hands. So encouraged, he fell
again and got up. She was still sitting there.

Shel, said Peacock, aloud to the Queen, has often acted before royalty.
He's in Hollywood now, having left me to settle all his tax affairs.
Hundreds of documents. All lies, of course. And there is this case for
alimony going on. He's had four wives, he said to Queen Victoria. That's
the side of theatre life I couldn't stand, even when we were boys. I could
see it coming. But – watch me, he said.

And delightfully he crumpled, the perfect backwards spin. Leaning up
on his elbow from where he was lying he waited for her to speak.

She did not speak, but two or three other queens joined her, all
crowding and gossiping together, as Peacock got up. The Royal Box! It
was full. Cars hooting outside the window behind the velvet curtains had
the effect of an orchestra and then, inevitably, those heavy green curtains
were drawn up. A dark, packed and restless auditorium opened itself to
him. There was dense applause.

Peacock stepped forward in awe and wholeness. Not to fall, not to fall,
this time, he murmured. To bow. One must bow and bow and bow and
not fall, to the applause. He set out. It was a strangely long up-hill journey
towards the footlights and not until he got there did it occur to him that
he did not know how to bow. Shel had never taught him. Indeed, at the
first attempt the floor came up and hit him in the face.

When My Girl Comes Home

She was kissing them all, hugging them, her arms bare in her summer dress, laughing and taking in a big draught of breath after every kiss, nearly knocking old Mrs Draper off her feet, almost wrestling with Mrs Fulmino, who was large and tall. Then Hilda broke off to give another foreign-sounding laugh and plunged at Jack Draper ('the baby') and his wife, at Mr Fulmino, who cried out 'What again?' and at Constance, who did not like emotion; and after every kiss, Hilda drew back, getting her breath and making this sound like 'Hah!'

'Who is this?' she said, looking at me.

'Harry Fraser,' Mr Fulmino said. 'You remember Harry?'

'You worked at the grocer's,' she said. 'I remember you.'

'No,' I said, 'that was my brother.'

'This is the little one,' said Mrs Fulmino.

'Who won the scholarship,' said Constance.

'We couldn't have done anything without him,' said Mr Fulmino, expanding with extravagance as he always did about everything. 'He wrote to the War Office, the Red Cross, the Prisoners of War, the American Government, all the letters. He's going to be our Head Librarian.'

Mr Fulmino loved whatever had not happened yet. His forecasts were always wrong. I left the library years ago and never fulfilled the future he had planned for me. Obviously Hilda did not remember me. Thirteen years before, when she married Mr Singh and left home, I was no more than a boy.

'Well, I'll kiss him too,' she said. 'And another for your brother.'

That was the first thing to happen, the first of many signs of how her life had had no contact with ourselves.

'He was killed in the war, dear,' said Mrs Fulmino.

'She couldn't know,' said Constance.

[441]

'I'm sorry,' said Hilda.

We all stood silent, and Hilda turned to hold on to her mother, little Mrs Johnson, whose face was coquettish with tears and who came only up to Hilda's shoulder. The old lady was bewildered. She was trembling as though she were going to shake to pieces like a tree in the autumn. Hilda stood still, touching her tinted brown hair which was done in a tight high style and still unloosened, despite all the hugs and kissings. Her arms looked as dry as sand, her breasts were full in her green, flowered dress and she was gazing over our heads now from large yellow eyes which had almost closed into two blind, blissful curving lines. Her eyebrows seemed to be lacquered. How Oriental she looked on that first day! She was looking above our heads at old Mrs Draper's shabby room and going over the odd things she remembered, and while she stood like that, the women were studying her clothes. A boy's memory is all wrong. Naturally, when I was a boy I had thought of her as tall. She was really short. But I did remember her bold nose – it was like her mother's and old Mrs Draper's; those two were sisters. Otherwise I wouldn't have known her. And that is what Mr Fulmino said when we were all silent and incredulous again. We had Hilda back. Not just 'back' either, but 'back from the dead', reborn.

'She was in the last coach of the train, wasn't she, Mother?' Mr Fulmino said to Mrs Johnson. He called her 'mother' for the occasion, celebrating her joy.

'Yes,' said Mrs Johnson. 'Yes.' Her voice scraped and trembled.

'In the last coach, next the van. We went right up the platform, we thought we'd missed her, didn't we? She was,' he exclaimed with acquisitive pride, 'in the First Class.'

'Like you missed me coming from Penzance,' said Mrs Fulmino swelling powerfully and going that thundery violet colour which old wrongs gave her.

'Posh!' said Hilda. And we all smiled in a sickly way.

'Don't you ever do it again, my girl! Don't you ever do it again,' said her mother, old Mrs Johnson, clinging to her daughter's arm and shaking it as if it were a bellrope.

'I was keeping an eye on my luggage,' Hilda laughed.

Ah! That was a point! There was not only Hilda, there was her luggage.

Some of it was in the room, but the bigger things were outside on the landing, piled up, looking very new, with the fantastic labels of hotels in Tokyo, San Francisco, and New York on it, and a beautiful jewel box in white leather on top like a crown. Old Mrs Draper did not like the luggage being outside the room in case it was in the way of the people upstairs. Constance went out and fetched the jewel box in. We had all seen it. We were as astonished by all these cases as we were by Hilda herself. After thirteen years, six of them war, we recognised that the poor ruined woman we had prepared for had not arrived. She shone with money. Later on, one after the other of us, except old Mrs Draper who could not walk far, went out and looked at the luggage and came back to study Hilda in a new way.

We had all had a shock. She had been nearly two years coming home from Tokyo. Before that there was the occupation, before that the war itself. Before that there were the years in Bombay and Singapore, when she was married to an Indian they always called Mr Singh. All those years were lost to us. None of us had been to India. What happened there to Mr Singh? We knew he had died – but how? Even if we had known, we couldn't have imagined it. None of us had been to Singapore, none of us to Japan. People from streets like Hincham Street do go to such places – it is not past belief. Knock on the doors of half the houses in London and you will find people with relations all over the world – but none of us had. Mention these places to us, we look at our grey skies and see boiling sun. Our one certainty about Hilda was what, in fact, the newspaper said the next day, with her photograph and the headline: *A Mother's Faith. Four Years in Japanese Torture Camp. London Girl's Ordeal.* Hilda was a terrible item of news, a gash in our lives, and we looked for the signs of it on her body, in the way she stood, in the lines on her face, as if we were expecting a scream from her mouth like the screams we were told Bill Williams gave out at night in his sleep, after he had been flown back home when the war ended. We had had to wait and wait for Hilda. At one time – there was a postcard from Hawaii – she was pinned like a butterfly in the middle of the Pacific Ocean; soon after there was a letter from Tokyo saying she couldn't get a passage. Confusing. She was travelling backwards. Letters from Tokyo were still coming after her letters from San Francisco.

We were still standing, waiting for Constance to bring in the teapot, for the tea was already laid. The trolley buses go down Hincham Street. It is a mere one hundred and fifty yards of a few little houses and a few little shops, which has a sudden charmed importance because the main road has petered out at our end by the Lord Nelson and an enormous public lavatory, and the trolley buses have to run down Hincham Street before picking up the main road again, after a sharp turn at the convent. Hincham Street is less a street than an interval, a disheartened connection. While we stood in one of those silences that follow excitement, a trolley bus came by and Hilda exclaimed:

'You've still got the old trams. Bump! Bump! Bump!' Hilda was ecstatic about the sound. 'Do you remember I used to be frightened the spark from the pole would set the lace curtains on fire when I was little?'

For, as the buses turned, the trolley arms would come swooping with two or three loud bumps and a spit of blue electricity, almost hitting Mrs Draper's sitting-room window which was on the first floor.

'It's trolleys now, my girl,' said old Mrs Draper, whose voice was like the voice of time itself chewing away at life. 'The trams went years ago, before the war.'

Old Mrs Draper had sat down in her chair again by the fire which always burned winter and summer in this room; she could not stand for long. It was the first remark that had given us any sense of what was bewildering all of us, the passing of time, the growing of a soft girl into a grown, hard-hipped woman. For old Mrs Draper's mind was detached from events around her and moved only among the signal facts and conclusions of history.

Presently we were, as the saying is, 'at our teas'. Mr Fulmino, less puzzled than the rest of us, expanded in his chair with the contentment of one who had personally operated a deeply British miracle. It was he who had got Hilda home.

'We've got all the correspondence, haven't we, Harry?' he said. 'We kept it – the War Office, Red Cross, Prisoner of War Commission, everything, Hilda. I'll show it to you.'

His task had transformed him and his language. Identification, registration, accommodation, communication, rehabilitation, hospitalisation, administration, investigation, transportation – well we had all dreamed of Hilda in our different ways.

'They always said the same thing,' Mrs Fulmino said reproachfully. 'No one of the name of Mrs Singh on the lists.'

'I wrote to Bombay,' said Mr Fulmino.

'He wrote to Singapore,' said Mrs Fulmino.

Mr Fulmino drank some tea, wiped his lips and became geography.

'All British subjects were rounded up, they said,' Mrs Fulmino said.

We nodded. We had made our stand, of course, on the law. Mrs Fulmino was authority.

'But Hilda was married to an Indian,' said Constance.

We glanced with a tolerance we did not usually feel for Constance. She was always trying to drag politics in.

'She's a British subject by birth,' said Mrs Fulmino firmly.

'Mum,' Hilda whispered, squeezing her mother's arm hard, and then looked up to listen, as if she were listening to talk about a faraway stranger.

'I was in Tokyo when the war started,' she said. 'Not Singapore.'

'Oh Tokyo!' exclaimed Mr Fulmino, feeling in his waistcoat for a pencil to make a note of it and, suddenly, realising that his note-taking days were over.

'Whatever the girl has done she has been punished for it,' came old Mrs Draper's mournful voice from the chair by the fire, but in the clatter no one heard her, except old Mrs Johnson, who squeezed her daughter's arm and said:

'My girl is a jewel.'

Still, Hilda's words surprised us. We had worked it out that after she and Mr Singh were married and went to Bombay he had heard of a better job in the state railway medical service and had gone to Singapore where the war had caught her. Mrs Fulmino looked affronted. If Mr Fulmino expanded into geography and the language of state – he worked for the Borough Council – Mrs Fulmino liked a fact to be a fact.

'We got the postcards,' said Mrs Fulmino sticking to chronology.

'Hawaii,' Mr Fulmino said. 'How'd you get there? Swim, I suppose.' He added, 'A sweet spot, it looks, suit us for a holiday – palms.'

'Coconuts,' said young Jack Draper, who worked in a pipe factory, speaking for the first time.

'Be quiet,' said his wife.

'It's an American base now,' said Constance with her politically sugared smile.

We hesitated but let her observation pass. It was simple to ignore her. We were happy.

'I suppose they paid your fare,' said Jack Draper's wife, a north-country woman.

'Accommodation, transportation,' said Mr Fulmino. 'Food, clothing. Everything. Financed by the international commission.'

This remark made old Mrs Johnson cry a little. In those years none of us had deeply believed that Hilda was alive. The silence was too long; too much time had gone by. Others had come home by the thousand with stories of thousands who had died. Only old Mrs Johnson had been convinced that Hilda was safe. The landlord at the Lord Nelson, the butcher, anyone who met old Mrs Johnson as she walked by like a poor, decent ghost with her sewing bundles, in those last two years, all said in war-staled voices:

'It's a mother's faith, that's what it is. A mother's faith's a funny thing.'

She would walk along, with a cough like someone driving tacks. Her chest had sunk and under her brown coat her shoulder blades seemed to have sharpened into a single hump. Her faith gave her a bright, yet also a sly, dishonest look.

'I'm taking this sewing up to Mrs Tracy's. She wants it in a hurry,' she might say.

'You ought to rest, Mrs Johnson, like the doctor said.'

'I want a bit of money for when my girl comes home,' she said. 'She'll want feeding up.'

And she would look around perhaps, for a clock, in case she ought, by this time, to have put a pot on the stove.

She had been too ill, in hospital, during the war, to speak about what might have happened to Hilda. Her own pain and fear of dying deafened her to what could be guessed. Mrs Johnson's faith had been born out of pain, out of the inability – within her prison of aching bones and crushed breathing – to identify herself with her daughter. Her faith grew out of her very self-centredness. And when she came out from the post office every week, where she put her savings, she looked demure, holy and secretive. If people were too kind and too sympathetic with her, she shuffled and looked mockingly. Seven hospitals, she said, had not killed *her*.

Now, when she heard Mr Fulmino's words about the fare, the clothes, the food, the expense of it all, she was troubled. What had she worked for – even at one time scrubbing in a canteen – but to save Hilda from a charity so vast in its humiliation, from so blank a herding mercy. Hilda was hers, not theirs. Hilda kept her arm on her mother's waist and while Mr Fulmino carried on with the marvels of international organisation (which moved Mrs Fulmino to say hungrily, 'It takes a war to bring it out'), Hilda ignored them and whispered to comfort her mother. At last the old lady dried her eyes and smiled at her daughter. The smile grew to a small laugh, she gave a proud jerk to her head, conveying that she and her Hil were not going to kowtow in gratitude to anyone, and Hilda, at last, said out loud to her mother what, no doubt, she had been whispering:

'He wouldn't let me pay anything, Mum. Faulkner his name was. Very highly educated. He came from California. We had a fancy dress dance on the ship and he made me go as a geisha . . . He gave me these . . .' And she raised her hand to show her mother the bracelets on it.

Mrs Johnson laughed wickedly.

'Did he . . . ? Was he . . . ?' said Mrs Johnson.

'No. Well, I don't know,' said Hilda. 'But I kept his address.'

Mrs Johnson smiled round at all of us, to show that in spite of all, being the poorest in the family and the ones that had suffered most, she and Hilda knew how to look after themselves.

This was the moment when there was that knock on the door. Everyone was startled and looked at it.

'A knock!' said Mr Fulmino.

'A knock, Constance,' said young Mrs Draper who had busy north-country ears.

'A knock,' several said.

Old Mrs Draper made one of her fundamental utterances again, one of her growls from the belly of the history of human indignation.

[447]

'We are,' she said, 'in the middle of our teas. Constance, go and see and tell them.'

But before Constance got to the door, two young men, one with a camera, came right into the room, without asking. Some of us lowered our heads and then, just as one young man said, 'I'm from the *News*,' the other clicked his camera.

Jack Draper said, nearly choking:

'He's taken a snap of us eating.'

While we were all staring at them, old Mrs Draper chewed out grandly:

'Who may they be?'

But Hilda stood up and got her mother to her feet, too. 'Stand up all of us,' she said eagerly. 'It's for the papers.'

It was the Press. We were in confusion. Mrs Fulmino pushed Mr Fulmino forward towards the reporter and then pulled him back. The reporter stood asking questions and everyone answered at once. The photographer kept on taking photographs and, when he was not doing that, started picking up vases and putting them down and one moment was trying the drawer of a little table by the window. They pushed Hilda and her mother into a corner and took a picture of them, Hilda calling to us all to 'come in' and Mr Fulmino explaining to the reporters. Then they went, leaving a cigarette burning on one of old Mrs Draper's lace doyleys under the fern and two more butts on the floor. 'What did they say? What did they say?' we all asked one another, but no one could remember. We were all talking at once, arguing about who had heard the knock first. Young Mrs Draper said her tea was spoiled and Constance opened the window to let the cigarette smoke out and then got the kettle. Mr Fulmino put his hand on his wife's knee because she was upset and she shook it off. When we had calmed down Hilda said:

'The young one was a nice-looking boy, wasn't he, Mum?' and Mr Fulmino, who almost never voiced the common opinion about anything but who had perhaps noticed how the eyes of all the women went larger at this remark, laughed loudly and said:

'We've got the old Hilda back!'

I mention this because of the item in the papers next day: A Mother's Faith. Four Years in Japanese Torture Camp. London Girl's Ordeal.

Wonderful, as Mr Fulmino said.

To be truthful, I felt uncomfortable at old Mrs Draper's. They were not my family. I had been dragged there by Mr Fulmino, and by a look now and then from young Mrs Draper and from Constance I had the feeling that they thought it was indecent for me to be there when I had only been going with Iris, Mr Fulmino's daughter, for two or three months. I had to be tolerated as one more example of Mr Fulmino's uncontrollable gifts – the gift for colonising.

Mr Fulmino had shot up from nothing during the war. It had given him personality. He was a short, talkative, heavy man of forty-five with a wet gold tooth and glossy black hair that streamlined back across his head from an arrow point, getting thin in front. His eyes were anxious, overworked and puddled, indeed if you had not known him you would have thought he had had a couple of black eyes that had never got right. He bowled along as he walked like someone absorbed by fondness for his own body. He had been in many things before he got to work for the Council – the army (but not a fighting soldier) in the war, in auctions and the bar of a club. He was very active, confiding and enquiring.

When I first met him I was working at the counter of the Public Library, during the war, and one day he came over from the Council Offices and said, importantly:

'Friend, we've got a bit of a headache. We've got an enquiry from the War Office. Have you got anything about Malaya – with maps?'

In the next breath he was deflating himself:

'It's a personal thing. They never tell you anything. I've got a niece out there.'

Honesty made him sound underhand. His manner suggested that his niece was a secret fortification somewhere east of Suez. Soon he was showing me the questionnaire from the Red Cross. Then he was telling me that his wife, like the rest of the Drapers, was very handsome – 'a lovely woman' in more ways, his manner suggested, than one – but that since Hilda had gone, she had become a different woman. The transition from handsome to different was, he suggested, a catastrophe which he was obliged to share with the public. He would come in from fire-watching, he said, and find her demented. In bed, he would add. He and I found ourselves fire-watching together, and from that time he started facetiously calling me 'my secretary'.

'I asked my secretary to get the sand and shovel out,' he would say about our correspondence. 'And he wrote the letter.'

So I was half a stranger at Hilda's homecoming. I looked round the room or out at the shops opposite and, when I looked back at the family several times, I caught Hilda's eyes wandering too. She also was out of it. I studied her. I hadn't expected her to come back in rags, as old Mrs Draper had, but it was a surprise to see she was the best-dressed woman in the room and the only one who looked as if she had ever been to a hairdresser. And there was another way in which I could not match her with the person Mr Fulmino and I had conjured. When we thought of everything that must have happened to her it was strange to see that her strong face was smooth and blank. Except for the few minutes of arrival and the time the reporters came, her face was vacant and plain. It was as vacant as a stone that has been smoothed for centuries in the sand of some hot country. It was the face of someone to whom nothing had happened; or, perhaps, so much had happened to her that each event wiped out what had happened before. I was disturbed by something in her – the lack of history, I think. We were worm-eaten by it. And that suddenly brought her back to me as she had been when she was a schoolgirl and when my older brother got into trouble for chasing after her. She was now sharper in the shoulders and elbows, no longer the swollen schoolgirl but, even as a girl, her face had the same quality of having been fixed and unchangeable between its high cheek bones. It was disturbing, in a face so anonymous, to see the eyes move, especially since she blinked very little; and if she smiled it was less a smile than an alteration of the two lines at the corners of her lips.

The party did not settle down quite in the same way after the reporters had been and there was talk of not tiring Hilda after her long journey. The family would all be meeting tomorrow, the Sunday, as they always did, when young Mrs Jack Draper brought her children. Jack Draper was thinking of the pub which was open now and asking if anyone was going over. And then, something happened. Hilda walked over to the window to Mr Fulmino and said, just as if she had not been there at the time:

'Ted – what did that man from the *News* ask you – about the food?'

'No,' said Mr Fulmino widening to a splendid chance of not giving the facts. 'No – he said something about starving the prisoners. I was telling him that in my opinion the deterioration in conditions was inevitable after the disorganisation in the camps resulting from air operations . . .'

'Oh, I thought you said we starved. We had enough.'

'What?' said Mr Fulmino.

'Bill Williams was a skeleton when he came back. Nothing but a bowl of rice a day. Rice!' said Mrs Fulmino. 'And torture.'

'Bill Williams must have been in one of those labour camps,' said Hilda. 'Being Japanese I was all right.'

'Japanese!' said Mr Fulmino. 'You?'

'Shinji was a Japanese,' said Hilda. 'He was in the army.'

'You married a Japanese!' said Mrs Fulmino, marching forward.

'That's why I was put in the American camp, when they came. They questioned every one, not only me. That's what I said to the reporter. It wasn't the food, it was the questions. What was his regiment? When did you hear from him? What was his number? They kept on. Didn't they, Mum?'

She turned to her mother who had taken the chance to cut herself another piece of cake and was about to slip it into her handkerchief, I think, to carry to her own room. We were all flabbergasted. A trolley bus went by and took a swipe at the wall. Young Mrs Draper murmured something and her young husband Jack said loudly, hearing his wife:

'Hilda married a Nip!'

And he looked at Hilda with astonishment. He had very blue eyes.

'You weren't a prisoner!' said Mrs Fulmino.

'Not of the Japanese,' said Hilda. 'They couldn't touch me. My husband was Japanese.'

'I'm not stupid. I can hear,' said young Mrs Draper to her husband. She was a plain-spoken woman from the Yorkshire coalfields, one of a family of twelve.

'I've nowt to say about who you married, but where is he? Haven't you brought him?' she said.

'You were married to Mr Singh,' said Mrs Fulmino.

'They're both dead,' said Hilda, her vacant yellow eyes becoming

[451]

suddenly brilliant like a cat's at night. An animal sound, like the noise of an old dog at a bone, came out of old Mrs Draper by the fire.

'Two,' she moaned.

No more than that. Simply, again: 'Two.'

Hilda was holding her handbag and she lifted it in both hands and covered her bosom with it. Perhaps she thought we were going to hit her. Perhaps she was going to open the bag and get out something extraordinary – documents, letters, or a handkerchief to weep into. But no – she held it there very tight. It was an American handbag – we hadn't seen one like that before, cream-coloured, like the luggage. Old Mrs Johnson hesitated at the table, tipped the piece of cake back out of her handkerchief on to a plate, and stepped to Hilda's side and stood, very straight for once, beside her, the old blue lips very still.

'Ted,' accused Hilda. 'Didn't you get my letters? Mother,' she stepped away from her mother, 'didn't you tell them?'

'What, dear?' said old Mrs Johnson.

'About Shinji. I wrote you. Did Mum tell you?' Hilda appealed to us and now looked fiercely at her mother.

Mrs Johnson smiled and retired into her look of faith and modesty. She feigned deafness.

'I put it all in the post office,' she said. 'Every week,' she said. 'Until my girl comes home, I said. She'll need it.'

'Mother!' said Hilda, giving the old lady a small shake. 'I wrote to you. I told you. Didn't you tell them?'

'What did Hilda say?' said Mr Fulmino gently, bending down to the old lady.

'Sh! Don't worry her. She's had enough for today. What did you tell the papers, Ted?' said Mrs Fulmino, turning on her husband. 'You can't ever keep your big mouth shut, can you? You never let me see the correspondence.'

'I married Shinji when the war came up,' Hilda said.

And then old Mrs Draper spoke from her armchair by the fire. She had her bad leg propped up on a hassock.

'Two,' said Mrs Draper savagely again.

Mr Fulmino, in his defeat, lost his nerve and let slip a remark quite casually, as he thought, under his voice, but everyone heard it – a remark that Mrs Fulmino was to remind him of in months to come.

'She strikes like a clock,' he said.

We were stupefied by Mr Fulmino's remark. Perhaps it was a relief.

'Mr Fraser!' Hilda said to me. And now her vacant face had become dramatic and she stepped towards me, appealing outside the family. 'You knew, you and Ted knew. You've got all the letters . . .'

If ever a man looked like the Captain going down with his ship and suddenly conscious, at the last heroic moment, that he is not on a ship at all, but standing on nothing and had hopelessly blundered, it was Mr Fulmino. But we didn't go down, either of us. For suddenly old Mrs Johnson couldn't stand straight any longer, her head wagged and drooped forward and, but for a chair, she would have fallen to the ground.

'Quick! Constance! Open the window,' Mrs Fulmino said. Hilda was on her knees by her mother.

'Are you there, Hilly?' said her mother.

'Yes, I'm here, Mum,' said Hilda. 'Get some water – some brandy.' They took the old lady next door to the little room Hilda was sharing with her that night.

'What I can't fathom is your aunt not telling me, keeping it to herself,' said Mr Fulmino to his wife as we walked home that evening from Mrs Draper's, and we had said 'Good-bye' to Jack Draper and his wife.

He was not hurt by Mrs Johnson's secretiveness but by an extraordinary failure of co-operation.

It was unwise of him to criticise Mrs Fulmino's family.

'Don't be so smug,' said Mrs Fulmino. 'What's it got to do with you? She was keeping it from Gran, you know Gran's tongue. She's her sister.' They called old Mrs Draper Gran or Grandma sometimes.

But when Mr Fulmino got home he asked me in so that we could search the correspondence together. Almost at once we discovered his blunder. There it was in the letter saying a Mrs Singh or Shinji Kobayashi had been identified.

'Shinji!' exclaimed Mrs Fulmino, putting her big index finger on the page. 'There you are, plain as dirt.'

[453]

'Singh,' said Mr Fulmino. 'Singh, Shinji, the same name. Some Indians write Singh, some Shinji.'

'Aud what is Kobayashi? Indian too? Don't be a fool.'

'It's the family name or Christian name of Singh,' said Mr Fulmino, doing the best he could.

Singh, Shinji, Shinji, Singh, he murmured to himself and he walked about trying to convince himself by incantation and hypnosis. He lashed himself with Kobayashi. He remembered the names of other Indians, Indian cities, mentioned the Ganges and the Himalayas; had a brief, brilliant couple of minutes when he argued that Shinji was Hindu for Singh. Mrs Fulmino watched him with the detachment of one waiting for a bluebottle to settle so that she could swat it.

'*You* thought Kobayashi was Indian, didn't you, Harry?' he appealed to me. I did my best.

'I thought,' I said weakly, 'it was the address.'

'Ah, the address!' Mr Fulmino clutched at this, but he knew he was done for. Mrs Fulmino struck.

'And what about the Sunday papers, the man from the *News*?' she said. 'You open your big mouth too soon.'

'Christ!' said Mr Fulmino. It was the sound of a man who has gone to the floor.

I will come to that matter of the papers later on. It is not very important.

When we went to bed that night we must all have known in our different ways that we had been disturbed in a very long dream. We had been living on inner visions for years. It was an effect of the long war. England had been a prison. Even the sky was closed and, like convicts, we had been driven to dwelling on fancies in our dreary minds. In the cinema the camera sucks some person forward into an enormous close-up and holds a face there yards wide, filling the whole screen, all holes and pores, like some sucking octopus that might eat up an audience many rows at a time. I don't say these pictures aren't beautiful sometimes, but afterwards I get the horrors. Hilda had been a close-up like this for us when she was lost and far away. For myself, I could hardly remember Hilda. She was a collection of fragments of my childhood and I suppose I had expected a girl to return.

My father and mother looked down on the Drapers and the Johnsons.

Hincham Street was 'dirty' and my mother once whispered that Mr Johnson had worked 'on the line', as if that were a smell. I remember the old man's huge crinkled white beard when I was a child. It was horribly soft and like pubic hair. So I had always thought of Hilda as a railway girl, in and out of tunnels, signal boxes and main line stations, and when my older brother was 'chasing' her as they said, I admired him. I listened to the quarrels that went on in our family – how she had gone to the convent school and the nuns had complained about her; and was it she or some other girl who went for car rides with a married man who waited round the corner of Hincham Street for her? The sinister phrase 'The nuns have been to see her mother' stuck in my memory. It astonished me to see Hilda alive, calm, fat and walking after that, as composed as a railway engine. When I grew up and Mr Fulmino came to the library, I was drawn into his search because she brought back those days with my brother, those clouts on the head from some friend of his, saying, 'Buzz off. Little pigs have big ears,' when my brother and he were whispering about her.

To Mrs Fulmino, a woman whose feelings were in her rolling arms, flying out from one extreme to another as she talked, as if she were doing exercises, Hilda appeared in her wedding clothes and all the sexuality of an open flower, standing beside her young Indian husband who was about to become a doctor. There was trouble about the wedding, for Mr Singh spoke a glittering and palatial English – the beautiful English a snake might speak, it seemed to the family – that made a few pock marks on his face somehow more noticeable. Old Mrs Draper alone, against all evidence – Mr Singh had had a red racing car – stuck to it that he was 'a common lascar off a ship'. Mrs Fulmino had been terrified of Mr Singh – she often conveyed – and had 'refused to be in a room alone with him'. Or 'How can she let him touch her?' she would murmur, thinking about that, above all. Then whatever vision was in her mind would jump forward to Hilda, captured, raped, tortured, murdered in front of her eyes. Mrs Fulmino's mind was voluptuous. When I first went to Mr Fulmino's house and met Iris and we talked about Hilda, Mrs Fulmino once or twice left the room and he lowered his voice. 'The wife's upset,' he said. 'She's easily upset.'

We had not all been under a spell. Not young Jack Draper nor his wife, for example. Jack Draper had fought in the war and where we thought of the war as something done to us and our side, Jack thought of it as something done to everybody. I remember what he said to his wife before the Fulminos and I said 'Good night' to them on the Saturday Hilda came home.

'It's a shame,' said Jack, 'she couldn't bring the Nip with her.'

'He was killed,' said his wife.

'That's what I mean,' said Jack. 'It's a bleeding shame she couldn't.'

We walked on and then young Mrs Draper said, in her flat, northern laconic voice:

'Well, Jack, for all the to-do, you might just as well have gone to your fishing.'

For Jack had made a sacrifice in coming to welcome Hilda. He went fishing up the Thames on Saturdays. The war for him was something that spoiled fishing. In the Normandy landing he had thought mostly of that. He dreamed of the time when his two boys would be old enough to fish. It was what he had had children for.

'There's always Sunday,' said his wife, tempting him. Jack nodded. She knew he would not fall. He was the youngest of old Mrs Draper's family, the baby, as they said. He never missed old Mrs Draper's Sundays.

It was a good thing he did not, a good thing for all of us that we didn't miss, for we would have missed Hilda's second announcement.

Young Mrs Draper provoked it. These Sunday visits to Hincham Street were a ritual in the family. It was a duty to old Mrs Draper. We went there for our tea. She provided, though Constance prepared for it as if we were a school, for she kept house there. We recognised our obligation by paying sixpence into the green pot on the chiffonier when we left. The custom had started in the bad times when money was short; but now the money was regarded as capital and Jack Draper used to joke and say, 'Who are you going to leave the green pot to, Mum?' Some of Hilda's luggage had been moved by the afternoon into her mother's little room at the back and how those two could sleep in a bed so small was a question raised by Mrs Fulmino whose night with Mr Fulmino required room for struggle, as I know, for this colonising man often dropped hints about how she swung her legs over in the night.

'Have you unpacked yet, Hilda?' Mrs Fulmino was asking.

'Unpacked!' said Constance. 'Where would she put all that?'

'I've been lazy,' said Hilda. 'I've just hung up a few things because of the creases.'

'Things do crease,' said Mrs Fulmino.

'Bill Williams said he would drop in later,' said Constance.

'That man suffered,' said Mrs Fulmino, with meaning.

'He heard you were back,' said Constance.

Hilda had told us about Shinji. Jack Draper listened with wonder. Shinji had been in the jute business and when the war came he was called up to the army. He was in 'Stores'. Jack scratched with delight when he heard this. 'Same as I tried to work it,' Jack said. Shinji had been killed in an air raid. Jack's wife said, to change the subject, she liked that idea, the idea of Jack 'working' anything, he always let everyone climb up on his shoulders. 'First man to get wounded. I knew he would be,' she said. 'He never looks where he's going.'

'Is that the Bill Williams who worked for Ryan, the builder?' said Hilda.

'He lives in the Culverwell Road,' young Mrs Draper said.

Old Mrs Draper, speaking from the bowels of history, said:

'He got that Sellers girl into trouble.'

'Yes,' exclaimed Hilda, 'I remember.'

'It was proved in court that he didn't,' said Constance briskly to Hilda. 'You weren't here.'

We were all silent. One could hear only the sounds of our cups on the saucers and Mrs Fulmino's murmur, 'More bread and butter?' Constance's face had its neat, pink, enamelled smile and one saw the truthful blue of her small eyes become purer in colour. Iris was next to me and she said afterwards something I hadn't noticed, that Constance hated Hilda. It is one of the difficulties I have in writing, that, all along, I was slow to see what was really happening, not having a woman's eye or ear. And being young. Old Mrs Draper spoke again, her mind moving from the past to the present with that suddenness old people have.

'If Bill Williams is coming, he knows the way,' she said.

Hilda understood that remark for she smiled and Constance flushed. (Of course, I see it now: two women in a house! Constance had ruled old Mrs Draper and Mrs Johnson for years and her money had made a big difference.) They knew that one could, as the saying is, 'trust Gran to put her oar in'.

Again young Mrs Draper changed the subject. She was a nimble, tarry-haired woman, impatient of fancies, excitements and disasters. She liked things flat and factual. While the family gaped at Hilda's clothes and luggage, young Mrs Draper had reckoned up the cost of them. She was not avaricious or mean, but she knew that money is money. You know that if you have done without. So she went straight into the important question being (as she would say), not like people in the South, double-faced Wesleyans, but honest, plain and straight out with it, what are they ashamed of? Jack, her husband, was frightened by her bluntness, and had the nervous habit of folding his arms across his chest and scratching fast under his armpits when his wife spoke out about money; some view of the river, with his bait and line and the evening flies, came into his panicking mind. Mr Fulmino once said that Jack scratched because the happiest moments of his life, the moments of escape, had been passed in clouds of gnats.

'I suppose, Hilda, you'll be thinking of what you're going to do?' young Mrs Draper said. 'Did they give you a pension?'

I was stroking Iris's knee but she stopped me, alerted like the rest of them. The word 'pension' is a very powerful word. In this neighbourhood one could divide the world into those who had pensions and those who hadn't. The phrase 'the old pensioner' was one of envy, abuse and admiration. My father, for example, spoke contemptuously of pensioners. Old Mrs Draper's husband had had a pension, but my father would never have one. As a librarian (Mr Fulmino pointed out), I would have a pension and thereby I had overcome the first obstacle in being allowed to go out with his daughter.

'No,' said Hilda. 'Nothing.'

'But he was your husband, you said,' said Constance.

'He was in the army, you say,' said young Mrs Draper.

'Inflation,' said Mr Fulmino grandly. 'The financial situation.'

He was stopped.

'Then,' said young Mrs Draper, 'you'll have to go to work.'

'My girl won't want for money,' said old Mrs Johnson, sitting beside her daughter as she had done the day before.

'No,' said young Mrs Draper. 'That she won't while you're alive, Mrs Johnson. We all know that, and the way you slaved for her. But Hilda wants to look after you, I'm sure.'

It was, of course, the question in everyone's mind. Did all those clothes and cases mean money or was it all show? That is what we all wanted to know. We would not have raised it at that time and in that way. It wasn't our way – we would have drifted into finding out – Hilda was scarcely home. But young Mrs Draper had been brought up hard, as she said, twelve mouths to feed.

'*I'm* looking after *you*, Mum,' said Hilda, smiling at her mother.

Mrs Johnson was like a wizened little girl gazing up at a taller sister.

'I'll take you to Monte Carlo, Mum,' Hilda said.

The old lady tittered. We all laughed loudly. Hilda laughed with us.

'That gambling place!' the old lady giggled.

'That's it,' laughed Hilda. 'Break the bank.'

'Is it across water?' said the old lady, playing up. 'I couldn't go on a boat. I was so sick at Southend when I was a girl.'

'Then we'll fly.'

'Oh!' the old lady cried. 'Don't, Hil – I'll have a fit.'

'"The Man Who Broke the Bank at Monte Carlo",' Mr Fulmino sang. 'You might find a boy friend, Mrs Johnson.'

Young Mrs Draper did not laugh at this game; she still wanted to know; but she did smile. She was worried by laughter. Constance did not laugh but she showed her pretty white teeth.

'Oh, she's got one for me,' said Mrs Johnson. 'So she says.'

'Of course I have. Haven't I, Harry?' said Hilda, talking across the table to me.

'Me? What?' I said completely startled.

'You can't take Harry,' said Iris, half frightened.

'Did you post the letter?' said Hilda to me.

'What letter?' said Iris to me. 'Did she give you a letter?'

Now there is a thing I ought to have mentioned! I had forgotten all about the letter. When we were leaving the evening before, Hilda had called me quietly to the door and said:

'Please post this for me. Tonight.'

'Hilda gave me a letter to post,' I said.

'You did post it?' Hilda said.

'Yes,' I said.

She looked contentedly round at everyone.

'I wrote to Mr Gloster, the gentleman I told you about, on the boat. He's in Paris. He's coming over at the end of the week to get a car. He's taking Mother and me to France. Mr Gloster, Mum, I told you. No, not Mr Faulkner. That was the other boat. He was in San Francisco.'

'Oh,' said Mrs Johnson, a very long 'oh,' and wriggling like a child listening to a story. She was beginning to look pale, as she had the evening before when she had the turn.

'France!' said Constance in a peremptory voice.

'Who is Mr Gloster – you never said anything,' said Mrs Fulmino.

'What about the currency regulations?' said Mr Fulmino.

Young Mrs Draper said, 'France! He must have money.'

'Dollars,' said Hilda to Mr Fulmino.

Dollars! There was a word!

'The almighty dollar,' said Constance, in the cleansed and uncorrupted voice of one who has mentioned one of the commandments. Constance had principles; we had the confusion of our passions.

And from sixteen years or more back in time or perhaps it was from some point in history hundreds of years back and forgotten, old Mrs Draper said: 'And is this Indian married?'

Hilda – to whom no events, I believe, had ever happened – replied: 'Mr Gloster's an American, Gran.'

'He wants to marry her,' said old Mrs Johnson proudly.

'If I'll have him!' said Hilda.

'Well, he can't if you won't have him, can he, Hilda?' said Mrs Fulmino.

'Gloster. G-L-O-S-T-E-R?' asked Mr Fulmino.

'Is he in a good job?' asked young Mrs Draper.

Hilda pointed to a brooch on her blouse.

'He gave me this,' she said.

She spoke in her harsh voice and with a movement of her face that in anyone else one would have called excited, but in her it had a disturbing lack of meaning. It was as if Hilda had been hooked into the air by invisible wires and was then swept out into the air and back to Japan, thousands of miles away again, and while she was on her way, she turned and knocked us flat with the next item.

'He's a writer,' she said. 'He's going to write a book about me. He's very interested in me . . .'

Mrs Johnson nodded.

'He's coming to fetch us, Mum and me, and take us to France to write this book. He's going to write my life.'

Her life! Here was a woman who had, on top of everything else, a life.

'Coming *here?*' said Mrs Fulmino with a grinding look at old Mrs Draper and then at Constance, trying to catch their eyes and failing; in despair she looked at the shabby room, to see what must be put straight, or needed cleaning or painting. Nothing had been done to it for years for Constance, teaching at her school all day, and very clean in her person, let things go in the house and young Mrs Draper said old Mrs Draper smelled. All the command in Mrs Fulmino's face collapsed as rapidly, on her own, she looked at the carpets, the lino, the curtains.

'What's he putting in this book?' said young Mrs Draper cannily.

'Yes,' said Jack Draper, backing up his wife.

'What I tell him,' Hilda said.

'What she tells him,' said old Mrs Johnson sparkling. Constance looked thoughtfully at Hilda.

'Is it a biography?' Constance asked coldly. There were times when we respected Constance and forgot to murmur 'Go back to Russia' every time she spoke. I knew what a biography was and so did Mr Fulmino, but no one else did.

'It's going to be made into a film,' Hilda replied.

'A film,' cried Iris.

Constance gleamed.

'You watch for American propaganda,' said Constance. There you are, you see: Constance was back on it!

'Oh, it's about me,' said Hilda. 'My experience.'

'Very interesting,' said Mr Fulmino, preparing to take over. 'A Hollywood production, I expect. Publication first and then they go into production.'

He spread his legs.

None of us had believed, or even understood what we heard, but we looked with gratitude to Mr Fulmino for making the world steady again.

Jack Draper's eyes filled with tears because a question was working in him but he could not get it out.

'Will you be in this film?' asked Iris.

'I'll wait till he's written it,' said Hilda with that lack of interest we had often noticed in her, after she had made some dramatic statement.

Mrs Fulmino breathed out heavily with relief and after that her body seemed to become larger. She touched her hair at the back and straightened her dress, as if preparing to offer herself for the part. She said indeed:

'I used to act at school.'

'She's still good at it,' said Mr Fulmino with daring to Jack Draper who always appreciated Mr Fulmino, but seeing the danger of the moment hugged himself and scratched excitedly under both armpits, laughing.

'You shouldn't have let this Mr Gloster go,' said Constance.

Hilda was startled by this remark and looked lost. Then she shrugged her shoulders and gave a low laugh, as if to herself.

Mr Fulmino's joke had eased our bewilderment. Hilda had been our dream but now she was home she changed as fast as dreams change. She was now, as we looked at her, far more remote to us than she had been all the years when she was away. The idea was so far beyond us. It was like some story of a bomb explosion or an elopement or a picture of bathing girls one sees in the newspapers – unreal and, in a way, insulting to being alive in the ordinary daily sense of the word. Or, she was like a picture that one sees in an art gallery, that makes you feel sad because it is painted.

After tea when Hilda took her mother to the lavatory, Constance beckoned to Iris and let her peep into the room Hilda was sharing, and young Mrs Draper, not to be kept out of things, followed. They were back in half a minute:

'Six evening dresses,' Iris said to me.

'She said it was Mr Faulkner who gave her the luggage, not this one who was going to get her into pictures,' said Mrs Fulmino.

'Mr Gloster, you mean,' said Constance.

Young Mrs Draper was watching the door, listening for Hilda's return.

'Ssh,' she said, at the sound of footsteps on the stairs and, to look at us, the men on one side of the room and the women on the other, silent, standing at attention, facing each other, we looked like soldiers.

'Oh,' said Constance. The steps we had heard were not Hilda's. It was Bill Williams who came in.

'Good afternoon one and all,' he said. The words came from the corner of a mouth that had slipped down at one side. Constance drew herself up, her eyes softened. She had exact, small, round breasts. Looking around, he said to Constance: 'Where is she?'

Constance lowered her head when she spoke to him, though she held it up shining, admiring him, when he spoke to us, as if she were displaying him to us.

'She'll be here in a minute,' she said. 'She's going into films.'

'I'll take a seat in the two and fourpennies,' said Bill Williams and he sat down at his ease and lit a cigarette.

Bill Williams was a very tall, sick-faced man who stooped his shoulders as if he were used to ducking under doors. His dry black hair, not oiled like Mr Fulmino's, bushed over his forehead and he had the shoulders, arms and hands of a lorry driver. In fact, he drove a light van for a textile firm. His hazel eyes were always watching and wandering and we used to say he looked as though he was going to snaffle something but that may simply have been due to the restlessness of a man with a poor stomach. Laziness, cunning and aches and pains were suggested by him. He was a man taking his time. His eyebrows grew thick and the way one brow was raised, combined with the side-slip of his mouth, made him look like some shrewd man about to pick up a faulty rifle, hit the bull's eye five times running at a fair and moan afterwards. He glanced a good deal at Constance. He was afraid of his manners before her, we thought, because he was a rough type.

'Put it here,' said Constance, bringing him an ashtray. That was what he was waiting for, for he did not look at her again.

Bill Williams brought discomfort with him whenever he came on Sundays and we were always happier when he failed to come. If there was anything private to say we tried to get it over before he came. How a woman like Constance, a true, clean, settled schoolteacher who even spoke in the clear, practical and superior manner of someone used to the voice of reason, who kept her nails so beautifully, could have taken up with him, baffled us. He was very often at Mrs Draper's in the week, eating with them, and Constance, who was thirty-five, quarrelled like a girl when she was getting things ready for him. Mrs Fulmino could not bear the way he ate, with his elbows out and his face close to the plate. The only good thing about the affair was that, for once, Constance was overruled.

'Listen to her,' Bill Williams would say with a nod of his head. 'A rank red Communist. Tell us about Holy Russia, Connie.'

'Constance is my correct name, not Connie,' she said.

Their bickering made us die. But we respected Constance even when she was a trial. She had been twice to Russia before the war and though we argued violently with her, especially Mr Fulmino who tried to take over Russia, and populate it with explanations, we always boasted to other people that she'd been there.

'On delegations,' Mr Fulmino would say.

But we could *not* boast that she had taken up with Bill Williams. He had been a hero when he came back from Japan, but he had never kept a job since, he was rough and his lazy zigzagging habits in his work made even Constance impatient. He had for her the fascination a teacher feels for a bad pupil. Lately their love affair had been going better because he was working outside London and sometimes he worked at week-ends; this added to the sense of something vague and secretive in his life that had attracted Constance. For there was much that was secret in her or so she liked to hint – it was political. Again, it was the secretiveness of those who like power; she was the schoolmistress who has the threat of inside knowledge locked up in the cupboard. Once Mrs Fulmino went purple and said to her husband – who told me, he always told me such things – that she believed Constance had lately started sleeping with Bill Williams. That was because Constance had once said to her:

'Bill and I are individuals.'

Mrs Fulmino had a row with Iris after this and stopped me seeing her for a month.

Hilda came back into the room alone. Bill Williams let his mouth slip sideways and spoke a strange word to her, saying jauntily to us: 'That's Japanese.'

Hilda wasn't surprised. She replied with a whole sentence in Japanese.

'That means' – but Bill Williams was beaten, but he passed it off. 'Well, I'd best not tell them what it means,' he said.

'East meets East,' Mr Fulmino said.

'It means,' said Hilda, 'you were on the other side of the fence but now the gate is open.'

Bill Williams studied her inch by inch. He scratched his head.

'Straight?' he said.

'Yes,' she said.

'Stone me, it was bloody closed when we were there,' said Bill Williams offensively, but then said: 'They fed her well, didn't they, Constance? Sit down.' Hilda sat down beside him.

'Connie!' he called. 'Seen these? Just the job, eh?' He was nodding at Hilda's stockings. Nylons. 'Now,' he said to Hilda, looking closely at her. 'Where were you? It got a bit rough at the finish, didn't it?'

Jack Draper came close to them to hear, hoping that Hilda would say something about what moved him the most: the enemy. Bill Williams gave him a wink and Hilda saw it. She looked placidly at Bill Williams, considering his face, his neck, his shoulders and his hands that were resting on his knees.

'I was okey doke,' she said.

Bill Williams dropped his mouth open and waggled the top of his tongue in a back tooth in his knowing manner. To our astonishment Hilda opened her mouth and gave a neat twist to her tongue in her cheek in the same way.

Bill Williams slapped his knee and, to cover his defeat in this little duel, said to all of us:

'This little girl's got yellow eyes.'

All the colour had gone from Connie's face as she watched the meeting.

'They say you're going to be in pictures,' said Bill Williams.

And then we had Hilda's story over again. Constance asked what papers Mr Gloster wrote for.

'I don't know. A big paper,' said Hilda.

'You ought to find out,' Constance said. 'I'll find out.'

'Um,' said Hilda with a nod of not being interested.

'I could give him some of my experience,' said Bill Williams. 'Couldn't I, Connie? Things I've told you – you could write a ruddy book.'

He looked with challenge at Hilda. He was a rival.

'Gawd!' he exclaimed. 'The things.'

We heard it again, how he was captured, where his battery was, the long march, Sergeant Harris who was hanged, Corporal Rowley bayoneted and left to die in the sun, the starvation, the work on the road that killed half of them. But there was one difference between this story and the ones he had told before. The sight of Hilda altered it.

'You had to get round the guards,' he said with a wink. 'If you used your loaf a bit, eh? Scrounge around, do a bit of trade. One or two had Japanese girls. Corporal Jones went back afterwards trying to trace his, wanted to marry her.'

Hilda listened and talked about places she had lived in, how she had worked in a factory.

'That's it,' said Bill Williams, 'you had to know your way around and talk a bit of the lingo.'

Jack Draper looked with affection and wonder at the talk, lowering his eyes if her eyes caught his. Every word entered him. The heat! she said. The rain. The flowers. The telegraph poles! Jack nodded.

'They got telegraph poles,' he nodded to us.

You sleep on the floor. Shinji's mother, she mentioned. She could have skinned her. Jack, brought up among so many women, lost interest, but it revived when she talked of Shinji. You could see him mouthing his early marvelling sentence: 'She married a Nip,' but not saying it. She was confirming something he had often thought of in Normandy; the men on the other side were married too. A bloody marvel. Why hadn't she brought him home? He would have had a friend.

'Who looked after the garden when Shinji was called up?' he asked. 'Were they goldfish, ordinary goldfish, in the pond?'

Young Mrs Draper shook her head.

'Eh,' she said. 'If he'd a known he'd have come over to change the water. Next time we have a war you just let him know.'

Mrs Fulmino who was throbbing like a volcano said:

'We better all go next time by the sound of it.'

At the end, Bill Williams said:

[466]

'I suppose you're going to be staying here.'

'No,' said Constance quickly, 'she isn't. She's going to France. When is it, Hilda? When is Mr Gloster coming?'

'Next week, I don't know,' said Hilda.

'You shouldn't have let him go!' laughed Bill Williams. 'Those French girls will get him in Paree.'

'That is what I have been saying,' said Constance. 'He gave her that brooch.'

'Oh ah! It's the stockings I'm looking at,' said Bill Williams. 'How did you get all that stuff through the customs? Twenty cases, Connie told me.'

'Twelve,' said Hilda.

Bill Williams did not move her at all. Presently she got up and started clearing away the tea things. I will say this for her, she didn't let herself be waited on.

Iris, Mr and Mrs Fulmino and the young Drapers and their children and myself left Hincham Street together.

'You walk in front with the children, Iris,' said Mrs Fulmino. Then they turned on me. What was this letter, they wanted to know. Anyone would have thought by their questions that I ought to have opened it and read it.

'I just posted it at the corner.' I pointed to the pillar box. Mrs Fulmino stopped to look at the pillar box and I believe was turning over in her mind the possibility of getting inside it. Then she turned on her husband and said with contemptuous suspicion: 'Monte Carlo!' As if he had worked the whole thing in order to go there himself.

'Two dead,' she added in her mother's voice, the voice of one who would have been more than satisfied with the death of one.

'Not having a pension hasn't hurt her,' said Mrs Draper.

'Not a tear,' said Mrs Fulmino.

Jack and Mr Fulmino glanced at each other. It was a glance of surreptitious gratitude: tears – they had escaped that.

Mr Fulmino said: 'The Japanese don't cry.'

Mrs Fulmino stepped out, a bad sign; her temper was rising.

'Who was the letter to?' she asked me. 'Was the name Gloster?'

'I didn't look,' I said.

[467]

Mrs Fulmino looked at her husband and me and rolled her eyes. Another of our blunders!

'I don't believe it,' she said.

But Mrs Fulmino *did* believe it. We all believed and disbelieved everything at once.

I said I would come to the report in the *News*. It was in thick lettering like mourning, with Hilda's picture: A Mother's Faith. Four Years in Japanese Torture Camp. London Girl's Ordeal. And then an account of how Hilda had starved and suffered and been brain-washed by questioners. Even Hilda was awed when she read it, feeling herself drain away, perhaps, and being replaced by this fantasy; and for the rest of us, we had become used to living in a period when events reduced us to beings so trivial that we had no strong feeling of our own existence in relation to the world around us. We had been bashed first one way, then the other, by propaganda, until we were indifferent. At one time people like my parents or old Mrs Draper could at least trust the sky and feel that it was certain and before it they could have at least the importance of being something in the eye of heaven.

Constance read the newspaper report and it fulfilled her.

'Propaganda,' she said. 'Press lies.'

'All lies,' Mr Fulmino agreed with wonder. The notion that the untrue was as effective as the true opened to him vast areas to his powers. It was like a temptation.

It did not occur to us that we might be in a difficult situation in the neighbourhood when the truth came out, until we heard Constance and Bill Williams had gone over to the Lord Nelson with the paper and Constance had said, 'You can't believe a word you read in the capitalist press.'

Alfred Levy, the proprietor and a strong Tory, agreed with her. But was Hilda criticised for marrying an enemy? The hatred of the Japanese was strong at this time. She was not. Constance may not have had the best motives for spreading the news, we said, but it did no harm at all. That habit of double vision affected every one publicly. We lived in the true and the untrue, comfortably and without trouble. People picked up the paper, looked at her picture and said, 'That's a shocking thing. A

British subject,' and even when they knew, even from Hilda's own lips the true story, they said, congratulating themselves on their cunning, 'The papers make it all up.'

Of course, we were all in that stage where the forces of life, the desire to live, were coming back, and although it was not yet openly expressed, we felt that curiosity about the enemy that ex-soldiers like Jack Draper felt when he wondered if some Japanese or some Germans were as fed up as he was on Saturdays by missing a day's fishing. When people shook Hilda's hand they felt they gave her life. I do not say there were not one or two mutterings afterwards, for people always went off from the Lord Nelson when it closed in a state of moralisation: beer must talk; the louts singing and the couples saying this or that 'wasn't right'. But this gossip came to nothing because, sooner or later, it came to a closed door in everybody's conscience. There were the men who had shot off trigger fingers, who had got false medical certificates, deserters, ration frauds, black marketeers, the pilferers of army stores. And the women said a woman is right to stand by her husband and, looking at Hilda's fine clothes, pointed out to their husbands that that kind of loyalty was sometimes rewarded; indeed, Mrs Fulmino asserted, by law.

We had been waiting for Hilda; now, by a strange turn, we were waiting for Hilda's Mr Gloster. We waited for a fortnight and it ran on into three weeks. George Hartman Gloster. I looked up the name on our cards at the library, but we had no books of his. I looked up one or two catalogues. Still nothing. It was not surprising. He was an American who was not published in this country. Constance came in and looked too.

'It is one of those names the Americans don't list,' she said. Constance smiled with the cool air of keeping a world of meaningful secrets on ice.

'They don't list everything,' she said.

She brought Bill Williams with her. I don't think he had ever been in a public library before, because his knowing manner went and he was overawed. He said to me:

'Have you read all these books? Do you buy them secondhand? What's this lot worth?'

He was a man always on the look-out for a deal; it was typical of him that he had come with Constance in his firm's light-green van. It was not like Constance to travel in that way. 'Come on,' he said roughly.

[469]

The weather was hot; we had the sun blinds down in the Library. We were in the middle of one of those brassy fortnights of the London summer when English life, as we usually know it, is at a standstill, and everyone changes. A new grinning healthy race with long red necks sticking out of open shirts and blouses appears, and the sun brings out the variety of faces and bodies. Constance might have been some trim nurse marching at the head of an official procession. People looked calm, happy and open. There was hardly ever a cloud in the sky, the slate roofs looked like steel with the sun's rays hitting them, and the side streets were cool in sharp shadow. It was a pleasant time for walking, especially when the sky went whitish in the distances of the city in the evening and when the streets had a dry pleasant smell and the glass of millions of windows had a motionless but not excluding stare. Even a tailor working late above a closed shop looked pleased to be going on working, while everyone else was out, wearing out their clothes.

Iris and I used to go to the park on some evenings and there every blade of grass had been wire-brushed by sunlight; the trees were heavy with still leaves and when darkness came they gathered into soft black walls and their edges were cut out against the nail varnish of the city's night. During the day the park was crowded. All over the long sweeps of grass the couples were lying, their legs at careless angles, their bottoms restless as they turned to the horseplay of love in the open. Girls were leaning over the men rumpling their hair, men were tickling the girls' chins with stalks of grass. Occasionally they would knock the wind out of each other with plunging kisses; and every now and then a girl would sit up and straighten her skirt at the waist, narrowing her eyes in a pretence of looking at some refining sight in the distance, until she was pulled down again and, keeping her knees together, was caught again. Lying down you smelt the grass and listened to the pleasant rumble of the distant traffic going round like a wheel that never stopped.

I was glad to know the Fulminos and to go out with Iris. We had both been gayer before we met each other, but seriousness, glumness, a sadness came over us when we became friends – that eager sadness that begins with thoughts of love. We encouraged and discouraged these thoughts in each other yet were always hinting and the sight of so much love around us turned us naturally away from it to think about it privately the more. She was a beautifully-formed girl as her mother must have once been, but slender. She had a wide laugh that shook the curls of her thick black hair. She was being trained at a typing school.

One day when I was sitting in the park and Iris was lying beside me, we had a quarrel. I asked her if there was any news of Mr Gloster – for she heard everything. She had said there was none and I said, sucking a piece of grass:

'That's what I would like to do. Go round the world. Anywhere. America, Africa, China.'

'A chance is a fine thing,' said Iris, day dreaming.

'I could get a job,' I said.

Iris sat up.

'Leave the Library?' she said.

'Yes,' I said. 'If I stay there I won't see anything.' I saw Iris's face change and become very like her mother's. Mrs Fulmino could make her face go larger and her mouth go very small. Iris did not answer. I went on talking. I asked her what she thought. She still did not answer.

'Anything the matter?' She was sulking. Then she said, flashing at me:

'You're potty on that woman too. You all are. Dad is, Jack is; and look at Bill Williams. Round at Hincham Street every day. He'll be having his breakfast there soon. Fascinated.'

'He goes to see Constance.'

'Have you seen Constance's face?' she jeered. 'Constance could kill her.'

'She came to the Library.'

'Ah,' she turned to me. 'You didn't tell me that.'

'She came in for a book, I told you. For Mr Gloster's books. Bill Williams came with her.'

Iris's sulk changed into satisfaction at this piece of news.

'Mother says if Constance's going to marry a man like Mr Williams,' she said, 'she'll be a fool to let him out of her sight.'

'I'll believe in Mr Gloster when I see him,' Iris said. It was, of course, what we were all thinking. We made up our quarrel and I took Iris home. Mrs Fulmino was dressed up, just putting the key in the door of her house. Iris was astonished to see her mother had been out and asked where she had been.

[471]

'Out,' said Mrs Fulmino. 'Have I got to stay in and cook and clean for you all day?'

Mrs Fulmino was even wearing gloves, as if she had been to church. And she was wearing a new pair of shoes. Iris went pale at the sight of them. Mrs Fulmino put her gloves down on the sitting-room table and said:

'I've got a right to live, I suppose?'

We were silenced.

One thing we all agreed on while we waited for Mr Gloster was that Hilda had the money and knew how to spend it. The first time she asked the Fulminos and young Drapers to the cinema, Mrs Fulmino said to her husband:

'You go. I've got one of my heads.'

'Take Jack,' young Mrs Draper said. 'I've got the children.'

They were daring their husbands to go with her. But the second time, there was a party. Hilda took some of them down to Kew. She took old Mrs Johnson down to Southend – and who should they meet there but Bill Williams who was delivering some goods there, spoiling their day because old Mrs Johnson did not like his ways. And Hilda had given them all presents. And two or three nights a week she was out at the Lord Nelson.

It was a good time. If anyone asked, 'Have you heard from Mr Gloster yet?' Hilda answered that it was not time yet and, as a dig at Constance that we all admired, she said once: 'He has business at the American Embassy.' And old Mrs Johnson held her head high and nodded.

At the end of three weeks we became restless. We noticed old Mrs Johnson looked poorly. She said she was tired. Old Mrs Draper became morose. She had been taught to call Mr Gloster by his correct name, but now she relapsed.

'Where is this Indian?' she uttered.

And another day, she said, without explanation:

'Three.'

'Three what, Gran?'

'There've been two, that's enough.'

No one liked this, but Mrs Johnson understood.

'Mr Gloster's very well, isn't he, Hil? You heard from him yesterday?' she said.

'I wasn't shown the letter,' said old Mrs Draper. 'We don't want a third.'

'We don't,' said Mrs Fulmino. With her joining in 'on Gran's side', the situation changed. Mrs Fulmino had a low voice and the sound of it often sank to the floor of any room she was in, travelling under chairs and tables, curling round your feet and filling the place from the bottom as if it were a cistern. Even when the trolley bus went by Mrs Fulmino's low voice prevailed. It was an undermining voice, breaking up one's uppermost thoughts and stirring up what was underneath them. It stirred us all now. Yes, we wanted to say, indeed, we wanted to shout, where is this Mr Gloster, why hasn't he come, did you invent him? He's alive, we hope? Or is he also – as Gran suggests – dead?

Even Mr Fulmino was worried.

'Have you got his address?' he asked.

'Yes, Uncle dear,' said Hilda. 'He'll be staying at the Savoy. He always does.'

Mr Fulmino had not taken out his notebook for a long time but he did so now. He wrote down the name.

'Has he made a reservation?' said Mr Fulmino. 'I'll find out if he's booked.'

'He hasn't,' said Bill Williams. 'I had a job down there and I asked. Didn't I, Connie?'

Mrs Fulmino went a very dark colour. She wished she had thought of doing this. Hilda was not offended, but a small smile clipped her lips as she glanced at Connie:

'I asked Bill to do it,' she said.

And then Hilda in that harsh lazy voice which she had always used for announcements: 'If he doesn't come by Wednesday you'll have to speak for me at your factory, Mr Williams. I don't know why he hasn't come, but I can't wait any more.'

'Bill can't get you a job. You have to register,' said Constance.

'Yes, she'll have to do that,' said Mr Fulmino.

'I'll fix it. Leave it to me,' said Bill Williams.

'I expect,' said young Mrs Draper, 'his business has kept him.' She was sorry for Hilda.

'Perhaps he's gone fishing,' said Jack Draper, laughing loudly in a kind way. No one joined in.

'Fishing for orders,' said Bill Williams.

Hilda shrugged her shoulders and then she made one of those remarks that Grandma Draper usually made – I suppose the gift really ran through the family.

'Perhaps it was a case,' she said, 'of ships that pass in the night.'

'Oh no, dear,' said Mrs Johnson trembling, 'not ships.' We went to the bus stop afterwards with the Fulminos and the young Drapers. Mrs Fulmino's calm had gone. She marched out first, her temper rising.

'Ships!' she said. 'When you think of what we went through during the war. Did you hear her? Straight out?'

'My brother Herbert's wife was like that. She's a widow. Take away the pension and they'll work like the rest of us. I had to.'

'Job! Work! I know what sort of work she's been doing. Frank, walk ahead with Iris.'

'Well,' said young Mrs Draper, 'she won't be able to go to work in those clothes and that's a fact.'

'All show,' said Mrs Fulmino triumphantly. 'And I'll tell you something else – she hasn't a penny. She's run through her poor mother's money.'

'Ay, I don't doubt,' said young Mrs Draper, who had often worked out how much the old lady had saved.

Mr Gloster did not come on Wednesday or on any other day, but Hilda did not get a job either, not at once. And old Mrs Johnson did not go to Monte Carlo. She died. This was the third, we understood, that old Mrs Draper had foreseen.

Mrs Johnson died at half past eight in the morning just after Constance had gone off to school, the last day of the term, and before old Mrs Draper had got up. Hilda was in the kitchen wearing her blue Japanese wrap when she heard her mother's loud shout, like a man selling papers, she said, and when Hilda rushed in her mother was sitting up in bed. She gripped Hilda with the ferocity of the dying, as if all the strength of her whole life had come back and she was going to throw her daughter to the ground. Then she died. In an hour she looked like a white leaf that has been found after a lifetime pressed between the pages of a book and as delicate as a saint. The death was not only a shock: from the grief that spread from it staining all of us, I trace the ugly events that followed. Only the frail figure of old Mrs Johnson, with her faith and her sly smile, had protected us from them until then, and when she went, all defence went with her.

I need not describe her funeral – it was done by Bickersons: Mr Fulmino arranged it. But one thing astonished us: not only our families but the whole neighbourhood was affected by the death of this woman who, in our carelessness, we thought could hardly be known to anyone. She had lived there all her life, of course, but people come and go in London, only a sluggish residue stay still; and I believe it was just because a large number of passing people knew just a little about her, because she was a fragment in their minds, that her death affected them. They recognised that they themselves were not people but fragments. People remembered her going into shops now and then, or going down to the bus stop, passing down a street. They remembered the bag of American cloth she used to carry containing her sewing – they spoke for a long time afterwards about this bag, more about it, indeed, than about herself.

Bickersons is a few doors from the Lord Nelson, so that when the hearse stood there covered with flowers everyone noticed it, and although the old lady had not been in that public house for years since the death of her husband, all the customers came out to look. And they looked at Hilda sitting in her black in the car when the hearse moved slowly off and all who knew her story must have felt that the dream was burying the dreamer. Hilda's face was dirty with grief and she did not turn her head to right or left as they drove off. I remember a small thing that happened when we were all together at old Mrs Draper's, after we had got her back with difficulty up the stairs.

'Bickersons did it very well,' said Mr Fulmino, seeking to distract the old lady who, swollen with sadness, was uncomfortable in her best clothes. 'They organise everything so well. They gave me this.'

He held up a small brass disc on a little chain. It was one of those identity discs people used to wear on their wrists in the war.

'She had never taken it off,' he said. It swung feebly on its chain. Suddenly, with a sound like a shout Mr Fulmino broke into tears. His face caved in and he apologised: 'It's the feeling,' he said. 'You have the feeling. You feel.' And he looked at us with panic, astonished by this discovery of an unknown self, spongy with tears, that had burst out and against whom he was helpless.

Mrs Fulmino said gently:

'I expect Hilda would like to have it.'

'Yes, yes. It's for her,' he said, drying his eyes and Hilda took it from him and carried it to her room. While she was there (and perhaps she was weeping too), Mr Fulmino looked out from his handkerchief and said, still sobbing:

'I see that the luggage has gone.'

None of us had noticed this and we looked at Constance who said in a whisper: 'She is leaving us. She has found a room of her own.' That knocked us back. 'Leaving!' we exclaimed. It told against Hilda for, although we talked of death being a release for the dead person we did not like to think of it as a release for the living; grief ought to hold people together and it seemed too brisk to have started a new life so soon. Constance alone looked pleased by this. We were whispering but stopped when we heard Hilda coming back.

Black had changed her. It set off her figure and although crying had hardened her, the skin of her neck and her arms and the swell of her breasts seemed more living than they had before. She looked stronger in body perhaps because she was shaken in mind. She looked very real, very present, more alive than ourselves. She had not heard us whispering, but she said, to all of us, but particularly to Mr Fulmino:

'I have found a room for myself. Constance spoke to Bill Williams for me, he's good at getting things. He found me a place and he took the luggage round yesterday. I couldn't sleep in that bed alone any more.'

Her voice was shaky.

'She didn't take up much room. She was tiny and we managed. It was like sleeping with a little child.'

Hilda smiled and laughed a little.

'She even used to kick like a kid.'

Ten minutes on the bus from Hincham Street and close to the centre of London is a dance hall called 'The Temple Rooms'. It has two bands, a low gallery where you can sit and a soft drink bar. Quite a few West Indians go there, mainly students. It is a respectable place; it closes at eleven and there is never any trouble. Iris and I went there once or twice. One evening we were surprised to see Constance and Bill Williams dancing there. Iris pointed to them. The rest of the people were jiving, but Bill Williams and Constance were dancing in the old-fashioned way.

'Look at his feet!' Iris laughed.

Bill Williams was paying no attention to Constance, but looking around the room over her head as he stumbled along. He was tall.

'Fancy Auntie Constance!' said Iris. 'She's getting fed up because he won't listen.'

Constance Draper dancing! At her age! Thirty-eight!

'It's since the funeral,' said Mr Fulmino over our usual cup of tea. 'She was fond of the old lady. It's upset her.'

Even I knew Mr Fulmino was wrong about this. The madness of Constance dated from the time Bill Williams had taken Hilda's luggage round to her room and got her a job at the reception desk in the factory at Laxton. It dated from the time, a week later, when standing at old Mrs Draper's early one evening, Constance had seen Hilda get out of Bill Williams's van. He had given her a lift home. It dated from words that passed between Hilda and Constance soon afterwards. Hilda said Williams hung around for her at the factory and wanted her to go to a dance. She did not want to go, she said – and here came the fatal sentences – both of her husbands had been educated men. Constance kept her temper but said coldly:

'Bill Williams is politically educated.'

Hilda had her vacant look.

'Not his hands aren't,' she said.

The next thing, Constance – who hardly went into a pub in her life – was in the Lord Nelson night after night, playing bar billiards with Bill Williams. She never let him out of her sight. She came out of school and instead of going home, marking papers and getting a meal for herself and old Mrs Draper, she took the bus out to the factory and waited for him to come out. Sometimes he had left on some job by the time she got there and she came home, beside herself, questioning everybody. It had been her habit to come twice a week to change her library books. Now she did not come. She stopped reading. At The Temple Rooms, when Iris and I saw her, she sat out holding hands with Bill Williams and rubbing her head into his shoulder, her eyes watching him the whole time. We went to speak to them and Constance asked:

'Is Hilda here tonight?'

'I haven't seen her.'

'She's a whore,' said Constance in a loud voice. We thought she was drunk.

It was a funny thing, Mr Fulmino said to me, to call a woman a whore. He spoke as one opposed to funny things.

'If they'd listened to me,' he said, 'I could have stopped all this trouble. I offered to get her a job in the Council Offices but,' he rolled his eyes, 'Mrs F. wouldn't have it and while we were arguing about it, Bill Williams acts double quick. It's all because this Mr Gloster didn't turn up.'

Mr Fulmino spoke wistfully. He was, he conveyed, in the middle of a family battle; indeed, he had a genuine black eye the day we talked about this. Mrs Fulmino's emotions were in her arms.

This was a bad period for Mr Fulmino because he had committed a folly. He had chosen this moment to make a personal triumph. He had got himself promoted to a much better job at the Council Offices and one entitling him to a pension. He had become a genuine official. To have promoted a man who had the folly to bring home a rich whore with two names, so causing the robbery and death of her mother, and to have let her break Constance's heart, was, in Mrs Fulmino's words, a crime. Naturally, Mr Fulmino regarded his mistakes as mere errors of routine and even part of his training for his new position.

'Oh well,' he said when we finished our tea and got up to pay the bill, 'it's the British taxpayer that pays.' He was heading for politics. I have heard it said, years later, that if he had had a better start in life he would have gone to the top of the administration. It is a tragic calling.

If Hilda was sinister to Constance and Mrs Fulmino, she made a different impression on young Mrs Draper. To call a woman a whore was neither here nor there to her. Up North where she came from people were saying that sort of thing all day long as they scrubbed floors or cleaned windows or did the washing. The word gave them energy and made things come up cleaner and whiter. Good money was earned hard; easy money went easy. To young Mrs Draper Hilda seemed 'a bit simple', but she had gone to work, she earned her living. Cut off from the rest of the Draper family, Hilda made friends with this couple. Hilda went with them on Saturday to the Zoo with the children. They were looking at a pair of monkeys. One of them was dozing and its companion was awake, pestering and annoying it. The children laughed. But when they moved on to another cage, Hilda said, sulkily:

'That's one thing. Bill Williams won't be here. He pesters me all the time.'

'He won't if you don't let him,' said young Mrs Draper.

'I'm going to give my notice if he doesn't stop,' said Hilda. She hunched a shoulder and looked around at the animals.

'I can't understand a girl like Constance taking up with him. He's not on her level. And he's mean. He doesn't give her anything. I asked if he gave her that clip, but she said it was Gran's. Well, if a man doesn't give you anything he doesn't value you. I mean she's a well-read girl.'

'There's more ways than one of being stupid,' said young Mrs Draper.

'I wonder she doesn't see,' said Hilda. 'He's not delivering for the firm. When he's got the van out, he's doing something on the side. When I came home with him there was stuff at the back. And he keeps on asking how much things cost. He offered to sell my bracelet.'

'You'd get a better price in a shop if you're in need,' said young Mrs Draper.

'She'd better not be with him if he gets stopped on the road,' said Jack, joining in. 'You wouldn't sell that. Your husband gave it you.'

'No. Mr Faulkner,' said Hilda, pulling out her arm and admiring it.

Jack was silent and disappointed; then he cheered up.

'You ought to have married that earl you were always talking about when you were a girl. Do you remember?' he said.

'Earls – they're a lazy lot,' said young Mrs Draper.

'I did, Jack,' said Hilda. 'They were as good as earls, both of them.'

And to young Mrs Draper she said: 'They wouldn't let another man look at me. I felt like a woman with both of them.'

[479]

'I've nowt against that if you've got the time,' said young Mrs Draper. She saw that Hilda was glum.

'Let's go back and look at the giraffes. Perhaps Mr Faulkner will come for you now Mr Gloster hasn't,' young Mrs Draper said.

'They were friends,' said Hilda.

'Oh, they knew each other!' said young Mrs Draper. 'I thought you just . . . met them . . .'

'No, I didn't meet them together, but they were friends.'

'Yes. Jack had a friend, didn't you?' said Mrs Draper, remembering.

'That's right,' said Jack. He winked at Hilda. 'Neck and neck, it was.' And then he laughed outright.

'I remember something about Bill Williams. He came out with us one Saturday and you should have seen his face when we threw the fish back in the water.'

'We always throw them back,' said young Mrs Draper taking her husband's arm, proudly.

'Wanted to sell them or something. Black market perch!'

'He thinks I've got dollars,' said Hilda.

'No, fancy that, Jack – Mr Gloster and Mr Faulkner being friends. Well, that's nice.' And she looked sentimentally at Hilda.

'She's brooding,' young Mrs Draper said to Mrs Fulmino after this visit to the Zoo. 'She won't say anything.' Mrs Fulmino said she had better not or *she* might say something. 'She knows what I think. I never thought much of Bill Williams, but he served his country. She didn't.'

'She earns her living,' said Mrs Draper.

'Like we all do,' said Mrs Fulmino. 'And it's not men, men, men all day long with you and me.'

'One's enough,' said young Mrs Draper, 'with two children round your feet.'

'She doesn't come near me,' said Mrs Fulmino.

'No,' Mr Fulmino said sadly, 'after all we've done.'

They used to laugh at me when I went dancing with Iris at The Temple Rooms. We had not been there for more than a month and Iris said: 'He can't stop staring at the band.'

She was right. The beams of the spotlights put red, green, violet and orange tents on the hundreds of dancers. It was like the Arabian Nights. When we got there, Ted Coster's band was already at it like cats on dustbins and tearing their guts out. The pianist had a very thin neck and kept wagging his head as if he were ga-ga; if his head had fallen off he would have caught it in one of his crazy hands and popped it on again without losing a note; the trumpet player had thick eyebrows that went higher and higher as he tried and failed to burst; the drummers looked doped; the saxophone went at it like a man in bed with a girl who had purposely left the door open. I remember them all, especially the thin-lipped man, very white-faced, with the double bass drawing his bow at knee level, to and fro, slowly, sinful. They all whispered, nodded and rocked together, telling dirty stories until bang, bang, bang, the dancers went faster and faster, the row hit the ceiling or died out with the wheeze of a balloon. I was entranced.

'Don't look as though you're going to kill someone,' Iris said.

That shows how wrong people are. I was full of love and wanted to cry.

After four dances I went off to the soft drink bar and there the first person I saw was Bill Williams. He was wearing a plum-coloured suit and a red and silver tie and he stood, with his dark hair dusty-looking and sprouting forward as if he had just got out of bed and was ducking his head on the way to the bathroom.

'All the family here?' he asked, looking all round.

'No,' I said. 'Just Iris and me.'

He went on looking around him.

'I thought you only came Saturdays,' he said suspiciously. He had a couple of friends with him, two men who became restless on their feet, as if they were dancing, when I came up.

'Oh,' said Bill Williams. Then he said, 'Nicky pokey doda – that's Japanese, pal, for keep your mouth shut. Anyone say anything, you never see me. I'm at Laxton, get me? Bill Williams? He's on night shift. You must be barmy. OK? Seeing you,' he said. 'No sign of Constance.'

And he walked off. His new friends went a step or two after him, dancing on their pointed shoes, and then stopped. They twizzled round, tapping their feet, looking all round the room until he had got to the carpeted stairs at the end of the hall. I got my squash and when I turned round, the two men had gone too.

But before Bill Williams had got to the top of the stairs he turned round to look at the dancers in one corner. There was Hilda. She was dancing with a young West Indian. When I got back to our table she was very near.

I have said that Hilda's face was eventless. It was now in a tranced state, looking from side to side, to the floor, in the quick turns of the dance, swinging round, stepping back, stepping forward. The West Indian had a long jacket on. His knees were often nearly bent double as though he were going to do some trick of crawling towards her, then he recovered himself and turned his back as if he had never met her and was dancing with someone else. If Hilda's face was eventless, it was the event itself, it was the dance.

She saw us when the dance was over and came to our table breathlessly. She was astonished to see us. To me she said, 'And fancy you!' She did not laugh or even smile when she looked at me. I don't know how to describe her look. It was dead. It had no expression. It had nothing. Or rather, by the smallest twitch of a muscle, it became nothing. Her face had the nakedness of a body. She saw that I was deaf to what Iris was saying. Then she smiled and in doing that, she covered herself.

'I am with friends over there' – we could not tell who the friends were – then she leaned to us and whispered:

'Bill Williams is here too.'

Iris exclaimed.

'He's watching me,' Hilda said.

'I saw him,' I said. 'He's gone.'

Hilda stood up frowning.

'Are you sure? Did you see him? How long ago?'

I said it was about five minutes before.

She stood as I remember her standing in Mrs Draper's room on the first day when she arrived and was kissing everyone. It was a peculiar stance because she usually stood so passively; a stance of action and, I now saw, a stance of plain fright. One leg was planted forward and bent at the knee like a runner at the start and one arm was raised and bent at the elbow, the elbow pushed out beyond her body. Her mouth was open and her deep-set yellow eyes seemed to darken and look tired.

'He was with some friends,' I said and, looking back at the bar, 'They've gone now.'

'Hah!' It was the sound of a gasp of breath. Then suddenly the fright went and she shrugged her shoulders and talked and laughed to all of us. Soon she went over to her friends, the coloured man and a white couple; she must have got some money or the ticket for her handbag from one of them, for presently we saw her walking quickly to the cloak-room.

Iris went on dancing. We must have stayed another half an hour and when we were leaving we were surprised to see Hilda waiting in the foyer. She said to me:

'His car has gone.'

'Whose?'

'Bill Williams's car.'

'Has he got a car?' Iris said.

'Oh, it's not his,' said Hilda. 'It's gone. That's something. Will you take me home? I don't want to go alone. They followed me here.'

She looked at all of us. She was frightened.

I said, 'Iris and I will take you on our way.'

'Don't make me late,' said Iris crossly. 'You know what Mum is.' I promised. 'Did you come with him?'

'No, with someone else,' Hilda said, looking nervously at the glass swing door. 'Are you sure his friends went too? What did they look like?'

I tried to describe them.

'I've seen the short one,' she said, frowning, 'somewhere.'

It was only a quarter of an hour's ride at that hour of the night. We walked out of The Temple Rooms and across the main road to the bus stop and waited under the lights that made our faces corpse-like. I have always liked the hard and sequinned sheen of London streets at night, their empty dockyard look. The cars come down them like rats. The red trolley bus came up at last and when we got in Hilda sat between us. The bus-load of people stared at her and I am not surprised. I have said what she looked like – the hair built up high, her bright green wrap and red dress. I don't know how you would describe such clothes. But the people were not staring at her clothes. They were staring at her eyebrows. I said before that her face was an extension of her nudity and I say it again. Those eyebrows of hers were painted and looked like the only things she had on – they were like a pair of beetles with turned-up tails that had settled on her forehead. People laughed under their hands and two or three youths at the front of the bus turned round and guffawed and jostled and whistled; but Hilda, remember, was not a girl of sixteen gone silly, but a woman, hard rather than soft in the face, and the effect was one of exposure, just as a mask has the effect of exposing.

We did not talk but when the trolley arm thumped two or three times at a street junction, Hilda said with a sigh, 'Bump! Bump! Bump!' She was thinking of her childhood in old Mrs Draper's room at Hincham Street. We got off the bus a quarter of a mile further on and, as she was stepping off, Hilda said, speaking of what was in her mind, I suppose, during the ride:

'Shinji had a gold wrist-watch with a gold strap and a golden pen. They had gone when he was killed. They must have cost him a hundred pounds. Someone must have stolen them and sold them.

'I reported it,' Hilda said. 'I needed the money. That is what you had to do – sell something. I had to eat.'

And the stare from her mask of a face stated something of her life that her strangeness had concealed from us. We walked up the street.

She went on talking about that watch and how particular Shinji was about his clothes, especially his shirts. All his collars had to be starched, she said. Those had gone too, she said. And his glasses. And his two gold rings. She walked very quickly between us. We got to the corner of her street. She stopped and looked down it.

'Bill Williams's van!' she said.

About thirty houses down the street we could indeed see a small van standing.

'He's waiting for me,' she said.

It was hard to know whether she was frightened or whether she was reckoning, but my heart jumped. She made us stand still and watch. 'My room's in the front,' she said. I crossed over to the other side of the street and then came back.

'The light is on,' I said.

'He's inside,' she said.

'Shall I go and see?' I said.

'Go,' said Iris to me.

Hilda held my wrist.

'No,' she said.

'There are two people, I think, in the front garden,' I said.

'I'm going home with you,' Hilda said to Iris decisively. She rushed off and we had to race after her. We crossed two or three streets to the Fulminos' house. Mrs Fulmino let us in.

'Now, now, Hilda, keep your hair on. Kill you? Why should he? This is England, this isn't China . . .'

Mr Fulmino's face showed his agony. His mouth collapsed, his eyes went hard. He looked frantic with appeal. Then he turned his back on us, marched into the parlour and shouted as if he were calling across four lines of traffic:

'Turn the wireless off.'

We followed him into the room. Mrs Fulmino, in the suddenly silent room, looked like a fortress waiting for a flag to fall.

We all started talking at once.

'Can I stay with you tonight?' she said. 'Bill Williams has broken into my house. I can't go there. He'll kill me.' The flag fell.

'Japan,' said Mrs Fulmino disposing of her husband with her first shot. Then she turned to Hilda; her voice was coldly rich and rumbling. 'You've always a home here, as you well know, Hilda,' she went on, giving a very unhomely sound to the word. 'And,' she said, glancing at her neat curtains to anyone who might be in ambush outside the window, 'if anyone tries to kill you, they will have to kill,' she nodded to her husband, 'Ted and me first. What have you been doing?'

'I was down at The Temple. Not with Bill Williams,' said Hilda. 'He was watching me. He's always watching me.'

'Now look here, Hilda, why should Bill Williams want to kill you? Have you encouraged him?'

'Don't be a fool!' shouted Mrs Fulmino.

'She knows what I mean. Listen to me, Hilda. What's going on between you and Bill Williams? Constance is upset, we all know.'

'Oh keep your big mouth shut,' said Mrs Fulmino. 'Of course she's encouraged him. Hilda's a woman, isn't she? I encouraged you, didn't I?'

'I know how to look after myself,' said Hilda, 'but I don't like that van outside the house at this hour of night, I didn't speak to him at the dance.'

'Hilda's thinking of the police,' ventured Mr Fulmino.

'Police!' said Mrs Fulmino. 'Do you know what's in the van?'

'No,' said Hilda. 'And that's what I don't want to know. I don't want him on my doorstep. Or his friends. He had two with him. Harry saw them.'

Mrs Fulmino considered.

'I'm glad you've come to us. I wish you'd come to us in the first place,' she said. Then she commanded Mr Fulmino: 'You go up there at once with Harry,' she said to him, 'and tell that man to leave Hilda alone. Go on, now. I can't understand you' – she indicated me – 'running off like that, leaving a van there. If you don't go I'll go myself. I'm not afraid of a paltry . . . a paltry . . . what does he call himself? You go up.'

Mrs Fulmino was as good a judge of the possibilities of an emotional situation as any woman on earth: this was her moment. She wanted us out of the house and Hilda to herself.

We obeyed.

Mr Fulmino and I left the house. He looked tired. He was too tired to put on his jacket. He went out in his shirt sleeves.

'Up and down we go, in and out, up and down,' said Mr Fulmino. 'First it's Constance, now it's Hilda. And the pubs are closed.'

'There you are, what did I tell you?' said Mr Fulmino when we got to Hilda's street. 'No van, no sign of it, is there? You're a witness. We'll go up and see all the same.'

Mr Fulmino had been alarmed but now his confidence came back. He gave me a wink and a nod when we got to the house.

'Leave it to me,' he said. 'You wait here.'

I heard him knock at the door and after a time knock again. Then I heard a woman's voice. He was talking a long time. He came away.

He was silent for a long time as we walked. At last he said:

'That beats all. I didn't say anything. I didn't say who I was. I didn't let on. I just asked to see Hilda. "Oh," says the landlady, "she's out." "Oh," I said, "that's a surprise." I didn't give a name – "Out you say?

When will she be back?" "I don't know," said the landlady, and this is it, Harry – "she's paid her rent and given her notice. She's leaving first thing in the morning," the landlady said. "They came for the luggage this evening." Harry,' said Mr Fulmino, 'did Hilda say anything about leaving?'

'No.'

'Bill Williams came for her luggage.'

We marched on. Or rather we went stealthily along like two men walking a steel wire of suspicion. We almost lost our balance when two cats ran across the street and set up howls in a garden, as if they were howling us down. Mr Fulmino stopped.

'Harry!' he said. 'She's playing us up. She's going off with Bill Williams.'

'But she's frightened of him. She said he was going to kill her.'

'I'm not surprised,' said Mr Fulmino. 'She's been playing him up. Who was she with at the dance hall? She's played everyone up. Of course she's frightened of him. You bet. I'm sorry for anyone getting mixed up with Bill Williams – he'll knock some sense into her. He's rough. So was her father.'

'Bill Williams might have just dropped by to have a word,' I said.

'Funny word at half past eleven at night,' said Mr Fulmino. 'When I think of all that correspondence, all those forms – War Office, State Department, United Nations – we did, it's been a poor turn-out. You might say,' he paused for an image sufficiently devastating, 'a waste of paper, a ruddy wanton waste of precious paper.'

We got back to his house. I have never mentioned, I believe, that it had an iron gate that howled, a noise that always brought Mrs Fulmino to her curtains, and a clipped privet hedge, like a moustache, to the tiny garden.

We opened the gate, the gate howled, Mrs Fulmino's nose appeared at the curtains.

'Don't say a word,' said Mr Fulmino.

Tea – the room smelled of that, of course. Mrs Fulmino had made some while we were out. She looked as though she had eaten something too. A titbit. They all looked sorry for Mr Fulmino and me. And Mrs Fulmino *had* had a titbit! In fact I know from Iris that the only thing Mrs Fulmino had got out of Hilda was the news that she had had a postcard from Mr Faulkner from Chicago. He was on the move.

'Well?' said Mrs Fulmino.

'It's all right, Hilda,' said Mr Fulmino coldly. 'They've gone.'

'There,' said Mrs Fulmino, patting Hilda's hand.

'Hilda,' said Mr Fulmino, 'I've been straight with you. I want you to be straight with me. What's going on between you and Bill Williams . . . ?'

'Hilda's told me . . .' Mrs Fulmino said.

'I asked Hilda, not you,' said Mr Fulmino to his wife, who was so surprised that she went very white instead of her usual purple.

'Hilda, come on. You come round here saying he's going to kill you. Then they tell me you've given your notice up there.'

'She told me that. I think she's done the right thing.'

'And did you tell her why you gave your notice?' asked Mr Fulmino.

'She's given her notice at the factory too,' said Mrs Fulmino.

'Why?' said Mr Fulmino.

Hilda did not answer.

'You are going off with Bill Williams, aren't you?'

'Ted!' Hilda gave one of her rare laughs.

'What's this?' cried Mrs Fulmino. 'Have you been deceiving me? Deceit I can't stand, Hilda.'

'Of course she is,' said Mr Fulmino. 'She's paid her rent. He's collected her luggage this evening – where is it to be? Monte Carlo? Oh, it's all right, sit down,' Mr Fulmino waved Mrs Fulmino back. 'They had a row at the dance this evening.'

But Hilda was on her feet.

'My luggage,' she cried, holding her bag with both hands to her bosom as we had seen her do once before when she was cornered. 'Who has touched my luggage?'

I thought she was going to strike Mr Fulmino.

'The dirty thief. Who let him in? Who let him take it? Where's he gone?'

She was moving to the door. We were stupefied.

'Bill Williams!' she shouted. Her rage made those artificial eyebrows look comical and I expected her to pick them off and throw them at us. 'Bill Williams I'm talking about. Who let that bloody war hero in? That bitch up there . . .'

'Hilda,' said Mr Fulmino. 'We don't want language.'

'You fool,' said Mrs Fulmino in her lowest, most floor-pervading voice to her husband. 'What have you been and done? You've let Bill Williams get away with all those cases, all her clothes, everything. You let that spiv strip her.'

'Go off with Bill Williams!' Hilda laughed. 'My husband was an officer.'

'I knew he was after something. I thought it was dollars,' she said suddenly.

She came back from the door and sat down at the table and sobbed.

'Two hundred and fifty pounds, he's got,' she sobbed. It was a sight to see Hilda weeping. We could not speak.

'It's all I had,' she said.

We watched Hilda. The painted eyebrows made the grimace of her weeping horrible. There was not one of us who was not shocked. There was in all of us a sympathy we knew how to express but which was halted – as by a fascination – with the sight of her ruin. We could not help contrasting her triumphant arrival with her state at this moment. It was as if we had at last got her with us as we had, months before, expected her to be. Perhaps she read our thoughts. She looked up at us and she had the expression of a person seeing us for the first time. It was like an inspection.

'You're a mean lot, a mean respectable lot,' she said. 'I remember you. I remember when I was a girl. What was it Mr Singh said, I can't remember – he was clever – oh well, leave it, leave it. When I saw that little room they put my poor mother in, I could have cried. No sun. No warmth in it. You just wanted someone to pity. I remember it. And your faces. The only thing that was nice was,' she sobbed and laughed for a moment, 'was bump, bump, bump, the trolley.' She said loudly: 'There's only one human being in the whole crew – Jack Draper. I don't wonder he sees more in fish.'

She looked at me scornfully. 'Your brother – he was nice,' she said. 'Round the park at night! That was love.'

'Hilda,' said Mrs Fulmino without anger. 'We've done our best for you. If we've made mistakes I hope you haven't. We haven't had your life. You talk about ships that pass in the night, I don't know what you mean, but I can tell you there are no ships in this house. Only Ted.'

'That's right,' said Mr Fulmino quietly too. 'You're overwrought.'

'Father,' said Mrs Fulmino, 'hadn't you better tell the police?'

'Yes, yes, dear,' agreed Mr Fulmino. 'We'd better get in touch with the authorities.'

'Police,' said Hilda, laughing in their faces. 'Oh God! Don't worry about that. You've got one in every house in this country.' She picked up her bag, still laughing, and went to the door.

'Police,' she was saying, 'that's ripe.'

'Hilda, you're not to go out in the street looking like that,' said Mrs Fulmino.

'I'd better go with her,' said Mr Fulmino.

'I'll go,' I said. They were glad to let me.

It is ten years since I walked with Hilda to her lodgings. I shall not forget it, and the warm, dead, rubbery city night. It is frightening to walk with a woman who has been robbed and wronged. Her eyes were half-closed as though she was reckoning as she walked. I had to pull her back on to the pavement or she would have gone flat into a passing car. The only thing she said to me was:

'They took Shinji's rings as well.'

Her room was on the ground floor. It had a divan and a not very clean dark green cover on it. A pair of shoes were sticking out from under it. There was a plain deal cupboard and she went straight to it. Two dresses were left. The rest had gone. She went to a table and opened the drawer. It was empty except for some letters.

I stood not knowing what to say. She seemed surprised to see me there still.

'He's cleared the lot,' she said vacantly. Then she seemed to realise that she was staring at me without seeing me for she lowered her angry shoulders.

'We'll get them back,' I said.

'How?' she said, mocking me, but not unkindly.

'I will,' I said. 'Don't be upset.'

'You!' she said.

'Yes, I will,' I said.

I wanted to say more. I wanted to touch her. But I couldn't. The ruin had made her untouchable.

[490]

'What are you going to do?' I said.

'Don't worry about me,' she said. 'I'm okey-doke. You're different from your brother. You don't remember those days. I told Mr Gloster about him. Come to that, Mr Faulkner too. They took it naturally. That was a fault of Mr Singh' – she never called him by his Christian name – 'jealousy.'

She kicked off her shoes and sat down on the cheap divan and frowned at the noise it made and she laughed.

'One day in Bombay I got homesick and he asked me what I was thinking about and I was green, I just said "Sid Fraser's neck. It had a mole on it" – you should have seen his face. He wouldn't talk to me for a week. It's a funny thing about those countries. Some people might rave about them, I didn't see anything to them."

She got up.

'You go now,' she said laughing. 'I must have been in love.'

I dreamed about Hilda's face all night and in the morning I wouldn't have been surprised to see London had been burned out to a cinder. But the next night her face did not come and I had to think about it. Further and further it went, a little less every day and night, and I did not seem to notice when someone said Bill Williams had been picked up by the police, or when Constance had been found half dead with aspirins, and when, in both cases, Mr Fulmino told me he had to 'give assistance in the identification', for Hilda had gone. She left the day after I took her to her room. Where she went no one knew. We guessed. We imagined. Across water, I thought, getting further and further away, in very fine clothes and very beautiful. France, Mr Fulmino thought, or possibly Italy. Africa, even. New York, San Francisco, Tokyo, Bombay, Singapore. Where? Even one day six months after she had left when he came to the library and showed me a postcard he had had from her, the first message, it did not say where she was and someone in the post office had pulled off the stamp. It was a picture of Hilda herself on a seat in a park, sitting with Mr Faulkner and Mr Gloster. You wouldn't recognise her.

But Mr Gloster's book came out. Oh yes. It wasn't about Japan or India or anything like that. It was about us.

The Necklace

———

'Just checking up on a necklace your wife took to Cleaver's,' the older
of the two detectives said to me when I got to the police station. He was
sucking a peppermint and was short of breath. The younger one kept his
hands in his raincoat pockets and didn't say a word, and neither did I.
We went into an inner room and sat down. I was afraid of having a smile
too big for my face; my mouth was watering. All the time, I could feel
the words swelling up in me: 'We only did our duty.' If you find something
in the street, you take it to the police. Of course, if it's valuable you may
get a reward. But not necessarily. Anyway, you don't do it for the reward.
But all that week I'd kept my eyes open for a notice saying 'Reward'.
Then the young detective pulled the necklace out of his pocket and put
it on the table. 'Do you recognise this, Mr Drayton?' he asked.

I recognised it at once. 'That's it,' I said. 'I found it Saturday.'

Exactly where, they asked, and what time? I told them.

'Do you know who it belongs to?' they asked.

'If I'd known, I would have taken it to them,' I said. It was a silly
question, and the next ones were silly, too.

'It doesn't belong to you?' the young one asked.

'Or your wife?' asked the older one.

'Definitely not,' I said. 'I found it in the street, I told you.'

'Do you know a Mrs Faber?' the young one asked me.

'No,' I said. 'What's she got to do with it?'

'You're a window cleaner, aren't you?' asked the older one. 'She lives
at 17 Launceston Road. Do you do a job there?'

'No,' I said. 'I do 24, 51, and the flats at the end. What's the idea?'

'And you say you found it at the corner of Alston Street and the
Promenade on Saturday?'

'That's it. I just told you,' I said.

'Just checking up. We have to check up on all lost property,' said the older one. And the young one must have had a nod from him, because he got up and left the room. I looked up at the dark green, glossy walls and the frosted window, and then I heard Nell's voice and her heels on the floor outside in the passage.

I sat there trying to remember everything as her voice came nearer, but there wasn't time. The one thing I could think of was Saturday, 11th January: all that rain, and the football match – we beat Hopley Rangers, 3–0. Even when I have been going over it since, my mind gets stuck there. Saturdays, in the season, I used to pack up the job early and go home to my dinner, and when Plushy came round – my mate, Plushy Edwards – we would go off. We'd both been playing for the Rovers a couple of years. Nell sometimes came, too, but she didn't take to Plushy much. Come to that, she must have hated him. It went back to the time when she first met me, and Plushy told her I was a married man with two children and not to break up a happy home. Plushy was always having a lark like that with her. 'I don't like men who tell lies,' Nell said. It worried her when people made jokes. She really believed them.

But as I say: Saturday, football, I am coming round Alston Street off the Promenade, on my way home, and there it is: a necklace with three strands of big pearls, lying in the gutter. I looked up and down the Promenade. The weather was squally; the rain had browned the pebbles on the beach and had softened the sishing of the sea. The only moving things in sight were the back of a bus that had passed, and two or three children running out of the rain a long way off, and the seagulls. I looked down at the gutter again. It surprised me the necklace was still there. I propped my bike against a lamp and went back and picked the thing up. The pearls were hard and cold, like rice, but wet. I wiped the dirt off them and looked up at the windows of the houses. If there had been someone looking out, I would have shouted, 'Anyone lost anything?' There was no one. I don't mind admitting that seeing a thing like this upset me. In this job, you see money, watches, and rings left about on desks and dressing tables the whole time. It doesn't worry me, but it annoys me. People miss something, and the next thing they're saying, 'It's the window cleaner.' I put the necklace into my pocket and I got on my bike. But the rain started coming down hard now, and I thought,

'This means no blooming football.' Plushy was waiting at my house already, just as fed up as I was about the weather. The necklace went out of my head.

'Here, lay off. I'm a bachelor,' said Plushy when I kissed my wife.

'You're late,' she said to me. She always said that. 'You two aren't playing football in this, are you? You're wet.'

'Yes, look at his hair. That German crop never suited him, did it, Nell?' said Plushy, starting his usual larks, and pretending to dribble a ball round our kitchen as he spoke. 'And where have you been? Hill Street? That blonde at 27, I bet. Look at his face! No, he's not been near Hill Street – oh, no! Dear, oh dear, oh dear!'

'I did Launceston Road this morning,' I said.

'I thought you were going up the Avenue,' my wife said. Her grey eyes looked empty and truthful.

'I did the Avenue yesterday,' I said.

We had been married two years, and this was her way of loving me – knowing everything I did. Now and then, she overloved me by getting it wrong. When I was out on the job, I would have the idea she was with me, because I was always thinking of her. So when she said she thought I was up the Avenue, I felt confused, as if she had been up there and I hadn't spotted her; or as if I ought to say I had been up the Avenue, so that she wouldn't have missed me. See what I mean? Sounds silly. I was so soppy about her that I didn't know which was me and which was Nell.

'Coming to the game, Nell?' Plushy asked her, and when she said she had something better to do than stand in the mud and the rain, Plushy left me alone and started on her. 'What's she up to, Jim?' he asked me.

'Ironing,' she said. 'I'm sorry for the poor girl who has to do yours. Have you found her?'

'There'll be no tears at Plushy's wedding,' I said. It was one of my mother's sayings.

'It'll be more like a court case,' Nell said seriously.

'Jim, she means it,' said Plushy.

I changed my clothes, and at two o'clock Plushy and I went off.

I took up window cleaning when I came out of the Army. Plushy persuaded me into it. The money was good. He said he'd heard women all over the country crying out loud in every street to get their windows cleaned. 'Just count the windows in this town,' he said to me. 'More windows than people. Every window a ruddy SOS. Someone's got to do them.' But Plushy got fed up with it after a year. The women got him down. 'They're screaming all day for you,' he said. 'You turn up and it's the wrong time. Women at you all day long – following you round the house, watching to see you don't mark their curtains or spoil their carpets, calling upstairs to someone to lock the drawers: "It's the window cleaner." Like they'd got the burglars in.' Plushy went off to work in a factory, but I liked being on my own. I stayed on, took over some of his customers. That is how I met Nell.

'Bad luck to see the new moon through glass,' Plushy said when I told him about meeting her, and she did look sort of moony. She was in the back bedroom of a house in the Avenue, fixing her ear-rings and doing up her face, when I came up the ladder outside. She had reddish hair brushed up so that it was like new copper lit by electric light. Her face was broad, calm, and white. It was my sister who started me using the word 'empty' about Nell's grey eyes. It was not the word I would have used myself, but her eyes did make me feel I was going to fall clean through them. When she looked up and saw me (my washleather had squeaked on the pane), I nearly fell off the ladder. She took her hand from her ear so quickly that she knocked a scent bottle over, and at the same time she shut one of the drawers with her knee.

A man like Plushy, who upset some of the customers by singing non-stop while he worked, would have taken his comb out and run it through his hair and gone on singing. So he made out when I told him. It's a lie. He would have done just what I did. I opened the window and climbed in and said, 'Sorry, miss. Let me wipe it up with the leather. If your old lady carries on, say it was the window cleaner.'

She stood over me, looking insulted, and watched me wipe the scent off the carpet with the leather. The only thanks I got was 'Close the window when you go out. My Aunt Mary won't mind about the rug.' I swear she said 'My Aunt Mary', but afterward she swore she didn't. The woman she worked for was misnamed Mrs Merry – a gloomy lady in a houseful of books (I never saw so many), with a voice like a high-class ship going out to sea, very snobby – so I might have made a mistake.

But it took a bit of time for me to get it into my mind that Nell was not the niece of this rich old bookworm.

Fate is a funny thing. Once it gets going, it never stops. I'd been working at different houses in the Avenue for more than a year and I had never set eyes on Nell, but now I seemed to run across her one day after the other. I asked her if her aunt had been angry about the scent.

'No,' Nell said. 'She didn't mind. That's not my aunt. My aunt's in Manchester. I'm the maid.'

I felt a fool trying to puzzle this out. Nell looked up and down the street, as if she were looking for someone. 'I told her,' she said. 'She didn't mind.'

'The lady you work for, you mean?' I asked.

'No, my Aunt Mary, in Manchester,' she said. 'I tell her everything.'

I asked her to come out with me, but she changed her mood and said her aunt in Manchester would not like that, and neither would Mrs Merry.

In those early days, it was always the same. This aunt of Nell's in Manchester wouldn't let her do anything. And to talk to Nell was like talking to two people, for she would turn her head aside when I said anything, as if she were discussing it with this old aunt of hers or someone else before she answered. I couldn't make out what age Nell was, either. To see her – short and solid and with her chin up – marching in slow, long steps down the street, she looked obstinate, like a schoolgirl; other times, when we were talking at a street corner, she had a small, disbelieving smile at the corner of her mouth, like a woman of thirty. She confused me. She was one person one minute and another the next. In the end, she said she would come out to the pictures with me, but I had to ask Mrs Merry first.

I have said Mrs Merry was like a ship. She bumped alongside her dining-room table when she came in, and docked at last in an armchair. Not in dry dock – she was rocking a large glass of gin. She asked me a lot of questions about myself, my mother, and my sister, in a hooting sort of voice, and said Nell was a refined, quiet girl and that she didn't like her going out. 'She is an orphan you know,' Mrs Merry said loudly. 'I understand her aunt brought her up. Very carefully – you can see. Her aunt in Manchester.'

When Nell and I left the house, I could hardly speak for the idea that her Aunt Mary was walking beside us. And later I could pretty well feel her sitting beside us at the pictures. I got fed up. We went to a milk bar afterward, and Nell took her coat off. She showed me her bracelet and her wrist-watch.

'Aunt Mary, I bet,' I said.

'Yes,' Nell said, with her nose in the air. 'Aunt Mary.' Her voice was small and soft, and seemed to me to come very clearly from a long way off.

There was no getting away from this aunt of hers. She lived in a huge house, Nell said, that had an enormous lawn in the shape of an oval, with a gravel path round it and a deodar at one end.

'What's a deodar?' I asked.

'A deodar? A tree,' she said. 'In the summer, she used to lie in a hammock under it. She taught me French.' She was an educated girl; you could see that.

But I expect you're thinking what I was thinking: If Nell's aunt was so rich and classy, why was an educated girl like Nell down in this place working as an ordinary maid? I came straight out with it.

'No,' said Nell. She began a lot of remarks with 'No' when I asked her things. 'There was trouble.'

'You got into trouble?' I asked.

'No,' she said. 'Her husband did.'

So Aunt Mary was married. She had got married only two years back, Nell told me. He was an elderly clergyman. I asked Nell what the trouble was. 'It's private,' she said. She just waved her hands. I had expected her to have broad, flat, strong hands, but they were small and plump; when she saw me looking at them, she put them in her lap and folded her fingers into her palms. But I had seen. She had a bad habit: she bit her nails.

I used to remember this when I got to taking her home to see my mother and sister.

'Class – that's all it is,' my sister said. 'Loaded down with Aunt Mary's jewellery and lying in bed all day long doing her face.' She did not like Nell's ladylike accent.

One Saturday, after football, I told Plushy about Nell's Aunt Mary and the clergyman. 'Do you reckon Nell's hiding something?' I asked. 'Has she been in trouble?'

'No,' he said. 'She just doesn't see the funny side.'

'What's funny in it?' I asked.

'Clergyman,' Plushy said.

So on Sunday I decided to get at it, and I asked Nell again about the clergyman.

'No,' she said, in her usual way. 'He was jealous of her giving me things. He had two children of his own. I couldn't stay after that. I can't bear jealousy.'

'What was the clergyman's name?' I asked.

'No, you're going to cause trouble.'

'How could I do that?'

'I don't know,' she said. 'You could. If you go and see him and tell him anything, I'll never speak to you again.'

'I never want to hear the name of Aunt Mary again,' I said. Then I calmed down. 'What about you and me – you know – sort of getting fixed up, married?'

Nell was watching me as if I were trying to steal something from her. She sat there – we were sitting in a shelter by the sea – and she was two girls, one of them looking insulted. I oughtn't to have said that about her aunt. She got up and walked off. It was dark, and she didn't speak all the way home and she shook my hand off her arm when I touched it.

The next morning at eight o'clock, she was outside our house. I went to the gate, and she ran and banged her head hard against my ribs, nearly knocking the wind out of me, and put her arms round me. She was crying. I took her in at the front door into our sitting-room and told the others to keep away.

'She's dead,' she said, sitting back from me. 'Aunt Mary's dead. I told you a lie. She died last year. I couldn't bear her to be dead. She was going to look after me, and she left all her money – everything – to that clergyman. I didn't want her money, but I couldn't bear it. My father's dead, my mother's dead – I couldn't bear any more.'

'There's me,' I said. 'Forget it.'

'I told you a lie,' she sobbed in my arms.

It wasn't long before Plushy came in and we were all laughing – my mother, my sister, even Nell.

'Blooming murderer,' said Plushy when he heard it. 'Look at him. No conscience. Kills a poor girl's auntie just to get his way.'

'Shut up, Plushy,' said my mother. 'The girl's upset.'

'It's easy for you, Ma,' Plushy said. 'But I was getting fond of Aunt Mary.'

Nell gaped at him.

'Well, Nell,' Plushy said. 'He'll have to be your Aunt Mary now.'

And so I was, for, except for some worry about where the clergyman had moved to and how he ought to do something for her – but all this was my mother's argument – Aunt Mary was a back number. Nell and I got married and we were on our own.

The rain stopped in the afternoon on that Saturday when I found the necklace. There was a lot of arguing when we got to the ground about whether we should play, because of the mess the field was in, and when we did start playing, it was a question of which side could stand up. Even chaps who were standing still suddenly fell down. The crowd was killing itself with laughter; you kicked the ball and you were flat on your back. Plushy and three others slid for yards into the Hopley goal and couldn't stop themselves; the Hopley goalie came out at them and went ahead first at Plushy. Their two heads cracked, wood against wood; you could hear it across the field. Plushy lost on this deal. It knocked him out for a few minutes. That is why, after the game, he went to the doctor's instead of coming home and having his tea with Nell and me, as he usually did.

I went back home alone. There was a change in Nell. She had done her ironing and she had put on her blue dress and she had done her hair. I don't mean that sort of change, though. She didn't often laugh, but now she came to me nearly laughing. She had the hot look of too much love. She even had some love left over for Plushy, and was very upset when I told her about him. She couldn't keep still. She rubbed against me like a cat when I sat down to tea, and then she leaned forward to me, pushing her plate nearer, looking at me while I was telling her about the game. Once or twice she interrupted me. 'Sorry, I love you,' she said.

I went on telling her about the game. Presently she sat back and said, 'Haven't you forgotten something?'

She was smiling, but it was a heavy, greedy, large-eyed smile, as if her own natural smile had been made larger by a reflector.

'Have I left the bike out?' Sometimes I forgot to put the bike away.

'Think,' she said. Since we had got married, she liked giving orders. Slowly the smile went.

'No,' she said shortly, and left the room. She really marched out of it. She went into the bedroom. I waited for her to come back, and when she didn't I called out, "I want some more tea!'

She did not answer. I pushed back my chair and went into the bedroom. She was standing at attention, with her back to me, in the middle of the room, doing nothing, with her hands at her sides. She did not turn round. Often when I didn't guess what she was thinking, she used to run off in this way and stand in the next room, stiff and sulking. It would take a long time finding out what was the matter, for the only person she was on speaking terms with was herself. It happened a lot before we were married. But now, when she turned round suddenly, her face was half smiling and appealing. She was wearing the necklace.

When women put on something new, they look high and mighty, as if you had got to get to know them all over again. I don't like it. They also look ten years older. The pearls made Nell's neck look thick. They also made her look as if she wasn't married any longer, unless you could afford to pay the extra. I wished I was rich and could have bought pearls for her – well, not bought them myself but sent her in somewhere to buy them. I don't like those shops.

She came towards me with half a clever tear in one eye. I call it clever; it wasn't real.

'Sorry, sorry,' she said. 'Don't be cross with me. I couldn't help it. The necklace fell out of your pocket . . . It fell out of your pocket when I was putting your overalls away. I wasn't going through your pockets, I swear, if that's what you think. It fell out onto the bed.' And she stepped to the bed and pointed to the place on the green quilt where it had fallen.

Some joke Plushy had once made about his landlady going through his pockets came back to me. For the first time, I knew that Nell had been going through my pockets on and off ever since we were married.

'Nell,' I said, 'that's not a present for you. I didn't buy it. I found it in

the gutter in Alston Street, coming home, dinner-time. You thought it
was for you.'

'Who is it for?' she asked, all her newness going. 'You found it – lying
in the street?'

'It isn't for anyone,' I said. 'I don't know who it belongs to. We'd best
take it to the police station.'

'Police,' she said, frightened.

'Yes,' I said. 'Some poor kid must have dropped it.'

Her face hardened. 'You weren't in Alston Street,' she said. 'You told
Plushy you were in Hill Street. I heard you.'

'No, I didn't,' I said. 'Plushy said that.'

'No, tell me the truth. You're hiding something,' she said. 'Where did
you find it?'

'Easy on,' I said. 'I told you. I found it in the gutter in Alston Street.'

'Then why didn't you tell me? Hiding it in your pocket!'

'I wasn't hiding it. I just put it there.'

'No, tell me the truth,' she said again.

'I am,' I said. 'I'm going to take it round. I forgot it. Some poor kid's
mother is carrying on, I bet.'

'Her mother!' she said. 'Whose mother? Jim, you've bought it for some
girl.' She put her hands to her neck, took the necklace off, and threw it
on the bed. 'Oh!' she cried out. 'You've bought it for some girl! That's
why you were hiding it!' And then she gave a howl and fell sideways on
the bed, crying into the pillow, with her blue dress drawn up above her
knees, and her legs coming out of it in a way so ugly and awful I could
not believe it. I'd seen my mother do this once years ago, and, of course,
I'd seen my sister do it often. She was a past-master; the whole house
stood still when my sister took a dive. But I thought it was the sort of
thing that only went on in our family when I was a child. I said to myself,
'So this is the girl whose aunt used to lie in a hammock under a deodar,
talking French. Class – there's nothing in it!' I wished the time was two
hours ago and I was playing football. I wished Plushy would come round.

'My tea's getting cold,' I said after a bit. It must have been the way I
said it. She sat up at once and came to the kitchen. She poured out the
tea and sat down in front of me, and I liked her better with the necklace
off, but her round face had become square and her white skin was thickly

red down to her neck. Her mouth was as small as a penny. She had picked up the necklace and put it beside her plate.

'I'm waiting,' she said.

'Plushy got hurt this afternoon,' I said. 'He got a crack on the head. You could hear it right across the field.'

She did not answer for a long time, and then she said, 'You told me that.'

I remembered I had.

'How can you tell such lies?' she said. '"Hear it across the field"! No, I'm sick of Plushy. Who are you married to? Is Plushy dead? I hope so.'

'Oh dear, oh dear,' I said.

'Stop talking like Plushy,' she said. 'Who is it for? Who did you buy it for? What's her name? I want the truth!'

'I've told you,' I said.

'Aunt Mary warned me about you,' she said.

'Your Aunt Mary never saw me,' I said. 'Aunt Mary's dead anyway.'

'Before she died,' she said.

Aunt Mary had come back into our lives. It had been so long since we had even mentioned her or her husband that I could hardly remember who she was for the moment. I realised what a long way we had travelled since Aunt Mary's time, and I thought of what my mother had once said about how quickly the dead drop back into the past. But having her brought back like this from the grave, in this tone, woke up my old jealousy. I admit it; I was jealous of Aunt Mary.

'Please, Jim,' Nell said, in a softer, pleading voice. 'Who did you buy it for? Why did you do Hill Street this morning?'

So we went over the streets again: Launceston Road, the Promenade, Alston Street, across the High Street . . .

'You bought it at Cleaver's,' she said.

'Learn some geography,' I said. 'I wasn't near Cleaver's.'

'Learn it!' she sobbed. 'That's all I do. I sit here all day thinking of where you are – one girl after another, just like Plushy.'

'You're jealous,' I said.

'Of course I'm jealous!' she shouted, in a thick, curdled voice like a man's.

'Now look –' I said. I put my hand on hers, and she did not take it away. She turned her head from me and then said quietly, as though she were speaking to the necklace, 'I know you found it, Jim. I'm sorry, I'm sorry.'

I didn't say anything, and after a moment she said softly, 'A valuable thing like that.'

'It's just Woolworth trash,' I said.

'Look at the clip,' she said fearfully, handing the necklace to me. 'It's worth hundreds.'

'Get away!' I said.

'It is. I know it is,' she said.

I picked up the necklace. The clip meant nothing to me, but, hearing her soft, truthful voice again, I felt sad. 'Put it on again,' I said. 'You looked nice in it.'

'Oh, I couldn't do that,' she said. 'It isn't ours.'

'Go on. You put it on before. Let's see you. Just once more,' I said. 'It's yours,' I said, laughing. I have explained she did not like jokes. She frowned. Then she leaned nearer to me but not looking at me – as if not to see me. 'Jim,' she said, in a very low voice. 'You didn't find it in the street. Truthfully, you didn't, did you? I won't say anything.'

'What do you mean?'

'You knocked it off,' she said.

The way she said this, as if she were whispering in my ear in the dark, frightened and excited me. Now she was searching my face for some hint or clue. There was a long silence between us.

I reached for the necklace and said, 'I'm going round to the police with it now. I'm not a thief.' But as I reached, there was a flash in her eyes and she snatched at it, too, as quickly as a cat.

'There'll be a reward!' she said, jumping up and standing away from me. We must have both caught the necklace, because it snapped and all the pearls scattered onto the carpet and over the lino. It was like during the war, when our corporal got his false teeth knocked out in the street. They went everywhere.

We were both down on our hands and knees at once. She was on the carpet. I was on the lino, by the dresser. This was how Plushy found us. There was a big piece of plaster on his forehead, under the curl of his black hair, where the goalie's head had cracked him.

'Don't step on them!' my wife called out.

'There's always something going on here,' Plushy said.

'Stand still,' we both said, straightening up.

'Let us pray,' said Plushy, kneeling down, too. 'What is it?'

Nell told him.

'Found it?' said Plushy sarcastically, getting up and standing above us. 'What? Finds a necklace in the gutter with no neck in it! Doesn't tell his best friend!'

'Have you got the clip?' my wife asked me.

'Got a clip, too?' said Plushy. 'Diamonds, I bet. Proper window cleaner's story. Lost your voice, Jim? Can't you sing?'

Nell reached up from the floor and put some of the pearls into a saucer.

'I bet he only whistles,' Plushy said. 'Whistling isn't strong enough. Jim, you know that. Whistling doesn't keep it off.'

'Help us,' said Nell. 'Stop talking.'

'Temptation,' said Plushy, bending down to look. 'By rights, I ought to be singing now, in case I slip one into my pocket. Remember old Charlie, Jim? He used to whistle like a canary. He was up someplace – Hill Street, 27. You know it, Jim – 27 – don't put on that face with me. Charlie started whistling the moment he put the ladder up. Ground floor, he's whistling fine; first floor, OK; second floor, getting short of breath, whistle gets weak. What happens? Lady's diamond ring comes clean across from the other side of the room to him. He tries to blow it back. He can't. It comes clean through the glass. He can't get a sound out, leans back and back. Falls off the ladder, three weeks in hospital.'

'Get on with the job, mate. Have you got the clip, Nell?' I said.

'I'm looking.'

'I reckon singing's better. We always used to sing when we were working together, didn't we, Jim? Remember your lady, Nell, at the Avenue?' Plushy put on the high-class hoot of Mrs Merry. '"Why doesn't someone stop that man singing?" Well, I did stop. I stopped right in the middle of a bar. Next thing, a five-pound note starts talking to me out of her handbag other side of the room and waving its hands about. Just like I'm talking to you now.'

'Her watch, you mean,' said Nell, getting up.

[504]

'Her watch?' said Plushy.

'Yes,' said Nell. 'I mean her watch. She missed a watch. I thought I'd never hear the last of it. Nothing funny about that, Plushy. I could have lost my place.'

Plushy did not like this.

'What d'you mean, Nell?' I asked.

'It was all right. I found it for her,' Nell said.

'Oh,' said Plushy sarcastically. 'That's something off my mind.' Those two hated each other.

'We can't take it round like this,' Nell said when we all stood up and looked at the saucer full of pearls. She dropped the clip on top.

'Too true you can't,' said Plushy. 'Looks too much like a ruddy shareout.'

We argued about it for a long time. I was the only one in favour of taking it round and telling the police what happened. I did not want a valuable thing like this in the house, and we couldn't go round to Cleaver's or someplace like that and get them re-strung until Monday. It would be the end of the week before we could get them to the police.

'But Plushy's a witness,' said Nell. 'He'll tell them you found it and we broke it by mistake.'

'Yes,' said Plushy. 'And you'll get a reward. What do I get?'

'Ten pounds,' said Nell.

'Twenty,' said Plushy. 'First instalment on a motor bike. Pop up to London for the week-ends.'

'No. Aunt Mary's was worth hundreds,' said Nell.

'Oh,' said Plushy. 'Got Nell's Aunt Mary back to stay with you?' he said to me. 'You never told me. Is she comfortable? A bit cramped in here for her, isn't it?'

Nell put her chin up and looked like the geography teacher at our school when I was a boy. Nell really did hate Plushy, and getting a crack on the head had livened him up even more. He was a lad. We'd made Aunt Mary comfortable in the bath, according to him, or on top of a cupboard, and then he made up a long tale of how she wasn't getting on with the clergyman. His children got on her nerves and she wanted a rest, Plushy said. Nell struggled against it, and then she couldn't hold out any longer. She started to laugh. She laughed as I had never seen her, doubling up over the arm of a chair, and then, suddenly, she got angry. 'Stop telling lies, Plushy!' she called out.

On Monday, Nell took the pearls down to Cleaver's to be re-strung.

'Sit down, Mrs Drayton,' the older detective said to Nell, and the young one went out and came back in a moment with two cups of tea. When Nell came into any room where I was, the place was changed, and where I was, who I was, and what I was would get mixed up in my mind. It was like beginning to get drunk. Nell pushed the cup of tea away scornfully.

'It's just routine,' the older one went on. 'We've been asking your husband about the necklace you took round to Cleaver's to be re-strung.'

'It broke,' I said.

'Just a minute, son,' the detective said. And to Nell, 'Now, you say it is your necklace – your own property? Like you said to Mr Cleaver, "It is mine"? Is that correct?'

I had half got up from my chair and had tried to catch her eye when she walked in, but she came in warily, not looking at me but into each corner of the room and then up at the window and back at the door. I might have been a stranger. When she looked in my direction, she didn't see me; at any rate, she quickly turned her head to one side.

'That's correct,' she said.

I think my mouth stuck wide open.

'Just a minute!' the young detective said to me sharply, shutting me up.

'But your husband says he found it at the corner of Alston Street and the Promenade,' the other said to her.

She looked at the young detective, then at the older one, then at me. I used to say that she confused me because she was like a couple of girls whispering secrets to each other, but now she was one woman, clear and decisive and firm in voice. There was nothing a long way off in it. It rang, and rang true and harsh.

'That's a bloody lie,' said Nell.

'Nell!' I cried. I had never heard Nell use language before in my life.

'It's mine!' Nell shouted at me. 'You know it is. Mr Cleaver knows it is. I asked him what it was worth. He's repaired it for me before. He recognised it. It's been in my family for years. It belonged to my Aunt Mary. I told Mr Cleaver. He knows. Bring him here. He knows it came to me when she died two years ago. She brought me up. Ask her husband, the Reverend Dickens. He lives in Manchester.'

'Nell –' I said.

'What's the address of the Reverend Dickens?' asked the older detective.

'Find out. You're so bloody clever,' said Nell. If she was more than one girl, I had never seen this one before – red and square in the face and her eyes moving like knife tips.

'Well,' said the dick, 'it's exactly like a necklace lost by a Mrs Faber.'

'Is it?' snapped Nell. 'Well, it isn't hers. It's mine. It was my Aunt Mary's, I told you. She gave it to me. She gave me everything, all the things I have.'

'Oh,' said the detective. 'Other things. What were they?'

'That's my business,' said Nell.

'Mrs Drayton,' said the detective, 'you haven't got an aunt, and you never did have, did you? Your father and mother live in London, don't they?'

'They're dead,' I said. 'Killed in the war. What's that got to do with it? Nell, what's going on?'

Nell suddenly took notice of me, as if she were seeing me for the first time. Her expression went through three changes. It was like seeing three photographs of a person quickly. The first was the square, raging face; the second lost its colour and softened; the third looked pale and sly. This one spoke to me in a low voice across the table, as if we were sharing a secret. 'You silly sucker,' she half whispered. 'You're covering up for Plushy. I won't have Plushy.'

And then she shouted at the detective, 'Plushy whipped it off Mrs Faber! Out with Plushy! Out! Out! My husband knows it.' She got up and rushed for the door, but the young one was standing there.

I've left the window-cleaning trade now. I gave it up after the case. I had to. There was too much talk. Nell got three months. She was mad. She must have been – that's the only thing I can think. But she didn't look mad in court. She had just one word for all of us, the police, me, Plushy, old Cleaver, everybody: liars. The only straight people in the world were her and her Aunt Mary. It came out in court that she'd worked this Aunt Mary game a couple of times before she met me. Once in Deptford and another time at a place near Bristol. But for that she might have got off – first offence. 'Her old auntie got around,' Plushy whispered to me when the police were reading her record out to the judge. 'Tiring, at her age.'

The last I saw of Nell was going downstairs out of the dock with the wardress. She didn't even look at me. I couldn't believe it. I still can't believe it. My mind goes back to the first time I saw her, through the back-bedroom window at Mrs Merry's, fixing the ear-rings – not hers but Mrs Merry's – and I say to myself, '11th January we beat Hopley, three-nought,' and I get stuck there.

Just a Little More

===

They were speaking in low voices in the kitchen.

'How is he? Has he said what he is going to do?' she asked her husband. 'Is there any news?'

'None at all,' her husband whispered. 'He's coming down now. He says he just wants a house by the sea, in a place where the air is bracing and the water's soft and there's a good variety of fish.'

'Sh-h-h! Why do we whisper like this? Here he comes. Get the plates.'

A moment later, the very old gentleman, her father-in-law, was standing in the doorway, staring and smiling. He was short and very fat, and one of the things he liked to do was to pause in the doorway of a room and look it over from ceiling to floor. In the old days, his family or his workers at the factory used to stiffen nervously when he did this, wondering where his eye would stop.

'Excuse me being rude,' he said at last. 'What a lovely smell.'

'Take your father in,' the wife said. 'These plates are hot. Go into the dining-room, Grandpa.'

'I'm just looking at your refrigerator, darling,' the old gentleman said. 'Very nice. It's a Pidex, I see. Is that a good make? I mean is it good – does it work well? . . . I'm glad to hear that. Did you get it from the Pidex people? . . . Ah, I thought you did. Good people.'

The son, who was in his fifties, took the old gentleman by the elbow and moved him slowly into the dining-room. The old gentleman blew his nose.

'No. Your mother's hands were as cold as ice when I got to her,' said the old gentleman, astonished by a memory. 'But she had gone. Where do I go? Do I sit here?'

He sat down very suddenly at the table. Although he weighed close to two hundred pounds, his clothes hung loosely on him, for he had once weighed much more. His nostrils had spread and reddened over a skin

[509]

that was greenish and violet on the cheeks but as pale and stringy as a chicken's at the neck.

His daughter-in-law and two grandchildren brought in the joint and the vegetables. The grandchildren were called Richard and Helen. They were in their teens. Their mouths watered when they saw the food on the table, and they leaned towards it, but kept their eyes politely on the old man, like elderly listeners.

'I hope you haven't cooked anything special for me,' the old man said. 'I was just saying I talk too much when I come for a week-end here, and I eat too much. It's living alone – having no one to talk to, and so forth, and you can't be bothered to eat – that's the point. What a lovely piece of beef that is! Wonderful. I haven't seen a joint of beef like that for centuries. A small bit of loin of lamb we might have, but my wife can't digest it.' He often forgot that his wife was dead. 'And it doesn't keep. I put it in the larder and I forget and it goes wrong.' His big face suddenly crinkled like an apple, with disgust.

'Well, well, I don't know, I'm sure,' he went on, gazing at the beef his son was now carving. 'I suppose it's all right. What do you call a joint like that?' He pointed across the table to his grandson. 'We used to have beef when your father was a boy, Richard. Your father was a boy once. You can't imagine that, can you? Aitchbone, was it? I can't remember. I don't know where your mother used to get it. Bell's, I suppose. I don't know what we paid for it. Sixpence a pound, perhaps. We can't do it now; it's the price.'

His son passed him a plate. The old man hesitated not knowing whether to pass it on and not wanting to. 'If this is for me, don't give me any more,' he said. 'I hardly eat anything nowadays. If I could have just a little fat . . .' Relieved, he kept the plate.

'Pass the vegetables to Grandpa,' said his daughter-in-law to Helen.

'Grandpa, vegetables?' Helen said, looking younger now as she spoke.

'Oh,' said the old gentleman. He had gone into a dream. 'I was just watching you carving,' he said to his son. 'I was looking at your face. You've got just the expression of your great-grandfather Harry. I remember him when I was a little boy. Father took me to see him – it was one morning. He took me down to a warehouse, would it be? – in the docks or harbour – a factory, perhaps – and he lifted me up to a window and I saw him, just his face, it was only a minute. He was slitting up herrings; it was a curing place.'

'Fish! I knew it.' His daughter-in-law laughed.

'The sea is in our blood,' said her husband. Everyone was laughing.

'What is this? What are you laughing at? What have I said?' the old gentleman asked, smiling. 'Are you getting at me?'

'That is where you get your taste for kippers,' said his daughter-in-law to her husband.

'Ah, kippers!' said the old gentleman, delighted by his strange success. 'How are you for fish in this neighbourhood? Do you get good fish? I sometimes feel like a piece of fish. But there doesn't seem to be the fish about, these days. I don't know why that is. No, I went up to the fishmonger on Tuesday and I looked. He came up to me, and I said "Good morning", "Good morning, Mr Hopkins," he said. "What can I do for you?" "Do for me?" I said. "Give me a fortnight in Monte Carlo." He exploded. I said, "What's happened to you? What's wrong?" "What do you mean, Mr Hopkins?" he said. "I mean, where's your fish?" I said. "That's not what I call fish. Not f-i-s-h." He knew what I meant. "Sole," he said. "Dover sole," I said. "Mr Hopkins," he said, "I haven't had a Dover sole for a fortnight. Not one I'd sell *you*. Lemon sole," he said, and something – grayling did he say? Well, that's the way it is. And so we go on.

'No,' the old man said after a moment. 'Kitty, your mother, my wife, was very fond of fish. When we were first married, and so forth, we came down from the north – How old are you, my boy? Fifty-seven? You're not fifty-seven! – it was just before you were born, and my wife said, "I'd give anything for an oyster." The train didn't get in till eight, but we were young and reckless in those days. I didn't care a damn for anyone. I was ready to knock the world over. I was in a good crib, five pounds a week at Weekley's – before Hollins took them over. All expenses. I thought I was Julius Caesar – marvellous, isn't it? Do I mean him? And we went across the road and your mother said, "Come on –"'

The son interrupted, picking up the story. 'And a bus driver leaned out of his cab and said, "Watch out, lady. Babies are scarce this year." Mother told me.'

'I'm sure she didn't,' said the old gentleman, blushing a little. 'Your father's imagination, Richard!'

'Yes, but what happened?' asked his daughter-in-law.

'And there was a little place, a real old London fish place – sawdust on the floor, I suppose they had in those days. Crossfield ... Cross ... Crofty – I forget the name – and we had a dozen oysters each, maybe I had a couple of dozen; I don't remember now, I couldn't say. Frederick's – that was the name of the place. Frederick's. And I suppose we must have followed it with Dover sole. They used to do a wonderful Welsh rabbit.'

'And that is how I was born,' said the son. 'Let me give you some more beef, Father.'

'Me? Oh, no. I don't eat what I used to. It's living alone, and these new teeth of mine – I've had a lot of trouble with them. Don't give me any more. I don't mind a couple of slices – well, just another. And some fat. I like a piece of fat. That's what I feel. You go home and you get to the house, and it's dark. And it's empty. You go in and the boiler's low – I don't seem to get the right coke. Do you get good coke here? You look at it all and you look in the larder and you can't be bothered. There's a chop, a bit of bread and cheese, perhaps. And you think, well, if this is all there is in life, you may as well finish it. I'm in a rut down in that place. I've got to get away. I can't breathe there. I'd like to get down to the sea.'

'I think you ought to go where you have friends,' said his daughter-in-law.

The old gentleman put his knife and fork down. 'Friends?' he said, in a stern voice, raising his chin. 'I have no friends. All my friends are dead.' He said this with indignation and contempt.

'But what about your friend Rogers, in Devonshire?' said his son.

'Rogers? I was disappointed in Rogers. He's aged. He's let himself go. I hadn't seen him for twenty-five years. When I saw him, I said to him, "Why, what's the matter with you? Trying to pretend you are an old man?" He looked at me. He'd let his moustache go long and grey. I wouldn't have known him. And there was something else. A funny thing. It upset me.' The old gentleman's jolly face shrivelled up again, with horror. 'The hairs in his nose had gone grey!' he said. 'I couldn't bear it.

[512]

He was very kind, and his wife was. We had lunch. Soup of some kind – tomato, or maybe oxtail – and then a piece of lamb, potatoes, and cauliflower. Oh, very nice. I've forgotten what the dessert was – some cream, I suppose, they have good cream there – and coffee, of course. Cheese . . . I don't remember. Afterwards – and this is what upset me about old people – they wanted a rest. Every day, after lunch, they go off and have a sleep – every day. Can you imagine that? I couldn't stand that. Terrible.'

'It's good to have a siesta,' said the son.

'I couldn't. I never have. I just can't,' said the old gentleman, in a panic. 'The other afternoon after lunch, I forget what I had, a chop, I think – I couldn't be bothered to cook vegetables, well, on your own you don't, that's the point – I dropped off. I don't know for how long, and when I woke up it was dark. I couldn't see anything. I didn't know where I was. "Where am I?" I said. "What day is it?" And I reached out for my wife. I thought I was in bed, and I called out, "Kitty, Kitty, where are you?" and then I said, "Oh." It came back to me. I'm here. In this room. I couldn't move. I got up and put on the light. I was done up. I poured myself out a small glass of port. I felt I had to. It was shocking. And shocking dreams.'

He stared and then suddenly he turned to his daughter-in-law and said, in another voice, 'Those sandwiches I shan't forget. Egg, wasn't it? You remember?' He wagged a finger at Helen. 'Helen, your mother is a wonder at egg sandwiches. It was the first time in my life I'd ever eaten them. The day we put Kitty away, you remember she came down and made egg sandwiches. What is the secret of it? She won't tell. Butter, I suppose? Richard, what is the word I want? You know – "smashing", I suppose you'd call them.'

He paused, and his eyes grew vaguer. 'No,' he went on, 'I don't know what I'll do. I think I shall go to the sea and look around. I shall get a list of houses, and put my furniture in store. I could live with your brother John, or you. I know I could, but it would be wrong. You have your own lives. I want my independence. Life is beginning for me – that is what I feel. I feel I would like to go on a cruise round the world. There was a house at Bexhill I saw. They wanted seven thousand for it. I felt it would suit me.'

[513]

'Seven thousand!' said his son, in alarm. 'Where would you get seven thousand from?'

'Oh,' said the old gentleman sharply, 'I should raise it.'

'Raise it!' exclaimed the son. 'How?'

'That's just it,' said the old gentleman cheerfully. 'I don't know. The way will open up. You perhaps, or John.'

Husband and wife looked down the table at each other in consternation.

'Shall we go upstairs and have some coffee?' she said.

'That son of yours, that Richard – did you see what he ate?' said the old gentleman as he got up from the table. 'Marvellous, isn't it? Of course, things are better than when I was a boy. I feel everything is better. We used to go to school with twopence for a pie. Not every day – twice a week. The other days, we just looked at the shop window. Pies piled up. And once a week – Friday, I expect – it was herrings in the evening. The fisherwoman came calling them in the street, eighteen a shilling, fresh fish out of the sea. Salmon I used to be fond of. D'you ever have salmon?'

He paused in the doorway and looked at the carpet on the stairs and at the wallpaper. 'I like rich things,' he said, nodding to the carpet. 'That gravy was good. Luscious grapes, pears, all large fruits I like. Those Christmas displays at the meat market – turkeys and geese by the thousand there used to be. I always used to bring your mother something. A few chops, two or three pairs of kippers. And so forth. I don't know what.'

'Upstairs to the sitting-room, Father,' said the son. 'I'm coming in a minute with the coffee.'

The son went into the kitchen, and the whispering began again.

'Seven thousand!' he said. 'Seven million wouldn't keep him!'

'Sh-h-h,' said his wife. 'It's a day-dream.'

'But what are we going to do?'

In a few minutes, he took the coffee upstairs. The old gentleman was sitting down, with his waistcoat undone and his thumbs twiddling on his stomach.

'I've been thinking about you,' the old gentleman said rebukingly. 'You've lost weight. You don't eat. You worry too much. My wife used to worry.'

The son passed a coffee cup to him.

'Is there a lot of sugar in it? Thank you,' the old man said. He gave it a stir, took a sip, and then held the cup out. 'I think I'll have a couple of spoonfuls more.'

The Snag

The marriage of middle age, the mad impromptus of reason, are the satisfying ones. By that time our obsessions have accumulated and assert their rights, and we find peace in the peculiarities of others. I am thinking of Mrs Barclay and myself. Our difficulty was the common one of turning a love affair into a marriage.

Sophia was a rattled woman of forty, with a pretty nose, when I met her. We had both gone to Percy Oblong's wedding party in Holland Park. She belonged to that set. Until I was crushed into a corner with her in one of the crowded rooms, and questioned her, I knew hardly any of the guests. There were, it seems, several important politicians, two or three titles, actors, actresses, authors; a large number of people known to the glossy magazines and, of the rest, there were scarcely any – according to the lively Mrs Barclay – without some well-known tale attached to them. It was Percy's third marriage and she pointed out to me that a feature of the party was its half a dozen youngish women who had known Percy too well and were prowling about with champagne glasses in their hands and with beautiful expressions of perturbed wistfulness, rather ostentatiously breathing out the news that emotional fulfilment had come to them after – thank God – giving Percy up. They were saying, as Sophia did, that he looked fatter. Among people shouting to be heard as the packed evening went on, Sophia's animated and gloomy mumble was refreshing and audible. We were both looking for a chance to get away from each other, when suddenly she pulled my sleeve so hard that I almost fell on her.

'Don't move,' she said sharply. 'Don't go. Stand still. Stand there. Talk. There's someone I don't want to see. Don't turn round.'

That is what started it – I mean started our affair. A conspiracy had begun. I was at once attracted to her. I asked her who she was hiding from and she said she would tell me later. The danger did not abate –

and the longer it lasted the more attractive I found her. Eventually I was offering to spy out the land. Then I had to get her out of the corner, out of the room, down the stairs, out of the house. The manœuvre was a triumph. As we stood in the cool black damp of the London night I knew that I had found at last my real gift. I was a rescuer. Fatal discovery. I got a taxi and took Sophia back to her flat and, that evening, and in the weeks that followed, I discovered calamity was what she lived by.

I shall always remember Sophia's flat. All day and half the night it rattled with the sound of electric trains; and all day and half the evening the telephone rang in it. She lived among a lot of expensive art books and pictures of the ballet and in a luxury that betrayed the deserted woman who had wrung out of interior decoration the things that she had failed to get from marriage. But the whole place shook. And her life – as she took pride in confiding – shook too. Never missing a party, eager to be at the centre of other people's love affairs and – she admitted – careless about her own, she was the centre of a lot of gossip. My instincts as a rescuer became stronger and stronger. Two months after Percy Oblong's wedding I was talking of the supreme act of life-saving: marriage. Sophia, between telephone calls, responded warmly to this idea; for her, it had the lure of a suicide. But there was an obstacle. She had been divorced in a noisy way, many years before – she could quote from the papers and remembered what she wore in court – and to this divorce she clung. It had sacred implications. She behaved about it like a cautious widow whose little capital was this shaming and perfect disaster. '*You* have not been divorced,' she said. She meant that I had no disaster of my own to put into a settlement.

And here we stuck, talking and talking, and the trains went by. And then, my luck turned. Calamity occurred. The seeds of it had been sown at our first meeting. Six months after that scene at Percy Oblong's wedding, in a week when I was away, Sophia landed herself with a slander action. Her telephone calls were all law and lawyers. She spoke lines that could have been convincing only on the stage. Nothing I could do when I came back could stop her and for three farcical days the British public were laughing about 'the Barclay case'. I saw this was the supreme test. Here was the dramatic setting we needed. Sophia was ill. She was frightened by what she had let herself in for. I must get her out of the

[517]

limelight, I thought. I must save her, restore her reputation. I talked her down and took action. She surrendered. It was August. I found a cottage in Wales where we could escape for a month. The Monday after the case I went up to get it ready. On the Wednesday I was to return to London and fetch her and we were to get married.

The cottage was a simple, cream-painted gate lodge with sharp Gothic windows. It was darkened by one of those tall firs that are often seen in rectory gardens and which are sometimes called Clergyman trees. One felt almost married standing under it. There was one advantage in the place from my point of view: it had no telephone. In our London days, Sophia's telephone had been my malignant rival, for Sophia lived by it. A few hours before my return to London to fetch her and on the day when I considered myself to be officially 'running away with Mrs Barclay' a boy arrived with a telegram from her. It told me to wait because she had decided to drive up to me. I had forgotten about telegrams. I saw that now I was not, in the strictest sense, 'running off with Mrs Barclay'. The struggle for power had begun.

And so I see her as she was, on that day, driving towards me in the Border country. Sophia was a single-minded driver, but the mind she used was the unconscious. I see her green car unpredictable in the traffic lanes, waltzing at corners. I hear her shouted at by other motorists, I see her chancing the yellow light, parking in the wrong place at Cheltenham, backing into the traffic stream at the narrow end of Worcester, making cyclists swerve. She had a small pink hat half hidden in her hair, at an angle which gave her pale face the look of folly the waning moon has in a windy sky. I could imagine the restlessness of her pretty and conversible shoulders. I did not know what to do with myself until two o'clock when she was to arrive and the changeable August sun made the hours slower. Over and over again I looked at flowers I did not know the name of in the garden. That tedium was broken. Telegrams began to arrive as suddenly as telephone calls. Two came from London, altering the time of departure. One came from Kidderminster saying she had taken the wrong road. And a final one from a town in Shropshire telling me to ring the hotel. I drove to the nearest telephone box.

'My dear,' she said with her low, fussed, guttural emphasis on the second word. 'Avoid me. Keep out of my way. I am poison. Ugh.'

I could imagine her shaking her head in a disgust with herself which used to please me.

'You know what has happened? It is unbelievable. Tyre burst!' She added that there was an awful man in shorts staring at her.

This, I knew, would be untrue. While she was telephoning Sophia would be regarding the man in shorts. Her ice-blue eyes would be staring in a rude, incredulous way; she was hypnotised by the sight of men, of terrible men. I suppose I describe myself.

'Stay where you are,' I said. 'Don't worry. Rest. I will come and fetch you.'

'Yes,' she said. 'I must rest. I'm half dead.'

It took me no more than half an hour to drive to the town. She was in the white lounge. She was wearing a grey suit and was sitting, slim and very upright, with a silk scarf round her long and beautiful throat and she was wearing the foolish hat on her greying hair. She was looking severely amused but when she saw me, she put all her vanity into a deep, laughing groan.

'My dear,' she said in an exhausted voice when she took my hand. Her hand was small, nervous and brittle, as if it would break.

'You're a saint. What is it that happens to me? I wreck everything. Why did I take that wrong road at Kidderminster? What *made* me?'

We were neither of us any longer young. Explanations were a game which gave us the illusion of youth and made our troubles and our past sparkle. We had grown up at the time when simplicity went out.

'You were trying not to come,' I said.

That kind of remark delighted her. It pleased me too. We felt younger. A belief in fate was her form of hypocrisy.

'Have you had tea? If you have, let's go. I've got my car,' I said.

'In two cars?' she said. 'Don't be silly. You see what a muddle it is. We must talk.'

'Not,' I said, 'with all these people. They are too interested. And why talk?'

'Look at them,' she said. 'I can't believe it.'

We were sitting in a zoo. The lounge of the hotel smelled of white paint, of tea, new carpet and roses and there was a long beam of sunny blue cigarette smoke slanting between us and one of the sofas. Arranged in their armchairs were a number of what looked like dressed-up animals. There were giraffes, tigresses, monkeys, birds, dogs and even a camel; they were middle-aged ladies, knitting or reading, and acutely interested in human nature, that is to say, Sophia and me. The only persons not listening to us had their backs to us. There was a man on the sofa beyond the beam of smoke with strong grey hair as thick as a schoolboy's. Near him sat a youth of sixteen wearing a school blazer and flannels. He wore spectacles. Of the man I could see only the sunburned neck and the shoulders of his tweed jacket. The youth was gazing at Sophia and turned his head, blushing, when I caught his look. He had a red notebook on his knee.

The man had a book too. Suddenly he slapped it on his knee and said in a ringing and confident voice:

'We're absolutely stumped, old boy.'

The zoo looked up from their knitting needles.

'Ssh!' said Sophia to me. 'Listen. It's fascinating. It's the man I told you about – the one in shorts who was staring at me.'

'Umph!' said the boy in a voice that was far more elderly than the man's.

'He's a professor or something,' Sophia said. 'Anyway, he knows a lot of women professors. He's on holiday. That is his son. They're on a bus tour. He was looking at me as if he knew me.'

'You are not a woman professor,' I said. 'How d'you know all that?'

Sophia was annoyed by this; she seriously liked to be whatever was going, if a man was concerned.

'He's been telling us all. Listen,' she said.

'That boy will know you again,' I said.

Sophia stared back at the boy in a prim and amused way that crushed him once more.

The man cleared his throat and the boy said something to his father obviously about us. The father spoke again. He was making a speech to the room. The pitch of his voice was exacting. It was the good-humoured voice of a humourless man, questing, inflected by a note that blended educated anxiety with the exhilaration which is shared by sea lions and great bores. It was a voice both specifically victimising and blandly generic. It was the voice of a university.

[520]

'The twenty-sixth,' it said. 'That's where we're sunk.'

'No bus,' the boy said.

'Let's have a look at your book again,' said the father.

Sophia sighed.

There was a pile of guide-books and timetables on the table beside the boy among the magazines. He handed the red notebook to his father.

'I don't see,' said the father, opening the book and turning the pages, 'how we've slipped up. We've done exactly what we planned.' He took a pencil and ticked pages of the book, item by item: 'August 16th. Leave Trigorin 8.15, arrive Llandor 11.30. Church, museum, sandwiches. Stay George and Dragon – all right?'

He ticked these items in the book.

'August 19th,' he continued. 'Leave nine ... what's this? I can't read your writing. You must learn to write figures in a clear, uneducated hand – ha! ha! I can't tell whether this is a three or a five ...'

'Five,' said the boy. 'We've done that.'

'I know, I know,' said the father. 'But I like things right. We may want to look this up in years to come. Now. Nine-five.' He altered the figure. The boy looked towards us with shame.

'August 19th,' said the father. 'Leave Llandor, arrive Creep 11.20. Visit castle, query dungeon. Yes, we did the dungeon. Early lunch Globe, another castle, bus 2 o'clock to Bronwen, waterfall, tea, stay Crown ...'

'That poor boy,' I said.

'There's a lot more, the whole holiday,' said Sophia. 'Day by day. Why poor? That's exactly what one ought to do.'

'Well, his poor wife,' I said. 'I can't see you doing it.'

'That's where we're wrong,' Sophia said. And then: 'She's not with them. She's dead.'

The certainty of Sophia made me laugh.

'Obviously she's dead,' she said and there was that dry, seductive, low-spirited choke in her throat, that grimace of ironical horror, that small, practical, disposing movement of the chin which indicated that Sophia was facing a decisive and disagreeable interment.

Sophia's words made me look more closely at the man. I picked up a magazine and looked over the top of it. I stopped smiling. Now I knew why I had noticed a peculiar quality in his voice. It was not generic. It was specific. I knew him. His wife *had* died. She had died three years before. It was a man called Charles Chaucer. I whispered this to Sophia.

'Ssh!' she said. 'Listen.'

'I know him,' I repeated. 'It is Charles Chaucer.'

Sophia paid no attention. She was listening to Chaucer, who was still speaking.

Rather than dismay, I felt laughter rise through my feet and grow inside my body, getting deeper and deeper until I was submerged in it. Sophia believed in Fate and so did I. But my notion was different from hers. Her belief enabled her to make a devious escape into a melancholy which permitted her to get out of anything she wanted to get out of. For me – I had only to look at Chaucer – Fate was then asinine. At forty-five I found my cheeks burning because the world's oldest joke was being played on me and, as always, at the time of crisis. To have met anyone, at this moment, would have been awkward. To meet Chaucer was farce.

For a little while I thought of getting away unseen. I studied the room. There was only one door in the middle. I had come in by this door unseen – else Chaucer would have sprung at once. There was no escape. I put down the magazine and stared at Chaucer's neck, daring him to look round.

Chaucer was farce because he was what is called my 'oldest friend'. I do not mean that he was a friend in any serious sense. His role in life was to be the oldest friend of everyone, the man who crops up in one's life on and off for twenty years and always at the unguarded moments. At Dieppe when one is sneaking out; at Dover when one is sneaking happily back. It is his knock at the door that stops the domestic quarrel, that interrupts the love affair or makes one put the pistol back in the drawer. Chaucer arrived in my life, every few years, like a clown or a conscience, innocently, creating guilt. His innocence lay in his efficiency in pursuing the single purpose of his life: 'I like to keep in touch.' The kiss is killed, the suicide misses his moment. Chaucer saves us.

'And you see what the 26th means,' Chaucer was saying. 'I can't believe that they don't run a bus every day – but here it is as plain as anything. Thursdays only. What a day to run a bus anyway. It's a real headache.'

The boy murmured.

'The snag is,' Chaucer said, 'that it knocks Snowdon clean out.'

[522]

He said this as if he had brought the whole mountain down on top of himself.

The idea of Snowdon, the highest mountain in Britain, being 'knocked clean out' made several ladies in the lounge look with the *de haut en bas* expression of English unbelief. There were snobbish smiles, but two ladies looked at Chaucer with sympathy. One of these was Sophia.

But there Snowdon rose implacably out of Chaucer's timetable, a mountain not subject to the climbing boots of poets like the mountains of the Lake District, not fatal to clerks, like Ben Nevis, but well clambered by lawyers, doctors, professors and undergraduates, injuring its half dozen, even killing its occasional woman schoolteacher every year, often in the headlines, sold to publicity. It rose out of Chaucer's timetable in the drifting Welsh rain, encircled by teams of cyclists, belted by motor coaches; the steep side falling into cones of scree, the sheep bleating like Wesleyan ministers on the gentler slopes, the farmers glowering at the tourists over the stone walls at the bottom, and the excursions from Manchester going up the long slope on foot or by the light railway to the café in the inevitable cloud at the summit. There they waited for the famous view, while the professional classes were roped on the chimney or the rock face. It stood there rather wet, very lordly in its rock, hostile to Chaucer's passion for contact.

'We'll have to miss it,' the boy said in a false voice.

The sympathetic lady and Sophia, too, looked sorry for the boy.

'Miss it!' cried the dogged Chaucer. 'But we can't miss Snowdon.'

'Suppose we make it Wednesday,' said the boy.

'No good,' said the father looking at the timetable. 'The eleven-twenty misses the connection by a quarter of an hour.'

'No co-operation,' said the boy.

I changed my mind. This seemed the moment to slip out.

'Darling,' I said, 'let's go.'

'All right,' said Sophia with resignation.

'Unless, unless,' said Chaucer. 'Here's an idea. Wait. Let me think.'

Sophia had moved and the boy now gasped as if he were about to miss the biggest chance of his life. Agitatedly he tried to attract his father's attention. In the silence of Chaucer's thinking I heard the boy mutter:

'Dad! Dad! That's the woman in the Barclay case.'

'Damn!' I said. 'That boy reads the papers.'

'Where?' said Sophia, looking round the room. She was paying no attention to me.

'Just a moment,' said Chaucer. 'I think I've got it. We don't go to Canwer, we take the early bus.' (I did not catch the name of the place.) 'Look at the timetable.'

The boy rummaged among the books but did not take his eyes off Sophia.

'We can't do that,' said the boy.

'We can. We can,' cried Chaucer. 'Why go to the *top* of Snowdon? We can work it if we go half-way up. What's wrong with that? Snowdon, half-way,' he declared. 'That's the idea.'

There was a sigh from the snobbish ladies. They were satisfied. The gentler ones saw the wish to protect Chaucer made irrelevant. Sophia, who had been rapt and ironical, made her grimace and was suddenly set in the gloom I feared in her. I squeezed her hand.

'What's the *good* of going to the top, old boy? What's the point?' said Chaucer. 'It's no different from other mountains. You get much the same view half-way.'

'OK,' said the boy, getting out his pencil.

Chaucer sat forward on the sofa, elated.

'The important thing in life is to ask the right questions,' he said.

Sophia sat back and picked up the magazine and leaned towards me. Looking at the advertisement of a fur coat, she said:

'How right he is! I've been going to the top, going to the limit all my life. Why? It is just as good half-way. That's why I am such a mess. I mean – take the case. Why did I go on with it? Why didn't you stop me?'

'I tried to,' I said. 'But there's no stopping you, you know, once you're set. You're stubborn.'

'I need someone to stop me,' she said. 'You know who that man is?'

'I have just been telling you. It's Chaucer.'

'Don't be silly. I'm serious,' she said. 'It's my husband, to the life.'

We were back where we had so often been before – to the sacredness of Sophia's divorce.

'Listen,' I said. 'I'm telling you. It's a man called Chaucer, a friend of mine. I know him. What do we do now?'

'Oh no!' she exclaimed, opening her handbag and getting out her mirror. 'Why on earth didn't you tell me! Let's go and speak to him. What an extraordinary man you are.'

At this the unmistakable voice of my oldest friend spoke out.

'The Barclay case? Why didn't you tell me? Where?'

Chaucer stood up and recognised me at once. His face was as pink as his neck. His blue eyes shone.

'How absolutely splendid,' he cried.

We went to him at once; Sophia still had the magazine in her hand as I introduced her.

'Marvellous,' said Chaucer. 'This is my son.'

Chaucer's face did not astonish me. It was young, it was sunburned to the neck. What astonished me were his clothes. Perhaps because of the mild youthfulness of his face, they seemed to overpower and astonish and magnify him. A stupendous tropical butterfly in tweed had broken out of the chrysalis of mourning. I had never seen this Chaucer before. Fresher and even younger after grief, he now wore a blatant black, red and green jacket in wide check. A blue and white check open shirt seemed to boil on his chest and a few chest hairs showed like a whiff of steam at the neck. His khaki shorts made his pink knees look wilful, like smooth supernumerary faces, tripling his powers of observation; the dark red stockings with the green scout tabs to the garters added a Tyrolean friskiness. In his ordinary crisis get-up he had been a grey figure. Now he was sporting and as blatant as a poster. A desire for publicity had been submerged in him.

'How d'you do?' he was saying to Sophia, holding her hand and turning to his son to say:

'Janet Forth was here this afternoon, wasn't she, old boy? You remember?' (This to me.) 'She was up at Newnham and went to the Foreign Office until she left for Athens – the British School. Got a CBE – did you know? You've only just missed her.'

At least we had not been his first prey that day.

'Took a First in History,' he went on to Sophia, at last releasing her hand. 'Sit down,' he said. 'This is splendid.'

We did not sit down.

'Trust C.C.,' I said to Sophia, 'to remember the learned ladies.'

Chaucer laughed shyly and innocently, giving Sophia a look that searched her face for her academic distinction. For Chaucer was Don Juan – but not the ordinary version of that character. He was the pursuer of academic women. To their persons and their sex he was indifferent: his lust and single-minded quest was for their intellectual particulars. Where had they been to school? To which university? In what year? With whom? When had they got their degrees? In what subjects? Had they taken a First or a Second? A large procession of educated women had given their academic all to Chaucer's amorous mind. Some had even become Dames. He sent blue-eyed glances at Sophia who suddenly became gay. What small academic jewel did she possess? An intermediate perhaps? A mere diploma? It was an academic undressing. I grinned. There was not a trace of intellect, beyond the usual socialite pickings, in Sophia. If she had graduated anywhere it was in the Courts – the Divorce Court and the Queen's Bench. Her only distinction was public scandal. Chaucer's son, standing back and unable to close his mouth, knew that. He was overcome.

In the meantime, Chaucer was eagerly telling us what we knew already.

'Snowdon,' he said. 'We've run into a spot of bother there. I thought of dropping in on Mary Cumberland . . .'

He was off again on his quest. He gave me a knowing look as he drew once more on the notorious provender of his power to bore. Then without warning, he said genially to Sophia:

'My son was just telling me he was sure he knew you. He saw your picture in the papers . . . the Barclay case.'

I could not speak. The son could not speak. All the ladies in the room – the giraffe, the dogs, the tigress and the camel – put down their books and stared.

'I expect he did,' Sophia said. 'It was everywhere. Which one did you see?' She put this question to the boy.

She was delighted and proud and radiant; and there was a pout of reproach at my annoyed face. I was depriving her of the only gain the case had brought her: publicity.

'I got my damages,' she said impudently with a new defiant look at me.

'I know. A farthing,' said the boy, an addict of fact.

Sophia saw my fidgeting shame. She knew the damages were contemptuous and that the case had been a calamity to her reputation.

'Splendid!' Chaucer said to her in his eager, pointless way. She was even more pleased. She turned to look at the ladies in the lounge and for a long time I had not seen her eyes so brilliant or heard her answering voice so vivacious. For myself, my worst memories of the scene in court were re-enacted. I expected to hear the judge, who looked like some moralising old woman in a red bathrobe and curlers – I expected to hear the judge say again:

'You may think the defendant is a woman of evil mind . . . On the other hand you may think that Mrs Barclay is not a woman for whom discretion means very much and that she has shown a general disposition to meddle and to make much of very little. You have seen her in the witness-box. You may ask if she is to be relied upon . . .'

And I could hear myself saying to Sophia before the action:

'Leave it alone. The woman is a spy. She has got her friends to watch you. People like that destroy themselves. Let them. It can't hurt you.'

'Unelevating society . . . frivolous action . . . storm in a teacup . . . ill-advised ladies . . .'

I could hear the judge going on. His voice melted into the voice of Chaucer who never dropped a piece of research.

'Who was the judge?' he asked.

Sophia told him.

'He was up at Magdalen with me,' cried the ecstatic Chaucer, rumpling the rug at his feet.

Sophia liked a social titbit like that. She would have gone to the scaffold with pleasure if, on the way, she could have picked up a bit of gossip about the hangman. Her pleasure and Chaucer's were complete.

'Now tell me about your holiday,' she said to the boy. 'Let me see your marvellous book.'

She rummaged among the magazines and soon had the table in disorder. She found his notebook.

'Ah, this is where you write it all down. What a good idea,' she said. 'You like to have everything planned.'

The boy was ashamed.

'Dad does,' said the boy.

'So do I,' said Sophia.

I gaped at her.

'I wish I wrote everything down,' she said. 'You know where you are. There is nothing to worry about. You've got it all except for one day.' She changed her lively manner and her argument. 'Isn't it rather thrilling? Not knowing? I mean unless you'd planned all the others, this one wouldn't be so thrilling?'

The youth looked suspiciously at her.

'Now then you two,' said Chaucer. 'Sorry to break it up.'

Chaucer's face was so sunburned, his son's face so pale, that he looked as if he had taken all the sunshine of their holiday for himself; now he was taking Sophia's kindness. I was relieved that it was he who was breaking up our meeting. I feared it would last forever.

'*En route*,' he said to his son. 'Leave the books there. Five-thirty. We've just got time for the Castle. Let's meet later on at dinner.'

I murmured something and they went.

'I hope not,' I said to Sophia. She was looking for her magazine in the muddle she had made on the table. She picked it up.

'Now,' I said. 'I suppose that was all right.'

'Let's sit down,' she said. Her gaiety had gone. 'I feel so low.'

'Those clothes of his. That suit! I love you,' I said.

We sat down where Chaucer had been sitting. The seat was warm with him still.

'What about his clothes?' said Sophia. 'You men are sweet. Straighten the rug, my dear. Did you see him, how he drew the rug up between his feet when he was talking to us? I was fascinated. He had almost worked it up to his knees in a heap. Is he always confident like that?'

'I didn't notice,' I said. 'That wasn't confidence – it was nerves.'

'Oh no! I could not look at anything else. I can't bear men who stand still,' she said.

I straightened the rug.

'You did not tell me he was your oldest friend,' she said.

'He isn't,' I said. 'But I have always known him.'

I gave her my reflections on oldest friends. She did not laugh.

'How little I know about you,' she said. 'You don't really know me.'

'We've known each other a long time,' I said.

'Nearly a year,' she said. 'He's like my husband.'

[528]

'Yes – you said. That was a bit of a shock, you know. Did he live on the examination papers of female dons?'

'Certainly not,' said Sophia, flashing in defence of her husband. 'Remember, I've been married. You have not.'

'I'm glad for your sake.'

'Why for mine?'

'You might have been jealous,' I said.

'Are you?' she said.

Sophia's husband had been a bond between us. His gratifying stupidity, his dullness, his baldness, his obstinacy had convinced me of my power over all the gossip about her. I had failed, of course, to stop her from going on with the silly slander action and I was put out by the scene with Chaucer which had shown me that, unrepentantly, she enjoyed the fight for its own sake and expected to be admired for it. What disturbed me was that Sophia's husband was an abstraction no longer. He was real. Possibly he wore a loud sports jacket and shorts and said things like 'Absolutely splendid'.

'Darling,' I said, 'I did not come here to sit in this hotel but to take you home. We are going to be married.'

'My dear,' she said, drawing away. 'We must talk.'

'Talk,' I said. 'What for? What about? We've done all the talking. I said . . . marry.'

She took my hand and squeezed it.

'I'm worn out,' she said. 'I'm so bewildered. I feel so numb.'

'We shall be quiet and peaceful,' I said.

'Peace – how I want it,' she said.

'Look, I'll see about your car and we'll go home.'

'I'm terribly sorry,' she said. 'This is not what I intended but I'm utterly whacked. I haven't slept for nights. And then Kidderminster . . .'

'Now, you've told me about Kidderminster. I'll go and see about the car.'

'My dear,' she said. 'I can't. It wouldn't be fair.'

'What do you mean?'

'I'll be better in the morning,' she said hurriedly. 'It's just the journey and we must talk.'

'Talk?' I said with exasperation.

'I promise you, in the morning,' she said. 'I'm going to stay here tonight. I've got a room. I'm sorry.'

'Sophia!'

She became very pale.

'I know,' she said. 'Forgive me.'

'But I've got the cottage. You let me get the cottage ready.' I was angry. 'When did you get a room here?' I asked. 'If you stay, I stay.'

'Oh, no, you can't do that,' she said in a prudish fluster that I had always found attractive. 'It wouldn't do.'

She looked nervously at the row of women in the room. 'You mustn't.'

'Darling,' I said. 'I love you. You've come all this way to love me.'

'You did not come to London for me,' she said.

'Darling! Your telegram,' I said. 'You told me not to.'

'Did I? Do you always do as you are told? Darling, your face. It looks so tragic. Don't, please, look like that. I can't bear it. It's only women, my dear. Oh lord, I'm always doing this.'

'Always?' I said sharply.

Her husband had become real. Now all the scandals became real also. The judge returned in his red bathrobe.

'Unreliable . . . frivolous . . .' he was still saying.

She listlessly picked up her magazine and she looked at me.

'I'm telling you the truth,' she said. 'Do you think I tell you the truth, always?'

'Yes,' I said. Afterwards, very often afterwards, puzzling about this question of hers, I remembered a movement of her lower lip when I answered. It was a movement of disappointment. She wanted me to say that I knew she was telling a lie. She badly wanted to be seen through, but despair had made me blind.

'I'm going to get the car,' I said decisively and getting up I walked out of the lounge into the hall and asked for the name of the garage. I was not away for more than a quarter of an hour.

When I came back she had gone. She had left a message with the hall porter saying that she would ring me in the morning.

'Madame said she was feeling tired,' said the porter in a voice of pious intimacy.

'Give me the telephone.'

'There are no telephones in the rooms,' he said with pride.

Sophia and I had certainly moved into a different world.

The man gave me her room number and, with disapproval, watched me walk up the shabby stairs. Her room was number eight on the first floor. I went up, crossed a landing which contained the largest case of stuffed seabirds I had ever seen. It gave a dead marine odour to the passage. I knocked. The door opened and there stood Chaucer.

'Splendid man!' cried Chaucer. 'Come in. We're just back. Where's Mrs Barclay? Let's all go and have a drink.'

I looked at the number of the door. It was 18. The one had been badly defaced.

'She's gone to bed very tired,' I had the resource to say. 'I'm just going home.'

Chaucer gave me a sly look that only the professional oldest friend can give. He knows the world is full of happenings he can only be on the edge of. He conveys: 'Between us it is unnecessary to say anything, but I think you are being very unwise.'

'She's in number eight,' he said enthusiastically. 'I looked it up if you want her.'

'No, no. I'm just going home,' I repeated.

'Well then, one for the road. You must,' he said.

He marched me down the stairs.

'There's meeting you to celebrate,' he said at the bar. 'So many years . . .' he said. 'Not,' he said with a killing blue-eyed glance, 'since Dieppe.'

It was a sharp blow. Whatever else he was, Chaucer was a professional and efficient. I had been running off with a schoolteacher in those days. He had met us on the boat going over. He and she had had a most satisfying talk about the year she had taken her diploma.

There was a change in Chaucer's conversation now we were at the bar. Academic research vanished. He was blatant.

'Interesting case the Barclay case,' he said. 'Why did she do it?'

I headed him off. He was on at once to libel and slander. I headed him off again on to his holiday, but the taste for crime and law was growing fast in him. It was new interest suddenly born. They had passed (he said) the mill at Duffin, the scene of the Purdom murder.

'The farmer's wife who poisoned her husband,' he explained. There was a don at Queen's or somewhere who had been disqualified from driving. He had only once been to the Law Courts in his life, Chaucer said (and he gleamed with the intention of never missing a case now), and that was to hear an appeal. The appellant was the member of a gang of safe breakers.

'It just shows you what a small place the world is. The man sitting next to me in court knew the prisoner. "Pal of mine. Pal of mine," he kept saying.' Chaucer was enjoying himself. He looked younger and younger with every crime he mentioned.

He had actually been sitting next to somebody else's oldest friend. Chaucer's son had joined us now and blurted out:

'I don't think that woman doctor will get off, do you?'

'The husband of your chemistry mistress is a QC, isn't he?' Chaucer asked proudly of his son. Chaucer's age dropped to the early thirties.

Chaucer insisted on seeing me off to the door of my car. I was obliged to drive off. I drove out of the town to the bridge over the river and looked at the mild evening water where one or two men were fishing . . . I was waiting for the moment when Chaucer and his son would be safely at dinner before I returned.

In an hour I was in Sophia's room. She was lying in bed.

'Didn't you get my message?' she said.

'You can't ring me. No telephone,' I said.

'Silly,' she said. 'Come for me in the morning, early.'

'About eleven?' I said, knowing her habits.

'Earlier,' she said.

'Ten-thirty?' I laughed.

'No, ten,' she said.

This was an old game of ours and it soothed me. I was restored.

'Ring me from the call box,' she said. 'I'll come down.'

When I got back to the cottage and saw its white solitary walls in the August moonlight, I saw she had been playing with me. Up and down stairs to the telephone she would go, yes; but she had been too 'low' to come here. One gets jealous of ridiculous things. She would do anything for a telephone. I had a bad night and, to teach her, I waited until eleven o'clock before I drove back those ten miles to the hotel.

The porter was standing outside his desk as if waiting for me.

'Mrs Barclay,' he sneered even before I asked him, 'has gone. She went out at half-past nine. There's a note for you.'

I took the letter and went out into the street to read it. I was not going to allow the porter to gaze at my destruction from the whited sepulchre of his old age. I was back instantly. Sophia said she had by mistake picked up Chaucer's little red exercise book, the bible of his journey, the chart of his life, with her magazine, and had only found it this morning. She had gone after him with it.

'I'm death,' she said.

The Chaucers had left by bus an hour earlier and no one knew where. On the wall of the office was the calendar. The figures 26 stood out large.

When I look back at this period of Sophia Barclay's life and of my own the fatal difference between us is clear. I had no unconscious mind; Sophia had no conscious mind. When I waited at the hotel for her to ring up or to come back, listening to the combustion of the summer traffic passing to the holiday mountains, I had leisure to go through her character inch by inch. It is a delusion that distance or waiting breed mystery and encourage desire. At the end of an hour there was little of Sophia's character left. I knew that when she returned I would start putting it together again and the knowledge made me laugh. I was laughing at Chaucer. Sophia had really brought off her most brilliant coup. To take away the planner's plan, to make away with the policy of the most insured man on earth – this was dazzling of her. I imagined the moment of discovery, the recriminations between father and son. Chaucer would be defeated. Without his book he would not know whether he was to eat a sandwich or have the hotel lunch anywhere. He would be faced by a waterfall when he had expected a castle. It would be anarchy. For the first time he would be out of touch. Unless – and I laughed even more when I imagined Sophia saying this to him as she certainly would – that his unconscious had been at work. For what phenomenal motive, in obedience to what primitive force, had he left the twenty-sixth blank?

On that decisive morning in our lives Sophia was true to herself. She

[533]

had as little idea of where she was as she had of the whereabouts of the Chaucers. Her inevitable telephone calls conveyed this. I damned his little red book. She called me intolerant.

'I must put this right. It's frightful of me. It is not as if they were friends,' she said.

And the next call:

'Still no luck. They must have gone on to Snowdon.'

'But that's a terribly long way. Come back.'

'I can't wreck their holiday,' she said.

'What about us?' I said. 'Are you running off with me or with Chaucer *père et fils?*'

'Speaking French does not make it funny,' she said. 'People are serious,' she added censoriously.

'Not Chaucer,' I said.

'His wife is dead. He's a widower,' she said.

Like divorce, death brought out all Sophia's profound feeling for the respectable. I was made to feel outside the pale of the central glooms of life.

I found out where she was.

'I'm coming for you,' I said.

'Two cars again. Don't be silly,' she said. 'I'm going to Snowdon.'

'So am I then,' I said. 'I can't wait wondering what all this chasing after widowers is about.'

Her voice changed.

'All what?' she said very coldly.

'This,' I said.

I recognised as I drove after her that what I had just said was disastrously wrong. I recognise after five years that it was one of those unforgivable mistakes one makes in one's life. Sophia was always doing the wrong thing but to call it 'all this' was to make her feel in the right about it. I had once called the Barclay case 'all this'. I spent the rest of the journey trying not to see the ludicrous side of our situation: the Chaucers voyaging without chart, Sophia pursuing them without knowing where they were and myself pursuing her, and all of us not meeting at the mountain sacred to Welsh tourism. I was wrong.

The first thing I saw at that point of the mountain where the light railway starts for the summit was Sophia's small green car. Near it stood Chaucer's son. Round-shouldered, thin, pale, glum, he was staring enviously at the heavy motor traffic on the road.

I got out of my car. 'Where are you all?' I asked.

He watched a motor cycle go roaring by and out of sight before he could collect himself to answer. He was deeply enjoying noise.

'Hullo,' he said passively. 'Dad's with Mrs Barclay. They told me to wait here in case you came.'

'Where are they?'

'Gone up,' he said, nodding to the mountain. 'Dad's taken her. We were in a mess. Dad couldn't find our book. She had taken it. We missed two buses.'

He spoke in the relieved manner of one who was grateful that his father had missed something for once.

'If Mrs Barclay hadn't found it and brought it we wouldn't have got here. She was very decent, she gave us a lift – that little Humber can shift when she steps on it.'

But I was looking up the green slopes and hard shoulders of the mountain. I was listening for her chatter.

'You won't see them,' he said.

'I'm sorry I've made you miss the trip. Why didn't you go?'

'Doesn't interest me,' said the boy. 'My idea was to take the motor bike to France. They didn't want me.'

'How long have they gone?'

'I don't know. They're going right up to the top though. When she gave us a lift that is what she said: "Now we can all go right up to the top." Dad and I were only going half-way. You see, she said she'd give us a lift on afterwards. She said she'd never been to the top of a mountain before in her life.'

The boy was grinning but he stopped shyly and frowned at me thoughtfully. Then he burst out:

'Do you think she got a fair deal in that case? She was telling Dad about it, he knows the judge. He said she ought to have got a thousand pounds. That woman doctor has, in the paper this morning. Do you think the law's always right? I've never met anyone who's been in a case before. There was trouble about a water burst in Dad's office and Mother wanted

[535]

him to bring a case, but he wouldn't, so we didn't get anything. I agree with Mrs Barclay, you've got to go all out.'

All out with Chaucer!

Many hours passed before they came down the mountain. Sophia was hot and blushed when she saw me. I had hardly ever seen her look so impudent. At half past six that evening I was following them all as she drove them a few miles on to their next stopping place and, as usual, she was soon out of sight. When I caught them up she had run into the bus from Llanberis. They spent the night of the twenty-sixth in hospital. It was the beginning of their courtship.

Chaucer never loses touch with old friends. After their marriage I had no sight of Sophia or Chaucer for a good five years. But then, one evening in London, when I was standing in a cinema queue trying to calm a girl I was with, who was making a scene, I heard the well-known voice drilling through the traffic noises of a London Saturday night: Chaucer. There was no escape. I dined with them. It was for them an elated dinner party. Thank heaven there were other guests.

No rattling electric trains near Chaucer's well-found house. No frantic decoration on its walls. There was not a touch of Sophia's in the place. From his previous marriage Chaucer has accumulated much of the larger mahogany and she had become larger to match it – larger, plump and silently contented. He looked down the table at her with pride. There were university couples at dinner – not at all Sophia's set – but there was no talk of academic women. Chaucer gossiped as if he had been the second cousin of a peer. He was on to judges, courts, queer cases, points of law. At first I was amused; then I realised Chaucer was exhaustive. I became alarmed. Rightly. The great bores are men of mastery and nerve.

'That is how we got married,' he was shouting to us all, pointing a hurrahing finger at her down the table. 'She nearly killed me. Stole my papers, crashed into a bus and the next thing I was at the altar. I could have brought a case. And there's an interesting point. The insurance company fought. There was a point of law. It's the only time my picture has been in the papers.'

I saw it on her face. They were two blissful news items. Publicity, scandal, had been Chaucer's craving.

'Or mine,' she said submissively.

'Oh, how can you say that!' protested Chaucer, with pride on her behalf. 'The Barclay case, don't be shy, tell them about it.'

'No, you,' she said.

'It's your story – still, if you won't, I must.'

'And don't forget the little red book,' she said with a voluptuous wriggle.

I couldn't believe my ears. There was a pause in which they both glanced at me, she satisfied and fulfilled; he slyly and, what was worse, protectively. The glance conveyed that she was the scandal I could never have made the most of and I was the hole-in-corner despair from whom he had saved her. But for him she might now be having rows with me in cinema queues on Saturday nights.

On the Scent

———

A big, oblong man, Manningtree gets out of bed in the morning briskly, straightens up at once, yawns, blows out his chest, then puts on a violet silk dressing-gown and is about to shout joyfully:

'Wakey, wakey! Rise and shine! Lash up and . . .' but no! He looks across to the bed where his gnat of a wife is sleeping under a little fizz of dyed red hair, with her busy mouth wide open, even in sleep, and he stops. Putting on a stealthy look and lifting his knees high he tiptoes out of the room. Manningtree's face is important. It has a quality that can only be called blatantly public, like a statue's; this is his fortune and his calamity. He is tall. He is handsome. At sixty-two, he still has beautifully polished fair hair, a pink, boyish skin, and still blue eyes and, at times, total calm. This is his fortunate side. His stealthy, dramatic look as he tiptoes out of the room is an aspect of the calamitous one; it empties clubs and bars, it empties sofas and corners of rooms at parties, it has emptied messes in two world wars. It is the look of the relentless, booming, whispering, story-teller.

Take getting up in the morning.

'I arise,' he says – making his blue eyes go very small – 'from my humble couch' – pulling down the corners of his mouth to mock pathos – 'and poop along' – he is confiding – 'to the end of the passage' – he is now secretive – 'to get in the milk and the papers.' Then he makes a peculiar movement of his lower jaw which shoots out sideways, at the same time almost closing his mouth so that he speaks a little grindingly through his teeth and conveys a lurking, better-not-be-caught-red-handed impression. He continues in a tone now sordid, 'To see what's going on in the world,' and, at this, his face becomes handsome, nearly blank – 'to see,' he says disparagingly, 'if there is anything of interest.'

He stares at you when he says this for a long time and most people have to lower their eyes as one does after looking at the blind statue of some soldier or politician. And then the conspiring look comes on again, he leans towards you with his jaw shooting sideways, driving you bit by bit into your corner until you want to put up your hands and surrender and he goes very mean and nasty about the mouth. 'And pick up the post to see if the Manningtree millions have turned up,' he adds.

So he describes the first half hour of the day. His wife, who does not sleep well in spite of doctors and pills of all kinds, is awake, but keeps her eyes closed because she has seen and heard this performance every morning of her married life – except for the war – but she opens them when he brings in her breakfast, keen and singing.

'No luck, old girl! No Manningtree. Boo hoo hoo,' he says, collapsing his face.

She could scream.

'Bunny's a fool, an ass, a dolt!' she tells her friends and all her little bits of jewellery repeat the message in flashes from her neck, her ears, her fingers. 'I think I shall go mad. We live in two pokey little rooms. I have nothing to put on. He hasn't even got a pension. Go to London! Go to Paris! My dear, we can't afford the bus fare to go to the cinema. That gas fire is the only comfort I've got in life.' She lowers her voice to a dirty whisper – 'As for you know what – we gave that up two years after we were married.'

And then she tells them the story of this disastrous marriage. There she was, a woman with brains, attractive too. Men with brains, she never could resist them: Angus, Charles, Duncan, Max – look what they have done. Angus an Admiral, Max, Governor of somewhere – but just because she was potty about a shifty and brilliant painter who jilted her for an Irish waitress--she had to go and marry Bunny Manningtree on the rebound. He worked for a travel agency and was hopeless at it.

'Of course,' she says, pulling herself together. 'He is a Manningtree. Lord Manningtree is his cousin. They are all bankers, shipbuilders, Cabinet Ministers, worth millions.

'I always have a look at *The Times* to see if any of them have died,' she says, twisting her little face, for she has caught something of his habits after twenty-five years, 'but the fool! He even says he doesn't think he's any relation at all, won't even write a letter and here we stick in this hole. And I had talent! We scrape, we sit. I stay in bed half the day and he comes in the evening with his library book – and he reads bits out to me. History! Mexico! That's the latest thing. The Aztecs.'

She gives an hysterical laugh.

'D'you know – I asked what he wanted to do when he was a boy – do you know what he said: an Aztec priest!!!'

She is wrong about this. After breakfast Manningtree walks across the park to earn, as he puts it, 'the sordid daily crust'. He has an excellent figure, he is presentably dressed, he has the serene, dummy-like expression that would delight any tailor. She is wrong about his wanting to be an Aztec; that was years ago, before the war. He has moved southward since then, across Panama, down the Andes. He is with the Incas, these days. After a few hundred yards, his face attracts attention from passers-by. It has begun to move. It is dramatising certain arguments about the Virgins of the Sun. He is going over their chief temples, their convents set apart from the Inca towns. He arrives eventually at Macchu Picchu. One hundred female skeletons have been found at that Inca hide-out – were they Virgins of the Sun or were they Manco II's concubines or simply Indians who had fled with him from the Spaniards? Manningtree has doubts. He scents a mystery and his blue eyes go very small. The only way to clear it up is to go back to the sixteenth century. He does this. He has got out of Cuzco unobserved by the Spaniards and although he knows the Inca roads well, the stone causeways six feet wide, scratched on the sides of the Andes or choked by the jungle, he also knows that the only safe, secret way is to go by the Urabamba River. He sets off, with a machete – but back he has to come because the old, old question has arisen. How is he dressed? How is he disguised? At this word, the artfulness of his face is so blatant that children fifty yards away think he is going to eat them.

Alas, Manningtree has now to postpone the answer. He has arrived. He straightens his face and goes into a doorway marked *Staff Only*, in the Hildegarde Memorial Museum.

This museum had been the white elephant of the city for two generations. The Council would have liked to have sold it or pulled it down; they could not do so. But fashions change. Once deserted except on rainy days, the museum is now visited by thousands of people every year.

It is a fantastic, cream-washed neo-Gothic mansion built about 1820 in the park – which was attached to it – by an Austrian Archduke for his mistress, the twelfth Duchess of Taxminster. There is a Byron story about her. After the Archduke died it was taken over, in the late 'seventies, by the intellectual son of the steel magnate Rudolf Dabchild and his crippled wife, Hildegarde von Hochfeld-Mannheim, who inherited the Kreutzer fortune. These two beetle-like creatures were compulsive, voracious, indiscriminate collectors. Trainloads, vanloads of remarkable furniture, armour, Spanish choir stalls, icons, Italian ceilings, porcelain, tapestries, pictures, weapons, costumes of all the ages, Chinese, Japanese and Indian objects, archaeological relics, and the usual cases of Polynesian masks, canoes, poisoned arrows and stuffed birds and so on, arrived at the mansion and choked it. When Dabchild's wife died, he unloaded it on the appalled city and called it the Hildegarde Memorial Museum. Fortunately a rich Trust supported it. It was run by antiquarians originally but, lately, since the dissolution of the British Empire, people who would have been Generals or Governors of African and Indian provinces in earlier days now dominate the committee. One of these, remembering Manningtree's record in the war, got him his job. Or rather his wife did, by circulating the gossip that he was a connection of the great Manningtrees.

Even now, Bunny Manningtree won't say what he was doing in the war. He simply says he was sitting on his bottom in the Shetlands, 'pooped around' for a few months in the United States and had something to do with one or two 'wheezes'. 'No initiative,' his wife says. 'He let them push him into Supply.' 'Supplying wheezes,' he explains. The word 'wheeze' comes out with a lingering malicious glee as if he were a schoolboy who has just bought a trick glass of beer at a joke shop or written to another boy in invisible ink. All the same, bits of the war, he says, 'had an interest'. Up in the Shetlands, for example, he got friendly with the seals and collected moss.

Whatever it was, it was a dead end, as far as his peacetime prospects were concerned. He stands (it must be said that is one thing he can do: stand properly. Few people can), about ten yards inside the main entrance of the Hildegarde, looking at the moons of his nails.

Once or twice a year an old acquaintance spots him:

'Good heavens, Manningtree? What are you doing here?'

'On the strength,' says Manningtree calmly. And then his other face jostles the calm one away and he narrows his blue eyes, slips his lower jaw sideways and says in a chewing, secretive and sordid voice: 'Actually – guide. I show the *hoi polloi* round. Coach parties. It's terrifying.' Then his face changes and he straightens to mention the finer aspects of his job.

'VIPs too. French mayors, Siamese Ambassador, Russians.'

He puts his hand to his mouth and coarsely whispers again:

'Minister of Labour last Tuesday.'

'There are one or two things worth a look,' he says. He leads his friends down the fantastic corridors, passing statues, Japanese paintings, Indian carvings, cases of porcelain. He comes to a door and a sly look comes on.

'Private apartments of the Archduke,' he says. The friends admire.

'Hoovered three times a week,' he says to the ladies. He beckons them on to the centre piece. It is, of course, the canopied bed of the Archduke.

'See the little secret staircase?' he says, nodding to a corner by the bed. He looks noble. His friends grin. He is disappointed by the blatancy of the universal reaction, especially if one of the men lags behind for a second look at the staircase and says, 'Very convenient.'

Manningtree's sinister face comes on, reprovingly. He nods to the staircase.

'That is why Bismarck tore up the Treaty.'

No one has any idea what he is talking about.

Afterwards, as the party leaves, Manningtree shakes hands and they go off saying, 'Poor old Bunny.'

At five o'clock he collects a book or two from the Library, goes home and after dinner he reads. Suddenly he may say to his wife:

'Here's another so-called explorer repeating the same cock-eyed idea. No Inca in his senses would have built a fort there, where it could be dominated by any enemy outside. It wasn't a fort, it was a holy city. The rising sun strikes through the slit on the Intihuatana sundial.'

No answer.

'Another howler,' he says. 'The saddle is not ten thousand feet up. I'd put it nearer eight thousand.'

'Perhaps it's grown since you were there,' his wife says.

One Monday – Mondays are usually quiet in the winter – a foreigner comes to the Hildegarde Museum. He is a tall, well-built German with clipped grey hair, cold, wide grey eyes, straight-nosed, straight-lipped, easy in carriage. He buys a guide-book at the counter, walks past Manningtree and sets off round the museum on his own. As he passes he leaves behind him a worldly smell of cigar, caraway and some other smell – a scent. The scent disturbs Manningtree. It makes him feel cold. Having nothing to do, he strolls off from room to room, looking for a sunny window. Once or twice he sees the foreigner in the distance. Manningtree's nose twitches. He moves to another room.

'Got it,' he says at last. '*Vol de nuit.*'

The foreigner can be seen distantly through three doorways. Manningtree dreams.

'Hun. Baron, I suppose. Baltic family. Query, born Lubeck. Staff Officer in war. No, not Staff Officer. Heidelberg, Oxford. Berliner. Villa in Dahlem, pretty district. Take a bus from the Kurfürstendamm. Forget the number.'

Manningtree moves on. There is more sun in the south of the building. He goes to his favourite room – ancient costumes. His mind travels.

In those days, he recapitulates, the Incas must have held the roads they scratched on the mountains and they certainly had fortified places. They once shelled the Spaniards in Cuzco with white-hot stones. (That, by the way, does not excuse the public rape of several hundred Virgins of the Sun.) Anyone trying to get the gen on Macchu Picchu and to see what Manco II's boys are up to had better take to the jungle following the Urabamba through its gorges. Have to be fit, of course.

Manningtree takes to the jungle. He slips below the fortified line. He has jungle cunning. In the hot depths of the gorges he can keep alive on bananas. He finds a deserted hut and there at night he hangs his shirt over the entrance to keep out the night air of the Andes. After sixty miles on foot, swollen with bites, he is at the base of Macchu Picchu two thousand feet above him. Up he goes; as he gets nearer he sees a sight to shake the spirit of any man. Two bodies come hurtling through the air, pass over him and crash into the gorge. Ah ha! The High Priest has caught a couple trying to get to the Virgins of the Sun. Manningtree pauses to consider the old, old problem. How is he dressed? Inca robes? But did the Incas wear Inca robes? Didn't the Spaniards make them wear

Spanish costume? And what was Spanish costume in Extremadura in the sixteenth century? An idea comes to Manningtree, a wheeze. Suppose he appears in Macchu Picchu dressed as he is now, in a navy blue suit with light chalk stripes, white collar, school tie? Why not? Take them by surprise, eh? Probably run away. That is exactly what happens. Men posted at the main gate make a bolt for it. He walks in and catches a boy – always ask a boy – *Donde està* the High Priest? – always make for a priest. Nasty sight here, by the way, two more men tied by their heels and hanging head down over the precipice – two more cases of trying to get to the Virgins of the Sun. A whole crowd of High Priests come along. They rush him. He is arrested at once. He is tried in the Court House – usual charge, Virgins of the Sun again; and, by the way, archaeologists are wrong, the courtyard described as residence of Manco II is actually *below* the residence – the military fellers get out their clubs and prepare to beat him to death and then pitch his body into the gorge.

A nasty fix this but Manningtree has an answer to it. He worked that one out when he was settling the dress problem a few hours ago when he was climbing up the hill. Manningtree's face takes on one of its most public leers of profound cunning, visible (one would guess), but for the Andes, as far away as the Pacific Ocean.

'Oh, High Priest,' Manningtree says. 'Throttle down a moment. I've been having a peep at your sundial. Art thou not all het up about sunrise and sunset, and what-have-you – Time in short? Am I right? Splendid! Well, let me put a little problem to you, something to think over. I come from the future. You're yesterday as far as I am concerned, I'm tomorrow. Tomorrow's sun has already risen before today's has set. D'you follow?'

One of the enclosed Virgins of the Sun stops weaving vicuna and looks out of a window and exclaims:

'Oh Thou!'

The fellows put down their clubs and they start a pi-jaw nineteen to the dozen – not loudly, by the way. At that altitude, the air is thin and voices are soft, a curious point. Manningtree takes his opportunity and talks in signs to the Virgin of the Sun. Where does that road lead to? he signals. She replies, by signs. To the real secret city. Manningtree thought as much. He has always held that Macchu Picchu was an outpost, a decoy.

He memorises her information. Never write anything down! He has always memorised everything.

The German visitor to the Hildegarde has come back to the room where Manningtree has been standing and has been watching him for several minutes. He has noticed that Manningtree is standing in front of a large glass case containing Spanish costumes and at first the German thinks Manningtree is talking to someone. Then he has the idea that since no one is visible the person must be hidden in the glass case. This does not startle him. He is alerted. He has recognised an interesting idea, a possible experience – it has, unfortunately, been used in films. He feels drawn to Manningtree and approaches him.

'Excuse me, sir,' he says in rather stiff, good English, 'are you by any chance the Head Director of the museum?'

Manningtree puts on his blank face at once.

'No, I'm not, I'm sorry. Can I be of any help?'

'I wonder if you could direct me to the archaeological section?' says the German. 'Are you an official?'

Manningtree's nose twitches. He has smelled *Vol de nuit* again. He has a strange cold feeling of being carried into the past.

'Oh no,' says Manningtree. 'I'm just a sort of chap keeping a sort of an eye.' And, in fact, he opens one eye to significant wideness.

'I beg your pardon,' says the German. 'You are a visitor like myself.'

'Oh no,' says Manningtree. 'For my sins this is where I earn the daily crust. Follow me. I'll show you.'

The German stares at him; then he smiles. He remembers. He remembers what the English are like; very soon, as the textbooks say, Manningtree is likely to make a joke. The German prepares himself for this. They walk in a friendly fashion across the room together, and nodding to the cases, Manningtree says in his sinister voice, 'This is where we keep the *disguises*.'

'The disguises?' the German repeats politely. Somewhere here, at any moment, will come the joke.

'The costumes,' says Manningtree with wonderful coolness.

'Ah!' The German is relieved. The joke has been accomplished. Manningtree becomes friendly.

'Have you seen the Private Apartments?'

'Yes. Of little interest,' says the German. 'Just the little incident of Bismarck and the Treaty.'

Manningtree is delighted. One does not often meet the man with inside knowledge. But he is still worried by the smell of *Vol de nuit*.

'Here,' he says, 'this is what you want. Archaeology. There are two rooms. Early British village?' Manningtree offers. 'The Western lake culture?'

'Africa?' He hesitates shyly, 'Inca?'

The German shrugs his shoulders and walks brusquely forward.

'This is what I want.' He opens his catalogue. 'The Mayas.'

Vol de nuit! Maya! Manningtree suddenly knows something. His face closes. He had been right first go off.

'You speak English very well. You were up at Oxford?' he asks.

'Yes. I had been at Heidelberg. My family comes from Lubeck, but I live in Berlin now.'

'Dahlem,' says Manningtree.

'Yes,' says the German warmly.

'Lovely trees. You can get a bus, I seem to remember, from the Kurfürstendamm, I forget the number – was it 86?'

'Interesting,' says the startled German. 'When were you there last?'

'Never,' says Manningtree. 'Not actually, ever.'

'This is extraordinary,' says the German.

Manningtree puts on his most asinine, blushing, apologising face.

'Always interested in places, local buses, trains, I collected timetables at school. I used to play at running goods trains all over Europe – the world actually. Fun. Something of interest.'

The German is puzzled and takes a long look at Manningtree. He is weighing up the question of madness for Manningtree looks very childish, stupid, his chin dropping, his mouth open. Manningtree changes the subject.

'I'm not a Maya man,' he says. 'I'm afraid I'll be no good to you,' Manningtree apologises. 'I moved on to the Incas.

'The Incas, now, that's another thing,' he goes on. 'I mean I'm not a scholar. I just potter. The priesthood, the roads. Clever people. Time, for example. They understood it.'

The German edges away. Manningtree follows him closer.

'And another thing – how they got the information through the Andes. Two thousand miles, three more like it. No writing, no letters, no telephone – memorised it.' He pauses. 'What was their secret?'

His face is blameless.

'No radio,' he concludes.

The German gives a sharp turn of his head. He is uncertain. Is Manningtree mad? Manningtree is now studying the cases of Mayan objects.

'Mayas are interesting too. You know them well?' says Manningtree humbly.

'Yes,' said the German.

'I tried it, before the war. There were too many problems,' says Manningtree. 'I moved out of Mexico on to the Incas. For instance, here's a thing I bet you can tell me, the sort of detail that I get stuck in; I mean, fed up with. The Palace at Mitla – you know the Palace at Mitla? I mean the second Incan palace.'

'But you *do* know the Mayas!' says the German suspiciously.

'Nothing,' says Manningtree. 'I mean the High Priest had put the wind up the Kings and all that and the Kings got very cunning.'

Manningtree begins his well-known jaw-sliding and significant eye-rollings.

'They cut three back doors so that they could nip out fast before the old boy could spot them – rather neat? The snag is – and this is where I stick – if you go to Mitla today there are no back doors. And, what's more, if you look up your Father Bourgoa you'll see he says there were six rooms. Actually there are only four. What d'you make of that?'

'Bourgoa's sources were unreliable,' says the German affably. 'He was repeating hearsay. What year were you there?'

'Alas and lackaday, never,' says Manningtree. 'Never had the where-withal. I just go pooping around old books.'

'Pooping!' exclaims the German.

'Just pooping and pottering,' says Manningtree.

'Pooping – I don't understand that English word,' says the German. 'I have heard it . . . yes . . .'

The German, who up to now has had simply a sharp intelligent German face, like thousands of others one sees along the Baltic, suddenly has a memory and *his* face changes. He seems to put on weight as if he had just eaten too much. His cheeks swell over his jaw which fattens, tears like juices come into his eyes which nearly close and look sly. At the sight of this, Manningtree's pink face blushes, his eyes begin watering too. He also fattens. The two men stand melting in front of each other like blushing snowmen as though the temperature of the room has shot up twenty degrees.

'I envy you going to Mexico,' says Manningtree.

'Oh, I haven't been there either,' says the German. The German goes on and, for the first time, his English syntax is clumsy.

'But it is always historical that makes for you the interest? I don't think so. When we met on the night train from New York to Chicago in December 1940, was that pooping, Captain Manningtree? You were interested in the Virgins of the Sun.'

Manningtree stares at him.

'I was a pooper, too!' exclaims the German with delight, extending his hand. 'Hochstadt.'

'Hochstadt!' nods Manningtree. And then he winks at the German.

'*Vol de nuit*, a great mistake, old boy. Terrible giveaway. We followed you all over the States. It clings. No offence. What are you up to now?'

The German looks humble.

'I have a small cinema,' he says sadly. 'Not Dahlem any more.'

'*Hoi polloi*, eh? Well, I suppose,' says Manningtree, 'it brings in the daily crust.'

And, in sympathy, he looks over the floors, walls and ceilings of the Hildegarde Memorial Museum with disgust.

'By the way, I always wondered,' says Manningtree, 'how did you manage after we got your radio?'

'Like the Incas,' says the German. He has got his revenge. He has made a joke.

The Hildegarde Museum closes. Manningtree walks home across the park. He tells his wife about the encounter.

'I recognised him the moment he came in,' he says. 'Smelt him. I didn't let on. I didn't say anything. Ah ha! I thought. Baron von Trondheim, I says to meself! I just lay low.' He crouches. 'I shammed dead.' He closes his eyes. 'Memory got busy. He recognised me too. I don't know how, deep fellow.'

'I wonder!' says his wife.

'Ah,' says Manningtree screwing up one eye and rubbing a finger joint on a thoughtful tooth. 'Still an agent, I think. He gave the name Hochstadt.'

Manningtree's pleasure fades. He looks gloomy.

'Manningtree millions not arrived, I suppose? No. Ah well. Have to wait for another war, but I'll be past it. My memory's going. I couldn't remember the number of the Dahlem bus. Bad show.'

Citizen

I wonder if you go to picture exhibitions and if you saw the drawings at the W Gallery a month or so ago. Italian drawings, by a woman – Effie Alldraxen. Very good notices the critics gave her. Very gratifying to me. She is my daughter. There was one large drawing that several of our friends mentioned – typically Italian, the picture of one of those palazzo courtyards in Rome with a statue in it. It was one she called 'The Father'. She caught the feeling that you have in Rome, of statues being everywhere – stone people (do you know?), threatening, appealing, almost walking about, crowding in, pushing the living off the pavement. One of the critics said she made the figure live – a curious statement, I thought, because stone and bronze are dead, aren't they? Of course, I don't know anything about art. I'm just a layman, a doctor. My business is illness. What interested me when I went to look at Effie's show was that the child was ill when she was doing the best of that stuff. I say 'child' – a father's slip of the tongue; she is turned forty.

I shall hope not to sound harsh, but Effie has not been an easy child. I would describe myself as detached. I see so many sick people. She has been sending us telegrams all her life, and before I opened the one she sent from Rome, where she was doing that picture, I thought: Now what mess has she got into? Effie's telegrams read as though she is doing her face in the mirror – a dab here, a dab there, but with words. It went, 'In hospital, motor accident. No bones, not serious, don't worry, just bad breakdown. Can you come immediately, not to bother, please if possible. Very well.'

Children tear at one's bowels. In eight hours I was out of the London rain and sitting by Effie's bedside in Rome, listening to her childish voice. She had not been in a motor accident. She had been pushed by the bumper of a slow-moving car in the Corso and had been knocked down by a bicycle.

[550]

'I think –' she said after we had gone over the incident several times. 'I think,' she said, stubbornly putting up her chin, 'I must have been trying not to get married.'

Effie is a small woman, and although she is growing plump, she looks younger than she is. She will be forty-one next June. She was sitting up in bed, and she had the pleased, shining, new, ashamed look, rather wet and cunning, of a golden spaniel that has been dressed up in shawls by children and is presently going to make a bolt for it into the garden.

'To Mr Wilkins,' she said.

'And who is he?' I asked.

'He was on the train when you saw me off from London. Schoolmaster,' she said. For testing one out, she has a small, high, plaintive voice.

'I don't remember him,' I said. 'But what's the matter? Is he married already?' One of the difficulties of Effie's life has been her love of other women's husbands.

'Oh no!' said Effie, giving a squeal of pleasure. She loved this kind of conversation. 'He hasn't got a wife.' Then she looked at me slyly. Effie is proud of her turbulent history. 'I suppose his not being married is the trouble,' she said.

Effie has two voices and two kinds of laughter. Her usual voice is small and sweet – the matter-of-fact voice of a girl of five, and she uses it for things that are true. The laughter that goes with it is the high squeal that used to enchant us when she was little. This voice is, no doubt, too arch for a woman of her age. Her other voice is dry, abrupt, grown-up, bold, and mannish, and it drops to short, doggish barks of laughter. In this voice, Effie does not often tell the truth. I knew now that Effie was going to tell me a lie next, because she arranged her bedclothes and looked me gruffly in the eye.

'You are going to be cross with me,' she said, in the brisk manner. 'I've started doing it again.'

'What?'

'Making happenings,' she said. She blushed.

I did not answer.

'I'm being followed,' said Effie.

'By Mr Wilkins?' I said, guessing.

'Oh no, no,' she barked.

'By some Italian?' I said.

Effie was so startled that she stopped laughing. I could see that I had put an idea into her head, perhaps for use in the future. There is something innocent about her. She had been a fortnight in Italy and it had not occurred to her that an Italian might follow her in the street, though she knew they followed other women. She had not thought of this because it was she who, in her day-dreams, was always the follower.

'Oh no,' she said. 'Not a man.' And then she added primly, correcting me, 'Not followed. Accompanied.'

After a moment, she went on. 'Everywhere,' she said. 'In the street. I have to make room. I have to step out of the way. That's how I got knocked down. There wasn't room.'

Effie stared at my stare. 'I can't see whether you're looking at me, Daddy,' she said. 'The light is on your glasses.'

'But who accompanies you?' I said.

'Oh, I knew you'd understand! Give me my drawings from the table,' she said. 'I'll show you. No, all of them. Not this one. Not this – flowers, rather nice, don't you think? Here it is. This one.' She pointed. 'It comes with me.'

There was simply a drawing of the courtyard of a Roman palace, but there was no one in it.

'The statue,' she said. 'It walks with me everywhere I go.' There was certainly a statue in the foreground of the drawing. She broke into real tears. 'Silly?' she sniffed. 'It came . . . here . . . this morning. But it's gone, now you're here. Not a fool – I, not you. I mean me – I'm not. It's true.' And then she said, with a touch of aesthetic shame, 'It's bronze, very late, 1884.'

I suppose I owe my great influence with my daughter to the fact that I have made it an absolute rule to believe everything she says. I have never known her to be unpractical. She is brisk and domestic – a drawer-tidier, a sock-darner, a saucepan-buyer (one would say) – and she is pretty. Her fair hair is duller than it used to be, and she has eyes the colour of dark ginger. A poet might call them 'orbs'. She dresses oddly, as spinsters do, but that is because her practical instinct makes her do a little something different with everything. She was now doing something with a statue.

[552]

'It must make a terrible noise,' I said.

'Frightful,' she said. 'And such a bad period.'

The effect that Italy has upon Anglo-Saxons is always impressive. In a couple of days, when Effie's temperature was down, I went to look at her persecutor. The palazzo is on the street that leads to the bridge you cross to get to San Angelo. There is a wide entrance smelling of cold candle smoke, and then one walks between double rows of columns into the courtyard beyond, where the colonnade continues on three sides of the building. On the fourth is the higher brick wall of some large house, relieved by creepers and fountains. After the hot street, this courtyard is cool and enchanting.

Which of the figures had Effie's wanton mind chosen? I looked at them. The statues were set off in arches or placed among shrubs. They stood amid the dark gloss of creepers and beside fountains. The chief fountain was against the back wall, where three Tritons, the mask of disaster upon their spreading mouths, spouted into the tank beneath them; in the corners of the court two other pipes of water spoke out in higher voice beneath the hanging foliage. The air was as still and cool and golden as white wine; the place was filled with the sounds of water notes, high and low, like faraway talk and quiet laughing. One could fancy that this sound was the classical jargon of the figures standing near or posed under the twenty arches of the colonnade. Apollo, conceited in cheek and buttocks – was it he Effie had chosen? Or Mercury, off on one of his record flights? The Venus, vacant-minded, or that careerist Diana? Which, of all those white, finger-pointing gods and goddesses, those stooping nymphs and skilful boys, with their grubby, blind eyes and stone-deaf ears? As I entered the courtyard, my steps seemed to have frozen the movements of immortals, who, once my back was turned, would resume their irreconcilable and impossible lives.

I come out of this disturbing episode in the life of my family so much better than anyone else that I have no reluctance now about describing the large bronze statue that was obviously Effie's. It stood on a high plinth in the middle of the courtyard. Bronze. More than life-size, it was the naked figure of a man; on the pedestal was boldly cut out a name and, beneath it, the words 'CITTADINO ESEMPLARE' – 'The Exemplary Citizen'. He was a man in the prime of life – a merchant, a burgher, a city father of some kind. His features were strong, his body muscular, boldly veined, broad-chested, overbearing. The legs were powerful; the expression of the face tragic, jealous, authoritative, unreasonable, and morose. The large hands were the open hands of a maker – a bread-winner's hands, which could stun an enemy or drive a woman. The Citizen was the not-to-be-questioned head of a large family (one would guess), a master of the marriage bed, the married man in absolute degree.

Mr Wilkins came with me on this visit to the courtyard – the Mr Wilkins Effie had spoken of when I got to the hospital, and whom I had made it my business to get in touch with. I glanced at Mr Wilkins. I stared again at the statue. What a rival!

I must describe Mr Wilkins. If my portrait appears to be unfavourable, it is because Mr Wilkins was one of those men who enter enthusiastically into the art of making an unfavourable impression. He was a tall man, fortyish, with dry hair, wearing a light grey suit and a school tie. He had a difficulty with the letter 'i'. We first met in the bar of my hotel to drink what he called 'a glass of wain'.

'Ai run a school,' he said. He bent down and up from his thin waist as he talked – a habit picked up from talking to little boys – keeping his hands fidgeting frivolously in his pockets as he did so. A friendly man, fizzing with descriptive talk, he was always in steadily rising spirits, but before he reached his limit, something checked him, his throat gave a click, and tears of apology came into his eyes. Unfairly, this suggested the shadiness of a double life.

I would have known him from Effie's account of him; she is a cruel mimic. He had been on the train when it left London, and on the motor coach from Paris across the Alps. They were in sight of Turin, she said, when Wilkins, who was sitting behind her, put his hand round the side of the high seat and tapped her on the shoulder. 'Castle,' said Wilkins. There are often white chapels on the tops of the steep hills of the lower Alpine valleys.

Effie bent forward to look up. 'Shrine, I think,' said Effie, who was working on her guide-book.

'Bai Jove!' said Wilkins. 'You're raight, shraine.'

A little later there was another tap. Then another. From Turin to Milan, and then on to Bologna and Florence, she said, Mr Wilkins must have tapped away at her shoulder dozens of times. First she had to twist her neck towards him as he put his face round the side of the seat, then she had to turn her back and twist forward, craning to see what he was talking about, after that she had to twist back towards him to make a comment. She would see a head of dry hair, and the head would be zigzagging, nose down, towards her, behind a ragged moustache. Her replies were usually corrections, for, in an educated way, Mr Wilkins was often mildly wrong in his information. In moments of rest, she would hear him making a sishing noise behind her. He made this sound, she discovered later, by rubbing his hands up and down the thighs of his trousers, like a boy who is just about to be caned. After Florence, her neck was stiff and her right shoulder was hunched inward at an uncomfortable angle from her efforts to avoid Mr Wilkins's tap. In her hotel, when she undressed, she looked on her delicate skin for the mark.

I understood Wilkins at once. His distortion of the letter 'i' was not due to affectation. It sounded like a family piety, a deference to a dear, dead, cultured sister; or it may have been due to catarrh, for he spoke like a person holding an inhaler to one nostril in order to keep on terms with a distant cold. A woman can conceal her life, but Wilkins could not hide his out-of-date appearance, his overfriendly guiltiness. In his one sided way, he had an air, but pinned to his back there seemed to hang a notice that Effie must have read at once: 'Frantically Desires Some Woman to Pull Him Together'.

From shoulder-tapping, Effie said, Wilkins moved to a feeble squeezing of the upper arm. Effie likes a strong hand. In Milan, the party they were travelling with went to the opera, and Wilkins slept through the first act, making a personal sound, with his free nostril, that was just above the note of the violins.

'Ai feah,' Wilkins apologised to Effie, 'Ai overdid the wain at luncheon.'

They went to the cathedral in Milan. 'Ai adore baroque,' said Wilkins.

'Gothic,' Effie said sharply.

'Mai word, Miss Alldraxen,' Wilkins said with appetite, 'Ai love it when you are severe. You're taking me in hand.'

Before Leonardo da Vinci in Bologna it was, 'Now you're going to put me through it.' And in Rome, to the party at large as they sat at luncheon,

Wilkins announced, 'Bai Jove, Miss Alldraxen gave me some punishment in the Vatican this morning. It is what Ai need.'

The actual proposal of marriage was made, Effie said, in the Colosseum at night. The floodlighting there penetrates the upper arches and turns the high brick colander into a place of strong-smelling shadows. There is a hoarse whispering of voices from invisible tourists. Across the brown darkness came the nasal syllables of guides.

'Torn – er – to peeces – er – by wild – er – animalls,' a guide was saying as Wilkins took Effie's hand.

Effie said, 'Don't be stupid,' and got back, in a temper, to the motor coach, which was hooting for them. She has told me that the moment Wilkins declared himself a sharp pain went into her shoulder and stayed there like a nail. It was, so to say, his last tap, and he had driven it home. She was annoyed as she took her seat in the coach, and then the annoyance went. I can see her looking with pride at the women of the party, who were already gossiping about Mr Wilkins and herself. 'My rheumatism,' her expression would signal to them. 'I knew it would come.'

I have seen Effie in love a great many times. I do not mean that she was now in love, but she was – as she likes to be – adjacent to love. When this happens, her nature changes; she even changes shape. Her bosom rises, her back straightens, she puffs out softly. Her voice becomes sad and wise, and has a peculiar soft hoot, a flutelike sound. Glumly, her head is raised. She feels she has the weight of the air before a thunderstorm upon her, the oppression that makes people complain of their heads, retire to a darkened room, and sicken. For to Effie love is illness. The sacred illness. Attentive doctors and pained nurses gather about an imaginary bed, which is not the bed of ecstasy but the bed of some satisfying ailment.

I will skip the passions of her childhood, but there was Mr Lucas at the art school when she was eighteen. Mr Lucas's wife would not divorce him; Effie became ill with a strained heart. Then there was a man called Bobby, who said, 'It was only a passade.' Effie with a year's neuralgia. Sinclair, wife and three: bronchitis. Allardyce, Roman Catholic, judicial separation: migraines. Macdonald, wife in India: imaginary pregnancy. I could go on. If there was an unmarriageable man in love with someone else, Effie's hospital instinct would find him at once. If an unmarried man fell in love with her, as Wilkins did, she bit his head off.

Effie knows all this very well. I had it out with her six or seven years ago – once and for all, as I thought – after she had sat for three days with a packed suitcase containing towels, sheets and dishcloths on the stairs outside the studio of a painter called Gotloff, whom she planned to move in on, but who had gone off in time to Paris. I found her in hospital recovering from what she pretended was an attempt at suicide. I shall not forget the long, promiscuous smile on her face and the bark of satisfied laughter she gave as I went to her bedside. 'It is really marriage I am in love with, not men,' she said then.

So Effie was well equipped for the Wilkins affair. At luncheon on the day after Wilkins had proposed, she was telling the party about 'my old pain' – the pain in her shoulder. The women were soon offering her remedies. After each suggestion, the pain would change its nature. It shot from shoulder to head, from head to stomach, from stomach to knees. Was it the food? Was it the wine? Was it the water? Was it the Tiber, or Roman fever, or the drains? The women gave orders to Wilkins, who went out to the pharmacy and came back with a collection of medicines – poultices, headache pills, throat pastilles, indigestion tablets, liver pills, drugs, purges, and tonics. Also a kilo of cotton wool – his own idea. The party went to the catacombs in the afternoon, and Effie and Wilkins stayed behind at the hotel. 'No thermometer!' she said. Out Wilkins went again. When he got back, Effie said, she was alone in the lounge.

'I am dying of thirst,' she said. 'Is there any mineral water?'

Hearing a precise request, Wilkins was impelled to go one better. He sent for brandy. When it was brought, he sat beside Effie, with his hands on his long thighs, regarding her with enthusiasm; illness in women was a form of surrender. In actual fact, of course, *he* was surrendering. In her bounteous complaints, Effie was giving him something to surrender to. He saw – I have no doubt – a house, a lifetime marked by journeys up and down stairs to the body of the holy object, with trays and bottles. He may even have imagined the spit of temper and reprimand.

The brandy improved Effie; its subtle medicinal evocation of the beauty of past illnesses must have warmed her. She looked at Mr Wilkins, who was waiting for more punishment.

'I suddenly saw,' she said to me, 'that he really meant it. I mean, he really did want to marry me.' He was, to all appearances, what she had been looking for all her life since the age of three – a husband. They sat in the lounge on a deep, hot sofa. Holding her glass, leaning her head back and looking at the ceiling, she talked. Out of imitative sympathy, aroused by his love, Wilkins leaned back and looked at the ceiling also. They exchanged untrue versions of their own early lives. Mr Wilkins stopped looking at the ceiling and gazed at Effie with headlong admiration.

'Bai Jove!' he exclaimed. 'Ai have never really had a past.'

It was not a boast; it was not a confession. It was said in the dashing and reckless manner of one who, as far as pasts were concerned, was agog to spend the future living in hers. I am pretty certain that until this sentence of his Effie had no interest at all in Mr Wilkins; the unlucky man had been damned in her eyes by his marriageable condition. But now he had revealed a difficulty; he was too utterly marriageable, and difficulty was indispensable to her.

I listened to Effie as she sat up in bed telling her story in her evasive, upside-down way. Her wet handkerchief was screwed up in one hand. She was laughing one minute and dabbing her eyes the next, while the nun kept coming into the room at the wrong moment and the Italian cars changed gears on the hill outside. She told me that Mr Wilkins's words had made her compare their two cases. She must have paused to consider whether to re-edit her life story and to appear no longer in the role of the victim of other people's marriages but as an innocent waiting, neatly and circumspectly, for 'love to come' at last. Effie was as good as any woman at altering the play she was acting in. I don't know – she didn't tell me this – but I don't mind betting that Effie replied, 'I haven't had a real past, either.'

But I wasn't there to speculate, so I asked her, 'Yes, but what did you say to him? Did you tell him you would marry him?'

'Oh no!' She squealed with the pleasure of maddening me. 'You are funny. I told him I would have to think.'

Everyone who has heard Effie say the word 'think' agrees it has a musical sound that takes all suggestion of the process called 'thought' out of it. To see her 'thinking' is delightful. She looks as though she is listening to a voice singing on a distant mountain. But she is practical. Oh, always practical. She went off into the streets of Rome with her sketchbook, looking for something – some person, some place on which to drape her thoughts. She found the palazzo and its courtyard. Why did she choose the courtyard?

'It was so quiet, so expectant,' she said to me.

Yes, I thought, and it had an obvious difficulty and flaw – The Exemplary Citizen. There was something terribly wrong about 'Cittadina Esemplare', 1844. He was an aesthetic mistake – the wrong period, on the wrong scale. Wherever one stood, that gloomy, dictatorial male rose like an implacable obstacle.

She sat down to draw. 'I had a really big think,' she said. 'About Mr Wilkins, about me – about everything.' As her pencil worked, her mind undoubtedly set off on a number of short trips into Wilkins's future life. She was in Warwickshire, the headmaster's wife; she was wearing a new sage-green tweed, with a yellow scarf, unmistakably smarter than the wives of the masters. She saw her shoes – red, I expect, to make people talk. At the school, she introduced progressive ideas – mixed-coloured sweaters for the boys, perhaps a French afternoon in her drawing-room, more Creative Art. There was a master – young, satanic, modern languages, shadows under his eyes, unhappy with a wife not quite his class. He avoided Effie at first. She said, 'Why do you avoid me?' Frankly, he looked as though he would kill her, and then suddenly 'it all came out'. They watched football matches while he told her, under his breath, things that (she told him) he ought not to say. Difficult. She looked at his dark palm; the lines of two major love affairs were deeply cut under the little finger.

She shifted her thoughts to the matrons. One of them had to go – one whose nose was out of joint. The woman had obviously been in love with Mr Wilkins for years, and, besides, where did the sherry go? There was also a sad one who made a hysterical scene about the school secretary and 'poured out her heart' into Effie's lap. Effie was also getting to know the Christian names of the boys, tiptoeing in to give a pat to a pillow of a new boy who was crying. One who stole she saved, by timely psychiatry, from kleptomania.

It was twelve o'clock in the palazzo courtyard, Effie told me. She had heard the midday siren of some factory. The morning had passed quickly, and art is exhausting. She had been sitting on a stone step, and she was stiff. She got up and looked at the enormous statue from a new angle and then at her drawing. It was wrong. It was awful. Apart from anything else, the feet were wrong. She had not made them stand squarely on the plinth; the figure was half in the air. I have no doubt she was giddy with hunger, but she felt, she said, that she was going to cave in with a sense of incompetence and failure. She walked to the plinth and looked at the Citizen's feet, and saw the sculptor had easily succeeded where she had failed.

'Damn! I can't even draw now! I shall have to marry him!' she said aloud, in an irritable and snapping voice.

She must have spoken louder than she knew, for she was startled to hear the walls of the courtyard echo her words. Among those statues, she had the impression of being overheard. She was even more startled to feel one of those well-known taps on her shoulder. She was horrified. Mr Wilkins! He had followed her! He had heard!

'I was so ashamed I couldn't move,' Effie said. 'I mean I really couldn't move. I was fixed to the spot. He was holding me. He was hurting. I could hardly turn my head, and when I did, I saw –'

Effie began to cry again. I think *I* had better describe what she says she saw. The hand on her shoulder was not the familiar hand of the schoolmaster. It was not a pink and playful human hand. It was far too large. The fingers were of metal, glossy and greenish black; the back of the hand was black, polished, and had bold, sculptured veins. It was the hand of the Citizen. And at once, leaning half his weight on her, he got clumsily down from his plinth, with a clang loud enough to bring all that part of Rome to its windows. Moving his hand to her neck, he gave her a shove forward and, without pause, marched her stumbling out of the courtyard and on to the pavement, naked and twice life-size as he was. Clang, clang, clang, through half a mile of street, he made for the hotel. It was lunchtime. The crowds on the pavement and at street corners were thick, the sunlight was blinding and sickening, but the exemplary male barged on. Effie had to step out into the street to save herself from being trodden on by him. She collided with people. And they, the whole lunch-time crowd, treated the thing in the traditional manner of the Italian nation – they stared at the woman and not at the man. At last the Citizen got her to the Corso, and made to cross over to the Galleria, where – and how she dreaded it! – Mr Wilkins was to be waiting. The traffic was heavy and fast, but the Citizen, that ungovernable married man, marched deafeningly across, now pushing his way ahead. He hauled her into the middle of the street, right in front of a car, and trod clean through a bicycle – a father not to be obstructed.

'But Mr Wilkins – didn't he help? Didn't he see? What did he do?' I asked.

Mr Wilkins did not have a chance. Nor did the police, the crowd, or the ambulance men. The statue even got into the ambulance when she was picked up.

'No one could stop him,' Effie sobbed. 'He came to the hospital. He came to this room. He was here all the time. He wouldn't let Mr Wilkins in.'

Effie stopped crying and lowered her eyes demurely. 'He told me – Mr Wilkins,' she said, 'that I'd overdone the wine.'

She raised her eyes again. Even Effie must have seen that she had gone too far. She quickly put out her hand and took mine.

'I'm sorry, Daddy dear,' she said. 'He's gone. It's over. You came, and he went.'

The Key to My Heart

W hen Father dropped dead and Mother and I were left to run the business on our own, I was twenty-four years old. It was the principal bakery in our town, a good little business, and Father had built it up from nothing. Father used to wink at me when Mother talked about their 'first wedding'. 'How many times have you been married? Who was it that time?' he used to say to her. She was speaking of the time they first ventured out of the bakery into catering for weddings and local dances. For a long time, when I was a child, we lived over the shop; then Mother made Father take a house down the street. Later still, we opened a café next door but two to the shop, and our idea was to buy up the two little places in between. But something went wrong in the last years of Father's life. Working at night in the heat and getting up at the wrong time of day disorganised him. And then the weddings were his downfall. There is always champagne left over at weddings, and Father got to like it and live on it. And then brandy followed. When Mr Pickering, the solicitor, went into the will and the accounts, there was muddle everywhere, and bills we had never heard of came in.

'Father kept it all in his head,' Mother said, very proud of him for that. Mr Pickering and I had to sort it all out, and one of the things we discovered was that what we owed was nothing to what people owed us. Mother used to serve in the shop and do the books. She did it, we used to say, for the sake of the gossip – to day-dream about why the schoolmistress ordered crumpets only on Thursdays, or guessing, if someone ordered more of this kind of cake or that, who was going to eat it with them. She was generally right, and she knew more about what was going on in the town than anyone else. As long as the daily and weekly customers paid their books, she didn't bother; she hated sending bills, and she was more pleased than upset when Mr Pickering told her there was a good six hundred pounds owing by people who either hadn't been asked to pay or who were simply not troubling themselves. In a small business, this was a lot of money. It was the rich and the big pots in the county who were the worst of these debtors. Dad and Mother never minded being owed by the rich. They had both grown up in the days when you were afraid of offending people, and to hear my mother talk you would have thought that by asking the well-off to fork out you were going to kill the goose that lays the golden egg, knock the bottom out of society, and let a Labour government in.

'Think of what they have to pay in taxes,' she would say, pitying them. 'And the death duties!' And when I did what Mr Pickering said, and sent out accounts to these people, saying politely that it had no doubt been overlooked, Mother looked mournful and said getting a commission in the Army had turned my head. The money came in, of course. When Colonel Williams paid up and didn't dispute it, Mother looked at his cheque as if it were an insult from the old gentleman and, in fact, 'lost' it in her apron pocket for a week. Lady Littlebank complained, but she paid all the same. A few did not answer, but when I called at their houses they paid at once. Though the look on Mother's face was as much as to say I was a son ruining her lifework and destroying her chances of holding her head up in society. At the end of two or three months, there was only one large account outstanding – a Mrs Brackett's. Mrs Brackett did not answer, and you can guess Mother made the most of this. Mother spoke highly of Mrs Brackett, said she was 'such a lady', came of a wonderful family, and once even praised her clothes. She was the richest woman in the county, and young. She became my mother's ideal.

Mrs Brackett was married to a pilot and racing motorist known in the town as Noisy Brackett; it was she, as my mother said, nodding her head up and down, who 'had the money'. Noisy was given a couple of cars and his pocket money, but, having done that, Mrs Brackett paid as little as she could, as slowly as she could, to everyone else. When I talked about her account to other shopkeepers in the town, they put on their glasses, had a look at their books, sniffed, and said nothing. Every shopkeeper, my father used to say, woke up in the early hours of the morning thinking of how much she owed him, and dreaming of her fortune. You can work out how long her bill with us had run on when I say it was nearly two hundred and thirty pounds. The exact sum was two hundred and twenty-eight pounds fourteen and fourpence. I shall always remember it.

The first time I made out Mrs Brackett's bill, I gave it to Noisy. He often came into the café to flirt with the girls, or to our shop to see Mother and get her to cash cheques for him. He was a thin little man, straight as a stick and looked as brittle, and covered (they said) with scars and wounds from his crashes. He had curly shining black hair, the face of a sick gipsy, and the lines of a charmer all over it. His smiles quickly ended in a sudden, stern twitching of his left cheek and eye, like the crack of a whip, which delighted the women. He was a dandy, and from Mother he had the highest praise she could give to any man. He was, she said, 'snobby'.

When I gave Noisy our bill, he handed it back to me at once. 'Be a sweetie-pie,' he said, 'and keep it under your hat until the day after tomorrow. Tomorrow's my pay-day, and I don't want the Fairy Queen to get her mind taken off it – d'you follow? Good! Fine! Splendid fellow! Bang on!' And, with a twitch, he was back in his long white Bentley. 'Bring it yourself,' he said, looking me up and down. I am a very tall man, and little Noisy had a long way to look. 'It'll do the trick.'

Noisy did not hide his dependence on his wife. Everyone except the local gentry liked him.

So on the Thursday, when the shop was closed and I could leave the café to the waitresses – a good pair of girls, and Rosie, the dark one, very pretty – I took the station wagon and drove up to Heading Mount, four miles out of the town. It was June; they were getting the hay in. The land in the valley fetches its price – you wouldn't believe it if I told you what a farm fetches there. Higher up, the land is poor, where the oak woods begin, and all that stretch belonged to old Mr Lucas, Mrs Brackett's father, who had made a fortune out of machine tools. The estate was broken up when he died. I came out of the oak woods and turned into the drive, which winds between low stone walls and tall rhododendron bushes, so that it is like a damp, dark, sunken lane, and very narrow. Couples often walked up on Sundays in June to see the show of rhododendrons on the slopes at Heading; the bushes were in flower as I drove by. I was speeding to the sharp turn at the end of the drive, before you come to the house, when I had to brake suddenly. Mrs Brackett's grey Bentley was drawn broadside across it, blocking the drive completely. I ought to have seen this was a bad omen.

To leave a car like that, anywhere, was typical of Mrs Brackett. If there was a traffic jam in the town, or if someone couldn't get into the market, nine times out of ten Mrs Brackett's car was the cause. She just stepped out of it wherever it was, as if she were dropping her coat off for someone else to pick up. The police did nothing. As she got back in, she would smile at them, raise one eyebrow, wag her hips, and let them see as much of her legs as she thought fit for the hour of the day, and drive off with a small wave of her hand that made them swell with apologies and blow up someone else. Sometimes she went into a rage that was terrifying coming from so small a person.

Now, in her driveway, I left my wagon and walked round her car towards the house. It was an old L-shaped house, sheltered by sycamores and built in the grey flaking stone of our part of the country. They say her father paid only twelve thousand pounds for it, and that included two or three cottages and farm buildings. The kitchens and servants' rooms and garages were at one side of the L – modern buildings, screened by laurels. Not that there were often any servants there. There was a small circle of lawn in the front of the house, with a statue in the middle of it.

As I walked across the lawn, I realised I had missed the back lane to the house, and that I ought to have driven along a wire-fenced road across the fields to the farm and the kitchen, where the housekeeper lived. But I had not been up there for several years, and had forgotten it. As I walked towards the white front door, I kicked a woman's shoe – a shoe for a very small foot. I picked it up. I was a few yards from the door when Mrs Brackett marched out, stopped on the steps, and then, as sharp as a sergeant, shouted, 'Jimmy!' She was looking up at the sky, as though she expected to bring her husband down out of it.

She was barefooted, wearing a blue-and-white checked shirt and dusty jeans, and her short fair hair untidy, and she was making an ugly mouth, like a boy's, on her pretty face. I was holding out the shoe as I went forward. There was no answer to her shout. Then she saw me and stared at the shoe.

'Who are you? What are you doing with that?' she asked. 'Put it down.'

But before I could answer, from the other side of the buildings there was the sound of a car starting and driving off on the back road. Mrs Brackett heard this. She turned and marched into the house again, but in a few seconds she returned, running past me across the lawn. She jumped into her car, backed – and then she saw mine blocking the drive. She sounded her horn, again and again. A dog barked, and she jumped out and bawled at me. 'You bloody fool!' she shouted. 'Get that van of yours out of the way!'

The language that came out of her small mouth was like what you hear in the cattle market on Fridays. I slowly went up and got into my van. I could hear her swearing and the other car tearing off; already it must have turned into the main road. I got into mine, and there we sat, face to face, scowling at each other through our windscreens. I reversed down the long, winding drive, very fast, keeping one eye on her all the time, and turned sharply off the road at the entrance. I don't mind saying that I was showing off. I can reverse a car at speed and put it anywhere to within an inch of where I want to. I saw her face change as she came on, for in her temper she was coming fast down the drive straight at me, radiator to radiator. At the end, she gave one glance of surprise at me, and I think held back a word she had ready as she drove past. At any rate, her mouth was open. Half a dozen cows started from under the trees and went trotting round the field in panic as she went, and the rooks came out of the elms like bits of black paper.

By bad luck, you see, I had arrived in the middle of one of the regular Brackett rows. They were famous in the neighbourhood. The Bracketts chased each other round the house, things came out of windows – clothes, boots, anything. Our roundsman said he had once seen a portable radio, playing full on, come flying out, and that it had fallen, still playing, in the roses. Servants came down to the town and said they had had enough of it. Money was usually at the bottom of the trouble. There was a tale going round that when a village girl who worked there got married, Mrs Brackett gave her a three-shilling alarm clock for a wedding present.

The rows always went the same way. A car would race out of the drive with Noisy in it, and five minutes later Mrs Brackett would be in her car chasing him, and no one was safe on the roads for twenty miles around. Sometimes it might end quietly in a country pub, with Mrs Brackett in one bar and Noisy in the other, white-faced and playing hymns on the piano to mock her until she gave in. Other times, it might go on through the night. Noisy, who raced cars, was the better driver, but she was wilder. She would do anything – she once cut through the footpath of the cemetery to catch him on the other side. She sometimes caught him, but more than once her meanness about money would leave her standing. There would be a telephone call to Briggs' garage: Mrs Brackett had run out of petrol. She was too mean ever to have much more than a gallon in the tank.

'Bless her,' Noisy used to say if anyone mentioned these chases to him. 'I always rely on the Fairy Queen to run out of gas.'

Noisy was a woman-hater. His trouble was his habit of saying 'Bless you' to the whole female sex.

'Well, I hope you're satisfied,' my mother said when I got home. I put Mrs Brackett's shoe on the table.

'I've made some progress,' I said.

My mother looked at the shoe for a long time. Now that I had got something out of Mrs Brackett, Mother began to think a little less of her. 'You'd think a woman with feet like that would dress better,' she said.

But what annoyed me was that at some stage in the afternoon's chase Noisy had slipped in and got Mother to cash him a cheque for twenty pounds.

June is the busy time of the year for us. There are all the June weddings. Noisy and Mrs Brackett must have settled down again somehow, because I saw them driving through the town once or twice. I said to myself, 'You wait till the rush is over.'

In July, I went up to the Bracketts' house a second time. Rosie, the dark girl who works in our café, came with me, because she wanted to meet her aunt at the main-line station three or four miles over the hill beyond Heading Mount, and I was taking her on there after I had spoken to Mrs Brackett. I drove up to the house. The rhododendrons had died, and there were pods on them already going brown. The sun struck warm in front of the house. It was wonderfully quiet.

I left the girl in the car, reading a book, and was working out a sentence to say, when I saw Mrs Brackett kneeling by a goldfish pond, at the far side of the great lawn. She turned and saw me. I did not know whether to go over the lawn to her or to wait where I was. I decided to go over, and she got up and walked to me. Mother was right about her clothes. This time she was wearing a gaudy tomato-coloured cotton dress that looked like someone else's, and nothing on underneath it. I do not know why it was – whether it was because I was standing on the grass she was walking over, whether it was my anxiety about how to begin the conversation, or whether it was because of her bare white arms, the dawdling manner of her walk, and the inquisitiveness of her eyes – but I thought I was going to faint. When she was two yards away, my heart jumped, my throat closed, and my head was swimming. Although I had often seen her driving through the town, and though I remembered our last meeting all too well, I had never really looked at her before. She stopped, but I had the feeling that she had not stopped but was invisibly walking on until she walked clean through me. My arms went weak. She was amused by the effect she had on me.

'I know who you are,' she said. 'You are Mr Fraser's son. Do you want to speak to me?'

I did, but I couldn't. I forgot all the sentences I had prepared. 'I've come about our cheque,' I said at last. I shouted it. Mrs Brackett was as startled by my shout as I was. She blushed at the loudness and shock of it – not a light blush but a dark, red, flooding blush on her face and her neck that confused her and made her lower her head like a child caught stealing. She put her hands behind her back like a child. I blushed, too. She walked up and down a yard or two, her head still down, thinking. Then she walked away to the house.

'You'd better come inside,' she called back in an offhand way.

You could have put our house into the hall and sitting-room of Heading Mount. I had been in that room when I was a boy, helping the waitress when my father was there doing the catering for a party. I do not know what you'd have to pay for the furniture there – thousands, I suppose. She led me through the room to a smaller room beyond it, where there was a desk. I felt I was slowly walking miles. I have never seen such a mess of papers and letters. They were even spread on the carpet. She sat down at the desk.

'Can you see the bill?' she muttered, not looking at me and pointing to the floor.

'I've got it here,' I said, taking the bill out of my pocket. She jerked her head. The flush had gone, and now she looked as keen as needles at me.

'Well, sit down,' she said.

She took the bill from me and looked at it. Now I could see that her skin was not white but was really pale and clay-coloured, with scores of little cracks in it, and that she was certainly nearer forty than thirty, as Mother always said.

'I've paid this,' she said, giving the bill a mannish slap. 'I pay every quarter.'

'It has been running for three and a half years,' I said, more at ease now.

'What?' she said. 'Oh, well, I paid something, anyway. This isn't a bill. It's a statement.'

'Yes,' I said. 'We have sent you the bills.'

'Where's the date? This hasn't got any date on it.'

I got up and pointed to the date.

'It ought to be at the top,' she said.

My giddiness had gone. Noisy came into the room. 'Hullo, Bob,' he said. 'I've just been talking to that beautiful thing you've got in the car.' He always spoke in an alert, exhausted way about women, like someone at a shoot waiting for the birds to come over. 'Have you seen Bob's girl, darling?' he said to her. 'I've just offered her the key to my heart.' And he lifted the silk scarf he was wearing in the neck of his canary-coloured pullover, and there was a piece of string round his neck with a heavy old door key hanging from it. Noisy gave a twitch to one side of his face.

'Oh God, that old gag,' said Mrs Brackett.

'Not appreciated, old boy,' said Noisy to me.

'Irresistible,' said Mrs Brackett, with an ugly mouth. She turned and spoke to me again, but glanced shrewdly at Noisy as she did so. 'Let me try this one on you,' she said. 'You've already got my husband's cheques for this bill. I send him down to pay you, and he just cashes them?'

'I'm afraid not, Mrs Brackett,' I said. 'That wouldn't be possible.'

'You can't get away with that one, my pet,' said Noisy. 'Are you ready to go out?' He looked at her dress, admiring her figure. 'What a target, Bob,' he said.

'I don't think we will ask Mr Fraser's opinion,' she said coldly, but very pleased. And she got up and started out of the room, with Noisy behind her.

'You had better send me the bills,' she called back to me, turning round from the door.

I felt very, very tired. I left the house and slammed the car door when I got in. 'Now she wants the damn bills,' I said to Rosie as I drove her up to Tolton station. I did not speak to her the rest of the way. She irritated me, sitting there.

When I got home and told my mother, she was short with me. That was the way to lose customers, she said. I was ruining all the work she and Dad had put into the business. I said if Mrs Brackett wanted her bills she could come and get them herself. Mother was very shocked.

She let it go for a day or two, but she had to bring it up again. 'What are you sulking about?' she said to me one afternoon. 'You upset Rosie this morning. Have you done those bills for Mrs Brackett yet?'

I made excuses, and got in the car and went over to the millers and to the people who make our boxes, to get away from the nagging. Once I was out of the town, in the open country, Mrs Brackett seemed to be somewhere just ahead of me, round a corner, over a hill, beyond a wood. There she was, trying to make me forget she owed us two hundred and twenty-eight pounds fourteen and fourpence. The moment she was in my head, the money went out of it. When I got back, late in the evening, Mother was on to me again. Noisy had been in. She said he had been sent down by his wife to ask why I had not brought the bills.

'The poor Wing Commander,' my mother said. 'Another rumpus up there.' (She always gave him his rank if there was a rumour of another quarrel at Heading.) 'She never gives him any peace. He's just an errand boy. She does what she likes with him.'

'He's been offering you the key to his heart, Mother,' I said.

'I don't take any stock of him,' Mother said. 'Or that pansy "sweetheart" stuff. Dad was the one and only for me. I don't believe in second marriages. I've no time for jealous women; they're always up to something, like Mrs Doubleday thinking I spoke to her husband in the bank and she was caught with the chemist, but you always think the Fairy Prince will turn up – it's natural.'

It always took a little time getting at what was in Mother's mind, yet it was really simple. She was a good churchwoman, and she thought Noisy was not really married to Mrs Brackett, because he had been divorced by his first wife. She did not blame Noisy for this – in fact, she admired it, in a romantic way – but she blamed Mrs Brackett, because, by Mother's theories, Mrs Brackett was still single. And Mother never knew whether to admire single women for holding out or to suspect them of being on the prowl. One thing she was certain of. 'Money talks,' she said. The thing that made Noisy respectable for her, and as good as being married in church, was that he had married Mrs Brackett for her money.

She talked like this the night we sat up and did that month's bills, but the next day – and this was the trouble with Mother – it ended in a row. I sent the bills up to Mrs Brackett by our delivery van.

'That is not the way to behave,' Mother said. 'You should have taken them yourself.'

And before the day was out, Mother was in a temper again. Mrs Brackett had spoken to her on the telephone and said she had been through the bills and that we had charged her for things she hadn't had, because she'd been in the South of France at the time.

'I told you to go,' Mother said to me.

I was angry, too, at being called dishonest. I got out the van and said I was going up at once.

'Oh, that's how it is,' said my mother, changing round again. 'Her Ladyship snaps her fingers and you go up at once. She's got you running about for her like Noisy. If I ask you to do anything, you don't pay any attention to me. But Mrs Brackett – she's the Queen of England. Two of you running after her.'

Mother was just like that with Father when he was alive. He took no notice. Neither did I. I went up to Heading. A maid let me in, and I sat there waiting in the drawing-room. I waited a long time, listening to the bees coming down the chimney, circling lower and lower and then roaring out into the room, like Noisy's car. I could hear Mrs Brackett talking on the telephone in her study. I could hear now and then what she was saying. She was a great racing woman, and from words she said here and there I would say she was speaking to a bookmaker. One sentence I remember, because I think it had the name of a horse in it, and when I got back home later I looked up the racing news to see if I could find it. 'Tray Pays On,' she said. She came out into the room with the laughter of her telephone call still on her face. I was standing up, with our account book in my hand, and when she saw me the laughter went.

I was not afraid of her any more. 'I hear there is some trouble about the bills,' I said. 'If you've got them, you can check them with the book. I've brought it.'

Mrs Brackett was a woman who watched people's faces. She put on her dutiful, serious, and obedient look, and led me again to the little room where the papers were. She sat down and I stood over her while we compared the bills and the book. I watched the moving of her back as she breathed. I pointed to the items, one by one, and she nodded and ticked the bills with a pencil. We checked for nearly half an hour. The only thing she said was in the middle of it – 'You've got a double-jointed thumb. So have I' – but she went right on.

'I can see what it is,' I said at the end. 'You've mistaken 1953 for '54.'

She pushed the book away, and leaned back in the chair against my arm, which was resting on it.

'No, I haven't,' she said, her small, unsmiling face looking up into mine. 'I just wanted you to come up.'

She gazed at me a long time. I thought of all the work Mother and I had done, and then that Mother was right about Mrs Brackett. I took my hand from the chair and stepped back.

'I wanted to ask you one or two things,' she said, confidingly, 'about that property next to the shop. I'll be fair with you. I'm interested in it. Are you? All right, don't answer. I see you are.'

My heart jumped. Ever since I could remember, Father and Mother had talked of buying this property. It was their day-dream. They simply liked little bits of property everywhere, and now I wanted it so that we could join the shop and the café.

'I asked because . . .' She hesitated. 'I'll be frank with you. The bank manager was talking about it to me today.'

My fright died down. I didn't believe that the bank manager – he was Mr Pickering's brother-in-law – would let my mother down and allow the property to go to Mrs Brackett without giving us the offer first.

'We want it, of course,' I said. And then I suspected this was one of her tricks. 'That is why I have been getting our bills in,' I said.

'Oh, I didn't think that was it,' she said. 'I thought you were getting married. My husband says you are engaged to the girl you brought up here. He said he thought you were. Has she any money?'

'Engaged!' I said. 'I'm not. Who told him that?'

'Oh,' she said, and then a thought must have struck her. I could read it at once. In our town, if you cough in the High Street the chemist up at the Town Hall has got a bottle of cough mixture wrapped up and waiting for you; news travels fast. She must have guessed that when Noisy came down dangling the key to his heart, he could have been round the corner all the time, seeing Rosie.

'I'm glad to hear you're not engaged,' Mrs Brackett said tenderly. 'I like a man who works. You work like your father did – God, what an attractive man! You're like him. I'm not flattering you. I saw it when you came up the first time.'

She asked me a lot of questions about the shop and who did the baking now. I told her I didn't do it and that I wanted to enlarge the restaurant. 'The machine bakeries are getting more and more out into the country,' I said. 'And you've got to look out.'

'I don't see why you shouldn't do catering for schools,' she said. 'And there's the Works.' (Her father's main factory.) 'Why don't you get hold of the catering there?'

'You can only do that if you have capital. We're not big enough,' I said, laughing.

'How much do you want?' she said. 'Two thousand? Three? I don't see why we couldn't do something.'

The moment she said 'we', I came to my senses. Here's a funny turnout, I thought. She won't pay her bills, but first she's after these shops, and now she's waving two thousand pounds in my face. Everyone in our town knew she was artful. I suppose she thought I was green.

'Not as much as two thousand,' I said. 'Just the bill,' I said, nodding at it.

Mrs Brackett smiled. 'I like you. You're interested in money. Good. I'll settle it.' And, taking her cheque-book from the top of the desk, she put it in her drawer. 'I never pay these accounts by cheque. I pay in cash. I'll get it tomorrow at the bank. I'll tell you what I'll do. You've got a shoe of mine. Bring it up tomorrow evening at, say, half past eight. I'll be back by then and you can have it.' She paused, and then, getting up, added quickly, 'Half tomorrow, half in October.'

It was like dealing with the gipsies that come to your door.

'No, Mrs Brackett,' I said. 'I'd like all of it. Now.' We stared at each other. It was like that moment months ago when she had driven at me in her car and I had reversed down the drive with one eye watching her and one on the road as I shot back. That was the time, I think, I first noticed her – when she opened her mouth to shout a word at me and then did not shout. I could have stayed like this, looking into her small, pretty, miser's blue eyes, at her determined head, her chopped-off fair hair, for half an hour. It was a struggle.

She was the first to speak, and that was a point gained to me. Her voice shook a little. 'I don't keep that amount of money in the house,' she said.

I knew that argument. Noisy said she always had two or three hundred pounds in the safe in the wall of her study, and whether this was so or not, I could not help glancing towards it.

'I don't like being dictated to,' she said, catching my glance. 'I have told you what I will do.'

'I think you could manage it, Mrs Brackett,' I said.

I could see she was on the point of flying into one of her tempers, and as far as I was concerned (I don't know why), I hoped she would. Her rows with Noisy were so famous that I must have wanted to see one for myself. And I didn't see why she should get away with it. At the back of my mind, I thought of all the others down in the town and how they would look when I said I had got my money out of Mrs Brackett.

Yet I wasn't really thinking about the money at all, at this moment. I was looking at her pretty shoulders.

But Mrs Brackett did not fly into a temper. She considered me, and then she spoke in a quiet voice that took me off my guard. 'Actually,' she said, lowering her eyes, 'you haven't been coming up here after money at all, have you?'

'Well –' I began.

'Sh-h-h!' she said, jumping up from her chair and putting her hand on my mouth. 'Why didn't you ring me and tell me you were coming? I am often alone.'

[574]

She stepped to the door and bawled out, 'Jimmy!' as if he were a long way off. He was – to my surprise, and even more to hers – very near.

'Yes, ducky?' Noisy called back from the hall.

'Damn,' she said to me. 'You must go.' And, squeezing my hand, she went through the drawing-room into the hall.

'What time do we get back tomorrow evening?' she said boldly to Noisy. 'Half past eight? Come at half past eight,' she said, turning to me, for I had followed her. 'I'll bring back the cash.'

The sight of Noisy was a relief to me, and the sound of the word 'cash' made Noisy brighten.

'Not lovely little bits of money!' he exclaimed.

'Not you,' said Mrs Brackett, glaring at him.

'How did you work it, old boy?' said Noisy later, giving me one of his most quizzical twitches as he walked with me to my van. When I drove off, I could see him still standing there, watching me out of sight.

I drove away very slowly. My mind was in confusion. About half a mile off, I stopped the car and lit a cigarette. All the tales I had heard about Mrs Brackett came back into my mind. It was one thing to look at her, another thing to know about her. The one person I wished I had with me was Noisy. He seemed like a guarantor of safety, a protection. To have had my thoughts read like that by her filled me with fear.

I finished my cigarette. I decided not to go straight home, and I drove slowly all along the lower sides of the oak woods, so slowly and carelessly that I had to swerve to avoid oncoming cars. I was making, almost without knowing it, for the Green Man, at Mill Cross. There was a girl there I had spoken to once or twice. No one you would know. I went in and asked for a glass of beer. I hardly said a word to her, except about the weather, and then she left the bar to look after a baby in the kitchen at the back. That calmed me. I think the way she gave me my change brought me back to earth and made me feel free of Mrs Brackett's spell. At any rate, I put the threepence in my pocket and swallowed my beer. I laughed at myself. Mrs Brackett had gypped me again.

When I got home it was late, and my mother was morose. She was wearing a black dress she often wore when she was alone, dressed up and ready to go out, yet not intending to, as if now that my father was dead she was free if someone would invite her. Her best handbag was beside her. She was often waiting like this, sitting on the sofa, doing nothing but listening to the clock tick, and perhaps getting up to give a touch to some flowers on the table and then sitting down again. Her first words shook me.

'Mrs Brackett was down here looking for you,' she said sharply. 'I thought you were with her. She wants you to be sure to go up tomorrow evening to collect some money when she comes back from Tolton. Where have you been?'

'Let the old bitch post it or bring it in,' I said.

Mother was horrified at the idea of Mrs Brackett soiling her hands with money.

'You'll do as I tell you,' she said. 'You'll go up and get it. If you don't, Noisy will get his hands on it first. You'd think a woman with all that money would go to a decent hairdresser. It's meanness, I suppose.'

And then, of course, I saw I was making a lot of fuss about nothing. Noisy would be there when I went up to Heading. Good old Noisy, I thought; thank God for that. And he'll see I get the money, because she said it in front of him.

So the next evening I went. I put my car near the garage, and the first person I saw was Noisy, standing beside his own car. He had a suitcase in his hand. I went over to him.

'Fairy Queen's been at work,' he said. He nodded at his tyres. They were flat. 'I'm doing some quick thinking.'

At that moment, a top window of the house was opened and someone emptied a suitcase of clothes out of it, and then a shower of cigarettes came down.

'She's tidying,' he said. 'I've got a quarter of an hour to catch the London train. Be a sweetie-pie and run me over there.'

I had arrived once more in the middle of one of the Brackett rows. Only this time Noisy was leaving it to me. That is how I felt about it. 'Hop in,' I said.

And when we were off and a mile from Heading, he sat up in the seat and looked round. 'Nothing on our tail,' he said.

'Have you ever heard of a horse called Tray?' I asked him. 'Tray Pays something? Tray Pays On – that can't be it.'

'Tray Pays On?' repeated Noisy. 'Is it a French horse?'

'I don't know,' I said.

'Bloody peasant? Could be,' said Noisy. 'Sounds a bit frog to me.'

We got to Tolton station. Noisy was looking very white and set with hatred. Not until he was standing in the queue getting his ticket did it occur to me what Noisy was doing.

'The first time I've travelled by train for fifteen years,' he called to me across from the queue. 'Damned serious. You can tell her if you see her' – people stared – 'the worm has turned. I'm packing it in for good.'

And as he went off to the train he called, 'I suppose you're going back? No business of mine, but I'll give you a tip. If you do, you won't find anything in the kitty, Bob.' He gave me his stare and his final twitch. It was like the crack of a shot. Bang on, as he would have said. A bull's-eye.

I walked slowly away as the London train puffed out. I took his advice. I did not go back to Heading.

There were rows and rows between the Bracketts, but there was none like this one. It was the last. The others were a chase. This was not. For only Mrs Brackett was on the road that night. She was seen, we were told, in all the likely places. She had been a dozen times through the town. Soon after ten o'clock she was hooting outside our house. Mother peeped through the curtains, and I went out. Mrs Brackett got out of her car and marched at me. 'Where have you been?' she shouted. 'Where is my husband?'

'I don't know,' I said.

'Yes, you do,' she said. 'You took him to Tolton, they told me.'

'I think he's gone to London,' I said.

'Don't be a damn liar,' she said. 'How can he have? His car is up there.'

'By train,' I said.

'By train,' she repeated. Her anger vanished. She looked at me with astonishment. The rich are very peculiar. Mrs Brackett had forgotten people travel by train. I could see she was considering the startling fact. She was not a woman to waste time staying in one state of mind for long. Noisy used to say of her, 'That little clock never stops ticking.'

'I see,' she said to me sarcastically, nodding out the words. 'That's what you and Jimmy have been plotting.' She gave a shake to her hair and held her chin up. 'You've got your money and you don't care,' she said.

'What money is that?' I said.

'What money!' she exclaimed sharply, going over each inch of my face. What she saw surprised her at first. Until then she had been fighting back, but now a sly look came to her; it grew into a smile; the smile got wider and wider, and then her eyes became two curved lines, like crow's wings in the sky, and she went into shouts of laughter. It sounded all down the empty street. She rocked with it.

'Oh no!' she laughed. 'Oh no, that's too good! That's a winner. He didn't give you a penny! He swiped the lot!'

And she looked up at the sky in admiration of that flying man. She was still grinning at me when she taunted breathlessly, 'I mean to say – I mean to say –'

I let her run on.

'It was all or nothing with you, wasn't it?' she said. 'And you get nothing, don't you?'

I am not sure what I did. I may have started to laugh it off and I may have made a step towards her. Whatever I did, she went hard and prim, and if ever a woman ended anything, she did then. She went over to the car, got in, and slammed the door.

'You backed the wrong horse when you backed Jimmy,' she called out to me.

That was the last of her. No more Mrs Brackett at the shop. 'You won't hear another word from her,' my mother said.

'What am I supposed to do – get her husband back?' I said.

By the end of the week, everyone in the town was laughing and winking at me.

'You did the trick, boy,' the grocer said.

'You're a good-looking fellow, Bob,' the ironmonger said.

'Quite a way with the girls,' the butcher said. 'Bob's deep.'

For when Mrs Brackett went home that night, she sat down and paid every penny she owed to every shopkeeper in the town. Paid everyone, I say. Bar me.

Noisy Flushes the Birds

T hings were quiet in the town; they'd been quiet for a year.

'You put on your clothes,' Mother said one evening, after we had closed the shop, 'and it isn't worth it.' That hat she bought in Ainsworth, she said, the blue one – she'd only worn it once.

But it was September now and, in our part of the country, if anything happens, September is the time for it. The harvest is in, people have nothing to do, except think of how they can annoy one another. I have heard holiday visitors put this down to the strong air, the variable warm Atlantic winds that send us half asleep so that we don't know whether we are alive or dreaming; Miss Croggan, the headmistress of the girls' school, says it's the Celtic blood taking time off to stir up old feuds. But nothing has happened, so far, this year. There was nothing to compare, for example, with the week Teddy Longfellow introduced two lunatics to the town and persuaded Major Dingle – Nigerian police, retired, and a stickler for the 'right people' – that they were a pair of baronets looking for a large property in the neighbourhood. The year before that, there was Hoblin, the farmer, who used disguised voices on the telephone, pretending that he was the Chief Constable, an official from the Ministry of Agriculture, the County Medical Officer, and so on, enquiring into a report that Teddy Longfellow had been watering his milk; he kept the story up for days, until Teddy nearly pulled his red beard off with panic.

And to move from fiction to fact, we had had no scandal to match the break-up of the Brackett marriage. No Bentleys about at night, I mean. No Noisy Brackett roaring through the town, followed a few minutes later by his wife chasing him. Their married life had been, for us, like one of those air displays when suddenly a pair of jets scream the place down, vanish into a whistle and, then, silence; suddenly, five minutes later, they are back again, down your neck, like wasps. Mother and I

[579]

closed the shop in the evening, as I say, and we sat down doing nothing.

'Can't you talk?' she said. 'Your father used to.'

'I've been on my legs all day,' I said.

Like an enormous, simple-minded cheese the September moon came slowly over the houses opposite and we stared at it. The size of it, Mother said, upset her.

And then – as if the moon had started them off – things began to happen. One thing after another. I caught it first. I went out to a dance on the Saturday night and, driving back, I got engaged to a girl called Claudia Dingle. I knew before I went that it was ten to one I would get engaged to someone or other. Claudia was the daughter of Major Dingle up at the Old Rectory, the man Teddy Longfellow had made a fool of. She was a tall girl with a small cloudy head of golden hair that seemed to be blowing off her head like flame, yet with a voice as cool as a water ice. She was so slight that I thought she would snap in two when she laughed. She had just come back from a finishing school in Switzerland. You should have heard the band play up at the Old Rectory and at our house, too! Mother pretended not to hear first of all when I told her and then said, 'Every time you go to a dance you get engaged.' When I said 'Only twice,' Mother said:

'They don't get their bread from us; they deal with Higgs.'

Up at Claudia's house the Major said:

'That hulking lad who comes round the back door with the bread and works in the café! Is the girl out of her mind?'

'Anyway,' said Claudia on the second day, 'it'll be divine to work in the shop. And you don't always have to be a baker.'

'Actually, my sweet,' I said, putting on a drawling voice like hers, 'I do.'

She said she didn't mean it that way. She said it wasn't her fault she was upper class and she'd adore to go out in the van with me.

Any time I got engaged it always upset me. It upset other people, too, and Mother got moody; and Claudia had no tact either, coming in and out of the shop and wanting to look at the bakehouse and saying how divine it was, when we were busy, and upsetting the girls. But the thing that set Mother against her was saying she was going to have the announcement put in *The Times*. Mother thought she meant the *County Times* and so did I, but Claudia meant the London *Times*.

'Everyone does,' Claudia said.

'I never heard of it in this town yet,' I said. 'I'd look a damn fool.'

Mother said it was daft; no one in the town would know. I argued this with Claudia.

'I meant *people*, not the town,' said Claudia. She didn't mean any harm; her finishing school had finished her.

The announcement went into the London *Times*.

One evening when I had been out at her house I came back home early and Mother was sitting at the window.

'What are you sitting there for; you can't see to read,' I said to her.

'Troubling about me – that is new,' Mother said. 'I've had my life.' And then she said, changing her voice to something like Mrs Dingle's refined accents, and mocking:

'We've had another of your old lady friends in this afternoon – Mrs Brackett. It never rains but it pours.'

My heart gave a jump like a fish.

'What did she want – credit?' I said.

'She's asked you and this girl – what is her name? – Claudia – to dinner,' said my mother. 'She asked me. No, I said, not me. I never go out, not since Dad died.' Mother thought eating with anyone but our relations a wickedness and only went to their houses because it was painful; and she looked like the Ten Commandments at anyone else who invited her to go out.

'She read about it in that London paper,' Mother said, accusing Claudia and me. And then we had the usual line about making your bed and lying on it.

'You can go and see the nobs if you like,' she said. 'And feast yourself on all this getting engaged and getting divorced. Dad was the one and only for me and we were true. You think you want the Fairy Prince, it's womanlike – but it's all soft pansy nonsense. I blame *her*; you don't know whether she's married or single; lady she may call herself, but I don't see she's even a woman, not a real woman.' And Mother added: 'She's got stout.'

[581]

The women in our town got stout or thin from day to day, according to Mother's moods. Father used to say he never knew a town where the weight and measurements of women changed so often and where an ordinary dress or coat was ever of the right length.

I switched on the light and I saw Mother's face looking square and offended, suspicion puffing it out. I expected her to look sulky, but I was astonished to see it was worse than that. She looked insulted and miserable.

'She paid her bill,' Mother said bitterly. She might have been looking at her grave in the churchyard. She was also suspicious.

'We had a long chat,' Mother said. 'She came inside.' (Mother referred to the room at the back of the shop which was a mixture of sitting-room, store-room and office. When Mother came out of it with anyone who had been 'asked inside' she always had a peculiar look on her face – pleased and unnatural. You could never get her to say what 'they' had said.)

I was as surprised as Mother that Mrs Brackett had paid. And I was suspicious, too.

'After five years, about time, too,' I said. 'I wonder what put that idea into her head?' I said.

'Why ask me?' said Mother. 'I'm not getting engaged to all these girls; you were the one chasing after her, driving her husband out of the house.'

'Chasing after Mrs Brackett!' I said.

Mother was on to her old tale. You won't believe it, but she blamed me for Mrs Brackett's divorce! Just because I ran into Noisy Brackett that evening a year before and he asked me to give him a lift to the station. How did I know he was leaving his wife?

We sat saying nothing.

'Well,' said Mother, 'you've come in. Haven't you any news?'

News! We had it next day in the lunch hour when the shop was closed. I was eating a chop when something went by with a roar. I mean something in the street. There was a screech at the sharp left bend at the church and then a noise like someone tumbling dustbins over. I put my knife and fork down.

'Sit down,' said Mother, getting up herself and going to the window. 'That's Noisy Brackett. He's back.'

Mother was holding the curtains. She was lit up with excitement. Even her brown hair shone.

'I knew he'd come back,' she cried. And she touched her hair here and there and brushed the crumbs off her dress.

'If it's Noisy he's hit something,' I said, getting up again.

'Sit down,' she said. She turned on me in a temper.

'People leave cars all over this town, no wonder there are accidents. The police ought to stop it,' she shouted.

Mother had always thought that all cars should be cleared out of the town so that Noisy Brackett could have a clear run through at ninety miles an hour. Mother smiled again. She was in heaven. If it had been anyone else but Noisy she would have screamed, pushed me to the door, pulled me back – but not for Noisy. He was a god; he could do anything.

I didn't believe it was Noisy; I think I know a Bentley when I hear one. But when I went up the street I found out Mother was right. People were still looking at the tyre marks on the street and the pavement. A couple of shopkeepers were looking at the back doors of their vans that had been cannoned down the hill. It was Noisy, they said. He had gone off now, nobody knew where. But the police, of course, had got him somewhere outside the town.

At first Mother was upset that Noisy had gone clean through the town without stopping for a word with us. But when Mother heard that he had been summoned for dangerous driving she was in Paradise. He would be back! He would be up before the court. And if any of those stuffed animals on the Bench dared to do anything to her Noisy she would put arsenic in their bread, she would tell their wives all she knew, and so on. But, underneath and more powerful, her feeling was different. You have got to know Mother. Noisy was back. That meant, for her, that 'they' – Mrs Brackett and Noisy – were reconciled. The divorce was off. '*He* loved *Her*.' He was back in Heading, that beautiful house, full of those things worth thousands, life was normal; love – 'the one and only' – was triumphant after all. And, to crown it, that dear sweet girl Claudia and I were invited there to dinner at the very throne of matrimonial happiness, an object lesson to us all. In the week following my engagement and

Noisy's summons to appear in court on a charge of 'wanton driving to the public danger' I have not known Mother so suddenly turn to happiness since Father's death.

All the same, Mrs Brackett did not turn up at the court when Noisy's case came on. Mother was a bit put out by this when I told her, but she said that it never looks nice when women are mixed up in the law; her own father left it in his will that no woman should go to his funeral. But I'll tell you who did turn up – I mean aside from half the town, and someone from the Ainsworth Press – Teddy Longfellow. He was Noisy's witness. He had been in the car at the time. Teddy was a funny man. He had a loud reddish suit on, with yellow squares on it, but it was not that – people said he got himself up to look like Satan. It was the way his hair came to a point in front and stood up in a couple of horns at the sides; and his beard. It was his stammer that made people say he had been a German spy.

But we had come to look at Noisy, to see how he would get out of it. The police had got him thoroughly tied up. There he was, the same old Noisy. Small, thin – 'his poor chest', Mother used to say – with a head of oily crinkly black hair, his gypsyish skin and always the dandy. He was all nerves and illness in an electric way and the women loved him for that. And there was that sudden twitch to one side of his face. It pulled the skin down from the eye, which seemed to stare out from the middle of calamity like the end of a pistol, before his face went back into dozens of soft smiling wrinkles. We knew he'd get off somehow, but how we could not imagine. He denied, of course, that he was doing fifty, because, as he said, he knew that corner by heart. And Teddy Longfellow denied it also.

'I was practically at a standstill, sir,' Noisy said to the Bench, with a shocked, polite glance at the police. 'But an extraordinary thing happened. I've never known it happen before in twenty-five years of driving; Le Mans, Monte Carlo, Brooklands. I sneezed, sir, just on the turn. A blinding sneeze, sir, without warning, quite extraordinary, like an explosion, like a bomb flash. Visibility absolutely nil. I didn't know where I was. I lost control. Never done it before. It was a mercy I was only doing twenty-two at the time, as Teddy, I mean the witness has just said. Perhaps I ought to say I suffer from hay fever. I got it in India.'

And when he said 'sneeze' Noisy's face gave one of his twitches and sudden stares with his left eye, as if he were going to produce a sample sneeze in court, a final burst, to make sure. The Chairman even started to raise his hand to ward it off. Well, the Bench hummed and ha'ed, but, of course, Noisy got off. Afterwards, at the Red Lion, he did one or two of these sneezes to show us; one of his Squadron Leaders during the war, he said, could do it with a monocle in his eye, without dropping it.

'I must pop in and have a word with your mama, Bob,' Noisy said to me. And when he came to the shop he gave Mother a kiss and said:

'What's happened? You look ten years younger, Mrs Fraser. I wonder if you would add to all your kindnesses and cash me a teeny weeny little cheque. Yes? You're quite sure? Now, isn't that like old times?'

'Come inside,' Mother said, blushing with happiness, leading him to the room at the back. 'I'm ashamed of you.' They stayed inside talking quite a while and when they came out Mother's face was blissful.

'Now remember your promise! Go and see,' said my mother, and she walked with him to the doorstep of the shop.

'I will. You bet I will, Mrs Fraser. Bang on.' Noisy smiled and waved to her. I walked a few yards with him. His face changed, he gave a serious twitch and said, in a dead, quizzing voice:

'How is she? How's the Fairy Queen? Have you seen her?'

'Not to speak to,' I said.

He looked as though he didn't quite believe me.

'I hear she paid her bill,' he said.

'Yes,' I said.

'Lovely money,' he said. 'I've got a spot of trouble there. Keep it under your hat – she's got her tiny little hands on my birds. She won't give them up. You don't know my birds! Yes, you do. That big case of birds that stands inside the door at Heading. Tropical birds. They're mine.'

I didn't remember them. Heading was so full of things.

'She can have what she likes, but she's not going to have my birds,' said Noisy. 'I'm going to get them. I've got to. I've sold them. I need the cash.' Noisy's face was now hard and serious; he lit a cigarette and wagged it up and down on his lips, studying my van. 'Wonderful woman, the Fairy Queen, really one of the best. But there's going to be a burglary.'

We got to his car and Teddy Longfellow was there.

[585]

'Take a look at this. T'that's what we w'want,' Teddy said. He was nodding to our van, which was parked behind his car. 'Take out the shelves and Bob's your uncle.'

'Hear that?' said Noisy to me. 'He's a natural car thief, that's how he made all his money. See you one of these days.' They got into Noisy's car, Noisy turned to give a tremendous sneeze for my benefit, there was the lovely throb of his engine and he was off.

You pass Teddy Longfellow's house on the Ainsworth road. It stands on a hill, one of those modern houses of glass and steel with a spiral staircase enclosed in a glass tower in front and something like the top of a lighthouse on the roof. It was built just as the war broke out and people said Longfellow had built it so that he could signal to the Germans from it. Claudia and I drove past once or twice and I was telling her that Teddy had made a fortune out of cotton and was a damn good farmer, the only up-to-date farmer in the district. I started telling her about the two fake baronets he had introduced to the town. The place, I said, is full of snobs. Of course, there I put my foot in it. I'd clean forgotten that Claudia's father, the Major, had been Teddy's victim. Class is a funny thing. Claudia was a pretty girl, no brain as Mother said, I give you that; but sweet and she stood up to the old Major and her mother with a will of her own; but when it came to class and family – well, she was her mother all over again. I've seen it since. I got the lot. Teddy was not a gentleman; he was just a shot-up businessman – at the word 'business' her face went sick – pretending to be a country gentleman and trying to buy his way in. He was loud. He was vulgar. He was rude. Of course, he wasn't a German, but loads of Germans came to visit him after the war. They came, Claudia said, to look at his pictures.

'They're worth a lot, aren't they?' I said.

'You're always talking about money,' Claudia said.

'It's what I live on,' I said.

'I don't know how much they're worth,' said Claudia. 'And I'm not interested. I only know my parents took Mrs Brackett over there one day and she proved to him his big Cézanne was fake. He's never forgiven her.'

'Cézanne – who's he?' I said.

'French, a painter,' she said. 'A very great painter.'

'Oh,' I said. 'Must be, if he's a friend of Mrs Brackett's. I'm ignorant.'

As I say, she was a sweet girl; you couldn't blame her. We had a bit of a quarrel on the way home. She told me her father had tried to stop her from driving with me on the bread round. He told her she was breaking the law, because of the licence. Of course, Mrs Dingle had put the Major up to that. I, like a fool, not thinking, said I'd often taken our girls out in it, the girls from the shop.

'And Mrs Brackett, I suppose,' said Claudia sulkily.

'Old Mrs B., the Fairy Queen!' I said. 'I'm not a bloody fool.'

'She's not old,' said Claudia.

'No, I suppose she isn't,' I said. 'She *looks* young. Very young sometimes.'

'Young!' exclaimed Claudia. 'Thirty-eight – I don't call that young.'

That was another thing my father used to say about the women of our town. They changed their age faster than in any other place he had ever known. A woman might be thirty in the morning and fifty-six by six in the evening or vice versa.

'Like bread,' he used to say. 'You see it rise, then it goes flat.'

The last thing I wanted to do was to go to have dinner with Mrs Brackett. The idea that just because I was engaged to Claudia Dingle I had to be paraded before the friends of her family, and Mrs Brackett above all, preyed on my mind. I had scarcely seen Mrs Brackett for a year, not since the time she came down to our house shouting and asking what I'd done with her husband. I had kept out of her way. Claudia was dragging me into this and I couldn't help saying to Mother: 'That's the last time I get engaged at a dance.'

'It is,' said Mother. 'Who's in a mood now?'

But the day before the dinner I was walking up the town and just as I got to the garage petrol pumps I saw Mrs Brackett. I was going to dodge into the paper shop, but I went on because I saw at once something was happening. Something that nearly made me laugh out loud. I had caught Mrs Brackett on the point of cheating the garage hand. It was the prettiest sight in the world. She had just had a gallon of petrol put in her car and the garage hand – it was Johnny Gibbs – was standing there with her money in his open hand and telling her that the price was a penny more.

She was cocking an eyebrow at him, which she well knew how to do, and gave a glance up and down the street. She was beginning to blush. Then she saw me. She turned her back on Johnny and came slowly towards me, like a cat. She was a small woman and I felt the old empty feeling I always had when I saw her walk; that she was going to dawdle her way clean through me.

'Hullo, stranger,' she said in a pleased, ringing, boyish voice. 'I've been in twice to congratulate you, but you weren't there.' Mother had not told me about the second time.

Mrs Brackett held out her hand. It was a small, square hand and strong; Claudia's hands were long and limp and you could feel the bones in them.

I didn't say much. I didn't know what to say.

'I'm glad you've shaved off your moustache,' she said, looking me over. She had pretty blue eyes.

Even I noticed that Mrs Brackett had altered. She still had something of the impudent twelve-year-old boy about her, but a boy who had tidied himself up. In Noisy's time she looked like what they call a 'young varmint', with her hair chopped as if she had cut it herself, her red check shirt and her dusty old jeans and the lipstick always hit or miss. Now she was wearing a dress, terrible colours, of course – geranium with yellow flowers on it – but a dress and smart shoes and she had been to the hairdresser's. And she had got her figure down. I don't say she looked pretty, because the bones of her face were too strong, but she looked alive. And something else – I couldn't make it out. When I said this to Mother, later on, Mother said:

'It's the divorce. Mrs Gordon was the same when she was divorced. She's trying to look respectable and sort of sad. A woman has to think.'

That wasn't my idea of Mrs Brackett. I thought she looked more like a woman, I mean one with a brain.

'Thanks for settling the bill,' I said. I wanted to show her I had won in the end and that I was glad all that nonsense was over.

Mrs Brackett didn't like that. She flushed. And she bent forward her head and studied her shoes for quite a while. Her dress was cut very low. Then she looked up quickly and caught me looking.

'Weddings are expensive,' she said, very cool. I laughed.

'The bride's parents pay,' I said.

[588]

Mrs Brackett gave a shake to her head, as if a bullet had whizzed near her.

'I bet you've told Claudia that,' she said, mocking me, but she was laughing. 'You are a one, aren't you?' And her little eyes closed into slits of glee as she laughed.

'Tomorrow night,' she said. She stepped into her car and she was off.

Johnny Gibbs stood there with his hand open. Both of us watched her go up the town and then stared at each other; he was damn nearly accusing me of plotting robbery.

Claudia was hanging about for me at home and when she had gone Mother said:

'Why are you so rude to that poor girl? What is the matter with you?'

'You heard her,' I said. 'She's trying to improve me,' for I had told them about meeting Mrs Brackett, and Claudia had been asking what I was going to wear. I had led her on and she was frightened I was just going to walk out of the bakehouse at seven o'clock in my overalls covered in flour and go up to Heading as I was.

'Why have I got to go up there anyway?' I said to Mother.

'The gardens are beautiful. Dad and I used to go up every spring when the rhododendrons were out. They'll take you round the gardens,' said Mother, daydreaming.

'You keep on saying "they" – I bet you anything you like Noisy won't be there,' I said. 'And it's September – the rhododendrons were over four months ago.'

'You needn't be rude to me,' Mother said. 'He will be there. He promised me.'

I told her about Johnny Gibbs and the penny.

'She's always up to something,' I said.

'I bet she is,' said Mother gaily. 'You take up with the nobs and get yourself engaged. What d'you expect? Dad and I were content to be in business.'

'Ah,' I said, remembering. 'That's a word Claudia doesn't like. Teddy Longfellow's in *business*. She doesn't like that.'

'There's a lot of things girls don't like they have to get used to,' said Mother.

But Mother was as agitated as I was, when the day for Mrs Brackett's party came. One of her suspicious moods set in. It began with her suspecting the cash register and the bills for flour; she suspected one of the waitresses at our café; women who came into the shop began to put on weight – always a bad sign with Mother – and the colours of their clothes didn't suit them. The men looked shifty, she said; she didn't like a bank manager who drank and she was furious that the butcher opposite was having his shop painted – what a time of year! She was sharp with the girls at the shop – Rosie, the dark one, was almost in tears – and all three girls kept half-turning their heads and walked about round-shouldered because they knew Mother was watching them. If I came out of the bakery into the office or the shop, Mother stopped serving and watched me, too. The worst of all was that she suddenly did not trust Noisy.

'He's a man,' she said.

'They're out for what they can get, both of them,' she said. She suddenly remembered Mrs Brackett had once talked of buying the property next door to us and she was glad anyway that we had stepped in and bought it a few months before.

'There is always a plot between those two,' she said.

'You didn't tell me Mrs Brackett had been in twice,' I said.

'I did,' said Mother. 'Are you starting calling everyone a liar? Even your own mother!'

I didn't think of it at the time – I never did think until after these moods were over – but I remember Dad used to say to her when she was like this:

'What's on your conscience, Mother?'

I'll come to that later.

Still she made an effort when I picked up Claudia at the Old Rectory and brought her back to show to Mother. Claudia was wearing a pale blue dress and her hair was cloudy and lovely. Mother wiped a tear at the sight of her and she was laughing when we waved goodbye; but when I turned back I saw Mother's face looking black with wretchedness as if she had seen us off to our execution or that we had left her to hers. I had the terrible feeling that we were off to the other side of the world and would never see her again and I blamed Claudia for this.

It was a light evening with a mackerel sky, the glimmer of the moon beginning on the stubble, and glinting on the heavy trees and the warm air smelled of the harvest. I was telling Claudia what the Government subsidy meant to the farmers who were complaining, though, for a fact, I could name three who had ten thousand in the bank . . .

'Look,' said Claudia interrupting. A soft owl flew over the lane.

'And that's not counting Teddy Longfellow,' I said. 'He must be worth a quarter of a million.'

'When you used to come up here to see the Bracketts was Rosie the one you took with you?' Claudia asked. 'The poor girl has got spots.'

'I took her to see her brother,' I said. 'I think it was her brother.'

'Oh, look,' said Claudia, 'another owl. They're like ghosts.' And took her hand from mine. She was a jealous girl.

But we were at Heading, driving through the deep walls of rhododendrons.

What a change: not in the house itself – it was a long L-shaped stone house with a wing making the angle – but in the garden. The lawn in front was rough; the mower had not been over it for months; one of the two climbing roses that had spread along the building had fallen off in a heap that entangled the flower-beds. They had not been weeded or touched – all so trim and well looked after in Noisy's time – but now let go. There was a stack of logs beside the wide front door, no one had bothered to move them in. Mrs Brackett's car, in need of a wash, stood near, and there was a station wagon not far from it.

'Whose is that?' I asked.

Claudia didn't know.

We went into the house. The door was open and Claudia called out. We were in the wide hall room that went to the back of the house. Then a tall, fair-haired man with a broken nose and wearing plimsolls came out of the drawing-room.

'Hullo,' he said. 'My name's Fobham, not that it matters. They're upstairs having a jaw.'

It was Lord Fobham. He lived at Abbey Moor. He took Claudia's coat and then said something to me that I didn't hear. I was standing there staring. For – against the wall was Noisy's case of birds. It was about four feet high, mounted on a stand, and contained a strange collection of stuffed birds perched on branches – birds of paradise, a pair of parrots, a golden pheasant, an oriole, an Indian kingfisher – so Lord Fobham said later. I was gaping at them. I was thinking Noisy must be mad to suppose he could walk in and lift a case like that.

'Awfully pretty. Victorian,' said Lord Fobham to me. He had a busy manner, never standing still, as if he were shaking his bones up.

'It must weigh a lot,' I said.

'Take a couple of footmen to lift it,' said Lord Fobham.

'I didn't mean weigh,' I said, confused. 'I mean they must be worth a bit.' Claudia bit her lip.

'No, don't think so, twenty-five quid the lot, no more. You pick them up anyway,' said Lord Fobham briskly. Claudia said, to put me in my place:

'They're beautiful. They're priceless.'

'You mean collectors after them?' said Lord Fobham, getting interested in Claudia. 'What would they give for a case like that?' Claudia studied them. She gave a severe glance at me and said:

'You'd better ask my father – but I'd say a hundred pounds.'

'I'd give a hundred and fifty pounds,' I said to annoy her.

'What!' said Lord Fobham, getting keen. 'You mean that?' Lord Fobham was always selling off bits of family property, pictures and heirlooms. At this Mrs Brackett and Lady Fobham came downstairs.

'What's this lot worth, Sally?' said Lord Fobham. 'Mr Fraser will give you a hundred for it.'

'It was me,' said Claudia.

'I wouldn't take three,' said Mrs Brackett.

'Well,' said Lord Fobham to me, 'if it's worth that to her I bet you'd easily find an American who'd give you twice that. What about your cousin?' he said to his wife.

'Don't be silly. He hasn't got a penny,' said Lady Fobham. 'It would smash if you moved it.'

'Don't be a damn fool. Pack it properly, case it up. Like we did with all that china,' said Lord Fobham to his wife. 'Use your brain. Look. It's light.' And he put his hands under the stand to tilt it.

'Come and have a drink and have a look at the other lots before you make up your mind,' said Mrs Brackett sarcastically.

'Damn funny. I never knew it, did you?' said Lord Fobham to me, looking back covetously at the case as we went into the drawing-room. 'Probably worth eight hundred pounds.'

'Where did you get it from?' he called to Mrs Brackett.

'It was my father's,' said Mrs Brackett.

'Darling,' said Lady Fobham. 'He'd sell me.'

'No offers,' said Lord Fobham. 'Are you in the business?' he said eagerly to me.

'No, Mr Fraser's a baker,' said Mrs Brackett.

'Ah, you can tell me,' said Lord Fobham, 'something I've always wanted to know. Why can't I get a decent crust on a loaf nowadays? Bread never has any crust.'

'Go to Mr Fraser and you'll get all the crust you want,' said Mrs Brackett, going over to Claudia. 'Darling, what a pretty dress. What are you drinking?'

'Ha! Ha! Ha!' Lady Fobham laughed. 'Are you a baker? What fun! I thought bakers were little men. You're as tall as my husband.'

'Taller. Use your eyes,' said Lord Fobham to his wife. 'God, how much gin did you put in this, Sally?' Mrs Brackett talked to me.

'Gosh, she's pretty. Gosh, she's young,' she said. 'You know how to pick them. Have you known each other long?'

'Why does your father stuff his birds?' Lord Fobham was saying to Claudia. 'I always shoot 'em.'

'He doesn't stuff birds,' said Claudia.

'Oh,' said Lord Fobham. 'Where does he shoot? Not up at Teddy Longfellow's, I hope. He shot a fox.' And to me he said: 'I always ask Sally about the gin – she waters it.'

'I do think Sally's wonderful about clothes,' said Lady Fobham to me, when Mrs Brackett poured out more drinks. 'She's got the most marvellous lack of colour sense I ever saw – tomato red – it's her personality brings it off. How do you do it, Sally?'

'It's easy,' said Mrs Brackett. 'I don't wear anything underneath.'

'Really!' said Lady Fobham.

'No one to speak to Alice,' Lord Fobham commanded, jerking a thumb at his wife. 'A couple of martinis and she goes middle class.'

I don't know how long we sat there. In spite of what Lord Fobham said the drinks were not watered this evening. They were strong. We went at last to dine in the large kitchen. Mrs Brackett rarely had servants. Lord Fobham poured the wine.

'Oh, how lovely. The '53,' said Claudia, clapping her hands and nodding to me. 'Look,' she said to me.

'It was the '51 I poured over Noisy,' said Mrs Brackett.

'Sally,' said Lord Fobham, who had drunk quite a lot. 'I never liked him.'

'You're wrong there,' said Mrs Brackett. '*I* liked him a lot. Mr Fraser likes Noisy, don't you?'

She looked at me innocently. I started to tell them about the way Noisy sneezed in court, but a look from Claudia showed me I ought not to have begun it. I went on all the same. But they were all beginning to shout.

'He's trying to tell a story. Everyone keep quiet,' said Lady Fobham kindly, flashing rings at me.

'I can't see it,' said Lord Fobham to me when I had done. 'You mean he sneezed his hands off the wheel? He was plastered.'

'I sneeze very loudly,' said Claudia, helping.

'You ask yourself,' said Lord Fobham, picking out a large potato from a dish and adding, 'Go on, pick one yourself,' to his wife. 'You ask yourself what makes a man attractive to a woman . . .'

'No one asked,' said Lady Fobham.

'Claudia knows,' said Mrs Brackett.

Lord Fobham poured the wine. We were making a terrible noise.

'All I can say . . .' Lord Fobham said. 'All I can say . . .' but he couldn't get a word in edgeways.

'All you can say – what?' said Lady Fobham.

'Why are your kitchen chairs so hard?' he said to Mrs Brackett. 'My bottom's got points on it. No', he went on. 'All I can say is I'm not like Teddy Longfellow, an atheist, reads Darwin, thinks you can go to bed with any man's wife. I believe in humility.'

'What!' cried Mrs Brackett. 'Humble – you!'

'I said humility,' said Lord Fobham drunkenly. 'Not humble. Don't be so damn middle class. There's a difference.'

'There's no place like home,' Lady Fobham began to sing, but stopped. 'Why are you looking so surprised, all of you?'

Everyone became quiet. There was a silence broken only by the sound of the coffee-pot sizzling. There were candles on the table. The curtains were not drawn. Outside the night was dark. The mackerel sky had thickened.

Presently Mrs Brackett said in a conversational voice:

'There's a man looking through the window.' We had drunk so much that we all laughed together.

'A man,' said Lady Fobham. 'How nice.'

'Through the end window,' said Mrs Brackett.

'I don't blame him,' said Lord Fobham. 'I went to dine with a fellow in Rio and half-way through dinner his wife said, "There's a man walking round the ceiling". You're plastered, Sally.'

'I'm tight, but I'm not plastered,' said Mrs Brackett. We all turned to look at the windows. There was nothing to see, but by her voice I knew Mrs Brackett was not joking.

'I'll go and look,' I said and left the room. I went out in the passage, through a large farm scullery to the back door and out into the garden. This part of the garden was sheltered by a high yew hedge and the light from the dining-room lit it fairly well. The night was dark. I was in the shadow, but I could see no one. I was just going inside again when I saw what looked like a large dog jump to the hedge. I went across to look. No sign of a dog. I went right up to the hedge: it was too dense for any dog to get through. And then, as I moved, I trod on something soft. I looked down and there was a man lying under the hedge with his hands hiding his head. I was treading on him. I stepped back.

'Get up,' I said.

But before I knew what to do, the man jumped to his feet and paused to stare. That curly hair, that twitch to the face was unmistakable. It was Noisy. He gave a leap and ran to the gate and was out of the garden before I could do anything. I didn't know what to do. Then I shouted to him. My shout brought out Lord Fobham and Mrs Brackett, too.

'Who was it?' she said.

'I don't know,' I said. 'He looked like a gypsy.'

'Get after him,' they cried. So I ran and I could see Noisy dodging along the shadows of the barns; he vaulted a five-barred gate and into the field beyond it. I let him, of course; anyway, though I've got long legs I've never been much of a runner. Noisy was small, he sprinted fast.

I got to the last lot of outbuildings and Mrs Brackett was coming up, shouting, 'Where is he?'

'He's over the gate and into the field,' I said. In fact, I had not seen where he went.

Mrs Brackett and I started for the field, when we heard a car starting up on the other side of the house. 'That's Bertie Fobham,' said Mrs Brackett, climbing over the gate, but at that very moment Lord Fobham came walking up to us.

Mrs Brackett had been grinning so far. She loved a hunt. But at this sound of a car driving off and with Lord Fobham beside us her grin went and a look of excited awakeness came to her boyish face.

'Quick,' she said, pulling me by the coat. We started back. She rushed back through the yard and garden to the house and through it. And then we both stopped. The front door was wide open and where Mrs Brackett's case of birds had stood there was now only the stand.

'It's Noisy. He's got them,' said Mrs Brackett.

'He can't have done it alone,' I said.

We rushed out on to the drive. Lord Fobham's car was there and so was hers.

'Get in,' she said. 'Bertie's a dead loss. I bet he's in the water butt.'

Far away, a good three-quarters of a mile across the flat fields, we could see the red tail-light of a car turn into the main road and its headlights fan northwards.

'There are two cars,' I said, pointing to the splashes of light on the trees.

Mrs Brackett was a fast driver. We were out of the long deep drive between the rhododendrons, past the estate cottages and in a little more than a minute were going northward on the winding road. Sometimes we saw the tail-light of the other car, sometimes we saw lights daubing the trees. There is a cross-roads not far off and when we were a quarter of a mile off we saw the car turn. As it turned it was picked out by the light of another car which turned in the opposite direction.

'There you are, two. That's our van,' I said. Distinctly I saw our green van.

'What is our van doing up here?'

Mrs Brackett did not answer. She had the racing instinct. Given a choice

[596]

between chasing a van and a racing car, she chose the latter. At the cross-roads we let the van go. There is a high ridge of open common with a narrow, bumpy but straight road rising and falling for miles, running through scattered coppices of ghostly beeches, leaning and flattened, although we were far inland, by the Atlantic winds. The little dot of light in the distance led us on.

'That's Noisy,' she said. I said nothing. I was sure it wasn't.

For Mrs Brackett it must have been like the old days, the revival of those fierce pursuits of her married life. Her cheek bones were set, her eyes were happy. The wind blew her hair back and I saw her strong straight forehead; and all the time she drove, she was turning her head and talking to me, but in an inspired way, keeping an eye on the leaping road.

'Where did you meet Claudia?' she said as the needle rose steadily on the speedometer. 'At a dance, I see. Which dance? When was that? And then you took her home? Is that when you got engaged? In the car? How old is she? Gosh, she's young.'

I answered the questions. Suddenly Mrs Brackett turned her head and came out with a blunt question.

'You're not in love with her, are you?' she said. 'All right, you don't want to talk about it. I don't think you are in love with her. They've no money, you know.'

'I'm not interested in money,' I said violently.

'Keep your hair on,' she said. Her voice changed and became nervous. 'You don't like me, do you? All right, don't answer that one. When are you going to be married?'

'Not for a long time,' I said to stop her talking.

'I think you're wise,' she said. 'It'd be unfair on her. We're gaining.'

And we were. The other car was not more than half a mile ahead. I had been trying to get a real sight of it for a long time. I was trying to think whose car it was for I was convinced that Noisy was in our van, though how he had got it unless, of course, he had pitched some tale to Mother, I couldn't imagine.

'We've got him,' said Mrs Brackett and, in her excitement, squeezed my hand. I squeezed hers. Almost at once, the engine spluttered, our speed died. Within fifty yards we stopped and the other car was away over the brow of the next hill.

The silence of the country flowed in on us.

'Well?' said Mrs Brackett.

'Sorry,' I said and let Mrs Brackett's hand go. I don't know why I had held it.

'Thank you,' said Mrs Brackett, taking her hand away. No petrol. It was the old story: Mrs Brackett was too mean to fill up her car. It had happened over and over again in her pursuits of Noisy. We all knew it. I smiled. She looked small, indignant and surprised, like a child. We sat there staring on the dead road, in the night silence of the Common, listening to the engine cool and to the small movements of animals in the gorse.

'Bad luck,' said Mrs Brackett. 'Damn.' She pulled her dress down over her knees.

'Bertie Fobham will be along in a minute,' she said.

'If he got out of the water butt,' I said. 'He's probably followed the van.'

'Yes, the van. What's going on between you and Noisy?' she said.

'Nothing,' I said.

She studied me. Then she gave that small shake to her head which either meant she was changing her mind about something or telling a whopper. She sat up straight.

'All right,' she said. 'Have it your own way. I'll tell you something. They're *his* bloody birds. Not mine. I kept them. I knew he'd come for them. I wanted him to, that's why I kept them. Now he's got them, he can keep them. That's funny – I don't want to see him any more. He's sweet, I was mad about him and I was damn pretty when I married him – but from a woman's point of view, he's no good. He wants a mother. Someone to pet him,' she said slyly, 'and cash his cheques.'

'He told me he was going to get the birds. I thought it was one of his jokes,' I said. I told her the story.

'Honour bright?' she said, like a schoolgirl. Then she added, 'Typical Noisy to come and peep through the window. I expect he's fallen for your Claudia.'

She glanced shrewdly to see how I would take that.

'All right,' she said. 'Another failure. Wash it out. That's the rotten attractive thing about him – he likes risk.'

It was no good sitting there. Lord Fobham was obviously not coming to look for us. There were never any cars on that road at this time of night. It was unlikely there would even be a night lorry. It was four miles to Tolton, the nearest garage. I moved to get out.

'Where are you going?' she said, pulling my arm.

'I'm going to walk to Tolton to get some petrol,' I said.

'I'm not going to stay here alone to be raped by some gamekeeper and I'm not going to walk,' she said, 'not in these shoes.' I sat back.

'So that's that,' I said. 'What are we going to do?'

'That's that,' she said. 'What are you worrying about?'

'Claudia,' I said. 'Who's going to take her home?' She considered this.

'The Major,' she said. 'I'm sure he clocks her in and out, doesn't he?'

'Yes, he does.'

Mrs Brackett moved towards me.

'Poor Mr Fraser,' she said putting her arm in mine and resting her head on my shoulder. 'Always in car trouble.'

Yes, I thought, the Major will fetch her. And with that, my conscience was set free. I moved Mrs Brackett's arm away and she sat up with annoyance for a second, then I put my arm round her and she put her head on my shoulder again.

'Mr Fraser,' she said. 'You're an old hand, aren't you? I bet you'll kiss me next.'

I did kiss her.

'Well that took a long time,' she said. 'About a year by my reckoning. All right, don't speak.' She suddenly laughed.

'Do you know, when Bertie Fobham offered me fifty pounds for those birds I nearly closed on it. We could have loaded them up our-selves.'

I kissed her again. She drew away from me and said:

'I suppose you know what you're doing?'

'No, I don't,' I said and I was speaking the truth. I tried to pull her to me, but adroitly she opened the door of the car and stepped out.

[599]

'Let us walk up and down,' she said, 'and listen to the owls.' And so we walked up and down a hundred times, I should think, asking me questions about myself, the shop and about Mother; she talked about the first time I went up to Heading to ask her to pay her bill.

'Gosh!' she said.

'You're lucky,' she went on. 'You've got your head screwed on.'

We must have walked up and down until two in the morning and then there were lights on the road. A lorry came along after all. We siphoned some petrol and then drove back.

'You drive,' she said and I did, with my arm round her waist. I could feel the heat of her face through my jacket. There was no one at Heading, of course, when we got there. At a quarter to three Claudia rang up while Mrs Brackett and I were having a drink. I explained to Claudia what had happened. She said simply:

'Oh! Why aren't you at home?'

And rang off.

I don't know what time I got home. Now and then through the breaking mackerel sky, the September moon dodged in and out as I drove back. No longer the big yellow moon of the night when I got myself engaged to Claudia, but white, half gone and tipped up. It seemed as it went in and out of the clouds to be turning towards me and turning away, like Mrs Brackett's busy, chattering head when the chase was on. The next morning Claudia broke off our engagement. Mrs Dingle and the Major sent the announcement to *The Times*.

Mother didn't say anything until the afternoon. She shut herself up in the office and went through the bills.

'Staying out all night round the lanes with a married woman ten years older than yourself,' Mother said. 'I don't blame the girl.'

The word 'lanes' meant only one thing to Mother.

'Two pounds three – what is this?' said Mother, reading from a bill. 'I'm glad you're out of it. Now we'll get some work done.'

'I'd still be in it,' I said, 'if you hadn't let Noisy wheedle the van out of you.'

'He brought it back. It's in the garage, you can see it. He thanked me. I don't often get thanks.'

She looked wistfully at another bill and then at me.

'I don't know what he is up to and I wouldn't believe him if he told me. I knew he'd break his promise and not go back to her.' She sighed with pleasure. 'A woman's a fool who believes a word that comes out of Noisy.'

Then Mother took off her glasses and began a tirade.

'And another thing. I may be an old woman – but don't think I'm blind. Don't think I don't know what brought Mrs Brackett down here, paying her bill, as large as life, asking you up there and all that la-di-da soft soap about how pleased I must be and that this Claudia was the most wonderful girl in the world. I said to her, "Well, Mrs Brackett, it will work itself out one way or the other, won't it? I could put my oar in, but I won't. It never lasts with him and I'm not breaking my heart."'

Mother paused. A memory distracted her.

'The second time she came, she bought three dozen meringues,' she said. 'Did she give you any last night? Well, they keep.'

'But,' said Mother, getting up from Father's old desk and flushing up with temper. 'If you think I talked Mrs Brackett into breaking it up, you're a very wicked boy . . .'

'I didn't say anything of the sort,' I said.

'Think, I said, not say,' said Mother.

And after that, I did begin to think and the more I thought the more I remembered what Father used to say about Mother's conscience.

Mother put her hand on the desk.

'Oh, you've upset me, with all this love,' she said. She had gone pale. She had frightened herself.

'And now I suppose it will be Mrs Brackett down here day and night, forty-five if she's a day, buying meringues and congress tarts until she's sick, and you'll be hiding, all innocent, in the bakehouse, leaving it to your mother. I wouldn't be that woman's dressmaker.'

Mother went to the mirror over the mantelpiece and fiddled with her hair. 'Age is what you feel,' she said, getting ready for the battle.

Noisy in the Doghouse

'Sorry to hear about you and Claudia, Bob,' Noisy Brackett said, finishing a glass of beer and leaving me at the Crown one morning. 'The Fairy Queen on the job again, I suppose? Take a tip from me. The next time you get engaged to a lovely thing like Claudia, steer clear of Fairy Queens. They turn funny when they see another girl get her man. Their little brains start working.'

Noisy knew the whole story. Everyone in our town knew it. When I walked up the street, everyone from the dogs upward was silently giving me advice: 'Fall for a divorced woman, ten years older than yourself [and some said twenty] – don't be a fool, boy!' I despised them all, but not Noisy. He had been married to her, I was in love with her; he and I were the only normal men in the town, and that was a thought I clung to. For the more I loved her the more I wanted to be saved from her, and Noisy was a living example of that salvation.

One good thing – the weather broke. Gales blew over the countryside and tore down the telephone wires. We were cut off from Heading for a day or two. Mother had a fright when the chimney caught fire at the back of our bakery; she thought the shop had gone. This, and the sign blowing off at the café, kept me outside and out of her sight. She had got as nervy as the weather. When I got in, I would find her sitting beside Father's photograph, which stood on a table by the window. She would get up and move about the room, trying the brown leather chair of the three-piece first, but it disagreed with her in some way. She moved to the next chair and glared back at the other as if it had deceived her. But now her arms couldn't settle to this one either, and she lifted her elbow to see why. Then her knees got annoyed, and with a groan she got up and returned to the upright chair by the window and turned Father's photograph an inch or so to the light, as if she were trying to shake him into talking to her.

This happened night after night. While Mother was doing this, I had one eye on her and one on the newspaper, but my mind was four miles away, up at Heading with Mrs Brackett, trying to catch sight of her face as it floated by, but all I could see was the drawing-room there and its three white-painted doors – the door she and I had come in by that night, the open door leading to the room where her farming papers were scattered over the floor, and a third door at the end of the room, which was closed. I never knew a door so closed. It watched us like a conscience. It seemed even to watch me now when I was at home. I could hear Mrs Brackett saying, 'What are you doing here at this time of night, Mr Fraser?' But the only thing I could remember was the parting in her hair, for she had kept her head lowered when she was sitting beside me. After that, I would try without any luck to see again that small movement in the pupils of her blue eyes, a movement as tiny as the click of a camera shutter, when she looked up to say goodbye. I was going to say, 'Where does that door lead to?' but the sight of her eyes taking a cool snapshot of what was going on inside me stopped me, and like a fool, I left.

I used to look at Mother over my paper. She would be staring at me, afraid of me and herself. We could not go on like this. So one evening when I came in from the Crown, I dived into it. I thought I would make her laugh. 'Major Dingley says I ought to be horsewhipped,' I said.

No answer from Mother.

'He said it to Lord Fobham over at the Crown. Noisy told me,' I said.

Mother was still silent, but when Noisy's name came up she reached for her handbag and looked for the mirror.

'Lord Fobham said –' I went on.

'I don't want to know what Lord Fobham or any of those pots said,' Mother said.

And she didn't. Mother thought it was wrong to know what people like that talked about, just as she mistrusted foreigners. They were 'daft', and she was sorry for them.

'He said, Lord Fobham said,' I went on, '"Can't do that. Can't horsewhip a man any more. No horses. Nothing but cars. The roads weren't made for them."'

'Where's the cleverness in that?' Mother said. 'We know who needs the tanning. The telephone's working again. She's been on the line three times this morning. I told her you were out.'

Mrs Brackett, of course! She was after me!

'What did she order?' I said, playing it light.

'Order!' said Mother. 'She was a good customer till you and her husband went stark staring mad.'

We were silent again. I thought of something else; I had heard a rumour going round.

'Teddy Longfellow says Noisy's got an Argentine girl now – an air hostess,' I said. 'They say he's going to marry her.' I couldn't have said anything worse if I'd tried. I thought Mother was going to hit the ceiling, burst, have a heart attack, or die. I'd never seen her face go so purple, then almost black. It nearly doubled its size. Her voice was always loud, but now she shouted, 'I won't have you going over to the Red Lion like this.' (I don't know why she always called the Crown the Red Lion.) 'You know what drink did to your father. Teddy Longfellow was a German spy in the war. He signalled. Don't ask me who he signalled to, but he signalled. Everyone knows he signalled.'

And Mother jumped up, went to the window, and pulled the blind down three inches, as if she, too, were signalling, but for the Army or someone to come and help her defend the country. If she had seen Noisy, or if she had seen Teddy Longfellow scratching his beard – he always picked at his beard at one corner of his mouth when he talked – she would have called out, 'Help! I'm signalling. Didn't you see it? I'm signalling. Come in. You've upset me, both of you.'

'Chinese air hostess!' she turned, raging on me. 'There aren't any Chinese here. Don't be a fool.'

'Argentine,' I said.

'You're always contradicting what I say,' she said. She sat down and became fretful. 'He can't,' she said. 'He's a married man.'

'He's divorced,' I said.

'You keep telling me that. I'm not deaf,' she said. 'The rat – why did he let her?'

There was a long silence; she was frightened by what she had said. At last she became calm. She took out her handkerchief, in case she was going to need it.

'I didn't mean that – not rat,' she said. She put her handkerchief back in her bag. Then she scowled. 'Argentine meat,' she said mournfully. 'Your father would never touch it.'

And then Mr Pickering, the solicitor, came over to see us.

'Good evening, Mrs Fraser,' said Mr Pickering. 'The wind's still bad, but you've got the bloom of spring on you.'

His nose, Mother said to me afterwards, had the bloom on it, too. We were waiting for him; in fact, that is why Mother had on her dark-blue dress and had her handbag beside her. A lucky thing had happened, and if it hadn't I think I might have gone mad with my mind fixed on Mrs Brackett. The Mill House at Galeford Priors had come up for sale privately, and Mother and I jumped at the chance of it – Mother because she liked a bit of property, and I because I knew it was cheap and because, as Father used to say, 'Nothing clears the mind like buying property. It sobers you up.'

But buying the Mill House gave us only a small respite. Since the night Claudia had broken our engagement I had neither seen nor spoken to Mrs Brackett. I did everything to stop myself. I'd go out in the car and make it go the other way. I'd walk up to the telephone and all round it, but I never lifted the receiver. I spent my time thinking of new things to do. I mended the sign on the café. I even whitewashed one wall of the garage, and though I thought I had painted her out with every brushstroke, she came up through the paint. But that evening, after Mr Pickering left, I had almost come to the end of everything that could prevent me trying to see her. I tried the usual little actions. I went round to the bakehouse to talk to the men. I came back and washed and shaved. I changed out of my working clothes. I put on my grey suit, but nothing happened, so I changed out of it into my brown. I came downstairs. There was only one thing left for me. I said to Mother, 'Let's go into Wetherington to the pictures.'

'Get me my coat,' Mother said. 'I'm going out. Don't gape at me. I suppose your mother can go out, too?'

Mother's temper was the worst side of her; it is the same with me.

'Go on, get out!' she cried. 'Go and chase your fancy woman. I'm not stopping you. I want to telephone.'

Every family has its terrible sentences. Mother did not often answer the telephone, except in the shop, and when I was a child, if Mother announced she wanted to 'use the telephone' she meant that everyone must get out of the house. Father used to say she would like the street cleared, too.

I left her, but you see the situation I was in; there was nothing to stop me going up to see Mrs Brackett. Nothing at all. I got out my car, but I was too startled to know where to drive, and, in fact, I just drove to the end of the town, then round it, and came back again to the cross-roads near our house to see if the lights were on. I drove out of the town again and then did the same journey once more, because I couldn't remember *which* lights were on. The second time they were all out.

All idea of going up to Mrs Brackett's went. Mother's mysteriousness saved me. I found myself going south to Wetherington at last and I was glad. Mrs Brackett's house was in exactly the opposite direction, and every mile I put between her and myself made me gladder. It was one of those clear black evenings when the sky has been cleaned up by the wind and the stars have been brushed as bright as buttons, and if you had asked me after half an hour where I was going, I would have said I didn't know, I was just letting the car take me where it wanted.

Then I woke up. I had seen a signpost and I knew suddenly where I had been going all the time, where I had been thinking of going for a week or more without knowing it. I was going to see Noisy. I was only two miles from his new house. I drove faster. All the feelings that had weighed me down for a couple of weeks fell off. Good old Noisy! Once I saw him I would be all right. If there was one person who could save me from Mrs Brackett, it was her ex-husband.

There is a stony lane up to Noisy's cottage. I had never been there in his time, but I knew where it was. I had once sheltered there with Claudia in a storm when it was a ruin. I remember she had been afraid there would be bats when we went upstairs, but there weren't. This cottage was on Teddy Longfellow's estate and stood under a row of beeches that sighed all the time – very rare trees in our part of the country. The land around it used to be grazing land, but Teddy had changed all that. Noisy had been living there for the best part of a year, after the divorce, rebuilding the place on his own. He was good with his hands and very patient.

I drove up to the cottage. It lay back behind new high wooden palings with a wide gate. The first thing I saw gave me a start; it was Brewster's cab and Teddy Longfellow's car beyond it. Beery Brewster was the taxi-driver in our town. I got out and went to open the gate, but I couldn't open it. I switched on my torch. I saw through a crack that there was a sort of lever and a bolt on it, and, on the gatepost, a bell. A bell in the country! And then I saw there was a wire running from the other side of the gate to an upper window of the cottage. I pressed the bell. A light came on over the front door and then another in the bedroom above, and the bedroom window opened and a grey-haired old woman with a shawl over her put her head out.

'Who is it?' she screeched in a nasal voice.

'Bob Fraser!' I called out. I put the light of my torch on her face. It gave a sudden twitch to the left eye that I would have recognised anywhere.

'Put that light out!' Noisy called out in his wartime voice. The wire squeaked, the gate opened. I went in, and Noisy was at the door with a wig in his hand and the shawl on his shoulders.

'Come in. We've quite a party in here. Welcome to the doghouse. Why didn't *you* bring your mother? Old Brewster's dead drunk in the kitchen. She had a terrible drive.'

Sitting by the fire in Noisy's little sitting-room, comfortable and happy, was Mother, with a glass of whisky in her hand.

'Oh, put that silly wig away,' Mother said, laughing at him. 'You frightened me out of my life. I hate those things. No!' screamed Mother. For Noisy had put the wig on again.

'It keeps away the undesirables,' Noisy said to me, underlining the word, giving a twitch to his face. 'Request permission to land. Permission refused.' He took the wig off and admired it. 'The old lady is like a mother to me. I'll get you a drink.'

I sat down next to Mother, and she muttered, 'What are you following me about for? Who looks a fool now?' And she nodded at the wig. 'Argentine hostess – *you'd* believe anything.'

And Mother laughed, united with herself and comfortable for the

[607]

first time for weeks. 'Teddy Longfellow's here,' she whispered to me, anxious to make her call on Noisy at this hour respectable. And she straightened her dress. 'What have you come here for? Haven't I got a life?'

Mother gave me a short, sharp rap on the knee to stop me replying, for Teddy Longfellow came in.

'Here, Teddy,' said Noisy, handing him a drink.

'You haven't cut down those blasted f-fir trees yet, I see,' said Teddy, fingering his beard at the end of his lower lip. His stammer, Noisy said, was worth ten thousand a year to him; it doubled his consonants and his income.

Teddy Longfellow scared everyone in our neighbourhood and enjoyed doing it. With his beard and the twist he gave to his hair and his eyebrows, he indeed looked like the devil. He used to alarm the parson during the war by praising Hitler, and annoy the hunting people by calling foxhounds 'those ruddy useless dogs'. Teddy liked causing trouble; it was he who had started this tale about Noisy's Argentine girl and – it turned out – had given him the wig. And, of course, he helped Noisy get his case of stuffed birds back from Heading, from under Mrs Brackett's nose, and had pinched our van to do it. As he sat there he eyed Mother and me to see if he could see any more chances of annoying us.

'I said when are you going to c-c-cut down those firs?' Teddy said.

'No can do,' said Noisy. 'Useful for emergency landings in poor visibility. When I get them in line I know I'm bang on the runway.'

'You won't get off the ground when the bomb drops anyway,' said Teddy.

'You don't think there will really be a bomb, do you, Mr Longfellow?' Mother said anxiously to Teddy.

'Bob,' said Noisy. 'Come out here. I'll show you the place. I can't bear to see that swine falling for the woman I love.'

And Noisy gave me a peculiar look. I have often thought of it since. I got up and went out of the room with him.

'Now,' said Noisy. 'Here's the passage. All my own work. I did every bit myself. I put in those two doors. These stairs were rotten; I had to replace half the treads. Come up. Oak, my boy, solid oak. Yes, I did all the painting. Made a bathroom. The geyser was falling to bits. I got a nice lad down at the airport to fix it for me. See? Hot. Cold. I did all the plumbing.'

He turned on the taps. All the pipes in the house jumped, whistled, and thundered.

'Beautiful sound, isn't it? Nothing like your own plumbing. Don't go away,' he said. 'Look at this. You sit in the bath, pull this ring – front gate closed, no one can get in. Pull this – open it. Front door, too. Wonderful what you can do if there are no women about. You see the idea? They can't get at you. Radio silence.'

He led the way downstairs.

'Follow me,' he said. 'You haven't seen all. I've got something rather special here. You'll appreciate it.'

He led the way down the passage to a locked door. It had a small shuttered hole in the middle of it. He unlocked the door. Inside was a tiny room, no larger than a keep pantry. It contained an armchair as wide as the room, a shelf with a gramophone on it, a wireless, a book or two, a few tins of food, and a lot of tools neatly arranged on the walls.

'What are these?' I said.

'Those? Wire clippers. Got them in the service; you can cut through a half-inch bar with them. Very useful.'

There were indeed several wires running through carefully made holes in the walls. He pulled one or two wires.

'Puts on red light outside. Warns them off . . . Shuts up garage . . . Turns on bath . . . Opens shutter on door, so you can see who's there. Press button, klaxon goes off in their face – no spies.' Noisy stood back and made a statement. 'You see the idea? Doghouse. Every house ought to have one. Make your own doghouse comfortable.'

But I was looking at something else. There was hardly space for the two of us to stand in the little room, but against the wall was the life-size figure of a young girl in uniform, cut out of cardboard – an air hostess advertising the Argentine Air Lines, smiling at us. She was beckoning.

'Ah,' said Noisy. 'You've seen her! What a peach, Bob! What a dish! Never says a word, just stands there day and night, always a welcome.'

Noisy stopped and looked at me, in a way half threatening, for he stuck out his thin chest. 'Don't go near her,' he said, 'or I'll kill you.'

And then slowly a dry grin came to one side of his mouth. 'If you're ever in trouble – you know what I mean, the only trouble there is – here you are. Just pop-along to the doghouse. I mean it. I trust you. Come along. I mean if the Fairy Queen gets on your tail, starts throwing the television about or burning your clothes on the sitting-room fire or trying to get your medals into slot machines. I say just let the air out of her tyres and buzz off down here. It's all yours. I've packed in all that sort of thing now. There's my girl now.' He pointed to the cardboard figure. 'I've given her the key to my heart.' He had hung that large rusty key on a nail stuck in the back of the model. 'And, by the way, that reminds me! Testing, testing, testing, zero, one, two, three, four – she rang up to see if you were here an hour ago.'

'Who?' I said.

'My ex-wife,' said Noisy, giving me the pistol shot with his eye.

He stared at me as if waiting for me to fall. Then he laughed. 'It's all right. I told her you weren't here. And, that's funny, you weren't! Be a good fellow, for God's sake, and ring her up or something. I don't want her blinding down here in the middle of the night looking for you. Go *now*,' he said. 'You know what women are. I had to put up the barricades when my other wife – the first one – dropped down here six months ago. She'd heard I was nesting. She brought two kids with her. I don't know where she got them. Now let's see what that swine Teddy is up to.'

We went into the sitting-room just as Mother was saying, 'If you could only tell the future, I mean, Mr Longfellow, you would know what was going to happen.'

She glared at me when I came into the room. She was on to her old subject, and Teddy was politely nodding.

'Bob's got to go off,' said Noisy, but I sat down. I didn't leave at once, and when I did I took Mother with me. She was upset.

'I could wring that Noisy's neck,' she said in the car. 'I could limb him, playing a trick like that. Spreading all that daft stuff with a wig. No woman would go and live at a place like that. What were you doing outside?'

'Looking for the air hostess,' I said.

'That's all pansy stuff. What's clever in it?'

So I said nothing, for now that she was with me she was fighting herself again.

Something must have happened to me at Noisy's – I don't know what – but the next evening I went up to Mrs Brackett's. I didn't even ring her first. I just went.

It was always quiet up at Heading. Through the trees by the house you could see the stars, and the grey stone was lit by them. There was a smell of cows and wood smoke, and there was a touch of frost in the air. I passed the maid going home on her bicycle as I was going up. The curtains were not drawn, and I could see two lamps burning in the long sitting-room. The front door was open, and after I had rung the bell I walked in the wide hall where Noisy's case of birds had once stood – the marks of the stand were still on the carpet – and I called out, 'Anyone at home?'

All the white doors in the hall were closed except one leading to the drawing-room. I listened. Then I heard talking; Mrs Brackett was speaking on the telephone. I went farther in and I heard her say, 'There's someone here,' but she still went on talking. More I couldn't catch until two or three words made me stop. She was saying the name of that horse again: 'Tray [or something or other] Pays On.' Exactly the words she had said two years or more ago, the second time I came up to ask her to pay our bill, and when she made all the trouble about it and I was afraid of her. I wasn't afraid of her now and I wasn't afraid of the house and all its things. The three or four big pictures in the room even looked smaller and the chairs rather shabby.

I heard her ring off and she came out fast from the room. When she saw me, the telephone look went dead on her face. She hesitated and then said, 'Hullo! That was Kitty Fobham.' Then she shook her head and said, 'Actually, it wasn't.'

Does that make two lies? I don't know: the moment she boldly said them she lowered her head and put out a foot as if she were sketching something in a hurry on the carpet, and then took a few steps aside before she looked at me again. She had a real liar's walk. It was her body that told the lies – I mean the way she walked, how her hips moved and her arms. Her tongue, I must say, usually told the truth. If it didn't, her head gave that shake to warn you she was going to try something on. That

was why people who spread stories about her really liked her. And when
I say her body told lies, I mean they were the kind of lies any man likes
to hear.

'They told me you telephoned,' I said.

'Why didn't you ring me back?' she said.

'I've come instead,' I said.

'You don't say! Well, sit down. I've been washing my hair,' she said.
She pointed to the deep, green settee where we had sat the night that had
ended my engagement with Claudia. It was too low for me; I'm tall.

Mrs Brackett looked plain. There was a line across her forehead, and
her hair was darker because it was wet. It ended in rat-tails, just like the
hair of a maid we used to have years ago. Mrs Brackett went to the far
side of the fireplace and held her hair down to dry it by the fire. We both
spoke at once.

She said, in her cattle dealer's voice, 'I wanted to see you. I expect you
think it was my fault Claudia broke up with you. I'm sorry.'

I said, 'What is this "Pays On"? "Say Pays On"? "Tray Pays On"?
You said it on the telephone.'

'Pays on?' she said, throwing her hair back and looking at me. 'What
d'you mean? On the blower – I said that?'

'I don't know,' I said. 'You said it once before, when I came up here
years ago, as well, about the bill.'

She smiled. 'Still on about the bill,' she said. 'What's the matter? Haven't
you paid your water rates? I don't know what you're talking about. "Pays
on"? Never heard of it.' And she lowered her head to the fire. 'I'll never
get this dry,' she said.

'That's it. Pays On,' I said. 'Is it a horse? Noisy said it was a horse.'

She sat up and again threw her hair back from her broad low forehead
when she heard Noisy's name.

'When I came up here,' I went on. 'Noisy said it sounded like one of
those French horses.'

'A French horse? I never heard . . .' She stopped. She opened her
mouth and put her tongue in her cheek, like a child caught stealing. She
got up and walked over to a side table where the drinks stood. I watched
the way she walked. She was wearing one of her terrible dresses of blue
stuff with little yellow and red daisies on it. It looked like someone else's.

And a tomato-coloured cardigan. I remember her saying, the night when Claudia and I had dinner there, that it puts a woman 'one up in the conver' if you give a man a shock at the sight of your clothes and it 'makes the other women look sick'.

'A horse.' She laughed. 'What will you have to drink?' she said, turning round. 'Noisy told you that?'

'Yes.'

'Well,' she said. 'I will tell you.' And she spoke like someone spelling out to a child. 'It's not a horse, it's a man. A Frenchman who lives in the country. It's French.'

'Nothing for me,' I said. 'Why talk in French? Is it smart or something?'

'You're a suspicious character, Bob,' she said. 'You sound sore. What's the matter? Has flour gone up? Can't you sell your cream puffs?'

I kept my temper, because her voice had changed and was soft.

'Let's see,' I said. 'He's a man. And he's French. And he lives in the country. He wouldn't be a peasant, would he?'

'Good!' she said, laughing. 'That's it – a French peasant. A real peasant.'

I nodded. '"Bloody peasant," Noisy said,' I said, giving a scratch behind my ear.

She gave me a long look, which died away, and she said outright, 'All right, you win. I was talking about you.'

'That's funny,' I said. 'Noisy thought it was a horse.'

'Noisy has better manners than me. Can we drop it?'

'What?' I said. 'Is it something insulting? I didn't know that. What's wrong with it? It's no worse than silly bitch, is it?'

I thought Mrs Brackett was going to fly at me, but she didn't. She stuck her chin out. She said quietly, seriously, 'I apologise.'

'That's all right,' I said. 'It's best to begin with a row.'

'Damn, damn, damn,' she said. 'I really do apologise. Honour bright.' And then her eye gave that little flick. 'Begin what?' she said.

I got up to walk over to the table to her.

'No,' she said. 'Stay where you are. If you don't want a drink, I do.' I sat down again, but when she brought her drink, she came over to my side of the fireplace and sat on the stool there. We were silent for quite a time.

'I've bought the Mill House,' I said.

'That's nice of you,' she said. 'You've changed the subject. How did you hear about it?'

She was sharp where there was a question of a deal. I told her about it. I said I thought of turning it into an hotel, and we argued about that a long time – how you'd never get a manager in a place like that.

'How much did you give for it?' she said.

I didn't answer, but – it just came into my head, and I didn't mean it – I said, 'How would *you* like to manage it?'

She was as surprised as I was. 'I don't like being mocked,' she said. 'Is that what you came up to say? Of course I wouldn't manage your hotel. Anyway, it's a crime to do anything like that with that place. D'you always go about sitting in cars with women and then ask them to manage hotels? Did you ask Claudia? Why are you so mad about money?'

Jealous! I pricked up my ears. The room seemed to smile at me. There was a picture on one of the walls of a lot of cardinals drinking wine, and the central one had his smiling face turned towards us. Even the white door at the end of the room might have opened; I wouldn't have been surprised.

'She was only a girl of nineteen,' I said. 'Since Father died, I am responsible.'

'Pooh. You're only twenty-two yourself.'

'Thirty,' I said.

'How old d'you think I am?' she said, putting her head back and moving to the sofa. In a way, she looked her worst, but I wasn't looking at her face. I remember Noisy once saying he was twenty-three hundred years old and that she was twelve.

'Twelve,' I said.

'I'm thirty-three,' she said, giving the short shake to her head. 'Actually, thirty-six. And don't copy Noisy.'

Thirty-six, I was thinking – that will be something to tell Mother the next time she starts on me about Mrs Brackett's age. When I looked at her again, she was very friendly.

'I'm selling this house, if you're in the buying mood,' she said. 'I can't afford it.'

I shook my head. 'Why don't you sell it to Teddy Longfellow?' I said. 'I saw him at Noisy's last night. He's rich.'

She started. 'The liar!' she said, blushing. 'Noisy said you weren't there.'

'I wasn't when you rang,' I said.

She smiled and leaned toward me. 'Did you see this girl of his, the Argentine girl everyone is talking about?'

I was the biggest fool in the world, I felt so confident of her.

'Yes,' I said carelessly, and I laughed.

'What is she like – young? I'm glad he's got a girl.'

I was in it; I had to go on. 'Yes, young,' I said.

'Is she tall?' Mrs Brackett moved nearer to me. 'Tell me what she's like.'

'Dark,' I said. 'Yes, tall.'

'Taller than me? Pretty? What is she like? What did she say?' She started arranging her hair as she talked.

'Taller,' I said. 'A bit – kind of stiff. I've only seen her in uniform. She didn't say much. No, I don't think she said anything. Teddy Longfellow was there, and Mother. Something dead about her.'

'Is she working? I mean is she air-hostessing still?'

I was beginning to enjoy this.

'I think they've grounded her.'

'Why?' Mrs Brackett said anxiously.

'I don't know,' I said.

'You must have some reason,' she said.

'She just looked grounded.'

'How can anyone look grounded? She sounds like a dummy to me,' said Mrs Brackett, with an unnatural laugh. 'Stiff as a board, in uniform. Doesn't she speak? Poor Noisy – serves him right. He likes a chat.'

She put her hand on my arm and said excitedly, 'I'll tell you what we'll do. Let's go and see them. I'll ring him up.'

'No,' I said, alarmed by what I'd said.

'Yes,' she said, moving away, but I caught her arm and held her.

'My hair is wet,' she said, shaking to get away, but I held her arm and presently she stopped pulling.

'Please,' she said. 'You're hurting me.' I slackened my hold and she got up at once. She was a trickster.

'I'm going to see them,' she said, looking at her watch and going toward the door.

'It's ten o'clock,' I said. 'They'll be in bed.'

Mrs Brackett stopped at the door. She went very white. With her hair plastered down and her mouth suddenly small and her eyes startled as if I had hit her, she looked ugly.

'That,' she said, coming back a step to me, 'was a dirty remark.'

'Trays Pays On,' I said.

She looked as if she would throw something, if there had been anything near. Then her eyes almost closed and she laughed and laughed and came and sat down near me. 'You're not the same as when you first came up here. What has happened to you?' she said softly to me.

'Nor are you,' I said, moving toward her.

She began pulling at the thread of the settee as she had done before. I can't remember what we said, but we did get on to the subject of the door at the end of the room and where it led to. To the second staircase, she said. And one thing led to another.

The next morning, when I had seen to the vans, I rang her. I was mad to hear her voice. There was no reply. Several times I rang, and there was no answer. Mother came into the room behind the shop to look at me, and every time the phone rang, she and I moved to it. At last I had to go to Wetherington in the afternoon – it was early closing with us, and Mother wanted to come with me and go shopping. There was something secretive about Mother, because she wouldn't, as she usually did, tell me where to pick her up in the town. Usually, I found her outside the biggest draper's, but today she wouldn't say for a long time, and then she said, 'In the station yard.' This puzzled me. She had what we used to call her broody look, like a hen sitting heavily, and occasionally she'd break out into the first line of a song, but stop because she could never remember the others. In the end, I met her at the station, looking comfortable and sly, as though she had eaten something good, and when we drove away, she was soft-tempered and dreamy. She had got her week of anger off her mind. We had been driving for twenty minutes when she said, 'They don't tell you anything. It's daft. Your Uncle Dan in Canada has been dead for years.'

She had been to a fortune-teller.

'Well, who else could it be?' she said.

We got back to the shop, and I drove into the yard at the side and straight for the garage, which I had left open. It was dark now, and I had put the headlights full on. Just as the car was going into the garage, Mother clutched my arm and cried out, 'Stop, Bob! There's a woman there!'

She was right. There, standing against the whitewashed wall, stood a tall young girl, smiling. For a moment I thought it was Molly Gibson; she was dark. Then I looked again. It was not a girl – not a living girl. It was Noisy's cardboard girl from the Argentine Air Lines.

'Oh, it gave me a turn, I thought you'd kill her,' Mother said. 'What is it? Who put it there?'

We got out. Mother looked at me suspiciously. It was what the fortune-teller had said, she told me: there'd be a visitor from overseas.

I examined the figure. 'It's Noisy's,' I said. 'It's got the key to his heart hanging on the back.'

Mother came and looked. Her face darkened. 'You've upset Noisy. You don't listen to me. You've upset him. I could see it the other night.' And Mother marched out of the yard, down the street to our house.

I knew Noisy was always playing the fool, but there was always something behind his jokes. And then – it was natural – I felt a bit uneasy about Noisy ever since I had fallen in love with Mrs Brackett. He was friendly, but he had changed. I had once or twice caught him giving me a strange look, his face not twitching, but still as stone; his eyes very sharp, sarcastic.

I went to the bakehouse, but the men didn't know anything about the dummy. I went along to the café and asked the two girls there. Had Noisy been in, I asked the first girl.

'No,' she said.

'Are you sure?' I asked.

The other girl came out of the kitchen.

'Has Noisy been in today? Any time?'

'No,' said the girls.

I told them there was a poster in the garage.

'Oh,' said the eager girl from the kitchen. 'That was Mrs Brackett. She left it this afternoon.' And she gave me a knowing smile; I did not like it.

'Did she leave a message?' I said, not letting on. 'You're sure it was Mrs Brackett?'

'Yes,' they said. And there was no message.

They were grinning behind my back when I left. I saw them in the mirror. You can imagine what was going on in my head. I didn't mind the joke, but Mrs Brackett and Noisy in it together!

I went back to our house.

'Mrs Brackett brought it,' I said to Mother.

Mother ignored this. Her temper was rising. 'Trying to make a laughing-stock of your mother!' she said. 'Telling me he had an Argentine girl up there! Do you think anyone in his senses would believe a twopenny tale like that?'

'I didn't make it up,' I said.

'I'm sure you didn't,' she said. 'You haven't the brains. All this love has made you stupid. Going about with your mouth wide open, you'd swallow anything, and the business goes to ruin. Two customers complained the bread was burned yesterday – the whole lot. The whole town's laughing at you. Noisy's taken your measurements, my boy. Running after another man's wife! They've made fools of you. And I am glad. It will teach you a lesson. And don't ask me to be sorry. I told you this divorcing was all my eye. Oh, I wish your father was alive!'

'Why would they put it there?' I said. 'Anyway, it was Mrs Brackett.'

I was going to say more; I was in a temper, too. I went round to the shop again and I sat at the desk staring at the telephone, and then I rang Mrs Brackett.

'I have been trying to ring you,' I said.

'That is a change,' she said. 'Is anything the matter?'

Her voice sounded cold.

I laughed. It was so lovely to hear her. 'Well,' I said. And I laughed again.

'What is the joke?' she said.

I was still laughing as I began. 'I –'

'Are you ringing me up about that dummy?' she said sharply. 'You are? You found it? Bad luck for you. Listen. I don't like being mocked. I had ten years of that kind of thing with Noisy.'

God, I thought. Mother storming at me at home, and Mrs Brackett shouting from up on the hill.

'I don't want any more stableboy jokes.' Mrs Brackett had a temper. We all had tempers, I suppose – Mother, me, Mrs Brackett, and all of us.

She slammed down the telephone.

I would have let her temper go and waited for her to cool off and to come running down. What stopped me was not my own temper, but what was clearer every moment I thought of it: that she and Noisy had got together again, for how else could she have got hold of the dummy?

I ran into the yard, and that damn silly thing was still smiling at me as I got into the car. I drove up to Heading. I was mad. The servant was coming down on her bicycle, just as I had seen her two days before. This time I could have gladly knocked her over.

But Mrs Brackett was not at Heading. She had gone out. I came slowly back to the shop. I did not know what to do. Several times my hand went to the telephone. I was tempted to ring Noisy to tell him what I thought of him, but I couldn't. I went over to the Crown.

And there I heard something that changed my mind. Teddy Long-fellow was in the bar talking to the landlord, who was polishing glasses and lifting each one to his eye to see if it was clean as he listened.

'They cut fifty pounds' worth of wire,' Teddy was saying.

'He told me that on the phone,' said the landlord.

'Hullo, Bob,' said Teddy. 'Did you hear this?'

'What was that? Have they cut your wire?' I said to Teddy. He often had trouble with hooligans who let his cattle out.

'Up at Mr Brackett's,' said the landlord.

'Noisy's had burglars,' said Teddy.

I looked at the landlord, for I never believed any tale that Teddy came along with, but the landlord put a glass down and said: 'This afternoon. When he was out.'

'Well, they wouldn't do it when he was in!' said Teddy scornfully.

Yes. Out (I thought). With Mrs Brackett, delivering that poster to me, but Teddy's next words put another light on it.

'I told Noisy just now it sounds like the job of a sex maniac to me,' said Teddy to the landlord, 'cutting all that wire, smashing a kitchen window – all to get at a woman! I told Noisy months ago it was a mistake to keep a foreign woman up there.'

'What woman?' said the landlord.

'Bob knows her, don't you, Bob?' said Teddy.

That was enough for me. Noisy had not been with Mrs Brackett; in fact it was clear from the far-away tone of Teddy's voice that he was going to spread the rumour that *I* was with her. He was picking away at his beard fast, delighted with himself. It was clear he had had a peep into my garage.

What puzzles me now is why I didn't let it go at that. I suppose I was so relieved to see that Noisy and Mrs Brackett were not in this together that I didn't stop to ask myself 'Whose side are you on?' but went straight off eagerly to ring up Noisy. If only I hadn't rung him!

'This is going to cost you a pretty penny, Bob,' Noisy said before I could get a word in. 'A hundred feet of wire chopped up to bits, two locks gone, kitchen window smashed, geyser not working – add the men's time at union rates . . .'

'I don't know what you're talking about.'

'And then,' Noisy went on. 'There's the emotional side. No one thinks of that nowadays. That's what I can't get over. Bob, you rotten free-lance, breaking up a happy home. Think of all those poor children crying, "Where's Mummy? When's she coming back from the Argentine?" Tragedy of easy divorce, divided homes, one more little delinquent attacking women in parks, Father's sad evidence –'

'Listen, Noisy –'

'Bob, you bloody daylight burglar. Over.'

'I've got her,' I said. 'She put her in our garage.'

'Who did?'

'Your wife.'

'My ex-wife, if you please,' said Noisy.

'We found her when we got back from Wetherington this afternoon.'

'Who's we?' said Noisy.

'Mother and I,' I said.

'Mother in it, too,' said Noisy. 'My God! Radio silence, old boy. I'll be over in five minutes.'

He came with his usual roar. 'Let me see her,' he said, and we went into the garage. He sniffed the air. 'It's damp in here. Bad for the poor girl's chest.' He looked at her proudly. 'Isn't she a peach? Now, my sweetie,' he said to her, 'you stay where you are, do as you are told. It will be all right. We're going to lock you in, so you don't get up to tricks.' And he closed the garage door.

'Aren't you going to take her back?' I said, as he locked the door himself.

'Bob,' he said very seriously, 'when Teddy Longfellow and I broke into Heading that time and got my case of birds back, they were my birds, weren't they? We didn't steal anything, did we? We didn't touch a thing that wasn't our own – right? We didn't do any damage, did we? We didn't break a kitchen window and leave filthy footmarks on the floor, did we? One of the cleanest jobs you ever saw, I bet, wasn't it? And we didn't lift anything lying about, like a pair of service wire clippers, for example?' He was scowling. 'Oh, yes,' he said, 'we're going to get them back. Jump in. I know her hideouts. We'll buzz up to Heading to see if the clippers are there, but if they're not they'll be in her car. And remember, Bob, for future reference' – he gave that twitch to his eye as he turned his head to me – 'when the Fairy Queen takes off she's never got more than a gallon of gas in the tank. That cuts the target area down to eleven miles. She can't be at the Fobhams', for instance.'

We were off. The roar of Noisy's car was unmistakable in our town, and of course it brought Mother to the door.

We tried Heading first – 'the ancestral home', Noisy said – and drew nothing, then to the Duck outside Tolton, the Lamb at Forth Hill, then the Aylesbury Arms, the Green Man, and the Sailor's Return.

'Bob,' said Noisy, getting whiter in the face after every pub, 'the Fairy Queen is not one of those who, in the normal free-for-all, can dish it out but can't take it. Something must have got her on the raw.'

I told him the story – well, three-quarters of it.

'Tall, dark girl, you said. Didn't talk much, you said? Very nice,' he said, grinning. 'Anything else?'

'I said I thought she was grounded,' I said.

Noisy laughed loudly. 'Wrong there, Bob,' he said. 'She's in uniform.'

He became thoughtful. 'Of course, I can see she was getting her own back on me, but why dump that lovely creature at *your* place? That's what foxes me.'

We drove on, missing the Harrow at Denton Bridge, because the man there watered the gin. 'There's only one more chance,' Noisy said, driving now on the wrong side of the road. 'Play the game or get out of the bed!' he shouted at a passing car.

We seemed to lose our way in by-lanes. Suddenly he pulled up at a pub called the Fox and stopped in the yard. We did not get out.

'The only thing I can think of, Bob, is you were making a pass at her. Yes, that's what it must have been,' Noisy said as we sat there. 'Never make a joke when you're making a pass at a woman. They don't like it. You're right down the drain if you do. And let me tell you, I don't care a damn if you *are* down the drain. But I want my wire clippers back. They've been with me in France, in Egypt, in India, and I've never seen the man who'd dare lay a finger on them.'

We looked round the yard.

'What did I tell you?' said Noisy suddenly. 'See that? She's here.'

He pointed to Mrs Brackett's car. We sat gazing at it.

'Keep your eyes skinned, Bob,' said Noisy at last. He got out and went over to her car, opened the door, and looked around inside. He came back with the heavy pair of service wire clippers in his hand.

'Mission accomplished,' he said. 'Let's get drunker.'

We considered the peaceful white walls of the inn, the bare trees, the lights shining behind the curtained windows.

'It brings back memories,' said Noisy. 'Many's the time we've finished up here, the Fairy Queen and I, after a row. Funny to think she's in there now, all on her own, knocking them back. Mind if I come in, too, for old time's sake?'

For I had begun to move for the door.

There was a loud noise coming from the bar, where the locals were, but we went into the small one. Sitting alone in a chair by the bar was Mrs Brackett.

'Scotland Yard,' said Noisy thickly, turning back the lapel of his coat.

Mrs Brackett put her drink down and, looking at Noisy, she blushed. 'I see you've brought the Sergeant,' she said, glancing coldly at me.

'We didn't know whether this was going to be a strong-arm job, did we, Bob?' said Noisy. 'It's all right. We're both drunk.'

'Mr Fraser's quite free with his arms, too,' said Mrs Brackett primly. 'Why doesn't he sit down? Is he going?' For Noisy had sat down beside her.

'I'm mad about her, aren't you, Bob?' said Noisy. 'A real bit of old Newgate, isn't she? No, Bob's not going.'

'Well, why doesn't he join in the conversation?' said Mrs Brackett. 'Has flour gone up again? Or is he worried about his new girl?'

'Oh,' cried Noisy, 'has Bob got a new girl? He didn't tell me that. Bob, what's this, you rotten seducer? You never told me.'

'A foreign girl – Argentine, I believe,' said Mrs Brackett. 'Very dark, very tall. They'll make a handsome pair. She used to be an air hostess, isn't that so, Mr Fraser? Grounded . . .'

'Much better grounded,' said Noisy. 'You know where they are.'

'A bit stiff in her uniform,' said Mrs Brackett.

'That will wear off when they get married,' said Noisy.

I laughed, but Noisy didn't and neither did Mrs Brackett when she looked at me.

'With a fine fellow like Bob, of course it will,' said Noisy. 'Good-looking, too.'

'Yes,' said Mrs Brackett. 'And doing well. He's just bought the Mill House. He asked me to manage it. It's going to be an hotel.'

'Go on!' said Noisy. 'What? Eight ten a week and all found?'

'You won't know him in ten years' time. He'll have bought the town,' said Mrs Brackett.

'Well, all I can say,' said Noisy, 'I hope he's found the right woman.'

'She sounds absolutely cut out for him,' said Mrs Brackett. 'Has she got any money, Mr Fraser?'

'*Mr* Fraser, *Mr* Fraser!' said Noisy in a shocked way. 'You don't seem to know each other too well. Come and sit over here, Bob, and get acquainted. This is Mrs Brackett. Will you excuse me a minute?'

And Noisy went out.

'I love you,' I said to Mrs Brackett. 'Let us go. Now.'

Mrs Brackett's face softened.

'I've been in love with you since I first saw you,' I said.

[623]

'I was mad about *you*, actually,' said Mrs Brackett. 'But' – giving a shake to her head – 'I don't like technique.'

'It was just a joke.'

'Really?' said Mrs Brackett. 'Well, I haven't got a sense of humour. Ask Noisy.'

'But last night you loved me,' I said.

'Hold it a minute,' she said. 'I'll tell you.'

She got up and went to the street door. 'Noisy's a long time,' she said. 'Has he gone? I didn't hear him.'

Then Noisy came in and met her there.

'I thought you'd gone,' said Mrs Brackett.

'No, my sweet, just taking the air,' said Noisy, taking her arm. 'Nice to be missed.'

Mrs Brackett hesitated.

'I'm going home,' she said and suddenly pushed violently past him out of the pub.

We stared at the closed door. The closed door in the sitting-room at Heading came into my mind. I don't know what was in Noisy's, but we both went after her. At once we heard a shout from her across the yard.

'Bloody funny!' she shouted and came marching in a fury across the yard, opened the door of Noisy's car, and got in and slammed it. Noisy sauntered up to her.

'You damn well drive me!' she shouted at him.

Noisy turned to me, shrugged, and beckoned, but I was staring at her car. Someone had let the air out of her two back tyres. Suddenly, I heard Noisy's car roar. He had taken off.

Mrs Brackett's car stood in our garage at home for three weeks. It took me twenty minutes to pump its tyres, and where she and Noisy went that night I do not know. I went after them. They weren't at Heading. They weren't at his cottage. Nor in the days, even the weeks that followed. The Post Office said they had gone abroad. The damp got into the hostess of the Argentine Air Lines. She peeled and she buckled and fell over. I told one of the men to pitch her in the dustbin. He brought the key hanging on the back to me, and I told him to throw that away, too. On second thoughts, I broke up the dummy girl myself.

Mother said nothing, but once or twice she goes on about the future – the usual thing. 'If you knew what was going to be you'd act differently,' she says. 'People ought to tell you, then you'd know,' she says. And then she gets on to Teddy Longfellow saying there isn't any future, and I tell her I agree with him. A few weeks ago, Heading came up for sale. Mother says the class of trade is changing in our town.

Blind Love

───

'I'm beginning to be worried about Mr "Wolverhampton" Smith,' said Mr Armitage to Mrs Johnson who was sitting in his study with her notebook on her knee and glancing from time to time at the window. She was watching the gardener's dog rooting in a flower-bed. 'Would you read his letter again: the second paragraph about the question of a partnership.'

Since Mr Armitage was blind it was one of Mrs Johnson's duties to read his correspondence.

'He had the money – that is certain; but I can't make out on what conditions,' he said.

'I'd say he helped himself. He didn't put it into the business at Ealing – he used it to pay off the arrears on the place at Wolverhampton,' she said in her cheerful manner.

'I'm afraid you're right. It's his character I'm worried about,' said Mr Armitage.

'There isn't a single full stop in his letter – a full page on both sides. None. And all his words are joined together. It's like one word two pages long,' said Mrs Johnson.

'Is that so?' said Mr Armitage. 'I'm afraid he has an unpunctuated moral sense.'

Coming from a blind man whose open eyes and face had the fixed gleam of expression you might have seen on a piece of rock, the word "unpunctuated' had a sarcasm unlike an ordinary sarcasm. It seemed, quite delusively, to come from a clearer knowledge than any available to the sighted.

'I think I'll go and smell out what he's like. Where is Leverton Grove? Isn't it on the way to the station? I'll drop in when I go up to London tomorrow morning,' said Mr Armitage.

The next morning he was driven in his Rolls-Royce to Mr Smith's house, one of two or three little villas that were part of a building speculation that had come to nothing fifty years before. The yellow brick place was darkened by the firs that were thick in this district. Mrs Johnson, who had been brought up in London places like these, winced at the sight of them. (Afterwards she said to Mr Armitage, 'It brings it back.' They were talking about her early life.) The chauffeur opened the car door, Mrs Johnson got out saying, 'No kerb', but Armitage, waving her aside, stepped out unhelped and stood stiff with the sainted upward gaze of the blind; then, like an army detail, the party made a sharp right turn, walked two paces, then a sharp left to the wooden gate which the chauffeur opened, and went forward in step.

'Daffodils,' said Mrs Johnson noting a flower-bed. She was wearing blue to match her bold, practical eyes, and led the way up the short path to the door. It was opened before she rang by an elderly, sick-looking woman with swollen knuckles who half-hid behind the door as she held it, to expose Smith standing with his grey jacket open, his hands in his pockets – the whole man an arrangement of soft smiles from his snowball head to his waistcoat, from his flies to his knees, sixteen stone of modest welcome with nothing to hide.

'It is good of you to come,' he said. He had a reverent voice.

'On my way to the station,' said Armitage.

Smith was not quite so welcoming to Mrs Johnson. He gave her a dismissive frown and glanced peremptorily at his wife.

'In here?' said Mrs Johnson briskly taking Armitage's arm in the narrow hall.

'Yes,' he said.

They all stood just inside the doorway of the front room. A fir tree darkened it. It had, Mrs Johnson recorded at once, two fenders in the fireplace, and two sets of fire-irons; then she saw two of everything – two clocks on the mantelpiece, two small sofas, a dining-table, a small table folded up, even two carpets on the floor, for underneath the red one, there was the fringe of a worn yellow one. Mr Smith saw that she noted this and, raising a grand chin and now unsmiling, said, 'We're sharing the 'ouse, the house, until we get into something bigger.'

And at this, Mrs Smith looked with the searching look of an agony in her eyes, begging Mrs Johnson for a word.

[627]

'Bigger,' echoed Mrs Smith and watched to see the word sink in. And then, putting her fingers over her face, she said: 'Much bigger', and laughed.

'Perhaps,' said Mr Smith, who did not care for his wife's laugh, 'while we talk – er . . .'

'I'll wait outside in the car,' said the decisive Mrs Johnson and when she was in the car she saw Mrs Smith's gaze of appeal from the step.

Half an hour later, the door opened and Mrs Johnson went to fetch Mr Armitage.

'At this time of the year the daffodils are wonderful round here,' said Armitage as he shook hands with Smith, to show that if he could not see there were a lot of things he knew. Mr Smith took the point and replaced his smiling voice with one of sportive yet friendly rebuke, putting Mr Armitage in his place.

'There is only one eye,' he stated as if reading aloud. 'The eye of God.'

Softly the Rolls drove off, with Mrs Smith looking at it fearfully from the edge of the window curtain.

'Very rum fellow,' said Armitage in the car. 'I'm afraid he's in a mess. The Inland Revenue are after him as well. He's quite happy because there's nothing to be got out of him. Remarkable. I'm afraid his friends have lost their money.'

Mrs Johnson was indignant.

'What's he going to do down here? He can't open up again.'

'He's come here,' Armitage said, 'because of the chalk in London water. The chalk, he says, gets into the system with the result that the whole of London is riddled with arthritis and nervous diseases. Or rather the whole of London is riddled with arthritis and nervous diseases because it believes in the reality of chalk. Now chalk has no reality. We are not living on chalk nor even on gravel: we dwell in God. Mr Smith explains that God led him to manage a chemist's shop in Wolverhampton, but to open one of his own in Ealing without capital was a mistake. He now realises that he was following his own will not the will of God. He is now doing God's work. Yesterday he had a cable from California. He showed it to me. "Mary's cancer cured gratitude cheque follows." He's a faith-healer.'

'He ought to be in gaol,' said Mrs Johnson.

'Oh no. He's in heaven,' said Armitage. 'I'm glad I went to see him. I didn't know about his religion, but it's perfect: you get witnesses like him in court every day, always moving on to higher things.'

The Rolls arrived at the station and Mr Armitage picked up his white stick.

'Cancer today. Why not blindness tomorrow? Eh?' he said. Armitage gave one low laugh from a wide mouth. And though she enjoyed his dryness, his rare laugh gave a dangerous, animal expression to a face that was usually closed. He got out of the car and she watched him walk into the booking-hall and saw knots of people divide to make way for him on the platform.

In the damp town at the bottom of the hills, in the shops, at the railway station where twice a week the Rolls waited for him to come back from London, it was agreed that Armitage was a wonder. A gentleman, of course, they said; he's well-off, that helps. And there is that secretary-housekeeper, Mrs Johnson. That's how he can keep up his legal business. He takes his stick to London, but down here he never uses it. In London he has his lunch in his office or in his club, and can manage the club stairs which worry some of the members when they come out of the bar. He knows what's in the papers – ever had an argument with him? – of course Mrs Johnson reads them to him.

All true. His house stood, with a sudden flash of Edwardian prosperity, between two larch coppices on a hill five miles out and he could walk out on to the brick terrace and smell the lavender in its season, and the grass of the lawns that went steeply down to his rose garden and the blue tiles of his swimming-pool boxed in by yew.

'Fabian Tudor. Bernard Shaw used to come here – before our time, of course,' he would say, disparaging the high, panelled hall. He was really referring to his wife who had left him when he was going blind twenty-two years ago. She had chosen and furnished the house. She liked leaded windows, brass, plain velvet curtains, Persian carpets, brick fireplaces and the expensive smell of wood smoke.

'All fake,' he would say, 'like me.'

You could see that pride made him like to embarrass. He seemed to know the effect of jokes from a dead face. But, in fact, if he had no animation – Mrs Johnson had soon perceived in her common-sensical way – this was because he was not affected, as people are, by the movements on other faces. Our faces, she had learned from Armitage, threw their lives away every minute. He stored his. She knew this because she stored hers. She did not put it like this, in fact what she said appeared to contradict it. She liked a joke.

'It's no good brooding. As Mother used to say, as long as you've got your legs you can give yourself an airing.'

Mrs Johnson had done this. She had fair hair, a good figure and active legs, but usually turned her head aside when she was talking as if to an imaginary friend. Mrs Johnson had needed an airing very badly when she came to work for Mr Armitage.

At their first interview – he met her in the panelled hall.

'You do realise, don't you, that I am totally blind? I have been blind for more than twenty years,' he said.

'Yes,' she said. 'I was told by Dr James.' She had been working for a doctor in London.

He held out his hand and she did not take it at once. It was not her habit to shake hands with people; now, as always, when she gave in she turned her head away. He held her hand for a long time and she knew he was feeling the bones. She had heard that the blind do this and she took a breath as if to prevent her bones or her skin passing any knowledge of herself to him. But she could feel her dry hand coming to life and she drew it away. She was surprised that, at the touch, her nervousness had gone.

To her, Armitage's house was a wonderful place. The space, the light made friendly by the small panes of the tall leaded windows, charmed her.

'Not a bit like Peckham,' she said cheerfully.

Mr Armitage took her through the long sitting-room where there were yellow roses in a bowl, into his study. He had been playing a record and took it off.

'Do you like music?' he said. 'That was Mozart.'

'I like a bit of a sing-song,' she said. 'I can't honestly say I like the classical stuff.'

He took her round the house, stopped to point to a picture or two and, once more down in the long room, took her to a window and said,

'This is a bad day for it. The haze hasn't lifted. On a clear day you can see Sevenham Cathedral. It's twelve miles away. Do you like the country?'

'Frankly I've never tried it.'

'Are you a widow, Mrs Johnson?'

'No. I changed my name from Thompson to Johnson and not for the better. I divorced my husband,' said Mrs Johnson crisply.

'Will you read something to me – out of the paper,' he said. 'A court case.'

She read and read.

'Go on,' he said. 'Pick out something livelier.'

'Lonely monkeys at the zoo?'

'That will do.'

She read again and she laughed.

'Good,' he said.

'As father used to say "Speak up ..."' she began, but stopped. Mr Armitage did not want to hear what father said.

'Will you allow me,' Armitage said, getting up from his desk. 'Would you allow me to touch your face?'

Mrs Johnson had forgotten that the blind sometimes asked this.

She did not answer at once. She had been piqued from the beginning because he could not see her. She had been to the hairdresser's. She had bought a blouse with a high frilled neck which was meant to set off the look of boyish impudence and frankness of her face. She had forgotten about touch. She feared he would have a pleading look, but she saw that the wish was part of an exercise for him. He clearly expected her to make no difficulty about it.

'All right,' she said, but she meant him to notice the pause, 'if you want to.'

She faced him and did not flinch as his hand lightly touched her brow and cheek and chin. He was, she thought, 'after her bones' not her skin and that, though she stiffened with resistance, was 'OK by her'. When, for a second, the hand seemed to rest on her jaw, she turned her head.

'I weigh eight stone,' she said in her bright way.

'I would have thought less,' he said. That was the nearest he came to

[631]

a compliment. 'It was the first time,' she said afterwards to her friend Marge in the town, 'that I ever heard of a secretary being bought by weight.'

She had been his secretary and housekeeper for a long time now. She had understood him at once. The saintly look was nonsense. He was neither a saint nor a martyr. He was very vain; especially he was vain of never being deceived, though in fact his earlier secretaries had not been a success. There had been three or four before her. One of them – the cook told her – imagined him to be a martyr because she had a taste for martyrdom and drank to gratify it; another yearned to offer the compassion he hated, and muddled everything. One reckoning widow lasted only a month. Blatantly she had added up his property and wanted to marry him. The last, a "lady", helped herself to the household money, behind a screen of wheezing grandeur and name-dropping.

Remembering the widow, the people who came to visit Mr Armitage when he gave a party were relieved after their meeting with Mrs Johnson.

'A good honest to God Cockney' or 'Such a cheery soul'. 'Down to earth,' they said. She said she had 'knocked about a bit.' 'Yes, sounds as if she had': they supposed they were denigrating. She was obviously not the kind of woman who would have any dangerous appeal to an injured man. And she, for her part, would go to the pictures when she had time off or simply flop down in a chair at the house of her friend, Marge, and say:

'Whew, Marge. His nibs has gone to London. Give me a strong cuppa. Let's relax.'

'You're too conscientious.'

'Oh, I don't mind the work. I like it. It occupies your mind. He has interesting cases. But sometimes I get keyed up.'

Mrs Johnson could not herself describe what keyed her up; perhaps, being on the watch? Her mind was stretched. She found herself translating the world to him and it took her time to realise that it did not matter that she was not 'educated up to it'. He obviously liked her version of the world, but it was a strain having versions. In the mornings she had to read his letters. This bothered her. She was very moral about privacy. She had to invent an impersonal, uninterested voice. His lack of privacy irked her; she liked gossip and news as much as any woman, but here it lacked the salt of the secret, the whispered, the found out. It was all information and statement. Armitage's life was an abstraction for him. He had to know what he could not see. What she liked best was reading legal documents to him.

He dressed very well and it was her duty to see that his clothes were right. For an orderly practical mind like hers, the order in which he lived was a new pleasure. They lived under fixed laws: no chair or table, even no ashtray must be moved. Everything must be in its place. There must be no hazards. This was understandable: the ease with which he moved without accident in the house or garden depended on it. She did not believe when he said 'I can hear things before I get to them. A wall can shout, you know.' When visitors came she noticed he stood in a fixed spot: he did not turn his head when people spoke to him and among all the head-turning and gesturing he was the still figure, the law-giver. But he was very cunning. If someone described a film they had seen, he was soon talking as if he had been there. Mrs Johnson, who had duties when he had visitors, would smile to herself at the surprise on the faces of people who had not noticed the quickness with which he collected every image or scene or character described. Sometimes, a lady would say to her: 'I do think he's absolutely marvellous', and, if he overheard this – and his hearing was acute – Mrs Johnson would notice a look of ugly boredom on his face. He was, she noted, particularly vain of his care of money and accounts. This pleased Mrs Johnson because she was quick to understand that here a blind man who had servants might be swindled. She was indignant about the delinquency of her predecessor. He must have known he was being swindled.

Once a month Mrs Johnson would go through the accounts with him. She would make out the cheques and take them to his study and put them on his desk.

The scene that followed always impressed her. She really admired him for this. How efficient and devious he was! He placed the cheque at a known point on his blotter. The blunt fingers of his hairless hands had the art of gliding and never groping, knowing the inches of distance; and then as accurately as a geometrician, he signed. There might be a pause as the fingers secretly measured, a pause alarming to her in the early days, but now no longer alarming; sometimes she detected a shade of cruelty in this pause. He was listening for a small gasp of anxiety as she watched.

There was one experience which was decisive for her. It occurred in the first month of her employment and had the lasting stamp of a revelation. (Later on, she thought he had staged the incident in order to show her what his life was like and to fix in her mind the nature of his peculiar authority.) She came into the sitting-room one evening in the winter to find a newspaper and heard sharp, unbelievable sounds coming from his study. The door was open and the room was in darkness. She went to it, switched on the light, and saw he was sitting there typing in the darkness. Well, she could have done that if she had been put to it – but now she *saw* that for him there was no difference between darkness and light.

'Overtime, I see,' she said, careful not to show surprise.

This was when she saw that his mind was a store of maps and measured things; a store of sounds and touches and smells that became an enormous translated paraphernalia.

'You'd feel sorry for a man like that,' her friend Marge said.

'He'd half kill you if you showed you were sorry,' Mrs Johnson said. 'I don't feel sorry. I really don't.'

'Does he ever talk about his wife?'

'No.'

'A terrible thing to do to leave a man because he's blind.'

'She had a right to her life, hadn't she?' said Mrs Johnson flatly. 'Who would want to marry a blind man?'

'You are hard,' Marge said.

'It's not my business,' said Mrs Johnson. 'If you start pitying people you end up by hating them. I've seen it. I've been married, don't forget.'

'I just wish you had a more normal life, dear.'

'It suits me,' said Mrs Johnson.

'He ought to be very grateful to you.'

'Why should he be? I do my job. Gratitude doesn't come into it. Let's go and play tennis.'

The two women went out and played tennis in the park and Mrs Johnson kept her friend running all over the court.

'I smell tennis balls and grass,' said Mr Armitage when she returned.

In the March of her third year a bad thing happened. The winter was late. There was a long spell of hard frost and you could see the cathedral tower clearly over the low-lying woods on most days. The frost coppered the lawns and scarcely faded in the middle of the day. The hedges were spiked and white. She had moved her typing table into the sitting-room close to the window to be near a radiator and when she changed a page she would glance out at the garden. Mr Armitage was out there somewhere and she had got into the habit of being on the watch. Now she saw him walk down the three lawns and find the brick steps that led to the swimming-pool. It was enclosed by a yew hedge and was frozen over. She could see Armitage at the far side of it pulling at a small fallen branch that had been caught by the ice. His foot had struck it. On the other side of the hedge, the gardener was cutting cabbage in the kitchen garden and his dog was snuffling about. Suddenly a rabbit ran out, ears down, and the dog was yelping after it. The rabbit ran through the hedge and almost over Armitage's feet with the dog nearly on it. The gardener shouted. The next moment Armitage who was squatting had the dog under his legs, lost his balance and fell full length through the ice into the pool. Mrs Johnson saw this. She saw the gardener drop his knife and run to the gap in the hedge to help Armitage out. He was clambering over the side. She saw him wave the gardener's hand away and shout at him and the gardener step away as Armitage got out. He stood clawing weed off his face, out of his hair, wringing his sleeves and brushing ice off his shirt as he marched back fast up the garden. He banged the garden door in a rage as he came in.

'That bloody man. I'll have that dog shot,' shouted Armitage. She hurried to meet him. He had pulled off his jacket and thrown it on a chair. Water ran off his trousers and sucked in his shoes. Mrs Johnson was appalled.

'Go and change your things quickly,' she said. And she easily raced him to the stairs to the landing and to his room. By the time he got there she had opened several drawers, looking for underclothes, and had pulled out a suit from his cupboard. Which suit? She pulled out another. He came squelching after her into the room.

'Towel,' she cried. 'Get it all off. You'll get pneumonia.'

'Get out. Leave me alone,' shouted Armitage who had been tugging his shirt over his head as he came upstairs.

She saw, then, that she had done a terrible thing. By opening drawers and putting clothes on the bed, she had destroyed one of his systems. She saw him grope. She had never seen him do this before. His bare white arms stretched out in a helpless way and his brown hands pitiably closed on air. The action was slow and his fingers frightened her.

'I told you to leave me alone,' he shouted.

She saw she had humiliated him. She had broken one of the laws. For the first time she had been incompetent.

Mrs Johnson went out and quietly shut the door. She walked across the landing to the passage in the wing where her own room was, looking at the wet marks of his muddy shoes on the carpet, each one accusing her. She sat down on the edge of her bed. How could she have been such a fool! How could she have forgotten his rule? Half-naked to the waist, hairy on the chest and arms, he shocked because the rage seemed to be not in his mind but in his body like an animal's. The rage had the pathos of an animal's. Perhaps when he was alone he often groped; perhaps the drilled man she was used to, who came out of his bedroom or his study, was the expert survivor of a dozen concealed disasters?

Mrs Johnson sat on her bed listening. She had never known Armitage to be angry; he was a monotonously considerate man. The shout abashed her and there was a strange pleasure in being abashed; but her mistake was not a mere mistake. She saw that it struck at the foundation of his life and was so gross that the surface of her own confidence was cracked. She was a woman who could reckon on herself, but now her mind was scattered. Useless to say to herself 'What a fuss about nothing,' or 'Keep calm.' Or, about him, 'Nasty temper.' His shout: 'Get out. I told you to leave me alone' had, without reason (except that a trivial shame is a spark that sets fire to a long string of greater shames), burned out all the security of her present life.

She had heard those words, almost exactly those words, before. Her husband had said them. A week after their wedding.

Well, *he* had had something to shout about, poor devil.

She admitted it. Something a lot more serious than falling into a pond and having someone commit the crime of being kind to you and hurting your silly little pride.

She got up from the bed and turned on the tap of the wash-basin to cool down her hot face and wash her hands of the dirt off the jacket she had brought upstairs. She took off her blouse and as she sluiced her face she looked through the water at herself in the mirror. There was a small birthmark, the size of a red leaf, which many people noticed and which, as it showed over the neck of the high blouses she usually wore, had the enticement of some signal or fancy of the blood; but, under it, and invisible to them, were two smaller ones and then a great spreading ragged liver-coloured island of skin which spread under the tape of her slip and crossed her breast and seemed to end in a curdle of skin below it. She was stamped with an ineradicable bloody insult. It might have been an attempt to impose another woman on her. She was used to seeing it, but she carried it about with her under her clothes, hiding it and yet vaunting.

Now she was reaching for a towel and inside the towel, as she dried herself, she was talking to Armitage.

'If you want to know what shame and pride are, what about marrying a man who goes plain sick at the sight of your body and who says "You deceived me. You didn't tell me".'

She finished drying her face and put the towel on the warm rail and went to her dressing-table. The hairbrush she picked up had been a wedding present and at each hard stroke of the brush on her lively fair hair, her face put up a fight, but it exhausted her. She brushed the image of Armitage away and she was left staring at the half-forgotten but never forgotten self she had been.

How could she have been such a fool as to deceive her husband? It was not through wickedness. She had been blinded too – blinded by love; in a way, love had made her so full of herself that, perhaps, she had never seen *him*. And her deceptions: she could not stop herself smiling at them, but they were really pitiable because she was so afraid of losing him and to lose him would be to lose this new beautifully deluded self. She ought to have told him. There were chances. For example, in his flat with the grey sofa with the spring that bit your bottom going clang, clang at every kiss, when he used to carry on about her wearing dresses that a man couldn't get a hand into. He knew very well she had had affairs with men, but why, when they were both "worked up", wouldn't she undress and go to the bedroom? The sofa was too short. She remembered how shocked his face looked when she pulled up her skirts and lay on the floor. She said she believed in sex before marriage, but she thought some things ought to wait: it would be wrong for him to see her naked before their wedding day. And to show him she was no prude – there was that time they pretended to be looking out of the window at a cricket match; or Fridays in his office when the staff was gone and the cleaners were only at the end of the passage.

'You've got a mole on your neck,' he said one day.

'Mother went mad with wanting plums when she was carrying me. It's a birthmark.'

'It's pretty,' he said and kissed it.

He kissed it. He kissed it. She clung to that when after the wedding they got to the hotel and she hid her face in his shoulder and let him pull down the zip of her dress. She stepped away and pretending to be shy, she undressed under her slip. At last the slip came off over her head. They both looked at each other, she with brazen fear and he – she couldn't forget the shocked blank disgust on his face. From the neck over the left shoulder down to the breast and below, and spreading like a red tongue to the back was this ugly blob – dark as blood, like a ragged liver on a butcher's window, or some obscene island with ragged edges. It was as if a bucket of paint had been thrown over her.

'You didn't tell me,' he said. If only she had told him, but how could she have done! She knew she had been cursed.

'That's why you wouldn't undress, you little hypocrite.'

He himself was in his underpants with his trousers on the bed and with his cuff-links in his hand which made his words absurd and awful. His ridiculous look made him tragic and his hatred frightening. It was terrible that for two hours while they talked he did not undress and worse that he gave her a dressing-gown to cover herself. She heard him going through the catalogue of her tricks.

'When . . .' he began in a pathetic voice. And then she screamed at him.

'What do you think? Do you think I got it done, that I got myself tattooed in the Waterloo Road? I was born like it.'

'Ssh,' he said, 'you'll wake the people in the next room.'

'Let them hear. I'll go and show them,' she screamed. It was kind of him to put his arm around her. When she had recovered, she put on her fatal, sporty manner.

'Some men like it,' she said.

He hit her across the face. It was not then but in the following weeks when pity followed and pity turned to cruelty he had said:

'Get out. Leave me alone.'

Mrs Johnson went to her drawer and got out a clean blouse.

Her bedroom in Armitage's house was a pretty one, far prettier than any she had ever had. Up till now she had been used to bed-sitters since her marriage. But was it really the luxury of the house and the power she would have in it that had weighed with her when she had decided to take on this strange job? She understood now something else had moved her in the low state she had been in when she came. As a punished and self-hating person she was drawn to work with a punished man. It was a return to her girlhood: injury had led her to injury.

She looked out of the window at the garden. The diamond panes chopped up the sight of the frozen lawns and the firs that were frost-whiskered. She was used to the view. It was a view of the real world; that, after all, was her world, not his. She saw that gradually in three years she had drifted out of it and had taken to living in Armitage's filed memory. If he said, for example, 'That rambler is getting wild. It must be cut back,' because a thorn caught his jacket, or if he made his famous remark about seeing the cathedral on a clear day, the landscape limited itself to these things and, in general, reduced itself to the imposed topographical sketch in his mind. She had allowed him, as a matter of abnegation and duty, to impose his world on hers. Now this shock brought back a lost sense of the right to her own landscape; and then to the protest that this country was not hers at all. The country bored her. The fir trees bored her. The lanes bored her. The view from this window or the tame protected view of the country from the Rolls-Royce window bored her. She wanted to go back to London, to the streets, the buses and the crowds, to crowds of people with eyes in their heads. And – her spirits rising – 'to hell with it, I want people who can *see* me'.

She went downstairs to give orders for the carpet to be brushed.

In the sitting-room she saw the top of Armitage's dark head. She had not heard him go down. He was sitting in what she called the cathedral chair facing the window and she was forced to smile when she saw a bit of green weed sticking to his hair. She also saw a heavy glass ashtray had fallen off the table beside him. 'Clumsy,' she said. She picked it up and lightly pulled off the piece of weed from his hair. He did not notice this.

'Mr Armitage,' she said in her decisive manner. 'I lost my head. I'm sorry.'

He was silent.

'I understand how you feel,' she said. For this (she had decided in her room) was the time for honesty and for having things out. The impersonality could not go on, as it had done for three years.

'I want to go back to London,' she said.

'Don't be a damn fool,' he said.

Well, she was not going to be sworn at.

'I'm not a damn fool,' she said. 'I understand your situation.' And then, before she could stop herself, her voice shaking and loud, she broke out with: 'I know what humiliation is.'

'Who is humiliated?' said Armitage. 'Sit down.'

'I am not speaking about you,' she said stiffly.

That surprised him, she saw, for he turned his head.

'I'm sorry. I lost my temper,' he said. 'But that stupid fellow and his dog . . .'

'I am speaking about myself,' she said. 'We have our pride, too.'

'Who is we?' he said, without curiosity.

'Women,' she said.

He got up from his chair, and she stepped back. He did not move and she saw that he really had not recovered from the fall in the pool, for he was uncertain. He was not sure where the table was.

'Here,' he said roughly, putting out a hand. 'Give me a hand out of this.'

She obediently took him by the arm and stood him clear of the table.

'Listen to me. You couldn't help what happened and neither could I.

There's nothing to apologise for. You're not leaving. We get on very well. Take my advice. Don't be hard on yourself.'

'It is better to be hard,' she said. 'Where would you have been if you had not been hard? I'm not a girl. I'm thirty-nine.' He moved towards her and he put his hand on her right shoulder and she quickly turned her head. He laughed and said, 'You've brushed your hair back.'

He knew. He always knew.

She watched him make for his study and saw him take the wrong course, brush against the sofa by the fireplace, and then a yard or two farther, he shouldered the wall.

'Damn,' he said.

At dinner conversation was difficult. He offered her a glass of wine which she refused. He poured himself a second glass and as he sat down he grimaced with pain.

'Did you hurt your back this afternoon?' she asked.

'No,' he said. 'I was thinking about my wife.'

Mrs Johnson blushed. He had scarcely ever mentioned his wife. She knew only what Marge Brook had told her of the town gossip: how his wife could not stand his blindness and had gone off with someone and that he had given her a lot of money. Someone said, ten thousand pounds. What madness! In the dining-room Mrs Johnson often thought of all those notes flying about over the table and out of the window. He was too rich. Ten thousand pounds of hatred and rage, or love, or madness. In the first place, she wouldn't have touched it.

'She made me build the pool,' he said.

'A good idea,' she said.

'I don't know why. I never thought of throwing her into it,' he said.

Mrs Johnson said: 'Shall I read the paper?'

She did not want to hear more about his wife.

Mrs Johnson went off to bed early. Switching on the radio in her room and then switching it off because it was playing classical music, she said to herself: 'Well, funny things bring things back. What a day!' and stepped yawning out of her skirt. Soon she was in bed and asleep.

An hour later, she woke up, hearing her name.

'Mrs Johnson. The water got into my watch, would you set it for me.' He was standing there in his dressing-gown.

'Yes,' she said. She was a woman who woke up alert and clear-headed.

'I'm sorry. I thought you were listening to a programme. I didn't know you were in bed,' he said. He was holding the watch to his ear.

'Would you set it for me and put my alarm right?' He had the habit of giving orders. They were orders spoken into space – and she was the space, non-existent. He gave her the watch and went off. She put on her dressing-gown and followed him to his room. He had switched on the light for her. She went to the bedside table and bent down to wind the clock. Suddenly she felt his arms round her, pulling her upright, and he was kissing her head. The alarm went off suddenly and she dropped the clock. It went on screeching on the floor at her feet.

'Mr Armitage,' she said in a low angry voice, but not struggling. He turned her round and he was trying to kiss her on the lips. At this she did struggle. She twisted her head this way and that to stop him, so that it was her head rather than her body that was resisting him. Her blue eyes fought with all their light, but his eyes were dead as stone.

'Really, Mr Armitage. Stop it,' she managed to mutter. 'The door is open. Cook will hear.'

She was angry at being kissed by a man who could not see her face, but she felt the shamed insulted woman in her, that blotched inhabitant, blaze up in her skin.

The bell of the alarm clock was weakening and then choked to a stop and in her pettish struggle she stepped on it; her slipper had come off.

'I've hurt my foot.' Distracted by the pain she stopped struggling and Armitage took his opportunity and kissed her on the lips. She looked with pain into his sightless eyes. There was no help there. She was terrified of being drawn into the dark where he lived. And then the kiss seemed to go down her throat and spread into her shoulders, into her breasts and branch into all the veins and arteries of her body and it was the tongue of the shamed woman who had sprung up in her that touched his.

'What are you doing?' she was trying to say, but could only groan the words. When he touched the stained breast she struck back violently saying: 'No, no.'

'Come to bed with me,' he said.

'Please let me go. I've hurt my foot.'

The surprising thing was that he did let her go and as she sat panting and white in the face on the bed to look at her foot, she looked mockingly at him. She forgot that he could not see her mockery. He sat beside her but did not touch her and he was silent. There was no scratch on her foot. She picked up the clock and put it back on the table.

Mrs Johnson was proud of the adroitness with which she had kept men away from her since her marriage. It was a war with the inhabitant of the ragged island on her body. That creature craved for the furtive, for the hand that slipped under a skirt, for the scuffle in the back seat of a car, for a five-minute disappearance into a locked office.

But the other Mrs Johnson, the cheerful one, was virtuous. She took advantage of his silence and got quickly up to get away; she dodged past him, but he was quick too. He was at the closed door. For a moment she was wily. It would be easy for her to dodge him in the room. And, then, she saw once more the sight she could not bear that melted her more certainly than the kisses which had filled her mouth and throat: she saw his hands begin to open and search and grope in the air as he came towards the sound of her breathing. She could not move. His hand caught her. The woman inside her seemed to shout 'Why not? You're all right. He cannot see.' In her struggle she had not thought of that. In three years he had made her forget that blindness meant not seeing.

'All right,' she said and the virtue in Mrs Johnson pouted. She gently tapped his chest with her fingers and said with the sullenness of desire, 'I'll be back in a minute.'

It was a revenge: that was the pleasure.

'Dick,' she called to her husband, 'look at this,' when the man was on top of her. Revenge was the only pleasure and his excitement was soon over. To please him she patted him on the head as he lay beside her and said, 'You've got long legs.' And she nearly said, 'You are a naughty boy' and 'Do you feel better?' but she stopped herself and her mind went off on to what she had to do in the morning; she listened and wondered how long it would be before he would fall asleep and she could stealthily get away. Revenge astonished by its quickness.

She slyly moved. He knew at once and held her. She waited. She wondered where Dick was now. She wished she could tell him. But presently this blind man in the bed leaned up and put both his hands on her face and head and carefully followed the round of her forehead, the line of her brow, her nose and lips and chin, to the line of her throat and then to her nape and shoulders. She trembled, for after his hands had passed, what had been touched seemed to be new. She winced as his hand passed over the stained shoulder and breast and he paused, knowing that she winced, and she gave a groan of pleasure to deceive him; but he went on, as if he were modelling her, feeling the pit under the arms, the space of ribs and belly and the waist of which she was proud, measuring them, feeling their depth, the roundness of her legs, the bone in her knees until, throwing all clothes back, he was holding her ankle, the arch of her foot and her toes. Her skin and her bones became alive. His hands knew her body as she had never known it. In her brief love affairs which had excited her because of the risk of being caught, the first touch of a man stirred her at once, and afterwards left her looking demurely at him; but she had let no one know her with a pedantry like his. She suddenly sat up and put her arms round him and now she went wild. It was not a revenge now; it was a triumph. She lifted the sad breast to his lips. And when they lay back she kissed his chest and then – with daring – she kissed his eyes.

It was six o'clock before she left him and when she got to her room the stained woman seemed to bloom like a flower. It was only after she had slept and saw her room in daylight again that she realised that once more she had deceived a man.

It was late. She looked out of the window and saw Armitage in his city clothes talking to the chauffeur in the garden. She watched them walk to the garage.

'OK,' she said dryly to defend herself. 'It was a rape.' During the day there would be moments when she could feel his hands moving over her skin. Her legs tingled. She posed as if she were a new-made statue. But as the day went on she hardened and instead of waiting for him to return she went into the town to see Marge.

'You've put your hair up,' said Marge.

'Do you like it?'

'I don't know. It's different. It makes you look severe. No, not severe. Something. Restless.'

'I am not going back to dinner this evening,' she said. 'I want a change. Leonard's gone to London.'

'Leonard!' said Marge.

Mrs Johnson wanted to confide in Marge, but Marge bored her. They ate a meal together and she ate fast. To Marge's astonishment she said, 'I must fly.'

'You *are* in a mood,' Marge said.

Mrs Johnson was unable to control a longing to see Armitage. When she got back to the house and saw him sitting by the fire she wanted him to get up and at least put his arms round her; but he did not move, he was listening to music. It was always the signal that he wanted to be alone.

'It is just ending,' said Armitage.

The music ended in a roll of drums.

'Do you want something, Helen?' he said.

She tried to be mocking, but her voice could not mock and she said seriously: 'About last night. It must not happen again. I don't want to be in a false position. I could not go on living in the house.'

She did not intend to say this; her voice, between rebuke and tenderness, betrayed this.

'Sit down.'

She did not move.

'I have been very happy here,' she said. 'I don't want to spoil it.'

'You are angry,' he said.

'No, I'm not,' she said.

'Yes you are; that is why you were not here when I got back,' he said.

'You did not wait for me this morning,' she said. 'I was glad you didn't. I don't want it to go on.'

He came nearer to her and put his hand on her hair. 'I like the way your hair shows your ears,' he said. And he kissed them.

'Now, please,' she said.

'I love you,' he said and kissed her on the forehead and she did not turn her head.

'Do you? I'm glad you said that. I don't think you do. When something has been good, don't spoil it. I don't like love affairs,' she said.

And then she changed. 'It was a party. Good night.'

'You made me happy,' he said, holding on to her hand.

'Were you thinking about it a long time?' she said in another voice, lingering for one more word.

'Yes,' he said.

'It is very nice of you to say that. It is what you ought to say. But I mean what I said. Now, really, good night. And,' giving a pat to his arm, she said: 'Keep your watch wound up.'

Two nights later he called to her loudly and curtly from the stairs: 'Mrs Johnson, where are you?' and when she came into the hall he said quietly, 'Helen.'

She liked that. They slept together again. They did not talk.

Their life went on as if nothing had happened. She began to be vain of the stain on her body and could not resist silently displaying, almost taunting him, when she undressed, with what he could not see. She liked the play of deceiving him like this; she was paying him out for not being able to see her; and when she was ashamed of doing this the shame itself would rouse her desire: two women uniting in her. And fear roused her too; she was afraid of his blindness. Sometimes the fear was that the blind can see into the mind. It often terrified her at the height of her pleasure that she was being carried into the dark where he lived. She knew she was not but she could not resist the excitement of imagining it. Afterwards she would turn her back to him, ashamed of her fancies, and as his finger followed the bow of her spine she would drive away the cynical thought that he was just filing this affair away in one of the systems of his memory.

Yet she liked these doubts. How dead her life had been in its practical certainties. She liked the tenderness and violence of sexual love, the simple kindness of the skin. She once said to him, 'My skin is your skin.' But she stuck to it that she did not love him and that he did not love her. She wanted to be simply a body: a woman like Marge who was always talking about love seemed to her a fool. She liked it that she and Armitage were linked to each other only by signs. And she became vain of her disfigurement and, looking at it, even thought of it as the lure.

'I know what would happen to me if I got drunk,' she thought at one of Armitage's cocktail parties, 'I'm the sort of woman who would start taking her clothes off.' When she was a young woman she had once started doing so and someone, thank God, stopped her.

But these fancies were bravado.

They were intended to stop her from telling him.

On Sundays Mrs Johnson went to church in the village near the house. She had made a habit of it from the beginning, because she thought it the proper thing to do: to go to church had made her feel she need not reproach herself for impropriety in living in the same house as a man. It was a practical matter: before her love affair the tragic words of the service had spoken to her evil. If God had done this to her, He must put up with the sight of her in His house. She was not a religious woman; going to church was an assertion that she had as much right to fair play as anyone else. It also stopped her from being "such a fool" as to fall to the temptation of destroying her new wholeness by telling him. It was "normal" to go to church and normality had been her craving ever since her girlhood. She had always taken her body not her mind to church.

Armitage teased her about her church-going when she first came to work for him; but lately his teasing had become sharper.

'Going to listen to Dearly Beloved Brethren?' he would say.

'Oh leave him alone,' she said.

He had made up a tale about her being in love with the vicar; at first it was a joke, but now there was a sharp edge to it.

'A very respectable man,' he said.

When the church bells rang on Sunday evening he said: 'He's calling to you.' She began to see that this joke had the grit of jealousy in it; not of the vicar, of course, but a jealousy of many things in her life.

'Why do you go there? I'd like to understand, seriously,' he said.

'I like to get out,' she said.

She saw pain on his face. There was never much movement in it beyond the deepening of two lines at the corners of his mouth: but when his face went really dead, it was as sullen as earth in the garden. In her sense, she knew, he never went out. He lived in a system of tunnels. She had to admit that when she saw the grey church she was glad, because it was not his house. She knew from gossip that neither he nor his wife had ever been to it.

There was something else in this new life; now he had freed her they were both more watchful of each other. One Sunday in April she saw his jealousy in the open. She had come in from church and she was telling him about the people who were there. She was sitting on the sofa beside him.

'How many lovers have you had?' he said. 'That doctor you worked for, now?'

'Indeed not,' she said. 'I was married.'

'I know you were married. But when you were working for those people in Manchester and in Canada after the war?'

'No one else. That was just a trip.'

'I don't believe you.'

'Honestly, it's true.'

'In court I never believe a witness who says "Honestly".'

She blushed for she had had three or four lovers, but she was defending herself. They were no business of his.

The subject became darker.

'Your husband,' he said. 'He saw you. They all saw you.'

She knew what he meant, and this scared her.

'My husband. Of course he saw me. Only my husband.'

'Ah, so there were others.'

'Only my husband saw me,' she said. 'I told you about it. How he walked out of the hotel after a week.'

This was a moment when she could have told him, but to see his jealousy destroy the happiness he had restored to her made her indignant.

'He couldn't bear the sight of me. He had wanted,' she invented, 'to marry another woman. He told me on the first night of our marriage. In the hotel. Please don't talk about it.'

'Which hotel was this?' he said.

The triviality of the question confused her.

'In Kensington.'

'What was the name?'

'Oh, I forget, the something Royal . . .'

'You don't forget.'

'I do honestly . . .'

'Honestly!' he said.

He was in a rage of jealousy. He kept questioning her about the hotel, the length of their marriage. He pestered for addresses, for dates and tried to confuse her by putting his questions again and again.

'So he didn't leave you at the hotel!' he said.

'Look,' she said. 'I can't stand jealous men and I'm not going to be questioned like one of your clients.'

He did not move or shout. Her husband had shouted and paced up and down, waving his arms. This man sat bolt upright and still, and spoke in a dry exacting voice.

'I'm sorry,' he said.

She took his hand, the hand that groped like a helpless tentacle and that had modelled her; it was the most disturbing and living thing about him.

'Are you still in love with your husband?'

'Certainly not.'

'He saw you and I have never seen you.' He circled again to his obsession.

'It is just as well. I'm not a beautiful woman,' she laughed. 'My legs are too short, my bottom is too big. You be grateful – my husband couldn't stand the sight of me.'

'You have a skin like an apple,' he said.

She pushed his hand away and said, 'Your hands know too much.'

'*He* had hands. And he had eyes,' he said in a voice grinding with violence.

'I'm very tired. I am going to bed,' she said. 'Good night.'

'You see,' he said. 'There is no answer.'

He picked up a Braille book and his hand moved fast over the sheets.

She went to her room and kicked off her shoes and stepped out of her dress.

'I've been living in a dream,' she thought. 'Just like Marge, who always thinks her husband's coming back every time the gate goes.'

'It is a mistake,' she thought, 'living in the same house.'

The jealous fit seemed to pass. It was a fire, she understood, that flared up just as her shame used to flare, but two Sundays later the fit came on again. 'He must hate God' she thought and pitied him. Perhaps the music that usually consoled him had tormented him. At any rate, he stopped it when she came in and put her prayer book on the table. There was a red begonia which came from the greenhouse on the table beside the sofa where he was sitting very upright, as if he had been waiting impatiently for her to come back.

'Come and sit down,' he said and began kindly enough. 'What was church like? Did they tell you what to do?'

'I was nearly asleep,' she said. 'After last night. Do you know what time it was?' She took his hand and laughed.

He thought about this for a while. Then he said. 'Give me your hands. No. Both of them. That's right. Now spit on them.'

'Spit!'

'Yes, that is what the Church tells you.'

'What *are* you talking about?' she said trying to get her hands away.

'Spit on them.' And he forced her hands, though not roughly, to her lips.

'What are you doing?' She laughed nervously and spat on her fingers.

'Now – rub the spittle on my eyes.'

'Oh no,' she said.

He let go of her wrist.

'Do as I tell you. It's what your Jesus Christ did when he cured the blind man.'

He sat there waiting and she waited.

'He put dust or earth or something on them,' he said. 'Get some.'

'No,' she said.

'There's some here. Put your fingers in it,' he said shortly. She was frightened of him.

'In the pot,' he insisted as he held one of her wrists so that she could not get away. She dabbed her wet fingers in the earth of the begonia pot.

'Put it on my eyes.'

'I can't do that. I really can't,' she said.

'Put it on my eyes,' he said.

[650]

'It will hurt them.'

'They are hurt already,' he said. 'Do as I tell you.' She bent to him and, with disgust, she put her dirty fingers on the wet eyeballs. The sensation was horrible and when she saw the dirty patches on his eyes, like two filthy smudges, she thought he looked like an ape.

'That is what you are supposed to do,' he said.

Jealousy had made him mad.

'I can't stay with a madman,' she thought. 'He's malicious.' She did not know what to do, but he solved that for her. He reached for his Braille book. She got up and left him there.

The next day he went to London.

His habits changed. He went several times into the nearby town on his own and she was relieved that he came back in a silent mood which seemed happy. The horrible scene went out of her mind. She had gone so far as to lock her bedroom door for several nights after that scene, but now she unlocked it. He had brought her a bracelet from London; she drifted into unguarded happiness. She knew so well how torment comes and goes.

It was full undreaming June, the leaves in the garden still undarkened, and for several days people were surprised when day after day the sun was up and hot and unclouded. Mrs Johnson went down to the pool. Armitage and his guests often tried to persuade her to go in; she always refused.

'They once tried to get me to go down to Peckham Baths when I was a kid, but I screamed,' she said.

The guests left her alone. They were snobbish about Peckham Baths.

But Mrs Johnson decided to become a secret bather. One afternoon when Armitage was in London and the cook and gardener had their day off, she went down with the gardener's dog. She wore a black bathing-suit that covered her body and lowered herself by the steps into the water. Then she splashed at the shallow end of the pool and hung on to the rail while the dog barked at her. He stopped barking when she got out and sniffed round the hedge when she pulled down her bathing-dress to her waist and lay down to get sun-drunk on her towel.

She was displaying herself to the sun, the sky and the trees. The air

[651]

was like hands that played on her as Armitage did and she lay listening to the snuffles of the dog and the humming of the bees in the yew hedge. She had been there an hour when the dog barked at the hedge. She quickly picked up a towel and covered herself and called to the dog: 'What is it?'

He went on barking and then gave up and came to her. She sat down. Suddenly the dog barked again. Mrs Johnson stood up and tried to look through one of the thinner places in the hedge. A man who must have been close to the pool and who must have passed along the footpath from the lane, a path used only by the gardener, was walking up the lawns towards the house carrying a trilby hat in his hand. He was not the gardener. He stopped twice to get his breath and turned to look at the view. She recognised the smiling grey suit, the wide figure and snowball head: it was "Wolverhampton" Smith. She waited and saw him go on to the house and ring a bell. Then he disappeared round the corner and went to the front of the house. Mrs Johnson quickly dressed. Presently he came back to look into the windows of the sitting-room. He found the door and for a minute or two went into the house and then came out.

'The cheek,' she said. She finished dressing and went up the lawn to him.

'Ah, there you are,' he said. 'What a sweet place this is. I was looking for Mr Armitage.'

'He's in London.'

'I thought he might be in the pool,' he said. Mr Smith looked rich with arch, smiling insinuation.

'When will he be back?'

'About six. Is there anything I can do?'

'No, no, no,' said Mr Smith in a variety of genial notes, waving a hand. 'I was out for a walk.'

'A long walk – seven miles.'

'I came,' said Mr Smith modestly lowering his eyes in financial confession, 'by bus.'

'The best way. Can I give you a drink?'

'I never touch it,' Mr Smith said putting up an austere hand. 'Well, a glass of water perhaps. As the Americans say "I'm mighty thirsty". My wife and I came down here for the water, you know. London water is chalky. It was very bad for my wife's arthritis. It's bad for everyone really. There's a significant increase in neuralgia, neuritis, arthritis in a city like London. The chalky water does it. People don't realise it,' and here Mr Smith stopped smiling and put on a stern excommunicating air.

'If you believe that man's life is ruled by water. I personally don't,' he said.

'Not by water only, anyway,' said Mrs Johnson.

'I mean,' said Mr Smith gravely, 'if you believe that the material body exists.' And when he said this, the whole sixteen stone of him looked scornfully at the landscape which, no doubt, concealed thousands of people who believed they had bodies. He expanded: he seemed to threaten to vanish.

Mrs Johnson fetched a glass of water. 'I'm glad to see you're still there,' she laughed when she came back. Mr Smith was resting on the garden seat.

'I was just thinking – thank you – there's a lot of upkeep in a place like this,' he said.

'There is.'

'And yet – what is upkeep? Money – so it seems. And if we believe in the body, we believe in money, we believe in upkeep and so it goes on,' said Mr Smith sunnily, waving his glass at the garden. And then sharply and loftily, free of this evil: 'It gives employment.' Firmly telling her she was employed. 'But,' he added, in warm contemplation, putting down his glass and opening his arms, gathering in the landscape, 'but there is only one employer.'

'There are a hell of a lot of employers.'

Mr Smith raised an eyebrow at the word "hell' and said: 'Let me correct you there. I happen to believe that God is the only employer.'

'I'm employed by Mr Armitage,' she said. 'Mr Armitage loves this place. You don't have to see to love a garden.'

'It's a sweet place,' said Mr Smith. He got up and took a deep breath. 'Pine trees. Wonderful. The smell! My wife doesn't like pine trees. She is depressed by them. It's all in the mind,' said Mr Smith. 'As Shakespeare says. By the way, I suppose the water's warming up in the pool? June – it would be. That's what I should like – a swim.'

'He *did* see me!' thought Mrs Johnson.

[653]

'You should ask Mr Armitage,' she said coldly.

'Oh no, no,' said Mr Smith. 'I just *feel* that to swim and have a sun-bathe would be the right idea. I should like a place with a swimming-pool. And a view like this. I feel it would suit me. And, by the way,' he became stern again, 'don't let me hear you say again that Mr Armitage enjoys this place although he doesn't see it. Don't tie his blindness on him. You'll hold him back. He *does* see it. He reflects all-seeing God. I told him so on Wednesday.'

'On Wednesday?'

'Yes,' he said. 'When he came for treatment. I managed to fit him in. Good godfathers, look at the time! I've got to get the bus back. I'm sorry to miss Mr Armitage. Just tell him I called. I just had a thought to give him, that's all. He'll appreciate it.

'And now,' Mr Smith said sportively, 'I must try and avoid taking a dive into that pool as I go by, mustn't I?'

She watched his stout marching figure go off down the path.

For treatment! What on earth did Mr Smith mean? She knew the rest when Armitage came home.

'He came for his cheque,' he said. 'Would you make out a cheque for a hundred and twenty pounds . . .'

'A hundred and twenty pounds!' she exclaimed.

'For Mr Smith,' he repeated. 'He is treating my eyes.'

'Your eyes! He's not an ophthalmic surgeon.'

'No,' said Armitage coldly. 'I have tried those.'

'You're not going to a faith-healer!'

'I am.'

And so they moved into their second quarrel. It was baffling to quarrel with Armitage. He could hear the firm ring of your voice but he could not see your eyes blooming wider and bluer with obstinacy; for her, her eyes were herself. It was like quarrelling with a man who had no self or, perhaps, with one that was always hidden.

'Your Church goes in for it,' he said.

'Proper faith-healing,' she said.

'What is proper?' he said.

[654]

She had a strong belief in propriety.

'A hundred and twenty pounds! You told me yourself Smith is a fraud. I mean, you refused his case. How can you go to a fraud?'

'I don't think I said fraud,' he said.

'You didn't like the way he got five thousand pounds out of that silly young man.'

'Two thousand,' he said.

'He's after your money,' she said. 'He's a swindler.'

In her heart, having been brought up poor, she thought it was a scandal that Armitage was well off; it was even more scandalous to throw money away.

'Probably. At the end of his tether,' he said. He was conveying, she knew, that he was at the end of his tether too.

'And you fall for that? You can't possibly believe the nonsense he talks.'

'Don't you think God was a crook? When you think of what He's done?'

'No, I don't.' (But in fact, the stained woman thought He was.)

'What did Smith talk about?'

'I was in the pool. I think he was spying on me. I forget what he was talking about – water, chalky water, was it?'

'He's odd about chalk!' Armitage laughed. Then he became grim again: 'You see – even Smith can see *you*. You see people, you see Smith, everyone sees everything and so they can afford to throw away what they see and forget. But I have to remember everything. You know what it is like trying to remember a dream. Smith is right, I'm dreaming a dream,' Armitage added sardonically. 'He says that I'm only dreaming I cannot see.'

She could not make out whether Armitage was serious.

'All right. I don't understand, but all right. What happens next?'

'You can wake up.' Mr Armitage gave one of his cruel smiles. 'I told you. When I used to go to the courts I often listened to witnesses like Smith. They were always bringing "God is my witness" into it. I never knew a more religious lot of men than dishonest witnesses. Perhaps they were in contact with God.'

'You don't mean that. You are making fun of me,' she said. And then vehemently: 'I hate to see you going to an ignorant man like that. I thought you were too proud. What has happened to you?'

She had never spoken her mind so forcibly to him before.

'If a man can't see,' he said, 'if you couldn't see, humiliation is what you'd fear most. I thought I ought to accept it.'

He had never been so open with her.

'You couldn't go lower than Mr Smith,' she said.

'We're proud. That is our vice,' he said. 'Proud in the dark. Everyone else has to put up with humiliation. You said you knew what it was – I always remember that. Millions of people are humiliated: perhaps it makes them stronger because they forget it. I want to join them.'

'No you don't,' she said.

They were lying in bed and leaning over him she put her breast to his lips, but he lay lifeless. She could not bear it that he had changed her and that she had stirred this profound wretchedness in him. She hated confession; to her it was the male weakness – self-love. She got out of bed.

'Come to that,' she said. 'It's you who are humiliating me. You are going to this quack man because we've slept together. I don't like the compliment.'

'And you say you don't love me,' he said.

'I admire you,' she said. She dreaded the word "love". She picked up her clothes and left the room. She hadn't the courage to say she hadn't the courage. She stuck to what she had felt since she was a child: that she was a body. He had healed it with his body.

Once more she thought, 'I shall have to go. I ought to have stuck to it and gone before. If I'd been living in the town and just been coming up for the day it would have been OK. Living in the house was your mistake, my girl. You'll have to go and get another job.' But, of course, when she calmed down, she realised that all this was self-deception: she was afraid to tell him. She brusquely drove off the thought and her mind went to the practical.

That hundred and twenty pounds! She was determined not to see him swindled. She went with him to Mr Smith's next time. The roof of the Rolls-Royce gleamed over the shrubbery of the uncut hedge of Mr Smith's house. A cat was sitting on the window-sill. Waiting on the doorstep was the little man, wide-waisted and with his hands in his optimistic pockets, and changing his smile of welcome to a reminder of secret knowledge when he saw her. Behind the undressing smile of Mr Smith stood the kind, cringing figure of his wife, looking as they all walked into the narrow hall.

'Straight through?' said Mrs Johnson in her managing voice. 'And leave them to themselves, I suppose?'

'The back gets the sun. At the front it's all these trees,' said Mrs Smith encouraged by Mrs Johnson's presence to speak out in a weak voice, as if it was all she did get. 'I was a London girl.'

'So am I,' said Mrs Johnson.

'But you've got a beautiful place up there. Have you got these pine trees too?'

'A few.'

'They give me the pip,' said Mrs Smith. 'Coffee? Shall I take your coat? My husband said you'd got pines.'

'No thank you, I'll keep it,' said Mrs Johnson. 'Yes, we've got pines. I can't say they're my favourite trees. I like to see leaves come off. And I like a bit of traffic myself. I like to see a shop.'

'Oh you would,' said Mrs Smith.

The two women looked with the shrewd London look at each other.

'I'm so busy up there I couldn't come before. I don't like Mr Armitage coming alone. I like to keep an eye on him,' said Mrs Johnson set for attack.

'Oh yes, an eye.'

'Frankly, I didn't know he was coming to see Mr Smith.'

But Mrs Johnson got nothing out of Mrs Smith. They were both half listening to the rumble of men's voices next door. Then the meeting was over and they went out to meet the men. In his jolly way Mr Smith said to Mrs Johnson as they left: 'Don't forget about that swim!'

Ostentatiously to show her command and to annoy Armitage, she armed him down the path.

'I hope you haven't invited that man to swim in the pool,' said Mrs Johnson to Mr Armitage on the way home.

'You've made an impression on Smith,' said Armitage. 'No, *I* haven't.'

'Poor Mrs Smith,' said Mrs Johnson.

Otherwise they were silent.

She went a second then a third time to the Smiths' house. She sat each time in the kitchen talking and listening to the men's voices in the next room. Sometimes there were long silences.

'Is Mr Smith praying?' Mrs Johnson asked.

'I expect so,' said Mrs Smith. 'Or reading.'

'Because it *is* prayer, isn't it?' said Mrs Johnson.

Mrs Smith was afraid of this healthy downright woman and it was an effort for her to make a stand on what evidently for most of her married life had been poor ground.

'I suppose it is. Prayer, yes, that is what it would be. Dad' – she changed her mind – 'my husband has always had faith.' And with this, Mrs Smith looked nervously at being able loyally to put forward the incomprehensible.

'But what does he actually *do?* I thought he had a chemist's shop,' pursued Mrs Johnson.

Mrs Smith was a timid woman who wavered now between the relics of dignity and a secretive craving to impart.

'He has retired,' said Mrs Smith. 'When we closed the shop he took this up.'

She said this hoping to clutch a certainty.

Mrs Johnson gave a bustling laugh.

'No, you misunderstand me. What I mean is, what does he actually *do?* What is the treatment?'

Mrs Smith was lost. She nodded as it were to nothingness several times.

'Yes,' she said. 'I suppose you'd call it prayer. I don't really understand it.'

'Nor do I,' said Mrs Johnson. 'I expect you've got enough to do keeping house. I have my work cut out too.'

They still heard the men talking. Mrs Johnson nodded to the wall.

'Still at it,' said Mrs Johnson. 'I'll be frank with you Mrs Smith. I am sure your husband does whatever he does do for the best . . .'

'Oh yes, for the best,' nodded Mrs Smith. 'It's saved us. He had a writ out against him when Mr Armitage's cheque came in. I know he's grateful.'

'But I believe in being open . . .'

'Open,' nodded Mrs Smith.

'I've told him and I've told Mr Armitage that I just don't believe a man who has been blind for twenty-two years . . .'

'Terrible,' said Mrs Smith.

'. . . can be cured. Certainly not by – whatever this is. Do you believe it, Mrs Smith?'

Mrs Smith was cornered.

'Our Lord did it,' she said desperately. 'That is what my husband says . . .'

'I was a nurse during the war and I have worked for doctors,' said Mrs Johnson. 'I am sure it is impossible. I've knocked about a lot. You're a sensible woman, Mrs Smith. I don't want to offend you, but you don't believe it yourself, do you?'

Mrs Johnson's eyes grew larger and Mrs Smith's older eyes were helpless and small. She longed for a friend. She was hypnotised by Mrs Johnson whose face and pretty neck grew firmly out of her frilled and high-necked blouse.

'I try to have faith . . .' said Mrs Smith rallying to her husband. 'He says I hold him back. I don't know.'

'Some men need to be held back,' said Mrs Johnson and she gave a fighting shake to her healthy head. All Mrs Smith could do in her panic was to watch every move of Mrs Johnson's, study her expensive shoes and stockings, her capable skirt, her painted nails. Now, at the shake of Mrs Johnson's head, she saw on the right side of the neck the small petal of the birth-mark just above the frill of the collar.

'None of us are perfect,' said Mrs Smith slyly.

'I have been with Mr Armitage four years,' Mrs Johnson said.

'It is a lovely place up there,' said Mrs Smith, eager to change the subject. 'It must be terrible to live in such a lovely place and never see it . . .'

'Don't you believe it,' said Mrs Johnson. 'He knows that place better than any of us, better than me.'

'No,' groaned Mrs Smith. 'We had a blind dog when I was a girl. It used to nip hold of my dress to hold me back if it heard a car coming when I was going to cross the road. It belonged to my aunt and she said, "that dog can see. It's a miracle".'

[659]

'He heard the car coming,' said Mrs Johnson. 'It's common sense.'

The words struck Mrs Smith.

'Yes, it is really,' she said. 'If you come to think of it.'

She got up and went to the gas-stove to make more coffee and new courage came to her. 'We know why she doesn't want Mr Armitage to see again!' she was thinking: the frightening Mrs Johnson was really weak. 'Housekeeper and secretary to a rich man, sitting very pretty up there, the best of everything. Plenty of money, staff, cook, gardener, chauffeur, Rolls-Royce – if he was cured where would her job be? Oh, she looks full of herself now, but she is afraid. I expect she's got round him to leave her a bit.'

The coffee began to bubble up in the pot and that urgent noise put excitement into her and her old skin blushed.

'Up there with a man alone. As I said to Dad, a woman can tell! Where would she get another man with that spot spreading all over. She's artful. She's picked the right one.' She was telling the tale to herself.

The coffee boiled over and hissed on the stove and a sudden, forgotten jealousy hissed up in Mrs Smith's uncertain mind. She took the pot to the table and poured out a boiling hot cup and as the steam clouded up from it, screening her daring stare at the figure of Mrs Johnson, Mrs Smith wanted to say: 'Lying there stark naked by that swimming-pool right in the face of my husband. What was he doing up there anyway?'

She could not say it. There was not much pleasure in Mrs Smith's life; jealousy was the only one that enlivened her years with Mr Smith. She had flown at him when he came home and had told her that God had guided him, that prayer always uncovered evil and brought it to the surface; it had revealed to him that the Devil had put his mark on Mrs Johnson, and that he wouldn't be surprised if that was what was holding up the healing of Mr Armitage.

'What were you doing,' she screamed at him, 'looking at a woman?'

The steam cleared and Mrs Smith's nervousness returned as she saw that composed face. She was frightened now of her own imagination and of her husband's. She knew him. He was always up to something.

'Don't you dare say anything to Mr Armitage about this,' she had shouted at him.

But now she fell back on admiring Mrs Johnson again.

'Settled for life,' she sighed. 'She's young. She is only fighting for her own. She's a woman.'

And Mrs Smith's pride was stirred. Her courage was fitful and weakened by what she had lived through. She had heard Mrs Johnson was divorced and it gave Mrs Smith strength as a woman who had "stuck to her husband". She had not gone round taking up with men as she guessed Mrs Johnson might have done. She was a respectable married woman.

Her voice trembled at first but became stronger.

'Dad wanted to be a doctor when he was a boy,' Mrs Smith was saying, 'but there wasn't the money so he worked in a chemist's, but it was always church on Sundays. I wasn't much of a one for church myself. But you must have capital and being just behind the counter doesn't lead anywhere. Of course I tried to egg him on to get his diploma and he got the papers – but I used to watch him. He'd start his studying and then he'd get impatient. He's a very impatient man and he'd say "Amy, I'll try the Ministry" – he's got a good voice – "Church people have money".'

'And did he?'

'No, he always wanted to, but he couldn't seem to settle to a church – I mean a religion. I'll say this for him he's a fighter. Nixon, his first guv'nor, thought the world of him: quick with the sales. Nixon's Cough Mixture – well, he didn't invent it, but he changed the bottles and the labels, made it look – fashionable, dear – you know? A lot of Wesleyans took it.'

Mrs Smith spread her hands over her face and laughed through her fingers.

'When Nixon died someone in the Church put up some money, a very religious, good man. One day Dad said to me – I always remember it – "It's not medicine. It's faith does it." He's got faith. Faith is – well, faith.'

'In himself?' suggested Mrs Johnson.

'That's it! That's it!' cried Mrs Smith with excitement. Then she quietened and dabbed a tear from her cheek. 'I begged him not to come down here. But this Mrs Rogers, the lady who owns the house, she's deaf and on her own, he knew her. She believes in him. She calls him Daniel. He's treating her for deafness, she can't hear a word, so we brought our things down after we closed up in Ealing, that's why it's so crowded, two of everything, I have to laugh.'

[661]

'So you don't own the house?'

'Oh no, dear – oh no,' Mrs Smith said, frightened of the idea. 'He wants something bigger. He wants space for his work.'

Mrs Smith hesitated and looked at the wall through which the sound of Mr Smith's voice was coming. And then, fearing she had been disloyal, she said: 'She's much better. She's very funny. She came down yesterday calling him. "Daniel, Daniel. I hear the cuckoo". Of course I didn't say anything: it was the man calling out "Coal". But she is better. She wouldn't have heard him at all when we came here.'

They were both silent.

'You can't live your life from A to Z,' Mrs Smith said, waking up. 'We all make mistakes. We've been married for forty-two years. I expect you have your troubles too, even in that lovely place.'

After the hour Mr Smith came into the kitchen to get her.

'What a chatter!' he said to her. 'I never heard such a tittle-tattle in my life.'

'Yes, we had a fine chat, didn't we?'

'Oh yes,' said Mrs Smith boldly.

'How is it going on?' said Mrs Johnson.

'Now, now,' Mr Smith corrected her. 'These cases seemingly take time. You have to get to the bottom of it. We don't intend to, but we keep people back by the thoughts we hold over them.'

And then, in direct attack on her. 'I don't want you to hold no wrong thoughts over me. You have no power over Divine Love.'

And he turned to his wife to silence her.

'And how would I do that?' said Mrs Johnson.

'Cast the mote out of thine own eye,' said Smith. 'Heal yourself. We all have to.' He smiled broadly at her.

'I don't know what all this talk about Divine Love is,' said Mrs Johnson. 'But I love Mr Armitage as he is.'

Smith did not answer.

Armitage had found his way to the door of the kitchen. He listened and said: 'Good-bye, Mrs Smith.'

And to Mr Smith: 'Send me your bill. I'm having the footpath closed.'

They drove away.

"I love Mr Armitage as he is". The words had been forced out of her by the detestable man. She hated that she had said to him what she could not say to Armitage. They surprised her. She hoped Armitage had not heard them.

He was silent in the car. He did not answer any of her questions.

'I'm having that path closed,' he repeated.

'I know!' she thought. 'Smith has said something about me. Surely not about "it"!'

When they got out of the car at the house he said to the chauffeur: 'Did you see Mr Smith when he came up here three weeks ago? It was a Thursday. Were you down at the pool?'

'It's my afternoon off, sir.'

'I know that. I asked whether you were anywhere near the pool. Or in the garden?'

'No, sir.'

'Oh God,' Mrs Johnson groaned. 'Now he's turned on Jim.'

'Jim went off on his motor-bike. I saw him,' said Mrs Johnson.

They went into the house.

'You don't know who you can trust,' Armitage said and went across to the stairs and started up. But instead of putting his hand to the rail which was on the right, he put it out to the left and, not finding it, stood bewildered. Mrs Johnson went to that side of him and nudged him in the right direction.

When he came down to lunch he sat in silence before the cutlets on his plate.

'After all these years! I know the rail is on the right and I put out my left hand.'

'You just forgot,' she said. 'Why don't you try forgetting a few more things?'

She was cross about the questioning of the chauffeur.

'Say, one thing a day,' she said.

He listened and this was one of those days when he cruelly paused a long time before replying. A minute went by and she started to eat.

'Like this?' he said, and he deliberately knocked his glass of water over. The water spread over the cloth towards her plate.

'What's this silly temper?' she said and lifting her plate away, she lifted the cloth and started mopping with her table napkin and picked up the glass.

'I'm fed up with you blind people,' she said angrily. 'All jealousy and malice, just childish. You're so clever, aren't you? What happened? Didn't that good Mr Smith do the magic trick? I don't wonder your wife walked out on you. Pity the poor blind! What about other people? I've had enough. You have an easy life; you sail down in your Rolls and think you can buy God from Mr Smith just because – I don't know why – but if he's a fraud you're a fraud.' Suddenly the wronged inhabitant inside her started to shout: 'I'll tell you something about that Peeping Jesus: he saw the lot. Oh yes, I hadn't a stitch on. The lot!' she was shouting. And then she started to unzip her dress and pull it down over her shoulder and drag her arm out of it. 'You can't see it, you silly fool. The whole bloody Hebrides, the whole plate of liver.'

And she went to his place, got him by the shoulder and rubbed her stained shoulder and breast against his face.

'Do you want to see more?' she shouted. 'It made my husband sick. That's what you've been sleeping with. And,' she got away as he tried to grip her and laughed: 'you didn't know! *He* did.'

She sat down and cried hysterically with her head and arms on the table.

Armitage stumbled in the direction of her crying and put his hand on her bare shoulder.

'Don't touch me! I hate your hands.'

And she got up, dodged round him to the door and ran out sobbing: slower than she was, he was too late to hear her steps. He found his way back to the serving hatch and called to the cook.

'Go up to Mrs Johnson. She's in her room. She's ill,' he said.

He stood in the hall waiting; the cook came downstairs and went into the sitting-room.

'She's not there. She must have gone into the garden.' And then she said at the window: 'She's down by the pool.'

'Go and talk to her,' he said.

The cook went out of the garden door and on to the terrace. She was a thin round-shouldered woman. She saw Mrs Johnson move back to the near side of the pool; she seemed to be staring at something in the water. Then the cook stopped and came shouting back to the house.

'She's fallen in. With all her clothes on. She can't swim. I know she can't swim.'

And then the cook called out 'Jim, Jim,' and ran down the lawns.

Armitage stood helpless.

'Where's the door?' he called. There was no one there.

Armitage made an effort to recover his system, but it was lost. He found himself blocked by a chair, but he had forgotten which chair. He waited to sense the movement of air in order to detect where the door was, but a window was half open and he found himself against glass. He made his way feeling along the wall, but he was travelling away from the door. He stood still again and smelling a kitchen smell he made his way back across the centre of the long room and at last found the first door and then the door to the garden. He stepped out, but he was exhausted and his will had gone. He could only stand in the breeze, the disorderly scent of the flowers and the grass mocking him. A jeering bird flew up. He heard the gardener's dog barking below and a voice, the gardener's voice, shouting 'Quiet!' Then he heard voices coming slowly nearer up the lawn.

'Helen,' called Armitage, but they pushed past him. He felt her wet dress brush his hand and her foot struck his leg; the gardener was carrying her.

'Marge,' Armitage heard her voice as she choked and was sick.

'Upstairs. I'll get her clothes off,' said the cook.

'No,' said Armitage.

'Be quiet,' said the cook.

'In my room,' said Armitage.

'What an idea!' said the cook. 'Stay where you are. Mind you don't slip on all this wet.'

He stood, left behind in the hall, listening, helpless. Only when the doctor came did he go up.

She was sitting up in bed and Armitage held her hand.

'I'm sorry,' she said. 'You'd better fill that pool up. It hasn't brought you any luck.'

Armitage and Mrs Johnson are in Italy now; for how long it is hard to say. They themselves don't know. Some people call her Mrs Armitage, some call her Mrs Johnson; this uncertainty pleases her. She has always had a secret and she is too old, she says, to give up the habit now. It still pleases Armitage to baffle people. It is impossible for her to deny that she loves Armitage, because he heard what she said to Smith; she has had to give in about that. And she does love him because his system has broken down completely in Italy.

'You are my eyes,' he says. 'Everything sounds different here.'

'I like a bit of noise,' she says.

Pictures in churches and galleries he is mad about and he likes listening to her descriptions of them and often laughs at some of her remarks, and she is beginning, she says, to get 'a kick out of the classical stuff' herself.

There was an awkward moment before they set off for Italy when he made her write out a cheque for Smith and she tried to stop him.

'No,' he said. 'He got it out of you. I owe you to him.'

She was fighting the humiliating suspicion that in his nasty prying way Smith had told Armitage about her before *she* had told him. But Armitage said, 'I knew all the time. From the beginning. I knew everything about you.'

She still does not know whether to believe him or not. When she does believe, she is more awed than shamed; when she does not believe she feels carelessly happy. He depends on her entirely here. One afternoon, standing at the window of their room and looking at the people walking in the lemonish light across the square, she suddenly said: 'I love you. I feel gaudy!' She notices that the only thing he doesn't like is to hear a man talk to her.

The Nest Builder

I have lost Ernest. We had been partners for a long time but, after a difficult year and the fiasco at Albine Rise, he went. Interior decoration is a hard, even a savage, trade; customers come to us not quite knowing what they want, but they know (and we know) that they want Perfection. That is very expensive. And there is a sad side to Perfection; there are losses, as you see around you in this shop now. They are Ernest's losses.

The two cabinets in yellow lacquer, for example – Mrs Cross, I call them. They were sent back by Mr Cross, just when Ernest had finished the Chinese drawing-room for her. Mr Cross divorced her. There is Mrs Raddock – the Empire sofa and the three chairs. She divorced Mr Raddock actually before we got the marble pillars into Mr Raddock's study. The Hepplewhite fourposter, waiting to go into Cheyne Row while Ernest was still getting the Italian bathroom right – Mr Fortescue died. A tragic business – but we get that, too, in the trade. The mirrors and consoles are Mrs Hunstable, Mrs Smith, and Lady Hatch, mirrors being a fate with Ernest. The moment he puts gilded mirrors with branches, cherubs, angels, scrolls, shells, or lions into a house, someone falls down the stairs, or there is a sarcastic scene between husband and wife or mother and daughter, and high talk of vanity, adultery, loss of looks or figure, even of camp or chichi; the next thing one hears is that the lease is for sale, then the accounts are disputed and the goods come back. The doctor or the lawyer, they say, sees deepest into the secrets of people's lives. I do not agree.

Yet it wasn't because of these losses that Ernest left us. They in fact stimulated his creative gift. When lacquer cabinets, Hepplewhite beds, mirrors, and so on, come back, he stands there stroking his small, soft beard, gazing at them at first as if personally affronted. Then one eyebrow goes up and he recognises with admiration their extraordinary power to wreck human lives, and turns on me a gentle, conspiring worldly young eye.

'George, dear boy!' he says. 'Mrs Grant, I think – don't you?' Or 'Who was that woman who rang up yesterday?' And he would pay me a compliment, too. 'George,' he often said to me, 'what a nose you have for booty!'

He would be thinking of times when I came back from some place in the country with an Adam fireplace, a triptych, a gout stool, or a big chunk of Spanish choir stall, or had added to our collection of rare cattle pictures. My task was to go round to the auctions, to get into early-Industrial Revolution houses in the North, to smell round rectories, look into the stabling of country houses, squint into the family detritus. That is, when I had the time, for I also had to deal with the trouble Ernest created for builders and painters, and his sneers at surly architects. It was Ernest – and this I gladly say – who brought the ideas to our business.

'My dear,' I once said to him, 'there are only two men in London who could turn a revolting Baptist chapel with Venetian excrescences into a Chinese pagoda. And you are both of them.'

'You mean a Turkish bath, dear boy,' he said. 'Why two men?'

'One to think up the ghastly idea, the other to persuade the people to have it.'

'D'you know, you've got very bald since Easter,' he said. 'Shall we have a little Mozart?'

Ernest at work was a frightening sight. Generally, he did not like me to come with him, but I've seen him at it more than once. He is a slender, shortish man, with carefully styled hair – neither fair nor grey, but in some subtle pastel shade, as soft as moleskin. It fits his head like an old-fashioned ink pad. His beard is itself one of those small *objets d'art* that women itch to touch. He has a voice as soft as cigarette smoke, an utterly insincere listening manner – the head a little inclined – and when, to take an example, Mrs Raddock talked pell-mell about enlarging her dining-room bookcases, he nodded with the air of a dignified mourner who is not a close friend of the family. This habit of grieving distantly and respectfully (after a wild, wheeling look at the ceiling, walls, and windows of the room, and with one rather cruel roll of the eye at the door he had just come through) had the effect of inducing dismay in many women. They would give a touch to their hair and a glance at their clothes, in order to recover fortitude; they had not realised, until that moment, that their dining-room, their drawing-room, their whole house, was dead, the interment long overdue.

'Yes, I see exactly what you mean, Mrs Raddock. The thing that worries me is the height of the folding doors.' Mrs Raddock, a confusing talker, foolish and flirtatious but a woman of will who until then had known what she wanted, was torpedoed at once by this shot. Ernest's words showed her her personal disaster: it was not that she had been three times married but that she had never noticed the height of her folding doors. And Ernest struck again. 'It is a pity the original chimneypiece has gone,' he accused.

'My husband found this one down in Wiltshire,' said Mrs Raddock, desperately pushing whatever blame that might arise on to him. Already Ernest was dividing husband and wife.

'Houses like this, so purely Regency, are getting rarer and rarer,' said Ernest sadly. 'So many are let go. I have been doing a library in Gloucestershire, a rather nice Georgian house – a room with a cupola, a small domed ceiling, you know?'

Mrs Raddock blushed at her lack of cupola.

'I'd better measure the height of the door,' Ernest said. 'The top moulding of your bookcase cannot possibly be below it. These houses put formality and balance first.'

Ernest's steel ruler whizzed up the jamb of the door and lashed there for a second or two, then slipped back with a hiss into its holder. Mrs Raddock stepped back. Formality and balance – how did you guess (her eager look seemed to say) that that is what I need in my life? She covered her defeat with a look of experienced irony at Ernest, but also of appeal. As I followed them around, I could hardly conceal my desire to protect the lady and Ernest from each other, and Ernest knew this. As we left the room to go upstairs to the drawing-room, he gave me a glare. 'Keep out of this,' the look said, for I had the weakness of comforting suggestion to our customers. (At the shop, he once said to me, crossly, 'You are so tall, dear boy. It makes you look dispassionate.')

Now we were at the top of red-carpeted stairs outside Mrs Raddock's drawing-room. The door was open. We could just see in. Ernest paused and turned his back as if he had seen something dreadful, and nodded downstairs to the room we had just left. 'Was it your idea or your husband's to have a black dining-room?' said Ernest. He spoke of every-thing with the suggestion that it belonged to a past the customer was anxious to forget.

'Oh, mine,' said Mrs Raddock, making a guilty effort to take the blame herself this time. 'Ten years ago,' she said, breaking helplessly into autobiography, 'when we moved up from the country.'

'Ten.' Ernest nodded. 'That would be about the date.' And Mrs Raddock sank once more.

In two more visits, she was holding his arm, as he gazed up at the mouldings of the ceiling and she gazed at his little beard, trying to formalise herself. The case of Mrs Raddock differs little from that of Mrs Cross, Mrs Hunstable, or, indeed, all the others. Ernest seized their flats and their houses with the ruthless hands of the artist, shook the interiors of their own windows, and re-created them. He was really shaking his clients out of the windows, too. Dark rooms appeared as monkey-haunted jungles; light was dispensed from chaste or unchaste vases, dripped like expensive tears, or shot out at piercing, agony-creating angles. Ceilings went up or down, alcoves appeared on blank walls. He had once a line in Piranesi dining-rooms and in hairy pagan bedrooms where furs and lewd hints of the goat's foot tossed around. He did sickening things with shot birds, which made the ladies scream at first; put down tigerish carpets, which gave them voluptuous shudders. He created impudent or intimate congeries of small furniture, and could make a large piece look like an Italian church. A pushing career woman like Mrs Greatorex was given a satiny nest of such kittenishness that it suggested to the visitor that here lived some delicate hypochondriac with little bones and sad pink rims to her sensitive eyes, instead of – as she was – a brassy, hard-bloused lady bawling down the telephone. Ernest penetrated to the hidden self of his client, discerned her so-far frustrated dream of perfection. And then a sudden practicality sprang up in his apparently passive personality and he took rough charge. It was they who then watched him – startled at first, then attentively, then gravely, then longingly. Here was the nest builder, and without realising it they grew irritable with their husbands, who came home – or what used to be home – to find the place half-closed or in chaos. These moneyed brutes trod on paint. The wives screamed out 'Don't go in there! Be careful! Ernest has moved the banisters.'

"Ernest" – husbands wearied of the name. One or two coarse ones – Raddock and Cross were like this – threw out doubts about his sex. The ladies made a face, wriggled their shoulders, and sighed that men like Ernest understood what most men forget – that women are not merely female – they are feminine. The time came when a flat or a house was finished. There was Mrs Cross's Chinese boutique. She stood entranced, hardly able to take a step, hardly able to see because of the sparkle that came to her excited eyes, which themselves looked jewel-like in this moment. She saw not only her house but herself, perfected. But, as always in the face of perfection, a mysterious sadness misted those eyes. There was the sense of loss that angels are said to have when they look back from Heaven upon the earth. A hunger made Mrs Cross go limp, opened Mrs Hunstable's uneasy mouth, brought a shiver to Mrs Raddock's nervous bosom. Their houses were now perfect, but one thing was missing. What was it?

It was Ernest. They wanted him. For weeks he had been in and out, caressing yet masterful. The creation was empty without the creator. Mrs Raddock rubbed herself against him; Mrs Cross muttered in a low voice, leading him to the bedroom, where she had a final question to ask. Mrs Greatorex frankly galloped at him. Our bad year began. Mrs Raddock left her third husband; a load of chandeliers came back. Mr and Mrs Cross broke up, after years of bickering in which the Chinese drawing-room had been a last emotional bid; the lacquer cabinets were returned. Mrs Greatorex went to Greece. Letters came in from bank managers and lawyers. There were last longing looks of farewell at Ernest. Some had wanted him socially, as a sparkler; others had wished to be sisters to him; others had wanted him as confidant, as an annoyance to their husbands. But why particularise? They wanted him. The final blow in that year came from Mrs Hunstable. This florid and open-hearted lady, whose upper part suggested a box at the opera in which she was somehow living and sitting, and who spoke in a jolly mixture of aria and ravening recitative – this lady was caught, actually caught, lying rather sideways on a Récamier couch, having her tears wiped by Ernest while she stroked his neat pad of hair.

Mr Hunstable caught them. She said she was comforting him.

'I was telling him,' cried Mrs Hunstable, jumping up and taking her

[671]

husband in her arms and wiping her tears at the same time, 'I was telling him he must not worry because he is different from other men. Ernest's on the point of breakdown.'

Mr Hunstable looked operatically doubtful.

'They feel it, Harry, you know,' she appealed.

'Ernest feels it. They all do.'

Mrs Hunstable was as near to telling the truth as a woman thinks necessary. The only correction needed here is that Ernest was comforting her. Ernest rarely spoke to me of his end-of-contract crises, but rumours are soon out. The telephone never stops in our trade, and more than half the calls are gossip. I often had to sweep up after Ernest emotionally. But Mrs Hunstable was not easily put off. She came to the office when Ernest was out, her mouth wide open, her breasts in disorder, demanding to know more. She tried to ransack me. She was all out for confession. Naturally, I said nothing. 'I see,' she said to me with a cold smirk. 'You hang together.' She became the mortally insulted mother whose sons will not confide in her. She turned on us and sold the house, her husband landed the stuff back on us, and they went off violently to the Bahamas, leaving us to their lawyers. The Hunstable episode was a shock to Ernest, and it worried me. As I say, it was the last one in a bad year. Until then I would have said that Ernest's successes with our clients depended on his skill in turning their desires into a ballet-like partnership from which he escaped by some beautifully timed leap, so to say, into the wings. But Mrs Hunstable was no dancer. The world was no stage to her; it was property. It was to be owned. I confess that working with an artist like Ernest is apt to make a man at the business end, like myself, fall back on a vulgar tone in a crisis.

'It's a pity, dear boy ... I mean – well, look, Ernest, let's not beat about the bush. Have another drink,' I said. I stopped and gave a loud laugh.

'I mean,' I said, 'it's a pity you couldn't, just for once ...'

'Be as other men?' Ernest said.

'I was only joking, dear boy.'

'Not with Mrs Hunstable,' Ernest said. 'Perhaps you, my dear –'

'Ernest,' I said. 'I'm sorry. I suppose we have to look at this in perspective.

I've often wondered whether we realise what we are doing. I don't think you do – or perhaps you do?'

'Our mistake is that we deal with people,' Ernest said.

'What a horrible thing to say,' I said.

'People with inner lives,' he said.

'You mean who send things back?' I said.

'Oh, all right!' he said angrily. 'What d'you want me to do – the Flashback Bar, Nasty's Steak House? Or some self-service counter? Or the Svengali Room at the Metropole?'

'You cannot send a bar back. You can't return a restaurant,' I said. 'What happened at the Sea Urchin?' It was six o'clock in the evening, December, a wet day. I had persuaded him to see what the manager of the Sea Urchin wanted, and he had just come back.

'They want fishermen's nets on the ceiling. That was OUT ten years ago. They're going to sit on capstans.'

'Not sit, surely, Ernest,' I said.

'I don't know – perhaps it was anchors,' Ernest said, covering his face with his hands.

I went to the cupboard in our office and reached for the bottle of gin, and as I did so the telephone rang. Ernest picked it up.

'My name is Richards. I wrote you a letter . . .'

I could hear a jubilant voice, fermenting like a small vat.

'Men! I'm sick of them,' Ernest said, handing the telephone to me.

'Richards, Gowing, and Cloud,' the happy voice went on.

'Lawyers,' I whispered to Ernest.

'You wrote us a letter? Oh dear,' I said.

I found the letter on my desk. It was one I had not had the heart to answer, and I passed it to Ernest – or, rather, I dangled it before him. I have, as Ernest says, a suicidal voice, and now I used it. 'Mr Richards,' I said to Ernest, 'is engaged to be married shortly to a divine girl called Miss Staples and has taken one of those little musical boxes on Albine Rise. It's all here in the letter.'

Then I turned back to the telephone.

'Why, of course, Mr Richards,' I said. 'When would you like us to come?' And when he rang off I looked strictly at Ernest. 'Eleven tomorrow morning,' I said. 'Ernest, it's this or the Sea Urchin.'

You find little enclaves like Albine Rise all over London if you know where to look. It was a group of nine small early-Victorian houses, enclosed in a terrace of weeping elms on an expensive hill. 'Musical box' is the word for any one of them. Only three hundred yards from a thundering and whining main road, but set above it, they seem – to a London ear – to tinkle together in rural quiet. One glance must have told Ernest when we arrived that there was little for us here: the couple had bought Perfection already. I turned away from it to study them.

Mr Richards, of the Queen's Bench voice, was a set piece: bowler hat, black coat, striped trousers, old Etonian tie. Miss Staples was the shock. She was a fat little thing with a ruddy face, dressed in hairy brown tweed – a girl with a decided look and a hard handgrip. She said little except that she was in a hurry and must get to something she called the Dairy Show. We went into the house. 'I just want it done in white!' she shouted.

'White?' said Ernest.

'All this chichi off. I want plain white,' said Miss Staples. Mr Richards looked at Ernest with appeal. 'Save me from plain white,' the look said. 'White?' said Ernest. 'Do you mean chalk or ivory or –'. 'Just white. Any white. White!' shouted Miss Staples cheerfully.

'Like sheep – clean ones,' said Mr Richards with fruity sarcasm, but also with a glance at Ernest screaming in a gentlemanly way for help. Ernest took in the pretty sitting-room and the pretty staircase outside, but he was looking with astonishment at the vigorous, golden, untidy hair of Miss Staples, at her cheeks as fresh as ham, her eyes as blue as blackbirds' eggs.

He was astounded. Most women, however bold their faces, were put in the wrong by him, but he failed – no, he did not even try – to put Miss Staples in the wrong. She was, he must have seen at once, his opposite – not a decorator but a de-decorator. 'White? Very chaste,' Ernest said in a louder voice than usual.

'Isn't that rather personal?' she said archly. Ernest was taken aback. Miss Staples showed small white teeth. 'Let me show you what the frightful people did – the people who had the place before,' she said, leading him up the stairs and showing him the bathroom. 'It may be OK for Cleopatra and her asp, but I keep dogs.'

'In the bathroom?' said Ernest.

'They scratch at the door,' said Miss Staples heartily. 'All this,' she said, pointing round the room, 'will have to go.'

'We have dogs,' apologised Mr Richards. Ernest looked at him. Mr Richards was a stout, pale young man choking with legal deprecation. The sentence sounded like 'M'lud my information is that my client keeps dogs.'

'That bloody traffic,' said Miss Staples from the window. One could scarcely hear the traffic.

'Better than calving cows,' said Mr Richards.

'Jerseys have such pretty eyes,' said Ernest. I was dumbfounded.

'Yes,' said Miss Staples. 'We've got fifty – two more coming this week. It's not the eyes, it's the yield! Isn't it Robert? I want this place for Robert during the week. I hate London.'

'This is where I shall be stabled,' said Robert.

'We're keeping the oats in the country,' Miss Staples snapped back offhand to her fiancé but gazing at Ernest. Ernest was entranced.

And so was Miss Staples.

Robert hated Ernest; Ernest despised Robert. Miss Staples looked Ernest over with open admiration, but with an occasional critical glance, her head on one side. 'What a frightful tie you're wearing,' she said. It struck me she was seeing what might, here and there, be altered. And Ernest was going over her in the same way, and was clearly finding, for the first time in his life, nothing that should be changed.

'The trees are very . . .' began Ernest, waving his hand at the weeping elms outside, but he was clearly indicating the waves of her hair.

'Give me twenty-five acres of kale any day,' said Miss Staples.

'Me, too,' said Ernest. I had never before heard Ernest lie.

'I'm afraid my wife – er, my future wife, it would be more correct to say – has rather drastic ideas. I hope Ernest will be able to exert an influence. In fact, that's why I asked . . .' Mr Richards whispered to me.

'I've got to go. You'd better come down for the week-end,' Miss Staples ordered. 'There are the fox masks, the antlers, one or two prize cups – I don't see anywhere here to put a saddle.'

'You're damn right there isn't,' said Ernest, marvelling at her.

This interview took place on a Tuesday. The following week-end, Ernest went to stay with Miss Staples and Mr Richards at her parents' house in the country. On Monday, he came back. He came into the shop about twelve. His usual quiet gravity had gone. He walked up and down and said, 'Stuffy in here. No air. I'll open the door.' It was a cold day.

'We shall die,' I said as the wind blew four yards of brocade off a screen and took the screen with it to the floor.

'What were they like, the older Stapleses?' 'Wonderful,' said Ernest. 'Like moulting owls. Perfect . . . Blast this stuff,' said Ernest, and he did something terrible. He kicked the brocade out of the way as it lay crouching on the floor – kicked it with boots that had obviously been in some country lane. I could have screamed, brocade at the price it is. There were probably not another four yards of that quality and colour in London, and it takes months to get it from France.

'The order's off,' Ernest said at last. 'Albine Rise. We had a flaming row. Robert and Joanna . . .'

'Joanna?'

'Miss Staples. She's broken it off. He said he'd allow the hunting prints, if she insisted, but he bloody well wasn't going to have the heads of stinking dead animals and photographs of the Chester Cattle Show. And filthy white paint.'

'Thank heaven, dear boy, it happened now, not later,' I said.

'What d'you mean?' said Ernest curtly.

We moved into the inner office to get out of the wind while Ernest told me more. 'Dear boy,' I said, 'what have you done to your eye?'

'Nothing,' said Ernest. One eye was ringed in green and purple. 'I was sawing a branch off a tree for her. She let go of the branch. It was too heavy for her. It sprang back and hit me in the eye. Wonderful girl. She didn't make a fuss.'

'And I suppose she kissed it better and Robert saw you?' I said.

And then we heard a shout and dogs barking in the shop. We went to see what had happened. In at the open door came two dogs, fighting. One ran under the Chinese lacquer cabinet, and after them came Miss Staples with a leash and collars in her hand.

'Shut that bloody door! They've slipped their collars!' Miss Staples shouted at us. I shut the door, Ernest caught one dog by the neck. Miss Staples seized the other.

[676]

Reddened by the struggle, Ernest and Miss Staples stood excitedly looking at each other, with dogs' dribble on their clothes.

'Joanna and I are going out to lunch,' Ernest said to me. 'Do you mind if we shut Sydney and Morris in the office? Good fellow.'

So our partnership ended. Ernest is farming now. Their house is terrible. It is the sort of house where dogs have their puppies on the sofa, where you can't see across the room for wood smoke, where the fake Jacobean furniture and brass trays are covered with old copies of the *Farmers Weekly*, where dogs' bones are found under rugs, where fox masks look down on you, where you can't see to read because the lamps are in the wrong place, and where Ernest sits in his gum-boots reading the local paper and Joanna sits with a transistor mewing out the news in Welsh while she sews some awful cotton dresses.

'She's dead right here, isn't she? Exactly what a place like this needed,' Ernest said to me, a flicker of the forgotten artist in him coming out – I flatter myself – at the sight of me. She had redecorated him.

A Debt of Honour

Mrs Thwaite got off the bus and turned the street corner, holding her key ready to get into her new flat. Every evening for months now, she was eager to be home, to sniff the new paint and to stand looking at the place, wanting to put her arms round it. She ran up the stairs, let herself in and threw her old fur coat on the divan in the sitting-room, put the gas poker in the fire and drew the curtains which did not quite meet, as if – by her intention – they had been carelessly made so as to let in a little of the shabby square and a stare of the London night into the flat. Then she went into the bedroom to see to the bed she had left unmade all day; almost at once she was sitting on the edge of it laughing, and telephoning to dear Argo – as she called him – to ask him to guess what she had found: his wristwatch under the pillow! And in a lower voice:

'Oh, wasn't it lovely?'

She was swinging the wristwatch in her hand, Argo was saying he would be round, as usual, at half past seven and just then the doorbell gave its ugly little buzz.

'Hold on a minute, darling. Someone at the door.' When she got there, still dangling the watch, she saw a man with his hat in his hand standing there, a short figure with silver hair brushed straight back and wearing a silvery grey overcoat. His face looked like a white blown-out paper bag. Long afterwards, she used to say he had the gleam of a simulacrum or a ghost. Then the paper bag burst and he showed his teeth in a smile. She instantly hid the watch in her hand. The teeth were unmistakable. They were not false teeth, but they looked false because they were not closely set; they were a squad of slight gaps, but the gaps were a little wider now than they had been nine years ago in her short married life. Her husband was standing there.

'Hullo, Phoebe,' he said and, with that, he marched in past her across the little hall into the middle of the sitting-room. He was much shorter than she was. She was a very tall woman and instinctively she stooped (as she had always done with him), when she followed the gleam of his overcoat into the room. He turned round and said at once:

'Nice place. Newly decorated. Frankly I didn't expect it in a neighbourhood like this.'

He marked at once his disappointment with her. After nine years, he conveyed, she had gone downhill.

Mrs Thwaite could not speak. A long scream seemed to be frozen in her. The shock was that, but for his teeth, Charles Thwaite was unrecognisable. She might have been telling lies about him for years.

He had been a bland little dark-haired pastry-fed fellow from the North when they had first gone off together, her fur coat collar sticking to the frost inside the window of the night train. What a winter that was! He was a printer but had given that up, a man full of spit when he talked and his black eyebrows going up like a pair of swallows. The kind of man who said, 'When I believe in a thing I put everything on it. Every penny in the bank, house, wife, children, shirt – everything.' Even in those days his face had been blown out. Under the eyebrows there were a pair of earnest eyes fixed in an upward look, the eyes of a chapel-going boy caught with a finger in the jampot; under them were curious, almost burned scoops of brown shadow – trade marks of a fate, the stamp of something saleable they had seemed to her. She could never stop wondering what it was.

But now, as she stood there with her hands clenched upon Argo's watch, and looking down at her husband she saw that age had efficiently smoothed him. The stains were like hard coins; his effect was metallic. He looked collected, brisk and dangerous. And she had forgotten how short he was, for her Argo was a tall man.

What came back to her in the instant of this meeting was the forgotten, indignant girlish feeling – which living with Argo had cured her of – that she was lanky and exposed. If she had been able to move from where she was standing she would have made a grab at her coat in order to cover herself and especially to cover her legs. She had the sensation that she had become a joke once more.

For, to start with, her height had always been ridiculous. Men passing in the street turned to look up at her, startled and in dismay, and she was not a beauty; her features were too large. And jokes attract jokes; only stumpy little fellows – her husband was one of them – ever looked twice at her, and with a very trying ambition or impudence puffing themselves out. She had had the timid impression that men were playing a game of hide and seek round her, as boys playing in the street sometimes did still. This made her either stare crushingly over their heads or droop like a schoolgirl. In her early meetings with Charles she had got into the habit of finding a long low seat and at a distance from him, where she could sit down, draw up her long legs, and listen on the same level as his. Being tall had turned her into a believer and listener, listening being a kind of apology; and she would look covertly down at her legs with a reproach that would change to a pout; for – when she had been with Charles – she was proud of the dashing way in which her legs had rushed her into this love affair and marriage and had disorganised her life. Nowadays, even with Argo, she would look at her legs with fear, thinking they belonged to someone else or were a pair of fine but disobedient daughters. What they had done to her, carrying her into that story of disaster! But the story itself, of course, had attracted Argo and she had come to feel that she had the grand distinction of being a woman to whom happiness and good luck were pettily irrelevant. One Sunday Argo looked at his feet sticking out boastfully from the bottom of the bed and said:

'Don't talk nonsense. Nine years is a long time. Your husband may be dead.'

'Oh no!'

She still wanted her husband to be alive – and not for the sake of vengeance only.

'If he were, we could get married. Anyway, the law could presume death . . .' Argo went on.

She was happy with Argo after years of misery. But she wouldn't have *that*. She did not quite want to lose the gamble, the incompleteness – so breathlessly necessary to her – of her history.

History was standing there at ease, looking at the flat. 'I've given you a surprise,' her husband said.

'What do you want?' She could speak at last. 'I can't have you here. I have people coming.'

'May I take my coat off?' he said and taking it off put it down beside hers on the divan.

'New?' he said, looking at hers.

At that her courage returned to her.

'That's the only thing you left me with,' she almost shouted and was ready to fly at him if he touched it. For in this frightened moment the coat, poor as it was, seemed to be her whole life – more than the office she worked in, more than Argo, more than her marriage. It was older than any of them. It was herself; it had known her longer than anything in the room.

Her husband turned away contemptuously and while she unclenched her hands and put Argo's watch on the mantelpiece he sat down in an armchair. As his eyes stripped the room, he said:

'Very nice, very nice. Kitchen there, I suppose. Bedroom through the door. Is that rug Chinese? I'm glad you're comfortable. You haven't changed. I must say you're very beautiful. By the way, I think you've left the telephone off in the bedroom – I can hear it crackling. Put it back, will you? Naturally I want to say a few words, to explain . . .'

'Say a few words' – how the phrase came back! There would be a lot of phrases.

She was determined not to sit down. The crackling of the telephone made her feel Argo was near.

An explanation! She wanted to demand it, rage for it, but she could not get the word out. She wanted to say 'Why? I just want to know why you left me. Don't imagine that I care, but I have a right to know. Then go.'

'I found the address in the telephone book,' he said, noting how well the world was organised. Then he made his announcement. It was more; it was a pronouncement, made with the modesty of an enormous benefactor.

'I have come back to you,' he said.

'Argo, he's going to kill us,' she wanted to cry out and moved behind her chair for protection. The chair, the whole room seemed to be sickening, sliding her into the past, out of the window, into the flat she and her husband had had – the flat at the top of the small hotel she had bought for them with her own money – to those terrible scenes, to the sight of him opening the drawers of her desk in the little office, to that morning

[681]

when she had unlocked the safe and found all the money gone – eight hundred pounds. Two of her father's pictures as well – but he left the frames behind! – and with them the foreign girl in number seven. She held the chair tightly to hold the drifting room still. There he sat and, by merely sitting, occupied more and more of the room until only the few inches where she stood belonged to her. Nothing in the room, the pictures, the tables, the curtains, chairs, not even the little blue pot on the mantelpiece with pencils in it, came to her help. She would have to pass him to shout from the window.

'You are a very beautiful woman,' he said in his praying, looking-skyward manner, but now the look was obsequious.

'You are the most beautiful woman I have ever known. You are the only woman I have been in love with.'

'You cannot break into my life like this,' she said. 'I have never been taken in by flattery.'

'You are my wife,' he said.

'I am certainly not,' she said. 'What is it you want?' And then she felt tears on her cheeks, ruinous tears; for this was the moment when he would get up and put his arms round her and she would be helpless. She tried to glare through her tears and did not know that this made her look brilliant, savage and frightening, indeed not helpless at all.

'I want *you*,' he said, without moving.

It was so wonderfully meaningless to hear him say this. Her tears stopped and she laughed loudly and did not know she was laughing. The laughter chased the fright out of her body. The joke restored her. That was the rock she stood on: a joke had been played on her when she was a child. She must put up with being a collection of jokes, but this joke was so preposterous that it drove all the others out. She could feel her laughter swallowing the little man up. It was wonderful also to see how her laughter took him aback and actually confused him so that he raised his chin and held up his hand to silence her. He had a small white hand. She remembered that this meant he was going to make a moral statement.

'I am a man who has sacrificed himself to women,' he said, pointing to this as one of his unanswerable historic benefactions.

Another of his sayings! How she longed for Argo to come in and hear it. Charles was a man who had always gone blandly back to first principles. Argo never quite believed the things she said about her marriage.

'"I am a man who has sacrificed myself to women" – it was one of the first things he said to me when I met him. It was that cold winter – the worst winter for seventeen years – I told you my coat stuck to the frosty window in the train – shall I tell you about it? You don't mind? There was an election. He was – you won't believe, but it is true, it was one of his "ideas" – standing for Parliament. Can you see him? He was standing as an Independent Republican – can you imagine it – in England, in the twentieth century! A gang of youths went round his meetings and sang *Yankee Doodle* when he was speaking. Of course he didn't get in. He got two hundred and thirty-five votes. He lost his deposit. There was a row in the town. They were afraid he was splitting the vote. Splitting – he didn't even touch it! I was staying at the only hotel, a freezing cold place. I had gone north to see my brother who was in hospital. Charles was always rushing in and out of the hotel, telephoning to his wife in London who was behaving very well – they were being divorced but she was holding the divorce up to stop the scandal – and to his mistress who was very tiresome. You could hear what he was saying all over the hotel because the telephone box was in the hall and he came out of it one evening and knew that I had heard. I was sitting wrapped up because I couldn't get near the fire.

'"You look warm," he said and then he looked back at the telephone box and said – well, that sentence. His set piece: "I've sacrificed myself to women".'

(What she did not tell Argo was that the remark was true. The scoundrel had 'sacrificed' himself to women and that this was what had attracted her. She really had wanted in her naïve way to be the chief altar.)

'I told my brother when I went to the hospital. He said "He certainly doesn't sacrifice himself to anything else".'

Now, as he sat there in her flat and her laughter was warming her, Charles went one better.

'Everything I have done,' he said, 'I have done for you. Oh yes, I have. You have been the cause and inspiration of it. You are the only woman who has influenced my mind. You changed my life. You were the making of me. When I went to South America . . .'

'Not South America!' she said. 'Really! Think of something better than that. Monte Carlo. Cape Town.'

'Buenos Aires first of all, then Chile – the women have beautiful voices there: it is the German and English influence,' he went on, taking no notice of her. 'Colombia – there's a culture that has collapsed. Bolivia, an extreme revolutionary situation, Ecuador, Indians in trilby hats looking like wood. I met the President. I've just come from Baranquilla. I flew.'

'With that girl?' she said. A bad slip. He'd be the first to note her jealousy and mock it.

'Of course not,' he said. He had a flat Yorkshire accent. 'I have always been interested as you know in the Republican experience. You remember the book you made me write?'

'You didn't write it!' she said.

It was fabulous, after nine years, to see again his blank, baby-like effrontery, to hear his humourless, energetic innocence. He wasn't joking: the scoundrel *was* seriously, very seriously interested in Republics! In a moment, he would tell her that he had stolen eight hundred pounds from her and deserted her out of a pure, disinterested passion for a harem of Republics in South America!

The dangerous thing was that he was manœuvring her back to the time of their marriage. She could feel him recreating their marriage, against all her resistance, so that the room was filling with it. She feared he would wait for some sign of weakness, and then leap at her; the little man was very strong. She saw that he was already undressing the years from her and taking her back to her naked folly and credulity; until, if she was not careful, he would bring her to the point of the old passion. The Republic – it was incredible to remember – he had caught her with it.

It was a shock to her to remember what she had been like in those days – for example, how for years she had nursed her mother and had no friends. Every day she pushed the old lady down the sea front in her chair. Men looked at her or rather stepped back in half-grinning astonishment at a young woman so lanky, so gauche and shy and craving. The sight of her scared them. When her mother died, she got away to London. She had a little money which she knew she must be careful with and tried to find a job. Living alone, she simply read. Her tallness made her crave and since no man came near her, she craved for an idea.

So she was divided now between impatience and the memory he was rousing in her. She saw a half-empty room in that Town Hall in the North and him on the platform, uttering the fatal word, at the end of his speech. Republic: all men equal – equal height, perhaps that was the lure? – and so on. Quoted Plato even: 'Love the beloved Republic.' In a small industrial town, the war just over, snow frozen to black rock for six weeks on the pavements outside; and the small audience of men just back from the war, breaking up, drifting out, the gang of louts singing their *Yankee Doodle*. She saw herself, exalted, turning in anger on the bored people around who were so rudely getting out and clattering their chairs; and, gazing back at him, she signalled to him, 'Yes, yes, yes, the Republic!' And when he lost, she really felt *she* would be the Republic! She had told Argo about this. 'How I hate that word now. I can't even bear to read it in the newspapers. I was mad,' she said. Argo could be very nasty sometimes. He said, 'I thought it was only men who went to bed with an idea.'

She had to admit, as she listened, that dear Argo knew little about women. She had had two triumphs in her marriage: she had won a short period of power over her husband by persuading him that if he thought so much about Republics he ought to write a book about them. She put her money into a small London hotel and drove him off to the British Museum to write it. If she had thought, she would have seen it was the ideal place for picking up foreign girls; but never mind about that. The other triumph was more important. She had beaten those two women, his wife in London and his mistress who was there in the North working for him. She – and the winter – had frozen them out.

Her husband was now in San Tomas – was it? – and in the midst of the mulatto problem.

'Where did you get the money?' she said coldly.

'Money?' he said. 'I went back to the printing trade.'

It was the first hint of reproach. She had persuaded him to give up that trade. Once she had got him she had been going to turn him into a political thinker. She had always said grandly to her friends: 'He's in politics.' Now she noticed a little colour come to his face and that he was patting his small hand up and down on the arm of the chair, in a dismissing way, as he had always done when money was mentioned. She had asked, she knew, the right question: indifference had made her intelligent.

'The heat was awful,' he was saying. 'When you go out into the street it is like a wall standing against you – I was glad you weren't there' – he had the nerve to say – 'it shuts you in. I used to change my clothes four or five times a day . . .'

'Expensive,' she said. 'I couldn't have afforded it.' He ignored this: no irony ever touched him.

'The only air-conditioned place was the casino and the cinema. The printing press was always breaking down. I was doing repairs half the time. I've not much use for casinos but I used to go there to cool off.'

He raised his eyes seriously in the manner of the schoolboy now licking the spoon – who was he raising them to? Some feared schoolmaster, preacher or father? – and she remembered with pleasure that this presaged the utterance of some solemn, earnestly believed untruth.

'I have never been a gambling man,' he said, 'as you know – but there, the casino is packed every night. You have to get a permit, of course. Thousands change hands. I used to watch the tables and then go home along the shore road. I used to listen to the sea; you couldn't see the waves, except sometimes a flash of white, like Robin Hood's Bay on a rough night – remember, lass?' – dropping into broad Yorkshire. 'Listen to this. One night when I went to the casino I had a shock: I saw *you*. I could have sworn it was you. You were standing there by one of the tables with a man, some politician: I knew him, the cousin of a man who owned one of the local papers. It was you, tall, beautiful, even the way you do your hair. I shan't forget the look in your eyes when you saw me. I thought "My God. I didn't do the right thing by her. I took her money. I have been a swine. I'll get the money and go back to her. I'll go down on my knees and beg her to take me back." You don't know what remorse is.'

'Oh, so you've come to pay me back?' she said.

'I knew it wasn't you, but it showed how you've haunted my mind every night for the last nine years,' he said. 'I couldn't take my eyes off that woman. She was playing. I went close to her and I played. I followed her play and won. I kept winning. Her husband came and joined us and we were all winning and I thought all the time "This is for her. For her".'

'For whom?' asked Mrs Thwaite.

[686]

'For you.'

'Did you sleep with her?'

'You can't sleep with those women. I was sleeping with an Indian girl,' he said impatiently. 'Don't interrupt me. It was for you. And then we started losing. I borrowed from her husband – he was excited like me. We all were. I'm not hiding anything. I lost everything I had. More than I had. A very large sum. I was ruined. Well, people are rich there. There was a thunderstorm that night. I couldn't pay for a taxi. The rain came down in sheets and the lightning was dancing about over the water in the streets. The whole place looked violet and yellow. I never saw anything like it. I wish you could have seen it. I stood there watching. You could see the sea, waves shooting up high, like hands. I thought "What have I done? What have I done to her?".'

'Who?' she said.

'*You*. I thought "My God, suppose she is dead!" I've never spent such a night in my life. At the door of the casino I heard that woman's voice, I thought it was yours. I went out. I went searching among the cars.'

'And she wasn't there?'

'I was drenched. I was out in it for half an hour. I didn't know what I was doing.'

'How did you pay back the money?' she said. '*Did* you pay it back?'

'Naturally,' he said with stupendous coldness. 'I had borrowed it from her husband. It was a debt of honour.'

'Oh honour,' she said. 'And what about the lady?'

It shocked her that she felt that not quite conquerable disloyalty of the body when he mentioned the woman.

She had long ago admitted to herself that jealousy had been the foundation of her love for him. At the first sight of him in that hotel in the North, she had seen him sitting with three or four people near the fire. There was a cheerful vulgar fellow with drink-pimpled skin – his agent, no doubt. There was an elderly man who looked at him with a noble pathos and two grey-haired women who watched him with mistrust. They were talking about the meeting in the Town Hall and one said 'In this weather there'll be a poor turnout.' A very thin young woman in a cheap black coat came in from the street kicking snow off her shoes and carrying a roll of posters which were packed in wet newspaper. Her

[687]

stockings were wet. He went up to her quickly, scowling (but smiling too), and after taking the posters, he led the wretched girl by the arm not to the fire, but to the street door, speaking in a loud official voice about canvassing in the morning; at the door, he lowered his voice and said, shadily and sharply and intimately, looking into her defiant eyes: 'I told you not to come here.'

An intrigue! She heard it. A flare of desire to be part of it, and of jealousy, went through her, a sudden hungry jealousy. She had never felt like this until then, not at any rate since she was a child. She felt she had been set alight.

Now, nine years later, she said:

'I don't know what you want. Why you're telling me this tale. It's all a lot of lies I know. I never wanted to see you again, but now I'm glad you've come. Where are you staying? Give me your address. I want a divorce. I shall divorce you. It's not a question of what you want. It is what I want now.'

She was fighting for Argo and herself.

'Just a moment,' he said. 'I haven't come to talk about divorces.'

'You can't stay here,' she said. 'I won't have you here.'

'Let me speak,' he said. 'I haven't come here to quarrel.' And shyly – how extraordinary to see him shy, for once – 'I want your help. I know I must have made you suffer. You have something rare in a woman: integrity. You tell the truth.'

'I'm certainly not going to help you about anything,' she said.

'Divorce,' he said. 'Of course, I hadn't thought of that. It's natural, of course: I'm a Catholic, but still . . .'

'Yes?' she said.

He tapped one of his teeth with his finger, thoughtfully.

'Let's get to the point. I'm in a little difficulty. Let me go on with what I was telling you. I've saved the printers a great deal of money – the firm in San Tomas. They were going to be forced to buy a new machine in New York, but I told them to wait, to let me work on it. That's what I've been doing. I've saved them thousands. These South Americans are no good at machinery. They just say "Buy a new one" – like that. They've got piles of money.'

Perhaps he *has* come to pay me back? Is that the idea – buying me back? she wondered. The white hand went slowly up and down on the arm of the chair.

'What is it you really came here for?' she said reasonably. A full smile of pure, admiring pleasure made his white skin shine, a smile of polite tenderness and discreet thanks.

'I want twelve hundred pounds,' he said. 'I had to borrow it from the firm to pay that man – as I told you just now. I want it rather quickly. The accountants come in at the end of the month. I want you to lend it to me.'

He said this in a voice of stupefying kindness and seriousness as if he were at last atoning for what he had done, unasked, in real friendship and generosity. It would, he gravely conveyed, be the most binding of ties. It would remind her of those happy days – ah, he too wished them to return! – when he had had money from her before. He conveyed that she would instinctively see the beauty of it – that he had come to her, the perfect woman, a second time; that she was, in truth, the only woman in his life, that of no one else would he ask such a thing.

And the strange part of it was that as she gasped at the preposterous suggestion and was about to turn on him, a small thrill went through her. She was a prudent woman, if anything a shade mean about the little money left to her, but he brought back to her the sense of unreason and danger that had turned her head when she had first met him. He brought back to her the excitement of the fact that he was – as she knew – unbelievable. It enhanced some quality of her own character: she was the kind of woman to whom mad things happened. And she saw herself running to Argo with her astounded mouth open and telling him, telling everyone. And, for a few seconds, she admired her husband. Twelve hundred pounds! In nine years his price had gone up!

'You stole twelve hundred pounds?' she said. 'Fiddled the books?'

'Stole?' he said. 'I don't like to hear you use a word like that. I borrowed it. I told you. It was a debt of honour.'

'You must be mad to think I would be such a fool. I haven't got twelve hundred pence. I've never had such a sum in my life.'

Stole! Arrest! Prison! Perhaps he had already been in prison? Was that why he was so pale? She was not frightened, but his case seemed to taint herself.

'But you can raise it,' he said briskly, dismissing what she said.

'I work for my living. I go to my office every day. I've had to. Where do you think I could get the money?'

There was a silence filled by the enormity of that sum. He was proposing to come here, settle here, and tie that huge debt to her neck, like a boulder. Argo must turn him out. He must come and turn him out.

'I was very sorry to see – when was it? I saw an English paper over there – that your aunt had died,' he said in a changed and sorrowful voice. 'I think you *can* raise it', he said suddenly, coolly threatening.

'Ah!' she woke up to it. '*Now* I see why you have come back to me. You thought I had just come into her money. You saw it in the paper and you came rushing back.'

'It was coming to you. I remember you telling me. And I am your husband.'

'Well, if you want to know, it did *not* come to me. When you left me, she blamed me not you. But do you think even if I had, I would give it to you? She left it to her brother.'

'Your brother?' he said sharply.

'No, *her* brother,' she said triumphantly.

'Is that true?'

'Ask him.'

He took out a pocket note book and turned over a page or two. 'The one in Newcastle?' he said. He had obviously been checking her family.

'You got nothing at all?' he said.

'No.' And this time she really did shout at him.

'I can't believe it,' he said curtly. 'I just can't believe you can have been such a damn fool.'

She could see he was affronted and injured. 'I offer you everything,' he seemed to say. 'And you give me nothing.'

There was a sneer on his papery face. The sneer she knew concealed desperation and she felt the beginnings of pity, but she knew now – what she had not known nine years ago – that this pity was dangerous to her; he would see it at once, and he would come towards her, grip her arm, press upon her, ignoring her mind but moving her body. He had a secret knowledge of her, for he had been the first to know that her body was wild.

She was frightened of herself. She had to get out of the room, but each

[690]

room was a trap. The only hope was the most dangerous room: the bedroom. It had a telephone in it.

'Argo, Argo, please come. Hurry,' she was crying to herself. But her husband did not step towards her, he went over to the mantelpiece and he was looking at something on it. He picked up Argo's watch. She moved to snatch it from him but he closed his hand. She actually touched his sleeve: touching him made her feel sick.

'Beginning all over again, I see,' he said. 'Does he live here?'

'That's my business.'

'Snug under the coat?' he laughed and let the watch dangle by its strap. She was blushing, and almost gasping, fearing he would now attack her.

But he did not.

'You realise, I hope, that you are committing adultery?' he said stiffly. 'I don't understand what has happened to you. You seem to have gone to pieces since I left you. I was surprised to see you living in a low-class district like this – what is he? Some clerk? You can't even manage your own money. Left it to her brother! How often I've told you – you never had any sense of reality. And by the way,' he went on angrily, 'if you had not left all your money in the safe, none of this would have happened. You should have paid it into the bank.'

'He is not a clerk,' she said. 'He's a professor in the university.' He laughed.

'That's what you wanted me to be. You are just romantic. The printing trade was not good enough for the lady.'

'I didn't want you to be a professor.'

'Write about the Republic. What Republic?' he jeered.

'It was your idea,' she said.

'Sitting in the British Museum, coming round to you for my money. I sacrificed myself to you. Why? I have always sacrificed myself to women. I loved you and you ruined me.'

'I don't believe you ever went to the Museum,' she said, 'except to pick up girls.'

'To think of my wife committing adultery!' he exclaimed. And – she could not believe her luck – he put the watch back on the mantelpiece with disgust. He ran his fingers on the mantelpiece and saw dust on his fingers.

'You don't look after your things. There are cigarette burns on this mantelpiece. I don't like your pictures, one, two, three nudes. Indecent. I don't like that. I suppose that is how you see yourself.'

He mooched about the flat and pointed at the frayed lining of her coat on the divan.

'That ought to have gone to the furriers,' he said. He stared at the coat and his temper quietened.

'It was a very cold winter, wasn't it?' he said. 'The worst winter for years. It cut down the canvassing, I couldn't get people to the polls. It wasn't that though. Do you know what lost me that election? Your coat. That was a true thing Jenny said after you saw me tell her to keep out of the hotel. "We're up against those hard-faced Tory women in their mink".'

'It's not mink,' she said.

'Whatever it is. Of course she was suspicious. But that wasn't the trouble. She was just freezing cold. Her room was an icebox. She couldn't stand it. She was coughing even when she started. She went off.'

He suddenly laughed.

'She was frozen out. You had a fur coat, she hadn't. Your coat won. Fourteen Purser Street, do you remember? – it kept us warm, after she had gone?'

'She didn't go for a week,' she said. After all, she had sat her rival out. But Mrs Thwaite was watching for her opportunity. How to get past him and snatch back the watch? She saw her chance and grabbed it. He was taken by surprise and did not, as she feared he would, catch her arm.

'I feel sick,' she said and rushed with her handkerchief to her mouth to the bedroom.

She sat on the bed and heard the crackling of the telephone receiver which she had not replaced. She put it back and then took it off to dial Argo's number, looking in fear at the door she had left open.

'Darling, darling. Charles has come back. My husband, yes. Yes, he's here. I am frightened. He won't go. I can't get him out. Please come, he's horrible. What are we to do? No, if he sees you he will go. Call the police? How can I do that? He's my husband. He's in the sitting-room, he's moving about. I can hear him. Get a taxi. I'm afraid. I'm afraid of what he'll do. I can't tell you. Get him out? How can I? Oh, please, thank you, darling, thank you, I love you . . . He's horrible.'

She put down the telephone and moved away, standing with her back to the window. If he came into the bedroom she would open the window and jump out. But he did not. He seemed to be picking up things in the sitting-room. She went back boldly now. He had picked up her coat and was holding it by the shoulders.

'Get out. Put that down. Get out. I have my own life now. I never want to set eyes on you again. I'm going to divorce you. I have rung for help.'

She was astonished by her own power and the firmness of her voice.

'Yes, I heard you,' he said. He had put his overcoat on again.

'And put my coat down,' she shouted again.

They stood outstaring each other. He was half smiling with passing admiration.

'No,' he said, 'I'll take it with me. A souvenir. Goodbye.'

She was flabbergasted to see him walk past her out of the room, open the door of the flat and go downstairs with her coat on his arm.

'Charles.' She ran to the door. 'Charles.' He went on.

'Charles, come back here.'

She was down at the street door, but, already, he was twenty yards away, crossing the street. He looked not so much ridiculous as luxurious carrying the coat. She felt he was carrying her off too. She shouted again but not loudly for she did not want people to stare at them in the street. She was about to run after him when she saw the blind man who lived farther down come tapping towards her with his white stick. He slowed down, sensing disturbance. He paused like a judgment. And in her pause of indecision, she saw her husband get to the bus stop and instantly, as if he were in league with buses and had bribed one or got it by some magic, a bus floated up beside him and he was off on it.

He had taken the last thing she had, he had taken twenty years of her life with him. She watched the bus until it was out of sight.

She went back to her door and she climbed the stairs and got inside and looked at the room where he had stood; it seemed to her that it was stripped of everything, even of herself. It seemed to her that she was not there. 'Why are women so mad about furs?' he had once said to her. 'To keep warm? No, so that they can feel naked'. One of his 'sayings'. But that was what she felt as she sat waiting for Argo to come; her husband had taken her nakedness.

Argo found her sitting there. When she stopped crying in his arms he said:

'He won't come back. I'll get on to the police.'

'Oh no.'

'He'll sell it. He was just after anything he could get. He might get fifty pounds for it.'

'He was very jealous. He used to try to make me say some man had given it to me.' She was proud of that. 'He's a funny man. He may not sell it.'

'You mean,' said Argo who, though placating, had his nasty side, 'he'll give it to one of his girl friends?'

'No,' she said angrily. She was not going to have that! An old feeling, one she used to have, that there was something stupid about very tall men like Argo, came back to her.

In the night she lay awake, wondering where her husband was. Perhaps everything he said had been true: that he did love her more than any of the women he had known, that he did want to be forgiven, that she had been hard and was to blame from the beginning. He had remembered Purser Street. Perhaps he *had* been in South America. She wished she had had twelve hundred pounds to give him. She would never forgive herself if he were arrested. Then her thoughts changed and she fell into thinking in his melodramatic way: he had taken her youth, her naked youth, with him and left her an old woman. She got up in the night and went to her mirror to see how much grey there was in her hair. She was not very much younger than Charles. She went back cold to bed and put her arms round Argo.

'Love me. Love me,' she said.

She hated Argo for saying that her husband had given the coat to another woman.

In the morning she went to her office.

'Someone walked into my flat yesterday and stole my fur coat,' she said.

What a life, they said, that poor woman has had; something is always happening to her. It never ends. But they saw her eyes shining brilliantly within their gloom.

The Cage Birds

J ust as he was getting ready to go to his office, the post came.

'A card from Elsie,' Mrs Phillips said. '"Come on Wednesday. All news when we meet. I've got Some Things. Augusta".' She turned the card over. There was a Mediterranean bay like a loud blue wide open mouth, a small white town stretching to a furry headland of red rocks. A few villas were dabbed in and a large hotel. The branch of a pine tree stretched across the foreground of the picture splitting the sea in two. Her husband had been brushing his jacket and stopped to look at the card: he started brushing again. In ten years, it seemed to her, he had brushed half the suit away, it was no longer dark grey but a parsimonious gleam.

They looked at each other, disapproving of the foreign scene; also of the name Elsie had given herself: Augusta. They had never got used to it.

'Ah ha! The annual visit! You'd better go,' he said. And then he laughed in his unnatural way, for he laughed only when there was no joke, a laugh that turned the pupils of his eyes into a pair of pin-heads. 'Before her maid gets hold of the things.'

'I'll have to take the boy. It's a school holiday.'

'Half fare on the bus,' he said. 'She always gives you something for the fare.'

And he laughed at this too.

'She forgot last year,' she said.

He stopped laughing. He frowned and reflected.

'You shouldn't let her forget. Fares have gone up. All across London! When I was a boy you could do it for sixpence. Get off at Baker Street – that'll save fourpence.'

He put the brush down. He was a youngish man whose sleeves were too short, and he was restlessly rubbing his red hands together now, glistering at the thought of the economy; but she stood still, satisfied.

When they were first married his miserliness had shocked her, but now she had fallen into abetting it. It was almost their romance; it was certainly their Cause. When she thought of the mess the rest of her family was in, she was glad to have years of girlhood anxiety allayed by a skinflint. She knew the sharp looks the shopkeepers and neighbours gave him when his eyes filled with tears as he haggled over a penny or two, and counted the change in his open martyred hand. But she stood by him, obstinately, raising her chin proudly when, giving his frugal laugh, he cringed at a counter or a ticket office. He had the habit of stroking his hands over the legs of his trousers and smiling slyly at her when he had saved a penny, and she, in ten years of marriage, had come to feel the same small excited tingle in her own skin as he felt in his.

'Get out of my way. We're going to Auntie's tomorrow,' she said to the boy when he came back from school in the afternoon. 'Here' – and she gave him the postcard – 'look at this.'

She was in the kitchen, a room darkened by the dark blobs of the leaves of a fig tree hanging their tongues against the window. It was an old tree, and every year it was covered with fruit that looked fresh and hopeful for a few weeks, and then turned yellow and fell on to the grass, because of the failure of the London sun. The dirty-minded woman next door said those leaves put ideas into your head, but Mrs Phillips couldn't see what she meant. Now she was ironing a petticoat to put on for the visit tomorrow and the boy was looking at the mole on her arm as it moved back and forth, her large grey eyes watching the iron like a cat. First the black petticoat, then her brassière, then her knickers; the boy watched restlessly.

'Mum. Where is Auntie's house?' the boy said looking at the card.

'There,' she said, straightening up and dashing a finger at random on the card.

'Can I swim?'

'No, I told you. We're not going there. We haven't got the money for holidays. That's where Auntie Elsie lives in the summer.'

'Where's Uncle Reg?'

That was the trouble: the kid asking questions.

'I told you. He's gone to China, Africa – somewhere. Stop kicking your shoes. They're your school shoes. I can't afford any more.'

[696]

Then she put down the iron with a clump and said: 'Don't say anything about Uncle Reg tomorrow, d'you hear? It upsets Auntie.'

'When are we going to see her?'

'Tomorrow. I keep telling you.'

'On a bus?'

'On a bus. Here,' she said, 'give me those shirts of yours.'

The boy gave her the pile of shirts and she went on working. She was a woman who scarcely ever sat down. She was wearing a black petticoat like the one she had ironed, her arms were bare and when she lifted up a garment he could see the hair in her armpits; hair that was darker than the tawny hair that was loose over her sweating forehead. What disturbed the boy was the way she changed from untidy to tidy and especially when she put on her best blouse and skirt and got ready to go out. The hours he had to wait for her when, going to the cupboard and looking at the dresses hanging there, she changed herself into another woman!

She was this other woman the next day when they went off to the bus stop. She was carrying a worn, empty suitcase and walked fast so he had almost to run to keep up with her. She was wearing a navy blue dress. She had tied a grey and white scarf round her head so that the pale face looked harder, older and emptier than it was. The lips were long and thin. It was a face set in the past; for the moment it was urging her to where she was going but into the past it would eventually fall back. At the bus stop she simply did not see the other people standing there. The boy looked at her raised chin with anxiety and when the bus came, she came down out of the sky and pushed the boy on and put the case under the stairs.

'You sit there,' she said. 'And see no one takes it.'

The annual visit! Her sister had come over from that island in June this year, early for her. It used to be Christmas in Reg's time and, for that matter, in the time of that other man she had never met. This new one had lasted three years; he was called Williams and he was buying the headland on the postcard, and he was a June man. He couldn't stand the mosquitoes. Her sister said: 'They suck his blood. He's like beef to them.' But who was the blood-sucker? You ask *him*! Those women have to get it while they can. At the Ritz one minute – and the next, where are they?

She called herself Augusta now. But Grace stuck to calling her Elsie: it was virtuous.

London was cabbaged with greenery. It sprouted in bunches along the widening and narrowing of the streets, bulging at corners, at the awkward turnings that made the streets look rheumatic. There were wide pavements at empty corners, narrow ones where the streets were packed. Brilliant traffic was squeezing and bunching, shaking, spurting, suddenly whirling round bends and then dawdling in short disorderly processions like an assortment of funerals. On some windows the blinds of a night worker were drawn and the milk bottle stood untouched at the door; at the Tube, papers and cigarette litter blowing, in the churchyards women pushing prams. The place was a fate, a blunder of small hopes and admired defeats. By the river one or two tall new buildings stuck up, prison towers watching in the midst of it. The bus crossed the river and then gradually made north to the Park and the richer quarters.

'There's your dad's shop,' she said to the boy. They passed a large store.

'There's his window, first floor,' she pointed up. That was where he worked in the week.

Now the streets were quieter, the paint was fresher, the people better dressed. By a church with a golden statue of St George and the Dragon outside it, she got the boy off the bus and walked to a new building where there was a man in blue uniform at the door.

In this instant the boy saw his mother change. She stopped, and her grey eyes glanced to right and then to left fearfully. Usually so bold, she cringed before the white building and its balconies that stuck out like sun decks. She lowered her head when the porter with the meaty despising nose opened the door into the wide hall. She was furtive and, in the lift, she tried to push the suitcase out of sight behind the boy; she felt ashamed. She also nervously trembled fearing to be suspected of a crime.

'Take your cap off in the lift when you're with a lady,' she said to the boy, asserting to the porter that she was respectable. With both hands the startled boy clawed the cap off his head.

The porter was not going to let them out of his sight. On the eleventh floor the door slid open. Across the hall of carpet and mirrors which made her feel she was a crowd of women at many doors and not one, he led her to the door. The boy noticed it had no knocker. No bang, bang, bang, iron on iron, as on their door at home; a button was pressed and a buzz like hair spray at the barber's could be heard. There were he noticed white bars behind the figured glass on the door where ferns were frosted.

Presently a maid wearing a pretty apron opened the door and let them in, looking down at their shoes. A green carpet, mirrors framed in mirror again, hotel flowers, lilies chiefly, on a glass-topped table of white metal: the flat was like the hall outside. It smelled of scent and the air stood warm and still. Then they were shown into a large room of creamy furniture, green and white satin chairs. There were four wide windows, also with white metal strips on them, beyond which the fat trees of the Park lolled. Did Auntie own them? At one end of the room was a small bar of polished bamboo. Then out of another room came Auntie herself taking funny short steps which made her bottom shake, calling in a little girl's voice 'Grace!' She bent down low to kiss him with a powdery face, so that he could see the beginning of her breasts. Her brooch pricked his jersey, catching it. 'Oh, we're caught.' She disentangled it.

'It's torn my jersey,' the boy whined.

'There you are. Look. I'll take it off and put it here.' She put the brooch on the table.

'Umph. Umph,' she said going back to him and kissing him again. Auntie had the tidiness of a yellow-haired doll. She was as pink as a sugared almond and her kiss tasted of scent and gin.

'You've lost a lot, Grace,' she said to her sister. 'Look at me. It's that French food. I've put on seven pounds. It shows when you're small. Mr Williams is coming today. I flew in yesterday from Paris. I've got some lovely things. It's no good anyone thinking they can leave me in Paris on my own.'

'Is Uncle Reg in Paris?' said the boy.

His mother blushed.

'Keep quiet. I told you,' she said with a stamp.

Elsie's round blue eyes looked at the boy and her lips pouted with seductive amusement. She wriggled a shoulder and moved her hips. The boy grew up as she looked at him.

'What do you like for tea? I've got something for you. Come with me and see Mary. Sit down, Grace.'

[699]

When the boy had gone the two sisters took up what they felt to be their positions in the room. Grace refused to take off her scarf and refused, also out of dread of contamination from the expense of the satin, to sit back on the sofa; she kept to the edge from where she could get a good view of everything. Elsie sat with her beautiful silk legs drawn up on the seat of a chair and lit a cigarette and touched the hair that had been made into a golden crust of curls that morning.

Grace said: 'The carpet's new.'

'They never last more than a year,' Elsie said with a cross look. She was pretty, therefore she could be cross. 'People drop cigarettes. I had the whole place done.' And with that she restlessly got up and shut the window.

'The curtains as well. Mr Williams paid five hundred pounds for the curtains alone! I mean – you've got to be kind to yourself. No one else will be. We only live once. He spent nearly as much in the bedroom. I saw the bills. Come and look at it.'

She got up and then sat down again. 'We'll see it in a minute.'

'You're all barred in,' Grace said.

'We had burglars again. I just got in – Mr Williams took me to Ascot. He likes a bit of racing – and I rushed back, well, to tell you the truth I must have eaten something that didn't agree with me, duck pâté I think that's what it was, and I had to rush. He must have followed me in, this man, I mean, and when I came out my handbag was open and he had cleared one hundred and fifty pounds. Just like that.' She lowered her voice. 'I don't like the man on the lift. Then at Christmas when we were on the island they came in again. The staff here were off duty, but you'd have thought people would see. Or hear ... That's what staff is like these days.'

'What happened?'

'They took my mink coat and the stole, and a diamond clasp, a diamond necklace and Mr Williams's coat, a beautiful fur-lined coat – he carried on, I can tell you – and all my rings. Well, not all. We got the insurance but I don't keep anything here now except what I'm wearing. The brooch – did you see it? Mr Williams gave it to me as a consolation, I was so upset. Pictures – that's where he puts his money usually. Everything's going up. You want to put your money into things. That's why we put those bars on the door and the windows. And – come here, I'll show you.'

They walked into the bedroom and on the door that gave on to the balcony there was a steel grille that closed like a concertina.

'You're caged in,' said Grace.

Elsie laughed.

'It's what Mr Williams said. Funny you should say it. He likes a joke – Reg could never see one, d'you remember? "Birdie – we'll keep you in a cage." Ah now,' she pointed to the white bed where dresses were laid out. 'Here it all is. I've picked them all out.'

But Grace was looking at a white cupboard with a carved and gilded top to it. The doors were open and thrown inside was a pile of summery hats, some had fallen out on to the violet carpet of the bedroom. Half of them were pink – 'My colour.'

'Oh,' said Elsie in a bored voice, already tired of them. 'That's what I got in Paris. I told you. On the way back.'

Elsie led her sister out of the bedroom again.

The cringing had gone; Grace sat stiffly, obstinately, hardened, without curiosity, looking at the luxury of the room.

'I heard from Birmingham the day before yesterday,' she said in a dead voice.

Elsie's pretty face hardened also.

'Mother's ill,' said Grace.

'What is it?' said Elsie.

'Her legs.'

'I hope you didn't tell her this address,' Elsie accused.

'I haven't written yet.'

'Grace,' said Elsie in a temper, 'Mother has her life. I have mine. And she never writes.'

She went to the bar, saying in the middle of her temper, 'This is new. I know it's no good asking you,' and she poured herself a glass of gin and vermouth and then resumed her temper, raising her small plump doll's chin so that Grace should know why her chin and throat and shoulders could, when her lips pouted and her eyes moistened, draw men's eyes to the hidden grave eyes of her breasts. Men would lower their heads as if they were going to charge and she kept her small feet nimble and ready to dodge. It was a dogma in the minds of both sisters that they were (in different but absolute ways) who they were, what they were, on their own and immovable in unwisdom.

This was their gift, the reward for a childhood that had punished them.

'Listen,' said Elsie in her temper, 'you haven't seen me. "How is Elsie?" "I don't know. I don't know where she is." I've got my life. You've got yours. If Dad had been alive things would be different.'

'I never say anything,' said Grace grimly. 'I mind my own business. I wouldn't want to say anything.'

Suddenly Elsie became secretive.

'Mary,' she nodded to the room where the maid and the boy were, 'always has her eye on the clothes. I don't trust anybody. You know these girls. You have to watch them. "Where's my red dress?" "At the cleaner's, ma'am." I wasn't born yesterday. But you can *use* them, Grace, I *know*. Let's go and look.'

Gay and confiding she took Grace back to the bedroom and looked at the dresses spread out on the bed. She held up a blue one.

'It's funny, I used to be jealous of your clothes. When we went to church,' Elsie said. 'Do you remember your blue dress, the dark blue one with the collar? I could have killed you for it and the bank manager saying, "Here comes the blue bird of happiness." Aren't kids funny? When you grew out of it and it came down to me, I hated it. I wouldn't put it on. It was too long. You were taller than me then, we're the same now. Do you remember?'

'And here is a black,' she said holding up another. 'Well, every picture tells a story. Mr Williams threw it out of the window when we were in Nice. He has a temper. I was a bit naughty. This one's Italian. It would suit you. You never wear anything with flowers though, do you?'

She was pulling the dresses off the bed and throwing them back again.

'Reg was generous. He knew how to spend. But when his father died and he came into all that money, he got mean – that's where men are funny. He was married – well, I knew that. Family counted for Reg. Grace, how long have you been married?'

'Ten years,' said Grace.

Elsie picked up a golden dress that had a paler metallic sheen to it, low in the neck and with sleeves that came an inch or two below the elbow. She held it up.

[702]

'This would suit you, Grace. You could wear this colour with your hair. It's just the thing for cocktails. With your eyes it would be lovely. Mr Williams won't let me wear it, he hates it, it looks hard, sort of brassy on me – but you, look!'

She held it against her sister.

'Look in the mirror. Hold it against yourself.'

Against her will Grace held it to her shoulders over her navy woollen dress. She saw her body transformed into a sunburst of light.

'Grace,' said Elsie in a low voice. 'Look what it does to you. It isn't too big.'

She stepped behind and held the dress in at the waist. Grace stood behind the dress and her jaw set and her bones stiffened in contempt at first and then softened.

'There's nothing to be done to it. It's wonderful,' said Elsie.

'I never go to cocktail parties,' said Grace.

'Look. Slip it on. You'll see.'

'No,' said Grace and let go of a shoulder. Elsie pulled it back into place.

'With the right shoes,' Elsie said, 'that will lift it. Slip it on. Come on. I've never seen anything like it. You remember how things always looked better on you. Look.'

She pulled the dress from Grace and held it against herself.

'You see what I look like.

'No,' she went on, handing it back. She went to the bedroom door and shut it and whispered, 'I paid two hundred and forty pounds for it in Paris – if you're not going to wear it yourself you can't have it. I'll give it to Mary. She's had her eye on it.'

Grace looked shrewdly at Elsie. She was shocked by her sister's life. From her girlhood Elsie had wheedled. She had got money out of their aunt; she drew the boys after her but was soon the talk of the town for going after the older men, especially the married. She suddenly called herself Augusta. It baffled Grace that men did not see through her. She was not beautiful. The blue eyes were as hard as enamel and she talked of nothing but prices and clothes and jewellery. From this time her life was a procession through objects to places which were no more than objects, from cars to yachts, from suites to villas. The Mediterranean was something worn in the evening, a town was the setting for a ring, a café was a looking glass, a night-club was a price. To be in the sun on a beach was to have found a new man who had bought her more of the sun.

Once she giggled to Grace:

'When they're doing it – you know what I mean – that's when I do my planning. It gives you time to yourself.'

Now, as Grace held the golden dress and Elsie said in her cold baby voice: 'If you don't keep it to wear I'll give it to Mary,' Grace felt their kinship. They had been brought up poor. They feared to lose. She felt the curious pleasure of being a girl again, walking with Elsie in the street, and of being in the firm humouring position of the elder sister of a child who, at that time, simply amused them all by her calculations. Except for their father, they were a calculating family. Calculation was their form of romance. If I put it on, Grace thought, that doesn't mean I'll keep it for myself. I'll sell it with the rest.

'All right. I'll just try it,' she said.

'I'll unzip you,' said Elsie, but let Grace pull her dress over her head, for the navy wool disgusted her. And Grace in her black slip pouted shyly, thinking "Thank heavens I ironed it yesterday." To be untidy underneath in an expensive flat like this – she would have been shamed.

She stepped into the golden dress and pulled it up and turned to the long mirror as she did this, and at once to her amazement, she felt the gold flowing up her legs and her waist, as if it were a fire, a fire which she could not escape and which, as Elsie fastened it, locked her in. The mirror she looked in seemed to blaze.

'It's too long.'

'We're the same height. Stand on your toes. Do you see?'

Grace felt the silk with her fingers.

'Take off your scarf.'

Grace pulled it off.

Her dead hair became darker and yet it, too, took on the yellow glint of the flame.

'It's too full,' said Grace for her breasts were smaller than Elsie's.

'It was too tight on me. Look!' Elsie said. She touched the material here and there and said, 'I told you. It's perfect.'

Grace half smiled. Her face lost its empty look and she knew that she was more beautiful than her sister. She gazed, she fussed, she pretended, she complained, she turned this way and that. She stretched out an arm to look at the length of the sleeve. She glowed inside it. She saw herself in Elsie's villa. She saw herself at one of those parties she had never been to. She saw her whole life changed. The bus routes of London were abolished. Her own house vanished and inside herself she cried angrily, to her husband looking at the closed door of the bedroom, so that her breasts pushed forward and her eyes fired up with temper:

'Harry, where are you? Come here! Look at this.'

At that very moment, the bedroom door was opened. The boy walked in and a yard behind him, keeping not quite out of sight, was a man.

'Mum,' the child called with his hands in his pockets, 'there's a man.'

The boy looked with the terror of the abandoned at the new woman he saw and said:

'Where's Mum?' looking at her in unbelief.

She came laughing to him and kissed him. He scowled mistrustfully and stepped back.

'Don't you like it?'

As she bent up from the kiss she had a furtive look at the man in the room: was it Mr Williams? He was gazing with admiration at her.

But Elsie was quick. She left Grace and went into the sitting-room and Grace saw her sister stop suddenly and heard her say, in a voice she had never heard before – a grand stagey voice spoken slowly and arrogantly as if she had a plum in her mouth, her society voice:

'Oh you! I didn't invite you to call this afternoon.' The man was dark and young and tall, dandified and sunburned. He was wearing a white polo neck jersey and he was smiling over Elsie's golden head at Grace who turned away at once. Elsie shut the bedroom door. As she did so, Grace heard her sister say:

'I have got my dressmaker here. It's very inconvenient.'

To hear herself being called "my dressmaker" and not "my sister," and in that artificial voice, just at the moment of her stupefying glory, to have the door shut in her face! She stared at the door that separated them, and then in anger went over to the door and listened. The boy spoke.

'Ssh,' said Grace.

'I am annoyed with you. I told you to telephone,' Elsie was saying. 'Who let you in?'

Grace heard him say: 'Get rid of her. Send her away.'

But Elsie was saying nervously, 'How *did* you get in?'

And quite clearly the man said:

'The way I went out last night, through the kitchen.' Grace heard a chair being pushed and Elsie say:

'Don't, I tell you. Mr Williams will be here. Stop.'

'Here, help me,' said Grace to the boy. 'Pick them up.' She had the suitcase on the bed and quickly started to push the dresses into her case. 'Come on.'

She tried to unzip the yellow dress but she could not reach.

'Damn this thing,' she said.

'Mum, you said a word,' said the boy.

'Shut up,' she said. And, giving up, she pushed the navy dress she had taken off into the case, just as Elsie came back into the room and said to the boy: 'Go and talk to the gentleman.' The boy walked backwards out of the room, gaping at his mother and his aunt until Elsie shut the door on him.

'Grace,' she said in an excited, low voice, wheedling. 'Don't pack up. What are you doing? You're not going? You mustn't go.'

'I've got to get my husband his supper,' said Grace sharply. Elsie opened her handbag and pulled out a five-pound note and pushed it into Grace's hand. 'There's time. That's for a taxi. Something awkward's happened. Mr Williams will be here in a minute and I can't get rid of this man. I don't know what to do. It is a business thing about the villa and he's pestering me and Mr Williams loathes him. I met him on the 'plane. I was very very silly. If Mr Williams comes, I'll say he's come with you from the dress shop. And you can leave with him.'

'You *said* Mr Williams knew him,' said Grace with contempt.

'Did I? I was a bit silly,' Elsie wheedled. 'You know what a fool I am – I let this gentleman drive me from the airport – well, that's harmless, I mean . . . Grace, you look wonderful in that dress. I only mean go out of the flat *with* him.' She looked slyly and firmly at Grace.

Into Grace's mind came that scene from their girlhood outside their school when Elsie made her stand with a young man and hold his arm to prevent him getting away while she fetched a new red coat. The young man had a marvellous new motor-bike. It was the first time Grace had held a young man's arm. She would never forget the sensation and the youth saying:

'She's a little bitch. Let's go.'

And how, just as she was going to say wildly, 'Oh yes' and he squeezed her arm, Elsie came running back and pulled him to the motor-bike and shouted to Grace: 'So long.'

Grace hesitated now, but then she remembered Elsie's society voice: 'My dressmaker.' And with that she had a feeling that was half disgust and half fear of being mixed up in Elsie's affairs. For Grace the place was too grand. The lies themselves were too grand. And there was this revelation that for years in every annual visit, Elsie had concealed and denied that they were sisters, just as she denied the rest of the family.

'No, Elsie,' Grace said. 'I've got to get back to Harry.'

She was tempted to leave the suitcase, but she thought, "She'd only think I'm a fool if I leave it."

'I'll take the case and I'd best go. Thanks, though, for the taxi.'

'Good-bye ma'am,' she said to Elsie in a loud, proud voice as they went into the sitting-room.

'Come on,' she called to the child. 'Where are you?'

He was sitting on a chair staring at the man, and particularly at his jacket, as if his eyes were microscopes. The man had walked over to the window.

Grace took the boy by the hand.

'Say Good-bye to the lady,' Grace said, pulling the boy who, scared still by the strangeness of his mother in her glory, said:

'Good-bye, Auntie.'

They sat in the taxi.

'Sit down,' said Grace to the boy. He had never been in a taxi before. He took a timid look at her. She was overpowering.

'I haven't been in a taxi since your dad and I came back from our honeymoon,' she said. London had changed. There were only doors to look at, doors at first of the rich houses in the park, and herself arriving at them, being taken into drawing-rooms. She wished her suitcase was not so shabby. She would go into the doorways of hotels; palaces seemed familiar; streets wider; she looked at the windows of shoe shops. She looked at the handbags women were carrying. The taxi came to the river and there she gleamed, as she passed over the sad, dirty, dividing water, but through the poorer streets, past the factories, the railway arches, the taxi went fast, passing the crowded buses. She was indignant with traffic lights that stopped them.

'Mum,' said the boy.

She was day-dreaming about the effect she would have on her husband when she opened the gate of her house.

'Do you like it?' she said.

'Yes. But mum . . .'

'Look,' she said, excited. 'We're nearly there. There's Woolworth's. There's Marks's. Look, there's Mrs Sanders. Wave to Mrs Sanders. I wonder if she saw us.'

Then the taxi stopped at the house. How mean it looked! 'Your dad is home,' she said as she paid the driver and then opened the gate and looked at the patch of flower-bed. 'He's been watering the garden.' But when she was paying the taxi driver the door of the house opened and her husband stood there with his eternal clothes-brush held in horror in the air. He gaped at her. His eyes became small.

'You took a cab!' he said, and looked as if he were going to run after it as it grunted off. 'How much did you give him?'

'She paid,' she said.

'Come in,' he said. 'Come in.' And he went into the dark hall, put the brush down and rubbed his hands as she lifted the suitcase into the house. The boy crept past them.

'What did he charge?' her husband said.

Not until then did he see the dress.

'Couldn't you get it into the case?' he said when they were in the small room that was darkened by the drooping bodies of the leaves of the fig tree. 'That colour marks easily.'

'That's why I took the cab.'

She watched her husband's eyes as she posed, her own eyes getting larger and larger, searching him for praise.

'It wants the right shoes,' she said. 'I saw some as we came back just now, in Walton's.'

She looked at him and the ghost of her sister's wheedling attitude came into her head as she let it droop just a little to one side.

'And my hair done properly. It blew about in the taxi. Jim was at the window all the time.'

Her husband's eyeballs glistered with what looked like tears.

'You're not thinking of keeping it for yourself?' he said, his face buckling into smiles that she knew were not smiles at all.

'Why not?' she said, understanding him. 'There's eighty pounds worth in the case there.'

'You're rich,' he said.

She opened the case.

'Look,' she said.

'You'd better get it off, you'll mark it cooking,' he said, and went out of the room.

From her bedroom she saw him in the back garden spraying his roses and brushing the green fly off with his finger. He was shaking the syringe to see if there was a drop more in it and she heard him ask the boy if he had been playing with the thing and wasting the liquid.

She gave a last look at herself in the mirror. She despised her husband. She remembered the look of admiration on the face of the man in her sister's flat. She took off the dress and pulled her woollen one out of the case and put it on. The golden woman had gone.

That evening as they sat at their meal, her husband was silent. He grunted at her account of the visit. She did not tell him she had been called "the dressmaker". Her husband was sulking. He was sulking about the dress. She tried to placate him by criticising her sister.

There was a man there, someone she picked up on the 'plane. She was trying to get rid of him because this man with all the property, Mr Williams, was expected. I don't envy her. She lives in a cage. Two burglaries they've had.'

'They're insured.' His first words.

She could still feel some of the gold of the dress on her skin, but as she went on about her sister, the grey meanness which in some way was part of her life with her husband, which emanated from him and which, owing to the poverty of her life as a girl, seemed to her like a resource – this meanness crept over her and coated her once more.

'And you talk of wearing the dress of a woman like that,' he said. And then the boy said, with his mouth full of potato:

'The man took Auntie's brooch off the table. I saw him. The pin was sticking out of his pocket. I saw it. It tore my best jersey.'

'Tore your jersey!' said her husband.

'What's this?' they both said together, united. And they questioned the child again and again.

Husband and wife studied each other.

'That wasn't a pin,' the father said to the boy.

'No,' said his wife, in her false voice. 'She'd got the brooch on.' And she signalled to her husband, but her husband said to the boy:

'Did he come in the taxi with you?'

'No,' said the boy and his mother together.

'I asked the boy.'

'No,' said the boy.

'Just as well,' he said to his wife. 'You see what they might say when they find out. I told you I don't like you going to that place. You lose your head.'

The next day she packed the gold dress with the rest and sold them all, as usual, to the dealers.

The Skeleton

====

Awful things happen to one every day: they come without warning and – this is the trouble, for who knows? – the next one may be the Great Awful Thing. Whatever that is.

At half past seven, just as the new day came aching into the London sky, the waiter-valet went up in the old-fashioned lift of the service flats with a tray of tea to Mr Clark's flat on the top floor. He let himself in and walked down the long, tiled hallway, through part of Mr Clark's picture collection, into the large sitting-room and, putting the tray down on the desk, drew back the curtains and looked down on the roofs. Arrows of fine snow had shot along the slate, a short sight of the Thames between the buildings was as black as iron, the trees stuck out their branches like sticks of charcoal and a cutting wind was rumbling and occasionally squealing against the large windows. The man wiped his nose and then went off to switch on one bar of the electric fire – he was forbidden to put on two – and moved the tray to a table by the fire. He had often been scolded for putting the tray upon Clark's valuable Chippendale desk, and he looked around to see if anything else was out of place in this gentlemanly room where every flash of polish or glass was as unnerving to him as the flash of old George Clark's glasses.

With its fine mahogany, its glazed bookcases which contained a crack regiment of books on art in dress uniform, its Persian rugs, its bronzes, figurines and silken-seated chairs and deep sofa that appeared never to have been sat on, and on the walls some twenty-five oil-paintings, the room had the air of a private museum. The valet respected the glass. He had often sat for a while at Mr Clark's desk gossiping with one of the maids while he saw to it that she did not touch the bronze and the Chinese figures – 'He won't allow anyone to touch them. They're worth hundreds – thousands,' – and making guesses at what the lot would fetch when the

[711]

old man died. He made these guesses about the property of all the rich old people who lived in the flats.

The girls, an ignorant lot, Irish mainly these days, gaped at the pictures.

'He's left them all to the nation,' the valet would say importantly. He could not disguise his feeling that the poor old nation had a lot to put up with from the rich. He could always get in a sexy word to the maids when they looked at the cylindrical nude with a guitar lying across her canister-like knees. But the other pictures of vegetation – huge fruits, enormous flowers that looked tropical with gross veins and pores on stalk and leaves – looked humanly physical and made him feel sick. The flowers had large evil sucking mouths; there were veined intestinal marrows; there was a cauliflower like a gigantic brain that seemed to swell as you looked at it. Nature, to this painter, was a collection of clinical bodies and looked, as Seymour said, 'Nood.' The only living creature represented – apart from the cylindrical lady – was a fish, but it, too, was over-sized and gorged. Its scales, minutely enumerated, gave Seymour "the pip". It was hung over the central bookcase.

'It doesn't go with the furniture,' Seymour had often said. The comforting thing to him was that, at any rate, the collection could not move and get at him. Like the books, the pictures, too, were cased behind glass.

'All by the same man. Come into the bedroom. Come on. And don't touch anything there because he'll notice. He sees everything,' he'd say.

In the bedroom he would show the girls the small oil-painting of the head of a young man with almost white hair standing on end, and large blue eyes.

'That's the bloke,' the valet would say. 'He did it himself. Self-portrait. John Flitestone – see, the name's at the bottom – cut his throat. You watch – his eyes follow you,' he would say, steering the girl. 'He used to come here with the old man.'

'Oh,' the girls were apt to gasp.

'Stop it, Mr Seymour,' they added, taken off their guard.

'Years ago,' Seymour said, looking pious after the pinch he'd given them.

The valet left the room and went down the passage to George Clark's bedroom. Carpet stopped at the door of the room. Inside the room the curtains were blowing, the two sparse rugs lifting in the draught on the polished floor and snow spitting on the table beside the bed. He caught the curtains and drew them back and tried to shut the heavy window. The room contained a cheap yellow wardrobe and chest of drawers which old George Clark had had since he was a boy. The sitting-room was luxurious but his bedroom was as bleak as a Victorian servant's. On a very narrow iron bedstead he lay stiff as a frozen monk and still as a corpse, so paper thin as to look bodiless, his wiry black hair, his wiry black moustache and his greenish face and cold red nose showing like a pug's over the sheet. It sneered in sleep.

'Seven-thirty, sir. Terrible morning,' he said. There was no answer. 'By God,' the valet said after a pause, 'the old man's dead.' In death – if that was what it was – the face on the pillow looked as if it could bite. Then the old man gave a snuffle.

The old man opened a wicked eye.

'The old bastard,' murmured the valet. Often the old boy had terrified and tricked him with his corpse-like look. It was Clark's opening victory in a day, indeed a life, devoted to victory. Then he woke up fully, frightened, reaching for his glasses, to see Seymour's blood-coloured face looking down at him.

'What?' George Clark said. And then the valet heard him groan. These groans were awful.

'Oh my God!' George Clark groaned, but spoke the words in a whisper.

'It's a terrible morning. Shall I put on the fire?'

'No.' The old man sat up.

The valet sighed. He went and fetched a cup of tea.

'You'll need this,' he put on his bullying voice. 'Better drink it hot in here. You'd better have your lunch here today. Don't you go to the club. It's snowing, the wind's terrible.'

George Clark got out of bed in his flannel pyjamas. He stepped barefooted to the window, studying the driving grey sky, the slant of snow and the drift of chimney smoke.

'Who closed the window?' he said.

'Oh dear,' said the valet to himself, 'now he's going to begin. The snow was coming in, Mr Clark. You'll get pneumonia. Please, sir.'

Clark was upright and tall. His small head jerked when he talked, on a long, wrinkled neck. His voice was naturally drawling but shortness of

breath was in conflict with the drawl and the sounds that came out were
jerky, military and cockerel-like. At eighty-two he looked about sixty,
there was hardly any grey in his moustache, the bridge of his gold-framed
glasses cut into his red nose. Seymour who was fifty was humped and
lame and looked seventy. In a fight old George would win and he gave
a sniff that showed he knew it. In fact, he got up every day to win;
Seymour knew that and accepted it.

What reduced him to misery was that the old man would *explain* his
victories. He was off on one now.

'No, I won't get pneumonia,' old George snapped. 'You see,
Seymour, it's a north wind. The north wind doesn't touch me. There's
no fat on me, I'm all bones. I'm a skeleton, there's nothing for it to bite
on.'

'No, sir,' said Seymour wretchedly. Ten to one George Clark would
now mention his family. He did.

'My father was thin, so was my grandfather, we're a thin family. My
youngest sister – she's seventy-eight – she's all bones like me.'

Oh God (Seymour used to moan to himself), I forgot – he's got a
sister! Two of them! He moved to get out of the room, but the old man
followed him closely, talking fast.

'One day last week I thought we were going to catch it, oh yes. Now
we're going to get it, I said! Awful thing! That clean white light in the
sky, stars every night, everything clear, everything sparkling. I saw it and
said, Oh no! No, no. I don't like this, oh no.'

He had now got Seymour in the doorway.

'You see – I know what *that* means.'

'Yes, sir.'

'East wind,' said George victoriously.

'That's it, sir.'

'Ah, then you've got to look out, Seymour. Oh yes. Awful business.
That's what finishes old people. Awful thing.' He drove Seymour forward
into the sitting-room and went to this window, studying the sky, and
sniffed two or three times at it.

'We're all right, Seymour. You see, I was right. It's in the north. I shall
have lunch at the club. Bring my cup in here. Why did you take it to the
bedroom?'

[714]

It was a cold flat. George Clark took a cold bath, as he had done ever since his schooldays. Then he ate a piece of toast and drank a second cup of tea and looked eagerly to see what was annoying in the papers – some new annoyance to add to a lifetime's accumulation of annoyances. It was one of the calamities of old age that one's memory went and one forgot a quite considerable number of exasperations and awful things in which, contrary to general expectation, one had been startlingly right. This forgetting was bad – as if one were the Duke of Wellington and sometimes forgot one had won the Battle of Waterloo.

In fact, George sat in comfort in a flat packed with past rows, annoyances and awful things, half-forgotten. It was an enormous satisfaction that many of his pictures annoyed the few people who came to see him nowadays. The Flitestones annoyed violently. They had indeed annoyed the nation to such an extent that, in the person of a "nasty little man" called Gaiterswell, the nation had refused them. (Seymour was wrong there.) George was very proud of this: his denunciation of Gaiterswell was one of the major victories of his life. George had been the first to buy Flitestones and even Flitestone himself, and had warned the vain and swollen-headed young man against Gaiterswell, years and years ago.

'Modish, Jack, he's merely modish. He'll drop you when it suits him.'

At twelve o'clock George walked across the Park to one of his clubs. He belonged to three. The Park was empty. He blew across it like a solitary, late leaf. The light snow was turning Whitehall black, and spat on his gold glasses; he arrived, a little breathless, but ready to deal with that bugbear of old men: protective sympathy.

'George! You ought not to be out on a day like this!' several said. One put his arm round his shoulder. They were a sneezing and coughing lot with slack affectionate faces, and friendly overburdened bellies, talking of snowed-up roads, late trains and scrambles for taxis.

'You *walked* through this! Why didn't you make your chauffeur bring you?'

'No car.'

'Or a cab?'

'Fares have gone up. I'm too mean.'

'Or a bus?'

'Oh no, no, you see,' said George glittering at them. 'I don't know if I told you' – he had told them innumerable times – 'when you're brought up by a rich brute of a father, as I was – oh yes, he was very rich – you get stingy. I'm very stingy. I must have told you about my father. Oh well, now, there's a story,' he began eagerly. But the bar was crowded; slow to move, George Clark found his listener had been pushed away and had vanished. He stood suddenly isolated in his autobiography.

'Oh God,' he groaned loudly, but in a manner so sepulchral and private that people moved respectfully away. It was a groan that seemed to come up from the earth, up from his feet, a groan of loneliness that was raging and frightening to the men around him. He had one of those moments which, he had to admit, were much commoner than they used to be, when he felt dizzy; when he felt he was lost among unrecognisable faces, without names, alone, in the wrong club, at the wrong address even, with the tottering story of his life, a story which he was offering or, rather, throwing out as a life-line, for help. His hand shook as he finished his glass of sherry. The moment passed and, recovering and trembling, he aged as he left the bar and crossed the hall to the dining-room, saying aloud to himself, in his fighting drawl: 'Now, now, now, we must be careful.'

The side tables were already taken but there were gaps at the two long tables. George stood blinking at the battle field. He had in the last years resigned from several clubs. Sometimes it was because of bridge, central heating, ventilation, smoking, about house committees, food and servants, usually over someone who, unknowingly, had become for a period uncommonly like the Arch Enemy, but who turned out to be no more than an understudy for the part. After a year or so George would rejoin the club. For him the dining-room was one more aspect of the general battle field. Where should he place his guns? Next to Doyle? No, he was "a Roman". George hated "Romans". He hated "Protestants' too. He was an atheist who never found anyone sufficiently atheistical. George was tired of telling Doyle how he had happened to be in Rome in '05 staying with one of the great families ('she was a cousin of the Queen's') and had, for a year, an unparalleled inside view of what was going on in the Vatican. 'Oh yes, you see, a Jesuit, one of their relations, became a great friend and exposed the whole hocus-pocus to me. You see, I have often been in a position to know more of what is going on than most people. I was close to Haig in the war.' There was Gregg, the painter; but it was intolerable to listen to academicians; there was Foster who had been opposed to Munich and George could not stand that. There was Macdonald – but Scots climb. Look at Lang! There was Jefferies, such a bore about divorce reform: the bishops want it but daren't say so. 'I told the Archbishop in this club that the moment you drag in God you lose your reason. My mother ought to have got a divorce. You should have seen his face. Oh no, he didn't like it. Not a bit.'

George looked at the tops of heads and the table-loads of discarded enemies, casualties of his battles, with a grin. At last, glancing around him, he chose a seat beside a successful, smirking pink man of fifty whose name he had forgotten. 'Pretty harmless,' muttered George. 'He thinks Goya a great painter when we all know he is just a good painter of the second rank. Ah, he's eating oysters.' This stirred a memory. The man was talking to a deaf editor but on the other side there were empty chairs. It was against George's military sense to leave an exposed flank but the chance of attacking the club oysters was too good to miss.

'I see you've risked the oysters. I never eat oysters in this club,' said George, sitting down. 'Poisonous. Oh yes, yes – didn't I tell you? Oh you see, it was an awful thing, last year . . .'

'Now George' said the man. 'You told me that story before.'

'Did I? Nothing in that' sniffed George. 'I always repeat myself, you see I make a point of telling my stories several times. I woke up in the night . . .'

'Please George,' said the man more sternly. 'I want to enjoy my lunch.'

'Oh ah, ah, ah,' said George sniffing away. 'I'll watch your plate. I'll warn you if I see a bad one.'

'Oh, really George!' said the young man.

'You're interrupting our conversation, George,' the editor called across. 'I was telling Trevor something very interesting about my trip to Russia.'

'I doubt if it is interesting,' said George in a loudish whisper to the other man. 'Interesting! I never found a Whig interesting.'

'Dear George is old. He talks too much,' said the deaf editor speaking louder than he knew.

'Not a lot of rot,' said George in a loud mutter.

[717]

'What's he say?' said the deaf editor.

'You see,' George continued to interrupt. 'I talk a lot because I live alone. I probably talk more than anyone in this club and I am more interesting than most people. You see, I've often been in a position to know more than most people here. I was in Rome in '05 . . .'

But George looked restlessly at the vacant chair beside him. 'I hope,' he said, suddenly nervous, 'some awful bore is not going to sit here. You never know who, who – oh no, oh no, no . . .'

It happened as simply as that, when one was clean off one's guard. Not a single awful thing: but the Great Awful Thing. He saw a pair of small, polished, sunburned hands with soft black hair on them pull back the chair and then a monkeyish man of seventy, with wretched eyes and an academic heaving up of the right shoulder, sat beside him.

'Good morning, George,' uttering the name George as if it contained a lifetime's innuendo.

'Oh God,' George said.

The man was the Arch Enemy and in a form he had never expected. Out of the future he should have come, a shape at a slowly opening door, pausing there, blocking it, so that one could not get out. Who he would be, what he would be, was unknown: he was hidden in next week, next year, as yet unborn.

But this man was known. He had sneaked in not from the future, but from the past. It was Gaiterswell.

'Just the man I want to speak to,' said Gaiterswell, picking up the menu in hands that George could only think of as thieving.

'I didn't know you were a member,' George choked out in words like lead shot.

'Just elected.'

George gave a loud sniff.

'Monstrous,' said George, but, holding on to manners, said it under his breath. He grasped his table napkin, ready to fly off and, at once, resign. It was unbelievable that the Committee, knowing his feelings as they must do, had allowed this man in. Gaiterswell who had stolen Flitestone from him: who had turned down Flitestone; who had said in *The Times* – in a letter above all – that George's eccentric tastes had necessarily taught him nothing about the chemical composition of oil-paint; Gaiterswell of the scandalous official appointment!

George had forgotten these Waterloos; but now the roar of them woke up in his brain. The fusillades he had let off in committees were heard again. The letters to *The Times* were shot off once more. Gaiterswell had said there were too many "gentlemen" in the art world. It was a pity (he was known to have said), it was a pity that the Empire had gone and there were no more natives for them to pester. George had replied, around the clubs, that the "nasty little man" suffered glaringly from merit and the path of the meritorious was strewn with the bodies they had kicked down the ladder as they climbed.

After he had said things like this, George considered that Gaiterswell was dead. The body could no doubt be found still lying, after twenty-five years, in that awful office of his with the fake Manet – of course it was a fake – on the wall.

'Just the man I want to speak to,' Gaiterswell said to the menu. (You noticed he never looked you in the face.)

'Wants to speak to me. For no good reason,' George murmured loudly to the man sitting on the other side of him.

'I bet you won't guess who came to see me the other day,' Gaiterswell said. 'Gloria Archer, Stokes that was. She's married to a Frenchman called Duprey. You remember her? What are you eating? The pie! Is it any good? She's got a lot of poor Jack Flitestone's letters. She's short of money. You wrote the *Memoir*, didn't you, George? Charming little book, charming. I told her to drop in on you. I said you'd be delighted to see her.'

George was about to put a piece of pie into his mouth. He put his fork down. He was shaking. He was choking.

'Drop in!' he said, astounded. 'Drop in?'

'Look here,' he called out, pushing his chair from the table. 'Oh, this is monstrous.' And he called to one of the waiters who rushed past and ignored him. 'Look here, I say, why do we have to have meat like this in this club . . . It's uneatable . . . I shall find the Secretary . . .'

And getting up, with his table napkin waving from his hand, he hurried to the end of the room, the light tossing in his glasses, and then, after wild indecision, left the room.

'Where has George Clark gone?' said an old gentleman who had been sitting opposite. 'He never finishes a meal.'

'It's his teeth', the deaf editor said.

George had made for the morning-room of the club where he circled like a dog.

'What manners!' he said to the portraits of dead members on the wall. Happier than he, they were together, he was alone. He was older than most of them had been and, with a flick of ironic pride which never quite left him in any distress, he could not but notice that he was rather better connected and had more inside knowledge than most of them had had. He addressed them again:

'Drop in! What manners! I shall resign.'

The Arch Enemy had appeared in a fashion unpredictable: from the past – and now he saw – not as a male but as a female. Gloria Archer – as he had always said: 'What a name!' It recalled (as he firmly pronounced it), the "Kinema", striking a blow for classical scholarship. Her portrait, if one could call it that, was in his sitting-room, cylindrical and naked. It had been there for over twenty-five years, with the other Flitestones, and he had long ago stopped remembering her or even Flitestone himself as human beings he had known. They were not life; they were art – not even art now, but furniture of his self-esteem. He had long ago closed his mind to them as persons. They had become fossilisations of mere anecdote. Now that damn little shot-up official, Gaiterswell who had been polished off long ago, had brought first Gloria back to life, and the name of Gloria had brought Flitestone back. The seals of anecdote were broken; one of the deepest wounds of George's existence was open and raw again. A woman's work; it was Gloria who had shown how dangerous Flitestone was to him: it was Gloria who had shown him the chaos of his heart.

He left the morning-room, got his hat and coat, buttoned himself up to the neck, and walked out into the street where the snow was coming in larger shots. At once he felt something like a film of ice form between his shirt and his bony chest and he stepped back afraid.

'No, no,' he said very loudly and passers-by raised their ducked heads thinking he was talking to them. But he was speaking to the wind: it had gone round to the east.

[720]

Seymour met him in the lift at the flat. He smelled of beer.

'You shouldn't have gone out, sir,' said Seymour.

Seymour looked murderous with self-righteousness.

George sat down on his sofa, frightened and exhausted. He was assaulted by real memories and was too weak to fend them off: he had felt frightened to death – he now admitted – in that so enjoyable 1914 war. Flitestone's pictures took on life. Flitestone, too. The cliché vanished – 'Not a bad minor painter, like a good many others ruined by the school of Paris' – the dangerous Flitestone appeared. He saw again the poor boy from a Scottish mill town, with gaunt cheeks, light blue eyes and almost white hair that stood up like a dandelion clock – ("took hours brushing it, always going to expensive hairdressers"). A pedant, too, with morbid and fanatical patience: it took him longer to paint a picture than anyone George Clark had ever known; the young man was rather deaf which made him seem to be an unworldly, deeply innocent listener, but there was – as George Clark saw – nothing innocent about him, there was a mean calculating streak – ('After all he realised I was a rich man', George swaggered) and he was soon taken up by wealthy people. He was clever and made them laugh. He was in trouble all the time with women, chasing them like a maniac and painting them with little heads and large bottoms, like pairs of enormous pink poppies.

('Now, there's a bloody fine bottom, George.')

Very annoying he was, too, especially when he got into Society. That was one thing George Clark knew all about and to be told about Lord This or That or a lot of duchesses, by a crude young genius from the slums, was infuriating.

'He's got five bloody great castles . . .'

'Only one. Forstairs and Aldbaron belong to his half-brother who married Glasnevin's sister. Jack, I wish you wouldn't pick your teeth at meals. I can't bear it. It's such frightful manners.'

'Lord Falconer does. He's got a gold toothpick.'

But these squabbles were merely annoying. Flitestone was the only human being George ever loved. Jealously loved. He was his prize and his possession. And the boy liked him. Here was the danger. George had dreaded to be liked. You lose something when people like you. You are in danger of being stripped naked and of losing a skin. With Flitestone he felt – ah there was the danger: he did not know what he felt except that it was passion. He could listen to him for hours. For eleven years, George had the sensation that he had married late in life someone who, fortunately, did not exist, and that Flitestone was their fantastic, blindly-invented son. Like a son he clawed at George's bowels.

His love affairs? Well, one had to avert the eye. They were, nevertheless, an insurance against George's instant jealous fear: that Flitestone would marry. The thought of that made George shrink. 'Marriage will ruin you' – he nagged at it. And that was where Gloria came in.

When Gaiterswell spoke of Gloria, a shot of jealous terror and satisfaction had gone through George. She bored him, of course. Yet in the last years of their friendship, Flitestone's insane love for this girl who would have nothing to do with him was the real guarantee. George even admired the young girl for the cruelty of her behaviour, for being so complete an example of everything that made women impossible. He was so absorbed in this insurance that he forgot the obvious: that Gloria might marry. She did. In a month on the rebound, Flitestone had married some milky, student girl whose first act was to push her husband into the influence of Gaiterswell. For Gaiterswell was the nation. A breach with George was inevitable.

He went to his desk and started writing to Gaiterswell. *I shall be obliged if you will inform Miss Stokes, Mrs Archer or whatever her name is, that I have no desire to meet her or enter into correspondence* . . . His hand shook. He could not continue.

'Awful business' was all he could say. The Arch Enemy had deprived him even of the power to talk to himself.

The east wind. Impossible to go out to any of his clubs that night. After dinner, he poured himself a very large whisky and left the bottle, uncorked, on his desk – a sinister breach of habit, for he always locked up his drink.

'I always reckon to be rather drunk every evening,' George used to say. It was a gesture to the dignity of gentlemanly befuddlement. But now, he felt his legs go; he was rapidly very drunk. He tottered to his bedroom, dropped his clothes on the floor and got into bed with his shirt, collar and tie on and was asleep at once. Often at night he had enjoyable dreams of social life at Staff HQ in the 1914 war. Haig, Ronnie Blackwater and others would turn up. A bit of gunfire added an interest: but this night he had a frightful dream. He dreamed that at the club, before all the members, he had kissed the teeth of George the Fifth.

This woke him up and he saw that it was daylight. His heart was racing. He could not find his glasses. He got out of bed. The room was getting light; he wondered if he were dead and he pulled back the curtain and what he saw convinced him that he was. The snow had stopped, the sky was hard and clear, and the sun was coming up in a gap between two high buildings. It was still low and this made it an enormous raw yellow football that someone had kicked there, without heat or radiance yet. It looked like a joke or some aimless idea; one more day (George realised as he became more conscious) had begun its unsolicited course over the blind slates of the city. 'Old men are lonely,' he often said but now he saw a greater loneliness than his own.

'I want those letters.' The desire came out before he could stop it. 'I must see Gloria. I must get Gaiterswell's dirty little hands off them.' He was longing for the past. Then he saw he was wearing his day shirt, his collar and tie.

'Oh God,' he said. And he got into his pyjamas and back into bed before Seymour should catch him.

At half past seven Seymour let himself into the flat. His demeanour was of one whose expectations were at last being fulfilled. He had warned several of the old people in the flats about the weather; he had seen Mr Clark come back yesterday exhausted when, against all advice, he had gone to the club. Reaching the sitting-room, Seymour saw a decanter of whisky standing on the table. This was a sight that he had thirsted for for years and he gazed at it entranced, unbelieving and with suspicion. He listened. There was no sound. Seymour made a grab at the decanter and took a long swig, letting a drop rest on his chin while he replaced what he had drunk with water from the hot-water pot on the tea-tray. He stood still trying to lick the drip off his chin but, failing, he wiped it off with his sleeve and, after looking at the letters on Mr Clark's desk, walked confidently to Mr Clark's bedroom.

'Good morning, Seymour. Half past seven,' said George. He was sitting up in bed. Seymour heard this reversal of their usual greeting with alarm.

He stood well away and slopped the tea in its saucer. He was even more alarmed to see Mr Clark had switched on his own fire and that his clothes were dropped in a muddle on the floor. George caught his glance and got out of bed to show that he was properly dressed and stood with one foot on his rumpled jacket. Panic and the whisky brought guilt into Seymour's face: he suddenly remembered he had made a disastrous mistake. He had forgotten to give Mr Clark a message.

'A lady rang last night, sir, when you were at dinner.'

'A lady – why didn't you tell me?'

'The head waiter took the call. He said you were out. She didn't leave a name.'

To distract an angry question, Seymour looked at the clothes on the floor.

'Dear, dear, dear, what a way to leave a suit.' He pulled the trouser leg from under George's foot and held the trousers up. 'Look at it.'

'What lady?' said George.

'She didn't leave a name. She said she'd drop in.'

'Drop in!' The horrible phrase.

'That's what she said, she'd drop in.'

'Who was it?'

'I don't know, sir. I never took the message. I told you – it was the new head waiter.'

'Don't stand there waving my trousers about like a fool, Seymour. It's your business to know.'

'They're all foreigners downstairs.'

George had his glasses on now and Seymour stepped away. In his panic he took a gamble.

'Might have been Miss Stokes,' he said. He had read the name on George's unfinished letter. The gamble was a mistake.

'Archer!' cried George. 'Where is the head waiter?' And hurrying to the sitting-room, he started banging the telephone. There was no answer.

'What time do the servants come on?' he called to Seymour. Seymour came in and listened to George banging away. He was very scared now. He dreaded that the head waiter would answer.

'They come when it suits them, now. They suit themselves,' said Seymour putting on a miserable manner. And then he got in his blow, the sentence he often used to the old people in the flats when they got difficult. It always silenced them.

'Might just as well sell the place,' he said.

'Sell!' George was silenced, too. He stared at Seymour who straightened himself and said, accusingly:

'Where's the jacket of this? Dear, dear, I suppose that's on the floor too.' And walked out, leaving George shivering where he stood.

'Sell?' said George.

On a long ledge of the stained building opposite, thirty or forty dirty pigeons were huddled, motionless, with puffed-out feathers, too cold to fly.

'Out on the street! Homeless.' Like Stebbing-Walker crippled and deaf who had married Kempton's half-sister – she was a Doplestone – and now lay in his nursing home, or Ronnie Blackwater who sat paralysed in the army infirmary. Sell – it was the awful word anxiously whispered in the lift by the old ladies, as they went up and down to their meals. Was the place being sold? Were the rents going up? Were they going to pull the whole place down? For months there would be silence; everyone breathed again; then once more, mostly from Seymour, the rumours began. Fear made them sly and they believed Seymour rather than the management. He moved among them like a torment.

George Clark went down early to luncheon, to get in before the restaurant vanished; rushed upstairs afterwards to barricade himself, so to speak, in his flat. There were few pigeons on the ledge now. What? Had tenancy gone out of Nature too? At seven o'clock he went to dinner. Instead of the two or three tables of old doll-like couples in the middle of the room, there was a large table at which ten large young men, loud and commercial, were laughing together. One or two had brief-cases with them. Obviously this was the group who were going to pull down the flats. George raced through the meal, feeling that, possibly, even before the apples and custard, he might be sitting out alone on a vacant site. George's fighting spirit revived over his wine. 'Ha,' he sneered at them as he left the table and went to the lift, 'I'll be dead before you can turn me out.'

The lift wheezed and wobbled upwards, making the sound of all the elderly throats in the building. He was startled to see the door of his flat open and, for a moment, thought the men had broke in already; but Seymour was standing in the cold hall. His heavy face looked criminal. In an insinuating, lugubrious voice he said:

'The lady's waiting to see you, sir.'

'Seymour, I've told you, never . . .' George hurried to his sitting-room. Gloria was standing by his desk reading the letter he had begun so often. *'Dear Gaiterswell, I would have thought that common decency . . .'*

'Oh, oh, no, no, I say,' said George greeting her, but was stopped.

A fur coat and a close-fitting black hat like a faded turban with brass colour hair sticking out of it rushed at him, a hot powdery face kissed him with a force that made him crack in his joints like a stick.

'Oh George, darling, I dropped in.' Gloria shouted at him through large stained teeth and laughed.

All he could see was these teeth and lipstick and blue eyes and she was laughing and laughing as she wiped the lipstick off his face.

'Oh well,' he said, 'they're selling the place . . .' Then she stood back in a pair of cracking shoes.

'George,' she said in a Cockney voice. 'It's marvellous. You haven't changed at all. You're not a day older.'

And she let her fur coat fall open and slip back on her shoulders and he saw the cigarette ash and one or two marks on the bosom of her black dress. She was a big woman.

'Oh,' George recovered and gave a victorious sniff. 'I'm eighty-two.'

'You're a boy,' she cried.

'Oh no, don't think I'm deceived by that sort of talk – er, well, you see I mean . . .' George nearly smiled. By his reckoning she was in her fifties and he could see what she wanted, what all women wanted, compliments. He was not, at his age, going to fall for that old game. She sat down on the sofa so as to show off her fine legs.

'Did you recognise me?' she asked.

'Oh well, you know . . .'

'Oh come on, George.'

'I dare say I – er – might have done. You see, I forget names and faces, it's an awful business . . . old people . . . they're selling this place . . .'

'Oh you crusty old thing. What do you mean – selling?' she said. 'You always were crusty. I knew you'd be at dinner, so I got that man to bring me up. What is his name? Is he all right? I didn't feel very comfortable with him in the lift.'

She moved her body and pouted.

'When your lady friends call you ought to tell them to keep an eye – well, George, how are you? How many years is it? It must be twenty-five. You weren't living here then.'

'It was the beginning of the war,' said George, but he could not remember. He had discarded memory as useless a long time back. He had seen her a lot, yet one of his few clear recollections was of sitting with Flitestone in the old Café Royal waiting for her to come in and arguing with him that she was not a woman who would stick to any man: he remembered her really as an absence.

'You've put on weight,' he said. But she hadn't changed much.

'Yes,' she said. 'I like it, don't you?'

The Cockney voice came warm and harsh out of the wide mouth. Her skin was rougher and was now looser on her bones but still had a wide-pored texture and the colourlessness which Flitestone used to say was like linen. One spot of colour in her cheeks and Flitestone would probably never have fallen for her. 'She's like a canvas. I'd like to paint *on* her,' Flitestone used to say to George. He did remember. The bare maleness of face on a girlish body was still there on the body of the full woman.

George stood, shaking at the sight of her.

'You're still an old bachelor, George?' she said. 'You didn't marry?'

'No,' said George with a grin of victory. 'You see, in my day, one never met any girls, everyone was chaperoned, you couldn't speak and we had no one to the house, oh no, my father wouldn't allow anyone, and then the war, and all that. I told you about my father, oh, now, there's a story ...'

'Oh, I've been. Three times,' she cut in, parading herself.

'Oh three! Well, that's interesting. Or I suppose it is. It doesn't surprise me. Please sit down. Let me get you a drink. Now let me see, keys. I have to keep it locked, well with the servants it isn't fair to leave drink about. Ah, in this pocket. I keep them here.'

[727]

He fussed at the cupboard and brought out a bottle of whisky and a bottle of sherry.

'Oh gin please,' she said. 'Can I help?'

'No, no, it's here. I keep it at the back. I'll put this bottle down here, yes, that's the way . . .' he chattered to himself.

Gloria walked across the room to look at the pictures, but stopped instead to look at her reflection in the glass of the bookcases and to rearrange the frilled neck of her dress. Then she looked up at the large picture of the fish.

'George! You've got my fish.'

'Ah yes, the fish. He painted four fish pictures. One is in the Tate, one is . . . now where is it?'

'*My* fish, I mean', she said. 'Don't you remember, it's the one I made you carry to Jack's place and the paper came off . . .'

'No, no,' said George.

'Yes, you must remember. You're not still cross, are you? You looked so funny.'

She took a deep breath in front of the picture, inhaling it. 'I don't know why we didn't eat it.'

'Ah yes. Awful business. Café Royal,' said George, a memory coming back.

She turned to the cylindrical woman in a shift, with enormous column-like legs, who was playing a guitar, and looked with flirtatious annoyance at it, paying off an old score.

'That's me,' she said.

'Oh no,' said George sarcastically. He was beginning to enjoy himself. 'It was done in Paris.'

'It's me,' said Gloria. 'But they're Violet's legs.' Gloria turned abruptly away, insulted, and taking her drink from George went back to the sofa. Once more she gave a large sigh and gazed with admiring calculation at the room. She leaned her head to one side and smiled at George.

'You are a dear, George. How cosy you are. It's wonderful to see old friends,' said Gloria sweetly. 'It brings it all back.'

She got up and put more gin in her drink and then leaned over his chair as she passed him and kissed the top of his head.

'Dear George,' she said and sat down. 'And you live here, all alone!

Well, George, I've brought the letters, all Jack's letters to me. I didn't know I had them. It's a funny thing: François found them, my husband, he's French. We live in France and he has an antique business. He said "They ought to fetch a bit," you know what the French are about money, so I remembered Monkey . . .'

'Monkey?'

'Monkey Gaiterswell, I always used to call him Monkey. We used,' said Gloria very archly, 'to be friends and he said "Sell them to America". Do you think he's right – I mean Monkey said you'd written a book about Jack and you'd know? He said I'd get five hundred pounds for them. I mean they're all about painting, famous people, the whole circle . . .'

Ah, it was a plot!

'Five hundred,' said George. 'You won't get five pounds. No one has ever heard of Flitestone in America. None of his pictures went there.'

'But the letters are very *personal*, George. Naturally you're in them.'

'I doubt it.'

'Oh you are. I remember. I know you are. You were his best friend. And you wrote so beautifully about him. Monkey says so.'

Obviously there was a plot between Monkey and Gloria.

'I've no doubt they are full of slanders. I should tear them up,' said George shortly.

'George,' she appealed. 'I need the money. François has gone off with some woman and I'm broke. Look.'

She opened her black shopping bag and took out a parcel of crumpled brown paper and put it on George's desk.

'Open it. I'll leave them with you to look at. You'll see.'

'Oh no. I can't do that,' said George. 'I don't care to be responsible. It leads to all sorts of awful business.'

'Read them. Open it. Here.'

She put down her empty glass and untied the string. A pile of letters of all sizes in Flitestone's large hand, each word formed carefully like the words of a medieval manuscript, slid on to George's desk.

George was sitting there and he withdrew his hand so as not to touch the letters. They brought Jack Flitestone into the room. George wanted them. He knew now what was meant when she said *he* was in them. It was not what *she* meant. The letters contained the, to him, affronting fact that he had not after all succeeded in owning his own life and closing it to others; that he existed in other people's minds and that all people dissolved in this way, becoming fragments of one another, and nothing in themselves. He had known that once, when Jack Flitestone had brought him to life. He knew, too, that he had once lived or nearly lived. Flitestone, in his dangerous way, had lived for him. One letter had fallen to the floor and Gloria read aloud:

> '. . . *Archie's car broke down outside Medley and we didn't get to Gorse until the middle of dinner. La Tarantula was furious and I offered to eat in the kitchen and the Prime Minister who was already squiffy . . .*'

'There you are, George. The Prime Minister,' cried Gloria.

George took the letter in the tips of his fingers and Gloria helped herself to another drink.

'Jack was an awful snob,' said George, but admiringly, putting the letter back. 'No manners, writing about people when he was a guest.'

'Oh come off it, George,' said Gloria, picking out one or two more. 'You know, I haven't read them for years. Actually Jack frightened me. So morbid. Here's one. Oh, this is good. It's about the time you and Jack went to Chartres. The tie drawer, George!'

The new blow from the past struck him. He remembered it: the extraordinary thing about small French hotels: they never gave you a drawer for your ties. He took the letter and read:

> '. . . *George surpassed himself this morning . . .*'

He had walked down the corridor to Flitestone's room and knocked.

'Here. I say, Jack. I want to speak to you.'

'What is it?' Flitestone called. Ordinary manners, one would have thought, would at least have led Flitestone to open the door, Jack was so *thoughtless.*

'Jack, Jack, I've no tie drawer in my room.'

Flitestone came to the door naked and pushed a drawer from his wardrobe into George's hand.

'Take mine.'

'Jack, here I say, dear fellow. Chambermaid.'

'Umph,' said George to Gloria. 'Inaccurate.'

He reached out for the next letter she offered to him. He looked at it distantly, read a few lines and stopped.

'Here, I say, I can't read this. It is to you,' he sneered a little.

'They're all to me.'

'Yes, but this is – er – private, personal.'

George looked quizzically and sternly at her; it was "not done" to look into another's moral privacy. It was also shameless and woman-like to show letters like these to him. But the phrases he had run into head-on had frightened him, they brought back to him the danger he had once lived in: his heart had been invaded, he had been exposed once to a situation in which the question of a victory or a defeat vanished.

'You see,' he said turning his head away nervously from her as he handed back the letter to her.

Gloria took it. She put on her glasses and read. Immediately she smiled. The smile became wider and she gave pleased giggles. She was blushing.

'Jack ought to have been a writer,' she said. 'I hated his paintings. It's quite true what he says, George. I was very attractive. I had marvellous legs.'

She turned to look at her reflection in the glass of the bookcase and took her fur coat off and posed. Gradually she lifted her skirt above her knees and pleased by what she saw, she lifted her skirt higher, putting one leg forward, then the other.

'Look, George,' she said. 'Look. They're still good. There aren't many women of my age with legs like these. They're damn fine, George. You've never seen a pair like that.' She turned sideways and pranced with pleasure.

'Gloria, please,' said George sharply.

But she marched over to the picture of the woman with cylindrical legs and said:

'I could have killed him for that. What's the matter with painters? Didn't he have enough to eat when he was a boy? He was always carrying on about his hard times.'

She lowered her dress and sat down to go on reading the letter.

'The pink peony, did you get to that?' she said. 'Really, Jack's ideas! Not very nice, is it? I mean, not in a letter. He wasn't very . . .' she stopped and was sad. 'No,' she checked herself. 'I'll tell you something, George: we only went to bed together once . . .'

'Gloria,' said George in agitation. 'Give me the letter. I'll put it with the others . . .'

She was making Flitestone far too alive.

'It was your fault, George. It was the dinner you gave us that night, the night I bought the fish. You say you don't remember? At the Café Royal. I made you go off to the Café Royal kitchen and get the largest fish they had. I don't know why. I wanted to get rid of you and I thought it would annoy you. I was getting plastered. Don't you remember? I said: "Tell them we want it for our cat. Our cat is enormous. It eats a salmon a day." And Jack kept on saying – we were both drunk – "I want to paint a large salmon. You're bloody stingy, George, you won't buy me a salmon."'

'Awful business,' snapped George. 'Jack never understood money.'

'You remember! Isn't that wonderful?' cried Gloria pulling off her hat and looking into her empty glass.

'You followed us out of the restaurant, all up Shaftesbury Avenue, and he was going to show me his new pictures. You had no tact, George. He was carrying the fish and he suddenly gave it to you and made you carry it and the paper blew off. George,' she said, 'do you mind if I have just a teeny-weeny one? There's a letter about it.'

And she pushed him aside and got at the parcel on his desk.

'I think you've had enough, Gloria.'

'For old times' sake,' said Gloria, filling her glass. She unfolded the parcel again and scattered the letters. George looked at the clock.

'I can't find it,' she said. 'It's here somewhere.'

'Gloria, I don't want drink spilled on my desk. I've forbidden Seymour . . .'

Gloria stopped and, now red in the face, smiled amorously. 'That man?' she said. 'Is he here?'

'Gloria,' said George. 'I'll have to – er – I'll have to – It's eleven o'clock, I . . .'

Gloria replied with dignity.

'Jack had no sense of behaviour. I could see it was spoiling your suit. I begged him, begged him,' she said grandly, 'to carry it himself. I was furious with him. He could see you had an umbrella as well, you always carried one and wore a bowler hat. He said "Stick it on the umbrella." I was terribly upset when he slammed the door in your face when we got to the studio. We had a terrible row and I made him swear to go round to your flat and apologise. It was awful, George. What did you do?'

'I took a cab, of course,' said George.

'Well, I mean, you couldn't leave a salmon in the street,' said Gloria. 'It was a suit like the one you are wearing now, dark grey. That isn't the one, is it? It can't be.'

'Gloria, I am sorry, but . . .'

Gloria frowned.

'I am sure it's there,' she said and went to the letters on the desk again. 'No, not that. Not that,' she began throwing the letters on the floor. 'Ah, here.'

She waved the letter and looked through it in silence until she read aloud:

'. . . *I apologised to George and he said he had left the fish with the hall porter, so I went down there. We had a bit of a row about my low class manners. I said I thought half the salmon in England had been to Eton. He told me to ask Seymour, the hall porter, for it . . .*'

'Inaccurate,' interrupted George. 'Seymour was never hall porter.'

'. . . *I said I have called for the specimen I loaned to Sir George Clark, the marine biologist, who is doing research on spawn . . .*'

'You see, George,' she said. She went back to the sofa. 'Come and sit here, George, don't be so stuffy. We can talk, can't we, after all these years? We are friends. That is what we all need, George, friends. I'm serious, George.' She had tears in her eyes.

'It was wicked of Jack to call you stingy. You gave him money. You bought his pictures.'

'But I *am* stingy,' said George. 'You see, rich people never give their children a penny. We never had anyone to the house at Maddings . . .'

'It was his jealousy,' said Gloria darkly. 'He was jealous of you.'

'Oh well, class envy . . .' George began.

'No, of you and me,' she said. 'Oh yes, George, he really was. That's why he tried to shake you off, that night, that's why we had such terrible scenes ... You were rich ...'

'Don't be ludicrous, Gloria.'

'Letters by every post, pursuing, bombarding me, I couldn't stand it.'

'Nonsense.'

'It isn't nonsense. You were very blind, George. And so you live in this place, alone. Jealous men are so *boring*, George. I've had four. I said "Oh to hell" and I went off to France. Vive de Gaulle! You know?' she said, raising her glass.

'To *les feuilles mortes d'automne*,' she said. 'That's what my husband says.'

He bent to take her glass to prevent her drinking more and she stroked his spiky hair. He put the glass away out of reach.

'That is why Jack married that stupid student girl,' she said in a suddenly sharp calculating voice. 'That broke up you and Jack, didn't it?'

'I don't wish to talk about it,' said George. 'It ruined him. Marriage is the ruin of painters.'

'George, come clean. After all, we all know it. You were in love with him, weren't you?'

There was a silence.

'Weren't you?' she persisted.

He recovered and achieved his worldly drawl.

'Oh I know there's a lot of that sort of thing about, was in my time, too. I paid no attention to it ... Women don't understand talent. I understood Jack's talent. Women ruined it.'

'Jack said you'd never been to bed with a woman in your life,' she said.

'It wasn't possible, it wasn't possible,' said George angrily. 'Not in my day. Not for a gentleman.' And he turned on her. 'I won't be questioned. I should burn those letters. You treated him badly. You killed his imagination. It's obvious in his work.'

He looked at the clock.

'George,' she said. 'You don't mean that. You don't know what you are saying. You were always so sweet to me.'

'I do mean what I said. Read your letters,' said George. And briskly he collected them off the floor and packed them up and tied the parcel. He was going to turn her out now.

She was staring stupidly.

'You don't want them?' she said. 'Monkey said you'd jump at them.'

'You've got one in your hands,' he said. 'No, I won't give a penny for them. I won't be blackmailed.'

Gloria got up to give the letter to him. She could not walk and put her hand on the table beside the sofa. It fell over, carrying her glass with it.

'What's that man Seymour doing in here? Tell him to get out. Out with Seymour,' she suddenly shouted. 'Out. Out. What d'you mean? Stop playing the innocent. You've never lived. That's you, George, that fish?' And she tried to point at the picture.

'Gloria, I won't have this,' shouted George. 'You're drunk.'

'You won't have it? You've never had it. My coat, who's taken that?'

But when she turned she fell heavily on to the sofa, twisted her body, with her skirt above her knees and one majestic leg trailing on the floor.

'Gloria. How dare you! In my house!'

'Darling,' she smiled and fell asleep instantly.

'Women,' George always said, glittering dryly, 'they contribute nothing.' She was contributing a stentorian snore.

He had couples up after dinner sometimes, elderly friends, and you could see how it was: they either couldn't let their husbands speak – poor Caldicott, for instance – or they sat as stupid as puddings. The men aged as they sat: rather them than me. Eighty-two and not a day's illness.

Gloria was contributing more than a snore. She was contributing an enormous haunch, an indecent white thigh – "Really". He would have to cover it. Couldn't she pull her skirt down. Couldn't she be drunk like a – like a lady! She contributed brutality, an awful animality to the room.

He went over and tried to pull her skirt down.

'Gloria,' he shouted.

He couldn't move the skirt. He gave her a shake. It stirred an enormous snore and a voluptuous groan and it seemed that she was going to roll off the sofa on to the floor. He couldn't have women lying on the floor in his flat. He could never get her up. He moved a chair against the sofa.

He sat down and waited. Gaiterswell was responsible for this. In the promiscuous Bohemian set he had lived in, the dirty little man would be used to it.

George could not ring for Seymour. Think of the scandal. She had trapped him. He hated her for what she had done to Jack, driving him out of his mind with jealousy of other men, encouraging him, evading him, never letting go. She, more than his expensive wife, was responsible for Jack's suicide. Gloria had paralysed him. You could see it in his paintings, after they had broken up: the paintings had become automatic, academic, dead, without air, without life. There were ten drawings of that fish. He had become obsessed with it.

It was a death of the heart; of George's heart as well. This body lying in the room was like the brutal body of his father. The old brute with his rages and his passions, his disgraceful affairs with governesses and maids in the very next room to where he slept as a boy – awful business – he would never forget that – the manners! – the shouts, his terrible behaviour to his wife: it had paralysed the whole family. They all hated him so violently, with a violence that so magnetised them all, that none of them had heart for others. He had killed their hearts; not one of them had been able to love. For a moment, George left these exact memories and went off into anecdotes about how he fought back against his father, sniffing triumphantly, as he did at the club. But the sight of Gloria there smashed the anecdotal in him. He recognised that he had *not* fought back and had not been victorious. He had risked nothing. He had been whipped into the life of a timid, self-absorbed scholar.

He poured himself a large whisky. It was gone midnight. Perhaps by the time he checked up on the windows in the flat and saw all the doors were closed, she would wake up. He carried his glass to his bedroom and put it by the bedside; and there exhaustion drove him to his habits. He took off his watch and put it on the table. He forgot why he had come into the room. It was not what he intended to do but he was tired, murmuring to himself 'Coat, hanger, shirt, trousers, shoes, socks,' he undressed and shivering he got into bed. He finished his whisky, turned out the light and – Gloria forgotten – he was at once asleep. And at once dreaming he was back in the sitting-room, parcelling the letters, watching her. He dreamed that he called Seymour who got a taxi and they hauled her into it. But as fast as they got her into the cab she was back upstairs on the sofa and his father and Jack were there too, but ignoring him, standing a yard or two away, though he shouted at them to help. And then the awful thing happened. He picked her up himself. He was at a railway station: he could go no farther: he dropped her. With an appalling noise, the enormous body fell just as a train came, steaming, blasting, wheels grinding, a massive black engine, advancing upon him. He gave a shout. It had hit him and crushed him. He was dying. He had had a heart attack. He screamed and he woke up shouting, sitting up in bed.

In the bedroom Gloria was standing in her stockinged feet and her petticoat, holding her skirt in her hand, her hair in disorder.

'What's the matter, George?' she said thickly. George could not speak.

'What is it? I woke up. I heard you shout.' Her breathing was heavy, it was the sound of the engine he had heard. George gaped at her.

'Are you ill?' she said. 'I passed out.'

'I, I, I . . . ,' he could say nothing more. He got out of bed. George was shuddering. 'What's the time?'

'Get into bed. You're freezing. You're ill.' She came over and took him by the arm and he allowed himself to be put back to bed.

'What an ice-box,' she said. She shut the window, switched on the fire.

'I'd better get a doctor,' she said.

'No,' said George. 'I'm all right.' He was panting. She felt his head.

'Where's my watch?'

'It's half past three nearly. George, for God's sake don't do that again. Have you got any aspirins? What happens when you're alone and there is no one here?'

'Ah, you see, I have an arrangement with the . . .'

'What? The doctor?'

'The telephone,' said George.

'The telephone? What the hell's the good of that? You might die, George. Where are those aspirins, be a dear and tell me. I'm sorry, George. You screamed. God, I hadn't time to put a skirt on,' she said archly.

'Oh well, so I see,' said George sarcastically.

'Ah, thank God,' said Gloria sighing. 'Now you sound more like yourself. You gave me a turn. I would have fallen on the floor if you hadn't put the chair there. I'll make you a cup of tea. Can you make tea in this awful museum?'

'No,' said George victoriously. 'You can't. I never keep tea here. Tea, I never drink it. Seymour brings it.'

'Well, my God, how you live, George, in this expensive barn,' she said, sitting on the bed.

'Awful business. Awful dream,' said George, coming round. 'I had an awful dream the other night, oh yes . . .'

'You look green, George. I'll get you a drink.'

She brought it to him and watched him drink it. 'I've been round your flat. There are no beds. If you don't mind I'll go back to the sofa. Now, stop talking.'

For George was off on some tale of a night in the war.

'This is the only bed,' he said. 'I used to keep a spare bed but I stopped that. People exploit you. Want to stay the night. It upsets the servants here.'

'There's not room for two in it, George,' she said. George stopped his drink.

'Gloria,' he stammered in terror of her large eyes. She came closer and sat on the bed. She took his free hand.

'You're cold,' she said.

'No,' he said. 'I'm not. All bone, you see, skeleton. My sister . . .'

She stood up and then bent over him and kissed him.

'I'll find a blanket,' she said. 'I'll go back to the sofa. I'm terribly sorry, George. George, I really am.'

'Well,' said George.

'George, forgive me,' she said and suddenly kneeled at the bed and put her arms round him. 'Let me warm you.'

'Oh no, no. No. Awful business,' said George.

She went away. George heard her opening cupboards, looking for blankets. He listened to every movement. He thought, Seymour will find her in the morning. Where could he hide her? Could he make her go to the bathroom and stay there till Seymour left? No, Seymour always ran his bath. He was trapped. He heard her go to the sitting-room. It was six before he fell asleep again.

At half past seven she came to his room with Seymour.

'My brother was taken very ill in the night,' she was saying to Seymour. 'I cannot find out who his doctor is? He oughtn't to be alone like this. At his age.'

'No ma'am,' said Seymour, looking guilty.

'Bring me his tea. Where does he keep his thermometer? Get me one.'

'I told him not to go out ma'am,' said Seymour.

'Thank heaven I came in.'

When Seymour left she said to George:

'Don't talk. It's tiring. A little scandal would have done you good, George, but not at your age.'

'Umph,' said George. 'That man knows my sister. She's as thin as a pole. She's meaner than me,' he cackled. 'She never tips anyone.'

'I told him I was the fat one,' she said. 'You stay there. I'm calling a doctor.'

Waiting for him to come was a nuisance. 'Awful business' having a woman in the house. They spend half their lives in the bathroom. You can't get into it. When George did get to it he was so weak he had to call for her. She was sitting in a chair reading Flitestone's letters and smiling. She had – George had to admit – made herself presentable.

'You're right, George,' she said. 'I'm going to keep them. He was so full of news. They're too,' she said demurely '. . . personal.'

And then the doctor came.

At the club George was sitting at luncheon.

'You're looking well, George,' said the academician who had just passed him the decanter.

'I never drink until the evening. I always reckon to drink a bottle of wine at dinner, a couple of glasses of port. I usually have a whisky here and one more back at the flat when I get home. I walk home, taxis are expensive and oh, oh, oh, I don't like the underground. Oh no, I don't like that.'

'You're looking fine.'

'I have been very ill. I had pneumonia. I was taken very ill a month ago, in the night. Luckily my sister has been looking after me. That is the trouble with old people who live alone, no one knows. They can't reach the bell. I told you about that awful night when I ate the oysters . . .'

'George, not now, please. I didn't know you had a sister?'

'Oh yes, oh yes. Two,' said George sharply. 'One is very thin, all bones like me, the other very fat.'

'But you're better? You look fine. I hear, by the way, that Sanders is getting married.'

'Oh, I knew about that. I advised him to, at his age. I warned him about the loneliness of bachelors in old age. I'm used to it. Keep occupied. See people. That's the secret. Oh yes, I worked it out. My father lived till he was ninety. You see, when I was young one never met any women. Just girls at deb parties, but speak to them, oh dear no. Not done. That's a big change. The bishops don't like sex, though Canterbury is beginning to come round. The Pope will have to make a move, he's been the stumbling block. A scandal. Oh yes, I happened to be in Rome in '05, staying with a Papal Count, and, well, I was able to tell him the whole inside story at the Vatican, you see I knew a very able Jesuit who was very frank about it privately . . .'

'What happened about Gloria?' said a voice. It was the Arch Enemy, sitting opposite.

'Hah,' said George. 'I recommended her not to sell. She offered to give me the letters, but I didn't care to take them. They were very intimate, personal.'

'I thought her husband had left her and she was short of money?'

'That's not the worst thing to be short of,' sniffed George.

'The trouble with Gloria was that she was also so sentimental,' said the Arch Enemy. 'The moment she sees a man her mind simply goes. Still does, and she must be sixty if she's a day,' he said, looking at George.

By God, George thought, the Arch Enemy is a fool.

The Speech

'It's a funny turn out. You don't know what front to take up for the best,' the chatty doorman replied to the big-bellied woman as he opened the door and let her and the other speakers into the hall.

'You'd better bloody well make your mind up or you'll be dead,' she said to him with a grin over her shoulder as she passed and followed the others up the steps on to the cold, dusty platform. And she said to the young man with heavy fair hair who was next to her when they sat down:

'That's this place for you. Did you hear him? It's dead. They've had the bomb already.' A man's voice shouted from the audience, just before Lord Birt got up to introduce the speakers:

'Good old Sally.'

No smile of pleasure moved her double chin, nor did she nod. She was counting. That one shout echoed. It revealed the emptiness of the hall. It would hold eight hundred; she had seen in her time twice that number fighting their way in. Now (she reckoned it up), there were no more than fifty or sixty.

The weather, the sleet whipping across all day (the secretary had said), not having had longer notice, couldn't get through to headquarters on the phone. A lot of people on short time. Excuses. They had even spelled her name wrong on the notice outside: Sally Proser, leaving out the second "s" and the sleet spitting on it made the red ink run into the blue as if the poster was sobbing and ashamed of them all. They couldn't get her name right, even in her own town.

Lord Birt had sat down. The first speaker was up.

'Friends,' he was saying, 'I shall not take up your time . . .' She looked at her watch.

'We'll be here half the night,' she said to the young man next to her. He was trying to keep a piercing look on his face. 'Who is he?'

'Doctor,' hissed the young man, crossing his legs. 'Quaker. Liberal.'

'God,' she said very audibly.

It was a large hall, a yawning historic fake in a Gothic baronial style, built out of cotton profits a hundred years before, shabbied by hundreds, thousands of meetings, the air staled and exhausted by generations of preachers, mayors and politicians. The damp had brought out a smell made of floor boards, the municipal disinfectants, the sweet, sooty cellulose effluence of the city. It was a smell provided by a dozen mills whose tall chimneys pencilled the pink fume of the sky, and by something of the fouled, milky green industrial river and the oily canal.

A mist hung across the middle of the hall like breath left behind for years and although all the chandeliers were lit, the light fell yellowish and weak on the audience sitting in their overcoats in the first five rows and on the long funereal stretch of empty chairs behind. One person after another turned around in discomfort looking at the distant glass doors at the back and then at the side, to see where the Arctic draught came from; and then, reproaching themselves, lifted their chins stiffly and stared with resentment at the platform.

The doctor was still going on. He was a tall, very thin man, vain of his eagle face, his blossom of white hair, his gentle, high-pitched, doubting vocables. They were moving equably out of 'the situation before all of us today'; then went on derisively to 'the international plane' and 'the lessons of history': (his past); to what he had said 'in this very hall' (references to local elections thirty years ago), and emerged into the benignancy of the 'moral issue' and circled impatiently to what he had 'always said'. Beside him sat young Lord Birt, ace flyer, Matisse owner, lecturer in America, with a dark, prompt electric black moustache, like a too recent political decision, and next to him the very young man.

'It's a scandal, a meeting like this,' Mrs Prosser was saying to him audibly through the doctor's speech. 'I'll take it up with headquarters. Where have they put you up – in an hotel? I was out last night, God knows where, in the Treasurer's house, and there's been a death in the family. Imagine the atmosphere.'

'Someone just died?' said the young man, astonished.

'Twenty-five years ago!' she said sarcastically. 'I've made fourteen speeches on this tour, in the last six days, and they hadn't the decency to put me into an hotel. It's all wrong.'

And Mrs Prosser's head, mouth and jaws, even her big arms, seemed to gather themselves together until she looked like a fist.

'What about Hungary?' shouted a man from the audience.

'Yes, what about Hungary?' shouted two or three others.

'They're waking up,' said the young man.

'I'm glad you asked me that question,' said the doctor, going on.

'No, it's nothing,' she said, giving an experienced glance at the shouters. 'They're dead. How did you get here? They didn't even have a car, borrowed it from the Treasurer's son, it broke down. We sat on the road for half an hour, on a night like this. Ah, well, the old bastard is drying up. It's you.'

The young man got up.

'Ladies and Gentlemen,' he began.

(Oh God, thought Mrs Prosser, but forgave him.) He had learned his speech, he was sawing it off, it fell in lumps to the floor. The women looked sympathetically, the men looked ironical, one or two of the shouters leaned forward to egg him on at first, and then leaned back, with their hands on their knees, giving up. Handsome, his hair flopping, he seemed to have some invisible opponent in front of him whom he was angrily trying to push away, so that he could see the audience. He struggled and at last he stopped struggling. He came to an end, looked back nervously to see if his chair was still there and when the audience clapped he looked back at them with suspicion and anger.

'I made a mess of it,' he murmured to Mrs Prosser as he sat down.

'Here we go,' Mrs Prosser ignored him. 'Watch me, if I don't wet my drawers before I've done with this bloody lot . . .'

She was up, adroitly slipping her old fur coat off her shoulders and into the hands of the young man, stepping in one stride to the edge of the platform. She stared at the audience, let them have a good look at her. She was a short woman of forty-seven. Robust. She was wearing a tan jumper that was low on her strong neck and pulled on anyhow, and a shabby green skirt. She had big breasts, which she had been ashamed of in her young days, wanting to hide them, but that was before she joined the Movement; a stout belly, hard as a drum, which made her laugh when she got up in the morning. Her face was round and she had a

[743]

double chin and the look on her face said: "Go on! Take a good look. It's your last chance."

Suddenly she let out her voice.

'Fellow workers,' she shouted. The words, slow, deep and swinging in delivery, rocked them. They stopped fidgetting and coughing. She heard with pleasure her full plain northern voice sweep out over them and to the back of the hall, filling it to the baronial beams and spreading over the seats and into the empty galleries.

'Good old Sally,' shouted a man.

'Come on Sally,' shouted another, wet-lipped with love at the sight of her and nudging his neighbour. She paused in the middle of her sentence and smiled fully at him – the first broad smile of the night.

She loved these opening minutes of her speeches. 'I'm an old potato,' she thought, 'but my hair is brown and alive and I've got a voice. I can do anything with it.' It was as powerful as a man's, yet changeable. Now it was soft, now violent; riotous in argument yet simple; always firm and disturbing. It could be blunt and brutal and yet it throbbed. It had sloshed its way through strikes and mass meetings; it had rebounded off factory walls, it had romped and somersaulted over thousands of heads. It had rung bitterly out through the Spanish War, when she was a young woman; through rows of the Second Front, the Peace Campaigns, the Hungarian quarrel; it was all out now for Banning the Tests. It had never worn out, never coarsened, never aged; in these first few minutes it was her blood, the inner, spontaneous fountain of her girlhood, something virginal she would never lose. At every meeting it was reborn.

Even her shrewd brown eyes were bemused by her utter pleasure in hearing this voice, so that all of her early sentences surprised her by their clarity and the feeling that was in them; she was proud to feel her lungs heave, to watch the next thought form in her brain, the next argument assemble, the words, the very vowels and consonants fall into place. It was thrilling to pause and throw in a joke, a flash of hate or a line of wit that would sometimes recklessly jump into her head and make it itch with pleasure. This was the moment when she caught the crowd, played with them and made them hers. It was the time, for her, of consciousness, like a sudden falling in love, when the eyes of the audience answered her signals, when she could look carelessly from face to face, watching her words flick like an angler's line over them, looking for the defaulter. And, picking this man or this woman out, she would pause, as it were, to ask the audience to watch her make her catch, as if she had come down off the platform to be down among them with an intimacy that teased them and made their minds twist and flick and curl with fear and pleasure.

And then – it happened: the break, almost painful for her. The virginal voice that was so mysteriously herself would separate from her and perform alone as if it had nothing to do with her at all. It became, simply, the Voice. It left her, a plain, big-bellied, middle-aged woman, a body, to stand there exposed in all the woundedness of her years, while it went off like some trained dog barking round the audience, rounding them up, fetching in some stray from the back, flinging itself against the rows of empty chairs.

'And I say and I say again: we've got to stop those tests! We tell the Americans to stop these tests. We tell this Tory government that if it does not stop these tests . . .'

Now it was barking down derisively from the gallery at the end of the hall, barking at the City Arms, at fire extinguishers, at the Roll of Honour in gold, at the broom left by the cleaner, at the draught coming in at the doors, it was barking round walls below and the feet of the audience.

The light went out of Mrs Prosser's face. She let the Voice carry on and she looked with boredom at the people. There was the elderly man, deaf and impatient; there was the big married woman with folded arms who kept glancing down her row to see everyone was listening, like a policewoman. There were the two girls, shoulder to shoulder, with pretty false faces, waiting for a chance to whisper. There was a woman with mouth open, ravenous, as if she were going to rush the platform and kiss her. There were the threes or fours of men frosted with self-respect. There was the man who seemed, nowadays, to come to all her meetings, a man neither young nor old, listening with one ear, and sly, who sat at the end of a row with one bent leg sticking out of the neat block of the audience and who glanced often at the side door, as if he were waiting his chance or for a sign, to make a bolt for it. For what? For the pubs before they closed, for the last tram, to meet someone, even just to stand in the street – why? Had he got – a life? It always troubled her. She wanted to follow him. And there was that swing door which kept gulping like a sob, as someone pushed in and gave a glance at the meeting and then went out and the door gave another gulp like the noise of a wash-basin as if all the words of that Voice of hers were going down a drain. She heard the Voice go on:

'For you can take it from me, if the Americans don't stop these tests, if the Russians don't stop these tests, if the Tory party just sits on its bum . . .'

Loud cheers. That was a word made for the North. Mrs Prosser grinned at the Voice's joke. She had a good big bum herself.

The Voice went on. It carried nearly thirty years of her life. At a meeting like this – no, not like this, but much larger and in the open streets, in the Blackshirt days, she had met her husband. There was a shouting, arm-wrenching tearing, kicking fight with the police. What solid lumps their bodies were! She (when she remembered it) had felt as light as air. A gale had lifted her suddenly so that she, like the rest of the scattering and re-forming crowd, was blown about and with a force in her big arms and body that was exalted. Bodies swung about like sacks of meal. The houses and all their windows seemed to buckle and bulge towards her, the cobbled street heaved up and down like a sea. You could pick up the street in your hands. A young man near her gave a shout and she shouted, too, and her shout was his and his was hers, for an extraordinary few moments they had the same body. A policeman struck at the young man, the blow fell on his neck and *she* felt the pain. She could not remember how – but she was clawing at the policeman and the young man's blood struck her cheek. They spent that night in prison.

The pupil teacher at the Adderdale Road School (Girls) to be in prison! That was when the hate started – her mother saying she would never hold her head up again – they had always been decent people. The father saying: 'All stuck-up with those books and too good for her own family.' And now she had disgraced them. If young Prosser, the little weed, came round the house again – the father said – he'd belt him. In this very city. They sacked her from the school. From that time on her life had been committees, lectures, meetings. Always travelling, always on platforms, her husband at one end of the country and she at the other. He with the shout on his face and she with the shout on hers, a drawing back of the lips over the teeth: that was their love, too. Love a shout, marriage a shout. They saw each other for an hour or two, or a day or two, eating anything, anywhere, usually a sandwich or a few bars of chocolate. It was the chocolate that had made her put on weight. 'I'm a fighting sweet-shop.' At first, he had been the nimble one, the leader, wearing himself out and often ill; he had the ideas; then, one week, when he was sick with an ulcer, she had taken a meeting – and the Voice, this strange being inside her, came out and now it was she who not only commanded him, but audiences by the hundred, then the thousands. The Voice took over her own and her husband's life.

And they stick me at a place nine miles outside the city (her body, her bullying breasts and affronted belly were saying), in weather like this! I don't say I wasn't comfortable. That'd be a lie. I was glad to see a coal fire. Three-piece suite too and the telly on, very nice. You wouldn't have seen that in our home when I was a girl. We had a laugh too about Lord Birt's house, all those chimneys. Mrs Jenkins was a maid there when she was a girl and they used to bless those chimneys! My husband and I did our courting up there in the woods above. Mrs Jenkins and I had a good laugh about old times. And then the old lady, Mr Jenkins's mother, got restless. 'Eh,' says Mrs Jenkins, 'Mother wants her telly. We turned it off when you came. She sits there in front of it, tapping her toes on the floor when the cowboys go by rocking up and down.' 'You want to get on your horse and ride the range, Gran, don't you?' says Harry Jenkins, the lad. 'Gran's in her saddle, reaching for her gun when the Westerns come on. She gets excited, don't you Gran?' Of course, the old lady was stone deaf and couldn't hear a word he said. But she looks at me and says, suddenly:

'That's Sally Gray.' Just like that, her eyes like pistols. 'That's Sally Gray.'

'No, Gran, that's Mrs Prosser. Excuse her, Mrs Prosser, the mind . . . she's failing.'

'It's Sally Gray,' says the old lady.

'Now, Gran!' says Mrs Jenkins. 'You be a good girl.'

'It's the girl that killed our Leslie. It's Sally Gray that sent our boy to Spain and killed him.'

'Gran,' says Mrs Jenkins. 'Stop that. I won't have you upset us. Excuse her, Mrs Prosser. My husband's brother was killed in the Spanish war. She doesn't forget it.'

"It's Sally Gray, the school teacher, who went to prison and got her name in the papers and broke poor Mrs Gray's heart.' The old lady stands flapping her little hands about and turning round and round like a dog.

The atmosphere – you can imagine it!

'Now Gran, Mrs Prosser didn't do anything to Les. It's a long time ago.'

'Tuesday, we heard,' the old lady said.

'Gran,' says the lad, taking the old lady's arm to steady her, 'don't carry on. It'd be a bad day for the workers if they didn't fight for themselves. Uncle Les was an idealist.'

Nine miles outside the town in weather like this!

'I'm sorry Mrs Prosser,' says Mrs Jenkins. 'Switch on the telly, Harry. She's a great problem. Definitely. I could kill her,' says Mrs Jenkins standing up stiff. And she suddenly picks up the teapot and rushes out of the room, crying.

'Excuse us,' says Mr Jenkins giving the old lady a shake.

What a committee to put me in a house like that with a mad old woman. Where's the consideration? And they bring me here in a borrowed car that breaks down and we stand there on the moor, with the sleet coming through my stockings. And they spell your name wrong and scrape up an audience of ten or twenty people.

There was a cheer from the audience. The Voice had got into them. Mrs Prosser paused: she was startled herself. She paused for the cheer and the Voice cracked a thin joke about the Foreign Secretary: 'They fly about from Bonn to Washington, from Washington to London; you don't see them flying down here. They're afraid of getting their feathers dirty,' and got a laugh from them, a dirty, draughty laugh, which gave the man at the end of the row a chance to inch his leg out farther and get ready to make a bolt for it; and at that very second she saw the dead white face of the clock at the end of the hall, its black hands like a jack knife, opening.

Twenty to nine! Her husband down at Plymouth, the other end of the country. And Jack? Where is Jack? But as her Voice picked up its freedom again and sailed on, she silently asked the audience: 'Where's my son?

What have you done with my son? A year ago I could tell you what he was doing. He'd come home from school, get himself some supper, that boy could cook, oh yes, and clean up afterwards – and then settle to his homework. He could look after himself, better than a grown man. From the age of nine he could manage on his own. My husband and I could leave him a week at a time and he didn't mind. And I'll tell you something else: a boy with a real political conscience!'

You've done it – her body was shouting to the audience – *you've* done it! For twenty-five years my husband and I have been fighting for *you*, fighting the class enemy, getting justice for you, and you sit there – what is left of you – pulling in the big money, drunk on Hire Purchase, mesmerised by your Tellys and your Pools – and what do you do for us? When I knew I was going to have that boy I said to my husband: 'We won't let this stop the work.' And we didn't. But you and your rotten society just did nothing. A year ago he was the best boy in this country and you couldn't stand it. No. You had to get him out and start him drinking with a lot of thieving hooligans, you put a knife in his hand. You know what he said to his father? 'Well, you were in prison, you and Mother, you told me.' 'Son,' his father said, 'we were fighting for justice for the people.' 'Oh that crap!' he says. That's what the great British people did while we were working for them. Those people out there lost a son twenty-five years ago in Spain. I want to tell you I lost mine last year – killed by his own side.

'Good old Sally,' the audience shouted. 'Hit 'em. Listen to her.'

Mrs Prosser paused with a smile of victory.

'But, my friends, you will say to me,' the Voice suddenly became quiet and reasonable, 'this government cannot act alone. It has got to consider the American government and the Russian government. You will say the British people cannot isolate itself from the human family . . .'

But Mrs Prosser was saying to them:

'Before I came here this evening they took me to this Lord Birt's house, the one I told you about with all those chimneys; very friendly those chimneys looked when we were courting in the woods above. My husband and I used to look down at the house. And the time I liked the best was when the smoke was going up straight from them in the autumn. Some week-ends when there was company at the house the smoke went up from many of them like it does from his Lordship's mills, but pleasanter, homey. You'd see rooks turning round and round over it and hear a dog drag its chain and bark, or hear pails clash where they were washing the car or swooshing out the yard at the back: I always wanted to see inside when I was a girl. Well today I saw it. Oh yes! There I was inside sitting by the fire with a cat on my knees. Can you see me with a cat? There were some people there and after we'd had our meal this young man who just made that bad speech was there looking at the books in the white bookcases. And there was a young girl, plump with brown hair, talking to him about them. Lord Birt asked him where they'd been that morning and they said: "Up in the woods at the back." I'll tell you something. I was jealous. I was jealous of that young girl talking to that young man. I felt old and ugly and fat. Mind you, I don't like the way these girls wear trousers, so that they look as naked as the tadpoles we used to catch when we were kids. I'd split them myself, you'd have a laugh – but it wasn't that that made me jealous. I couldn't *talk* about anything. That lad can't make a speech, but he can talk and so could the girl. I sat there dumb and stupid. Every day, morning and evening, year after year, generation after generation, this was a home and they could talk about a subject in it. If you talked about a subject in my home when I was a girl they'd call you "stuck up". All I can do is to make bloody fine speeches in bloody empty halls like this.'

There was coughing in the audience and now the Voice was quieter. The man sitting at the end of the row with his leg out made up his mind. He got both legs out and, bending slightly, thinking to make himself invisible, he slowly tiptoed out across the bare space to the door at the side. And half those forty or fifty heads, in the midst of their coughing, turned to watch, but not that widely smiling woman who was still looking ravenously up at the platform as if she were going to rush at Mrs Prosser and swallow her.

Mrs Prosser saw the man tiptoeing out to that life of his and she did what she always could do, at any meeting, startle it out of its wits with a sudden shout, and make any escaper stop in his absurd delinquent steps.

'Fellow workers' (the Voice rang out), 'don't kid yourselves. You won't escape. It is you and your children who are being betrayed by this cowardly government. It is you . . .'

[750]

But her life was the forty-seven-year-old body with the big white mournful bottom saying to them:

And if you want to know what I thought when I passed the long mirror in the hall of Lord Birt's house when we were getting in the car to come to this place where I was born and brought up and where you can't even spell my name, if you want to know what I thought, I can tell you. It's you have made me ugly! Working for you! You never gave me a minute to read a book, look at a picture or feed the spirit inside me. It was you who made me sit dumb as an old cow back there. You fight for justice and you lose half your life. You're ugly and you've made me as ugly as you are.

The applause went up sharp and short near the platform and echoed in the emptiness behind the audience. Chairs shifted. Mrs Prosser sat down. Lord Birt and the young man congratulated her. She looked scornfully and boastfully at them.

'I've wet them,' she said to the young man as they walked away down the steps off the platform. Out of the little crowd of people who had stayed behind to talk to the speakers, the young girl came forward and secretively, not to embarrass him, squeezed the young man's arm and said 'You were wonderful.' He hardly listened but was looking eagerly into the crowd that surrounded Mrs Prosser.

'We'll wait for her,' he said fiercely. 'She had them' – he held out his cupped hand – 'like that.' And he clenched his fist.

The Liars

'We're all dressed up today,' said the landlady, going downstairs to her husband in the kitchen, from the old lady's room. 'Diamond rings, emerald necklace – she's put the lot on. I said to her: "You're all dressed up for company, I see." "Yes," she said, "Harry's coming." I mean, it's childish. I don't trust that man. He'd stop at nothing and he tells lies. And do you know what she said?'

'What did she say?' said the landlady's husband.

'It's Thursday, Mrs Lax, she says. It's my day for telling lies.'

It was a February afternoon. Under her black wig, the old lady upstairs was sitting up in bed reading her father's *Baudelaire*. She read greedily; her eyes, enlarged by her glasses, were rampaging over the lines; with her long nose and her long lips sliding back into her cheeks, she looked like a wolf grinning at the smell of the first snow and was on the hunt restlessly among the words.

> '*Vous que dans votre enfer mon âme a poursuivies*
> *Pauvres soeurs, je vous aime autant que je vous plains*'

she was murmuring avidly as she read. All over the bed were books, French and English, papers, detective novels that she had picked up and pushed away. On and off, in the long day, she had looked to see what was going on in the street; sleet had emptied it. The only thing that still caught her eye was an old blackbird gripping the branch of the plane tree outside her window; its wings hanging down, alone.

'You're late,' said the old lady, pulling her shawl violently round her arms, taking off her glasses and showing her strong, expectant teeth, when Harry came up to her room at four o'clock. The bold nose was naked and accusing.

Harry put the library books he had brought for her on the table under the window by her bedside. He was a tall, red-faced man with the fixed look of moist astonishment at having somehow got a heavy body into his navy-blue suit and of continually hearing news.

'I had my hair cut,' he said, moving a small cane-seated chair out of the muddle of furniture into the middle of the room. The old lady waited impatiently for him to sit down.

'No,' he said. The old lady took a deep breath and gave a small hungry smile.

'No,' he said. 'A terrible thing happened when I came out of the barber's.' The old lady let out her breath peacefully and let her head slip aside on her pillow in admiration.

'I saw my double,' Harry said.

Two years ago she had been in hospital, but before that Harry had the job of pushing her along the sea front in a bath chair on fine mornings. When she had been taken ill, he had started working in the bar and dining-room of the Queens Hotel. Now that she was bedridden he brought her books. First of all, in the days when he used to wheel her out, it was 'Yes, Miss Randall' or 'Is that a fact, Miss Randall?' while she chattered about the town as it was when she was a child there, about her family – all dead now – and about her father, the famous journalist, and what he had done at Versailles after the 1914 war and his time in the Irish troubles, and her London life with him. And Harry told her about himself. 'I was born in Enniskillen, ma'am.' 'Now that's a border town, isn't it Harry?' 'It's like living on a tightrope ma'am. My father fought against the British.' 'Very foolish of him,' said the old lady. 'Oh, it was,' said Harry. 'He had us blown up.' 'The British *bombed* you, Harry?' 'Not at all, it was one of father's bombs, home-made thing, it went off in the house.' 'Were you hurt, Harry?' 'I was at my Auntie's. So I went to sea.' 'So you did, you told me, and the ship blew up too.' 'No ma'am it was the boiler. It was a Liverpool ship, the *Grantham*.' 'Two explosions, I don't believe you, Harry.' 'It's God's truth ma'am. It was in New York harbour. But I'd left her in Buenos Aires – there was always trouble on her.' 'And then you went to that hacienda – no, you got a job in an hotel first of all – isn't that it?' 'Yes, in two or three hotels, ma'am, until this American lady took me up to her hacienda.' 'To look after the horses?' 'That is correct.' 'This was the lady who rode her horse up the steps into the dining-room?' 'No ma'am,' said Harry, 'she rode it right inside and up the marble staircase into her bedroom.' 'She couldn't Harry. A mule yes, but not a horse.' 'That part was easy for her, ma'am, it was getting the horse down that was the trouble. She called us, the Indian boy and myself, and we had to do that. Down twenty-five marble steps. She stood at the top shouting at us "Mind the pictures".' 'I suppose there was an explosion there, too, Harry?' 'No ma'am, but there were butterflies as large as plates flying through the air, enough to knock you down' . . . 'Harry,' said the old lady one day, 'you're as big a liar as my sister's husband used to be.'

Harry looked at her warily, then around him to see if there was anyone he could call to for help if there was trouble.

'It's God's truth,' said Harry rapidly and anxiously.

'There's truth and there's God's truth,' said the old lady. It was after this that she had to be taken off to hospital.

'So you saw your double, Harry,' the old lady said. 'Stand up and let me look at you.'

Harry stood up.

'They've cropped you at the back, you're nearly blue. I'll tell you whose double you are, Harry. My sister's husband. He was in the hotel business like you.'

'Is that a fact?' said Harry. 'Did your sister marry?'

'I've been thinking about it ever since you went to work at the Queens,' said the old lady. 'He was taller and broader than you and he had fair hair, not black like yours, and a very white face, a London night face – but the feet were the same, like yours, sticking out sideways. Sit down, Harry.'

'I suppose,' said Harry, who had heard versions of this story before. 'I suppose he'd be the manager?'

'Manager!' shouted the old lady. 'He wouldn't have considered it! Ambassador, Archbishop, Prime Minister, more like it. That is what he sounded like and what he looked like – anyway what we *thought* he was. He was the head waiter at a night-club.'

She stared herself into silence.

'No, it's God's truth,' said Harry, taking his chance. 'I was coming out of the barber's and I forgot your books and went back for them and when I came to cross the street, the lights changed. There was a crowd of us there on the kerb and that was when I saw this fellow. He was standing on the other side of the street waiting to cross. I stared at him. He stared at me. We were the double of each other. I thought I was looking in a mirror.'

The old lady let her head slip back peacefully on the pillow, a happy smile came on her face and she took a biscuit from the tin.

'Same clothes?' said the old lady slyly.

'Except for the hat,' said Harry. 'Same height. He was staring at me. Same nose, eyes, everything. And then the lights changed and he stepped off the kerb and I stepped off and we were still staring at each other. But when we got to the middle I couldn't look at him any longer and I looked away. We passed each other and I felt cold as ice down one side of my body.'

'Did he turn round? Did *he* recogniseyou?'

'He did not. But after we passed I looked back and he wasn't there. No sign of him at all. I got to the kerb and I had a second look. He'd gone.'

'He was lost in the crowd.'

'He was not. There wasn't a crowd. He was the only one crossing from that side of the street. Except for the hat, it was me.'

The pupils of Harry's eyes were upright, brown ovals. He had been wronged, so wronged that he looked puffed out, full of wind.

'It was like passing an iceberg in the Atlantic. Or a ghost,' Harry said.

'You could say Deb's husband was a ghost,' said the old lady. 'He was living upstairs in the flat above us for three years before we met him. We used to hear his taxi at four in the morning. He was out all night and we were out all day. Deb at her art school and I worked on the paper my father used to work on.'

'You mightn't have met at all,' Harry said. 'I never saw the night porter at the Queens for a year.'

'I wish we hadn't,' said the old lady.

'It would be accidental if you did. Would there have been an accident?' Harry said, putting on an innocent look. 'When I was working on that hacienda with the American lady, the one with the horse in her bedroom . . .'

'There was an accident!' said the old lady. 'You know there was. I told you, Harry.'

'He left the stopper in his basin,' Harry said.

'With the tap dripping,' the old lady said. 'Deb got home one evening and heard the water dripping through the ceiling on to father's desk. She

put a bowl underneath it and it splashed all over father's books – we had
a very pleasant flat, not like this. Father left us some very beautiful things.
When I got home I was angry with Deb. She was a very dreamy girl.
"Why didn't you get the housekeeper up instead of letting it ruin
everything?" I said. *I* had to ring for him – stone deaf, like your cook.
Didn't you say the explosion on that ship, the *Cairngorm*, made your cook
stone deaf?'

'On the *Grantham*', Harry said.

'You told me the *Cairngorm* before,' said the old lady. 'But never mind.
He got his keys and went upstairs to see what was going on. That flat,
Harry. It was empty. When I say empty, just the lino on the floor . . .'

'I've got lino at the Queens,' said Harry. 'Brown with white flowers.'

'Nothing – nothing but a table and a bed and a couple of chairs. It was
like a cell. It was like a punishment hanging over us. Not a book. There
was a parcel of shirts from the laundry on the bed – that would have told
us something if we'd looked.'

'It would,' said Harry.

'Four o'clock in the morning,' said the old lady, 'he came home. The
taxi ticking down below in the street! Like a ghost in the night. Of course
he came next day to apologise about the water. Harry, the moment he
stood in the room, I knew I'd seen him before! I said to my sister "I've
seen that man somewhere." The way he stopped in the doorway, looking
across the room at Deb and me and the chairs, nodding at them as if he
were telling us where to sit, the way he held his hands together as he
spoke with his head bent. He had one of those kissing mouths – like a
German. He looked at the books that had been splashed and said, "Balzac
and Baudelaire, very great men," and looked fatter in the face after he
said it. More important. We said they were father's books and my sister
said "Father was a special correspondent. Perhaps you've heard of him."
He said he'd heard people mention him at his club and it sounded as if
he'd eaten father.' The old lady laughed out loud at this idea of hers and
left her mouth open for a while after she had laughed. 'I'll tell you who
he was like,' she said excitedly, 'that statue of George II. Or do I mean
the Duke of Bedford?

'I wanted to get rid of him: he was so large and serious and he sounded
as if he was making a speech to Parliament about what some painter he

knew had said about art and the public. He knew a lot of people – cabinet ministers, actors, judges. Well, I said, when he'd gone, I don't know who he is but he's a man "in the know!" Deb did not like my saying this. "He's a journalist, I expect." Before he went Deb asked him to have a drink with us one day. "Let me look at my diary. Thursday I'm free and Sundays, unless I go away to stay," he said. "Come on Sunday," Deb said. He came. We had people there. The first thing he did was to start handing round the drinks. It was *his* party. He owned us. He'd eaten us too. I couldn't take my eyes off him. One or two people were as curious as I was. "Who is he? The editor of *The Times?* What does he do?" He wasn't like any of our friends, we were all younger. You know what I think drew us to him – girls are such fools – his conceit! He was as conceited as a gravestone. I watched him moving about. There was his round white face, rather puffy, and his head bowing like the whole of the House of Hanover – the House of Hanover were very stiff, I know, Harry, but you know what I mean – and talking about the Prime Minister and politics in a pooh-poohing way; but down below were his feet sticking out sideways and scampering about beneath him – like messenger boys. "Which paper do you work for?" I asked him. "I'm not a journalist," he said. "Oh", I said, "the housekeeper said you were a journalist on night work. We hear your taxi every night. And do you know what he said? "I asked the housekeeper about *you* when I took my flat here. I wanted to be sure it was a quiet house. He said you were two ladies out all day." Snubs to us, I said to my sister after he had gone, but she said "Fancy him asking about us!" and she danced round the room singing up at the ceiling "I'm a lady out all day." We could hear him upstairs walking about.'

'Yes, but that's what I can't make out about this man,' said Harry. 'I was thinking about it yesterday. Why wouldn't he tell you what his job was?'

'He thought we were a pair of snobs,' said the old lady. 'I expect we were.'

'Out all night, he could have been a printer,' said Harry.

'Or the post office! Or the police! Nightwatchman. Actor. We thought of that,' the old lady raced along. 'It was clever of him: you see what he did. He didn't tell a single lie but he started us imagining things and telling lies to ourselves. Deb couldn't leave it alone. Every time he dodged our questions, she made something up.'

The old lady pulled her arms out of the shawl and spread her arms wide.

'Burglar came into *my* head,' she shouted. 'I came home from the office one evening and there they were, both of them, sitting on the sofa, and he was saying he had heard on the "highest authority" – the highest authority, he actually used those words, I always called him the highest authority after that to annoy Deb – that the Cabinet had decided to legalise street betting. When he left I said to Deb "Deb, that man is not in politics: he is in crime." "I can tell you he is *not* in crime," Deb said, "I asked him straight out."

Harry leaned forward and began to rub his hands up and down his sleeves making a sound like breath.

'"I asked him straight out what he did," Deb said, and he said he was very sorry but it was secret work, something he couldn't talk about, but not crime. He made her promise not to ask or try to find out, but he said he would tell her when he was free to say.'

'If you'd looked at those shirts on his bed you'd have known the answer,' Harry said. 'Dress shirts.'

'The head waiter at a smart night-club,' the old lady said.

'And earning good money, I suppose,' said Harry. 'That is where he picked up his talk.'

'I've told you all this before, Harry,' said the old lady.

'Things come back,' said Harry.

'The chief steward on the *Grantham*,' said Harry, 'used to pass himself off as the Captain when he went ashore. That was to girls too.'

'Oh he talked very well and took us in. You can call him a waiter if you like but you know what I call him? Bluebeard.'

'Bluebeard?' said Harry, very startled. 'Was he married?'

'No, but he had Bluebeard in him,' said the old lady. 'A girl will do anything to find out a secret.'

'That's true,' said Harry.

The old lady stared at Harry, weighing him up. Then she said, in a lower voice: 'I can talk to you, Harry. You're a married man. I mean you've been a married man. Show me your wife's picture again.'

Harry opened his wallet and took out an old snapshot of a young girl with smooth dark hair drawn in an old-fashioned style round an oval face.

'She was pretty, Harry. Deb was fair and a bit plump.' She looked at the photograph a long time and then gave it back to Harry who put it in his wallet again.

'You miss her, Harry.'

'I do that.'

'You would have had a home,' said the old lady. 'I haven't got a home. You haven't got a home – and yet, years ago, before we moved to London, my family had a large house in this town.'

The old lady suddenly changed her mood and her voice became sarcastically merry.

'Bluebeard! Oh, we were all mystery! Secret service, Russian spies. When Deb went to bed at night, she started drawing back the curtains, turning out the lights and undressing by the light of the street lamp down below. And she would open the window wide – in the winter! The fog blowing in! She would stand in her nightdress and say "Can't you feel the mystery of London? I want to feel I am everywhere in London seeing what everyone is doing this minute. Listen to it." "You'll get pneumonia," I said. But it was love. He came down to see us very often now. One day he was saying something about the French Ambassador and French foreign policy, it sounded boastful and I said (I remember this) "Father was one of Clemenceau's very few English friends' – which wasn't true. I told you he made us tell lies. That impressed him because before he went he asked us both out to dinner – at the Ritz! The Ritz! And that was where something funny happened – only a small thing. A party at another table started staring at him and I was sure I heard someone mentioned his name. I'm sure I heard one of the men say "There's Charles," and I said to him: "Someone knows you over there." "No," he said. "They were talking about you. They were saying it was unfair a man taking out two pretty sisters." Deb was very pleased. "He's very well known," she said. "In case, he can't be secret, can he?" I said.

'He never took us out again.'

The old lady scowled.

'After that it was champagne, caviar, lobster. Up in his flat and Deb took her gramophone – I never went. "He must be a cook," I said and she said "No, he sends out for it" and wouldn't speak to me for a week afterwards. She was clean gone. She gave up her classes because she couldn't see him during the day except on Thursdays and Sundays. She was mad about him. And she got very secretive, hiding things, not like her at all. I told her she'd have a bigger secret than she bargained for.'

The old lady sniggered.

'I was jealous,' said the old lady in a moping voice.

'Ah you would be I expect,' Harry agreed.

'Yes,' moped the old lady.

'And then,' said Harry giving a loud slap to his knee. 'There was this ring at the bell . . .'

The old lady looked suspiciously at him.

'The same as the time I told you about, when we docked at Marseilles – with that Algerian. Short black socks he had on and . . .'

The old lady woke up out of her moping, offended.

'Algerian! He was not an Algerian. He was a Cypriot. I was very surprised to hear a ring at that time of the evening. I thought it must have been one of those Jehovah's Witnesses. I went to the door and there he was, this little dark Cypriot with a bottle sticking out of his pocket – I thought he was drunk. He asked for Mr Charles. "There is no Mr Charles here," I said. "What number do you want?" "Six", he said.'

'And you were four!' said Harry.

'This is four,' I said pointing to the number on the door. Well you'd think people could read. Number six is upstairs.' And I shut the door quickly, I was frightened.'

'You can mark a man with a bottle,' said Harry. 'I've seen that too.'

'I heard him ring the bell upstairs. I heard talking. And then it was all quiet. Then suddenly I heard a shout and I thought the ceiling was coming down, like furniture being thrown about.'

'An argument?' said Harry.

'An argument,' said the old lady. She tightened her shawl round her and leaned back as if she were warding off blows.

'Screams, Harry! Lobster, Harry! Glass! And Deb rushing out to the landing making a horrible squeal like a dog being run over. I rushed out of our flat and up the stairs and there was Deb in her petticoat shrieking and just as I got to her the Cypriot rushed out with ketchup or blood, I don't know which, on his boots and ran downstairs. I pulled Deb out of the way. Her scream had stopped in her wide open mouth and she was pointing into the lobby of the flat. There was Charles getting up from the floor, in his shirt sleeves with blood all over his face. You couldn't walk for glass.'

The old lady stared at Harry and, picking up Baudelaire's poems, contemptuously threw them to the end of the bed. Then slowly she smiled and Harry smiled. They smiled at each other with admiration.

'Yes,' said Harry with a nod. 'It's feasible.' The old lady nodded back.

'It's feasible all right,' Harry said. 'The same as I was saying happened in Marseilles when I was in the *Grantham* – Egyptian onions from Alexandria – you could smell us all over the port. I went ashore with the second mate and we were having a drink in one of those cafés with tables on the street – only there five minutes and this Algerian comes in, a young fellow. He walks straight between the tables to the head waiter who was flicking flies off the fruit and shoots him dead. Not a word spoken. Same idea. The head waiter had been fiddling chicken and brandy, selling it on the side, and when the boss tumbled to it, the waiter said this Algerian kitchen boy – that is what he was – had done it and the boss fired him. Same story. They're very hot-blooded down there. It was all in the papers.'

'The Cypriot was kitchen boy at the club. Champagne, lobster, caviar, it all came from there! Week after week,' said the old lady.

'Yes,' said Harry.

'We kept it out of the papers, of course,' said the old lady loftily.

'You don't want a thing like that in the papers,' Harry agreed. 'Just sweep up and say nothing, like that time at the Queens when Mr Armitage . . .'

'We had a reason,' said the old lady. 'I'll tell you something I never told you before. When Deb came screaming to the door, I didn't tell you – she had a broken bottle in her hand.'

'Is that so!' said Harry very startled.

'It's true. That is what happened. It was Deb that did the fighting not the Cypriot. It was Deb.'

'God Almighty,' said Harry. 'And she married him after that!'

'She didn't marry him,' said the old lady. 'I know I said she did, but she didn't. "I wouldn't marry a man who cheated like that," she said. She wouldn't speak to him. Or look at him. She wouldn't get a doctor to look after him. He had a terrible cut on his forehead. I had to clean it and bandage it and get him to the hospital and nurse him. She wouldn't go near him. And it wasn't because he'd cheated. Now she knew about him, the secret, she didn't want him. She was a girl like that. It was a pity. He did well for himself. I showed you the postcard of his hotel – it must be one of the biggest in Cannes. When you sit like that with your feet turned out, you remind me of him. He could tell the tale too,' she suddenly laughed. 'You're the double.'

And then the landlady came in with tea and put the tray across the old lady's lap.

'There,' she said. 'Tea for two as the saying is. And don't you tire her out, Mr O'Hara. Another quarter of an hour.'

The old lady frowned at the closed door when the landlady went and listened for her steps going down the stairs.

'I *could* have married him,' the old lady said.

'Now this woman, Harry,' she said quickly. 'With the horse. She was after you, wasn't she? Why did she make you come up and get that horse down? Why couldn't she ride it down, she rode it up. You're trying to throw dust in my eyes . . .'

'No, it was a fine horse and Irish bred,' said Harry. 'She bought it off a man who had lost his leg . . .'

The afternoon had darkened. The bird that had been sitting on the tree all day had gone. Harry said 'Good-bye' to the old lady. 'See you next Thursday,' he said.

'And don't be late. Don't let that woman at the Queens keep you. It's your day off,' she called as he stood by the open door at the top of the stairs.

He went back along the front, listening to the laughter of the sea in the dark, and then into the bar of the Queens Hotel. But because it was his half day off, on the other side of it, as a customer, drinking a small whisky and listening to what people had to say.

Our Oldest Friend

'Look out!' someone said. 'Here comes Saxon.'

It was too late. Moving off the dance floor and pausing at the door with the blatant long sight of the stalker, Saxon saw us all in our quiet corner of the lounge and came over. He stopped and stood with his hands on his hips and his legs apart, like a goalkeeper. Then he came forward.

'Ah! This *is* nice!' he crowed, in the cockerel voice that took us back to the Oxford years. He pulled up a chair and placed it so that none of us could easily get out. It passed through our heads that we had seen that dinner-jacket of his before. He must have had it since the last term at school. It was short, eager and juvenile in the sleeves and now his chest had bolstered it, he seemed to be bursting with buns and toffee. A piece of stiff fair hair stuck up boyishly at the back. He crossed his short legs and squeezed them with satisfaction as his sharp blue eyes looked around our circle over his strong glasses.

'How awfully nice.' For niceness was everything for him. 'Everyone is here,' he said and nodded back to the people on the dance floor. 'Jane Fawcett, Sanderson-Brown, Tony Jameson and Eileen – I just missed them in Brussels, they'd just left for Munich – very nice catching them here. With the Williamsons!'

He ran off a list of names, looking over one lens of the glasses that were not quite straight on his young enthusiastic nose as he spoke them, and marking each name with a sly look of private knowledge. We were the accused – accused not so much of leaving him out of things, as of thinking, by so doing, that he *was* out of them. His short, trotting legs infallibly took him to old acquaintance. Names from the past, names that we had forgotten from school and then Oxford came out, and made our wives look across at us at first with bewilderment and then set them to whispering and giggling.

'What are you doing, Saxon?' someone said. 'Are you still on the Commission?'

'In principle yes, in practice,' said Saxon, uttering his favourite words, 'I'm the liaison between Ways and Means and the Working Party.'

'The liaison!' one of the wives said.

'Yes. It's awfully nice. It works very well. We have to keep in touch with the sub-committees. I saw the Dustman the other day. He's a Trustee now, he came in from Arbitration.'

'The Dustman?' Mrs Selby said to her husband.

'Oxford,' said Selby. 'Lattersmith. Economist. Very old. He was called the Dustman because he was very dirty.'

'Tessa's father,' Saxon said. And as he shot the name of Tessa at us, he grinned at each one of us in turn to see what could be found in our faces. There are things in the past that become geological. Selby's face became as red as Aberdeen marble; some of us turned to sandstone; one or two to millstone grit or granite; that was how alarm and disclaimer took us.

'Your oldest friend,' said Mrs Selby to her husband, grinding out the phrase.

'In principle yes, in practice no,' said Selby bitterly mocking Saxon's well-known phrase.

'*My* oldest friend, if you please,' said Thomas, always a rescuer.

'And mine!' two of us said together, backing him up.

'Is she yours?' said kind Jenny Fox to me.

'She is the "oldest friend" of all of us.'

We laughed together loudly, but not in unity of tone. Hargreaves was too loud, Fox was too frivolous, Selby was frightened and two or three laughs were groans. There was something haphazard, hollow, insincere and unlasting about our laughter, but Day saved us by saying in his deep grave voice to Saxon:

'We ought to settle this. Who *is* Tessa's oldest friend? When did *you* meet Tessa, Saxon?'

'Selby and I were at school with her, at Asaph's.'

'You didn't tell me that,' said Selby's wife to her husband.

'I tried to get her to come tonight,' said Saxon. 'She's gone out with the Dustman. He said they might drop in later.'

Our wives put on stiff faces: one or two picked up their handbags and looked at the door on to the dance floor, as if they were going to search it, and even the building. The incident was one of Saxon's always unanswerable successes but once more Thomas saved us. He said to Saxon:

'So *you're* her oldest friend.'

And Selby said grimly: 'Yes, you were at Asaph's a year before me.'

'Saxon! You've been holding out on us,' we said with false jollity.

One of the ladies nodded at us and said to her neighbour: 'They seem to be a club.'

The pious pretence on the part of our wives that they did not know Tessa Lattersmith was, in its way, brilliant in our embarrassed state. It brought out the hypocrisy in Harry James who said in a light-headed way:

'She's married now, I suppose?'

'Oh no,' said Saxon. 'She's carrying on.' And he meant carrying on, as it were, in the sense of working hard on the joint committee, himself informed because he was, after all, the liaison.

'You mean,' said Mrs Selby, 'she hasn't found anyone's husband willing?'

'Shame!' said Saxon as at an annual general meeting. 'Shame.'

'Perhaps,' said the kind young Jenny Fox, 'she doesn't want to be married.'

'She's very rich,' said James.

'Very attractive,' said Day.

'Big gobbling eyes.'

'Lovely voice.'

'I don't agree,' said Fox. 'It bodes. It comes creeping into you. It gets under your shirt. It seems to come up from the floor. Expensive clothes, though.'

'Not like the Dustman's!' shouted Thomas, rescuing us again. 'D'you remember? I used to see him at the station waiting for the Oxford train. He used to walk up to the very last bench on the platform, and flop down. I thought he was a tramp kipping down for the night, the first time. His clothes were creased as though he'd slept in them. He had that old suitcase, made of cardboard I should say, tied with string – and parcels of books tied up. Like Herbert Spencer. You know Herbert Spencer had to have everything tied to him? He sat there looking wretched and worn out, with his mouth open and his thick hair full of dust – a real layabout from the British Museum. He hardly got his feet off the ground when he walked, but sort of trudged, as if he was wading through sand. He must be well past seventy.'

'No, he's barely sixty. Tessa's only thirty-two.'

'Thirty-seven,' said Mrs Selby.

'He's sixty-two,' said Saxon. 'Tessa is a year younger than me.'

'The Lattersmiths were rich,' said James again. 'I mean compared with the rest of us.'

'The Dustman's wife had the money,' said Thomas. 'She belonged to one of those big shipping families. Did you ever see her? She's like Tessa – oh, she comes after you with those big solemn eyes.'

'We went to see her, didn't we?' Day said to his wife. 'She saw Diana's necklace, her eyes were fixed on it . . .'

'*And* my rings!'

'She just wanted them. Greedy. She couldn't bear it that Diana had something that she hadn't got.'

'She wanted you as well,' said Diana.

'Oh,' said Tom, the rescuer. 'There's nothing in that. Old Ma Dustman wanted me too, in fact she wanted all of us. "I am so worried about Tessa, I wish she'd settle down. I wish she'd find a nice husband – now *you*, you're fond of Tessa, I'm sure".'

'Shame!' called Saxon again.

We had forgotten about him; he was sweating as he watched us with delight.

'No, it's true,' I said to Saxon.

'And she couldn't have them, poor things,' one of the wives said and the others joined in laughing at us.

James once more pushed us into trouble.

'Did you ever go on a picnic with them? I mean when they came down to School? No? Saxon, didn't you and Selby? Didn't you? None of your camp fires with damp sticks, thermos bottles and tea slopping over the tomato sandwiches. Oh no! And it never rained: old Ma Dustman had ordered sun down from Fortnum and Mason's. They brought the Daimler and the butler came – how did they fit him in, I wonder? I bet he went ahead in the Rolls. He set tables and chairs. Silver teapot, the best Rockingham . . .'

'Not Rockingham, it can't have been.'

'Well old Spode. Something posh. The butler handed round the stuff. I only just knew Tessa then. I had brought a girl called Sadie and Tessa brought a girl called Adelaide with her and Tessa said "I want you to meet Harry James. He's my oldest friend." Sadie looked sick.'

'It had started then?' some of our wives cried out.

'Long before that,' I said. 'In the cradle.'

'Exactly what she said just before we were married when you introduced me,' said Mrs Day to her husband.

'She said it to me at our wedding,' said Mrs Selby and, glaring at her husband, 'I don't know *why*.'

'I don't get what her fascination for you all was!' said sly Mrs James.

'Oh,' we all said largely, in a variety of voices, 'I don't know . . . She was about . . .'

'You know, I think it was sex,' said Jenny Fox.

'Was it sex?' we looked at each other, putting as much impartiality as we could into the enquiry.

'Sex! Of course it was sex,' said Mrs Selby, putting her chin up and gripping her handbag on her knee.

'Not for me,' said Harry James.

'Nor me.' One wife squeezed her husband's hand. 'Why not?'

This dumbfounded us. We huddled together. Why had none of us made a pass? Were we frightened?

'You took her to picture galleries,' said Mrs Selby.

'Yes,' said Selby. 'She did nothing but talk about a man called Cézanne.'

'That's it. A whole party of us went to Parma and she did nothing but talk of a man called Fabrice,' said Tom.

'Fabrice?'

'Stendhal,' said Saxon.

'I had Lawrence in Rome.'

'There was always another man. Anyone have Picasso? Or Giacometti?' said James.

'Who did you have, Selby? Russell? Einstein?'

Selby had had enough. With the treachery of the desperate, he said: 'She talked of nothing but you, James.'

'No,' said Tom the rescuer. 'You can't have had. *I* had you, James.'

'I had Tom.'

'Day was my trouble.'

'With me it was Bill.'

'What a lovely daisy chain,' one of the wives said. 'The whole distinguished lot of you. Who's missing?'

'Saxon,' Jenny Fox said.

We all stared accusingly at him. Saxon went on squeezing himself. He looked archly over his glasses.

'I had the Dustman,' he said complacently.

We laughed but Mrs Selby silenced us and said to Saxon: 'Go on. You're the only one who's telling the truth.'

'She was always very worried about the Dustman,' he said. 'They're a wretched family. He scarcely ever goes home.'

And at this, the band started again and Saxon got up and asked my wife to dance. We were left with Saxon's picture of that rich girl alone in the world. Before the evening was out he had danced with each one of our wives. We all grinned and said 'Look at old Saxon at the end of term dance.'

If there was one non-dancer on the floor it was he. His feet, rather like the Dustman's, trudged, in straight, fated lines, deep in sand; enthusiastically deep. He danced, as it were, in committee. Our wives found themselves in the grip of one who pushed them around, all the time looking askance from side to side as if they were sections or sub-sections for which he was trying to find a place in some majority report. They lost their power to dance. The matter had become desperately topographical to them; while he, as he toiled on, was running off the names of people.

'I saw him in Paris on the second day of the conference.' Or 'They were in New York when Foreign Relations met the working party.'

Or 'They ran into one another in Piccadilly when the delegation met the Trustees. Thompson, Johnson, Hobson, Timson, Richardson, Wilkinson' – our wives returned to us like new editions of *Who's Who*.

Except Mrs Selby. She was much taller than he and on the floor she had the prosecuting look of one who was going to wring what she wanted out of Saxon. She did not look down at him but over his head at the piece of fair hair that stuck up at the back of his head. He soon had to give up his committee style. She got a grip of him, got him into corners, carried him off to the middle, turned savagely near the band and in this spot, she shouted to him:

'What's all this stuff about Tessa and the Dustman?'

And as she said it, seeing him turn to the right, she swung him round to the left and when the dancers were thinning on the floor she planted him in a quiet spot in the middle.

'Tessa's slept with all of you, hasn't she?' she said.

'Shame!' Saxon said, stopping dead. He took off his glasses and there was a sudden change in him. Often since, seeing that naked look on his face, I have thought: 'How he must have hated us.' I remember at school how we stuffed sausage down his neck and how he just let us do it. Sausage after sausage went down. Then off came the glasses and he backed to an open window. Now, on the dance floor, with his glasses off, Saxon suddenly began to dance – if that is the word for it – as if he had been stung. Where had he learned these extraordinary steps? – that sudden flinging wide of his short legs and arms, that strange buckling and straightening of the body, the thrusting forward and back of his punch-ball head, those sudden wrenchings of Mrs Selby back and forth, and spinning her round, that general air of looking for a knockout in the rebound off the ropes. Mrs Selby's firm eyes were disordered as she tried to foresee his movements, and amid the disorder, she was magnetised by the fiendish rhythm of his feet and by the austere look of his unforgiving face.

'Hasn't she?' called Mrs Selby, in a last piteous attempt. The band stopped and she stood there getting her breath in the middle of the floor. Saxon, without music, dropped back into the goalkeeper stance we knew so well, with his hands on his hips and short legs apart. She was staring at Saxon, he was staring at her. It was a long stare. Selby and his partner passed them and he saw what Mrs Selby saw: obstinate tears were forming in Saxon's naked eyes; water filled them; it dropped on his pink cheeks. He took out his glasses and pretended to wipe them with his handkerchief and put them on. He was sternly, silently, crying. Mrs Selby put out her hand repentantly; no doubt he did not see her hand but walked with her off the floor. We were clapping in the silly way people do and someone called out:

'Where did you learn that one, Saxon?'

He looked with bewilderment at us.

'I'll be back in a minute,' he said and walked across the room to the outer hall of the hotel.

Mrs Selby put herself with kind Jenny Fox and whispered to her for a long time and Mrs Fox said:

'It's not your fault. How could you know?'

'I only *said* it,' Mrs Selby said wretchedly, looking at the swing door that let cold air in from the outer hall when it flashed round and where Saxon had gone.

'What was the matter with Saxon?' Selby accused.

'He's upset – nothing,' said Mrs Fox turning to Selby as she patted Mrs Selby's hand. And then, arguing for herself, Mrs Selby told us.

Presently the swing door flashed and Saxon came back and three of us got up to offer him a chair. We gave him the best one, beside a low table which had a brilliant lamp on it. Instantly it threw his shadow on the white wall – a shadow that caricatured his face – the long nose, the chin that receded, the glasses tilted as he looked askance at us, the sprig of schoolboy hair.

'They haven't turned up yet,' he said.

We looked at our Saxon with awe. It was obvious he was in love with that rich, beautiful woman. He must always have been in love with her. We had pulled her to pieces in front of him. What he must have been feeling as he pretended and as he submitted to our joke. And, after all this, she had not come. Where was she? One or two of us wanted to get up and find her. Where would she be? We could not guess. We had to admit that Tessa merely slummed with us. She would never think of coming to a second-rate hotel like this or to an old Asaphians' reunion. She'd be at some smart dinner party, something very grand – she certainly had "oldest friends" in very grand circles. One could imagine her long neck creeping up close to the conscience of an Archbishop. Or disturbing the shirt of an Ambassador, or her boding voice creeping up the sleeve of a banker who would be saying: "Young lady, what are all your hippie friends up to nowadays?" at one of old Ma Dustman's dinner parties. *She* would be stripping the jewellery off the women and telling Sir Somebody Something that one would be a fool to sell one's Matisses yet. The Dustman would not be there. We tried not to look at the unmarriageable silhouette of Saxon's head on the wall.

'Where did you pick up that wonderful step, Saxon?' Mrs Selby said gaily, to make amends.

Saxon gave a forgiving glance. He had recovered.

'At the Cool It,' he said.

'What's the Cool It?' Thomas said.

'A club,' said Saxon.

'Never heard of it.'

'In the docks,' said Saxon.

'The docks?'

Saxon in the docks! The liaison committees in the docks! Saxon in low life! Saxon a libertine!

'What on earth takes you to the docks? Research? Come clean. Having fun?'

In our repentance, we made a hero of him. The old sly Saxon, pleased and pink, was with us again.

'In principle, yes,' said Saxon. 'I sometimes go with the Dustman.'

We could not speak. Saxon and the Dustman in the docks!

'What is it – a cellar?'

'It's a sewer,' said Saxon complacently. 'Tessa goes there with her father.'

'The Dustman takes his daughter to a place like that!'

'He says it will loosen her up,' said Saxon, looking for hope in our eyes. 'You see he wants her to get married.'

Saxon settled back, impudently, comfortably, in the chair. The brocade enriched him and he maliciously considered us one by one.

'To a stoker?' said Selby.

'No,' said Saxon. 'To me – in principle. That's why I go down there. You see, she's worried about him. We go down to see he doesn't get into trouble. I had to pull him out of a nasty fight last week. We got him out. We got him home. To her place. He hates going to his.'

The notion of Saxon fighting was as startling as his dance.

'She must be very grateful to you,' we said politely.

[771]

'Why do you say "marry in principle"?' said Selby.

'He means,' Mrs Selby explained sharply to her husband, disliking the mockery, 'the Dustman is her oldest friend, older even than Saxon is. Isn't that so, Saxon?'

'In practice, yes,' said Saxon, entirely forgiving her. 'I'll go and have another look for them. They promised to come. The Dustman said it would be awfully nice to see us all again. I'll just go and see.'

And he got up and trotted across the yards of hotel carpet that had a pattern of enormous roses. It seemed that their petals were caressing him on his way to the door. The door spun round and Saxon vanished.

Our wives said: 'What a sad story!' and 'What a bitch that girl is.' But we thought: 'Good old Saxon.' And 'He's suffering for us.' Selby put it crudely saying: 'That lets us off the hooks.' And then our feelings changed. There was Saxon sitting like a committee on his own feelings, delegating them incurably to sub-committees, and sitting back doing nothing, relying on an amendment. He must have been doing this for the last eight years. But this led us to another feeling. *We* would never have behaved as Saxon behaved. Each of us saw that beautiful girl in our minds and thought we would have soon pulled her out of this ridiculous obsession with the Dustman and his low life. And how often we had heard of coquettes like Tessa settling down at last in their thirties with faithful bores like Saxon, men they had snubbed over and over again before that alarming age caught them out.

We kept our eyes on the main door of the hotel and were so fixed on it that we did not notice, at once, a figure crossing the dance floor at our side and looking in at us.

'Well!' we heard Tessa's slow, only too well-known voice, dwelling raffishly on the word so that it meant "What are you up to? You didn't think you could keep me out of this." Her large solemn eyes, as forcefully short-sighted as Saxon's were, put their warning innuendo to each of us in turn and the mouth of a beautiful Persian cat possessed us one by one. The spell was on us. A comfortable mew to each of our wives indicated that she had known us years before they had.

We were nearly screaming for help. It was for Thomas, the rescuer, to save us.

'Saxon has just gone out looking for your father.'

[772]

She was up from her chair at once and making for the main door. She had fine legs, a fast passionate step, and Mrs Selby said of her dress:

'It's expensive, but pink is hopeless if you're putting on weight.'

But Selby, over-eager for any hope that could be got out of the situation, said:

'Did you see her when she came in? It was exactly like Saxon. Hunting. You know – in principle yes, but in practice – well. She's a liaison too. I think the Dustman's loosened her up and found the man for her.'

But no one paid much attention to Selby for the swing doors flashed and across the hall came the Dustman, Saxon and Tessa together.

'Look, daddy,' she said to the old man. He had not, of course, changed into a dinner-jacket and his tweed jacket was done up on the wrong button. His trudging step, I now thought, was not so much a trudge as a scraping caused by the probability that he was swinging by an invisible rope hooked to the seat of his learned trousers.

'Look,' she said, 'all my oldest friends!'

And Saxon stood apart with his hands on his hips, watching, his legs apart, keeping goal, wistful, admiring, triumphant.

'Who's dancing?' piped the old man. And soon all of us were on the floor, the Dustman shoving Mrs Selby along as if to her doom, and Tessa following him with her eyes all the time, as Saxon leapt into his passionate, dreadful and unavailing antics all round her. Once in a while she would note where he was, open her mouth to say something pleasant, and then coldly change her mind.

The Honeymoon

The ceremony was over. We were married. The registrar, who had done seventeen weddings that morning and who stood at a table between two vases of chrysanthemums, said:

'It is the custom, if the parties so desire, to embrace.' Victoria, who was very small and hated anyone telling her to do anything, tipped her head back to avoid being kissed but I bent down and gave her two pecks on the brim of her hat and one, at last, on her cheek. Surprised, she kissed me. Mistrustful of our Town Hall my mother-in-law said:

'They have wallpaper on the walls in these places.' We signed and then Victoria and I went out first down the long corridor and since I felt I was walking three inches above the floor I was puzzled by the marble echoes raised by my shoes. A photographer walked backwards before us. Outside, our party stood in two rows on the steps and we were photographed again, Harry – the best man – standing at the back. On the wall of a warehouse across the street I saw a notice saying, Do Not Obstruct this Entrance.

Then we drove off to my mother-in-law's house and I don't remember much more about it all, except a rather sudden unimportance, and Harry saying, when we got to the wedding-cake stage: 'When she cuts, clap.' The photographs were rushed round in the afternoon and it is all a blank until we went off to the station to catch the London train. Harry did something I would never have thought him capable of: it was the sort of thing he detested: he led the confetti-throwing. It snowed on us. He flung it, in contempt I suppose. He tried to stuff some down my neck. It was very dry and thick. He went mad, is all I can say. Something broke in me too. My teeth were wet. I suddenly hated Harry; it was a hatred stored up for two years; I went for him with my umbrella chasing him back from the gate into the house. I think I would have half-killed him or, at any rate, made him bleed, if my father had not dragged me back to the car. As we drove off, I opened the car window and shouted: 'My umbrella! My umbrella!' They had taken it from me and I could see my father propping it carefully against some shrubbery.

'The swine!' I said, brushing off the confetti, and then I looked at Victoria's face and stopped. 'My wife,' I thought. I couldn't believe it; she looked so sweet and tender as a kitten; she was pouting and blushing and when I put my arm round her waist I could feel the layers of silk moving over her soft body. How heavenly women are! For two years she had held out against marrying me; but now, in a mere three hours, she had softened and changed into mine.

When I look back on it I see the idea that I should marry Victoria was not mine alone. All her relations and friends wanted me to marry her. Harry wanted it most of all and everyone agreed with Harry that he should *not* marry her. The opposition came from Victoria. Harry was the man she wanted and Harry wanted only himself. He loved his own rich black hair, his own fawn complexion, his own romantic lips, his satanic side-glances, his clothes. He was a dandy and more than that. He loved himself as he was, as he would be and even as he had been in history. We worked in a big shoe shop in the town and when there were no customers and we had nothing to do, he used to make drawings of himself as Sir Walter Raleigh, in Indian ink, on old shoe boxes.

One day he said to me, eyeing me sideways and stroking his chin, as if he had a pointed beard on it:

'One of my ancestors was executed. He was a conspirator.'

At the end of my first day, when I was taken on at the shop, Harry said to me:

'I've got my motor-bike at the back. Let's go somewhere. I'll take you home.' Victoria who worked in the cash desk must have heard him, but I didn't realise the mistake I was making.

'I believe in being in the crowd but not of the crowd,' Harry called back to me, as I sat behind him.

The next day I saw that Victoria hated me. Harry usually took *her* home. This slight made her snap and raise her very small nose sharply so that I got to know her nose very well, especially the tiny nostrils. It was a dogmatic, sad little nose and that is where I began to fall in love with her – from the nose downwards. But after I had gone out once or twice more with Harry, Victoria's mind was made up. She did all she could to get me the sack. She made trouble between me and the manager by making mistakes on the bills and telling me, in front of customers, that I had got prices wrong. One day a woman came in and said I had sent her one crocodile and one lizard shoe: Victoria had changed the shoes. These tricks made me laugh and when I laughed she was astonished and all the more determined. Girls always go too far. The manager was no fool. One afternoon she saw the foot of the step ladder, which was used to get the shoes from the upper shelves, sticking out beyond the corner of the stock-room door. She gave it a push – she was very small but she was very strong – thinking I was up there getting a pair of 8½ brogues for a man who had come in with fishing rods. But it was Harry who was on the ladder. Down he fell and a whole pile of boxes with him.

'And what is all this?' the manager said, pointing to one of Harry's drawings of Sir Walter Raleigh.

'My ancestor,' said Harry scornfully.

It was he who was sacked. He was very pleased.

'She's a nice girl but I can't bear her. She once threw bread at me at a dance,' Harry said. 'I shall go to London.'

And so Victoria and I were left dumbfounded together. This changed her. She stopped quarrelling with me. I walked home with her several times. I enjoyed the clatter her heels made on the pavement, the way she drove her mother out of the room, the way she spoke to dogs. I stroked her neck in the park and this made her arch her back with pleasure. She sat on my knee in my lodgings, holding me tight enough to strangle me – and started telling me how much she loved Harry, ever since school, for years.

'Harry,' I said. 'You mean Sir Walter Raleigh.' She stiffened.

'He has proof,' she said. 'I couldn't love you.' This is where her friends came in and her mother.

'Don't worry,' they said. 'It's all silliness. She's difficult. Be patient. Be gentle.' But Harry was in London, far away. He came back once for Easter. The three of us went to a café.

'London,' said Harry looking darkly at me, 'is the most dangerous city in the world. You have to know your way about. But one can be in the crowd and yet not of it.'

It was a favourite sentence of his.

'Stop saying One as if you were a dummy,' Victoria said. Harry looked sideways at himself in the café mirror, raised an elaborate eyebrow and smiled at himself.

Victoria picked up the remains of her ice-cream and intended to throw it all at the mirror so that (she said afterwards) he could not see himself: it hit the glass but splashed over his grey suit. Later, he said to me, sarcastically:

'I congratulate you. Victoria is getting over that nonsense about me. She used to throw bread before.' He was wrong. Victoria had not changed. In the next two months I lost twenty pounds in weight and had pains in the back. The manager asked me to his house to supper and his wife told my fortune. A whole hand of spades came out and I dropped the Queen on the carpet.

'You're surrounded by enemies,' she said. This was not true. I had too many friends. Within the week I got a letter from Harry telling me of a job in London at nearly twice the salary.

I was getting tired of Harry, Harry, Harry from Victoria with her arms round my neck and when I heard the news I saw the truth. I had never been in love with her. I even loved the shoe trade better than I loved her, being on my own, away from my parents, too. I got sly. I told Victoria I was leaving the town for good and going to London, that no doubt I should see Harry and I would make him realise what a wonderful girl she was. I was enthusiastic about this. Victoria's reply exploded inside me:

'When do you go? At the end of the month?' she asked. 'We'll get married next week. We'll go to London for our honeymoon, that will save money.'

I could not believe it. I went to London to fix up the job. She made me promise to come back, the same day. When I returned tired out on the train that did not get in until eleven at night, Victoria was on the platform waiting for me. She rushed at me. She even grabbed me.

'I was worried to death. I'll never let you out of my sight again,' she said.

I was appalled.

'I've found an hotel for us,' I said.

'So have I,' she said. 'Isn't it wonderful.'

'Harry told me,' I said.

'Harry told me too,' she said. 'I telephoned to him.' Harry was making sure. It was he who got us married.

So there we were, married, sitting in the train going to London. I shall not forget the journey – four hours: it seemed like a fortnight. Fields, fields, people picking mushrooms, factories, telegraph poles, fields, towns, back gardens, junctions. We had a compartment to ourselves. I pulled the blinds on the corridor side after the ticket inspector had been and then I moved to kiss Victoria. She had changed into a tweed suit and she stiffened. The pout had gone from her lips. Her nose was raised.

'You haven't labelled your case,' she said looking up at the luggage rack.

'I did it this morning when you reminded me,' I said, putting my arm round her.

'I can't see it,' she said. I laughed.

'It's at the back,' I said. And I turned the case round to show her the label hanging down.

She still did not believe me.

'Look,' I said. She was small enough to lift on to the seat and I lifted her to see the label.

'It's what I thought,' she accused. 'You've put on the wrong label.'

'I haven't,' I said. I read out '"The Austin Hotel, Barnaby Street."'

'We're staying at Frenns,' she said. And she showed me the label on hers.

'You have made a mistake,' I said. 'Harry told me – the Austin.'

'Frenns, he said. You know he did,' she said.

'I beg your pardon, it was the Austin.'

Austin, Frenns, Frenns, Austin – so we went on. She got angry.

'Mother said you were obstinate,' she said.

The train slowed down beside a goods train carrying calves which were lowing.

'Those poor things. Prisoners!' cried Victoria. 'Look at them.'

She turned on me accusingly.

'Our honeymoon and you don't know where we're going.'

'The Austin Hotel,' I said. 'Here's the letter confirming our reservations.'

I showed her the letter. The Austin Hotel was printed at the top of the paper. Victoria was a suspicious girl. She took the paper and read it carefully from the very top edge to the bottom, twice. And then turned it over in case something was written on the other side.

'You see,' I said.

'You did this behind my back,' she said.

'I'll alter your labels,' I said, getting out my pen.

'Don't touch them,' she said, taking my pen from me. 'After what he's done to me, do you think I would go to a place Harry suggested.'

'He suggested both.'

'One to me, one to you,' she said.

'I know why his ancestor was executed,' I said. 'Still he was only giving us a choice.'

'A choice,' she said. 'You think it's funny, don't you? What choice has anyone got?' I glanced out of the window.

'A pheasant. Quick. Look,' I called to her. She turned her head. 'Two,' she said and sat gloomily looking at her hands in her lap. Once more I put my arm round her. 'Nature is a trap,' she said, moving away from me. 'Leave me alone.'

She closed her eyes. She could not get comfortable. Crossly she put her head on my shoulder. Suddenly a red-faced young soldier who was shouting to several others slid our door back, gave us a look, winked at me and made a lewd noise, 'Clop, clop,' with his tongue and went off shouting to his friends.

'Don't touch me, I said,' said Victoria.

'What is the matter?' I asked.

'Oh, stop asking me what is the matter. You whine. Talk to me. Don't ask me questions.'

The soldiers were bollocking about down the corridor. Of course, when Victoria said 'Talk to me' that put every idea out of my head. She was silent most of the way to London. What was on her mind? I knew what was on mine.

Villas began to thicken. The train shrieked at thousands of them. I saw a bus with the name Victoria on it. I nudged her in my excitement. She did not look. We went into tunnels and London flung smoke at us.

'We are nearly there,' I shouted with excitement. She did not speak. She said nothing when we got out of the train at the station but it was she who said sharply to the cab driver before I could open my mouth: 'The Austin Hotel.'

'Where's that, miss?' said the cab driver.

'Barnaby Street,' I called, over her head.

London seemed to smell of cold escaping gas and the houses looked like hundreds of dirty sparrows and the sky like a rag, as we drove to the hotel.

There must have been a dozen little brown houses converted into hotels in the street where the Austin was – Linden, Stella Maris, Northern, Fitzroy, Malvern, I noticed the names. They looked friendly all together; one had blue and yellow lights round its windows; ours was next door, the brick work painted green from the basement to the first floor. The Austin, it said. Private Hotel. Private – how nice! Victoria had said it made her sick when the manager at the shoe shop had told us that he and his wife had the Bridal Suite at the large hotel in Ventnor thirty years ago.

'Did you pay the taxi driver enough? I don't like the way he's looking at us,' Victoria said to me, when the driver had put our luggage out.

'He's looking at the hotel,' I said.

An Irish maid came up from the basement to the door, eating something, and said 'Sign here' and 'Up to the top to number twelve,' and hearing a whistle from below, she said 'Wait till I put me bloody kettle off.'

We went upstairs. It was a tidy, well-polished place, nicely painted, with a fern in a brass pot on every landing. It was wonderfully private and quiet. A girl in a dressing-gown and with a comb in her hand looked out of a door on the second floor and gaped at Victoria and me.

'I thought it was Gladys, sorry,' she said. Friendly people. And we heard the Irish maid say to her, as she came up at last: 'It's the honeymoon couple.'

My heart was banging and I felt hungry: there was a smell of steak pudding coming up the stairs, but at the top landing, it had gone. The maid pushed open the door. The room had a double bed with a pretty pink cover and there was a fancy kind of net curtain at the window, with rabbits and daffodils on it.

'Ah, look at me, leaving that this morning,' said the Irish girl, taking away the floor mop she had left beside the dressing-table.

I waited for the door to close and then I stepped out to kiss Victoria, saying, 'It's clean. It's at the front.'

'We must unpack,' she said, stepping back.

My father's words came back to me. 'It may sound a funny thing to say but when your mother and I were first married, I was taking my shoes off, I'd never been in an hotel with your mother before . . .' Well, that is what I felt like when Victoria said she must unpack. I had never seen her unpack. I'd never seen any woman unpack.

First she went all round the room to every corner and cupboard in it, like a cat. And opened all the drawers. She unlocked her cases and out came her dresses. She spread them on the bed and straightened them, one by one. Out came the new brushes her aunt had given her. Then things for her dressing-table. Then she started hanging dresses and going back to give them a pull or change the coat hanger. Every time she walked across the room (and it must have been a hundred times), the windows shook. I had put a brown suit and a tweed jacket on a chair.

'If you're not wearing those, hang them. They'll get out of shape,' she said.

I did not know where to hang them, so I hung them over the door of a cupboard.

'They don't leave you much room,' she said. 'What have you done with your shoes? Look what you're doing! Sweep it up.'

I had taken off my jacket and one more shower of Harry's confetti went on to the floor.

'What with?' I said and went to look out of the window. An oldish man and a young woman were getting out of a taxi and came into our hotel: father and daughter, I thought. The evening was beginning and the neon lights from the Court Hotel opposite began to turn one of our walls red and made Victoria look as if she were blushing. She had finished unpacking.

'You leave your things everywhere,' she said. 'I am going to wash.'

She took off her jacket and her blouse and went to the basin. I was suddenly frightened of her, or perhaps it was of the hooks of her brassière.

'And then we'll go and look at London,' I said, exhausted, and sat on the edge of the bed. The next thing she was asking me for her brown shoes and as I went to look for them she went to the cupboard, stepped out of her skirt and was half-way into a new dress when I looked round.

Suddenly she pulled it off and rushed to the basin.

'Go away. Quickly. I feel sick,' she said.

'I'll open the window,' I said. 'It's stuffy in here.'

She wasn't sick. I helped her to the bed.

'Go out. Go for a walk,' she said.

'No,' I said. 'We'll go out together. We'll have a bit of air and a drink. You'll feel better.'

'No,' she said.

I waited. Outside the taxis were passing.

'How do you feel now?' I asked.

'Oh, do stop asking me how I feel. All right. Let us go out.'

So we went out. When we got downstairs we met the landlady. She had very large blue eyes and bleached hair.

'Comfortable, dear?' she said as she went coldly and rapidly over everything Victoria had got on.

'Going to take some air,' I said.

'Nothing like it,' said the landlady.

Victoria must have been studying her for when she got outside she said: 'She's been drinking.'

'She looked like a sofa standing up on end,' I said. Victoria did not laugh.

'Perhaps,' I said, 'she'd lost a castor.' Victoria did not smile.

Where we went I could not tell you. London looked heavy. There was nothing but streets of closed shops. I read out the names of them. We passed restaurants. We went to a pub but Victoria would not drink anything.

'Aren't you going to eat?' she said.

'They don't serve food here,' I said.

'Oh! Then why did we come here?' Of course, as Harry said, you've got to know London. He could have told us where to eat. I ought to have asked him.

'There's a place,' she said, pointing to a lit-up cafeteria. And on our way to it, she heard a cat miaow and we stopped in an office doorway while she stroked it. It tried to follow us.

'Go back,' she said. 'Go back. It will get run over. Please!' Victoria was almost in tears and we stood there coaxing the cat. Its fur was gritty. I tried to grab it and it jumped from me and raced clean across the street.

Victoria gave a shriek. Fortunately it got across safely and went into a doorway opposite and stared at us.

'Suppose it tries to get back,' she said. Her nails were digging into my arm where she was holding it. Well, in the end, I had a poached egg at the cafeteria. Victoria would not touch hers. And we went back to the Austin. My heart was hammering. A radio was playing on the second floor. I went to the bathroom. When I got back to our room the light was off. I thought Victoria must be in bed, but she was not. The window was wide open and the curtain blowing far into the room. She had gone. And then I saw her. She was sitting in her night-gown on the window with both legs over the sill. I rushed over to her.

'I can't, I can't!' she cried as I caught her. I had quite a fight getting her in.

'I don't love you,' she said. 'I never loved you. It is Harry. I'm sorry, I'm sorry. But I can't.' She cried and she clung.

'I thought I could, but I can't.' It was just like our early days but now Harry was cut off from her by our marriage.

I could not believe what I heard. I wanted her more than I can say, for her grief and tears, the ugliness of it, and the anger I felt, made her more desirable.

'I never wanted to marry you. They made me. You forced me into it.'

The little twister, I thought.

'It's a pity Harry isn't here,' I said bitterly.

'That's a dirty remark,' she said fiercely and she stopped crying.

Well, I thought, I have heard of this happening to people but fancy it happening to me. I saw years of empty life ahead of me. Suddenly she said:

'I wonder whether that poor cat was locked out?' and we started talking about cats, her mother's cats, the cats that stalked one another on the garden walls at the back of her mother's house. She became calm.

'You are so understanding,' she said. 'I have done something terrible to you. That is what is so unfair.'

'Get into bed. I'll go and sit over there,' I said. 'You'll catch cold.'

She obeyed. Exhausted, I went and sat in the chair by the window.

It was a narrow, grey armchair of the furry kind and the fur pricked through my trousers and my sleeves. Do you know what she did, within five minutes? She fell asleep. The wedding night! I could hear the whistling noise from her open mouth. There was her whistle, the whipping of the cars going by, the ticking of taxis outside, the hotels, the voices of the drunks after the pubs had closed. It had seemed a quiet street and a quiet hotel, but now bedroom doors were banging, lavatories and basins were flushed, pipes jumped. Even at two in the morning people were coming in. On our floor you could hear boots coming off, throats being cleared, the high laugh of a woman once or twice and heavy bumps on mattresses as if enormous bodies, too big for the beds, had flopped on them.

I thought: 'I will wait. She didn't mean it,' and took off my collar and tie and loosened my shoes. I was tired out. I must have dozed off. I was dreaming we were in the train and that suddenly I was being sucked out of the window by an overpowering voice that said:

'I am Sir Walter Raleigh.'

And in a second I was fighting for my life with the manageress of the hotel who was naked and covered with grease. I woke up in terror. And then I heard shouts coming from the street. Screams were coming from the stairs of the hotel. I looked out of the window and down below in the street I saw police. They were pushing two or three women into a van. Then I saw a policeman ushering out the manageress of our hotel. She was calling back, I suppose, to the Irish maid:

'Ring my solicitor. Phone him up.'

Suddenly the door of our room was opened. I turned and a policeman stood there.

'Come on. Out of this,' he said, ignoring me and giving the bed a shake.

'Here!' I shouted.

Victoria woke up and shouted: 'Harry!'

'You keep out of this, Harry,' said the policeman to me.

'What do you want? This is my wife.'

'Come on, miss,' said the policeman to Victoria. The cab driver had called her "miss' too.

The voice of the Irish maid came up the stairs.

'It's the honeymoon couple.' She got to the room.

'It's the honeymoon couple,' she said. The policeman looked around the room, at my brown suit and the extra jacket hanging on the cupboard. Then he saw the confetti on the floor.

'Here's our reservation,' I said, pushing the letter at him. 'What's this all about? What do you mean by breaking in?'

The policeman went out to the passage.

'Here, who's this?' he called down the stairs. Someone answered and he came back. He looked at me contemptuously:

'You ought to know better than to bring your wife to a place like this. Take my tip and clear out by the morning unless you want trouble.'

'How dare you. My husband is the assistant manager at Walgrave's,' shouted Victoria and got out of bed to fly at him, in her night-dress.

'Ma'am!' said the policeman, averting his face, 'Please go back to bed.'

And he hurried from the room.

'Why,' cried Victoria to me, 'did you let him insult me? Why didn't you hit him? Get dressed. I'm going to ring up the police.'

'That was the police,' I said.

'I'm not blind,' she shouted.

'Funny places for Harry to know about,' I said. 'Come and look.'

They were just closing the door of the police van as we looked out of the window. Then we saw people looking out of windows opposite. They were not looking at the police van. They were looking at us. We both drew our heads in and pulled the curtains across.

'This was your hotel, not Harry's,' she said. 'You stayed here.

'I've never stayed in London in my life,' I said.

'Harry said Frenns.'

Frenns, Austin, Austin, Frenns – we were off again.

'Harry told us both of them,' I said. 'There must be something wrong with Harry.'

'What?' she defied.

'He is in the world but not of it.' She went to the chest of drawers and began taking her clothes out.

'I'm going now,' she said.

'Where, at three in the morning?'

'I'm going. Get my dresses. Don't drag them on the floor. Look what you've done.'

She dressed. We packed everything up. We carried our luggage downstairs. The bedroom doors were open. In the manageress's office a policeman was sitting with the Irish maid. They looked at us in silence, but afterwards I heard them laughing, the maid was peeping through the curtains as we got into the street.

We walked. I was lugging the cases and Victoria had one of hers. My arms ached as we trudged. There was no one about. We did not know where we were going.

'I wish we had Harry here,' I said. 'He could carry one of these. Wait.'

I put the cases down and changed loads.

'And he knows London,' I said. 'Come on.'

'Where are we going?' Victoria said weakly.

'Where did that cat live?' I said. We passed a small open square with a seat in it.

'This will do,' I said.

'We can't stay out,' she said. At last I saw a taxi coming slowly towards us like a housefly along the black, glassy street. I hailed him. I told him to go to the station we had arrived at.

'I'll put you back on the morning train,' I said. 'You can have a sleep at the Station Hotel. I need a sleep myself. I'll get a couple of rooms.'

And that is what we would have done but when we got there I didn't like to ask for two singles: it didn't seem respectable and I didn't like the look the night clerk gave us. We were too tired to undress but slept in our clothes until midday the following day: Sunday.

They do a lot of shunting at the main line stations on Sundays; the night mail comes in, the sleepers go out to the siding. As for us, we got rid of Harry for good.

The Chain-Smoker

The important thing was to stop Magnolia going to Venice. 'That I won't have,' Karvo said. 'Where is Chatty? Never here when he is wanted. Drunk, I suppose. Or in bed. I bet he's at his aunt's. Get him.'

At that very moment Chatterton came into the office, opening the door only about a foot and sliding in.

'Chatty!' Karvo made a sound like a wounded bull, indeed almost wept. 'You've heard the news?' Karvo waved the others out of the office and Chatty sat down on the sofa opposite Karvo's enormous desk; or, rather, he folded up there like a small piece of human trellis that smoked, squeaked and coughed. He was an illness in itself.

'Yes,' Chatty said. 'She has heard the doctor has stopped you flying. She's heard you and Maureen are picking up the train in Paris. She rang me half an hour ago.'

'Chatty, you've got to stop her. I won't have that woman in Venice,' Karvo said. 'You've got to keep her in London. I tried to get you last night. Where were you?'

'I was with her,' said Chatty. 'At the Spangle.'

'I'm very grateful to you,' said Karvo, calming down.

Chatty swallowed a couple of pills off the palm of his hand. 'The fog got into my chest,' he said. 'She's still going to court. But she doesn't know whether she will shoot you or commit suicide. What she wants to do is to commit suicide first, then shoot you and then sue the company for breach of contract. Somewhere along the line she has got to fit in a scene at some place like the Caprice in which she tears Maureen's dress off her back. She would like to see blood – not pools of it, but visible nail-stripes on Maureen's face, any-where it will show – say on the upper part of the back. She doesn't know whether it would be better to do this in the restaurant – I told her it had been done too often in restaurants – or in court, but I

[787]

pointed out that Maureen was not a material witness and would not be there.'

Karvo paid no attention. He was looking at the script on his desk, but glancing up said, considerately:

'Chatty, are you all right? I can hear your chest from here. You're not going to crack up again?'

'I've been up half the night three nights running. She never wants to go to bed.'

'I didn't have *that* trouble with her,' Karvo grunted boastfully, looking at the script again.

'I made a mistake about Magnolia,' Karvo went on. 'I thought she would lift the whole story. She has the finest pair of arms I've ever seen in pictures, but she can't move them except up and down slowly like a cop holding up traffic. She can't move anything. You saw her. I thought she was Life. She's as dead as the Venus de Milo.'

'It has no arms,' said Chatty. 'Magnolia *is* Life. I told her so last night. I said "Magnolia, you're Life . . ."'

'*You* said that to her?' said Karvo suspiciously.

'Yes. She said you said she was Life. I said "He was right. You're Life itself." Actually, larger.'

'It's no good in pictures,' Karvo said.

'It's terrible out of pictures,' Chatty said. 'Awful in the evenings.'

'You've got to stop her. I don't care how,' Karvo said, shouting again.

'I know' said Chatty. 'I'm having lunch with her.' And he got up and used one of the telephones on Karvo's desk. 'No. I know the time of the train, sweetie' he said in the murdered voice of the sick. 'Bring me the Continental timetable in your own little loving hands.'

'Why do you want that?' said Karvo, suspicious again.

'I was brought up on it; it's the only book I can read now without having a heart attack,' said Chatty. The girl brought the book into the office and Chatty's face broke into dozens of small smiling lines, like a cracked plate, and he did two or three more coughs. The girl looked protectively at him.

'What I dream of is a beautiful sanatorium with you looking after me,' he said to the girl who said: 'Oh Mr Chatterton, no.'

Karvo shook his head.

'You ought to stop smoking, Chatty.'

'I appeal to the mother in them,' said Chatterton. 'If I stopped coughing I'd be useless to the firm. I'll try and get Magnolia down to the farm, Tony.'

'That's a good idea,' said Karvo generously. 'It will do you good. You need pure air.'

'I'm working on the idea that her ancestors travelled in cattle trucks. I doubt if it will work.'

Karvo went very red. The innuendo reflected on his tastes. He was going to make a speech, but Chatty looked at his watch, said 'I'll be late,' and went.

Magnolia was not Karvo's first mistake. Art is the residue of innumerable rejections; so, in fact, is love. So is everything. Some rejections are more difficult than others. Karvo was the godhead of the organisation; Chatty had had to give up years ago, after his first breakdown, but Karvo clung to him. He had drifted into becoming the oilcan of the machine, the worn-out doctor. Sooner or later, everyone from the doorman upwards was bound to turn to Chatty: the shrunk face, the one-lung chest, the shaky hand, the sad busy eyes, the weak, grating voice that seemed to contain the dregs of all the rumours in the world, concealed a dedication to all the things the machine had forgotten to do. The very weakness of the voice contained a final assuring sense that the situation, whatever it was, had hit bottom and that he had fallen back on forces only he was in touch with. What his official job was, neither he nor anyone knew. Except that he had to put everything right.

In black moments, he would say, 'I'm the company's hangman.' A shrewd actress would know she was losing her part if she found herself dining at Claridges alone with Chatty, with champagne on the table. One or two of Karvo's wives had had the disturbing experience of seeing Chatty arrive at the house with flowers and were alarmed by his tête-à-têtes. In the middle of an evening's drinking, actors would suddenly wonder why Chatty was telling them, again and again, that they were very great artists. Diners at the Spangle or the Hundred and Five would notice how a neat, sick man, darkened by sun lamp, so often seemed to be at a certain table with a girl who was leaning close to him and pouring out what was, momentarily, her heart, while he nodded and filled up her glass. They had seen some girls with elbows on the table, with tears running down their cheeks, and next to them, elbows on table too, not in tears, but wearing his wrecked expression, Chatty stroking a hand, listening, nodding, squeezing and – when a waiter passed – giving an efficient nod at the bottle. It would be replaced. Some held his arm. Others, once every half hour, he lightly kissed on the bare shoulder. He might ask to look at a ring. Or, gazing at their palms, tell their fortunes. To others he whispered a scandal: they leaned back open-mouthed and when he had finished they leaned towards him and went back satisfied to their own tale. In certain cases, the difficult ones, he might be driven almost to the edge (but never further) of his own secret. Very rarely, they laughed; occasionally simple ones would put an arm round his neck and rest a head on his shoulders, not thinking about him at all, their soft hunting eyes gazing round the restaurant, and he would sit back happily, giving only an occasional glance at them. His job was done.

So now he was with Magnolia. She was a woman who easily changed size. She could inflate or contract. At the moment, not touching her smoked salmon, she was contracting. The large mouth had become no more than a slot, her large eyes a collection of flints, her flowing brows had stiffened and had the boding look of moustaches, her noble breasts were like a pair of grenades with the pins out; and those arms, usually so still and statuesque, now swiped about like Indian clubs as she talked. And Karvo said she could not move! Chatty, sitting beside her, came only up to her shoulder, and when she looked down at him, she looked as though she was planning eventually to get up and tread on him, affecting not to see he was there.

'These things never last with Karvo,' he persisted, worn out, tasting the wine and pouring her a glass. She looked at it with hatred. 'A girl like that can't hold him.'

'A television starlet from Walsall,' she sneered. 'She can't act. And she smells. Ask the camera men. Something's happened to Karvo – what is it? You know him. His wife is at the back of this. Well, he's not going to get away with it. I'll kill her. Chatty, I'm going on that train. Why doesn't he fly?'

'The doctor stopped him.'

'We always flew. He needs more than a doctor. I shall be on that train.'

Her mouth widened and she started to eat. It looked as though she were eating what she had just killed.

'You know, Nolly,' said Chatty, 'you're a superb girl. Shall I tell you something? I found you, didn't I? Oh yes, I did. I saw you in *Potter's Clay* years before Karvo. It's all my fault. I made Karvo take you. I showed him what you were. I said "She will lift the whole show, get it right off the ground." You'll sit there like a goddess. When you move, just as you are doing now . . .'

She was putting a piece of smoked salmon towards her mouth but stopped and put her fork back to look at him.

'There,' he exclaimed, 'that movement! What you did that very minute! A small thing like that: you're a lady. There's breeding in it. I'll tell you something I never told you. When you and he went off that first evening I knew something was on; I came in here and I got plastered.' She was bored.

'Why?'

Chatty turned his head away.

'Stop bitching. You know why.'

And he turned his head back again and gazed at her and blinked. He had sunk lower on the banquette so that she now swelled enormously over him, and as she swelled, so he sank lower, reached for his glass and drained it recklessly and stared up at her through the glass he drank. She studied him with the slow astonishment of a cat that is not quite sure whether she has a mouse beside her; then with horror; then with the look of a mother who says to her baby 'I could eat you,' but a mother who is going to do it, and not eat, but gnaw. He put out his small brown hand and rested it on her leg and controlled his surprise at the monumental size of it.

Chatty rarely had to go as far as this; most girls – and Magnolia was one – could recognise the difference between the pass direct and a pinch that was the retraction of a careless preceding remark. With Magnolia his normal methods had failed: expressing unbelief, then sympathy, then fierce indignation at the man – he was cracking up, had lost his reason, it was "his age" etc. etc. – Chatty would then attack the other woman, mentioning false or disorganised teeth, affected voice and adding minutiae of his own: rubbing calves, perhaps, or inturned toes. He would throw in the name of some interesting man ('not in the theatre, darling') and drop into a word or two of French. *Tout passe, tout casse, tout lasse* – wasted, by the way, on Magnolia who did not speak French. He would then, if they were still difficult, move on towards his own secret. He was a waif: they were both lonely waifs. Chatty's secret: that was what everyone wanted to know and they became alert at this stage. Why wasn't he married? Was he queer? Was he nothing? Mother's boy? Auntie's boy? He evaded these insinuations by talking about his farm. Ah, but what went on at that farm? Who was this woman he called Aunt Laura down at the farm? There were times when it seemed that only the desperate pass, what he called the final solution, would do.

'Darling I want to bite that lovely shoulder. Come down to the farm with me.'

They were almost agog. What orgies went on there? They would discover the secret. Discreetly he moved to enthusiastic anti-climax.

'We shall be on our own. There's only Aunt Laura there. She's deaf. Looking after her bed-ridden sister. Very religious. I'll show you my Hereford herd. We can cut down nettles. Aunt Laura's woman who used to come up from the village to cook is in hospital, but we'll manage. It's the simple life. Just ourselves. What d'you say?'

He had never known them not to say 'No'. Very apologetically too. Apologising calmed them. Then he would pay the bill, drop them in the firm's car, saying 'In the old days I used to slip away to Paris.' Just the idea! But not with him, oh dear God no! They could do better than that – and sometimes did, and when he dropped them at their flat, he had dissolved an illusion and given them a new one.

But Chatty did not offer Aunt Laura to Magnolia. He had seen that this case was too desperate: also, what would any sane woman sooner do – go to Venice or to Wiltshire? No press in Wiltshire. So when he said 'Stop bitching' and there was no answering twitch of her leg to his hand, he took a long and conquering breath.

'I know how you feel,' he said. 'I feel as you do. I said to Karvo "You don't understand Magnolia. She's virginal. There's an inner chastity, something single-hearted, when she loves she loves once and for all. I feel it, you feel it, the audience feels it. She's a one-man woman. Bucky and the Bronsinki boy – oh yes, I know about *them*, but that doesn't alter the inner truth".'

Magnolia looked strangely at him. The idea that she had an inner nature was new to her, that it was virginal, amazed. Her mouth started to become its normal size, her brows began to curve – at the recollection, of course, of Bucky and the Bronsinki boy – and she looked with the beginning of curiosity at Chatty: she had the sensation that he was revealing an unsuspected vacancy in her life. Chatty, always sensitive to hopeful change, took his hand off her leg – a good move: Magnolia tried out a feeling of austerity. It made her feel important. Still, her refrain did not change, except in tone. There was a just detectable new note of self-sacrifice.

'I'm going on that train. I hate trains. Why doesn't he fly? Well, I'm going on it. I've got my reservation.'

Was a moral nature being born? Chatty put his hand back quickly.

'We'll go together,' he said. 'I've got a reservation too.'

'You? You have? Here,' she said coarsely, 'what's the bloody idea? Is this one of Karvo's bloody tricks?' A dangerous moment! Moral natures are not born suddenly. Chatty gave a violent grip of righteousness to her leg. He spoke in a righteous voice, not forgetting to put some of the ginger of the underhand in it.

'My job's at stake, too,' he said out of the corner of his mouth. 'I don't know about you, but I know what I'm doing. We're going together to rescue him. We've got to save that man, between us. It's worth ten thousand a year to me. But money's nothing. I don't know why I should save him – well, I do know. It's for you.'

'I'm going to raise hell at the Gare de Lyon,' she stuck to it. 'I've got their seat numbers. I'll turn the dining-car upside down. I'll . . .'

'No, darling, listen to me. Wait till we get to Venice. The Paris Press is no good to you. They'll be in Venice, anyway.'

Chatty made one of his body-wrecking efforts and sent up a hard stare into Magnolia's eyes. He noted, with satisfaction, as the stare continued, that when she removed his hand from her leg, she did so with a primness which must have been a new thing for her.

Months afterwards Chatty told Karvo that until the Magnolia episode, and in spite of all his experience, he had never realised what genius owes to lucky insights. The plan was clumsy and full of risks. You had to choose between evils. Better a scene at the Gare de Lyon – without the Press – than a scene at Venice; the thing to avoid was something, thank God, that had not got into Magnolia's stupid head. She could easily have flown to Venice on her own and waited to trap him at the Gritti as he arrived. Why didn't she think of that?

'I tumbled on the obvious,' Chatty said. 'My task was to encourage this new growth of virtue in Magnolia. There is a detective in every virtuous woman – you know, "I'm having my husband followed." It was the idea of *following* you that had narrowed her mind.'

He clinched with Magnolia quickly.

'Show me that ticket,' he snapped at her. Half-bewildered she got it out of her bag. He took it and said:

'We'll scrap this part. Let me have it. We'll fly to Paris while Maureen is being sick in the Channel and pick up the train there.'

Magnolia got up from the table and had a look of dawning righteousness on her face. ('She looked ready to sing *Fight the good fight*,' Chatty said.)

'I admit,' she said to Chatty, 'I was wrong about you.'

Chatty went back to Karvo.

'Well?' said Karvo vehemently.

'We're going *with* you. I can't stop her.'

'Chatty,' shouted Karvo.

'Listen. The first principle in dealing with problems is to break them into their parts. First of all, I am restoring her virginity. I am doing that for self-protection.'

'Stop being so clever. I have to think of the Press. She can't come with me. That's the whole point.'

Chatty began a long fit of coughing. He coughed up and down the sofa.

'There's nothing to be done about that. I've gone the whole hog with her.'

Karvo looked cynically and despisingly at Chatty. Chatty understood the look.

'No, I agree, not that. Loyalty to the company does not go as far as that,' said Chatty, wiping his eyes.

Karvo growled at him.

'We shall travel in the back part of the train,' said Chatty.

'That won't do, I tell you,' shouted Karvo. 'This is serious.'

'Tony, pictures have destroyed your intelligence. You're going to Venice, aren't you? You leave Paris on the *Adriatique* at 15.30. Right? So Magnolia and I have to be on it. I have got our reservations, but by some mistake, in the office – I don't know who the girl is who looks after your reservations, but you ought to sack her – Magnolia and I are leaving Paris at 7.36 in the morning, on the Geneva non-stop.'

'You're not going to Venice?'

'We *think* we are going to Venice. Spiritually Magnolia is travelling in the last coach on your train. Physically we shall be in Geneva.'

'Why Geneva, for God's sake,' said Karvo.

'The lake, the mountains, William Tell.'

'She can fly from Geneva!' said Karvo.

'I am going to be very ill,' said Chatty.

'Ill?' said Karvo. 'Your mind's ill. Your brain has gone soft. You've made a mess of this. I shall fly. I shall have to fly and you know what the doctor said. Come to my funeral.'

'I'll be laid out in Geneva,' said Chatty, 'a good half-day before you and Maureen get to Venice. Come to mine.'

Chatty (Karvo used to say) would never have been one of the great directors; he always preferred the trees to the wood. An obscurantist. His plots were always entangled. He never thought things out. But he had two great gifts: a talent for confusing issues and above all for illness. This gave him the invalid's mastery of detail. When Chatty sickened he was inspired.

Before the flight to Paris he did not go to bed at all; he was on the telephone to Magnolia and drinking hard. It made him sound sincere. Take the calls to Magnolia first:

'Magnolia. Something terrible has happened. That Miss What's-her-name in the office must have spilled the beans. Karvo's heard something. The swine's catching the *morning* train to Venice.'

He waited and prayed. No. Thank God! Magnolia did not say 'There's no morning train to Venice.'

'The 7.36. We've got to be there. We're flying tonight. I'm changing the tickets now.'

'Call it off,' said Magnolia suspiciously.

'No,' shouted Chatty. 'I'm getting on that train and so are you. I've got the tickets in my pocket. You're not going to let them get away with it. They're committing *adultery*, Magnolia!'

'You're drinking, Chatty.'

'Of course I'm drinking,' said Chatty. 'I'll have the car for the airport at 1.15. They must be in Paris already. No. I don't know where.'

This decided Magnolia: that woman, in Paris!

As for illness, indispensable to the refinements of strategy: Chatty was a wreck when he got Magnolia into the 'plane. Only his fevered eyes seemed to be alive: they seemed to drag his body after them.

In the 'plane he muttered on and off during the flight. Halfway across the Channel he began fidgetting in his seat, going through his pockets and wearing Magnolia down with the words 'I've forgotten my pills. I can't move without them.' Magnolia was frightened by his state: the dawn gave him an awful yellow look. He collapsed into a chair at the Café at the Invalides and sent a waiter to see if there was a pharmacy open and told Magnolia the man could easily make a fatal mistake. She must go with him. No pharmacies were open. Magnolia's ignorance of French brought out her aggression.

'My friend is very ill,' she said in English to the waiter. He did not understand.

'My husband is dying,' she shouted. This episode made the arrival of Chatty and Magnolia at the Gare de Lyon seem like an ambulance party rushing to hospital with three minutes to spare before the train left or the patient died. Chatty was not going to have Magnolia running loose on the platform for half an hour scrutinising every coach or finding out they were on the Geneva train.

They sat breathless in the compartment. Chatty had a wide range of coughs, from the short, dry hack to the display that came up from the ankles and seemed to split his eyes.

'A little more air.' He got up to open the window.

'Sit down,' said Magnolia. She was frightened. Her strong arms drew down the heavy window of the French train herself.

Then she watched. When he stopped coughing at last he told a terrible story about an injection for tetanus he had been given when he was a schoolboy, as the train moved off, and laughed.

'Stop laughing,' she said. 'You'll bring it on again.'

Her face, he was pleased to see, had grown severe. A firm, almost chaste look of moral reprimand was growing on it. He got out a cigarette.

'Don't smoke,' she said, and repeated with appeal:

'Chatty, *please* don't smoke.' He put his cigarettes away.

'You're right,' he said.

'Try and sleep.'

'I wish I could. People keep passing in the corridor. Do you mind if we pull down the blind.'

'*I'll* do it,' she said, commanding.

'Magnolia,' he said. 'You're being extraordinarily good to me. You're a saint. I'm sorry, I seem to be making a mess of this.'

'It's not your fault,' she said.

'It is.'

'No, it's mine,' she said on a note of noble confession. But she gave a grind to her teeth. 'I ought to have flown.' Oh God, thought Chatty, she's off again.

'If you had I would have gone with you,' he said. 'I'm going to see you through this thing. When I think of that bastard twelve coaches up the train...'

'Twelve?' she said, uncrossing her legs and frowning.

'You can imagine how I feel,' he said. 'I look at you and I see a woman he has never seen.'

'Sleep,' she said sternly.

'I can't,' he said.

'You must.'

'I've made a mess of my life. I'm sorry for a lot of things I've done. Why did I let him take you?'

Chatty closed his eyes but not completely. He had to keep an eye on her. He was not going to have her slipping out into the corridor, searching the coaches or talking to informative strangers. He was surprised to discern, though mistily through his lashes, that she was looking neither restless nor relaxed, but sat there rigidly gazing at him with apprehension. A novel combination of feelings was growing in her. As virtue was increased by her mission and by looking after him, so a new fear was born too: the fear that is native to virtue. She was travelling alone in a railway compartment with a man in a chaotically disturbed state – a man who, so he said, had repressed certain feelings for years. She was in his hands. And in a foreign country too. As she watched the French meadows and the licentious woodlands go by, she wondered if he would go mad and attack her. These were pleasant sensations; they made her feel prim. What did she, what did anyone know about Chatty? In sleep he looked very ugly.

At Dijon he opened his eyes and sneezed.

'When the sun rises the moon sneezes,' he said. 'Old Chinese proverb.'

He laughed. She did not like that. He *was* mad! She sat back and squeezed her legs together tightly.

The ticket inspector came in.

'What did he say? He was looking at me,' asked Magnolia, afterwards.

'He said he had seen you in a picture. "Disarmed".'

Magnolia looked happy for the first time.

'I wish I spoke French like you do,' she said. 'Teach me some words.' And taking out her mirror made up her face.

'And,' said Chatty, leering, as the train clattered through the long sidings and went out of Dijon, 'he was looking at the drawn blinds. The frogs never miss anything. They have imagination.'

Magnolia closed her bag and was on guard.

'I can't eat,' said Chatty when he heard the luncheon bell tinkle. 'But I'll take you along. You must eat something.'

'No,' she said. 'I don't want anything.'

She was either not being distracted from her revenge or she was becoming increasingly the nurse. Chatty wished he knew which it was.

Hours passed sleepily and then, seeing her restive, he told her about his Aunt Laura. She used to go to Aix where the waters are good for the kidneys. The doctors could not decide whether she had two or two and a half kidneys. Many people, he said, have extra rudimentary organs. Magnolia saw herself approaching his secret.

'Two and a half! Is she really your aunt?' she said.

'I will tell you the honest truth,' said Chatty.

'Yes?'

'I don't really know. We were brought up to call her Auntie. She has been like a mother to us. And yet more like a nun than a mother. Something must have happened to her; some disappointment – she gave up everything for us.'

Magnolia found herself wondering how she would look as a nun.

Chatty said, 'Say what you like, there is *something* about nuns. I can see it in you,' he was saying. 'All women have a nun inside them.' It was pleasant to hear and made her idly double her watch on Chatty.

'Those poor nuns in Africa,' she said, ready to put up a fight if he sprang at her.

Chatty was, of course, thinking of the approaching crisis. It would come when they got to Geneva. The question was whether she would see what had happened, at the station; or whether he might hold out until they saw Lake Léman. He was occupied with the fantasy that he might palm off the lake as the Mediterranean. He rejected it. He plumped for a terrible scene at the station. He would stagger off the train and simply collapse on the platform. 'Get a doctor. Get an ambulance,' he would shout. He suddenly heard Magnolia say irritably:

'When do we get to Venice?'

'An hour and a half, I should say.'

'Don't you know?' said Magnolia getting crosser. And ruining everything, two inspectors slid back the door of the compartment, a young one and an old one. The old one had spread the news that Magnolia was on the train.

'When do we get to Venice?' she called out in English to the older one.

'Venice?' said the older inspector in English, too. 'We are going to Geneva.'

'Chatty!' shouted Magnolia.

'This is the Geneva train,' said the younger inspector in French.

'Good lord,' said Chatty. 'They've put us on the wrong train.'

'Give me those tickets,' Magnolia shouted again.

The speed at which Magnolia left her religious order was something Chatty always remembered. Her face became crimson, then violet, marked by changing dabs of green; she swelled up, she rose up. She pushed Chatty aside and started on the inspectors. The older one stepped back and pushed the young one forward: the young one made a speech. She flew at Chatty:

'What is he saying?'

And not waiting for an answer, she declaimed that she was due at Venice that very moment, to receive the Festival prize; that the train must be put into reverse; that a 'plane be brought instantly into the compartment; that the train itself must, if necessary, fly. The young inspector gazed at the fling of Magnolia's white arms from armpit to wrist, the terrifying spread of her fingers, the rise and fall of her volcanic bosom, the blue eyes that ripped him, the throat that boiled, the nostrils that went in and out like bellows, until tears of admiration formed in his young eyes. Chatty raised his eyebrows at the older inspector, who raised his eyes in profound understanding at Chatty. The lips of the young one did not speak, but they moved with unconscious, unavailing kisses.

'Can't act?' thought Chatty. 'There ought to have been a train sequence in the film. Lift? She's lifting the train off the rails.'

Of course, he reflected, Magnolia was life not art: that is what had got Karvo and what horrified Chatty. In his quick croak he made several speeches in French, conveying that, in the present misunderstanding, the French railways were not to blame. Exchanging glances the two inspectors conveyed that the next hour and a half would be hell. They showed eagerness to share this opportunity with Chatty, even to exchange places. The desire to experience hell with Magnolia shone in the eyes of the younger man. The older one's face indicated that, in the well-known relations between men and women, it is the nuance that is always interesting. They congratulated Chatty silently on his fortune. Think – they signalled to each other – of the reconciliation! Sadly, looking restlessly at each other, they went away to the end of the coach and glanced up the corridor to see if anything was happening yet and if their moment might come. Once, the older man went up to the compartment and then hurried back to report: the blinds which had shot up in the dispute were down again. The young man sighed sadly. The reconciliation already?

No, not the reconciliation. Magnolia was crying, letting tears bowl down her cheeks – if only she could have done that on the set! – she had tried to hit Chatty twice but in the swaying of the train she had missed. He said nothing but, lighting a cigarette, fell into a run of quiet coughing. He had pulled down the blinds so that she could have a good cry undisturbed. After about fifty coughs the irritating sound made her forget to sob and reach for her handbag.

'You are a dirty swine. Karvo put you up to this,' she said.

'There was no other way of getting you away from that man,' he said. 'I wanted you to myself.'

'Don't you dare touch me,' she said as he moved to the seat beside her. The fear she had amused herself with in the early part of the journey now became real. He was abducting her. This was a rape. Chatty innocent? Chatty ill? Chatty, the orphan bachelor shedding a tear about his Aunt Laura? Aunt Laura my eye. He was nothing more than a dirty rapist. A new layer of virginity formed over her, icing her completely.

'Have you ever been to Geneva?' Chatty said.

'Don't insult me,' said Magnolia.

'Beautiful lake,' said Chatty.

No answer.

'Mont Blanc, not far,' said Chatty.

No answer.

'I haven't been there for fifteen years,' Chatty said. 'Not since I was up at Appol in the sanatorium.'

No comment.

'I left a lung up there.'

'I'm getting a 'plane,' said Magnolia. Chatty lit another cigarette.

'That's five you've smoked in the last half-hour. Look at the floor,' said Magnolia. There was, Chatty noted, just a tiny bit of the nurse left in her. He tactfully picked up the cigarette stubs and put them in the ash tray and sat down again. There was nothing like a little tidying for getting a woman through a crisis.

'I've never told anyone this,' he said. 'I've got to tell you. Well, no, you won't be interested?'

'What?' she snapped.

[801]

Chatty sighed.

'It's too painful,' he said. 'Some things one never gets over. Just a German girl I knew there – I mean there, Geneva.'

'What German girl?' Magnolia sneered.

'Up at Appol, in the sanatorium where I was. We both were. She was very ill. It went on for months. We used to go for walks – not very far. We had one pair of lungs between us – it wasn't too bad. It was in May – flowers, you know, lambs – spring: we couldn't stand it. One morning we got into the funicular and said: "Let's go off," just like that, no luggage, just as we were. We were laughing all the way down. I got a car to drive us to Geneva. We went to an hotel, an old-fashioned one. Our room had two marble-encased wash-basins side by side, very handsome ones. Two people could stand there and wash together. You could wash each other – Swiss idea of marriage I suppose.'

'Don't be disgusting,' said Magnolia.

'We laughed so much at those basins,' Chatty said, 'that the first thing we did was to stand there splashing water at each other. We soaked the place. We couldn't stop laughing. I was drying myself with a big towel: I'd got my head in it. Suddenly I noticed she'd stopped laughing and I pulled the towel away from my face. She was leaning over the basin. It was splashed all over with blood. It was coming out of her mouth. A haemorrhage.'

Magnolia leaned back to get farther away from him.

'I'd killed her,' he said. 'She died up at Appol two months later. I've never told anyone.'

How often she had heard: "No one knows anything about Chatty".

'It wasn't your fault,' she said at last.

'We were sex mad,' he said. 'I never slept with her.'

'Oh,' said Magnolia.

'You can live without it,' said Chatty.

'What was her name?'

'Greta.'

A shot of jealousy hit Magnolia. The hills were turning into mountains, the fields were steeper, she strained to see if there was yet a sight of the Alps. She wanted to be high up in them.

'Where's Appol?' she said.

'High up,' he said. 'There's an enormous lake at Geneva. We used to walk there. I shot a picture there once before I cracked up. I've always had the idea of doing *William Tell.*'

Magnolia's business sense woke up.

'I've never told anyone this. I never told Karvo – he's not the kind of a man who would understand. You're the only person who knows. You have sympathy. You know what it is to lose someone. Now you know why I cheated about the tickets. I wanted you to see the place and walk by the lake.'

Magnolia's mind was still in Appol. How wonderful to be like Greta and die slowly, untouched, by the lake: Chatty attending her and telling Karvo the news.

Brusquely Chatty said:

'Forget it. I've got us rooms at the Splendide. We'll be there in twenty minutes. We'll have a drink. The Press will be there. I lined that up in London.'

Magnolia came down from the high snows.

It *was* an abduction. She saw herself defending a virtue made absolute. It was a sensation she had not had since she was a girl of fifteen when she had knocked a man off his bicycle who had chased her across a common: a superb feeling.

In the taxi that took them from the railway station in Geneva to the hotel, she said to Chatty:

'The first thing to do is to find out about the 'plane to Venice.'

'Wait,' said Chatty, 'till you see the view. I want to show you Greta's grave.'

An hour later she was standing at the window of her hotel room looking out at that view. There was no 'plane until the morning. She would have to hold out all night. She could hear Chatty moving in the room next door. Presently there was a knock at her door: Chatty advancing already upon her?

She called out: 'You can't come in.'

But the door was open and the chambermaid was there. The gentleman in number sixty-seven next door, the maid said, had been taken very ill; would she come at once? Chatty was lying on his bed with his shoes off and a hole in the toe of one of his socks. He had a handkerchief to his mouth. He reached for her hand.

'Greta,' he said. 'A doctor.'

Chatty is up at Appol. He reports to Karvo on the telephone.

'Just the rest I needed. I was coming here anyway. Magnolia was an angel. She still is. What she needs is a part as a nurse. When she visits me she comes into the room on tip-toe. She's bought a dress that looks like a uniform. She's got exactly the face that goes with high necks and starch. And she is full of suffering – no Karvo, suffering for *me*. Did I say nurse. A nun, that's her part.'

And two or three weeks later:

'I'm getting out soon. She wants to move me down to Geneva to an old hotel – that place with double wash-basins, do you know? Remind me to tell you. It's a very morbid idea actually, but she is in that mood at the moment. It does her good to be morbid for a bit.'

And later again:

'Yes. I've moved. No, *she's* got the wash-basin room. I'm on the same floor though. She comes along with a nice man called Ronzini or Bronzoni or something: she met him, yes, of course, in the bar. The uniform has gone – I miss it. Well, what did I tell you? It's all right now. She's just been in to say do I mind if Bronzoni drives her to Garda for a couple of days. Well, I don't mind, but I wonder what she has been telling that Italian. He said to me "She needs rest Mr Chatterton. You have caused her a lot of anxiety." I have an idea she has told him she doesn't feel safe with me. No need for you to make funny remarks. I had a very trying job restoring her virginity: the sort of job that's beyond you, Karvo. You wouldn't recognise the girl who is going off to Garda for a couple of days. Exalted. I'll be back in London at the end of the month. For God's sake send me some money. Prices are very high here.'

The Last Throw

The new week began for Karvo. For him weeks were always new. Cheered by the doorman, receptionists, secretaries, he went voluptuously into purdah in the lift; on the silent top floor he came out, all animal, on to the stretches of green carpet which seemed to grow like the lawns of the country house life he had just left. He raced to his enormous desk on which lay an elephant's foot mounted on silver presented to him by an African ruler after his latest film, and he pressed a button. The call was answered by the fit of dry coughing that contained Chatterton.

'Chatty,' Karvo began vigorously. Then, reproachfully, 'I thought you had given up smoking?'

'I have,' said Chatty. 'That was nostalgia. I live in the past.'

'Can you spare a minute?'

It always took Chatty longer to get to Karvo than Karvo could bear. Passing the open doors of offices, meeting people in the corridors, anywhere in the building Chatty paused and, with the cough and the ravaged smile of dandyish human wreckage, asked people how they were. How far downhill on the way to dilapidation are you, when shall we all be human souls together? his large eyes seemed to ask. One or two hypochondriacs would tell him. Why does this preposterous organisation run so well, Chatty sometimes asked himself – for he had the vanity of casualties, and replied: 'I am the oil in the wheels, the perambulating clinic, the ambulance, the Salvation Army, the conscience – if it has one – kept alive by a sunlamp, an expensive tailor and dozens of teeny weeny little pills.' And with the air of one saying 'Good-bye' to himself, Chatty walked on.

Also, he added honestly, kept alive by Karvo, King of Kings, the Elephant's Foot, the Life Force. Now for the Monday morning shot! At board meetings Chatty often doodled pictures of Karvo as an elephant sitting in the studio with a crown on his head, a cigar in his mouth and a sceptre in his hand, while a naked cast of well-known actors, actresses and teams of cameramen the size of ants crawled before him. Now Chatty slipped into Karvo's room like a well-dressed fever and saw Karvo in clothes that Karvo supposed were the right thing for high life in the English countryside. He was sitting in front of a very fat book that looked like the Family Bible and there was an uncommon expression of piety or, at any rate, of elevation on his large, unmanageable face.

'When did you go to the doctor last?' said Karvo kindly, but passed immediately to what he loved to do on Mondays: his weekend.

Karvo was at that period in his life when the tide of democracy and cinema had floated him into the private boscage where peers, millionaires and merchant bankers spent their lives. Chatty sat down on a sofa and waited to be carried into Karvo's dreamland. At once Karvo was on to the Hamilton-Spruces for a second, advanced to the Holinsheds and then, after a long detour among the connections of the Esterhazys, the Radziwills, the Hohenzollerns, the Hotspurs, Talbots, Buckinghams, the Shakespearean cast of the English counties, finally swerved to France to meet the Albigenses.

'Aren't they cousins of the Radziwills?' Karvo wanted to know.

'No,' said Chatty. 'The Albigenses were a persecuted race. They are extinct.'

Karvo turned to the title page of the book before him. It was not the Bible; it was not the Almanach de Gotha. It was a bound typescript.

'They were massacred,' said Chatty. 'In the South of France. About the twelfth century. Because of their religion.'

'The South of France,' said Karvo. His eyes switched on a sharp commercial light. 'How many were massacred?'

He was thinking of a crowd scene.

'I don't know – a million; no, perhaps only a few hundred thousand,' said Chatty.

'The French Ambassador gave this manuscript to me at the Hamilton-Spruces'. His wife wrote it,' said Karvo. 'Will you have a look at it?' Chatty had one more of his coughing fits as he took the manuscript.

'You *haven't* given up,' Karvo accused him. 'Cheating never pays.'

'It's your cigar,' said Chatty.

Chatty went to his office, opened the bottom drawer of his desk where he kept his dozens of bottles of pills and rested his feet on the open drawer as he sat down to read. First he looked up the name of the

Ambassador. Then he studied the name on the title page. As he expected, the author could not possibly be the wife of the French Ambassador. In the hot house of Society, Karvo usually misnamed the blooms. The name of that lady was not even in the long list of acknowledgements which began with a few eminences, went on to the Bibliothèque Nationale, the British Museum, combed the universities, and ended with inexhaustible gratitude to a dearest husband without whose constant advice and patience, etc. etc. The dedication read 'To Doggie from Pussy'.

Chatty studied the index and appendices and then, rearranging his feet on the drawer, was unable to prevent himself from memorising 600 pages of historical research. On Friday he went in to see Karvo.

'I'm just off to the country,' he said. 'I've read that thing. The author is Christine Johnson, a learned woman, first-class historian – no doubt about that. If you're interested in the Albigenses, this is the last word. You'll be glad to hear about the Cathari heresy. You know, of course, that the Cathari were dualists. Early dieters too; fast Monday, Wednesday and Friday every week. This annoyed the pope. I think she'll have trouble all the same in Chapters Nine and Ten. Speaking as an historian . . .'

Karvo looked up from the script he was reading.

'Thank you,' said Chatty. 'Speaking as an historian I would say she is entirely speculative in Chapter Ten. Mad, I'd say. Massacres, of course. Several. The Albigenses were exterminated. There's nothing in it for us.'

'Massacres?' said Karvo again. 'What's the story?'

'Page 337. Incest,' said Chatty. 'Brother and sister, separated at birth by religious fanatics, meet again, don't know each other, get married – not knowing that, after she's been raped in Toulouse and as they escape over the Pyrenees, that a woman called Clothilde de San Severino has betrayed them to the Inquisition, who torture both. Roughly that.'

'Torture,' said Karvo looking up. 'What kind? Incest? Have you marked the pages I'd like to see?'

He softened. 'My sister would never have let you get into the state you're in, Chatty. Would you mind seeing this woman – just politeness – tact, you know.'

'All right,' said Chatty.

Karvo's face blurred into one of his occasional looks of shame.

'Do you know her?' Chatty said.

Karvo shrugged.

The woman, Christine Johnson, had gone to her house in Paris but came to Chatty's office a fortnight later. Chatty spent an hour and a half with her. Late in the afternoon he went to Karvo's office, opening the door wide instead of sliding in, and shutting it with careful ceremony. He sat down on Karvo's distant sofa, put his feet up and said nothing.

'You're quiet,' said Karvo.

'Have you ever experienced a miracle?' said Chatty.

'Many,' said Karvo.

'Yes, I know. So have I. I'll put it another way. Have you ever met again, or accidentally passed in the street, your first girl friend whom you haven't seen or heard of for fifteen or twenty years?'

'Mine was in my pram,' said Karvo. 'I don't remember.'

'I'm not talking of childish vice. I mean your first adult girl friend. Have you seen her since, even at a distance?'

'That's a miracle I've avoided.'

'Why?' said Chatty. 'I can see her: short, very fat, strong glasses, a touch of something on the skin, spots perhaps, dirty raincoat, sullen with congested virtue, round-shouldered. (There's nothing against that. A lot of girls go in for being round-shouldered; they are trying out ways of being important or graceful, learning the job.) But wearing a seaman's heavy black jersey, no breasts or, rather, creased woollen bumps. The jersey is too large. Walking as if still marching into the classroom. "Girls! Forward March! Follow Diana." Another thing – you could never see her alone. She was always with some other girl – very pretty, but for some insane reason the pretty one didn't appeal to you.'

'Come to the point,' said Karvo.

'And I don't suppose you've ever seen her years later with the man she married eventually. You imagined he was a weed who kept a small electrical shop or something like that and they lived out at – well, you know those places – with four children who have kicked the garden to pieces. Informative, rebuking, that's what she was. Always ticking you off – "No, Karvo. Stop it, Karvo."'

'I remember that,' said Karvo, putting on his martyred face. 'Stop wasting my time. Kitchen sink is finished in pictures – you know that, Chatty.'

'I've just met mine,' said Chatty. 'Can I have a drink? No, don't ring for it. I'll get it myself.'

Chatty went to Karvo's drink cabinet. It was large and designed to look like the west front of a Gothic cathedral but without the saints.

'I can see why you shy off the subject,' said Chatty. 'I would have done so two hours ago, until Christine walked into my office. Except for the electrician and the four children, she used to be exactly as I have told you – but, my God! A butterfly has risen from that awful chrysalis. If it had been her pretty friend Ann I would not have been surprised – but Christine! The miracle has happened. As a matter of fact I must have changed too. Down at reception she told the girl she had an appointment with Sir Arthur Chatterton. She is not the wife of the French Ambassador.'

'Who said she was?' said Karvo.

'Sweet Jesus – but let it pass.'

'She's not only exquisite. She has brains.' Chatty's voice became sad. 'More than brains. Considering what she's got – what a waste.'

'How d'you mean?' said Karvo. 'Many women have first-class minds.'

'I wasn't thinking of her mind,' said Chatty. 'I was thinking of her money. She's rich. I was thinking of her clothes. How many distinguished lady historians do you know with emeralds on their fingers, who have sacked Paris for their clothes, whose hats seem to have blown over from the Place Vendôme and who, besides owning houses in London and Paris, spend their winters on their dear, dear brother's estate in Toulouse?

'She was wearing a hat like a birthday cake made of air and a very short dress. I suppose it was a dress? She seemed to be getting out of it rather than wearing it – pretty well succeeded on the left thigh and the right shoulder. A hot-house flower with large glasses like windows. All the fat gone. A butterfly – but what am I talking about? A dragonfly,' he said.

Chatty coughed.

'You oughtn't to talk so much,' said Karvo.

'I knew her by her teeth,' Chatty said sadly. 'And her voice. It used to come out frosted out of the heart's deep freeze. It still does. Oh dear, it brought it all back. Christine and then her pretty friend Ann and me all sitting in Lipps,' said Chatty.

'Is she married?' said Karvo.

'To a man in the Foreign Office, an adviser, whatever that is. Ronnie,' said Chatty.

'So,' said Karvo. 'You've missed the boat.'

'Oh no,' said Chatty, 'they've asked me to dinner the week after next when they come back from Scotland. They're staying with the Loch Lomonds.'

Karvo raised both his chins.

'I've stayed with the Loch Lomonds,' he said.

'So what was it like?' Karvo sneered. 'Bollinger, Mouton Rothschild . . .'

Chatty was lying once more on the sofa in Karvo's room.

'You remember the husband of your first girl friend,' said Chatty. 'The man with the small electrical shop or television rentals, if you like, the man who replaced you in the loving heart you broke . . .'

'I never broke any girl's heart,' said Karvo looking up from his letters. 'Accountants break mine.'

'Imagine you are back in Paris. Now here's a girl, Cambridge, double first, ruins her poor pink-rimmed eyes in the Bibliothèque Nationale, borrows the occasional ten or twenty francs from you because she's hungry – you see her, this Miss Sorbonne in her chrysalis days, your friend, suddenly avoiding you in the Boulevard Saint Germain, walking by night, in silence, except that she scrapes a foot. She is with a tall young man who keeps bumping his dirty raincoat into hers because he walks aslant and bends to talk down into the top of her head, as if he were trying to graze there – not that there was much to graze on, her hair was very thin. He edges her towards the gutter or into those walls saying Défense d'Afficher, as the case may be, talking about the Guermantes, say . . . And you say bitterly to yourself, "Two pairs of strong glasses, two sets of rabbit teeth have felt an irresistible attraction."'

One of Karvo's telephones rang.

'Karvo,' said Karvo, heaving half of his body over the desk and in a voice suddenly plaintive said:

'No, my darling. Yes my darling. You'd better not, my darling. In that case you must, my darling.'

And then put down the telephone and got his body back on to the chair, breathless, his eyelids blinking, paler than his face. He had his crucifixion look and he said to Chatty:

'What were you saying? That was Dolly.'

'I was saying,' said Chatty sitting up and raising his voice, 'they now live in a bloody mansion! Cézannes, Picassos, Soutines, Renoirs, up the stairs, everywhere. From the drawing-room window you can see all the most expensive flowering shrubs and trees in bloom in the Crescent. A manservant brings in the champagne and in comes the adviser to the Foreign Office.'

'Who is that?'

'I've told you,' said Chatty. 'Ronnie.

'There he is,' said Chatty. 'And he leans down and starts grazing on *your* hair now. He is young but has gone bald early, very confidential and nods at every word you say. Congratulating himself. As she floats into the room, he says, "It's a winner, isn't it!"'

'She is wearing a dress made of two sheets of flame. One of the flames appears to be looped between her legs, but of course that can't be true and for the rest of the evening you keep trying to work out how she got it on. And she says, as she comes in: "Doggie!" And he looks at her and says "Pussy!" They've come back from Scotland via Vienna and Paris.'

'Who else was at the party?' said Karvo thirstily.

'No party,' said Chatty. 'Just his sister Rhoda. Up from the country for a couple of days shopping. A nice pensive woman, older than her brother, looking like an engraving of George Eliot, heavy dark hair peacefully parted in the middle, Victorian brooch, a long romantic poem. A woman you see talking to gardeners, walking on lawns, driving off in a little car to local education committees. A botanist too, in a religious way. We talked about a bowl of white peonies in the drawing-room. "Paeonia," she said. She was very reserved and shy. She said the plant had been introduced into Cornwall by the Brethren of Saint Michael. In the thirteenth century. She wouldn't interest you, Karvo, she's a good woman.'

'She doesn't,' said Karvo.

'Quite a medieval evening up till then,' said Chatty. Suddenly Ronnie, the husband, says, "Pussy, you must *show* them!" As he says this he gives a lick of glee to his lips and his hands jump about in his trouser pockets. "Oh Doggie," she says. "Shall I be naughty? It's dreadful, dearest Chatty.

Hats, Chatty! I've robbed the Place Vendôme. Bring your champagne."'

And Chatty told how her weak thin hand took his – he could feel all the bones in it – attached to an arm of steel. He was nearly dead, he said, by the time they all got up the long curving staircase, not from the climb so much as from sinking almost to the ankles in the hush of a deep-yellow stair-carpet. The four of them arrived in a large bedroom that had three high wide windows, the bay swelling over the lawn of the Crescent. But Chatty imagined from what was going on on the walls of the room that he was in the Burmese jungle. He wouldn't have been surprised, he said, to see the violet bottoms of mandrills sitting in the branches. Furry animals, like animal royalty, were spread on the floor. There was a golden bed, a Cleopatra's barge. Ronnie's sister stood apart. She had obviously seen it all before and, as beauties often do, looked unwell. Ronnie's face had stopped nodding. His mouth opened and he looked like a man congratulating himself on being about to be turned into a tiger, for Christine took a little run, almost a flight, to a wardrobe . . .

'Don't bother about the wardrobe,' said Karvo.

'. . . she pulled the doors open and out fell an enormous heap of hats, like a cloud of petals on the floor. About eighty of them. I spilled my champagne down my tie,' said Chatty. 'It was the least I could do. Let me go on. "She'll wear them all," Ronnie says. "Pussy, is your back tired? She has to rest her back." "Doggie," she says and pouts. Rhoda, the sister, is still standing apart. She is not drinking. She is a healthy woman who likes country walks but when the hats came tumbling out she expands and goes red in the face as if she is struggling against a pain in the chest. The stairs of course. Heart, I suppose – all those stairs.'

So, Chatty said, he tried to calm her by asking where she lived in the country and she said she lived this side of Bath and he told her his aunt had a farm on the far side of the city and how he went down there for weekends.

'"It's your part of the country too," I said to Christine. How nice, how strange.

'Always be careful when you talk to girls, Karvo,' said Chatty. 'Profit by my experience. She said I was mixing her up with Ann. Ann came from Bath. *She* came from Yorkshire.'

'What of it?' said Karvo.

'Didn't your first girl friend ever slice you in half with a look?' said Chatty.

Karvo had stopped listening so Chatty got down to business.

'We went downstairs to the Albigenses.'

Ronnie edged him into a wall against a small Soutine as if about to give him extremely private information about a foreign government.

'"The return to the twelfth century," Ronnie says. "It's absolutely *the* modern subject. It's the world today. Religious wars, mass murder, the crushing of small cultures. The Inquisition. It went on for a century. They appealed to the pope of course." "Dear dreadful Pope Innocent," Christine called across. "The Stalin of the time," says Ronnie bearing down closer. "Tortures. The Provençal nobility appear in crowds on the scene."'

Chatty gathered there was a sort of liberal called the Duc d'Aquitaine, trying to keep the peace, but the murder of Peter of Castelnau brought Pope Innocent's storm troops down from the north.

'"Castelnaus, weren't they cousins?" says Christine to her husband. And to Chatty, "The Johnsons came originally from Toulouse."'

'The sister interrupts. "Putney," she says.

'"You'll find it in the Cistercian records," says Christine. "Or you can look it up in Schmidt or in Vaissete."

'It was a piquant moment,' Chatty said. 'There you had on the one hand a scholarly genealogist who could slip back to the twelfth century as easy as pie but who, to be frank, was a *belle laide*, especially when she showed her teeth, being challenged by a peaceful botanist who had a corner in monkish gardening.

'I enjoyed it,' said Chatty to Karvo. 'It took me back to the old days in Paris. I'm afraid the two ladies don't get on.'

Karvo put on his martyred look.

'It was all right,' said Chatty. 'Ronnie saved the situation. A born diplomat. He started telling me about the children of light and the children of darkness and finished up talking about the Perfecti.'

Karvo looked up.

'It's not a cigar,' said Chatty.

The Johnsons asked Karvo to dinner.

'That woman's electric. You're wrong about her book,' said Karvo to

[813]

Chatty when he came back. 'I read the passages you marked. Wow! There's a story. She's going places.'

When the mid-Atlantic slick flooded into Karvo's English, Chatty knew that one of what he called Karvo's Seasons was about to begin.

'I think,' said Karvo, 'you offended her. Did you say something?'

'Something rude about the twelfth century, I expect,' said Chatty.

'No, something's bugging her,' said Karvo.

'I left with Rhoda that evening. We walked down the side of the park under the trees,' said Chatty. 'Perhaps it was that. Now Rhoda, there's a woman. She knows the names of flowers. Too plump for you, Karvo. And forty. She's the complete English lady. So beautifully conventional and uncandid, quiet but deep – you know – when they talk about their neighbours you aren't sure whether they are people or rhododendrons; whether the Winstanleys, say, are a breed of cattle or the county education committee or an asparagus bed. A good green-fingered woman – knows what is ranunculaceous and what is not. In human life, I mean. The only trouble is that they are always doing something for others. Lovely summer night and all she can do is to ask me the name of Christine's professor in Paris. One of her neighbours wants to send her daughter there.'

'What are you talking about?' said Karvo.

'I'm talking about love,' said Chatty. 'Not as you know it. I could love a woman like that.'

'I want a treatment for this story,' said Karvo. And with that Karvo's Albigensian period began. The word 'massacre' had caught him. So had 'torture'. So had 'incest'. So had Christine. His head filled up with crime, sex and churches, romanesque towers, medieval obscenities, antiques. After a month he bought a Van Gogh – and wouldn't say what he gave for it – one of the painter's swirling cornfields, done in the asylum. It matched his mood. He galloped over the Pyrenees with the incestuous rebel couple. Everywhere he went – to expensive restaurants, embassies and house parties – Christine and her husband were there. They gave enormous parties.

'They never ask me,' said Chatty.

'You know, of course,' Karvo said, 'she's a Castelnau. That's why she wrote the book.'

'No,' said Chatty. 'That's her husband.'

'I don't take to him,' said Karvo. 'You've got it wrong.'

'I think,' said Chatty, 'they're both Castelnaus. There's a Castelnau Road in Putney.'

'That's not surprising,' said Karvo, briefly an historian. 'The survivors and descendants of the Albigenses split up, half joined up with the Huguenots and went to Bordeaux and the other half to England. They made a fortune in cotton. That's where she gets her money. She told me her brother's still got the place in Toulouse.'

'Incidentally, the Castelnaus were on the wrong side – in the pay of the pope. Did she mention it?' said Chatty. 'Of course I know one should never trust one's ancestors. Does Dolly get on with her?' Chatty asked, speaking of Karvo's latest wife.

'You know what women are about clothes. I'm taking Dolly to Paris,' said Karvo.

'My aunt is not well. I'm off to the country,' Chatty said.

There were long seasons in Karvo's life; there were short ones when he was between pictures. Seasons were apt to turn into cycles. The summer passed. The winds of early September were bashing the country gardens. 'The hollyhocks are flat on their backs,' Rhoda wrote in a note to Chatty. She added a postscript saying, 'I discovered the Professor's name – it was Ducros.' Grit was blowing into Chatty's office window as he read the treatment.

'The story has no shape or end,' he said to Karvo. 'What does it mean, what is the message?'

Karvo spread his arms wide and held them in the air. Seeing nothing in them he began to reach for a button on his desk.

'I'll tell you what it means, what we have got to bring out,' Chatty said. He stood up and recited: 'The massacre of the Albigensians meant the final disappearance of the great medieval culture of Provence. It was lost for ever to European civilisation.'

Karvo was suspicious, then appalled. He changed physically before Chatty's eyes. The word 'culture' piled up like a wall that got larger every day. He stared at all that masonry and boredom settled on him.

'Funny,' he said, 'those are the very words Christine used.'

'They're in the script,' said Chatty.

'It is true,' he went on, looking at a pill on the palm of his hand and then swallowing it. 'Nothing lasts.'

[815]

The learned Christine had cooked her goose, so Chatty said, with a phrase. In the following weeks she and the Albigensian heresy were done for.

'Write her a note,' said Karvo. 'There's a good fellow.'

'No,' said Chatty. 'She's your baby. She dropped me. I burn with resentment. I still can't think what I did.'

'It's personally embarrassing,' said Karvo, lifting his blotter and pretending to look for something.

'Much more for me – old time's sake, you know,' said Chatty. 'Get Phillips to do it.' Phillips managed Karvo's company. 'Dear Mrs Johnson, we have now had a full breakdown of the costs, etc. etc . . . He is a master of the commercial lament.'

The letter was sent and Chatty returned the manuscript.

'My office seems empty without it – modern almost,' said Chatty. 'Sad. You meet your childhood sweetheart again and then – nothing.'

He waited for the inevitable aftermath of Karvo's dreams; he would hear Christine's syllables freezing the man who ignorantly rejected Provençal culture and the birthplace of the Castelnaus.

But there was no reply. After a few weeks the manuscript was returned by the post office.

'Unknown' was written across it in pencil by an enthusiastic hand.

Chatty telephoned to the house. No manservant answered. He heard the voice of the cook. She had come in, she said, to collect her things before the removal men got them. You could trust no one today. The Johnsons had gone to their house in Paris and Mrs Johnson had gone to Toulouse – her brother had died – such difficulties about the estate! The cook did not know the address. The London house had been sold. She was damping the telephone wires with her tears.

'Such troubles,' she said.

An inexplicable hole had opened in London social life. It was as if whole streets, indeed the Crescent itself, had been removed, as if the map had been changed, without consultation, overnight, and nonentity had supervened.

'Anyone could see there was trouble there,' Karvo said. 'Ronnie Johnson was an adventurer. He came in, stripped her of every cent she had. I heard him talking to a Greek banker at the Holinsheds about the trouble she was having about getting money out of France.'

'I'll find out where she is from Rhoda,' said Chatty.

'Forget it,' said Karvo.

'I don't want to talk about it on the telephone. May I come and see you?' Chatty heard Rhoda's clear harvesting voice gathering sheaves of moral beauty as it came across the hills, the fields and the woods, the gardens and the village churches from the borders of Somerset. Partridge shooting had begun.

When Chatty was clearing up after Karvo's passages through people's lives he usually took the grander casualties to the Hundred and Five, but it was closed for redecoration and Chatty was obliged to ask Rhoda to the Spangle. This little club was hardly the place for a lady from the country and one who could never be a casualty. The Spangle would be packed with people whose cheques bounced and whom 'one had never met'. By nine in the evening couples were hunched and whispering nose to nose across the gingham cloth of their tables, listening not to each other, but for erotic news from the table behind them. It was a place for other people's confessions. There was the hope of being refreshed by scenes breaking out now and then. Les, the proprietor, who wore a cowboyish shirt, was a big-bellied, soft man with heavy spongy arms, white as suet pudding. He was in his sixties and was damp and swollen with the public secrets of his customers. Most people came in asking for someone else.

'Was John in last night?'

Les would perhaps reply, 'Sarah was asking for him', or 'I had a card from Flo. She's in Spain', or 'Phil can't leave his dog', or, flatly, 'Ada's barred.'

Rhoda was wearing a cardigan, a green blouse, a tweed skirt and good walking shoes, but Chatty saw her face had changed. The sad George Eliot gaze had gone. The thick smooth black hair had been cropped into a variety of lengths so that she looked as if she had been pulled – not unwillingly – through a hedge – that is to say, younger. Victory, even giddiness, was in her beautiful brown eyes. Les stared with suspicion and offence at any new woman guest brought into the club and scarcely nodded to her when Chatty introduced her, but Rhoda did not mind. She sat down, after an efficient look around her, and said:

'What a killing place.'

[817]

The word 'killing' made Chatty happy; it was so lyrically out of date. 'Tell me who everyone is,' she said.

'Les is in a bit of a mood tonight,' Chatty began by apologising for Les. 'He's on the watch for people who forgot to bring him a present for his birthday. He used to be an actor.'

So Chatty and Rhoda fell to whispering and looking around like everyone else. He thought he was in for a restful evening and started talking about his farm. He looked at her and saw starlings flocking, avenues of elms. Rhoda allowed this, then abruptly she said: 'So you turned down Christine's film?'

Chatty's face twitched. Experienced in consoling discarded actresses and mistresses, he had little experience in consoling authors. He certainly did not know how to begin with authors' relatives.

'The sad fact is,' he said, 'that the best films are made out of bad books, not out of good ones.'

He saw the formidable Rhoda appear.

'That is not true,' she said with the quiet authority of a thoughtful life. He now saw himself in for an ethical evening. But he was wrong again. She was too firm or too gentle to argue. He ordered their meal and he saw her pursuing truth placidly on her own through a large plate of whitebait, a fish that would have given him gout within an hour.

'It is always embarrassing turning down the work of a friend,' he said. 'One always does it at the wrong moment. Family crisis, brother dying – actually dead, I believe. I hear Christine's in Toulouse. For the funeral, I suppose.'

Rhoda, a frugal woman, scrupulously ate the last small fish and then drank a glass of white wine straight off. He noted the care of the first operation, the abandon of the second.

'That is what I want to talk to you about,' she said.

Les was calling to a young woman: 'Hello, darling. Where's Stephen? Andrew was asking for him.'

'Stephen,' whispered Chatty, 'has forgotten Leslie's birthday.'

But Rhoda had lost interest in the killing aspect of the club.

'They are not in Toulouse,' she said.

'Perhaps it was Paris, I forget,' said Chatty.

'Christine's brother is not dead. She hasn't got a brother.'

'But surely!' Chatty said. If there was one thing he remembered about the Christine of so many years ago, it was Christine telling him of her brother, retired from the Navy, living in the South of France, growing his own wine: 'the head of the family'. With its old-fashioned overtones of solid money, family counsels, trusts, wills, marriages, crests on the silver and so on and the weary care of her voice as she threw away her brother's distinctions, the phrase had stuck with him. He had read it in novels. To hear it spoken had been one of those instances of a forgotten piece of social history flying out of the past into the present like a stone coming through a window.

'Paul, the head of the family,' said Chatty.

Seeing Rhoda's eyes studying him he lost his confidence.

'Perhaps it was Ann's brother. One of them had a brother. It's a long time ago,' he said.

'I've never met Ann,' said Rhoda. 'But I am quite certain Christine hasn't got a brother.'

Chatty backed out, for he saw the truth-seeker in Rhoda's eyes.

'Or I may be mixing it up with the book,' he said. 'The girl who went off with her brother.'

'I haven't read the book,' said Rhoda with a flick of the whip in her voice.

Chatty started telling the story but she interrupted.

'There is *no* family,' she said.

'But she comes from the north,' Chatty said. 'Yorkshire or somewhere. She said so at dinner. Her mother died, the father was killed in an air raid. There was just this brother.'

'Her mother died,' said Rhoda, 'but her father and her stepmother are still alive. Not in the north of England. They've never been near it. They live less than twenty miles from you, the other side of Bath. They run a small public house.'

Chatty saw that pile of pink, white and lacy hats come tumbling out of her wardrobe like butterflies and heard Christine's voice saying:

'No, I am a Yorkshire woman. You're thinking of Ann.'

'I have been to see them,' said Rhoda. 'They haven't seen or heard of Christine for sixteen years. Her father used to be a seed salesman. They haven't heard a thing about her since she was a student in Paris. They didn't even know she was married. Their name is Till. She has a sister who runs the place, a nice girl, but it's an awful pub. The father retired there to drink the profits. He said "Tell that girl if she comes near here I'll get my belt out."'

The waitress brought Boeuf Bourguignon for Rhoda and, for Chatty, a sole. What an appetite she had! Rhoda continued her pursuit of the truth in silence through the food. Chatty gaped at his fish.

'This is good,' she said at last. 'You're letting yours get cold. I found them through the headmistress of her school. I am on the Education Committee. She said Christine was the cleverest girl they had ever had.'

It was a principle of Chatty's to believe everything he was told, but now the very fish on his plate seemed opposed to him. It had been served on the bone and he hesitated to put his knife to it for fear of what he would find inside. He moved his mind to Paris. He saw a heavy black sweater, a pair of twisted stockings, a student's notebook on a café table.

'I can't believe it,' said Chatty. 'Hundreds of girls leave home, I know ... They turn up in this place ...'

'The London house is sold, the bailiffs have the pictures. Ronnie is at home with us. He has left her – thank God.'

'Oh dear,' said Chatty.

'The film,' said Rhoda, 'was her last throw. In the last ten years she has run through more than £100,000 of Ronnie's money,' said Rhoda. 'One hundred thousand.'

Rhoda changed before Chatty's eyes. The twined leafy branches that had seemed to frame the pensive face of the rural botanist dissolved. He saw instead the representative of a huge family trust.

'Where is she now?' he said.

'In a nursing home,' she snapped at him. 'I know where I'd put her!'

Chatty put down his knife and fork. He could not bear the sad colour of the fish.

'Poor Christine,' he said looking at it.

'Poor Christine!' said Rhoda loudly, indeed addressing the club. The quiet oval face became square and the country skin flushed to a dark red. 'Poor Ronnie, you mean. She has ruined him.'

'They were rather going it, of course,' said Chatty. 'I suppose Ronnie knew what he was doing. What does he say?'

'He knew nothing until ten days ago. Nothing at all about her. Lies from the beginning to the end.'

And when she said, 'Lies,' Rhoda shouted.

The customers of the Spangle looked up and glanced at one another with joy. A row! That shout was in the genuine tradition of the club. Everyone was at home. At such moments the quarrelling parties usually called for more drink. Les stepped behind the bar ready to get it. Rhoda corrected herself.

'Lies,' she said quietly. 'Pure invention.'

'Ronnie *must* have known,' Chatty said. 'How did he find out?'

'He didn't. I did. Ronnie knew nothing, absolutely nothing. I had had my suspicions when he brought her down to stay before they were married; I couldn't stand her delivery.'

Chatty raised the bottle to Rhoda's glass and he filled his own.

'It took time,' said Rhoda. 'You've known her longer than any of us,' she said, 'did she ever say or do . . .'

She stopped. She saw Chatty's face, so rakishly marked by the lines of his illnesses, smooth out and another face set very hard upon it. She was going to accuse him next. The pursuit of truth was going too far. Rhoda's voice had lost its note of moral beauty. He was thinking of the post-scripts to her note: 'The name of the Professor is Ducros.' She had been hunting then.

'Mr Chatterton,' she said. 'I love my brother. He is everything to me. He always will be. We have always been close all our lives since we were children. He is something very rare – a good man. I would die for him. I knew I was right about that girl. He is easily deceived. It isn't the money. I hate what she has done to him. I love my brother more than anything in the world.'

How many times Chatty had heard the word 'love' spoken at the Spangle by girls with globes of tears hanging in their eyes, by girls with their teeth set, by girls with their mouths twisted by rage. He patted their hands, told their fortunes, made up love affairs of his own – generally the most successful way of soothing them. He had the sad story of the girl who was in a Swiss sanatorium with him; they had both lost a lung. Such affectionate creatures all these girls were! They forgot their rages when they heard this and, looking at him with contented superstition, as if he were a talisman, their eyes cleared, glanced around the room and began their eternal quest once more.

But Rhoda was not in their case. She gazed at him, not asking for help, but with the self-possession of one born for a single passion. In twenty years' time that look would be unalterably there. She not only loved; she was avenged. She had not given up until she had got her brother back. Chatty wished that victory in love would look more becoming.

'It is extraordinary, I agree, and I am sure if you say so, it is true,' said Chatty.

'Every word,' said Rhoda.

'And a hundred thousand pounds is a lot of money.'

'It's not only the money,' she said.

'Well, I don't see really, if you think about it, what harm has been done. Ronnie was having the time of his life. He obviously adored her . . .'

'He was tricked.'

'. . . buying her houses, taking her round, enjoying a splash, showering her with Renoirs and hats. With a brain like hers she might still be sitting on the steps of the British Museum eating a sandwich out of a paper bag. He must have liked it. Quite frankly she isn't a beauty. Ronnie created her.'

'She deceived him.'

'I think he knew,' said Chatty. 'I expect he'd been bored up to then. Boredom makes you close your eyes and take the plunge.'

'She's such a snob. That accent!' said Rhoda.

'Pedantic,' he said. 'Scholars often are. Anyway one gets used to accents in the theatre.'

He saw he was annoying her.

'It's really a fairy tale isn't it?' he said. 'Ronnie waved a wand.'

For a moment he thought she was going to lean across the table and hit him. He sat back and recited:

'The Owl and the Pussy Cat went to sea
In a beautiful sea-green boat.
They took some honey and plenty of money
Wrapped up in a five pound note.'

The poem was too much for her. A tear dropped down her cheek.

'You've got the line wrong,' she said, struggling against the pain. 'It was a *pea*-green boat.'

'It was all those scholarships that gave her away. I traced them back,' she said bitterly.

The situation became too clear for Chatty. He did not wish to see, too distinctly, the good woman who in a passion of jealousy had hunted her sister-in-law down. He was disturbed by a wish that Christine and not Rhoda were sitting before him. He gave a number of dry coughs, but he could not cough the wish away.

'Diana,' Chatty called the waitress, an overworked girl who had the habit of keeping a cigarette burning on a saucer by the kitchen hatch, 'if you'll bring me a packet of cigarettes I'll marry you.'

'You, Mr Chatterton!' said the girl. 'That'll be the day.'

'It's desperate.'

The girl saw Rhoda's tears and pulled a face. The Spangle liked tears. She fetched the cigarettes. Chatty stood the packet on end considering it, not with passion but with lust. Rhoda saw the packet through her tears.

'You can't! You mustn't,' she said strictly. Chatty picked up the packet and held it to his nose.

'Lovely temptation,' he said, touching the packet with his lips and putting it down again. Rhoda's tears had stopped. In none of Chatty's experiences at the Spangle had he ever known that a packet of cigarettes could bring tears to a sudden end.

'Did they have any children?' Chatty asked.

'No – that is one blessing.'

'Perhaps that was the trouble?' said Chatty.

The expression on the good woman's face was one of horror so deep that she was silent.

And now Les came to their table, ignoring Rhoda.

'How's Karvo?' he asked. 'Maggy was asking for him.'

'Oh God!' said Chatty.

'Who is Maggy?' asked Rhoda when Les walked off.

'It's a long story. Too personal. Some other time. I'm thinking about Christine. What a performance – one has to admit.'

'I don't think that remark is appropriate,' said Rhoda. 'There's a time when sympathy stops. I think of her sometimes. What a hell she must have lived in knowing every day for years that she might be found out.'

The satisfaction of Rhoda's voice shocked Chatty. He gave up trying to charm her.

'Oh I don't think conscience troubled her at all,' he said gaily. 'I don't think she was in hell. That is what I mean by performance. She knew her part in every detail. It must have thrilled her to act it, adding a little touch every day. Only an academic could do that! It's a pretty commonplace everyday story really, but to her – what a triumph! What documentation! Imagine her memory! And making Ronnie love it.'

'Not now,' said Rhoda. 'She has lost him for good.'

'That is true,' said Chatty. 'The really sad thing is that she has lost Paul.'

'You are infuriating,' said Rhoda. 'He *never existed*, I tell you.'

'I know. She invented him. That is what makes it worse. She has lost her only real friend.'

Chatty was glad to see that the perfect Rhoda looked troubled.

'What you are saying is that I did wrong,' she said.

'I think you did what you *wanted* to do,' said Chatty.

'I can see,' she said, 'that you don't like me. Hasn't anyone any moral sense nowadays? You knew her. I thought it was my duty to tell you. That was my only motive.'

Rhoda picked up her handbag.

'Diana, my sweetheart,' Chatty called to the waitress. 'I seem to want my bill.'

They sat silently until the bill came and then Rhoda said:

'Thank you for a lovely evening. You must drive over and see us some time. Ronnie would like that.'

Karvo said to Chatty:

'A hundred thousand pounds? Who told you?'

'Clothilde,' said Chatty. 'She was on the pope's side. You remember the Albigensians . . .'

'We didn't make it,' said Karvo.

'I know,' said Chatty. 'I mean the escape of the lovers over the Pyrenees, but Clothilde is with them. She has tracked down the incest story and she betrays them to the Inquisition out of jealousy. Rhoda Johnson. Another tragedy in my life. I've seen into the heart of a good woman. Never do that.'

Karvo ignored this.

'It was a Swedish story really,' said Karvo furtively. 'The Swedes could do it.'

'No, not Swedish, not even Albigensian – very English, West Country. The brother's name was Paul, purely imaginary. Still his estate was useful as capital security, especially when he died.'

'Who are we talking about?' said Karvo.

'Christine's brother Paul,' said Chatty.

'But he's dead.'

'You don't listen,' Chatty said. 'Think of what he was going to leave her. Did she ever mention it to you?'

'Yes,' said Karvo, surprised. 'She did. Why?'

'Historians go mad. All that research and detail work gets them down. They crack up. Get delusions of grandeur and, in two minutes, they are popping in their personal story. They're badly paid, too. She needed the money. You can't blame them,' said Chatty.

'When did the Johnsons leave?' said Karvo.

'They didn't leave. She's had a breakdown. She is in a nursing home.'

'Yes, you told me – when was that?'

'Weeks and weeks ago,' Chatty took out his diary, 'October fourth.'

Then Chatty saw Karvo do an extraordinary thing. The man who couldn't remember his wife's birthday, the martyr who was always in trouble because he could not remember the dates of his several wedding anniversaries, the man for whom everything was done by secretaries, the man who was entirely public, surprised Chatty by the secretive way in which he now performed a private action. He took out a pocket diary. Chatty had seen Karvo do this only once before when he was ill; indeed Karvo had shown him a page with an X and a figure written against it. The first Tuesday in every month he recorded his weight. He opened the diary now and said:

'October fourth – that's what *I've* got. Why did you make a note of it?'

'A sense of loss,' said Chatty. 'She'd gone.'

'I didn't know she meant anything to you,' said Karvo bashfully.

'There it is,' said Chatty. 'Nor did I. One thinks of it at night.'

[825]

'Chatty . . .' Karvo began. 'Well, no – I don't want to pry into your private affairs.'

'Oh no, there was nothing like that in it. I liked her best when she was dirty and fat. I asked them both down to the farm but she wouldn't come. It rather hurt at the time, but I see it now. It might have saved them, even both of them.'

Karvo pressed the button and asked for his chauffeur to be sent round.

'A hundred thousand pounds,' said Karvo, but in the fond, impersonal, admiring manner of one who sees yet one more piece of financial history pass down the Thames, under the bridges and out to sea.

'Tell the chauffeur to wait,' said Chatty. 'Karvo, I don't want to pry into your private affairs. I want to ask you about ours – yours and mine.'

Karvo saw no escape from Chatty when the lines of his face smoothed out.

'All right, if that is what you want to know, she's as frigid as stone,' said Karvo. 'I tried – well, not actually tried – at the Holinsheds'.'

'Oh I know *that*,' said Chatty. 'I discovered that in Paris years ago. I was just finding out when Ronnie Johnson knocked at my door. A very innocent fellow – he didn't realise what was going on. Or perhaps he did. I remember he nodded. Don't let's talk about it. What I want to know is how much she touched you for on October fourth? She got £50 out of me. I made a note of it.'

'You fool,' boasted Karvo. 'She got £750 out of me, guaranteed by the estate.'

'Paul's,' said Chatty.

Karvo had a special way of falling into speechlessness. He would lean back in his chair, then would seem to be making a quick inventory of everything in the office, then close his eyes. It was as if he was under an anaesthetic at the dentist's. His inner life would become brilliant with ridiculous dramas and when he came round, panting, he would see what he must do. He came round now.

'I can get it off expenses,' he said. 'Why did you do it, Chatty?'

'Oh, you know – the pathos of the rich.'

Karvo grunted and got up.

'Can I drop you anywhere?'

'No,' said Chatty. 'I'm going to try and see Christine.'

'Don't be a fool,' said Karvo. 'You'll never get it back.'

'That is not what I'm going for,' said Chatty. 'She's alone.'

The Camberwell Beauty

August's? On the Bath Road? Twice-five August – of course I knew August: ivory man. And the woman who lived with him – her name was Price. She's dead. He went out of business years ago. He's probably dead too. I was in the trade only three or four years but I soon knew every antique dealer in the South of England. I used to go to all the sales. Name another. Naseley of Close Place? Jades, Asiatics, never touched India; Alsop of Ramsey? Ephemera. Marbright, High Street, Boxley? Georgian silver. Fox? Are you referring to Fox of Denton or Fox of Camden – William Morris, art nouveau – or the Fox Brothers in the Portobello Road, the eldest stuttered? They had an uncle in Brighton who went mad looking for old Waterford. Hindmith? No, he was just a copier. Ah now, Pliny! He was a very different cup of tea: Caughley ware. (Coalport took it over in 1821.) I am speaking of specialities; furniture is the bread and butter of the trade. It keeps a man going while his mind is on his speciality and within that speciality there is one object he broods on from one year to the next, most of his life; the thing a man would commit murder to get his hands on if he had the nerve, but I have never heard of a dealer who had; theft perhaps. A stagnant lot. But if he does get hold of that thing he will never let it go or certainly not to a customer – dealers only really like dealing among themselves – but every other dealer in the trade knows he's got it. So they sit in their shops reading the catalogues and watching one another. Fox broods on something Alsop has. Alsop has his eye on Pliny and Pliny puts a hand to one of his big red ears when he hears the name of August. At the heart of the trade is lust but a lust that is a dream paralysed by itself. So paralysed that the only release, the only hope, as everyone knows, is disaster; a bankruptcy, a divorce, a court case, a burglary, trouble with the police, a death. Perhaps then the grip on some piece of treasure will weaken and fall into the watcher's hands and even if it goes elsewhere he will go on dreaming about it.

[827]

What was it that Pliny, Gentleman Pliny, wanted of a man like August who was not much better than a country junk dealer? When I opened up in London I thought it was a particular Staffordshire figure, but Pliny was far above that. These figures fetch very little though one or two are hard to find: The Burning of Cranmer, for example. Very few were made; it never sold and the firm dropped it. I was young and eager and one day when a collector, a scholarly man, as dry as a stick, came to my shop and told me he had a complete collection except for this piece, I said in my innocent way: 'You've come to the right man. I'm fairly certain I can get it for you – at a price.' This was a lie; but I was astonished to see the old man look at me with contempt, then light up like a fire and, when he left, look back furtively at me; he had betrayed his lust.

You rarely see an antique shop standing on its own. There are usually three or four together watching one another: I asked the advice of the man next door who ran a small boatyard on the canal in his spare time and he said, 'Try Pliny down the Green: he knows everyone.' I went 'over the water', to Pliny; he was closed but I did find him at last in a sale-room. Pliny was marking his catalogue and waiting for the next lot to come up and he said to me in a scornful way, slapping a young man down, 'August's got it.' I saw him wink at the man next to him as I left.

I had bought myself a fast red car that annoyed the older dealers and I drove down the other side of Newbury on the Bath Road. August's was one of four little shops opposite the Lion Hotel on the main road at the end of the town where the country begins and there I got my first lesson. The place was closed. I went across to the bar of the hotel and August was there, a fat man of sixty in wide trousers and a drip to his nose who was paying for drinks from a bunch of dirty notes in his jacket pocket and dropping them on the floor. He was drunk and very offended when I picked a couple up and gave them to him. He'd just come back from Newbury races. I humoured him but he kept rolling about and turning his back to me half the time and so I blurted out:

'I've just been over at the shop. You've got some Staffordshire I hear.'

He stood still and looked me up and down and the beer swelled in him.

'Who may you be?' he said with all the pomposity of drink. I told him. I said right out, 'Staffordshire. Cranmer's Burning.' His face went dead and the colour of liver.

'So is London,' he said and turned away to the bar.

'I'm told you might have it. I've got a collector,' I said.

'Give this lad a glass of water,' said August to the barmaid. 'He's on fire.'

There is nothing more to say about the evening or the many other visits I made to August except that it has a moral to it and that I had to help August over to his shop where an enormous woman much taller than he in a black dress and a little girl of fourteen or so were at the door waiting for him. The girl looked frightened and ran a few yards from the door as August and his woman collided belly to belly.

'Come back,' called the woman.

The child crept back. And to me the woman said, 'We're closed,' and, having got the two inside, shut the door in my face.

The moral is this: if The Burning of Cranmer was August's treasure, it was hopeless to try and get it before he had time to guess what mine was. It was clear to him I was too new to the trade to have one. And, in fact, I don't think he had the piece. Years later, I found my collector had left his collection complete to a private museum in Leicester when he died. He had obtained what he craved, a small immortality in being memorable for his relation to a minor work of art.

I know what happened at August's that night. In time his woman, Mrs Price, bellowed it to me, for her confidences could be heard down the street. August flopped on his bed and while he was sleeping off the drink she got the bundles of notes out of his pockets and counted them. She always did this after his racing days. If he had lost she woke him up and shouted at him; if he had made a profit she kept quiet and hid it under her clothes in a chest of drawers. I went down from London again and again but August was not there.

Most of the time these shops are closed. You rattle the door handle; no reply. Look through the window and each object inside stands gleaming with something like a smile of malice, especially on plates and glass; the furniture states placidly that it has been in better houses than you will ever have, the silver speaks of vanished servants. It speaks of the dead hands that have touched it; even the dust is the dust of families that have gone. In the shabby places – and August's was shabby – the dealer is like a toadstool that has grown out of the debris. There was only one attractive object in August's shop – as I say – he went in for ivories and on a table at the back was a set of white and red chessmen set out on a board partly concealed by a screen. I was tapping my feet impatiently looking through the window when I was astonished to see two of the chessmen had moved; then I saw a hand, a long thin work-reddened hand appear from behind the screen and move one of the pieces back. Life in the place! I rattled the door handle again and the child came from behind the screen. She had a head loaded with heavy black hair to her shoulders and a white heart-shaped face and wore a skimpy dress with small pink flowers on it. She was so thin that she looked as if she would blow away in fright out of the place, but instead, pausing on tiptoe, she swallowed with appetite; her sharp eyes had seen my red car outside the place. She looked back cautiously at the inner door of the shop and then ran to unlock the shop door. I went in.

'What are you up to?' I said. 'Playing chess?'

'I'm teaching my children,' she said, putting up her chin like a child of five. 'Do you want to buy something?'

At once Mrs Price was there shouting:

'Isabel. I told you not to open the door. Go back into the room.'

Mrs Price went to the chessboard and put the pieces back in their places.

'She's a child,' said Mrs Price, accusing me.

And when she said this Mrs Price blew herself out to a larger size and then her sullen face went blank and babyish as if she had travelled out of herself for a beautiful moment. Then her brows levelled and she became sullen again.

'Mr August's out,' she said.

'It is about a piece of Staffordshire,' I said. 'He mentioned it to me. When will he be in?'

'He's in and out. No good asking. He doesn't know himself.'

'I'll try again.'

'If you like.'

There was nothing to be got out of Mrs Price.

In my opinion, the antique trade is not one for a woman, unless she is on her own. Give a woman a shop and she wants to sell something; even that little girl at August's wanted to sell. It's instinct. It's an excitement.

[830]

Mrs Price – August's woman – was living with a man exactly like the others in the trade: he hated customers and hated parting with anything. By middle age these women have dead blank faces, they look with resentment and indifference at what is choking their shops; their eyes go smaller and smaller as the chances of getting rid of it became rarer and rarer and they are defeated. Kept out of the deals their husbands have among themselves, they see even their natural love of intrigue frustrated. This was the case of Mrs Price who must have been handsome in a big-boned way when she was young, but who had swollen into a drudge. What allured the men did not allure her at all. It is a trade that feeds illusions. If you go after Georgian silver you catch the illusion, while you are bidding, that you are related to the rich families who owned it. You acquire imaginary ancestors. Or, like Pliny with a piece of Meissen he was said to keep hidden somewhere – you drift into German history and become a secret curator of the Victoria and Albert Museum – a place he often visited. August's lust for 'the ivories' gave to his horse-racing mind a private oriental side; he dreamed of rajahs, sultans, harems and lavish gamblers which, in a man as vulgar as he was, came out, in sad reality, as a taste for country girls and the company of bookies. Illusions lead to furtiveness in every-day life and to sudden temptations; the trade is close to larceny, to situations where you don't ask where something has come from, especially for a man like August whose dreams had landed him in low company. He had started at the bottom and very early he 'received' and got twelve months for it. This frightened him. He took up with Mrs Price and though he resented it she had made a fairly honest man of him. August was to be *her* work of art.

But he did not make an honest woman of her. No one disapproved of this except herself. Her very size, growing year by year, was an assertion of virtue. Everyone took her side in her public quarrels with him. And as if to make herself more respectable, she had taken in her sister's little girl when the sister died; the mother had been in Music Hall. Mrs Price petted and prinked the little thing. When August became a failure as a work of art, Mrs Price turned to the child. Even August was charmed by her when she jumped on his knee and danced about showing him her new clothes. A little actress, as everyone said, exquisite.

It took me a long time to give up the belief that August had the

Cranmer piece – and as I know now, he hadn't got it; but at last I did see I was wasting my time and settled in to the routine of the business. I sometimes saw August at country sales and at one outside Marlborough something ridiculous happened. It was a big sale and went on till late in the afternoon and he had been drinking. After lunch the auctioneer had put up a china cabinet and the bidding was strong. Some outsider was bidding against the dealers, a thing that made them close their faces with moral indignation; the instinctive hatred of customers united them. Drink always stirred August morally; he was a rather despised figure and he was, I suppose, determined to speak for all. He entered the bidding. Up went the price: 50,5,60,5,70,5,80,5,90. The outsiders were a young couple with a dog.

'Ninety, ninety,' called the auctioneer.

August could not stand it. 'Twice-five,' he shouted.

There is not much full-throated laughter at sales; it is usually shoppish and dusty. But the crowd in this room looked round at August and shouted with a laughter that burst the gloom of trade. He was put out for a second and then saw his excitement had made him famous. The laughter went on; the wonder had for a whole minute stopped the sale. 'Twice-five!' He was slapped on the back. At sixty-four the man who had never had a nick-name had been christened. He looked around him. I saw a smile cross his face and double the pomposity that beer had put into him and he redoubled it that evening at the nearest pub. I went off to my car and Alsop of Ramsey, the ephemera man who had picked up some Victorian programmes, followed me and said out of the side of his mouth:

'More trouble tonight at August's.'

And then to change the subject and speaking for every dealer south of the Trent, he offered serious news.

'Pliny's mother's dead – Pliny of the Green.'

The voice had all the shifty meaning of the trade. I was too simple to grasp the force of this confidence. It surprised me in the following weeks to hear people repeat the news: 'Pliny's mother's dead' in so many voices, from the loving memory and deepest sympathy manner as much suited to old clothes, old furniture and human beings indiscriminately, to the flat statement that an event of business importance had occurred in my eventless trade. I was in it for the money and so, I suppose, were all the rest – how else could they live? – but I seemed to be surrounded by a dreamy freemasonry, who thought of it in a different secretive way.

On a wet morning the following spring I was passing through Salisbury on market day and stopped in the square to see if there was anything worth picking up at the stalls there. It was mostly junk but I did find a pretty Victorian teapot – no mark, I agree – with a chip in the spout for a few shillings because the fever of the trade never quite leaves one even on dull days. (I sold the pot five years later for £8 when the prices started to go mad.) I went into one of the pubs in the square, I forget its name, and I was surprised to see Marbright and Alsop there and, sitting near the window, Mrs Price. August was getting drinks at the bar.

Alsop said to me:

'Pliny's here. I passed him a minute ago.'

Marbright said: 'He was standing in Woolworth's doorway. I asked him to come and have one, but he wouldn't.'

'It's hit him hard his mother going,' Marbright said. 'What's he doing here? Queen Mary's dead.'

It was an old joke that Gentleman Pliny had never been the same since the old Queen had come to his shop some time back – everyone knew what she was for picking up things. He only opened on Sundays now and a wealthy crowd came there in their big cars – a new trend as Alsop said. August brought the drinks and stood near, for Mrs Price spread herself on the bench and never left much room for anyone else to sit down. He looked restless and glum.

'Where will Pliny be without his mother,' Mrs Price moaned into her glass and, putting it down, glowered at August. She had been drinking a good deal.

August ignored her and said, sneering:

'He kept her locked up.'

There is always a lot of talking about 'locking up' in the trade; people's minds go to their keys.

'It was kindness,' Mrs Price said, 'after the burglars got in at Sampson's, three men in a van loading it up in broad daylight. Any woman of her age would be frightened.'

'It was nothing to do with the burglary,' said August, always sensitive when crime was mentioned. 'She was getting soft in the head. He caught her giving his stuff away when she was left on her own. She was past it.'

Mrs Price was a woman who didn't like to be contradicted.

'He's a gentleman,' said Mrs Price, accusing August. 'He was good to his mother. He took her out every Sunday night of his life. She liked a glass of stout on Sundays.'

This was true, though Mrs Price had not been to London for years and had never seen this event; but all agreed. We live on myths.

'It was her kidneys,' moaned Mrs Price. One outsize woman was mourning another, seeing a fate.

'I suppose that's why he didn't get married, looking after her,' said Marbright.

'Pliny! Get married! Don't make me laugh,' said August with a defiant recklessness that seemed to surprise even himself. 'The last Saturday in every month like a clock striking he was round the pubs in Brixton with old Lal Drake.'

And now, as if frightened by what he said, he swanked his way out of the side door of the pub on his way to the Gents.

We lowered our eyes. There are myths, but there are facts. They all knew – even I had heard – that what August said was true, but it was not a thing a sensible man would say in front of Mrs Price. And – mind you – Pliny standing a few doors down the street. But Mrs Price stayed calm among the thoughts in her mind.

'That's a lie,' she said peacefully as we thought, though she was eyeing the door waiting for August to come back.

'I knew his father,' said Alsop.

We were soon laughing about the ancient Pliny, the Bermondsey boy who began with a barrow shouting 'Old Iron' in the streets, a man who never drank, never had a bank account – didn't trust banks – who belted his son while his mother 'educated him up' – she was a tall woman and the boy grew up like her, tall with a long arching nose and those big red ears that looked as though his parents had pulled him now this way now that in their fight over him. She had been a housekeeper in a big house and she had made a son who looked like an old family butler, Cockney to the bone, but almost a gentleman. Except, as Alsop said, his way of blowing his nose like a foghorn on the Thames, but sharp as his father. Marbright said you could see the father's life in the store at the back of the shop; it was piled high with what had made the father's money, every kind of old-fashioned stuff.

'Enough to furnish two or three hotels,' Alsop said. Mrs Price nodded.

'Wardrobes, tables . . .' she said.

'A museum,' said Marbright. 'Helmets, swords. Two four-posters the last time I was there.'

'Ironwork. Brass,' nodded Mrs Price mournfully.

'Must date back to the Crimean War,' said Marbright.

'And it was all left to Pliny.'

There was a general sigh.

'And he doesn't touch it. Rubbish he calls it. He turned his back on it. Only goes in for the best. Hepplewhite, marquetries, his consoles. Regency.'

There was a pause.

'And,' I said, 'his Meissen.'

They looked at me as if I were a criminal. They glanced at one another as if asking whether they should call the police. I was either a thief or I had publicly stripped them of all their clothes. I had publicly announced Pliny's lust.

Although Mrs Price had joined in the conversation, it was in the manner of someone talking in her sleep; for when this silence came, she woke up and said in a startled voice:

'Lal Drake.'

And screwing up her fists she got up and, pausing to get ready for a rush, she heaved herself fast to the door by which August had left for the Gents, down the alley a quarter of an hour before.

'The other door, missis,' someone shouted. But she was through it.

'Drink up,' we said and went out by the front door. I was the last and had a look down the side alley and there I saw a sight. August with one hand doing up his fly buttons and the other arm protecting his face. Mrs Price was hitting out at him and shouting. The language!

'You dirty sod. I knew it. The girl told me.' She was shouting. She saw me, stopped hitting and rushed at me in tears and shouted back at him.

'The filthy old man.'

August saw his chance and got out of the alley and made for the cars in the square. She let me go and shouted after him. We were all there and in Woolworth's doorway was Pliny. Rain was still falling and he looked wet and all the more alone for being wet. I walked off and, I suppose, seeing me go and herself alone and giddy in her rage she looked all round and turned her temper on me.

'The girl has got to go,' she shouted.

Then she came to her senses.

'Where is August?'

August had got to his car and was driving out of the square. She could do nothing. Then she saw Pliny. She ran from me to Pliny, from Pliny to me.

'He's going after the girl,' she screamed.

We calmed her down and it was I who drove her home. (This was when she told me, as the wipers went up and down on the windscreen, that she and August were not married.) We splashed through hissing water that was like her tears on the road. 'I'm worried for the child. I told her, "Keep your door locked." I see it's locked every night. I'm afraid I'll forget and I won't hear him if I've had a couple. She's a kid. She doesn't know anything.' I understood that the face I had always thought was empty was really filled with the one person she loved: Isabel.

August was not there when we got to their shop. Mrs Price went in and big as she was, she did not knock anything over.

'Isabel?' she called.

The girl was in the scullery and came with a wet plate that dripped on the carpet. In two years she had changed. She was wearing an old dress and an apron, but also a pair of high-heeled silver evening shoes. She had become the slut of the house and her pale skin looked dirty.

'You're dripping that thing everywhere. What have you got those shoes on for? Where did you get them?'

'Uncle Harry, for Christmas,' she said. She called August Uncle Harry. She tried to look jaunty as if she had put all her hope in life into those silly evening shoes.

'All right,' said Mrs Price weakly, looking at me to keep quiet and say nothing.

Isabel took off her apron when she saw me. I don't know whether she remembered me. She was still pale, but had the shapeliness of a small young woman. Her eyes looked restlessly and uncertainly at both of us, her chin was firmer but it trembled. She was smiling too and, because I was there and the girl might see an ally in me, Mrs Price looked with half-kindness at Isabel; but when I got up to go the girl looked at me as if she would follow me out of the door. Mrs Price got up fast to bar the way. She stood on the doorstep of the shop watching me get into the car, swollen with the inability to say 'Thank you' or 'Goodbye'. If the girl was a child, Mrs Price was ten times a child and both of them standing on the doorstep were like children who don't want anyone to go away.

I drove off and for a few miles I thought about Mrs Price and the girl, but once I had settled into the long drive to London, the thought of Pliny supplanted them. I had been caught up by the fever of the trade. Pliny's mother was dead. What was going to happen to Pliny and all that part of the business Pliny had inherited from his father, the stuff he despised and had not troubled himself with very much in his mother's time. I ought to go 'over the water' – as we say in London – to have a look at it some time. In a few days I went there; I found the idea had occurred to many others. The shop was on one of the main bus routes in South London, a speckled early Victorian place with an ugly red brick store behind it. Pliny's father had had an eye for a cosy but useful bit of property. Its windows had square panes (1810) and to my surprise the place was open and I could see people inside. There was Pliny with his nose which looked servile rather than distinguished, wearing a long biscuit-coloured tweed jacket with leather pads at the elbows like a Cockney sportsman. There, too, was August with his wet eyes and drinker's shame, Mrs Price swelling over him in her best clothes, and the girl. They had come up from the country and August had had his boots cleaned. The girl was in her best too and was standing apart touching things in the shop, on the point of merriment, looking with wonder at Pliny's ears. He often seemed to be talking at her when he was talking to Mrs Price. I said:

'Hullo! Up from the country? What are you doing here?' Mrs Price was so large that she had to turn her whole body and place her belly in front of everyone who spoke to her.

'Seeing to his teeth,' she said nodding at August and, from years of habit, August turned too when his wife turned, in case it was just as well not to miss one of her pronouncements, whatever else he might dodge. One side of August's jaw was swollen. Then Mrs Price slowly turned her whole body to face Pliny again. They were talking about his mother's death. Mrs Price was greedy, as one stout woman thinking of another, for a melancholy tour of the late mother's organs. The face of the girl looked prettily wise and holiday-fied because the heavy curls of her hair hung close to her face. She looked out of the window, restless and longing to get away while her elders went on talking, but she was too listless to do so. Then she would look again at Pliny's large ears with a childish pleasure in anything strange; they gave him a dog-like appearance and if the Augusts had not been there, I think she would have jumped at him mischievously to touch them, but remembered in time that she had lately grown into a young lady. When she saw him looking at her she turned her back and began writing in the dust on a little table which was standing next to a cabinet; it had a small jug on it. She was writing her name in the dust I S A B . . . And then stopped. She turned round suddenly because she saw I had been watching.

'Is that old Meissen?' she called out, pointing to the jug.

They stopped talking. It was comic to see her pretending, for my benefit, that she knew all about porcelain.

'Cor! Old Meissen!' said August pulling his racing newspaper out of his jacket pocket with excitement, and Mrs Price fondly swung her big handbag; all laughed loudly, a laugh of lust and knowledge. They knew, or thought they knew, that Pliny had a genuine Meissen piece somewhere, probably upstairs where he lived. The girl was pleased to have made them laugh at her; she had been noticed.

Pliny said decently: 'No, dear. That's Caughley. Would you like to see it?'

He walked to the cabinet and took the jug down and put it on a table.

'Got the leopard?' said August, knowingly. Pliny showed the mark of the leopard on the base of the jug and put it down again. It was a pretty shapely jug with a spray of branches and in the branches a pair of pheasants were perching, done in transfer. The girl scared us all by picking it up in both hands, but it was charming to see her holding it up and studying it.

'Careful,' said Mrs Price.

'She's all right,' said Pliny.

Then – it alarmed us – she wriggled with laughter.

'What a funny face,' she said.

Under the lip of the jug was the small face of an old man with a long nose looking sly and wicked.

'They used to put a face under the lip,' Pliny said.

'That's right,' said August.

The girl held it out at arm's length and, looking from the jug to Pliny, she said: 'It's like you, Mr Pliny.'

'Isabel!' said Mrs Price. 'That's rude.'

'But it is,' said Isabel. 'Isn't it?' She was asking me. Pliny grinned. We were all relieved to see him take the jug from her and put it back in the cabinet.

'It belonged to my mother,' he said. 'I keep it there,' Pliny said to me, despising me because I had said nothing and because I was a stranger.

'Go into the back and have a look round if you want to. The light's on.'

I left the shop and went down the steps into the long white store-room where the white-washed walls were grey with dust. There was an alligator hanging by a nail near the steps, a couple of cavalry helmets and a dirty drum that must have been there since the Crimean War. I went down into streets of stacked up furniture. I felt I was walking into an inhuman crypt or worse still one of those charnel houses or ossuaries I had seen pictures of in one of my father's books when I was a boy. Large as the store was, it was lit by a single electric light bulb hanging from a girder in the roof and the yellow light was deathly. The notion of 'picking up' anything at Pliny's depressed me, so that I was left with a horror of the trade I had joined. Yet feelings of this kind are never simple. After half an hour I left the shop. I understood before that day was over and I was back in the room over my own place that what had made me more wretched was the wound of a sharp joy. First, the sight of the girl leaving her name unfinished in the dust had made my heart jump, then when she held the vase in her hands I had felt the thrill of a revelation; until then I had never settled what I should go in for but now I saw it. Why not collect Caughley? That was it. Caughley; it was one of those inspirations that excite one so that every sight in the world changes; even houses, buses and streets and people are transfigured and become unreal as desire carries one away – and then, cruelly, it passes and one is left exhausted.

The total impossibility of an impatient young man like myself collecting Caughley which hadn't been made since 1821 became brutally clear. Too late for Staffordshire, too late for Dresden, too late for Caughley and all the beautiful things. I was savage for lack of money. The following day I went to the Victoria and Albert and then I saw other far more beautiful things enshrined and inaccessible. I gazed with wonder. My longing for possession held me and then I was elevated to a state of worship as if they were idols, holy and never to be touched. Then I remembered the girl's hands and a violent day dream passed through my head; it lasted only a second or two but in that time I smashed the glass case, grabbed the treasure and bolted with it. It frightened me that such an idea could have occurred to me. I left the museum and I turned sourly against my occupation, against Marbright, Alsop and above all Pliny and August, and it broke my heart to think of that pretty girl living among such people and drifting into the shabbiness of the trade. I S A B – half a name, written by a living finger in dust.

One has these brief sensations when one is young. They pass and one does nothing about them. There is nothing remarkable about Caughley – except that you can't get it. I did not collect Caughley for a simple reason; I had to collect my wits. The plain truth is that I was incompetent. I had only to look at my bank account. I had bought too much. At the end of the year I looked like getting into the bankruptcy court unless I had a stroke of luck. Talk of trouble making the trade move; I was Trouble myself, dealers could smell it coming and came sniffing into my shop and at the end of the year I sold up for what I could get. It would have been better if I could have waited for a year or two when the boom began. For some reason I kept the teapot I had bought in Salisbury to remind me of wasted time. In its humble way it was pretty.

In the next six months I changed. I had to. I pocketed my pride and I got a dull job in an auctioneer's; at least it took me out of the office when I got out keys and showed people round. The firm dealt in house property and developments. The word 'develop' took hold of me. The firm was a large one and sometimes 'developed' far outside London. I was told to go and inspect some of the least important bits of property that were coming into the market. One day a row of shops in Steepleton came up for sale. I said I knew them. They were on the London Road opposite the Lion Hotel at the end of the town. My boss was always impressed by topography and the names of hotels and sent me down there. The shops were in the row where August and one or two others had had their business, six of them.

What a change! The Lion had been re-painted; the little shops seemed to have got smaller. In my time the countryside had begun at the end of the row. Now builders' scaffolding was standing in the fields beyond. I looked for August's. A cheap café had taken over his place. He had gone. The mirror man who lived next door was still there but had gone into beads and fancy art jewellery. His window was full of hanging knick-knacks and mobiles.

'It's the tourist trade now,' he said. He looked ill.

'What happened to August?'

He studied me for a moment and said, 'Closed down', and I could get no more out of him. I crossed the street to the Lion. Little by little, a sentence at a time in a long slow suspicious evening, I got news of August from the barmaid as she went back and forth serving customers, speaking in a low voice, her eye on the new proprietor in case the next sentence that came out of her might be bad for custom. The sentences were spoken like sentences from a judge summing up, bit by bit. August had got two years for receiving stolen goods; the woman – 'She wasn't his wife' – had been knocked down by a car as she was coming out of the bar at night – 'not that she drank, not really drank; her weight really' – and then came the final sentence that brought back to me the alerting heat and fever of its secrets: 'There was always trouble over there. It started when the girl ran away.'

'Isabel?' I said.

'I dunno – the girl.'

I stood outside the hotel and looked to the east and then to the west. It was one of those quarters of an hour on a main road when, for some reason, there is no traffic coming either way. I looked at the now far-off fields where the February wind was scything over the grass, turning it into waves of silver as it passed over them. I thought of Isab . . . running with a case in her hand, three years ago. Which way? Where do girls run to? Sad.

I went back to London. There are girls in London too, you know. I grew a beard, reddish: it went with the red car which I had managed to keep. I could afford to take a girl down to the south coast now and then. Sometimes we came back by the Brixton road, sometimes through Camberwell and when we did this I often slowed down at Pliny's and told the girls, 'That man's sitting on a gold mine.' They never believed it or, at least, only one did. She said: 'Does he sell rings? Let us have a look.'

'They're closed,' I said. 'They're always closed.'

'I want to look,' she said, so we stopped and got out.

We looked into the dark window – it was Saturday night – and we could see nothing and as we stared we heard a loud noise coming, it seemed, from the place next door or from down the Drive-in at the side of Pliny's shop, a sound like someone beating boxes or bath tubs at first until I got what it was: drums. Someone blew a bugle, a terrible squeaky sound. There was heavy traffic on the street, but the bugle seemed to split it in half.

'Boys' Brigade, practising for Sunday,' I said. We stood laughing with our hands to our ears as we stared into the dark. All I could make out was something white on a table at the back of the shop. Slowly I saw it was a set of chessmen. Chess, ivories, August – perhaps Pliny had got August's chessmen.

'What a din!' said the girl. I said no more to her for in my mind there was the long forgotten picture of Isabel's finger on the pieces, at Steepleton.

When I've got time, I thought, I will run over to Pliny's; perhaps he will know what happened to the girl.

And I did go there again, one afternoon, on my own. Still closed. I rattled the door handle. There was no answer. I went to a baker's next door, then to a butcher's, then to a pub. The same story. 'He only opens on Sundays,' or, 'He's at a sale.' Then to a tobacconist's. I said it was funny to leave a shop empty like that, full of valuable stuff. The tobacconist became suspicious.

'There's someone there all right. His wife's there.'

'No she's not,' his wife said. 'They've gone off to a sale. I saw them.' She took the hint.

'No one in charge to serve customers,' she said.

I said I'd seen a chessboard that interested me and the tobacconist said: 'It's dying out. I used to play.'

'I didn't know he got married,' I said.

'He's got beautiful things,' said his wife. 'Come on Sunday.'

Pliny married! That made me grin. The only women in his life I had ever heard of were his mother and the gossip about Lal Drake. Perhaps he had made an honest woman of *her*. I went back for one last look at the chessmen and, sure enough, as the tobacconist's wife had hinted someone had been left in charge, for I saw a figure pass through the inner door of the shop. The watcher was watched. Almost at once I heard the tap and roll of a kettle drum, I put my ear to the letter box and distinctly heard a boy's voice shouting orders. Children! All the drumming I had heard on Saturday had come from Pliny's – a whole family drumming. Think of Pliny married to a widow with kids; he had not had time to get his own. I took back what I had thought of him and Lal Drake. I went off for an hour to inspect a house that was being sold on Camberwell Green, and stopped once more at Pliny's on the way back. On the chance of catching him. I went to the window: standing in the middle of the shop was Isabel.

Her shining black hair went to her shoulders. She was wearing a red dress with a schoolgirlish white collar to it. If I had not known her by her heart-shaped face and her full childish lips, I would have known her by her tiptoe way of standing like an actress just about to sing a song or give a dance when she comes forward on the stage. She looked at me daringly. It was the way, I remembered, she had looked at everyone. She did not know me. I went to the door and tipped the handle. It did not open. I saw her watching the handle move. I went on rattling. She straightened and shook her head, pushing back her hair. She did not go away. She was amused by my efforts. I went back to the window of the shop and asked to come in. She could not hear, of course. My mouth was opening and shutting foolishly. That amused her even more. I pointed to something in the window, signalling that I was interested in it. She shook her head again. I tried pointing to other things: a cabinet, an embroidered firescreen, a jar three feet high. At each one she shook her head. It was like a guessing game. I was smiling, even laughing, to persuade her. I put my hands to my chest and pretended to beg like a dog. She laughed at this and looked behind, as if calling to someone. If Pliny wasn't there, his wife might be, or the children. I pointed upwards and made a movement of my hands, imitating someone turning a key in a lock. I was signalling, 'Go and get the key from Mrs Pliny,' and I stepped back and looked up at a window above the shop. When I did this Isabel was frightened; she went away shouting to someone. And that was the end of it; she did not come back.

I went away thinking, Well, that is a strange thing!

What ideas people put into your head and you build fancies yourself – that woman in the bar at Steepleton telling me Isabel had run away and I imagining her running in those poor evening shoes I'd once seen, in the rain down the Bath Road, when what was more natural in a trade where they all live with their hands in one another's pockets – Pliny had married, and they had taken the girl on at the shop. It was a comfort to think of. I hadn't realised how much I had worried about what would happen to a naïve girl like Isabel when the break-up came. Alone in the world! How silly. I thought, one of these Sundays I'll go up there and hear the whole story. And I did.

There was no one there except Pliny and his rich Sunday customers. I even went into the store at the back, looked everywhere. No sign of Isabel. The only female was a woman in a shabby black dress and not wearing a hat who was talking to a man who was testing the door of a wardrobe, making it squeak, while the woman looked on without interest, in the manner of a dealer's wife; obviously the new Mrs Pliny. She turned to make way for another couple who were waiting to look at it. I nearly knocked over a stack of cane chairs as I got past.

If there was no sign of Isabel, the sight of Pliny shocked me. He had been a dead man, permanently dead as wood, even clumsy in his big servile bones, though shrewd. Now he had come to life in the strangest, excited way, much older to look at, thinner and frantic as he looked about him this way and that. He seemed to be possessed by a demon. He talked loudly to people in the shop and was suspicious when he was not talking. He was frightened, abrupt, rude. Pliny married! Marriage had wrecked him or he was making too much money; he looked like a man expecting to be robbed. He recognised me at once. I had felt him watching me from the steps going down to the store. As I came back to the steps to speak to him he spoke to me first, distinctly in a loud voice:

'I don't want any of August's men here, see?'

I went red in the face.

'What do you mean?' I said.

'You heard me,' he said. 'You know what he got.'

Wells of Hungerford was standing near, pretending not to listen. Pliny was telling the trade that I was in with August – publicly accusing me of being a fence. I controlled my temper.

'August doesn't interest me,' I said. 'I'm in property. Marsh, Help and Hitchcock. I sold his place, the whole street.'

And I walked past him looking at a few things as I left.

I was in a passion. The dirty swine – all right when his mother kept an eye on him, the poor old woman, but now – he'd gone mad. And that poor girl! I went to the tobacconist for the Sunday paper in a dream, put down my money and took it without a word and was almost out of the door when the wife called out:

'Did you find him? Did you get what you wanted?' A friendly London voice. I tapped the side of my head.

'You're telling me,' the wife said.

'Well, he has to watch everything now. Marrying a young girl like that, it stands to reason,' said the wife in a melancholy voice.

'Wears him out, at his age,' suggested the tobacconist.

'Stop the dirty talk, Alfred,' said the wife.

'You mean he married the *girl*?' I said. 'Who's the big woman without a hat – in the store?'

'What big woman is that?' asked the tobacconist's wife. 'He's married to the girl. Who else do you think – there's no one else.'

The wife's face went as blank as a tombstone in the sly London way.

'She's done well for herself,' said the tobacconist. 'Keeps her locked up like his mother, wasn't I right?'

'He worships her,' said the woman.

I went home to my flat. I was nauseated. The thought of Isabel in bed with that dressed-up servant, with his wet eyes, his big raw ears and his breath smelling of onions! Innocent? No, as the woman said, 'She has done well for herself.' Happy with him too. I remembered her pretty face laughing in the shop. What else could you expect, after August and Mrs Price.

The anger I felt with Pliny grew to a rage but by the time I was in my own flat Pliny vanished from the picture in my mind. I was filled with passion for the girl. The fever of the trade had come alive in me; Pliny had got something I wanted. I could think of nothing but her, just as I remember the look August gave Pliny when the girl asked if the jug was Meissen. I could see her holding the jug at arm's length, laughing at the old man's face under the lip. And I could see that Pliny was not mad; what was making him frantic was possessing the girl.

I kept away from Pliny's. I tried to drive the vision out of my mind, but I could not forget it. I became cunning. Whenever my job allowed it – and even when it didn't – I started passing the time of day with any dealer I had known, picked up news of the sales, studied catalogues, tried to find out which ones Pliny would go to. She might be with him. I actually went to Newbury but he was not there. Bath he couldn't miss and, sure enough, he was there and she wasn't. It was ten in the morning and the sale had just started. I ran off and got into my car. I drove as fast as I could the hundred miles back to London and cursed the lunchtime traffic. I got to Pliny's shop and rang the bell. Once, then several long rings. At once the drum started beating and went on as if troops were marching. People passing in the street paused to listen too. I stood back from the window and I saw a movement at a curtain upstairs. The drumming was still going on and when I bent to listen at the letter box I could hear the sound become deafening and often very near and then there was a blast from the bugle. It was a misty day south of the river and for some reason or other I was fingering the grey window and started writing her name, I S A B . . . hopelessly, but hoping that perhaps she might come near enough to see. The drumming stopped. I waited and waited and then I saw an extraordinary sight: Isabel herself in the dull red dress, but with a lancer's helmet on her head and a side drum on its straps hanging from her shoulders and the drum sticks in her hand. She was standing upright like a boy playing soldiers, her chin up and puzzling at the sight of the letters BASI on the window. When she saw me she was confused. She immediately gave two or three taps to the drum and then bent almost double with laughter. Then she put on a straight face and played the game of pointing to one thing after another in the shop. Every time I shook my head, until at last I pointed to her. This pleased her. Then I shouted through the letter box. 'I want to come in.'

'Come in,' she said. 'It's open.'

The door had been open all the time; I had not thought of trying it. I went inside.

'I thought you were locked in.'

She did not answer but wagged her head from side to side.

'Sometimes I lock myself in,' she said. 'There are bad people about, August's men.'

She said this with great importance, but her face became ugly as she said it. She took off the helmet and put down the drum.

'So I beat the drum when Mr Pliny is away,' she said. She called him Mr Pliny.

'What good does that do?'

'It is so quiet when Mr Pliny is away. I don't do it when he's here. It frightens August's men away.'

'It's as good as telling them you are alone here,' I said. 'That's why I came. I heard the drum and the bugle.'

'Did you?' she said eagerly. 'Was it loud?'

'Very loud.'

She gave a deep sigh of delight.

'You see!' she said, nodding her head complacently.

'Who taught you to blow the bugle?' I said.

'My mother did,' she said. 'She did it on the stage. Mr Pliny – you know when Mr Pliny fetched me in his motor-car – I forgot it. He had to go back and get it. I was too frightened.'

'Isab . . .' I said.

She blushed. She remembered.

'I might be one of August's men,' I said.

'No you're not. I know who you are,' she said. 'Mr Pliny's away for the day but that doesn't matter. I am in charge. Is there something you were looking for?'

The child was gone when she put the drum aside. She became serious and practical: Mrs Pliny! I was confused by my mistake in not knowing the door was open and she busied herself about the shop. She knew what she was doing and I felt very foolish.

'Is there something special?' she said. 'Look around.' She had become a confident woman. I no longer felt there was anything strange about her.

I drifted to look at the chessmen and I could not pretend to myself that they interested me, but I did ask her the price. She said she would look it up and went to a desk where Pliny kept his papers and after going through some lists of figures which were all in code she named the sum. It was enormous – something like £275 and I said, 'What!' in astonishment. She put the list back on the desk and said, firmly:

'My husband paid £260 for it last Sunday. It was carved by Dubois. There are only two more like it. It was the last thing he did in 1785.'

(I found out afterwards this was nonsense.)

She said this in Pliny's voice; it was exactly the sort of casual sentence he would have used. She looked expressionlessly and not at all surprised when I said, 'Valuable,' and moved away.

I meant, of course, that she was valuable and in fact, her mystery having gone, she seemed conscious of being valuable and important herself, the queen and owner of everything in the shop, efficiently in charge of her husband's things. The cabinet in the corner, she said, in an offhand way, as I went to look at it, had been sold to an Australian. 'We are waiting for the packers.' We! Not to feel less knowing than she was, I looked around for some small thing to buy from her. There were several small things, like a cup and saucer, a little china tray, a christening mug. I picked things up and put them down listlessly and, from being indifferent, she became eager and watched me. The important, serious expression she had had vanished, she became childish suddenly and anxious: she was eager to sell something. I found a little china figure on a shelf.

'How much is this?' I said. It was Dresden; the real thing. She took it and looked at the label. I knew it was far beyond my purse and I asked her the price in the bored hopeless voice one puts on.

'I'll have to look it up,' she said.

She went to the desk again and looked very calculating and thoughtful and then said, as if naming an enormous sum:

'Two pounds.'

'It can't be,' I said.

She looked sad as I put it back on the shelf and she went back to the desk. Then she said:

'I tell you what I'll do. It's got a defect. You can have it for thirty-five shillings.'

I picked it up again. There was no defect in it. I could feel the huge wave of temptation that comes to one in the trade, the sense of the incredible chance, the lust that makes one shudder first and then breaks over one so that one is possessed, though even at that last moment, one plays at delay in a breathless pause, now one is certain of one's desire.

I said: 'I'll give you thirty bob for it.'

Young Mrs Pliny raised her head and her brown eyes became brilliant with naïve joy.

'All right,' she said.

The sight of her wrapping the figure, packing it in a box and taking the money so entranced me that I didn't realise what she was doing or what I had done. I wasn't thinking of the figure at all. I was thinking of her. We shook hands. Hers were cold and she waved from the shop door when I left. And when I got to the end of the street and found myself holding the box I wondered why I had bought it. I didn't want it. I had felt the thrill of the thief and I was so ashamed that I once or twice thought of dropping it into a litter box. I even thought of going back and returning it to her and saying to her: 'I didn't want it. It was a joke. I wanted you. Why did you marry an awful old man like Pliny?' And those stories of Pliny going off once a month in the old days, in his mother's time, to Lal Drake that old whore in Brixton, came back to me. I didn't even unpack the figure but put it on the mantelpiece in my room, then on the top shelf of a cupboard which I rarely used. I didn't want to see it. And when in the next months – or even years – I happened to see it, I remembered her talking about the bad people, August's men.

But, though I kept away from Pliny's on Sundays, I could not resist going back to the street and eventually to the shop – just for the sight of her.

And after several misses I did see her in the shop. It was locked. When I saw her she stared at me with fear and made no signals and quickly disappeared – I suppose into the room at the back. I crossed the main road and looked at the upper part of the house. She was upstairs, standing at a window. So I went back across the street and tried to signal, but of course she could only see my mouth moving. I was obsessed by the way I had cheated her. My visits were a siege for the door was never opened now. I did see her once through the window and this time I had taken the box and offered it to her in dumb show. That did have an effect. I saw she was looking very pale, her eyes ringed and tired and whether she saw I was remorseful or not I couldn't tell, but she made a rebuking yet defiant face. Another day I went and she looked terrified. She pointed and pointed to the door but as I eagerly stepped towards it she shook her head and raised a hand to forbid me. I did not understand until, soon, I saw Pliny walking about the shop. I moved off. People in the neighbourhood must often have seen me standing there and the tobacconist I went to gave me a look that suggested he knew what was going on.

Then, on one of my vigils, I saw a doctor go to the side door down the Goods Entrance and feared she was ill – but the butcher told me it was Pliny. His wife, they said, had been nursing him. He ought to convalesce somewhere. A nice place by the sea. But he won't. It would do his wife good. The young girl has worn herself out looking after him. Shut up all day with him. And the tobacconist said what his wife had said a long time back. 'Like his poor mother. He kept *her* locked in too. Sunday evening's the only time she's out. It's all wrong.'

I got sick of myself. I didn't notice the time I was wasting for one day passed like a smear of grey into another and I wished I could drag myself away from the district, especially now Pliny was always there. At last one Saturday I fought hard against a habit so useless and I had the courage to drive past the place for once and did not park my car up the street. I drove on, taking side streets (which I knew, nevertheless, would lead me back), but I made a mistake with the one-ways and got on the main Brixton road and was heading north to freedom from myself.

It was astonishing to be free. It was seven o'clock in the evening and to celebrate I went into a big pub where they had singers on Saturday nights; it was already filling up with people. How normal, how cheerful they were, a crowd of them, drinking, shouting and talking; the human race! I got a drink and chose a quiet place in a corner and I was taking my first mouthful of the beer, saying to myself: 'Here's to yourself, my boy,' as though I had just met myself as I used to be. And then, with the glass still at my lips, I saw in a crowd at the other end of the bar Pliny, with his back half-turned. I recognised him by his jug-handle ears, his white hair and the stoop of a tall man. He was not in his dressy clothes but in a shabby suit that made him seem disguised. He was listening to a woman who had a large handbag and had bright blonde hair and a big red mouth who was telling him a joke and she banged him in the stomach with her bag and laughed. Someone near me said: 'Lal's on the job early this evening.' Lal Drake. All the old stories about Pliny and his woman came back to me and how old Castle of Westbury said that Pliny's mother had told him, when she was saying what a good son he was to her, that the one and only time he had been with a woman he had come home and told her and put his head in her laps and cried 'like a child' and promised on the Bible he'd never do such a thing again. Castle swore this was true.

I put down my glass and got out of the pub fast without finishing it. Not because I was afraid of Pliny. Oh no! I drove straight back to Pliny's shop. I rang the bell. The drum started beating a few taps and then a window upstairs opened.

'What do you want?' said Isabel in a whisper.

'I want to see you. Open the door.'

'It's locked.'

'Get the key.'

She considered me for a long time.

'I haven't got one,' she said, still in a low voice, so hard to hear that she had to say it twice.

'Where have you been?' she said.

We stared at each other's white faces in the dark. She had missed me!

'You've got a key. You must have,' I said. 'Somewhere. What about the back door?'

She leaned on the window, her arms on the sill. She was studying my clothes.

'I have something for you,' I said. This changed her. She leaned forward trying to see more of me in the dark. She was curious. Today I understand what I did not understand then; she was looking me over minutely, inch by inch – what she could see of me in the sodium light of the street lamp – not because I was strange or unusual – but because I was not. She had been shut up either alone or with Pliny without seeing another soul for so long. He was treating her like one of his collector's pieces, like the Meissen August had said he kept hidden upstairs. She closed the window. I stood there wretched and impatient. I went down the Goods Entrance ready to kick the side door down, break a window, climb in somehow.

[851]

The side door had no letter box or glass panes, no handle even. I stood in front of it and suddenly it was opened. She was standing there.

'You're *not* locked in,' I said.

She was holding a key.

'I found it,' she said.

I saw she was telling a lie.

'Just now?'

'No. I know where he hides it,' she said lowering her frank eyes.

It was a heavy key with an old piece of frayed used-up string on it.

'Mr Pliny does not like me to show people things,' she said. 'He has gone to see his sister in Brixton. She is very ill. I can't show you anything.'

She recited these words as if she had learned them by heart. It was wonderful to stand so near to her in the dark.

'Can I come in?' I said.

'What do you want?' she said cautiously.

'You,' I said.

She raised her chin.

'Are you one of August's men?' she said.

'You know I'm not. I haven't seen August for years.'

'Mr Pliny says you are. He said I was never to speak to you again. August was horrible.'

'The last I heard he was in prison.'

'Yes,' she said. 'He steals.'

This seemed to please her; she forgave him that easily. Then she put her head out of the doorway as if to see if August were waiting behind me.

'He does something else, too,' she said.

I remembered the violent quarrel between August and poor Mrs Price when she was drunk in Salisbury – the quarrel about Isabel.

'You ran away,' I said.

She shook her head.

'I didn't run away. Mr Pliny fetched me,' she said and nodded primly, 'in his car. I told you.'

Then she said: 'Where is the present you were bringing me?'

'It isn't a present,' I said. 'It's the little figure I bought from you. You didn't charge me enough. Let me in. I want to explain.'

I couldn't bring myself to tell her that I had taken advantage of her ignorance, so I said:

'I found out afterwards that it was worth much more than I paid you. I want to give it back to you.'

She gave a small jump towards me. 'Oh please, please,' she said and took me by the hand. 'Where is it?'

'Let me come in,' I said, 'and I will tell you. I haven't got it with me. I'll bring it tomorrow, no not tomorrow, Monday.'

'Oh. Please,' she pleaded. 'Mr Pliny was so angry with me for selling it. He'd never been angry with me before. It was terrible. It was awful.'

It had never occurred to me that Pliny would even know she had sold the piece; but now, I remembered the passions of the trade and the stored-up lust that seems to pass between things and men like Pliny. He wouldn't forgive. He would be savage.

'Did he do something to you? He didn't hit you, did he?'

Isabel did not answer.

'What did he do?'

I remembered how frantic Pliny had been and how violent he had sounded, when he told me to get out of his shop.

'He cried,' she said. 'He cried and he cried. He went down on his knees and he would not stop crying. I was wicked to sell it. I am the most precious thing he has. Please bring it. It will make him better.'

'Is he still angry?'

'It has made him ill,' she said.

'Let me come in,' I said.

'Will you promise?'

'I swear I'll bring it,' I said.

'For a minute,' she said, 'but not in the shop.'

I followed her down a dark passage into the store and was so close that I could smell her hair.

Pliny crying! At first I took this to be one of Isabel's fancies. Then I thought of tall, clumsy, servant-like Pliny, expert at sales with his long-nosed face pouring out water like a pump, repentant, remorseful, agonised like an animal, to a pretty girl. Why? Just because she had sold something? Isabel loved to sell things. He must have had some other reason. I remembered Castle of Westbury's story. What had he done to the girl?

Only a cruel man could have gone in for such an orgy of self-love. He had the long face on which tears would be a blackmail. He would be like a horse crying because it had lost a race.

Yet those tears were memorable to Isabel and she so firmly called him 'Mr Pliny'. In bed, did she still call him 'Mr Pliny'? I have often thought since that she did; it would have given her a power – perhaps cowed him.

At night the cold white-washed store-room was silent under the light of its single bulb and the place was mostly in shadow, only the tops of stacked furniture stood out in the yellow light, some of them like buildings. The foundations of the stacks were tables or chests, desks on which chairs or small cabinets were piled. We walked down alleys between the stacks. It was like walking through a dead, silent city, abandoned by everyone who once lived there. There was the sour smell of upholstery; in one part there was a sort of plaza where two large dining tables stood with their chairs set around and a pile of dessert plates on them. Isabel was walking confidently. She stopped by a dressing-table with a mirror on it next to a group of wardrobes, and turning round to face it, she said proudly:

'Mr Pliny gave it all to me. And the shop.'

'All of this?'

'When he stopped crying,' she said.

And then she turned about and we faced the wardrobes. There were six or seven, one in rosewood and an ugly yellow one, and they were so arranged here that they made a sort of alcove or room. The wardrobe at the corner of the alley was very heavy and leaned so that its doors were open in a manner of such empty hopelessness, showing its empty shelves, that it made me uneasy. Someone might have just taken his clothes from it in a hurry, perhaps that very minute, and gone off. He might be watching us. It was the wardrobe with the squeaking door which I had seen the customer open while the woman whom I had thought to be Mrs Pliny stood by. Each piece of furniture seemed to watch – even the small things, like an umbrella stand or a tray left on a table. Isabel walked into the alcove and there was a greeny-grey sofa with a screwed-up paper bag of toffees on it and on the floor beside it I saw, of all things, the lancer's helmet and the side drum and the bugle. The yellow light scarcely lit this corner.

'There's your drum,' I said.

'This is my house,' she said, gaily now. 'Do you like it? When Mr Pliny is away I come here in case August's men come . . .'

She looked at me doubtfully when she mentioned that name again.

'And you beat the drum to drive them away?' I said.

'Yes,' she said stoutly.

I could not make out whether she was playing the artless child or not, yet she was a woman of twenty-five at least. I was bewildered.

'You are frightened here on your own, aren't you?'

'No l am not. It's nice.'

Then she said very firmly:

'You will come here on Monday and give me the box back?'

I said: 'I will if you'll let me kiss you. I love you, Isabel.'

'Mr Pliny loves me too,' she said.

'Isab . . .' I said. That did move her.

I put my arm round her waist and she let me draw her to me. It was strange to hold her because I could feel her ribs, but her body was so limp and feeble that, loving her as I did, I was shocked and pulled her tightly against me. She turned her head weakly so that I could only kiss her cheek and see only one of her eyes and I could not make out whether she was enticing me, simply curious about my embrace or drooping in it without heart.

'You *are* one of August's men,' she said getting away from me. 'He used to try and get into my bed. After that I locked my door.'

'Isabel,' I said. 'I am in love with you. I think you love me. Why did you marry a horrible old man like Pliny?'

'Mr Pliny is not horrible,' she said. 'I love him. He never comes to my room.'

'Then he doesn't love you,' I said. 'Leaving you locked up here. And you don't love him.'

She listened in the manner of someone wanting to please, waiting for me to stop.

'He is not a real husband, a real lover,' I said.

'Yes, he is,' she said proudly. 'He takes my clothes off before I go to bed. He likes to look at me. I am the most precious thing he has.'

'That isn't love, Isabel,' I said.

'It is,' she said with warmth. 'You don't love me. You cheated me. Mr

[855]

Pliny said so. And you don't want to look at me. You don't think I'm precious.'

I went to take her in my arms again and held her.

'I love you. I want you. You are beautiful. I didn't cheat you. Pliny is cheating you, not me,' I said. 'He is not with his sister. He's in bed with a woman in Brixton. I saw them in a pub. Everyone knows it.'

'No he is not. I *know* he is not. He doesn't like it. He promised his mother,' she said.

The voice in which she said this was not her playful voice; the girl vanished and a woman had taken her place and not a distressed woman, not a contemptuous or a disappointed one.

'He worships me,' she said and in the squalid store of dead junk she seemed to be illumined by the simple knowledge of her own value and looked at my love as if it were nothing at all.

I looked at the sofa and was so mad that I thought of grabbing her and pulling her down there. What made me hesitate was the crumpled bag of toffees on it. I was as nonplussed and, perhaps, as impotent as Pliny must have been. In that moment of hesitation she picked up her bugle, and standing in the aisle, she blew it hard, her cheeks going out full and the noise and echoes seemed to make the shadows jump. I have never heard a bugle call that scared me so much. It killed my desire.

'I told you not to come in,' she said. 'Go away.'

And she walked into the aisle between the furniture, swinging her key to the door.

'Come back,' I said as I followed her.

I saw her face in the dressing-table mirror we had passed before, then I saw my own face, red and sweating on the upper lip and my mouth helplessly open. And then in the mirror I saw another face following mine – Pliny's. Pliny must have seen me in the pub.

In that oblong frame of mahogany with its line of yellow inlay, Pliny's head looked winged by his ears and he was coming at me, his head down, his mouth with its yellowing teeth open under the moustache and his eyes stained in the bad light. He looked like an animal. The mirror concentrated him and before I could do more than half turn he had jumped in a clumsy way at me and jammed one of my shoulders against a tall-boy.

'What are you doing here?' he shouted.

[856]

The shouts echoed over the store.

'I warned you. I'll get the police on you. You leave my wife alone. Get out. You thought you'd get her on her own and swindle her again.'

I hated to touch a white-haired man but, in pain, I shoved him back hard. We were, as I have said, close to the wardrobe and he staggered back so far that he hit the shelves and the door swung towards him so that he was half out of my sight for a second. I kicked the door hard with my left foot and it swung to and hit him in the face. He jumped out with blood on his nose. But I had had time to topple the pile of little cane chairs into the alleyway between us. Isabel saw this and ran round the block of furniture and reached him and when I saw her she was standing with the bugle raised like a weapon in her hand to defend the old man from me. He was wiping his face. She looked triumphant.

'Don't you touch Mr Pliny,' she shouted at me. 'He's ill.'

He *was* ill. He staggered. I pushed my way through the fallen chairs and I picked up one and said: 'Pliny, sit down on this.' Pliny with the bleeding face glared and she forced him to sit down. He was panting. And then a new voice joined us; the tobacconist came down the alley.

'I heard the bugle,' he said. 'Anything wrong? Oh Gawd, look at his face. What happened, Pliny? Mrs Pliny, you all right?' And then he saw me. All the native shadiness of the London streets, all the gossip of the neighbourhood came into his face.

'I said to my wife,' he said, 'something's wrong at Pliny's.'

'I came to offer Mr Pliny a piece of Dresden,' I said, 'but he was out at Brixton seeing his sister, his wife said. He came back and thought I'd broken in and hit himself on the wardrobe.'

'You oughtn't to leave Mrs Pliny alone with all this valuable stock, Mr Pliny. Saturday night too,' the tobacconist said.

Tears had started rolling down Pliny's cheeks very suddenly when I mentioned Brixton and he looked at me and the tobacconist in panic.

'I'm not interested in Dresden,' he managed to say.

Isabel dabbed his face and sent the tobacconist for a glass of water.

'No, dear, you're not,' said Isabel.

And to me she said: 'We're not interested.'

That was the end. I found myself walking in the street. How unreal people looked in the sodium light.

The Diver

In a side street on the Right Bank of the Seine where the river divides at the Ile de la Cité, there is a yellow and red brick building shared by a firm of leather merchants. When I was twenty I worked there. The hours were long, the pay was low, and the place smelled of cigarettes and boots. I hated it. I had come to Paris to be a writer but my money had run out, and in this office I had to stick. How often I looked across the river, envying the free lives of the artists and writers on the other bank. Being English, I was the joke of the office. The sight of my fat pink innocent face and fair hair made everyone laugh; my accent was bad, for I could not pronounce a full 'o'; worst of all, like a fool, I not only admitted I hadn't got a mistress, but boasted about it. To the office boys this news was extravagant. It doubled them up. It was a favourite trick of theirs, and even of the salesman, a man called Claudel with whom I had to work, to call me to the street door at lunchtime and then, if any girl or woman passed, they would give me a punch and shout:

'How much to sleep with this one? Twenty? Forty? A hundred?' I put on a grin, but, to tell the truth, a sheet of glass seemed to come down between me and any female I saw.

About one woman the lads did not play this game. She was a woman between thirty and forty I suppose, Mme. Chamson, who kept the menders and cleaners down the street. You could hear her heels as she came, half-running, to see Claudel, with jackets and trousers of his on her arm. He had some arrangement with her for getting his suits cleaned and repaired on the cheap. In return – well, there was a lot of talk. She had sinfully tinted hair built up high over arching, exclaiming eyebrows, hard as varnish and when she got near our door there was always a joke coming out of the side of her mouth. She would bounce into the office in her tight navy blue skirt, call the boys and Claudel together, shake hands with them all, and tell them some tale which always ended, with a dirty glance around, in whispering. Then she stood back and shouted with laughter. I was never in this secret circle and if I happened to grin, she gave me a severe and offended look and marched out scowling. One day, when one of her tales was over, she called back from the door:

'Standing all day in that gallery with all those naked women, he comes home done for, finished.'

The office boys squeezed each other with pleasure. She was talking about her husband who was an attendant at the Louvre, a small moist-looking fellow whom we sometimes saw with her, a man fond of fishing, whose breath smelled of white wine. Because of her arrangement with Claudel, and her stories, she was a very respected woman.

I did not like Mme. Chamson; she looked to me like some predatory bird; but I could not take my eyes off her pushing bosom and her crooked mouth. I was afraid of her tongue. She caught on quickly to the fact that I was the office joke, but when they told her on top of this I wanted to be a writer, any curiosity she had about me was finished. 'I could tell him a tale,' she said. For her I didn't exist. She didn't even bother to shake hands with me.

Streets and avenues in Paris are named after writers; there are statues to poets, novelists and dramatists, making gestures to the birds, nurse-maids and children in the gardens. How was it these men had become famous? How had they begun? For myself, it was impossible to begin. I walked about packed with stories, but when I sat in cafés or in my room with a pen in my hand and a bare sheet of paper before me, I could not touch it. I seemed to swell in the head, the chest, the arms and legs, as if I was trying to heave an enormous load on to the page and could not move. The portentous moment had not yet come. And there was another reason. The longer I worked in the leather trade and talked to the office boys, the typists there and Claudel, the more I acquired a double personality; when I left the office and walked to the Metro, I practised French to myself. In this bizarre language the stories inside me flared up, I was acting and speaking them as I walked, often in the subjunctive: but when I sat before my paper, the English language closed its sullen mouth.

And what were these stories? Impossible to say. I would set off in the morning and see the grey, ill-painted buildings of the older quarters leaning together like people, their shutters thrown back, so that the open

[859]

windows looked like black and empty eyes. In the mornings the bedding was thrown over the sills to air and hung out, wagging like tongues about what goes on in the night between men and women. The houses looked sunken-shouldered, exhausted, by what they told; and crowning the city was the church of Sacré Coeur, very white, standing like some dry Byzantine bird, to my mind, hollow-eyed and without conscience, presiding over the habits of the flesh and – to judge by what I read in newspapers – its crimes also; its murders, rapes, its shootings for jealousy and robbery. As my French improved the secrets of Paris grew worse. It amazed me that the crowds I saw on the street had survived the night and many indeed looked as sleepless as the houses.

After I had been a little more than a year in Paris, fourteen months in fact, a drama broke the monotonous life of our office. A consignment of dressed skins had been sent to us from Rouen. It had been sent by barge – not the usual method in our business. The barge was an old one and was carrying a mixed cargo and, within a few hundred yards from our warehouse, it was rammed and sunk one misty morning, by a Dutch boat taking the wrong channel. The manager, the whole office, especially Claudel, who saw his commission go to the bottom, were outraged. Fortunately the barge had gone down slowly near the bank, close to us; the water was not too deep. A crane was brought down on another barge to the water's edge and soon, in an exciting week, a diver was let down to salvage what he could. Claudel and I had to go to the quay and, if a bale of our stuff came up, we had to get it to the warehouse and see what the damage was.

Anything to get out of the office. For me the diver was the hero of the week. He stood in his round helmet and suit on a wide tray of wood hanging from four chains and then, the motor spat, the chains rattled and down he went with great dignity under the water. While the diver was under the water, Claudel would be reckoning his commission over again – would it be calculated only on the sale price or on what was saved? 'Five bales so far,' he would mutter fanatically. 'One and a half per cent.' His teeth and his eyes were agitated with changing figures. I, in imagination, was groping in the gloom of the river bed with the hero. Then we'd step forward; the diver was coming up. Claudel would hold my arm as the man appeared with a tray of sodden bales and the brown water streaming off them. He would step off the plank on to the barge where the crane was installed and look like a swollen frog. A workman unscrewed his helmet, the vizor was raised and then we saw the young diver's rosy, cheerful face. A workman lit a cigarette and gave it to him and out of the helmet came a long surprising jet of smoke. There was always a crowd watching from the quay wall and when he did this, they all smiled and many laughed. 'See that?' they would say. 'He is having a puff,' and the diver grinned and waved to the crowd.

Our job was to grab the bale. Claudel would check the numbers of the bales on his list. Then we saw them wheeled to our warehouse, dripping all the way, and there I had to hang up the skins on poles. It was like hanging up drowned animals – even, I thought, human beings.

On the Friday afternoon of that week, when everyone was tired and even the crowd looking down from the street wall had thinned to next to nothing, Claudel and I were still down on the quay waiting for the final load. The diver had come up. We were seeing him for the last time before the weekend. I was waiting to watch what I had not yet seen: how he got out of his suit. I walked down nearer at the quay's edge to get a good view. Claudel shouted to me to get on with the job and as he shouted I heard a whizzing noise above my head and then felt a large, heavy slopping lump hit me on the shoulders. I turned round and the next thing I was flying in the air, arms outspread with wonder. Paris turned upside down. A second later, I crashed into cold darkness, water was running up my legs swallowing me. I had fallen into the river.

The wall of the quay was not high. In a couple of strokes I came up spitting mud and caught an iron ring on the quay wall. Two men pulled my hands. Everyone was laughing as I climbed out.

I stood there drenched and mud-smeared, with straw in my hair, pouring water into a puddle that came from me, getting larger and larger.

'Didn't you hear me shout?' said Claudel.

Laughing and arguing, two or three men led me to the shelter of the wall where I began to wring out my jacket and shirt and squeeze the water out of my trousers. It was a warm day and I stood in the sun and saw my trousers steam and heard my shoes squelch.

'Give him a hot rum,' someone said. Claudel was torn between looking after our few bales left on the quay and taking me across the street to a bar. But, checking the numbers and muttering a few more figures to himself, he decided to enjoy the drama and go with me. He called out that we'd be back in a minute.

We got to the bar and Claudel saw to it that my arrival was a sensation. Always nagging at me in the office, he was now proud of me.

'He fell into the river. He nearly drowned. I warned him. I shouted. Didn't I?'

The one or two customers admired me. The barman brought me the rum. I could not get my hand into my pocket because it was wet.

'You pay me tomorrow,' said Claudel, putting a coin on the counter.

'Drink it quickly,' said the barman.

I was laughing and explaining now.

'One moment he was on dry land, the next he was flying in the air, then plonk in the water. Three elements,' said Claudel.

'Only fire is missing,' said the barman.

They argued about how many elements there were. A whole history of swimming feats, drowning stories, bodies bound, murders in the Seine, sprang up. Someone said the morgue used to be full of corpses. And then an argument started, as it sometimes did in this part of Paris, about the exact date at which the morgue was moved from the island. I joined in but my teeth had begun to chatter.

'Another rum,' the barman said.

And then I felt a hand fingering my jacket and my trousers. It was the hand of Mme. Chamson. She had been down at the quay once or twice during the week to have a word with Claudel. She had seen what had happened.

'He ought to go home and change into dry things at once,' she said in a firm voice. 'You ought to take him home.'

'I can't do that. We've left five bales on the quay,' said Claudel.

'He can't go back,' said Mme. Chamson. 'He's shivering.'

I sneezed.

'You'll catch pneumonia,' she said. And to Claudel: 'You ought to have kept an eye on him. He might have drowned.'

She was very stern with him.

'Where do you live?' she said to me.

I told her.

'It will take you an hour,' she said.

Everyone was silent before the decisive voice of Mme. Chamson.

'Come with me to the shop,' she ordered and pulled me brusquely by the arm. She led me out of the bar and said, as we walked away, my boots squeaking and squelching:

'That man thinks of nothing but money. Who'd pay for your funeral? Not he!'

Twice, as she got me, her prisoner, past the shops, she called out to people at their doors:

'They nearly let him drown.'

Three girls used to sit mending in the window of her shop and behind them was usually a man pressing clothes. But it was half past six now and the shop was closed. Everyone had gone. I was relieved. This place had disturbed me. When I first went to work for our firm Claudel had told me he could fix me up with one of the mending girls; if we shared a room it would halve our expenses and she could cook and look after my clothes. That was what started the office joke about my not having a mistress. When we got to the shop Mme. Chamson led me down a passage inside which was muggy with the smell of dozens of dresses and suits hanging there, into a dim parlour beyond. It looked out on to the smeared grey wall of a courtyard.

'Stay here,' said Mme. Chamson planting me by a sofa. 'Don't sit on it in those wet things. Take them off.'

I took off my jacket.

'No. Don't wring it. Give it to me. I'll get a towel.'

I started drying my hair.

'All of them,' she said.

Mme. Chamson looked shorter in her room, her hair looked duller, her eyebrows less dramatic. I had never really seen her closely. She had become a plain, domestic woman; her mouth had straightened. There was not a joke in her. Her bosom swelled with management. The rumour that she was Claudel's mistress was obviously an office tale.

'I'll see what I can find for you. You can't wear these.'

I waited for her to leave the room and then I took off my shirt and dried my chest, picking off the bits of straw from the river that had stuck to my skin. She came back.

'Off with your trousers, I said. Give them to me. What size are they?'

My head went into the towel. I pretended not to hear. I could not bring myself to undress before Mme. Chamson. But while I hesitated she bent down and her sharp fingernails were at my belt.

'I'll do it,' I said anxiously.

Our hands touched and our fingers mixed as I unhitched my belt. Impatiently she began on my buttons, but I pushed her hands away.

She stood back, blank-faced and peremptory in her stare. It was the blankness of her face, her indifference to me, her ordinary womanliness, the touch of her practical fingers that left me without defence. She was not the ribald, coquettish, dangerous woman who came wagging her hips to our office, not one of my Paris fantasies of sex and danger. She was simply a woman. The realisation of this was disastrous to me. An unbelievable change was throbbing in my body. It was uncontrollable. My eyes angrily, helplessly, asked her to go away. She stood there implacably. I half-turned, bending to conceal my enormity as I lowered my trousers, but as I lowered them inch by inch so the throbbing manifestation increased. I got my foot out of one leg but my shoe caught in the other. On one leg I tried to dance my other trouser leg off. The towel slipped and I glanced at her in red-faced angry appeal. My trouble was only too clear. I was stiff with terror. I was almost in tears.

The change in Mme. Chamson was quick. From busy indifference, she went to anger.

'Young man,' she said. 'Cover yourself. How dare you. What indecency. How dare you insult me!'

'I'm sorry. I couldn't help . . .' I said.

Mme. Chamson's bosom became a bellows puffing outrage.

'What manners,' she said. 'I am not one of your tarts. I am a respectable woman. This is what I get for helping you. What would your parents say? If my husband were here!'

She had got my trousers in her hand. The shoe that had betrayed me fell now out of the leg to the floor.

She bent down coolly and picked it up.

'In any case,' she said and now I saw for the first time this afternoon the strange twist of her mouth return to her, as she nodded at my now concealing towel – 'that is nothing to boast about.'

My blush had gone. I was nearly fainting. I felt the curious, brainless stupidity that goes with the state nature had put me in. A miracle saved me. I sneezed and then sneezed again; the second time with force.

'What did I tell you!' said Mme. Chamson, passing now to angry self-congratulation. She flounced out to the passage that led to the shop and coming back with a pair of trousers she threw them at me and, red in the face, said:

'Try those. If they don't fit I don't know what you'll do. I'll get a shirt,' and she went past me to the door of the room beyond saying:

'You can thank your lucky stars my husband has gone fishing.'

I heard her muttering as she opened drawers. She did not return. There was silence.

In the airless little salon, looking out (as if it were a cell in which I was caught) on the stained smudgy grey wall of the courtyard, the silence lengthened. It began to seem that Mme. Chamson had shut herself away in her disgust and was going to have no more to do with me. I saw a chance of getting out but she had taken away my wet clothes. I pulled on the pair of trousers she had thrown; they were too long but I could tuck them in. I should look an even bigger fool if I went out in the street dressed only in these. What was Mme. Chamson doing? Was she torturing me? Fortunately my impromptu disorder had passed. I stood listening. I studied the mantelpiece where I saw what I supposed was a photograph of Mme. Chamson as a girl in the veil of her first communion. Presently I heard her voice:

'Young man,' she called harshly, 'do you expect me to wait on you. Come and fetch your things.'

Putting on a polite and apologetic look, I went to the inner door which led into a short passage only a yard long. She was not there.

'In here,' she said curtly.

I pushed the next door open. This room was dim also and the first thing I saw was the end of a bed and in the corner a chair with a dark skirt on it and a stocking hanging from the arm, and on the floor a pair of shoes, one of them on its side. Then, suddenly, I saw at the end of the bed a pair of bare feet. I looked at the toes; how had they got there? And then I saw: without a stitch of clothing on her, Mme. Chamson – but could this naked body be she? – was lying on the bed, her chin propped on her hand, her lips parted as they always were when she came in on the point of laughing to the office, but now with no sound coming from them; her eyes, generally wide open, were now half-closed, watching me with the stillness of some large white cat. I looked away and then I saw two other large brown eyes gazing at me, two other faces: her breasts. It was the first time in my life I had ever seen a naked woman, and it astonished me to see the rise of a haunch, the slope of her belly and the black hair like a moustache beneath it. Mme. Chamson's face was always strongly made up with some almost orange colour, and it astonished me to see how white her body was from the neck down, but not the white of statues, but some sallow colour of white and shadow, marked at the waist by the tightness of the clothes she had taken off. I had thought of her as old, but she was not; her body was young and idle.

The sight of her transfixed me. It did not stir me. I simply stood there gaping. My heart seemed to have stopped. I wanted to rush from the room, but I could not. She was so very near. My horror must have been on my face but she seemed not to notice that, but simply stared at me. There was a small movement of her lips and I dreaded that she was going to laugh; but she did not; slowly she closed her lips and said at last between her teeth in a voice low and mocking:

'Is this the first time you have seen a woman?'

And after she said this, a sad look came into her face.

I could not answer.

She lay on her back and put out her hand and smiled fully.

'Well?' she said. And she moved her hips.

'I,' I began, but I could not go on. All the fantasies of my walks about Paris, as I practised French, rushed into my head. This was the secret of all those open windows of Paris, of the vulture-like head of Sacré Coeur looking down on it. In a room like this, with a wardrobe in the corner and with clothes thrown on a chair, was enacted – what? Everything – but, above all, to my panicking mind, the crimes I read about in the newspapers. I was desperate as her hand went out.

'You have never seen a woman before?' she said again.

I moved a little and out of reach of her hand I said, fiercely:

'Yes, I have.' I was amazed at myself.

'Ah!' she said and when I did not answer, she laughed: 'Where was that? Who was she?'

It was her laughter, so dreaded by me, that released something in me. I said something terrible. The talk of the morgue at the bar jumped into my head.

I said coldly: 'She was dead. In London.'

'Oh my God,' said Mme. Chamson sitting up and pulling at the coverlet, but it was caught and she could only cover her feet.

It was her turn to be frightened. Across my brain newspaper headlines were tapping out.

'She was murdered,' I said. I hesitated. I was playing for time. Then it came out.

'She was strangled.'

'Oh no!' she said and she pulled the coverlet violently up with both hands, until she had got some of it to her breast.

'I saw her,' I said. 'On her bed.'

'You *saw* her? *How* did you see her?' she said. 'Where was this?'

Suddenly the story sprang out of me, it unrolled as I spoke.

'It was in London,' I said. 'In our street. The woman was a neighbour of ours, we knew her well. She used to pass our window every morning on her way up from the bank.'

'She was robbed!' said Mme. Chamson. Her mouth buckled with horror.

I saw I had caught her.

'Yes,' I said. 'She kept a shop.'

'Oh my God, my God,' said Mme. Chamson looking at the door behind me, then anxiously round the room.

'It was a sweets shop,' I said, 'where we bought our papers too.'

'Killed in her shop,' groaned Mme. Chamson. 'Where was her husband?'

'No,' I said, 'in her bedroom at the back. Her husband was out at work all day and this man must have been watching for him to go. Well, we knew he did. He was the laundry man. He used to go in there twice a week. She'd been carrying on with him. She was lying there with her head on one side and a scarf twisted round her neck.'

Mme. Chamson dropped the coverlet and hid her face in her hands; then she lowered them and said suspiciously:

'But how did *you* see her like this?'

'Well,' I said, 'it happened like this. My little sister had been whining after breakfast and wouldn't eat anything and Mother said, "That kid will drive me out of my mind. Go up to Mrs Blake's" – that was her name – "and get her a bar of chocolate, milk chocolate, no nuts, she only spits them out." And Mother said, "You may as well tell her we don't want any papers after Friday because we're going to Brighton. Wait, I haven't finished yet – here take this money and pay the bill. Don't forget that, you forgot last year and the papers were littering up my hall. We owe for a month."'

Mme. Chamson nodded at this detail. She had forgotten she was naked. She was the shopkeeper and she glanced again at the door as if listening for some customer to come in.

'I went up to the shop and there was no one there when I got in . . .'

'A woman alone!' said Mme. Chamson.

'So I called, "Mrs Blake," but there was no answer. I went to the inner door and called up a small flight of stairs, "Mrs Blake" – Mother had been on at me as I said, about paying the bill. So I went up.'

'You went up?' said Mme. Chamson, shocked.

'I'd often been up there with Mother, once when she was ill. We knew the family. Well – there she was. As I said, lying on the bed, naked, strangled, dead.'

Mme. Chamson gazed at me. She looked me slowly up and down from my hair, then studied my face and then down my body to my feet. I had come barefooted into the room. And then she looked at my bare arms, until she came to my hands. She gazed at these as if she had never seen hands before. I rubbed them on my trousers, for she confused me.

'Is this true?' she accused me.

'Yes,' I said, 'I opened the door and there . . .'

'How old were you?'

I hadn't thought of that but I quickly decided.

'Twelve,' I said.

Mme. Chamson gave a deep sigh. She had been sitting taut, holding her breath. It was a sigh in which I could detect just a twinge of disappointment. I felt my story had lost its hold.

'I ran home,' I said quickly, 'and said to my mother, "Someone has killed Mrs Blake." Mother did not believe me. She couldn't realise it. I had to tell her again and again. "Go and see for yourself," I said.'

'Naturally,' said Mme. Chamson. 'You were only a child.'

[868]

'We rang the police,' I said.

At the word 'police' Mme. Chamson groaned peacefully.

'There is a woman at the laundry,' she said, 'who was in the hospital with eight stitches in her head. She had been struck with an iron. But that was her husband. The police did nothing. But what does my husband do? He stands in the Louvre all day. Then he goes fishing, like this evening. Anyone,' she said vehemently to me, 'could break in here.'

She was looking through me into some imagined scene and it was a long time before she came out of it. Then she saw her own bare shoulder and pouting she said, slowly:

'Is it true you were only twelve?'

'Yes.'

She studied me for a long time.

'You poor boy,' she said. 'Your poor mother.'

And she put her hand to my arm and let her hand slide down it gently to my wrist; then she put out her other hand to my other arm and took that hand too, as the coverlet slipped a little from her. She looked at my hands and lowered her head. The she looked up slyly at me.

'You didn't do it, did you?' she said.

'No,' I said indignantly, pulling back my hands, but she held on to them. My story vanished from my head.

'It is a bad memory,' she said. She looked to me, once more, as she had looked when I had first come with her into her salon soaking wet – a soft, ordinary, decent woman. My blood began to throb.

'You must forget about it,' she said. And then, after a long pause, she pulled me to her. I was done for, lying on the bed.

'Ah,' she laughed, pulling at my trousers. 'The diver's come up again. Forget. Forget.'

And then there was no more laughter. Once in the height of our struggle I caught sight of her eyes; the pupils had disappeared and there were only the blind whites and she cried out: 'Kill me. Kill me,' from her twisted mouth.

Afterwards we lay talking. She asked if it was true I was going to be a writer and when I said, 'Yes,' she said:

'You want talent for that. Stay where you are. It's a good firm. Claudel has been there for twelve years. And now, get up. My little husband will be back.'

She got off the bed. Quickly she gave me a complete suit belonging to one of her customers, a grey one, the jacket rather tight.

'It suits you,' she said. 'Get a grey one next time.'

I was looking at myself in a mirror when her husband came in, carrying his fishing rod and basket. He did not seem surprised. She picked up my sodden clothes and rushed angrily at him:

'Look at these. Soaked. That fool Claudel let this boy fall in the river. He brought him here.'

Her husband simply stared.

'And where have you been? Leaving me alone like this,' she carried on. 'Anyone could break in. This boy saw a woman strangled in her bed in London. She had a shop. Isn't that it? A man came in and murdered her. What d'you say to that?'

Her husband stepped back and looked with appeal at me.

'Did you catch anything?' she said to him, still accusing.

'No,' said her husband.

'Well, not like me,' she said, mocking me. 'I caught this one.'

'Will you have a drop of something?' said her husband.

'No, he won't,' said Mme. Chamson. 'He'd better go straight home to bed.'

So we shook hands. M. Chamson let me out through the shop door while Mme. Chamson called down the passage to me, 'Bring the suit back tomorrow. It belongs to a customer.'

Everything was changed for me after this. At the office I was a hero.

'Is it true that you saw a murder?' the office boys said.

And when Mme. Chamson came along and I gave her back the suit, she said: 'Ah, here he is – my fish.'

And then boldly: 'When are you coming to collect your things?'

And then she went over to whisper to Claudel and ran out.

'You know what she said just now,' said Claudel to me, looking very shrewd: 'She said "I am afraid of that young Englishman. Have you seen his hands?"'

[870]

Did You Invite Me?

Rachel first met Gilbert at David and Sarah's, or it may have been at Richard and Phoebe's – she could not remember – but she did remember that he stood like a touchy exclamation mark and talked in a shot-gun manner about his dog. His talk jumped so that she got confused; the dog was his wife's dog but was he talking about his dog or his wife? He blinked very fast when he talked of either. Then she remembered what David (or maybe Richard) had told her. His wife was dead. Rachel had a dog, too, but Gilbert was not interested.

The bond between all of them was that they owned small, white stuccoed houses, not quite alike – hers alone, for example, had Gothic churchy windows which, she felt, gave her point – on different sides of the park. Another bond was that they had reached middle life and said nothing about it, except that Gilbert sharply pretended to be younger than the rest of them in order to remind them they had arrived at that time when one year passes into the next unnoticed, leaving among the dregs an insinuation that they had not done what they intended. When this thought struck them they would all – if they had the time – look out of their sedate windows at the park, the tame and once princely oasis where the trees looked womanish on the island in the lake or marched in grave married processions along the avenues in the late summer, or in the winter were starkly widowed. They could watch the weekend crowds or the solitary walkers on the public grass, see the duck flying over in the evenings, hear the keeper's whistle and his shout, 'All Out,' when the gates of the park closed an hour after sunset; and at night, hearing the animals at the zoo, they could send out silent cries of their own upon the place and evoke their ghosts.

But not Gilbert. His cry would be a howl and audible, a joint howl of himself and this dog he talked about. Rachel had never seen a man so howling naked. 'Something must be done about him,' she thought every time she met him. Two years ago, Sonia, his famous and chancy wife, had died – 'on the stage', the headlines in the London newspapers said, which was nearly true – and his eyes were red-rimmed as if she had died yesterday, his angry face was raw with drink or the unjust marks of guilt and grief. He was a tall man, all bones, and even his wrists, coming out of a jacket that was too short in the sleeve, seemed to be crying. He had also the look of a man who had decided not to buy another suit in his life, to let cloth go on gleaming with its private malice. It was well known – for he boasted of it himself – that his wife had been much older than he, that they quarrelled continually and that he still adored her.

Rachel had been naked too, in her time when, six or seven years before, she had divorced her husband. Gilbert is 'in the middle of it', she thought. She had been 'through it' and had 'come out of it', and was not hurt or lonely any more and had crowded her life with public troubles. She was married to a newspaper column.

'Something really *must* be done about him,' she said at last out loud to David and Sarah, as she tried to follow Gilbert's conversation that was full of traps and false exit lines. For his part, he sniffed when he spoke to them of Rachel.

'Very attractive woman. Very boring. All women are boring. Sonia was a terrible bore sometimes, carrying on, silly cow. What of it? You may have remarked it: I'm a bore. I must go. Thank you Sarah and David, for inviting me and offering me your friendship. You did invite me, didn't you? You did? I'm glad. I have no friends. The friends Sonia and I invited to the house were hers not mine. Old codgers. I must go home and feed her dog.'

They watched him go off stiffly, a forty-year-old.

An outsider he was, of course, because of loss. One feels the east wind – she knew that. But it was clear – as she decided to add him to her worries – that he must always have been that. He behaved mechanically, click, click, click, like a puppet or an orphan, homelessness being his vanity. This came out when David had asked Gilbert about his father and mother in her presence. From David's glances at his wife Rachel knew they had heard what he said many times before. Out came his shot, the long lashes of his childish eyes blinking fast.

'Never met the people.' He was showing contempt for a wound. He was born in Singapore, he said. One gathered the birth had no connection with either father or mother. She tried to be intelligent about the city.

'Never saw the place,' he said. The father became a prisoner of the Japanese; the mother took him to India. Rachel tried to be intelligent about India.

'Don't remember it,' he said. 'The old girl' – his mother sent him home to schools and holiday schools. He spent his boyhood in camps and dormitories, his army-life in Nissen huts. He was twenty when he really 'met' his parents. At the sight of him they separated for good.

No further answers. Life had been doled out to him like spoonfuls of medicine, one at a time; he returned the compliment by doing the same and then erected silences like packs of cards, watching people wait for them to fall down.

How, Rachel asked, did the raw young man come to be married to Sonia, an actress at the top of the tree, fifteen years older than he? 'The old girl knew her,' he said; she was his mother's friend. Rachel worried away at it. She saw, correctly, a dramatic woman with a clever mouth, a surrogate mother – but a mother astute in acting the part among her scores of grand and famous friends. Rachel had one or two famous friends too, but he snubbed her with his automatic phrase:

'Never met him.'

Or

'Never met her.'

And then Rachel, again correctly, saw him standing in the doorway of Sonia's drawing-room or bringing drinks perhaps to the crowd, like an uncouth son; those wrists were the wrists of a growing boy who silently jeered at the guests. She heard Sonia dressing him down for his Nissen hut language and his bad manners – which, however, she encouraged. This was her third marriage and it had to be original. That was the heart of the Gilbert problem; Sonia had invented him; he had no innate right to be what he appeared to be.

So Rachel, who happened to be writing an article on broken homes, asked him to come round and have a drink. He walked across the park from his house to hers. At the door he spoke his usual phrase:

'Thank you for inviting me. You did invite me, didn't you? Well, I thank you. We live on opposite sides of the park. Very convenient. Not too near.'

He came in.

'Your house is white and your dog is white,' he said.

Rachel owned a dog. A very white fox terrier came barking at him on a high, glassy note, showing a ratter's teeth. Rachel was wearing a long pale blue dress from her throat to the tips of her shoes and led him into the sitting-room. He sank into a soft silky sofa with his knees together and politely inspected her as an interesting collection of bones.

'Shall I ever get up from this?' he said patting the sofa. 'Silly question. Yes I shall, of course. I have come, shortly I shall go.' He was mocking someone's manners. Perhaps hers. The fox terrier which had followed him into the small and sunny room sniffed long at Gilbert's shoes and his trouser legs and stiffened when he stroked its head. The dog growled.

'Pretty head,' he said. 'I like dogs' heads.' He was staring at Rachel's head. Her hair was smooth, neat and fair.

'I remarked his feet on the hall floor, tick, tick tick. Your hall must be tiled. Mine is carpeted.'

'Don't be so aggressive, Sam,' said Rachel gravely to the dog.

'Leave him alone,' said Gilbert. 'He can smell Tom, Sonia's bull terrier. That's who you can smell isn't it? He can smell an enemy.'

'Sam is a problem,' she said. 'Everyone in the street hates you, Sam, don't they? When you get out in the garden you bark and bark, people open their windows and shout at you. You chase cats, you killed the Gregory boy's rabbit and bit the Jackson child. You drive the doctor mad. He throws flower pots at you.'

'Stop nagging the poor animal,' said Gilbert. And to the dog he said: 'Good for you. Be a nuisance. Be yourself. Everyone needs an enemy. Absolutely.'

And he said to himself: 'She hasn't forgiven her husband.' In her long dress she had the composure of the completely smoothed-over person who might well have nothing on underneath. Gilbert appreciated this, but she became prudish and argumentative.

'Why do you say "absolutely",' she said, seeing a distracting point for discussion here. 'Isn't that relative?'

'No,' said Gilbert with enjoyment. He loved a row. 'I've got an enemy at my office. Nasty little creepy fellow. He wants my job. He watches me. There's a new job going – promotion – and he thinks I want it. So he watches. He sits on the other side of the room and is peeing himself with anxiety every time I move. Peeing himself, yes. If I leave the room he goes to the door to see if I'm going to the director's office. If I do he sweats. He makes an excuse to go to the director to see if he can find out what we've been talking about. When I am working on a scheme he comes over to look at it. If I'm working out costs he stares with agony at the lay-out and the figures. "Is that Jameson's?" He can't contain himself. "No, I'm doing my income tax," I tell him. He's very shocked at my doing that in office hours and goes away relieved. He'll report that to the director. Then a suspicion strikes him when he is half-way back to his desk and he turns round and comes over again panting. He doesn't believe me. "I'm turning inches into centimetres," I say. He still doesn't believe me. Poor silly bugger.'

He laughed.

'Wasn't that rather cruel?' she said. 'Why centimetres?'

'Why not? He wants the French job. Boring little man. Boring office. Yes.'

Gilbert constructed one of his long silences. Rachel saw skyscrapers, pagodas, the Eiffel Tower and little men creeping up them like ants. After a while Gilbert went on and the vision collapsed:

'He was the only one who came from the office to Sonia's funeral. He brought his wife – never met her before – and she cried. The only person who did. Yes. He'd never missed a show Sonia was in.'

'So he isn't an enemy. Doesn't that prove my point,' she said solemnly. Gilbert ignored this.

'They'd never met poor Sonia,' he said. And he blinked very fast.

'I never met your wife either, you know,' said Rachel earnestly. She hoped he would describe her; but he described her doctors, the lawyers that assemble after death.

'What a farce,' he said.

He said: 'She had a stroke in the theatre. Her words came out backwards. I wrote to her two husbands. Only one replied. The theatre sent her to hospital in an ambulance – the damn fools. If you go to hospital you die of pneumonia, bloody hospital won't give you enough pillows, you lie flat and you can't get your breath. What a farce. Her brother came and talked, one of those fat men. Never liked the fellow.'

She said how terrible it must have been.

'Did she recover her speech? They sometimes do.'

'Asked,' he said, 'for the dog. Called it god.'

He got up suddenly from the sofa.

'There! I have got up. I am standing on my feet. I am a bore,' he said. 'I shall go.'

As he left the room the terrier came sniffing at his heels.

'Country dogs. Good ratters. Ought to be on a farm.'

She plunged into a confidence to make him stay longer.

'He used to be a country dog. My husband bought him for me when we lived in the country. I know' (she luxuriated in a worry) 'how important environment is to animals and I was going to let him stay – but when you are living alone in a city like London – well there are a lot of burglaries here.'

'Why did you divorce your husband?' he asked as he opened the front door. 'I shouldn't have asked. Bad manners. I apologise. I was rude. Sonia was always on to me about that.'

'He went off with a girl at his office,' she said staunchly.

'Silly man,' said Gilbert looking at the dog. 'Thank you. Goodbye. Do we shake hands? You invited me, now it is my turn to invite you. That is the right thing, of course it is. We must do the right thing. I shall.'

Weeks passed before Gilbert invited Rachel. There were difficulties. Whatever he decided by day was destroyed by night. At night Sonia would seem to come flying out of the park saying the house had belonged to her. She had paid for it. She enumerated the furniture item by item. She had the slow, languid walk of her stage appearances as she went suspiciously from room to room, asking what he had done with her fur coats and where her shoes were. 'You've given them to some woman.' She said he had a woman in the house. He said he asked only David and Sarah; she said she didn't trust Sarah. He pleaded he had kept the dog. When he said that, her ghost vanished saying he starved the poor thing. One night he said to her, 'I'm going to ask Rachel, but you'll be there.'

'I damn well will,' she said. And this became such a dogma that when, at last, he asked Rachel to come, he disliked her.

His house was not so sedate as hers which had been repainted that year – his not. His windows seemed to him – and to her – to sob. There was grit on the frames. When he opened the door to her she noted the brass knocker had not been polished and inside there was the immediate cold odour of old food. The hall and walls echoed their voices and the air was very still. In the sitting-room the seats of the chairs, one could see, had not been sat on for a long time, there was dust on the theatrical wallpaper. Hearing her, Sonia's dog, Tom, came scrabbling the stair carpet and rushed into the room hysterically at both of them, skidding on rugs, snuffling, snorting, whimpering and made at once for her skirts, got under her legs and was driven off on to a sofa of green silk, rather like hers, but now frayed where the dog's claws had caught.

'Off the sofa, Tom,' said Gilbert. The dog ignored this and snuffled from its squat nose and gazed from wet eyes that were like enormous marbles. Gilbert picked up a rubber bone and threw it to the dog. Down it came and the racing round the room began again. Rachel held her glass in the air for safety's sake and the dog jumped at it and made her spill whisky on her dress. In this confusion they tried to talk.

'Sonia liked being photographed with Tom,' he said.

'I only saw her on the stage once. She was very beautiful,' she said. 'It must have been twelve years ago. Gielgud and another actor called Slade were in it. Was it Slade? Oh dear! My memory!'

'Her second husband,' he said.

He picked up the dog's rubber bone. The dog rushed to him and seized it. Man and dog pulled at the bone.

'You want it. You won't get it,' said Gilbert while she seemed to hear her husband say: 'Why can't you keep your mouth shut if you can't remember things?' And Gilbert, grinning in his struggle with the dog, said:

'Sonia always had Tom to sleep on our bed. He still does. Won't leave it. He's on it even when I come back from the office.'

'He sleeps with you?' she said with a shudder.

'I come home. I want someone to talk to.'

'What d'you do with him when you go to your office?' The dog pulled and snorted. 'The woman who comes in and cleans looks after the dog,' he said. And went on: 'Your house has three storeys, mine has two, otherwise the same. I've got a basement full of rubbish. I was going to turn it into a flat but Sonia got worse. Futile. Yes, life is futile. Why not sell the damn place. No point. No point in anything. I go to the office, come back, feed the dog and get drunk. Why not? Why go on? Why do *you* go on? Just habit. No sense in it.'

'You *do* go on,' she said.

'The dog,' he said.

I must find some people for him to meet. He can't live like this, she thought. It is ghastly.

When she left, he stood on the doorstep and said:

'My house. Your house. They're worth four times what we gave for them. There it is.'

She decided to invite him to dinner to meet some people – but who could she ask? He was prickly. She knew dozens of people but, as she thought of them, there seemed, for the first time, to be something wrong with all of them. In the end she invited no one to meet him.

'On a diet, silly cow,' he thought when she came to the door but he fell back on his usual phrase as he looked about the empty room.

'Did you invite me? Or shall I go away? You *did* invite me. Thank you. Thank you.'

'I've been in Vienna with the Fladgates. She is a singer. Friends of David and Sarah.'

'Fladgates? Never heard of the people,' he said. 'Sonia insulted someone in Vienna. I was drunk. Sonia never drank anything – that made her insults worse. Did your husband drink?'

'Indeed not.'

He sat down on the sofa. The evening – Sonia's time. He expected Sonia to fly in and sit there watching this woman with all her 'problems' hidden chastely except for one foot which tipped up and down in her shoes under her long dress. But – to his surprise – Sonia did not come. The terrier sat at Rachel's feet.

'How is your enemy?' she said as they drank. 'The man in the office.'

'He and his wife asked me to dinner,' he said.

'That's kind,' she said.

'People are kind,' he said. 'I've remarked that.'

'Does he still watch you?'

'Yes. You know what it was? He thinks I drink too much. He thinks I've got a bottle in my desk. It wasn't the job that was worrying him. We are wrong about people. I am. You are. Everyone is.'

When they went in dinner candles were on the table.

'Bloody silly having candles,' he said to himself. And when she came in with the soup, he said:

'We had candles. Poor Sonia threw them out of the window once. She had to do it in a play.'

The soup was iced and white and there was something in it that he could not make out. But no salt. That's it, he thought, no salt in this woman. Writing about politics and things all day and forgets the salt. The next course was white too, something chopped or minced with something peculiar, goodness knew what. It got into his teeth. Minced newsprint, he thought.

'Poor Sonia couldn't cook at all,' he said, pushing his food about, proud of Sonia. 'She put dishes on the floor near the stove, terrible muddle, and rushed back to hear what people were saying and then an awful bloody stink came from the kitchen. I used to go down and the potatoes had burned dry and Tom had cleared the plates. Bloody starvation. No dinner.'

'Oh no!' she said.

'I live on chops now. Yes,' he said. 'One, sometimes two, every day, say ten a week. Am I being a bore? Shall I go?'

Rachel had a face that had been set for years in the same concerned expression. That expression now fell to pieces from her forehead to her throat. Against her will she laughed. The laugh shook her and was loud; she felt herself being whirled into a helpless state from the toes upwards. Her blood whirled too.

'You laughed!' he shouted. 'You did not protest. You did not write an article. You laughed. I could see your teeth. Very good. I've never seen you laugh before.'

And the dog barked at them.

'She laughed,' he shouted at the dog.

She went out to make coffee, very annoyed at being trapped into laughing. While he waited, the dog sat undecided, ears pricked, listening for her and watching him like a sentry.

'Rats,' whispered Gilbert to the dog. It stood up sharply.

'Poor bastard. What a life,' he said.

The dog barked angrily at him and when she came in, he said: 'I told your dog he ought to be on a farm.'

'You said that before,' she said. 'Let us have coffee next door.' They moved into the next room and she sat on the sofa while she poured the coffee.

'Now *you* are sitting on the sofa. I'm in this armchair,' he said, thinking of life tactically. 'Sonia moved about too. I used to watch her going into a room. Where will she sit next? Damned if I ever got it right. The same in restaurants. Let us sit here, she'd say, and then when the waiter came to her chair, she'd say, "No, not here. Over there." Never knew where she was going to settle. Like a fly. She wanted attention. Of course. That was it. Quite right.'

'Well,' she said coldly, 'she was an actress.'

'Nothing to do with it,' he said. 'Woman.'

'Nonsense,' she said, hating to be called a woman and thought, 'It's my turn now.'

'My husband,' she said, 'travelled the whole time. Moscow, Germany, Copenhagen, South Africa, but when he got home he was never still, posing to the animals on the farm, showing off to barns, fences, talking French and German to birds, pretending to be a country gentleman.'

'Let the poor man alone,' he said. 'Is he still alive?'

'I told you,' she said. 'I won't bore you with it all.'

She was astonished to find herself using his word and that the full story of her husband and herself she had planned to tell, and which she had told so many people, suddenly lost interest for her. And yet, anyway, she thought, why shouldn't I tell this man about it? So she started, but she made a muddle of it. She got lost in the details. The evening, she saw, was a failure. He yawned.

If there was one thing Rachel could honestly say it was that she had not thought of her husband for years. She had not forgotten but he had become a generality in the busyness of her life. But now, after the evening when Gilbert came to dinner, her husband came to life and plagued her. If an aeroplane came down whistling across the wide London sky, she saw him sitting in it – back from Moscow, Capetown, Copenhagen, descending not upon her, but on another woman. If she took the dog for a run in the park, the cuddling couples on the grass became him and that young girl; if babies screamed in their prams they were his children; if a man threw a ball it was he; if men in white flannels were playing cricket, she wondered if he was among them. She imagined sudden, cold meetings and ran through tirades of hot dialogue. One day she saw a procession of dogs, tails up and panting, following a bitch, with a foolish grin of wet teeth in their jaws, and Sam rushed after them; she went red in the face shouting at him. And yet she had gone to the park in order to calm herself and to be alone. The worst thing that could happen would be to meet Gilbert, the cause of this, but, like all malevolent causes, he never showed his face. She had wished to do her duty and be sorry for him, but not for him to become a man. She feared she might be on the point of talking about this to a woman, not a woman she knew well – that would be disastrous – but, say, to some woman or girl sitting alone on a park seat or some woman in a shop; also a confidence she would regret all her life. She was touchy in these days and had a row with the doctor who threw flower pots at her dog. She petted the animal. 'Your head is handsome,' she said, stroking its head, 'but why did you go after that silly bitch?' The dog adored her when she said this. 'You're vain,' she said to it.

Gilbert *did* go to the park but only on Saturdays when the crowds came. He liked seeing the picnics, the litter on the grass; he stood still with pleasure when babies screamed or ice-cream dripped. He grinned at boys throwing water from drinking fountains and families trudging, drunks lying asleep, and fat girls lying half on top of their young men and tickling their faces with grass. 'The place is a damn bedroom. Why not? Where else can they go? Lucky, boring people. I've got a bedroom and no one in it.'

One Saturday, after three days of rain, he took his dog there and – would you believe it? – there the whole crowd was again, still at it, on the wet grass. The trouble with Sonia was that she thought the park was vulgar and would never go there – went once and never again, hadn't brought the right shoes.

He remarked this to his dog as he let it off its leash. The animal scampered round him in wide circles; came back to him and then raced off again in circles getting wider and wider, until it saw a man with string in his hand trying to fly a kite. The kite was flopping on the ground, rose twenty or thirty feet in the air and then dived again. The dog rushed at the kite, but the man got it up again, higher this time. Gilbert walked towards the man. 'Poor devil, can't get it up,' he said as he walked. He got near the man and watched his struggles.

Then the kite shot up high and Gilbert watched it raving there until suddenly it swept away higher still. Gilbert said: 'Good for him.' The boredom of the grey afternoon was sweet. He lit a cigarette and threw the empty packet on the grass and then he found he had lost sight of the dog. When he saw it again it was racing in a straight line towards a group of trees by the lake. It was racing towards another dog. A few yards away from the dog it stopped and pranced. The dog was a terrier and stopped dead, then came forward. They stood sniffing at each other's tails and then jumped round muzzle to muzzle. They were growling, the terrier barked and then the two dogs flew at each other's necks. Their play had turned to a war, their jaws were at each other's necks and ears. Gilbert saw at once it was Rachel's dog, indeed Rachel was running up shouting, 'Sam. Sam.' The fight was savage and Tom had his teeth in.

'Stop them,' Rachel was shouting. 'Stop them. They'll kill each other. He's got him by the throat.'

And then she saw Gilbert: 'You!'

Gilbert was enjoying the fight. He looked around and picked up a stick that had fallen from a tree.

'Stop them,' she shouted.

'Get yours by the collar, I'll get mine,' he shouted to her.

'I can't. Sam! Sam! They're bleeding.'

She was dancing about in terror, trying to catch Sam by the legs.

'Not by the legs. By the collar, like this, woman,' he shouted. 'Don't put your arms round him, you idiot. Like this. Stop dancing about.'

He caught Tom by the collar and lifted him as both dogs hung on to each other.

'You're strangling him. I can't, I can't,' she said. Gilbert brought his stick down hard on the muzzles of the dogs, just as she was trying to grasp Sam again.

'You'll kill them.'

He brought the stick down hard again. The dogs yelped with pain and separated.

'Get the leash on,' he said, 'you fool.'

Somehow she managed it and the two dogs now strained to get at each other. The terrier's white neck and body were spotted with blood and smears of it were on her hands.

Gilbert wiped their spit off his sleeve.

They pulled their dogs yards apart and she stared at him. It infuriated her that he was laughing at her with pure pleasure. In their stares they saw each other clearly and as they had never seen each other before. To him, in her short skirt and her shoes muddied by the wet grass, her hair disordered and the blood risen to her pale face, she was a woman. The grass had changed her. To her he was not a pitiable arrangement of widower's tricks, but a man on his own. And the park itself changed him in her eyes; in the park he, like everyone else there, seemed to be human. The dogs gave one more heave to get at each other.

'Lie down, Sam,' Gilbert shouted.

She lifted her chin and was free to hate him for shouting at her animal.

'Look after yours. He's dangerous,' she called back, angered by the friendliness of his face.

'Damn silly dogs enjoyed it. Good for them. Are you all right? Go up to the kiosk and get a drink – if I may I'll follow you up – see you're all right.'

'No, no,' she put out a loud moan – far too loud. 'He's bleeding. I'll take him home,' and she turned to look at the park. 'What a mess people make.' And now walking away shouted a final accusation: 'I didn't know you brought your dog here.'

He watched her go. She turned away and dragged the struggling terrier over the grass uphill from the lake. He watched her walking unsteadily.

'Very attractive figure,' he thought. 'Silly cow. Better go home and ring her up.'

He turned and on the way back to his house he could still see her dancing about on the grass and shouting. He went over the scene again and repeated his conclusion. 'She's got legs. Never seen them before. A woman. Must be. Full of life.' She was still dancing about as he put a bowl of water down for the dog. It drank noisily and he gave it another bowl and then he washed the dog's neck and looked at its ear. 'Nothing much wrong with you,' he said. He fed the animal and soon it jumped on the sofa and was instantly snorting, and whimpering and shaking into sleep.

'I must ring her up, yes, that is what I must do.'

But a neighbour answered and said Rachel had gone to the vet and she had come back in a terrible state and had gone to bed with one of her migraines.

'Don't bother her,' he said. 'I just rang to ask how the dog was.'

Rachel was not in bed. She was standing beside the neighbour and when the call was over, she said:

'What did he say?'

'He asked about the dog.'

'Is that all?'

'Yes.'

This flabbergasted her.

In the middle of the night she woke up and when her stupefaction passed she damn well wished he was there so that she could say, 'It didn't occur to you to apologise. I don't like being called a fool. You assume too much. Don't think I care a damn about *your* dog.' She was annoyed to feel a shudder pass through her. She got out of bed and, looking out of her window at the black trees, saw herself racing across the park to his house and pulling that dog of his off his bed. The things she said! The language she used! She kicked the dog out of the room and it went howling downstairs. She went back to bed weak and surprised at herself because, before she realised it, Sam became Tom in her hand. She lay there stiff, awake, alone. Which dog had she kicked? Sam or Tom?

In his house Gilbert locked up, poured himself a strong whisky, then a second, then a third. Uncertain of whom he was addressing, Rachel or Sonia, he said, 'Silly cow,' and blundered drunkish to bed. He woke up at five very cold. No dog. The bed was empty. He got out of bed and went downstairs. For the first time since Sonia had died the dog was asleep on the sofa. He had forgotten to leave his door open.

In the morning he was startled to hear Sonia's voice saying to him in her stage voice: 'Send her some flowers. Ask her to dinner.'

So he sent the flowers and when Rachel rang to thank him he asked her to dinner – at a restaurant.

'Your house. My house,' he said. 'Two dogs.'

There was a long silence and he could hear her breath bristling.

'Yes, I think it has to be somewhere else,' she said. And added: 'As you say, we have a problem.'

And after this dinner and the next, she said:

'There are so many problems. I don't really know you.'

They talked all summer and people who came regularly to the restaurant made up stories about them and were quite put out when in October they stopped coming. All the proprietor had heard was that they had sold their houses – in fact he knew what they'd got for them. The proprietor had bought Sonia's dog. There was a terrier, too, he said, but he didn't know what had happened to that.

The Rescue

After the bad spring, the first two or three weeks of that summer turned on a sudden blaze and the pain went out of Mother's shoulder, and she let me buy the shortest mini-skirt in town. My tall brother and his taller friend George came down from Cambridge with beards like barley, and when I went out with them my golden hair seemed to flow from shop window to shop window as we walked by. The sunlight sparkled like the cymbals and trumpets of a regimental band in the park, celebrating a triumph. And it *was* a time of victory in our family, especially for Mother. Why had we got a Socialist mayor at last? Why had the Council given in after years of speeches, committee meetings, votes and letters to the papers and agreed to turn the lake in the park into a lido? Who was behind all this but Mother? On top of this, there was the annual pageant; she ran that, too.

'You ought to take a rest,' people said to her. There was always someone at the door – people rushed in to see her while she sat at the typewriter, made her lists, jumped to the telephone.

'Get on!' she would call to us. 'Get on with it. Don't stop.' She was short, stout and bouncing – born to rule.

This year she was putting on King Arthur and the Knights of the Round Table – nothing to do with the history of the town, but pageants were an annual holiday for Mother. Instead of bossing the Council, she would take a breath for a day or two, then start organising the past. I was to be one of Guinevere's ladies. Every day, new bundles of plastic shields, helmets, spears, swords and dresses were dumped in the house, so that there was hardly room to sit down. And when my brother and George came, they added Africa to it; thump, boom and howls came off the records, and they larked about, dressing-up in robes and swinging swords at each other.

Get on? We would have done that much faster but for the people she

[886]

brought in to help. She rarely came home without some new adherent; her strong glasses picked them out as she raced down the street on her short legs or looked out of the car window. She caught people suddenly, as a frog catches flies, and digested them without a blink. Just at our busiest time she brought home the slowest young man in the town, a real plague called Ellis, a boy of twenty. He worked in the library; I had often seen him there when she sent me for books on the costumes of King Arthur's time.

'We want him for advice,' Mother said. Ellis was Advice in person. Once he was in the house we could not get rid of him; he sat among the helmets on one of the sofas, gazing at Mother, worshipping her, and, between long silences, uttering deep opinions that came up from his boots. In this hot weather he wore a thick suit, a waistcoat, and woollen socks. Having got him for advice, Mother never listened to him. The only thing I ever remember her saying to him was, 'Why don't you take your jacket off?' We said she'd brought him home to get him to undress.

'Your boy friend is in there,' we'd say when she came in with a new pile of costumes for the procession.

'Tell Ellis to count these,' she said.

I would go up to him, shake my long hair from one shoulder to the other and say, 'For you. To count.'

One evening I accidentally let out our secret joke about him: 'Count these, Lancelot.'

Ellis ignored this. He lived for opinion, not for action.

The Lancelot joke had started because soon after Ellis had adopted us, Mother lost the man who was going to take the part of Lancelot in the pageant. 'Every year an accident,' Mother said. 'That is life.'

This year's Lancelot had been knocked off his bicycle by a dog and had broken his ankle.

'Don't worry,' George said. 'You've got a Lancelot here. Promote Ellis.'

Mother ignored this but kept on worrying about her difficulty for days.

'Ellis for Lancelot,' we kept on at her.

'Don't be malicious,' Mother said, at her typewriter. 'He lives alone in lodgings.'

What was the real Lancelot like? Tall, I thought, with a fair beard and cool blue Cambridge eyes, like George's. But George said, 'Don't be a nit. Arthur's knights were dwarfs. Bad food in the Middle Ages made everyone short.'

Perhaps he was right. Our Lancelot was a stump, not more than five feet two inches high, with a low forehead and heavy arms. His habit of uttering opinions was a way of making himself seem taller. He hauled up his views from some deep mine inside him and as they came up he stood on tiptoe and his chest swelled and, ignoring us, he unloaded them like coals for Mother alone.

Our joke did not make Ellis wince or laugh. Rather, it made him grow in importance and gaze even more profoundly at Mother, labouring at something he would sooner or later bring out, and when Mother came in and said she had found someone exactly fitted for the part, we saw Ellis looking scornfully at us and even more admiringly at Mother.

'I'm glad,' he said. 'If you had asked me, I would have had to refuse.'

'Refuse Mother!' We were amazed.

'On principle,' he said.

We were putting the helmets into boxes and we stopped.

'He was an adulterer,' Ellis said.

We all laughed, except Mother.

'It happens to be a fact,' Ellis said.

'But –,' we all shouted together. We were soon at it, shouting about history, art and life, love and sex.

'Let him speak,' said Mother, getting on with her work.

'It has nothing to do with history,' he said. 'If I had my way, I would pass a law making adultery illegal. If a man or woman committed it, they would be brought to the courts, tried, fined two hundred pounds, and imprisoned for two years.'

'Why two hundred?' my brother said.

'Back to the Middle Ages,' said George. 'You say you're not influenced by history!'

'And when they came out of jail, I would have them branded on the back of the hand.'

'With the letter "A" like in Nathaniel Hawthorne,' I said. I had read him that term at school.

Ellis looked at me and for the first time smiled, congratulating me for having read the book.

'That's right,' he said.

'You mean you'd make Lancelot march in the pageant wearing a letter "A" on his hand?' George said.

'Yes,' said Ellis.

'You'd make it fashionable,' said my brother.

'Anyone like to join the club?' said George, dancing about and waving his hands. 'I've got my "A". I see you've got yours. What about it?'

Because George did this and to show I was on his side and to make him take notice of me instead of going off with my brother all the time, I went to the desk by the window and drew a large 'A' on the back of my hand.

'Look,' I said, showing my hand to all of them. '"A".'

'You won't get that off in a hurry, my girl – it's marking ink,' said Mother. George looked coldly at me.

The strange thing was that, having uttered his thoughts and seeing us make fun of them, Ellis went flat and bewildered. He looked at Mother in appeal. He sat back on the sofa, astonished at the ruin of his ideas.

'Do you think it would make it popular?' he asked Mother simply.

Mother was holding up a red robe against George. 'Is this too long for Kate Mason?' she said. 'I haven't been listening.' And to be kind to Ellis she changed the subject and said to him: 'The mayor's opening the lido tomorrow, three o'clock. Bring your trunks.'

It is strange to see adoration harden into fear. Ellis seemed to step back to the shadows of his lodgings suddenly, away from us.

'I can't get off from the library tomorrow,' he said.

A simple statement, of course, but a contradiction of Mother's order. She was not used to being refused anything. She put the robe down. 'I will speak to Mrs Lowkes,' Mother said. Mrs Lowkes was the librarian and when Mother said 'speak' she meant she would require Mrs Lowkes to do as she was told.

One shock leads to another. Ellis stood up and looked fiercely at me and obstinately at Mother. 'I haven't got a suit,' he said.

'There are plenty here,' said Mother.

'I can't swim,' said Ellis, drawing on hidden capital.

[889]

'That doesn't matter,' said Mother. 'We'll teach you.'

Ellis moved back towards the door of the room.

'No one can teach me,' he said, heaving up a load of pride into his chest. 'I hate water. My father was a sailor. *He* couldn't swim. He drowned.'

'How awful,' I said.

He turned to me and said: 'He left my mother. She died.'

Until now we had never thought of Ellis as a member of a family. We hadn't even thought of him as being human, except in a general way. Seeing he had silenced us, he added information that built up the tragic distinction of his family. 'Very few sailors can swim,' he said. 'They are fatalists.'

Ellis, our fatalist!

Mother saved us. 'Don't worry,' she said. 'There'll be a crowd there tomorrow.'

But having made his stand, Ellis got even bolder with Mother. 'I don't like crowds,' he said. 'They'll ruin the lake.'

Her adorer was telling her that she was wrong – she who had fought for eight years to get the lido for the town! He was defying her and was appealing to me.

Mother was at her sewing machine. 'You mustn't hate so many things, Ellis,' she said.

After he left I said: 'He looked as though he was going to cry.'

'No. His eyes just swell up when he looks at you,' my brother said.

'I'll say!' said George.

I knew that. Ellis had very large eyes and they did swell whenever he saw me come into the library. I used to make up questions about books until I made him leave his desk and say, 'I'll get that book for you.'

I used to have a special look that said, 'You can do better than that,' or 'Why do you do what you are told?' And I had another, very long look that said, 'I know that when you are saying things to Mother you are really saying them to me. You are frightened of me.' And I would run my forefinger slowly down the edge of his desk as we talked. At sixteen, a girl likes to see what a young man will do. I hung about while other people came to the desk because I could see I was embarrassing him. Then I went off. Once when I turned round as I got to the door and caught him looking at me he dropped five books he had in his hands. There was a noise that made everyone stare. A thrilling noise, like a tyre-burst.

Mother got her way with the librarian, of course. Ellis was forced to come with us to the lake. As Socialists, she said, it was our duty to see that all mankind was happy. We drove to the park gate, left the car, and walked the last two hundred yards across the grass. George and my brother ran on fast to get into the water. I raced with them – for I liked giving Ellis a distant view of myself – and left him and Mother dawdling behind. Ellis had the bathing trunks under his arm; the bundle looked like a book he was going to read. Presently Mother broke into a trot to make up for lost time, talking as she ran. Ellis trotted, too.

'I can't run in these shoes. I've ricked my shoulder,' said Mother as she puffed up to me. She sat on a stone bench on the stretch of concrete where the diving board and the newly built changing rooms were. She shook her shoulder to get her breath back and as she gazed at the lido she said: 'Have you ever seen anything so wonderful?'

I went off and got changed. The lake was a sight! I don't exaggerate. There were thousands of people – well, no, hundreds – in the water already, others queueing up at the gate, and others lined up two deep to get at the diving board. A flag was flying over one of the buildings. For years the lake, which is large and with willows hanging over the far bank, was simply ornamental and empty except for a few ducks quacking on it. Now it was striped with bodies near the water's edge and farther out there were hundreds of what looked like coconuts – the heads of the swimmers. Half the town was there.

Ellis's first words were: 'They've smashed it up.' A good description. Usually still or rippling, the water was now like a splintered mirror and there was scarcely a yard between any of the people – at any rate, not near the shore.

'A mob,' Ellis said, opining.

Mother said: 'Ellis, you mustn't be a snob.'

Ellis heaved up a thought. 'I prefer nature,' he said.

'But people are nature, Ellis,' Mother said.

Ellis was taken aback. He frowned. One more opinion had been ruined. His love for Mother had gone.

'Come on,' said Mother to Ellis, taking off her glasses and greedy for the water. 'Get your things off.' And she went off to change. I had already changed, as I have said, and was made to stand guard over Ellis who did not move. I saw he was plotting to slip away when we had gone in.

'I took a walk here last night. I often go for a walk,' he said quietly to me. 'It was still light. No one was about – only a dog. You could see every branch, every leaf of the trees reflected in the water, going down and down and down.'

'It's only ten feet deep in the middle,' I said.

'Ten feet!' he said and stepped back, wiping his forehead with the back of his hand.

He was disappointed with me when I laughed.

There were shouts from the diving board where a very thin man with his trunks flapping on his bones was bouncing up and down; then up went his heels. George and my brother followed him. I was longing to go. At last Mother came out, bulging in her old-fashioned black suit – an embarrassing sight. 'Please get into the water quick,' I wanted to say to her. But she waited to say to Ellis, 'Why haven't you changed?'

Ellis gave her a lover's last pleading look and then went off miserably.

'He is scared,' I said. 'He thinks he'll sink through to Australia.'

'Look after him and see he goes in,' said Mother who was off at once to the diving board. She went in with a thump and a man said: 'Wait for the tidal wave on the other side.'

I was tired of waiting, but when Ellis came out, changed, I cheated. 'Good,' I said and left him.

I was soon in the water. George and my brother were swimming out beyond the thick crowd along the shore. Mother was following them and I raced after them.

'Where's Ellis?' shouted Mother when I caught up.

'He's back there.'

'You oughtn't to leave him like that. It's selfish.'

'He can't swim.'

'Teach him,' Mother said. 'I'll be along in a minute.'

Mother was always on at me about my selfishness. So after a while I swam back and waded through the crowd.

'Good!' I shouted.

[892]

Ellis was in, all right. He was standing scarcely waist-deep in the brown water. It was strange to see only half of Ellis; it made him seem more human. People bumped into him and every time this half-Ellis was bumped he turned his head as if to say a few words. He was standing lost, as puzzled as a bust by what was going on around him. Then his arm moved; he scooped up some water in his hand and had a look at it, as if to say something about water to anyone near. But since everyone was tumbling and splashing about him, he glumly tipped the handful of water back. When he saw me, he waded back three yards to the rocky bank, with the sudden vainglory of one baptised late in life, and got out. He stood with the water pouring off his thick white body and making a pool around him. He had the furtive look of one who has done half his duty. I had done mine. I left him and went off to the diving board.

The crowd was still pouring in at the gate. The queues for the high-diving platform and the diving board were long and busy. I joined one of them and looked out for Mother and after a long wait I saw her. She was coming in. You couldn't miss her black suit in the crowd, and when she got to the shallow water she stood up, looking for Ellis. Then she ducked under, somersaulted and tumbled about like a kid. She was enjoying herself. Someone turned round and saw her bottom and gave it a slap. I wished she wouldn't make an exhibition of herself, but no one in the water noticed her much. They were all packed together, splashing.

I went for the high-diving platform. On my way up the crowded ladder, where people were so slow, I looked again for Mother and Ellis. I didn't see her at first, but I saw him. He was still standing on the bank, dripping, with three or four youths near by. He was touching one or two of them on their arms, to make them listen to him. They nodded and turned away. Then he pulled at them again and started pointing. I got slowly higher up the ladder. Ellis had not got the attention of the group and his opinions were increasing. He was still pointing. Presently his shoulders straightened and his chest filled out; an enormous opinion was coming out of him – one that made them draw away, gaping shiftily at one another. And then I saw Mother. I saw her face as she rolled over on her back in the water. Her mouth was open and her face was dirty at the lips and both her legs came up in the air. Her eyes were closed. A girl next to me on the ladder said: 'Look – that woman down there is in trouble. She's drowning.'

Although there were several people only a yard or so away from her – two of them were actually throwing a ball over her – no one paid any attention. I pushed my way back down the ladder and then I saw Ellis turn and shout to the group that had moved back to consider her. I saw him step down in the water and wade towards her. He was alongside her, trying to get his arms round her body. She rolled out of them and then I saw mud on her feet. He was wrestling with her and calling to a man to hold her, but the man's hand slithered. Then Ellis at last got her by the slippery waist, blew out his chest, and in a struggling lunge lifted her, heaved her, blundered with her, dragging her to the bank.

I was down from the ladder and was rushing to the spot where a policeman was saying, 'Put her over there,' and there was Ellis alone, carrying Mother – the whole of her! – to a bench against the wall, with a trail of water following him and, after the water, a cortège of respectful people. I pushed my way among them and bumped into Ellis, who, being short, was shoved away by the crowd from the bench where Mother lay.

'She's all right,' he said importantly.

Then George and my brother ran up and pushed their way into the scrum.

I can't give a clear account of what happened. I got to Mother. She looked so slimy and wet and swollen in the face. A lot of people were saying what a scandal it was – a woman drowning a few feet from the shore in a crowd like that and no one taking any notice of her, and arguments about what is nearest to the eye is hardest to see, and strong swimmers are always the weakest, and the same thing happened to a child at the town swimming bath last year, there ought to be a law, and an argument about who pulled her out. Mother came back to life quickly and the crowd thinned away, moralising. When we got her wrapped up and sitting up, she was soon herself and very angry. I took her to the changing-room and got her dressed.

'Horrible little man with his arms round me,' she said. 'Quite unnecessary.'

'It was Ellis.'

'No, it wasn't,' Mother said. She'd been pulled out by some brute who tore the shoulder strap of her suit, she said. We got the car round and put her into it. Ellis was alone and stood ashamed, at a distance. He conveyed that he had not intended to intrude in a family matter.

'Come on, Ellis,' my brother called.

Ellis did not answer; he looked crushed. What he wanted to do was to stand there and give a full account of what had passed while he stood arguing with the youths at the water's edge. We pushed him into the car and Mother said irritably as we drove off, 'Ellis, why don't you take off your waistcoat?'

She glowered and when we got home and gave her a drink she went on glowering. She hated anyone to take charge of her and she hated our few cautious jokes. 'My shoulder went and I lost my balance,' she said. She was firm that whoever interfered and brought her in it was not Ellis. He had the tact to say nothing and we were obliged to thank him with our glances.

But slowly, as we began to think back on the incident, we came round, as always in self-defence, to Mother's point of view. We stopped murmuring thanks to Ellis; it was not quite right that an outsider should rescue Mother. And there was a change in him. He had lost his habit of gazing at Mother and all desire to have an opinion seemed to have gone out of him. Before long, we were relieved to hear him say he must go. We didn't want him there all night. I went with him to the door.

'See you soon,' I said putting out my hand.

He took my hand and held it hard. His hand was not like George's or my brother's.

'Three feet of water,' he said. 'Three feet of water. Muddy at the bottom.' Not in self-disparagement, not an opinion, though perhaps a criticism of something.

Whatever it was, we both gave a shout of laughter and shut the door, and I walked to the gate with him, laughing, and the laughter so shook me from head to toes that I suddenly kissed him in a 'Now-what-do-you-think-of-that?' way. All he said was, 'Come out.'

'I'll walk with you to the corner.'

We marched down the street, silent as soldiers. We said nothing and we could hear only the sound of our shoes. It was as if our feet were talking. At the corner, where the main road begins, cars were rushing by.

'Come on,' he said. And again his hand gripped mine and all the houses I knew in that street began to look different. We walked on and suddenly Ellis gave a peculiar jump, like a frog, and we laughed to the next turning and the next, from street to street, bumping together.

'Where are we going?'

'To the park.'

'It's closed.'

'I know a place where you can get in.'

And so we did get in. The everyday smell of the pavements went and we stood in the night glow of the grass under the trees, which were as black as men against the town lights. The sky was like pink water above us and we were sinking, sinking, sinking. My heart thumping for breath, at the bottom of the world, until somewhere near the trees Ellis stopped his little jumps and I sat down exhausted. I was clutching at him, pulling him under with me and struggling with the kisses that came out of him and throwing my hair back to get more. He looked wicked in the dark.

The next day, to the bang, bang, bang of the band, we marched in the pageant. It banged the way my heart banged in the park. I wore a high conical hat with a veil hanging from it. Ellis had a green jerkin and carried a pikestaff. I could hardly bear to look at him for fear of laughing, but when we got near the town hall and the band stopped, I said: 'Well, Lancelot, show me the back of your hand.'

'It's not the same thing,' said Ellis and started to explain, but I stopped him.

I taught him to swim that summer.

The Marvellous Girl

The official ceremony was coming to an end. Under the sugary chandeliers of what had once been the ballroom of the mansion to which the Institute had moved, the faces of the large audience yellowed and aged as they listened to the last speeches and made one more effort of chin and shoulder to live up to the gilt, the brocaded panels of the walls and the ceiling where cherubs, clouds and naked goddesses romped. Oh, to be up there among them, thought the young man sitting at the back, but on the platform the director was passing from the eternal values of art to the 'gratifying presence of the Minister', to 'Lady Brigson's untiring energies', the 'labours of Professor Exeter and his panel' in the Exhibition on the floor below. When he was named the Professor looked with delight at the audience and played with a thin gold chain he had taken from his pocket. The three chandeliers gave a small united flicker as if covering the yawns of the crowd. The young man sitting at the back stared at the platform once more and then, with his hands on his knees, his elbows out and his eye turned to the nearest door, got ready to push past the people sitting next to him and to be the first out – to get out before his wife who was on the platform with the speakers. By ill-luck he had run into her before the meeting and had been trapped into sitting for nearly two hours, a spectator of his marriage that had come to an end. His very presence there seemed to him an unsought return to one of those patient suicides he used to commit, day after day, out of drift and habit.

To live alone is to expose oneself to accident. He had been drawing on and off all day in his studio and not until the evening had he realised that he had forgotten to eat. Hunger excited him. He took a bus down to an Italian restaurant. It was one of those places where the proprietor came out from time to time to perform a private ballet. He tossed pancakes almost up to the ceiling and then dropped them into a blaze of brandy in the pan – a diversion that often helped the young man with the girls he now sometimes took there. The proprietor was just at the blazing point when two women came into the restaurant in their winter coats and stood still, looking as if they were on fire. The young man quickly gulped down the last of a few coils of spaghetti and stood up and wiped his mouth. The older, smaller of the two women was his wife and she was wearing a wide hat of black fur that made her look shorter than he remembered her. Free of him, she had become bizarre and smaller. Even her eyes had become smaller and, like mice, saw him at once and gave him an alert and busy smile. With her was the tall, calm girl with dark blue eyes from their office at the Institute, the one she excitedly called 'the marvellous girl', the 'only one I have ever been able to get on with'.

More than two years had gone by since he and his wife had lived together. The marriage was one of those prickly friendships that never succeeded – to *his* astonishment, at any rate – in turning into love, but are kept going by curiosity. It had become at once something called 'our situation'; a duet by a pair of annoyed hands. What kept them going was an exasperated interest in each other's love affairs, but even unhappiness loses its tenderness and fascination. They broke. At first they saw each other occasionally, but now rarely; except at the Institute where his drawings were shown. They were connected only by the telephone wire which ran under the London pavements and worried its way under the window ledge of his studio. She would ring up, usually late at night.

'I hope it's all right,' she'd say wistfully. 'Are you alone?'

But getting nothing out of him on that score, she would become brisk and ask for something out of the debris of their marriage, for if marriages come to an end, paraphernalia hangs on. There were two or three divans, a painted cupboard, some rugs rolled up, boxes of saucepans and frying pans, lamps – useful things stored in the garage under his studio. But, as if to revive an intimacy, she always asked for some damaged object; she had a child's fidelity to what was broken: a lampshade that was scorched, an antique coal bucket with one loose leg, or a rug that had been stained by her dog Leopold whose paws were always in trouble. Leopold's limp had come to seem to the young man the animal's response to their hopeless marriage. The only sound object she had ever wanted – and got into a temper about it – was a screwdriver that had belonged to her father whom she detested.

Now, in the restaurant, she put up a friendly fight from under the wide-brimmed hat.

'I didn't know you still came here,' she said.

'I come now and again.'

'You must be going to the opening at the Institute.'

'No,' he said. 'I haven't heard of it.'

'But I sent you a card,' she said. 'You must go. Your drawings are in the Exhibition. It's important.'

'Three drawings,' said the girl warmly.

'Come with us,' his wife said.

'No. I can't. I'm just going to pay my bill.'

A lie, of course. She peered at his plate as if hoping to read his fortune, to guess at what he was up to. He turned to the girl and said with feeling:

'Are you better now?'

'I haven't been ill,' said the girl.

'You said she'd been in hospital,' he said to his wife.

'No I didn't,' she said. 'She went to Scotland for a wedding.'

A quite dramatic look of disappointment on the young man's face made the girl laugh and look curiously at him. He had seen her only two or three times and knew nothing much about her, but she was indeed 'marvellous'. She was not in hospital, she was beautiful and alive. Astounding. Even, in a bewildering way, disappointing.

The waiter saved him and moved them away.

'Enjoy yourselves,' said the young man. 'I'm going home.'

'Goodbye,' the girl turned to wave to him as she followed his wife to the table.

It was that 'goodbye' that did for him. It was a radiant 'goodbye', half laughing, he had seen her tongue and her even teeth as she laughed. Simply seeing him go had brought life to her face. He went out of the restaurant and in the leathery damp of the street he could see the face following him from lamp to lamp. 'Goodbye, goodbye,' it was still saying. And that was when he changed his mind. An extraordinary force pulled his scattered mind together; he determined to go to the meeting and to send to her, if he could see her in the crowd, a blinding, laughing, absolute Goodbye for ever, as radiant as hers.

Now, as he sat there in the crowded hall there was no sign of her. He had worn his eyes out looking for her. She was not on the platform with his wife and the speakers of course. The director, whose voice suggested chocolate, was still thanking away when, suddenly, the young man did see her. For the light of the chandeliers quivered again, dimmed to a red cindery glow and then went out, and as people gasped 'Oh', came on strongly again and one or two giggled. In that flash when everyone looked up and around, there was a gap between the ranks of heads and shoulders and he saw her brown hair and her broad pale face with its white rose look, its good-humoured chin and the laugh beginning on it. She turned round and she saw him as he saw her. There are glances that are collisions, scattering the air between like glass. Her expression was headlong in open conniving joy at the sight of things going wrong. She was sitting about ten rows in front of him but he was not quick enough to wave for now, 'plonk', the lights went out for good. The audience dropped *en masse* into the blackness, the hall sank gurgling to the bottom of the sea and was swamped. Then outside a door banged, a telephone rang, feet shuffled and a slow animal grunting and chattering started everywhere and broke into irreverent squeals of laughter.

Men clicked on their lighters or struck matches and long anarchic shadows shot over the walls. There was the sudden heat of breath, wool, fur and flesh as if the audience had become one body.

'Keep your seats for a moment,' the director said from the darkness, like God.

Now was the time to go. Darkness had wiped out the people on the platform. For the young man they had become too intimate. It had seemed to him that his wife who sat next to her old lover, Duncan, was offering too lavish a sight of the new life she was proposing to live nowadays. Duncan was white-faced and bitter and they were at their old game of quarrelling publicly under their breath while she was tormenting him openly by making eyes at the Professor who was responding by making his gold chain spin round faster and faster. The wife of the director was studying all this and preparing to defend her husband in case the longing in those female eyes went beyond the Professor and settled on *him*.

How wrong I was about my wife's character, the young man thought. Who would have thought such wistful virginity could become so rampant.

The young man said: 'Pull yourself together, Duncan. Tell her you won't stand any more of it. Threaten her with Irmgard . . .'

Darkness had abolished it all.

It was not the darkness of the night outside. This darkness had no flabby wet sky in it. It was dry. It extinguished everything. It stripped the eyes of sight; even the solid human rows were lumped together invisibly. One was suddenly naked in the dark from the boots upwards. One could feel the hair on one's body growing and in the chatter one could hear men's voices grunting, women's voices fast, breath going in and out, muscles changing, hearts beating. Many people stood up. Surrounded by animals like himself he too stood up, to hunt with the pack, to get out. Where was the girl? Inaccessible, known, near but invisible. Someone had brought a single candle to the desk at which the director stood like a spectre. He said:

'It would seem, ladies and gentlemen, that there has been a failure of the . . . I fear the . . . hope to procure the . . .'

There was a rough animal laugh from the audience and, all standing up now, they began to shuffle slowly for the doors.

'Get out of my way. Please let me pass,' the young man shouted in a stentorian voice which no one heard for he was shouting inside himself. 'I have got to get to a girl over there. I haven't seen her for nearly a year. I've got to say "Goodbye" to her for the last time.'

And the crowd stuck out their bottoms and their elbows, broadened their backs and grew taller all around him, saying:

'Don't push.'

A man, addressing the darkness in an educated voice, said: 'It is remarkable how calm an English crowd is. One saw it in the Blitz.'

The young man knocked over a chair in the next row and in the next, shoving his way into any gap he could find in the clotted mass of fur and wool, and muttering:

'I've only spoken to her three times in my life. She is wearing blue and has a broad nose. She lives somewhere in London – I don't know where – all I know is that I thought she was ill but it turns out that she went to a wedding in Scotland. I heard she is going to marry a young man in Canada. Think of a girl like that with a face as composed as a white rose, but a rose that can laugh – taking her low voice to Canada and lying at night among thousands of fir trees and a continent of flies and snow. I have got to get to the door and catch her there and say "Goodbye".'

He broke through four rows of chairs, trod on feet and pushed, but the crowd was slow and stacked up solid. Hundreds of feet scraped. Useless to say to them:

'A fox is among you. I knew when I first saw this girl that she was to be dreaded. I said just now in a poetic way that her skin is the colour of a white rose, but it isn't. Her hair has the gloss of a young creature's, her forehead is wide and her eyebrows are soft and arching, her eyes are dark blue and her lips warm and helpless. The skin is really like bread. A marvellous girl – everyone says so – but the sure sign of it is that when I first saw her I was terrified of her. She was standing by an office window watching people in the street below and talking on the telephone and laughing and the laughter seemed to swim all over her dress and her breasts seemed to join in and her waist, even her long young legs that were continuing the dance she had been at – she was saying – the night before. It was when she turned and saw me that my sadness began.

'My wife was there – it was her office – and she said to me in a whisper:

'"She is marvellous, isn't she? The child enjoys herself and she's right. But what fools girls are. Sleep with all the boys you like, don't get married yet, it's a trap, I keep telling her."

'I decided never to go to that office again.'

The crowd shuffled on in the dark. He was choking in the smell of fur coats, clamouring to get past, to get to the door, angrily begging someone to light one more match – 'What? Has the world run out of matches and lighters?' – so that he could see her, but they had stopped lighting matches now. He wanted to get his teeth into the coat of a large broad woman in front of him. He trod on her heels.

'I'm sorry,' he wanted to say. 'I'm just trying to say "Goodbye" to someone. I couldn't do it before – think of my situation. I didn't care – it didn't matter to me – but there was trouble at the office. My wife had broken with that wretched man Duncan who had gone off with a girl called Irmgard and when my wife heard of it she made him throw Irmgard over and took him back and once she'd got him she took up with the Professor – you saw him twiddling his gold chain. In my opinion it's a surprise that the Exhibition ever got going, what with the Professor and Duncan playing Cox and Box in the office. But I had to deliver my drawings. And so I saw this girl a second time. I also took a rug with me, a rug my wife had asked for from the debris. Oh yes, I've got debris.

'The girl got up quickly from her desk when she saw me. I say *quickly*. She was alone and my sadness went. She pointed to the glass door at the end of the room.

'"There's a Committee meeting. She's in there with her husband and the others."

'I said – and this will make you laugh Mrs Whatever-your-name-is, but please move on – I said:

'"But *I* am her husband," I said.

'With what went on in that office how could the girl have known? I laughed when I said this, laughing at myself. The girl did not blush; she studied me and then she laughed too. Then she took three steps towards me, almost as if she was running – I counted those steps – for she came near enough to touch me on the sleeve of my raincoat. Soft as her face was she had a broad strong nose. In those three steps she became a woman in my eyes, not a vision, not a sight to fear, a friendly creature, well-shaped.

'"I ought to have known by your voice – when you telephone," she said.

'Her mistake made her face shine.

'"Is the parcel for the Exhibition?" she said.

'I had put it on a chair.

'"No, it's a rug. It weighs a ton. It's Leopold's rug."

'"I've got to go," I said. "Just say it's Leopold's. Leopold is a dog."

'"Oh," she said. "I thought you meant a friend."

'"No. Leopold wants it, apparently. I've got a lot of rugs. I keep them in the garage at my studio. You don't want a rug, do you? As fast as I get rid of them some girl comes along and says, 'How bare your floor is. It needs a rug,' and brings me one. I bet when I get back I'll find a new one. Or, I could let you have a box of saucepans, a Hoover, a handsaw, a chest of drawers, firetongs, a towel rail . . ."

'I said this to see her laugh, to see her teeth and her tongue again and to see her body move under its blue dress which was light blue on that day. And to show her what a distance lay between her life and mine.

'"I've got to go," I said again but at the door I said,

'"Beds too. When you get married. All in the garage."

'She followed me to the door and I waved back to her.'

To the back of the fur-coated woman he said, 'I can be fascinating. It's a way of wiping oneself out. I wish you'd wipe yourself out and let me pass. I shall never see her again.'

And until this night he had not seen her again. He started on a large design which he called *The Cornucopia*. It was, first of all, a small comic sketch of a dustbin which contained chunks of the rubbish in his garage – very clever and silly. He scrapped it and now he made a large design and the vessel was rather like the girl's head but when he came to drawing the fruits of the earth they were fruits of geometry – hexagons, octagons, cubes, with something like a hedgehog on top, so he made the vessel less like a girl's head; the thing drove him mad the more he worked on it.

September passed into October in the parks and once or twice cats on the glass roof of the studio lost their balance and came sliding down in a screech of claws in the hurly-burly of love.

One night his wife telephoned him.

'Oh God. Trouble,' he said when he heard her plaintive voice. He had kept out of her way for months.

'Is it all right? Are you alone?' she said. 'Something awful has happened. Duncan's going to get married again. Irmgard has got her claws into him. I rang Alex – he always said I could ring – but he won't come. Why am I rejected? And you remember that girl – she's gone. The work piles up.'

'To Canada?' he said.

'What on earth makes you say that?' she said in her fighting voice.

'You said she was.'

'You're always putting words into my mouth. She's in hospital.'

'Ill,' he said. 'How awful. Where is she?'

'How do I know?' she said. 'Leopold,' and now she was giggling. 'Leopold's making a mess again. I must ring off.'

'I'm sorry,' he said.

Ill! In hospital! The picture of the girl running towards him in the office came back to him and his eyes were smeared with tears. He felt on his arms and legs a lick of ice and a lick of fire. His body filled with a fever that passed and then came back so violently that he lost his breath. His knees had gone as weak as string. He was in love with the girl. The love seemed to come up from events thousands of years old. The girl herself he thought was not young but ancient. Perhaps Egyptian. The skin of her face was not rose-like, nor like bread, but like stone roughened by centuries. 'I am feeling love,' he said, 'for the whole of a woman for the first time. No other woman exists. I feel love not only for her face, her body, her voice, her hands and feet but for the street she lives in, the place she was born, her dresses and stockings, her bus journeys, her handbags, her parties, her dances. I don't know where she is. How can I find out? Why didn't I realise this before?'

Squeezed like a rag between the crowd he got to the doorway and there the crowd bulged and carried him through it backwards because he was turning to look for her. Outside the door was an ambitious landing. The crowd was cautiously taking the first steps down the long sweep of this staircase. There was a glimmer of light here from the marble of the walls and that educated man gripped his arm and said, 'Mind the steps down,' and barred the young man's way. He fought free of the grip and stood against the wall. 'Don't be a damn fool,' said the educated man, waving his arms about. 'If anyone slips down there, the rest of you will pile on top of them.' The man now sounded mad. 'I saw it in the war. A few at a time. A few at a time,' he screamed. And the young man felt the man's spit on his face. The crowd passed him like mourners, indecipherable, but a huge woman turned on him and held him by the sleeves with both hands. 'Thornee! Thornee! Where are you? You're leaving me,' she whimpered. 'Dear girl,' said a man behind her. 'I am here.' She let go, swung round and collided with her husband and grabbed him. 'You had your arm round that woman,' she said. They faded past. The young man looked for a face. Up the stairs, pushing against the procession going down, a man came up sidling against the wall. Every two or three steps he shouted, 'Mr Zagacheck?' Zagacheck, Zagacheck, Zagacheck came nearer and suddenly a mouth bawled into the young man's face with a blast of heavily spiced breath.

'Mr Zagacheck?'

'I am not Mr Zagacheck,' said the young man in a cold clear voice and as he said it the man was knocked sideways. A woman took the young man's hand and said:

'Francis!' and she laughed. She had *named* him. It was the girl, of course. 'Isn't this wild? Isn't it marvellous? I saw you. I've been looking for you,' she said.

'I have been looking for you.'

He interlaced his fingers with her warm fingers and held her arm against his body.

'Are you with your wife?' she said.

'No,' he said.

She squeezed his hand, she lifted it and held it under her arm.

'Are you alone?' he said.

'Yes.'

'Good,' he said. 'I thought you'd gone.' Under her arm he could feel her breast. 'I mean for good, left the country. I came to say "Goodbye".'

'Oh yes!' she said with enthusiasm and rubbed herself against him. 'Why didn't you come to the office?'

He let go of her hand and put his arm round her waist.

'I'll tell you later. We'll go somewhere.'

'Yes!' she said again.

'There's another way out. We'll wait here and then slip out by the back way.'

The crowd pressed against them. And then, he heard his wife's voice, only a foot away from him. She was saying: 'I'm not making a scene. It's you. I wonder what has happened to the girl.'

'I don't know and I don't care,' the man said. 'Stop trying to change the subject. Yes or no? Are you?'

The young man stiffened: 'This is the test. If the girl speaks the miracle crashes.'

She took his arm from her waist and gripped his hand fiercely. They clenched, sticking their nails into each other, as if trying to wound. He heard one of the large buttons on his wife's coat click against a button of his coat. She was there for a few seconds; it seemed to him as long as their marriage. He had not been so close to his wife for years. Then the crowd moved on, the buttons clicked again and he heard her say:

'There's only Leopold there.'

In a puff of smoke from her cigarette she vanished. The hands of the girl and Francis softened and he pressed hard against her.

'Now,' he whispered. 'I know the way.'

They sidled round the long wall of the landing, passing a glimmering bust – 'Mr Zagacheck,' he said – and came to the corner of a corridor, long and empty, faintly lit by a tall window at the end. They almost ran down it, hand in hand. Twice he stopped to try the door of a room. A third door opened.

'In here,' he said.

He pulled her into a large dark room where the curtains had not been drawn, a room that smelled of new carpet, new paint and new furniture. There was the gleam of a desk. They groped to the window. Below was a square with its winter trees and the headlights of cars playing upon them and the crowd scattering across the roads. He put his arms round her and kissed her on the mouth and she kissed him. Her hands were as wild as his.

'You're mad,' she said. 'This is the director's room,' as he pushed her on to the sofa but when his hands were on the skin of her leg, she said, 'Let's go.'

'When did you start to love me?' he said.

'I don't know. Just now. When you didn't come. I don't know. Don't ask me. Just now, when you said you loved me.'

'But before?'

'I don't know,' she said.

And then the lights in the building came on and the lights on the desk and they got up, scared, hot-faced, hot-eyed, hating the light.

'Come on. We must get out,' he said.

And they hurried from the lighted room to get into the darkness of the city.

The Spree

The old man – but when does old age begin? – the old man turned over in bed and, putting out his hand to the crest of his wife's beautiful white rising hip and comforting bottom, hit the wall with his knuckles and woke up. More than once during the two years since she had died he had done this and knew that if old age vanished in the morning it came on at night, filling the bedroom with people until, switching on the light, he saw it staring at him; then it shuffled off and left him looking at the face of the clock. Three hours until breakfast; the hunger of loss yawned under his ribs. Trying to make out the figures on the clock he dropped off to sleep again and was walking up Regent Street seeing, on the other side of it, a very high-bred white dog, long in the legs and distinguished in its step, hurrying up to Oxford Circus, pausing at each street corner in doubt, looking up at each person as he passed and whimpering politely to them: 'Me? Me? Me?' and going on when they did not answer. A valuable dog like that, lost! Someone will pick it up, lead it off, sell it to the hospital and doctors will cut it up! The old man woke up with a shout to stop the crime and then he saw daylight in the room and heard bare feet running past his room and the shouts of his three grandchildren and his daughter-in-law calling, 'Ssh! Don't wake Grandpa.'

The old man got out of bed and stood looking indignantly at the mirror over the washbasin and at his empty gums. It was awful to think, as he put his teeth in to cover the horror of his mouth, that twelve or fourteen hours of London daylight were stacked up meaninglessly waiting for him. He pulled himself together. As he washed, listening to the noises of the house, he made up a speech to say to his son who must be downstairs by now.

'I am not saying I am ungrateful. But old and young are not meant to be together. You've got your life. I've got mine. The children are sweet – you're too sharp with them – but I can't stand the noise. I don't want to live at your expense. I want a place of my own. Where I can breathe.

Like Frenchy.' And as he said this, speaking into the towel and listening to the tap running, he could see and hear Frenchy who was his dentist but who looked like a rascally prophet in his white coat and was seventy if he was a day, saying to him as he looked down into his mouth and as if he was really tinkering with a property there:

'You ought to do what I've done. Get a house by the sea. It keeps you young.'

Frenchy vanished, leaving him ten years younger. The old man got into his shirt and trousers and was carefully spreading and puffing up the sparse black and grey hair across his head when in came his daughter-in-law, accusing him – why did she accuse?

'Grandpa! You're up!'

She was like a soft Jersey cow with eyes too big and reproachful. She was bringing him tea, the dear sweet tiresome woman.

'Of course I'm up,' he said.

One glance at the tea showed him it was not like the tea he used to make for his wife when she was alive, but had too much milk in it, tepid stuff, left standing somewhere. He held his hairbrush up and he suddenly said, asserting his right to live, to get out of the house, in air he could breathe:

'I'm going in to London to get my hair cut.'

'Are you sure you'll be all right?'

'Why do you say that?' he said severely. 'I've got several things I want to do.'

And, when she had gone, he heard her say on the stairs:

'He's going to get his hair cut!'

And his son saying, 'Not again!'

This business, this defiance of the haircut! It was not a mere scissoring and clipping of the hair, for the old man. It was a ceremonial of freedom; it had the whiff of orgy; the incitement of a ritual. As the years went by, leaving him in such a financial mess that he was now down to not much more than a pension, it signified desire – but what desire? To be memorable in some streets of London, or at least, as evocative as an incense. The desire would come to him, on summer days like this, when he walked in his son's suburban garden, to sniff and to pick a rose for his buttonhole;

and then, already intoxicated, he marched out of the garden gate on to the street and to the bus stop, upright and vigorous, carrying his weight well and pink in the face. The scents of the barbers had been creeping into his nostrils, his chest, even went down to his legs. To be clipped, oiled and perfumed was to be free.

So, on this decent July morning in the sun-shot and acid suburban mist, he stood in a queue for the bus, and if anyone had spoken to him, he would have gladly said, to put them in their place:

'Times have changed. Before I retired, when Kate was alive – though I must honestly say we often had words about it – I always took a cab.'

The bus came and whooshed him down to Knightsbridge, to his temple – the most expensive of the big shops. There, reborn on miles of carpet he paused and sauntered, sauntered and paused. He was inflamed by hall after hall of women's dresses and hats, by cosmetics and jewellery. Scores of women were there. Glad to be cooled off, he passed into the echoing hall of provisions. He saw the game, the salmon and the cheese. He ate them and moved on to lose twenty years in the men's clothing department where, among ties and brilliant shirts and jackets, his stern yet bashful pink face woke up to the loot and his ears heard the voices of the rich, the grave chorus of male self-approval. He went to the end where the oak stairs led down to the barbers; there, cool as clergy they stood gossiping in their white coats. One came forward, seated him and dressed him up like a baby. And then – nothing happened. He was the only customer and the barber took a few steps back towards the group saying:

'He wasn't at the staff meeting.'

The old man tapped his finger irritably under his sheet. Barbers did not cut hair, it seemed. They went to staff meetings. One called back:

'Mr Holderness seconded it.'

Who was Holderness?

'Where is Charles?' said the old man to call the barbers to order. Obsequiously, the man began that pretty music with his scissors.

'Charles?' said the barber.

'Yes. Charles. He shaved me for twenty years.'

'He retired.'

Another emptiness, another cavern, opened inside the old man.

'Retired? He was a child!'

'All the old ones have retired.'

The barber had lost his priestly look. He looked sinful, even criminal, certainly hypocritical.

And although the old man's head was being washed by lotions and oils and there was a tickling freshness about the ears and his nostrils quickened, there was something uneasy about the experience. In days gone by the place had been baronial, now it seemed not quite to gleam. One could not be a sultan among a miserable remnant of men who held staff meetings. When the old man left, the woman at the desk went on talking as she took his money and did not know his name. When he went upstairs, he paused to look back – no, the place was a palace of pleasure no longer. It was the place where – except for the staff – no one was known.

And that was what struck him as he stepped out of the glancing swing doors of the shop, glad to be out in the July sun, that he was a sultan, cool, scented and light-headed, extraordinary in a way, sacred almost, ready for anything – but cut off from expectancy, unknown now-a-days to anybody, free for nothing, liberty evaporating out of the tips of his shoes. He stepped out on the pavement dissembling leisure. His walk became slower and gliding. For an hour shop windows distracted him, new shops where old had been shocked him. But, he said, pulling himself together, I must not fall into *that* trap. Old people live in the past. And I am not old! Old I am not! So he stopped gliding and stepped out wilfully, looking so stern and with mouth turned down, so corrupt and purposeful with success, that he was unnoticeable. Who notices success?

It was always – he didn't like to admit it – like this on these days when he made the great stand for his haircut and the exquisite smell. He would set out with a vision, it crumbled into a rambling dream. He fell back, like a country hare, on his habitual run, to the shops which had bought his goods years ago, to see what they were selling and where he knew no one now: to a café which had changed its decor, where he ate a sandwich and drank a cup of coffee; but as the dream consoled, it dissolved into final melancholy. He with his appetite for everything, who could not pass a shop window, or an estate agent's, or a fine house, without greed watering in his mouth, could buy nothing. He hadn't the cash.

There was always this moment when the bottom began to fall out of his haircut days. He denied that his legs were tired, but he did slow down.

It would occur to him suddenly in Piccadilly that he knew no one now in the city. He had been a buyer and seller, not a man for friends; he knew buildings, lifts, offices, but not people. There would be nothing for it but to return home. He would drag his way to the inevitable bus-stop of defeat and stand, as so many Londoners did, with surrender on their faces. He delayed it as long as he could, stopping at a street corner or gazing at a passing girl and looking around with that dishonest look a dog has when it is pretending not to hear its master's whistle. There was only one straw to clutch at. There was nothing wrong with his teeth, but he could ring up his dentist. He could ring up Frenchy. He could ring him and say: 'Frenchy? How's tricks?' Sportily. And (a man for smells) he could almost smell the starch in Frenchy's white coat, the keen, chemical, hygienic smell of his room. The old gentleman considered this and then went down a couple of disheartened side streets. In a short *cul de sac*, standing outside a urinal and a few doors from a dead-looking pub, there was a telephone box. An oldish, brown motor coach was parked empty at the kerb by it, its doors closed, a small crowd waiting beside it. There was a man in the telephone box, but he came out in a temper, shouting something to the crowd. The old man went into the box. He had thought of something to say:

'Hullo, Frenchy! Where is that house you were going to find me, you old rascal?'

For Frenchy came up from the sea every day. It was true that Frenchy was a rascal, especially with the women, one after the other, but looking down into the old man's mouth and chipping at a tooth he seemed to be looking into your soul.

The old man got out his coins. He was tired but eagerness revived him as he dialled.

'Hullo, Frenchy,' he said. But the voice that replied was not Frenchy's. It was a child's. The child was calling out: 'Mum. Mum.' The old man banged down the telephone and stared at the dial. His heart thumped. He had, he realised, not dialled Frenchy's number, but the number of his old house, the one he had sold after Kate had died.

The old gentleman backed out of the box and stared, tottering with horror, at it. His legs went weak, his breath had gone and sweat bubbled on his face. He steadied himself by the brick wall. He edged away from the bus and the crowd, not to be seen. He thought he was going to faint. He moved to a doorway. There was a loud laugh from the crowd as a young man with long black hair gave the back of the bus a kick. And then, suddenly, he and a few others rushed towards the old man, shouting and laughing.

'Excuse us,' someone said and pushed him aside. He saw he was standing in the doorway of the pub.

'That's true,' the old man murmured to himself. 'Brandy is what I need,' and, at that, the rest of the little crowd pushed into him or past him. One of them was a young girl with fair hair who paused as her young man pulled her by the hand and said kindly to the old man:

'After you.'

There he was, being elbowed, travelling backwards into the little bar. It was the small Private Bar of the pub and the old man found himself against the counter. The young people were stretching their arms across him and calling out orders for drinks and shouting. He was wedged among them. The wild young man with the piratical look was on one side of him, the girl and her young man on the other. The wild young man called to the others: 'Wait a minute. What's yours, Dad?'

The old man was bewildered. 'Brandy.'

'Brandy,' shouted the young man across the bar.

'That's right,' said the girl to the old man, studying his face. 'You have one. You ought to have got on the first coach.'

'You'd have been half-way to bloody Brighton by now,' said the wild young man. 'The first bloody outing this firm's had in its whole bloody history and they bloody forgot the driver. Are you the driver?'

Someone called out: 'No, he's not the driver.'

'I had a shock,' the old man began, but crowded against the bar no one heard him.

'Drink it up then,' the girl said to him and, startled by her kindness, he drank. The brandy burned and in a minute fire went up into his head and his face lost its hard bewildered look and it loosened into a smile. He heard their young voices flying about him. They were going to Brighton. No, the other side of Brighton. No, this side – well to bloody Hampton's mansion, estate, something. The new chairman – he'd thrown the place open. Bloody thrown it, laughed the wild man, to the Works and the Office and, as usual, 'the Works get the first coach'. The young girl leaned down to smell the rose in the old man's buttonhole and said to her young man, 'It's lovely. Smell it.' His arm was round her waist and there were the two of them bowing to the rose.

'From your garden?' said the girl.

The old man heard himself, to his astonishment, tell a lie.

'I grew it,' he said bashfully.

'We shan't bloody start for hours,' someone said. 'Drink up.'

The old man looked at his watch; a tragic look. Soon they'd be gone. Someone said: 'Which department are you in?' 'He's in the Works,' someone said. 'No, I've retired,' said the old man, not to cause a fuss. 'Have another, Dad,' said the young man. 'My turn.'

Three of them bent their heads to hear him say again, 'I have retired,' and one of them said: 'It was passed at the meeting. Anyone retired entitled to come.'

'You've made a mistake,' the old man began to explain to them. 'I was just telephoning to my dentist . . .'

'No,' said one of the bending young men, turning to someone in the crowd. 'That bastard Fowkes talked a lot of bull but it passed.'

'You're all right,' the girl said to the old man.

'He's all right,' said another and handed the old man another drink. If only they would stop shouting, the old man thought, I could explain.

'A mistake . . .' he began again.

'It won't do you any harm,' someone said. 'Drink up.'

Then someone shouted from the door. 'He's here. The driver.'

The girl pulled the old man by the arm and he found himself being hustled to the door.

'My glass,' he said.

He was pushed, holding his half empty glass, into the street. They rushed past him and he stood there, glass in hand, trying to say, 'Goodbye,' and then he followed them, still holding his glass, to explain. They shouted to him 'Come on' and he politely followed to the door of the bus where they were pushing to get in.

But at the door of the bus everything changed. A woman wearing a flowered dress with a red belt, a woman as stout as himself, had a foot on the step of the bus and was trying to heave herself up, while people ahead of her blocked the door. She nearly fell.

[914]

The old man, all smiles and sadness, put on a dignified anger. He pushed his way towards her. He turned forbiddingly on the youngsters.

'Allow me, madam,' he said and took the woman's cool fat elbow and helped her up the step, putting his own foot on the lower one. Fatal. He was shoved up and himself pushed inside, the brandy spilling down his suit. He could not turn round. He was in, driven in deeply, to wait till the procession stopped. 'I'm getting out,' he said.

He flopped into the seat behind the woman.

'Young people are always in a rush,' she turned to say to him.

The last to get in were the young couple.

'Break it up,' said the driver.

They were slow for they were enlaced and wanted to squeeze in united.

The old man waited for them to be seated and then stood up, glass in hand, as if offering a toast, as he moved forward to get out.

'Would you mind sitting down,' said the driver. He was counting the passengers and one, seeing him with the glass in his hand, said, 'Cheers.'

For the first time in his adult life, the old man indignantly obeyed an order. He sat down, was about to explain his glass, heard himself counted, got up. He was too late. The driver pulled a bar, slammed the door, spread his arms over the wheel and off they went, to a noise that bashed people's eyeballs.

At every change of the gears, as the coach gulped out of the narrow streets, a change took place in the old man. Shaken in the kidneys, he looked around in protest, put his glass out of sight on the floor and blushed. He was glad no one was sitting beside him for his first idea was to scramble to the window and jump through it at the first traffic lights. The girl who had her arm round her young man looked round and smiled. Then, he too looked around at all these unknown people, belonging to a firm he had never heard of, going to a destination unknown to him, and he had the inflated sensations of an enormous illegality. He had been kidnapped. He tipped back his hat and looked bounderish. The bus was hot and seemed to be frying in the packed traffic when it stopped at the lights. People had to shout to be heard. Under cover of the general shouting, he too shouted to a couple of women across the gangway:

'Do we pass the Oval?'

The woman asked her friend, who asked the man in front, who asked the young couple. Blocks of offices went by in lumps. No one knew except someone who said: 'Must do.' The old man nodded. The moment the Oval cricket ground came into sight, he planned to go to the driver and tell him to let him off. So he kept his eyes open, thinking:

What a lark. What a thing to tell them at home. 'Guess what? Had a free ride. Cheek, my boy,' he'd say to his son, 'that's what you need. Let me give you a bit of advice. You'll get nowhere without cheek.'

His pink face beamed with shrewd frivolity as the coach groaned over the Thames that had never looked so wide and sly. Distantly a power station swerved to the west, then to the east, then rocked like a cradle as the young girl – restless like Kate she was – got out of her young man's arms and got him back into hers, in a tighter embrace. Three containers passed, the coach slackened, then choked forward so suddenly that the old man's head nearly hit the back of the head of the fat lady in front. He studied it and noticed the way the woman's thick hair, gold with grey in it, was darker as it came out of her neck like a growing plant and he thought, as he had often done, how much better a woman's head looks from behind, the face interferes with it in front. And then his own chin went slack and he began a voluptuous journey down corridors. One more look at the power station which had become several jumping power stations, giving higher and higher leaps in the air, and he was asleep.

A snore came from him. The talking woman across the gangway was annoyed by this soliloquising noise which seemed to offer a rival narrative; but others admired it for its steadiness which peacefully mocked the unsteady recovery and spitting and fading energy of the coach and the desperation of the driver. Between their shouts at the driver many glanced admiringly at the sleeper. He was swinging in some private barber's shop that swerved through space, sometimes in some airy corridor, at other times circling beneficently round a cricket match in which Frenchy, the umpire, in his white linen coat, was offering him a plate of cold salmon which his daughter-in-law was trying to stop him from eating; so that he was off the coach, striking his way home on foot at the tail of the longest funeral procession he had ever seen, going uphill for miles into fields that were getting greener and colder and emptier as snow came on and he sat down plonk, out of breath, waking to hear the weeping of the crowds, all weeping for him, and then, still walking, he saw himself outside the tall glass walls of a hospital. It must be a hospital for inside two men in white could be clearly seen in a glass-enclosed room, one of them the driver, getting ready to carry him in on a stretcher. He gasped, now fully awake. There was absolute silence. The coach had stopped; it was empty: he was alone in it, except for the woman who, thank God, was still sitting in front of him, the hair still growing from the back of her neck.

'Where . . .' he began. Then he saw the hospital was, in fact, a garage. The passengers had got out, garagemen were looking under the bonnet of the bus. The woman turned round. He saw a mild face, without make-up.

'We've broken down,' she said.

How grateful he was for her mild face. He had thought he was dead.

'I've been asleep,' he said. 'Where are we?'

He nearly said: 'Have we passed the Oval?' but swallowed that silly question.

'Quarter past three,' he said. Meaning thirty miles out, stuck fast in derelict country at a cross roads, with a few villas sticking out in fields, eating into the grass among a few trees, with a hoarding on the far side of the highway saying, blatantly, 'Mortgages', and the cars dashing by in flights like birds, twenty at a time, still weeping away westwards into space.

The woman had turned to study him and when he got up, flustered, she said in a strict but lofty voice:

'Sit down.'

He sat down.

'Don't you move,' she said. 'I'm not going to move. They've made a mess of it. Let them put it right.'

She had twisted round and he saw her face, wide and full now, as meaty as an obstinate country girl's, and with a smile that made her look as though she were evaporating.

'This is Hampton's doing,' she said. 'Anything to save money. I am going to tell him what I think of him when I see him. No one in charge. Not even the driver – listen to him. Treat staff like cattle. They've got to send another coach. Don't you move until it comes.'

Having said this she was happy.

'When my husband was on the Board nothing like this happened. Do you know anyone here – I don't. Everything's changed.'

[917]

She studied his grey hair.

The old man clung for the moment to the fact that they were united in not knowing anybody. His secretiveness was coming back.

'I've retired,' he said.

The woman leaned further over the back of the seat and looked around the empty bus and then back at him as if she had captured him. Her full lips were the resting lips of a stout woman between meals.

'I must have seen you at the Works with John,' she said. 'It was always a family in those days. Or were you in the office?'

'I must get out of this,' the old man was thinking and he sat forward nearer to her, getting ready to get out once more. 'I must find out the name of this place, get a train or a bus or something, get back home.' The place looked nameless.

But, since his wife had died, he had never been as near to a strange woman's face. It was a wide, ordinary, baby-like face damp in the skin, with big blue eyes under fair, skimpy eyebrows, and she studied him as a soft, plump child would study – for no reason, beyond an assumption that he and she were together in this; they weren't such fools, at their ages, to get off the coach. It was less the nearness of the face than her voice that kept him there.

It was a soft, high voice that seemed to blow away like a child's and was far too young for her, even sounded so purely truthful as to be false. It came out in deep breaths drawn up from soft but heavy breasts that could, he imagined, kick up a hullabaloo, a voice which suggested that by some silly inconsequent right she would say whatever came into her head. It was the kind of voice that made the old man swell with a polite, immensely intimate desire to knock the nonsense out of her.

'I can smell your rose from here,' she said. 'There are not many left who knew the firm in John's time. It was John's life work.'

He smiled complacently. He had his secret.

She paused and then the childish voice went suddenly higher. She was not simply addressing him. She was addressing a meeting.

'I told him that when he let Hampton flatter him he'd be out in a year. I said to John, "He's jealous. He's been jealous all the time."'

The woman paused. Then her chin and her lips stuck out and her eyes that had looked so vague began to bulge and her voice went suddenly deep, rumbling with prophecy.

'"He wants to kill you," I said. You,' said the woman to the old man, 'must have seen it. And he did kill him. We went on a trip round the world, America, Japan, India,' her voice sailed across countries. 'That's where he died. And if he thinks he can wipe out that by throwing his place open to the staff and getting me down there, on show, he's wrong.'

My God, she's as mad as Kate's sister used to get after her husband died, thought the old man. I'm sitting behind a mad woman.

'Dawson,' she said and abruptly stood up as the old man rose too. 'Oh,' she said in her high regal style gazing away out of the window of the bus. 'I remember your name now. You had that row, that terrible row – oh yes,' she said eagerly, the conspirator. 'You ring up Hampton. He's afraid of you. He'll listen. I've got the number here. You tell him there are twenty-seven of his employees stranded on the Brighton road.'

The old man sighed. He gave up all idea of slipping out. When a woman orders you about, what do you do? He thought she looked rather fine standing there prophetically. The one thing to do in such cases was to be memorable. When is a man most memorable? When he says 'No'.

'No, I wouldn't think of it,' he said curtly. 'Mr Hampton and I are not on speaking terms.'

'Why?' said the woman, distracted by curiosity.

'Mr Hampton and I,' he began and he looked very gravely at her for a long time. 'I have never heard of him. Who is he? I'm not on the staff. I've never heard of the firm.' And then like a conjuror waving a handkerchief, he spread his face into a smile that had often got him an order in the old days.

'I just got on the coach for the ride. Someone said "Brighton". "Day at the sea," I said. "Suits me."'

The woman's face went the colour of liver with rage and unbelief. One for the law, all the rage she had just been feeling about Hampton now switched to the old man. She was unbelieving.

'No one checked?' she said, her voice throbbing. She was boiling up like the police.

The old gentleman just shook his head gently. 'No one checked' – it was a definition of paradise. If he had wings he would have spread them,

taken to the air and flown round her three times, saying, 'Not a soul! Not
a soul!'

She was looking him up and down. He stood with a plump man's
dignity, but what saved him in her eyes were his smart, well-cut clothes,
his trim hair and the jaunty rose; he looked like an old rip, a racing man,
probably a crook; at any rate, a bit of a rogue on the spree, yet innocent
too. She studied his shoes and he moved a foot and kicked the brandy
glass. It rolled into the gangway and he smiled slightly.

'You've got a nerve,' she said, her smile spreading.

'Sick of sitting at home,' he said. Weighing her up – not so much her
character but her body – he said: 'I've been living with my daughter-in-law
since my wife died.'

He burst out with confidence, for he saw he had almost conquered her.

'Young and old don't mix. Brighton would suit me. I thought I would
have a look around for a house.'

Her eyes were still busily going over him.

'You're a spark,' she said, still staring. Then she saw the glass and bent
down to pick it up. As she straightened she leaned on the back of the seat
and laughed out loud.

'You just got on. Oh dear,' she laughed loudly, helplessly. 'Serves
Hampton right.

'Sit down,' she said. He sat down. She sat down on the seat opposite.
He was astonished and even shy to see his peculiar case appreciated and
his peculiarity grew in his mind from a joke to a poem, from a poem to
a dogma.

'I meant to get off at the Oval, but I dropped off to sleep,' he laughed.

'Going to see the cricket?' she said.

'No,' he said. 'Home – I mean my son's place.'

The whole thing began to appear lovely to him. He felt as she laughed
at him, as she still held the glass, twiddling it by the stem, that he was
remarkable.

'Years ago I did it once before,' he said, multiplying his marvels. 'When
my wife was alive. I got a late train from London, went to sleep and
woke up in Bath. I did. I really did. Stayed at the Royal. Saw a customer
next day. He was so surprised to see me he gave me an order worth
£300. My wife didn't believe me.'

'Well, can you blame her?' the woman said.

The driver walked from the office to the garage and put his head into the coach and called out:

'They're sending a new bus. Be here four o'clock.'

The old man turned: 'By the way, I'm getting off,' he shouted to the driver.

'Aren't you going on?' said the woman. 'I thought you said you were having a trip to the sea.'

She wanted him to stay.

'To be frank,' said the old man. 'These youngsters – we'd been having a drink – they meant no harm – pushed me on when I was giving you a hand. I was in the pub. I had had a bit of a shock. I did something foolish. Painful really.'

'What was that?' she said.

'Well,' said the old man swanking in his embarrassment, and going very red. 'I went to this telephone box, you know, where the coach started from, to ring up my dentist – Frenchy. I sometimes ring him up, but I got through to the wrong number. You know what I did? I rang the number of my old house, when Kate – when my wife – was alive. Some girl answered, maybe a boy, I don't know. It gave me a turn, doing a thing like that. I thought my mind had gone.'

'Well, the number would have changed.'

'I thought, I really did think, for a second, it was my wife.'

The traffic on the main road sobbed or whistled as they talked. Containers, private cars, police cars, breakdown vans, cars with boats on their roofs – all sobbing their hearts out in a panic to get somewhere else.

'When did your wife die?' said the woman. 'Just recently?'

'Two years ago,' he said.

'It was grief. That is what it was – grief,' she said gravely and looked away from him into the sky outside and to the derelict bit of country.

That voice of hers, by turns childish, silly, passing to the higher notes of the exalted and belligerent widow – all that talk of partners killing each other! – had become, as his wife's used to do after some tantrum, simply plain.

Grief. Yes it was. He blinked away the threat of tears before her understanding. In these two years he seemed, because of his loneliness, to be dragging an increasing load of unsaid things behind him, things he had no one to tell. With his son and his daughter-in-law and their young friends he sat with his mouth open ready to speak, but he could never get a word out. The words simply fell back down his throat. He had a load of what people called boring things which he could not say; he had loved his wife; she had bored him; it had become a bond. What he needed was not friends, for since so many friends had died he had become a stranger: he needed another stranger. Perhaps like this woman whose face was as blank as his was, time having worn all expression from it. Because of that she looked now, if not as old as he was, full of life you could see; but she had joined his lonely race and had lost the look of going nowhere. He lowered his eyes and became shy. Grief – what was it? A craving. Yet not for a face or even a voice or even for love, but for a body. But dressed. Say, in a flowered dress.

To get his mind off a thought so bold he uttered one of his boring things, a sort of sample of what he would have said to his wife.

'Last night I had a dream about a dog,' he began to test her out as a stranger to whom you could say any damn silly thing. A friend would never listen to damn silly things.

The woman repeated, going back to what she had already said, as women do:

'Remembering the telephone number – it was grief.'

And then went off at a tangent, roughly. 'Don't mention dreams to me. Last week at the bungalow I saw my husband walk across the sitting-room clean through the electric fire and the mirror over the mantelpiece and stand on the other side of it, not looking at me, but saying something to me that I couldn't hear – asking for a box of matches I expect.'

'Imagination,' said the old man, sternly correcting her. He had no desire to hear of her dead husband's antics, but he did feel that warm, already possessive desire, to knock sense into her. It was a pleasant feeling.

'It wasn't imagination,' she said, squaring up to him. 'I packed my things and went to London at once. I couldn't stand it. I drove in to Brighton, left the car at the station and came up to London for a few days. That is why when I heard about Hampton's party at the office I took this coach.'

'Saved the train fare. Why shouldn't Hampton pay?' she grinned. 'I told him I'd come to the party, but I'm not going. I'm picking up the car at Brighton and going home to the bungalow. It's only seven miles away.'

She waited to see if he would laugh at their being so cunningly in the same boat. He did not laugh and that impressed her, but she sulked. Her husband would not have laughed either.

'I dread going back,' she said sulkily.

'I sold my place,' he said. 'I know the feeling.'

'You were right,' said the woman. 'That's what I ought to do. Sell the place. I'd get a good price for it, too. I'm not exactly looking forward to going back there this evening. It's very isolated – but the cat's there.'

He said nothing. Earnestly she said:

'You've got your son and daughter-in-law waiting for you,' she said, giving him a pat on the knee. 'Someone to talk to. You're lucky.'

The driver put his head into the door and said:

'All out. The other coach is here.'

'That's us,' said the woman.

The crowd outside were indeed getting into the new coach. The old man followed her out and looked back at the empty seats with regret. At the door he stepped past her and handed her out. She was stout but landed light as a feather. The wild young man and his friends were shouting, full of new beer, bottles in their pockets. The others trooped in.

'Goodbye,' said the old man, doing his memorable turn.

'You're not coming with us?' said the woman. And then she said, quietly, looking around secretively, 'I won't say anything. You can't give up now. You're worried about your daughter-in-law. I know,' she said.

The old man resented that.

'That doesn't worry me,' he said.

'You ought to think of them,' she said. 'You ought to.'

There was a shout of vulgar laughter from the wild young man and his friends. They had seen the two young lovers a long way off walking slowly, with all the time in the world, towards the coach. They had been off on their own.

'Worn yourselves out up in the fields?' bawled the wild young man and he got the driver to sound the horn on the wheel insistently at them.

'You can ring from my place,' said the woman.

The old man put on his air of being offended.

'You might buy my house,' she tempted.

The two lovers arrived and everyone laughed. The girl – so like his wife when she was young – smiled at him.

'No. I can get the train back from Brighton,' the old man said.

'Get in,' called the driver.

The old man assembled seventy years of dignity. He did this because dignity seemed to make him invisible. He gave a lift to the woman's elbow, he followed her, he looked for a seat and when she made room for him beside her, invisibly he sat there. She laughed hungrily, showing all her teeth. He gave a very wide sudden smile. The coach load chattered and some began to sing and shout and the young couple, getting into a clinch again, slept. The coach started and shook off the last of the towny places, whipped through short villages, passed pubs with animal names, The Fox, The Red Lion, The Dog and Duck, The Greyhound and one with a new sign, The Dragon. It tunnelled under miles of trees, breathed afresh in scampering fields and thirty miles of greenery, public and private; until, slowly, in an hour or so, the bald hills near the sea came up and, under them, distant slabs of chalk. Further and further the coach went and the bald hills grew taller and nearer.

The woman gazed disapprovingly at the young couple and was about to say something to the old man when, suddenly, at the sight of his spry profile, she began to think – in freezing panic – of criminals. A man like this was just the kind, outwardly respectable, who would go down to Hampton's Garden Party to case the place – as she had read – pass as a member of the staff, steal jewellery, or plan a huge burglary. Or come to her house and bash her. The people who lived only a mile and a half from where she lived had had burglars when they were away; someone had been watching the house. They believed it was someone who had heard the house was for sale. Beside her own front door, behind a bush, she kept an iron bar. She always picked it up before she got her key out – in case. She saw herself now suddenly hitting out with it passionately, so that her heart raced, then having bashed the old man, she calmed down; or rather she sailed into one of her exalted moods. She was wearing a heavy silver ring with a large brown stone in it, a stone which looked violet in some lights, and she said in her most genteel, faraway voice:

'When I was in India, an Indian prince gave this ring to me when my husband died. It is very rare. It is one of those rings they wear for protection. He loved my husband. He gave it to me. They believe in magic.'

She took it off and gave it to the old man.

'I always wear it. The people down the road were burgled.'

The old man looked at the ring. It was very ugly and he gave it back to her.

'What fools women are,' he thought and felt a huge access of strength. But aloud he said:

'Very nice.' And not to be outdone, he said: 'My wife died in the Azores.'

She took a deep breath. The coach had broken through the hills and now cliffs of red houses had built up on either side and the city trees and gardens grew thicker and richer. The sunlight seemed to splash down in waves between them and over them. She grasped his arm.

'I can smell the sea already!' she said. 'What are you going to tell your daughter-in-law when you ring up? I told the driver to stop at the station.'

'Tell them?' said the old man. A brilliant idea occurred to him. 'I'll tell them I just dropped in on the Canary Islands,' he said.

The woman let go of his arm and, after one glance, choked with laughter.

'Why not?' he said grinning. 'They ask too many questions. Where have you been? What are you doing? Or I might say Boulogne. Why not?'

'Well, it's nearer,' she said. 'But you must explain.'

The wild young man suddenly shouted:

'Where's he taking us now?' as the coach turned off the main road.

'He's dropping us at the station,' the woman called out boldly. And indeed, speeding no more, grunting down side streets, the coach made for the station and stopped at the entrance to the station yard.

'Here we are,' she said. 'I'll get my car.'

She pulled him by the sleeve to the door and he helped her out.

They stood on the pavement, surprised to see the houses and shops of the city stand still, every window looking at them. Brusquely cutting them off, the coach bumped away at once downhill and left them to watch it pass out of sight. The old man blinked, staring at the last of the coach, and the woman's face aged.

It was the moment to be memorable, but he was so taken aback by her heavy look that he said:

'You ought to have stayed on, gone to the party.'

'No,' she said, shaking brightness on to the face. 'I'll get my car. It was just seeing your life drive off – don't you feel that sometimes?'

'No,' he said. 'Not mine. Theirs.' And he straightened up, looked at his watch and then down the long hill. He put out his hand.

'I'm going to have a look at the sea.'

And indeed, in a pale blue wall on this July day, the sea showed between the houses. Or perhaps it was the sky. Hard to tell which.

She said, 'Wait for me. I'll drive you down. I tell you what – I'll get my car. We'll drive to my house and have a cup of tea or a drink and then you can telephone from there and I'll bring you back in for your train.'

He still hesitated.

'I dreaded that journey. You made me laugh,' she said.

And that is what they did. He admired her managing arms and knees as she drove out of the city into the confusing lanes.

'It's nice of you to come. I get nervous going back,' she said as they turned into the drive of one of the ugliest bungalows he had ever seen, on top of the Downs, close to a couple of ragged firs torn and bent by the wind. A cat raced them to the door. Close to it, she showed him the iron bar she kept behind the bush. A few miles away between a dip in the Downs was the pale blue sea again, shaped like her lower lip.

There were her brass Indian objects on the wall of the sitting-room; on the mantelpiece and, leaning against the mirror he had walked through, was the photograph of her husband. Pull down a few walls, reface the front, move out the furniture, he thought, that's what you'd have to do, when she went off to another room and came back with the tea tray, wearing a white dress with red poppies on it.

'Now telephone,' she said. 'I'll get the number.' But she did not give him the instrument until she heard a child answer it. That killed her last suspicion. She heard him speak to his daughter-in-law and when he put the telephone down:

'I want £21,000 for the house,' she said grandly.

The sum was so preposterous that it seemed to explode in his head and made him spill his tea in his saucer.

'If I decide to sell,' she said, noticing his shock.

'If anyone offers you that,' he said drily, 'I advise you to jump at it.'

They regarded each other with disappointment.

'I'll show you the garden. My husband worked hard in it,' she said. 'Are you a gardener?'

'Not any longer,' he said as he followed her sulking across the lawn. She was sulking too. A thin film of cloud came over the late afternoon sky.

'Well, if you're ever interested let me know,' she said. 'I'll drive you to the station.'

And she did, taking him the long way round the coast road and there indeed was the sea, the real sea, all of it, spread out like the skirt of some lazy old landlady with children playing all along the fringes on the beaches. He liked being with the woman in the car, but he was sad his day was ending.

'I feel better,' she said. 'I think I'll go to Hampton's after all,' she said watching him. 'I feel like a spree.'

But he did not rise. Twenty-one thousand! The ideas women have! At the station he shook hands and she said:

'Next time you come to Brighton . . .' and she touched his rose with her finger. The rose was drooping. He got on the train.

'Who is this lady-friend who keeps ringing you up from Brighton?' his daughter-in-law asked in her lowing voice several times in the following weeks. Always questions.

'A couple I met at Frenchy's,' he said on the spur of the moment.

'You didn't say you'd seen Frenchy. How is he?' his son said.

'Didn't I?' said the old man. 'I might go down to see them next week. But I don't know. Frenchy's heard of a house.'

But the old man knew that what he needed was not a house.

Our Wife

I agree that my wife is a noise and a nuisance, especially in a seaport and sailing place like Southampton. Even her little eyes long for trouble. People come down to sail at the weekend, clumping about in gum boots and sweaters, and they hear Molly's voice and ridicule by the quay: 'Stupid yachting people! Look at *him*. He's missed the mooring twice. They can't even sail.'

In the restaurant – it is called The Ship – it is ten to one she will be shouting, and then she'll stop dead. 'Why does everyone stare?' she says.

'I expect it is because your conversation is more interesting than theirs,' I say.

And Trevor, who is with us, of course, and who always repeats her last phrase or mine, slaps his eager knee and says, 'Yes, more interesting.'

'After all, you *were* talking about my first wife,' I say.

Another slap from Trevor, who grins and says, 'Your first wife!'

Molly is as noisy as a guttersnipe. Or as Jack (I remember) once said, 'As noisy as a blowlamp, but pretty.' Jack was her first husband.

The noise is what has attracted us all to her. We have loved it. She has opinions about everything. She loves an argument. Anything will do. In the old days, I remember, she started a row about whether Jack and I were the same height. He was, in fact, exactly the same height as myself – six feet one and a half inches. She wouldn't have it. About height she is a fanatic. She is under five feet high, and one of her boasts is that her father was the shortest captain in the Royal Navy. I can see her getting up on a chair in the sitting-room to peer at the pencil marks we had made on the wall. Standing on the chair, she was the same height as ourselves. This wonder silenced her, but when I helped her down she was arguing again. Our ruler was wrong and so was the tape measure – the taunts shot up at us like a boy's pellets. Jack and I stood looking like a pair of fools who had outgrown our strength, while she went on to say that most of the weights and measures used in shops were fraudulent.

[928]

'They probably are,' Jack said.

'There you are,' she jeered at me.

'Jack's right,' I said.

She gaped at us. 'I see,' she said. 'You've fixed it between you.'

Those were happy days.

That memory of Jack and me standing against the wall ten years ago takes me to something else – what he said in a pub in the little place on the Kent coast where they then lived. She was sitting on a bar stool between two men who were arguing with her about sailing – her father, the Captain, had been a tartar about boat behaviour when she was a child, and she hated sailing more than anything – and Jack and I heard her say to one of them, 'You want cooling down', and she put her hand out for the ice bucket. If she had been tall enough, she would have reached it and emptied it over their heads.

Jack was ill, as he often was in those days. In the lazy detached, speculative voice of the very sick, he said, 'See that? Two of them. Molly is a girl who needs two husbands at a time.'

He had seen something I had never noticed, and he said this with a little malice. He was either warning or defining me – or even arranging for the succession.

I am a construction engineer and I was working near their village on a new dock for tankers that were being built in this marsh country. I was a widower living in lodgings, without much to do in my spare time except play about with my boat. All those attacks on people who sailed were really attacks on me. It was one of the bonds between us – her hatred of my boat. She and Jack lived in an old house in the village that had become a hell of trucks and bulldozers on the way to the dock. I got to know Jack and Molly when a big tree was blown down in a gale in their garden and made a large gash in a brick wall. I talked to them and very soon I was offering to clear up the mess. Molly's husband was not strong enough. He was hacking at the tree with a weak man's fury, and was soon exhausted. I got a machine from the dock, and soon they were watching me work. I am a practical man. I'm good at things like that. The noise of the machine drowned her opinion of what I was doing. All she could do was to shake her brown hair.

In the following evenings, I rebuilt the wall and she stood arguing that it was 'only a theory' that plumb lines hang straight. After that job was done I was captured. It was an old house, and soon I was mending doors, unstopping drains, relagging pipes, putting in washers, repairing their car. I even painted a door bright blue after she and Jack quarrelled about the colours. And all the time she was arguing about how our dock would pollute the river, destroy the countryside, and drive away the bird life.

'Think of the tankers bringing oil for your car,' I'd say.

Then she would turn on Jack's doctors, on hospitals, and then on Jack and me. Men were always up to something. 'You can't deny it,' she would say. 'Look at Jack. Look at you. It's guilt.'

I don't know what she meant by 'guilt' and I don't think Jack did, either, but it made us feel more interesting. She'd get on to 'guilt' and say Jack was oversexed, or turn about and say he was undersexed. Or that he threw money away. Or never spent a penny. Or was shut up in himself. Or perpetually running after other women. She wore her hair short and had the habit of giving a nervous sniff in the middle of her sentences – an original and wistful sound in the general clatter which attracted me – and her face would go very red, while her mouth went sputtering gaily away like a little motor-bike. Jack listened to her, blinking busily as if he were taking notes. After a tirade, he'd get up, give a nod, and say quietly, 'She's an old character.' And he would go off, leaving me with her. I would often get up to go with him but she would stop me.

'Stay here. He's going to sit on the seawall. Leave him alone. It may be a poem.'

For Jack was a poet; here was the fascination for me. In my trade I'd never run across a poet. Goodness knows how they lived – he read for publishers, I think – but every so often he would go up to his room or sit on the seawall and, as if he were some industrious hen, he would (as I once said) lay a poem. Molly was angry with me when I said that. She allowed no one to make jokes about his poems except herself.

I wish I had not made this joke, for in a few months his health got very bad. He collapsed. It was I who took him to hospital. I thought he simply had an ulcer. He sat up in bed with a tube in his mouth and I tried to cheer him up.

'You must not make me laugh,' he said. 'It will tear the stitches.'

In a few days he came home, walked down the village street, and took a glass of whisky when he got back, and that night he died.

The first thing Molly said to me was indignant. 'He borrowed five pounds from me this morning,' she said.

Then she became exalted and tender. 'It was wonderful that he left the hospital the day before that nurse who was so good to him was leaving. She couldn't bear the matron. No one could.'

Then her grief overcame her. 'I can't bear it,' she wept. 'I can't believe he isn't upstairs now.'

'Neither can I,' I said. 'I've never felt like this before.'

I loved Jack. I loved her. I had, I felt, been married to both of them.

'The lock on the wardrobe door has gone again,' she suddenly said, angrily weeping and accusing me.

I put my arm round her shoulders. She had become motionless and heavy as lead with grief, and she shook my arm off.

'I'll go and look at it,' I said. 'Leave it to me.'

For a poor man, Jack had occasional reckless fits. He hankered after expensive antiques. This wardrobe I knew well, for I had three or four times tried to repair the lock for them. Owing to the weight of the doors, it was often going wrong. It was a huge oaken piece brought over from France by Huguenots – so Molly swore – in the seventeenth century and it stood in their bedroom. It was the first of Jack's purchases and she and he had a monumental row about it. She had been going to send it back to the shop, but Jack saved it in a very clever way; he wrote a poem about it. This made it sacred in her eyes. After this, he became a secret furniture buyer and had to store the stuff out of her sight, and once or twice I collected it for him.

'So that is what you and Jack were up to,' she said after he died. She admired our shadiness. To punish me – and Jack, too – she sold the lot, but not the wardrobe.

The furniture episode became another bond between us, especially because of the toings and froings of the sale, during the time of her grief. Her grief recalled mine when my wife had died, and we often talked about it. She would gaze and nod and talk quietly. She became, except for the tiny sniff, a soundless person. Slowly her grief passed. After a year, my

job at the dock came to an end. I was to be moved to the London office
and I started packing.

Molly's character suddenly returned to her when she saw my clothes
stacked on the table in my lodgings. 'It's a good thing!' she said. 'It will
get you away from that idiotic boat.'

My transfer to London was a victory for her opinion. She glittered with
victory.

'I'll take you out in it,' I said, 'for a last sail.'

I was astonished, even moved, by her reply. 'All right!' she said
defiantly, but I could see that, despite her victory, her lip was trembling.
I could see that she did not want me to leave, and I didn't want to leave
her. I knew that when we were out on the water and I was, perhaps,
coming about and making her duck the boom, I would be able to say
what I could not say to her on land. We set off, but soon it began to
blow, the sails rapped out, and the wind carried away everything she said.
She was indignant and frightened. When we got ashore, she said, 'You're
a masochist, like Jack. It is all guilt.'

'I'm going to sell her,' I said, looking down at the boat from the quay
wall. While we were out and I was putting in a reef, I had asked her to
marry me.

'When you sell it,' she said.

I sold it.

Unluckily for her, we hadn't been married for three months when the
firm moved me from London back to Southampton. There was the sea
again. There were those detested, lovely white tents dotted over the
water.

'All yachtsmen are liars,' she said when she saw them, accusing me of
arranging my transfer. I paid no attention to her; in fact, the trouble we
had moving the furniture to our house took her mind off it.

Our house at Southampton was small. I wanted to put the wardrobe –
she called it the *armoire* – on the ground floor, but she said it must go into
the bedroom. To get it up there I had to take out a tall window and put
a hoist in from an attic. The thing weighed a ton. It took two days and
three men to get it into the bedroom. It had been Jack's first extravagance
and Molly was very proud of the difficulty it caused. She stood in the
garden shouting at the men and came peering at it, to see they did not

damage it. In fact, the lock did scrape the brickwork when the thing was halfway in.

The scrape on the brickwork must have weakened the lock, or perhaps the damp summer affected the doors in some way, for they did not easily close. In the winter, there would be a sudden click and one door would swing forward. I put it right, and then, after a malicious lull, the wardrobe – the *armoire* I should say – would come open again. Sometimes I worked on the lock; sometimes I wedged and re-wedged the feet, blaming the slope of the floor.

In the end, I succeeded, and for a long time the thing was quiet. But one night when I was making love to Molly the door came groaning open like a hound.

'What's that?' said Molly pushing me away.

I paused in my efforts. 'It's only Jack,' I said. 'It's haunted.'

Now, why on earth I should have said such an appalling thing, and at such a moment, I cannot think. If there is one thing we all know, it is that you should never make a joke – if you call that a joke – when you are making love. I would have given anything to take the words back. Perhaps it was a sign that I was beginning to want help, as Jack had done. Hadn't he said she was a woman who needed two husbands?

The effect on Molly was surprising. She sat up, put on the light, and looking excitedly at the door, she laughed. '"Haunted" – that's very perceptive of you,' she said, admiring me.

I was shocked by her laugh and pushed her down again. (But, to be frank, love was a fitful thing with Molly. Now that we were married, she said I bullied her into it.) She got free of my arms, put on the light once more, gave herself a little shake like a dog, and gazed in a rapture of importance. 'It's weird,' she said. 'It *could* be haunted. Jack always said nothing is forgotten.'

Molly loved to sit up arguing in the middle of the night when I was exhausted. She said that all things were permeated by the people who had touched them. Now I made my second mistake. I said the *armoire* was probably alive with the hands of Huguenots. This idea annoyed her.

'It's very funny about you,' she said. 'I didn't know you were a jealous man. Or are you trying to change the subject?'

'Jack! Huguenots! All of you! Listen to this! I want help!' I cried to myself.

We were still arguing at three o'clock, when she changed round and said, 'I'm glad you're not a jealous man. That means a lot to me.'

I was carried away by this compliment and the softness of her voice. Only exhaustion could have put me off my guard.

Working in Southampton, I could see from my office window the sloping funnels of liners, the cranes dipping towards them, and, beyond that, the water. As I have said, there was always a sail or two in sight, and on week-ends there were scores of them. I had sometimes to go to the boatyards and there I would look with longing at some craft with beautiful lines on the stocks outside the sheds. The wings of the angry gulls and their quarrelling voices made me think of Molly with love, and it was while I was gazing in this weak mood at a beautiful, dark-blue thirty-foot sloop one afternoon that a man climbed out of her. He was a tall, lazy-voiced fellow, with a tired face, very slim and fair.

'She's lovely,' I said.

'Lovely,' he said.

'Cigarette?' I said.

'Cigarette? Thanks,' he said. 'I am selling her.'

'Selling her?' I said.

He nodded. I nodded. An interesting fellow – quiet, a listener. We walked round the boat and had a look inside.

'Frankly,' he said. 'I can't afford her. I've got to give her up. I've just bought an Aston-Martin. I can't run both.'

Speed was what he liked, he said. He liked to *move*. He gave a lick to his lip; he was a man like myself, a man giving up one thing for another. I sighed at our singular unity.

'We might do a deal – if I can persuade my wife,' I said.

'Ah,' he said, 'your wife.'

His name was Trevor. I asked him to come up to the house later and have a drink. 'But not a word,' I said.

Trevor was an understanding man.

'Who is this man you're bringing up here?' my wife said when I told her. 'One of your sailing friends – I know! What are you and he up to?'

'No,' I said. 'He's given up sailing. He can't afford it.'

One more victory was in my wife's small eyes. And when Trevor arrived, wearing a white pullover under his dandyish long jacket, and very narrow trousers, she looked from one to the other of us to see who was the taller. I saw her immediate interest. Without realising it, I was at the beginning of a masterstroke. I had brought to the house a tall man who had given up boats. She was excited by the arrival of an ally.

'My husband's mad about them, quite out of his mind,' she said to Trevor. 'He's thinking of them all the time. He's always up to something, hanging around boatyards – don't think I don't know. He pretends he's at the engineer's, but it's always a boat.'

'A boat,' said Trevor. There was a gentle, weary note in his voice, and it conveyed to her that mine was one of those infantile and tedious vices that afflict so many men and from which he was now free.

'Better than chasing women,' I said.

'Women!' she said. 'It's a substitute! Don't tell me.'

Trevor listened to us with appreciation as we wrangled. He lived alone, and he looked with pleasure at the excitements of home life. My wife, walking up and down and clattering on, with a glass in her hand, was adding to her victories, and Trevor occasionally glanced at me with private congratulation.

'I'll tell you what happened the other night!' she cried.

'We've got an old French *armoire* in our bedroom and the lock keeps going wrong. He makes out he's repaired it, but I don't know – it's weird! It opens every time we get into bed. Do you know what Tom said? He said, "I bet that's my first wife again." ' She gave a loud laugh. 'Look at his face. Guilt.'

'Guilt it must be,' I said.

'You've been married before?' said Trevor – his first original sentence. I felt gratitude to him for saying this; it created an intimacy.

'Of course he has,' said my wife. 'He keeps quiet about it. That's what is infuriating about him. He keeps so quiet.'

'Jack was quiet,' I said.

'No need to bring up Jack,' she said in her sacred voice.

'Who was Jack?' said Trevor.

'He was my husband,' she said, stopping with dignity. And then she turned on me. 'Tell him about your wife's iron boot,' she jeered.

'Iron boot!' said Trevor. He was overjoyed by her.

But she saw she had gone too far and calmed a little. 'Not actually an iron boot,' she said, and when she laughed her eyebrows were like a pair of wings. 'Her skates. He took her roller-skating – roller-skating, my dear! – and one came off and she fell over and he got engaged. Poor Tom.'

Then Trevor uttered his next original sentence to me: Why don't you mend the lock?'

'He's always mending it – or says he is,' she said. 'He's useless with his hands.'

'It's a French thing, very heavy, eighteenth century,' I said.

'Seventeenth,' she said. 'The Huguenots brought it over.'

'Full of Huguenots,' I said.

Trevor heard out this dispute, and then he uttered three original sentences. 'My mother has got one,' he said. 'We had a lot of trouble with it. I got it right in the end.'

I gazed at Trevor's hands. Like his voice they were limp and tired. They were long and thin.

'I wish you'd mend ours,' Molly said to him in a businesslike way. 'And then we'd get some sleep.' She gave me a sharp look.

'It's probably like my mother's,' Trevor said. 'They're all alike. I don't mind having a go. Tomorrow?'

I saw that I had found a treasure. The boat was as good as mine, if Trevor and I worked together on it. And there was more to it than the boat.

'There you are!' said Molly, sneering gaily at me at having an order obeyed as simply as that.

The following evening I found Trevor on the sofa in our sitting-room with a large broken-veined bruise on his forehead. He had mended the lock, but he had moved my wedges, and just as he was testing it the door swung open and hit him on the head. Molly was mopping the wound.

I elected him at once as Molly's additional husband.

Our life – or rather my life – is more peaceful now. I don't mean less noisy or less of a wrangle, but simply that Trevor now bears some of the burden. He comes round most evenings and if he misses a few days she is out after him to find out what he is up to.

'He has girls in his flat,' she says angrily when she comes back. 'I know! Making out he stays in and listens to records. He never listens to ours!'

'He likes noise,' I tell her. 'He said so last time when he was here. It's company.'

Trevor turns up again, and he and I say nothing about our transaction. She has been out with him in his racing car, which terrifies her, and to me she says: 'It's nothing but sex. A substitute. You defend him, of course.'

It is true that when he runs her up to London for the day I go sailing. When he brings her back, she says: 'Racing drivers are a lot of impotent morons.'

I say to Trevor: 'She's an old character.'

'Character,' says Trevor, slapping his knee at the word. Then, with a sly look at me – for he likes danger as much as I do – he perhaps says, 'Let's go and eat at The Ship.' (It is near the mooring where I keep my secret boat.)

We drive down, and at the first sight of a sail she starts about 'the stinking yachtsmen'. At dinner, she says, in a voice that makes everyone in the restaurant stop eating and stare at us, 'Guilt, that is what it is! There is something going on between you two. Men!'

And when her voice drops for a second, she entrances both of us with that other noise, the little dog-like sniff.

The Lady from Guatemala

Friday afternoon about four o'clock, the week's work done, time to kill; the editor disliked this characterless hour when everyone except his secretary had left the building. Into his briefcase he had slipped some notes for a short talk he was going to give in a cheap London hall, worn by two generations of protest against this injustice or that, before he left by the night plane for Copenhagen. There his real lecture tour would begin and turn into a short holiday. Like a bored card player he sat shuffling his papers and resented that there was no one except his rude, hard-working secretary to give him a game.

The only company he had in his room – and it was a moody friend – was his portrait hanging behind him on the wall. He liked cunningly to draw people to say something reassuring about the picture. It was 'terribly good', as the saying is; he wanted to hear them say it lived up to him. There was a strange air of rivalry in it. It rather overdid the handsome mixture of sunburned satyrlike pagan and shady jealous Christian saint under the happy storm of white hair. His hair had been grey at thirty; at forty-seven, by a stroke of luck, it was silken white. His face was an actor's, the nose carved for dramatic occasions, the lips for the public platform. It was a face both elated and ravaged by the highest beliefs and doubts. He was energised by meeting this image in the morning and, enviously, he said goodbye to it at night. Its nights would be less tormented than his own. Now he was leaving it to run the paper in his absence.

'Here are your tickets,' his secretary breezed into the room. 'Copenhagen, Stockholm, Oslo, Berlin, Hamburg, Munich – the lot,' she said. She was mannerless to the point of being a curiosity.

She stepped away and wobbled her tongue in her cheek. She understood his restless state. She adored him; he drove her mad and she longed for him to go.

'Would you like to know what I've got outside?' she said. She had a malicious streak. 'A lady. A lady from Guatemala. Miss Mendoza. She has got a present for you. She worships you. I said you were busy. Shall I tell her to buzz off?'

The editor was proud of his tolerance in employing a girl so sportive and so familiar; her fair hair was thin and looked harassed, her spotty face set off the knowledge of his own handsomeness in face and behaviour.

'Guatemala! Of course I must see her!' he exclaimed. 'What *are* you thinking about? We ran three articles on Guatemala. Show her in.'

'It's your funeral,' said the girl and gave a vulgar click with her tongue. The editor was, in her words, 'a sucker for foreigners'; she was reminding him that the world was packed with native girls like herself as well.

All kinds of men and women came to see Julian Drood: politicians who spoke to him as if he were a meeting, quarrelling writers, people with causes, cranks and accusers, even criminals and the mad. They were opinions to him and he did not often notice what they were like. He knew they studied him and that they would go away boasting: 'I saw Julian Drood today and he said . . .' Still he had never seen any person quite like the one who now walked in. At first, because of her tweed hat, he thought she was a man and would have said she had a moustache. She was a stump, as square as a box, with tarry chopped-off hair, heavy eyebrows and yellow eyes set in her sallow skin like cut glass. She looked like some unsexed and obdurate statement about the future – or was it the beginning? – of the human race, long in the body, short in the legs and made of wood. She was wearing on this hot day a thick, bottle-green velvet dress. Indian blood obviously; he had seen such women in Mexico. She put out a wide hand to him; it could have held a shovel; in fact she was carrying a crumpled brown-paper bag.

'Please sit down,' he said. A pair of heavy feet moved her with a surprisingly light skip to a chair. She sat down stiffly and stared without expression, like geography.

'I know you are a very busy man,' she said. 'Thank you for sparing a minute for an unknown person.' She looked formidably unknown.

The words were nothing; but the voice! He had expected Spanish or broken English of some grating kind, but instead he heard the small, whispering, birdlike monotone of a shy English child.

'Yes, I *am* very busy,' he said. 'I've got to give a talk in an hour and then I'm off to lecture in Copenhagen . . . What can I do for you?'

'Copenhagen,' she said, noting it.

'Yes, yes, yes,' said the editor. 'I'm lecturing on apartheid.'

There are people who listen; there are people upon whom anything said seems not to be heard but, rather, to be stamped or printed. She was also receiving the impress of the walls, the books, the desk, the carpet, the windows of the room, memorising every object. At last, like a breathless child, she said: 'In Guatemala I have dreamed of this for years. I'm saying to myself, "Even if I could just see the *building* where it all happens!" I didn't dare think I would be able to *speak* to Julian Drood. It is like a dream to me. "If I see him I will tell him," I said, "what this building and what his articles have done for my country."'

'It's a bad building. Too small,' he said. 'We're thinking of selling it.'

'Oh no,' she said. 'I have flown across the ocean to see it. And to thank you.'

The word thank came out like a kiss.

'From Guatemala? To thank me?' The editor smiled.

'To thank you from the bottom of our hearts for those articles.' The little voice seemed to sing.

'So people read the paper in Guatemala,' said the editor, congratulating that country and moving a manuscript on to another pile on his desk.

'Only a few,' she said. 'The important few. You are keeping us alive in all these dark years. You are holding the torch of freedom burning. You are a beacon of civilisation in our darkness.'

The editor sat taller in his chair. Certainly he was vain, but he was a good man. Virtue is not often rewarded. A nationalist? Or not? he wondered. He looked at the ceiling, where, as usual – for he knew everything – he found the main items of the Guatemalan situation. He ran over them like a tune on the piano. 'Financial colonialism,' he said, 'foreign monopoly, uprooted peasants, rise of nationalism, the dilemma of the mountain people, the problem of the coast. Bananas.

'It is years since I've eaten a banana,' he said.

The woman's yellow eyes were not looking at him directly yet. She was still memorising the room and her gaze now moved to his portrait.

He was dabbling in the figures of the single-crop problem when she interrupted him.

'The women of Guatemala,' she said, addressing the portrait, 'will never be able to repay their debt to you.'

'The women?'

He could not remember; was there anything about women in those articles?

'It gives us hope. "Now," I am saying, "the world will listen,"' she said. 'We are slaves. Man-made laws, the priests, bad traditions hold us down. *We* are the victims of apartheid, too.'

And now she looked directly at him.

'Ah,' said the editor, for interruptions bored him. 'Tell me about that.'

'I know from experience,' said the woman. 'My father was Mexican, my mother was an English governess. I know what she suffered.'

'And what do you *do?*' said the editor. 'I gather you are not married?'

At this sentence, the editor saw that something like a coat of varnish glistened on the woman's wooden face.

'Not after what I saw of my mother's life. There were ten of us. When my father had to go away on business, he locked her and all of us in the house. She used to shout for help from the window, but no one did anything. People just came down the street and stood outside and stared and then walked away. She brought us up. She was worn out. When I was fifteen, he came home drunk and beat her terribly. She was used to that, but this time she died.'

'What a terrible story. Why didn't she go to the Consul? Why –'

'He beat her because she had dyed her hair. She had fair hair and she thought if she dyed her hair black like the other women he went with, he would love her again,' said the childish voice.

'Because she dyed her hair?' said the editor.

The editor never really listened to astonishing stories of private life. They seemed frivolous to him. What happened publicly in the modern world was far more extravagant. So he only half listened to this tale. Quickly, whatever he heard turned into paragraphs about something else and moved on to general questions. He was wondering if Miss Mendoza had the vote and which party she voted for. Was there an Indian bloc? He looked at his watch. He knew how to appear to listen, to charm, ask a jolly question and then lead his visitors to the door before they knew the interview was over.

'It was a murder,' said the woman complacently.

The editor suddenly woke up to what she was saying.

'But you are telling me she was *murdered*!' he exclaimed.

She nodded. The fact seemed of no further interest to her. She was pleased she had made an impression. She picked up her paper bag and out of it she pulled a tin of biscuits and put it on his desk.

'I have brought you a present,' she said, 'with the gratitude of the women of Guatemala. It is Scottish shortbread. From Guatemala.' She smiled proudly at the oddity of this fact. 'Open it.'

'Shall I open it? Yes, I will. Let me offer you one,' he humoured her.

'No,' she said. 'They are for you.'

Murder. Biscuits, he thought. She *is* mad.

The editor opened the tin and took out a biscuit and began to nibble. She watched his teeth as he bit; once more, she was memorising what she saw. She was keeping watch. Just as he was going to get up and make a last speech to her, she put out a short arm and pointed to his portrait.

'That is not you,' she pronounced. Having made him eat, she was now in command of him.

'But it is,' he said. 'I think it is very good. Don't you?'

'It is wrong,' she said.

'Oh.' He was offended and that brought out his saintly look.

'There is something missing,' she said. 'Now I am seeing you I know what it is.'

She got up.

'Don't go,' said the editor. 'Tell me what you miss. It was in the academy, you know.'

He was beginning to think she was a fortune teller.

'I am a poet,' she said. 'I see vision in you. I see a leader. That picture is the picture of two people, not one. But you are one man. You are a god to us. You understand that apartheid exists for women too.'

She held out her prophetic hand. The editor switched to his wise, pagan look and his sunny hand held hers.

'May I come to your lecture this evening?' she said. 'I asked your secretary about it.'

'Of course, of course, of course. Yes, yes, yes,' he said and walked with her to the outer door of the office. There they said goodbye. He watched her march away slowly, on her thick legs, like troops.

The editor went into his secretary's room. The girl was putting the cover on her typewriter.

'Do you know,' he said, 'that woman's father killed her mother because she dyed her hair?'

'She told me. You copped something there, didn't you? What d'you bet me she doesn't turn up in Copenhagen tomorrow, two rows from the front?' the rude girl said.

She was wrong. Miss Mendoza was in the fifth row at Copenhagen. He had not noticed her at the London talk and he certainly had not seen her on the plane; but there she was, looking squat, simple and tarry among the tall fair Danes. The editor had been puzzled to know who she was for he had a poor visual memory. For him, people's faces merged into the general plain lineaments of the convinced. But he did become aware of her when he got down from the platform and when she stood, well planted, on the edge of the small circle where his white head was bobbing to people who were asking him questions. She listened, turning her head possessively and critically to each questioner and then to him, expectantly. She nodded with reproof at the questioner when he replied. She owned him. Closer and closer she came, into the inner circle. He was aware of a smell like nutmeg. She was beside him. She had a long envelope in her hand. The chairman was saying to him:

'I think we should take you to the party now.' Then people went off in three cars. There she was at the party.

'We have arranged for your friend . . .' said the host. 'We have arranged for you to sit next to your friend.'

'Which friend?' the editor began. Then he saw her, sitting beside him. The Dane lit a candle before them. Her skin took on, to the editor's surprised eye, the gleam of an idol. He was bored; he liked new women to be beautiful when he was abroad.

'Haven't we met somewhere?' he said. 'Oh yes. I remember. You came to see me. Are you on holiday here?'

'No,' she said. 'I drink at the fount.'

He imagined she was taking the waters.

'Fount?' said the editor, turning to others at the table. 'Are there many spas here?' He was no good at metaphors.

He forgot her and was talking to the company. She said no more during the evening until she left with the other guests, but he could hear her deep breath beside him.

'I have a present for you,' she said before she went, giving him the envelope.

'More biscuits?' he said waggishly.

'It is the opening canto of my poem,' she said.

'I'm afraid,' said the editor, 'we rarely publish poetry.'

'It is not for publication. It is dedicated to you.'

And she went off.

'Extraordinary,' said the editor, watching her go; and, appealing to his hosts, 'That woman gave me a poem.'

He was put out by their polite, knowing laughter. It often puzzled him when people laughed.

The poem went into his pocket and he forgot it until he got to Stockholm. She was standing at the door of the lecture hall there as he left. He said: 'We seem to be following each other around.'

And to a minister who was wearing a white tie: 'Do you know Miss Mendoza from Guatemala? She is a poet,' and escaped while they were bowing.

Two days later, she was at his lecture in Oslo. She had moved to the front row. He saw her after he had been speaking for a quarter of an hour. He was so irritated that he stumbled over his words. A rogue phrase had jumped into his mind – 'murdered his wife' – and his voice, always high, went up one more semitone and he very nearly told the story. Some ladies in the audience were propping a cheek on their forefinger as they leaned their heads to regard his profile. He made a scornful gesture at his audience. He had remembered what was wrong. It had nothing to do with murder; he had simply forgotten to read her poem.

Poets, the editor knew, were remorseless. The one sure way of getting rid of them was to read their poems at once. They stared at you with pity and contempt as you read and argued with offence when you told them

which lines you admired. He decided to face her. After the lecture he
went up to her.

'How lucky,' he said. 'I thought you said you were going to Hamburg.
Where are you staying? Your poem is on my conscience.'

'Yes?' the small girl's voice said. 'When will you come and see me?'

'I'll ring you up,' he said, drawing back.

'I'm going to hear you in Berlin,' she said with meaning.

The editor considered her. There was a look of magnetised inhuman
committal in her eyes. They were not so much looking at him as reading
him. She knew his future.

Back in the hotel, he read the poem. The message was plain. It began:

I have seen the liberator
The foe of servitude
The godhead.

He read on, skipping two pages and put out his hand for the telephone.
First he heard a childish intake of breath, and then the small determined
voice. He smiled at the instrument; he told her in a forgiving voice how
good the poem was. The breathing became heavy, like the sound of the
ocean. She was steaming or flying to him across the Caribbean, across
the Atlantic.

'You have understood my theme,' she said. 'Women are being history.
I am the history of my country.'

She went on and boredom settled on him. His cultivated face turned
to stone.

'Yes, yes, I see. Isn't there an old Indian belief that a white god
will come from the East to liberate the people? Extraordinary, quite
extraordinary. When you get back to Guatemala you must go on with
your poem.'

'I am doing it now. In my room,' she said. 'You are my inspiration. I
am working every night since I saw you.'

'Shall I post this copy to your hotel in Berlin?' he said.

'No, give it to me when we meet there.'

'Berlin!' the editor exclaimed. Without thinking, without realising what
he was saying, the editor said: 'But I'm *not* going to Berlin. I'm going
back to London at once.'

'When?' said the woman's voice. 'Could I come and talk to you now?'

'I'm afraid not. I'm leaving in half an hour,' said the editor. Only when he put the telephone receiver back did the editor realise that he was sweating and that he had told a lie. He had lost his head. Worse, in Berlin, if she were there, he would have to invent another lie.

It *was* worse than that. When he got to Berlin she was not there. It was perverse of him – but he was alarmed. He was ashamed. The shadiness of the saint replaced the pagan on his handsome face; indeed, on the race question after his lecture, a man in the audience said he was evasive.

But in Hamburg at the end of the week, her voice spoke up from the back of the hall: 'I would like to ask the great man who is filling all our hearts this evening whether he is thinking that the worst racists are the oppressors and deceivers of women.'

She delivered her blow and sat down, disappearing behind the shoulders of bulky German men.

The editor's clever smiles went; he jerked back his heroic head as if he had been shot; he balanced himself by touching the table with the tips of his fingers. He lowered his head and drank a glass of water, splashing it on his tie. He looked for help.

'My friends,' he wanted to say, 'that woman is following me. She has followed me all over Scandinavia and Germany. I had to tell a lie to escape from her in Berlin. She is pursuing me. She is writing a poem. She is trying to force me to read it. She murdered her father – I mean, her father murdered her mother. She is mad. Someone must get me out of this.'

But he pulled himself together and sank to that point of desperation to which the mere amateurs and hams of public speaking sink.

'A good question,' he said. Two irreverent laughs came from the audience, probably from the American or English colony. He had made a fool of himself again. Floundering, he at last fell back on one of those drifting historical generalisations that so often rescued him. He heard his voice sailing into the eighteenth century, throwing in Rousseau, gliding on to Tom Paine and *The Rights of Man*.

'Is there a way out of the back of this hall?' he said to the chairman afterwards. 'Could someone keep an eye on that woman? She is following me.'

They got him out by a back door.

At his hotel, a poem was slipped under his door.

Suckled on Rousseau
Strong in the divine message of Nature
Clasp Guatemala in your arms.

'Room 363' was written at the end. She was staying in the same hotel! He rang down to the desk, said he would receive no calls and demanded to be put on the lowest floor, close to the main stairs and near the exit. Safe in his new room he changed the time of his flight to Munich.

There was a note for him at the desk.

'Miss Mendoza left this for you,' said the clerk, 'when she left for Munich this morning.'

Attached to the note was a poem. It began:

Ravenous in the long night of the centuries
I waited for my liberator
He shall not escape me.

His hand was shaking as he tore up the note and the poem and made for the door. The page boy came running after him with the receipt for his bill which he had left on the desk.

The editor was a well-known man. Reporters visited him. He was often recognised in hotels. People spoke his name aloud when they saw it on passenger lists. Cartoonists were apt to lengthen his neck when they drew him, for they had caught his habit of stretching it at parties or meetings, hoping to see and be seen.

But not on the flight to Munich. He kept his hat on and lowered his chin. He longed for anonymity. He had a sensation he had not had for years, not, indeed, since the pre-thaw days in Russia: that he was being followed not simply by one person but by dozens. Who were all those passengers on the plane? Had those two men in raincoats been at his hotel?

He made for the first cab he saw at the airport. At the hotel he went to the desk.

'Mr and Mrs Julian Drood,' the clerk said. 'Yes. Four-fifteen. Your wife has arrived.'

'My wife!' In any small group the actor in him woke up. He turned from the clerk to a stranger standing at the desk beside him and gave a yelp of hilarity. 'But I am not married!' The stranger drew away. The editor turned to a couple also standing there. 'I'm saying I am not married,' he said. He turned about to see if he could gather more listeners.

'This is ludicrous,' he said. No one was interested and loudly to the clerk he said: 'Let me see the register. There is no Mrs Drood.'

The clerk put on a worldly look to soothe any concern about the respectability of the hotel in the people who were waiting. But there, on the card, in her writing, were the words: Mr and Mrs J. Drood – London.

The editor turned dramatically to the group.

'A forgery,' he cried. He laughed, inviting all to join the comedy. 'A woman travelling under my name.'

The clerk and the strangers turned away. In travel one can rely on there being one mad Englishman everywhere.

The editor's face darkened when he saw he had exhausted human interest.

'Four-fifteen. Baggage,' called the clerk.

A young porter came up quick as a lizard and picked up the editor's bags.

'Wait. Wait,' said the editor. Before a young man so smoothly uniformed he had the sudden sensation of standing there with most of his clothes off. When you arrived at the Day of Judgment there would be some worldly youth, humming a tune you didn't know the name of, carrying not only your sins but your virtues indifferently in a couple of bags and gleaming with concealed knowledge.

'I have to telephone,' the editor said.

'Over there,' said the young man as he put the bags down. The editor did not walk to the telephone but to the main door of the hotel. He considered the freedom of the street. The sensible thing to do was to leave the hotel at once, but he knew that the woman would be at his lecture that night. He would have to settle the matter once and for all now. So he turned back to the telephone box. It stood there empty, like a trap. He walked past it. He hated the glazed, whorish, hypocritically impersonal look of telephone boxes. They were always unpleasantly warmed by random emotions left behind in them. He turned back: the thing was still empty. 'Surely,' he wanted to address the people coming and going in the foyer, 'someone among you wants to telephone?' It was wounding that not one person there was interested in his case. It was as if he had written an article that no one had read. Even the porter had gone. His two bags rested against the desk. He and they had ceased to be news.

He began to walk up and down quickly but this stirred no one. He stopped in every observable position, not quite ignored now, because his handsome hair always made people turn.

The editor silently addressed them again. 'You've entirely missed the point of my position. Everyone knows who has read what I have written, that I am opposed on principle to the whole idea of marriage. That is what makes this woman's behaviour so ridiculous. To think of getting *married* in a world that is in one of the most ghastly phases of its history is puerile.'

He gave a short sarcastic laugh. The audience was indifferent.

The editor went into the telephone box and, leaving the door open for all to hear, he rang her room.

'Julian Drood,' he said brusquely. 'It is important that I should see you at once, privately, in your room.'

He heard her breathing. The way the human race thought it was enough if they breathed! Ask an important question and what happens? Breath. Then he heard the small voice: it made a splashing, confusing sound.

'Oh,' it said. And more breath: 'Yes.'

The two words were the top of a wave that is about to topple and come thumping over on to the sand and then draws back with a long, insidious hiss.

'Please,' she added. And the word was the long, thirsty hiss.

The editor was surprised that his brusque manner was so wistfully treated.

'Good heavens,' he thought, 'she *is* in that room!' And because she was invisible and because of the distance of the wire between them, he felt she was pouring down it, head first, mouth open, swamping him. When he put the telephone down, he scratched his ear; a piece of her seemed to be coiled there. The editor's ear had heard passion. And passion at its climax.

[949]

He had often heard of passion. He had often been told of it. He had seen it in opera. He had friends – who usually came to him for advice – who were entangled in it. He had never felt it and he did not feel it now; but when he walked from the telephone box to the lift, he saw his role had changed. The woman was not a mere nuisance – she was something like Tosca. The pagan became doggish, the saint furtive as he entered the lift.

'Ah,' the editor burst out aloud to the liftman. '*Les femmes.*' The German did not understand French.

The editor got out of the lift and, passing one watchful white door after another, came to 415. He knocked twice. When there was no answer, he opened the door.

He seemed to blunder into an invisible wall of spice and scent and stepped back, thinking he had made a mistake. A long-legged rag doll with big blue eyes looked at him from the bed, a half-unpacked suitcase was on the floor with curious clothes hanging out of it. A woman's shoes were tipped out on the sofa.

And then, with her back to a small desk where she had been writing, stood Miss Mendoza. Or, rather, the bottle-green dress, the boxlike figure were Miss Mendoza's; the head was not. Her hair was no longer black; it was golden. The idol's head had been chopped off and was replaced by a woman's. There was no expression on the face until the shock on the editor's face passed across to hers; then a searching look of horror seized her, the look of one caught in an outrage. She lowered her head, suddenly cowed and frightened. She quickly grabbed a stocking she had left on the bed and held it behind her back.

'You are angry with me,' she said, holding her head down like an obstinate child.

'You are in *my* room. You have no right to be here. I *am* very angry with you. What do you mean by registering in my name – apart from anything else it is illegal. You know that, don't you? I must ask you to go or I shall have to take steps . . .'

Her head was still lowered. Perhaps he ought not to have said the last sentence. The blond hair made her look pathetic.

'Why did you do this?'

'Because you would not see me,' she said. 'You have been cruel to me.'

'But don't you realise, Miss Mendoza, what you are doing? I hardly know you. You have followed me all over Europe; you have badgered me. You take my room. You pretend to be my wife . . .'

'Do you hate me?' she muttered.

Damn, thought the editor. I ought to have changed my hotel at once.

'I know nothing about you,' he said.

'Don't you want to know about me? What I am like? I know everything about you,' she said, raising her head.

The editor was confused by the rebuke. His fit of acting passed. He looked at his watch.

'A reporter is coming to see me in half an hour,' he said.

'I shall not be in the way,' she said. 'I will go out.'

'*You* will go out!' said the editor.

Then he understood where he was wrong. He had – perhaps being abroad addressing meetings, speaking to audiences with only one mass face had done this – forgotten how he dealt with difficult people.

He pushed the shoes to one end of the sofa to find himself a place. One shoe fell to the floor, but after all it was his room, he had a right to sit down.

'Miss Mendoza, you are ill,' he said.

She looked down quickly at the carpet.

'I am not,' she said.

'You are ill and, I think, very unhappy.' He put on his wise voice.

'No,' she said in a low voice. 'Happy. You are talking to me.'

'You are a very intelligent woman,' he said. 'And you will understand what I am going to say. Gifted people like yourself are very vulnerable. You live in the imagination, and that exposes one. I know that.'

'Yes,' she said. 'You see all the injustices of the world. You bleed from them.'

'I? Yes,' said the editor with his saint's smile. But he recovered from the flattery. 'I am saying something else. Your imagination is part of your gift as a poet, but in real life it has deluded you.'

'It hasn't done that. I see you as you are.'

'Please sit down,' said the editor. He could not bear her standing over him. 'Close the window, there is too much noise.'

She obeyed. The editor was alarmed to see the zipper of her dress was half undone and he could see the top of some garment with ominous lace on it. He could not bear untidy women. He saw his case was urgent. He made a greater effort to be kind.

'It was very kind of you to come to my lectures. I hope you found them interesting. I think they went down all right – good questions. One never knows, of course. One arrives in a strange place and one sees a hall full of people one doesn't know – and you won't believe me perhaps because I've done it scores of times – but one likes to see a face that one recognises. One feels lost, at first . . .'

She looked hopeful.

This was untrue. The editor never felt lost. Once on his feet he had the impression that he was talking to the human race. He suffered with it. It was the general human suffering that had ravaged his face.

'But, you know,' he said sternly, 'our feelings deceive us. Especially at certain times of life. I was worried about you. I saw that something was wrong. These things happen very suddenly. God knows why. You see someone whom you admire perhaps – it seems to happen to women more than men – and you project some forgotten love on him. You think you love him, but it is really some forgotten image. In your case, I would say, probably some image of your father whom you have hated all these years for what he did when you were a child. And so, as people say, one becomes obsessed or infatuated. I don't like the word. What we mean is that one is not in love with a real man or woman but a vision sent out by oneself. One can think of many examples . . .'

The editor was sweating. He wished he hadn't asked her to close the window. He knew his mind was drifting toward historic instances. He wondered if he would tell her the story of Jane Carlyle, the wife of the historian, who had gone to hear the famous Father Matthew speak at a temperance meeting and how, hysterical and exalted, she had rushed to the platform to kiss his boots. Or there were other instances. For the moment he couldn't remember them. He decided on Mrs Carlyle. It was a mistake.

'Who is Mrs Carlyle?' said Miss Mendoza suspiciously. 'I would never kiss any man's feet.'

'Boots,' said the editor. 'It was on a public platform.'

'Or boots,' Miss Mendoza burst out. 'Why are you torturing me? You are saying I am mad.'

The editor was surprised by the turn of the conversation. It had seemed to be going well.

'Of course you're not mad,' he said. 'A madwoman could not have written that great poem. I am just saying that I value your feeling, but you must understand I, unfortunately, do not love you. You *are* ill. You have exhausted yourself.'

Miss Mendoza's yellow eyes became brilliant as she listened to him.

'So,' she said grandly, 'I am a mere nuisance.'

She got up from her chair and he saw she was trembling.

'If that is so, why don't you leave this room at once?' she said.

'But,' said the editor with a laugh, 'if I may mention it, it is mine.'

'I signed the register,' said Miss Mendoza.

'Well,' said the editor smiling, 'that is not the point, is it?'

The boredom, the sense of the sheer waste of time (when one thought of the massacres, the bombings, the imprisonments in the world) in personal questions, overcame him. It amazed him, at some awful crisis – the Cuban, for example – how many people left their husbands, wives or lovers, in a general post; the extraordinary, irresponsible persistence of outbreaks of love. A kind of guerilla war in another context. Here he was in the midst of it. What could he do? He looked around the room for help. The noise of the traffic outside in the street, the dim sight of people moving behind office windows opposite, an advertisement for beer were no help. Humanity had deserted him. The nearest thing to the human – now it took his eye – was the doll on the bed, an absurd marionette from the cabaret, the raffle or the nursery. It had a mop of red hair, silly red cheeks and popping blue eyes with long cotton lashes. It wore a short skirt and had long insane legs in checked stockings. How childish women were. Of course (it now occurred to him), Miss Mendoza was as childish as her voice. The editor said playfully: 'I see you have a little friend. Very pretty. Does she come from Guatemala?' And frivolously, because he disliked the thing, he took a step or two towards it. Miss Mendoza pushed past him at once and grabbed it.

'Don't touch it,' she said with tiny fierceness.

She picked up the doll and, hugging it with fear, she looked for somewhere to put it out of his reach. She went to the door, then changed her mind and rushed to the window with it. She opened the window; as the curtains blew, she looked as if a desperate idea had occurred to her – to throw herself and the doll out of the window. She turned to fight him off. He was too bewildered to move and when she saw that he stood still, her frightened face changed. Suddenly, she threw the doll on the floor and, half falling on to a chair near it, her shoulders rounded, she covered her face with her hands and sobbed, shaking her head from side to side. Tears crawled through her fingers down the backs of her hands. Then she took her hands away and, soft and shapeless, she rushed to the editor and clawed at his jacket.

'Go away. Go away,' she cried. 'Forgive me. Forgive. I'm sorry.' She began to laugh and cry at once. 'As you said – ill. Oh, please forgive. I don't understand why I did this. For a week I haven't eaten anything. I must have been out of my mind to do this to you. Why? I can't think. You've been so kind. You could have been cruel. You were right. You had the courage to tell me the truth. I feel so ashamed, so ashamed. What can I do?'

She was holding on to his jacket. Her tears were on his hands. She was pleading. She looked up.

'I've been such a fool,' she said.

'Come and sit here,' said the editor, trying to move her to the sofa. 'You are not a fool. You have done nothing. There is nothing to be ashamed of.'

'I can't bear it.'

'Come and sit here,' he said putting his arm on her shoulder. 'I was very proud when I read your poem. Look,' he said, 'you are a very gifted and attractive woman.'

He was surprised that such a heavy woman was not like iron to the touch but light and soft. He could feel her skin, hot through her dress. Her breath was hot. Agony was hot. Grief was hot. Above all, her clothes were hot. It was perhaps because of the heat of her clothes that for the first time in years he had the sensation of holding a human being. He had never felt this when, on a few occasions, he had held a woman naked in her bed. He did something then that was incredible to himself. He gently kissed the top of her head on the blonde hair he did not like. It was like kissing a heated mat and it smelled of burning.

At his kiss she clawed no longer and her tears stopped. She moved away from him in awe.

'Thank you,' she said gravely and he found himself being studied, even memorised, as she had done when she had first come to his office. The look of the idol was set on her again. Then she uttered a revelation. 'You do not love anyone but yourself.' And, worse, she smiled. He had thought, with dread, that she was waiting to be kissed again, but now he couldn't bear what she said. It was a loss.

'We must meet,' he said recklessly. 'We *shall* meet at the lecture tonight.'

The shadow of her future passed over her face.

'Oh no,' she said. She was free. She was warning him not to hope to exploit her pain.

'This afternoon?' he said trying to catch her hand, but she drew it away. And then, to his bewilderment, she was dodging round him. She was packing. She began stuffing her few clothes into her suitcase. She went to the bathroom, and while she was there, the porter came in with his two bags.

'Wait,' said the editor.

She came out of the bathroom looking very pale and put the remaining things into her suitcase.

'I asked him to wait,' the editor said.

The kiss, the golden hair, the heat of her head, seemed to be flying round in the editor's head.

'I don't want you to leave like this,' the editor said.

'I heard what you said to the man,' she said hurriedly shutting the suitcase. 'Goodbye. And thank you. You are saving me from something dreadful.'

The editor could not move when he saw her go. He could not believe she had gone. He could feel the stir of her scent in the air and he sat down exhausted but arguing with his conscience. Why had she said that about loving only himself? What else could he have done? He wished there were people there to whom he could explain, whom he could ask. He was feeling loneliness for one of the few times in his life. He went to the window to look down at the people. Then, looking back to the bed, he was astounded by a thought, 'I have never had an adventure in my life.' And with that, he left the room and went down to the desk. Was she still in the hotel?

'No,' said the desk clerk. 'Mrs Drood went off in a taxi.'

'I am asking for Miss Mendoza.'

'No one of that name.'

'Extraordinary,' lied the editor. 'She was to meet me here.'

'Perhaps she is at the Hofgarten, it's the same management.'

For the next hour he was on the telephone, trying all the hotels. He got a cab to the station; he tried the airlines and then, in the afternoon, went out to the airport. He knew it was hopeless. 'I must be mad too,' he thought. He looked at every golden-haired woman he could see: the city was full of golden-haired women. As the noisy city afternoon moved by, he gave up. He liked to talk about himself but here was a day he could never describe to anyone. He could not return to his room but sat in the lounge trying to read a paper, wrangling with himself and looking up at every woman who passed. He could not eat nor even drink and when he went out to his lecture he walked all the way to the hall on the chance of seeing her. He had the fancy once or twice, which he laughed at bitterly, that she had just passed and had left two or three of her footprints on the pavement. The extraordinary thing was that she was exactly the kind of woman he could not bear: squat, ugly. How awful she must look without clothes on. He tried to exorcise her by obscene images. They vanished and some transformed idealised vision of her came back. He began to see her tall and dark or young and fair; her eyes changing colour, her body voluptuously rounded, athletically slim. As he sat on the lecture platform, listening to the introduction, he made faces that astonished the audience with a mechanical display of eagerness followed by scorn, as his gaze went systematically from row to row, looking for her. He got up to speak. 'Ladies and gentlemen,' he began. He knew it would be the best lecture he had ever given. It was. Urging, appealing, agonising, eloquent. It was an appeal to her to come back.

And then, after a lot of discussion which he hardly heard, he returned to the hotel. He had now to face the mockery of the room. He let himself in and it did mock. The maid had turned the bed back and on it lay the doll, its legs tidied, its big ridiculous eyes staring at him. They seemed to him to blink. She had forgotten it. She had left her childhood behind.

On the Edge of the Cliff

———

The sea fog began to lift towards noon. It had been blowing in, thin and loose for two days, smudging the tops of the trees up the ravine where the house stood. 'Like the cold breath of old men,' Rowena wrote in an attempt at a poem, but changed the line, out of kindness, to 'the breath of ghosts', because Harry might take it personally. The truth was that his breath was not foggy at all, but smelt of the dozens of cigarettes he smoked all day. He would walk about, taking little steps, with his hand outstretched, tapping the ash off as he talked. This gave an abstracted searching elegance which his heavy face and long sentences needed. In her dressing gown Rowena went to his room. His glasses were off and he had finished shaving and he turned a face savaged to the point of saintliness by age, but with a heavy underlip that made him look helplessly brutal. She laughed at the soap in his ears.

'The ghosts have gone,' she said poetically. 'We can go to Withy Hole! I'll drive by the Guilleth road, there's a fair there. They'll tell our fortunes.'

'Dull place,' he said. 'It used to be full of witches in the sixteenth century.'

'I'm a witch,' she said. 'I want to go to the fair. I saw the poster. It starts today.'

'We'll go,' he said, suspicious, but giving in.

He was seventyish, and with a young girl of twenty-five one had, of course, to pretend to be suspicious. There are rules for old men who are in love with young girls, all the stricter when the young girls are in love with them. It has to be played as a game.

'The sea pinks will be out on the cliffs,' he said.

'You old botanist!' she said.

He was about to say 'I know that' and go on to say that girls were like flowers with voices and that he had spent a lot of his life collecting both, but he had said these things to her often before and at his age one had to avoid repeating oneself, if possible. Anyway, it was more effective as a compliment when other people were there and they would turn to look at her. When young girls turned into women they lost his interest: he had always lived for reverie.

'So it's settled,' she said.

Now he looked tragic as he gazed at her. Waving his razor, he began his nervous trick of taking a few dance-like steps and she gave him one of her light hugs and ran out of the room.

What with his organising fusses and her habit of vanishing to do something to a drawing she was working on, the start was late.

'We'll have to eat something,' she said, giving an order.

But it was his house, not hers. He'd lived alone long enough not to be able to stand a woman in his kitchen, could not bear to see her cut a loaf or muddle the knives and forks or choke the sink with tea leaves.

'Rowena and I,' he said to people who came to see them, in his military voice, 'eat very little. We see no one.'

This was not true, but like a general with a literary turn, he organised his imagination. He was much guided by literature. His wife had gone mad and had killed herself. So in the house he saw himself as a Mr Rochester, or in the car as Count Mosca with the young duchess in *La Chartreuse de Parme*; if they met people, as Tolstoy's worldly aunt. This was another game: it educated the girl.

While he fussed between the kitchen and the room they ate in, she came down late and idled, throwing back her long black hair, lassoing him with smiles and side glances thrown out and rushed at him while he had a butter plate in his hand and gave him another of her light engulfing hugs and laughed at the plate he waved in the air.

'Rowena!' he shouted, for she had gone off again. 'Get the car out.'

The house was halfway up the long ravine, backed and faced by an army of ash trees and beeches. There was the terrace and the ingenious steep garden and the plants that occupied him most of the day, and down from the terrace he had had to cut the twenty or thirty steps himself, heaving his pickaxe. Rowena had watched his thick stack of coarse grey hair and his really rather brutal face and his pushed-out lips, as he hacked and the pick hit the stones. He worked with such anger and pride, but he looked up at her sometimes with appealing, brilliant eyes. His furious ancient's face contained pain naturally.

She knew he hated to be told to be careful when he came down the steps. She knew the ceremony of getting him into the car, for he was a tall, angular man and had to fold himself in, his knees nearly touching his chin, to which the long deep despondent lines of his face ran heavily down. It was exciting for her to drive the old man dangerously fast down the long circling lane through the trees, to show how dangerous she could be, while he talked. He would talk nonstop for the next hour, beginning, of course, with the country fair.

'It's no good. Plastic, like cheap food. Not worth seeing. The twentieth century has packaged everything.'

And he was on to the pre-Roman times, the ancient spirit of carnival, Celtic gods and devils, as they drove out of the ravine into deep lanes, where he could name the ferns in the stone walls, and the twisting hills and corners that shook the teeth and the spine. Historical instances poured out of him. He was, she said, Old Father Time himself, but he did not take that as a joke, though he humoured her with a small laugh. It was part of the game. He was not Father Time, for in one's seventies, one is a miser of time, putting it by, hiding the minutes, while she spent fast, not knowing she was living in time at all.

Guilleth was a dull, dusty, Methodistical little town with geraniums in the windows of the houses. Sammy's Fair was in a rough field just outside it, where dogs and children ran about. There was only one shooting gallery; they were still putting up the back canvas of the coconut shy. There were hoopla stalls, a lot of shouting and few customers. But the small roundabout gave out its engine whistle and the children packed the vulgar circle of spotted cows with huge pink udders, the rocking horses, the pigs, the tigers and a pair of giraffes.

The professor regarded it as a cultural pathos. He feared Rowena. She was quite childishly cruel to him. With a beautiful arrogance that mocked him, she got out of the car and headed for ice cream. He had to head her off the goldfish in their bowls. She'd probably want to bring one home.

'Give me some money,' she said, going to the roundabout. There was a small crowd near that. 'I'm going on the giraffe. Come on.'

'I'll watch you,' he complained and cleaned his glasses.

There she was, riding a giraffe already, tall and like a schoolmistress among the town children, with her long hair, which she kept on throwing back as she whirled round, a young miracle, getting younger and younger. There were other girls. There were town youths and there was an idiotic young man riding backwards on a cow, kicking out his legs and every now and then waving to the crowd. Rowena on her giraffe did not smile, but as she came round sedately, waved to the old man as she sailed by.

He looked at his watch. How much longer?

'I'm going on again,' she called, and did not get off.

He found himself absurdly among the other patient watchers, older than all, better dressed too, on his dignity, all curiosity gone. He moved away to separate himself from his bunch of them, but he had the impression they all moved with him. There was a young woman in a bright-red coat who always seemed to be in the next bunch he joined. Round came the giraffe: round came the young man on the cow. The young woman in red waved. Seeing that to wave was the correct thing, the old man too waved at the giraffe. The woman waved again a moment later and stared at him as if annoyed. He moved a yard from her, then five yards, then to the other side of the roundabout. Here he could wave without being conspicuous, yet the woman was standing close to him once more. She was small with reddish hair, her chin up, looking at him.

'You don't remember me,' she accused him in a high voice. Her small eyes were impudent. He stepped back, gaping.

'Daisy Pyke,' she said.

Pyke? Pyke? He gaped at her briefly, his mind was sailing round with Rowena.

'George's wife,' she said, challenging his stupidity.

'George . . .' But he stopped. George Pyke's wife must be fifty by now. This woman could not be more than thirty. Her daughter – had they had a daughter?

'Have I changed as much as that?' she said. Her manner was urchin-like and she grinned with pleasure at his confusion and then her mouth drooped at the corners plaintively, begging. Nowadays he thought only of Rowena's wide mouth, which made all other women vague to him. And then the hard little begging, pushing mouth and its high voice broke into his memory. He stepped back with embarrassment and a short stare

[960]

of horror which he covered quickly, his feet dancing a few steps, and saying with foolish smiles, 'Daisy! I thought ... I was watching that thing. What are you doing here?'

Now that he remembered, he could not conceal a note of indignation and he stood still, his eyes peered coldly. He could see this had its effect on her.

'The same as you,' she said in that curt off-hand voice. 'Waiting. Waiting for them to come off.' And she turned away from him, offended, waved wildly at the roundabout and shouted, 'Stephen, you fool!' The young man riding backwards on the cow waved back and shouted to her.

What an appalling thing! But there it is – one must expect it when one is old: the map in one's head, indeed the literal map of the country empties and loses its contours, towns and villages, and people sink out of sight. The protective faces of friends vanish and one is suddenly alone, naked and exposed. The population ranked between oneself and old enemies suddenly dissolves and the enemy stands before one. Daisy Pyke!

The old man could not get away. He said as politely as he could manage, 'I thought you went abroad. How is George?'

'We did. George,' she said, 'died in Spain.' And added briskly, 'On a golf course.'

'I'm sorry. I didn't know.'

She looked back at the roundabout and turned again to say to him, 'I know all about you. You've got a new house at Colfe. I've still got the old house, though actually it's let.'

Forty miles lay between Colfe and Daisy Pyke – but no people in between! Now the roundabout stopped. There was a scramble of children getting on and getting off, and the local watchers moved forward too.

'I must get Rowena,' he said ruthlessly and he hurried off, calling out in his peremptory voice, 'Rowena!'

He knew that Daisy Pyke was watching him as he held out a hand to help Rowena off, but Rowena ignored it and jumped off herself.

'Rowena. We must go.'

'Why? It was lovely. Did you see that ridiculous young man?'

'No, Rowena,' he said. 'Where?'

'Over there,' she said, 'with the girl in red, the one you were chatting up, you old rip. I saw you!' She laughed and took his arm. 'You're blushing.'

'She's not a girl,' he said. 'She's a woman I used to know in London twenty years ago. It was rather awful! I didn't recognise her. I used to know her husband. She used to be a friend of Violet's.'

'Violet's!' said Rowena. 'But you *must* introduce me.' She was always eager to know, as if to possess, everyone he had ever known, to have all of him, even the dead. Above all Violet, his wife. Rowena longed to be as old as that dead woman.

'Really, Harry, you are frightful with people.'

'Oh, well . . . But she's appalling. We had a terrible row.'

'One of your old loves,' she teased.

'I had to throw her out of the house,' he said. 'She's a liar.'

'Then I *must* see her,' said Rowena. 'How thrilling.'

'I think they've gone,' he said.

'No,' said Rowena. 'There they are. Take me over.'

And she pulled him towards the hoopla stall where Daisy Pyke and the young man were standing. There lay the delightfulness of Rowena: she freed him from the boredom into which his memories had set and hardened. He had known many young girls who in this situation would be eagerly storing opportunities for jealousy of his past life. Rowena was not like that.

At the stall, with its cunningly arranged bowls, jugs, and toys, the young man with the yellow curling hair was pitching rings onto the table, telling Daisy to try and altering the angle of the ring in her hand.

'Choose what you want, hold the ring level and lightly, don't skim fast. Don't bowl it like that! Like this.'

Daisy's boldness had gone. She was fond and serious, glancing at the young man before she threw.

'Daisy,' said the old man, putting on a shady and formal manner as if he were at a party, 'I have brought Rowena to meet you.'

And Rowena stepped forward gushingly. 'How d'you do! I was telling Harry about the young man on the cow.'

'Here he is,' said Daisy stiffly. 'Stephen!'

The young man turned and said 'Hello' and went on throwing rings. 'Like that,' he said.

[962]

Rowena watched him mockingly.

'We are just off,' said Harry.

'I've heard a lot about you,' said Daisy to Rowena.

'We're going to walk along the cliffs,' said Harry.

'To Withy Hole,' said Rowena.

'It was extraordinary meeting you here,' said Harry.

'Perhaps,' said Daisy, 'we'll meet again.'

'Oh, well – you know we hardly see anyone now,' said Harry.

Daisy studied Rowena impudently and she laughed at the boy, who had failed again.

'I won a goldfish once,' said Rowena, laughing. 'It died on the way home.'

'Extraordinary,' the old man said as he and Rowena walked away. 'That must be George's son, but taller. George was short.'

When she got him back into the car she saw by his leaden look that the subject was closed. She had met one more of his friends – that was the main thing.

The hills seemed to pile up and the sea to get farther and farther away and then, suddenly, as they got over the last long hill, they passed the caravan sites that were empty at this time of the year and looked like those flat white Andalusian towns he remembered, from a distance. The old man was saying, 'But we have this new rootless civilisation, anarchic but standardised' – suddenly the sea appeared between the dunes below, not grey and choppy, but deep blue, all candour, like a young mouth, between the dunes and beyond it, wide and still and sleepily serene. The old man was suddenly in command, fussing about the exact place where they could leave the car, struggling over the sand dunes dotted with last year's litter, on to the huge cliffs. At the top there they could look back and see on the wide bay the shallow sea breaking idly, in changing lines of surf, like lips speaking lines that broke unfinished and could not be heard. A long way off a dozen surfers were wading out, deeper and deeper, towards the bigger waves as if they were leaving the land for good and might be trying to reach the horizon. Rowena stopped to gaze at them, waiting for one of them to come in on a long glissade, but the old man urged her on to the close turf of the cliffs. That is what he had come for: boundlessness, distance. For thirty miles on a clear day in May like this, one could walk without meeting a soul, from headland to headland, gazing through the hum of the wind and under the cries of the dashing gulls, at what seemed to be an unending procession of fading promontories, each dropping to its sandy cove, yet still riding out into the water. The wind did not move the old man's tough thatch of hair but made his big ears stick out. Rowena bound her loose hair with a scarf. From low cliff to high cliff, over the cropped turf, which was like a carpet, where the millions of sea pinks and daisies were scattered, mile after mile in their colonies, the old man led the way, digging his knees into the air, gesticulating, talking, pointing to a kestrel above or a cormorant black as soot on a rock, while she followed lazily yards behind him. He stopped impatiently to show her some small cushioned plant or stood on the cliff's edge, like a prophet, pointing down to the falls of rock, the canyons, caverns, and tunnels into which the green water poured in black and was sucked out into green again and spilled in waterfalls down the outer rocks. The old man was a strong walker, bending to it, but when he stopped he straightened, and Rowena smiled at his air of detachment as he gazed at distant things as if he knew them. To her he looked like a frightening mixture of pagan saint and toiling animal. They would rest at the crest of a black cliff for a few minutes, feel the sun burn their skin, and then on they went.

'We can't see the bay any more,' she said. She was thinking of the surf-riders.

'The cliff after the next is the Hole,' he said and pulled her to her feet.

'Yes, the Hole,' she said.

He had a kind of mania about the Hole. This was the walk he liked best and so did she, except for that ugly final horror. The sea had tunnelled under the rock in several places along this wild coast and had sucked out enormous slaty craters fifty yards across and this one a hundred and eighty feet deep, so that even at the edge one could not see the water pouring in. One stood listening for the bump of hidden water on a quiet day: on wild ones it seethed in the bottom of the pot. The place terrified Rowena and she held back, but he stumbled through the rough grasses to the edge, calling back bits of geology and navigation – and to amuse her, explained how smugglers had had to wait for the low wave to take them in.

[964]

Now, once more, they were looking at the great meaningless wound. As he stood at the edge he seemed to her to be at one with it. It reminded her of his mouth when she had once seen it (with a horror she tried to wipe from her mind) before he had put his dentures in. Of her father's too.

Well, the objective was achieved. They found a bank on the seaward side out of the wind where the sun burned and they rested.

'Heaven,' she said and closed her eyes.

They sat in silence for a long time but he gazed at the rising floor of eventless water. Far out, from time to time, in some small eddy of the wind, little families of whitecaps would appear. They were like faces popping up or perhaps white hands shooting out and disappearing pointlessly. Yes, they were the pointless dead.

'What are you thinking about?' she asked without opening her eyes.

He was going to say 'At my age one is always thinking about death,' but he said 'You.'

'What about me?' she said with that shamelessness of girls.

'Your ears,' he said.

'You are a liar,' she said. 'You're thinking about Daisy Pyke.'

'Not now,' he said.

'But you must be,' she said. She pointed. 'Isn't the cove just below where you all used to bathe with nothing on? Did she come?'

'Round the corner,' he said, correcting her. 'Violet and I used to bathe there. Everyone came. Daisy came once when George was on the golf course. She swam up and down, hour after hour, as cold as a fish. Hopeless on dry land. Gordon and Vera came, but Daisy only once. She didn't fit in – very conventional – sat telling dirty stories. Then she went swimming, to clean up. George was playing golf all day and bridge all evening; that didn't go down well. They had a dartboard in their house: the target was a naked woman. A pretty awful, jokey couple. You can guess the bull's-eye.'

'What was this row?' she said.

'She told lies,' he said, turning to her. And he said this with a hiss of finality which she knew. She waited for one of his stories, but it did not come.

'I want to swim in the cove,' said Rowena.

'It's too cold this time of the year,' he said.

'I want to go,' she said.

'It's a long way down and hard coming back.'

'Yes, but I want to go – where you all used to go.'

She was obstinate about this, and of course he liked that.

'All right,' he said, getting up. Like all girls she wanted to leave her mark on places. He noticed how she was impelled to touch pictures in galleries when he had taken her to Italy. Ownership! Power! He used to dislike that but now he did not; the change was a symptom of his adoration of her. And she did want to go. She did want to assert her presence on that empty sand, to make the sand feel her mark.

They scrambled the long way down the rocks until the torn cliffs were gigantic above them. On the smooth sand she ran barefoot to the edge of the sea rippling in.

'It's ice!' she screamed.

He stood there, hunched. There was a litter of last year's rags and cartons near the rocks. Summer crowds now swarmed into the place, which had been secret. He glowered with anger at the debris.

'I'm going to pee,' he said.

She watched the sea, for he was a long time gone.

'That was a big one,' she shouted.

But he was not there. He was out on the rocks, he had pulled off his clothes. He was standing there, his body furred with grey hair, his belly wrinkled, his thighs shrunk. Up went his bony arms.

'You're not to! It will kill you! Your heart!' she shouted.

He gave a wicked laugh, she saw his yellow teeth, and in he dived and was crawling and shouting in the water as he swam out farther, defying her, threshing the water, and then as she screamed at him, really frightened, he came crawling in like some ugly hairy sea animal, his skin reddened with cold, and stood dripping with his arms wide as if he was going to give a howl. He climbed over the rocks and back to the sand and got his clothes and was drying himself with his shirt.

'You're mad,' she said. 'You're not to put that wet thing on.'

'It will dry in this sun,' he said.

'What was all that for?' she said. 'Did you find her?'

'Who?' he said, looking round in bewilderment. He had dived in

[966]

boastfully and in a kind of rage, a rage against time, a rage against Daisy Pyke too. He did not answer, but looked at her with a glint of shrewdness in his eyes. She was flattered by the glitter in this look from a sometimes terrifying old man.

He was tired now and they took the short inland road to the car close to those awful caravans, and when she got him into the car again he fell asleep and snorted. He went to his room early but could not sleep; he had broken one of his rules for old men. For the first time he had let her see him naked. He was astounded when she came into his room and got into his bed: she had not done this before. 'I've come to see the Ancient Mariner,' she said.

How marvellous. She is jealous, after all. She loves me, he went about saying to himself in the next weeks. She drove to what they called 'our town' to buy cakes. 'I am so thin,' she said.

The first time she returned saying she had seen his 'dear friend Daisy.' She was in the supermarket.

'What's she doing there?' he said. 'She lives forty miles away. What did she say?'

'We did not speak. I mean, I don't think she saw me. Her son was with her. He said hello. He'd got the hood of the car up. She came out and gave me a nod – I don't think she likes me,' she said with satisfaction.

The next week she went again to get petrol. The old man stayed at the house, shook one or two mats, and swept the sitting-room floor. It was his house and Rowena was untidy. Then he sat on the terrace, listening for her car, anxiously.

Presently he picked up the sound, much earlier than her usual time, and saw the distant glint in the trees as the car wound its way up. There she was, threading her beauty through the trees. He heard with alarm the sudden silences of the car at some turn in the hill, then heard it getting louder as it turned a corner, then passing into silence again. He put his book down and went inside in a dutiful panic to put the kettle on, and while he waited for it to boil he took the cups out pedantically, one by one, to the table on the terrace and stood listening again. Now it was on the last stretch, now he heard a crackling of wheels below. He ran in to heat the teapot and ran out with his usual phrase: 'Did you get what you wanted?'

Then, puffing up the last steps, she came. But it was not she; it was a small woman, bare-legged and in sandals, with a swaggering urchin grin on her face, pulling a scarf off her head. Daisy!

'Gosh!' she said.

Harry skipped back a yard and stood, straightening and forbidding. 'Daisy!' he said, annoyed, as if waving her off.

'Those steps! Harry!' she said. 'Gosh, what a view.'

She gave a dry dismissive laugh at it. She had, he remembered, always defied what she saw. The day when he had seen her at the fair seemed to slide away under his feet and years slid by, after that, following that day.

'What –' he began. Then in his military way, he jerked out, 'Rowena's gone into town. I am waiting for her.'

'I know,' said Daisy. 'Can I sit down and get my breath? I know. I saw her.' And with a plotting satisfaction: 'Not to speak to. She passed me. Ah, that's better.'

'We never see people,' said Harry sternly. 'You see I am working. If the telephone rings, we don't answer it.'

'The same with us. I hope I'm not interrupting. I thought – I'll dash up, just for a minute.'

'And Rowena has her work . . .' he said. Daisy was always an interrupter.

'I gave you a surprise,' said Daisy comfortably. 'She is lovely. That's why I came. You're lucky – how d'you do it? Where did you find her? And what a place you've got here! I made Stephen go and see his friends. It was such a long time – years, isn't it? I had to come. You haven't changed, you know. But you didn't recognise me, did you? You were trying not to see me, weren't you?'

Her eyes and her nose were small. She is at her old game of shock tactics, he thought. He looked blankly at her.

'I explained that,' he said nervously. 'I must go and turn the kettle off,' he said. He paused to listen for Rowena's car, but there was no sound.

'Well,' she said. 'There you are. Time goes on.'

When he came back with a teapot and another cup, she said, 'I knew you wouldn't come and see me, so I came to see you. Let me see,' she said and took off the scarf from her head. 'I told you George died, didn't I? Of course I did,' she said briskly.

'Yes.'

'Well . . .' she said. 'Harry, I had to see you. You are the only wise man I know.' She looked nervously at the garden and across to the army of trees stacked on the hill and then turned to him. 'You're happy and I am happy, Harry. I didn't come to make a scene and drag it all up. I was in love with you, that was the trouble, but I'm not now. I was wrong about you, about you and Violet. I couldn't bear to see her suffer. I was out of my mind. I couldn't bear to see you grieving for her. I soon knew what it was when poor George died. Harry, I just don't want you to hate me any more. I mean, you're not still furious, are you? We do change. The past is past.'

The little liar, he thought. What has she come up here for? To cause trouble between himself and Rowena as she had tried to do with his wife and himself. He remembered Daisy's favourite word: honesty. She was trying for some reason to confuse him about things he had settled a long time ago in his mind.

He changed the subject. 'What is –' – he frowned – 'I'm sorry, I can't remember names nowadays – your son doing?'

She was quick to notice the change, he saw. Nothing ever escaped Daisy.

'Oh, Tommy, the ridiculous Tommy. He's in Africa,' she said, merrily dismissing him. 'Well, it was better for him – problems. I'm a problem to him – George was so jealous too.'

'He looks exactly like George,' Harry said. 'Taller, of course, the curly hair.'

'What are you talking about? You haven't seen him since he was four.' She laughed.

'Don't be stupid, Daisy, we saw him last week at that – what is the name of the place? – at the fair.'

The blood went from Daisy's face. She raised her chin. 'That's a nasty one,' she said and gave her head a fierce shake. 'You meant it to, didn't you? That was Stephen. I thought you'd be the last to think a thing like that, with your Rowena. I expect people say it and I don't care and if anyone said it to him he wouldn't know what they were talking about. Stephen's my lover.'

The old sentimental wheedling Daisy was in the coy smile that quickly followed her sharpness. 'He's mad about me,' she said. 'I may be old enough to be his mother, but he's sick of squealing, sulky girls of seventeen. If we had met years ago, he would have hated me. Seriously, Harry, I'd go down on my knees to him.'

'I am sorry – I – that's why I didn't recognise you. You can ask Rowena. I said to her, "That's Daisy Pyke's daughter," Harry said, 'when I saw you.'

Daisy gaped at him and slowly her lips curled up with delight. 'Oh, good! Is that true? Is it? You always told the truth. You really thought that! Thank you, Harry, that's the nicest thing you ever said to me. I love you for it.'

She leaned forward, appealing to him quietly.

'George never slept with me for seven years before he died. Don't ask me about it, but that's the truth. I'd forgotten what it was. When Stephen asked me I thought it was an insult – you know, all this rape about. I got into the car and slammed the door in his face and left him on the road – well, not on the road, but wherever it was – and drove off. I looked back. He was still standing there. Well, I mean, at my age! That next day – *you* know what it is with women better than anyone – I was in such a mood. When I got back to the house I shouted for George, howled for him to come back and poured myself a tumblerful of whisky and wandered about the house slopping it on the carpet.' She laughed. 'George would have killed me for *that* if he had come – and I went out into the garden and there was Stephen, you won't believe it, walking bold as brass up from the gate. He came up quickly and just took the glass from me very politely – the stuff was pouring down my dress – and put it on the grass and he wiped my blouse. That's what did it.'

She paused thoughtfully and frowned. 'Not there,' she said prudishly, 'not at the house, of course. I wanted to get away from it. I can't bear it. We went to the caravan camp. That's where he was living. I don't know why I'm telling you this. I mean, there's a lot more.'

She paused. 'Love is something at our age, isn't it? I mean, when I saw you and Rowena at Guilleth – I thought I must go and talk to you. Being in the same boat.'

'We're not,' he said, annoyed. 'I am twenty years older than you.'

'Thirty, if you don't mind,' she said, opening her bag and looking into her mirror. When she had put it away with a snap she looked over the flowers in the steep garden to the woods. She was listening for the sound of a car. He realised he had stopped listening for it. He found himself enjoying this hour, despite his suspicions of her. It drove away the terrors that seemed to dissolve even the trees of the ravine. With women, nature returned to its place, the trees became real trees. One lived in a long moment in which time had stopped. He did not care for Daisy, but she had that power of enticement which lay in stirring one with the illusion that she was defying one to put her right. With Rowena he had thrown away his vanity; with Daisy it returned.

'Where did you and Rowena go the day we saw you?' she asked suddenly.

'Along the cliffs,' he said.

'You didn't go to the cove, did you? It's a long way. And you can't swim at this time of the year.'

'We went to the cove and I *did* swim,' he said. 'I wouldn't let Rowena.'

'I should hope not! You don't forget old times, do you?' She laughed coolly. 'I hope you didn't tell Rowena – young girls can be so jealous. I *was* – d'you remember? Gosh, I'm glad I'm not young still, aren't you?'

'Stop being so romantic, Daisy,' said the old man.

'Oh, I'm not romantic any more,' she said. 'It doesn't pay else one would pity *them*, Rowena and Stephen. So you did go to the cove – did you think of me?'

'I only think of death now,' he said.

'You always were an interesting man, the type that goes on to his nineties, like they do now,' she said. 'I never think about it. Stephen would have a fit. He doesn't even know what he's going to do. Last week he thought he'd be a beach guard. Or teach tennis. Or a singer! He was surfing on the beach when I first saw him. He was living at the camp.'

She paused, offended. 'Did you know they switch off the electric light at ten o'clock at the office in those places? No one protests. Like sheep. It would make me furious to be treated like that. You could hear everyone snoring at once. Not that we joined in, I must say. Actually, we're staying in his mother's house now, the bunks are too narrow in those caravans, but she's come back. So we're looking for something – I've let my house. The money is useful.'

The old man was alarmed. He was still trying to make out the real reason for her visit. He remembered the old Daisy – there was always a hidden motive, something she was trying out. And he started listening urgently again for Rowena's car. I know what it is, he thought; she wants to move in here!

'I'm afraid it would be impossible to have you here,' he said.

'Here, Harry?' she said, astonished. 'None of that! That's not what I came for. Anyway,' she said archly, 'I wouldn't trust you.'

But she considered the windows and the doors of the house and then the view. She gave a business-like sniff and said seriously, 'You can't keep her a prisoner here. It won't last.'

'Rowena is not a prisoner. She can come and go when she likes. We understand that.'

'It depends what you mean by coming and going,' said Daisy shrewdly. 'You mean you are the prisoner. That is it! So am I!'

'Oh,' said Harry. 'Love is always like that. I live only for her.'

'That is it! I will tell you why I came to see you, Harry. When I saw Rowena in town I kept out of her way. You won't believe it – I can be tactful.'

She became very serious. 'Because I don't want us to meet again.' It was an open declaration. 'I mean not see you for a long time, I mean all of us. You see, Rowena is so beautiful and Stephen – well, you've seen him. You and I would start talking about old times and people, and they'd be left out and drawn together – now, wouldn't they? I just couldn't bear to see him talking to her, looking at her. I wish we had not met down at the fair. It's all right now, he's with his surfing friends, but you understand?'

She got up and said, 'I mean it, Harry. I know what would happen and so do you and I don't want to *see* it happen.'

She went up to him because he had stood up and she tapped him hard on the chest with her firm bold finger. He could feel it on his skin, a determined blow, after she had stepped away.

'I know it can't last,' she said. 'And you know it can't. But I don't want *you* to see it happen,' she said in her old hard taunting style. 'We never really use your town anyway. I'll see *he* doesn't. Give me your word. We've got to do this for each other. We've managed quite well all these years, haven't we? And it's not saying we'll *never* meet someday, is it?'

'You're a bitch, Daisy,' he said, and he smiled.

'Yes, I'm a bitch still, Harry,' she said. 'But I'm not a fool.'

She put out her hand again and he feared she was going to dig that hard finger in his chest again, but she didn't. She tied her scarf round her hair. 'If anything happened I'd throw myself down Withy Hole.'

'Stop being so melodramatic, Daisy,' he said.

'Well, I don't want you conniving,' she said coarsely. 'I don't want any of your little arrangements.'

And she turned to the ravine and listened. 'Car coming up,' she said.

'Rowena,' he said.

'I'll be off. Remember.'

'Be careful at the turns,' he said helplessly. 'She drives fast. You'll pass her on the road.'

They did not kiss or even shake hands. He listened to her cursing the steps as she went down and calling out, 'I bet you dug out these bloody steps yourself.'

He listened to the two cars whining their way towards each other as they circled below, now Rowena's car glinted, now Daisy's. At last Rowena's slowed down at the steps, spitting stones.

Rowena came up and said, 'I've just passed Daisy on the road.'

'Yes, she's been here. What a tale!'

She looked at the empty cups. 'And you didn't give your dearest friend any tea, you wretch.'

'Oh, tea – no – er – she didn't want any,' he stammered.

'As gripping as all that, was it?' she laughed.

'Very,' he said. 'She's talking of marrying that young man. Stephen's not her son.'

'You can't mean that,' she said, putting on a very proper air. 'She's old enough –' but she stopped, and instead of giving him one of her light hugs, she rumpled his hair. 'People do confide in you, I must say,' she said. 'I don't think I like her coming up here. Tell me what she said.'

[973]

A Family Man

―――――

Late in the afternoon, when she had given him up and had even changed out of her pink dress into her smock and jeans and was working once more at her bench, the doorbell rang. William had come, after all. It was in the nature of their love affair that his visits were fitful: he had a wife and children. To show that she understood the situation, even found the curious satisfaction of reverie in his absences that lately had lasted several weeks, Berenice dawdled yawning to the door. As she slipped off the chain, she called back into the empty flat, 'It's all right, Father. I'll answer it.'

William had told her to do this because she was a woman living on her own: the call would show strangers that there was a man there to defend her. Berenice's voice was mocking, for she thought his idea possessive and ridiculous; not only that, she had been brought up by Quakers and thought it wrong to tell or act a lie. Sometimes, when she opened the door to him, she would say, 'Well! Mr Cork,' to remind him he was a married man. He had the kind of shadowed handsomeness that easily gleams with guilt, and for her this gave their affair its piquancy.

But now – when she opened the door – no William, and the yawn, its hopes and its irony, died on her mouth. A very large woman, taller than herself, filled the doorway from top to bottom, an enormous blob of pink jersey and green skirt, the jersey low and loose at the neck, a face and body inflated to the point of speechlessness. She even seemed to be asleep with her large blue eyes open.

'Yes?' said Berenice.

The woman woke up and looked unbelievingly at Berenice's feet, which were bare, for she liked to go about barefoot at home, and said, 'Is this Miss Foster's place?'

Berenice was offended by the word 'place'. 'This is Miss Foster's residence. I am she.'

'Ah,' said the woman, babyish no longer but sugary. 'I was given your address at the College. You teach at the College, I believe? I've come about the repair.'

'A repair? I make jewellery,' said Berenice. 'I do not do repairs.'

'They told me at the College you were repairing my husband's flute. I am Mrs Cork.'

Berenice's heart stopped. Her wrist went weak and her hand drooped on the door handle, and a spurt of icy air shot up her body to her face and then turned to boiling heat as it shot back again. Her head suddenly filled with chattering voices saying, Oh, God. How frightful! William, you didn't tell her? Now, what are you, you, you going to do. And the word 'Do, do' clattered on in her head.

'Cork?' said Berenice. 'Flute?'

'Florence Cork,' said the woman firmly, all sleepy sweetness gone.

'Oh, yes. I am sorry. Mrs Cork. Of course, yes. Oh, do come in. I'm so sorry. We haven't met, how very nice to meet you. William's – Mr Cork's – flute! His flute. Yes, I remember. How d'you do? How is he? He hasn't been to the College for months. Have you seen him lately – how silly, of course you have. Did you have a lovely holiday? Did the children enjoy it? I would have posted it, only I didn't know your address. Come in, please, come in.'

'In here?' said Mrs Cork and marched into the front room where Berenice worked. Here, in the direct glare of Berenice's working lamp, Florence Cork looked even larger and even pregnant. She seemed to occupy the whole of the room as she stood in it, memorising everything – the bench, the pots of paintbrushes, the large designs pinned to the wall, the rolls of paper, the sofa covered with papers and letters and sewing, the pink dress which Berenice had thrown over a chair. She seemed to be consuming it all, drinking all the air.

But here, the disorder of which she was very vain, which indeed fascinated her, and represented her talent, her independence, a girl's right to a life of her own and, above all, being barefooted, helped Berenice recover her breath.

'It is such a pleasure to meet you. Mr Cork has often spoken of you to us at the College. We're quite a family there. Please sit. I'll move the dress. I was mending it.'

But Mrs Cork did not sit down. She gave a sudden lurch towards the bench, and seeing her husband's flute there propped against the wall, she grabbed it and swung it above her head as if it were a weapon.

'Yes,' said Berenice, who was thinking, Oh, dear, the woman's drunk, 'I was working on it only this morning. I had never seen a flute like that before. Such a beautiful silver scroll. I gather it's very old, a German one, a presentation piece given to Mr Cork's father. I believe he played in a famous orchestra – where was it? – Bayreuth or Berlin? You never see a scroll like that in England, not a delicate silver scroll like that. It seems to have been dropped somewhere or have had a blow. Mr Cork told me he had played it in an orchestra himself once, Covent Garden or somewhere . . .'

She watched Mrs Cork flourish the flute in the air.

'A blow,' cried Mrs Cork, now in a rich voice. 'I'll say it did. I threw it at him.'

And then she lowered her arm and stood swaying on her legs as she confronted Berenice and said, 'Where is he?'

'Who?' said Berenice in a fright.

'My husband!' Mrs Cork shouted. 'Don't try and soft-soap me with all that twaddle. Playing in an orchestra! Is that what he has been stuffing you up with? I know what you and he are up to. He comes every Thursday. He's been here since half past two. I know. I have had this place watched.'

She swung round to the closed door of Berenice's bedroom. 'What's in there?' she shouted and advanced to it.

'Mrs Cork,' said Berenice as calmly as she could. 'Please stop shouting. I know nothing about your husband. I don't know what you are talking about.' And she placed herself before the door of the room. 'And please stop shouting. That is my father's room.' And, excited by Mrs Cork's accusation, she said, 'He is a very old man and he is not well. He is asleep in there.'

'In there?' said Mrs Cork.

'Yes, in there.'

'And what about the other rooms? Who lives upstairs?'

'There are no other rooms,' said Berenice. 'I live here with my father. Upstairs? Some new people have moved in.'

Berenice was astonished by these words of hers, for she was a truthful young woman and was astonished, even excited, by a lie so vast. It seemed to glitter in the air as she spoke it.

Mrs Cork was checked. She flopped down on the chair on which Berenice had put her dress.

'My dress, if you please,' said Berenice and pulled it away.

'If you don't do it here,' said Mrs Cork, quietening and with tears in her eyes, 'you do it somewhere else.'

'I don't know anything about your husband. I only see him at the College like the other teachers. I don't know anything about him. If you will give me the flute, I will pack it up for you and I must ask you to go.'

'You can't deceive me. I know everything. You think because you are young you can do what you like,' Mrs Cork muttered to herself and began rummaging in her handbag.

For Berenice one of the attractions of William was that their meetings were erratic. The affair was like a game: she liked surprise above all. In the intervals when he was not there, the game continued for her. She liked imagining what he and his family were doing. She saw them as all glued together as if in some enduring and absurd photograph, perhaps sitting in their suburban garden, or standing beside a motorcar, always in the sun, but William himself, dark-faced and busy in his gravity, a step or two back from them.

'Is your wife beautiful?' she asked him once when they were in bed.

William in his slow serious way took a long time to answer. He said at last, 'Very beautiful.'

This had made Berenice feel exceedingly beautiful herself. She saw his wife as a raven-haired, dark-eyed woman and longed to meet her. The more she imagined her, the more she felt for her, the more she saw eye to eye with her in the pleasant busy middle ground of womanish feelings and moods, for as a woman living alone she felt a firm loyalty to her sex. During this last summer when the family were on holiday she had seen them glued together again as they sat with dozens of other families in the aeroplane that was taking them abroad, so that it seemed to her that the London sky was rumbling day after day, night after night, with matrimony thirty thousand feet above the city, the countryside, the sea and its beaches where she imagined the legs of their children running across the sand, William flushed with his responsibilities, his wife turning to brown her back in the sun. Berenice was often out and about with her many friends, most of whom were married. She loved the look of harassed contentment, even the tired faces of the husbands, the alert looks of their spirited wives. Among the married she felt her singularity. She listened to their endearments and to their bickerings. She played with their children, who ran at once to her. She could not bear the young men who approached her, talking about themselves all the time, flashing with the slapdash egotism of young men trying to bring her peculiarity to an end. Among families she felt herself to be strange and necessary – a necessary secret. When William had said his wife was beautiful, she felt so beautiful herself that her bones seemed to turn to water.

But now the real Florence sat rummaging in her bag before her, this balloon-like giant, first babyish and then shouting accusations, the dreamt-of Florence vanished. This real Florence seemed unreal and incredible. And William himself changed. His good looks began to look commonplace and shady: his seriousness became furtive, his praise of her calculating. He was shorter than his wife, his face now looked hang-dog, and she saw him dragging his feet as obediently he followed her. She resented that this woman had made her tell a lie, strangely intoxicating though it was to do so, and had made her feel as ugly as his wife was. For she must be, if Florence was what he called 'beautiful'. And not only ugly, but pathetic and without dignity.

Berenice watched warily as the woman took a letter from her handbag.

'Then what is this necklace?' she said, blowing herself out again.

'What necklace is this?' said Berenice.

'Read it. You wrote it.'

Berenice smiled with astonishment: she knew she needed no longer defend herself. She prided herself on fastidiousness: she had never in her life written a letter to a lover – it would be like giving something of herself away, it would be almost an indecency. She certainly felt it to be very wrong to read anyone else's letters, as Mrs Cork pushed the letter at her. Berenice took it in two fingers, glanced and turned it over to see the name of the writer.

'This is not my writing,' she said. The hand was sprawling; her own was scratchy and small. 'Who is Bunny? Who is Rosie?'

Mrs Cork snatched the letter and read in a booming voice that made the words ridiculous: '"I am longing for the necklace. Tell that girl to hurry up. Do bring it next time. And darling, don't forget the flute!!! Rosie." What do you mean, who is Bunny?' Mrs Cork said. 'You know very well. Bunny is my husband.'

Berenice turned away and pointed to a small poster that was pinned to the wall. It contained a photograph of a necklace and three brooches she had shown at an exhibition in a very fashionable shop known for selling modern jewellery. At the bottom of the poster, elegantly printed, were the words

Created by Berenice

Berenice read the words aloud, reciting them as if they were a line from a poem: 'My name is Berenice,' she said.

It was strange to be speaking the truth. And it suddenly seemed to her, as she recited the words, that really William had never been to her flat, that he had never been her lover, and had never played his silly flute there, that indeed he was the most boring man at the College and that a chasm separated her from this woman, whom jealousy had made so ugly.

Mrs Cork was still swelling with unbelief, but as she studied the poster, despair settled on her face. 'I found it in his pocket,' she said helplessly.

'We all make mistakes, Mrs Cork,' Berenice said coldly across the chasm. And then, to be generous in victory, she said, 'Let me see the letter again.'

Mrs Cork gave her the letter and Berenice read it and at the word 'flute' a doubt came into her head. Her hand began to tremble and quickly she gave the letter back. 'Who gave you my address – I mean, at the College?' Berenice accused. 'There is a rule that no addresses are given. Or telephone numbers.'

'The girl,' said Mrs Cork, defending herself.

'Which girl? At Enquiries?'

'She fetched someone.'

'Who was it?' said Berenice.

'I don't know. It began with a W, I think,' said Mrs Cork.

'Wheeler?' said Berenice. 'There is a Mr Wheeler.'

'No, it wasn't a man. It was a young woman. With a W – Glowitz.'

'That begins with a G,' said Berenice.

'No,' said Mrs Cork out of her muddle, now afraid of Berenice. 'Glowitz was the name.'

'Glowitz,' said Berenice, unbelieving. 'Rosie Glowitz. She's not young.'

'I didn't notice,' said Mrs Cork. 'Is her name Rosie?'

Berenice felt giddy and cold. The chasm between herself and Mrs Cork closed up.

'Yes,' said Berenice and sat on the sofa, pushing letters and papers away from herself. She felt sick. 'Did you show her the letter?' she said.

'No,' said Mrs Cork, looking masterful again for a moment. 'She told me you were repairing the flute.'

'Please go,' Berenice wanted to say but she could not get her breath to say it. 'You have been deceived. You are accusing the wrong person. I thought your husband's name was William. He never called himself Bunny. We all call him William at the College. Rosie Glowitz wrote this letter.' But that sentence, 'Bring the flute,' was too much – she was suddenly on the side of this angry woman, she wished she could shout and break out into rage. She wanted to grab the flute that lay on Mrs Cork's lap and throw it at the wall and smash it.

'I apologise, Miss Foster,' said Mrs Cork in a surly voice. The glister of tears in her eyes, the dampness on her face, dried. 'I believe you. I have been worried out of my mind – you will understand.'

Berenice's beauty had drained away. The behaviour of one or two of her lovers had always seemed self-satisfied to her, but William, the most unlikely one, was the oddest. He would not stay in bed and gossip but he was soon out staring at the garden, looking older, as if he were travelling back into his life: then, hardly saying anything, he dressed, turning to stare at the garden again as his head came out of his shirt or he put a leg into his trousers, in a manner that made her think he had completely forgotten. Then he would go into her front room, bring back the flute and go out to the garden seat and play it. She had done a cruel caricature of him once because he looked so comical, his long lip drawn down at the mouthpiece, his eyes lowered as the thin high notes, so sad and lascivious, seemed to curl away like wisps of smoke into the trees. Sometimes she laughed, sometimes she smiled, sometimes she was touched, sometimes angry and bewildered. One proud satisfaction was that the people upstairs had complained.

[980]

She was tempted, now that she and this clumsy woman were at one, to say to her, 'Aren't men extraordinary! Is this what he does at home, does he rush out to your garden, bold as brass, to play that silly thing?' And then she was scornful. 'To think of him going round to Rosie Glowitz's and half the gardens of London doing this!'

But she could not say this, of course. And so she looked at poor Mrs Cork with triumphant sympathy. She longed to break Rosie Glowitz's neck and to think of some transcendent appeasing lie which would make Mrs Cork happy again, but the clumsy woman went on making everything worse by asking to be forgiven. She said 'I am truly sorry' and 'When I saw your work in the shop I wanted to meet you. That is really why I came. My husband has often spoken of it.'

Well, at least, Berenice thought, she can tell a lie too. Suppose I gave her everything I've got, she thought. Anything to get her to go. Berenice looked at the drawer of her bench, which was filled with beads and pieces of polished stone and crystal. She felt like getting handfuls of it and pouring it all on Mrs Cork's lap.

'Do you work only in silver?' said Mrs Cork, dabbing her eyes.

'I am,' said Berenice, 'working on something now.'

And even as she said it, because of Mrs Cork's overwhelming presence, the great appeasing lie came out of her, before she could stop herself. 'A present,' she said. 'Actually,' she said, 'we all got together at the College. A present for Rosie Glowitz. She's getting married again. I expect that is what the letter is about. Mr Cork arranged it. He is very kind and thoughtful.'

She heard herself say this with wonder. Her other lies had glittered, but this one had the beauty of a newly discovered truth.

'You mean Bunny's collecting the money?' said Mrs Cork.

'Yes,' said Berenice.

A great laugh came out of Florence Cork. 'The big spender,' she said, laughing. 'Collecting other people's money. He hasn't spent a penny on us for thirty years. And you're all giving this to that woman I talked to who has been married twice? Two wedding presents!'

Mrs Cork sighed.

'You fools. Some women get away with it, I don't know why,' said Mrs Cork, still laughing. 'But not with my Bunny,' she said proudly and as if with alarming meaning. 'He doesn't say much. He's deep, is my Bunny!'

'Would you like a cup of tea?' said Berenice politely, hoping she would say no and go.

'I think I will,' Mrs Cork said comfortably. 'I'm so glad I came to see you. And,' she added, glancing at the closed door, 'what about your father? I expect he could do with a cup.'

Mrs Cork now seemed wide awake and it was Berenice who felt dazed, drunkish, and sleepy.

'I'll go and see,' she said.

In the kitchen she recovered and came back trying to laugh, saying, 'He must have gone for his little walk in the afternoon, on the quiet.'

'You have to keep an eye on them at that age,' said Mrs Cork.

They sat talking and Mrs Cork said, 'Fancy Mrs Glowitz getting married again.' And then absently, 'I cannot understand why she says "Bring the flute."'

'Well,' said Berenice agreeably, 'he played it at the College party.'

'Yes,' said Mrs Cork. 'But at a wedding, it's a bit pushy. You wouldn't think it of my Bunny, but he *is* pushing.'

They drank their tea and then Mrs Cork left. Berenice felt an enormous kiss on her face and Mrs Cork said, 'Don't be jealous of Mrs Glowitz, dear. You'll get your turn,' as she went.

Berenice put the chain on the door and went to her bedroom and lay on the bed.

How awful married people are, she thought. So public, sprawling over everyone and everything, always lying to themselves and forcing you to lie to them. She got up and looked bitterly at the empty chair under the tree at first and then she laughed at it and went off to have a bath so as to wash all those lies off her truthful body. Afterwards she rang up a couple called Brewster who told her to come round. She loved the Brewsters, so perfectly conceited as they were, in the burdens they bore. She talked her head off. The children stared at her.

'She's getting odd. She ought to get married,' Mrs Brewster said. 'I wish she wouldn't swoosh her hair around like that. She'd look better if she put it up.'

The Spanish Bed

Out of the stream of cars with boats on their trailers that drive out from Colchester towards the giddy light of the sea, only one or two will turn off at a fingerpost marked To Villas. The drivers find themselves at a small house that until some twenty years ago was the home of John Osorio Grant, the novelist. It is a small place, painted in a fresh grey that gleams in the sun, rather like the silvery mud banks of the estuary when the tide is low, and is really three little villas with pinched bay windows, which Grant knocked into one somewhere about 1912 while living there for forty years with his sister. The house then passed to an enterprising man in the oyster trade who made money in a fashionable restaurant in London and was admired in the village for taking the mean little bays out of the house and putting in two long landscape windows in their place, a man greedy for views. But he tired of the country, as Londoners do, and sold the house to the present occupier, a Dr Billiter, a retired mining engineer and mineralogist from the North who has lived a wandering working life in Chile, Bolivia and for a long time in Mexico.

The doctor is a big man, overweight, as soft as an elephant, his jacket and trousers hanging on him like a hide. He walks in a creeping way, stooping as very tall men do, as if he were following a scent, often nibbling a biscuit. In the village it is felt to be unnatural for a man of his size to be living alone. 'Pure accident' he says has brought him to the village and he waves a heavy arm to give himself the careless, even frivolous air of a balloon that has slipped its mooring and taken off into the sky. What he means is that there are 'pure' accidents and 'vulgar' accidents; the pure accidents occur only to a scientific mind which has been long-headedly prepared for them.

He had been reading the novels of John Osorio Grant over and over again as a recreation in the lonely evenings of a life on mining sites where one gets sick of the company around one. A good detective story is like

[983]

the detective work of mineralogy in a brisker, more relaxing form. His revered, though very trying mother had often kept house for him during long spells of his career and it was on the last of his exasperating trips with her to the silver mines at Guanajuato – where her mania for buying unwanted, picturesque rubbish in Mexican markets was getting on his nerves – that she redeemed herself by an astonishing discovery.

In a pile of rotting paperbacks she spotted a book called *A Visit to the Osorio Mines*. Printed in Mexico City in 1902 and full of misspellings, it was Grant's first book, written when he was nineteen and had been sent out to learn Spanish by his family, who were Osorio's agents in England. A juvenile book of fifty pages, it had never been published anywhere else and was unknown in Grant's list of works. The doctor became, in that instant, a potential bibliophile: he had a treasure.

A second accident occurred – it must be an example of the 'impure', for it could happen to any of us – about a year before his retirement, when he was planning to return to England and live in the country with his mother, in one of those English villages that are the scene of Grant's novels: places equipped with a squire, a clergyman, spinsters, a dubious City man, a vigilant postmistress and a house with a panelled library, gleaming with the knowledge and the corpses it had seen. But his dear mother died. Mexico became suddenly empty: he packed and went to comfort himself in his dreamed-of England, but there the emptiness of his dream made him fretful. It was at one of his lowest moments, when he was cheering himself with a dozen oysters in a London restaurant, that he found himself talking to the oysterman who owned Villas. The ghost of Grant suddenly came in to occupy the empty stool beside the doctor at the bar. In the course of a few weeks he ate dozens of oysters and found himself buying Villas, and Grant's ghost came down with him.

The doctor was lonely no more. From that time he talked and hummed to himself, throbbing with the sensation that he was a miracle. It cannot be said that he 'heard' Grant telling him to put the place back into the state it had been in *his* time, for there was nothing mystical in the doctor; despite his slothful look, he was a restless, practical man. He was certainly 'impelled' to tear out the blatant landscape windows the oysterman had put in, to put back the narrow bay windows so as to darken the house, and to uncover the stone floor that lay under the oysterman's chic parquet, as a beginning. He had always been called 'the Doctor' in Mexico because of his distinction in his science; now he felt an exuberant desire for distinction in a new field. He had no friends, but he boldly created the at first imaginary Friends of John Osorio Grant Society. After a year or so they numbered about seven. They wrote to him and one or two called and he slowly got together material for a pamphlet saying that Grant was a shamefully neglected figure in the history of the detective novel, the creator of the famous Detective Inspector Coffin.

As he wrote and rewrote his sentences, a pencil drawing of Grant, which he had found at a bookseller's in Colchester, looked down and seemed to say, 'Enough of Inspector Coffin. What about me?' Grant had been eclipsed by his sister, the marvellous gardener and Queen of Flower Shows, in local memory, just as the doctor had been dominated by his mother.

In the bluster of a spring morning another example of 'pure accident' occurred. The doctor was working in the room he called his 'office', which used to be Grant's study, when he heard a loud jangling noise in the bedroom above. Slates blown off? A gutter gone? Water coming through? Burglars? (On this, particularly, he was sensitive. Villas had been burgled after Grant had died.) In the manner of Inspector Coffin, the doctor went up the uncarpeted stairs to his bedroom and caught the village girl who came in to clean bouncing saucily on the high iron bed, a decorative Spanish object with a tin panel, lacquered in black and yellow triangles at the head, and very loose, which had belonged to Grant and which the doctor had found rusting in a garden shed. Caught out, red as puberty in the face, the girl got off the jangling bed, picked up a broom and pretended to sweep the tiled floor. Shy as he was large, the doctor jerked a big thumb at the room in a general apologetic way, and went away humming.

He wished that the girl's mother still worked for him and had not pushed this impertinent daughter into the job, for she always gaped at his size, which put her into a state of swallowed giggles. But this incident changed her. From that morning she became timorous and propitiating – she was frightened that he would tell her mother. Nervously she watched him. She was all 'Yes, Doctor' and 'No, Doctor'. She brought him apples, she brought him biscuits – he liked nibbling biscuits, for he was a hungry hypochondriac who thought that with the exception of oysters, a square meal made him put on weight. In a week or two she came in with a Christmas card in an envelope with a long-out-of-date stamp on it.

'Very pretty,' he said.

'See what it says,' she said. 'It was in Gran's cardboard box.' Gran was long ago dead.

The doctor opened the card and then looked at the girl, who seemed to him suddenly rooted in genius or complicity. Villagers often showed him useless antiques in the hope of turning a penny or merely to show that they knew more about the place than he would ever know. Did the girl know the importance of what she had pilfered? He hoped not. But she had done what no publisher, no library, no Record Office or correspondent had been able to do. The faded ink on the card said: 'Love to you, Gran dear, and all your family. Clarissa Ward.' And, thank God, there was an address. He had discovered what people in the village either did not know or had forgotten, a detail which he had longed to know ever since he took the house: the address of Grant's widow.

Apart from that boyish visit to Mexico there was only one odd incident in Grant's life. As the doctor used to say lightly to any member of the Society who came to the house, 'We know that he returned to England. We know that he settled here with his sister. Then there are two missing years during which, as the records show, he married a Miss Ward. Who she was, what happened to her, no one knows. The marriage lasted two years. She vanished and his sister returned. No one in the village remembers Miss Ward. It looks as though –' he would add roguishly, 'as if the two ladies did not get on. Anyway, Miss Ward seems to have been unimportant.'

The word 'unimportant' was slurred over. As a mineralogist the doctor believes that no fact, however small, is unimportant. Put all the facts together and one gets the whole: think of the hundreds of now precisely known facts about the formation of crystals that explain the unanswerable existence of metals. It irked him as it would have irked Inspector Coffin, that a small fact about Grant eluded him and, as he looked at the card, he already felt the itch for an erotic secret that comes even to amateur biographers.

The doctor did nothing about the card at first, for the picture of Grant rebuked him. On the other hand, Inspector Coffin egged him on. Eventually the inspector won and the doctor sat at his typewriter, writing and rewriting a letter to Miss Ward. With a tact that seemed to him enormous and painful he said nothing about Grant. He simply wrote that he was the owner of Villas and was writing an account of the house because of its unique historic interest. He understood that she had once lived there and he would be grateful if she would consent to see him. When the letter was done, he fell into melancholy. The woman was probably dead. No reply came. After a few weeks he wrote a second letter, enclosing a copy of the first. Still no reply. Hope died. Then it occurred to him to write in his own naked hand: the clumsy personal hand, he had found, often achieved what the machine could not. He came out into the open: he said that in Mexico he had come across a little book written by John Osorio Grant which had never been published in England. He would be delighted to show it to her. This brought a reply at once from a Miss Carter saying that Miss Ward, who was seriously ill, asked her to thank him and to say she received no visitors.

Dr Billiter rushed from his house and walked down the short rough path to the village, down the street and then up again, his face shining like the face of a euphoric but silent town crier, waving an arm boastfully. 'Miss Ward, once the wife of John Osorio Grant, is alive! She exists! No one but myself knows it. You've been hiding this from me but I've found out for myself.'

The only question was: Did the child know what she had done? No doubt she had eavesdropped and heard him mention the name to visitors. Still, to be certain, he bought her some sweets in the village shop. She was a hungry child.

More important was the question of the race with death. Miss Ward was old; she was ill. By the end of the week he could stand his torment no more. He set out on the drive across the middle of England to Nottingham and stood on Miss Ward's doorstep.

The house was small and trim – not in the mining or lace-making districts. He rang the bell and a small woman with grey hair pulled back painfully from a bony forehead opened the door. He jerked a thumb at the traffic and people passing in the street as if throwing them and himself away and becoming nothing.

'My name is Billiter – Dr Billiter,' he began. 'I have been in correspondence with a Miss Carter . . .'

The woman looked back into the hall of the house and then gazed at him, taking in his size very much in the stupefied way of the village girl at Villas. Then she tried to enlarge herself, and in a grand voice with a tremor in it she said, 'We always have Dr Gates. Why did he send *you*? It's too late. I was telephoning all day yesterday to the hospital and in the end I had to get the ambulance myself. It is a scandal. Miss Carter is in hospital. I am Miss Ward and I shall report the matter to the authorities.' At that word the small woman's neck quivered.

'Miss Ward!' cried the doctor. His thick lips parted, his mouth was wet with wonder. For a moment he wanted to pick her up and carry her off, the treasure, ten times more precious than all the silver in Mexico. 'But it is you I wanted to see,' he marvelled.

She pushed her head back and looked up at him with suspicion. He saw this and spoke in his natural voice, which was as soft and polite as the buzzing of a large bee. 'Miss Carter wrote to say *you* were ill and I feared –'

Miss Ward addressed the street. 'I am not ill,' she said. 'I'm in very good health.'

'I apologise for the intrusion,' he said. 'I happened to be passing. I am sorry to hear Miss Carter is in hospital. I really came about our correspondence. By the way, I am not a doctor.'

'Then why do you call yourself one?' she said.

'Not a medical doctor. I am a mineralogist.' He began to fiddle with the zipper of his briefcase. 'It's about Villas,' he said, appealing to her.

'What villas?' said Miss Ward. 'Miss Carter is my secretary. I am not interested in buying villas or anything –'

'No,' he said. 'Let me explain. It's the name of my house. I am a great admirer of the work of John Osorio Grant and I am working on . . .'

He had by now got his pamphlet and the letters out of his case.

Miss Ward had bold, grey-greenish, salty eyes, and at the name of Grant the lid of her right eye slowly drooped and closed until it looked like a small ivory ball, and the left one like the tip of a pistol. 'There's no one of that name here. I do not let rooms,' she said. And with that she closed the door in his face. Just before it was completely closed, he heard her say loudly to someone he supposed to be in the hall, 'Damn you.'

The doctor stared at the red brick of the house. 'Glazed midland clay,'

[988]

he muttered, 'probably a hundred years old; it never weathers.' It was as implacable as the woman had been. He got back into his car, wagging his head, jerking his thumb at passing cars, humming to himself, 'Poor John. Poor John.' Privately he always called Grant by his Christian name when he thought of him. John had become part of himself, like a brother.

When he saw the village girl next day he lied to her, unnecessarily. He said, 'Yesterday I had to go to London.'

One of the small annoyances of receiving visitors at Villas, even members of the Society and especially their wives, is that they are far more interested in the garden than in the house when the summer comes. He is obliged to listen to their botanical comments and hear them say, 'She was a wonderful gardener.'

The garden has little interest for him: it had meant nothing to John. It was the sister's empire. The doctor is proud of having filled in the oysterman's tiled swimming pool and shows you that the old pond reappeared afterwards from the spring which had fed the vulgar pool. That proves a point.

'You remember the pond in *Death Among the Lilies*?' he says.

He leads you back along a brick path. The ladies say it is a pity that the place has 'been let go so wild' and crowd around some unusual rose or lily or shrub they have detected. At the end of a brick path they notice two statues – or rather, there are two plinths. On one, a goddess-like figure in graceful robes is placed, rather blotched by lichen in the face and looking ill-used and sulky. On the other plinth there is only a pair of feet. The figure was knocked down by the motor mower of the oysterman's gardener. The odd thing is that visitors often tactfully avert their eyes from the feet and replace the missing statue in their minds.

'Are *they* anyone in particular?' visitors often ask.

This annoys the doctor. He dismisses the figures. No, he says, they are only ornamental. Grant's sister picked up a taste for garden statues in Italy and she bought a pair from Stillbury Manor when the Electricity Board took over the big house. She got them for a pound apiece. It is a small satisfaction to him that here he can refer to a document; he nods to the house and says, 'I can show you the receipt inside.' Often as he walks around he picks up a stone and throws it into a flower bed. One has the impression that he is throwing it at someone – possibly Grant's sister.

Once he gets people back into the house his eager pride comes back. He looks down, confiding, into the face of anyone who asks a question. 'The last man put parquet floors down in the rooms downstairs,' he says. 'This is the original stone floor.' He has ripped out the modern fireplaces, of course. Furniture, he says, was a difficulty. Grant's sister, they say, had one or two valuable family things – two or three of the smaller pieces had been stolen by burglars who had broken in after John's death. But Grant's taste was for the plain and useful. Chic modern wallpaper has been scraped off. Whitewash returned, good clean whitewash.

You follow the doctor's pachydermic figure. It darkens the passages or the stairs, fussing over what relics he has found and what he is going to find. He jerks a thumb as you pass a chair, a table, a rug or a picture and says 'Chair' or 'Table' or 'Rug,' and so on. He is all modesty in his passion for the obvious. Looking out of a window he may say 'Garden' or 'Bird in apple tree' or 'Field' or 'Boy kicking football.' Outside of his science he has a kind of compassion for facts, hoping they may divulge something privately to him one day.

His most apologetic moment is in Grant's study – no original furniture, but it is redeemed by his collection of Grant's novels and the files and the pencil portrait. Lately he has found out that the dealer has lied to him: the portrait is not of Grant. So the doctor says 'Probably Grant' and likes to think that it will somehow turn into Grant's likeness if it is kept long enough. He gets the visitors out of this room quickly to Grant's severe bedroom. This has been perfectly reconstructed. Spanish- or Mexican-looking tiles are back on the floor and there is the Spanish bed – the one the village girl was caught lying on.

After the defeat at Nottingham and when the year climbed into the summer, the doctor took to going to the sailing club, the only place where Grant had not been effaced by his sister, but the sole interest of the raconteurs of that place was how much any figure of the past had drunk or what sort of boat he had had. About this there were arguments: none could remember. To one story he did listen carefully. The tale was that Grant had gone out one afternoon and, in classic fashion, had got stuck in the mud in a falling tide and had had to sit there half the night. They added that a girl was in the boat: this is a common myth in English estuaries. Still – you never know.

Then one day – late in August – the doctor was seen skipping fast to the post office to send a telegram.

Another example of 'pure' accident had occurred. He had received a letter with a Nottingham postmark. He studied the envelope and postmark several times before he opened it. It was addressed in a large hand that rushed downhill almost off the envelope. The letter was from Miss Ward. He raced through it, missing most of what it said the first time, and then he read it slowly again. The striking thing was that all the t's were crossed with long lines so that a squall of sleet seemed to be blowing across the page.

'Dear Dr Billiter,' the letter began, 'I do not know if you recollect our meeting, the other day . . .'

The other day! It was five months ago!

'. . . but I do apologise for the confusion, due to the sad circumstances of my friend's sudden illness.'

She went on to say that she would so much like to see the pamphlet about Villas he had mentioned and thought there were many things she remembered about the place, although it was years since she had been there. Would he send her a copy? Or if he were over in Nottingham, she hoped he would call.

Going over the letter once more, the doctor saw it was dated three weeks before the postmark on the envelope. There was a postscript squeezed on to the bottom of the page and the last word had been crowded out:

'I am grieved to say that poor Miss Carter has d –'

Two days after his telegram, not waiting for a reply, the doctor drove to Nottingham yawning with appetite. He finished a packet of biscuits and had to stop to buy a cake before he got once more to Miss Ward's doorstep.

For a few seconds he could not believe he was looking at the same woman. The grey hair was not drawn back but was now loose and blond. She was wearing a violet jacket and bright-pink trousers which showed she had a droll little belly and was plumper and younger. He remembered meagre eyelashes; now they were long. Only the drooping of the right eyelid convinced him she was the same woman. Her shoes had high heels and she had a prowling step as she led him into a pretty room at the back of the little house, and when they sat down he noticed the high-arch shoe. She gazed at him with a doll-like satisfaction and did not listen at all to his explanations and politenesses, waving them away in a chatting fashion. But when he said how sorry he was to hear about her poor friend, her voice changed and she gave a short shake of her head. 'Don't speak of it,' she said in a reciting voice and choosing her words sadly and carefully: 'It was a stroke.'

Suddenly she stopped reciting. 'So you live at Villas? How extraordinary. How time passes. And you knew *dear* Ossy? Where did you meet? In Mexico?'

'Dear Ossy!' The pet name shocked him. Obviously she had not taken in what he had just told her. 'Dear Ossy' – how lightly a husband is thrown away.

'John,' he said, staking his claim to the man. 'No. I never met him. I found his book – or rather my mother did – as I told you. I was in Mexico long after his time. I've brought the book to show you.'

She merely glanced at it and put it on the table. 'It's a paperback,' she said. 'I thought you said it was in leather – valuable.'

'Oh, but it *is* valuable: a rarity. These things are often worth a great deal.'

'How much?' she said. 'Thousands?'

'Oh no, not thousands – perhaps fifty or a hundred. I wasn't thinking of the money.'

'You should,' she said and began to wag her foot up and down. Afterwards he remembered the sudden small frenzy of her foot and, once more, that drooping eyelid that gave him the impression he was talking to two women at once.

'Anyway,' she said and the eye opened, 'you live in that awful house, those mean miserly little windows! And those stone floors! It was so damp! It was ruining his books – he'd lived there for years. The chimney smoked too. Poor Ossy, he ought to have been a priest. But I heard some rich man bought the place and made a lot of improvements, made it fit to live in. Ossy was very – you know – close.'

The doctor was annoyed to hear his dream attacked. 'I've put the bay windows back. They give the place its date – 1820 – its character. And the stone floors too; of course, I put in a damp course. I wanted it to be as it was in John's time,' he said stoutly. And he went on to describe all the things he had done, room by room, until he saw again that she was not listening to him but studying him in detail, with a pleased ironical flirtatious smile on her face. She interrupted him.

'Does your wife like it?' she said. 'Are you married?'

'Oh no, not actually,' said the doctor, finding himself to his surprise apologising.

'Why do you say "not actually"?' She laughed. 'I mean, it's not my business,' said Miss Ward.

The biographer did not like being questioned. He jerked a thumb at his life as he did at things. He explained about his mother.

'Those mothers!' she said. 'Was she an invalid?'

He decided to stop her questions and to get *his* life out of the way as quickly as possible by a comic exaggeration. 'She had enormous, one might almost say preposterous, good health. Her death was a shock.' For he himself still felt an emptiness he was fighting to fill.

'It's so unfair. It leaves guilt. One is always a prisoner,' she said and her little mouth – a spoiled mouth, he thought – slipped at the corners. Then she brightened.

'You know, Ossy and I were only married two years,' she said invitingly. 'I do not use his name.'

'Yes, I gathered . . . I was going to ask you . . ."

'The traffic is terrible in this street. Can't you hear it, even at the back?' she said to the walls of the room.

'I can't say I do.'

'Humming?' she said.

This worried her, but defying the traffic, she burst out with: 'Two years! When I heard he was dying – I used to keep in touch with old Granny Blake in the village, I always sent a card every Christmas, she was really the only friend I had there – I felt I had to go and see him. Even after all those years one has a picture of people in one's head. I made Miss Carter drive me there. She tried to stop me, but I just had to go. Isn't that strange? After all, he had been my husband, in spite of everything, but leave that alone. It was really shocking – big gaps in the shelves in his library where I waited. Those stone floors. His sister wouldn't let me go up at first. She told Miss Carter I was drunk. I had to force my way upstairs. Miss Carter made her let me go. That room, that horrible bed – you know he had a terrible Spanish bed? – it was the bed that shocked me and the bedclothes had not been changed. He had died two hours before and, you won't believe it, they hadn't closed his eyes. Ossy was a big man, like you, and now his body was like an insect's. His teeth! He couldn't have minded if I was drunk, could he?'

Dr Billiter murmured. The stern Miss Ward he had met the first time appeared and the enamelled face cracked at the mouth into the lines of her age.

'If his sister had looked after him instead of that filthy garden, he wouldn't have died like that,' she said violently. 'And the roses smelled. There was no air. I couldn't stay in it. I went outside, walked among her rotten flowers in the rain.'

The passion of Miss Ward startled Dr Billiter. He had come for a pleasant biographical chat. There were so many things he wanted to ask her about the house if only she would let him direct the conversation.

'I'll show you something,' she said and went to an album which was lying on a table and put it on his knee. There was an old picture of a boat lying on the hard and John, a big man with a heavy moustache and wearing a yachting cap, was standing with his arm around a young girl – herself. He had a rudder in his free hand.

'His sister,' she said, 'wouldn't go near the water. Not after he got stuck on a mud bank all night with her once.'

'Ah now,' said the doctor. 'I remember hearing –'

'He didn't love her. He loved me,' she said.

This is embarrassing but better, thought the doctor nervously.

'I can prove it,' she said. 'Come here.' And she made him come to the French window that looked out on to a small paved garden with ferns planted against the walls and a pool with lilies in it. In the centre of the pool stood a stone figure.

'Ossy got Sidney McLaughlin to do it. Do you know his work?'

'I'm afraid I don't. You mean he did the statue?'

'Of course,' she said. 'It's me – soon after we were married.'

'Very nice. Very pretty,' he said politely.

'When I left his poor body in that room I walked up the path – you know the path, you must do – and there it was. He hadn't moved it. He'd kept it. After everything – bad things! That is love, isn't it?'

'You mean at Villas?' said Dr Billiter, so embarrassed by this talk of love that he had not been looking at the figure but at the paving, noting that it was sandstone. And then the meaning of her words hit him.

'At Villas. Of course,' she said.

Dr Billiter looked closely at the figure and became flabby with unbelief. He studied the figure in every detail. With scarcely any doubt the figure was the one missing from the plinth in his garden and he fingered the catch on the window. Or was it a copy? Perhaps these ornamental figures were manufactured by the score. He could not speak. He glanced at Miss Ward and saw she was watching him with a look, half complacent, half cunning, a look that brought the village girl who worked for him to his mind. He had to struggle against his whole training and nature, against years of looking at rock and automatically naming it. Miss Ward was a deluded woman. He could not say to her, 'I'm afraid you're mistaken or someone has taken you in. That figure is not you, it's one of a pair of ordinary ornamental figures that came from the garden at Stillbury Park. John's sister bought them. I've got the invoice in my papers.'

'Of course I was young,' she was now reciting calmly. 'Long dresses had just come in for the evenings and one wore one's hair long and tied like that.'

The doctor was helpless. Painfully he allowed himself to split in two. He allowed himself to drift away with her into fantasy. 'You must feel very happy to be remembered. It's charming.'

'And so *like*,' she insisted. 'You can see.' And she fetched the photograph and made him look again at it.

There was not the slightest resemblance between the face and body of the statue and the fat girl with short black hair and wearing a heavy jersey and clumsy gumboots.

She must be mad, he thought. There was only one truth he could tell. 'You have solved a mystery for me,' he said. 'I've often wondered what happened to the statue – you know, there is only the plinth there now, only the feet ...'

'What feet? It's got feet,' she said indignantly.

'I've asked everyone in the village what happened to it. No one knew.'

'Who did you ask?' she said sharply.

'Everyone. Gardeners. Builders,' he said. 'The pair must have looked rather nice together.'

'The pair?' she said. 'There was only me. No one else.'

Oh God, thought the doctor. I suppose people see only what they want to see.

'Anyway,' he said, 'it's the best piece of news I've had for a long time. To know it's safe. It's wonderful it came to you.'

'He left nothing to me.'

'Or perhaps his sister . . . ?' he suggested.

'His sister!' She laughed at that. '*You* didn't know her.'

The doctor made a last attempt. 'In the sale after he died?' he asked.

Miss Ward now laughed victoriously. Her fingers nipped his jacket by the sleeve and she drew him from the window. As he moved towards his chair she pulled his cuff tight and her fingers pinched as she made him flop beside her on the sofa. She leaned closely to him. 'I stole it,' she whispered.

'I don't believe you!' said Dr Billiter as playfully as he could in his heavy way.

'I did. I stole it.'

'A heavy thing like that,' he teased. 'You couldn't.'

'I have *friends*,' she said. And then she became querulous, talking to herself rather than to him; this talking, as if to someone else in the room, was one of the irritations in listening to her. She was saying, 'Ossy's family said, "Who are her people? Who are her friends?"' And then openly to him: 'Who wants people? I have *friends*, very good friends, very close friends.

'Oh, it would make a wonderful story for your book! His sister shut up the house but she forgot one thing – you can't shut up a garden! It was screamingly funny. I won't tell you who they were, but they were *friends*! They got into the garden at night by the back lane and pulled it out – into their car, of course. I can't go on calling you Doctor – what do your friends call you?'

'James,' he said, hating to give it to her.

'I shall call you Jimmy,' she said. 'Jimmy. It's such a thrill – stealing, don't you think? I bet you like stealing things?'

'I suppose the nearest I've come to it is forgetting to return a book. Sweets, of course, when I was a boy,' he said.

'There you are!' she said. 'You must call me Clarissa. When you were in the mines in Mexico, didn't you steal silver?'

'Of course not, Clarissa' – another surrender there – 'it's just lumps of crystal.'

'I would have!' she cried.

He was on the point of giving her a small lecture on the crystalline origin of ores, of striation, the seeping of water, the dead pressure of rock for hundreds of thousands of years – the knowledge was at his fingertips, but the faculty for uttering facts had left him. He was adrift in her imagination. There was a vacancy in his mind, and out of it, as her fingers pinched him, his mouth spouted one of the rare and reckless inspirations of his life. 'You were not *stealing*,' he said. 'You were only taking what was your own.'

'Yes,' she said firmly.

'You were,' he said, 'taking yourself.'

The moment he said this he couldn't believe that he had been capable of saying a thing so nonsensical and so cruelly untrue.

Miss Ward let go of his sleeve and moved away to look at him with wonder, a pretty wonder in which there was a tinge of morbid seductive gloom, like a shadow setting off a brilliant light. 'You are a very clever man, Jimmy,' she mumbled gravely. 'I'm so grateful to you. It's a long time, so long, long and long since I have been able to open my heart to someone who understands. I can *talk* to you. I'm so glad you've come.' She jumped up. 'We must drink to it! What will you drink? Champagne? Yes, let us have champagne – but you'll have to open the bottle. I can't stand noise.' She put her hands to her ears.

'It's rather early,' said Dr Billiter.

'It isn't! Don't move. I'll get it.'

He watched her walk out of the room and feared the prowl of her arching feet. He went to the French windows and once more his fingers went to the catch. Secretively he opened the door and stepped into the little flagged garden and looked closely at the figure. Now there was absolutely no doubt: the figure was not a copy, it *had* certainly come from Villas. The feet – left behind – had been replaced and were awkwardly held to the figure by a rusting iron band. The 'friends' had been in a hurry and careless, if what she said was true: there was a repaired crack across the waist. Very likely they had had to carry the statue in two pieces. His mind was wandering into the sadness of a hopeless lust and his hands itched. Morally the thing belonged to Villas and to him. He felt ashamed, now that he was alone, that he had not spoken out. Why should the delusions of others paralyse one's own desires? Why does one give in? A fantasy of his own jumped into his mind. He saw himself telling her the truth, bringing her to her senses. She gave in and begged him to take the thing, generously he offered her money – she refused – he wrapped the statue in sacking with his own hands, roped it, cased it, carted it into his car and saw the amazement of the village as, in a self-disparaging way and not to injure her – mustn't do that – he would say that he had managed to find the figure in some garden shop or stone mason's. In some way, John applauded . . .

The dream exhausted him. He heard Miss Ward's steps. He went back to the room. At least now, he hoped, they would settle down and he could ask her more questions.

'I was having another look at you,' he said, nodding to the garden, astounded to hear himself giving in to her once more as, carefully putting a napkin over his hand, he removed the wire from the cork of the bottle.

She put her hands to her ears. 'I don't think you were a miner or whatever you call it, Jimmy,' she said. 'I think you've been a waiter. Is it over?'

'There,' he said. And slowly poured out a glass.

'You're so attentive,' she said. 'I'm sure your real name is Charles. You were at the old Café Royal!'

'That's right!' He laughed. 'And you ordered *quenelles de brochet*. I remember it like yesterday.'

'Now you are making fun of me,' she said severely.

Oh dear, she was beginning again.

'I am not. To the two goddesses,' he said, raising his glass to her and to the figure.

'Whew!' she said when she drank and held out her glass for more. 'You are a strange man,' she said and her eyelid drooped. 'Tell me truthfully' – she spoke of truth-telling as an abnormality – 'why are you writing about Ossy, the house and everything? Changing it. Digging out that old Spanish bed?'

'I like doing things,' he said. 'That bed was a find.'

'Not for Ossy,' she said. 'Not for me.' She made a prudish horrified face. 'It clattered! The noise!' she said. 'I wasn't in love with him. He took me from my friends. I told you I had friends, a lot. He was years older than me and his sister watched me. If I was on the telephone, she always listened behind the door.'

The doctor was not sure that *he* ought to listen to her. And he wished she had not brought in the champagne.

'*I* know why you took the house. Why do you want to be Ossy? Why do you want to be someone else? Did you do something' – she pouted – '*wrong* in Mexico? I mean – police?'

'Indeed not!' he said shortly.

'I did,' she said proudly. 'Ossy went off to Holland on the boat and I didn't want to go. I sold all his books, his father's books, while he was away – the valuable ones, I mean.'

'I don't believe you,' he said.

'Don't pretend to be stupid,' she said. 'Four thousand pounds. Well, he didn't give me any money. And other things too.'

'I still don't believe you,' he said.

'So I know why you have come here. You want to take my statue away. Someone told you I'd got it. You want to put it back on those horrible feet in your garden. I saw it when you were looking at it. That is why you kept writing letters, isn't it? Why do you keep on humming?' Her voice was becoming a shout.

He had never seen suspicion, despair and anger so suddenly splinter a face so that she turned into the old woman he had seen on the step the first time. Her face was cracking like stone and then, to his eyes, there was the mica-like glister of tears on it.

She dropped her glance to the floor and put her hands to her ears. 'Stamp, stamp, stamp,' she shouted like a soldier.

'Clarissa,' he said. 'Please. I've not come for your statue. I told you I did not know it was here.'

She took her hands from her ears. 'What did you say? Feet are stamping,' she appealed to him.

[999]

'I said I haven't come for your statue.'

'Yes you have. Why don't you take *me*, not that thing. Take me back to Villas with you. I'm in prison here.' The eyelid did not droop: both eyes stared at him. 'But you won't take me, will you? Oh no, you're frightened,' she said slyly.

He was indeed frightened and appalled when she got up, thinking she was going to rush at him, but instead she went pathetically to the door and her hand struggled with the handle. Outside in the hall she called out, 'Miss Carter. Miss Carter.'

'She is mad,' the doctor said aloud; 'she is calling to the dead. She has got my book in her hand.'

He lumbered after her. What does one do with mad women? Shake them? Startle them? Shock them by an enormous shout? She was going up the stairs, holding on to the banister. One shoe had fallen off and, out of politeness, he picked it up.

'Clarissa!' he bellowed. 'You've got my book.'

And following her cautiously, fearing he might have to grapple with her, he heard a door open above and saw a frail old woman in a dressing gown looking over the banister. She was carrying a stick.

'What is it, darling?' the old woman said in a voice like a man's. 'Why are you dressed up like that? You know it's forbidden.' And dropping her stick, gripping the rail and in pain, one arm useless, the woman he had been told was dead grunted down the stairs.

'The police have come,' Miss Ward sobbed. 'Help me.'

The old woman stopped and called out, 'You are Dr Billiter. I told you not to come here. Look what you've done. Stay where you are.'

Miss Ward reached the old woman, who put her arm around her and said, 'There, darling. It's all right.'

'Let me help,' said Dr Billiter. 'I understood –'

'Go away,' called the old lady. 'She needs me. You don't understand. Please go. Go at once.'

'She said . . .' the doctor began. 'She has my book . . .'

'I know what she said,' the old woman said. 'You're a naughty girl, darling, dressing up like that. You know that as long as I am alive I'll look after you.'

'He's trying to take me away,' Miss Ward whispered. 'Make him

[1000]

go. I haven't done anything.' She let the book drop from her hand.

'You can do one thing,' the old woman called over Miss Ward's head to Dr Billiter. 'You can ring Dr Gates. The number's in the red book in the front room. He knows.'

And the old woman sat on the stairs holding Miss Ward as Dr Billiter crawled up after the book and put the shoe down. 'Shoe,' he said out of habit and went down to the telephone.

When he came back and stood on the linoleum in the hall, he saw there was no one on the stairs. The house was silent. He waited and then he tiptoed to the door and went out into the street and stood still, breathless, not knowing where he was, until he saw his car. It was a long time before he could recall how to drive it and where he was going, and when the cars raced past him, heading for God knows where, and as the fields and trees and towns lurched at him as if they were going to vomit over him, he could only think: Carter alive! Carter alive! He rustled the biscuit bag in his pocket, but could not eat. Three hours on the road! Turned sixty as he was, he wished his mother were fulminating beside him. When at last he got to Villas, its windows catching the sea-light of the evening, the sight calmed him, but once he was inside he was scared by the speechless doors in the rooms. He could not rid himself of the feeling that they were closed against him, that the place was not his and that Clarissa Ward would open them and even John himself would be in his study, laughing at his notes and files.

That night he did not sleep in the Spanish bed. In the morning, looking out of the spare-room window at the back he saw the empty plinth. Pointlessly he waved an arm at it, and then, at nine o'clock, the village girl came.

'When I come yes'day,' she said, accusing him, 'you wasn't there.' She had uttered, it seemed to him, a profound truth.

A month or so later there was a letter from Miss Carter enclosing a cutting from a Nottingham paper: 'Sept. 17th, Clarissa Ward, *tragically* . . .' He knew what the word meant. She had wanted that tragedy to occur at Villas!

The Wedding

————

The market was over. Steaming in the warm rain of the June day, the last of the cattle and sheep were being loaded into lorries or driven off in scattered troupes through the side streets of the town which smelt of animals, beer, small shops, and ladies. The departing farmers left, the exhaust of their cars hanging in the air.

Tom Fletcher, the forty-year-old widower with a wilful twist of chestnut hair over his forehead where the skin had a knot of intention in it, drove off but got out at the open door of The Lion, and putting his head down as if threatening to charge into the crowd there, shouted, 'Come on, Ted. Leave the women alone till Saturday,' and Ted Archer came out and sat very tall in the car.

'That used to be a terrible place,' Archer said. 'The new people have done it up.'

The pair drove twelve miles on the Langley road round the bottom of Scor, the hill which stuck up in a wooded lump over the slates of the town. To children of the town, Scor looked like the head of an old man, and that image sank into their minds like a kindness when they grew up. They thought the quarry carved out of the hill was his mouth. Today the rain ran off the woods into the streams that waggled below him.

Driving up the long rise to Poll Cross, the two men saw a woman come out of the larches, straight in the back and walking fast. She carried her head well.

'Effie Thomas must be hard up for it – going up the woods on a day like this,' said Ted.

'Bugger,' said Tom. He had the sly voice of someone enjoying a meal. 'Someone got his knees wet. What's the matter with you, Ted? That's not Effie, with a back like that. That's Mrs Jackson, the little bitch from the College, Mary's teacher. I'd give ten pounds to anyone who'd take her up Scor on a Sunday afternoon and pull her tights down. Filling my girl with a lot of parlez-vous. What's the good of French? Bugger, you can't talk French to your Herefords, Ted. Why don't you marry that teacher, Ted?'

'She's been married once already,' said Ted.

'I know she has. She'll miss it, won't she then?' said Tom.

They caught up with her and made her skip up on the bank. The young woman had a rude look – very alluring.

'Jump in, you're getting your pretty hair wet, Mrs Jackson,' said Fletcher, very courtly. 'Get in the back. We'll drop you. You'll be all right. I've got Ted in the front with me and I've tied his hands.'

'I have been enjoying my constitutional; but, well, thank you. Yes, I will avail myself . . .'

'Avail yourself of everything while you can. We dropped the pig at the market.'

'How do you do, Mrs Jackson,' said Ted when she got in and they drove on.

'Hear him?' said Tom. 'He speaks French. You ought to see his heifers go off round the fields when they hear him. Like a horsefly under their tails.'

'I can believe it,' said Mrs Jackson, who had a strict habit of giving a shake of her head for the sake of boldness. Fletcher was watching Mrs Jackson in the mirror. Her fair hair was drawn straight back from her forehead into a bun at the back. It was the kind of hair that frizzes and is almost white. She was a thin, plain young woman; her blue eyes were small.

'You'll be coming to the wedding, missus, Saturday?' said Fletcher.

'I am looking forward to it,' she said. 'Most kind of you to ask me.' Her pretty voice was cooled by all the knowledge in her head.

Fletcher dropped into country speech and said to Ted, 'Tha was at school with me, warn't 'e, Ted? He's nobbut a rough farmer's boy, missus. Remember, Ted, poor old Lizzie Temple? Us dropping peppermints down her blouse?' And then to Mrs Jackson: 'He'd begun already. That's thirty-five years ago. Never ride in the back of a car with him.'

'I will think of that when the temptation occurs,' Mrs Jackson said.

'When the temptation occurs. Did you hear that, Ted?'

Mrs Jackson said she had never seen the country so green and Tom said he had never seen Mrs Jackson's cheeks so blooming, which was a fancy, for she was as pale as a bone and her humour was dry.

They arrived at her little cottage, which stood back from the road on a short rise, and when she got out she thanked Fletcher and in her firm way she said, 'I haven't given Mary up.' The little blue eyes were determined.

Tom Fletcher gave one of his loud laughs and called to her as she crossed the road, 'Run in quick, missus, or Ted'll chase you upstairs.'

But when they drove off Ted said, 'I can't stand so much forehead in a woman.'

'It's the best part,' said Tom. 'But you wouldn't know that. But she's putting ideas into my Mary's head. It was all poor Doris's doing, sending the girl to a snobby college like that and now they want to send her to Oxford. Before Doris died I couldn't say anything, could I? But Doris has gone now. And Flo's getting married. I'll be alone in that house now, Ted, if I let Mary go.'

'That's right, Tom. You will.'

'It's all right for you, Ted, you dirty bugger, but I don't want my girl putting on airs and marrying a French professor. Where's the economics of it? Your family and mine, Ted, have farmed this land for two hundred years, haven't they? That's what I call economics. I want my girl at home talking English. And doing the wages. I've told old Mother Jackson so.'

'How old is Mrs Jackson?'

'Too old for you, Ted, you old bugger. Turned thirty, but I tell you if she hadn't been a friend of Doris's, I wouldn't have had her in the house, talking that classy stuff to Doris all day, about Louis IV, the pair of them – they did. Ted, as if they were married to him. She wanted us to call one of my bulls Napoleon . . .' Fletcher's temper blew away into laughter. 'No, I haven't anything against her. She's got a head on her. It's an education to listen to her. But her husband made a poor job of her. Ask me – she never had it. She sent me the bloody forms to fill up. I've got enough forms. Well – she's not going to get Mary.'

They got to Ted's place and they went in to see the boxing on television. It annoyed Tom that although Ted hadn't got *his* money (for he often calculated that), Ted's house was a fine white place, fit for a gentleman, with peaches on its walled garden, well run.

'You bachelors look after yourselves,' he said.

There was not a scratch on the paint inside the house, not a smear on the mahogany. If Ted hadn't won as many prize cups at the shows as he had, there was not a speck on his carpets. There were portraits of Ted's grandfather and grandmother on the wall of the dining-room; the decanters sparkled. A lot of money had gone down the drain in Ted's family, but the dining table could seat twenty-five and looked as if it was waiting for the whole tribe of Ted's forebears to come back and throw away more money if he reformed and got married.

'My place has been let go since Doris died,' he said jealously as he watched the boxing. 'Old Mrs Prosser comes in but she's past it. That was a low one, see that?'

They were watching the middle of a fight.

'It will be all right after the wedding,' said Ted.

'All right? What d'you mean? I'll be alone in the house like you, you bugger. His eye's cut.'

'Mary's a good girl. She's got brains,' Ted said. 'You'll have to look around, Tom.'

'Look at that – footwork, footwork. The lad'll never get anywhere with that. Hit him, boy. Look around? You haven't left much around, have you, you old sod.'

'There's old Mrs Arkwright. You'll have to do a deal,' said Ted slyly.

'Bugger that for a deal,' said Tom. 'She's had one of my tractors for a month up there. I'd sooner old Mrs Doggett. If she was twenty years younger, I'd have her. You remember how you lassoed her at Bill Hawkins's wedding? The old girl's got a kick on her.'

'She did the cancan,' shouted Ted, getting a drink. 'I bet your Mrs Jackson can do a cancan. She's been in Paris.'

The laughter stopped. A mean look came into Fletcher's face. 'She's been divorced,' he said. He stuck out his lip. 'They oughtn't to have a woman like that in the College. All the la-di-da did it. But we all know who she is.'

'Old Charlie Tilly's daughter,' said Ted.

'The seedsman who used to have The Lion till he drank it dry,' said Tom.

'News travels,' sighed Ted. 'There was no money there. She ran off with some society man.'

'If I'd been Charlie Tilly, I'd have tanned her arse. She never told him, just ran off and they didn't see or hear of her for twelve years,' said Tom.

'Mrs Tilly didn't know anything until she saw a picture of her in a magazine at the dentist's – all dolled up at Ascot races. High society,' said Ted.

'And comes back here as if nothing had happened.'

They sat in silence and then Fletcher said, 'She ran through twenty thousand pounds of her husband's money.' He swelled with satisfaction at the size of the sum and at the thought that a local girl could do that. 'She's got a brain. Ah now, look at that – he's marking him.'

They watched the fight to the end.

Messell, the art master at the College, came into Mrs Jackson's study. It had once been the housekeeper's room in the large country house which the College rented. For five years since she came out of the hospital after her divorce and the rest of her scandal, she had been teaching here.

Messell said, 'What's the matter with the town bull's daughter, Christine? I've just passed her in the corridor wiping her eyes.'

Mrs Jackson considered Messell for a while. 'Her sister is getting married. She is quarrelling with her father. I am going to the wedding,' she said.

'It's this place,' said Messell. 'It's too grand for them. How many of them have got ballrooms forty feet high with painted ceilings in their homes? They walk about dreaming they are duchesses.'

Messell was wearing a cape and a violet tunic done up with small buttons high on the neck, and there his round face rested on it like a detachable moon. His large round eyes were vain of their woes. It would be no surprise, she thought, to see him carrying his head in his hand, for he had the look of one wishing he had been executed in more dashing times than the present.

'Speak for yourself,' she said in her bossy way. 'Why shouldn't they think they are duchesses? I always wanted to be one. Girls are practical. A girl is a new thing: they have to invent themselves.'

'Did you invent yourself?' Messell said.

'Of course,' said Mrs Jackson.

Messell had the prowling gaze of one who is vain of seeing through people.

'Why,' he asked, 'why did we leave London for a dump like this?'

'We?' she said. 'I have to earn my living. What are you going to do this half-term?'

It was impossible to get anything out of Mrs Jackson.

'Sleep,' he said. 'Drink. What are you going to do?'

'I told you I'm going to the wedding tomorrow,' she said.

'Why are women so mad about weddings?' he sneered.

'We live for the future,' she said. 'Why don't you go to London and commit a sin?'

The sun was beginning to shimmer in the summer mists next morning as she drove towards the town.

When she had first come to teach at the College, five years ago, she was uneasy at the sight of the countryside she had left when she was a girl and rarely left the park that surrounded the place. She did not want to be seen. But after a year she drove defiantly into Langley; she had to face it. It was enemy country: the enemy was her childhood. When she saw Scor hill coming boldly out of the summer haze, and the slate roofs of the town in its hollow, every house, every window flashed old dull hatreds. In time they vanished and became no more than a tale – for the place emptied. The people in the shops and in the streets looked unreal. She seemed at once a ghost and yet the only real and living person there. It annoyed her that the people she passed and looked at so intensely did not ask to know who she was. She compelled herself on one of these early visits to stand in front of The Lion, where her father had brought her to live when she was six and he had married again. It was a mean little place but it sparkled now, and she looked at the top bedroom window at the front where she had so often stood, outstaring the dry, biblical brick of the Baptist chapel opposite, a building that seemed to forbid the thoughts in her head. It now looked feeble; she had outwitted it. How much shouting had gone on in the family. How proud she had been her name was Tilly and not the name of her handsome stepsisters, whose beauty had looked greedy and common to her. They had grown up and married now. The only unmarried one was living in another pub at Fenn twenty miles away, with her stepmother.

After one long compelled stare she did not visit the place again, but when she went to the town nowadays her ghost at the window of the place eyed her from the street she avoided. Guilt gave way to a new regret which went on for years – that she had never brought her husband to see the place where her plots and ambitions were born, because she was afraid. Once, on one of her low evenings this last year, she had been on the point of telling Messell her story, for in his prowling way he had sniffed out that she was a fellow casualty, but she stopped herself. He was not up to it. He was muddy with remorse about something: he lacked the secret pride of prodigals and had stopped at dressing up.

Today as she drove, Scor hill came up stealthily. She parked her car and went into the church she had not been in since she was a child. It looked smaller, of course, and the Latin inscriptions on the tablets of the stone walls seemed nearer. She read one, looking for howlers out of habit. The organ dribbled out a squealing flourish, and for a moment she could hear her husband's voice calling to her in that church at Toulon on their honeymoon: 'Here's one! Look at this.' They were looking for the tomb of Comte de Tillet. The Tillys were French émigrés! she had told him. The unforgivable thing about him was that he had the innocence of the rich and accepted her fantasies as a compliment to himself. But now the organ bellowed as if from all Tom Fletcher's herds, and Fletcher walked up the aisle with Mary's sister, the bride. He marched forward, correctly in step, with his crested head lowered, chin forward on his short strong neck, his brow knotting when his eyes marked the site of the altar as if he would pause to pad his feet and lower his shoulders and gallop the last three yards, catch the vicar and send him flying in his surplice. Yet he stopped with the ease of a man at the market.

'Doesn't it strike you,' she wanted to say to the congregation, to keep her distinction, 'doesn't it strike you as all rather indecent?'

But her question was sung down by the hymns, particularly by an aunt of the bride who was sitting behind her and by an uncle as pink-skinned as a salmon. The restiveness of the ceremony got into her waist and legs, and afterwards when she left the church she was smiling and excited by the chatter outside. She drove on to Fletcher's house and felt, for the first time since her divorce, unmarried. The eyes of the other women sparkled with the same brief hungry feeling themselves.

There was the marquee striped in red and white on the lawn – Mary had boasted that it would be. What a day for boasting! The scene was like a flower show and between the hats of the ladies she saw the long view of the fields and woods and hills buzzing in the sun, and the cattle down below slowly moving up the fields curiously, as excited as the crowd, to the garden hedge. It was astonishing to find herself among so many tall young men whose weathered necks stuck out of their white collars. The bride was in full folly, queening it before the groom, rushing him from one group to another as though she were going to eat them all. Fletcher stood confidently among his guests, shouting in his meaty way, yet bowing – really *bowing* – to the ladies, old and young. The tuneful aunt spoke to Mrs Jackson, and she, feeling that a fantasy of the learned kind was called for, said in a ringing voice, 'Mr Fletcher has the head of a Roman emperor.'

The aunt was baffled. Mrs Jackson explained, 'As it might be on a medallion.'

'He won two first prizes at Cottesbury,' said the aunt, who belonged enthusiastically to contemporary life.

Mrs Jackson repeated her remark to the vicar, who nodded, and she was inspired to develop the idea: 'One forgets how much of Roman wealth must have been in cattle.'

This news made the vicar anxious to move away and he adroitly introduced her to another aunt. 'This is Mary's famous Mrs Jackson,' he said.

'If only poor Doris could have seen this day. This is what Tom has just said to me. It is sad. She was the love of his life,' said the aunt.

That sentence rang through Mrs Jackson's head all afternoon. At some time or other everyone in the town and the countryside would take a long breath and utter it. Ted Archer had innumerable loves of his life; her stepsisters had been thick in the gossip of these loves. On every day of the week, except the day of the cattle market, the town was enthralled by love of every kind, even when money went over the counters in shops or ladies went to the library or drank their tea. Window blinds signalled it. One looked at the unlikely people, but the sentence ran from glance to glance.

Mrs Arkwright, colouring up with champagne in the heat and sitting in the tent on a chair that was sinking into the grass, uttered the sentence to Mrs Jackson: 'I lost my husband. He was the love of my life – I know. But we mustn't think of ourselves. It's Mary I'm worried about, losing a sister. Tom will be alone in the house. My heart bleeds for that man.' Mrs Arkwright was panting. 'I'm resting because of my leg. I must get some air.'

She obliged Mrs Jackson to help her into the garden. 'It's not like one of your London weddings,' she said. 'Ah, there's Tom, poor man. As I was saying, Mary ought to get away. I'm on your side. *You* understand.'

Mrs Arkwright threw away a cigarette and coughed into the flower bed and then turned to consider the pleasant house. 'It's sheltered,' she said, lighting another cigarette and giving a pull to her waist, for she was large, boxed into her clothes, dark-haired and brimming with fate. 'He's letting it go. I don't mean anything nasty, but the sitting-room paint! And then upstairs – you can see for yourself there's no woman. And Mary at the College: she is too young. Of course you can't say anything to *him*. But I agree with you.'

Mrs Jackson got away to the hedge at the bottom of the garden and Tom Fletcher came up to her.

'Is that Scor?' she said. 'What a lovely view.'

'Twenty miles of steak, missus,' Tom Fletcher said, and he called to Ted Archer, 'Come here, you bugger. Mrs Jackson wants you to take her up Scor hill.'

'I went up there when I was a child,' said Mrs Jackson primly.

Fletcher sent out one of his bellows of laughter. 'I never met a woman here who hasn't,' he shouted and gave Ted Archer a punch.

The afternoon moved on from laugh to laugh. There was silence for a speech about the secret of happiness. The bride laughed and pouted. The groom said, 'All I can say is, she is a smashing girl. She's the love of my life.' And that over, the men got into groups and talked about their farms and the children played hide-and-seek round the skirts of the women as the afternoon lolled in the fields and Scor became plainer and nearer, creeping up like the cattle. At last the women moved to the front door of the house, waiting for the couple to come down, and one or two young men shouted up at the window, 'Come on, Jim, can't you wait?'

Three men went into the drive to the car under the dusty elms and the young children now climbed on to the flint wall by the yard, the girls grabbing at the legs of the boys. The afternoon wheeled and cooled; short shadows edged their way out from the trees. Mrs Arkwright came slowly across the lawn and pushed her way to stake a claim in Fletcher in the crowd by the door. There was a scrimmage, the confetti flew, the photographers calmed them all down, there was a click as time stopped. Then shouts. Tom Fletcher went down with Mary and the couple to the car and he picked up a child that had fallen on the way. Ted Archer blew his hunting horn and off went the car and young men slapped on the roof. As it crawled out on to the lane a man suddenly scrambled on top of the roof and was carried away, banging violently on top of it. A bottle fell from his pocket and broke on the road.

'Who's that?' said Fletcher.

But the car had gone.

Oh, God, said Mrs Jackson to herself. Messell. He's drunk. How did he get here?

The young men went into the lane and watched, and after a long time, back came Messell without his cape, in his violet shirt, covered in dust and a trouser leg torn.

'It's all right,' he shouted. 'I'm impotent. I want Mrs Jackson. Where's Mrs Jackson?' he shouted as he stumbled into the drive.

Mrs Jackson dodged up the steps into the house. What a disaster! How had he got there? She hid in the bathroom; she could just see him swaying and talking among the men, who were looking at him in silence, and then she saw him sit on a grass bank. She came down into the large empty sitting-room. It had not changed since Doris's time. All those thin silver vases! And the photographs of the shows, the smell of roses and cigarettes, and the family chairs empty. The seats had slackened since Doris's time, helplessly. Peeping from the window, Mrs Jackson saw children watching Messell: he had got up again. She did not know where to go for safety. She went along to a room she remembered – the one Fletcher called his office. The blinds were down to keep out the sun, and in the low light she could see only the glimmer of the silver cups Fletcher had won. She went in and listened.

'Little Chris Tilly.'

She stiffened at the lazy, insinuating impertinence of his voice. She had not heard her maiden name spoken for years.

Fletcher was sitting at his desk looking at his wages sheets.

'Oh, I'm sorry,' said Mrs Jackson. 'I didn't see you. I came in to the cool.'

'Who are you chasing?' he said.

There was suddenly loud shouting from the yard.

'Stay there a minute,' he said. 'I want to say a word to you.'

He went out and soon came back. 'Did you bring that professor with you?'

'Certainly not.'

'I don't want any professors here. I've got enough trouble with government inspectors. You've got some funny people up at the College, missus.'

He stared at her rudely and she set her chin.

'Well, don't go. Sit down with me. Look at all this stuff. Forms, forms, forms. Buggered if I can read them. Mary'll have to do it. Have you taught her to read forms? How to pay wages – that's what a girl needs. That's education. Well, that's where it all goes,' he said and picked up the papers and dropped them into a wastepaper basket.

Mrs Jackson smiled, but Fletcher scowled slyly.

'*And* the forms you sent me, missus. My girl's staying here. No offence, missus, but you've had your turn; now it's mine.'

'Don't let us discuss it now. It's been a lovely wedding. Flo was so pretty. And such a nice young man.'

'He'll do if he can make anything out of a hundred acres. If she makes him work. You can have all the professors at Oxford and Cambridge, but my girl stays here, missus, and she knows it. You've got to tell her. If she won't listen to me, she'll listen to you.'

'She's got the best brain in the school,' she said. 'She's desperate. If you're not careful, you'll lose her altogether. Mrs Arkwright was talking to me ...'

Tom Fletcher reddened as he stared at her. 'Old Mother Arkwright doesn't know her arse from her elbow. My daughter's my business.'

'I don't think this is the time to talk about it,' said Mrs Jackson. 'Mary's a prizewinner.' And she waved towards the cups on his shelves. 'Like you. Don't you think she should choose?'

'No,' said Fletcher. 'I never chose. You didn't choose.'

'But I did.'

'So they tell me,' he said morosely. 'I haven't anything against you, missus. Your life's your own. But I've got fifteen hundred acres.' He looked round the room. 'Look at the state those cups are in. Old Mrs Prosser comes in, but now Flo's gone, who will clean them?'

Fletcher was himself startled by his own turn of mind. A shout from the yard disturbed him. Mary ran into the room. She stopped when she saw Mrs Jackson and her father. 'They're chasing Mr Messell, Mrs Jackson,' she said anxiously.

'Let 'em chase him,' said Fletcher, getting up. 'I've said all I want to say. Let's see what the lads are doing. Us country lads like a bit of sport. This isn't your first wedding here,' he shouted, and when he got up he gave her a slap on the bottom. 'Come on.'

He pushed Mrs Jackson to the door, and when they got out onto the steps of the house, there were Ted Archer and two or three others, in their black wedding clothes, but now with ropes in their hands. One of the farmers had flung out his rope and lassoed another who was getting out of it, just as Archer was sending out his own rope at Messell, who dodged. In a moment three men were out for Messell, who dodged again and backed to the yard wall and then suddenly slipped through a gap at the side of it. They were after him.

Cars started up. The guests were going. The young farmers came back, followed by Messell. They were tired of him and he flopped down again on the grass bank.

The children visited him from time to time with wonder: he was stretched out asleep on the grass. Tom Fletcher winked at Ted Archer, who sent out his rope and caught one of the aunts. She screamed with such pleasure that one of the men rushed at her, picked her up in his arms and carried her to the open trunk of his car and dumped her into it as she kicked up her legs. She climbed out and her hair came down. Three other ladies doubled up with inciting laughter and mocked the men. One by one the men chased and caught them.

[1013]

Tom Fletcher's red face swelled like a turkey cock's: he was shouting. 'Give us the cancan, Mrs Doggett,' he shouted as the old lady's legs went up in the air. The aunt with the beautiful voice climbed out of the trunk of a car and dared them to rope her again. Fletcher stood near Mrs Jackson and called out 'Go on!' to the men. The dust flew. The skirts went up, the hair came down. Then it all stopped and the women got together, panting, tidying their clothes and now daring Tom Fletcher himself, who had picked up a rope.

Mrs Jackson took the opportunity to go to Fletcher and in her politest manner said, 'Good-bye, Mr Fletcher. I'm afraid I have to go. I have an engagement. It has been a lovely wedding.'

'Go?' he said. 'You can't go.'

But she went off to her little car. He watched her. He levelled the rope.

'Mrs Jackson!' Mary called.

Fletcher's rope snaked out, knocked Mrs Jackson's hat over her eyes and was over her shoulders, pulling her hair down and biting on her waist. He pulled her stumbling towards him.

'Daddy!' shouted Mary.

Mrs Jackson's face hardened as she got her footing and showed her bold teeth at him. The other women had laughed when they were caught, but she did not. She pulled fiercely at the rope and she surprised him by a sharp pull that got it out of his hands. He made a grab at it and missed. He was stupefied as she stared at him. The aunts watched in silence. Slowly Mrs Jackson got out of the rope, carefully picked it up, and walked to her car. Mary rushed after her.

'Go away, child,' said Mrs Jackson, and the girl rushed back to her father with tears in her eyes and then ran into the house, red-cheeked with shame.

They saw Mrs Jackson arranging her hair in the car mirror while Fletcher stood there scowling and silent, and everyone stared at him. Ted Archer dropped his own rope. Fletcher grinned uncomfortably and then Mrs Jackson drove off fast. They stood listening to the sound of her car as it went over the hill behind the farm.

'Tom,' said Ted Archer. 'She's gone off with your rope.'

Five pigeons on the roof of the house flew off in a wide circle. They seemed to be following her.

Messell got up from the grass and walked towards Fletcher. 'Sir, that was not the act, that was not the act, act . . .' He could not go on.

'Bugger off,' said Fletcher and went sullenly into the house, shouting for his daughter.

'Intolerable,' Mrs Jackson muttered as she drove fast to the main road, looking into the mirror to see if she was followed.

'Little Chris Tilly' – the countryside had broken its long silence about her; he was mocking her, all those ridiculous women, so polite to her face, were mocking her. She did not mind, but to be roped in like that, by a man, with the lot of them, was too much. She could feel the blow of the dirty rope on her neck, feel its bite on her waist, and see the dusty marks on her dress, and despite her temper she felt weak. She looked in the mirror again and again, feared still that she was followed, and could not get his stare, as he threw the rope at her, out of her head. The fear was strong enough to make her get off the main road and take the long way home, looking for some private place where she could straighten her clothes, and when she found one she stopped her car and went nervously into the trees and pulled up her dress to see whether her skin was marked. There were no marks.

'All the same!' she protested and drove on more calmly, and she was left with impatience at the girl's tears.

'She'll have to fight for herself,' she said. 'I did. After this I'm not going to raise a finger for her. Anyway, she'll fall for the first man she sees and that will be the end of her.'

The evening clouded as she sat restlessly in her cottage trying to read and stopping to look from the windows as each car went by, and at last went into her back garden. The air was heavy, the trees were darkening and still. There was a large elm in the field beyond and it was oppressive in its huge, spreading silence, waiting.

She sat in a deck chair watching the grass grow dimmer. Presently an inexplicable eddy of wind passed across the field until, striking the elm, it swirled into the tree, lifting and parting the branches as if men had got into it and were tearing it; it heaved and swelled and raved for a full minute and then suddenly the wind passed.

'I shall go to London. I must get hold of someone. Who shall I ring?'

[1015]

she said. She went indoors and got out her suitcase and began getting dresses out of a closet, holding them up and then throwing them on the bed. Only one she picked up again.

'You little tart,' she said, 'where have you been?' And she threw it down again. There was a knock at her door.

'Fletcher,' she said and stood, all the strength running coldly out of her legs and then rushing back up her body and tossing in her heart.

'No, Messell of course,' she said to deceive herself. She looked out of the window and saw a bicycle standing against the garden wall.

'It's me. It's Mary,' the girl's voice called.

The girl stood white-faced and hot in the little sitting-room. She said, 'I'm not going back. Oh, Mrs Jackson, I've run away. I'll never forgive him.'

Mrs Jackson made her sit down and the girl cried on her shoulder.

'It was so insulting to you,' she was saying.

Why, thought Mrs Jackson as she listened to the girl, why have I got to relive my life?

And when she said this, sensations of triumph sparkled in her and her heart was warm. Years of self-accusation vanished from her and the headlong tenderness of being young flowed in.

'But I was not insulted at all. Surprised, yes, but it was rather a compliment,' she lied.

The girl looked gravely and mistrustfully at Mrs Jackson.

'Did you tell them you were coming here?'

'No,' said the girl.

'Good heavens,' said Mrs Jackson. 'We must get you back at once. I'll take you. They'll be out of their minds. At this hour.'

'I saw your face,' said the girl.

'You mustn't go by faces,' said Mrs Jackson. She went to her bookcase and picked out a book. 'This is what I promised to lend you. I was going to bring it this morning.'

The girl held the book in bewilderment.

'I shall tell your father you came for the book,' Mrs Jackson said.

She told the girl to read the book while she made some tea. It was called *Rambouillet: The Art of Conversation.*

'You wrote it!' exclaimed the girl.

'Yes, I did. I was going to bring it to give it to you at the wedding, but I forgot. Better late than never.'

She drove the girl back to the farm, where Ted Archer was standing at the door.

'She's here,' called Archer, and Fletcher came rushing out.

'Mrs Jackson forgot to give me this,' the girl said. 'I've been to fetch it.'

'At this hour?' said Fletcher as Mary kissed him.

'We've been all over the countryside looking for her,' said Ted Archer quietly to Mrs Jackson as they went inside. 'They had words.'

They sat on the large shabby chairs and Fletcher listened silently to Mrs Jackson's chatter about the wedding, staring at her, and when at last she made him laugh she put on a prudish, busy face and got up to go at once.

'I'll be up tomorrow for my rope,' he shouted from the doorstep as she switched on the car lights and drove off. It was the only time he spoke. His shout seemed to own the night.

When she got back to her cottage, she lay on her bed. 'Oh, no,' she said in the little hot room. A heavy night of throwing off bedclothes. Trivial dreams of voices and faces and Fletcher sitting in his chair and staring at her! And then – what a triumph – in the morning there was a mark on her waist: it had come up in the night. She would have liked to show it to him.

She had washed her hair and was sitting with a scarf around it, looking harsh and prim, when Fletcher came in the afternoon.

She put on an impudent mouth when he came to the door. She took the rope down from a hook. 'Here is what you came for.'

He took it and dropped it down outside on the step and then came in and sat down on the sofa.

'You've done something to this place since the old postman had it. It belonged to Randall; he was a fool to let it go. We got a bit rough, as Mary says. But I told her I could see you were on your way, and the best way to get a lady to stay is to stop her from going! I know, I know – the lads were rough.'

'Well,' said Mrs Jackson. 'I am not cattle. I suppose it was what one would have to call a country junket.'

'I can't bear the stuff,' said Fletcher innocently. 'We used to give it to the girls, with prunes, when they wanted loosening.'

Mrs Jackson sat very upright on her chair.

'I had an engagement,' she said.

'That's just what I said to Mary – she's been carrying on. I said you'd got an engagement.'

'How is Mary?' said Mrs Jackson.

'Girls get excited by weddings,' he said. 'You saw the heifers. News spreads. You've been married and so have I – it makes a difference. What's that?'

He pointed to a picture hanging on the wall beside the fireplace. It seemed to be a foam of pink cream and lace, and then he saw the vanishing chalk outline of a doll or a girl floating in the foam, possibly on a garden swing: there was a pink face, two indigo blurs for her eyes, the poppy-red of a drooping mouth. The creature was either just appearing or disappearing in the paint.

'It's a Vandenesse,' she said, recovering her grand voice. 'French.'

He nodded. 'Expensive, I expect,' he said.

'My husband gave seven hundred and fifty pounds for it,' said Mrs Jackson coldly.

Fletcher was silent, then he said, 'A rich man.'

'Very,' said Mrs Jackson.

'Yes, that's what I heard.'

Fletcher shifted on the sofa. 'Bugger, I sold a bull last week for two thousand pounds. Who is it supposed to be?'

'It's a portrait of the Comtesse de Tillet,' she said.

He nodded. 'It would look funny in a farmhouse,' he said.

'Yes, but this is not a farmhouse,' she said.

Mrs Jackson gave a shake of her head to change the subject. 'I was writing you a letter,' she said, pointing to the table by the window where she had been typing. 'But you throw letters away, don't you, so coming here you've saved me a sheet of paper. I have been thinking of what you said to me yesterday about Mary. I've changed my mind since last night. I agree with you. Mary's better off at home.'

'What's this?' said Fletcher, startled. 'Turnabout, I see. Are you telling me she's not good enough?'

'Oh, she's a clever girl,' said Mrs Jackson. 'Simply – I was mistaken.'

'You're saying she's not good enough.'

'Not at all. I've changed my mind.'

His face was amiable. 'I'll tell you what you are, missus. You're a bloody liar.' He laughed. 'And I'll tell you something else. That picture's not the countess of whatever you call her: it's you. Mary told me.'

'It is the title of the picture. I have the catalogue,' she said.

'It's you. Only he's taken all your bones out. He ought to have knocked something off for the price of that. When I am buying an animal I want to see how it stands. I look at its bones.'

'I am sure you do,' said Mrs Jackson sharply. 'But my husband was buying a work of art, not an animal. Don't you like it? The dress is very pretty, don't you think? I love the dress. I've got it upstairs. I was thinking of taking it to London tomorrow – very silly, of course, it's so out of date.'

It was delightful to sit there, looking so plain, and to mock him. She got to her feet. 'I'll get it,' she said.

'No,' he said, standing up, and he held both her arms. 'Stay where you are. You and me have got to do a deal. I want you over at the farm.'

'But I'm going to London. What deal? I know – you want me to clean all those cups.'

'I did them myself this morning,' he said intently. 'I want you down at the farm and we'll do what you like about Mary.'

In the cottage room the short man seemed to shut out the afternoon light. He was looking into her small blue eyes and she saw he dismissed the fight in them and in her chin. He let go of one arm and neatly pulled the scarf from her head, so that her damp fair hair straggled to her shoulders. She put on a face of horror that gave a twist to her parted lips, but the horror was growing into a pleasure in itself. It heated and was growing into a noise in her head as he stared at her, and yet in quick glances he was also taking in the room, the door, the furniture, the cushions, the books, and did not even spare the rugs on the floor. His stare was the stare of the hunt.

'Sit down. Please let me go,' she said.

She was astonished, she was disappointed, when he sat down.

'Tom,' she said. 'Me. On a farm. Are you mad?'

'You know my name, anyway,' he said. 'I'm not mad.' And then he said simply, 'You brought Mary home.'

'Of course I did. What do you imagine?' she said.

'You brought Mary home,' he said again.

'You don't know anything about me,' she said.

'I know everything about you.' He nodded at the picture. 'He's got your mouth.'

'My mouth?' she said. She could not resist turning to the picture and looking at it with a moment's pride, and then the horror came back into her face and she mocked again. 'You go by mouths, too,' she said.

'Yes,' he said and pulled her gently by the hand to the sofa, where she skilfully sat away from him.

'My hair is wet,' she said, pushing it back over her ears. 'What a sight I must be. Go on – what are you saying? You want a housekeeper? Now, there's Mrs Arkwright –'

He did not let her finish the sentence. She was pushing his hands away, his arms, opening her mouth to speak, her ears full of din and her eyes scattering her hatred until, in a pause, her skin burned and her eyes dulled as his were dulled and her lips drooped, when his kissing stopped.

'At least,' she said in a hard low voice into his coat, 'at least lock the door.'

There was a lot of talk at the shows that summer when Fletcher and she and sometimes Mary, too, drove off together. Ted Archer denied it all until Tom had his house repainted and Mrs Jackson left the College and sold her cottage. Messell went about saying Vandenesse was a third-rate painter with a knack of catching girls inventing themselves but no good when they had turned thirty.

The Worshippers

Eeles worshipped Lavender, Lavender worshipped Eeles but worshipped Gibbs absolutely – but what is worship? It is not love. To worship is to be put in a trance by an image. There is not much time for this commodity in the rag trade in that district of London that lies infested by anxiety between the north side of Oxford Street and the Middlesex Hospital.

At eight-fifteen every morning Lavender is sulking like a middle-aged schoolboy, head down, under his bowler hat, as he walks towards his office building. He affects a hump to his shoulders, but when he gets there, or rather, when he 'comes alongside' or smartly 'up to moorings' – as he still says after his time in the Navy years and years ago – he lowers his shoulders and gives a sway as he turns, feeling the roll of *Ripper*, the destroyer he was in, mostly in the Channel, or the French gunboat in which he served on the Yangtze. He is wearing an expensive suit and carrying a correctly rolled umbrella. Five seconds later Eeles, who has been standing in another doorway reading a newspaper and on the lookout for his boss, slips the paper in his pocket and follows Lavender up five flights of dirty stone stairs and joins him just as he is putting his key in a door lettered LAVENDER & COOK in black on the frosted glass, and follows him into the inner office. There Gibbs, Lavender's great-uncle, is waiting for them. Gibbs has been there all night, hanging on the wall, done in oils and heavily encrusted in a gold frame, three foot three by two foot nine, first shown publicly at the Royal Academy in 1882.

Eeles, short, going bald, and getting plump, but much younger than Lavender and nothing like as well-dressed, stands at attention as at an inspection of armoured cars in which he served in the war, while Lavender glances at Gibbs to see whether he is hanging straight. Then both men go to their desks.

'He's much better in this room than he was when we were in the front of the building,' Lavender has said more than once.

Once or twice Eeles has said, 'Much better now he's been cleaned up.'

Gibbs, in his eighties perhaps, is sitting with the difficulty of very stout men, at a desk. His white hair sticks up short like pig's bristles; his cheeks, chins, and the roll of fat around his neck are as pink as a baby's; his little blue eyes are bright and gluttonous. Below the neck the body rests like three balloons at bursting point, the last one resting on his legs. A watch chain travels across his waistcoat like a caravan of annual profits. The whole figure has the modesty and the anonymity of pork, for – as Lavender has many times told Eeles and others – Great-Uncle Gibbs had made a quarter of a million in the bacon trade and contained, even consumed, the firm of Drake, Feldström, Gibbs, and Schmidt (London, Colchester, Hamburg, and Copenhagen, Ltd.), and was the best judge of claret south of the Wash.

Eeles's worship of Lavender had begun when he first saw the portrait. The picture might be terrible, old Gibbs might be vulgar, but in him Lavender had an ancestor. Lavender was, therefore, a gentleman. Eeles decently agreed that to be a gentleman was an asset, though as one who could offer nothing like it in return, he privately thought the condition might not be worth the candle and could even be tragic. What was good for bacon was not necessarily good for the rag trade.

As for the credit side of the account, Eeles would never forget Lavender's handling of Cook. The title of the firm had become a commercial fantasy. Cook had been a non-worshipping man – a *haben Sie?* fellow, hand outstretched, as Lavender said, drawing on the three or four words of German he had picked up in the firm's connexions with Frankfurt – who had suddenly cleared out two years ago, taking customers with him and starting up in competition. Lavender's manner during this row reminded Eeles of Lavender's version of what happened to the officer commanding *Ripper* who, having scraped the hull of that destroyer against the wall of a Dutch harbour as a stick of bombs fell on it while getting a Royal person out safe and sound, received an engraved document from the Admiralty expressing 'Their Lordships' displeasure.' Lavender was a master of being as displeased as a lord, if the occasion arose.

Eeles said, 'I wanted to kick the bugger downstairs.'

This so pleased Lavender that his worship of Eeles began.

'S-s-so,' said Lavender, who stammered a little but mastered it by pulling a face and giving an attractive twist to his neck, 's-so did I.'

After Cook saw the red light and cut his losses, money was tight for Lavender and Eeles, and the firm moved into two smaller and cheaper office rooms at the back of the building. They looked over an alley where the light was dimmer but one could at any rate open a window and let what passed for air into the place. The two men cleaned up the rooms one Sunday. 'Operation Removal' began. Lavender stripped to his underpants, as he had often had to do when he was Ordinary Seaman 0267 etc. before he got a ring of gold braid and his commission. The dandy was surprisingly strong, hairless, and in good condition, no sign of fat on him except in the jowl; with his long lashes and thick dark hair he looked like a youth. He had been a pretty child. Eeles, who was much younger but was putting on weight, took off only his shirt and jacket and was sandy-haired and very pink – as pink as Gibbs, Lavender noticed. They swept down the dirty cream walls of the two rooms with brooms, Lavender being finicky about dust, then washed them. It was Lavender who, saying he had of course scrubbed decks and cleaned grease off propeller shafts, went down on his knees and scrubbed the lino left by the previous tenant, calling out that it was 'coming up' green as grass. Eeles protested at the sight of an older man like Lavender getting down on his knees – an officer too – but he remembered his major in the war who screamed like bloody hell if there was a speck of dirt on a tank. Lavender got up with his pail of filthy water from time to time and looked out of the window. He said it was a pity the street below was not the English Channel or the Yangtze. Eeles was nervous about this but controlled himself.

Then they moved the furniture. This Sunday was the most enjoyable day in the history of the firm: they talked often about it afterwards.

'Back a bit,' said Eeles as they heaved the two desks from the front of the building to the back.

'Mind the bloody door handles,' said Lavender, not concerned with Eeles's knuckles but with possible scratches on the wood. He was touchy about scratches. While they were lifting the metal filing cabinet two of the drawers slid open, letters and invoices showered on the floor. The two men put the thing down and picked up the papers.

'Good God, here's one from dear old Hauser,' said Lavender, picking it up. In more prosperous days they had had the Hauser agency for Swiss lace but had lost it when Hauser died. The letter was written in French, and Lavender started reading it aloud. Lavender had spent two years in a French silk factory, learning the trade, when he was young. Eeles did not understand French, had never met Hauser, but stood more or less at attention respectfully because Lavender's eyes were glistening with worship.

'After he died I stood outside Le Coq au Vin where we had dinner every time I was in Lausanne and I cried like a child,' he said. He had worshipped Hauser, Hauser's wife, Hauser's daughters and their husbands.

Eeles nodded his head and said to break the emotional moment, 'Now we come to the big stuff.'

There were heavy rolls of lace, brocades, and so on, eight feet long. To heave this dead weight down the corridor from the old office was like lifting dead bodies. There was nothing to grip. One had to cuddle the damn things. Lavender put his hand to his back. When he was a boy a Gibbs cousin of his, he said, had pushed him off a tree and he had nearly broken his back: he often got twinges there even now. Still, he did his part. After four in the afternoon the job was done except for the most important thing: hanging the picture of Great-Uncle Gibbs.

It was disturbing when you thought about it, Lavender said, that an old man who must have weighed two hundred and fifty pounds in life should weigh so little in a portrait, even allowing for the frame. A relief – as Eeles said. But to get at the right height on the wall above Lavender's desk called for ruler and pencil marking, arguments about the exact spot, Eeles holding the picture up for Lavender to consider and Lavender holding it up for Eeles, who said eventually, as his arms ached, that the old man had come to life and was making his weight felt. An hour passed before the wall was plugged and the picture was hung.

When they had washed and dressed they came back to the room and considered the picture again.

'It gives the room a glow,' Lavender said. 'Lights up the place.' It sometimes irritated him in the old office when the lights came on in the afternoon in the shops opposite, especially the neon lights, that they made the old man jumpy as if he were on the razzle. 'It made him look tired,' he added.

'He'll be quieter in here,' said Eeles.

Lavender smiled defensively. If a client came to the place and cracked a joke, such as 'It must have been years since the old boy saw his fly', Lavender would close his eyes, offended. A man, Eeles understood, could call his ancestors bastards if he liked, but strangers ought to keep their mouths shut; but he did venture a small joke. 'Pity he can't answer the phone.'

He and Lavender were usually out on their calls half the day.

'Yes,' said Lavender with a short laugh, 'it would save me quite a bit on the answering service.' Then he became serious and intimate. When he got back from Brussels, Frankfurt, or Belfast, he said, 'I always drop in here to look at him before I go on to the club. I don't know why.'

'Well,' said Eeles at last, 'I suppose I'd better get home to the wife and kids.'

'Yes,' said Lavender. 'Thanks for coming. You won't have a quick one round the corner?'

Eeles excused himself and Lavender said, looking doggish, 'D'you really mean that?'

'Yes,' said Eeles.

'Pity,' said Lavender. 'Oh well – gin and women, always my trouble, as the fellow said.'

Two months after the move, Lavender went on business to Hamburg and when he got back Eeles said, 'There's a letter from the bank.'

'Damn impudence,' said Lavender when he read it. 'They're all the same, afraid of Head Office. I'll go round in the morning. I'll tell him where he gets off.'

Eeles gaped. 'He's rung up three times. What are you going to say?' Eeles asked.

'Chop, chop, move the account,' said Lavender.

That is what Eeles admired: Lavender's nerve.

'Anything else?'

'Mrs Baum rang,' said Eeles.

After Eeles left that evening and when Lavender was unpacking his samples, a soft but mannish voice called from the door of the outer room. Lavender was raking up an old row he had had with his father and for the moment thought it must be he, although he had died years before.

Then he recognised the voice of Mrs Baum (Prunella Gowns. Wholesale Only). He had been as nervous of a visit from her as he used to be of his father when he was a boy. She was an old business friend and he had not told her that he had moved the office.

'B.,' she said – he hated to be called Bertrand: hell at school, 'effing B-B-Burlington Bertie' when he was in the Navy. Bloody sissy name, weak.

'Those stairs, B! Eeles told me you'd moved.'

She opened her fur coat to get her breath back. Her face looked wolfish in a good-natured way and made her look older than she was, but her eyes were dark and alive and sparkled like her rings.

'Sit down, sit down, I'll take your coat,' said Lavender.

'I'll keep it,' she said.

She was very much a woman, but her voice brought the pleasant chords of men's voices to Lavender's head – Eeles, for example, old Hauser, Alfie, her husband – a long procession going back to 'displeasure' Stamford of *Ripper*; and Law who 'opened his heart' to him when they were in the hospital in Bombay; Monnier in Saigon; Jack Gibbs; Porter the racing driver who had lost a leg and who had secretly taught him to drive when he was sixteen, which had led to that god-awful row with his father – all worshipped and worshipping. So that when Alfie Baum turned out to be a swine and left Jess Baum for a model at a trade show in Manchester and 'broke Jess's heart,' she took Alfie's place in the male procession. Lavender felt like marrying her himself in a kind of way; the difficulty was that by that time he was already married to Phyllis, whom Alfie and Jess, as worshippers, had warned him against.

'How is Eeles getting on?' said Mrs Baum.

'Hard-working. Loyal. Straight as a die,' said Lavender.

'What did I tell you?' she said possessively. 'If you had listened to me, you would have got rid of Cook years ago.'

'*Mauvais type*,' said Lavender. Mrs Baum made him feel Continental.

She ignored this and looked shrewdly at the bleak office. 'Who on earth's that?' she said, pointing to the picture.

'You've seen it before,' he said.

'Never.'

'Never? That's funny. It was in the old office. G-Great-Uncle Gibbs,' said Lavender.

'What's it doing here?'

'Phyllis won't have it in the house; her sister doesn't like it.'

Lavender gave the twist to his neck. For him the picture was the great test: by their response to it one knew who saw life as one saw it oneself. Neither Phyllis nor her sister did.

Mrs Baum sighed. Alfie had told the young Lavender, 'Never marry a girl from the same office; as bad as the girl next door.'

Then her eyes looked greedy and her face softened. 'You'd have to pay a fortune for a frame like that, B. It's Victorian. They don't even make them now. All that goldwork in it,' she said. 'You can see,' she added, 'it's a likeness. You told me about him, I know, but I never *pictured* him.'

A whole group of fat commercial men, bursting at the waist, came into her suddenly affectionate mind – Alfie, of course; then a cousin of his who was a theatrical agent; and on her side of the family, men whose knees she had sat on when she was a child. Her feelings were for the comforts and the sadness of the flesh. She was on the stout side herself.

'I don't see any of you in him,' she said. 'Not your figure, not your eyes. Not your father's side of the family. I don't see any Lavender in him, B.'

'Best judge of claret south of the Wash,' said Lavender. 'Left his money to the Lord's Day Observance Society.' And added, 'Gin and women, always my trouble. Negative father.'

Mrs Baum nodded. Baffled by this word the first time she had heard Lavender use it, she was proud now of knowing the code. Alfie had told her that it came from the days when ships used flag signals and ran up a flag with a X on it to signal: 'Cancel last message.'

'Not your father's side. Your mother's, I suppose.'

'N-no, no, no, no,' said Lavender softly as if conjuring up spirits. 'Frankly,' he said. 'Sort of. Let me see, grandmother's, sister's husband – what have you?'

Mrs Baum was a hard-headed woman but she loved his 'No. No. No. No's'; they enveloped him in a mist. The vagueness of Lavender had always attracted her – she seemed to glide with him towards the unknowable. A wave of comforting madness washed over her; her rings sparkled with sentiments and her lips loosened with appetite. She remembered large foggy photographs (but cocoa-coloured) in her home as a girl, and

[1027]

people looking silly in coloured snaps, but there was nothing as bold, bright, 'as large as life and twice as natural,' as her mother used to say, like a portrait framed in gold. Her heart – as she grew up – worshipped the sight of old men, pink as babies. They made her feel younger.

'You shouldn't keep a valuable picture like that here,' she said restlessly. 'Any burglar would lift it for the frame alone.'

'Phyllis hates it,' he said.

'How is Phyllis?' she asked, without interest.

'*Comme ci, comme ça,*' said Lavender. '*Plus ça change . . .*'

She liked his bits of French. They made her think she had just come back from Paris. As Alfie used to say, he ought to have been on the stage.

'No,' added Lavender, and to get off the subject of his wife he changed his face and manner. He became 'One' – she always admired that. Not only he, but his truly beautiful suits, seemed to be speaking. 'One gets off the boat train late at night, after a couple of double gins, drops the luggage in at the office. There he is, waiting,' he said. He waved a hand towards the picture. 'The longer one lives, the more one values someone to come back to.'

Mrs Baum felt a short ugly stab in the heart. She knew what he felt. Often she would leave her flat, she said, and go back to the showroom in the evening when the girls had gone and it was closed. 'And yet, B., you never knew him. I mean, he was dead before you were born. Life is funny the way it takes you . . .' She gazed at the portrait.

'There is more in life than one thinks,' said Lavender.

'You're right, B.,' said Mrs Baum. 'A picture like that can take you back.'

'Frankly,' he said. 'Yes and no.'

But Mrs Baum understood this. In her business-like way she thought that her life had begun when she was a very young woman and she really did look lovely: you knew it wouldn't last and you packed all you could into it – but men were different. A man like B. – like Alfie, too – never got beyond the time when they were boys and, damn them, it kept them young. It came to her as a revelation. B. did not see Gibbs when he looked at the picture: he was seeing his childhood.

This was the boring side of men and the damn thing was that they played on your feelings; she could feel this happening to her now. She kept quiet about this and changed the subject.

'How's business?' said Mrs Baum. 'I'll tell you what I came about. My niece, Zita, is getting married, and of all things, she wants to get married in Irish lace . . . I thought I'd pop round to see if you had any.'

'Foolish virgin,' said Lavender: 'Come in here.' And she followed him into the outer room. 'There you are.' And he pointed to the long rolls packed in oiled paper stacked against the walls. 'Take your pick. As the American said, "Brother, you want lace, we've got it."' And he dropped into his Irish turn as he looked at the labels and tried to lift the top parcel off. 'We're on strike, God help us, don't mind the broken windows but t'anks to the Blessed Virgin there's a darling piece for the dear child, me brother won't put a bomb under the place till after the wedding.'

Lavender tried to lift one more of the parcels.

Mrs Baum looked about the room. It was small, and stacks of samples rose halfway up to the window, so that there was scarcely any light. Against one wall there was a small typing desk and a chair.

'Look at that,' she said sentimentally, 'I had one like that when Alfie and I started up.'

The table, he said, was for a German secretary he sometimes had, one of the *haben Sie?*'s.

'Don't bother now,' she said.

'There's yards of it here, I know,' said Lavender, looking at the dust on his hands. 'Eeles has been in Belfast. I'll get him to find some.'

'Yes,' she said. 'Don't spoil that beautiful suit. Look at your hands. Let's go and have a drink.'

'Will do,' he said, relieved. 'This stuff weighs a ton, it gets you in the back. I'll wash this off.'

She liked the distress he showed when he looked at his blackened hands. He went to wash them in an alcove in his own office, and while she waited she went up to the portrait of Great-Uncle Gibbs and put a finger out and touched it. Lavender returned, and seeing her near the picture, straightened it and then put his blotter straight on his desk, saw that the telephone books were in the right order on Eeles's table. Then he got his coat from the coat stand, remarking that Eeles had only one bad habit: he often used Lavender's peg by mistake.

'Small things,' he said, 'irritate.'

Mrs Baum liked a man who fussed about small things. Alfie had fussed about his shirts.

Lavender gave one last look at the picture before they left. 'You can call it sentimental or what you like, but if I was down to my last penny, I wouldn't sell Great-Uncle Gibbs.'

'What's wrong with sentiment?' she said, taking his arm. He looked up and they walked to the stairs of the silent, empty building.

'Let's go to Giuseppe's.'

Giuseppe's was a bar in a large hotel a hundred yards around the corner, and still holding his arm, Mrs Baum felt what she always liked about Lavender. Cook had called him a snob and a fool, Alfie had told him to grow up, but Lavender was a gentleman who took your mind off things: he was like a whole crowd of men, yet blessed with a loneliness like her own. The street outside was empty at this time of the evening except for an occasional couple like themselves. Their footsteps echoed off the walls of the closed offices and the windows of closed sandwich bars, and were suddenly silent as they passed an empty, grave-like doorway.

They found themselves on the huge carpet of the hotel on which thousands of pairs of shoes without people in them might be treading. The place was empty now but notable for packed trade shows where she and Alfie and B. had often met. The lounge immediately inside was remarkable for a row of tall bronze dancers standing on marble pillars and each holding a tray or a brass tambourine over her head, presumably to cheer the models who arrived. Mrs Baum remembered sitting at a table there and Alfie telling her to give up her job in Birmingham and start up in his business with him; she had often mentioned this to Lavender. They went past this now empty hall, done in what Alfie had said was the Moorish style, into the enormous panelled bar, also empty, where the barman was reading a paper.

'*Il ne marche pas*,' said Lavender.

'It's dead,' she said. 'No trade since Giuseppe left.'

'Negative Giuseppe,' said Lavender, swinging her back to the doors.

'Let's go round to the flat,' she said scornfully to the empty bar.

'Hard to starboard,' he said, leading her out.

They arrived at her block of flats, built in white tiles suited to plumbing on a vast scale. He knew the place well.

The Worshippers

There was always something wrong in his cottage in the country when he got home on Saturday mornings. 'Poor Phyllis,' he said, always would put his piles of *Punch* in the wrong order, and never learned to draw a pair of curtains properly, and never put things away in the kitchen. After the Navy it drove him mad. She had a peculiar habit of standing behind him when he was reading which he could not cure her of, and it brought on the pain in his back because it reminded him of the time when Flo Gibbs, the sister of the superb Jack – much older than himself – whom he had worshipped, had pushed him off the tree. He ought to have married Flo but she was much too rich, or one of dear old Hauser's Swiss daughters, any one of them. They could run a house and old Hauser would have been in and out. He would have had a son whom he could have put into the Navy. A man's life, not like the rag trade.

Mrs Baum's three rooms, kitchen, and bathroom were spotless and would have passed an admiral's inspection. He liked the white curtains with their large tomato-like spots, the spongy leather sofa that slumped like the perfect substitute for Alfie in the room, suggesting that Mrs Baum had no intention, indeed no need of marrying again. He liked that: an ideal. He liked its rival, the blue, yellow, and white Chinese carpet, although the glass-topped dining table upset him. Sitting at it, one could see other people's feet. The place was so much fresher than it had been in Alfie's cigar-smoking time.

How often he and Mrs Baum had sat there talking of this and that! The sofa was made for going over the past.

'You go and get the drinks, B.,' called Mrs Baum from her bedroom. 'You know where they are.'

'Gin and women . . .' Lavender began. And when she came back and as they raised their glasses, he said, 'Happy nights.' 'And no regrets,' she said.

'So you're flying to Frankfurt again,' she said.

'Negative aircraft,' he said. 'By sea.'

She knew that, of course.

'No,' he said and told her what he had told her a dozen times before. She liked her flat to have someone else's voice saying the same things again and again.

'No,' he said, holding up his hand and closing his eyes for a second or two, so that his blank eyelids made him look as if he were going into a trance and that he was telling her not to interrupt him in a sacred matter. 'When Jack Gibbs retired he took a house in France for the winter and he always got a cabin on one of the *Queen*s as far as Cherbourg. "Only way to travel: see the Channel." Jack was right. I always go via Cherbourg.

'Last time I went an American said to me,' Lavender went on, '"Brother, if you're heading for Frankfurt, you're on the wrong ship." "Saves time," I said and told him. "Well, I'll be darned," he said.

'No,' said Lavender, defying reason in a way that gave Mrs Baum one more twinge of worship. 'One picks up the *Queen* at Southampton. Go straight to old Frank at the bar, pink gin, double of course. "Nice to see you again, sir. Blowy tonight." "Glad to hear it." "Bad for the bar, sir." "Only thing I miss, she doesn't roll. *Ripper* bucked like a horse. One misses that." "Not me, sir, I was in minesweepers." A few more double gins and in six hours one is at Cherbourg, wakey, wakey, Paris train waiting for you, cut across Paris in time for a bottle of Chablis at the Café de la Paix. "*La sole meunière comme toujours, Monsieur Lavandaire*," to the Gare de l'Est and you're in Frankfurt eleven o'clock. *Haben Sie?*'s all round you. It's the only way. One can argue that it takes longer and costs more . . .'

'Well, B., it does,' said Mrs Baum. 'It only takes an hour by air.'

'But people *know* one,' said Lavender, shutting his eyes again. 'You know where you are. Dear old Hauser, he wouldn't fly either. I was thinking of him. Swiss have no navy. Had to take the train from Zürich, but crossed Dover-Calais. Kept him young. And . . .'

'Help yourself to another,' said Mrs Baum. 'Nothing for me.'

'Great-Uncle Gibbs always took the boat to Copenhagen or the Hook even when he was turned eighty,' said Lavender, pouring himself a drink.

'Flying hadn't been invented. Alfie was never near a boat in his life,' said Mrs Baum.

'That's what was wrong with him,' said Lavender.

Mrs Baum switched on the television. 'Oh dear,' she said. 'Look at that. Another bomb in Belfast. I hope Eeles is all right.'

She switched it off. 'I can't stand it,' she said. 'You get your shop burned down – what for?'

'Eeles?' said Lavender, looking at his watch. 'He's on his way back by now. Nothing can touch Eeles anyway.

'No,' he went on. 'Up and down the Channel, bringing in a convoy at night with the fireworks going – Alfie would have enjoyed it. I think of it when I go to Cherbourg. One goes on deck and a flash of summer lightning brings it back, the sea lit up like an ice rink and some silly sod says "Where's the cat?" when the stuff comes over. Cat hated gunfire. Sunrise, all quiet, and the cat comes back and the signal comes through: "Thank you, *Ripper*, rather a nice party, I think." Stamford was always sloshed to the eyeballs when he went up to the bridge at Dover, stone sober when he got outside.'

Mrs Baum had heard this story very often and said pleasantly, 'Alfie always took our accounts down to the shelter in the war if anything happened. We moved the office to Bury St Edmunds. Wasn't that near your uncle's place?'

'Bury . . .' Lavender began, but stopped because the telephone rang.

Mrs Baum answered it. 'Who?' said Mrs Baum. 'No. I can't. I have people here.' And banged down the telephone in a sudden temper.

'What's that?' said Lavender.

'That's the trouble with this place, B.,' she said. 'It's not what it was. They've let a different class of people in, you don't know who they are. When you're on your own you feel nervous. I never used to feel like that. It is a man called Williams on the tenth floor. He keeps pestering me. He knocked on the door three nights ago. I keep the chain on now.'

Lavender tried to rise from the sofa. 'What's his number? I'll tell him where to get off,' he said and knocked his glass over.

'Stay where you are,' said Mrs Baum. 'Don't move till I get a cloth.'

'On your carpet,' said Lavender, getting up at last and following her, and when she came out of the kitchen he tried to pull the cloth from her.

'I'll do it,' she said. And got down on her knees and rubbed.

Lavender admired this. She was stout but looked very neat on her knees and her hair kept its shape. When she stood up, Lavender took the cloth from her and went down on his knees too and continued to rub. He even moved the sofa in case any of the drink had gone under it. 'Careful of your back,' Mrs Baum said. 'Don't spoil your suit.'

'Negative suit,' he said.

She fetched a clothes brush. She was impressed by his brushing: a fastidious man.

'Give yourself another drink,' she said.

Lavender got himself another large one and stood it carefully on the table, but did not drink. It stood there, still as an idol.

Her friendly voice suddenly had a note of accusation. 'I rang the club the other day and they said you weren't living there any more.'

Lavender's talking face became still and he stared at her a long time and then his voice took on the general, indignant noise of men grumbling at a bar. 'The food's gone off. Usual story. New chef. They put the prices up.'

'You resigned?' she said, shocked and insinuating.

'Yes and no. Sort of.'

He looked ashamed.

He had taken her to dinner there more than once on Ladies' Night. He must be doing well to belong to a club like this, she thought. Paintings of inhumanly tall field marshals, admirals, viceroys in splendid frames and with killing eyes, hung in the vast Dining Room. The effect of all this glorious manliness was girlish. It was like a dress show for men, a sunrise of hermaphrodites – it excited her. She admired especially the sapphire sash which one of those eminences was wearing across his breast – not this season's colour for women, too pale – but she found herself thinking more than once that a sash like that would have suited Lavender and that she could easily get one of the girls in the workroom to make him one. Blue, she had daydreamed, was the colour of Uncle Gibbs's eyes – *Great-* Uncle Gibbs, why did she always make that mistake and call him Uncle?

She always put on something fashionable, not in the shops yet, but in spite of the imperial splash on the walls, most of the tables were empty – only a few old people were there and the women looked proud of being dowdy in their biscuit-coloured cardigans. The room was cold and the waiters were negligent; all foreigners, she supposed, who couldn't understand Lavender's English. They fetched one who was baffled by his French. 'All *haben Sie?*'s,' he said. The good thing was the sight of Lavender blinking at the wine list as if it were sacred and then hearing him say, 'Châteauneuf-du-Pape – old Hauser drank nothing else.' But Gibbs was a claret man. So was Jack.

Now as they sat on the sofa in her flat, she said, 'They want to put my rent up. I haven't made up my mind. What were we talking about when that prowler Williams rang?'

For it struck her that Lavender was not touching his drink: giving up his room at the club, moving into a pokey office at the back of the building. Something wrong?

'Drink up,' she said gently. He drank.

'Bury, that was it,' he said. 'You mentioned Bury.'

'When Alfie and I were in Bury we drove out to a posh hotel in the country, with long crinkly chimneys. On a hill,' she said.

'Nor'west of Bury?' Lavender asked.

'I never know which is south, east or west,' she said, laughing. 'The name will come to me . . .'

Lavender ran off a list of small towns and villages: Flaxton, Pyke Market, Market Plympton, Bush Vale, Lord Beverley's place with the long grey wall which Lavender had climbed over to see the deer when he was a boy.

'Something Manor,' she said. 'Littlestone?' she said.

'Lytestone,' he corrected her.

He slipped into his tragic Saint Bernard look: his youthfulness vanished and he put his hand over his forehead.

'Don't go on,' he said. 'The Gibbs place.'

'That's what Alfie said. We had a lovely room,' she said, leading him on. (With all that Gibbs money behind him, why did he resign from the club?) 'With a balcony. The car park was packed. People coming and going all night. They couldn't complain of business. Fancy that belonging to your uncle. We wondered which room you had when you lived there. We were talking about you.'

Lavender watched the red spots on Mrs Baum's curtains arrange themselves in vertical lines and begin to move upwards, reach the rail and descend in a shower and then slowly move up again.

'*Great*-uncle,' Lavender corrected her. 'What room?'

'When you stayed; when you visited.'

He stared at her. The red tomato-like spots on the curtain began to rise faster like a reel unwinding.

'When you were a boy,' she said.

Lavender stared at Mrs Baum and his reddened face turned as pale as veined stone. His stare was concentrated, and if a minute before he was drunkish, he was now sober. He was accusing her, examining her, suspecting her, searching her with an intensity that made her uncomfortable. He waved a hand, waving her away, but she was still there. She wished she had not spoken.

'My room?' he said.

'Yes,' she teased. 'I bet they put you next door to your cousin Jack.'

'Flo,' he said sharply.

'Flo,' she said. 'I knew it. The one who pushed you off the tree. I can see it all. You've been a lucky devil, B. Fancy being brought up in that lovely place. The staircase! There was an old gardener who had been there when the family had it. You'd know him. He showed us round the garden. Have you ever been back? You ought to do that. It's interesting.'

Lavender looked away from her, but he put out his hand and gripped her by the wrist. His hand was large and strong and hurt her.

'What was the gardener's name?' he said.

'I don't remember – but he said he remembered you.'

'He's a bloody liar,' he said.

'You're hurting me, B. That's what he said. You ought to go and see it – you ought to see where I was brought up, Stepney! Alfie and I had to laugh. Well, the servants they must have had to run a place like that! We asked which room you had.'

He let go of her hand and turned to face her. He said in a jeering voice, hurrying over the words, 'Over the stables at the back. Sixteen months, Mother's cousin was cook there. I was ten.'

'You never told me that, B.,' said Mrs Baum, who loved exciting news. 'Alfie and I thought you were brought up there.'

'A fellow called Law, the best friend a man ever had, when we were in hospital in Bombay, he opened his heart to me. He came from Stepney. I told him. His mother was a cook. We used to go for walks and talk of this and that, private things,' he said, shutting his eyes.

'Well,' said Mrs Baum taking a big breath. 'We've come a long way, B. I wasn't prying into your private affairs.'

He got up and got himself another drink.

'You know your trouble, B. You've got a soft heart,' she said.

'No, no, no, no, no,' he said, cheering up as he created what she called his mist. And suddenly he said loudly, 'Lytestone taught me something. I made a vow...'

But the red tomato-like spots of the curtains started once more to stream upwards and he lost what he was going to say. He had a confused feeling that she might be Law. He wanted to tell her things he had told Law, but all he could remember was Jack Gibbs's playroom with a whole fleet of little lead models of ships set out on the floor. Not to be moved unless Jack said so, and he was older. Battle of Jutland. Then Jack letting him move one ship, then two, shouting to his sister Flo to clear out. That was why she pushed him off the tree, bang on his back, afterwards. Unconscious. Doctor. That's why they had to let him stay all that time.

He struggled to explain this to Mrs Baum (or was she Law?), that he worshipped Jack, as he tried to stop them becoming spots on the curtains. Only one thing was certain: 'Chop, chop,' he said. 'All gone. House sold. Auction.'

'B.,' she said. 'Sit down. I'll get us some coffee.'

'Wait,' he commanded. 'I bought the picture. Fifty pence. Damn shame. No one left in the family would touch it,' he said.

She was hurrying to the kitchen.

'Negative coffee,' he shouted to her. 'I made a vow . . .'

She looked back. 'I can hear, B.,' she said.

'To look after the poor old bastard,' he muttered to himself. He got up and made a wild swing towards the bottles and then wheeled back and flopped onto the sofa, astonished. She turned off the stove, but by the time she got to him he had passed out.

For a while she considered him. Once he seemed to speak.

'Gin and women. Chop. Chop,' he said.

She waited anxiously, but he said nothing else. She cautiously got a chair and put it near his feet and she lifted them on it. She opened the door to the bathroom and was in and out of the kitchen, eating a bun, watching him. His breathing became louder. There was a kind of happiness in seeing him there. It was like having Alfie back. After two hours she understood he was there for the night. She took off his shoes and got a rug to put over him. She turned down all lights except one, went to her own room and left her door ajar in case he stirred. For the first time since Alfie left her she felt safe for the night and slept deeply.

In the morning she heard him in the bathroom. She put on one of her gaudier dressing gowns and came in when he was dressed. He looked heavy in the face and flinched at the brilliant red-and-yellow garment, but said, 'Very sorry about last night. Something went wrong with the steering. Did I say anything?'

'That's all right – you never stopped,' she said, laughing.

He had folded the blanket neatly, straightened the sofa.

'Feeling better?'

She brought him a cup of coffee.

'Now,' she said firmly, 'when did you give up the club?'

'Two months ago,' he said.

'I don't mean that,' she said. 'Where have you been staying? At the cottage?'

'No, no, no, no, no,' he said quickly. 'Fares have gone up. Negative cottage.'

'Where, B.? With your sister?'

'Yes and no,' he said. 'At the office.'

'What!' she shouted.

'I've got a sleeping bag. By the way, don't tell Eeles. I put it away every morning before he comes. I walk up the street. Turn round. He's always there on time.'

'On the floor – with your back? What is wrong?' she said. 'Is it Eeles?'

Mrs Baum was perplexed by him and by herself: there was an expression of disaster concealed in Lavender's face which made her feel masterly and grand. She was prosperous: energy had flowed out of her after Alfie had left her, but she missed the sense of gamble that always seemed to hang about Alfie. It struck her as being rather fine that B. had rescued the picture of that ugly old man who was no connexion of his – it was silly but it showed a sort of decency – and that his mother's cousin had been a cook in that house.

'You haven't sacked Eeles, have you?' she said suspiciously.

'No,' said Lavender. 'He's been in Ireland settling the strike.'

Well, she thought, that's not what's on his mind. 'Has he settled it?'

'Yes and no. It settled itself. Depends which way you look at it. They pinched the looms out of the factory and two of the machines and put a bomb in it. Negative workshop. Bloody funny really. They're all on social security – except Eeles and me.'

'Why didn't you tell me last night?' she said to him. 'Was Eeles all right?'

'Oh yes,' said Lavender. 'Sergeant, ex-armoured cars. Straight as a die. You're all right there. You walk down the middle of the street with a bottle of whisky sticking out of your coat pocket. Like going up the Yangtze in the war – we always kept to the middle of the river. By the way, he'll have got the lace. He probably went round to the fellow who pinched it.'

'Well, thank you, but I can't spend the morning talking about the Yangtze,' Mrs Baum said. 'I've got to get to the showroom. When are you coming back from Frankfurt? None of this Cherbourg nonsense: take the plane. Cook left you holding the baby with that Irish business. You've lost a lot of money. Stick to Frankfurt. When are you coming back? Wednesday? Are you going home?'

'No, no, no, no, no,' said Lavender. 'Negative home.'

That 'negative' shocked her, but she shook off her pain.

'I sometimes feel sorry for your wife, B.,' she said. 'But you can't sleep on the floor in that office. I won't have it. You'd better come here. That will keep Williams quiet. And we've got to have a talk. You've got to cut down your expenses.'

They left the flats. The commissionaire gave a sort of salute and Mrs Baum held her chin up and looked very grand and very respectable. They parted at the street corner.

'What did you pay at the club?' she asked.

'One way and another, if you reckon it up –' he began.

'Tell me on Wednesday,' she said. 'You could bring Great-Uncle Gibbs.' And at that afterthought she sighed. It was the wrong thing to say.

'I don't think Eeles would like that,' he said sternly.

'Anyway . . .' she said and went away, saying to herself, 'I'm a fool.'

Outside the office Eeles was reading his paper, and though surprised to see Lavender coming up the street instead of coming down it, he followed him up the stairs into the office.

The Vice-Consul

Under the blades of the wide fan turning slowly in its Yes-No tropical way, the vice-consul sloped in his office, a soft and fat man, pink as a ham, the only pink man in the town, and pimpled by sweat. He was waiting for the sun to go down into the clouds over the far bank of the estuary, ten miles wide here, and to put an end to a bad week. He had been plagued by the officers and crew of a Liverpool ship, the *Ivanhoe*, smoking below in the harbour. There was trouble about shipping a puma.

His Indian clerk put his head in at the door and said in the whisper of the tropics, 'Mr McDowell's here.'

Years at this post on the river had reduced the vice-consul's voice also to the same sort of whisper, but he had a hoarseness that gave it rank. He believed in flying off the handle and showing authority by using allusions which his clerk could not understand.

'Not the bloody Twenty-third Psalm from that blasted tramp again,' he said and was glad McDowell heard it as he pushed in earnestly after the clerk. McDowell was a long-legged man with an unreasonable chin and emotional knees.

'I've brought Felden's licence,' he said.

'I ought to have had it a week ago,' said the vice-consul. 'Have you got the animal aboard yet? It was on the dock moaning away all day. You could hear it up here.'

'We've got it on deck,' said McDowell.

'Typical hunter,' said the vice-consul, 'thinking he could ship it without a licence. They've no feeling for animals and they're liars too.'

'No hearts,' said McDowell.

At this low hour at the end of the day, the vice-consul did not care to have a ship's officer trump his own feelings.

It was part of the vice-consul's martyrdom during his eight years at the port that he was, so to say, the human terminus on whom hunters, traders, oilmen, television crews, sailors whose minds had been inflated by dealing with too much geography, dumped their boasts. Nature in the shape of thousands of miles of jungle, flat as kale, thousands of miles of river, tributaries, drifting islands of forest rubbish, not to mention millions of animals, snakes, bloodsucking fish, swarms of migrating birds, butterflies and biting insects, had scared them and brought them down to the river to unload their fantasies.

'Take your boa constrictor . . .' they began. 'Take your alligator . . . Take your marching ant . . .'

Now he had to 'take' a man called Felden who had tried to stuff him up with the tale that his fourteen-year-old son had caught the beast on his fishing line in a backwater above Manaos.

The vice-consul was a sedentary man and longed to hear a fact. 'When do you sail?' he said when McDowell sat down on an upright chair which was too small for him.

'The day after tomorrow,' said McDowell.

'I can't say I'll be sorry to see you lot go,' said the vice-consul, making his usual speech to departing sailors. 'I'd like to know where the hell your company gets its crews.'

'I'm from Belfast,' said McDowell, placing his hands on those knees.

'Oh, nothing personal,' said the vice-consul. He stamped the licence, pushed it across his desk and stood up, but McDowell did not move. He leaned forward and said, 'Would you do me a favour?'

'What favour?' said the vice-consul, offended.

McDowell started to caress his knees as if to get their help. 'Would you be able to recommend a dentist in the town?' he said.

The vice-consul sat down, made a space on his desk and said, 'Well, that's a change. I thought you were going to tell me you had got yourself clapped like the rest of your crew and wanted a doctor. Dentist? Afraid not. There isn't a dentist in the place, not one I'd recommend, anyway. You've been here three weeks and can see for yourself. Half the population have no teeth at all. None of the women, anyway. Go down the street, and if you're not careful, you can walk straight down their throats.'

McDowell nodded. The vice-consul wanted more than a nod.

'It stands to reason,' he said, expanding. 'What do they get to eat? Dried meat and manioc covered in bird droppings, fish that tastes of newspaper from the bloody river. No fresh milk, no fresh meat, no fresh vegetables – everything has to be flown in and they can't afford it. It would kill them if they could.'

McDowell shook his head and kept his knees still. 'Catholic country,' he said.

'No topsoil,' said the vice-consul, putting on a swagger. 'If you've got a pain in the jaw, I'm sorry. Take my advice and do what I do. Get on the next plane to Miami. Or Puerto Rico if you like. It'll cost you a penny or two but it's the only way. Sorry for you. Painful.'

'Oh,' said McDowell, sitting back like an idol. 'My teeth are all right,' he said.

'Then what do you want a dentist for?'

'It's my dentures,' McDowell said, gleaming as he made the distinction.

'All right – dentures,' said the vice-consul.

'They've gone. Stolen.'

The vice-consul looked at McDowell for a long time. The jaws did not move, so he turned sideways and now studied McDowell, screwing up one annoyed eye. The man swallowed.

'Mr McDowell,' he said, taking the syllables one by one. 'Are you feeling the heat? Just give your mouth a tap. If I'm not mistaken, you're wearing them.'

McDowell let his arms fall to his sides and parted his lips: a set of teeth gleamed as white and righteous as a conjuring trick. 'I never sail without me spares,' he said.

The vice-consul wasn't going to stand funny business from British subjects. He had an air for this.

'Very wise,' he said. 'You fellows are always getting your teeth knocked out by your pals. Makes you careful, I suppose. What do you want *me* to do? You've got a captain, haven't you?' He became suspicious. 'I suppose you're not thinking of Filing an Official Complaint,' he said, pulling a form out of his drawer, waving it at McDowell and putting it back, 'because I can tell you, officially, that who pinches what from whom on the bloody *Ivanhoe* is no concern of mine, unless it's connected with mutiny, wounding, murder or running guns.'

The vice-consul knew this kind of speech by heart.

The sun had floundered down into the clouds; he shouted to his clerk to put on the light but switched it on himself. He decided to match McDowell on the meaning of words.

'You said "stole," McDowell. You must have some prize thieves in your crew. But will you tell me how you get a set of dentures out of a man's head against his will, even when he's asleep, unless he's drugged or tied up. Were you drunk?'

'I've never touched a drop in my life,' said McDowell.

'I suppose not,' said the vice-consul coldly.

'I took them out myself. I always put my dentures in a glass.'

'So I should hope,' said the vice-consul. 'Filthy leaving them in. Dangerous too. What else did they take? Watch? Wallet? Glasses?'

McDowell spoke carefully, picking over the peculiarity of an austere and personal case. 'Only my dentures,' he said. 'It wasn't the crew. I don't mix with them. They read magazines. They never think. I wasn't aboard,' he said softly, adding to his mystery. 'It wasn't at night. I was ashore. In the afternoon. Off duty.'

The Indian clerk put his head in at the door and looked anxiously from McDowell to the vice-consul.

'What do you want now? Can't you see I'm busy?' said the vice-consul.

The man's head disappeared and he shut the door.

McDowell stretched his long arms and placed his hands on his knees and his fingers began to drag at his trousers. 'I saw it with my own eyes,' he said. 'I saw this girl with them. When the rain started.'

'What girl?' the vice-consul said, lighting a cigar and putting a haze of smoke between himself and his torment. 'The rainy season started six weeks ago,' he swaggered. 'You get your thunderstorm every afternoon. They come in from the west and build up over the river at two o'clock to the minute and last till ten past three. You can set your watch by them.'

The vice-consul owned the climate.

'Tropical rain,' he said grandly, 'not the drizzle you get in Belfast. The rain comes down hot, straight out of the kettle, floods the streets and dries up in ten minutes, not a sign of it except the damn trees grow a foot higher. The trouble is that it doesn't clear the air: the heat is worse afterwards. You feel you're breathing – I don't know – boiled stair carpet my wife says, but that's by the way.' He waved at the smoke. 'You'll tear the knees of those trousers of yours if you don't leave them alone.'

A dressy man, he pointed his cigar at them. McDowell's knees stuck out so far that the vice-consul, who was a suspicious man, felt that they were making a displeasing personal claim on him. They indeed gave a jump when McDowell shouted in a voice that had the excitement of sudden fever, 'I can stand thunder. But I can't stand lightning, sheet or forked. It brings my dinner up. It gets under your armpits. A gasometer went up in Liverpool when I was a boy and was blown blazing across the Mersey —'

'I thought you said you came from Belfast,' said the vice-consul. 'Lightning never bothers me.'

'There was this thunderbolt,' said McDowell, ignoring him, and his voice went to a whisper. 'I'm in the entrance of this hotel, looking at the alligator handbags to take one home for my wife and I've just picked one up and down comes this bolt, screaming behind my back, with a horrible violet flame, and sends me flying headfirst up the passage. There's a girl there, polishing the floor, and all the lights go out. The next thing, I'm in an open doorway, I'm pitching headfirst on to a bed in the room and I get my head under the clothes. It's like the end of the world and I'm praying into the pillow. I think I am dead, don't I?'

'I don't know,' said the vice-consul coldly. 'But what do you do at sea? And where was this place?'

'It's natural at sea,' said McDowell, calming down. 'The Columbus. Yes, it would be the Columbus.'

'Never heard of it,' said the vice-consul.

'I don't know how long I am there, but when it gets quieter I look up, the lightning is going on and off in the window and that's when I see this girl standing by the mirror —'

'The one who was polishing the floor, I suppose,' said the vice-consul with contentment.

'No,' said McDowell, 'this one was in the bed when I fell on it, on top of her, I told you.'

'You didn't. You pulled her in,' said the vice-consul.

McDowell stopped, astonished, but went on, 'Standing by the mirror, without a stitch of clothing on her. Terrible. She takes my dentures out of the glass, and the next thing, she opens her mouth wide and she's trying to fit them, this way and that, to her poor empty gums.'

'You couldn't see all that in a flash of lightning. You must have switched the light on,' said the vice-consul.

McDowell slapped his knee and sat back in a trance of relief. 'You're right,' he said gratefully. 'Thank God you reminded me. I wouldn't want to tell a lie. The sight of her with her poor empty mouth destroyed me. I'll never forget it. It'd break a man's heart.'

'Not mine,' said the vice-consul. 'It's disgusting. Shows ignorance too. No two human jawbones are alike.'

'The pitiful ignorance, you're right!' said McDowell. 'I called out to her, "Careful what you're doing! You might swallow them. Put them back in the glass and come back to bed."'

The tropical hoarseness left the vice-consul's voice. 'Ah,' he shouted and put his cigar down. 'I thought we'd come to it. In plain English, you had come ashore to commit fornication.'

'I did not,' said McDowell, shocked. 'Her sister works for the airline.'

'Oh, it's no business of mine. I don't care what you do, but you were in bed with that girl. You said so yourself. But why in God's name did you take your dentures out? In the middle of the afternoon?'

McDowell was even more shocked. He sat back sternly in his chair. 'It would have looked hardly decent,' he said, 'I mean on an occasion like that, for any man to keep his teeth in when a poor girl had none of her own. It was politeness. You'd want to show respect. I've got my principles.'

He became confident and said, 'My dentures have gold clips. Metal attracts lightning – I mean, if you had your mouth open, you might be struck dead. That's another reason why I took them out. You never know who the Lord will strike.'

'Both of you, I expect,' said the vice-consul.

'Yes,' said McDowell, 'but you've got to think of others.'

The vice-consul got out his handkerchief and wiped his face and his head.

'You'd never get away with this twaddle in a court of law,' said the vice-consul. 'None of this proves she stole your dentures.'

'She had gone when I woke up, and they had gone. The rain was pouring down outside or I would have gone after her,' said McDowell.

'And you wouldn't have caught her if you had,' said the vice-consul with deep pleasure. 'She sold them before she got to the end of the street. You can say goodbye to that lot. You're wasting my time. I've got two other British ships docking in an hour. I've told you what to do. Keep clear of the police. They'll probably arrest you. And if you want a new set of dentures, go to Miami as I said.'

'But they're not for *me*,' exclaimed McDowell. 'I want them for this girl. I've got the money. It's wrong to steal. Her sister knows it and so does she. If you see a soul in danger, you've got to try and save them.'

'God help me,' said the vice-consul. 'I've got enough trouble in this port as it is, but as a matter of interest, who told you to go to this place – the Columbus – to buy handbags? You can get them at every shop in the town. The river's crawling with alligators.'

McDowell nodded to the outer office where the Indian clerk sat. 'That gentleman.'

'He did, did he?' said the vice-consul, laughing for the first time and achieving a louder shout to his clerk.

The Indian clerk came in. He loved to be called in when the vice-consul was talking business. He gleamed with the prestige of an only assistant. The vice-consul spoke to him in Portuguese with the intimacy of one who sketches his way through a language not his own. The clerk nodded and nodded and talked eagerly.

'My clerk says,' said the vice-consul, in his large way, 'that you came in at midday the day before yesterday and asked where you could get a girl. He says he knows the airline girl and her sister. He knows the whole family. The father has the barbershop opposite the church and he is a dentist too. He buys up teeth, mostly after funerals.'

The clerk nodded and added a few words.

'He says he fixed him up. He says this man's got the biggest collection of teeth in the town.'

The clerk's neck was thin; he was like wood. He opened his mouth wide with pride for McDowell to see. There were five sharp steel teeth and two with gold in them.

The vice-consul went on, 'He says he often sells them to missionaries. The Dominicans have a mission here. The poor devils come back from far up in the Indian settlements looking like skeletons after three years and with their teeth dropping out. I told you: no calcium. No fresh vegetables. No milk. The climate . . .'

The Indian said no more.

McDowell got up and moved towards the clerk suspiciously, setting his chin. 'What's he say about the Dominicans?' said McDowell in a threatening way.

The vice-consul said, 'He says you could go down to this man, this barber chap, and you might find your teeth.'

The Indian nodded.

'If you don't – well, they've been snapped up and are being flown up the river. Sorry, McDowell, that's all we can do. Take my advice and get back double-quick to your ship. Good day.'

The vice-consul picked up some papers and called to McDowell as he left the room, 'They'll be up there, preaching The Word.'

The following day the vice-consul went out to the *Ivanhoe* to have a last drink with the captain and to have a look at the puma, and grinned when it opened its mouth and snarled at him. The captain said McDowell would be all right once he got to sea, and went on to some tale about a man who claimed to have a cat that backed horses.

It's the bloody great river that does it, the vice-consul thought as he was put ashore afterwards and as he walked home in the dark and saw all the people whispering in their white cotton clothes, looking like ghosts. He was thinking it was only another year before his leave and that he was the only human being in the town.

The Accompanist

It was the afternoon. Joyce had been with me for nearly two hours when suddenly she leaned over me to look at my watch on the table.

'Half past four,' she cried in a panic. 'Stop it. I shall be late,' and scrambling out of bed, she started getting into her clothes in a rush. She frowned when she caught me watching her. I liked watching her dress: her legs and arms were thin, and as she put up her arms to fasten her bra and leaned forward to pull on her tights she seemed to be playing a game of turning herself into comic triangles. She snatched her pale-blue jersey and pulled it over her head, and when her fair hair came out at the top she was saying, 'Don't forget. Half past seven. Don't be difficult. You've got to come, William. Bertie will be upset if you don't. Ivy and Jim will be there and Bertie wants you to tell them about Singapore.'

In a love affair, one discovers a gift for saying things with two meanings.

'If they are going to be there, Bertie won't miss *me*,' I said. 'He used to be mad about Ivy, asked her to marry him once – you told me.'

'You are not to say that,' Joyce said fiercely as she dragged her jersey down. 'Bertie wanted to marry a lot of girls.'

So I said yes, I would be there. She put on her coat, which I thought was too thin for a cold day like this, and said, 'Look at the time. Hendrick will be so angry,' as she struggled away from my long kiss. Her skin burned and there were two red patches on her cheeks. Then she went.

It was only on her 'music days' when she was rehearsing with Hendrick that we were able to meet.

Afterwards I went to the window hoping to see her on the street, but I missed her. I pulled a cover over the bed, walked about and then I came across a shopping bag on the table. Joyce had forgotten it. I looked into the bag and saw it contained eight small apple pies packed in cartons: Joyce was a last-minute shopper and they were obviously meant for the dinner we were all going to eat that evening. Well, there was nothing to

[1048]

be done. I could hardly take them to Bertie's and say, 'Your wife left these at my place.' Before I left at seven o'clock I ate one. It was cold and dry, but after seeing Joyce, I always felt hungry.

It was a cross-London journey into the decaying district where she and Bertie lived. One had to take one bus, then wait for another. Their flat was on the ground floor of a once respectable Victorian villa. I was glad to arrive at the same time as four other guests, all of us old friends of Bertie's: André, an enormous young Belgian in a fur coat; his toy-like wife, Podge; an unmarried girl who adored Bertie and who rarely said anything; and a sharp dark political girl who worked on a review Bertie sometimes wrote for.

Bertie himself came to the door wearing old-fashioned felt slippers. It was odd to see them on a young man who was even younger than we were – not yet thirty. He had a copy of *Le Monde* in his hand and he waved it in the air as he shouted 'Well done!' to all of us in the voice of a housemaster at the School Sports. And as we went in he was jubilant, crowing like a cockerel. 'My errant spouse,' he said, 'is at this moment, I presume, toiling across the metropolis and will be here soon. You see, this is one of Joyce's music days. Hendrick's concert is coming on the week after next and he makes her rehearse the whole time, poor wretch. Of course, it's awfully nice for her.'

(Bertie loved things to be 'awfully nice.')

'He had discovered,' Bertie went on proudly, 'that she is the only accompanist he can work with. It's very useful, too' – Bertie looked over his glasses sideways at us – 'it brings in the pennies. And it gives me time to catch up on *The Times* and *Le Monde*.'

And he slapped the paper against his leg with something like passion. Then he led us into the bedroom where we were to leave our coats.

Except for André, we were all poor in those days. Flats were hard to find. It had taken Bertie and Joyce a long time to find this one – they had had to make do with Bertie's old room – and they had to wait for Bertie's family furniture to arrive out of storage from the North. As we took off our coats we felt the chill of the large room and I understood Joyce's embarrassed giggles when she spoke of it. It was, in the late-Victorian way, high and large; the mouldings on the ceiling, a thing now admired, looked like a dusty wedding cake with cracks in it. There was a huge marbled and empty fireplace, but – at variance with the period – brutal red tiles were jammed around it and it was like an enormous empty mouth, hungry for coal or the meals served there when the room had been the dining room of earlier generations. In front of it, without curb or fender, a very small electric fire – not turned on – stood like a modern orphan. Bertie was careful with money, and he and Joyce had not been able to afford to redecorate the room. One could detect small faded flowers in the grey wallpaper; in the bay window hung three sets of curtains: net for privacy, then a lighter greenish summer set, and over them heavy, once banana-coloured, curtains, faded at the folds, like the old trailing robes of a dead Edwardian lady.

But it was the enormous bed that, naturally, appalled me. The headboard was of monumental walnut, scrolled at the top, and there were legs murderous to a bare foot. Over the bed was spread a pink satiny coverlet, decorated by love knots and edged by lace from the days of Bertie's parents, even grandparents. It suggested to me a sad Arthurian barge, a washed-out poem from some album of the Love's Garland kind. There was, of course, a dressing table with its many little shelves, and one had the fear of seeing dead heroines in its mirrors and even, in the cold, seeing their breath upon the glass. I caught sight of my own face in it, looking Chinese and sarcastic: I tried to improve my expression. Faded, faded – everything faded. The only human things in the room were our coats thrown on the bed – I dropped mine out of pity on what I hoped was Joyce's side of it – and the hem of one of Joyce's dresses characteristically caught by the doors of a huge wardrobe. The sight of it made me feel the misty air of the room was quivering with Joyce's tempers and her tears.

But I exaggerate – there was one more human thing: Bertie's old desk from his Oxford days against the wall near the inner door, and his long bookcase. This was packed with books on modern history, politics and economics, and here it was that Bertie would sit typing his long articles on foreign politics. We all knew – and Joyce had told me – how she would go to sleep at night to the sound of 'poor Bertie's' typewriter. She was a simple girl, but Bertie was charged by a brain that had given him a Double First at Oxford, made him the master of six or seven languages, and kept him floating for years like an eternal student on scholarships, grants and endowments. In the corner stood stacks of *The Times, Le Monde* and other periodicals, on the floor.

'Haven't you caught up on these *yet?*' André said.

'You see, they're sometimes useful,' Bertie said. And he added with a stubborn laugh, 'Joyce, poor wretch, complains, but I tell her I don't *like* throwing things away.'

We moved into the other room.

When I was with Bertie I always felt protective of him, but this evening I did feel a jolt when I saw the dining table, which had been pushed into a far corner of the large room. Those apple pies! Moral questions I found had a way of putting out their noses in small ways in these days. But like everyone else I felt affection for Bertie. He loved his friends and we loved him: he was our possession, and in his shrewd collecting way he felt the same about us. His long nose, on which the glasses never sat straight, his pinkness, his jacket stuffed with papers, pens and pencils, his habit of standing with his hands on his hips as if pretending he had a waist, his short legs apart, his feet restless with self-confidence like a schoolboy, were endearing.

His sister-in-law, the only woman to wear a long dress, and her Australian husband were standing in the room.

'And this is William,' Bertie said, admiring me. 'He's just back from Singapore, idle fellow.'

'We have just hopped over from Rome,' said Ivy's husband.

Unlike Joyce, Ivy was almost a beauty, the clever businesswoman of the family, and the rest of the evening she seemed to be studying me – so much so that I wondered if Joyce had, in her thoughtless fashion, been talking about us.

We sat around on a deep, frayed sofa or in armchairs in which the cushions had red or green fringes, so that we seemed to be squatting on dyed beards, while Bertie kept us going about people he'd met at the embassy in Brussels, about the rows on the commission – the French delegate walking out in a huff – or a letter in *The Times* in which all the facts were wrong. The dark girl started an argument about French socialism and Bertie stopped it by saying he had got in an afternoon's tennis while he was over there.

He was still delighted with us and, swaying on his feet, keen on sending over a volley or smashing a ball over the net. His talk brought back to me the day he had asked Joyce to marry him. It was the only proposal of marriage I had ever heard. All of us, except Ivy and her husband, had been there. We had managed to get one of the public courts in the Park; on the other courts players were smartly dressed in their white shorts and we were a shabby lot. I could see Bertie, who was rolling about like a bundle in old flannels that were slipping down, and sending over one of his ferocious services; I could hear him shouting 'Well done!' or 'Hard luck, partner!' to Joyce, whose mind strayed if an airplane flew over. I remembered him sitting beside Joyce and Podge and me on the bench when our game was over, with one eye on the next game and the other eye reading a thick political review. It was the time of the year when the spring green is darkening with the London lead. Presently I heard him chatting to Joyce about some man, a cousin of André's who had found an 'awfully nice niche' in Luxembourg. At that time Bertie had found no 'niche' and was captivated by those who had. Joyce had only a vague idea of what a 'niche' was and first of all thought he was talking about churches, but then he was on to his annual dispute with his solicitor, who wanted him to get rid of his family's furniture because storage charges were eating up the trust.

'You see,' he said, talking across Joyce and Podge to me, 'I shall want it when I get my London base.'

Joyce laughed and said, 'But you *are* in London.'

'Yes,' said Bertie, 'but not as a *base*. My argument is that I must let the stuff stay where it is until I get married.'

André and his wife were playing and she had just skied her ball and, waiting for his moment, André smashed it over. Joyce cried out, 'Marvellous!' She had not really been listening to Bertie. And then she turned to him and said, 'I'm sorry. I was watching André – Bertie, I meant you – you're getting married! How wonderful. I am so pleased! Who is it? Do tell us.'

Bertie gave one of his side glances at Podge and me and then said to Joyce, 'You!'

It was really like that: Joyce saying 'Don't be silly, Bertie' and 'No, I can't. I couldn't . . . I . . .' He got hold of her hand and she pulled it away. 'Please, Bertie,' she said. She saw, we all saw, he meant it, and she was angry and confused; we saw the other couple coming towards us, their game over. She felt so foolish that she picked up her racket and ran – ran out of the court.

'What's the matter with Joyce?' said André.

Bertie stood up and stared after her and began beating a leg with the review. He appealed to all of us. 'I've just asked Joyce to marry me,' he said and reported his peculiar approach.

'And she said "No,"' I said with satisfaction. Love or marriage were far from my own mind; but hearing Bertie and seeing Podge run after Joyce in the Park, I felt a pang of jealousy and loss. In two days I would be far away from my friends, sweating in a job in Singapore. Bertie heard my words, and as always when he was in a jam, he slyly dropped into French. Lightly and confidently he said, '*Souvent femme varie.*'

Afterwards it struck me that Bertie's proposal was an appeal: it was the duty of all his friends to get him married. Indeed, Podge said she was afraid he was going to turn to her next. There was even an impression that he had proposed marriage to all of us; but I now see that he was a man with no notion of private life. The team spirit contained his passion, and knowing his exceptional case, he was making us all responsible as witnesses and as friends.

This passed through my mind as we all sat there in his flat listening for the distant ticking of a taxi stopping at the end of the street. Joyce was forbidden to spend money on taxis and would come running in breathlessly saying she had had to 'wait hours' for a bus.

Conversation came to a stop. Bertie had at last run down. Suddenly Ivy said, 'Bertie, how long was this awful furniture in storage?'

Bertie was not put out. He loved Ivy for calling it awful. He crossed his short, sausage-like legs and sat back with pride in which there was a flash of malice, and flicked his feet up and down.

'Twenty-seven years,' he said. 'No, let me see. Mother died when I was born, Father died the previous year, then my Aunt Pansy moved in for four or five years, that makes twenty-two years. Yes. Twenty-two.'

'I like it,' said Podge, defending him.

'But it's unbelievable,' said Ivy. 'It must have cost a fortune to store it.'

'That's what my guardian says,' said Bertie.

'Why didn't you make him sell it?' said André.

'I wouldn't let him,' said Bertie. 'You see, I told him it would be useful when I got married.'

We used to say that it must have been the thought of having Bertie's furniture hanging over them that had frightened off the many girls he had tried to marry. After all, a girl wants to choose.

Bertie's pink face fattened with delight at the attack. 'Joyce hates it,' he said comfortably. 'She thinks I ought to sell it.'

He was wrong; Joyce laughed at his furniture but she dreaded it.

'You'd make a fortune in Australia with furniture like this,' said Ivy's husband.

'No,' said Bertie. 'You see, it was left to me.'

He took off his glasses and exposed his naked face to us. I did not believe Joyce when she told me he cried when she had begged him to sell it, but now I did.

If the bedroom had the pathos of an idyll, the furniture in this living room was a hulking manufacture in which historic romance was martial and belligerent. Only in some lost provincial hotel which is putting up a fight against customers do you sometimes find oaken objects of such galumphing fantasy. There was a large armoire with knobs, like breasts, on its pillars, and shields on the doors. Under them, sprays of palm leaves had been carved; the top appeared to be fortified. The breast motif appeared on the lower drawers. The piece belonged to the time when cotton manufacturers liked to fancy they lived in castles.

There was a sideboard which attempted the voluptuous, but oak does not flow: shields appeared on its doors. There were more shields carved on two smaller tables; on the dining table, the curved edges would be dangerous to the knuckles, and its legs might have come from the thighs of a Teutonic giantess. The fireplace itself was a battalion of fire irons, toasting forks, and beside it, among other things, two brass scuttles (also with breasts, coats of arms and legs) that stood on claws. There was a general suggestion of jousting mixed with Masonic dinners and ye olde town criers.

'There ought to be a suit of armour,' said André.

The only graceful object was Joyce's piano, which had belonged to her mother. It stood there, defeated.

Bertie nodded stubbornly. 'You see,' he said, grinning at us, 'it's my *dot*.' And gave a naughty kick with his slippers.

Father dead before he was born, mother dead, aunt dead – Bertie was trebly an orphan. He had been brought up by a childless clergyman who was headmaster of a well-known school. There were photos of school and Oxford groups on the mantelpiece. André and I recognised ourselves in the latter: Bertie was an institutional man, his furniture was his only link with common human history. It was the sacred evidence not only of his existence but of the continuity of the bloodstream, the heartbeat and the inextinguishable sexual impulse of his family. He was a rarity, and our rarity too. We were a kind of society for cosseting him. Joyce, who loved him, felt this, and I did too.

But no Joyce came and André cast restless glances at the bottle of sherry, which was now empty. Bertie saw that a distraction was needed. 'We can't wait any longer,' he said. 'Let us eat.'

He jumped up, and putting on one of his acts of pantomime, he went to the dining table and picked up a carving knife and fork, and flinging his short arms wide, he pretended to sharpen the knife and then to carve an imaginary roast.

We laughed loudly and Ivy joined him. 'Come on!' she said, and pulling *Le Monde* out of his pocket, put it on the dish and said, 'Carve this.'

Bertie was hurt. 'Shame,' he said, putting the paper back in his pocket.

Fortunately the front door banged and in came Joyce, breathless, frightened, half laughing, kissing everyone and telling us that Hendrick was giving a lesson when she got there and then would not let her go. And, of course, she had to wait for hours at a bus stop.

'Poor Bertie,' she cried and kissed him on the forehead, and shaking her hair, stared back, daring us to say anything that would upset him. She went out to the kitchen and came back to whisper to her sister, 'I've got the chops, but I must have left the pud in the taxi. Don't tell him. What shall I do?'

She looked primly at me. She had not changed her clothes, but because she looked prim (and by one of those tricks of the mind) I suddenly saw her standing naked, her long arms freckled, all bones, and standing up to her knees in the water rushing over the rocks of a mountain stream in the North where she and Bertie and I and a climbing party had camped for the night. I was naked too and on the bank, helping her out while Bertie, who refused to go into the river, was standing fully dressed and already, at seven in the morning, with a book he had opened. Bertie was unconcerned.

Yes, I thought this evening as she looked at me – I had one of those revelations that come late to a lover. She stands with the look of a girl who has a strange shame of her bones. She pouts and looks cross as a woman does at an inquisitive, staring child: there is a pause when she does not know what to do, and then she pushes her bones out of her mind and laughs. But that pause has bowled one over. It was because Joyce was so funny to look at that I had become serious about her.

By the time we all sat down to the meal I had advanced to the fantasy that when she laughed, her collarbones laughed. She had quickly changed into a dress that was lower in the neck, so that one saw her long throat. The food was poor; she was no cook, but André had brought wine and soon we were all shouting. Bertie was in full cackle and Joyce was telling us about Hendrick, whom the rest of us had never met, and after dinner Bertie persuaded Joyce to go to the piano and sing one of her French songs.

'*Jeune fillette*,' he called. Quickly, with a flash of nervous intimacy in her glance of obedience, she sat at the piano and began: '*Jeune fillette, profitez du temps . . .*'

Bertie rocked his head as the song came out of her long throat. The voice was small and high, and it seemed to me that she carried it like a crystal inside her. The notes of the accompaniment seemed to come down her arms into her hands – which were really too big – and out of the fingers rather than from the piano. She sang and she played as if she did not exist.

'Her French,' André's wife whispered, 'is perfect, not like André's awful Belgian accent,' and said so again when the song was over.

Joyce had her strange sensual look of having done something wrong.

'She can't speak a word of French,' said Bertie enthusiastically. 'She was eight months in Paris, staying with Ivy, and couldn't say anything except "Yes" and "No."'

'"No,"' said André, swelling out to tell one of his long Belgian stories, 'is the important word.'

'You have Mother's voice,' Ivy said to Joyce. And to us: 'Mother's was small. And true too – and yet she was deaf for the last twenty years of her life. You won't believe it, but Father would sing the solo in church on Sundays and Mother rehearsed him all the week perfectly and yet she can't have heard a note. When she died, Joyce had to do it. And she hated it, didn't you?'

Joyce swung round on the stool and now we saw – what I had begun to know too well – a fit of defiance.

'I didn't hate *that*, Ivy,' she said. '*You* know what I couldn't bear! On Saturdays,' Joyce blurted to us all, daring Ivy to stop her, 'after lunch before anything was cleared away, he used to make me get the scissors and clip the hair out of his ears, ready for Sunday.'

'Joy!' said Ivy, very annoyed. 'You exaggerate.'

'I don't,' said Joyce. 'He used to belch and spit into the fireplace too. He was always spitting. It was disgusting.'

We knew that the girls were the daughters of a small builder who had worked his way up and was a mixture of religion and rough habits.

'And so,' said Bertie to save the situation, 'my future spouse began her *Wanderjahre*, abandoned all and ran away to Paris, where Ivy had established herself – and met the Baron!'

Ivy nodded gratefully. '*Your* Baron, Joyce!' she laughed.

'Who is the Baron?' the Australian asked.

Now Joyce appealed to Ivy not to speak, but Bertie told them, mentioning he had met the Baron since those days, in Paris and Amsterdam – Bertie kept in touch with everyone he had ever met. It is painful to hear someone amiably destroy one of the inexpressible episodes in one's life and I knew Joyce was about to suffer, for in one of our confiding afternoons she had tried to tell me. It was true that Ivy, the efficient linguist, had started a translation bureau in Paris and the so-called Baron, a Czech exile, used to dictate long political articles to Joyce. In the long waits while he struggled to translate into English, Joyce's mind was far away.

'He always asked for Joyce,' Ivy said. 'He used to say –'

'You are not to say it!' said Joyce.

But Ivy mimicked him. 'I vant ze girl viz ze beautiful ear. One year in Paris she knows no French, no languages – but she understands. How is zat? She does not listen to ze language. She listens to the Pause!'

'Well done!' cried Bertie.

'What the hell is "the Pause"?' said the Australian.

'Before he started dictating again,' I said brusquely.

Bertie looked at me sharply. I realised I had almost given Joyce away. What I think the Baron was trying to say (I told Joyce when she too had asked me what he meant, for she had grown fond of him and sorry for his family too, whom he had to leave in Prague) was that Joyce had the gift of discontinuity. She was in a dream until the voice that was dictating, or some tune, began again. She and I went on talking about this for a long time without getting any clearer about it, and I agree there was some conceit on my part in this theory: I saw myself as the tune she was waiting for.

'André,' Joyce called to hide her anger. 'Sing us your song. The awful one.'

'It's Bertie's song,' said André. 'It's his tour de force. Play on, Joyce – and put all the Pauses in.'

She could always take a joke from André, who looked like a mottled commissionaire. He had all the beer and Burgundy of Brussels in him, all those mussels, eels and oysters, and that venison.

Bertie's song was one more of his pantomime acts to which his long nose, his eyes darting side glances and his sudden assumption of a nasal voice gave a special lubricity. The song was a rapid cabaret piece about a wedding night in which the bride's shoulder is bitten through, her neck twisted and her arm broken and ends with her mother being called in and saying:

> *Ci-gît la seule en France*
> *Qui soit morte de cela.*

Bertie was devilish as Joyce vamped out the insinuating tune. We all joined in at the tops of our voices in the chorus at the end of each verse:

> *Ça ne va guère, ça ne va pas*

– even Joyce, her little blue eyes sparkling at the words she did not understand, though André had once explained them to her. In the last chorus she glanced back at me, sending me a reckless message. I understood it. From her point of view (and Bertie's), wedding nights were an academic subject. Bertie's enjoyment of the song was odd.

'Really, Bertie!' said the dark girl, who had argued with him about French socialism before dinner.

When she got up from the piano, Joyce looked enviously at her sister because her Australian husband had laughed the loudest and had given Ivy a squeeze. Then as Joyce caught my eye again her strange pout of sensual shame appeared and I felt I had been slapped on the face for having thoughts in my mind that matched her own. Her look told me that I could never know how truly she loved Bertie and feared him too, as she would love and fear a child. And she hated me for knowing what I would never have known unless she had mumbled the tale of tears of failure in the grey room next door.

And a glum stare from Podge, Bertie's oldest friend, showed me even more that I was an outsider.

The song had stirred Bertie's memory too, but of something more remote. He planted himself before me and sprang into yet another of his pantomime acts which the sight of me excited. He put on his baby voice: 'William and I didn't have our pudding! Poor Bertie didn't have his pudding.'

Joyce's face reddened. Their talk of food, money, their daily domestic life, was irritating in my situation. I lived by my desire; *they* had the intimacy of eating. I must have put on a mask, for Ivy said: 'William's all right. He's got his well-fed Chinese look.'

Even Joyce had once said that about me.

'How awful of me!' Joyce cried to all of us.

I thought we were lost, but she recovered in time.

'Bertie, isn't it terrible? I left it . . .' – she dared not say 'in the taxi' – 'I left it at Hendrick's.'

Bertie's jollity went. He looked as stubborn as stone at Ivy and Joyce. Then with one of his ingenious cackles he dropped into French, which was a sign of resolution in him. '*Tout s'arrange*,' he said. 'You can pick it up on Friday when you go there for rehearsal. By the way, what was it?'

'But, Bertie,' Ivy said. 'It will be stale or covered in mould by then. Apple tarts.'

We all saw a glitter of moisture in Bertie's eyes; it might have come from greed or the streak of miserliness in him – it might have been tears.

[1059]

'We must get them back,' said Bertie.

André saved Joyce by coming out with one of his long detailed stories about a Flemish woman who kept a chicken in her refrigerator for two months after her husband left her. It became greener and greener, and when he came back with his tail between his legs she made him eat it. And he died.

André's stories parodied one's life, but this one distracted Bertie while Joyce whispered to her sister, 'He means it.'

'Tell him Hendrick ate them. He *has* probably eaten them by now. Singers are always eating.'

'That would be worse,' said Joyce.

After that André bellowed out a song about his military service and the party broke up. We went into the bedroom and picked up our coats while Joyce stood there rubbing her arms and saying, 'Bertie, did you know you had turned out the fire?'

I was trying to signal Friday, Friday, Friday to her, but she took no notice. Of course her sister was staying on in London. How long for? What would that mean?

We all left the house. Bertie stood, legs apart, on the step, triumphant. I found myself having to get a taxi for the socialist girl.

'Where on earth are we?' she asked, looking at the black winter trees and the wet, sooty bushes of the gardens in the street. 'Have you known them a long time? Do you live in London?'

'No,' I said. 'I'm on leave. I work in Singapore.'

'What was all that extraordinary talk about the Baron?' She sent up a high laugh. 'And the Pause?'

I said it was all Greek to me. I was still thinking Friday, Friday, Friday. Joyce would come or she would not come: more and more reluctant as the day drew nearer, with a weight on her ribs, listening for her tune. And if she heard it, the bones in her legs, arms, her fingers, would wake up and she would be out of breath at my door without knowing it.

Tea with Mrs Bittell

She liked to say it was 'inconvenient,' on the general ground that a lady should appear to complain beautifully when doing a kindness to someone outside her own class; lately she had been keeping an afternoon for a rather 'quaint' person, a young man called Sidney, one of a red-jacketed ballet who hopped about at the busy tea counter in Murgatroyd and Foot's. He often chatted with her to annoy the foreign tourists who pushed and shouted at his counter. She discovered that he came on Sundays to her own church. Such a lonely person he was, sitting in his raincoat among the furs and black suits and in such a sad situation: his father had been in the hospital for years now – a coal miner – he had that dreadful thing miners get. It was so *good* that the young man came to church with a friend, another young man from the tea counter, and waking up from her snooze during the service, she often frowned with pleasure. She would say to her atheistical sister, 'The younger generation are hungry for Faith.' The second young man stopped coming after a month or two, and only Sidney was left. She astounded him by asking him to tea.

Mrs Bittell was sitting in her flat in the expensive block nearly opposite the church, among the wrongs and relics of her seventy years, when Sidney first came.

'Deliveries round the corner, second door,' the doorman said.

'I'm a friend of Mrs Bittell's,' said Sidney.

The doorman's chestload of medals flashed. 'Why didn't you say you were a friend?' he said, looking Sidney up and down. 'Seventh floor.'

'A very disagreeable man,' said Mrs Bittell when Sidney told her this, his wounded chin raised. She was a puddingy woman, reposing on a big sleepy belly; her hair was white and she had innocent blue eyes. She wore, as usual, a loosely knitted pink jersey, low in the neck, a heather-mixture skirt, flat-heeled shoes, and was very short. Her family had been Army people and at first she thought Sidney rather civilian in a disappointing way when he was not wearing the red jacket he wore in the shop, as she led him across the wide old-fashioned panelled hall of her flat into the full light of her large drawing-room, which, in addition to her furniture and pictures, owned a large part of the London sky where the clouds prospered: one looked down on the tops of three embassies and across to the creamy stucco of a long square.

Sidney sat looking at the distances between her sofas, her satiny chairs and other fine things. She remembered he had been so startled when she invited him to tea that he must be quite outside the concept of 'invitations'. Indeed, he had gone first of all to one of the large windows and searched the rooftops until he found the building where he and his family distantly lived. It was a high-rise block, a mile away, howling like cats, he told her, with the tenants' radios and television sets and children.

'We don't have anything to do with the neighbours,' he said complacently. 'Talk to the people next door, next thing they unscrew your front door or saw it off when you go out, and pinch the TV.'

He turned his head slowly to Mrs Bittell. He was a slow-talking young man, nearly handsome in a doleful way, and Mrs Bittell liked this; she was slow and melancholy herself. He gave a droll laugh when he spoke of doors being sawn off and took a mild pride in the fact.

He also added something about the nearest roofs. 'I can't stand slate,' he said. 'Slate is killing my father. The mine did it.'

Mrs Bittell murmured in her social way that, oh dear, she thought he had been a *coal* miner.

'No,' he said. 'Slate.'

He spoke in short sentences between disconcerting pauses. 'Dad took me down when I left school.'

'You worked there?' said Mrs Bittell.

'No,' he said fastidiously. 'Slate mines are cold. I don't like the cold.'

There was a long pause.

'The deeper you go, the colder it gets,' he said.

Mrs Bittell said her sister Dolly had had the same impression of the catacombs outside Rome, even though wearing a coat.

'I've heard of them,' he said.

From his account of the mine it seemed to her that he was describing the block of flats in which he was sitting with her, but upside down, under the earth. Yet the mine also seemed like a buried church with aisles, galleries, and side chapels, but in darkness and shaken by the noise of drilling holes for the sticks of dynamite and by the explosions in which the echoes pealed from cavern to cavern. The men worked with a stump of lighted candle on the peaks of their caps.

'Surely, Sidney, that is very dangerous, I've been told,' said Mrs Bittell. 'Not lamps?'

'No gas in the slate mines,' he said. But Sidney fell into a state of meditation. 'Splinters,' he said. 'A splinter drops from the roof and goes clean through your skull. You have to wear a helmet. Dad never wore a helmet.'

'Oh, dear, how thoughtless,' said Mrs Bittell.

'No. A splinter never got him.'

Sidney had a taste for horrors which he displayed as part of his family's limited capital. 'The dust got him,' said Sidney. 'He wouldn't wear a mask.

'So I went to work in "the grocery".'

Mrs Bittell was offering him a second cup of tea from her silver teapot. She held the cup above the slop basin.

'I forget, d'you like to keep your remains?'

He thought about this; a funeral appeared to him to be passing through his mind.

'I always keep mine,' she said.

'It's OK, Mrs Bittell,' he said.

She was trying to think of a tactful way of saying the accent was on the second syllable of her name.

After that, talk became much easier. His long face still mooned but he warmed, although they got at cross purposes when she thought he was talking about the church when he was talking about the shop. He said he enjoyed the smell of furs, scent – they were like the smell of provisions. He looked at her piano and said, 'Do you play it?'

Mrs Bittell had a wide peaceful white forehead with fine lines on it, her eyes were delicately child-like and her voice was graceful, but now the peacefulness vanished. Her face became square and stubborn, and because his pauses were so long she was tempted to fill them with troubles and horrors of her own: her late husband's atrocious behaviour – he had once hit her with a bedside lamp; the selfishness of her daughters, who had made such 'hopeless' marriages; the suspicions of her trustees, her income not a quarter of what it used to be; the wicked rise of taxes. Her wrongs settled like a migraine in fortified lumps on her forehead. But she did say to Sidney when he mentioned her piano that once one has got used to the big wrongs of life, little ones wake up, with their mean little teeth.

There had been a new wrong in her life in the last few months. The Misses Pattison on the floor below, she told him, the judge on the floor above, a Scottish 'banker person', the general across the landing, had complained about her playing the piano. Several tenants had sent notes protesting: the landlord and even a solicitor had been dragged in to remind her of Clause 15 in her agreement about the hours when the playing of musical instruments was permitted. She had stonewalled, argued and evaded, tried tears, saying they were depriving an old lady of the only pleasure she had left in life. But she had had to give in: she was allowed to play between two and four in the afternoon. Even the doorman had turned against her. She supposed, she said, Sidney had seen, in the entrance hall to the flats, the board with a sliding slot indicating whether tenants were 'In' or 'Out.' She was sure, she told Sidney, that the doorman changed her slot to 'Out' when she was 'In,' and to 'In' when she was 'Out.'

Sidney came to life when she said this; he exclaimed that the slot said 'Out' when he had arrived. Mrs Bittell had always loved a suspicion and she was impressed to find someone who shared one with her.

Before Sidney came to tea, on all his visits – Wednesday being his day off – Mrs Bittell sat at her piano, a little distant from it because of her bold stomach, making one more attempt at a bit of Debussy. The notes came slowly from her fingers, for she was not one to vary her pace through life, and with occasional vehemence when she was uncertain. Biting her lips, she tried a little Chopin, but that went too fast, so she moved at last to one of those Hebridean songs she had known since she was a girl of fourteen. Now the fine lines on her forehead cleared and softened, her look became faraway and serene, her eyes became heavenly, and she felt herself to be gliding like a lonely bird over the rocky Atlantic shore at Cranach, her grandmother's great house. She was back in her childhood, keeping her father's boat straight in the sea-loch as he stood up and cast his line. She remembered chiefly his moustache like a burn. As the song began to fall away to its end she ventured to sing faintly, her voice coming out strong with longing as she lingered over the last line:

'Sad am I without thee!'

Who was 'thee'? Certainly not her father with his shout of 'Keep your oars straight, girl'; certainly not her husband, who had helped himself to her money for years and left her contemptuously and gone to live only a mile away across the park to play bridge with his military friends, and die. Certainly not a lover, though she had once thought the best man at her wedding rather attractive. Not the baby she had lost, or the daughters, who had made such unsuitable marriages. Sometimes she thought of 'thee' as a girl – the self that had mysteriously slipped away when she was rushed into her marriage.

The buzzer sounded at the door. 'Thee', of course, was not Sidney.

He took off his raincoat, folded it carefully and put it on the chest in the dim hall. They were on closer terms now.

'I heard you playing when I was coming up in the lift,' he said.

'Oh, dear!' she said.

'Not to worry, Mrs Bittell. They can't touch you. It's five to four: you've got another five minutes.'

And he dawdled to allow her to dash back and get the last ounce of her rights.

He was at ease in the room now.

'Now tell me, how is your father today?' she said.

'The same,' he said. 'Round at the hospital. He goes three days a week. The doctors think the world of him; he's very popular.' He added lazily, 'X-rays. He must have had a hundred.'

'The family depends on you,' she said.

'Oh, no,' he said. 'There was the sickness benefit; the pension; the grant; he's an important case.' Sidney seemed to regard the illness as a profession, an investment.

'What a worry for your mother – but you have a sister, haven't you? How old is she? Has she got a job?'

Sidney looked wounded at the suggestion. He was careful to let the

[1065]

peculiarity of his family sink in. 'Seventeen,' he said. 'She sits on the sofa, sucking her thumb, like a baby, and looking at television. She's Mother's pet. They all sit looking at it. Dad too,' he said.

This pleased him as he sat thinking about it and he laughed. 'Mother goes out,' he said, 'and always comes back with a special offer she sees on the commercials or something from Bingo.

'That,' he added, studying the spaces between things in Mrs Bittell's flat, in which the well-mannered chairs and tables kept their distance from one another, 'is why we're so crowded in our place. You can't cross the room.'

Mrs Bittell said, politely evading comparison, 'You have long legs.'

'Yes,' said Sidney, shaking his head. 'Jennifer says, "You're always on about my legs, what about yours?"'

Sidney offered this information in a bemused way. Suddenly he woke up out of his own life and asked, 'Who is that gentleman over there?'

She was relieved to see he was looking at one of three portraits on the wall.

'Oh,' she said solemnly, 'I thought you meant someone had got into the flat.'

'No, hanging on the wall,' he said.

'Oh, that's just the old Judge. We call him the Judge – the red robe and the fur collar. It was from my mother's family,' said Mrs Bittell in a deprecating way. She had caught Sidney's taste for horrors: 'I fear not a very nice man. They say he sentenced his own son to death.'

'Oh,' Sidney nodded. 'History.'

'I suppose it is,' said Mrs Bittell. 'I like the next one to it, the boy in blue satin with his little sword – the Little Count. I don't know whether he was really a Little Count.'

'Is he the one that was sentenced to death?' said Sidney.

'Oh, no,' said Mrs Bittell protectively. 'The Little Count was the father of the Judge.' She had her own pride in her family's crimes.

'Are you interested in pictures?' She got up and he followed her to look more closely.

'Antique,' he said. 'They must be valuable.'

'So they say, but there is such a lot of that sort of thing about,' she said.

He gazed a long time at the Little Count and again at the Judge. He gave a sigh. '*The Battle of Waterloo* was on television last night. Did you see it?'

'I'm afraid not,' Mrs Bittell apologised. 'I haven't a television. I believe the Misses Pattison have. I can hear it at night.' Her wrongs woke up indignantly. 'I don't know why they should complain of my piano.'

Sidney ignored this. 'Do you think the Duke of Wellington was sincere?' he said.

'They say he was very witty,' said Mrs Bittell.

'But do you think he was sincere?'

'Sincere?' said Mrs Bittell. She was lost. 'I've never thought of that,' she said.

She saw he was struggling with a moral question, but what was it? She felt one of those violent sensations that swept through her nowadays since her quarrels about the piano. Did Sidney, who was older than she had at first thought, more than thirty, his dark hair receding, did Sidney feel too that sincerity, honesty, consideration, were wearing thin in modern life?

'I know what you mean,' said Mrs Bittell, who did not. She compared Sidney with her ancestors and even with the Duke of Wellington. Sidney was reaching towards the Light; she could not say her forebears had ever done so. She had known the family pictures all her life as furniture: they represented the boredom of centuries, of now meaningless anger. When her husband left her she had seen herself as a woman ruined by generations of reckless plunderers of land, putting down rebellions, fighting wars, gambling and drinking away their money, building big houses, losing their land to lawyers and farmers, grabbing the money of their wives and quarrelling with their children. She saw herself with unassuming pride as the victim of history. Even in the Mansions – her rising anger told her – her own class had betrayed her.

She calmed herself by showing him a photograph of a boy of ten. 'My only grandson,' she said. 'Of course he's grown up now. Rupert.'

'I've got a friend called Rupert,' Sidney said.

'Really. Such a nice name,' said Mrs Bittell, putting the photograph down.

[1067]

'He used to work at Murgatroyd's,' he said, suddenly eager. 'You must have seen him – tall, fair moustache. He left.'

'I don't remember,' she said. 'But wait – didn't you bring him to the church?'

'That's it,' said Sidney. 'He brought me. You don't often meet a man who has had an education. Every Sunday we used to go to a different church – St Paul's, Westminster Abbey. He knew about antiques too. Lunchtime and Saturdays we used to go to the National Gallery. He could see *into* pictures. If he was here now,' he said, surveying her pictures and her furniture, 'he'd have valued everything. It was very interesting.'

'Very,' said Mrs Bittell.

'I was in the National Gallery this morning,' he said. 'It's my day off. I had the idea I might find him there. I've been everywhere we went. Holborn Baths too, we used to go swimming.'

'And did you find him?' said Mrs Bittell.

'No,' said Sidney, looking aloof. 'I don't know where he is. He walked out of the shop last August; not a word.'

He paused in the midst of his mystery.

'He left the place where he lived. I went round, but he'd gone. The landlady didn't know. No address. Not a word.'

'Too extraordinary,' said Mrs Bittell.

'I mean, you'd think a friend wouldn't go like that. I thought he was sincerely my friend.' Sidney gazed at her for an answer. 'After three years,' he said.

He aged as he gazed. He sat there as if he were the last of a series of Sidneys who was now quite austerely alone, challenging her with a slight smile on his mouth, to see the distinction of his case.

'Oh, but there *must* be an explanation, Sidney,' said Mrs Bittell.

She had an inspiration. 'Was he married? I mean – or was he going to get married?'

Sidney looked at her disparagingly. 'Rupert would never marry,' he said. 'I know that. It was ruin, he always said; you were better alone.'

'If it's the wrong person,' said Mrs Bittell, nodding, 'but in the Kingdom of Heaven there is neither marriage nor giving in marriage,' she said. 'As the Bible says.' The tune of 'Sad Am I Without Thee' went through her head. Her words brought her to the point of confidence, but she did not give in to it.

Sidney considered her. He held his hurt face high. 'There was an American who used to come into Murgatroyd's. He was from the Bahamas,' he said. 'Or somewhere.'

'Ah, the Bahamas!' said Mrs Bittell. 'Then perhaps that's where your friend went? My husband's best man went to live in the Bahamas. Have you enquired? Business may have taken him to the Bahamas.'

Sidney's pale long face swelled and his mouth collapsed with agonised movements. Mrs Bittell was embarrassed to see tears on his face.

'I can't bear it, Mrs Bittell.' A loud howl like a dog's howling at the moon came out of him. He was sobbing.

'Oh, Sidney, what is it?' said Mrs Bittell, moving from her chair to the sofa where he sat.

The cry took her back years to a painful scene in Aldershot when a subaltern in her husband's regiment had suddenly sobbed like this about some wretched girl. He had actually cried on her shoulder. Sidney did more than this: his head was on her bosom, weeping. His dark hair had a peculiar smell, just like the subaltern's smell. She patted Sidney on the head, but she was thinking, I mustn't tell my sister Dolly about this, or my daughters. It would be terrible if her grandson suddenly came; he often dropped in.

'I am sure you'll hear from him,' she was saying.

'I loved him,' Sidney wept.

'Love is never lost. In the Kingdom of Heaven, love is never lost, Sidney dear,' said Mrs Bittell. 'I know how you feel. I have been through it too.' She was thinking of her children.

He sat back away from her. He seemed to be saying that whatever she had been through, it was nothing to what he had been through. She also saw that in some kind of craven way he was worshipping her. And even while she felt compassion, she felt disturbed. Why had it never occurred to her, in her miserable troubles with her husband, long ago over, but for which her daughters blamed her, that there had been no 'other woman'?

'We must turn to God,' she said, though she knew that years ago she had done nothing of the sort, that outrage had possessed her.

'We must pray,' she said. 'The Kingdom of Heaven is within us, Sidney.' And she declared, 'There is no separation for the children of God.'

Sidney looked round the room and then back to her, immovable in his gloom.

'We must not cling to our sorrows,' she said, for he looked vain of his, but he nodded in a vacant fashion. She smiled beautifully, for she felt that there was some hope in that nod. As he got up to go Sidney changed too. He walked with her into the dim hall, at home in her company now. As he picked up his raincoat he saw himself reflected in the glass of a very large old picture, the full-length portrait of a girl, it seemed, though scarcely visible except for the face.

'Who is that?' he said.

'Oh, just a family thing. It used to be at Cranach. I'll switch on the light.'

There was an overshadowing tree with leaves like hundreds of chattering tongues, a little stream in the foreground and a large grey mossy boulder. On it a sad, naked, wooden-looking nymph was sitting, the skin yellowed by time. In one corner of the picture was a little Cupid aiming an arrow at her.

Sidney gaped. 'Is that you?' he said.

Questions took a long time sinking into Mrs Bittell's head, which was clouded by kindness and manners and a pride in her relics. She herself had not 'seen' the picture for years. It was glazed and was hardly more than a mirror in which she could give a last look at her hat before she went out. She was not surprised by Sidney's remark.

'It doesn't really belong to me, it's really my sister's, but she doesn't like it, so I put it there.'

Sidney tried to cover his mistake. 'That is what I meant. Your sister,' he said.

'Oh, no,' said Mrs Bittell, waking up. 'It's Psyche, the goddess, the nymph, I believe. The Greek legend, Psyche – the soul. I really must get one of those lights they fix to frames. It's so hard to know what to do with big pictures, don't you find? Do you like it?'

'It's supposed to be by – Lely, is it?' said Mrs Bittell nervously. 'My husband said it was probably only a copy. My daughter tells me I ought to get it cleaned and hang it in the drawing-room, where one can see it more clearly.'

The idea appeared to shock Sidney. 'I've never seen one like that in a house before. In a gallery. Not in a house,' he said censoriously.

'I mean,' said Sidney. 'The man who painted it, was he sincere?'

Mrs Bittell was baffled again by the word and murmured politely. Her mind moved as slowly as her feet as she opened the door for him to leave and said, 'You must call me Zuilmah, Sidney dear. Remember I will pray for you and Rupert. Ring for the lift,' she said.

'I'll go down the stairs,' said Sidney. He was bewildered.

She went to the bathroom after he had left and saw from the window the top of the distant block of flats where he lived. Now that the evening was coming on, the block was a tall panel of electric light, standing up in the sky. A thought struck her: How absurd to say it's a portrait of Dolly – no resemblance at all.

She flushed the toilet.

For Mrs Bittell, Psyche was part of her furniture. She had not really looked at it since she was a girl at Cranach. Then she remembered that she and Dolly used to giggle and say it was Miss Potter, their governess, with nothing on. Mrs Bittell had long stopped noticing that Psyche was naked, and if she had been asked, would have said that the figure was wearing one of those gauzy scarves that pictures of nymphs wore in books. She had never even thought of naked statues as being naked. Men, she supposed, might think they were – they were so animal.

It came to her that Sidney was a man.

'How embarrassing,' she said. She imagined she had seen a hot, reddish cloud in Sidney's eyes. He had gaped, mouth open, at the picture, and his mouth looked angry and wet. She had once or twice seen her wretched husband looking at the picture, mouth open in the same way, though (as she remembered) he was short of money and said, 'We'd get a tidy price for it at Christie's,' and they had their lifelong quarrel. He was always itching to sell her things to pay his debts.

'You can't sell it, it's Dolly's,' she had said to him.

'Your bloody sister,' he said.

Now Mrs Bittell's peaceful face changed into a lump of fear. Sidney slipped into her husband's place and became dangerous. He had had an empty, staring expression when he looked at that body. And he had thought it was she herself! Things she had read in the papers rushed into her mind, tales of men breaking into houses and attacking women, grappling with them, murdering them. Sidney had cried on her shoulder. He had touched her hand. His was hot. The scene became transformed. She saw the struggle. She would scream – she looked at her table with a lamp on it – yes, she would hit him with a lamp. That was what her husband had used on her.

Mrs Bittell sat on the sofa opposite to the one Sidney and she had sat on and looked at the squashed cushions, her heart thumping. Slowly the panic quietened.

'How foolish,' she said.

She recovered and went to her piano. She played three or four notes secretively and sulkily, and the illicit sound restored her.

Of course – Psyche was the soul, a 'thee', the thee of her dead baby, herself as a young girl before she married, a loss, sadness. And Sidney too had a 'thee'. He must have been thinking of Rupert, poor young man.

I must pray. I must not let the Devil get hold of me, she thought. Sidney and Rupert are children of God made in His image and likeness.

And she closed her papery eyelids and prayed and pleasantly dropped off to sleep in the middle of the prayer.

For two weeks Sidney did not come to the church; then he reappeared and came to the flat again.

'I've been worrying about you,' she said.

Sidney had changed. She noticed, once he had got out of the dim hall into her drawing-room, that his hair was different. It was combed forward and he looked younger, leaner. She did not say anything; perhaps her prayers had been answered.

'I've been worrying about you,' she said again. 'Have you any news?'

'I made up my mind and packed the job in,' he said. He looked careless and grand.

'Sidney! From Murgatroyd's. Was that wise? Why did you do that?' Mrs Bittell was shocked.

'Undercurrents,' he said.

Mrs Bittell could understand that. There were undercurrents in the Mansions. There were even undercurrents at the church.

'No consideration,' he said lazily.

Mrs Bittell could understand that, too. Why was her youngest daughter so critical of her? Why did young people push past her in bus queues?

'What are you going to do?' she said.

'I'm in no hurry,' he said. 'I might go back to Reception. Hotels.'

'Is that better?' she said.

'Could be,' he said.

'That is where I first met him – Rupert – hotel.' He was off-hand, cool, disdainful.

'Do sit down and tell me,' she said.

He sat down. 'It's all this stealing that goes on I can't stand. It's not the customers – it's the staff. Food, clocks, rugs – anything. Six Persian rugs last week. You can see it being wheeled off to delivery and loaded onto vans in the bay. Tell the management, they don't want to know. Insured. Rupert couldn't stand it. I think that's why he left.'

'We live in a terrible world,' said Mrs Bittell.

'Bomb in that restaurant yesterday – did you read it in the paper? A woman had her hand blown off,' he said.

'How horrible,' said Mrs Bittell. His new haircut made it seem more horrible. 'Did they catch the men?'

'Tell the police, they don't want to know,' said Sidney.

One of those sudden rages which seized her flared up and made her heart thump; her stomach swelled and her sweet face became ugly. Rage was lifting her into the air. Once more all her wrongs came back to her. She felt herself to be united with him: he was no longer the 'quaint' young man. He was human and alone, as she was. And then her rage declined. No, she mustn't give in to anger; one had to face evil. A sentence from one of the vicar's sermons came back to her: she loved the way he said it. 'The darkest hour precedes the dawn.' This was a dark hour for the world and for Sidney.

'When everything is dark, Sidney dear,' she said, 'we must pour in more love. We must open the floodgates.' She was swimming in the growing exaltation of one who had sent out a message. She looked at his doubting face.

[1073]

A vulgar buzzer went at the door, which startled her.

'Oh, dear,' said Mrs Bittell. 'Now, who can that be? I hope it is not someone awkward.'

How often in her life she had expected a prayer to be miraculously answered when she opened her eyes.

Sidney and she looked at each other. Then her face became stubborn. 'How irritating,' she said. 'I'm losing my memory. It's Mr Ferney. I'd forgotten him. He's a friend of my sister's and we've drunk all the tea. How silly of me.'

'Shall I go to the door?' said Sidney possessively.

'No, I'll go. He's retired,' she called back as she went. 'Stay here. Would you do me a great kindness and put the kettle on? Wait – it's probably the doorman.'

Mr Ferney was at the door. Mr Ferney was a meaty middle-aged man with two reproachful chins and a loud flourishing voice.

'Dear Zuilmah,' he bawled. 'Always the same. Like your Psyche, with a lily in your hand, waiting for Cupid's arrow. Am I late?'

'We didn't wait for you,' said Mrs Bittell.

Since he had retired Mr Ferney's profession was having tea with ladies. He was on the verge of a belated search for a wife.

'You don't know Mr Taplow, a dear friend,' said Mrs Bittell.

Mrs Bittell went to make more tea.

'Tiplow,' said Mr Ferney. 'Somerset Tiplows?'

'Taplow,' said Sidney.

'Taplow, Tiplow, all Somerset names. Tiplawn, too. People couldn't spell in the past. You'll find Ferns, Fennys, de la Fresne and of course Ferness. I tell Mrs Bittell that she was a Battle,' he confided in a loud voice. 'Bataille.'

'What are you talking about?' said Mrs Bittell, returning with her silver teapot.

'Your horrible family, my dear,' said Mr Ferney. 'The rogues' gallery – that awful fellow.' He pointed to the Judge.

'Mr Taplow and I were talking about that the other day, weren't we, Sidney? Sidney was saying that History is coming back, wasn't that it? Tell Mr Ferney.'

'History always comes back. I can't afford it, can you?' said Mr Ferney.

Sidney's face became swollen on one side and he said, 'I'll be going then. I've got to get Father,' to Mrs Bittell.

'Must you? Oh, dear. Of course you must,' said Mrs Bittell. 'Mr Taplow's father is in the hospital.'

'Nothing serious, I hope.'

'I'm afraid it is,' said Mrs Bittell.

'Such a tiresome man, I'm so sorry,' she murmured as she took Sidney to the door. 'Remember, Sidney dear, what I said. Open the floodgates. Don't forget to come to church on Sunday.'

And seeing his unhappy look, she gave him a light kiss.

Sidney was shocked by the kiss.

'Who is that? What's he mean by "then"? I've seen him somewhere. It'll come back to me . . . Treplawn,' said Mr Ferney.

'He used to work at Murgatroyd and Foot's,' said Mrs Bittell. 'Terrible stories he's been telling me. I'm trying to help him.'

'Oh, I see,' said Mr Ferney, relieved, and passed his cup. 'What's he after? You do slave for people. I wish you'd slave for me.'

Thieves in Murgatroyd and Foot's, a shop known all over the world for generations! The building itself became a long flaunting wrong and, for her, London changed overnight. Even the gardens in the squares became suspect to her. The doors of pillared terraces looked dubious, embassies were whited sepulchres, the cars outside hotels carried loads of criminals away. Walking in her quiet way, in the past she had floated sedately above curiosity, merely noticing that the young rushed. But now she saw that the city had become a swarming bazaar: swarms of foreigners of all colours – Arabs, Indians, Chinese, Japanese, and all people jabbering languages she had never heard – came in phalanges down the pavements, their eyes avid for loot. If she paused because she heard an English voice, she was pushed and trodden on, more than once laughed at. In the once quiet streets, such as the one in which her sister lived, there were empty bottles of whisky and brandy rolling in the gardens.

She noticed these things now because for three weeks Sidney had not been to church and when she was out walking she was looking at all the faces thinking she might see him. He had disappeared in the flood.

Yet the more impossible it was for her to know where he was or what he was doing or why he did not come, the calmer she became; inevitably the divine will would be manifested and, indeed, she went so far as to stop praying; in a modest way the sensation was exalting.

At church she gave up looking for Sidney in the congregation when the hymns were sung – she was too short to see far when she was sitting. It must have been on the fifth Sunday, as she stood up for the second hymn and heard the mouths of the well-dressed congregation shouting forth, that she noticed two men across the aisle who were holding their hymnbooks high and not singing. Sidney – and who was the other man? She hardly remembered him – it *must* be Rupert!

Mrs Bittell stopped singing and said loudly, almost shouted 'No' to the will of God. She flopped into her seat and her umbrella went to the floor. The church seemed to roll like a ship; the altar shot up into the air. The powerful odour of the fur coat of the woman in front of her was suffocating. The miracle had occurred. Rupert had returned. Sidney was standing beside him. Prayer had been answered: it had swept Rupert back across the Atlantic. All the old prayers of her life that had never been answered became like rubbish. A real miracle had been granted to her.

Flustered, she got to her feet and started singing the last verse and looked across the aisle. The two young men had heard her umbrella fall and now they were both singing, and singing at her, at least Rupert's mouth was open but Sidney was half hidden, and Rupert's teeth flashed. She nodded curtly; she had only one desire: to go at once across the aisle in anger and say, 'Why didn't you tell Sidney you were going away? Why didn't you write? If he is sincerely your friend?'

When the service was over, they were ahead of her in the crowded aisle, but she found Sidney waiting for her on the pavement and Rupert a few yards away.

'He's back,' said Sidney, beckoning to Rupert, who stood politely aside. For a moment the young man still looked unlike a real man but more like some photograph of a man.

'What did I tell you, Sidney?' she said as Rupert came nearer.

Sidney stood back, gazing up at the hero, his eyes begging her to admire.

'I remember you, Mrs Bittell,' Rupert said.

'What a time it has been,' she said.

'What a time,' he said.

'Our bus,' said Sidney.

'You must tell me everything. Come to tea,' she pleaded. 'Monday? I don't want to lose you again.'

They looked at each other and glanced at the bus and agreed. How flat she felt, but as they ran for the bus they turned back to wave – how delightful to see a miracle running.

Mrs Bittell went beautifully and as if empowered to the door. There stood Sidney, so proud that he looked as if he would fall headfirst into the hall; behind him, stiffly controlled, stood Rupert, the answered prayer, perhaps rightly wearing dark glasses as if, as yet, shy of the spiritual life. She forgot to close the door and Rupert politely shut it for her.

'It gives a click,' she called back to him.

'It clicked,' he said.

Sidney went eagerly forward. They stood in the drawing-room.

'The Judge!' said Sidney, pointing to the picture. Rupert ignored this and looked round the room.

'Now,' said Mrs Bittell playfully, 'where is your sunburn?'

'He has been ill,' said Sidney. 'He's only just out of hospital.'

'I picked up one of those bugs,' said Rupert.

'Oh, dear. I hope it was not serious,' said Mrs Bittell.

'Two months,' said Sidney dramatically. What an emotional young man he was!

It was disappointing not to see the miracle in perfect health. His voice was hoarse, he brought a smell of cigarettes with him, and he had lost weight, so that his cocoa-coloured suit was loose on him. His thin face seemed to have a frost on it, and when he took his dark glasses off, he was obliged to narrow his eyes because of the light in the room. The thinness of the face made his mouth and lips too wide. There was grey in his hair. She noticed this because she had never been sure which of the young men at the tea counter he was. He sat so stiff and still, and despite his illness, his bones looked too heavy for the chair. He picked up one of the cups on the tea table and looked at the mark as Mrs Bittell went off to get her silver teapot.

'Now tell us all about the Bahamas,' said Mrs Bittell as she came back, and out came her story that her husband's best man at their wedding had been aide-de-camp to the governor, whose name she could not remember; it was a long time ago, of course.

'Who is governor now?'

The question made Rupert smile thoughtfully. 'McWhirter,' he said at last. 'He's retired, though – not very popular – the new man came after I left.'

'I must ask my sister. She'll tell us,' said Mrs Bittell.

This was disappointing. And Rupert's account of the Bahamas was bewildering. No Government House, no beaches, no palm trees. All Victorians, he said. Full of English stuff left by early settlers. Harmoniums everywhere, he said, grandfather's clocks. Fox-hunting pictures.

Sidney said enthusiastically that Rupert was 'in antiques'.

Mrs Bittell recovered. 'There used to be Bittells in sugar – though I believe that was in Jamaica.' She spoke disdainfully, admitting – to put Rupert at his ease – the shames that can occur in all families. She moved nearer home. 'You must be very thankful you left Murgatroyd's,' she said, admiring him. 'There were undercurrents, Sidney tells me.'

Rupert said, 'You could put it that way.'

'It takes courage,' she said, and she meant this for Sidney, for it seemed to her that Rupert was a decisive man, one who had struck out on his own.

'You have interesting things,' he said, nodding at her very fine bureau.

'Just old things from Cranach,' said Mrs Bittell, and she led them across the room.

'These are large flats,' he said. 'You've got a museum.'

'And there's the big picture in the hall,' said Sidney, the excited familiar of the place. 'Lily.'

They went out into the hall and Rupert looked closely at the picture. 'It could be a Lely,' he said.

An educated man!

And then Rupert said something which was not really very tactful. 'It would pay you to have this cleaned,' he said. 'Six by four,' he said, guessing the measurements. 'It needn't cost too much if you go to the right firm – Dolland's, say – they do a good job. I mean, it would bring it out.'

'I do not think my sister would care for that,' Mrs Bittell said. 'It has never been cleaned. You see, it's always been in the family. I believe it was always like that.'

She did not think Rupert knew her well enough to make suggestions about the tastes of the Bittells. They did not like things 'brought out'. She certainly did not wish to do anything as 'inconvenient' as that. It would be like asking Dolly to get herself 'brought out'.

'It's very suitable with the panelling,' she said.

'That's true enough,' said Rupert disparagingly.

And then Rupert made one more worrying remark about the picture. It was, she reported to her sister more than once afterwards, kindly meant, she was sure.

'That's interesting. There's one in the National Gallery like this, Sid.' (He called Sidney 'Sid'!) 'See the Cupid down there in the corner? See how he's holding his bow? He's going to miss. He won't get her in the heart. He'll catch her in the – er – leg,' he said. And he indicated the probable course of the arrow. And he gave a short laugh.

Over the years Mrs Bittell had not particularly noticed that Psyche had a leg. Surely it was quite wrong to believe that the soul had legs.

And she could not understand why Rupert laughed.

She said, in her social voice, as one asking for information, 'I always understood Cupid was blind.'

Rupert stopped his laugh and she was amazed to see him turn to Sidney and do a most disconcerting thing: he winked at Sidney. The answer to prayer had winked. Even Sidney, she saw, was shocked by this.

Soon after this they said good-bye.

The miracle had vanished. The flat was empty now. Rupert had come back. Sidney was happy. There was nothing for her to do. He did not come to church. His visits stopped.

'Sad am I without thee' – whoever 'thee' was – she sang on some days as she played her piano in the agreed hours. That last chord became more vehement. Mrs Bittell put jealousy into the chord. Surely Sidney could spare her one afternoon? The hardest aspect of the case was that she had no one left to pray for, but she was stubborn in her sense of loss and she began to feel, as her jealousy grew, that wherever Sidney was, whatever he was doing, she could still pray for the freedom of his soul. Freedom, of course, from that very puzzling love of that strange young man who had, after all, not been sincere.

It was a prayer without urgency. It would come into her head at night when she saw the lights of the flats where Sidney lived, or when she was visiting her sister, or sitting on the train coming home from one of those trying visits to her daughter.

On one of her returns, on a Sunday too, when she had been obliged to miss her church, at six in the afternoon – she was expecting her grandson. She feared she was late. She got to her flat. She *was* late. The boy was there. His suitcase was in the hall, open, in his untidy way and – strange – his shoes beside it.

'Rupert darling,' she called.

And when there was no answer, she called again. There was a strange smell in the flat. But then there were sounds; he must be in the bathroom. She went to the bathroom door and said quietly, 'Rupert. It's Granny.'

The door was open. He was not there. She went to her bedroom, where the door was half open, and there she saw a pair of stockinged feet and the cocoa-coloured trousers of a man kneeling at a drawer beside her bed.

'What *are* you doing, Rupert?' she said. The man got halfway to his feet.

She saw the face of Sidney's Rupert. His dark glasses were on her bed with some of her jewellery. A long smile split his face for a moment as he stood up. He had a bracelet in his hand.

'Put that down,' said Mrs Bittell. And called calmly, as if to her grandson, 'Rupert, there's a man in my bedroom.'

And with that she pulled the bedroom door to and turned the key in the lock.

'I've locked him in,' she called.

The man was wrenching at the door handle. Then she heard him open the window.

But now Mrs Bittell had exhausted the words she could speak. She opened her mouth to scream, but no sound came. Lead seemed to fill her legs, her heart thundered in her ears; she saw through the doorway of the drawing-room (miles away, it seemed) the telephone. She began a slow trudge that seemed to take hours, as in a dream, while the man

[1080]

returned to hammering at the door, shouting, 'I'll break your bloody neck, you silly old bitch.'

She was stupefied enough to turn and hear the sentence out. She got to the drawing-room, then to the hall, and what she saw there drove her back. Psyche was not there. The frame was empty. That sight drove her back, and giddily she went to her piano and banged away at the keys, defying the whole block of flats, banging as the man banged at the closed door. The telephone rang and rang, but still she banged and banged on the keys and then the man broke through the door and was coming at her, but in his stockinged feet; on the parquet at the edge of one of her rugs he skidded and fell flat on his back.

Mrs Bittell saw this. She had often, in her quiet way, thought of what she would do if someone attacked her. She had always planned to speak gently and to ask them why they were so unhappy and had they forgotten they were children of God. But a terrible thing had happened. She had wet herself, like a child, all down her legs. Red with shame, as he rushed and fell and was trying to get up, she tipped the piano stool over as he jumped at her. He stumbled over it. And this was the moment she had often imagined. She became as strong as History; she picked up the brass table lamp and bashed him on the neck, the head, anywhere. Not once, but twice or three times. And then fell back and fainted.

That is how the doorman, the general from across the landing, the Misses Pattison and her grandson found her, as Rupert, bleeding in the head, was trying to put on his shoes in the hall and run for it.

'Tell Sidney to come,' she was murmuring as they knelt beside her, and for a long time the telephone still went on ringing.

'A man called Sidney,' said the doorman, answering it. 'He's asking for her.'

He turned to the crowd. 'He says it's urgent.'

No one replied.

With pomp the doorman returned to the telephone and said, 'Mrs Bittell is indisposed.'

The Fig Tree

I checked the greenhouses, saw the hose taps were turned off, fed the Alsatian, and then put the bar on the main gate to the Nursery and left by the side door for my flat. As I changed out of my working clothes I looked down on the rows of labelled fresh green plants. What a pleasure to see such an orderly population of growing things gambling for life – how surprising that twenty years ago the sight of so much husbandry would have bored me.

When I was drying myself in the bathroom I noticed Sally's bathcap hanging there and I took the thing to the closet in the bedroom, and then in half an hour I picked up Mother at her hotel and drove her to Duggie and Sally's house, where we were to have dinner. I supposed Mother must have seen Sally's bathcap, for as we passed the Zoo she said, 'I do wish you would get married again and settle down.'

'Dutch elm disease,' I replied, pointing to the crosses on one of two trees in the Park.

The Zoo is my halfway mark when I go to Duggie and Sally's – what vestiges of embarrassment I feel become irrelevant when I have passed it.

'It worries your father,' Mother said.

Mother is not 'failing'. She is in her late seventies and Father was killed in the war thirty years ago, but he comes to life in a random way, as if time were circular for her. Father seems to be wafted by, and sows the only important guilt I have – I have so little memory of him. Duggie has said once or twice to Sally that though I am in my early forties, there are still signs that I lacked a father's discipline. Duggie, a speculative man, puts the early whiteness of my hair down to this. Obviously, he says, I was a late child, probably low in vitality.

Several times during this week's visit I have taken Mother round the shops she likes in London. She moves fast on her thin legs, and if age

has shortened her by giving her a small hump on her shoulders, this adds
to her sharp-eyed, foraging appearance. She was rude, as usual, to the
shop assistants, who seemed to admire this – perhaps because it reminded
them of what they had heard of 'the good old days'. And she dressed with
taste, her makeup was delicate, and if her skin had aged, it was fine as
silk; her nose was young, her eyes as neat as violets. The week had been
hot, but she was cool and slightly scented.

'Not as hot as we had it in Cairo when your father was alive,' she said
in her mannish voice.

Time was restored: Father had returned to his grave.

After being gashed by bombs during the war, the corner of early-
Victorian London where Duggie and Sally live has 'gone up'. Once a
neighbourhood of bed-sitters, now the small houses are expensive and
trim; enormous plane trees, fast-growing sycamores, old apple and pear
trees bearing uneatable fruit, crowd the large gardens. It was to see the
garden and to meet Duggie, who was over from Brussels on one of his
monthly trips, that Mother had really come: in the country she is an
indefatigable gardener. So is Sally, who opened the door to us. One of
the unspoken rules of Sally and myself is that we do not kiss when I go
to her house; her eyes were as polite as glass (and without the quiver to
the pupils they usually have in them) as she gave her hand to my mother.
She had drawn her fair hair severely back.

'Duggie is down in the garden,' Sally said to Mother and made a fuss
about the steps that lead down from her sitting-room balcony. 'These
steps my husband put in are shaky – let me help you.'

'I got used to companionways going to Egypt,' said Mother in her
experienced voice. 'We always went by sea, of course. What a lovely
garden.'

'Very wild,' said Sally. 'There used to be a lawn here. It was no good,
so we dug it up.'

'No one can afford lawns nowadays,' said my mother. 'We have three.
Much better to let nature take its course.'

It is a clever garden of the romantic kind, half of it a green cavern
under the large trees where the sun can still flicker in the higher branches.
You duck your way under untidy climbing roses; there is a foreground,
according to season, of overgrown marguerites, tobacco plants, dahlias,

irises, lilies, ferns – a garden of wild, contrived masses. Our progress was slow as Mother paused to botanise until we got to a wide, flagged circle which is shaded by a muscular fig tree. Duggie was standing by the chairs with a drink in his hand, waiting for us. He moved a chair for Mother.

'No, I must see it all first,' Mother said. 'Nice little magnolia.'

I was glad she noticed that.

There was a further tour of plants that 'do well in the shade' – 'Dear Solomon's-seal,' she said politely, as if the plant were a person. A bird or two darted off into other gardens with the news – and then we returned to the chairs set out on the paved circle. Duggie handed drinks to us, with the small bow of a tall man. He is lazily well-made, a bufferish fellow in his late fifties, his drooping grey moustache is affable – 'honourable' is how I would describe the broad road of sunburned baldness going over his head. His nose is just a touch bottled, which gives him the gentlemanly air of an old club servant, or rather of being not one man but a whole club, uttering impressions of this and that. Out of this club his private face will appear, a face that puts on a sudden, fishy-eyed stare, in the middle of one of his long sentences. It is the stare of a man in a brief state of shock who has found himself suspended over a hole that has opened at his feet. His job takes him abroad a good deal and his stare is also that of an Englishman abroad who has sighted another Englishman he cannot quite place. Not being able to get a word in while the two women were talking, he turned this stare on me. 'I missed you the last time I was home,' he said.

Again, it is my rule that I don't go to the house unless he is there.

'How is that chest of yours?'

I gave a small cough and he gave me a dominating look. He likes to worry about my health.

'The best thing your uncle ever did for you was to get you out of the city. You needed an open-air life.'

Duggie, who has had to make his own way, rather admires me for having had a rich uncle.

Was he shooting a barb into me? I don't think so. We always have this conversation: he was born to repeat himself – one more sign of his honourableness.

Duggie takes pride in a possessive knowledge of my career. He often says to Sally, 'He ought to put on weight – white hair at his age – but what do you expect? Jazz bands in Paris and London, hanging round Chelsea bars, playing at all that literary stuff, going into that bank – all that sort of nonsense.' Then he goes on, 'Mother's boy – marrying a woman twelve years older than himself. Sad that she died,' he adds. 'Must have done something to him – that breakdown, a year in the sanatorium, he probably gambled. Still, the Nursery has pulled him together. Characteristic, of course, that most of the staff are girls.'

'It's doing well,' he said in a loud confidential voice, nodding at the fig tree by the south wall, close to us.

'What a lovely tree,' Mother said. 'Does it bear? My husband will only eat figs fresh from the tree.'

'One or two little ones. But they turn yellow and drop off in June,' said Sally.

'What it needs,' Duggie said, 'is the Mediterranean sun. It ought to be in Turkey, that is where you get the best figs.'

'The sun isn't enough. The fig needs good drainage and has to be fertilised,' Mother said.

'All fruit needs that,' said Duggie.

'The fig needs two flies – the Blastophaga and, let me see, is it the Sycophaga? I think so – anyway, they are Hymenoptera,' Mother said.

Duggie gazed with admiration at my mother. He loves experts. He had been begging me for years to bring her over to his house.

'Well, we saved its life, didn't we, Teddy?' he said to me and boasted on his behalf and mine. 'We flagged the area. There was nothing but a lake of muddy water here. How many years ago was that?'

'Four or five,' I said.

'No!' said Duggie. 'Only three.'

Was he coming into the open at last and telling me that he knew that this was the time when Sally and I became lovers? I think not. The stare dropped out of his face. His honourable look returned.

Sally and Duggie were what I call 'Monday people' at the Nursery. There is a rush of customers on the weekend. They are the instant gardeners who drive in, especially in the spring and autumn, to buy everything, from plants already in bud and flowers, the potted plants, for balconies

of flats. The crowd swarms and our girls are busy at the counter we had
to install to save costs as the business grew. (The counter was Duggie's
idea: he could not resist seeing the Nursery as one of his colonies.) But
on Monday the few fanatic gardeners come, and I first became aware of
Sally because she was very early, usually alone, a slight woman in her
late thirties with her straw-blond hair drawn back from a high forehead
in those days, a severe look of polite, silent impatience which would turn
into a wide, fastidious grimace like the yawn of a cat if anyone spoke to
her. She would take a short step back and consider one's voice. She looked
almost reckless and younger when she put on glasses to read what was
on the sacks and packets of soil, compost, and fertiliser in the store next
to the office, happiest in our warm greenhouses, a woman best seen under
glass. Her eyebrows were softer, more downily intimate than anything
else about her. They reminded me when I first saw her of the disturbing
eyebrows of an aunt of mine which used to make me blush when I was
a boy. Hair disturbs me.

One day she brought Duggie to the Nursery when I was unloading
boxes of plants that came from the growers and I heard her snap at him,
'Wait here. If you see the manager, ask about grass seed and stop
following me round. You fuss me.'

For the next half-hour she looked round the seedlings or went into the
greenhouses while Duggie stood where he was told to stand. I was near
him when the lorry drove off.

'Are you being attended to?' I said. 'I'll call a girl.'

He was in his suspended state. 'No, I was thinking,' he said in the lazy
voice of a man who, home from abroad and with nothing to do, was
hoping to find out if there were any fellow thinkers about. 'I was thinking,
vegetation is a curious thing,' he said with the predatory look of a man
who had an interesting empire of subjects to offer. 'I mean, one notices
when one gets back to London there is more vegetation than brick. Trees,'
he said. 'Plants and shrubs, creeper, moss, ivy,' he went on, 'grass, of
course. Why this and not that? Climate, I suppose. You have laurels here,
but no oleander, yet it's all over the Mediterranean and Mexico. You get
your fig or your castor-oil plant, but no banana, no ginkgo, no datura.
The vine used to swarm in Elizabethan times, but rare now, but I hear
they're making wine again. It must be thin. The climate changed when

the Romans cut down the forests.' For a moment he became a Roman and then drifted on, 'Or the Normans. We all come down to grass in the end.'

He looked at our greenhouses.

'My job takes me away a lot. I spend half the year abroad,' he said. 'Oil. Kuwait.'

He nodded to the distant figure of his wife. She was bending over a bed of tobacco plants.

'We spent our honeymoon in Yucatán,' he said with some modest pomp. He was one of those colonising talkers, talking over new territory.

'But that is not the point,' he said. 'We can't get the right grass seed. She sows every year, but half of it dies by the time summer comes. Yet look at the Argentina pampas.' He was imposing another geography, some personal flora of his own, on my Nursery. Clearly not a gardener: a thinker at large.

I gave him the usual advice. I took him to a shed to show him sacks of chemicals. His wife came back from the flower beds and found us. 'I've been looking for you everywhere,' she said to him. 'I told you to wait where you were.' She sounded to be an irritable woman.

He said to me, in an aloof, conspiring way, ignoring her, 'I suppose you wouldn't have time to drop round and have a look at our lawn? I mean, in the next week or two –'

'It will be too late by then,' she interrupted. 'The grass will be dead. Come along,' and she made that grimace – a grimace that now struck me as a confidence, an off-hand intimation.

He made an apologetic gesture to me and followed her obediently out of the Nursery.

I often had a word or two with Sally when she came alone: grass seed seemed to be the couple's obsession. She said it was his; he said it was hers. I was a kind of umpire to whom they appealed when we met.

So one afternoon in November when I was delivering laurels to a neighbour of theirs down the street, I dropped in at their house.

A fat young man was sitting sedately on a motorbike outside it, slowly taking off a fine pair of gauntlets. Sitting behind the screen of the machine, he might have been admiring himself at a dressing-table mirror. In his white crash helmet he looked like a doll, but one with a small black moustache.

'Those lads get themselves up, don't they?' I said to Duggie, who came to the door.

'Our tenant,' Duggie said. 'He has the flat in the basement. He uses the side entrance. Under our agreement he does not use the garden. That is reserved for ourselves. Come through – I had these iron steps put in so that my wife has strictly private access to the garden without our interfering with him or he with us. My wife would have preferred a young married couple, but as I pointed out, there would be children. One has to weigh one thing against another in this life – don't you find?'

We went down to the garden. Their trouble was plain. The trees were bare. Half of the place was lifeless soil, London-black and empty. The damp yellow leaves of the fig tree hung down like wretched rags, and the rest had fallen flat as plates into a very large pool of muddy water that stretched from one side of the garden to the other. Overnight, in November, a fig collapses like some Victorian heroine. Here – as if she were about to drown herself. I said this to Duggie, who said, 'Heroine? I don't follow.'

'You'll never grow a lawn here. Too much shade. You could cut the trees down . . .'

At this moment Sally came down and said, 'I won't have my trees cut down. It's the water that's killing everything.'

I said that whole districts of London were floating on water. Springs everywhere, and the clay held it.

'And also, the old Fleet River runs underground in this district,' I said. 'The only thing you can do is to put paving down.'

'The Fleet River? News to me,' said Duggie, and he looked about us at other gardens and houses as if eager to call out all his neighbours and tell them. 'Pave it, you say? You mean with stones?'

'What else?' said Sally curtly and walked away. The garden was hers.

'But, my dear,' he called after her, 'the point is – what stones? Portland? Limestone?'

The coloniser of vegetation was also a collector of rock. A load of geology poured out of him. He ran through sandstone, millstone grit, until we moved on to the whinstone the Romans used on Hadrian's Wall, went on to the marble quarries of Italy and came back to the low brick wall of their garden, which had been damaged during the war.

Presently there was the howling and thumping of jazz music from the basement flat.

'I told you that man has girls down there,' Sally said angrily to her husband. 'He's just come in. He's turning the place into a discothèque. Tell him to stop – it's intolerable.'

And she looked coldly at me as if I too were a trespasser, the sort of man who would kick up a shindy with girls in a quiet house. I left. Not a happy pair.

I sent him an estimate for paving part of the garden. Several months passed; there was no reply and his wife stopped coming to the Nursery. I thought they were abroad. Then in the spring Duggie came to the Nursery with his daughter, a schoolgirl, who went off to make up confidently to a van driver.

Duggie watched her and then said to me, 'About those paving stones. My wife has been ill. I had a cable and flew home.'

'I hope it was not serious?'

He studied me, considering whether to tell me the details, but evidently – and with that kind of reluctance which suggests all – changed his mind. 'The iniquitous Rent Act,' he said disparagingly, 'was at the bottom of it.'

He gave an outline of the Act, with comments on rents in general. 'Our tenant – that boy was impossible, every kind of impertinence. We tried to get rid of him but we couldn't. The fellow took us to court.'

'Did you get an order against him?' I asked.

Duggie's voice hurried. 'No. Poor fellow was killed. Drove his motor-bike head-on into a lorry, a girl with him too. Both killed. Horrible. Naturally, it upset my wife: she blames herself. Imagination,' he apologised. Duggie spoke of the imagination accusingly.

'The man with the little black moustache?' I asked.

'She wouldn't have a married couple there,' he said.

'I remember,' I said. 'You mentioned it.'

'Did I?' he said. He was cheered by my remembering that.

'You see,' he said. 'It was clearly laid down in the agreement that he

[1089]

was not to go into the garden under any pretext, but he did. However, that is not what I came about. We're going to pave that place, as you suggested. It will take her mind off it all.' He nodded to the house. 'By the way, you won't say anything to her, will you? I'm away so much the garden is everything to her.'

Shortly after this I took one of our men over to the house. Duggie was stirred at the end of the first day when he came home from his London office to see we had dug up a lot of brick rubble – chunks of the garden wall which had been knocked down by blast during the war. On the second day he came back early in the afternoon and stood watching. He was longing to get hold of my man's pickaxe. The man put it down and I had turned around when I heard the dead sound of steel on stone and a shout of 'Christ!' from Duggie. He had taken the pickaxe and brought it down hard on a large slab of concrete and was doubled up, gripping his wrists between his legs, in agony. Sally came to the balcony and then hurried down the steps. Her appearance had changed. She was plumper than she had been, there was no sign of illness, and she had done her hair in a new way: it was loosened and she often pushed it back from her cheeks.

'You are a fool, Duggie,' she said.

The man was shovelling earth clear of the slab of concrete, which tilted down deep into the earth.

'It's all right. It's all right. Go away. I'm all right,' said Duggie.

'What is it?' he said.

'Bleeding air-raid shelter,' my gardener said. 'There's one or two left in the gardens round here. A gentleman down the road turned his into a lily pond.'

He went on shovelling and dug a hole. The concrete ended in a tangle of wire and stone. It had been smashed. He kneeled down on the ground and said, 'The end wall has caved in, full of wet muck.' He got up and said, disappointed, 'No one in it. Saved some poor bloke's life. If he copped it, he wouldn't have known, anyway.'

Sally made a face of horror at the gardener. 'Those poor people,' she said. 'Come indoors. What a fool you are, Duggie.'

Duggie refused to go. Pain had put him in a trance: one could almost see bits of his mind travelling out of him as he called triumphantly to her, 'Don't you see what we've got, my dearest?' he cried, excitement driving out his pain. He was a man whose mind was stored with a number of exotic words: 'We've got a *cenote*.'

How often we were to hear that word in the next few days! For months after this he must have continued startling people with it in his office, on buses, men in clubs, whoever was sitting next to him in aircraft on his way to Kuwait.

'What is a cenote?' I said, no doubt as they did.

'It's an underground cistern,' he said. 'You remember Yucatán, Sally – all those forests, yet no water. No big rivers. You said, "How did the Mayans survive?" The answer was that the Maya civilisation floated on underground cisterns.'

Duggie turned to me, calling me Teddy for the first time. 'I remember what you said about London floating on underground rivers – it's been on my mind ever since you said it. Something was there at the back of my mind, some memory, I couldn't get it. There it is: a cenote. That's where your fig tree has been drinking, Sally. You plant your fig tree on a tank of water and the rubble drains it.

'Sally and I saw dozens of cenotes, all sizes, some hundred feet deep on our honeymoon,' he confided to me.

Sally's eyes went hard.

'The Mayans worshipped them: you can see why. Once a year the priests used to cut out the heart of a virgin and throw it into the water. Propitiation,' he said.

'It's an act for tourists at the nightclubs there,' said Sally drearily.

'Yes,' Duggie explained to us and added to me, 'Fake, of course.'

Sally said, 'Those poor people. I shall never go into this garden again.'

In the next few days she did not come down while we turned the ruin into a foundation, and the following week Duggie superintended the laying of the stones. His right arm was in a sling.

When the job was finished Duggie was proud of the wide circle of stones we had laid down.

'You've turned my garden into a cemetery. I've seen it from the window,' Sally said.

Duggie and I looked at each other: two men agreeing to share the unfair blame. She had been ill; we had done this job for her and it had made things worse.

Imagination, as Duggie had said. Difficult for him. And I had thought of her as a calm, sensible woman.

It happened at this time I had to go to the Town Hall about a contract for replanting one of the neglected squares in the borough, and while I was there and thinking of Duggie and Sally I tried to find out who had lived in their house and whether there was any record of air-raid casualties. I went from office to office and discovered nothing. Probably the wrong place to go to. Old cities are piled on layer after layer of unrecorded human lives and things. Then Duggie sent a cheque for our work, more promptly too than most of our customers do. I thought of my buried wife and the rot of the grave as I made out a receipt. It occurred to me that it would be decent to do something for Duggie. I was walking around the Nursery one morning when I saw a small strong magnolia, a plant three feet high and already in bud. It was risky to replant it at this time, but I bound it, packed it, and put it in a large tub and drove to their house one Saturday with it, to surprise them. Sally came to the door with a pen in her hand and looked put-out by my sudden call. I told her I had the plant in the van.

'We didn't order anything. My husband is in Kuwait – he would have told me. There must be a mistake.'

The pen in her raised hand was like a funny hostile weapon, and seeing me smile at it, she lowered her hand.

'It's not an order. It's a present. In the van,' I said. She looked unbelieving at the van and then back at me. In the awkward pause my mind gave an unintended leap. I forgot about Duggie.

'For you,' I said. I seemed to sail away, off my feet.

'For me?' she said. 'Why for me?'

I was astonished. Her face went as white as paper and I thought she was going to faint. She stood there, trembling. The pen dropped out of her hand to the floor and she turned round and bent to pick it up and stood up again with a flustered blush as if she had been caught doing something wrong.

'You're the gardener,' I said. 'Come and look.'

She did not move, so I started off down the few steps to the gate. She followed me and I saw her glance, as if calling for protection to the houses on either side of her own.

[1092]

'Why should you do this?' she said in an unnatural voice. I opened the gate, but she made me go through first.

The swollen rusty-pink and skin-white buds of the plant were as bright as candles in the darkness of the van.

'Advertising,' I said with a salesman's laugh. She frowned, reproaching me doubtfully. But when she saw the plant she said, 'How lovely!'

My tongue raced. I said I had been thinking of the paved circle in the middle of the garden; the magnolia would stand there and flower before the trees shaded the place, and that it could be moved out of the tub wherever she wanted it in the garden later in the year.

'You mean that?' she said.

So I got out a trolley, put up a board, and wheeled the plant down from the van carefully. It was very heavy.

'Be careful,' she said. She opened the side entrance to the garden and followed me there.

'No muddy puddle now. It's gone,' I boasted. It was a struggle getting the heavy tub in place and she helped me.

'You've got a gardener's strong hands,' I said.

I looked around and then up at the trees. Her wide mouth opened with delight at the plant.

'How kind you are,' she said. 'Duggie will love it.'

I had never been alone with her in this garden and, I remember, this was privileged ground. She walked around and around the plant as if she were dancing.

'It will be in full bloom in ten days,' I said. 'It will cheer up the fig tree. It's trying to bud.'

'This time of the year,' she said, despising it, 'that tree looks like a chunk of machinery.'

A half-hour passed. We went back to the house and she thanked me again as I pushed the trolley.

'Leave it there,' she said. 'I must give you some tea or a drink. How lucky I was in. You should have telephoned.'

In the sitting-room she laughed as she looked back at the plant from the window. It was, I realised, the first time I had heard her laugh. It was surprising not to hear Duggie's voice. She went off to make tea and I sat in an armchair and remembered not to put my dirty hands on the arms.

Then I saw my footmarks coming across the carpet to me. I felt I had started on a journey.

I noticed she frowned at them and the cups skidded on the tray when she came back with the tea.

I said apologetically, 'My boots!'

Strange words, now that I think of it, for the beginning of a love affair; even she gaped at them as if they had given me away.

When she had only half filled my cup she banged the teapot down, got up and came across to squeeze my hand.

'Oh, you are so *kind, kind,*' she said and then stepped back to her chair quickly.

'You *are* a friend,' she said.

And then I saw tears were dropping down her cheeks. Her happy face had collapsed and was ugly. 'I'm sorry to be so silly, Mr Ormerod,' she said, trying to laugh.

Ten shelves of Duggie's books looked down, their titles dumb, but listening with all ears as I sat not knowing what to do, for, trying to laugh, she sobbed even more and she had to get up and turn her back to me and look out of the window.

'It's all right,' she said with her back to me. 'Don't let your tea get cold. My husband wanted to put an urn there,' she said. 'I suppose he told you.'

Duggie had not been able to control his drifting mind.

'This is the first time I've been in the garden since you were here last,' she said, turning round.

'By the way,' I said, 'if you're worrying about the shelter, I can tell you – I've looked up the records at the Town Hall. There were no casualties here. There was no one in the shelter.'

I did not tell her no records could be traced. Her tears had made my mind leap again.

'Why on earth did you do that?' she said, and she sat down again.

'I had the idea it was worrying you,' I said.

'No, not at all,' she said, shaking after her cry, and she put on an off-hand manner and did not look at me.

'The shelter? Oh, that didn't worry me,' she said. 'The war was thirty years ago, wasn't it? One doesn't have to wait for bombs to kill people.

They die in hospital, don't they? Things prey on my husband's mind. He's a very emotional man; you mightn't think it. I don't know whether he told you, we had trouble with a young man, a tenant. It made Duggie quite ill. They flew him home from Kuwait.'

I was baffled. She had exactly reversed the story Duggie had told me.

She said with the firm complacency of a married woman, 'He talks himself into things, you know.'

After she said this there was a question in her eyes, a movement like a small signal, daring me for a moment. I was silent and she began talking about everyday things, in a nervous way, and intimacy vanished.

She stood at the door and gave a half wave as I left, a scarcely visible wave, like a beckon. It destroyed me. Damn that stupid man, I thought when I got home and stood at the stove getting a meal together. The telephone rang and I turned the stove off. I thought the call was from my mother – it was her hour – but the voice was Sally's, firm but apologetic. 'You've left your trolley. I thought you might need it.'

O blessed trolley! I said I'd come at once. She said curtly she was going out. That, and the hope that she was not interrupting my dinner, were the only coherent, complete sentences she spoke in one of the longest calls I have ever had. On her side it was a collection of unfinished phrases with long silences between them, so that once or twice she seemed to have gone away – silences in which she appeared to be wrestling with nouns, pronouns, and verbs that circled round an apology and explanation that was no explanation, about making 'that silly scene'. No sooner was she at the point of explanation than she drifted off it. It struck me that listening to her husband so much, she had lost the power of talking.

There was something which, 'sometime in the future,' she would like to ask me, but it had gone from her mind. 'If there is a future,' she added too brightly. Her silences dangled and stirred me. The manner was so like Duggie's: it half exasperated me and I asked her if she would have dinner with me one day. 'Dinner?' This puzzled her. She asked if I had had my dinner. The idea died and so did the conversation. What affectation, I thought afterwards. Not on my side: desire had been born.

But on the following day I saw her waiting in one of our greenhouses. She was warmer under glass. I had collected my trolley. That, for some reason, pleased her. She agreed to have dinner with me.

'Where on earth are we going?' she said when we drove off.

'Away from the Nursery,' I said. I was determined to amuse her. 'To get away from the thieves.'

'What thieves?' she said.

'The old ladies,' I said.

It is well known, if you run a nursery, that very nice old ladies sometimes nip off a stem for a cutting or slip small plants into their bags. Stealing a little gives them the thrill of flirtation. I said that only this week one of them had come to me when I was alone in a greenhouse and said, 'Can I whisper something to you? I have a *dreadful* confession to make. I have been very naughty. I *stole* a snippet of geranium from you in the summer and it has struck!'

Sally said, 'And what about old men? Don't they steal?'

My fancy took a leap. 'Yes, we've got one,' I said, 'but he goes in for big stuff.'

There was a myth at our Nursery that when a box of plants was missing or some rare expensive shrub had been dug up and was gone, this was the work of a not altogether imaginary person called Thompson who lived in a big house where the garden abutted on our wall. Three camellias went one day, and because of the price he was somehow promoted by the girls and became known as 'Colonel' Thompson. He had been seen standing on a stepladder and looking over our wall. I invented a face for the colonel when I told Sally about this. I gave him a ripe nose, a bald head, a drooping moustache; unconsciously. I was describing Duggie. I went further: I had caught the colonel with one leg over the wall, and when I challenged him he said, 'Looking for my dog. Have you seen my dog?'

Sally said, 'I don't believe you.'

This was promising. A deep seriousness settled on us when we got to the restaurant. It was a small place. People were talking loudly, so that bits of their lives seemed to be flying around us, and we soon noticed we were the quietest talkers there, talking about ourselves, but to our plates or the tablecloth, crumbling bread and then looking up with sudden questions. She ate very fast; a hungry woman, I thought. How long, she asked suddenly, raising a fork to her mouth, how long had I known my wife before we were married? Four months, I said. She put her fork down.

'That was a rush,' she said. 'It took Duggie and me seven years.'

'Why was that?'

'I didn't want to get married, of course,' she said.

'You mean you lived together?' I said.

'Indeed not. We might not even have married *then*,' she said, 'but his firm was sending him to Mexico for three years. We knew each other very well, you know. Actually,' she mumbled now, 'I was in love with someone else.' She now spoke up boldly, 'Gratitude is more important than love, isn't it?'

'Is that the question you wanted to ask me,' I said, 'when you telephoned?'

'I don't think I said that,' she said.

I was falling in love with her. I listened but hardly heard what she said. I was listening only to my desire.

'Gratitude? No, I don't,' I said. 'Not when one is young. Why don't you go with him on his jobs?'

'He likes travel, I don't,' she said. 'We like each other. I don't mind being alone. I prefer it. You're alone, aren't you?'

Our conversation stopped. A leaden boredom settled on us like a stifling thundercloud. I whispered, looking around first to be sure no one heard me, and in a voice I scarcely recognized as my own, 'I want you.'

'I know,' she said. 'It's no good,' she said, fidgeting in her chair and looking down at the cloth. Her movement encouraged me.

'I've loved you ever since –'

She looked up.

'– since you started coming to the Nursery,' I said.

'Thank you, but I can't,' she said. 'I don't go to bed with people. I gave that up when my daughter was born.'

'It's Duggie?' I said.

She was startled and I saw the grimace I knew.

She thought a long time.

'Can't you guess?' she said. And then she leaned across and touched my hand. 'Don't look so gloomy. It's no good with me.'

I was not gloomy. That half wave of the hand, the boredom, the monotony of our voices, even the fact that the people at the next table had found us so interesting that they too had started whispering, made me certain of how our evening would end.

'Let us go,' I said.

I called a waiter and she watched me pay the bill and said, 'What an enormous tip.' In our heavy state, this practical remark lightened us. And for me it had possessive overtones that were encouraging; she stood outside, waiting for me to bring the car with that air women have of pretending not to be there. We drove off and when I turned into a shopping street almost empty at this hour I saw our heads and shoulders reflected in the windows of a big shop, mocking us as we glided by: two other people. I turned into a street of villas; we were alone again and I leaned to kiss her on the neck. She did not move, but presently she glanced at me and said, 'Are you a friend?'

'No,' I said. 'I'm not.'

'I think I ought to like that,' she said. And she gripped my arm violently and did not let it go.

'Not at my house,' she said.

We got to my flat and there she walked across the sitting-room straight to the window and looked down at the long greenhouses gleaming in the dark.

'Which is Colonel Thompson's house?' she said.

I came up behind her and put my arms round her and she watched my daring hands play on her breasts with that curiosity and love of themselves that women have, but there was a look of horror on her face when I kissed her on the mouth, a hate that came (I know now) from the years of her marriage. In the next hours it ebbed away, her face emptied, and her wide lips parted with greed.

'I don't do things like this,' she said.

The next day she came to me; on the third day she pulled me back as I was getting out of bed and said, 'Duggie's coming home. I have something bad to tell you, something shameful.' She spoke into my shoulder. 'Something I tried to tell you when I telephoned, the day you came with the plant, but I couldn't. Do you remember I telephoned to you?

'I told a lie to Duggie about that young man, I told Duggie he attacked me.' She said, 'It wasn't true. I saw him and his girl at night from my bedroom window going into the garden with their arms round each other, to the end of it, under the trees. They were there a long time. I imagined what they were doing. I could have killed that girl. I was mad with jealousy – I think I was really mad. I went out into the garden many nights to stop them, and in the afternoons I worked there to provoke him and even peeped into their window. It was terrible. So I told Duggie. I told him the boy had come up behind me and pulled at my clothes and tried to rape me. I tore my blouse to prove it. I sent a cable to Duggie. Poor Duggie, he believed me. He came back. I made Duggie throw the boy out. You know what happened. When the boy was killed I thought I would go out of my mind.'

'I thought you said Duggie was ill,' I said.

'That is what I'm ashamed of,' she said. 'But I was mad. You know, I hated you too when Duggie brought you in to do those stones. I really hated anyone being in the garden. That is why I made that scene when you brought the magnolia. When you came to the door I thought for an awful moment it was the boy's father coming for his things; he did come once.'

I was less shocked than unnerved. I said, 'The real trouble was that you were lying to yourself.' I saw myself as the rescuer for a moment.

'Do you think he believed you?' I said.

She put on the distant look she used to have when I first met her, almost a look of polite annoyance at being distracted from her story. Then she said something that was true. 'Duggie doesn't allow himself to believe what he doesn't want to believe. He never believes what he sees. One day I found him in the sitting-room, and he started to pull a book out of the bookcase and closed it with a bang and wiped his eyes. "Dust," he said. "Bad as Mexico." Afterwards I thought, He's been crying.'

'That was because he knew he was to blame,' I said.

I went to my window and looked at the sky. In the night he would be coming across it.

'What are we going to do?' I said. 'When shall I see you? Are you going to tell him?'

She was very surprised. 'Of course not,' she said, getting out of bed.

'But we must. If you don't, I shall.'

She picked up her dress and half covered herself with it. 'If you do,' she said, 'I'll never see you again, Colonel Thompson.'

'He'll find out. I want to marry you.'

'I've got a daughter. You forget that. He's my husband.'

'He's probably got some girl,' I said lightly.

The gentleness went out of our conversation.

'You're not to say that,' she said vehemently. We were on the edge of a quarrel.

'I have got to go,' she said. 'Judy's coming home. I've got to get his suits from the cleaners and there are some of yours.'

My suits and Duggie's hanging up on nasty little wire hangers at the cleaners!

We had a crowd of customers at the Nursery and that took my mind off our parting, but when I got back to my flat the air was still and soundless. I walked round my three rooms expecting to see her, but the one or two pictures stared out of my past life. I washed up our empty glasses. Well, there it is, I thought cynically. All over. What do you expect? And I remembered someone saying, 'Have an affair with a married woman if you like, but for God's sake don't start wanting to marry her.'

It was a help that my secretary was on holiday and I had to do all the paperwork at night. I also had my contract for re-planting the square the council had neglected and did a lot of the digging myself. As I dug I doubted Sally and went over what I knew about her life. How did she and Duggie meet? What did they say? Was Sally flaunting herself before her husband, surprising and enticing him? I was burned by jealousy. Then, at the end of the week, before I left for the square at half past eight, I heard her steps on the stairs to my office. She had a busy smile on her face.

'I've brought your suits,' she said. 'I'm in a rush.' And she went to hang them in their plastic covers on the door, but I had her in my arms and the suits fell to the floor.

'Is it all right?' I said.

'How do you mean?' she said.

'Duggie,' I said.

'Of course,' she said complacently.

I locked the door. In a few minutes her doubts and mine were gone. Our quarrel was over. She looked at me with surprise as she straightened her skirt.

Happiness! I took one of our girls with me to the square and stood by lazily watching her get on with her work.

After lunch I was back at the Nursery and I was alarmed to see Duggie's bald head among the climbing greenery of our hothouse. He was stooping there, striped by sunlight, like some affable tiger. I hoped to slip by unseen, but he heard me and the tiger skin dropped off as he came out, all normality, calling, 'Just the man! I've been away.'

I gave what must have been the first of the small coughs, the first of a long series with which I would always greet him and which made him put concern into his voice. I came to call it my 'perennial hybrid' – a phrase that struck him and which he added to his vocabulary of phrases and even to his reflections on coughs in general, on Arab spitting and Mexican hawking.

'I came over to thank you for that wonderful magnolia. That was very kind. I missed it in flower but Sally says it was wonderful. You don't know what it did for her. I don't know whether you have noticed, she's completely changed. She looks years younger. All her energy has come back.' Then in a louder voice: 'She has forgotten all that trouble. You must have seen it. She tells me she has been giving you a hand, your girl's away.'

'She was very kind. She took my suits to the cleaners.'

He ignored this. We walked together across the Nursery and he waved his hand to the flower beds. Did I say that his daughter was with him? She was then a fat girl of thirteen or fourteen with fair hair like her mother's.

'Fetched them,' said the pedantic child, and from that time her gaze was like a judgement. I picked a flower for her as they followed me to the door of my office.

'By the way,' he said, 'what did you do about that fellow who gets over the wall? Sally told me. Which wall was it?'

Sally seemed to tell him everything.

'He's stopped. That one over there.'

He stood still and considered it. 'What you need is a wire fence, with a three-inch mesh to it; if it was wider, the fellow could get his toe in. It would be worth the outlay – no need to go in for one of those spiked steel fences we put up round our refineries.' He went on to the general question of fences: he had always been against people who put broken glass on walls. 'Unfair,' he said. He looked lofty – 'Cruel, too. Chap who did that ought to be sent off the field.

'Come and have a drink with us this evening,' Duggie said.

I could think of no excuse; in fact I felt confident and bold now, but the first person I saw at the house was Duggie wearing a jacket far too small for him. It was my jacket. She had left his suits at my office and taken mine to her own house.

Duggie laughed loudly. 'Very fishy, I thought, when I saw this on my bed. Ha-ha! What's going on? It would be funnier still if you'd worn mine.'

Sally said demurely she saw nothing funny in that. She had only been trying to help.

'Be careful when Sally tries to help.' He was still laughing. The comedy was a bond. And we kept going back to it. Judy, her daughter, enjoyed this so much that she called out, 'Why doesn't Mr Ormerod take our flat?'

Our laughter stopped. Children recklessly bring up past incidents in their parents' lives. Duggie was about to pour wine into Sally's glass and he stopped, holding the bottle in the air. Sally gave that passing grimace of hers and Duggie shrank into instant protective concern and to me he seemed to beg us all for silence. But he recovered quickly and laughed again, noisily – too noisily, I thought.

'He has to live near the Nursery, don't you, Teddy? Colonel Thompson and all that.'

'Of course,' said Sally easily. 'Duggie, don't pour the wine on the carpet, please.'

It was a pleasant evening. We moved to the sitting-room and Sally sat on the sofa with the child, who gazed and gazed at me. Sally put her arm round her.

Three years have passed since that evening when Judy spoke out. When I look back, those years seem to be veiled or to sparkle with the mists of an October day. How can one describe happiness? In due time Duggie would leave and once more for months on end Sally and I would be free, and despite our bickerings and jealousies, our arguments about whether Duggie knew or did not know, we fell into a routine and made our rules. The stamp of passion was on us, yet there was always in my mind the picture of her sitting on the sofa with her daughter. I came to swear I would do nothing that would trouble her. And she and I seemed able to forget our bodies when we were all together. Perhaps that first comedy had saved us. My notion was that Duggie invented me, as he had invented her. I spend my time, she says, inventing Duggie. She invented neither of us.

Now I have changed my mind. After that evening when the child Judy said, 'Why doesn't Mr Ormerod take our flat?' I am convinced that Duggie *knew* – because of his care for Sally, even because he knew more than either of us about Sally and that tenant of theirs who was so horribly killed on his motorbike. When he turned us into fictions he perhaps thought the fiction would soon end. It did not. He became like a weary, indulgent, and distant emperor when he was home.

But those words of Judy's were another matter. For Duggie, Judy was not a fiction. She was his daughter, absolutely his, he made her. She was the contradiction of his failure. About her he would not pretend or compromise. I am now sure of this after one or two trivial events that occurred that year. One afternoon the day before he was due home – one of those enamelled misleading October days, indeed – Sally was tidying the bedroom at my flat. I was in the sitting-room putting the drinks away and I happened to glance down at the Nursery. I saw a young woman there, with fair hair, just like Sally's, shading her eyes from the sun, and waving. For a moment I thought it was Sally who had secretly slipped away to avoid the sad awkwardness of those business-like partings of ours. Then I saw the woman was a young girl – Judy. I stepped back out of sight. I called Sally and she came with a broom in her hand.

'Don't go near the window like that' – she was not even wearing a bra – 'look!'

'It's Judy! What is she up to? How long has she been there?' she said.

'She's watching us,' I said. 'She knows!'

Sally made that old grimace I now so rarely see.

'The little bitch,' she said. 'I left her at home with two of her school friends. She can't know I'm here.'

'She must do,' I said. 'She's spying.'

Sally said crisply, 'Your paranoia is a rotten cover. Do you think I didn't know that girl's got a crush on you, my sweetheart? Try not to be such a cute old man.'

'Me? Try?' I said jauntily.

And then, in the practical manner of one secure in the higher air of unruffled love, she said, 'Anyway, she can't see my car from there. She can't see through walls. Don't stand there looking at her.'

She went back to tidying the flat and my mind drifted into remembering a time when I was a boy throwing pebbles at the window of the girl next door. What a row there was with her mother!

I forgot Judy's waving arm. Duggie came home and I was not surprised to see him wandering about the Nursery two days later like a dog on one of his favourite rounds, circling round me from a distance, for I was busy with a customer, waiting for his chance. He had brought Judy with him. She was solemnly studying the girls, who with their order books and pencils were following undecided customers or directing the lost to our self-service counter inside the building. Judy was murmuring to herself as if imagining the words they said. She was admiring the way one of the girls ordered a youth to wheel a trolley-load of chrysanthemums to the main gate.

When I was free Duggie came quickly to me. 'That counter works well,' he said. He was congratulating himself, for the counter had been his idea, one item in his dreamy possession of the place. 'It has cut down the labour costs. I've been counting. You've got rid of three girls, haven't you?'

'Four,' I said. 'My secretary left last week to get married.'

Judy had stopped watching and came up with him. Yes, she had grown. The child whose face had looked as lumpish as a coffee mug, colourless too, had suddenly got a figure, and her face was rounded. Her eyes were moist with the new light of youth, mingling charmingly with an attempt at the look of important experience. She gazed at me until Duggie stopped talking, and then she said, 'I saw you the day before yesterday' – to show she had started to become an old hand – 'at your window. I waved to you.'

'Did you?' I said.

'You weren't in your office,' she said.

Cautiously I said, 'I didn't see you.'

'You were ironing your shirts.'

A relief.

'Not me. I never iron my shirts,' I said. 'You must have seen the man who lives in the flat below. He's always ironing his shirts, poor fellow. He usually does it at night.'

'On the third floor,' the girl said.

'I live on the fourth, dear,' I said.

'How awful of me,' the girl said.

To save her face Duggie said, 'I like to see women scrubbing clothes on stone – on a riverbank.'

'That's not ironing, Daddy,' she said.

There was the usual invitation to come to his house for a drink now that he was back. I did my cough and said I might drop in, though as he could see, we were in a rush. When I got to his house I found a chance to tell Sally. 'Clever of her,' I said. 'It was a scheme to find out which floor I live on.'

'It was not what you think,' Sally said.

The evening was dull and Sally looked unwell and went to bed early. Duggie and I were left to ourselves and he listened to me in an absent-minded way when I told him again about my secretary leaving. He said grumpily, 'You ought to leave the girls alone and go in for older women,' and went on to say that his sister-in-law was coming to stay, suggesting that married life also had its troubles. Suddenly he woke up, and as if opportunity had been revealed to him in a massive way he said, 'Come and have dinner with me at my club tomorrow.'

The invitation was half plea, half threat. *He* was being punished. Why not myself also?

Duggie's club! Was this to be a showdown? The club was not a bolt-hole for Duggie. It was an imperial institution in his life and almost sacred. One had to understand that, although rarely mentioned, it was head-quarters, the only place in England where he was irrefutably himself and at home with his mysteries. He did not despise me for not having a club myself, but it did explain why I had something of the homeless dog about me. That clubs bored me suggested a moral weakness. I rose slightly in his esteem once when I told him that years ago my uncle used to take me to *his* club. (He used to give me a lot to drink and lecture me on my feckless habits and even introduced me to one or two members – I suppose to put stamina in me.) These invitations came after my wife's death, so that clubs came to seem to me places where marriages were casketed and hidden by the heavy curtains on the high windows.

There was something formidable in Duggie's invitation, and when I got to his club my impression was that he had put on weight or had received a quiet authority from being only among men, among husbands, in mufti. It was a place where the shabby armchairs seemed made of assumptions in leather and questions long ago disposed of. In this natural home Duggie was no longer inventive or garrulous. Nods and grunts to the members showed that he was on his true ground.

We dined at a private table. Duggie sat with his back to an old brocade curtain in which I saw some vegetable design that perhaps had allayed or taken over the fantasies of the members.

A couple of drinks in the bar downstairs and a decanter of wine on the table eased Duggie, who said the old chef had had a stroke and that he thought the new chef had not got his hand in yet. The sweetbreads had been runny the last time; maybe it would be better to risk the beef.

Then he became confessional to put me at my ease: he always came here when his sister-in-law came to stay. A difficult woman – he always said to Sally, 'Can't you put her off? You'll only get one of your migraines after she has been.'

'I thought Sally didn't look too well,' I said.

'She's having a worrying time with Judy,' he said. 'Young girls grow up. She's going through a phase.'

'She is very lovely.'

He ignored this. 'Freedom, you know! Wants to leave school. Doesn't work. Messed up her exams.'

'Sex, I suppose,' I said.

'Why does everyone talk about sex?' said Duggie, looking stormy. 'She wants to get away, get a flat of her own, get a job, earn her living, sick of the old folks. But a flat of her own – at sixteen! I ask you.'

'Girls have changed.'

Duggie studied me and made a decision. I now understood why I had been asked.

'I wondered,' said Duggie, 'has she ever said anything to you – parents are the last to hear anything.'

'To me?'

'Friend of the family – I just wondered.'

'I hardly ever see her. Only when Sally or you bring her to the Nursery. I can't see the young confiding in me. Not a word.'

Duggie was disappointed. He found it hard to lose one of his favourite fancies: that among all those girls at the Nursery I had sublimated the spent desires of my youth. He said, taking an injured pride in a fate, 'That's it. I married into a family of gardeners.'

And then he came out with it – the purpose of this dinner: 'The girl's mad to get a job in your nursery. I thought she might have been sounding you out – I mean, waving to that fellow ironing his shirt.'

'No. Nothing,' I said.

'Mad idea. You're turning people away! I told her. By the way, I don't want to embarrass you. I'm not suggesting you should take her on. Girls get these ideas. Actually, we're going to take her away from that school and send her to school in Switzerland. Alps, skiing. Her French and German are a mess. Abroad! That is what she needs.'

Abroad! The most responsive string in Duggie's nature had been struck. He meant what he said.

'That will be hard on Sally,' I said. 'She'd miss her terribly.'

'We've got to do the best for the girl. She knows that,' said Duggie.

And without warning the old stare, but now it was the stare of the interrogator's lamp, turned on my face, and his manner changed from the brisk and business-like to the commandingly off-hand.

'Ironical,' he said. 'Now, if Sally had wanted a job at your nursery, that would be understandable. After all, you deal with all those Dutch and French, and so on. Her German's perfect. But poor Judy, she can't utter.'

'Sally!' I laughed. 'She'd hate it.'

Duggie filled my glass and then his own very slowly, but as he raised the decanter he kept his eye on me: quite a small feat, indeed like a minor conjuring trick, for a man who more than once had knocked a glass over at home and made Sally rush to the kitchen for a cloth.

'You're quite wrong,' he said. 'I happen to know.'

Know what? 'You mean *she's* mentioned it,' I said.

'No, no, of course not,' he said. 'But if you said the word, I'm certain of it. Not last year, perhaps. But if Judy goes to Switzerland, she'll be alone. She'd jump at it.'

Now the wine began to work on him – and on me, too – and Duggie's conversation lost its crisp manner. He moved on to one of his trailing geographical trances; we moved through time and space. The club became subtropical, giant ferns burst out of the club curtains, liana hung from the white pillars of the dining-room, the other members seemed to be in native dress, and threading through it all was the figure of Sally, notebook in hand. She followed us downstairs to the bar, which became a greenhouse, as we drank our port. No longer wretched because her daughter had gone, no longer fretting about the disastrous mess she had made of her life when she was young, without a mother's experience to guide her. I heard Duggie say, 'I know they're moving me to Brussels in a few months and of course I'll be over every weekend – but a woman wants her own life. Frankly,' he said with awe in his voice, 'we *bore* them.'

The club resumed its usual appearance, though with an air of exhaustion. The leather chairs yawned. The carpets died. A lost member rose from the grave and stopped by Duggie and said, 'We need a fourth at bridge.'

'Sorry, old boy,' said Duggie.

The man went off to die elsewhere.

'And no danger,' said Duggie, 'of her leaving to get married.'

And now, drunkish as we were, we brought our momentous peace conference to an end. The interrogator's lamp was switched on again just before we got to our feet and he seemed to be boring his way into my head and to say, 'You've taken my wife, but you're bloody well not going to get my daughter into your pokey little fourth-floor flat ironing your shirts.'

I saw the passion in his mottled face and the powerful gleam of his honourable head.

After Sally had put up a fight and I had said that sending Judy away was his revenge, Sally came to work for me. Duggie had married us and I became as nervous and obsequious as a groom. There was the awkwardness of a honeymoon. She dressed differently. She became sedate – no strokings and squeezes of love were allowed: she frowned and twisted away like a woman who had been a secretary all her life. She looked as young and cross as a virgin. She went back to her straight-back hair style; I was back in the period when I was disturbed by the soft hair of her eyebrows. Her voice was all telephone calls, invoices, orders, and snapping at things I had forgotten to do. She walked in a stately way to the filing cabinet. Only to that object did she bend: she said what a mess her predecessor or I had left it in. If she went downstairs to the yard when the lorries arrived, she had papers in her hand. The drivers were cocky at first and then were scared of her. And in time she destroyed our legend – the only unpopular thing she did – the legend of Colonel Thompson. Dog or no dog, he had never come over the wall. The thief, she discovered, had been one of our gardeners. So Colonel Thompson retired to our private life.

Before this, our life had been one of beginnings, sudden partings, unexpected renewals. Now it hummed plainly along from day to day. The roles of Duggie and myself were reversed: when Duggie came home once a week now from Brussels, it was he who seemed to be the lover and I the husband. Sally grew very sharp with both of us and Duggie and I stood apart, on our dignity.

I have done one thing for him. I took my mother to dine with him, as I have said.

'What a saintly man,' she said as we drove away. 'Just like your father. He's coming to see me next time they're at their cottage.'

A Careless Widow

———

After taking a two-mile walk across fields halfway up the headland, to break himself in, as he put it, on the first day of his holiday, Frazier got back to the hotel. He had a bath to get the last of London off his skin, then, avoiding the bar already crowded with golf players, he went out on to the terrace to be alone. He had been coming to this hotel for three or four years in the spring, a man who liked to stay in a place full of middle-aged people, many of them so well-known to one another that it was simple for him to avoid them and to be alone. Off he went to walk all day; off they went to the golf course or to drive about in their cars. If he was slightly known it was by his surname: 'Frazier with an "i"' he would say with a piercing pedantic stare, giving a roll to his stone-blue eyes as he said it, like a tall schoolmaster mocking a boy. He was, in fact, a hairdresser who came to this lonely part of the Atlantic coast to slough off the name of Lionel, as he was called at the rather expensive *salon de coiffure* in London, where he was eagerly sought after. ('You know,' ladies said, 'how difficult it is to get an appointment with Lionel.') He was a tallish, slender man, not one of your sunken-chested barbers, gesticulating with comb and scissors as they skate about you, grown cynical with the flatteries of the trade. On the contrary, despite his doll's head of grey hair and the mesh of nervous lines on his long face, he was as still and as dispassionate as a soldier.

At this moment, on the terrace, he was examining the distant clouds over the sea half a mile below the garden; and the few villas, watching the purple, the black, the dyed pink and the golden, as they restyled themselves in one of those spectacular sunsets common on this coast. He broke off to stretch out a hand and to glance at the palm and widely stretched fingers as if looking at a mirror. And then, after the lapse into this habit of his trade, he looked at the sky again, until the sound of the door opening on to the terrace made him turn. He saw a middle-aged woman and a young man standing there. He saw her snatch the young man's arm to reprimand him in a threatening way and then push the arm away. They moved to a table at the end of the terrace. Frazier, who preferred to be alone, thought this was the moment to go back inside, but the woman looked up as he got to the door.

'Lionel!' she called. Then she rushed at him. 'What on earth are you doing here? How extraordinary to find *you* at this hotel.'

'Mrs . . .' Frazier stood still and his eyes went wide with horror. 'Mrs Morris! I don't believe it. How did *you* find it? When did you arrive?' He pulled himself together and all those fine lines on his face switched to politeness. 'What an unexpected pleasure.'

With excitement she said: 'This is my son. He's come over from Canada.'

And to her son she said: 'Tom, I wrote to you about Lionel. I've told you how he saved my life when Alec was taken ill.'

The son was a tall, bulky young man who gave Frazier the worldly look of one more bored than surprised by his mother's habit of staring at men anywhere and, the next moment, going straight up to them and saying, 'We have met before.'

'I don't believe it, Lionel,' she said. And, almost archly, 'What a thrill!'

It would have been bad enough, Lionel thought, if Mrs Morris had been one of his customers. It was worse that she was a neighbour from the flat below his own in London whom (he thought) he had at last shaken off! Staying here! A woman who talked and talked, never finished her sentences. A floundering, overflowing, helpless widow, her face so dramatic as it shot out of her thick hair that was like an old black curtain round her cheeks.

Frazier did what he could to hide the shock of seeing her. And then he was certain she knew what he felt, for the dramatic look went. She now gazed at him humbly, guiltily, as one given to excesses of gratitude and saw the talent unwanted.

'As a matter of fact,' she said proudly, 'Tom and I are not staying at the hotel. It's too expensive. We have taken a flat in one of the villas down the road. We just dine here. I used to live in these parts years and years ago. When you were a boy, Tom. We have a lot of old friends here.'

And then she laughed away the shock she had seen on Lionel's face and said to her son: 'I know what Lionel is going to do! Walk and walk. I don't know how you do it, Lionel. I can't face hills any more. Do you know, Tom, he walks across Hyde Park twice a day to work – when he's on his feet all day! I see you going out every morning from my window, Lionel.'

'Oh,' said Frazier, ashamed now, for he liked her laugh. 'I'm sure we'll meet.'

'We're just going in to dinner. Early start tomorrow,' she said to her son. 'We're driving to Land's End.'

To escape, Lionel said he was going down the road to see what the tide was doing.

'I always like to check on the tide,' he said, as he opened the door for them and then left as they went into the dining-room.

Disaster! Friends here? I doubt it. She's on the war path, her non-stop tongue chasing him! Not staying, but dining *every night*. Oh God! His walk down to the sea was ruined. Had he let the name of the hotel slip out in those chats with her in London? At the salon he often chatted in a gossipy way about trips, hotels, countries, prices, as he stood behind his customers, feeling the heat of their scalps and seeing their torpid or fretful faces in the mirror. Women came to him to be changed, to be perfected. They arrived tousled and complaining and they left transfigured, equipped for the hunt again. They were simply top-knots to him. When they got up he was always surprised to see they had legs and arms and could walk. He sometimes, though not often, admired the opposite end of them: their shoes.

But Mrs Morris was not a customer. She was a close neighbour, a fellow leaseholder. For him she was virtually headless, a body, a part of the building and of ordinary life. He still thought of her after the death of her husband not as a person but simply as 'the couple downstairs', giving the name of Summers, who had lived for at least ten years in the flat below and who had only one head between them – her husband's, hers being disposable from a professional point of view. To Frazier her elderly husband had looked brutally placid and she as squashed as a cushion when he went up in the lift with them. What did one know about one's neighbours in a city? Nothing, until that Saturday afternoon when his doorbell rang and rang and rang and a woman was calling 'Mr Frazier. Mr Frazier.' The porter and others called him Frazer – she had at any rate had the merit, he remembered, of 'giving him the "i"'. He was marinating some breast of chicken in his perfect kitchen when he heard the bell, wearing an apron of dark blue and white stripes. He dried his hands, took the apron off and went to the door. There she was, with her winter coat open and her keys jingling from her hand.

'Mr Frazier! Please can you help me. I can't get a sound out of the porter. My husband's fallen out of bed; he's on the floor. He's had a stroke or a fit – I can't get him up from the floor. I've rung the doctor. Would you *please* help me? I am sorry . . .'

Nothing cushiony about her then. She had a tearing grip as hard as a child's on his coat and her nails pinched through to his arm; her black hair, which usually swung over her cheeks, was now pushed back from a high naked forehead which startled him by revealing the curl of a white scar on it.

'Of course, Mrs Summers,' he said (she was not Mrs Morris to him then). She dragged him to the lift but he pulled her away, saying the stairs would be quicker. He skipped down fast. She followed, more slowly, because her eyesight was not as good as his, calling out, 'He's been ill for a fortnight. He's such a weight. I found him when I came back. I went out to buy some fish because of his stomach. There was nothing in the fridge.' The door of the flat was open. He went into a thick smell, partly of spice, and upholstery that seemed vegetable and hot with marriage. He saw the open door of the bedroom – what awful curtains! – and there was Mr Summers, lying on his back on the floor with half the bedclothes dragged with him, blood on the sheet, a dribble of wet in one nostril and a pale belly with white hairs curling on it, half out of his pyjamas. The face was dark violet with a green streak in it and he had a look of disdain about the mouth. Mrs Summers was on her sharp knees beside him at once, holding her husband by the feet.

'Not his ankles!' said Lionel. He was taking the man's pulse.

'Put a pillow under his head. Pull those sheets away,' he said calmly. Frazier got his hands under the man's shoulders from behind and heaved him to a near sitting position.

'Sit up, soldier,' said Lionel. 'Hup. Hup.'

The man opened his eyes feebly.

'I'll hold him here,' Lionel said. 'You get him under the knees. Now, slowly.'

They raised the body and then let it to the floor again.

Mrs Summers stooped to pull up her husband's pyjamas. 'It's the weight,' she said again.

'Change round,' said Lionel. 'We'll get him nearer the bed.'

In the end, somehow or other, they manhandled the hot body and rolled it on to the bed, Frazier falling on top of him.

'We've got him the wrong way up. Now gently, your end.'

The man was awake now and grunted. 'Bloody Red Cross.' He closed his eyes and his breathing roared.

'He was in the army,' gasped Mrs Summers, apologising. 'Were you in the army?'

'Ambulance driver,' Frazier said.

She said: 'He's been climbing the wall, all these weeks. It's those pills. I found him when I got back.'

They sat, catching their breath. Frazier looked around the room. The Summerses were a heavy couple, with heavy furniture. The head of the wide bed was padded and crossed by two awful loops of pink satin. The padded part was stained by the grease marks left by two heads. Frazier had thought of her as a cushiony woman, but in the struggle, when their bodies or arms touched, he was shocked to feel the bones through the soft flesh. Those bones must be made of iron. He saw her roughly pull her hair back from her forehead, and now he knew why he had paid so little attention to her. The hair was dull black slow-growing stuff, hanging in loose ropes – perhaps she had had soft curls when she was young, but now her hair seemed to have been set in some out-of-date perm in a style she must have settled for once and for all years ago. Her strong nose stuck out boldly beyond the weak chin, as if they were staging another wilful life behind the curtain. The face reminded Lionel of an actor he used to see in his father's underground barber shop when he was a boy. The actor's eyes were large and brown and lamplike, as hers were.

'You would have done better to have put a blanket over him and to have left him on the floor,' the doctor said when he arrived, and he called an ambulance.

Down by the sea, because the heavy weeds were hanging from the rocks, scraps of this scene came to Frazier's mind as he stood for the moment watching the tide come in quietly, making a sound of sentences without words.

Poor Mr Summers had died in hospital. A crowd of friends came to console her after the funeral. She came up to thank and thank and thank him and admired his flat and the plants on the balcony. There was a look of hunger on her face as she looked back on it when she left.

Then, after a few weeks, she was at his door, asking him, with apologies, to witness her signature on some document. She was wearing a red suit as bright as a geranium – an improvement. He picked up the document and saw she had signed Pamela Morris. It turned out she was two persons, indeed three, for she was open-mouthed, eager to explain. The woman he had known as Mrs Summers had divorced a man called Morris, who had once hit her over the head with a bottle. Mr Summers had been her solicitor and had rescued her. She had met him in an hotel in Vichy when she was with her father, who lived there as a tax exile. Her tale began to ramble about Europe. At every pause, her mouth remained half open to mark the change to the next chapter, going back to Mr Morris, a man often on a yacht or at a race, while she looked after baby Tom in a house near the Lizard – 'You know the Lizard?' Which race and where was not clear to Frazier – she was calling him Lionel now. The bright red suit turned out to have been given to her by one of her rich women friends. The shoes, too. There was a moment in this talk when she became almost a customer in his eyes. No grief, no reality, her life like the shuffling of cards. The enormous distinction of Mr Summers and indeed of herself was that they had seen no point in marrying.

She paused as he got her a second glass of whisky and then said, 'What a lovely piece of cut glass. You have such lovely things.' And at this she was back to that awful night when he had been so kind, kind, kind, as if all the women in her were talking in turn. She became secretive. She repeated that she had left Mr Summers for a quarter of an hour, as she had told the doctor. But now '*not* to get fish!' He had been asleep and had suddenly woken up and asked her to fetch his wallet from his jacket hanging over a chair. He had pulled out a slip of paper. It was a betting slip. He had backed the winner in the afternoon's race at Newbury: he told her, ordered her, to go down to the betting shop to collect his winnings. Pamela Morris knew nothing about horse racing. The only quarrels she and Summers had – well, not the only ones – were about his betting. She knew he had not been out of the flat for ten days, but when she reminded him of this he boiled up in a temper and started getting out of bed. She was so frightened by his illness that she lost her head. Perhaps he *had* got out, somehow. Men did get out.

'I didn't look at the slip. I put on my coat – *you* saw me in my coat when I came up to your flat? – and went to the shop and when I gave the slip in, the man pushed it back at me. It was two years old!'

There was awe in her face as she stopped for breath: it turned into a sudden laugh hissing along her delighted teeth.

'The wrong slip?' said Lionel, who was a literal rather than a laughing man, and looked at the stretched fingers of his hand. Then he understood: her laugh showed a pride in the irresistible folly of Mr Summers. Lionel saw the first tear in her great still eyes. And, even more proudly, she said, 'I didn't want to make a fool of him in front of the doctor. Alec, you know, was a solicitor.'

As he listened Lionel became even more aware that Mrs Morris was a body. His clientele were no more than heads that he gardened as he gardened the plants on his balcony.

As he listened to her Lionel became aware that their physical struggle with Summers had created an unwanted bond. Headless she might be, from his professional point of view, but she was alive because she was deep in the belief in the plural quality of the first person singular.

Since she admired his flat – and goodness knows he admired it himself, never thought of anything else once he got home in the evenings – he showed her round it. It was not a stew of upholstery, a goulash of furniture, as hers was: every object had been picked up, collected with great care, and had had to show itself worthy: and, by the way, nothing, absolutely nothing, had come out of a boutique, nothing *outré*, jokey or licentiously odd. He showed her the perfect kitchen, installed by *himself*, and every glittering utensil.

'Alec would have loved this,' she said, conveying that it terrified her. 'He always did the cooking, never let me near the stove – never cleaned it, either. If he had a fault, he had a cook's temper.'

And she went on, in her way of begging for an answer to a question: 'I suppose that was why he was so jealous of my husband and hated poor Tom? Wouldn't have the poor boy in the flat?'

That, no doubt, was the measure of her love for the man.

[1116]

They went into the two other rooms, one of which he said he was going to redecorate.

'Lionel,' she said as she looked around and then went out, 'I wish you'd decorate my flat. Tell me what to do.'

(He ignored that at the time, but afterwards her words came back to him.)

He bent down and picked up a piece of cotton from the carpet in the hall and then simply gazed politely at her without replying. He was vain of living alone. He shopped, cooked, cleaned and polished. His cupboards were models of order. His glass was polished. His china gleamed. The jars and packets in his refrigerator were labelled. If anything broke or went wrong, he himself repaired it. He took her out to his balcony where his plants thrived. He showed her the glazed cabinet fixed to his wall, electrically heated, where he grew his seedlings. Redecorate? Advise? Certainly not. She was clearly incompetent. After the death of Summers the smells of saucepans burned out on the stove in her flat came up to his kitchen. Out of kindness he gave her a small plant in a pot for *her* balcony.

That was a mistake. In a couple of weeks, she came up with the dying plant. Overwatered. She sat with him for an hour. After this she started telephoning to him, about things that had gone wrong in her flat, and then, when he evaded her, she started slipping notes under his door. Once a week he did not mind seeing her, hearing about Summers's will, or her son, Tom, but twice in a week was too much. She sat on his sofa, often in that red coat and skirt which did not go at all with his room, talking away about everyday life.

'I love sitting here looking at everything,' she said, sighing naïvely. 'You are so cosy.'

'Cosy' was not a word he liked. He was a busy, practical man, not given to idle speculation.

'You ought to have been a decorator.' (Back on her theme again.)

He said as drily as possible, struck, however, by the thought, 'I suppose I am.'

He was thinking of his work at the salon.

'Of course! That is what you are!' And she laughed.

'I was never taught to do anything,' she said, but as usual the words suggested that her life was a string of accidents, for which she had been avid, and that when these were disastrous they left an aftermath of glee. The only subject which did not end in a laugh was her son, by Mr Morris. She had 'put' him firmly into a New Zealand bank and he had left that for a job in Canada. She was proud he had done that because her ex-husband, Mr Morris, had tried to stop him. Lionel said that boys change their minds and that he himself had wanted to go on the stage.

Lionel was a listener and was unprepared when this admission made her stop talking about herself.

'Why didn't you?'

'There was a boy at school called Archie. His father was a barber, like mine. He used to act in the school play. He would draw girls' heads on pictures of Vikings in the history books – the girls in the class.'

'And did he go on the stage?'

'He was older than me. Killed in the war,' said Lionel.

'Oh!' said Mrs Morris, eager to mourn. 'And is that why you became a hairdresser rather than an actor?'

Surprised by the intimacy of this Lionel said, not wishing to talk about Archie, who had come to life in his mind, 'No, nothing to do with it. I suppose I used to watch my mother doing her hair when I was a boy. Brushing it, with all those hairpins in her mouth, putting up a piece of hair on top of her head and holding it there. It used to fall down and I had to hold it for her, because it often fell down when she picked up another long piece from the other side, then she would start winding it round – it always came out all right in the end like a conjuring trick. She wouldn't let father touch it with his scissors when short hair came in. She kept hers long until she died.'

'I know,' said Mrs Morris. 'I used to see her when Alec and I moved into the flats and she was living with you.'

'That was when father died,' he said.

'You used to take her to the theatre,' said Mrs Morris fondly. 'You go to the theatre a lot, don't you?'

Lionel was alarmed when she said this. He wished he had not revealed anything about himself. The next thing, she would be getting round him to take her to a theatre. That evening she did something very tiresome as he stooped slightly to open the door to let her out of the flat.

'Poor Lionel,' she said. 'You were so good to your mother. Not every son is,' she said. And suddenly she kissed him on top of the head, rather greedily, and having ruffled his hair started to put it right.

That was too much. She was ordinary life and ordinary life always went too far. After this he made a point of putting her off when she telephoned or slipped another note under his door. He was going out, he said. Or he was washing paint, getting the spare room ready for his sister. Also, twice after Mrs Morris left, he had to get a cloth and wipe a stain of whisky from the seat of the velvet sofa she had been sitting on, and – as he said to one of his customers at the salon – he had to hunt for days all over London for something that really got stains off velvet, and in the end he had to get the sofa reupholstered. The expense! The visits stopped. If by chance he travelled up with her in the lift he felt that too much life was going up with him and – to judge by her plaintive expression – life abashed by its longing to *frequent*.

He got back to the hotel. She and her son were dining in a distant corner of the crowded room. A long time passed before he saw them leave, and they showed no sign of seeing him. He went up to his room. 'It will be intolerable. Why didn't I ask how long they were staying? I must get out.'

He lay on his bed looking at a guide for new places.

The danger on the next morning was that he might meet her near the villas on the road before they left for Land's End. Any one of them might be the one where she and her son were staying. But once he was on the beach below and had climbed to the cliff he knew he was safe for the day; and once his feet were on the close turf his mind scattered her as his restless eyes collected all the details of the long stretch of sea and the sky like another country hanging over it. No human voices, only the screams of gulls and the hum of the wind. Below him, the sea came pouring black as whales into the deep gullies between the rocks and was sucked out like suds and then hurled in again. These walks were personal victories for Lionel after the months of piddle-paddling (as he said) around all those ladies in the London salon. Occasionally he saw other men or women walking on some higher or lower ground keeping their distance as he kept his, or – if they chanced to walk close by – sticking, as he did, to passing like solitary clouds, un-marred by a muddling word. People really were like clouds in the sky, born out of the horizon, and as the hours went by they slowly joined the rising grey populations and processions that drifted away across the blue sky and the changing sunlight. Every year he felt re-born here. The sky was always young and ageless, the rocky land got older every day. Clip-clip-clipping in the salon, Lionel also aged with every day, but here, every hour made him younger as he aged.

When he got back to the hotel at the end of a day and went into the dining-room he was relieved to notice that Mrs Morris and her son were not back. What a fuss about nothing!

And so it went on – wet or fine, he was out, on top of this promontory or that, going further every day as if daring the Morrises. Four days passed. Not a sign of them. Had he been rude? What were they doing? Was she, in her slapdash way, being almost pompously discreet? He didn't want to chat, but he would have liked to tell her and her son about some of his discoveries. For example, terror. His life had been without it: hers must have had its precipitous moments, poor sentimental soul. The paths he followed from one cliff edge to the next would suddenly zigzag and turn inland and then seaward again, around appalling ravines whose black or lichened walls dropped sheer to inaccessible spits of sand below. Gulls and crows were often at their savage wars there. Sometimes there were bloody feathers torn from dead bodies on the grass. There was one particular place, close to an estuary, where the land was in a state of débâcle: huge blocks of rocks, the size of houses or fallen castles, had been torn off the cliffs and were stranded there in a chaos of spouting water. Closer to the shore here was a brutal coagulation of stranded rock which had astonished him when he saw it on his first holiday here – a year when he had had a row with one of the stylists at the salon. The rock looked like the body of a truncated man, arms chopped short, huge chest and head tipped back so that one saw only the underside of a chin – a giant in a barber's chair, tipped back and ready for a shave. He would have liked to tell Mrs Morris about rocks. She would stretch her eyes and give one of her amazed laughs, as she always did at grotesque things made half-true: that tale of her husband hitting her on the head with a bottle and leaving the scar had been told like a wonder she had had a gift for. Had *her* chin tipped back like that?

There was one more terror, for the collector of terrors, which Lionel called 'the black wall'. It was a ravine which he studied from one side and then the other. It dropped sheer to a spit of sand left by the tide where there was a narrow isolated rectangle of flat rock, like the hull of a lost ship or perhaps a table where fifty people could sit down to eat. He had often noticed that there were boulders just below the top of the wall and from below the boulders there was a thin irregular scratched line going steeply down, vanishing behind lower boulders and then beginning again. The scratch must once have been a path used by fishermen. He stepped down a yard or two, daring himself to go down then, frightened, crawled back.

'Better not,' Frazier said, looking at his hands. They were his living. He could not afford to break his fingers or his wrists on a giddy climb like that. Anyway, he had his eye on a black cloud coming dragging rain across the sea and he had no sooner turned back towards home than a squall did blow up and whipped him and soaked him before he was halfway back to the hotel six miles away. He broke his rule and went for a large whisky in the bar.

This was on the sixth evening.

'Hullo,' said Mrs Morris's son. He was sitting on a stool at the bar with a young girl wearing jeans, his hand on her knee. She was simply pretty, with her fair hair knotted up in a careless way.

'This is Sal,' said the son. 'Mr Frazier.'

'*You* live in Falmouth?' said the girl.

'Get clued up,' said the worldly young man. 'Mr Frazier is a friend of Ma's in London. That's someone else. I told you!'

'Sorry,' said the girl. 'Oh, I know! We *saw* you this afternoon, out on the cliff.'

'Coming up from the Coffin,' the young man said. 'How far did you get? Ma dropped us on the road and we came across the fields; it's only a mile. She'd gone to have her hair done and we had to bloody walk back. We got soaked. Did you? Did you get to the bottom? It's called the Coffin,' the boy said. 'I took Sal to look at it.'

'I didn't see you,' said Lionel. Watched!

'Ma used to take us on picnics down the path there when I was a kid, very sheltered down there. We used to have a house back on the road.' (Owning the place!) And to the girl he said: 'In Dad's time. I told you. Before they split up.' A young know-all, thought Lionel.

'Your mother took you down that wall!' said Lionel. 'It's impossible.'

[1121]

'A bit dizzy, but it used to be all right. I know what you mean – you can't get down now, the rock's fallen,' the boy said.

'Will you have a drink?' Lionel said.

'I think I'd better not. Sal's soaked through and I've got to drop her. Ma will be back. But thanks.'

Lionel watched them go.

'London friend'? 'Someone else'? What did the knowing boy mean? And where on earth could she get her hair done in this part of the world, not that that would bother her!

'Well,' thought Lionel, 'that lets me off the hook. I suppose I've been rather rude to the old bird.'

He found himself wishing to see the fat woman who had got down the 'black wall' when she was young.

He went into dinner. There were two or three large laughing parties of old friends in the middle of the crowded dining-room, and murmuring grey-haired couples at other tables. Corks popped. Between courses – slow in being served because he was alone – Lionel tried to see if she and her son and the girl had slipped in and were at the table at the other end of the room. They were not. The sun had long ago gone down, and that night the fine weather broke. When he got to his room he saw his windows were drenched, and water was gushing out of the gutters above his balcony.

In the morning, the wind was steadier, the rain quieter, but the sky was dirty and the sea looked like unwashed linen. The seagulls perched on aerials and chimneys, their indignant heads turned into the wind.

That was the trouble on this coast: fogs or rain would set in for days. The guests in the hotel turned their backs to the windows and sat hiding themselves behind newspapers: the heartier ones went boisterously out to their cars. One or two little groups sat around talking about their relations in the towns they came from, in the tones of people sitting after a funeral. Every now and then a golfer would come back from the main door dispirited. Lionel sat in the coffee room, which was usually empty in the morning. An expert in choosing chairs, he had marked one down on his first day. It was now unoccupied. He kept an eye on the puddles on the terrace and saw at last that the rain was stopping.

Then he heard a voice saying to one of the waiters: 'I wonder if I could have some coffee?'

Mrs Morris was standing there carrying a raincoat and wearing a white scarf round her head. She came at once to sit with him. She had come up, she said, because something had gone wrong with the electric power at her flat.

'Would you like me to come down and look at it?' he said at once – to make amends. He had once or twice put something right in the stove she maltreated at her London flat.

'No, it's the landlord's job to see to it,' she said. And then: 'No walking today?' – flirtatiously wagging a finger at him.

She did not take her scarf off, and although her face looked bare, it looked shapely with thoughts of her own.

'We went to Falmouth yesterday,' she said. 'The trees in the harbour are much better there than here. Taller, more sheltered.'

Then, relaxing: 'Tom said he saw you yesterday at the Coffin. Mr Morris, my husband, had a house a couple of miles away once,' she said.

She laughed. 'He wanted to show his girl the place where he was brought up. Especially,' she said, 'the Coffin.'

That word excited her and then she said: 'I dropped them there. It's a mistake to go back to the past. I mean at my age. Our age,' she said. 'Don't you think?' Yet she said this with the pride of one who had always chosen the mistake when she was young, and even now she had the warm wide open eyes of a woman hoping for another.

'Tom has got a very pretty girl,' Lionel said.

'Oh, I'm so relieved he's got a girl at last – I can't tell you! I'd begun to think . . .' she stopped. 'He just wasn't interested. I mean he's twenty-nine. Not afraid of them, always about with them, but – indifferent. I was afraid it was my fault.'

'They seemed full of themselves,' Lionel said.

'He's very good at his job,' she said.

'I was afraid,' she said, 'that the divorce had upset him. Alec hated him, I told you. It was so difficult. The funny thing is' – and it was clear she thought that this, being funny, was a revelation – 'Tom liked Alec! Liked him better than his own father. Tom was really sad when Alec died.'

'He was sad for you,' Lionel said, who suddenly remembered he himself had disliked Mr Summers. The man had looked so much like the soap-white bust of someone who had never existed. Perhaps there was something sexy in the blind, bland conceit of busts?

[1123]

Lionel waited. She would break off sentences as if beguiling herself with the dramas hidden beyond in the open-ended.

'You see, Lionel,' she suddenly said, 'my mother died when I was a girl, a child. Not died exactly, but "put away". I mean, I didn't know her. I'll never forget what you told me about your own mother doing her hair. When I grew up my father used to take me abroad with him on business. Norway, Sweden, France. He had a lot of business friends. He was in timber.'

'Lonely for a girl,' he said.

'Most people thought I was having a wonderful time, but you are right, Lionel. I *was* alone half the time, sitting in hotel rooms, reading novels. The novels I read! Eating. Talking to waiters. I used to think of my mother. Mr Morris was much older than me, in timber too, a friend of father's. After him, I mean after the divorce, I was afraid of Tom's *feeling* for me.'

She looked at him greedily, intently. Lionel saw she was working up to asking him why *he* hadn't married.

'Do you think a mother can be too frank?' she said.

Lionel was lost. He wondered if she could mean she had been chased all round Europe by her father's friends. He could see that she might have been a pretty girl, dangerous in her naïvety, either piling up daydreams or perhaps not innocent at all.

'Was it really because of your mother you took up doing women's hair?' she said, leaning forward, avid for a secret.

'No,' he said. 'Men's hairdressing was going downhill. More money in the women's trade.'

He was about to tell her about the rock that looked like a man tipped back waiting for a shave. Her habit of rambling from the point was infectious. But she was too quick.

'Ah,' she said, with all her breath. 'Money! That's it, isn't it? You had to look after your mother. I mean you had her to live with you. I remember when Alec and I moved into the flats. We used to see you both going out together.' Then, looking around the room to see if anyone had come in and could hear, she said in a low voice: 'Alec *did* something in the law, I never understood it – one of those things solicitors are supposed not to do. Horses – I don't know. I mean, when he died, he hardly left me anything. Well, thank goodness, the flat belongs to me until the lease runs out. I'm so grateful to Tom. He came over to sort things out. He thinks I should sell the lease. What d'you think, Lionel?'

What an extraordinary thing – Mrs Morris no longer there! New people. Builders, painters, hammering. How awful.

She glowed at the surprise she had given him.

'How much of your lease have you got left?' he said.

'I must ask Tom,' she said.

'I wouldn't do it if I were you, unless you know you've got a place to go to. Prices are still going up,' he warned her. In fact, not liking change himself, he wanted to stop her.

'I don't want to be a burden on Tom. He wants me to go to Canada with him. I suppose I could, but he's very serious about this girl,' she said. 'He's fallen flat for her these last weeks. Down here! He met her with an old friend of ours. I wish I had talked to you about this before, Lionel. I'm afraid I've been very stand-offish. You must have thought I was avoiding you, but it wasn't that. We were out all the time. I've known this friend most of my life, when his wife was alive. I told him about you and Alec. But I don't know whether I'd like to go back and live in the country again. Plants die when they see me!' Her eyes were brilliant when she laughed now.

'He'd miss his garden in London,' she added, looking around the room again. 'It's stuffy in here, isn't it?' And she began fidgeting with the knot on her scarf.

'He wants to marry me, but I don't know,' she said, whether offended with her scarf or the man, Lionel could not tell. 'He's coming over to dinner tomorrow night. I would love you to meet. You always know *what to do*!'

And then she tugged off her scarf. He had been looking only at a face: but now, as she shook back her hair he saw that half of what he had called the old rope had gone and that threatening parting with it. Her hair had been chopped into short curl-like lengths, her forehead was clear, her eyebrows had come to life.

'You've changed your hair,' he said. He nearly said 'You have come out into the open.' But the stylist added: 'But it's marvellous, so young.' Immediately he stopped saying 'I' and used the professional 'one'.

'One can see the ears and the neck, the forehead is rounded,' he said, and moved both his hands as if modelling the roundness himself.

'Not severe?' she said. 'Or gollywoggy? As though I'd fallen through a hedge?'

'It brings out the eyes,' he said. 'It's perfect. Slimming too.'

'You are a darling,' she said. 'I am so frightened. It shows the grey.'

It was perhaps a touch 'gollywoggy': he was silent about that. But he said a slight salting of grey gave dignity to the head.

'Now you have a head!' he said. 'I am jealous.'

'Ah?' she said curiously.

'I'm jealous of the man who did it. Where did you get it done?' he asked.

'Tom's girl friend found him for me,' she said, disappointed. 'Do you really think the forehead's all right?'

He knew she was thinking of the scar.

'Perfect,' he said. And in fact the scar did not show.

'It was rather an awful place really,' she said. 'Do you know a dog got in from the street and started eating the hair that had fallen on the floor? The poor thing might have choked to death.' She gazed. An omen? she seemed to ask.

'The time!' she said, getting up. 'I must get back. Look out of the window – there's a pair of wagtails jumping at the flies. They never fly straight. Thank you, thank you, Lionel. Between ourselves?' she said with a prudish glance. 'Don't say anything, will you?'

He walked through the foyer of the hotel to the door, where she refused to put her scarf on.

'I miss you,' she said and after a step or two she looked back at him with a pout of mock despair that seemed to implicate him in her continuing fate.

Another garrulous fragment of ordinary life was leaving him, going about its business. He was afloat in space, and below him he began to feel the cold air of an empty flat. There was selling and marrying in her eyes. At her age! He looked at the clouds and could not make up his mind which way to walk. More important: how was he to get out of that awful dinner tomorrow night?

Cocky Olly

━━━━

At the end of term I often give a lift to two or three of my students who are going back to London. They talk; I listen. Halfway, about forty miles from the city, where the motorway rises and slices through the Downs, cutting one off from the towns that are merely names on the road signs, I interrupt their chatter to point out one or two prehistoric barrows. The youngsters listen politely. When we pass the sign, 'NEXT EXIT FORDHAMPTON', where a winding side road drops itself into the wooded country, I have the impulse to say that down there is a turning to Clapton St Luke, Fogham, and the Marshes – one of the paradises of my childhood – but I check it. And farther on we pass Newford, where I was at school when I was a girl, forty years ago. One of these days, when there is no one with me, I plan to go and look at these places, but I never do. The main road whips it all away.

I hear Newford is larger now; people commute from there to London. Only a few used to take a train from Fordhampton, with its main street running down the hill to the small river, where we would lean from the bridge hoping to see the private trout in the pool where rich Londoners, one of them a Cabinet Minister, used to fish at weekends. On Monday mornings, when I was waiting at our station for the train to take me to school, the Cabinet Minister would be dressed in bowler hat, black coat, and striped trousers, and carrying his official case. Unlike the rest of the passengers, he would be trotting up to the end of the platform and back, often fifteen times: I counted. If my father drove me to the station he would give his big laugh and say loudly for anyone to hear, 'Bloody politician. Up to no good.' I was a weekly boarder at the school in Newford, and at first my mother drove me all the way and then would pick me up on Saturday mornings and drive me home to Upper Marsh, a different country, almost an island between the Downs, where the village people had a more drawling way of talking than the people in the towns. I had picked up the habit before my school days, from the children I played with on the farm near our house.

Marsh Hole really was like a deep hole, where four lanes met at a big farm. Our house was a mile up the road to Upper Marsh, a red mock-Tudor villa that I used to boast was Elizabethan. It was built between the wars. I also thought it was immense, but it was small. It looked out onto a large field of kale. At the back of our house (which my school friend Augusta called 'the eyesore') lay a two-mile stretch of water meadow that went to the foot of the bald Downs themselves. Rarely did one see anyone walking across it and not often any cattle grazing, either. The endless pampas (as I used to call it – one of my favourite words) was alive with insects in the spring and summer, and, from my bedroom, I used to feel I had only to stretch my finger to touch the prehistoric barrow at the top of the far-off hill and the curious chalk track that went in a zigzag scratch almost to the top. The water meadow began at a hedge at the bottom of our steep garden. I remember when I was thirteen gazing at it and feeling it all belonged to our family. This was because the people at Lower Marsh, half a mile farther down our lane, had exactly the same view, although we could not see their house even in the winter. A mound or tongue of coppice kept us from the sight of our nearest neighbours. Lower Marsh had a short avenue of elms leading to a farm where I used to play with the village boys. Lower Marsh House itself was large and grey, with big windows. The village boys said it was haunted. A strange tall man with a long black beard sometimes came out of it, and once I saw him in the road piddling into the hedge near our house. Another time, a funeral hearse went by and after that the black-bearded man did not appear again. But my mother told me I could not have seen all this, because I wasn't even born. Yet it is very vivid to me, and now I think I must have heard my parents talking of some such event much later.

But I know for a fact that years later Lower Marsh House was occupied by Major Short and his wife and a young boy, because I saw them hitting a shuttlecock in the air once or twice as we drove past. Often at weekends if we were walking by we could see two or three cars parked in the avenue of elms.

'Guests!' my mother would say.

'Weekend riffraff,' my father said. 'Gang of traitors. Pacifists, long-haired pansies, atheists, bathing stark naked in that swimming-pool. Friends of Hitler and Stalin. Calls himself a major.'

'Well, he was,' my mother would say.

'First World War,' said my father, who was a brigadier.

'But, Buzzer,' my mother said – Buzzer was my father's army nickname: they used to say he buzzed like a wasp – 'didn't Major Short do rather well in that war, got a medal and was badly wounded?'

'Got himself blown up, some fool dug him out.'

I always thought of the Major as a kind of fair-haired elephant, with a huge chest, lying under tons of French mud. My father had also been wounded. His left arm creaked and he wore a black glove on his artificial hand. He was a slight man with red hair and scalded patches on his face and a high, sandy kind of voice with grit in it, and when he talked of the Major he would get into a temper. Then he'd laugh in the middle of it, and more than once he added, 'Sends his boy to a god-awful boarding school in Dorset run by pansies and refugees wearing sandals, where the boys live in trees. Girls, too. No wonder the little bastard runs away.'

'Surely not in trees, Buzzer,' my mother would say in her high, thrilled, happy voice. I think that my mother and father were thrilled by each other.

'Ruined by that nanny they had, too,' Father went on. 'Not a lad I'd care to have in my command.'

These outbursts cheered my father. He was often up and down to the War Office in London or away fishing. At home he would either be ordering Mother's plants about in the garden or sitting for hours playing patience with his one hand. 'Crash, crash, tinkle, tinkle, tinkle,' he would call out as he put a winning deal down. He was thinking of glass flying about in French villages when shells burst during that war.

Another thing that annoyed my father was that the Shorts did not go to church. We were forbidden to know them. Mother said it was nothing to do with that old war. The real trouble was that our land almost joined theirs and that the Major had cut down several fir trees at the edge of it. My father, Mother said in her heavenly voice, liked cover.

As for myself, I often thought about 'the little bastard' Benedict, who not only lived in trees but was a 'run-away' as well: that worried Mother, too. In spite of the quarrel between the two men, I believed Mother and Mrs Short sometimes met in Newford. They belonged to a musical group, a quartet. More than once I saw the boy shopping with his father and mother in Fordhampton, jumping up and down with excitement as he called to them to look at the posters of a gangster film at the cinema and talking with a spluttering lisp. He had black hair like his mother's and her same sunburned toasted skin – because he lived in trees, perhaps – and he was handsome in his mother's way. I used to wonder if he had run away that very day. He was two years younger than I.

At fourteen, I was a studious girl. I longed to be a monitor at my school and I thought, as my father did, that Benedict was spoiled and that he ought to be 'taken in hand'. Often when I was out in our garden and looking at the Downs rising straight out of the marsh I was fascinated by the chalky track rising to the top and I would think of Benedict 'running' forty miles, at least, across country, and coming down that track as he came at last in sight of his home. I soon found out that in fact he did not run far. He had the nerve to telephone his father once he had escaped from that school of his and his father drove out at night, to pick him up outside some pub on the road. I was awed by this crime.

This and the thought of all those guests 'bathing naked' in the 'traitors'' house at Lower Marsh gripped me. In the holidays I would sometimes get through the hedge at the bottom of our garden and follow the rough ground until their house came into view and I would see the lawn of the Shorts' garden and keep an eye open for a sight of the runaway. Once, I thought I saw him with his mother walking across the water meadow picking wild flowers. Another time, he was coming in our direction and then drifted away. I used to think if he came near our garden I would shout out to him, 'What are you doing here? This is private property!' At last I decided to be illegal myself one weekend and to climb through our hedge and then walk cautiously all along the meadow till I could get a full view of the Shorts and their friends. Getting through the hedge always excited me. The air seemed freer on the other side, the smells different. I did this many times just for something to do, and at first went no nearer. I always took an apple with me, throwing it up and down as I walked, for I thought this would make the Shorts think I was passing by accident. Sometimes there was no one there, sometimes only Mrs Short digging in her garden. If it was a weekend there would be several men and women sitting in basket chairs on the long veranda or on the lawn. The lawn looked rough, but sometimes they played a mixture of bowls and croquet. In time I got bolder, passing within twenty yards of their garden. No sign of naked atheists or a swimming pool and only once a sight of Benedict, running from player to player. I heard the Major booming at him.

I gave up bothering about the Shorts. One hot and heavy afternoon at the end of that summer when the clouds hardly moved and the water meadow was as still as a photograph I got through our hedge again and walked across the water meadow, soon eating my apple, because I was thirsty. I looked at the St John's-wort, a yellow flower that swarms with disgusting caterpillars. The insects were biting and I kept brushing off the flies that were swirling round my head. I remember the swallows and crows were flying low. I was making for the wood at the bottom of the Downs and when I got there the wood pigeons had stopped cooing. Even the flies had gone. The wood had that cankered, damp smell – the smell of toadstools. It came into my head to see if there were any Red Blushers, which excited me, because there might be also what my fungus book called Poisonous or False Red Blushers – not that I would touch them but I liked to give myself a fright by staring at poisonous things and congratulating myself on knowing the difference. I didn't go too deeply into the wood but just shuffled through the dead leaves. The wood was darker, and presently I felt a big warm spit of rain on my face. Suddenly a shot went off, and I nearly jumped out of my skin and the silent wood pigeons came clattering out of the trees and went circling over the marsh. Then there was a long silence. I hurried out of the wood, and crackling sticks seemed to be coming after me. Suddenly the runaway came running out, carrying a gun. There were tears on his white face as he rushed at me.

'Quick! Quick!' he screeched. 'I've shot a bird. It's streaming with blood. It's frightful. It's still alive. It's flapping about.' And he grabbed hold of my arm.

I brushed back my hair. I heard myself saying in my father's voice, 'Stop waving that gun about. You can't leave a wounded bird.' I shook off his arm. 'Show me where it is,' I said.

'Up here! Up here!' he shouted out.

The bird was lying on the ground flapping one wing. There was blood on it and its white lids were closing upward. Benedict was afraid to touch it.

'It's got diphtheria,' he said. 'That's why I shot it.'

I knelt to pick it up.

'Birds don't get diphtheria,' I said.

'They *do*,' he screeched.

In a moment it was dead and horribly warm.

'We must bury it,' I said.

'No,' he said and stepped away. He was white and frantic.

'Come back,' I said. 'We can't leave it here. It's cruel.' When I was small we always buried a bird if we found one dead.

'You must bury it,' I ordered. 'Dig a hole.' He had no knife. Nor had I. I told him to get a stick. He obeyed and we started digging a hole in the soft ground.

'Make it deep,' he said. He was excited now. At last the hole was deep enough and I put the poor bird in and raked the earth back. 'More leaves, more leaves,' he said. 'In case a stoat digs it up.'

'Did you get permission to have that gun?' I said. We were very hot about 'getting permission' for things at school.

'It's Glan's,' he said. Glanville was his father. 'Is this your half-term?'

'No,' I said. 'I'm a weekly boarder.'

'The Devil lives here,' he said. He had decided to frighten me.

'That's stupid,' I said. 'He doesn't exist.'

'It's a she-devil,' he said and he started jumping about in a jeering way.

'You're dotty,' I said.

I now felt several drops of rain, then it was pattering down. This stopped us talking and we looked up. There was a strange change of light and then a rumbling noise. The air was hot and heavy. Thunder! We hurried out of the wood, which was filled with a new sour smell, and just as we got out of the trees there was a long yellow flash of lightning. The peal of thunder came at once.

Benedict gave one of his shrill laughs. 'We'll be struck dead,' he screeched.

'We must get away from the trees,' I said. And then the rain came drenching down so that we could hardly see his distant house through it.

We started to run. My blue-and-white cotton dress was soaked at once, and we were nearly blinded by the rain. There was another flash as we stumbled through the humps of the meadow and then mud splashed our legs. We were running towards the Shorts' house; thank goodness my father was away fishing. We got across the ditch onto Benedict's forbidden lawn and ran up to the veranda of the house. I looked around as we ran: no swimming-pool in sight. The Major's wife was standing there calmly, and then the Major came out.

'Ah,' he said in a calm, insinuating, conspiratorial voice. 'The frightful Benedict and who has he brought with him? Is it the apple girl? I wonder. Yes, it is the apple girl.'

I realised I had been watched from the house every time I walked past. I was afraid of him.

'Oh, Benedict, you're drowned,' his mother said. 'What a bore you are. What on earth got into your head, when you know the Crowthers and the others are coming any minute. And look at poor dear Sarah. Get inside.' How did she know my name?

'Shall I take the firearm?' said Glanville Short to Benedict. 'I wonder how it came into your possession?'

All houses have their smell. The Shorts' house was larger than ours and smelled of thyme and oil paint and old wood fires.

We were taken up the plain polished stairs of the house – the stairs of *our* house were carpeted – passing paintings of geometric faces which looked new. I remember two fat pink naked nymphs dancing on a big seashell and two naked young men standing looking at them. We passed a large room upstairs with bookcases going up to the ceiling and a picture of that tall man with the long black beard sitting in a basket chair and stroking a cat. I was pushed into a bathroom.

'Get it all off, I think, don't you, Sarah, my dear?' said Mrs Short, who had a book in her hand. 'While I see to Benedict.'

What a bathroom! There was a blown-up painting or photograph of an ancient ruin, which continued on three walls of the room from floor to ceiling. I rubbed myself with a towel. When Mrs Short came back I was staring at the painting.

'Is that the Roman Forum?' I said, showing off.

'No, that is Persepolis, my dear. In Persia.' She pointed to a figure on a grand but broken stairway. 'They say it is Darius – you remember? –

but it doesn't seem possible. Now, I don't know what we're going to fit you out with.' She had brought a bundle of shorts and jerseys with her.

'We were burying a dead bird,' I said.

'We could turn the legs up. Do you mind shorts?'

People coming, I thought, as I dried my hair. How awful.

'Please don't bother,' I said as I pulled on the shorts. 'May I ring my mother?'

'Now you're a boy – what do you make of that? Rather fun? How is your mother? I missed her at the chamber music last week.'

So that rumour was true! I had always suspected that although we were ordered by my father not to know the Shorts, she and my mother still met at Newford.

'Rather chic, I think,' she said, looking at me. 'You must come down and get warm.'

We went along the corridor and round corners to a second flight of stairs, down to a kitchen and through a cloakroom with a telephone in it, and then across the hall into a large morning room, where there was a music stand with a sheet of music on it near a large window, and a violin propped against one wall. A radio was on a big table with books and newspapers and also on the same table there was a large, unfinished jigsaw puzzle spread out.

And that is how I remember Emma Short always: a small woman with small, brown brilliant eyes, as dark as Benedict was, wearing a plain but pretty dress, chattering and eagerly questioning herself as she stands before the large puzzle of some famous picture – a cathedral or a castle perhaps, with a river in the foreground. This one also had the figure of a man with a boat on the river. She is standing there picking up a piece and saying, 'How beastly they are to put so much water in these things. It's cheating. What a bore. Ah, now – here, do you think? No. No. Ah, perhaps here? You must look at the little wiggles.' And she put a curly piece of the puzzle into its place.

'You must know Mrs Figg,' she said.

'She teaches us French,' I said, surprised.

'I *know*!' said Mrs Short with a laugh. 'Too extraordinary. What do you make of her? Odd, do you find? Her hats! Is Augusta a friend of yours? She's coming.'

Augusta Chambers, head girl of my school! Augusta – to see me dressed up like this!

I said again I must telephone to my mother to fetch me.

'Glan will do that,' she said. 'You must have some tea to warm you up.'

Through the window I saw two or three cars arrive. People and their children were soon jabbering in the hall. I heard Benedict screeching at them. As they came into the room Benedict was pulling Augusta's father by the wrist and saying, 'Foxey, Foxey, you're a murderer, a murderer. I'm going to report it to the police.'

'The number is 3052,' said Augusta's father. 'Shall I get it for you?'

There was a crowd of people taking off their coats in the hall. Benedict let Foxey's hand go, and Augusta came to me and said, 'What fun.' She whispered, 'Benedict is mad, as usual.'

I was muttering that I must go and getting nearer to the door to escape when Glanville Short stopped me. 'I have told your mother,' he said. 'You're staying to tea.'

Suddenly we were in a dining-room, sitting round a very large painted table, which seemed to be an astrological map.

'Your marvellous table,' said Augusta. And to me, 'Emma designed it. Isn't it wonderful?'

I was still embarrassed by my ridiculous clothes. I had never seen so many people in my life, all talking their heads off. At home we lived to ourselves, as my father said. Doors were always shut in our house. Here all the doors were open and names were flying about. Everyone was asking questions about other people. Benedict was screeching. The walls of the room were painted pale violet. A number of people I had never heard of were declared 'mad'. A Mary somebody was 'too extraordinary about her dogs'. There was news that someone called Stephanie had lost the manuscript of a novel she was writing, on a bus, for the second time.

'What do you make of Chester?' someone said.

The city or some person? I could not guess. I was out of my depth in this new language, but Benedict was listening eagerly, as if enchanted by mockery when his father spoke.

Augusta's handsome brother sat between me and Emma Short. He asked where I lived and went to school. When I told him about school, he said, 'Bad marks – it's on the Right Bank,' which amused him. It was a long time, almost a year, before I found out what he meant, and by then I was mad about him. People like the Shorts were sometimes called the Left Bank of an imaginary river like the Seine. Newford was very Right Bank, Fordhampton was very Left.

Suddenly tea was over. Emma Short groaned. 'It's still raining,' she said. 'What a bore. No croquet.'

'But Emma,' said Augusta's brother, 'we could take umbrellas.'

'Yes!' shouted Benedict, getting up. 'Umbrellas, umbrellas – we'll get umbrellas!'

'I think it will have to be Cocky Olly,' said Glan Short.

And they all shouted, 'Yes, Cocky Olly!'

'I don't know it,' I said.

'You do know it,' Benedict insisted. 'You must do. This is Cocky Olly Lane – everyone plays it. It's Prisoner's Base.'

'Cocky Olly' is the name that jumps into my mind even now when I drive past the signpost to Fordhampton. And when I look back on it who could have been more of a Cocky Olly than myself, chasing the runaway boy across the fields.

'Cocky Olly!' we all shouted.

'No one to go into the bedrooms,' said Emma Short. 'Library and bathrooms are free.'

'Including, I hope,' said Foxey, 'the pig's bathroom.' He meant that Glanville had kept half a pig in brine in one of the bathrooms during the war. I had heard of this at home, and I had been told that it was illegal to cure a pig without registering the fact with the agricultural inspector. My father always said Major Short ought to be reported to the inspector and sent to jail.

And so with Foxey as Cocky Olly to start us off, the grown-ups and we children raced up the stairs and hid all over the house. Soon we were shouting warning cries of 'Cocky Olly on the back stairs!' as everyone raced away. 'Cocky Olly in the library!' 'Cocky Olly in the passage!' 'Cocky Olly in Annie's room!' and we raced up another flight, and Augusta, who had been caught, was shouting, 'Rescue, rescue!' and

Benedict was crying for rescue, too. I got to him and touched him. He was free. He was the most excited of us all. Round the house, up and down, we went. On a desk in the library, where Glanville worked, I came upon a huge book called *The Building of the Pyramids*. It was written, Augusta told me, by that old man with the long black beard – the one I had seen peeing into the hedge, whose portrait was on the wall, not easy to see because the afternoon was dark. The rain was still coming down. Then the hue and cry came again, the sound of scattering people. I ran along the passage and made for a door where the passage turned a corner. Benedict had scooted there. We collided and stepped back into a small room where the curtains were drawn. Suddenly Benedict locked the door. 'That's not fair,' I said. I can hear myself, even now, saying it.

Benedict said in his shrill voice, 'There's a dead body in here.'

I was not going to be scared by him. I remembered what Foxey had done when Benedict called him a murderer.

'Yes,' I said. 'I know. I've reported it. It's on the floor. Give me the key or I'll put the light on.'

He gave me the key at once.

'This is your room,' I said.

'It isn't,' he said. 'It used to be Nanny's, but we threw her out.' I told him he couldn't scare me, and, in fact, after that I couldn't get rid of him. He followed me everywhere as we chased round in the game.

The grown-ups had gone down to the drawing room and eventually, hot and puffed, we went in to join them. It was a greenish silky room. Glanville was handing out orange juice to cool us down, and small glasses of gin, I suppose, to the grown-ups and to Augusta's brother, too. Glanville moved slowly, politely, with a sly conspiring look in his eyes as he gave us our drinks. He had been in the middle of telling a story when we rushed in, and now he continued. He had been on a jury at Winchester, he said, and there was evidence from a policeman who said he had seen the prisoner signalling to a confederate on a racecourse, and then the judge had said, 'A signal, officer? Would you be kind enough to do the signal for us?' and the officer made strange movements with his hand. The judge said, 'Officer, would you mind doing that again?'

Glanville had a gift for acting. He could make you feel guilty by rolling his eyes and looking mysterious. In a fish shop in Fordhampton when I was with my mother we once heard him saying in his quiet accusing voice to the fishmonger, 'Have you *fish?*'

I looked round at the pictures on the walls of the drawing room. There were two clowns and there was a painting of a sculptured head of a girl in profile, mounted on a short marble stand, a girl with large eyes, very beautiful.

'It's a Stolz,' Augusta whispered to me.

'No, it isn't,' said her brother. 'It's a Webb in her Stolz period.' And to me he said, in Mrs Short's manner, 'What do you make of it?'

'It looks chopped off,' I said. I saw Augusta's brother was disappointed in me.

I looked at the heads of all the people in the room. They seemed to be like people from another planet. I was in love with them all and did not want to leave. And then Foxey said, 'We must go,' and Augusta said to me, 'We'll drop you.'

'No, I'll walk. It's only up the lane.'

'You must come again,' said Mrs Short.

'I wonder whether we shall see more of the apple girl,' said Glan in his conspiring mocking tone. 'I think we shall.'

I remember sitting next to Augusta's brother in the back of the car and Benedict waving frantically to us.

'Where are your clothes?' my mother asked when I was dropped at our house.

I had forgotten them.

'What a sight you look.'

I could not stop talking about everything and everyone I had seen – the house, the huge tea table, the puzzle on Mrs Short's table, the Persepolis in the bathroom. I explained that it was not my fault I had gone there, but I was worried about what my father would say. Mother made light of it. All she wanted to know was whether Benedict had played his violin.

This startled me.

'He is going to be *good*,' my mother said in her thrilled voice. She was astonished that I did not know.

I could not go to sleep for thinking about it all: the rooms, the stairs, the girl's head, Benedict locking me in the room, and Augusta's brother.

I looked at my room and hated our furniture and the smell of polish, and wanted to run away.

It was only in the morning that I remembered I had not seen the swimming-pool.

I admit that I left my wet clothes behind so that I would be able to return. The following morning, I went back to Lower Marsh openly by the road and down the avenue of elms, with a bundle of the Shorts' clothes under my arm, but kept back the shirt until it could be washed. The air was fresher after the storm. The front door of the house was open. There was no bell or knocker. I could hear Glanville talking on the telephone, which perhaps for some secret reason was in the cloakroom. At our house we had a proper telephone fitted in our hall.

I heard Glanville say on the telephone, 'So you think well of Gentle Annie do you? I had rather fancied –' and I think he said 'Monte Cristo'. And then, 'Rather dangerous, do you think? The going will be heavy after all the rain. Well, we must hope.' Then he must have changed the subject, for in a conspiring, private voice he was saying, 'I am inclined to agree with you, Foxey. I fancy that Oedipus is coming into the open. He is digging a grave in the garden – indeed, *two* graves. But we don't despair, Foxey. There is a filly, and we're pinning our hopes there. We shall have to see how it goes. Goodbye, Foxey.'

Now what was that about?

Then he came out of the cloakroom and saw me.

'Ah, what have we here? The apple girl without her apple. She has brought a parcel. What can that be?'

He took the parcel and then, in his plotting way, said, 'We must discover where the frightful Benedict is. Do you think he may be in the garden? Shall we go and see?'

I had decided that when he was buried under tons of earth by a land mine, or whatever it was, in the First World War, Glanville must have saved his life by asking himself innumerable questions. Perhaps that is silly, but he always looked at me or anyone else so steadily as he spoke that he was outside time and his blue eyes cast a spell. This made me shy, because he was not an old man. Now he led me through the house onto the long veranda and we looked down across the lawn. No sign of Benedict, so we went round the side of the house and there, in the paddock, we saw him. He was digging with difficulty in the tufty grass, and when we got to him we saw he had taped out two long rectangles side by side and had dug a few spadefuls of earth out of the end of one. As we watched, Benedict stuck the garden fork into the ground and danced around it.

'Can he be looking for buried treasure?' the Major asked.

Benedict jumped about crying, 'Guess, guess, guess. Don't tell her, Glan.'

I said he was making a flowerbed.

'No, no, no,' he called out. 'Guess.'

Mrs Short came up from the garden and the Major explained why I was there. Benedict was annoyed because we were not talking to him.

'He says it is a swimming-pool – one for men, one for ladies,' said Mrs Short.

We all laughed.

Benedict looked from one to the other of us. 'I have changed it,' he said. 'It's an Egyptian tomb for Pharaoh.'

'And this one, perhaps, for his wife?' said the Major, pointing to the second rectangle.

'Where is the pyramid?' I said.

'It's going to be a barrow,' said Benedict. 'An ancient mound.'

The Major and his wife strolled away, and Benedict and I were left alone. I picked up the garden fork and tried to dig. 'Don't do that,' he said, and pulled the fork from me, rather frightened. 'It's boring,' he said.

It was a lazy morning, one of those long mornings – how long they are when one is young – when you wander about and every minute is as long as an hour.

'I'm going to see the dead bird,' he said at last.

I did not want to go home. I thought, This is where I want to stay, so I followed him. We crossed the hedge into the water meadow, where the air was cool, and listened to the swish of our shoes against the wiry grass and watched the insects jump away and stopped to listen to the larks singing like electric bells high up in the sky and tried to see them, and we seemed to walk from one electric bell to another. Like Benedict I was playing at running away. First he went ahead fast, but I soon caught up and passed him.

'Beat you,' I said, and rumpled his head as I passed. He began to chase me. We passed the end of the wood where the dead bird was and got across the stream, where we messed about with sticks in the water and startled birds. Then we began to climb. I wanted to get to the top of the barrow, but it was longer and higher than I had imagined it would be. The view grew wider and wider and went on for miles, and there was no sound now. We were high above the singing larks. I could see our house and Benedict's standing quiet with the sun on them. We stopped and sat down. We were sitting on the bones of people who had died *millions* of years ago. There was no sound here except the wind, but then we heard the baaing of a ram. It sounded to me like the voice of a buried man, but I did not say this. We got up from where we were sitting and looked for it but could see nothing. The sound must have come from the ram far below. I nearly said, 'The heights! How I love them!' but I didn't. Benedict, I thought, is too young; I was centuries older than he was. I wanted to stay there for ever – not with Benedict but, say, with Augusta's brother, and when we stood for a last look on the miles of flat fields and clumps of trees where there would be a church tower and little houses on the far side, with a road wriggling round a wood, I wanted to go there, too. Suddenly – I don't know why – thinking of Augusta's brother, I marched up to Benedict and kissed him and ran off. He didn't like this and picked up a thorny stick and chased after me.

I stopped. 'Why do you run away from school?' I asked severely.

'I hate it,' he said at once. 'It's boring. I'm not going back.'

The Devil was there, he went on. Benedict and the Devil! The Devil was dressed in red, he said. This time the Devil was the man who taught music there at his school. He was ignorant, stupid.

It was getting late. We went stumbling down the steep path, and as we got lower I could hear the skylarks again, no higher than my shoulder but far out over the fields below. I could almost have caught one of them.

When we got down to the meadow Benedict was angry when I said I had to get back home. 'Stay, stay,' he said, 'I'll let you dig.' But I said no, I didn't want to dig. He followed me across the meadow to our hedge, still saying 'Stay.' I said I had to pack up and go back to school in the afternoon. When I got through the hedge and called out 'Goodbye,' he shouted 'I hate you!' I saw him walking away and then suddenly he ran and then he was out of sight. I don't know why I kissed him when we were on the barrow.

Everything changed at my school in Newford after that party at Lower Marsh. Augusta, who was a good deal older than I and taller, had never taken much notice of me, but now she came floating round me like a swan. She had long golden hair and large grey dreaming eyes that narrowed and dwelled on you in an inspecting way. She said, 'I didn't know you knew the Shorts,' in a way that suggested I had hidden a secret from her. Her voice seemed to float on romantic secrets. She was also our chief mimic and gossip. She'd do Mrs Figg's sarcastic voice, and she knew which teacher was in love with an old don at Oxford who was married. She called two girls who doted on the art master 'Picasso's Doves', and the headmistress 'the blessed St Agnes'. To be with her was like reading a novel in serial parts; she paused and we knew there were chapters to come.

I told her that we did not really know the Shorts, though my mother, I thought, often met Mrs Short at a musical quartet at Newford.

She narrowed her questioning eyes. 'I adore Glan and Emma, don't you?'

And before I knew what I was saying I said there was some trouble about fir trees.

'Fir trees!' said Augusta with a laugh that egged me to go on, but I had come to a lame end.

We were going into supper and Mrs Figg passed us. 'Don't dawdle, Sarah,' she said.

I was not a dawdling girl, and I saw that I must have been copying Augusta's dawdling walk. It was new to me, and I felt I had grown up several months. As we separated and went to our different tables Augusta said, off-hand, 'Of course, Benedict's quite mad. My father says it goes back to that awful pious nurse he had. She used to tell him that the Devil would get him and that he would go to hell. And then there was that awful Webb business.' And, with that, she glided away.

But the phrase 'that awful Webb business' and Augusta walking away with her I-know-more-than-you-do look made me dog Augusta whenever I could. And I could see by her face that she noticed this. We went off the next day to play tennis on the school court. She was a slapdash tennis player, and even the few balls that came over the net seemed to know something. When we left the court and went to our dormitory to change

I said, 'My father didn't cut down those fir trees. It was old Webby who used to work for the Shorts as well as for us.'

Augusta stood there with her blouse off. Her grown-up breasts, larger than mine, seemed to be staring at me. The bell rang and we hadn't washed.

'Run along,' she said. 'Actually,' she said – we all said 'actually' in a cutting way in those days – 'I was talking about Glanville's first wife. She died years ago. She drowned.'

I felt I was like some silly fish dangling on a hook in hot air. I could not breathe.

'Come along, girls,' Mrs Figg called from the door of the dormitory. I choked my way into my clothes. I sluiced my face and through the water I saw the astonishing stone face of the drowning Webb in the drawing room at Lower Marsh.

Poor Benedict, I thought, and I ran down the clattering stairs to the dining room. I mumbled my way through grace and saw Augusta across the room saying grace beautifully, her lovely chin raised. Later she ate slowly, while I was racing through my food and spilled my milk. I was still wriggling on Augusta's hook. I was in her power.

But Augusta was merciful to me, or else, I suppose, she saw the kind of opportunity she loved. If she was dreamy, she was also crisp.

In our free time it was easy for girls to be in twos, lying in the grass, and at last I was able to say, 'Poor Benedict, his mother drowned.' This explained the strange things he did, and his talk of the body in the room.

'I did not say that,' said Augusta scornfully. 'Emma is his mother. Glan was married to Webb. *Then* he married Emma. What a thing to say! Did your father say that? If he did, it's very wicked,' she said sharply.

I said no, he'd never said anything like that, nor my mother, I swore. Augusta was still suspicious of this, but at last she saw how confused I was, and she forgave me. She said that Glanville had married a Miss Webb when he came home after the First World War; everyone was mad about her. It was not until much later that I began to wonder how Augusta knew the story. It must have happened *before* the war and she wasn't born then. But she said that Webb had gone off to Egypt with a painter called Stolz and that he had left her, and so she had come home and drowned herself in the river at Fordhampton.

The one where father can't afford to fish, I thought. And then I thought of Benedict digging a grave for Pharaoh and his wife in his garden.

I had already told Augusta about this the day after Cocky Olly, but when I mentioned it again now, Augusta cut the story short. 'That boy is always digging,' she said. 'He wants to be an archaeologist, like that man in Glanville's library.' And she said dreamily, 'I would never be a second wife, unless he was like Glanville.'

We got up from the grass laughing. I mean, *I* laughed; Augusta didn't. Anyway, she said, Emma and Glan were sending Benedict to the grammar school in Newford. That would stop him running away because he'd come home every day by train. And she gave me one of her narrow-eyed looks. The Shorts were her possession.

The long holidays began. My father took us to Devonshire to stay in a hotel near a place where he went fishing. Mother and I went on long walks, and the only event of the day was to come back by the bridge over the river to catch sight of him. We were not allowed to go near him when he was fishing. Once or twice we drove ten miles to a high red-faced cliff – they were not chalky cliffs as they are in our part of the country. The waves were forever staining the sand red near the shore. We used to park on the cliff with other cars and walk not too near the edge and look at the sea glittering some days and on others tumbling fast down the Channel. I loved the Channel because it was wider here. This was the only time I thought of the Shorts and Benedict, for they were in Brittany. *La mer*: what a beautiful word! We had a set book by Pierre Loti to read in the holidays. My mother said she, too, had had to read it at school when she was a girl, yet she was no help with the words I didn't know.

So, back home again. It seemed dull. I rushed to my post at the end of our garden and looked across the water meadow, but there was no sight of Benedict on the first day. In the middle of the week I did see him in the distance with a girl taller than he and making for his house. I waved. They did not see me, and I tried to make myself look larger when they came into closer view. I waved again. They still did not see me. I felt something like a red-hot electric wire run through me – a wire that seemed to turn into a flame, as if I were alight. Then I went icy cold. Benedict was with Augusta! I was flaming with jealousy. I watched till they went out of sight.

My father was in the garden talking to my mother, who was pulling up weeds. I got carried away and went out to the road and walked along to the Shorts' drive. There were cars outside the house, one of them Foxey's red car. A party. And I wasn't invited. I was stiff with misery. I went back to my room and tried to read, but I was listening, for hours it seemed to me, to hear the cars drive away. When I went to bed my jealousy went. I remembered that the next week I would see Benedict on the train to and from school.

But at first this was not so. On the first day of term Augusta told me that Benedict's mother was going to drive him to his grammar school and bring him back each day. So I became a parcel again on my weekly journey. On Monday mornings I saw the politician doing his morning trot up and down the platform, and weekend people going to London with their papers, and a few grammar-school boys who got in at King's Mill and played cards all the way. Their school caps had a yellow ring round them. On Saturday afternoons there was always a large crowd of them going back to their homes in King's Mill or Fordhampton. About a dozen of them would stand on the platform bashing one another with their cases, and checking the woman who ran the buffet. Sometimes she turned them out. They crowded round the slot machines and tried to force them to yield up coins. I used to sit on a seat watching them. The porters grinned at the boys, but the ticket inspector hated the way they pushed past him. Sometimes a boy would be pushed onto my seat and I would walk away higher up the platform. There was a fat boy who was always eating chocolate.

The first Saturday I saw Benedict on the platform, he was keeping clear of the other boys. 'Hullo,' he said eagerly in his high voice, and the fat boy mocked, 'Squeaky's got a little t-tart.'

They stared at us and then went on pushing one another around. Benedict was carrying his violin case. I had never seen that before. I asked him why he wasn't wearing the school cap.

'Because I hate it,' he said.

I can't remember what we talked about except that I told him that I had seen him with an old lady walking across the water meadow and had waved to him. He was startled.

'A witch,' he said.

'No, it wasn't,' I said. 'It was Augusta. Don't tell her I said that.'

'I'll tell,' he said.

I knew he would, because every now and then after our train came in and we took our seats he said, 'I'll tell, I'll tell.'

At Fordhampton, Glan was waiting for him, and my mother was there as well.

'Aha!' said Glanville in his insinuating way. 'The apple girl.'

'It seems damn silly,' said my father to my mother when I got home. 'Why couldn't he have given Sarah a lift and saved you the trouble? Save petrol, too. Typical socialist.'

'You don't give the boy a lift,' Mother said.

'Don't be an owl,' Father said. 'That man's got nothing to do.'

So every Monday and Saturday I travelled on the train with Benedict. He had become quieter and it seemed that he had settled into the school. It was 'beastly' there, of course, but chiefly, he said, because the music master was angry when he told him the school piano was out of tune. He also hated Prayers, and the fat boy who got into the train at King's Mill was the Devil. This came out one morning when a man across from us was reading a newspaper with a headline in big print: 'CLIFF MURDER: HUNT FOR BRIGHTON YOUTH.' Benedict began jumping up and down in his seat and said the fat boy had done it. 'It's Fatty! It's Fatty!' he said in a furious whisper. I told him not to be silly. At school I told Augusta this was now the only sign of Benedict's being mad, but she had changed this term. She said it was Glanville who put these ideas into his son's head. Foxey said so, too. But after this Benedict was calm. One day he brought his stamp collection and he showed it to me, and once I ruffled his black hair when he said I was as fat as Augusta. I knew what he meant: I was growing up. I told him Augusta would marry him if he was not careful, and I laughed because he looked scared. He was very polite after that.

I enjoyed those train rides and I missed him for two weeks when he had flu. I was glad to see him when he reappeared on the platform at Newford

Station. I had got there late because I had gone into one of the shops in the town to buy a lipstick like Augusta's. I had run all the way from the shop, frightened that I had missed the train. At first I didn't see Benedict. Some boys were crowded round the fat boy as usual, begging him to give them a bit of his chocolate. The fat boy was backing away from them and Benedict was watching. The fat boy was sly and stood back against the wall, looking around for some way of escape. One boy was pulling at his arm. Suddenly the fat boy broke from them and went up to Benedict, snatched his cap from his pocket, and cried, 'Put your cap on, Squeaky, or I'll report you.'

Benedict stood holding his violin case and did not put his cap on, and the fat boy suddenly stepped forward and pulled the cap down over Benedict's eyes and face. I called out, 'Leave him alone.'

And then I saw Benedict do a stupid thing. He pulled his cap off and sent it flying off the platform and onto the railway track, and then, white with fright, he dashed at the fat boy and struck him on the shoulder with his violin case, screeching out, 'I'll kill you!'

The fat boy moved away, frightened. Two women were watching us, and one of them said, 'I will report you to your headmaster,' and she said to her friend, 'It's Major Short's boy.' I got Benedict by the sleeve and we walked away from the crowd. I was giddy with temper and walked him far up the platform, and when I looked back I saw the boys gaping at the cap lying on the railway line. Two boys were beginning to follow us, but the others were still crowding round Fatty. And then the train came in. I got Benedict into a first-class carriage in front. Three of Fatty's crowd raced up looking for us, but I pulled down the blind. I could hear the porters bawling, and the boys ran back. We sat still; the compartment had a notice saying 'Ladies Only'. There was a long wait and a strange silence at our end of the train. I let down the window and saw some of the boys getting off the train, all laughing. I heard a porter shout, 'Not this train!' A whistle blew. The train, I saw, was much longer than the train we usually took.

'We're on the wrong train,' I said. 'It's the express. Quick. It doesn't stop at Fordhampton,' and I tried to open the door. Then the train – one of the new diesels – moved out fast. I turned round. Benedict was lounging back on the seat.

'I knew!' he said, laughing at me.

'You beast,' I said.

I was scared. I saw the last of the pink houses of Newford and heard the chime of the signal box, as final and frightening as if it were killing itself with laughter. My father and mother would be waiting for me at Fordhampton and the train would whiz through. And that woman from Lower Marsh who had heard me shout in the mixup with the boys – she would report it all to my father. I lost my head.

'Why didn't you tell me it was the wrong train?' I said. 'I hate you.'

'I'm running away,' he said, delighted by my terror. 'I hate that school. I hate Glanville. I'm not going back.'

There is a long wooded stretch outside Newford and all the leaves on the trees seemed to be talking about us. Had he planned it?

'Where are you going?' I said.

He was sitting there gloating and grinning. 'To London,' he said.

'But that's in the opposite direction. This train goes to Bath.'

'I'll get a London train there,' he said.

'You're mad. It's hundreds of miles away.'

What frightened me was that I had only two shillings on me.

'How much money have you got?' I said.

'My aunt lives in Bath. She'll give me the money,' he said.

The train was speeding. Two little stations went by like a shout.

'The Devil is on this train,' he said with glee. 'I saw him on the platform.'

I was standing up still, and the train swerved at King's Mill when it crossed the river. A man was fishing there. I fell onto my seat. I was tired of Benedict and his Devil.

'I'll rape you,' he said.

'You won't,' I said. 'Silly little Squeaky.' And I got up and rumpled his hair. 'You'd better look at your violin. You smashed it when you hit that boy.'

This stopped him. He opened his case and took out his violin and looked at it very carefully and then he took up his bow and played one or two notes. They sounded very sad. All this time I had been trying not to cry, and it was the sound of those notes, like someone speaking, that stopped me. In that moment I recovered my wits. I looked about the compartment and noticed the communication cord. A notice said

'Emergency. To Stop Train Pull the Cord. Penalty for Improper Use £5.'
I was scared. When the train got near Fordhampton I knew I was going to
pull the cord and make it stop there. I sat down and got out one of my school
books and pretended to read, but I was looking at the fields. When the train
got to Flour Mill I would get ready to pull the cord. This calmed me. I got
up and said, 'I am going to the lavatory.' I was dying to go. 'There's one for
you at the other end of the corridor,' he said.

There was the door marked 'Toilet Vacant'. I went in. The window
was of frosted glass so that I couldn't see out, but I could tell by the
sound of the train crossing the river where we were. We'd crossed one
bridge. There were two more to come. I knew how long that took. I
wasn't long in the lavatory before someone tried the door. I waited. Then
I pulled the catch. It had stuck. It wouldn't open at first; when it did there
was the ticket inspector on the other side. The inspector always tested
the door in order to catch any one hiding from him. He was a big man
with a red face and a black moustache like a wet paintbrush.

'Sorry, Miss. Ticket, please.'

'It's in my bag in the compartment,' I said. He looked at my hat – we
wore straw hats with a red band at my school – and slowly followed me
to the compartment. Benedict was not there, and as I opened my bag I
heard a deep rumbling noise, louder than the noise of river bridges. We
were rushing over the High Street at Fordhampton. The station platform
screeched at us, people flew away in a stream of dots, the green top of
the town hall danced away, and the brick orphanage on the outskirts of
the town looked down on us from fifty narrow windows. I had forgotten
this was an express train. With a final clap Fordhampton vanished, the
points clattered, and the oak woods closed in on us. Benedict came into
the compartment.

'Ticket,' the ticket inspector said to Benedict, who got out his train
pass.

'We're going to Bath,' Benedict said coolly.

'You're in first class!' said the inspector. 'Fordhampton, it says here.
That your violin? We've passed Fordhampton.'

He took my train pass and looked at it and said the same thing. Then
he sat down with us and got out a printed pad. 'Both going to Bath?
Plenty of room in third class in the next coach.'

He slowly turned the pages of his pad. 'You'll be owing me some money,' he said. 'Ten pounds each. You got in at Newford, I see. It comes expensive.' He looked very sly when he said this and then sighed and said sharply, 'First class – let me see. Fifteen pounds each, I make it. Holidays begun early, eh? Playing in a concert?' He was looking around in the compartment, and I knew he was trying to see if we had smashed the lightbulbs or slashed the seat.

'We got into the wrong train and some boys locked us in. We thought it was the Fordhampton train,' I said. 'My father is waiting for us. He's a brigadier. It's terrible. No one told us at Newford. I'm not going to Bath, and we missed our lunch.'

'Well, it will be a long wait,' said the inspector. 'But your friend's going to Bath. With his violin?'

'No, I'm going to London. I'm in the school orchestra,' Benedict said calmly.

I was so amazed I could only say, 'Benedict!'

'I am,' said Benedict.

'It's a funny way to go to London. Down to Bath, up to London, wrong way round. Cost you more. Twenty-five pounds, I make it.'

'Where is the buffet car?' said Benedict, putting on an important voice.

The inspector said it was two coaches back. 'Stay where you are,' he said. He got up slowly. He put his pad in his pocket and said he'd be back later on. We waited and waited.

'Why did you tell such lies? We'll be arrested.'

'Let's go to the buffet car,' Benedict said. 'I'm hungry.'

If only I hadn't bought that lipstick. With only my two shillings, we couldn't pay for lunch.

The train broke out of the Downs, where there was a white horse carved on the hill, and into unknown country, herds of cows in the fields, farms, chickens, horses galloping away. This flat country went on, mile after mile. Farther and farther. I worried where we would go in Bath, where we would sleep the night. Terrible tales came into my mind of girls attacked on trains. I was thinking about what my father had said about the Shorts.

'You're not giving a concert,' I said. 'You can't even play.'

'I can,' he said. He opened his case and got his violin out, but I asked if he had got any money. He pulled out a few coppers from his pocket. 'Come on,' he said. 'Let's go to the buffet car. I'll tell them to send the bill.'

But before we could move the inspector came back with a young man who stood in the doorway studying us and murmured something I couldn't catch.

'Stand up, Ben,' this man said.

'My name is Benedict,' said Benedict. He could be as cool and ironical as Glanville.

The young man said, annoyed, 'Where's your school cap?'

I burst out, 'A boy threw it on the line at Newford when the train was coming in.'

'What was his name?' asked the man.

'Fatty,' said Benedict.

'Better check at Castle Wadney,' said the young man to the inspector. They went off down the corridor.

The train was gliding past wide fields of mustard, a few big clouds were hanging still in the sky. Presently the train slowed down almost to a standstill, and when I looked out I saw a gang of men standing back: they were working on the line. I can still remember every one of their faces looking up at me. Then we crawled past watercress beds to Castle Wadney, a town on a hill but with no castle that I could see. The train had stopped.

'Police,' whispered Benedict excitedly.

The inspector came back and said, 'Soon get you back, Miss. You're getting out here.'

At that busy station porters were rolling milk cans down the platform. We were taken to the stationmaster's office, a dark room smelling of ink and tea. The stationmaster was drinking a cup in between talking on the telephone, and there was a machine somewhere that clicked dot, dot, dash. A man at another table called 'Brighton on the line for you' to a very clean young man with hair short at the neck, who went to the telephone.

One of these new men looked at our train passes and asked our names again. I showed him mine on my exercise book. Someone was having a row with the stationmaster, who held the phone away from his ear.

'Sure it's not Knowles?' the smooth young man asked Benedict.

'Short. Short. Short,' Benedict jeered.

'Short,' I joined in. 'I mean he's Short, I'm –'

'I'm asking him,' said the smooth young man. 'How do I know your name's Short, son?' he asked.

And then Benedict did a thing I'll never forget. He turned his back to the man and pulled the neck of his jacket clear of his neck until the name tape was showing.

The detective held the jacket and called to the two new men. 'Take a dekko at this.'

'"Short",' they both said. 'O K, Sonny.'

'Hold on, they're on the line,' said the stationmaster into the telephone. Then he beckoned to us.

Glanville was on the line. Emma, too. And my father. When we had stopped talking to them the two inspectors had gone and so had our train. We were going to be sent back on the 3.44.

One of the detectives said, 'Sorry, Miss.' And the other said, 'On the lookout for a lad from Brighton. You won't miss your concert,' he said to Benedict and went off.

'Watch out,' whispered Benedict. 'They'll follow us.' He was delighted.

The stationmaster took us to the buffet and told the woman there to give us what we asked for and to give the bill to him. He told Benedict his daughter was taking piano lessons. We were put on the 3.44 to Fordhampton, and I felt sad going back.

'It was the Brighton Cliff Murder,' said Benedict. 'They thought we were in on it.'

And indeed a youth had taken the hand brake off his parents' car, jumped out, and left them to go over the cliff. There was a picture of a boy very like Benedict with curly hair. We saw it all when a man got in at one of the stops with the picture on the inside page and a headline saying 'HUNT MOVES TO WEST COUNTRY'. I muttered to Benedict, 'Keep quiet or I'll strangle you.'

Benedict started bouncing with delight on his seat. He said that Glan had told him all about the murder. And he started to tell me. The Devil would be in it, I knew.

'*Stop it*,' I said. 'Not now. You promised me.'

The train was a slow one. The man got out at Stockney. And then I said, 'Why did you say you were going to Bath?'

'To see the Roman ruins,' he said.

'But you said London, too, to give a concert,' I said. I couldn't keep up with him.

'I am going to the College of Music next term,' he said.

I began to tease him. 'There was a devil on *this* train – it was you,' I said and gave him a push.

There is nothing to say about our arrival at Fordhampton, except that my mother was talking to Mrs Short, and Benedict was talking all the time to Glan, telling him how he had shown his name tape to the detective. Father was talking to the stationmaster, who was shaking his head.

'I gave the stationmaster at Newford a blowing up,' Father said. 'I mean, suppose they'd been troops?'

'It's the staff, you know what I mean,' said the stationmaster. 'Your daughter's here.'

'Oh,' said my father, astonished to see me. And then he saw Glanville and stiffened. 'All present and correct,' he said sarcastically.

In the car driving home I began telling my father and mother what had happened, but Father said, 'Wait till we get home.'

Mother said, 'You should have pulled the alarm cord.'

Father said, 'Costs five pounds. I haven't got five pounds.'

I didn't say anything about Benedict's saying he was running away. Father was already revelling in the war he was now beginning with the railway company. He was going to write to the chairman at once. He was going to get someone at the War Office to blow them up. Mother's eyes shone.

When I went to school on Monday Benedict was not on the train, but Mrs Figg had heard the story, because Mother had rung the school. Augusta knew, too. Then she told me that once a man had exposed himself in a train when she was there, in a full compartment!

What did she do? 'Nothing,' she said grandly. 'I turned my head away and looked out of the window.'

That weekend my mother picked me up at my school and Benedict at his and drove us back to the Shorts, and I was invited for tea. Father said it was the least they could do.

Mrs Short was standing by her puzzle when I got there, a new one of a castle.

'It's a beast,' she said. There were a dozen people at that beautiful table and Benedict was crowing and interrupting his father. Then it was Cocky Olly again and all of us racing around.

A Trip to the Seaside

After she had dropped her sister off at the hotel Sarah drove *Mr* Andrews (as she pointedly called him) along the sea front to the station. They were stiffened by silence. He got out and said coldly, 'Thank you. Goodbye,' but she got out too and said, 'Oh, no. I'm coming onto the platform to see you onto the train.' He looked at his watch: for seven minutes he would have to put up with her. She even stood close to him; until the London train came she was not going to let him out of her sight. Even when, to escape, he excused himself and went to the door marked 'Gentlemen' she marched with him and stood outside, vigilant. When he came out and the train arrived at last she almost pushed him into the nearest compartment, and would have closed the door but other passengers were crowding after him. Still she did not move, and at the open door she started muttering short sentences. She said: 'We don't want you down here messing up her life again and trading on her feelings.'

Andrews did not speak. He sat in his corner seat, his face as pink as Aberdeen granite, looking straight ahead of him, ignoring her, his chin raised, his nose on its dignity. She was a short and avid woman with dry grey hair and about his age. Just before the door was closed by a porter and the train gave a starting jolt she shouted: 'I hope we never set eyes on you again.'

Some passengers raised their newspapers after a glance at him. Others stared. In the first five minutes as the train picked up speed he sat without changing his expression. Then he got up and left the compartment with a look of contempt for everyone there and, checking his ticket, made for an empty compartment in the first-class coach. There he was alone, looking blankly at the villas, trees and fields wheeling back in the watery spring dusk.

That morning Andrews had arrived from London just to spend the day, even possibly a week if things went well. You could never tell. Anyway there would be a sniff of sea air to clean his kippered London lungs. He thought of fish as he walked from the station, had lunch at a hotel called the George, which seemed to be the best place, fancied oysters, a Dover sole, a glass of white wine, which brought out that pink in his face. Then, better dressed than the Easter crowd, he went for an inspecting stroll. He was a widower of sixty-five who had spent his business life in the carpet trade. It had struck him as a good omen and a compliment to his gifts as a salesman that the lounge of the hotel had a new chocolate-coloured carpet with a design of huge chrysanthemums on it – one of his 'lines', the Demeter Floral. It wore well. He had indeed the muted walk of a man for whom the streets were carpeted and the smile of a public benefactor with a quiet surprise in his pocket. He was looking for a wife. He looked at one or two houses that were for sale, for a house was what he wanted: a house by the sea. The prices were very high: the dream had to go. He turned off to the address of Miss Louisa Browder, who had been his secretary for years before his job had come to a sudden end. As he came up in the train he had thought of her as a possibility, if also a *faute de mieux*.

To call on Louisa Browder would require nerve, for she had walked out of his office after a row five years before, but he was not a man to entangle himself in the rights and wrongs of the past. He knew the trouble had started at a trade exhibition in Brighton – a much larger resort than this – and he put it down to her age, or perhaps her mother's death, to those family things like the bother with her jealous sister who had never liked him – things that upset women and make them take it out on others, just as his wife Daisy used to do. In *her* jealous way – jealousy her only fault – she would shout 'Louisa's a woman and don't you forget it.' Yet Louisa had often stayed for weekends at their house, almost a friend of the family. He was shocked that she had not written him a letter of condolence when his wife died. He sent her the newspaper notice of Daisy's death and, as a rebuke, with no comment of his own. There was no answer for a long time and then a short letter did come, signed formally Louisa Browder, saying she was sorry to read the sad news and that Daisy had been a 'loyal wife and a wonderful mother to his children'. The curt note could, of course, be called a riposte if you like to take it that way, but what struck him most was the cause of the delay in her reply. She had moved out of London. She had gone to live in this town in a house by the sea. The address transformed her: a new life in a pretty house with a sea view, that was what he repeated to himself like a song these days.

Andrews had not told Louisa he was coming: in dealing with women surprise was essential. He passed the sedate terrace houses of the sea front and was disappointed to find himself in a side street and standing at the door of a mean little villa, with no sea view and with the degrading word *Vacancies* on a card in the window. She had gone downhill. There was an old white car in the garage at the side of the place. The thumping and miauling of canned music was coming out of the front room as he pushed the door bell. There was no answer. He rang again. When the door was opened the music rushed out, swamping his voice, which he had to raise when he spoke to a gingery young man with a book in his hand. His long hair seemed to be dancing to the tune.

'Come along in,' the young man said and, bawling up the stairs 'Sally, an old gent for you,' went back to the front room. Andrews winced at the sight of linoleum on the floor of the hall. The house was cold and smelled of polish. Sarah – not Louisa – came to the top of the stairs and called out 'We're full up,' but came down, rubbing her hands together, half cringing, half ready for battle – the whole Browder family, even Louisa (Andrews remembered) had always cringed. She said again, 'I said we're full up.' And she shut the sitting-room door before she looked at him. Then she stepped back.

'*Mr* Andrews!' she said and seemed to swallow a huge lump of unbelief and suspicion. 'What do *you* want?'

Still a public benefactor, but now hard-eyed, Andrews said, 'I was hoping to see Louisa – I happened to be here on business and I thought I'd drop in for a moment.'

'She's gone out,' said the sister, studying him. 'What do you want to see her about if I may ask? Is she expecting you?'

'No,' he said. 'Just a little surprise. When will she be in? She wrote to me so kindly when Daisy died – my wife you know.'

'I know,' said the sister briskly. 'She showed me the letter.'

'I didn't know that she had moved down here,' he said.

'I suppose she can move if she wants to,' said the sister.

'A nice little town. Really,' he said boldly, 'I've been looking around for a place for myself. You look well, Sarah.'

She did not: she looked scrawny and yellow.

'A place here?' Sarah said. 'I told you we are full.' But now she looked frightened. She studied him from his nose to the tips of his shoes. 'You mean you're looking for a *house* here?' She hesitated. At that moment the telephone on the hall table rang. 'Come into the dining-room,' she said.

She pushed him into a room and said, 'Stay there.' The room had a french window looking onto a cold little garden. The spring plants, he saw, were late this year, held back by the east wind.

He heard her answering the call: then he heard footsteps in the room above and a rush down the stairs and Louisa's voice.

'Still a liar,' said Andrews.

The room was small. The furniture was of the kind that is bought at a discount. There was a polished oak table with a dispirited runner on it, chairs that stood at the table like orphans, a sideboard with a bottle of ketchup on it. On the mantelpiece was a vase of artificial flowers and a photograph of the old Browders standing in their garden like tired and hardened pensioners. They had been a poor family, supported by Louisa, the cleverer of the daughters. There was a bleak armchair with wooden arms that dared anyone to sit on it. Andrews accepted the dare and sat, patting the arms as he waited. The call stopped and he now heard the voices of the sisters: Sarah's voice came through the door as one whispering, arguing hiss: Louisa's, saying little in her practical way, a voice warm though with iron in it. He remembered how little she had moved her lips when she spoke; even in his harassed moments with her he had admired the way the voice tersely filled his office (and even the street outside when they left the place together) with proverbial facts to be borne in mind. She had been piquant in a spinsterish way, slender, mannish and brisk during the years she had worked with him in his office. It had always astonished him when his jealous wife said, 'She knows what she's after.'

Now the door was opened and in came Louisa alone, wearing a heavy grey overcoat and carrying a large handbag. It was a principle with Andrews, especially in dealing with women, to smile and put them in the wrong at once.

'Sarah told me you were out,' he said. 'I just dropped in' (this being his privilege).

'I was dressing to go out,' she said in her equally correcting way, but with a laziness that was new to him. 'Sarah says you're here on business.'

'Not really.' He smiled.

And then he came out with it, all charm: 'I came especially to see *you*, to know how things are. And to thank you for your letter.'

Except for the changeless voice, he could not believe that this dawdling woman was the Louisa he had known so well – even feared. All the way down in the train she had seemed to skip across the hedges and disappear into woods – a tall busy woman, often not more than a pair of eyebrows and big dutiful eyes. In the office she had skilfully drooped her shoulders, because he was shorter. Now, in this room, she seemed short and there was more engaging shape and body to her. Her hands, which she used to clench, were now open and at ease. Her glossy black hair was waved and though she had aged and now wore glasses, the two streaks of swan-white hair over her ears looked dashing and her lips were firm, her teeth were not set in the old attentiveness. With no desk to work at, no papers to hand to him, no telephone to answer, no memory of detail to store for him, she stood easily free. She had often worked late at the office with him because – as he knew – she hated going back to her home. She had been good-humoured but she rarely laughed. She had lived for the office, but now the nervous lines cut by office life had gone, her face was on holiday and open.

Still, after they had talked a little, she did say with an old school-teacher's satisfied mockery: 'So you are a widower, Morton.'

She spoke of him as a species. Morton was his second name. She had never used his first Christian name, which was Alfred. That belonged to his wife at home.

'Yes,' he said, rather boasting of the fact.

'It is hard,' she said, 'to lose someone you love. I know how I felt when Mother died. I appreciated what I had lost.'

Remarkable, when one thought of her complaints about her mother. He was annoyed that he had to grimace in order to indicate that he had a tear to hold back.

He'd forgotten Daisy's jealousy of Louisa and Louisa's silence about her – except for that letter of condolence. He suddenly found himself crumpling into an account of Daisy's long illness and her death, and how a week before she died her hair seemed to be golden again, as it had been when she was a girl and how her colour came back. The tear fell and slipped into the corner of his mouth.

'And you still live in that big house?' Louisa said.

He recovered.

'No, we moved into a smaller place five years ago, when I retired.'

Louisa approved of the smaller house. 'That was wise, I'm sure.

'How do you manage by yourself?' she said without concern. 'Who looks after you?'

He had not come to talk to Louisa about this, but since his wife's death he had taken to rambling on to local people in the shops, even in the street where he lived, to anyone, about the bemusing novelty of his new life. He could not stop himself. Grief had made him novel, and he called himself 'you'.

'You get up in the morning,' he was saying to Louisa, 'if you don't forget to set the alarm the night before, and you go down and potter about in the blessed kitchen, so to speak, getting a cup of tea, and you start taking it upstairs and then you stop: you see, you can have your tea where you like, upstairs or down, and you look into the refrigerator to see what is there – sometimes things smell, go wrong. You don't cook much, you fry something perhaps, there's no decent restaurant near where we live. You forget things – don't lay the table. The laundry's the bother – a girl comes in, but these girls never clean properly and' (suddenly making a face) 'her husband has a van or something, they're up all night dancing at clubs, gambling by the sound of it, bingo or whatever they call it, some such name. Can't make a bed. Comes when she thinks she will.' And, with passion, 'No idea how to brush a carpet.'

Andrews frowned at the wall.

The gingery young man next door had turned up the volume on his record-player and the music came whirling through the wall like a typhoon that blew through his clothes into his skin. It thumped and twanged and swirled in sounds nasal and self-pitying, men groaning, girls screaming their skirts off. He held up his hand to stop the noise. Raising his voice as if to order it to stop he said, embarrassed, 'Her husband knocks her about: she showed me the bruises on her leg and on her shoulder: "Look at these bruises, they come up black and blue in the night," right up her bare leg,' he said. 'These young people laugh. I don't know what the idea is.

'I've got to get rid of that girl!' He was shouting again. For the moment he was addressing Daisy, the town, the world, and he looked startled when he saw Louisa again.

'Girls are hard to get,' Louisa said placidly. 'Sarah can't get anyone.'

'I've got to get away, sell the house,' he said. 'I was saying to Sarah a town like this would suit me,' he said. 'A blow from the sea.'

'Houses are expensive here,' she said in her book-keeping voice. 'You'd better stay where you are. You'd miss your children.'

'They've got their own lives,' he said. And he made his message clear to her. 'One thing I've learned is that you can't live in the past.'

They had been standing, but now she sat down at the table while he went back to the armchair. She had loosened her overcoat, as if to let out the woman in her, but she held on to the handbag standing on the table. The music had stopped strangling the air but it had fallen into long hiccuping passages of monotonous indifferent drumming. The sound was like the sound of the wheels of the train when he had come up in the morning and when the trees had looked girlish in the fields and he had imagined her as she used to be, before the quarrel – a friend, more intelligent than poor Daisy had been. He had looked out of the window of the train, once just in time to catch sight of a wide estuary where the sailing boats were moored, and in that glimpse of the sea he saw it had lost its air of heaving and grieving at its stored-up deaths. It was waving like a flag. It had struck him when he walked up from the station that the shopping street of the town was full of men and women whose arms and legs had been coiled up in bed with one another all night. Scores of women passed him, women you didn't know but who might slap your face if you stopped them and explained your situation. Yet, as they hurried by, they seemed to ask you why you didn't. What could you say? How do you begin it? You have to get to know them – the boredom of that – at his age he hadn't time for that sort of thing. The one woman he knew was this Louisa – she knew him and he knew her. In a funny sort of way they had had years of marriage in the office.

In the room he was arguing with the drumming, which went on and on, and he was even tapping his foot. Louisa looked years away from him at the table. The crowds of women in the streets and shops had been too near, too sudden, but the distance of Louisa made him stop tapping his foot. He crossed his legs and felt the imposing stillness of a desire that he had never felt before. Desire in a cheap place like this!

He said, in an unnaturally high voice, going back to what he had already said, 'Sarah looks well, and so do you.'

'Thank you,' said Louisa. 'She is.'

'You must have a lot to do, running this place,' he said. 'She said you were full up.'

'I believe she is,' said Louisa. 'Everything in the town gets full up in the holidays. I don't *live* here, you know,' she said with a small condescending laugh.

'I thought you did,' he said, feeling in his pocket for her letter.

'No, I'm at the hotel,' she said. 'More comfortable. We sold the old house in London when Mother died.'

Moved to a hotel! She seemed to leave her distance and come closer to him. As a salesman he had spent so much of his life in hotels. He loved, of course, those great acres of carpets in the grand ones; hotels were palaces of pleasure and money. Their very upholstery sent messages of erotic sensation when one touched it. Even in the small hotel – in a town like this – the guests, the waiters, the servants and the clerks, were like figures in a dream as they walked silently from room to room. When telephones rang they carried voices from another world. One became a dream oneself.

'I was going to say,' he said, showing his new admiration of her worth, 'that this place did not seem like you.'

And he waved disparagingly at the furniture.

'You've done what I ought to do.' He shouted for a third time decisively at the music. 'Are you at the George?' he challenged. 'Don't tell me you're at the George!' He laughed. 'I had lunch there today. Very comfortable. Good fish. I didn't see *you*!'

He uncrossed his legs and felt himself become a wonder.

'No,' she said, smiling at him mischievously: her first real smile. 'I'm up the hill near the church. The Clarence. Quieter. More select.'

'Sea view?' he said greedily.

'Of course – every room – and a nice garden.'

It was yet another principle of his never to be at a loss. He pulled a list of local hotels from his pocket.

'Yes, here it is. The Clarence, thirty-seven rooms, all with sea view.'

Louisa said, 'Forty-five pounds a day. With bath. Service and V A T not included. Weekly terms.'

'That's right,' said Andrews. And, congratulating her: 'Pricey.'

'Not for what you get,' she said.

The Browders had been a poor skimping family, carefully putting money away. Extraordinary. Louisa must have saved a lot to be staying in an hotel like the Clarence.

'Why don't we have dinner there tonight? Let me buy you dinner,' he said grandly.

'I can't do that, Morton,' she said.

'Or at the George,' he said, 'if you want a change. Funny thing about the George – they have got that carpet, like the one I sold when we were at Brighton years ago, one of our lines, the Demeter Floral – chocolate and flowers. You remember it I'm sure. Chrysanthemums in an urn.'

He laughed eagerly.

'It will be just like old times.'

Louisa frowned at that.

'Morton, I'm not *staying* at the Clarence. I'm not a guest. I work there in the office. We're very busy. I've got to go in a minute and see about the dinners. Twelve Germans have just booked in. That was reception ringing up when you were talking to Sarah.'

Louisa diminished in his eyes. He gaped.

'Working there? Did you say working?' said Andrews. He was offended with her because he had made a mistake. He turned on the boy next door. 'I wish Sarah would make that boy stop his infernal noise. You can't hear what anyone says.'

Louisa frowned at him.

'Oh that! That's Peter, my step-son, he's working for his exams. He always puts his record-player on when he's working. I'm used to it, I suppose, but it gets on his father's nerves. That's why we send Peter down here to Sarah's, but he eats with us at the hotel. When you run a hotel you have to put the guests first.'

'Step-son?' he said.

The air seemed to go out of his lungs with a whistle and his voice went up high as a boy's, and she seemed to him to jump up and down, like a film gone wrong, between floor and ceiling.

[1163]

'I am a step-mother,' she pronounced, as one who was equipped with a two-fisted power.

Andrews felt himself clamped between the arms of the narrow chair. His mouth was left open with no words in it, a foolish red hole he could not close. It seemed to him that she was not one woman but had become part of the general chorus of women he had seen in the streets of the town, impersonally swinging their handbags and lugging their shopping bags, taunting him with their indifference. In his bewilderment he lost all sense of time as he often did through living alone, and was on the point of saying aloud 'Daisy will have a fit when I tell her this.'

He recovered enough to say, 'I don't believe you.'

A rival widower had stolen a march on him! There was also the affront that, as a former employee and office possession, she had not consulted him first.

He felt in his pocket for her letter, which lately he had taken to carrying about, as a kind of invoice. He took it out and, putting on his glasses, read it. Looking over the top of his glasses he said, 'You didn't say you were married here.'

It was signed with her maiden name.

'I wasn't married then,' she said, formally. 'Mr Forrester and I were married last year – when his divorce came through.'

Louisa fattened with pride when she threw out the word 'divorce'. She was conveying that she was not a consoling nurse or frustrated spinster, fit only for an enfeebled widower. She was not a victim! She had attracted a man so much that he had divorced his wife. There was a note of rebuke in this: what had Andrews done for her? Casually she dropped the subject.

'My husband *manages* the Clarence. We belong to a chain.' The word 'chain' enlarged her importance. 'So does the George. When we are full up we can always send people down there.'

Andrews could manage only a faint sarcasm.

'You seem to own the town,' he said.

Not leaving the matter there she pretended to be hurt. 'I don't know why you are so surprised, Morton. Actually you have *met* my husband.'

He was in the dock, accused. As coolly as he could he said: '*Met* him? I don't think I have – where – what is his name?'

'The same as mine,' she said. 'Forrester. Jack Forrester.'

He felt in his pocket again, but gave up.

'I don't remember any Forrester,' he said.

'Oh, Morton!' she said archly. 'Think! Brighton! June '74. The trade exhibition. When you got that big contract for Demeter Floral. You remember *that*, I'm sure.'

There they were, bang in the middle of their quarrel. Surely, after all these years, she was not going to drag that up?

'I remember I pulled off a £10,000 order,' he boasted.

He could at any rate dismiss her marriage.

'I am not talking about carpets,' she said between her teeth. Her eyes, which were made larger by her glasses, seemed to him to be rummaging into their working life together, as if it were a waste. A question was in her eyes, idly put there to gratify some private vanity.

He was not going to be fool enough, in his present situation, to gratify that.

He knew the stare was unforgiving, that she might force her question upon him. He had smoothed away all his memories of that incomprehensible time at Brighton but now he remembered going back to the hotel where they had been staying, and that she had been waiting in the foyer for him. He remembered her saying with excitement, 'Did you bring it off?' And he had said, 'Let's get out of this.' They had crossed the street to the promenade, and he remembered the long, gaudy, floodlit sea front with the flags flying from the hotels and from the tall lamp standards and how the lights had blacked out all sight of the sea. The front was like a stage set: the crowd looked clownish as they passed from lamp to lamp. She had put her arm on his as he talked about his success. Usually at trade exhibitions they dined at the hotel with people in the trade and early in the evening she left him with the men, but this night she had persuaded him to celebrate at a restaurant. They drank a glass or two of champagne and then they dawdled back to the hotel, and she had circumspectly taken her pinching hand from his arm as they went across the foyer to the lift; but there she held his arm again and squeezed it as they went up to their floor. At the door of her room, rather embarrassingly, she had kept him talking, her voice getting quieter. Her fingers pretended to pick a piece of cotton from the lapel of his jacket.

'Come in for a minute,' she mumbled, as if she were eating. And there was an eating look in her eyes.

Andrews had been startled. He remembered thinking he ought not to have let her drink champagne. He had looked at his watch and said: 'Good God! Do you know what time it is? I haven't rung Daisy yet to tell her the news. I'm late.'

It was then he saw her face turn and there had been a twist of anger on it. It became suddenly hard, empty-eyed, like a mask of brass in the sick yellow light of the hotel corridor as he said good night in a fatherly way and went down to his own room at the end of the corridor. He was surprised that she banged her door. He was glad: he couldn't sit up half the night with her talking about the troubles of the Browder family.

But the next day! Andrews had never been able to tell his wife what happened on the second evening. Daisy wouldn't have believed him. She would have shouted triumphantly that she had 'known it' for years. That evening contained a lump of his history, so heavy in his mind, so entangled in outrage and the inadmissible desire he had never recognised, that he had succeeded in locking it out of memory. Now, talking to this married Louisa, in this miserable little villa by the sea, every fragment of it came alive again.

The day after their 'celebration', Louisa was late at the firm's stand at the show. Not surprisingly, she had a headache. He told her to go and lie down. He himself was so taken up with the details of his sale that he didn't get back to his own room at the hotel until seven in the evening. When he got there the telephone was ringing. That pest Sarah! The Browder family up in arms! Where was Louisa? Sarah said she had been ringing all day. Their mother was ill again. Dying, of course. Old Mrs Browder was said to be dying in every call Sarah had made for years. Louisa must come home at once. If she did go, there was never anything wrong with Mrs Browder.

To cut Sarah short, he had said, 'I'm sure she's in her room. There must be some mistake. I'll go and see.'

And he did go and knocked and knocked at the door, for he could hear voices. He heard a man's voice call, 'Who the hell is that? Tell him to go away.'

Louisa came to the door in a yellow dressing-gown – very yellow.

'It's only Mr Andrews,' she called back to a red-haired man who came out of the bathroom, saying, 'Tell him to buzz off and mind his own business.'

The man had a necktie in his hand and was bare-footed. The scene had been so incredible to Andrews that he had scarcely recognised Louisa. He could not now remember if he said anything to her, but he congratulated himself on remembering the exact words he had said to the man: 'I am addressing my secretary. Her mother is very ill.'

'I'll ring Sarah later, Mr Andrews' was all Louisa said. 'She's always checking up on me.'

And she had shut the door in his face.

Even then he did not believe what he had seen. He went to his room. He rang Sarah and in a muddled way said first that Louisa was asleep and then that she was with friends.

'That's a lie,' said Sarah. 'She's with you. I can hear her. Do you think I don't know what's going on between you?'

Andrews had had enough of the Browders. He lost his temper.

'If you want to know, she's picked up some man in the bar,' he said.

Sarah astounded him by laughing.

'That will stop you messing about, won't it? I've always been sorry for your wife.'

Now, in Sarah's house, with the old Browders looking at him from their photograph on the mantelpiece, he saw Louisa was waiting for him to speak.

'You told Sarah you *had* met him,' she said. 'It was not very nice of you, Morton. He is my husband now, so really, you see, it might be awkward to have dinner with you. Really I don't think this town would suit you, do you? And now I must go and you must catch your train. Sarah's taking me to the Clarence and she'll drop you at the station. Was there anything else you wanted to ask me?'

'Nothing,' he said.

The handle of the door moved. Sarah, he guessed, had been listening at the door, for in she came and said, 'Now then, Louisa, your husband's rung again.'

In the car Louisa said to Sarah, 'Tell Peter to remember to put on a tie if he's coming up to dinner.'

Nothing more was said.

Andrews watched her go into the Clarence, of course – but nothing, nothing, nothing, the wheels of the train hammered, like Sarah's voice, as he was carried back to London. Passing the estuary in the dusk he saw the boats were flying no pennants and no flags.

[1167]

Things

I was out early practising my putting on the lawn, which I have brought
pretty well to perfection. This was the first time I had had a chance to
get out my clubs after a week of gales. They strike this jagged tip of
south-west England first, tear through the leaning trees and send the
fields and hedges streaming and the steep hills bowling across the map
into the Channel, and take your mind and the tears in your eyes away
with them. But now, as if the whole rumpus had not occurred, the sky
was cloudless and as still as glass, and the only sounds were the tap of
my club on the balls and the cries of the gulls ripping through the air.
The young gulls must have hatched and the parents were driving off the
crows. Probably next day there would be sea fog. We don't live on land
here, as my wife says, we live in weather. One lives from one hour to
the next, as they turn into days and weeks and the piled up years we
spent in Africa, Canada, Egypt and Hong Kong.

On this quiet day last April Rhoda rang up. It was the first time that
we had been able to have breakfast outside. As I say, I was out on the
lawn and I heard the telephone ring. I am supposed to be retired, but
the week rarely passes without two or three calls from the London office,
the dockyard or some Ministry about an oil rig or a dry dock or asking
me to go and serve on some commission of enquiry. I am a consultant
now, called in when something goes wrong – stress mostly.

I crossed the lawn. My wife, Miranda, was standing by an open window
answering the call. Not in her usual calm, practical voice, but in a high
thrilled rushing voice: 'Darling, how extraordinary! How marvellous!
Where are you? What are you doing? Why didn't you write? We've been
so worried about you. What *are* you doing . . .?' and so on, as she used
to do when she and I first met and she was in love. She looked younger
and warmer with every word.

Rhoda is her sister, who lives in Italy. Miranda was, I supposed, shouting to be heard in the Mediterranean. She always shouts on an international call. But she was really proclaiming, in her emotional way, across time, and that is why she was looking so young. We haven't seen Rhoda since we went to Hong Kong about ten years ago and, frankly, it's been a relief. She has never been one to write – a Christmas card every year, of course, but nothing more. When the long call came to an end Miranda stood staring out over the fields into the sky and to the sea. Then she came back out of time when she saw me.

I said: 'Has anything happened? Something wrong? It must have cost her a penny or two ringing from Italy.'

We often laughed at Rhoda's comic miserliness over small sums of money.

'She's not in Italy,' said Miranda, accusing Rhoda, me, and the view with one of her dramatic stares. 'She's on her way down from London. She's in Exeter. I've asked her to stay the night. She's sad the children are not here: she was longing to see them.'

There was a pause as her excitement died.

'She *is* incredible,' Miranda said. 'She said she didn't know they were both married. But I wrote her – you saw the letter – she even sent them wedding presents!'

'Typical Rhoda,' I said. 'She lives in the future.'

Miranda frowned at me. 'Be nice,' she pleaded.

I was going to say, 'I hope she's not bringing that awful man Sammy she's living with, the one with the wide trousers,' but I checked myself. I retreated into a joke that goes back to the time when I first met Miranda and when Rhoda was no more than a child.

'I wonder,' I said, 'what she *wants*,' pronouncing that word in Rhoda's baby-talk way when she was very determined, dwelling on it – 'wawnt'. Her telephone call had opened up the past for Miranda and me. Miranda laughed.

'I bet she'll *wawnt* our house,' I added.

Miranda said firmly, 'Well, she can't have that.'

We are very proud of our house. We are in our sixties, though Miranda does not look it: her hair is brown and has scarcely any grey, but the house has rejuvenated us. After working for so long abroad, living as we had to in hotels, company bungalows and other people's furnished flats

and villas, with nothing of our own there, now for about the first time
we have a place that is really our own and with our own things. New
sofas, beds, chairs – we are still as excited as if we were newly married.
We came here because Miranda was born and brought up in this part of
the country, in a house called Lodge seventeen miles away, a place which
had been in her family for something like a hundred years – or even
more, I suppose. We have the portrait of her great-great-grandfather the
'Trafalgar Captain', who retired from the Navy there after that war. The
picture hangs in our living-room now. Lodge is where I first met the
family during *our* war. In the invasion scare I was billeted in the stables.
We were wiring the beaches and building those concrete strong points –
pill-boxes – along the coast.

Miranda and I sometimes pass Lodge on our way to London. You can't
see it from the road because the trees and shrubberies are overgrown.
You can't even see the stump of brick tower that her grandfather built at
one end of the place, in a fit of pretension, for the house is no more than
a square farmhouse built of narrow slabs of brown and black stone. The
trees darkened the rooms even in Miranda's time, and the troops used to
get scared by the squeaking branches scraping the slates at night. Miranda
loved Lodge and was sad that the place, so settled and with windows that
still, for her, seemed to hold the faces that had looked through them, was
sold when her mother died. Rhoda detested it – or so she said.

Our own house is, I am glad to say, modern and pretty with its pink
walls, and I have improved it. I am efficient at this kind of thing, and
Miranda has furnished it with taste. Living here, we often say, is like
having a second honeymoon. We live for ourselves and know hardly any
of the summer people who come down, though I meet one or two on the
golf course. Of course we have our own children and grandchildren
down in the summer. Thick walls of flowering shrubs ten feet high –
which I keep well clipped – protect Miranda's garden where she is always
working when she is not painting a little. Painting got her through the
loneliness of being abroad. Here, since this is her own country and she
isn't lonely, she paints less. She says the light changes too fast for her
now.

So Rhoda came to stay.

We both say still that we did not recognise Rhoda, except for her walk on the gravel drive, perhaps. She trotted like a busy little girl as she got out of her car, went sniffing around it, peering in, seeing the doors were locked. (She kept everything locked when she was a child.) Then she stepped onto the lawn in the high-heeled shoes she always wears to give her height and stood back like an impertinent urchin staring at our house, counting the windows – she had always been a counting girl. Then, chin still lifted, her nose wriggled and she sniffed – a good sign with her: she admired the place! I was right: she was the old Rhoda, still 'wawnting' until plaintiveness quickly followed.

But she was not any of the series of Rhodas we have in our memory of her, certainly not the Rhoda I had last seen in my bank in London, ten years before, when she was off to Italy. Like Miranda's, her hair was brown when she was a girl, but in the bank it was yellow and on it she was wearing a small black flowerpot hat. She had always been one for a fashion that had gone out and with her smudged lipstick, her hit-or-miss eye-shadow, she looked at that time like a widow who had not yet mastered the part. Naturally: she was unmarried. There was a red-faced man with a hot-from-a-funeral look with her. (I will come back to Sammy later on.) But this was not the Rhoda we now saw on our lawn. We had expected sunburn, an Italian look, but instead her little face was scalded and she wore no makeup. The flowerpot hat had been replaced by a man's shabby brown beret, tipped forward on her head, and from under it poured a long stream of hair, grey as fog, over her shoulders and down her back. She was wearing something like a brown-striped football jersey and bright emerald-green trousers, and she now had a small belly full of impudence and authority. She looked like a witch out of a child's book. I did not say this to Miranda as we walked towards her, but I did say, 'Rhoda still wants justice.' (She had always said in her quarrels: 'It isn't fair. I want justice.')

Rhoda trotted up to us, the kissing began, and then abruptly she stepped back and considered me.

'You've grown a beard,' she mocked. (I have a pointed white beard.) 'You look pink and respectable.'

'Oh,' laughed Miranda, 'he's not as respectable as he looks.'

'You see?' cried Rhoda with glee, turning to me. 'She got her dig in.'

Rhoda has always been conspicuous for a few key words. After 'want' came 'dig': she loved to see people getting 'digs' in at each other. The next word came out when I asked, 'Where's your suitcase?' and looked into the back of her car. A pile of old cardboard boxes and tied-up packages had been tumbled in. On top of them were a radio, two umbrellas, a couple of pairs of slacks, an anorak, two tins of biscuits, Wellington boots and a stack of steel rods wrapped in canvas which looked like golf clubs. And a rolled-up sleeping-bag.

'I didn't know you played golf,' I said.

'No, that's my bed. I can't sleep in hotel beds. I put it on the floor. I stopped in Exeter on the way down.'

'Been making tea?' I asked. There was a teapot on the floor.

'I picked it up in Taunton market,' she said. She had a plastic bag in her hand.

'Nothing in the car?' I said.

'No, those are my *things*,' she said holding the bag tightly.

'Things' was another word that went back to her childhood. I remember the chest of drawers in her room at Lodge and – more important – one or two boxes containing her broken watches and dolls, strips of velvet or silk, patterns, knitting, sewing, badges, clips, combs, childish jewellery, letters, programmes, the crown of a hat she had once had, a mug, unused diaries and cracked snapshots, dozens of cotton reels. No one in the family – certainly not Miranda or a maid (there were maids when she was a child) – was allowed near the hoard. Once I remember her mother saying, 'You must clear this mess up. What's the good of *one* king?' – holding up a playing-card – and Rhoda snatched it from her mother, put it into a cardboard box and sat on it. 'It's mine.'

We were about to move into the house when she stopped and pointed back to our white gate. 'Philip,' she said, 'I say! Pebbles! Was that your idea?'

'It's the name of the house. What about it? Down the road there's Breakers, White Sands, Sea Spray, The Dunes.'

'Weird!' Rhoda mocked.

'I don't see anything weird in it,' I said. 'You have Bella Vista all over Italy.'

'Sammy and I live in a flat,' she said and then turned to Miranda and said, 'Sammy is my lover.'

'I know,' said Miranda. 'Philip told me.'

'Lover' is the last and most important of Rhoda's key words. She did not live in time, as we did; the coming and going of lovers marked the calendar for her. We did not know many of Rhoda's friends, but I cannot think of any man of whom she did not casually make this claim or, at any rate, did not consider whether she might wish to make it at some time or other. Sammy had lasted longer than most.

'I wish you'd brought Sammy,' said Miranda. 'I've never met him, you know. You didn't leave him in Exeter, did you?'

'No, he's in Rome. I expect he's still in bed. He was fast asleep when I left.'

'I'll get some tea,' I said.

'No, I want to see the house first. Everything,' said Rhoda and she put on her strong glasses for the inspection.

I let Miranda take her. I could hear them going from room to room upstairs, talking and laughing. I went up at last to see how they were getting on. They came out of a bedroom and I pointed to the radiators and said: 'Have you shown Rhoda the bathrooms?' They ignored me. I went along to the first bathroom and, since they didn't follow, I flushed the lavatory.

Rhoda said, 'Why did you do that?'

'He loves doing it,' said Miranda. 'He'll never stop being an engineer.'

'Not like those awful lavatories at Lodge,' I called, 'where the pipes clanked all over the house and you thought it was coming down, or like that one in Cairo: that was the worst.'

'It's like a second honeymoon being here,' said Miranda – *our* phrase.

'I never had one. Everything else, but not that. I mean you can't count Jeremy,' said Rhoda, walking slowly along the landing and peering at each engraving on the wall.

'"Poachers Netting Partridges at Night",' she read aloud. 'That was at Lodge. In the hall.'

We got down to the sitting-room – it was once two rooms and is now large, and from the two west windows there is a clear sight of the sea and the Pig Rock, lying two miles out with its moustache of surf. Some days when bad weather is coming the rock seems to move in, dark and near: on this afternoon it glittered and seemed farther away. It's the first thing I look at when I get up in the morning, better than a barometer.

I mentioned this, but Rhoda, who had not taken off her beret, did not reply. She was standing still in the sitting-room, which I consider Miranda's masterpiece: she ought to have been a decorator, she has such a gift for colour. Rhoda was counting again. In that jersey and those terrible emerald trousers, she stood out like a gypsy. Quick as a bird she picked out the one or two family things that had come to us from Lodge. She stared at the portrait of the Trafalgar Captain over the fireplace and said suddenly, 'I looked in on old George Ogbourne in Exeter.'

'I wondered why you stopped in Exeter,' Miranda said. 'You should have come straight through. Who is George Ogbourne?'

'Oh, you know him,' said Rhoda. 'He used to be at Raddles, the auctioneers who sold Lodge when the Bulwers bought it. Those auction people make the money! He went in for antiques. He remembers *you*, Miranda. And he remembered me. "Let me see, you must be Rhoda," he said.

'He's getting on,' she said. 'His son Peter runs the business now. He knows the Bulwers. You didn't tell me that Jeremy Bulwer had married again when his wife died – that fluffy little thing. What is the new one like?'

'We don't know the Bulwers,' I said. 'I just see him on the golf course sometimes. Very bald.'

'But Jeremy was my first lover!' she said, forgetting us and the room for a moment, and she took a step or two, looking at her feet as if talking to one foot and then the other, plotting. And then she said sentimentally, 'I think I'll drop in at the Lodge while I'm here. For old times' sake.'

This silenced us. I know that thirty years have passed and that, thank God, Rhoda's love affairs are no business of ours. But this was too near home. I could just imagine Rhoda 'dropping in' at Lodge and getting in a sizeable 'dig', saying what a funny thing it was – that Jeremy had been mad about her and they'd run off to London when he was engaged to his first wife, who in the end had taken him back. And then adding loudly what she used to say of all her early lovers – 'He was impotent' – to see how the Bulwers took that.

'We shall have to stop that,' I thought. Very embarrassing on a golf course. Almost as bad as the time I was persuaded to take Rhoda on in our London office and she fell for Doggett and his wife asked Miranda to intervene. If she *has* come back to start those old larks, I thought, I'll have something to say about it and she won't like it.

But Rhoda was chattering on.

'Peter Ogbourne says prices have gone sky high since we sold Lodge.' And looking at a china cabinet in the room she said, 'You'd get a thousand or more for a piece like that. I gave Peter a lift to Plymouth, his car had broken down. He was going to a sale.'

'I don't think we're selling anything, are we, Miranda?' I said coldly.

Miranda said, 'Why don't we all sit down?'

Rhoda studied the positions of the sofa and armchairs and then she looked closely at one of the chairs, which had a footstool under it.

'My darling little stool!' she cried. She darted to it, knelt down and pulled it out, and sat on it victoriously. I have never seen an object 'bagged' so quickly in my life.

'Yes,' said Miranda. 'Granny's little stool.' And to me: 'Rhoda and I used to fight for it. Granny made us take turns.'

'Granny always cheated,' said Rhoda, dropping her mouth open and looking from one to the other of us to see if the 'dig' had got home.

What I remembered, as I went out to get the tea tray, was Rhoda at the age of fifteen in school uniform sitting on the stool at Lodge before Miranda and I were married, staring at love, as we sat on a terrible prickly horsehair sofa, and Rhoda saying, 'Why don't you hold hands?' At fifteen she was a pest who followed us everywhere. She had just become very religious: one of the maids had converted her to the Plymouth Brethren. 'But, darling,' her mother said, 'they're not quite our class.' Rhoda's religious phase lasted until the second year of the war when the invasion scare came and the soldiers were billeted in the stables. One of them, a Captain Blake, called her the pocket Cleopatra. (It was in her Plymouth Brethren period that she had once left the room calling out 'Sexual intercourse is damnation'. She loved the phrase: it was directed at us.)

I put the tray down. Rhoda gazed at the silver teapot and then shook a passing fancy out of her head.

'If I had married Jeremy Bulwer I'd have had Lodge,' she said. And picking up a scone, she waved it at the room and said, 'Did you take all this to Africa?'

'No. Of course not. Most of it's new. We left one or two Lodge things with Philip's mother,' said Miranda. 'There wasn't much – the cabinet, the Trafalgar Captain, the secretaire . . .'

'I suppose you took everything to Italy,' Miranda said. 'It would be easier.'

'Oh no,' said Rhoda, buttering her scone. 'We sold it all.'

'Everything, after you left the Square when . . .' Miranda began nervously.

'Yes, Sammy and I sold the lot when we bought the hotel.'

'All of it? Oh, Rhoda!'

'We ought to have kept the silver,' Rhoda said. 'We'd have got ten times the price now. Money is money, isn't it? As Sammy says, no good hoarding everything. Things need a change. It cheers them up, he says.'

'It's cheered up the Captain coming here, I must say,' I said pointing to the portrait. 'You couldn't see him properly at Lodge. We had him cleaned.'

Rhoda sniffed at the Captain. 'Imagine the life of his wife, polishing all that stuff, chained to it, while he was at sea,' Rhoda said.

'But you used to love *things*, Rhoda,' said Miranda. 'It seems so sad but I suppose it was sensible. There wouldn't have been enough room in your hotel.'

'We've sold the hotel,' said Rhoda. 'All those tourists taking photographs and talking about "art". It was too much for Sammy's nerves – I mean the old people you get always complaining about their washbasins and quarrelling with one another, some are quite mad. And the bells going all day.'

Miranda said, in her discreet, orderly way, 'We've never been quite sure what Sammy *does*. I do so wish you'd brought him with you. What does he *do* now?'

Miranda had never quite believed my account of Sammy when I came back from our accidental meeting so long ago at my bank. What had struck me particularly in the fleshy young man was his trousers: his jacket was open and the trousers were braced high over his wide waist, almost to his ribs. He had black hair with a curl over his forehead and a damp, glistening crimson face, his fists, his nose, his lips were heavy; his body looked too full of blood, like that of a boxer or a publican or one of the security guards at the bank. Rhoda had said: 'I want you to meet Sammy. He's my lover.' They looked as though they had hired each other. He came forward and said 'Pleased to meet you,' in a confidential way that suggested: this bird and I have just done a deal. And he looked back shrewdly at the bank clerks at the main desk as he might have glanced back at a bar when he was going to offer a new pal a drink.

'We are in a rush,' Rhoda had said. 'We've only got half an hour to get to the airport. We're going to Italy.'

'S'right,' Sammy said.

Rhoda looked proudly amused by the disparity of their accents – a 'dig' at me, of course.

'Come on,' she said to Sammy, and he lazily followed her steps out of the bank.

Sammy called back to me, 'Be seeing you.'

One thing I was certain of: he was afraid of Rhoda.

Now, as Rhoda was passing her cup to Miranda, she said: 'He's got a nightclub now. It's much better for him. Poor Sammy, he's allergic to the sun in Italy. It upsets his eyes. He's shortsighted. He likes night work – he sleeps all day.'

I remembered how the hulking fellow blinked when he was introduced to me. I had said to Miranda when I got home, 'Rhoda's shortsighted too. They probably don't see each other.'

'We get a crowd,' Rhoda was saying now, 'especially at the week-ends.'

Her businesslike words brought to Rhoda's little eyes that miserly gleam the family used to tease her about at Lodge, which had evidently lasted: the clothes she was wearing looked cheap. But the plaintive drooping mouth of her 'wawnting' was not there. Her lips curled up happily when she talked of Sammy.

'Money is very necessary to Sammy, you know,' she said to me.

'We all need money nowadays,' I answered, laughing.

'You don't understand, Philip,' she said. 'He needs it for his gambling.'

'Oh, Rhoda, you don't mean you've got a gambling club?' cried Miranda.

'He doesn't drink. He doesn't even drink wine in Italy. He doesn't mind if I do. He needs to gamble,' Rhoda added, 'psychologically.'

'Oh, Rhoda, I don't know. Isn't it awful for you? I know those places make money, but they lose more. It's lucky you haven't a family.'

'But I have,' Rhoda said. 'There's Sammy's little boy. He's sweet. He calls me Mamita.'

'We didn't know Sammy was married before,' we said together.

'He wasn't. He had an Italian woman,' said Rhoda.

And she sat back looking from one to the other of us with a storyteller's glee. She sighed.

'How nice it is here. D'you remember how we used to go up the cliffs to watch the baby seagulls? Will you take me, Philip, while I'm here?'

'I am sure Philip will take you,' said Miranda. 'When he's done his letters.'

I took the hint and went to my study. There was a photograph of an oil rig being towed out to sea on one wall and a watercolour of boats on Hong Kong harbour, one of Miranda's, but all I could think of was Rhoda's long grey hair over her shoulders. 'She's mad. She's mad. It's the usual tale of an old woman trying to look young, being bled for her money by a layabout.' The scene in my bank kept racing across the page as I started to write a letter, and I had to give up. Perhaps Sammy had sent her over here to get money out of Miranda?

An hour went by and then Miranda opened my door and, looking back cautiously, said loudly, 'Are you ready now to take Rhoda to see the baby seagulls while I start cooking?'

Miranda looked behind her, listened, and then whispered, 'I think she's looking for a house.'

'Here? Oh, God! Not here!'

'She's on about starting an antique shop . . .' – but she stopped as we heard Rhoda's heels in the hall.

'He'd love to take you, Rhoda,' Miranda called.

Rhoda and I got into the car. When the sun goes down into the sea here it often sets off a firework display, sending out pink rockets, but this evening there was no more than a slow, yellowing light above a bank of low cloud that was coming in. The daylight was going and the sea was as dull as slate.

[1178]

'It's going to be too late to see the baby seagulls,' I said as we slowed down at the turning to the cliff.

'I don't care whether I see them or not,' Rhoda said. 'Peter and I will see them tomorrow – Peter Ogbourne. I've got to get off early. I'm picking up Peter and we're driving to Falmouth. He's got another sale there. Let's go to Lodge.'

So all this talk of seagulls was a trick to get me to Lodge, to 'drop in' on the Bulwers. I was not going to have that. 'Just to pass it,' she said wistfully. I was wrong.

So the drive was to be a sentimental trip on a cloudy evening. There is something bemusing about the narrow roads in this part of the country. A stranger can easily get lost in them, they wind between banks of stone slabs with high hedges on top of them, so that you are tunnelling and see nothing of the country, simply the sky. North, south, east and west vanish. At the sharp corners there are often signposts showing four ways, with different distances, for getting to the same village. Tourists laugh at them, forgetting these roads were built not for getting from village to village but from farm to farm. The only dramatic sight is the number of dead trees one passes, tall silver skeletons with their branching arms stuck up, like dead preachers.

Rhoda was counting the skeleton trees with excitement. She said, 'There is one at Lodge.'

And so there was.

'I'll slow down. I can't stop – it's a nasty corner,' I said, for I was still suspicious. 'You won't be able to see anything.'

'That's all right,' she said again. 'Just to feel myself passing it.'

The sight contented her, and very slowly we passed the gate of the overgrown drive.

The old concrete pill-box we had built just inside the drive during the war was still there, but with nettles growing out of it now. The sight of that pleased Rhoda too. She used to stand there watching us build it.

'I liked the war,' she said. 'It was fun. Very good for women.'

'Not for your mother or anyone with children,' I said. 'No more servants. They went into the factories.'

'That's what I mean,' she said. 'They got decent wages for once. Mother was hell to the village girls we had.'

'Women have a worse time now,' I said.

We got into the usual argument but she rattled on until she suddenly stopped and said, 'Do you remember Captain Blake? He turned me out of the tower. I was furious with him – putting a machine-gun post up there. Stupid idea. It was *my* room. I had all my things there. I think that's where I lost my Coronation mug.'

Her indignation died.

'Poor Captain Blake. Why did they *arrest* him?'

I could have said, 'You know why, Rhoda. Don't look so innocent,' but she carried on.

'I know he was rather – you know – but he really did *like* little girls. He was only cuddly. He called me the pocket Venus.'

I said I thought it was the pocket Cleopatra.

'No,' she said fiercely. 'It was Venus.'

We had now passed the gate, thank God, and had gone beyond the wood at the end of what used to be the garden.

She closed the window of the car and tidied her hair, spreading it carefully over her shoulders, looking like a witch once again, and said, 'By the way, Peter is not my lover. Actually I'm not interested in sex any more.'

This was the most startling remark I had ever heard Rhoda make.

'I didn't think he was,' I said laughing. 'You've only known him a day.'

'Two days,' she said.

We were back in the maze of high-banked lanes, and I put the headlights on.

'I showed the children to Peter,' she suddenly said. 'I've got them in the car.'

A home-going tractor with no lights came suddenly out of a blind side turning when she said this and I had to brake suddenly.

'Bloody fool,' I called out. 'What do you mean – children?'

'The Captain's children – the picture with his wife. They're in the back of my car. I brought them with me. Peter says I ought to take them to Sotheby's and get them valued, they'd fetch a good price. Did Miranda tell you? Sammy and I are going in for antiques – not in Italy, Italy's finished.'

And then she said, 'I *saw* that in Exeter.' She was talking to herself, not to me.

[1180]

'Saw' was a word of hers I had forgotten. It is really the most important. When Rhoda 'sees', she is having a sudden vision or revelation, which comes into her mind out of the blue, driving out all calculation for the moment. I think it must have started in her religious phase and was something she got from the Brethren, something like a 'call', although you hear a 'call' but you 'see' a vision. Miranda and I used to be distressed or angry about the mess she seemed to make of her life – those 'lovers' always left her, she did not leave them, and then her money was obviously being thrown away on Sammy; it seemed to us a bad end to it. What kept her going were these sudden 'seeings'.

'I don't know anything about shops. I'm an engineer. Don't shops require capital? I don't know anything about antiques.'

'But Peter does,' she said.

I knew what was going to happen as our headlights lit up our pink house. Rhoda would rush in to Miranda, alight with vision, and say that I had said the idea was splendid.

That is almost what happened when I was getting the drinks and Miranda came in from the kitchen. Miranda and I exchanged glances: What has she told you? What do you know? Did Miranda think Rhoda and Sammy were breaking up? What about this Peter? What was going on? Miranda was signalling: I don't know. Do you? We were like actors sketching our way through lines in a plot that only Rhoda knew. I said, to forestall Rhoda, 'No baby seagulls.'

'We went to Lodge,' said Rhoda.

'Just passed it,' I said, to calm Miranda.

Rhoda paid no attention to us.

'I'll get the children,' she said and carrying her drink with her, she went out to her car.

I said to Miranda quickly: 'The Captain's children. She's going to sell the picture.'

Rhoda returned, holding her glass high in one hand and carrying the picture, which was nearly as tall as herself. It was wrapped in old sacking and roughly tied. She put it against a chair and swallowed her drink, then she knelt down and started picking at the string. Bits of the dirty sacking made a mess on the carpet. I tried to pick it up. I hate a mess in a room. We saw the picture at last.

[1181]

Unlike our portrait of the Trafalgar Captain, this picture was quite large – we always said that was why Rhoda had chosen it. It was exactly as it had been at Lodge – darkened by age, which made the faces small and yellow. The Captain's wife was sitting on a stone bench, under a tree, and with her were three little girls in once-white dresses with blue ribbons, one child looking down at a little dog. A country scene but, rather absurdly, the painter had put in the mast of a ship in the background. Our Captain at any rate looked rosy and alive; his family were peaky and stiff, like dolls. Rhoda came to business. Peter had seen it and said, 'It's a primitive. Primitives fetch a price.' And what was certain, he said, was that it would fetch three times as much if the Captain was sold with it.

'Rhoda! What a sad thing to do with a family thing. Sell the children? You don't mean it,' Miranda said.

Rhoda watched our faces.

'Well, I can tell you this – we're not selling the Captain, are we, Miranda?' I said. Let Rhoda sell what she liked. My temper was rising at the sight of Rhoda proposing to sell our things under our noses and turning our house into a saleroom. Rhoda went one better.

'I'll sell them to you if you like,' Rhoda said, dropping her mouth open like a haggler.

'We don't want them,' I said. 'Do we, Miranda?'

'But Rhoda, the two pictures are not by the same painter,' Miranda said. 'You can see that by the signatures. The children were done by some local man – Barnes or something. Ours is a Drummond.'

Rhoda was startled but shook the idea out of her head.

'Peter says it's a Drummond,' she argued.

'Soon settle that – look at the signature.'

It was illegible. On the back a label said: 'Flora Barnes. Falmouth.'

Miranda said shrewdly, 'Does Sammy want you to sell it?'

Rhoda put on an airy manner and gave one of her dry cackles. 'Sammy doesn't know I've got it here,' she said. 'He'd go out of his mind. I packed it up when he was at the club or with that woman of his.'

Her eyes went into slits of pleasure at the memory of her trick.

Miranda said, 'Have you left Sammy?'

'I'll never leave Sammy,' Rhoda said. 'And Sammy won't leave me.

When he finds out I've got the picture and gets my letter about Peter and the prices things fetch he'll be over here on the next plane. Sammy will do anything for money. He'll bring the little boy.'

She went into a brisk dream.

'Gamblers love children and that woman hates them.'

'You mean and bring the – er – lady?'

Rhoda, Sammy, and his mistress on our doorstep!

'No,' said Rhoda. 'I don't mind what women he has, but he's had this one long enough. I know how to manage Sammy.'

Neither Miranda nor I could think of anything to say. Rhoda held out her glass and I gave her another drink. Rhoda saw that her proposal had failed and when her 'visions' fail, she always throws them away. She looked down at her shoes thoughtfully and said in her sly and deedy voice, very slowly sketching her way into a new idea: 'I actually don't think I will sell the picture when Sammy gets here. I haven't any children of my own. The boy is rather sweet. He likes the picture: he thinks they're mine.'

And then she said, shrewdly, 'Peter says when you go in for antiques it's always a good thing to have something you *won't* sell in a shop.'

And Rhoda knelt on the floor and began to put the picture back into its sacking. I helped her.

I said, 'I can't see Sammy in an antique shop. You can't sleep all day in a shop.'

'I'll run the shop,' she said. 'I'm going to talk to Peter tomorrow. He might come in with us. They'll get on – they're both keen on money – and he's younger than Sammy. That'll keep Sammy awake.'

We both shouted with laughter and Rhoda was surprised for a moment and then looked very clever. She went to sit on the stool.

Miranda said that dinner was ready and as she went into the kitchen called back, 'Is Peter married, Rhoda?'

'God, no,' Rhoda called back, and looked at me suggesting that there was something stupid in our married condition.

We went to eat in the alcove at the end of the room. When we were served she put her head almost down to her plate and looked up to see what our forks were putting into our mouths before she began.

There was no more talk about pictures or Peter or Sammy, but we

[1183]

laughed about old times at Lodge – the soldiers there, how kind Captain Blake was to her the night Plymouth was bombed and how Miranda had found her sitting on the captain's knee in her nightgown and she had fallen asleep and had a terrible dream that she was struggling with Miranda in the sea.

Rhoda said, 'I thought you were drowned. I was trying to save you.'

Miranda said drily, 'And you brought me a cup of tea every morning for a week afterwards. I wondered why.'

'It was weird,' said Rhoda, ignoring this. 'Mother was so upset. I was only talking to poor Captain Blake. He was only being cuddly – he wasn't my lover, you know . . .'

'I should hope not. You were only a child,' said Miranda.

'He was after *you* – but *you* had Philip,' Rhoda said and turned to me and said, 'What was all the fuss about? Anyway, he told me he was impotent . . .'

'Shut up, Rhoda,' I said.

She looked mischievously at me but obeyed.

After this there was no more fuss until bedtime. Then she insisted on having her travelling-bed put up alongside the empty bed in the spare room, and when this was done she complained that it blocked the way to the window. She said she would sooner sleep on the floor in the sitting-room, so we let her bring her sleeping-bag down, and we helped her dismantle her travelling-bed. She said she wanted to slip away in the morning without disturbing us.

'I will say goodbye now. I'll be off at six o'clock. I never eat breakfast,' she said.

Then she wanted a needle and cotton to mend the lining of her beret, which – it turned out – was Sammy's.

So we left her and went up to our room. I said to Miranda, 'Sammy must be a saint to live with a woman like that.'

'She *does* worry me,' Miranda said. 'That dream of hers about struggling with me in the sea. Do you think I was beastly to her when she was a child? I do hope she's comfortable.'

I could not get to sleep until three in the morning. I looked out of the window: the light from the sitting-room still lit up the lawn. When I woke up about seven I had an alarming thought about the Trafalgar

Captain. I went downstairs and was relieved to see he was still hanging on the wall. I went to the front door. Her car had gone but on the doorstep there was Granny's little stool propped up against the bootscraper. Had she thought of taking it? Had she forgotten or changed her mind?

Rhoda's voice buzzed in our ears in the next few days. She did not telephone or write. Months went by without news. I suppose we shall hear at Christmas. Miranda thinks Rhoda is like one or two of the old village people here who seem to be made of weather rather than flesh and blood. They live in their fancies and 'seeings', trying out their lives in the air, trying their feelings on the market, shrewdly watching the bidders.

'She was trying out herself and her ideas on us,' Miranda said. 'Crystal-gazing like a gypsy. Making up her mind about Sammy.'

I don't know. Six months after she left, that Peter Ogbourne fellow came to the house, touting for antiques, and I sent him away with a flea in his ear, but we did ask him about Rhoda.

'Very kind old lady,' he said politely. 'She gave me a lift to Plymouth.'

'I thought she was giving you a lift to Falmouth,' I said.

'The funny thing is I've never been to Falmouth in my life,' he said.

'She said something about showing you a picture of children – a Primitive,' I said.

'Not me. It must have been some other dealer. Or my father,' he said. 'But she did give me your address.'

A Change of Policy

———

Soon after six on a rainy London evening, when the traffic was clogged and bleating in the streets, Paula got back from Chelsea to her flat off Baker Street. She had been reading to a learned old lady whose sight was failing, a friend of her sister, and she was about to change from her red dress – the one with the large gilt buckle on it – when there was a long aggravating ring at the doorbell. No doubt some stupid messenger had mistaken her bell for that of the sportswear shop on the ground floor. She went down the steep stairs and when she opened the door there was the sharp back of a man with greying hair who was shouting at a woman who was trying to get her car into a parking place on the other side of the street. He turned around.

'Hullo, Paula,' he said. 'Usual thing. Can't keep my nose out of other people's troubles. That's a lie – protecting my property. Don't want that silly woman smashing into my car.'

Paula stared at him and, astonished, said, 'Mr Southey!'

'Same as the poet,' he said.

'George! I'm sorry, I didn't recognise you. Well, come in. You've grown a beard.'

As he followed her up the narrow staircase he said, 'I'm glad you noticed. A small Vandyke – keeping up with the lads at the works. Just got in from Munich – actually Istanbul.'

Paula's small sitting-room had tall windows and was made to look larger by a long discreet mirror that set off her height. A woman of taste: sets of small leatherbound books on the shelves on either side of the fireplace.

'Why didn't you telephone?' she said. She was easily irritated by people who dropped in. 'And *do* sit down.'

'I did,' he said. 'A message for me at the airport – from my brother – said the proofs of the *Quarterly* were two months late. I said, "That's not

[1186]

like Paula," saved time and went straight to the Prof Shop. No dice. They said you'd left, packed in the job, sent in your cards. Glowry gone, Featherstone too. New girl at reception.'

'Do sit down, George,' she said.

'I mean we've been printing the *Quarterly* for how long is it – years. What's going on?'

'I don't know,' she said. 'Yes, I did resign. I am not in touch with anyone there. There has been a change of policy.'

She wished he had not called the Institute 'the Prof Shop'. It was a learned institution, a century old, internationally respected.

'But you ran the place,' said George. 'Arranged all the foreign lectures, introduced them . . .'

'How did you know my address, George?' she asked. She was a woman for rules, and there *was* a rule that no private addresses could be given.

'That was easy,' he said. 'You've forgotten. I dropped you and your sister here one night, five years ago. After that lecture – Herr Doktor Wafflenbloater or something, on the Catholic Church and the Third Reich. You sneaked me in.'

'Dr Grein,' she said stiffly.

'There I go, flat on my face as usual. That's it – Grein, of course. I call them all Wafflenbloater. You introduced him, the only thing I understood. It was pouring with rain, like tonight, and your sister and some friend of his couldn't get a taxi afterward and I drove you here, all of you. I remembered you said there was an antique shop on the ground floor. I see it's a sports shop now. Things change.'

'I remember now; you were very kind,' she said. 'She was Dr Grein's wife, Sophie. And it is kind of you to come now.'

'You told me not to drive too fast,' he said. 'Not kind at all. Business is business. We're worrying about the contract for the *Quarterly* – we've had it for years. What do you mean you resigned? Did you storm out, or what?'

He had known her well once, in the early days of the *Quarterly*, when he used to bring in the proofs himself and they went through them together. She had been a tall, calm, rather distant young woman with a quiet, clear, serious voice.

'You have changed your hair style,' he said. He remembered she had dark hair that had gravely framed her head. He had heard a lady sitting next to him at that Grein lecture say she looked exactly like George Eliot, whoever that was – very calm and certain. Now her hair was shorter, freer. It even looked chopped and wild.

'You've come to life,' he said. 'What are you doing?'

'Nothing.'

She really had 'stormed out'. She remembered it all: how the chairman had called her to his grand office, where he sat with the large Edwardian portrait of the founder of the Institute and the small one of the first committee, looking portentous on the grey wall behind him. The chairman said that the committee had decided that the Institute must be modernised. They intended to go for something called Communications, and they had put in a popular journalist to turn the *Quarterly* into a magazine, with newsy extracts from lectures instead of the full text. The new man had already brought in a young woman to run Personality Closeups.

George listened to her without expression. 'His mistress, I suppose,' he said.

'I have no idea,' she said in her principled voice. 'That could possibly have been a consideration.'

'So you stormed out?' he said.

'They didn't *fire* me, George,' she said. 'They wanted me to run the library. The Old Folks Home, the Black Hole of Calcutta, we used to call it. No one ever used it. If they had asked me to go on the committee I would have stayed. Yes, I suppose I stormed.'

She was remembering how on the afternoon when she left the Institute a flight of pigeons clattered out of the square near the British Museum and, it seemed to her, flew the news of her angered virtue to those parts of London where standards and integrity still had meaning. She had influential, well-placed friends who had rallied to her in London and in the country, when she went there to stay. In those early weeks, she felt that she was walking a yard or two above the earth. The trouble was that her friends had outlived their influence; it had leaked away. When you lose an important job, there comes a time when there are silences: you embarrass, you find yourself in a limbo, you become a curiosity. Even the target of indignation loses its focus. After the promising interviews that, one by one, came to nothing, her story seemed to dissolve. Her money was running out. This very day, as she came back on the crawling bus from the old lady's flat, she had felt that the people who were crowding into restaurants and shops and bars or rushing along with parcels were employed. They had homes, and soon, if nothing happened, she would be forced to get out of hers.

'There was nothing personal in the reason for my leaving,' she said, annoyed by any insinuation that jealousy was at the heart of her decision.

He nodded. 'From our point of view, of course,' he said, 'it doesn't matter what the Institute wants. We print anything. That *Quarterly* gave us prestige. We took trouble with it. But if they want a comic, we can do it. If they want a colour magazine, we can do it. We print anything for anybody. Travel brochures, coloured wrappers, mottoes, anything from calendars to the Koran, printing for Eskimos, Malays, Arabs – we do a lot for Arabs. Even Old Masters, popular reproductions of the classy stuff. But why am I doing all the talking?'

'You do talk a lot, George,' she said, smiling at him. 'More than you used to in the old days, when you came in and we did the proofs.'

'That was because I couldn't make out what the *Quarterly* was about until you read out a sentence or some of those foreign names. What on earth are you doing reading to an old lady?' he said seriously. 'We've got to do something about that. I get ideas, you know. I run into a lot of people.'

The 'we' made her raise her fine eyebrows. She pointed to the typewriter on the table. She said she was doing some translation.

There he sat, not so much staring at her, she thought, as staring at himself in the tall mirror.

'You've changed,' she said. Working with him, she had taken him for granted as part of his trade. She had even felt she was, in some detached way, superior to him. But now, being in limbo, she began to see him as a man.

'As a matter of fact I have an offer to go to Kenya,' she said.

And it was true that the rich old lady had said to her in an erratic way, 'Why don't you come to Nairobi with me?' Clearly she didn't mean it; she was too old to move and was simply remembering her travels.

Why did I say that, Paula suddenly thought. I must be mad. She looked at his face. It was as set as a gambler's: he had drawn it out of her. She knew why she had talked. The virtue had gone out of her; the euphoria had disintegrated. If she could have got hold of that woman who had taken her job she would have slapped her face.

He seemed to know all this as he studied her.

'Derailed,' he said.

'I don't understand,' she said.

'Nothing. Old family saying. Didn't I tell you – my father worked in the shunting signal box at Euston when he started as a boy. First week, he put a truck of fish or something off the line. It upset him. He gave in his cards. Anyone loses their job in our family, like my sister's boyfriend not turning up on their wedding day, breaking the engagement – remind me to tell you about that – *derailed*, that's the word we use. I can hear him. Forget it – things come up in your mind.'

'You are ridiculous, George,' she said, and she laughed for the first time.

'It's true,' he said. 'That is what the old man used to tell us. Derailed. There it is.'

His excitement went. The flush went from his talking face and he stared at her. 'Come and have dinner with me,' he said.

'I can't,' she said. 'My sister will be here.'

'Bring her along. I remember her – she was with you when I picked you up after that meeting.'

Paula remembered her sister saying, 'Who was that awful little man – very kind, of course.' Just imagine it!

'Anyway, you've had a long flight. You must be exhausted. Your family is expecting you.'

'Oh, that's fixed,' he said. 'The boy's away at school.'

'But your wife . . .'

He looked at her steadily. 'No wife,' he said.

She waited for him to say more but he said nothing. He'd been married twice – he had told her. Separated? Surely he had not left that pretty, fair-haired girl who had worked in Reception and to whom they had all given a present when she married him? She remembered Featherstone, who was on the committee, saying in his disappointed way, 'I hope she doesn't regret it. The descendant of the poet is a bit of a rake.' But the laconic 'No wife' struck her as being a final refusal to speak.

'Don't you know?' he said.

'I don't know anything,' she said.

He had not been to the Institute more than once in the last two years. A young assistant had been sent in his place. She had supposed that was because he had become a partner in the firm, travelling about.

'If I may, I'd like to use your telephone to ring my son,' he said now. 'I always ring every day when I am away, to tell him where I am and when I'm getting back. I rang from Munich today – or yesterday – I've got the days all wrong. Boys worry. But they love long-distance telephone calls at school, it makes them feel important. I ring my wife first – I mean, I ring the hospital. My wife had a stroke nearly two years ago. She's at the Grafton Forster Hospital. She's been unconscious ever since. No change. She doesn't know who I am. No sign. I go and see her twice a week when I'm at home. Just lies there, eyes open. It happened when I was on the Australian trip. I came back at once.'

'George, why didn't you tell me? What a terrible story. I can't believe it . . . It must have been awful for you this time in Munich.'

'I had to go,' he said. 'You might as well be anywhere. I mean when you're nowhere . . .'

And she had been talking to him of the Institute, losing her job! Her limbo was petty compared with his.

He was totally transformed in her eyes. He was no longer the bouncing talker. That talk was hysteria. Even if she could not yet believe in the catastrophe, it had turned him from an actor into a human being who was himself. Even more terrible than the hospital visits were those daily telephone calls to the boy. She was ashamed of her own commonplace troubles.

And then her telephone rang. They both looked at the instrument on her desk.

'I gave the hospital this number,' he said. 'I always leave a number wherever I am. I'm a string of telephone numbers.'

She rushed to the telephone and answered it.

'Not for you,' she said, for George was on the edge of his chair. A man was talking.

She said dryly, 'You are a rare bird, aren't you? When did she let *you* out of the cage? No, I can't. I simply can't. Absolutely not. I have people here. Quite impossible.' And then she said, 'You should think of these things earlier.'

And then, rather grandly, glancing back at George she felt impelled to

[1191]

let George hear her telling a lie. It was like a confession. She seemed to grow taller.

'My sister and her husband are here, staying with me. We're going out to dinner. No, not tomorrow, I shall be in the country.' And putting down the receiver she looked angrily at it and said, 'I'm sorry.' She was blushing.

He was looking with admiration at her. 'I remember you at the Institute like that,' he said. 'Now you will have to say you will come to dinner with me. I have an idea. No need to go to Kenya. I know a Greek restaurant. We'll have to cross two parks to get there. It's a good place. Noisy. Full of young people. That means you can't hear what anybody is saying and they can't hear you. Very private. Real clatter.'

He got up and put out his hand to pull her up.

'All right,' she said, and, surprised, she let him pull her up. 'I am sure this is very bad for you. I'll just change into something.'

'May I telephone? The boy,' he said.

In the days when he used to come to the Institute she remembered she had seen him going off with one or the other of the girls at the reception desk of the office. Now, she thought as she went upstairs, he is not *that* man. She changed into a silk blouse that had a pattern of large green and blue leaves.

'Is this all right?' she asked when she returned.

'Just the job,' he said.

'Now,' she said when she was in his car and they drove out of her street, 'what was the news?'

'No change,' he said.

'The boy?' she said. 'Was he all right? What did he say? You didn't tell me his name.'

'Night jungle,' he said as they drove away, waving at the park. 'Rainy season. His name's Harry. The bother with boys is they're always asking questions. Mania for details.'

'I've got nephews,' she said.

'I had to go over the whole flight home. Change at Frankfurt – he never lets me miss out a change of plane. Wanted to know if I had seen any snakes in Munich. Mixing it up with when I came home from Australia two years ago. He's got snakes on his brain. Cobras or mambas. I cheated and said there was a dancing snake in the Munich Zoo that ends up hanging from the tree in a figure of eight. Actually, I think that's true,' he said. 'Now he's taken to horses, and I've taken up riding.'

He leaned forward, peering ahead as a traffic light changed. 'We'll skip Baker Street,' he said knowingly, 'and take a right. Fantastic dream.'

In the side streets she saw he was one of those drivers who cannot resist a sharp turn or a shortcut. Some passing motorist hooted at him.

'Now what did he mean by that?' he said.

'Your driving,' Paula said. 'You're not on a horse.'

Between a warehouse and a house with corrugated iron covering its windows was a door with a travel poster saying 'Come to Greece'. They had arrived.

He helped her out of the car, holding her arm. 'Mind you don't fall down the step.'

Noisy! She found herself ducking and going head first into a Greek song that swirled over her in the hot upper air. There was the sound of the open steaming kitchen, the open grill behind the distant counter, and, on either side of the narrow, pretty room, pairs of customers, most of them young. The youngest girls, bunched up in their jerseys and anoraks, were smiling and soundlessly talking.

'How comic,' she said. 'What is the song? Do you understand?'

'Not a word,' he said. 'It's probably about love, death, and goats.'

The young proprietor came up to him and said, 'Mr Southey,' and then murmured quietly, 'Any news?'

George shook his head. The proprietor raised his deploring hands.

In the middle of their meal George said, seriously, 'We've had a lot of bother in Munich. The Germans are very stubborn. We're doing a book on the Rubens in the old Pinakotek. The British publishers hate the translation. There's an idea – why don't you do it? Drop Kenya. You talk German. Come with me. You'll flabbergast them. Three or four days – call it five. There you are – a job. I'm serious. I'll see to it that my brother pays you decently. All expenses paid, of course – actually, it'll only take a couple of days. You can go to the Alps, see your old friends – the Greins and so on.'

'George, you are very kind. I'm very sorry, I could not possibly go there. I hate the place.'

'But you were there for two years. It's a fine city. You taught at the university.'

'No,' she said. 'I was *at* the university, but I taught at a school there. I was never so unhappy in my life. I never want to see the place again. I'm superstitious.'

The four men who were talking loudly near the counter suddenly shouted with laughter and two of them punched each other and went on laughing. She frowned at the noise. She felt it was splitting her in two and that part of herself was being dragged back into the past, and that George was not the person she could possibly tell about it.

'I see,' he said.

The two neutral words began to exasperate her because they were neutral. That 'I see' had turned him into a stranger. She ought to have turned him down flat. She had gone too far. And then her feeling changed. She thought of him making those calls to the hospital and to his son every day: he had not hidden his misery. The noise, the songs howling out their imaginary passions, all the more forceful for being meaningless, undermined her reserve.

'As I expect you know,' she said, '*I* nearly married a German.'

She waited for him to say 'Yes, I know.'

'I didn't know that,' he said. 'I don't know anything about you.'

'I thought perhaps you did,' she said.

'If I had I wouldn't have mentioned it.'

'Dr Grein,' she said.

'Waffen – Sorry – Grein! You mean the man who gave that lecture when I drove you and your sister home? Well, there I go, flat on my face again.'

'It was over then. He came with his wife. I was in love with him before he married, but it went wrong. There is no reason why I shouldn't tell you this, except you said your first wife was a German and a Catholic. Dr Grein's a Catholic.'

'You mean he wouldn't divorce his wife?' he said. 'You can if you know the ropes.'

The ropes!

'I was very young. People broke it up: his family, my sister.'

'Religion is a curse,' he said. 'I've seen too much of it. What it does to people.'

'That is simply not *true*,' she said sharply in her correcting way. 'My sister is a deeply religious woman. She objected because Heinrich's family were peasants. I'd written to my father and told him this. She read the letter to him. She sent me a telegram saying my father was very ill. I went home at once. He was going blind. I used to read to him. It went on for a month. I always seem to be reading to blind people! My father kept saying, "Where's this man? I want to have a look at him." But Heinrich didn't come. His father and mother were sweet, simple people. They were nice to me, but when I was away they warned him against me. All the little hill farms there look like children's toys, all the villages, too, so clean and bright, the fields so green climbing up to pinewoods, and after that the rock and the snow, the air so pure. It turned my head, I suppose.'

'There's nothing toylike about peasants,' he said. 'They're not children.'

'I know,' she said. 'I never want to see the place again. Thank you for asking me, if you really meant it.'

'Oh, well,' he said. 'My brother can settle it. Really, there's no need for anyone to go. The firm can do the job just as well in London.'

'That's much better, George,' she said. 'With all this worry about your wife it would be madness to go back to Munich. If I were in your position I would be thinking all the time, "Suppose she wakes up, suppose she dies." You've got back today, but every day you were away must have been awful.'

He said, looking like stone, 'I'm "away" here in London. I've been "away" for almost two years. I'm nowhere.'

'You're not really away, George. You take your love for your wife and your son with you everywhere.'

He sat back from the table as if to make himself distant and said, quietly, under the noise of the place, 'I didn't come to see you about the proofs. I came to see *you*. You are very beautiful. I want you.'

She could not stop the freezing lines of horror forming on her face – not at what he had said but horror of herself. She sat back looking nervously at the people in the restaurant, and in confusion she said, 'I'm not beautiful. I didn't think . . . I never thought . . . George, you must see – but thank you, George, please don't go on with this. I don't go in for that sort of thing. Even if I felt – You must see, I would not do that to your wife. Don't be angry. Any woman likes to hear it. I admire you, George, but I don't like messes. I couldn't – Oh damn, don't look so hurt, George. I envy your wife. She is a very lucky woman to be loved as you love her. I'm not a prude. I don't mean you are wrong. I mean that it would be wrong for me.'

'I see,' he said in his flat, maddening way and simply stared.

She said, looking down at her empty coffee cup with suppressed anger, 'It's natural. You want a woman.' And she looked up at him.

'You,' he said. 'I always have.'

'I don't like bedroom affairs,' she said, and suddenly burned with jealousy of George's wife, indeed of all the women in the restaurant. She could hear her sister saying, 'What is the matter with you? Why do you keep falling for impossible men?'

'Can we go?' she said.

He called for the bill. There was another loud shout of laughter from the men at the table in the corner of the bar and one of them reached for another bottle of wine.

The proprietor himself brought the bill, and after George paid it they got up and the proprietor followed them to the door. He said to George, 'I hope you have good news.' And to her, 'Thank you, my lady, and be careful of the step.'

They were out in the rainy drizzle and got into the car. He said, 'I've spoiled the evening. I'm sorry.'

Whatever was in her head, her body hated him to say that.

'You have a right to ask me. Everyone has a right.'

'Like the man who rang you at your flat?' he said.

'That was just an old friend,' she said sharply. Damn again: he had noticed that.

They drove back through the two parks, empty jungles, under the artificial pink city sky. They did not speak. It was awful that the talker did not speak. When he stopped outside her house she said, 'Thank you for dinner, George. You must get some sleep.'

'Sleep?' he said. 'I've the feeling that I've been standing up all night for years.'

Then he pointed. 'The usual London cat on your doorstep,' he said. 'Not yours?'

She got out and said 'Shoo' to the cat and then, 'You do promise to tell me, please, if there is good news. I'll pray for it.'

'Pray?' he said.

She watched the tail-light of his car getting smaller and smaller as he drove away down the street. It seemed to her that, like him, she had been standing up all night. He had not even said he loved her, thank heavens. Since Grein's time she had not loved any of her one or two lovers. She shivered at the appalling simplicity of George's situation.

The next day she was glad to go to read to the old lady.

'Something has happened to you,' the old lady said. 'I can tell by your voice. You have good news.'

The lines of the old lady's face lit up with conspiratorial pleasure. Paula was surprised at hearing herself say she had been offered an interpreting job in Munich but only for a few days.

The old lady said 'Munich!' and talked of the time she and her husband and a friend called Tregarron had been there before the war. The old lady scowled at a memory as she went on and then suddenly stopped. There was something like a harsh call to arms in the confused ruined corridors of the old lady's mind. She said sharply, 'That was where your silly sister had that stupid affair with some Nazi professor when she was at the university. Grein or something. Laborious fellow – common. You and your father had to go there and get her out of it.'

'Dr Grein was not a Nazi,' said Paula loudly. 'My sister did not have an affair with him. Who told you that? Professor Grein is a very distinguished, happily married man. You must be thinking of someone else. My sister would never do anything like that.'

The old lady was frightened. She offered Paula a piece of marzipan.

'Now, when are you going to Kenya?' Paula asked to distract her.

'Who told you I was going to Kenya?' asked the old lady.

'You did,' Paula said. 'You said you had a friend down there.'

A tear ran down the old lady's face. 'I have no friends,' she said. 'All my friends are dead. You are my only friend.'

I ought to have gone to see George's poor wife in hospital and stop wasting my time with old friends of my sister, Paula said to herself when she got back to her flat. Why didn't anyone at the Institute tell me that this had happened to the girl? It's the least I can do for that man. Such a pretty girl. She had always felt protective of those 'children', as she called the typists at the Institute. Perhaps the sight of someone she had known in the past would have the curing effect of shock.

Two days later, she put down her work and with mission in her eyes she took the train from London to the Sussex town. She felt exalted watching the green country wheel wider and wider as the train cut through it. But when the train gave out its electric howl as it rushed into the peremptory tunnel under the Downs and emerged at the station of the town, she suddenly thought, How awful of me. I ought to have asked George. What an intrusion. How awful if I met him in the street.

The town was bunched on a steep hill of confusing little streets. Halfway up the hill, the traffic was heavy as buses and trucks rumbled past to the coast. She remembered George telling her that the place was famous for its murder trials at the county court and its religious riots. One year, the Pope had been burned in effigy on Guy Fawkes Day, and George had made her laugh with the tale of a woman from the marshes who was known to stick pins into a doll on the window of her cottage and to shout 'Curse his name! Curse his name!' as she did it.

At last she got to the long red brick hospital and its car park. She gave the name of the patient she wanted to see to the clerk at the entrance and found herself in the waiting room sitting with a dozen other visitors, all silent, all staring at the door as they had done at the sight of her. We look like a coven of witches, she thought. She had imagined that she would have been taken immediately to the Sister and certainly the doctor. She sat there thinking of what she would say when she would be taken to see the patient. Someone said, 'The doctor's doing the wards,' and half an hour passed before her name was called. When she was led to the ward she asked, foolishly, 'May I speak to her?'

'Of course. The others do. She won't answer.'

'We used to work in the same office. She was my secretary,' said Paula humbly to the down-to-earth Sister who joined them for a moment as they stood looking at the now grey-haired woman lying unmoving, her eyes open. There was a sudden crash of oxygen cylinders that were being unloaded from a truck in the yard outside. The eyes did not move.

Suddenly it occurred to Paula to speak in a peremptory office voice: 'Ethel!' she said. 'The moment Mr Southey gets here, tell him that I have a message from your son Harry. Please bring him to my room at once.'

There was no movement of the eyes.

The Sister said, 'Mr Southey has been this morning. If he's away he always telephones.'

Once more there was the crash of the oxygen cylinders.

'Mr Southey's brother and his wife always call.'

As Paula left the hospital she saw new people in the waiting room. They seemed to be trying to read her face as she hurried to the door. She glanced at the marshes stretching to the foot of the Downs as she hurried back to the station. She wondered where George lived in the town. She went up to the end of the platform to be away from the other passengers waiting for the next train. It was market day in the town and she could hear the calves lowing in their pens. Then, sparkling with electric flashes, the plain yellow-faced London train came in. Not until it had taken her out through that dramatic short tunnel that seemed to her to pass under the hospital did she feel free and unwatched. Under the spell of the racing train, as the countryside circled and the bridges seemed to shout at her, and branch lines swerved away into places unknown to her, and the living sky seemed to ride with her, did she think, Why did I do that presumptuous, untruthful thing?

At last the train slowed down and rumbled over the Thames and squealed as it slowly turned into the terminus, and, released, she got up from her seat and joined the crowd that rushed to the barrier and, once past it, scattered with intent in their eyes. She threw away her usual prudence about money and took a taxi to her house. There she stood in her sitting-room, among her things, and looked at the assuring, demure white houses opposite, and then went up to her bedroom and changed her clothes and washed her hands and did her face and went down to her desk and telephoned to George and waited impatiently while a secretary went to look for him. At last he answered. 'Trouble with a machine,' he said.

'I hope you don't mind, George. I went down to the hospital this morning to see Ethel. I hope you don't think I was intrusive.'

'So the nurse said,' he said. His voice was dull. 'It was kind of you.'

'Not kind. It was terrible. George, I've just got back home.' And then, in a quieter voice, 'I think I have good news for you.'

'You've got a job?'

'No, no, George,' she said impatiently. 'You remember – what you were saying? When are you coming to London? We could talk. Not on the phone, not today. My sister is coming. Tomorrow, George. I can't tell you now.'

Soon the Hoover was howling in the flat. Her sister did not come.

On the Saturday evening, up the stairs he came, into the room. She sat on one of the small armchairs and he on the sofa, staring at her. In the small room the literal distance between them seemed to him to be enormous and to her puzzling. She had planned that he would be sitting on the chair and she would prop herself on the sofa; they were wrongly placed.

'George,' she said. 'I will.'

He stared at her and she said, 'I'm shy. Why don't you kiss me, George?'

He jumped up and went to her and was astonished that she turned her head this way and that to keep him away, so that they almost wrestled.

'We shall be on the floor,' she said with a laugh so harsh that he let her go.

'Not here,' she said, clutching his hand. 'Upstairs.'

She laughed as she pulled him up the stairs and then looked at him with a gloating defiant stare as she pulled off her clothes and he followed her to the bed.

'Printer!' she laughed. 'You are a snake. What are you doing here?'

Then, 'How thin you are.'

Then, 'How strong,' and she groaned, 'Go on, go on – you're killing me.' And then softly, 'Oh, darling,' and her eyes flooded with tears of pleasure. 'No more,' she said.

They lay in silence for a long time.

'When did you first think of me?' she asked.

'When I first saw you,' he said.

'That was years ago,' she said.

'When did you?' he said.

'I don't know – when you asked me.'

'Not before that?' he said.

'I think when you told me about ringing your son – I don't know,' she laughed. 'When you grew a beard, Mr Vandyke.'

And that was not the end of it. In the morning he was still asleep, with his mouth open. She smiled at that and kissed him on the forehead, but he did not move. She gathered her clothes together and went to the bathroom. The sound of running water did not disturb him. After a while he called. There was no answer. He slept again. And then there she was in the room, astonishingly wearing a hat and a light coat and carrying a handbag.

'Where are you going?' he said.

'Nowhere. I've just come back from church. Get up.'

'Church!' he said, astonished. 'To confession?' he mocked.

'Of course not,' she said sharply. 'I always go. I told you my father was a clergyman. I went to pray for your wife,' she said gravely. 'Have you rung the hospital?'

'Yes, I did when I woke up,' he said bluntly. 'Nothing.'

She wanted to rush at him and to kiss him, and not till they were eating breakfast at a little table in the living room did he say, 'It was lovely,' and she put her hand out to him and he kissed it.

'When are you going to ring your son?' she asked.

'Not on Sunday mornings. They're at church. I go riding. I'll get him at teatime.'

And he went on to explain that on Sundays his cleaning woman did not come and he had lunch at the hotel or at his brother's. 'When the Germans come over with the Munich book you must come down to the works. You must meet my brother, see my house.'

She interrupted sharply. 'You must understand, G, I could not possibly do *that*,' she said firmly.

They went to the park, where the sky was wide and open. There was a distant bellowing and screeching of animals from the zoo as they passed the absurd cricket matches and the couples clinging on the grass, the girls pulling down their dresses to their knees, and the older couples calling their dogs that raced away in wider and wider circles. A man was teaching his son to fly a kite; it twirled around and somersaulted again and again until at last it flew up high and twirled again and dived fast to the ground.

'My son is getting too old for kites. He wants an aeroplane,' George said.

They walked to the long lake where old ladies and children were feeding the ducks, and they laughed at the noisy parties in the rowing boats.

'I'm hungry,' she said. 'There's not much to eat in these cafés on Sundays.'

They went to a crowded place outside the park, and the day dawdled as he drove back to her flat.

'No,' she said. 'You're mad, George,' but he gripped her hand and they went upstairs.

The dark had come as she watched the red light of his car vanishing down the street.

She felt in their walk through the park that she belonged to the real world now and that George had renewed her life and that she was part of things that lived, the growing trees, even the grass, the birds flying over, even dogs racing, the children and every person she passed – even the people, unknown to her, who lived in the distant houses that surrounded the park, even people in the sky, as an occasional aeroplane passed across it, flying to the east, the west, the north, or the south. And, mysteriously, she felt at one with his wife and his son. Now she worked with heightened alacrity on the book she was translating; she loved seeing the German words turned into English, as if she were giving new birth to them. She was becoming useful again after that long period when she had left the Institute. Her anger had gone. She was needed.

George brought the news that two Germans from the firm publishing the Munich book were coming to his brother's works for the day and George wanted her to go down there to interpret. George's son would be there, too; it was the time of the boy's half-term holiday. George brought him to the station to meet her as she arrived. 'Here's Harry,' he said.

She saw a plump boy with reddish hair who stared at her defiantly when they shook hands.

'My mother is in hospital,' he said. 'She can't talk.'

'I know,' she said. 'I am very sorry. She and I used to work in the same office.'

'Dad said,' he said. 'Are you a German?'

'Oh no,' she said. 'But I speak German. That is why I have come.'

They went to the works. There was George's brother wearing a white dust coat. Two Germans stiffly bowed. The boy followed them round as they looked at the machines and listened to her speaking English and then German. He was awed by her, and whenever she spoke he moved his lips trying to copy her, saying the strange words. At last, since no one paid attention to him, he began quietly mocking her, saying, 'Vee fill, gobble, high Slosh, goramma de goramma, nine ten, volly gelob, Ya, Ya.'

'Shut up,' his father said.

So the boy followed them muttering. He hated her, and when they all went to look at a line of damp prints hanging on a line he gave her a sly kick on the shin. She glanced at him and said nothing. He was about to give her another kick when his father said, 'Stop that or you go home.' The boy was frightened and now followed her slowly.

'Your father says you have got a grass snake,' she said. 'Where do you keep it? Will you show it to me?'

'Ah,' said the younger of the Germans. *'Eine Ringelnatter.* Where is it?'

After that the boy was quiet, and he dropped out of the procession. When the visit was over, she went to the boy and asked, 'Where *is* your snake? Show it to me. What is its name?'

'Snakey,' he said.

The party walked to his uncle's house and the boy ran into the garden and came back with the snake, which had wound itself round his arm. A triumph.

'Oh, don't let it come near me!' Paula called out. 'It'll sting me.'

'It doesn't sting.'

The Germans laughed. Everyone laughed.

'Stroke it,' said the boy.

She touched it. 'Oh, it's cold!' she said.

The boy jumped about.

'Calm down,' said George. 'I think it wants to be in its box.'

'Come on. I'll show you where I keep it in the garden,' said the boy.

'Next time,' said his uncle, looking at his watch. 'We've got to get to Brighton for lunch. You've been very helpful,' he said to Paula. 'Why are you limping?'

'Oh, that,' she said. 'I knocked my shin against that machine.'

And so they went off to Brighton, over the Downs, to shouts of

'*Wunderbar!*' and jokes about the British Alps without any *Schnee*, and at last to the first sight of the sea flying out like a flag, and to lunch with speeches from the two Germans, and jokes about the esteemed lady, and glasses clinking and bows in all directions. They said how they would all meet in Frankfurt in a month's time – or was it a week's time? And when it was over and George was going to drive them to Gatwick airport, she begged him to put her on the train because her leg was painful.

'You'd better stay here. I'll get a room,' he said.

'Darling George,' she said. 'I can't. I'm exhausted. Drop me at the station. I must get back to London. Don't look so sad, George.'

'Trains every half hour,' he said. And he drove by a longer route on the outskirts of the town, passing a church in a long village street.

'Church,' he said, jerking his thumb. 'See that? Parson coming out – see that? Kids riding ponies. Cricket field at the back. Nice place to retire to.'

And then, after a steep climb, he got her to the station barrier, and there in the clanging of luggage trolleys she said, 'I loved seeing Harry. He's like you.' And she tapped him on the chest. 'When do you go to Frankfurt?'

He pulled out his diary and said, 'Ten days' time.'

She snatched it from him and, looking at it, said, 'All those "X"s. Who's that?'

'You,' he said. 'Let's get onto the platform.'

'No,' she said. 'I hate platform goodbyes.'

Five days later he rang her and was at her door in the afternoon. The trip to Frankfurt had been brought forward.

'It's tomorrow,' he said. 'Change your mind and come with me.'

'I can't possibly come. I've invited my sister,' she said. 'She'll be here while you're away. You are annoying, G.'

He looked at the small pile of typescript on her table and at the page that was sticking out of her typewriter and then at the open German book. 'Well, if you can't come, read some to me,' he said suddenly. 'I want to hear you speak it, like when the Germans were here, and then I'll think of it all the bloody week while I'm away. Anything, just to hear your beautiful voice.'

'G, how strange you are today.'

In the end she agreed and picked up the book, opened it at random, and read.

'A bit more,' he said.

So she read on and then laughed at him. 'You didn't understand a word.'

'I did. *Frauen* something.'

'*Frauenkirche,*' she said.

He said, 'That's it. The way your throat moved. Say it again.' And then he had his arm around her and she was struggling against him.

'You were thinking of your pretty German wife,' she said, and she struggled until she was helpless, as she had been that first time. 'Not here, George,' she said. 'No, not on the floor.'

And when she got up from it she said, 'Tell your son you're the snake. The German is *Schlange.*'

The next day he left for Frankfurt.

'Ring me when you get there!' she called after him.

'You bet,' he said.

She worked all day and that evening he rang her. 'It's hell,' he said. 'You'd hate it. Hundreds of publishers sniffing round one another like dogs. Chinese, Japanese, American, half Europe, all the disunited nations. How many pages have you done?'

'You love it, you old fraud,' she said. 'Have you rung the boy?'

'Yes,' he said.

The next evening he rang again, and the next day, he said there was going to be a trip down the Rhine.

On the third day he said he was calling to ask how many pages she had done. 'It's calming down here,' he said. 'Tomorrow there's going to be some excursion. I don't know where – to some wine place. No, wait a minute – that's the day after tomorrow. By the way, our German friends, especially the big one – you remember – want to be remembered to you. I think he's going to send you a present. I wonder what. How many pages?'

On the fourth day there was no call and she rang the hotel and someone said he was out at the museum, not in his room, and someone else said,

'Not at the museum, on the excursion.' There was a gabble of voices on the hotel exchange, and after a long time she heard a man who said he was the manager and asked who was speaking and she said, in German, 'I simply want to speak to Doctor Southey, with the British delegation, who is staying with you. It's urgent.' And she said vehemently, 'This is his wife, speaking from London.'

And she heard the man say to someone, 'You fool, why didn't you tell me this lady was his wife?' And she could clearly hear him say, 'You rang his brother? Where is his brother, at the hospital?'

She was trapped in a net of angry voices. And then the manager spoke again: 'Madame, we have supposed his brother must have told you. You must prepare yourself for bad news. I assure you we got in touch with his office at once. We supposed his brother would have passed the knowledge to you. Doctor Southey died in hospital yesterday, after a riding accident.'

'Get off the line!' she shouted. 'I am speaking to someone.'

The manager repeated his sentence. 'Not deaf,' he shouted. 'Dead. *Tod. Doktor Southey ist gestorben.*' And he repeated one of his long, riddlelike sentences.

Paula felt her face collapse. The strength went out of her hands and out of every object in the room, and indeed her whole body seemed to be jumping away from her and leaving her. She dropped the telephone, which hung squawking on its cord.

'George, you conceited fool –' she began.

'Stop that!' she shouted at the telephone.

She felt her body shrinking to nothing and then suddenly grossly bursting, as if to mock her. She seemed to hear George say those words that always annoyed her when he was caught out and was trying to smooth his way out of something – words that now grew fainter and fainter: 'There I go, flat on my face.'

'George, why didn't you tell me?' she whispered as if she were looking for him in the room.

And then the news became real to her. 'That poor boy,' she said. And now she did believe the news. 'His poor wife,' she said. 'This will kill her.'

She felt that half her life had been ripped out of her, that she was hanging in suspense between the present and her earlier memories of him, which became more vivid and real than the recent ones. Almost cautiously, she went from room to room, not able to believe that he would never again be sitting on that chair or this, or walk up the stairs. And then she could hear him making those telephone calls to the hospital and to his son at school.

Some days later a formal card announcing the memorial service arrived, saying 'Funeral Private'. With it there was a short typed letter from George's brother thanking Paula for her beautiful letter and the lovely wreath. Paula had also sent her love to the boy, and from him in time there came a letter written on lined paper from his school:

> Dear Mrs Paula. I hope you are quit well. A beastly dog got Snakey. I have got a new one.

A few years ago two new London ladies became noticeable in the village of X. They settled in a cottage near the church at the top of the long street and walked every day to the post office in the afternoons. In fact, only the tall gaunt one with the thick grey hair who takes long steps is, strictly speaking, a Londoner. The little one with the reddish dyed hair is well known to be the sister-in-law of the printer who lives two miles away on the outskirts of the town. She trots along with a scraping step, chattering to the tall one, who, when they first came to live there, was thought to be a nurse, for it was known that the little one had been for a long time in the hospital in the town, lying there in a coma for goodness knows how long, after a stroke. About that, she has nothing to say, of course, for that part of her life is missing, but what she does not fail to say, with pride, too, about herself and the tall one called Paula is that they had been friends since they worked in the same office in London, at a place called the Institute.

'When we were girls,' she says. 'That is where I met my husband.'

Her husband is buried in the new plot of land the church had taken over some years back: a man said to have been in his time a fast bowler in the village cricket team.

About Paula, the tall one, little is known beyond the fact that once or twice a week she drives in a small car to the university ten miles away. Three or four of the village people even went to a lecture she gave on

[1207]

some German subject at the Literary Society in the town. There was a poster on the door of the Village Hall, and the daughter of the woman who runs the post office and village shop and has a big black dog went to the lecture. And so, indeed, did the printer and his wife. The village also knows that it is Ethel's, the little one's, son who comes down at weekends. He is a good-looking young man who often goes for a walk up on the Downs with Paula. His mother goes only as far as the footpath at the end of the village because she can't manage the steep climb.

Their cottage is really two small flint-and-tiled cottages turned ingeniously into one. Ethel has a room on the ground floor, with a door giving onto the long lawn because she finds stairs tiring. Paula works in a room upstairs, where one wall is lined with books, and she sleeps in a narrow room that looks out onto the churchyard. Behind the house is a public footpath and a handsome row of sycamores and then the cricket field and the pink villas of the newer part of the village. In the afternoons and some evenings the two ladies sit in a sitting room, which is almost luxurious, for it is furnished with one or two treasures Paula brought down from her London flat there. There is a long, tall gilded mirror on one wall, a *chaise-longue*, and a cabinet with one or two pieces of china in it. The chairs are pleasantly low-seated, the windows are long and look out across the garden hedge to the public footpath, and it is pleasant to hear the gate slamming at the end of it and to see who has gone by.

Quite a number of distinguished visitors come to the house, especially one or two professors from Paula's university, and this is the time for Ethel to show her gift of bringing in large glasses, like globes, containing her speciality: well-iced and powerful gin-and-vermouths. When she comes into the room she always catches the ends of the sentences she hears and repeats them as if to give the impression that she had not been out of the room. If she hears a visitor saying 'In my opinion the film is a disaster to anyone who has read the book,' she glides in saying, '– To anyone who has read the book,' to join in the conversation. When her son is there and perhaps says, 'It was three-one at halftime,' she will eagerly repeat, 'Three-one at halftime.' She is making up for the time she was in hospital for all those years and heard nothing. She is particularly quick to pick up Paula's exclamations in the garden when Paula finds a climbing rose has gone wild and says, 'Nothing to be done with them. Cut them back or they go on, regardless, with ideas of their own.' Ethel says, with fervour, '– With ideas of their own.' When someone says, 'Munich has the finest collection of pictures in Europe,' she repeats, 'the finest in Europe,' as if she had been visiting there all her life.

Ethel's son has turned into a plump and dressy young man with the habit of making a hissing noise between his teeth when he is bored. On Saturdays there is sometimes a sharp bang, like a shot, from the gate to the footpath at the side of the house. The gate slams loudest when the children from the pony club ride through.

'I wish that woman from the riding school would take her horses some other way,' says Paula.

'– Her horses some other way,' says Mrs Southey as she limps into the room. She adds, 'The noise interferes with Paula's work. How can she concentrate?'

But both women are thinking of George's death. His widow says, 'It was all conceit. I could understand if he had had a woman – but a horse! I'm not being funny.'

And she rambles into memories of the Institute and says to Paula, 'Everyone thought you were going to marry Mr Featherstone. He made sheep's eyes at everyone. You don't know the whole of it.'

Her son listens. He would sooner be down at the village pub but he knows the ladies expect him to take them out to dinner on Saturdays at some restaurant or other. He likes his food and always wants to try a new place.

'Where shall we go?' Paula asks.

He pulls out his diary and looks down a list of telephone numbers.

'All those telephone numbers – just like George,' Paula says.

'I collect them,' he says. 'I started when I was at school. Dad used to ring me up from all over Europe.'

'Yes,' says Mrs Southey primly. 'We've got all his diaries, with numbers from all over the world.'

The shabby diaries are a guide to George's life when she was absent from it.

'He even telephoned from Turkey,' the young man said.

'And,' said Paula, 'sometimes from my house to the hospital and to your school.'

'Yes, you told me,' said Ethel, pitying her. 'He had no regard for anyone's convenience.'

The Image Trade

―――――――

What do you make of the famous Zut – I mean his stuff in this exhibition? Is he just a newsy collector of human instances jellied in his darkroom, or is he an artist – a Zurbarán, say, a priest searching another priest's soul? Pearson, one of a crowd of persons, was silently putting these questions to them on a London bus going north.

Last July, Pearson went on, he was at home. The front-door bell rang. 'He's here! On time!' his beautiful wife said. She was scraping the remains of his hair across his scalp. 'Wait,' she said, and turning him round, she gave a last sharp brush to his shoulders and sent him dibble-dabbing fast down three flights of stairs to the door. There stood Zut, the photographer, with his back to Pearson and on impatient feet, tall and thin in a suit creased by years of air travel. He was shouting to Mrs Zut, who was lugging two heavy bags of apparatus up the street to the house. She got there and they turned round.

As a writer, in the news too and in another branch of the human-image trade, Pearson depended on seeing people and things as strictly they are not. The notion that Zut and his wife could be a doorstep couple offering to buy old spectacles or discarded false teeth, a London trade, occurred to him, but he recovered and, switching on an eager smile, bowed them into the house. They marched past him down the hall, briskly, like a pair of surgeons, to the foot of the stairs and looked back at him.

'I hope you had no difficulty in finding this – er – place,' Pearson said, vain of difficulty as a sort of fame.

'None,' said Zut. 'She drives. I read the street map.' Mrs Zut had not put down her load. Zut seemed to ask, Are you the body?

Well, said Pearson spaciously, where did they want to 'do', or 'take' – he hesitated between saying 'it' or 'me'. He said this to all photographers, waving a hand, offering the house. Zut looked up at the stairs and the high ceiling.

Pearson said, Ground-floor dining room, tall windows, books? Upstairs by half-landing, a balcony, or would you say patio, flowers, shrubs, greenery, a pair of Chinese dogs in stone, view of neighbouring gardens? Down below, garden seat under tree, could sit there taking the air. And talking of air, have often been done – if that is the word – outside in the street, in overcoat and fur hat by interesting railings, coat buttoned or unbuttoned. No? Or first-floor sitting room. High windows again, fourteen feet in fact, expensive when curtaining, but chairs easy or uneasy, large mirror, peacock feathers on wife's desk, quite a lot of gilt, *chaise-longue* indeed. Have often been done there, upright or lying full length. *Death of Chatterton* style.

Zut said, 'Furniture tells me nothing. Where do you work?'

'Work?' said Pearson.

'Where you write,' said Zut.

'Oh, that,' said Pearson. 'You mean the alphabet, sentences? At the top. Three flights up, I'm afraid,' apologising to Mrs Zut. (Writer, writing at desk, rather a cliché for a man like Zut – no?)

Already Zut was taking long steps up the stairs, followed by Mrs Zut, who refused to give up her two rattling bags, Pearson looking at Mrs Zut's grey hair and peaceful back as he came after them. From flight to flight they went and did not speak until they were under a fanlight at the top. In a pause for breath Pearson said, 'Burglar's entry.'

Zut ignored this and, pointing to a door, 'In here?' he said.

'No, used to be children's bathroom. Other door.' The door was white on the outside, yellowing on the inside. They marched in.

'It smells of – what would you say? – decaying rhubarb, I'm afraid. I smoke a pipe.'

There was the glitter of permafrost in Zut's hunting eyes as he studied the room. There were two attic windows; the other three walls were blood red but stacked and stuffed with books to the ceiling. They were terraced like a football crowd, in varieties of anoraks, a crowd unstirred by a slow game going on among four tables where more books and manuscripts were in scrimmage.

'That your desk?' said Zut, pointing to the largest table.

'I'm a table man,' said Pearson, apologising, bending to pick up one or two matches and a paper clip from the floor. 'I migrate from table to table.' And drew attention to a large capsized photograph of the Albert Memorial propped on a chest of drawers. Accidentally, Zut kicked a metal wastepaper basket as he looked round. It gave a knell.

Yes, Pearson was inclined to say (but did not), this room has a knell. Authors die. Dozens of funerals of unfinished sentences here every day. It is less a study than a – what shall I say? – perhaps a dockyard for damaged syntax? Or, better still, an immigration hall. Papers arrive at a table, migrate to other tables or chairs, and, when they are rubber-stamped, get stuffed into drawers. By the way, outgoing mail on the floor. Observe the corner bookcase, the final catacomb – my file boxes. I like to forget.

Mrs Zut dropped to her knees near a window and was opening the bags.

Now (Pearson was offering his body to Zut), what would you like me to be or do? Stand here? Or there? Sit? Left leg crossed over right leg, right over left? Put on a look? Get a book at random? Open a drawer? Light a pipe? Talk? Think? Put hand on chin? Great Zut, make your wish known.

Talk, Zut. All photographers talk, put client at ease. Ask me questions. Dozens of pictures of me have been taken. I could show you my early slim-subaltern-on-the-Somme-waiting-to-go-over-the-top period. There was my Popular Front look in the Thirties and Forties, the jersey-wearing, all-the-world's-a-coal-mine period, with close-ups of the pores and scars of the skin and the gleam of sweat. There was the editorial look, when the tailor had to let out the waist of my trousers, followed by the successful smirk. In the Sixties the plunging neckline, no tie. Then back to collar and tie in my failed-bronze-Olympic period. Today I fascinate archaeologists – you know, the broken pillar of a lost civilisation. Come on, Zut. What do you want?

Zut looked at the largest table. It had a clear space among pots of pencils, ashtrays, paper clips, two piles of folders for the execution block – a large blotter embroidered by pen wipings, and on it was a board with beautiful clean white paper clipped to it.

'There,' said Zut, pointing to the chair in front of it. Zut had swollen veins on his long hands. 'Sit,' he said.

Pearson sat. There was a hiss from Mrs Zut's place on the floor, close to Zut. She had pulled out the steel rods of a whistling tripod. Zut gave a push to her shoulder. Up came a camera. She screwed it on and Zut fiddled with it, calling for more and more little things. What fun you have in your branch of the trade, said Pearson. You have little things to twizzle. Well, I have paper clips, pipe cleaners, scissors, paste. I try out pens, that's all – to save me from entering the wilderness, the wilderness of vocabulary.

But now Zut was pulling his creased jacket over his head and squinting through the camera at Pearson, who felt a small flake of his face fall off. And at that moment Zut gave Mrs Zut a knock on her arm. 'Meter,' he said. Then he let his coat slip back to his shoulders and stepped from the end of the table to where Pearson was sitting and held the meter, with shocking intimacy, close to Pearson's head. He looked back at the window, muttering a word. Was the word 'unclean'? And he turned to squint through the camera and looked up to say, 'Take your glasses off.'

My glasses. My only defence. Can't see a thing. He took them off.

Ah, Zut, I see you don't talk, because you are after the naked truth, you are a dabbler in the puddles of the mind. As you like, but I warn you I'm wise to that.

'Don't smile.'

I see, you're not a smile-please man, muttered Pearson. Oh, Zut, you've such a shriven look. If you take me naked, you will miss all the *et cetera* of my life. I am all *et cetera*. But Zut was back under his jacket, spying again, and then he did something presumptuous. He came out of his jacket, reached across the table, and moved a pot of pencils out of the way. The blue pot, that rather pretty *et cetera* that Pearson's wife had found in a junk shop next to the butcher's – now a pizza café – twenty-four years ago on a street not in this district. Zut, you have moved a part of my life to another table, it will hate being there, screamed Pearson's soul. How dare you move my wife?

Anything else?

'Not necessary,' said Zut and, reaching out, gave Mrs Zut a knock on the arm. 'Lamp,' he said between his teeth.

Mrs Zut scrabbled in the bag and pulled out a rubbery cord; at the end was a clouded yellow lamp, a small sickly moon. She stood up and held it high.

Zut gave another knock on her arm as he spied into the camera.

[1214]

'Higher,' he said.

Up went the lamp. Another knock.

'Keep still. You're letting it droop,' said Zut. Oh, Florence Nightingale, can't you, after all these years, hold it steady?

'Look straight into the camera,' called Zut from under his jacket.

'Now write,' said Zut.

'Write? Where?'

'On that paper.'

'Pen or pencil?' said Pearson. 'Write what?'

'Anything.'

'Like at school.'

Pearson tipped the board on the edge of the table.

'Don't tip the board. Keep it flat.'

'I can't write flat. I never write flat,' Pearson said. And I never write in public, if anyone is in the room. I grunt. I make a noise.

I bet you can't photograph a noise.

Pearson glanced at Zut. Then, sulking, he slid the board back flat on the table and felt the room tip up.

Zut, Pearson murmured. I shall write: Zut keeps on hitting his wife. Zut keeps on hitting his wife. Can't write that. He might see. Zut, I am going to diddle you. I shall write my address, 56 Hill Road Terrace, with the wrong post code – N6 4DN. Here goes: 56 Hill Road Terrace, 56 Hill Road Terrace . . .

'Keep on writing,' said Zut.

Pearson continued 56 Hill Road Terrace and then misspelled 'terrace'. Out of the corner of his eye he saw the little yellow lamp.

'Now look up at me,' said Zut.

The room tipped higher.

'Like that. Like that. Like that,' hissed Zut. 'Go on. Now go on writing.'

Click, click, click, went the shutter of the camera. A little toad in the lens has shot out a long tongue and caught a fly.

'You're dropping it again,' said Zut, giving Mrs Zut a punch.

'Good,' the passionate Zut called to Pearson, then came out of his jacket.

'My face has gone,' Pearson said.

But how do you know you've got *me?* My soul spreads all over my body, even in my feet. My face is nothing. At my age I don't need it. It is no more than a servant I push around before me. Or a football I kick ahead of me, taking all the blows, in shops, in the streets. It knows nothing. It just collects. I send it to smirk at parties, to give lectures. It has a mouth. I've no idea what it says. It calls people by the wrong names. It is an indiscriminate little grinner. It kisses people I've never met. The only time my face and I exchange a word is when I shave. Then it sulks.

Click, went the camera.

Pearson sat back and put down his pen and dropped his arm to his side.

'Will you do that again,' said Zut. 'The way you just dropped your arm,' Zut said.

Pearson did it.

'No,' said Zut. 'We've missed it.'

Pearson was hurt, and apologised to Mrs Zut, the dumb goddess. Not for worlds would he upset her husband. She simply gazed at Zut.

Zut himself straightened up. The room tipped back to its normal state. Pearson noticed the long lines down the sides of Zut's mouth, wondered why the jacket did not rumple his grey hair. Cropped, of course. How old was he? Where had he flown from? Hovering vulture. Unfortunate Satan walking up and down the world looking for souls. Satan on his treadmill. I bet your father was in, say, the clock trade, was it? – and when you were a boy you took his watch to pieces looking for Time. Why don't you *talk?* You're not like that man who came here last year and told me that he waited until he felt there was a magnetic flow uniting himself and me. A technological flirt. Nor are you like that other happy fellow with the waving fair hair who said he unselfed himself, forgot money, wife, children, all, for a few seconds to become me!

Zut slid a new plate into the camera and glanced up at the ceiling. It was smudged by the faint shadows of the beams behind it. A prison or cage effect. Why was he looking at the ceiling? Did he want it to be removed?

Pearson said, 'Painted only five years ago. And look at it! More expense.'

Zut dismissed this.

'Look towards the window,' said Zut.

'Which one?' said Pearson.

'On the right,' said Zut. 'Yes. Yes.' Another blow on that poor woman's arm.

'Lamp – higher. Still higher.'

Click, click from the toad in the lens.

'Again,' said Zut.

Click. Click. Another click.

'Ah!' said Zut, as if about to faint.

He's found something at last, Pearson thought. But, Zut, I bet you don't know where my mind was. No, I was not looking at the tree-tops. I was looking at a particular branch. On a still day like this, there is always one leaf skipping about at the end of a branch on its own while the rest of the tree is still. It has been doing that for years. Why? An *et cetera*, a distinguished leaf. Could be me. What am I but a leaf?

One more half-hearted click from the camera, and then Zut stood tall. He had achieved boredom.

'I've got all I want,' he muttered sharply to his wife.

All? said Pearson, appealing. There are tons of me left. I know I have a face like a cup of soup with handles sticking out – you know? – after it has been given a couple of stirs with a wooden spoon. A speciality in a way. What wouldn't I give for bone structure, a nose with bone in it!

Zut gave a last dismissive look around the room.

'That's it,' he said to his wife.

She started to dismantle the tripod. Zut walked to the photograph of the Albert Memorial on the chest near the door, done by another photographer, and studied it. There was an enormous elephant's head in the foreground. Zut pointed. 'Only one eye,' he said censoriously.

'The other's in shadow,' said Pearson.

'Elephants have two eyes,' said Zut. And then, 'Is there a . . .'

'Of course, of course, the door on the left.'

Pearson was putting the muscles of his face back in place. He was alone with Mrs Zut, who was packing up the debris of the hour.

'I have always admired your husband's work,' he said politely.

'Thank you,' she said from the floor, buckling the bags.

'Remarkable pictures of men – and, of course, women. I think I saw one of you, didn't I, in his last collection?'

'No,' she said from the floor, looking proud. 'I don't allow him to take my picture.'

'Oh surely –'

'No,' she said, the whole of herself standing up, full-faced, solid and human.

'His first wife, yes. Not me,' she said resolutely, killing the other in the ordinary course of life.

Then Zut came back, and in procession they all began thanking their way downstairs to the door.

At the exhibition Pearson sneaked in to see himself, stayed ten minutes to look at his portrait, and came out screaming, thinking of Mrs Zut.

An artist, he said. Herod! he was shouting. When the head of John the Baptist was handed to you on that platter, the eyes of that beautiful severed head were peacefully closed. But what do I see at the bottom of your picture. A high haunted room whose books topple. Not a room indeed, but a dank cistern or aquarium of stale water. No sparkling anemone there but the bald head of a melancholy frog, its feet clinging to a log, floating in literature. O Fame, cried Pearson, O Maupassant, O *Tales of Hoffmann*, O Edgar Allan Poe, O Grub Street.

Pearson rushed out and rejoined the human race on that bus going north and sat silently addressing the passengers, the women particularly, who all looked like Mrs Zut. The sight of them changed his mind. He was used, he said, to his face gallivanting with other ladies and gentlemen, in newspapers, books, and occasionally on the walls of galleries like that one down the street. Back down the street, he said, a man called Zut, a photographer, an artist, not one of your click-click men, had exhibited his picture, but by a mysterious accident of art had portrayed his soul instead of mine. What faces, Pearson said, that poor fellow must see just before he drops off to sleep at night beside the wise woman who won't let him take a picture of her, fearing perhaps the Evil Eye. A man in the image trade, like myself, Pearson called back as he got off the bus. Not a Zurbarán, more a Hieronymus Bosch perhaps. No one noticed Pearson getting off.

List of sources and dates

You Make Your Own Life – 1938
Sense of Humour; A Spring Morning; Main Road; The Evils of Spain;
Handsome Is As Handsome Does; The Aristocrat; The Two Brothers;
X-ray; The Scapegoat; Eleven o'Clock; The Upright Man; Page and
Monarch; Miss Baker; You Make Your Own Life.

It May Never Happen – 1945

The Sailor; The Lion's Den; The Saint; It May Never Happen; Pocock
Passes; The Oedipus Complex; The Voice; Aunt Gertrude; Many Are
Disappointed; The Chestnut Tree; The Ape; The Clerk's Tale; The Fly
in the Ointment; The Night Worker.

Previously uncollected stories appearing in:
1. *Collected Stories* – 1956

The Sniff – n.d.; The Collection – n.d.

2. *Collected Stories* – 1982

Things as They Are – in *Sailor, Sense of Humour & Other Stories*, Knopf,
1956.

3. *More Collected Stories* – 1983

Double Divan – 1946; The Landlord – 1948; Passing the Ball – 1950; A
Story of Don Juan – 1950; The Ladder – 1955; The Satisfactory – 1955.

When My Girl Comes Home – 1961

The Wheelbarrow; The Fall; When My Girl Comes Home; The Necklace;

Just a Little More; The Snag; On the Scent; Citizen; The Key to My Heart.

The Key to My Heart – 1963

Noisy Flushes the Birds; Noisy in the Doghouse. (This collection also contains the story 'The Key to My Heart.')

Blind Love – 1969

Blind Love; The Nest Builder; A Debt of Honour; The Cage Birds; The Skeleton; The Speech; The Liars; Our Oldest Friend; The Honeymoon; The Chain-Smoker.

The Camberwell Beauty – 1974

The Camberwell Beauty; The Diver; Did You Invite Me?; The Rescue; The Marvellous Girl; The Spree; Our Wife; The Last Throw; The Lady from Guatemala.

On the Edge of the Cliff – 1980

On the Edge of the Cliff; A Family Man; The Spanish Bed; The Wedding; The Worshippers; The Vice-Consul; The Accompanist; Tea with Mrs Bittell; The Fig Tree.

A Careless Widow – 1989

A Careless Widow; Cocky Olly; A Trip to the Seaside; Things; A Change of Policy; The Image Trade.

About the Author

═══════

V. S. PRITCHETT is one of the great literary men of our time, a critic, novelist, writer of short stories, biographer, and autobiographer. His most recent work is *Lasting Impressions: Essays 1961–1987*. Now in his ninetieth year, he is president of the Society of Authors, and a foreign honorary member of both the Academy of Arts and Letters and the Academy of Arts and Sciences. Pritchett was knighted in 1975. He lives in London with his wife, Dorothy.

Complete collected stories   S.S
   V.S. Pritchett

DATE DUE			
MAY	1991		
JUN 1	1991		
JUL	1991		
JUL 1	1991		
AUG 1	1991		
SEP 1	1991		